wwnorton.com/nawol

The StudySpace site that accompanies *The Norton Anthology of World Literature* is FREE, but you will need the code below to register for a password that will allow you to access the copyrighted materials on the site.

READ-WELL

THE NORTON ANTHOLOGY OF

WORLD LITERATURE

THIRD EDITION

VOLUME A

THE NORTON ANTHOLOGY OF WORLD LITERATURE

THIRD EDITION

MARTIN PUCHNER, *General Editor*
HARVARD UNIVERSITY

SUZANNE AKBARI
UNIVERSITY OF TORONTO

WIEBKE DENECKE
BOSTON UNIVERSITY

VINAY DHARWADKER
UNIVERSITY OF WISCONSIN, MADISON

BARBARA FUCHS
UNIVERSITY OF CALIFORNIA, LOS ANGELES

CAROLINE LEVINE
UNIVERSITY OF WISCONSIN, MADISON

PERICLES LEWIS
YALE UNIVERSITY

EMILY WILSON
UNIVERSITY OF PENNSYLVANIA

VOLUME A

W. W. NORTON & COMPANY | New York · London

W. W. Norton & Company has been independent since its founding in 1923, when William Warder Norton and Mary D. Herter Norton first published lectures delivered at the People's Institute, the adult education division of New York City's Cooper Union. The firm soon expanded its program beyond the Institute, publishing books by celebrated academics from America and abroad. By midcentury, the two major pillars of Norton's publishing program—trade books and college texts—were firmly established. In the 1950s, the Norton family transferred control of the company to its employees, and today—with a staff of four hundred and a comparable number of trade, college, and professional titles published each year—W. W. Norton & Company stands as the largest and oldest publishing house owned wholly by its employees.

Editor: Peter Simon
Assistant Editor: Conor Sullivan
Managing Editor, College: Marian Johnson
Manuscript Editors: Barney Latimer, Alice Falk, Katharine Ings, Michael Fleming, Susan Joseph, Pamela Lawson, Diane Cipollone
Electronic Media Editor: Eileen Connell
Print Ancillary Editor: Laura Musich
Editorial Assistant, Media: Jennifer Barnhardt
Marketing Manager, Literature: Kimberly Bowers
Senior Production Manager, College: Benjamin Reynolds
Photo Editor: Patricia Marx
Permissions Manager: Megan Jackson
Permissions Clearing: Margaret Gorenstein
Text Design: Jo Anne Metsch
Art Director: Rubina Yeh
Cartographer: Adrian Kitzinger
Composition: Jouve North America, Brattleboro, VT
Manufacturing: R. R. Donnelley & Sons—Crawfordsville, IN

The text of this book is composed in Fairfield Medium with the display set in Aperto.

Library of Congress Cataloging-in-Publication Data

The Norton anthology of world literature / Martin Puchner, general editor . . . [et al.].—3rd ed.
p. cm.
"Volume A."
Includes bibliographical references and index.
ISBN 978-0-393-91329-3 (v. A : pbk.)—ISBN 978-0-393-91330-9 (v. B : pbk.)—ISBN 978-0-393-91331-6 (v. C : pbk.)—ISBN 978-0-393-91332-3 (v. D : pbk.)—ISBN 978-0-393-91333-0 (v. E : pbk.)—ISBN 978-0-393-91334-7 (v. F : pbk.) 1. Literature—Collections. I. Puchner, Martin, 1969– II. Norton anthology of world masterpieces
PN6014.N66 2012
808.8—dc23

2011047211

W. W. Norton & Company, Inc., 500 Fifth Avenue, New York, NY 10110-0017
wwnorton.com
W. W. Norton & Company Ltd., Castle House, 75/76 Wells Street, London W1T 3QT

6 7 8 9 0

Contents

III. EARLY CHINESE LITERATURE AND THOUGHT 1311

Preface

In 1665, a Turkish nobleman traveled from his native Istanbul to Europe and recorded with disarming honesty his encounter with an alien civilization. Over the course of his life, Evliya Çelebi would crisscross the Ottoman Empire from Egypt all the way to inner Asia, filling volume after volume with his reports of the cities, peoples, and legends he came across. This was his first journey to Vienna, a longtime foe of the Ottoman Empire. Full of confidence about the superiority of his own culture, Evliya was nevertheless impressed by Vienna's technical and cultural achievements. One episode from his *Travels,* a charming moment of self-deprecation, tells us how, during his tour of Vienna's inner city, Evliya sees what he believes to be "captives from the nation of Muhammad" sitting in front of various shops, toiling away at mind-numbing, repetitive tasks. Feeling pity for them, he offers them some coins, only to find that they are in fact mechanical automatons. Embarrassed and amazed at the same time, Evliya ends this tale by embracing the pleasure of seeing something new: "This was a marvelous and wonderful adventure indeed!"

Throughout his travels, Evliya remained good-humored about such disorienting experiences, and he maintained an open mind as he compared the cultural achievements of his home with those of Vienna. The crowning achievement of Vienna is the cathedral, which towers over the rest of the city. But Evliya found that it couldn't compare with the architectural wonders of Istanbul's great mosques. As soon as he was taken to the library, however, he was awestruck: "There are God knows how many books in the mosques of Sultan Barqūq and Sultan Faraj in Cairo, and in the mosques of [Sultan Meḥmed] The Conqueror and Sultan Süleymān and Sultan Bāyezīd and the New Mosque, but in this St. Stephen's Monastery in Vienna there are even more." He admired the sheer diversity and volume of books: "As many nations and different languages as there are, of all their authors and writers in their languages there are many times a hundred thousand books here." He was drawn, naturally enough, to the books that make visible the contours and riches of the world: atlases, maps, and illustrated books. An experienced travel writer, he nonetheless struggled to keep his equilibrium, saying finally that he was simply "stunned."

Opening *The Norton Anthology of World Literature* for the first time, a reader may feel as overwhelmed by its selection of authors and works (from "as many different languages as there are") as Evliya was by the cathedral library. For most students, the world literature course is a semester- or year-long encounter with the unknown—a challenging and rewarding journey, not a stroll down familiar, well-worn paths. Secure in their knowledge of the culture of their upbringing, and perhaps even proud of its accomplishments, most students will discover in world literature a bewildering variety of similarly rich and admirable cultures about which they know little, or nothing. Setting off on an imaginative journey in an unfamiliar text, readers may ask themselves questions similar to those a traveler in a strange land might ponder: How should I orient myself in this unfamiliar culture? What am I not seeing that someone raised in this culture would recognize right away? What can I learn here? How can I relate to the people I meet? Students might imagine the perils of the encounter, wondering if they will embarrass themselves in the process, or simply find themselves "stunned" by the sheer number of things they do not know.

But as much as they may feel anxiety at the prospect of world literature, students may also feel, as Evliya did, excitement at the discovery of something new, the exhilaration of having their horizons expanded. This, after all, is why Evliya traveled in the first place. Travel, for him, became almost an addiction. He sought again and again the rush of the unknown, the experience of being stunned, the feeling of marveling over cultural achievements from across the world. Clearly Evliya would have liked to linger in the cathedral library and immerse himself in its treasures. This experience is precisely what *The Norton Anthology of World Literature* offers to you and your students.

As editors of the Third Edition, we celebrate the excitement of world literature, but we also acknowledge that the encounter with the literary unknown is a source of anxiety. From the beginning of our collaboration, we have set out to make the journey more enticing and less intimidating for our readers.

First, we have made the introductory matter clearer and more informative by shortening headnotes and by following a consistent pattern of presentation, beginning with the author's biography, then moving to the cultural context, and ending with a brief introduction to the work itself. The goal of this approach is to provide students with just enough information to prepare them for their own reading of the work, but not so much information that their sense of discovery is numbed.

The mere presentation of an anthology—page after page of unbroken text—can feel overwhelming to anyone, but especially to an inexperienced student of literature. To alleviate this feeling, and to provide contextual information that words might not be able to convey, we have added hundreds of images and other forms of visual support to the anthology. Most of these images are integrated into the introductions to each major section of the anthology, providing context and visual interest. More than fifty of these images are featured in six newly conceived color inserts that offer pictures of various media, utensils, tools, technologies, and types of writing, as well as scenes of writing and reading from different epochs. The result is a rich visual overview of the material and cultural importance of writing and texts. Recognizing the importance of geography to many of the works in the anthology, the editors have revised the map program so that it complements the literature more directly. Each of the twenty-six maps has been redrawn to help readers orient themselves in the many corners of the world to which this anthology will take them. Finally, newly redesigned timelines at the end of each volume help students see at a glance the temporal relationships among literary works and historical events. Taken together, all of these visual elements make the anthology not only more inviting but also more informative than ever before.

The goal of making world literature a pleasurable adventure also guided our selection of translations. World literature gained its power from the way it reflected and shaped the imagination of peoples, and from the way it circulated outside its original context. For this, it depends on translation. While purists sometimes insist on studying literature only in the original language, a dogma that radically shrinks what one can read, world literature not only relies on translation but actually thrives on it. Translation is a necessity, the only thing that enables a worldwide circulation of literature. It also is an art. One need only think of the way in which translations of the Bible shaped the history of Latin or English. Translations are re-creations of works for new readers. Our edition pays keen attention to translation, and we feature dozens of new translations that make classical texts newly readable and capture the originals in compelling ways. With each choice of translation, we sought a version that would spark a sense of wonder while still being accessible to a contemporary reader. Many of the anthology's most fundamental classics—from *Gilgamesh*, Homer's epics, the Greek dramatists, Virgil, the Bible, the *Bhagavad-Gītā*, and the Qur'an to *The Canterbury Tales*, *The Tale of Genji*, Goethe's *Faust*, Ibsen's *Hedda Gabler*, and Kafka's *Metamorphosis*—are presented in new translations that are both exciting works in English and skillful echoes of the spirit and flavor of the original. In some cases, we commissioned new translations—for instance, for the work of the South Asian poet Kabir, rendered beautifully by our South Asian editor and prize-winning translator Vinay Dharwadker, and for a portion of Çelebi's travels to Vienna by our Ottoman expert Gottfried Hagen that has never before been translated into English.

Finally, the editors decided to make some of the guiding themes of the world literature course, and this anthology, more visible. Experienced teachers know about these major themes and use them to create linked reading assignments, and the anthology has long touched on these topics, but with the Third Edition, these themes rise to the surface, giving all readers a clearer sense of the ties that bind diverse works together. Following is discussion of each of these organizing themes.

Contact and Culture

Again and again, literature evokes journeys away from home and out into the world, bringing its protagonists—and thus its readers—into contact with peoples who are different from them. Such contact, and the cross-pollination it fosters, was crucial for the formation of cultures. The earliest civilizations—the civilizations that invented writing and hence literature—sprang up where they did because they were located along strategic trading and migration routes. Contact was not just something that happened between fully formed cultures, but something that made these cultures possible in the first place.

Committed to presenting the anthology's riches in a way that conveys this central fact of world literature, we have created new sections that encompass broad contact zones—areas of intense trade in peoples, goods, art, and ideas. The largest such zone is centered on the Mediterranean basin and reaches as far as the Fertile Crescent. It is in this large area that the earliest literatures emerged and intermingled. For the Mediterranean Sea was not just a hostile environment that could derail a journey home, as it did for Odysseus, who took ten years to find his way back to Greece from the Trojan War in Asia Minor; it was a connecting tissue as well, allowing for intense contact around its harbors. Medieval maps of the Mediterranean pay tribute to this fact: so-called portolan charts show a veritable mesh of lines connecting hundreds of ports. In the reorganized Mediterranean sections in volumes A and B, we have placed together texts from this broad region, the location of intense conflict as well as friendly exchange, rather than isolating them from each other. In a similar manner, the two major traditions of East Asia, China and Japan, are now presented in the context of the larger region, which means that for the first time the anthology includes texts from Vietnam and Korea.

One of the many ways that human beings have bound themselves to each other and have attempted to bridge cultural and geographic distances is through religion. As a form of cultural exchange, and an inspiration for cultural conflict, religion is an important part of the deep history of contact and encounter presented in the anthology, and the editors have taken every opportunity to call attention to this fact. This is nowhere more visible than in a new section in volume C called "Encounters with Islam," which follows the cultural influence of Islam beyond its point of origin in Arabia and Persia. Here we draw together works from western Africa, Asia Minor, and South Asia, each of them blending the ideas and values of Islam with indigenous folk traditions to create new forms of cultural expression. The original oral stories of the extraordinary Mali epic *Sunjata* (in a newly established version and translation) incorporate elements of Islam much the way the Anglo-Saxon epic *Beowulf* incorporates elements of Christianity. The early Turkish epic *The Book of Dede Korkut* similarly blends Islamic thought and expression with the cultural traditions of the pre-Islamic nomadic tribes whose stories make up the bulk of the book. In a different way, the encounter of Islam with other cultures emerges at the eastern end of its sphere of influence, in South Asia, where a multireligious culture absorbs and transforms Islamic material, as in the philosophical poems of Tukaram and Kabir (both presented in new selections and translations). Evliya Çelebi, with his journey to Vienna, belongs to this larger history as well, giving us another lens through which to view the encounter of Islam and Christianity that is dramatized by so many writers elsewhere in the anthology (most notably, in the *Song of Roland*).

The new emphasis on contact and encounter is expressed not just in the overall organization of the anthology and the selection of material; it is also made visible in clusters of texts on the theme of travel and conquest, giving students access to documents related to travel, contact, trade, and conflict. The greatest story of encounter between peoples to be told in the first half of the anthology is the encounter of Europe (and thus of Eurasia) with the Americas. To tell this story properly, the editors decided to eliminate the old dividing line between the European Renaissance and the New World that had prevailed in previous editions and instead created one broad cultural sphere that combines the two. A (newly expanded) cluster within this section gathers texts immediately relevant to this encounter, vividly chronicling all of its willful violence and its unintended consequences in the "New" World. This section also reveals the ways in which the European discovery of the Americas wrought violence in Europe. Old certainties and authorities overthrown, new worlds imagined, the very concept of being human revised—nothing that happened in the European Renaissance was untouched by the New World. Rarely had contact between two geographic zones had more consequences: henceforth, the Americas would be an important part of the story of Europe.

For a few centuries European empires dominated global politics and economics and accelerated the pace of globalization by laying down worldwide trade routes and communication networks, but old empires, such as China, continued to be influential as well. A new section called "At the Crossroads of Empire" in volume E gathers literature produced in Vietnam, India, and China as Asian and European empires met and collided, vying for control not only of trade routes and raw materials but also of ideas and values. The writers included here felt the pressures of ancient traditions and new imperial powers and resisted both, crafting brave and imaginative responses to repressive conditions. Another new section, "Realism across the World," traces perhaps the first truly global artistic movement, one that found expression in France, Britain, Russia, Brazil, and Japan. And it was not just an effect of European dominance. Representing the daily experiences of people living in gritty urban poverty, for example, the Japanese writer Higuchi Ichiyō developed her own realism without ever having read a European novel.

In the twentieth century, the pace of cultural exchange and contact, so much swifter than in preceding centuries, transformed most literary movements, from modernism to postcolonialism, into truly global phenomena. At the end of the final volume, we encounter Elizabeth Costello, the title character in J. M. Coetzee's novel. A writer herself, Costello has been asked to give lectures on a cruise ship; mobile and deracinated, she and a colleague deliver lectures on the novel in Africa, including the role of geography and oral literature. The scene captures many themes of world literature—and serves as an image of our present stage of globalization. World literature is a story about the relation between the world and literature, and we tell this story partly by paying attention to this geographic dimension.

Travel

The accounts of Evliya Çelebi and other explorers are intriguing because they recount real journeys and real people. But travel has also inspired a rich array of fictional fabulation. This theme lived in past editions of the anthology, as indeed it does in nearly any world literature course in which Homer's *Odyssey*, Chaucer's *Canterbury Tales*, Cervantes' *Don Quixote*, Swift's *Gulliver's Travels*, and many other touchstones of the world literature canon are read. To further develop this theme in the Third Edition, the editors have added several new texts with travel at their center. Among them is the first and most influential Spanish picaresque novel, *Lazarillo de Tormes*, a fast-paced story that shows how fortune has her way with the low-born hero. Lazarillo's resilience and native smarts help him move from master to master, serving a priest, a friar, a chaplain, and an archbishop, all of whom seek to exploit him. The great Vietnamese epic *The Tale of Kiều*, another new selection, features an even greater survival artist. In this tale the heroine, repeatedly abducted and pressed into prostitution and marriage, survives because of her impeccable stoicism, which she maintains in the face of a life that seems shaped by cruel accidents and ill fortune. Even as these tales delight in adventures and highlight the qualities that allow their heroes to survive them, they are invested in something else: the sheer movement from one place to the next. Travel narratives are relentlessly driven forward, stopping in each locale for only the duration of an adventure before forcing their heroes to resume their wanderings. Through such restless wandering, travel literature, both factual and fiction, crisscrosses the world and thereby incorporates it into literature.

Worlds of the Imagination

Literature not only moves us to remote corners of the world and across landscapes; it also presents us with whole imagined worlds to which we as readers can travel. The construction of literary, clearly made-up worlds has always been a theme of world literature, which has suggested answers to fundamental questions, including how the world came into being. The Mayan epic *Popol Vuh,* featured in volume C, develops one of the most elaborate creation myths, including several attempts at creating humans (only the fourth is successful). In the same volume, Milton retells the biblical story of the Fall, but he also depicts the creation of new worlds, including earth, in a manner that is influenced by the discovery of the New World in the Western Hemisphere. For this new edition, the editors have decided to underline this theme, which also celebrates the world-creating power of language and literature, by placing a new cluster of creation myths, called "Creation and the Cosmos," at the very beginning of the anthology. The myths in this cluster resonate throughout the history of world literature, providing imaginative touchstones for later authors (such as Virgil, John Mandeville, Dante, and Goethe) to adapt and use in their own imaginative world-creation.

But world-creation, as highlighted in the new cluster, not only operates on a grand scale. It also occurs at moments when literature restricts itself to small, enclosed universes that are observed with minute attention. The great eighteenth-century Chinese novel *The Story of the Stone* by Cao Xuequin (presented in a new selection) withdraws to a family compound, whose walls it almost never leaves, to depict life in all its subtlety within this restricted space for several thousand pages. Sometimes we are invited into the even more circumscribed space of the narrator's own head, where we encounter strange and surreal worlds, as in the great modernist and postmodernist fictions from Franz Kafka and Jorge Luis Borges. By providing a thematic through-line, the new edition of the anthology reveals the myriad ways in which authors not only seek to explain our world but also compete with it by imagining new and different ones.

Genres

Over the millennia, literature has developed a set of rules and conventions that authors work with and against as they make decisions about subject matter, style, and form. These rules help us distinguish between different types of literature—that is, different genres. The broad view of literature afforded by the anthology, across both space and time, is particularly capable of showing how genres emerge and are transformed as they are used by different writers and for different purposes. The new edition of the anthology underscores this crucial dimension of literature by tracking the movement of genres—of, for example, the frame-tale narration from South Asia to northern Europe. To help readers recognize this theme, we have created ways of making genre visible. Lyric poetry is found everywhere in the anthology, from the foundational poetry anthologies of China to modern experiments, but it is the focus of specially designed clusters that cast light on medieval lyric; on how Petrarch's invention, the sonnet, is adopted by other writers; or, to turn to one of the world's most successful poetic genres, on the haiku. By the same token, a cluster on manifestos highlights modernism's most characteristic invention, with its shrill demands and aggressive layout. Among the genres, drama is perhaps the most difficult to grapple with because it is so closely entangled with theatrical performance. You don't understand a play unless you understand what kind of theater it was intended for, how it was performed, and how audiences watched it. To capture this dimension, we have grouped two of the most prominent regional drama traditions—Greek theater and East Asian drama—in their own sections.

Oral Literature

The relation of the spoken word to literature is perhaps the most important theme that emerges from these pages. All literature goes back to oral storytelling—all the foundational epics, from South Asia via Greece and Africa to Central America, are deeply rooted in oral storytelling; poetry's rhythms are best appreciated when heard; and drama, a form that comes alive in performance, continues to be engaged with an oral tradition. Throughout the anthology, we connect works to the oral traditions from which they sprang and remind readers that writing has coexisted with oral storytelling since the invention of the former. A new and important cluster in volume E on oral literature foregrounds this theme and showcases the nineteenth-century interest in oral traditions such as fairy and folk tales and slave stories. At the same time, this cluster, and the anthology as a whole, shows the importance of gaining literacy.

Varieties of Literature

In presenting everything from the earliest literatures to a (much-expanded) selection of contemporary literature reaching to the early twenty-first century, and from oral storytelling to literary experiments of the avant-garde, the anthology confronts us with the question not just of world literature, but of literature as such. We call attention to the changing nature of literature with new thematic clusters on literature in the early volumes, to give students and teachers access to how early writers from different cultures thought about literature. But the changing role and nature of literature are visible in the anthology as a whole. The world of Greek myth is seen by almost everyone as literary, even though it arose from ritual practices that are different from what we associate with literature. But this is even more the case with other texts, such as the Qur'an or the Bible, which still function as religious texts for many, while others appreciate them primarily or exclusively as literature. Some texts, such as those by Laozi (new addition) or Plato (in a new and expanded selection) or Kant (new addition) belong in philosophy, while others, such as the Declaration of Independence (new addition), are primarily political documents. Our modern conception of literature as imaginative literature, as fiction, is very recent, about two hundred years old. In this Third Edition, we have opted for a much-expanded conception of literature that includes creation myths, wisdom literature, religious texts, philosophy, political writing, and fairy tales in addition to plays, poems, and narrative fiction. This answers to an older definition of literature as writing of high quality. There are many texts of philosophy, or religion, or politics that are not remarkable or influential for their literary qualities and that would therefore have no place in an anthology of world literature. But the works presented here do: in addition to or as part of their other functions, they have acquired the status of literature.

This brings us to the last and perhaps most important question: When we study the world, why study it through its literature? Hasn't literature lost some of its luster for us, we who are faced with so many competing media and art forms? Like no other art form or medium, literature offers us a deep history of human thinking. As our illustration program shows, writing was invented not for the composition of literature, but for much more mundane purposes, such as the recording of ownership, contracts, or astronomical observations. But literature is writing's most glorious side-product. Because language expresses human consciousness, no other art form can capture the human past with the precision and scope of literature. Language shapes our thinking, and literature, the highest expression of language, plays an important role in that process, pushing the boundaries of what we can think, and how we think it. The other great advantage of literature is that it can be reactivated with each reading. The great architectural monuments of the past are now in ruins. Literature, too, often has to be excavated, as with many classical texts. But once a text has been found or reconstructed it can be experienced as if for the first time by new readers. Even though many of the literary texts collected in this anthology are at first strange, because they originated so very long ago, they still speak to today's readers with great eloquence and freshness.

Because works of world literature are alive today, they continue to elicit strong emotions and investments. The epic *Rāmāyana*, for example, plays an important role in the politics of India, where it has been used to bolster Hindu nationalism, just as the *Bhagavad-Gītā*, here in a new translation, continues to be a moral touchstone in the ethical deliberation about war. Saddam Hussein wrote an updated version of the *Epic of Gilgamesh*. And the three religions of the book, Judaism, Christianity, and Islam, make our selections from their scriptures a more than historical exercise. China has recently elevated the sayings of Confucius, whose influence on Chinese attitudes about the state had waned in the twentieth century, creating Confucius Institutes all over the world to promote Chinese culture in what is now called New Confucianism. The debates about the role of the church and secularism, which we highlight through a new cluster and selections in all volumes, have become newly important in current deliberations on the relation between church and state. World literature is never neutral. We know its relevance precisely by the controversies it inspires.

Going back to the earliest moments of cultural contact and moving forward to the global flows of the twenty-first century, *The Norton Anthology of World Literature* attempts to provide a deep history. But it is a special type of history: a literary one. World literature is grounded in the history of the world, but it is

also the history of imagining this world; it is a history n
pened, but also of how humans imagined their place in
We, the editors of this Third Edition, can think of no b
young people for a global future than through a deep and
tion of world literature. Evliya Çelebi sums up his explor
"marvelous and wonderful adventure"—we hope that reade
about the adventure in reading made possible by this antholo
to it for the rest of their lives.

also the history of imagining this world: it is a history not just of wh[illegible] pened, but also of how humans imagined their place in the midst of his[illegible] We, the editors of this Third Edition, can think of no better way to prepa[illegible] young people for a global future than through a deep and meaningful exploration of world literature. Evliya Çelebi sums up his exploration of Vienna as a "marvelous and wonderful adventure"—we hope that readers will feel the same about the adventure in reading made possible by this anthology and will return to it for the rest of their lives.

About the Third Edition

New Selections and Translations

This Third Edition represents a thoroughgoing, top-to-bottom revision of the anthology that altered nearly every section in important ways. Following is a list of the new sections and works, in order:

VOLUME A

A new cluster, "Creation and the Cosmos," and a new grouping, "Ancient Egyptian Literature" • Benjamin Foster's translation of *Gilgamesh* • Selections from chapters 12, 17, 28, 29, 31, and 50 of Genesis, and from chapters 19 and 20 of Exodus • All selections from Genesis, Exodus, and Job are newly featured in Robert Alter's translation, and chapter 25 of Genesis (Jacob spurning his birthright) is presented in a graphic visualization by R. Crumb based on Alter's translation • Homer's *Iliad* and *Odyssey* are now featured in Stanley Lombardo's highly regarded translations • A selection of Aesop's *Fables* • A new selection and a new translation of Sappho's lyrics • A new grouping, "Ancient Athenian Drama," gathers together the three major Greek tragedians and Aristophanes • New translations of *Oedipus the King*, *Antigone* (both by Robert Bagg), *Medea* (by Diane Arnson Svarlien), and *Lysistrata* (by Sarah Ruden) • A new cluster, "Travel and Conquest" • Plato's *Symposium* • A new selection of Catullus's poems, in a new translation by Peter Green • *The Aeneid* is now featured in Robert Fagles's career-topping translation • New selections from book 1 of Ovid's *Metamorphoses* join the previous selection, now featured in Charles Martin's recent translation • A new cluster, "Speech, Writing, Poetry," features ancient Egyptian writings on writing • A new tale from the Indian *Jātaka* • New selections from the Chinese *Classic of Poetry* • Confucius's *Analects* now in a new translation by Simon Leys • *Daodejing* • New selections from the Chinese *Songs of the South* • Chinese historian Sima Qian • A new cluster, "Speech, Writing, and Poetry in Early China," features selections by Confucius, Zhuangzi, and Han Feizi.

VOLUME B

Selections from the Christian Bible now featured in a new translation by Richmond Lattimore • A selection from book 3 of Apuleius's *The Golden Ass* • Selections from the Qur'an now featured in Abdel Haleem's translation • A new selection from Abolqasem Ferdowsi's *Shahnameh*, in a new translation by Dick Davis • Avicenna • Petrus Alfonsi • Additional material from Marie de France's *Lais*, in a translation by Robert Hanning and Joan Ferrante • An expanded selection of poems fills out the "Medieval Lyrics" cluster • Dante's *Divine Comedy* now featured in Mark Musa's translation • The Ethiopian

Kebra Nagast • An expanded selection from Boccaccio's *Decameron*, in a new translation by Wayne Rebhorn • A new translation by Sheila Fisher of Chaucer's *Canterbury Tales* • *Sir Gawain and the Green Knight* now featured in a new translation by Simon Armitage • Christine de Pizan's *Book of the City of Ladies* • A new cluster, "Travel and Encounter," features selections from Marco Polo, Ibn Battuta, and John Mandeville • New selections in fresh translations of classical Tamil and Sanskrit lyric poetry • New selections and translations of Chinese lyric poetry • A new cluster, "Literature about Literature," in the Medieval Chinese Literature section • Refreshed selections and new translations of lyric poetry in "Japan's Classical Age" • Selection from Ki No Tsurayuki's *Tosa Diary* • A new translation by Meredith McKinney of Sei Shōnagon's *Pillow Book* • A new, expanded selection from, and a new translation of, Murasaki Shikibu's *The Tale of Genji* • New selections from *The Tales of the Heike*, in Burton Watson's newly included translation.

VOLUME C

A new translation by David C. Conrad of the West African epic *Sunjata* • *The Book of Dede Korkut* • A new selection from Evliya Çelebi's *The Book of Travels*, never before translated into English, now in Gottfried Hagen's translation • New selection of Indian lyric poetry by Basavaṇṇā, Mahādevīyakkā, Kabir, Mīrabāī, and Tukaram, in fresh new translations • Two new clusters, "Humanism and the Rediscovery of the Classical Past" and "Petrarch and the Love Lyric," open the new section "Europe and the New World" • Sir Thomas More's *Utopia* in its entirety • Story 10 newly added to the selection of Marguerite de Navarre's *Heptameron* • *Lazarillo de Tormes* included in its entirety • A new cluster, "The Encounter of Europe and the New World" • Lope de Vega's *Fuenteovejuna* now featured in Gregary Racz's recent translation • A new cluster, "God, Church, and Self."

VOLUME D

A new section, "East Asian Drama," brings together four examples of Asian drama from the fourteenth through nineteenth centuries, including Zeami's *Atsumori*, Kong Shangren's *The Peach Blossom Fan* (in a new translation by Stephen Owen), and two newly included works: Chikamatsu's *Love Suicides at Amijima* and the Korean drama *Song of Ch'un-hyang* • A new cluster, "What Is Enlightenment?" • Molière's *Tartuffe* now featured in a new translation by Constance Congdon and Virginia Scott • Aphra Behn's *Oroonoko; or, The Royal Slave*, complete • New selections by Sor Juana Inés de la Cruz, in a new translation by Electa Arenal and Amanda Powell • An expanded, refreshed selection from Cao Xueqin's *The Story of the Stone*, part of which is now featured in John Minford's translation • Ihara Saikaku's *Life of a Sensuous Woman* • A new cluster, "The World of Haiku," features work by Kitamura Kigin, Matsuo Bashō, Morikawa Kyoriku, and Yosa Buson.

VOLUME E

A new cluster, "Revolutionary Contexts," features selections from the Declaration of Independence, the Declaration of the Rights of Man and of the Citizen, and the Declaration of Sentiments from the Seneca Falls convention, as well as pieces by Olympe de Gouges, Edmund Burke, Jean-Jacques Dessalines, William Wordsworth, and Simón Bólivar • New selection from book 2 of Rousseau's *Confessions* • Olaudah Equiano's *Interesting Narrative* • Goethe's *Faust* now featured in Martin Greenberg's translation • Selections from Domingo Sarmiento's *Facundo* • A new grouping, "Romantic Poets and Their Successors," features a generous sampling of lyric poetry from the period, including new poems by Anna Laetitia Barbauld, William Wordsworth, Samuel Taylor Coleridge, Anna Bunina, Andrés Bello, John Keats, Heinrich Heine, Elizabeth Barrett Browning, Tennyson, Robert Browning, Walt Whitman, Christina Rossetti, Rosalía de Castro, and José Martí, as well as an exciting new translation of Arthur Rimbaud's *Illuminations* by John Ashbery • From Vietnam, Nguyễn Du's *The Tale of Kiều* • A new selection and all new translations of Ghalib's poetry by Vinay Dharwadker • Liu E's *The Travels of Lao Can* • Two pieces by Pandita Ramabai • Flaubert's *A Simple Heart* • Ibsen's *Hedda Gabler*, now featured in a new translation by Rick Davis and Brian Johnston • Machado de Assis's *The Rod of Justice* • Chekhov's *The Cherry Orchard*, now featured in a new translation by Paul Schmidt • Tagore's *Kabuliwala* • Higuchi Ichiyō's *Separate Ways* • A new cluster, "Orature," with German, English, Irish, and Hawaiian folktales; Anansi stories from Ghana, Jamaica, and the United States; as well as slave songs, stories, and spirituals, Malagasy wisdom poetry, and the Navajo Night Chant.

VOLUME F

Joseph Conrad's *Heart of Darkness* • Tanizaki's *The Tattooer* • Selection from Marcel Proust's *Remembrance of Things Past* now featured in Lydia Davis's critically acclaimed translation • Franz Kafka's *The Metamorphosis* now featured in Michael Hofmann's translation • Lu Xun, *Medicine* • Akutagawa's *In a Bamboo Grove* • Kawabata's *The Izu Dancer* • Chapter 1 of Woolf's *A Room of One's Own* newly added to the selections from chapters 2 and 3 • Two new Faulkner stories: "Spotted Horses" and "Barn Burning" • Kushi Fusako, *Memoirs of a Declining Ryukyuan Woman* • Lao She, *An Old and Established Name* • Ch'ae Man-Sik, *My Innocent Uncle* • Zhang Ailing's *Sealed Off* • Constantine Cavafy • Octavio Paz • A new cluster, "Manifestos" • Julio Cortazár • Tadeusz Borowski's *This Way for the Gas, Ladies and Gentlemen*, in a new translation by Barbara Vedder • Paul Celan • Saadat Hasan Manto • James Baldwin • Vladimir Nabokov • Tayeb Salih • Chinua Achebe's *Chike's School Days* • Carlos Fuentes • Mahmoud Darwish • Seamus Heaney • Ama Ata Aidoo • V. S. Naipaul • Ngugi Wa Thiong'o • Bessie Head • Ōe Kenzaburō • Salman Rushdie • Mahasweta Devi's *Giribala* • Hanan Al-Shaykh • Toni Morrison • Mo Yan • Niyi Osundare • Nguyen Huy Thiep • Isabel Allende • Chu T'ien-Hsin • Junot Díaz • Roberto Bolaño • J. M. Coetzee • Orhan Pamuk.

Supplements for Instructors and Students

Norton is pleased to provide instructors and students with several supplements to make the study and teaching of world literature an even more interesting and rewarding experience:

Instructor Resource Folder

A new Instructor Resource Folder features images and video clips that allow instructors to enhance their lectures with some of the sights and sounds of world literature and its contexts.

Instructor Course Guide

Teaching with The Norton Anthology of World Literature: *A Guide for Instructors* provides teaching plans, suggestions for in-class activities, discussion topics and writing projects, and extensive lists of scholarly and media resources.

Coursepacks

Available in a variety of formats, Norton coursepacks bring digital resources into a new or existing online course. Coursepacks are free to instructors, easy to download and install, and available in a variety of formats, including Blackboard, Desire2Learn, Angel, and Moodle.

StudySpace (wwnorton.com/nawol)

This free student companion site features a variety of complementary materials to help students read and study world literature. Among them are reading-comprehension quizzes, quick-reference summaries of the anthology's introductions, review quizzes, an audio glossary to help students pronounce names and terms, tours of some of the world's important cultural landmarks, timelines, maps, and other contextual materials.

Writing about World Literature

Written by Karen Gocsik, Executive Director of the Writing Program at Dartmouth College, in collaboration with faculty in the world literature program at the University of Nevada, Las Vegas, *Writing about World Literature* provides course-specific guidance for writing papers and essay exams in the world literature course.

For more information about any of these supplements, instructors should contact their local Norton representative.

Acknowledgments

The editors would like to thank the following people, who have provided invaluable assistance by giving us sage advice, important encouragement, and help with the preparation of the manuscript: Sara Akbari, Alannah de Barra, Wendy Belcher, Jodi Bilinkoff, Freya Brackett, Psyche Brackett, Michaela Bronstein, Amanda Claybaugh, Rachel Carroll, Lewis Cook, David Damrosch, Dick Davis, Amanda Detry, Anthony Domestico, Merve Emre, Maria Fackler, Guillermina de Ferrari, Karina Galperín, Stanton B. Garner, Kimberly Dara Gordon, Elyse Graham, Stephen Greenblatt, Sara Guyer, Langdon Hammer, Iain Higgins, Mohja Kahf, Peter Kornicki, Paul Kroll, Lydia Liu, Bala Venkat Mani, Ann Matter, Barry McCrea, Alexandra McCullough-Garcia, Rachel McGuiness, Jon McKenzie, Mary Mullen, Djibril Tamsir Niane, Felicity Nussbaum, Andy Orchard, John Peters, Daniel Taro Poch, Daniel Potts, Megan Quigley, Imogen Roth, Catherine de Rose, Ellen Sapega, Jesse Schotter, Stephen Scully, Brian Stock, Tomi Suzuki, Joshua Taft, Sara Torres, Lisa Voigt, Kristen Wanner, and Emily Weissbourd.

All the editors would like to thank the wonderful people at Norton, principally our editor Pete Simon, the driving force behind this whole undertaking, as well as Marian Johnson (Managing Editor, College), Alice Falk, Michael Fleming, Katharine Ings, Susan Joseph, Barney Latimer, and Diane Cipollone (Copyeditors), Conor Sullivan (Assistant Editor), Megan Jackson (College Permissions Manager), Margaret Gorenstein (Permissions), Patricia Marx (Art Research Director), Debra Morton Hoyt (Art Director; cover design), Rubina Yeh (Design Director), Jo Anne Metsch (Designer; interior text design), Adrian Kitzinger (cartography), Agnieszka Gasparska (timeline design), Eileen Connell, (Media Editor), Jennifer Barnhardt (Editorial Assistant, Media), Laura Musich (Associate Editor; Instructor's Guide), Benjamin Reynolds (Production Manager), and Kim Bowers (Marketing Manager, Literature) and Ashley Cain (Humanities Sales Specialist).

This anthology represents a collaboration not only among the editors and their close advisors, but also among the thousands of instructors who teach from the anthology and provide valuable and constructive guidance to the publisher and editors. *The Norton Anthology of World Literature* is as much their book as it is ours, and we are grateful to everyone who has cared enough about this anthology to help make it better. We're especially grateful to the more than five hundred professors of world literature who responded to an online survey in early 2008, whom we have listed below. Thank you all.

Michel Aaij (Auburn University Montgomery); Sandra Acres (Mississippi Gulf Coast Community College); Larry Adams (University of North Alabama); Mary Adams (Western Carolina University); Stephen Adams (Westfield State

College); Roberta Adams (Roger Williams University); Kirk Adams (Tarrant County College); Kathleen Aguero (Pine Manor College); Richard Albright (Harrisburg Area Community College); Deborah Albritton (Jefferson Davis Community College); Todd Aldridge (Auburn University); Judith Allen-Leventhal (College of Southern Maryland); Carolyn Amory (Binghamton University); Kenneth Anania (Massasoit Community College); Phillip Anderson (University of Central Arkansas); Walter Anderson (University of Arkansas at Little Rock); Vivienne Anderson (North Carolina Wesleyan College); Susan Andrade (University of Pittsburgh); Kit Andrews (Western Oregon University); Joe Antinarella (Tidewater Community College); Nancy Applegate (Georgia Highlands College); Sona Aronian (University of Rhode Island); Sona Aronian (University of Rhode Island); Eugene Arva (University of Miami); M. G. Aune (California University of Pennsylvania); Carolyn Ayers (Saint Mary's University of Minnesota); Diana Badur (Black Hawk College); Susan Bagby (Longwood University); Maryam Barrie (Washtenaw Community College); Maria Baskin (Alamance Community College); Samantha Batten (Auburn University); Charles Beach (Nyack College); Michael Beard (University of North Dakota); Bridget Beaver (Connors State College); James Bednarz (C. W. Post College); Khani Begum (Bowling Green State University); Albert Bekus (Austin Peay State University); Lynne Belcher (Southern Arkansas University); Karen Bell (Delta State University); Elisabeth Ly Bell (University of Rhode Island); Angela Belli (St. John's University); Leo Benardo (Baruch College); Paula Berggren (Baruch College, CUNY); Frank Bergmann (Utica College); Nancy Blomgren (Volunteer State Community College); Scott Boltwood (Emory & Henry College); Ashley Bonds (Copiah-Lincoln Community College); Thomas Bonner (Xavier University of Louisiana); Debbie Boyd (East Central Community College); Norman Boyer (Saint Xavier University); Nodya Boyko (Auburn University); Robert Brandon (Rockingham Community College); Alan Brasher (East Georgia College); Harry Brent (Baruch College); Charles Bressler (Indiana Wesleyan University); Katherine Brewer; Mary Ruth Brindley (Mississippi Delta Community College); Mamye Britt (Georgia Perimeter College); Gloria Brooks (Tyler Junior College); Monika Brown (University of North Carolina–Pembroke); Greg Bryant (Highland Community College); Austin Busch (SUNY Brockport); Barbara Cade (Texas College); Karen Caig (University of Arkansas Community College at Morrilton); Jonizo Cain-Calloway (Del Mar College); Mark Calkins (San Francisco State University); Catherine Calloway (Arkansas State University); Mechel Camp (Jackson State Community College); Robert Canary (University of Wisconsin–Parkside); Stephen Canham (University of Hawaii at Manoa); Marian Carcache (Auburn University); Alfred Carson (Kennesaw State University); Farrah Cato (University of Central Florida); Biling Chen (University of Central Arkansas); Larry Chilton (Blinn College); Eric Chock (University of Hawaii at West Oahu); Cheryl Clark (Miami Dade College–Wolfson Campus); Sarah Beth Clark (Holmes Community College); Jim Cody (Brookdale Community College); Carol Colatrella (Georgia Institute of Technology); Janelle Collins (Arkansas State University); Theresa Collins (St. John's University); Susan Comfort (Indiana University of Pennsylvania); Kenneth Cook (National Park Community College); Angie Cook (Cisco Junior College); Yvonne Cooper (Pierce College); Brenda Cornell (Central Texas College); Judith Cortelloni (Lincoln College); Robert Cosgrove (Saddleback College); Rosemary Cox (Georgia Perimeter College);

Daniel Cozart (Georgia Perimeter College); Brenda Craven (Fort Hays State University); Susan Crisafulli (Franklin College); Janice Crosby (Southern University); Randall Crump (Kennesaw State University); Catherine Cucinella (California State University San Marcos); T. Allen Culpepper (Manatee Community College–Venice); Rodger Cunningham (Alice Lloyd College); Lynne Dahmen (Purdue University); Patsy J. Daniels (Jackson State University); James Davis (Troy University); Evan Davis (Southwestern Oregon Community College); Margaret Dean (Eastern Kentucky University); JoEllen DeLucia (John Jay College, CUNY); Hivren Demir-Atay (Binghamton University); Rae Ann DeRosse (University of North Carolina–Greensboro); Anna Crowe Dewart (College of Coastal Georgia); Joan Digby (C. W. Post Campus Long Island University); Diana Dominguez (University of Texas at Brownsville); Dee Douglas-Jones (Winston-Salem State University); Jeremy Downes (Auburn University); Denell Downum (Suffolk University); Sharon Drake (Texarkana College); Damian Dressick (Robert Morris University); Clyburn Duder (Concordia University Texas); Dawn Duncan (Concordia College); Kendall Dunkelberg (Mississippi University for Women); Janet Eber (County College of Morris); Emmanuel Egar (University of Arkansas at Pine Bluff); David Eggebrecht (Concordia University of Wisconsin); Sarah Eichelman (Walters State Community College); Hank Eidson (Georgia Perimeter College); Monia Eisenbraun (Oglala Lakota College/Cheyenne-Eagle Butte High School); Dave Elias (Eastern Kentucky University); Chris Ellery (Angelo State University); Christina Elvidge (Marywood University); Ernest Enchelmayer (Arkansas Tech University); Niko Endres (Western Kentucky University); Kathrynn Engberg (Alabama A&M University); Chad Engbers (Calvin College); Edward Eriksson (Suffolk Community College); Donna Estill (Alabama Southern Community College); Andrew Ettin (Wake Forest University); Jim Everett (Mississippi College); Gene Fant (Union University); Nathan Faries (University of Dubuque); Martin Fashbaugh (Auburn University); Donald J. Fay (Kennesaw State University); Meribeth Fell (College of Coastal Georgia); David Fell (Carroll Community College); Jill Ferguson (San Francisco Conservatory of Music); Susan French Ferguson (Mountain View Comumunity College); Robyn Ferret (Cascadia Community College); Colin Fewer (Purdue Calumet); Hannah Fischthal (St. John's University); Jim Fisher (Peninsula College); Gene Fitzgerald (University of Utah); Monika Fleming (Edgecombe Community College); Phyllis Fleming (Patrick Henry Community College); Francis Fletcher (Folsom Lake College); Denise Folwell (Montgomery College); Ulanda Forbess (North Lake College); Robert Forman (St. John's University); Suzanne Forster (University of Alaska–Anchorage); Patricia Fountain (Coastal Carolina Community College); Kathleen Fowler (Surry Community College); Sheela Free (San Bernardino Valley College); Lea Fridman (Kingsborough Community College); David Galef (Montclair State University); Paul Gallipeo (Adirondack Community College); Jan Gane (University of North Carolina–Pembroke); Jennifer Garlen (University of Alabama–Huntsville); Anita Garner (University of North Alabama); Elizabeth Gassel (Darton College); Patricia Gaston (West Virginia University, Parkersburg); Marge Geiger (Cuyahoga Community College); Laura Getty (North Georgia College & State University); Amy Getty (Grand View College); Leah Ghiradella (Middlesex County College); Dick Gibson (Jacksonville University); Teresa Gibson (University of Texas–Brownsville); Wayne Gilbert (Community College of Aurora); Sandra Giles (Abraham Baldwin Agricultural College); Pamela Gist (Cedar Valley College); Suzanne Gitonga (North Lake College); James Glickman (Community College of Rhode Island); R. James Goldstein (Auburn University); Jennifer Golz (Tennessee Tech University); Marian Goodin (North Central Missouri College); Susan Gorman (Massachusetts College of Pharmacy and Health Sciences); Anissa Graham (University of North Alabama); Eric Gray (St. Gregory's University); Geoffrey Green (San Francisco State University); Russell Greer (Texas Woman's University); Charles Grey (Albany State University); Frank Gruber (Bergen Community College); Alfonso Guerriero Jr. (Baruch College, CUNY); Letizia Guglielmo (Kennesaw State University); Nira Gupta-Casale (Kean University); Gary Gutchess (SUNY Tompkins Cortland Community College); William Hagen (Oklahoma Baptist University); John Hagge (Iowa State University); Julia Hall (Henderson State University); Margaret Hallissy (C. W. Post Campus Long Island University); Laura Hammons (Hinds Community College); Nancy Hancock (Austin Peay State University); Carol Harding (Western Oregon University); Cynthia Hardy (University of Alaska–Fairbanks); Steven Harthorn (Williams Baptist College); Stanley Hauer (University of Southern Mississippi); Leean Hawkins (National Park Community College); Kayla Haynie (Harding University); Maysa Hayward (Ocean County College); Karen Head (Georgia Institute of Technology); Sandra Kay Heck (Walters State Community College); Frances Helphinstine (Morehead State University); Karen Henck (Eastern Nazarene College); Betty Fleming Hendricks (University of Arkansas); Yndaleci Hinojosa (Northwest Vista College); Richard Hishmeh (Palomar College); Ruth Hoberman (Eastern Illinois University); Rebecca Hogan (University of Wisconsin–Whitewater); Mark Holland (East Tennessee State University); John Holmes (Virginia State University); Sandra Holstein (Southern Oregon University); Fran Holt (Georgia Perimeter College–Clarkston); William Hood (North Central Texas College); Glenn Hopp (Howard Payne University); George Horneker (Arkansas State University); Barbara Howard (Central Bible College); Pamela Howell (Midland College); Melissa Hull (Tennessee State University); Barbara Hunt (Columbus State University); Leeann Hunter (University of South Florida); Gill Hunter (Eastern Kentucky University); Helen Huntley (California Baptist University); Luis Iglesias (University of Southern Mississippi); Judith Irvine (Georgia State University); Miglena Ivanova (Coastal Carolina University); Kern Jackson (University of South Alabama); Kenneth Jackson (Yale University); M. W. Jackson (St. Bonaventure University); Robb Jackson (Texas A&M University–Corpus Christi); Karen Jacobsen (Valdosta State University); Maggie Jaffe (San Diego State University); Robert Jakubovic (Raymond Walters College); Stokes James (University of Wisconsin–Stevens Point); Beverly Jamison (South Carolina State University); Ymitri Jayasundera-Mathison (Prairie View A&M University); Katarzyna Jerzak (University of Georgia); Alice Jewell (Harding University); Elizabeth Jones (Auburn University); Jeff Jones (University of Idaho); Dan Jones (Walters State Community College); Mary Kaiser (Jefferson State Community College); James Keller (Middlesex County College); Jill Keller (Middlesex Community College); Tim Kelley (Northwest-Shoals Community College); Andrew Kelley (Jackson State Community College); Hans Kellner (North Carolina State); Brian Kennedy (Pasadena City College); Shirin Khanmohamadi (San Francisco State University); Jeremy Kiene (McDaniel College); Mary Catherine Kiliany (Robert Morris University); Sue Kim (Univ Birmingham); Pam Kingsbury (University of North Alabam (University of California, Santa Cruz); Lydia Kualapai (Schrein Kumar (University of Cincinnati); Roger Ladd (University Pembroke); Daniel Lane (Norwich University); Erica Lara Junior College); Leah Larson (Our Lady of the Lake Unive (Ocean County College); Shanon Lawson (Pikes Peak Co College); Michael Leddy (Eastern Illinois University); Eric Leuschner (Fort Hays State University); Patricia Licklider (John Jay College, CUNY); Pamela Light (Rochester College); Alison Ligon (Morehouse College); Linda Linzey (Southeastern University); Thomas Lisk (North Carolina State University); Matthew Livesey (University of Wisconsin–Stout); Vickie Lloyd (University of Arkansas Community College at Hope); Judy Lloyd (Southside Virginia Community College); Mary Long (Ouachita Baptist University); Rick Lott (Arkansas State University); Scott Lucas (The Citadel); Katrine Lvovskaya (Rutgers University); Carolin Lynn (Mercyhurst College); Susan Lyons (University of Connecticut—Avery Point); William Thomas MacCary (Hofstra University); Richard Mace (Pace University); Peter Marbais (Mount Olive College); Lacy Marschalk (Auburn University); Seth Martin (Harrisburg Area Community College–Lancaster); Carter Mathes (Rutgers University); Rebecca Mathews (University of Connecticut); Marsha Mathews (Dalton State College); Darren Mathews (Grambling State University); Corine Mathis (Auburn University); Ken McAferty (Pensacola State College); Jeff McAlpine (Clackamas Community College); Kelli McBride (Seminole State College); Kay McClellan (South Plains College); Michael McClung (Northwest-Shoals Community College); Michael McClure (Virginia State University); Jennifer McCune (University of Central Arkansas); Kathleen McDonald (Norwich University); Charles McDonnell (Piedmont Technical College); Nancy McGee (Macomb Community College); Gregory McNamara (Clayton State University); Abby Mendelson (Point Park University); Ken Meyers (Wilson Community College); Barbara Mezeske (Hope College); Brett Millan (South Texas College); Sheila Miller (Hinds Community College); David Miller (Mississippi College); Matt Miller (University of South Carolina–Aiken); Yvonne Milspaw (Harrisburg Area Community College); Ruth Misheloff (Baruch College); Lamata Mitchell (Rock Valley College); D'Juana Montgomery (Southwestern Assemblies of God University); Lorne Mook (Taylor University); Renee Moore (Mississippi Delta Community College); Dan Morgan (Scott Community College); Samantha Morgan-Curtis (Tennessee State University); Beth Morley (Collin College); Vicki Moulson (College of the Albemarle); L. Carl Nadeau (University of Saint Francis); Wayne Narey (Arkansas State University); LeAnn Nash (Texas A&M University–Commerce); Leanne Nayden (University of Evansville); Jim Neilson (Wake Technical Community College); Jeff Nelson (University of Alabama–Huntsville); Mary Nelson (Dallas Baptist University); Deborah Nester (Northwest Florida State College); William Netherton (Amarillo College); William Newman (Perimeter College); Adele Newson-Horst (Missouri State University); George Nicholas (Benedictine College); Dana Nichols (Gainesville State College); Mark Nicoll-Johnson (Merced College); John Mark Nielsen (Dana College); Michael Nifong (Georgia College & State University); Laura Noell (North Virginia Community College); Bonnie Noonan (Xavier University of Louisiana); Patricia Noone (College of

. Saint Vincent); Paralee Norman (Northwestern State University–Leesville); nk Novak (Pepperdine University); Kevin O'Brien (Chapman University); arah Odishoo (Columbia College Chicago); Samuel Olorounto (New River Community College); Jamili Omar (Lone Star College–CyFair); Michael Orlofsky (Troy University); Priscilla Orr (Sussex County Community College); Jim Owen (Columbus State University); Darlene Pagan (Pacific University); Yolanda Page (University of Arkansas–Pine Bluff); Lori Paige (Westfield State College); Linda Palumbo (Cerritos College); Joseph Parry (Brigham Young University); Carla Patterson (Georgia Highlands College); Andra Pavuls (Davenport University); Sunita Peacock (Slippery Rock University); Velvet Pearson (Long Beach City College); Joe Pellegrino (Georgia Southern University); Sonali Perera (Rutgers University); Clem Perez (St. Philip's College); Caesar Perkowski (Gordon College); Gerald Perkus (Collin College); John Peters (University of North Texas); Lesley Peterson (University of North Alabama); Judy Peterson (John Tyler Community College); Sandra Petree (Northwestern Oklahoma State University); Angela Pettit (Tarrant County College NE); Michell Phifer (University of Texas–Arlington); Ziva Piltch (Rockland Community College); Nancy Popkin (Harris-Stowe State University); Marlana Portolano (Towson University); Rhonda Powers (Auburn University); Lisa Propst (University of West Georgia); Melody Pugh (Wheaton College); Jonathan Purkiss (Pulaski Technical College); Patrick Quinn (College of Southern Nevada); Peter Rabinowitz (Hamilton College); Evan Radcliffe (Villanova University); Jody Ragsdale (Northeast Alabama Community College); Ken Raines (Eastern Arizona College); Gita Rajan (Fairfield University); Elizabeth Rambo (Campbell University); Richard Ramsey (Indiana University–Purdue University Fort Wayne); Jonathan Randle (Mississippi College); Amy Randolph (Waynesburg University); Rodney Rather (Tarrant County College Northwest); Helaine Razovsky (Northwestern State University); Rachel Reed (Auburn University); Karin Rhodes (Salem State College); Donald R. Riccomini (Santa Clara University); Christina Roberts (Otero Junior College); Paula Robison (Temple University); Jean Roelke (University of North Texas); Barrie Rosen (St. John's University); James Rosenberg (Point Park University); Sherry Rosenthal (College of Southern Nevada); Daniel Ross (Columbus State University); Maria Rouphail (North Carolina State University); Lance Rubin (Arapahoe Community College); Mary Ann Rygiel (Auburn University); Geoffrey Sadock (Bergen Community College); Allen Salerno (Auburn University); Mike Sanders (Kent State University); Deborah Scally (Richland College); Margaret Scanlan (Indiana University South Bend); Michael Schaefer (University of Central Arkansas); Tracy Schaelen (Southwestern College); Daniel Schenker (University of Alabama–Huntsville); Robyn Schiffman (Fairleigh Dickinson University); Roger Schmidt (Idaho State University); Robert Schmidt (Tarrant County College–Northwest Campus); Adrianne Schot (Weatherford College); Pamela Schuman (Brookhaven College); Sharon Seals (Ouachita Technical College); Su Senapati (Abraham Baldwin Agricultural College); Phyllis Senfleben (North Shore Community College); Theda Shapiro (University of California–Riverside); Mary Sheldon (Washburn University); Donald Shull (Freed-Hardeman University); Ellen Shull (Palo Alto College); Conrad Shumaker (University of Central Arkansas); Sara Shumaker (University of Central Arkansas); Dave Shuping (Spartanburg Methodist College); Horacio Sierra (University of Florida); Scott Simkins (Auburn University); Bruce

Simon (SUNY Fredonia); LaRue Sloan (University of Louisiana–Monroe); Peter Smeraldo (Caldwell College); Renee Smith (Lamar University); Victoria Smith (Texas State University); Connie Smith (College of St. Joseph); Grant Smith (Eastern Washington University); Mary Karen Solomon (Coloardo NW Community College); Micheline Soong (Hawaii Pacific University); Leah Souffrant (Baruch College, CUNY); Cindy Spangler (Faulkner University); Charlotte Speer (Bevill State Community College); John Staines (John Jay College, CUNY); Tanja Stampfl (Louisiana State University); Scott Starbuck (San Diego Mesa College); Kathryn Stasio (Saint Leo University); Joyce Stavick (North Georgia College & State University); Judith Steele (Mid-America Christian University); Stephanie Stephens (Howard College); Rachel Sternberg (Case Western Reserve University); Holly Sterner (College of Coastal Georgia); Karen Stewart (Norwich University); Sioux Stoeckle (Palo Verde College); Ron Stormer (Culver-Stockton College); Frank Stringfellow (University of Miami); Ayse Stromsdorfer (Soldan I. S. H. S.); Ashley Strong-Green (Paine College); James Sullivan (Illinois Central College); Zohreh Sullivan (University of Illinois); Richard Sullivan (Worcester State College); Duke Sutherland (Mississippi Gulf Coast Community College/Jackson County Campus); Maureen Sutton (Kean University); Marianne Szlyk (Montgomery College); Rebecca Taksel (Point Park University); Robert Tally (Texas State University); Tim Tarkington (Georgia Perimeter College); Patricia Taylor (Western Kentucky University); Mary Ann Taylor (Mountain View College); Susan Tekulve (Converse College); Stephen Teller (Pittsburgh State University); Stephen Thomas (Community College of Denver); Freddy Thomas (Virginia State University); Andy Thomason (Lindenwood University); Diane Thompson (Northern Virginia Community College); C. H. Thornton (Northwest-Shoals Community College); Elizabeth Thornton (Georgia Perimeter); Burt Thorp (University of North Dakota); Willie Todd (Clark Atlanta University); Martin Trapp (Northwestern Michigan College); Brenda Tuberville (University of Texas–Tyler); William Tucker (Olney Central College); Martha Turner (Troy University); Joya Uraizee (Saint Louis University); Randal Urwiller (Texas College); Emily Uzendoski (Central Community College–Columbus Campus); Kenneth Van Dover (Lincoln University); Kay Walter (University of Arkansas–Monticello); Cassandra Ward-Shah (West Chester University); Gina Weaver (Southern Nazarene University); Cathy Webb (Meridian Community College); Eric Weil (Elizabeth City State University); Marian Wernicke (Pensacola Junior College); Robert West (Mississippi State University); Cindy Wheeler (Georgia Highlands College); Chuck Whitchurch (Golden West College); Julianne White (Arizona State University); Denise White (Kennesaw State University); Amy White (Lee University); Patricia White (Norwich University); Gwen Whitehead (Lamar State College–Orange); Terri Whitney (North Shore Community College); Tamora Whitney (Creighton University); Stewart Whittemore (Auburn University); Johannes Wich-Schwarz (Maryville University); Charles Wilkinson (Southwest Tennessee Community College); Donald Williams (Toccoa Falls College); Rick Williams (Rogue Community College); Lea Williams (Norwich University); Susan Willis (Auburn University–Montgomery); Sharon Wilson (University of Northern Colorado); J. D. Wireman (Indiana State University); Rachel Wiren (Baptist Bible College); Bertha Wise (Oklahoma City Community College); Sallie Wolf (Arapahoe Community College); Rebecca Wong (James Madison University); Donna

Woodford-Gormley (New Mexico Highlands University); Paul Woodruff (University of Texas–Austin); William Woods (Wichita State University); Marjorie Woods (University of Texas–Austin); Valorie Worthy (Ohio University); Wei Yan (Darton College); Teresa Young (Philander Smith College); Darcy Zabel (Friends University); Michelle Zenor (Lon Morris College); and Jacqueline Zubeck (College of Mount Saint Vincent).

THE NORTON ANTHOLOGY OF

WORLD LITERATURE

THIRD EDITION

VOLUME A

I

Ancient Mediterranean and Near Eastern Literature

THE INVENTION OF WRITING AND THE EARLIEST LITERATURES

The word "literature" comes from the Latin for "letters." "Oral literature" is therefore a contradiction in terms. Most modern westerners assume that literature is something we read in books; it is, by definition, written language. But people told stories and sang songs long before they had any means to record them. Oral types of song, poetry, and storytelling are quite different from those produced by writing, and it is difficult for us, living in an age dominated by printed and digital language, to imagine a world where nobody could read or write. Preliterate societies had different intellectual values from our own. We tend to think that a "good" story or essay is one that is neatly organized, original, and free from obvious repetition; we think of clichés as a mark of bad writing. But people without literacy tend to love stock phrases, traditional sayings, and proverbs. They are an essential mechanism by which cultural memory is preserved. Before writing, there was no such thing as an "author"—a single individual who, all alone, creates a text to be experienced by a solitary, silent reader. Instead,

King Priam asks Achilles for the body of his son, Hector. From an archaic Greek bronze relief, ca. 570–560 B.C.E.

poets, singers, and storytellers echoed and manipulated the old tales and the inherited wisdom of their people.

Of course, without either writing or recording equipment, all oral storytelling is inevitably lost. The tales that were told before there was writing cannot be collected in any anthology. But they left their mark on the earliest works of written literature—and many subsequent ones as well. As one would expect, literacy did not take hold all at once; the transition was partial and gradual, and in much of the ancient world, poetry and storytelling were less closely associated with written texts than they are for us. **Plato's *Phaedrus*** gives us some indication that the ancient Athenians were conscious of the enormous cultural change involved in the invention of writing. Nostalgia for the days before literacy continued into the later ancient world. By the time of the early Roman Empire—whose culture was much more literate than that of classical Athens—poets could make self-conscious efforts to imitate oral gestures, as when **Virgil**, writing his ultraliterate epic, the ***Aeneid***, pretends to be an oral poet: "Wars and a man I sing."

An administrative tablet from Mesopotamia, ca. 3100–2900 B.C.E.

Writing was not originally invented to preserve literature. The earliest written documents we have contain commercial, administrative, political, and legal information. It was in the region of the Tigris and Euphrates rivers, Mesopotamia (which means "the place between the rivers"), that writing was first developed; the earliest texts date from around 3300 to 2990 B.C.E. The characters of this writing were inscribed on tablets of wet clay with a pointed stick; the tablets were then left in the sun to bake hard. The characters are pictographic: the sign for *ox* looks like an ox head and so on. The bulk of the texts are economic—lists of food, textiles, and cattle. But the script is too primitive to handle anything much more complicated than lists, and by 2800 B.C.E. scribes began to use the wedge-shaped end of the stick to make marks rather than the pointed end to draw pictures. The resulting script is known as cuneiform, from the Latin word *cuneus*, "a wedge." By 2500 B.C.E. cuneiform was used for many things beyond administrative lists: the texts preserved historical events and even, finally, literature. It was on clay tablets and in cuneiform script that the great Sumerian epic poem ***Gilgamesh*** was written down. This writing system was not, however, designed for a large reading public. Each sign denoted a syllable—consonant plus a vowel—which meant that the reader had to be familiar with a large number of signs. Furthermore, the same sign often represented two or more different sounds, and the same sound could be represented by several different signs. It is a script that could be written and read only by experts, the scribes, who often proudly recorded their own names on the tablets.

The writing system invented by the Egyptians was even more

A limestone stele (ca. fourth century B.C.E.) in the shape of the symbol of the Phoenician goddess Tanit, with Punic script (a derivative of Phoenician) carved into its surface.

esoteric than cuneiform. It is called hieroglyphic, an adjective formed from the Greek words for "sacred" and "carving." Although it appears on many different materials, its most conspicuous and continuous use was for inscriptions carved on temple walls and public monuments. It was pictographic, like the earliest Sumerian script, but the pictures were more elaborate and artistic. Unlike the Sumerian pictographs, they were not replaced by a more efficient system; the pictures remained in use for the walls of temples and tombs, while more cursive versions of hieroglyphics—the hieratic and demotic scripts—were developed for faster writing. But the Egyptians soon developed their system to include signs standing for sounds, as well as for single objects: for instance, the same sign could mean either "house," *pr*, or simply the sound *pr*. This was only one of many complications that made even the modified versions of the script a difficult medium of communication for anyone not trained in its intricacies. It is no wonder that one of the frequent figures to appear in Egyptian sculpture and painting is the professional scribe, his legs tucked underneath him, his writing material in his lap, and his brush in his hand.

There was one ancient writing system that, unlike cuneiform and hieroglyphic, was destined to survive, in modified forms, until the present day. It was developed by the Phoenicians, a Semitic trading people. The script consisted of twenty-two simple signs for consonantal sounds. Through trade, the Phoenician script spread all over the Mediterranean. It was adopted by the ancient Hebrews, among others. The obvious advantage of this system was that it was so easy to learn. But there was still one area of inefficiency in this system—namely, that the absence of notation for the vowels made for ambiguity. We still do not know, for example, what the vowel sounds were in the sacred name of God, often called the Tetragrammaton, because it consists of four letters; in our alphabet the name is written as YHWH. The usual surmise is Jahweh (*yá-way*), but for a long time the traditional English-language version was Jehovah.

One thing was needed to make the script fully efficient: signs for the vowels. This was the contribution of the Greeks, who, in the eighth or possibly the ninth century B.C.E., adopted the Phoenician script for their own language but used for the vowels some Phoenician signs that stood for consonantal combinations not native to Greek. They took over (but soon modified) the Phoenician letter shapes and also their names: *alpha*, a meaningless word in Greek, represents the original *aleph* ("ox"), and *beta* represents the original *beta* ("house"). The Greeks admitted their indebtedness; Greek myths told the story of Cadmus, king of Tyre, who taught the Greeks how to write, and, as the historian Herodotus tells us, the letters were called Phoenician. The Romans, who adapted the Greek alphabet for their own language, carved their inscriptions on stone in the same capital letters that we still use today.

ANCIENT NEAR EASTERN AND MEDITERRANEAN CULTURES

Modern, postindustrial societies depend, economically, on machines and sources of energy to operate them. We use complex devices to produce food and clothes, to build roads and cities, to excavate natural resources (such as oil or coal), to construct nonnatural materials (such as plastics), to get from place to place, and to communicate with others across the globe: by phone, television, computers, and the Internet. In the ancient world, most of these machines did not yet exist. Though metal was mined and worked, what we know as heavy industry did not exist. Coal and oil were not exploited for energy. War galleys were propelled by sail and human oarsmen; armies moved, sometimes vast distances, on foot. People therefore relied far more heavily on the kind of natural resources that can be easily accessed by human labor: no ancient city could be built far from fresh water and fertile soil, on which to grow crops and graze animals for meat and wool. Where we use machines and fossil fuel, all the advanced civilizations of the ancient world depended for their existence on slaves, who worked the land; took care of animals and children; dug the mines; built houses, temples, cities and pyramids; manufactured household goods (ranging from basic tableware to decorative artwork); performed housework; and provided entertainment. Modern Western societies exploit natural resources and harness them by using the cheap human labor available in less "developed" countries; most of the time, we do not even think about the people who made our clothes, phones, or cars or about the energy it takes to produce them and dispose of them. Similarly,

A relief from the Palace of Sargon, from the eighth century B.C.E. It shows the transport of large logs fueled by human rowers.

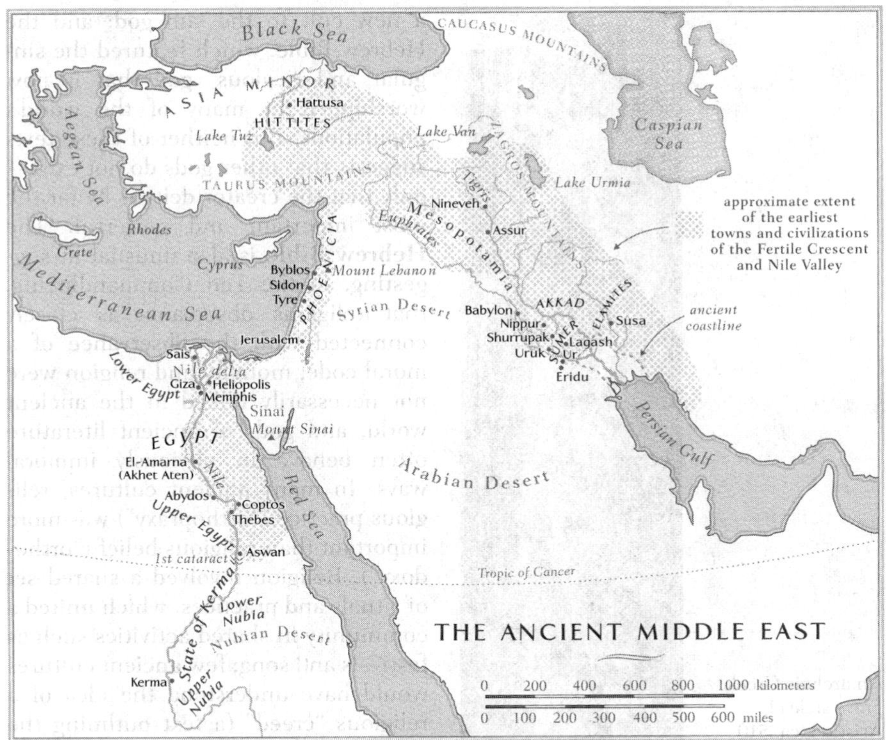

elite ancient Hebrews, Greeks, and Romans seem to have taken slaves almost entirely for granted. The existence of ancient slavery should remind us not to idealize ancient cultures (even those of the "great Western tradition") and to remember how easily human beings, ourselves included, can be blinkered about the forms of injustice and exploitation that are essential to their cultural existence.

Because ancient societies depended on the proximity of natural resources, especially well-irrigated, fertile soil, the first civilizations of the Mediterranean basin developed in two regions that were particularly receptive to agriculture and animal husbandry. These areas were the valley of the Nile, where annual floods left large tracts of land moist and fertile under the Egyptian sun, and the valleys of the Euphrates and Tigris rivers, which flowed through the Fertile Crescent, a region centered on modern Iraq. Great cities—Thebes and Memphis in Egypt and Babylon and Nineveh in the Fertile Crescent—came into being as centers for the complicated administration of the irrigated fields. Supported by the surplus the land produced, they became centers also for government, religion, and culture.

Later, from the second millennium B.C.E. onward, more cultures developed around the Mediterranean, including those of the Hebrews, the Greeks, and the Romans. These societies remained distinct from one another, and each included many separate social groups: we should be wary of generalizing about what "people in antiquity" believed or did. But it does make sense to consider the ancient Mediterranean and Near East as a single, albeit complex, unit, because there were large-scale cultural exchanges between these various peoples, as a result of trade, colonization, and imperialism. Greek sculpture

An archaic Greek grave stele of Aristion, ca. 510 B.C.E. This piece, although Greek, exhibits characteristics common to Egyptian and other Mediterranean and near Eastern sculpture.

and architecture of the seventh century B.C.E., for instance, show heavy debts to Egypt, and striking similarities between Greek and Near Eastern myths are probably the result of Mesopotamian influence.

Most ancient cultures were polytheistic (they believed in many gods); and since crosscultural religious influence was common, gods were often reinvented from one place to another. Ancient texts that emphasize a single deity over all others are rare: the most important exceptions to the polytheistic rule are the Egyptian ***Great Hymn to the Aten***, composed at a time when the Egyptian monarchy was setting up a new cult to the sun god; and the Hebrew Bible, which featured the singular and "jealous" god that is now worshipped by many of the world's populations. But neither of these texts suggests that other gods do not exist—only that the creator deity is by far the most important and powerful. The **Hebrew Bible** is also unusual in suggesting, in the Ten Commandments, that religious observance is closely connected with the observance of a moral code; morality and religion were not necessarily linked in the ancient world, and gods of ancient literature often behave in obviously immoral ways. In many ancient cultures, religious practice ("orthopraxy") was more important than religious belief ("orthodoxy"). Religion involved a shared set of rituals and practices, which united a community in shared activities such as festivals and song; few ancient cultures would have understood the idea of a religious "creed" (a text outlining the specific beliefs of a particular religious community, to which all members must subscribe). Cult practices were often highly localized. We should, then, be wary of assuming that the stories about gods that appear in literary texts are necessarily a record of the religious beliefs of a whole culture. Myths circulated in many different forms, changing from one place and time to another; in most ancient cultures, composing alternative stories about the gods does not seem to have been regarded as "heretical," as it might seem to a modern Jewish, Christian, or Muslim reader.

THE GREEKS

The origin of the peoples who eventually called themselves Hellenes is still a mystery. The language they spoke belongs clearly to the Indo-European family (which includes the Germanic,

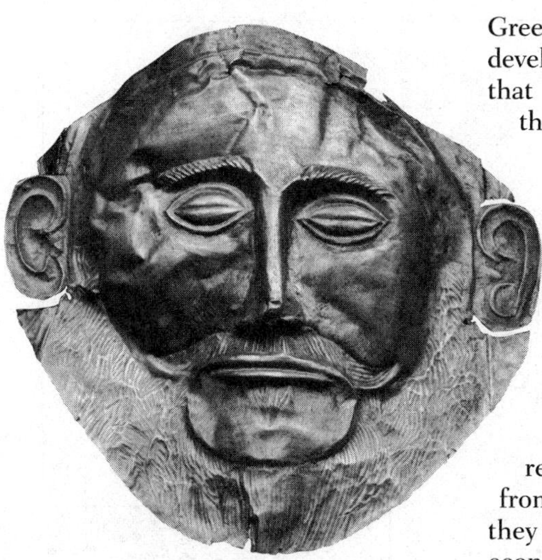

A gold "death mask" from Mycenae, ca. 1550–1500 B.C.E., sometimes referred to as the "mask of Agamemnon."

Celtic, Italic, and Sanskrit language groups), but many of the ancient Greek words and place names have terminations that are definitely not Indo-European—the word for sea (*thalassa*), for example. The Greeks of historic times were presumably a blend of native tribes and Indo-European invaders.

In the second millennium B.C.E., a brilliant culture, called Minoan after the mythical king Minos, flourished on the large island of Crete, centered around enormous palace structures; and the citadel of Mycenae and the palace at Pylos show that mainland Greece, in that same period, had a comparably rich culture, which included knowledge of a writing system called Linear B. But some time in the last century of the millennium, the great palaces were destroyed by fire. With them disappeared not only the arts and skills that had created Mycenean wealth but even the system of writing. For the next few hundred years, the Greeks were illiterate and so no written evidence survives for this time, known as the Dark Ages of Greece. During this time, the Greeks developed the oral tradition of poetry that would culminate in the ***Iliad*** and the ***Odyssey***.

The Dark Ages ended in the eighth century B.C.E., when Greece again became literate—but with a quite different alphabet, borrowed from the Phoenicians. At this time, Greece was still a highly fragmented place, made up of many small independent cities. These were known as "city-states" (a rendering of the Greek term *polis*, from which we get "politics"), because they were independent political and economic entities—not, like modern cities, ruled by a centralized national government. The geography of Greece—a land of mountain barriers and scattered islands—encouraged this fragmentation. The cities differed from each other in custom, political constitution, and even dialect: their relations with each other were those of rivals and fierce competitors. In the eighth and seventh centuries B.C.E., Greeks founded many new cities all over the Mediterranean coast, including some along the coast of Asia Minor. Many of these new outposts of Greek civilization experienced a faster economic and cultural development than the older cities of the mainland. It was in the cities founded on the Asian coast that the Greeks adapted to their own language the Phoenician system of writing, adding signs for the vowels to create their alphabet. The Greeks probably first used their new written language for commercial records and transactions, but as literacy became more widespread all over the Greek world in the course of the seventh century B.C.E., treaties and political decrees were inscribed on stone and literary works written on rolls of paper made from the Egyptian papyrus plant.

In the sixth century B.C.E., the Per-

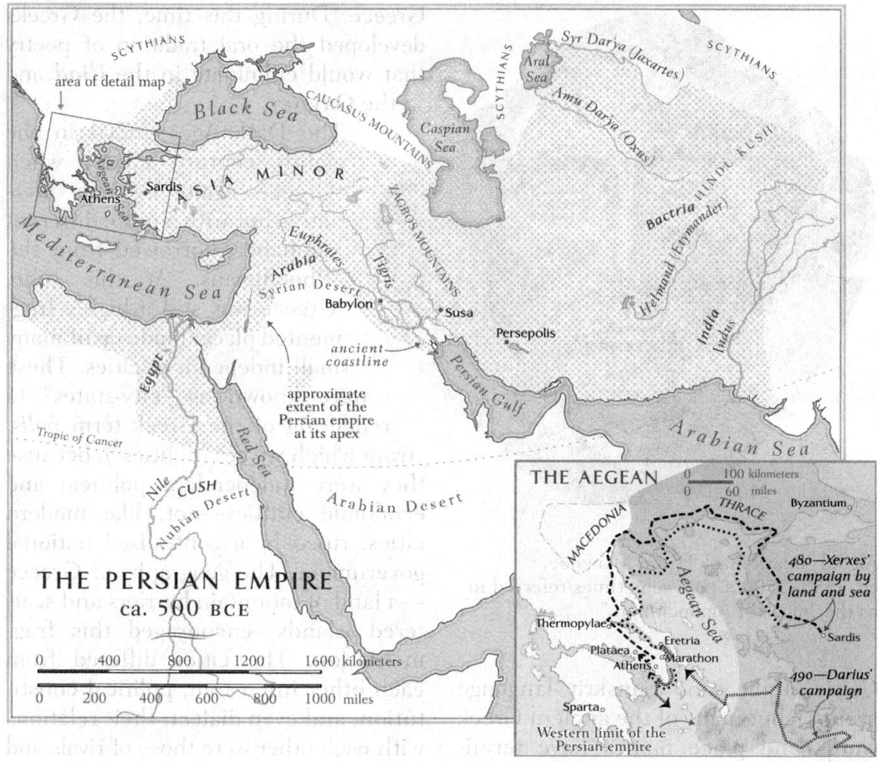

sian Empire dominated the Near East and Mediterranean areas, eventually becoming the largest empire in the ancient world. Millions of people lived under Persian control, and the ruling dynasty of Persia (the Achaemenids) conducted an expansionist policy, extending their domain from their center in Pasargadae (in modern Iran) east, as far as the Indus river, and west, into Egypt and Libya, as well as into the eastern parts of Greece, such as the cities of Ionia (in Asia Minor). The Persians had a sophisticated and globalized culture, influenced by elements from many of the other cultures they had encountered; their art was rich and intricate, and their architecture was impressively monumental. The empire was governed by a complex and highly developed political system, with the emperor at the top of the ladder. The Persian army was huge and expertly trained, and it included vast numbers of skilled cavalrymen and archers. By the beginning of the fifth century B.C.E., the Persian Empire must have seemed all but unstoppable; it would have been reasonable for the Persians to assume that they could dominate the remaining parts of Greece. But surprisingly, the Greeks—led by Athens and Sparta—managed to repel repeated Persian invasions in the years 490 to 479 B.C.E., winning decisive naval battles at Marathon and Salamis. Their astonishing victory over Persia boosted the confidence of the Greek cities in the fifth century. Free from the fear of foreign invasion, the Athenians produced their most important literary and cultural achievements.

Sparta was governed by a ruling elite, an oligarchy ("rule of the few") that used strict military discipline to maintain control over a majority underclass. By contrast, Attica—the city-state of which Athens was the leading city—was at this time a democracy, one of the first such states in the world. "Democracy," which means "rule by the people," did not imply that all adult inhabitants had the chance to vote; "the people" were a small subset of the population, since women, slaves, and metics (resident aliens) were all excluded from the rights of citizenship. The citizens of Attica in the fifth century probably numbered only about thirty thousand, while the total population may have been ten times that. Slaves had no rights at all; they were the property of their masters. Women, even free-born women, could not own property, hold office, or vote. The elite women of Athens had less autonomy than those in most Greek city-states, including Sparta (where women were allowed to exercise outside in the gymnasium); in Athens, they were expected to remain inside the house except for funerals and religious festivals, rarely seen by men other than their husbands or male relatives. Moreover,

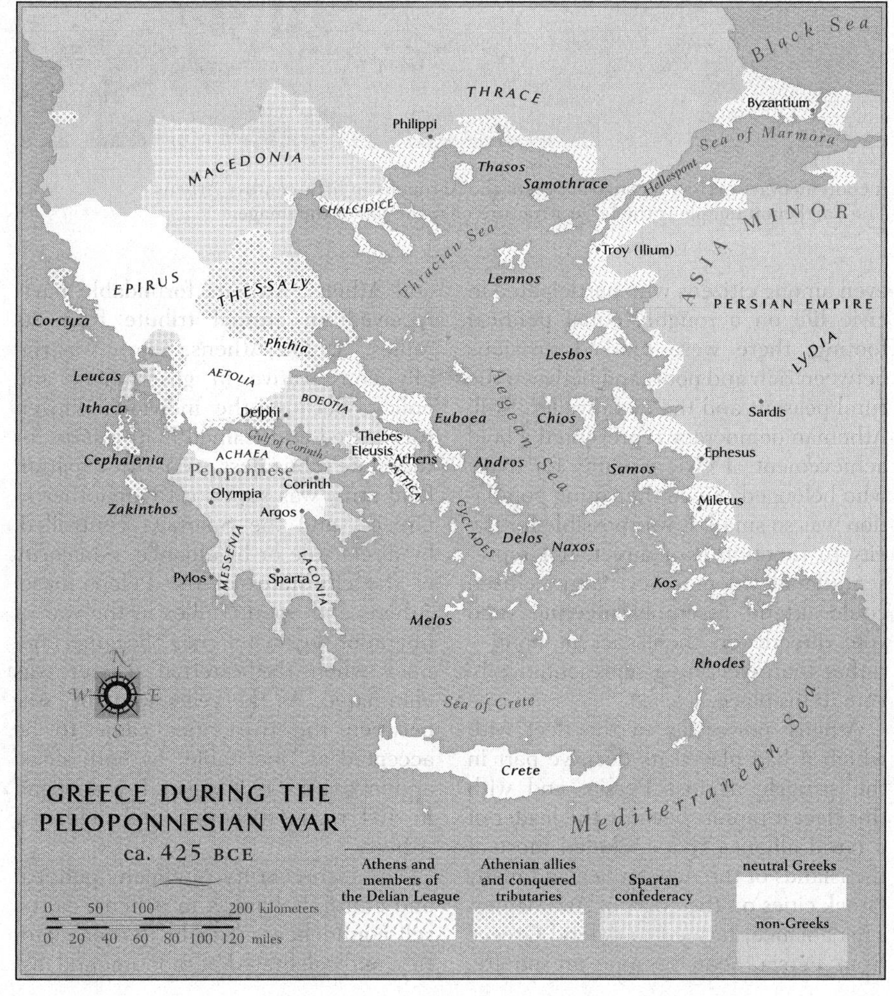

A contemporary artist's reconstruction of the Acropolis in fifth-century Athens. The Parthenon temple is the large structure near the top of the image.

even among citizens who participated in civic life on a roughly equal political footing, there were marked divisions between rich and poor, and between the rural peasant and the city dweller. Still, Athenian democracy represented a bold achievement of civic equality for those who belonged. Since the voting population was so small, it was possible for the city to function as a direct, not representational, democracy: any citizen could attend assembly meetings and vote directly on the issues at hand—rather than electing a representative to vote in his place.

Athens' power lay in the fleet with which it had played its decisive part in the struggle against Persia, and with this fleet it rapidly became the leader of a naval alliance that included most of the islands of the Aegean Sea and many Greek cities on the coast of Asia Minor. This alliance, formed to defend Greece from Persia, soon became an empire, and Athens, with its formidable navy, received an annual tribute from its "allies." Unlike Athens, Sparta was rigidly conservative in government and policy. Because the individual citizen was reared and trained by the state for the state's business, war, the Spartan land army was superior to any other in Greece, and the Spartans controlled, by direct rule or by alliance, a majority of the city-states of the Peloponnese. Athens and Sparta, allies in the war of liberation against Persia, became enemies when the external danger was eliminated. As the years went by, war between the two cities came to be accepted as "inevitable" by both sides, and in 431 B.C.E. it began. It was to end in 404 B.C.E. with the total defeat of Athens.

The fifth century saw many political and cultural changes in Athens, as the self-confidence roused by Persian victories, and celebrated by monumental displays of civic pride (such as the famous Parthenon temple to the city's goddess, Athena, completed in 438 B.C.E.), gave way to the increasing social tensions and anxieties of the war years. But throughout this century Athenian democracy provided its citizens with a cultural and intellectual environment that was without precedent in the ancient world. In the sixth century, Greeks on the Ionian coast had already begun to develop new, protoscientific ideas, alternatives to the old myths about how the world was made. Now many of the most original thinkers and writers from all over the Greek world began to gather in Athens. This time marked the beginning of new ways of thinking in many different areas. Greek doctors began to ask new questions about how the body works, including how environmental factors (such as climate and diet) affect health, and they supported their theories by observation. The first anthropological historian, **Herodotus**, analyzed and described how one culture differs from another (focusing on differences between Greeks, Persians, and Egyptians), while the first political historian, Thucydides, showed how economic and political factors could combine to cause war. These years marked the dawning of prose literature, in medicine, history, and philosophy. The fifth century was also the great age of Athenian theater: both tragedy and comedy developed and flourished at this time, and drama provided an essential outlet for the cultural confusions of the age.

Literary and intellectual changes accompanied changes in the ways that elite young men were educated. Throughout the Greek world, during the fifth century and beyond, children's education was based on the poems of Homer; Greek boys learned the tales of the *Iliad* and the *Odyssey* along with the alphabet, often from an educated slave tutor; sections of these poems were also performed, by trained actors (rhapsodes), as adult entertainment. But in the fifth century the education of adolescent boys changed. Intellectuals immigrating to Athens from other Greek cities met a new demand for their services as teachers, to train young men for public life, especially for the art of public speaking. These professional tutors, or Sophists ("wisdom teachers"), taught the techniques of rhetoric, as well as more substantial subjects like government, ethics, literary criticism, even astronomy.

The Sophists were popular, and many parents were willing to spend large sums to have their sons trained by them. But, perhaps inevitably, the new educational methods, combined with the new intellectual trends sweeping the city, resulted in a generation gap. Older men felt that the new teachers had corrupted their sons and led them to question the value of traditional religious beliefs and practices. These fathers saw the intellectual advances of the fifth century as morally corrupting: some feared the corrosion of moral certainty when teachers made claims like that of the Sophist Protagoras, that "Man is the measure of all things." The most famous of the Sophists, in his own day as well as later, was Socrates. Socrates was in some ways an unusual Sophist: unlike the majority of these teachers, he was an Athenian citizen, not an immigrant from another city; and unlike other Sophists he seems to have demanded no fee for his teaching. But we should not be too quick to accept the sharp distinction that his pupil and defender, Plato, made between the (supposedly fraudulent) Sophists and the (genuinely philosophical) Socrates. Contemporaries—including the comedian **Aristophanes**, who wrote a play attacking Socrates' dangerous sophistry (***Clouds***)—made no such distinction. Socrates's interests and methods seemed to overlap with those of other wisdom teachers: like Protagoras, he investigated ethics, politics, and truth through "dialectics," a

A mosaic from a villa in Pompeii from ca. 100 B.C.E. depicts a philosophical discussion in the Academy of Plato.

method of question and answer—although, unlike Protagoras, he apparently believed in the possibility of true goodness. Still, his extraordinary mind and personality made him by far the most influential intellectual of his time, and—largely through the work of his most brilliant student, Plato—Socrates became the starting point for all later Western philosophy.

In the last quarter of the fifth century, the whole traditional basis of individual conduct, which had been concern for the unity and cohesion of the city-state, was undermined. "In peace and prosperity," says Thucydides, "both states and individuals are actuated by higher motives; . . . but war, which takes away the comfortable provision of daily life, is a hard master, and tends to assimilate men's characters to their conditions." Growing aggressive in their desperation, the Athenians were aware that they were faring badly in the war and launched a disastrous naval campaign in Sicily (413 B.C.E.), in which many ships were lost and many men lost their freedom and their lives. Unstable political conditions followed, leading to a short-lived oligarchic revolution at home (411 B.C.E.). The war dragged on for another seven years, until finally Athens, her last fleet gone, surrendered to the Spartans. A pro-Spartan antidemocratic regime, the Thirty Tyrants, was installed but soon overthrown. Athens became a democracy again, but the confidence and unity of its great age were gone forever. One of the first actions of the new democratic government was to execute Socrates, who had been associated with Alcibiades and Critias and whose "corruption of the young" and unusual religious beliefs must have seemed to represent everything the city wanted to forget.

In the fourth century B.C.E., the Greek city-states became involved in constant internecine warfare. Politically and economically bankrupt, they fell under the power of Macedon in the north, whose king, Philip, combined a ferocious energy with a cynicism that enabled him to take full advantage of the disunity of the city-states. Greek liberty ended at the battle of Chaeronea in 338 B.C.E., and Philip's son Alexander inherited a powerful army and the political control of all Greece. He led his Macedonian and Greek armies against Persia, and in a few brilliant campaigns became master of an empire that extended into Egypt in the south and to the borders of India in the east. He died at Babylon in 323 B.C.E., and his empire broke up into a number of independent kingdoms ruled by his generals; modern scholars refer to the period that followed (323–146 B.C.E.) as the Hellenistic age. One of these generals, Ptolemy, founded a Greek dynasty that ruled Egypt until after the Roman conquest and ended only with the death of Cleopatra. The results of Alexander's fantastic achievements were more durable than might have been expected. Into the newly conquered territories came thousands of Greeks who wished to escape from the political futility and economic crisis of the homeland. Wherever they went, they took with them their language, their culture, and their typical buildings—the gymnasium and the theater. The great Hellenistic cities, though now part of kingdoms, grew out of the earlier city-state model and continued many of its civic and political institutions. At Alexandria, in Egypt, the

A detail from a mosaic (dating from ca. 80 B.C.E.) discovered in Pompeii that shows Alexander the Great on horseback in battle.

Britannia
Londinium
Gesoriacum
GERMANIA
Rhine
Elbe
Oder
Colonia Agrippina
Augusta Treverorum
Seine
Gallia
Loire
Danube
Carnuntum
Atlantic Ocean
ALPS
Sava
Lugdunum
Aquileia
Burdigala
Lacus Benacus
Verona
Po
Mantua
Ravenna
Massilia
Narbo
Salonae
Italia
Adriatic Sea
Douro
Ebro
Hispania
Tiber
Corsica
ROME
Sulmo
Tarraco
Tagus
Sardinia
Misenum
Brundisium
Tyrrhenian Sea
Baleares Major
Corduba
Sicily
Mediterranean
Gades
Syracusae
Tingi
Caesarea
Carthago
Mauretania
Africa
Malta
HIGH ATLAS MOUNTAINS
SAHARAN ATLAS MOUNTAINS
AENEAS' JOURNEY
Tiber
Rome
LATIUM
Cumae
THRACE
Aenea
Castrum Minervae
EPIRUS
Buthrotum
Troy
Mount Ida
PHRYGIA
Mount Etna
Eryx
Sicily
Delos
Strophades
Carthago
AFRICA
Pergamea
Crete

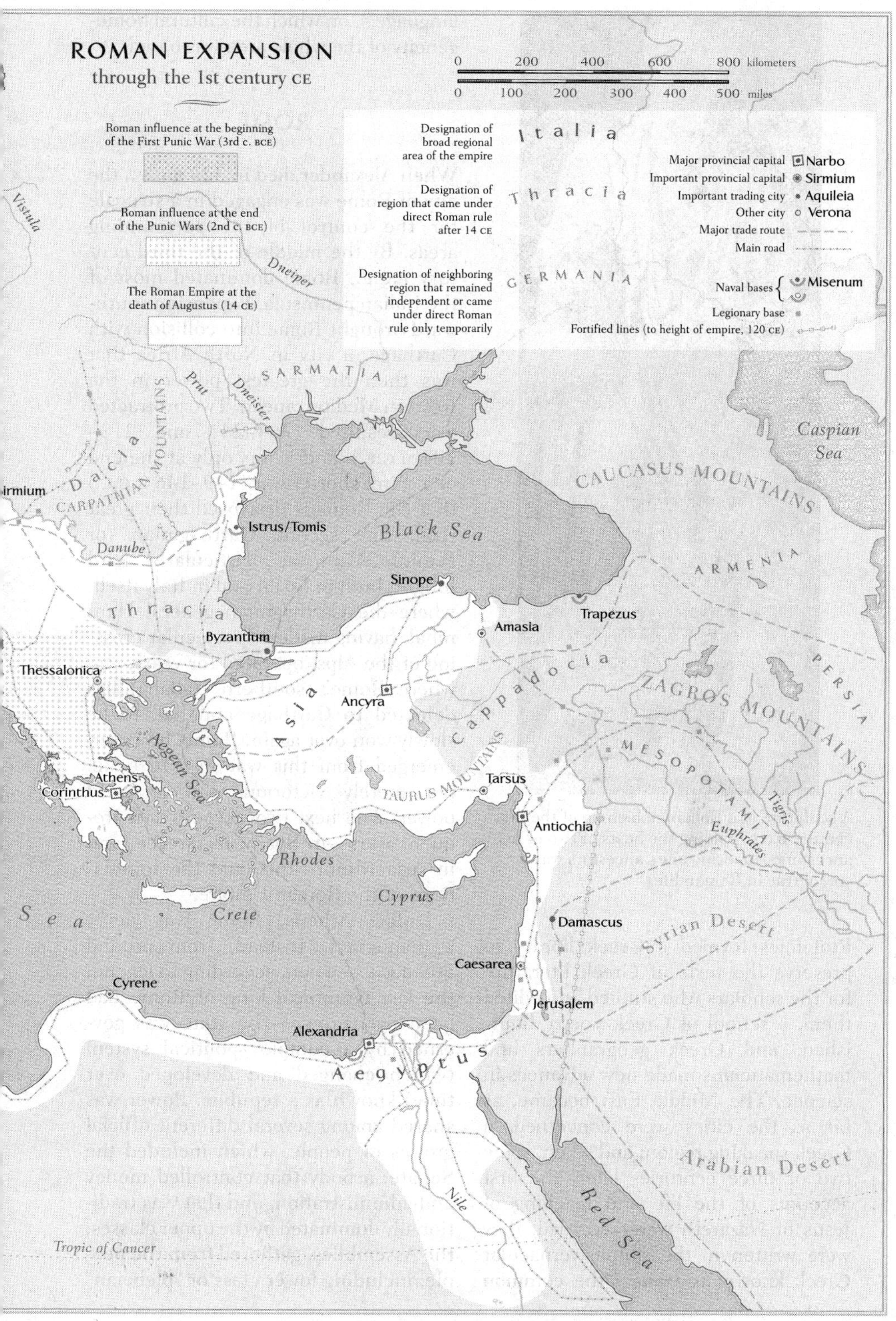
ROMAN EXPANSION
through the 1st century CE
0 200 400 600 800 kilometers
0 100 200 300 400 500 miles
Roman influence at the beginning of the First Punic War (3rd c. BCE)
Roman influence at the end of the Punic Wars (2nd c. BCE)
The Roman Empire at the death of Augustus (14 CE)
Designation of broad regional area of the empire
Italia
Designation of region that came under direct Roman rule after 14 CE
Thracia
Designation of neighboring region that remained independent or came under direct Roman rule only temporarily
GERMANIA
Major provincial capital Narbo
Important provincial capital Sirmium
Important trading city Aquileia
Other city Verona
Major trade route
Main road
Naval bases Misenum
Legionary base
Fortified lines (to height of empire, 120 CE)
Vistula
Dneiper
SARMATIA
Prut
Dneister
CARPATHIAN MOUNTAINS
Dacia
irmium
Danube
Istrus/Tomis
Black Sea
Caspian Sea
CAUCASUS MOUNTAINS
ARMENIA
Sinope
Trapezus
Amasia
Thracia
Byzantium
Thessalonica
Ancyra
Asia
Cappadocia
PERSIA
ZAGROS MOUNTAINS
MESOPOTAMIA
Tigris
Euphrates
Aegean Sea
Athens
Corinthus
TAURUS MOUNTAINS
Tarsus
Antiochia
Rhodes
Cyprus
Crete
Sea
Damascus
Syrian Desert
Caesarea
Jerusalem
Cyrene
Alexandria
Aegyptus
Nile
Red Sea
Arabian Desert
Tropic of Cancer

A sculpture of a Roman nobleman of the first century B.C.E. holding the busts of two of his ancestors. Honoring one's ancestors was a core virtue in Roman life.

Ptolemies formed a Greek library to preserve the texts of Greek literature for the scholars who studied and edited them, a school of Greek poetry flourished, and Greek geographers and mathematicians made new advances in science. The Middle East became, as far as the cities were concerned, a Greek-speaking region; and when, some two or three centuries later, the first accounts of the life and teaching of Jesus of Nazareth were recorded, they were written in the simple vernacular Greek known as *koine* ("the common language"), on which the cultural homogeneity of the whole area was based.

ROME

When Alexander died in 323 B.C.E., the city of Rome was engaged in a struggle for the control of the surrounding areas. By the middle of the third century B.C.E., Rome dominated most of the Italian peninsula. Expansion southward brought Rome into collision with Carthage, a city in North Africa that was then the greatest power in the western Mediterranean. Two protracted wars resulted (264–241 and 218–201 B.C.E.), and it was only at the end of a third, shorter war (149–146 B.C.E.) that the Romans destroyed their great rival. The second Carthaginian (or Punic) War was particularly hard fought, both in Spain and in Italy itself, where the Carthaginian general Hannibal, having made a spectacular crossing of the Alps, operated for years, and where Rome's southern Italian allies defected to Carthage and had to be slowly won over again. Rome, however, emerged from this war in 201 B.C.E. not merely victorious but a world power. The next two decades saw frequent wars—in Spain, in Greece, and in Asia Minor—that laid the foundations of the Roman Empire.

Unlike Athens, Rome was never a democracy. Instead, from around 509 B.C.E.—when, according to legend, the last tyrannical king of Rome had been overthrown—the state was governed by a complex political system (which changed and developed over time) known as a republic. Power was shared among several different official groups of people, which included the Senate, a body that controlled money and administration, and that was traditionally dominated by the upper classes; the Assemblies, gathered from the people, including lower class or "plebeian" citizens; and elected officials called Magistrates, the most important of whom were the two Consuls, elected every year. The system (one of the most important models for the United States Constitution many centuries later) was designed, above all, to prevent any single person or group from seizing total control. The republic would last until the time of the Roman civil wars, in the first century B.C.E.

The Greeks believed that arguing, strife, and competition can be good, since they inspire us to outdo others and improve ourselves. The Romans, by contrast, saw conflict as deadly: it was what, in Roman mythology, led the founder of their city, Romulus, to kill his twin brother, Remus. Whereas the Athenians prided themselves on adaptability, versatility, and grace, the Roman idea of personal and civic virtue was based on a sense of tradition, a myth of old Roman virtue and integrity. "By her ancient customs and her men the Roman state stands," wrote Ennius, a Roman epic poet, capturing an ethos that emphasized tradition (known as the *mos maiorum,* the custom of predecessors) and commended "seriousness" (*gravitas*), "manly courage" (*virtus*), "industry" (*diligentia*), and above all, "duty" (*pietas*). Roman power was built on efficiency, and strength through unity. The Romans organized a complicated yet stable federation that held Italy loyal to them in the presence of invading armies, and they developed a legal code that formed the model for all later European and American law. The achievements of the Romans, in conquest and in organizing their empire after victory, were due in large part to their talent for practical affairs. They built sewers, baths with hot and cold water, straight roads, and aqueducts to last two thousand years.

A Roman aqueduct, built in the first century B.C.E., still standing at Pont du Gard in France.

Given the Romans' pragmatism and adherence to tradition, one might expect their literature to be very dull. But this is not true at all. Roman poets often struggled with, or frankly rejected, the moral codes of their society. The poems of **Catullus**, an aristocratic young man who lived in the last years of the Roman Republic (first century B.C.E.), suggest a deliberate attempt to thumb his nose at the serious Roman topics of politics, war, and tradition. Instead, Catullus writes about love, sex, and feelings and satirizes the people he finds most annoying. A generation or two later, both **Virgil** and **Ovid** also question—in very different ways—whether unthinking loyalty to the Roman state is a desirable goal.

By the end of the first century B.C.E., Rome was the capital of an empire that stretched from the Straits of Gibraltar to Mesopotamia and the frontiers of Palestine, and as far north as Britain. While Greek history began with the epics of Homer (instrumental in creating a sense of Greek national identity that transcended the divisions of the many city-states), the Romans had conquered half the world before they began to write. Latin literature began with a translation of the *Odyssey*, made by a Greek prisoner of war; and, with the exception of satire, the model was always Greek. Roman authors borrowed wholesale from Greek originals, not furtively but openly and proudly, as a tribute to the source. But this frank acknowledgment of indebtedness should not blind us to the fact that Latin literature is original, and sometimes profoundly so. Catullus translated the Greek lyric poet **Sappho**, but he added to her evocation of agonizing jealousy a distinctively Roman anxiety about idleness. Ovid retold Greek myths, making them funnier by giving them a Roman rhetorical punch. Virgil based his epic, the *Aeneid*, on Homer, but he chose as his theme the coming of the Trojan prince Aeneas to Italy, where he was to found a city from which, in the fullness of time, would come "the Latin race . . . and the high walls of Rome."

The institutions of the Roman city-state proved inadequate for world government. The second and first centuries B.C.E. were dominated by civil war, between various factions vying for power: generals against senators and populists against aristocrats. Coalitions were formed, but each proved unstable. Julius Caesar, a successful Roman general, seized power (although he refused the title "king"); but he was assassinated in 44 B.C.E. by a party hoping to restore the old system of shared rule. More years of civil war followed, until finally, in 31 B.C.E., Julius's adoptive nephew, Octavian—who later titled himself Augustus—managed to defeat the ruler of the eastern half of the empire, Mark Antony, along with Antony's ally and lover, Cleopatra, queen of Egypt. Augustus played his hand carefully, claiming that he was restoring the Republic; but he assumed primary control of the state and became the first in the long line of Roman emperors.

For the next two hundred years the successors of Augustus, the Roman emperors, ruled the Mediterranean and Near Eastern world. The empire covered a vast area that included Britain, France, all southern Europe, the Middle East, and the whole of North Africa. Some native inhabitants, in all these areas, were killed by the Romans; others were enslaved; many, both slave and free, were Romanized, acculturated into the norms of the Roman people. Roman culture stamped this whole area of the world in ways that can still be discerned today: the Romans built roads, cities, public baths and theaters and brought their literature and language—Latin—to the provinces they ruled. All modern

Romance languages, including Spanish, French, and Italian, developed from the language spoken throughout the Roman Empire.

But controlling so many people, in so many different areas, from the central government in Rome was difficult and expensive. It could not be done forever. Marcus Aurelius (121–180 C.E.), who in his spare time wrote a beautiful book of thoughts about his struggle to live a good life (the *Meditations*), was the first emperor to share his power with a partner; this was the first official recognition that the empire was too big to be ruled by one man. The Romans fought a long losing battle against invading tribes from the north and east. When it finally fell, the empire left behind it the idea of the world-state, later adopted by the medieval church, which ruled from the same center, Rome, and which claimed a spiritual authority as great as the secular authority it replaced.

CREATION AND THE COSMOS

Cosmogonies—stories about how the world began—have been told by almost every culture in the world. They help people define their place in the universe, embedding the specifics of one human culture within a wider, "cosmic" pattern. The Greek word *cosmos* implies order and beauty, as well as universe: to compose a "cosmogony" is to describe how the world came to be a beautiful and well-ordered place. The genre includes some of the earliest texts in all surviving literature. These texts give us an idea of how human beings in premodern civilizations tried to make sense of their world, and how they answered questions that still puzzle scientists, philosophers, poets, and theologians today. Where does the world come from? What is it made of? Is there an order or pattern or purpose in the universe, or do things happen at random? Was there a god or gods who created or arranged the world? How did life on earth begin? How did human beings come into existence? Has there always been evil? If not, how did wickedness and conflict first begin?

These questions are profound, but the answers offered by ancient texts may strike modern readers as "primitive" or naive. Early cosmogonies provide mythical stories, involving divine personifications, instead of scientific theories (such as the big bang) about the beginnings and composition of the cosmos. But we should take these stories as a provocation to think harder about what "scientific" thinking really is. How are our beliefs about atomic particles different from ancient beliefs about the power of earth and sky? Clearly, the bards and poets who told most of these stories were not interested in conducting verifiable or falsifiable experiments to find out how the world works. In that sense, they were "unscientific." But it does not follow that they were unsophisticated in their thinking. Even the authors of the earliest surviving texts were already responding in complex ways to a long set of oral and written traditions.

Nor were these stories immediately supplanted by later ways of thinking and writing. Mythological traditions about the origins of the universe inspired the beginnings of science and informed later discussions of philosophy, history, and theology. The work of the early Greek thinkers who are often seen as the first scientists—the "pre-Socratics"—includes some critique of traditional theology and myth; **Xenophanes**, for instance, suggested that **Homer** and **Hesiod** (whose *Theogony* includes the earliest Greek myths about the origins of the gods) are both "impious" in their depiction of the gods committing adultery. The earliest "scientific" or "philosophical" thought still belongs to the tradition of Hesiod, although entities like "water," "fire," "air," and "mind" are substituted for the named deities who appeared in the archaic texts (like Gaia or Uranus). Much later,

A detail from the Hellenistic altar of Pergamon, ca. 164–156 B.C.E., that shows the giant Alcyoneus being forcibly separated from the earth goddess, Gaia, by Athena.

the Roman philosopher-poet **Lucretius** challenges the idea that we need to imagine divine creators for the (purely material) world, but he makes extensive poetic use of the cosmological tradition even as he rejects it.

This selection includes a range of texts, from the Babylonian creation epic ***Enuma Elish*** and the archaic Greek ***Theogony***, through fragments of Ionian "pre-Socratic" philosophy, and on to the poetry of Lucretius. The continuity of mythical elements across the Babylonian, Greek, and Roman cultures—including the story of divine creation followed by a massive flood—argues that the ancient Mediterranean world had a common heritage.

Ancient cosmogonies do not usually begin with creation *ex nihilo* ("from nothing"). Rather, they present some kind of primeval matter—often personified forms of earth, sky, and water—from which the world took shape; the Akkadian epic *Enuma Elish* begins by imagining a time before the heaven and earth had names, and the text tells a story of progressively more-detailed processes of naming. In several stories, like the ***Epic of Gilgamesh***, the separation of heaven and earth and their ensuing reunion fuel the creation of humankind and the development of civilization. These works also trace the ways that human life has changed since it began. The change may be presented, as in the **Hebrew Bible** and in the Greek myths of the Golden Age recorded by Hesiod, as a fall from a state of innocence and grace. Alternatively, contemporary culture may be imagined as an improvement on an old, primitive life, as in the Greek myth of Prometheus, who brought fire and technology to helpless humanity. Both these mythical patterns—the idea of decline and the idea of progress—are essential to the way that human beings imagine themselves and their place in the world.

The notion of a whole world is a relatively new one in human history. There is no word for the universe as one entity in Sumerian or Akkadian—the languages spoken by the most ancient Mesopotamian peoples (from the sixth millennium B.C.E. onward). Rather, the universe is conceived as a combination of several constituents and designated by terms such as *An-Ki* ("Heaven-Earth"). But even in these cultures, there was a developing notion of what the *Enuma Elish* calls "the entirety of all of everything." In trying to imagine the whole world, ancient peoples tended, naturally enough, to see their own place as the center and then construct stories about what might lie above, below, and beyond.

Cosmogonies frequently contain a political dimension. Descriptions of the great creator god may, by analogy, praise a human ruler who has an intimate relationship with his divine equivalent. These texts often feature stories of a primeval struggle between different generations of the gods, a "theomachy" (battle of the gods): in several cases, a younger male god (Marduk in the Babylonian stories, Zeus in the Greek myths) manages to destroy, castrate, or enslave the dominant figures of an earlier regime. This kind of story can be seen as the triumph of male power over an earlier time, imagined as matriarchal; as a prototype for how successful human rulers can replace warring factions or oligarchies; or as a mirror of the usual struggles in human families, in which the younger generation always, in the end, takes over from the older. Creation stories may also help establish the centrality of a particular place or culture within the whole world. For instance, by suggesting that the Babylonian deity Marduk played the most important part in the creation of humanity, the Babylonian poem *Enuma Elish* establishes Babylon as the most important culture.

A modern impression made from an Akkadian seal from ca. 2200 B.C.E. depicting the sun god riding a boat with a dragon head—suggesting how the civilized god has defeated and co-opted the forces of chaos (the dragon).

Cosmogonies tend to classify the world in a hierarchical structure. The upper world is the home of gods; the lower world, beneath the earth, is often a place of death, demons, gods, and ancestral spirits. The center of the world—in Egypt, Babylon, Israel, Greece, or Rome—is the most habitable area, suitable for humans; beyond it lie less hospitable lands, as well as the ocean, which most ancient Mediterranean peoples imagined as an endless expanse of water surrounding the whole mass of land. The terms in which people imagined creation, and the gods, varied with the landscape they inhabited. In the largely cloudless desert climate of Egypt, the night sky was particularly clear, and sunrise, along with the disappearance of the stars, was dramatic; in Egyptian texts, the creator god (sometimes presented as the only god that matters—an apparent precursor to monotheistic gods) is closely linked to the sun. In Mesopotamian, Greek, and Hebrew texts, by contrast, we find less emphasis on the sun and more attention paid to the sky in general and especially, to water as the element from which everything comes—and to which things may eventually return. Water is sometimes the source of all life; Apsu, the fresh-water ocean, appears as the "begetter of the gods" in *Enuma Elish.* The Greek man often known as the first philosopher, **Thales**, theorized that the whole world is made of water. But water—especially salt water—is also a locus for fear of the unknown, of the unpredictable, and of the gods' wrath. The story of Noah's flood is paralleled by several other flood myths from the ancient Mediterranean. In *Gilgamesh* (Tablet XI), the earth is conceived as a giant mountain emerging out of the primeval waters. In *Enuma Elish,* the ocean turns into a monster that has to be defeated by Marduk.

Poetic accounts of cosmogony played an important part in literature throughout antiquity: they are not confined to the distant past. From the beginning, composing stories about cosmic creation was intimately related to thinking about human acts of creation. Creation stories are meditations on the act of making, and we should remember that the Greek word for poetry, *poesis,* primarily means "making." Often some of the most self-aware works of literature, these stories raise questions about how human and divine agency relate to one another when we make up worlds of the mind. How do stories get shaped into a satisfying and beautiful arrangement? Is there a perfect or only partial analogy between the ordering of the cosmos and the ordering of a literary text?

CANNIBAL SPELL FOR KING UNIS

ca. 2325 B.C.E.

This is one of the earliest surviving long Egyptian texts. It was inscribed inside the pyramid of a dead king, in a place where it could never be read by human eyes after the building in which it was carved was completed. Full of violent imagery, it presents the deceased king as ascending to the sky and taking on the role of the creator god in a perpetual cycle defined by the daily rising of the sun and the corresponding disappearance of the night sky, imagined as the king's devouring of the stars, which are themselves deities and part of his kin group. By consuming the other deities, the king assimilated their magical powers. It has been suggested that the Cannibal Spell was composed to be recited during the sacrifice of a bull or ox before a ritual meal that would have formed part of the king's funeral ceremonies.

Cannibal Spell for King Unis[1]

The sky has grown cloudy, the stars obscured; the (sky's) arcs have quaked, the horizons' bones shaken; and those who move have grown still,[2] having seen Unis apparent and ba as the god who lives on his fathers and feeds on his mothers.

Unis is the lord of jackal-like rapacity, whose (own) mother does not know his identity:[3]

for Unis's nobility is in the sky and his power in the Akhet,[4] like Atum,[5] his father who bore him—and though he bore him, he is more powerful than he;

for Unis's kas[6] are about him, his guardian forces under his feet, his gods atop him, his uraei[7] on his brow;

for Unis's lead uraeus is on his forehead, ba when seen and akh[8] for shooting fire; for Unis's powers are on his torso.

1. Translated by James P. Allen.
2. The heavenly bodies stop moving in their awe at what is happening. Unis has appeared and he has ba-power. Ba is an aspect of the divine and human person and a principle of movement, primarily in the next world, as well as a concept of divine and royal power.
3. Knowing someone's identity or name gives one power over them. Even Unis's mother does not have such power.
4. The horizon, where the sun rises in the morning and sets in the evening. The word is related to *akh* (see below).
5. A creator god, identified as the old form of the sun god associated with sunset.
6. The principle of vitality handed down the generations in the male line; another aspect of the person. Deities and kings have many kas; human beings have one.
7. Rearing cobras, worn on the forehead by deities and kings, that protect the wearer by spitting fire. (*Uraeus*, below, is the singular form of the word.)
8. Both a word meaning "effective" and the form the deceased takes on in the next world as a transfigured soul. *Akhu* is one of the two words for magical power used in the text (the other is *heka*).

Unis is the sky's bull, with terrorizing in his heart, who lives on the evolution[9] of every god, who eats their bowels when they have come from the Isle of Flame[1] with their belly filled with magic.

Unis is an equipped one who has gathered his effectiveness, for Unis has appeared as the great one who has assistants, sitting with his back to Geb.[2]

Unis is the one whose case against him whose identity is hidden[3] was decided on the day of butchering the senior ones.

Unis is lord of offering, who ties on the leash (of the sacrificial animal), who makes his own presentation of offerings.

Unis is one who eats people and lives on gods, one who has fetchers[4] and sends off dispatches.

Grasper of Forelocks in the kettle is the one who lassoes them for Unis;

Serpent with Sweeping Head is the one who guards them for him and bars them for him;

Gory All Over is the one who binds them for him;

Courser, the lords' knife-bearer, is the one who will slit their throats for Unis and takes out for him what is in their belly—he is the messenger he sends to confront;

Shezmu is the one who will butcher them for Unis and who cooks a meal of them for him on his evening hearthstones.

Unis is the one who eats their magic and swallows their akhs,

for their adults are for his morning meal, their middle-sized ones for his evening meal, their little ones for his nighttime snack, their old men and women (fuel) for his ovens;

for the sky's great northerners[5] are the ones who set fire for him to the cauldrons containing them with the bones of their senior ones;

for those in the sky serve him, while the hearthstones are poked for him with the legs of their women;

for both skies[6] go around (in service) for him and the two shores serve him.

Unis is the most controlling power, who controls the controlling powers;

Unis is the sacred image who is most sacred of sacred images;

anyone he finds in his way he will devour.

for Unis's proper place is in front of all the privileged ones in the Akhet.

Unis is the god who is senior to the senior ones,

for thousands serve him and hundreds present offering to him;

9. "Evolution," which can also be rendered "manifestation," comprises the various forms that divine or human beings take on during their lifetime.

1. A place of transition in the celestial world.

2. The god of the earth. Unis sets his back to Geb because he has ascended to the sky.

3. Perhaps the principal creator. "Case against" is one of many examples of litigation in the next world. "Senior ones" are the oldest gods.

4. Unis has many assistants in his task of butchery. Five are given descriptive names in the following passage. The last of them, Shezmu, is a god associated with butchery and punishment.

5. The stars and constellations north of the ecliptic (the apparent path of the sun through the sky during a year) in the night sky, here envisaged as gods.

6. The two parts of the sky, north and south of the ecliptic. The "two shores" are those of the Nile. Both sky and earth are in the king's service.

for he has been given title as the greatest controlling power by Orion,[7] the gods' father;
for Unis has reappeared in the sky and is crowned as lord of the Akhet;
for the vertebrae of spines have been broken up for him and he has acquired the gods' hearts;
for he has eaten the red and swallowed the raw.

Unis will feed on the lungs of the experienced and grow content from living on hearts and their magic as well.

Unis will spit out when he licks the emetic parts in the red, for he is replete and their magic is in his belly.

Unis's privileges will not be taken from him, for he has swallowed the Perception of every god.[8]

Continuity is the lifetime of Unis, eternity is his limit, in his privilege of "When He Likes He Acts. When He Dislikes He Does Not Act," which is in the Akhet's limits forever continually.

For their ba is in Unis's belly and their akhs are with Unis, as the excess of his meal with respect to (that of) the gods, since it was heated for Unis with their bones.[9]
for their ba is with Unis, and (only) their shadows are (still) with their owners;
for Unis is in this (state), ever apparent, ever set.

Those who do (evil) deeds will not be able to hack up the place of Unis's heart among the living in this world forever continually.[1]

7. The constellation Orion is identified as a senior deity in the Pyramid Texts—texts carved into the walls and sarcophagi of pyramids of the Old Kingdom; in later periods Orion is associated with the god of the dead, Osiris.

8. Unis has consumed the mental capacities of the gods, and now he can outwit them.

9. Unis's meal consisted of the gods, including their *bas* and *akhs*, and so was in excess of anything they could have.

1. Unis commands this world as well as the celestial world and is perpetually immune to evil.

THE GREAT HYMN TO THE ATEN

ca. 1350 B.C.E.

Inscribed prominently at the entrance to the tomb of an important official in the new capital city of el-Amarna, this hymn celebrates the sun as creator and sustainer of the world and emphasizes the close connection between the god and his human counterparts, the king (Amenhotep IV) and queen (Nefertiti). The king initiated a religious and political revolution when he exclusively promoted the cult of the sun god, Aten, built a new capital, and changed his name to Akhenaten, which means "He who is effective for Aten." For a decade or two the old pantheon with numerous gods was neglected in favor of a new, singular creator god. Some scholars have seen the cult of Aten as an early type of monotheism, although this is much debated. The peaceful and lyrical tone of the hymn is at odds with the violence accompanying the changes that Akhenaten introduced, which were rejected within a few years of his death, when Egyptians abandoned the new capital, destroyed the king's monuments, and tried to erase his name from their society's memory.

Akhenaten and his family make an offering to Aten, the sun god.

The Great Hymn to the Aten[1]

Adoration of *Re-Harakhti-who-rejoices-in-lightland*[2] *In-his-name-Shu-who-is-Aten,* living forever; the great living Aten who is in jubilee, the lord of all that the Disk encircles, lord of sky, lord of earth, lord of the house-of-Aten[3] in Akhet-Aten; (and of) the King of Upper and Lower Egypt, who lives by Maat, the Lord of the Two Lands,[4] *Neferkheprure,*[5] *Sole-one-of-Re*; the Son of Re who lives by Maat,[6] the Lord of Crowns, *Akhenaten,* great in his lifetime; (and) his beloved great Queen, the Lady of the Two Lands, *Nefer-nefru-Aten Nefertiti,* who lives in health and youth forever. The Vizier, the Fanbearer on the right of the King, ——— Ay; he says:

Splendid you rise in heaven's lightland,
O living Aten, creator of life!
When you have dawned in eastern lightland,
You fill every land with your beauty.[7]
You are beauteous, great, radiant,
High over every land;
Your rays embrace the lands,
To the limit of all that you made.
Being Re, you reach their limits,
You bend them for the son whom you love;
Though you are far, your rays are on earth,
Though one sees you, your strides are unseen.

When you set in western lightland,[8]
Earth is in darkness as if in death;
One sleeps in chambers, heads covered,
One eye does not see another.
Were they robbed of their goods,
That are under their heads,
People would not remark it.
Every lion comes from its den,
All the serpents bite;
Darkness hovers, earth is silent,
As their maker rests in lightland.

1. Translated by Miriam Lichtheim.
2. The translation uses "lightland" for the Egyptian *akhet,* more often rendered "horizon." In the vision of Akhenaten, lightland was primarily on the east, where the sun rose. The two phrases in italics make up the formal name of Akhenaten's god, generally referred to as "(the) Aten." They are written in cartouches like kings' names.
3. Both the temple of the Aten in Akhet-Aten and the whole city as the god's estate.
4. A standard title of Egyptian kings. The Two Lands are Upper and Lower Egypt.
5. The name Akhenaten took when ascending the throne, before he initiated his revolution; it means "the perfect one of the manifestations of Re." Nefer-nefru-Aten is a comparable name given exceptionally to Akhenaten's queen, Nefertiti: "the perfect one of the perfection/beauty of Aten."
6. The most typical epithet of Akhenaten, who used the central Egyptian concept of Maat ("truth, order, justice") without clearly distinguishing it from its traditional meanings.
7. "Beauty" also means "presence."
8. Contrary to traditional Egyptian belief, the west, the normal abode of the dead, is seen in purely negative terms, as night and the absence of the god's protection.

Earth brightens when you dawn in lightland,
When you shine as Aten of daytime;
As you dispel the dark,
As you cast your rays,
The Two Lands are in festivity.
Awake they stand on their feet,
You have roused them;
Bodies cleansed, clothed,
Their arms adore your appearance.
The entire land sets out to work,
All beasts browse on their herbs;
Trees, herbs are sprouting,
Birds fly from their nests,
Their wings greeting your *ka*.[9]
All flocks frisk on their feet,
All that fly up and alight,
They live when you dawn for them.
Ships fare north, fare south as well,
Roads lie open when you rise;
The fish in the river dart before you,
Your rays are in the midst of the sea.

Who makes seed grow in women,
Who creates people from sperm;
Who feeds the son in his mother's womb,
Who soothes him to still his tears.
Nurse in the womb,
Giver of breath,
To nourish all that he made.
When he comes from the womb to breathe,
On the day of his birth,
You open wide his mouth,
You supply his needs.
When the chick in the egg speaks in the shell,
You give him breath within to sustain him;
When you have made him complete,
To break out from the egg,
He comes out from the egg,
To announce his completion,
Walking on his legs he comes from it.

How many are your deeds,
Though hidden from sight,
O Sole God beside whom there is none![1]
You made the earth as you wished, you alone,
All peoples, herds, and flocks;

9. *Ka* normally means the generative principle transmitted through the generations. Here it seems to mean simply the god's manifestation of himself in the sunrise.

1. This could mean either that no god can be compared with the Aten/Re or that he is the only god.

All upon earth that walk on legs,
All on high that fly on wings,
The lands of Khor and Kush,[2]
The land of Egypt.
You set every man in his place,
You supply their needs;
Everyone has his food,
His lifetime is counted.
Their tongues differ in speech,
Their characters likewise;
Their skins are distinct,
For you distinguished the peoples.

You made Hapy in *dat*,[3]
You bring him when you will,
To nourish the people,
For you made them for yourself.
Lord of all who toils for them,
Lord of all lands who shines for them,
Aten of daytime, great in glory!
All distant lands, you make them live,
You made a heavenly Hapy descend for them;
He makes waves on the mountains like the sea,
To drench their fields and their towns.
How excellent are your ways, O Lord of eternity!
A Hapy from heaven for foreign peoples,
And all lands' creatures that walk on legs,
For Egypt the Hapy who comes from *dat*.

Your rays nurse all fields,
When you shine they live, they grow for you;
You made the seasons to foster all that you made,
Winter to cool them, heat that they taste you.
You made the far sky to shine therein,
To behold all that you made;
You alone, shining in your form of living Aten,
Risen, radiant, distant, near.
You made millions of forms from yourself alone,
Towns, villages, fields, the river's course;
All eyes observe you upon them,
For you are the Aten of daytime on high.

2. Syria in the north and Sudan in the south.
3. Hapy is the inundation of the Nile, essential to life in Egypt; *dat* is Egyptian for "underworld," from which the inundation could be considered to emerge. Other lands that do not have the inundation must be content with rain as an equivalent from the sky; this is then characterized as another Hapy.

[. . .][4]

You are in my heart,
There is no other who knows you,
Only your son, *Neferkheprure, Sole-one-of-Re,*
Whom you have taught your ways and your might.
Those on earth come from your hand as you made them,
When you have dawned they live,
When you set they die;
You yourself are lifetime, one lives by you.
All eyes are on your beauty until you set,
All labor ceases when you rest in the west;
When you rise you stir everyone for the King,
Every leg is on the move since you founded the earth.
You rouse them for your son who came from your body,
The King who lives by Maat, the Lord of the Two Lands,
Neferkheprure, Sole-one-of-Re,
The Son of Re who lives by Maat, the Lord of crowns,
Akhenaten, great in his lifetime;[5]
(And) the great Queen whom he loves, the Lady of the Two Lands,
Nefer-nefru-Aten Nefertiti, living forever.

4. A broken and obscure passage omitted by the translator.
5. A special epithet adopted by Akhenaten. Nefertiti's epithet "living forever" is a standard one applied to both kings and queens.

THE BABYLONIAN CREATION EPIC (*ENUMA ELISH*)

Enuma Elish ("When on high"), titled from the opening words of the poem, is an Akkadian poem that may have originated as early as the eighteenth century B.C.E. (although some have dated it to the twelfth century B.C.E.). Even this ancient story combined several other, much earlier cosmogonies, from Sumerian, Old Akkadian, and West Semitic cultures, that told of the warrior god's struggle against the primeval female sea monster (Tiamat). The narrative structure of our text reflects a clear agenda: the author gives pride of place to the Babylonian god, Marduk, whose temple in Babylon becomes the religious and political center of the world. The story traces the world's creation: from the two primary personifications of ocean (fresh and salt, Apsu and Tiamat) out of which emerge the earliest gods—who fight against the fresh ocean, the father-figure Apsu, when he wants to destroy them and restore primeval silence. Then Marduk, the creator god, kills Tiamat and from her body fashions the world; he establishes the first city, Babylon, where he has his cosmic home in the Esagila temple. Marduk's father, Ea, creates the first humans out of the blood of Qingu, Tiamat's consort and general, and these are to serve the gods' many needs. Finally, Marduk creates the netherworld, providing a mythic space for human existence after death.

From The Babylonian Creation Epic (*Enuma Elish*)[1]

From *Tablet I*

When on high no name was given to heaven,
Nor below was the netherworld called by name,
Primeval Apsu was their progenitor.
And matrix-Tiamat was she who bore them all,[2]
They were mingling their waters together,
No canebrake was intertwined nor thicket matted close.[3]
When no gods at all had been brought forth,
Nor called by names, none destinies ordained,
Then were the gods formed within the(se two).

* * *

1. Translated by and with footnotes adapted from Benjamin R. Foster.
2. Before anything existed in the world, Mother Ocean, Tiamat, and Fresh Water, Apsu, mingled to produce the first pairs of gods.
3. Nothing divided or covered the waters.

From *Tablet V*

Marduk creates Babylon as the terrestrial counterpart to Esharra, abode of the gods in heaven. The gods are to repose there during their earthly sojourns.

Marduk made ready to speak and said
(These) words to the gods his fathers,
"Above Apsu, the azure dwelling,
"As a counterpart to Esharra, which I built for you,
"Below the firmament, whose grounding I made firm.
"A house I shall build, let it be the abode of my pleasure.
"Within it I shall establish its holy place.
"I shall appoint my (holy) chambers.
I shall establish my kingship.
"When you go up from Apsu to assembly,
"Let your stopping places be here, before your assembly.[4]
"When you come down from heaven to [assembly],
"Let your stopping places be there to receive all of you.
"I shall call [its] name [Babylon],
Houses of the Great Gods,[5]
"We shall all hold fe[stival]s with[in] it."
When the gods his fathers heard what he commanded,
They [. . .]
"Over all things that your hands have created,
"Who has [authority, save for you]?
"Over the earth that you have created,
"Who has [authority, save for] you?
"Babylon, to which you have given name,
"Make our [stopping place] there forever."

* * *

From *Tablet VI*

The rebellious gods are offered a general pardon if they will produce their leader. They produce Qingu, claiming that he started the war. He is sacrificed, and his blood is used to make a human being.

When [Mar]duk heard the speech of the gods,
He was resolving to make artful things:
He would tell his idea to Ea,[6]
What he thought of in his heart he proposes,
"I shall compact blood, I shall cause bones to be,
"I shall make stand a human being, let 'Man' be its name.

4. When the gods or their cult images traveled to Babylon, they could stay in chambers at Marduk's temple.
5. Original meaning of the name Babylon.
6. Before this text was written, creation in the Mesopotamian tradition was usually attributed to the Mother Goddess and Ea (or Enki), the god of wisdom and magic. In order to insert Marduk, the Babylonian city god, into this tradition, the text credits Marduk with giving Ea the idea for creating humankind.

"I shall create humankind,
"They shall bear the gods' burden that those may rest.
"I shall artfully double the ways of the gods:
"Let them be honored as one but divided in twain."[7]
Ea answered him, saying these words,
He told him a plan to let the gods rest,
"Let one, their brother, be given to me,
"Let him be destroyed so that people can be fashioned.
"Let the great gods convene in assembly,
"Let the guilty one be given up that they may abide."
Marduk convened the great gods in assembly,
He spoke to them magnanimously as he gave the command,
The gods heeded his utterance,
As the king spoke to the Anunna-gods (these) words,
"Let your first reply be the truth!
"Do you speak with me truthful words!
"Who was it that made war,
"Suborned Tiamat and drew up for battle?
"Let him be given over to me, the one who made war,
"I shall make him bear his punishment, you shall be released."
The Igigi, the great gods answered him,
To Lugaldimmerankia, counsellor of all the gods, their lord,
"It was Qingu who made war,
"Suborned Tiamat and drew up for battle."
They bound and held him before Ea.
They imposed the punishment on him and shed his blood.
From his blood he made humankind.
He imposed the burden of the gods and exempted the gods.
After Ea the wise had made humankind,
They imposed the burden of the gods on them!
That deed is beyond comprehension.
By the artifices of Marduk did Nudimmud create!

Marduk divides the gods of heaven and netherworld.
The gods build Esagila, Marduk's temple in Babylon

Marduk the king divided the gods,
The Anunna-gods, all of them, above and below,
He assigned to Anu[8] for duty at his command.
He set three hundred in heaven for (their) duty,
A like number he designated for the ways of the netherworld:
He made six hundred dwell in heaven and netherworld.
After he had given all the commands,
And had divided the shares of the Anunna-gods
of heaven and netherworld,
The Anunna-gods made ready to speak.
To Marduk their lord they said,

7. Reference to the two main divisions of the Mesopotamian pantheon: the supernatural "Anunna-gods" and the infernal "Igigi-gods."
8. The sky god who is supreme in the pantheon but remote from human affairs. The ancient city-state Uruk, where the great hero Gilgamesh was king, was known for its temple to Anu.

"Now, Lord, you who have liberated us.
"What courtesy may we do you?
"We will make a shrine, whose name will be a byword,
"Your chamber that shall be our stopping place,
    we shall find rest therein.
"We shall lay out the shrine, let us set up its emplacement,
"When we come (to visit you), we shall find rest therein."
When Marduk heard this,
His features glowed brightly, like the day,
"Then make Babylon the task that you requested,
"Let its brickwork be formed, build high the shrine."
The Anunna-gods set to with hoes,
One (full) year they made its bricks.
When the second year came,
They raised the head of Esagila,[9] the counterpart to Apsu,
They built the upper ziggurat of Apsu,
For Anu-Enlil-Ea[1] they founded his [. . .] and dwelling,
He took his seat in sublimity before them,
Its pinnacles were facing toward the base of Esharra.
After they had done the work of Esagila,
All the Anunna-gods devised their own shrines.

* * *

Marduk is made supreme god. Anshar gives him a second name, Asalluhi. Anshar explains Marduk's role among gods and men with respect to this second name.

After Anu had ordained the destinies of the bow,[2]
He set out the royal throne
    that stood highest among the gods,
Anu had him sit there, in the assembly of the gods.
Then the great gods convened,
They made Marduk's destiny highest, they prostrated themselves.
They laid upon themselves a curse (if they broke the oath),
With water and oil they swore, they touched their throats.[3]
They granted him exercise of kingship over the gods,
They established him forever
    for lordship of heaven and netherworld.
Anshar[4] gave him an additional name, Asalluhi,
"When he speaks, we will all do obeisance,
"At his command the gods shall pay heed.

* * *

9. Wordplay on the name of Marduk's temple, which means "house whose head is high."
1. Here three major gods of the Mesopotamian pantheon probably stand for the powerful Marduk.
2. Right before this passage, Marduk's bow is made into a star constellation by the god Anu.
3. A slashing gesture people performed when taking an oath to show what should happen to those who break it.
4. God of the second generation after the creator couple Tiamat and Apsu. Anshar, "Whole Heaven," is coupled with Kishar, "Whole Earth."

Beginning of the explanation of Marduk's fifty names. Names 1–9 are those borne by Marduk prior to this point in the narrative. Each of them is correlated with crucial points in the narrative as follows: his birth, his creation of the human race to provide for the gods, his terrible anger but his willingness to spare the rebellious gods, his proclamation by the gods as supreme among them, his organization of the cosmos, his saving the gods from danger, his sparing the gods who fought on the side of Tiamat, but his killing of Tiamat and Qingu, and his enabling the gods to proceed with the rest of what is narrated.

"Let us pronounce his fifty names,
"That his ways shall be (thereby) manifest, his deeds likewise(?):
MARDUK!
"Who, from his birth, was named by his forefather Anu,
"Establisher of pasture and watering place,
who enriches (their) stables,
"Who by his Deluge weapon subdued the stealthy ones,
"Who saved the gods his forefathers from danger.
"He is indeed the Son, the Sun,
the most radiant of the gods,
"They shall walk in his brilliant light forever.
"On the people whom he made,
creatures with the breath of life,
"He imposed the gods' burden, that those be released.
"Creation, destruction, absolution, punishment:
"Each shall be at his command, these shall gaze upon him.
"MARUKKA shall he be,
the god who created them (humankind),
"Who granted (thereby) the Anunna-gods contentment,
who let the Igigi-gods rest.
"MARUTUKKU shall be the trust of his land,
city, and people,
"The people shall heed him forever."
The rest of the fifty names of Marduk follow here.

* * *

From *Tablet VII*

Composition and purpose of this text, its approval by Marduk.

They must be grasped: the "first one"[5] should reveal (them),
The wise and knowledgeable should ponder (them) together,
The master should repeat, and make the pupil understand.
The "shepherd," the "herdsman" should pay attention,[6]

5. As in other Mesopotamian mythical stories, this part explains how the text originated and how it should be used by later ages. The "first one" probably refers to somebody who recites or "reveals" the text during a religious ceremony. This epilogue emphasizes the sacredness of the text—approved by Marduk himself—which should not be changed by future generations.

6. "Shepherd" is a cliché for king.

He must not neglect the Enlil of the gods, Marduk,
So his land may prosper and he himself be safe.
His word is truth, what he says is not changed,
Not one god can annul his utterance.
If he frowns, he will not relent,
If he is angry, no god can face his rage.
His heart is deep, his feelings all encompassing,
He before whom crime and sin must appear for judgment.
The revelation (of the names) that the "first one"
    discoursed before him (Marduk),
He wrote down and preserved for the future to hear,
The [wo]rd of Marduk who created the Igigi-gods,
[His/Its] let them [ ], his name let them invoke.
Let them sound abroad the song of Marduk,
How he defeated Tiamat and took kingship.

HESIOD

late eighth century B.C.E.

The *Theogony* and *Works and Days* are composed in the same meter and come from the same period as the Homeric epics—the late eighth century B.C.E. The *Theogony,* which means "birth of the gods," begins with the story of how the poem itself came into being, when the Muses inspired the poet Hesiod on Mount Helicon. The text tells how the Olympian gods, ruled by Zeus, emerged out of the earlier generations: Earth and Sky (Gaia and Ouranos) gave birth to the Titans, who were finally overthrown by Zeus. Hesiod also includes several stories about the prehistory of humanity, which address the origins of technology, sin, and suffering. These include the story of Prometheus, a clever Titan who tricked Zeus and stole fire from heaven to give to mankind; Zeus punished Prometheus with eternal pain and punished humanity by creating woman as a "tempting snare / from which men cannot escape." In *Works and Days*, a poem that combines mythical stories with injunctions about how to live, work, farm, and sail, Hesiod gives a different, somewhat less misogynistic version of the myth, in which a woman (Pandora, or "All Gifts") does not represent evil but accidentally brings evil into the world. Hesiod then offers yet another account of how suffering came to the world, this time without invoking gender at all: humans gradually degenerated, from the age of gold to the age of iron, in which we now live.

From Theogony[1]

I begin my song with the Helikonian Muses whose domain
is Helikon, the great god-haunted mountain;
their soft feet move in the dance that rings
the violet-dark spring and the altar of mighty Zeus.
They bathe their lithe bodies in the water of Permessos
or of Hippokrene or of god-haunted Olmeios.
On Helikon's peak they join hands in lovely dances
and their pounding feet awaken desire.
From there they set out and, veiled in mist,
glide through the night and raise enchanting voices
to exalt aegis-bearing Zeus and queenly Hera,[2]
the lady of Argos who walks in golden sandals;
gray-eyed Athena, daughter of aegis-bearing Zeus,
and Phoibos Apollon and arrow-shooting Artemis.
They exalt Poseidon, holder and shaker of the earth,
stately Themis and Aphrodite of the fluttering eyelids,
and gold-wreathed Hebe and fair Dione.[3]
And then they turn their song to Eos, Helios, and bright Selene,[4]
to Leto, Iapetos, and sinuous-minded Kronos,[5]
to Gaia, great Okeanos,[6] and black Night,
and to the holy race of the other deathless gods.
It was they who taught Hesiod beautiful song
as he tended his sheep at the foothills of god-haunted Helikon.
Here are the words the daughters of aegis-bearing Zeus,
the Muses of Olympos, first spoke to me.
"Listen, you country bumpkins, you pot-bellied blockheads,
we know how to tell many lies that pass for truth,
and when we wish, we know to tell the truth itself."
So spoke Zeus's daughters, masters of word-craft,
and from a laurel in full bloom they plucked a branch,
and gave it to me as a staff, and then breathed into me
divine song, that I might spread the fame of past and future,
and commanded me to hymn the race of the deathless gods,
but always begin and end my song with them.
Yet, trees and rocks are not my theme. Let me sing on!
Ah, my heart, begin with the Muses who hymn father Zeus
and in the realm of Olympos gladden his great heart;
with sweet voices they speak of things that are
and things that were and will be, and with effortless smoothness
the song flows from their mouths. The halls of father Zeus

1. Translated by Apostolos N. Athanassakis. *Theogony* means "birth of the gods" or "divine generation."

2. Zeus and Hera are the king and queen of the gods.

3. All gods and goddesses. Apollon, god of poetry, and Artemis, goddess of the hunt, are twins; Poseidon, brother of Zeus, causes earthquakes; Themis is goddess of justice (her name means "right" or "lawfulness"); Aphrodite is goddess of sexual desire; *Hebe* means "youth"; Dione is the mother of Aphrodite.

4. Personifications of dawn, sun, and moon.

5. Leto is the mother of Apollo and Artemis; Iapetos and Kronos are Titans (children of the earth and sky).

6. Earth and Ocean.

the thunderer shine with glee and ring, filled with voices
lily-soft and heavenly, and the peaks of snowy Olympos
and the dwellings of the gods resound. With their divine voices
they first sing the glory of the sublime race of the gods
from the beginning, the children born to Gaia and vast Ouranos[7]
and of their offspring, the gods who give blessings.
Then they sing of Zeus, father of gods and men—
they begin and end their song with him
and tell of how he surpasses the other gods in rank and might.
And then again the Olympian Muses and daughters of aegis-bearing Zeus
hymn the races of men and of the brawny Giants,
and thrill the heart of Zeus in the realm of Olympos.
Mnemosyne,[8] mistress of the Eleutherian hills,
lay with father Zeus and in Pieria gave birth to the Muses
who soothe men's troubles and make them forget their sorrows.
Zeus the counselor, far from the other immortals, leaped
into her sacred bed and lay with her for nine nights.
And when, as the seasons turned, the months waned,
many many days passed and a year was completed,
she gave birth to nine daughters of harmonious mind,
carefree maidens whose hearts yearn for song;
this was close beneath the highest peak of snowy Olympos,
the very place of their splendid dances and gracious homes.
The Graces and Desire dwell near them and take part
in their feasts. Lovely are their voices when they sing
and extol for the whole world the laws
and wise customs of all the immortals.
Then they went to Olympos, delighting in their beautiful voices
and their heavenly song. The black earth resounded with hymns,
and a lovely beat arose as they pounded their feet
and advanced toward their father, the king of the sky
who holds the thunderbolt that roars and flames.
He subdued his father, Kronos, by might and for the gods
made a fair settlement and gave each his domain.
All this was sung by the Olympian Muses,
great Zeus's nine daughters whose names are
Kleio, Euterpe, Thaleia, Melpomene,
Terpsichore, Erato, Polymnia, Ourania,
and Kalliope, preeminent by far,
the singers' pride in the company of noble kings.[9]
And if the daughters of great Zeus honor a king
cherished by Zeus and look upon him when he is born,
they pour on his tongue sweet dew
and make the words that flow from his mouth honey-sweet,
and all the people look up to him as with straight justice

7. Ouranos (Uranus) is Sky.
8. Memory.
9. The nine Muses preside over nine arts: Kleio over history, Euterpe over music, Thaleia over comedy, Melpomene over tragedy, Terpsichore over dance, Erato over lyric poetry, Polymnia over choral poetry, Ourania over astronomy, and Kalliope over epic.

he gives his verdict and with unerring firmness
and wisdom brings some great strife to a swift end.
This is why kings are prudent, and when in the assembly
injustice is done, wrongs are righted
by the kings with ease and gentle persuasion.
When such a king comes to the assembly he stands out;
yes, he is revered like a god and treated with cheerful respect.
Such is the holy gift the Muses give men.
The singers and lyre players of this earth
are descended from the Muses and far-shooting Apollon,
but kings are from the line of Zeus. Blessed is the man
whom the Muses love; sweet song flows from his mouth.
A man may have some fresh grief over which to mourn,
and sorrow may have left him no more tears, but if a singer,
a servant of the Muses, sings the glories of ancient men
and hymns the blessed gods who dwell on Olympos,
the heavy-hearted man soon shakes off his dark mood, and oblivion
soothes his grief, for this gift of the gods diverts his mind.
Hail, daughters of Zeus! Grant me the gift of lovely song!
Sing the glories of the holy gods to whom death never comes,
the gods born of Gaia and starry Ouranos,
and of those whom dark Night bore, or briny Pontos[1] fostered.
Speak first of how the gods and the earth came into being
and of how the rivers, the boundless sea with its raging swell,
the glittering stars, and the wide sky above were created.
Tell of the gods born of them, the givers of blessings,
how they divided wealth, and each was given his realm,
and how they first gained possession of many-folded Olympos.
Tell me, O Muses who dwell on Olympos, and observe proper order
for each thing as it first came into being.
Chaos[2] was born first and after it came Gaia
the broad-breasted, the firm seat of all
the immortals who hold the peaks of snowy Olympos,
and the misty Tartaros[3] in the depths of broad-pathed earth
and Eros,[4] the fairest of the deathless gods;
he unstrings the limbs and subdues both mind
and sensible thought in the breasts of all gods and all men.
Chaos gave birth to Erebos[5] and black Night;
then Erebos mated with Night and made her pregnant
and she in turn gave birth to Ether[6] and Day.
Gaia now first gave birth to starry Ouranos,
her match in size, to encompass all of her,
and be the firm seat of all the blessed gods.
She gave birth to the tall mountains, enchanting haunts
of the divine nymphs who dwell in the woodlands;
and then she bore Pontos, the barren sea with its raging swell.

1. Sea.
2. In Greek, "chaos" suggests a gap or chasm, not necessarily disorder.
3. An abyss beneath the earth.
4. Sexual desire.
5. Darkness.
6. The upper part of the sky.

All these she bore without mating in sweet love. But then
she did couple with Ouranos to bear deep-eddying Okeanos,
Koios and Kreios, Hyperion and Iapetos,
Theia and Rheia, Themis and Mnemosyne,
as well as gold-wreathed Phoibe and lovely Tethys.
Kronos, the sinuous-minded, was her last-born,
a most fearful child who hated his mighty father.
Then she bore the Kyklopes, haughty in their might,
Brontes, Steropes, and Arges of the strong spirit,
who made and gave to Zeus the crushing thunder.
In all other respects they were like gods,
but they had one eye in the middle of their foreheads;
their name was Kyklopes because of this single
round eye that leered from their foreheads,
and inventive skill and strength and power were in their deeds.
Gaia and Ouranos had three other sons, so great
and mighty that their names are best left unspoken,
Kottos, Briareos, and Gyges, brazen sons all three.
From each one's shoulders a hundred invincible arms
sprang forth, and from each one's shoulders atop the sturdy trunk
there grew no fewer than fifty heads;
and there was matchless strength in their hulking frames.
All these awesome children born of Ouranos and Gaia
hated their own father from the day they were born,
for as soon as each one came out of the womb,
Ouranos, with joy in his wicked work, hid it
in Gaia's womb and did not let it return to the light.
Huge Gaia groaned within herself
and in her distress she devised a crafty and evil scheme.
With great haste she produced gray iron
and made a huge sickle and showed it to her children;
then, her heart filled with grief, she rallied them with these words:
"Yours is a reckless father; obey me, if you will,
that we may all punish your father's outrageous deed,
for he was first to plot shameful actions."
So she spoke, and fear gripped them all; not one of them
uttered a sound. Then great, sinuous-minded Kronos
without delay spoke to his prudent mother:
"Mother, this deed I promise you will be done,
since I loathe my dread-named father.
It was he who first plotted shameful actions."
So he spoke, and the heart of giant Earth was cheered.
She made him sit in ambush and placed in his hands
a sharp-toothed sickle and confided in him her entire scheme.
Ouranos came dragging with him the night, longing for Gaia's love,
and he embraced her and lay stretched out upon her.
Then his son reached out from his hiding place and seized him
with his left hand, while with his right he grasped
the huge, long, and sharp-toothed sickle and swiftly hacked off
his father's genitals and tossed them behind him—
and they were not flung from his hand in vain.

Gaia took in all the bloody drops that spattered off,
and as the seasons of the year turned round
she bore the potent Furies and the Giants, immense,
dazzling in their armor, holding long spears in their hands,
and then she bore the Ash Tree Nymphs of the boundless earth.
As soon as Kronos had lopped off the genitals with the sickle
he tossed them from the land into the stormy sea.
And as they were carried by the sea a long time, all around them
white foam rose from the god's flesh, and in this foam a maiden
was nurtured. First she came close to god-haunted Kythera
and from there she went on to reach sea-girt Cyprus.
There this majestic and fair goddess came out, and soft grass
grew all around her soft feet. Both gods and men
call her Aphrodite, foam-born goddess, and fair-wreathed Kythereia;
Aphrodite because she grew out of *aphros,* foam, that is,
and Kythereia because she touched land at Kythera.
She is called Kyprogenes, because she was born
in sea-girt Cyprus, and Philommedes, fond of a man's genitals,
because to them she owed her birth. Fair Himeros[7] and Eros
became her companions when she was born and when she joined the gods.
And here is the power she has had from the start
and her share in the lives of men and deathless gods:
from her come young girls' whispers and smiles and deception
and honey-sweet love and its joyful pleasures.
But the great father Ouranos railed at his own children
and gave them the nickname Titans, Overreachers,
because he said they had, with reckless power, overreached him
to do a monstrous thing that would be avenged someday.
Night gave birth to hideous Moros and black Ker[8]
and then to Death and Sleep and to the brood of Dreams.

* * *

From Works and Days[1]

This is why Zeus devised sorrows and troubles for men.
He hid fire. But Prometheus, noble son of Iapetos,[2]
stole it back for man's sake from Zeus, whose counsels are many.
In the hollow of a fennel stalk he slipped it away,
unnoticed by Zeus, who delights in thunder.
So the cloud-gatherer in anger said to him:
"Son of Iapetos, craftiest of all,
you rejoice at tricking my wits and stealing the fire
which will be a curse to you and to the generations that follow.

7. Longing.
8. Doom and Fate.
1. Translated by Apostolos N. Athanassakis. Early in the poem, Hesiod urges his addressee to work hard; this passage explains why humans cannot simply live a life of ease.
2. Iapetos is a Titan, a child of the Earth and Sky, part of the generation of divine beings that preceded Zeus and the other Olympians.

The price for the stolen fire will be a gift of evil
to charm the hearts of all men as they hug their own doom."
This said, the father of gods and men roared with laughter.
Then he ordered widely acclaimed Hephaistos[3] to mix earth with water
with all haste and place in them human voice
and strength. His orders were to make a face
such as goddesses have and the shape of a lovely maiden;
Athena was to teach her skills and intricate weaving,
and golden Aphrodite[4] should pour grace round her head,
and stinging desire and limb-gnawing passion.
Then he ordered Hermes[5] the pathbreaker and slayer of Argos
to put in her the mind of a bitch and a thievish nature.
So he spoke, and they obeyed lord Zeus, son of Kronos.
Without delay the renowned lame god fashioned from earth,
through Zeus's will, the likeness of a shy maiden,
and Athena, the gray-eyed goddess, clothed her and decked her out.
Then the divine graces and queenly Persuasion
gave her golden necklaces to wear, and the lovely-haired Seasons
stood round her and crowned her with spring flowers.
Pallas Athena adorned her body with every kind of jewel,
and the Slayer of Argos—Hermes the guide—through the will
of Zeus whose thunder roars placed in her breast
lies, coaxing words, and a thievish nature.
The gods' herald then gave her voice and called this woman
Pandora[6] because all the gods who dwell on Olympos
gave her as a gift—a scourge for toiling men.
Now when the Father finished his grand and wily scheme
he sent the glorious Slayer of Argos and swift messenger
to bring the gift of the gods to Epimetheus,[7]
who did not heed Prometheus's warning never to accept
a gift from Olympian Zeus, but send it back,
for fear that some evil might befall mortals.
First he accepted it and then saw the evil in it.
Earlier, human tribes lived on this earth
without suffering and toilsome hardship
and without painful illnesses that bring death to men—
a wretched life ages men before their time—
but the woman with her hands removed the great lid of the jar
and scattered its contents, bringing grief and cares to men.
Only Hope stayed under the rim of the jar
and did not fly away from her secure stronghold,
for in compliance with the wishes of cloud-gathering Zeus
Pandora put the lid on the jar before she could come out.
The rest wander among men as numberless sorrows,

3. God associated with technological skill and craftsmanship.
4. The goddess of sexual desire. Athena is the goddess of handicrafts and wisdom.
5. Messenger god, who killed the many-eyed monster Argos.
6. The name means "all gift."
7. Brother of Prometheus. *Prometheus* suggests "forethought"; *Epimetheus*, "hindsight."

since earth and sea teem with miseries.
Some diseases come upon men during the day, and some
roam about and bring pains to men in the silence of night
because Zeus the counselor made them mute.
So there is no way to escape the designs of Zeus.
I will give you the pith of another story—if you wish—
with consummate skill. Treasure this thought in your heart:
men and gods have a common descent.
At first the immortals who dwell on Olympos
created a golden race of mortal men.
That was when Kronos was king of the sky,
and they lived like gods, carefree in their hearts,
shielded from pain and misery. Helpless old age
did not exist, and with limbs of unsagging vigor
they enjoyed the delights of feasts, out of evil's reach.
A sleeplike death subdued them, and every good thing was theirs;
the barley-giving earth asked for no toil to bring forth
a rich and plentiful harvest. They knew no constraint
and lived in peace and abundance as lords of their lands,
rich in flocks and dear to the blessed gods.
But the earth covered this race,
and they became holy spirits that haunt it,
benign protectors of mortals that drive harm away
and keep a watchful eye over lawsuits and wicked deeds,
swathed in misty veils as they wander over the earth.
They are givers of wealth by kingly prerogative.
The gods of Olympos made a second race
—a much worse one—this time of silver,
unlike the golden one in thought or looks.
For a hundred years they were nurtured by their prudent mothers
as playful children—each a big baby in his house—
but when they grew up and reached adolescence
they lived only for a short while, plagued by the pains
of foolishness. They could not refrain from reckless violence
against one another and did not want to worship the gods
and on holy altars perform sacrifices for them,
as custom differing from place to place dictates.
In time Zeus, son of Kronos, was angered and buried them
because they denied the blessed Olympians their due honors.
The earth covered this race, too;
they dwell under the ground and are called blessed mortals—
they are second but, still, greatly honored.
Zeus the father made a third race of mortals,
this time of bronze, not at all like the silver one.
Fashioned from ash trees, they were dreadful and mighty
and bent on the harsh deeds of war and violence;
they ate no bread and their hearts were tough as steel.
No one could come near them, for their strength was great
and mighty arms grew from the shoulders of their sturdy bodies.
Bronze were their weapons, bronze their homes,

and bronze was what they worked—there was no black iron then.
With their hands they worked one another's destruction
and they reached the dank home of cold Hades
nameless. Black death claimed them for all their fierceness,
and they left the bright sunlight behind them.
But when the earth covered this race, too,
Zeus, son of Kronos, made upon the nourishing land
yet another race—the fourth one—better and more just.
They were the divine race of heroes, who are called
demigods; they preceded us on this boundless earth.
Evil war and dreadful battle wiped them all out,
some fighting over the flocks of Oidipous
at seven-gated Thebes, in the land of Kadmos,
others over the great gulf of the sea in ships
that had sailed to Troy for the sake of lovely-haired Helen;
there death threw his dark mantle over them.
Yet others of them father Zeus, son of Kronos, settled at earth's ends,
apart from men, and gave them shelter and food.
They live there with hearts unburdened by cares
in the islands of the blessed, near stormy Okeanos,
these blissful heroes for whom three times a year
the barley-giving land brings forth full grain sweet as honey.
I wish I were not counted among the fifth race of men,
but rather had died before, or been born after it.
This is the race of iron. Neither day nor night
will give them rest as they waste away with toil
and pain. Growing cares will be given them by the gods,
and their lot will be a blend of good and bad.
Zeus will destroy this race of mortals
when children are born gray at the temples.
Children will not resemble their fathers,
and there will be no affection between guest and host
and no love between friends or brothers as in the past.
Sons and daughters will be quick to offend their aging parents
and rebuke them and speak to them with rudeness
and cruelty, not knowing about divine retribution;
they will not even repay their parents for their keep—
these law-breakers—and they will sack one another's city.
The man who keeps his oath, or is just and good,
will not be favored, but the evildoers and scoundrels
will be honored, for might will make right and shame will vanish.
Base men will harm their betters with words
that are crooked and then swear they are fair.
And all toiling humanity will be blighted by envy,
grim and strident envy that takes its joy in the ruin of others.
Then Shame and Retribution will cover their fair bodies
with white cloaks and, leaving men behind,
will go to Olympos from the broad-pathed earth
to be among the race of the immortals, while grief and pain
will linger among men, whom harm will find defenseless.

EARLY GREEK PHILOSOPHY[1]

seventh through fifth centuries B.C.E.

The earliest "scientific" thinkers of ancient Greece are known as the pre-Socratics, because historians have often seen a sharp break between their interests—mostly in the physical structure of matter—and those of philosophers after Socrates, who concentrated above all on ethics. Most of the thinkers quoted here lived in the Greek-speaking cities of Ionia, in modern Turkey. Unfortunately, we have access to the words and ideas of these people only in "fragments," which usually means that they were quoted or paraphrased by much later ancient authors. But it is clear, even from these fragmentary sources, that their ideas were revolutionary. Thales of Miletus (ca. 624–546 B.C.E.) was the first to suggest that the world is made of a single underlying substance, which he theorized was water. Thales made various mathematical discoveries and was probably the first person to predict a solar eclipse, in 585 B.C.E. Heraclitus (ca. 535–475 B.C.E.) was known for his obscurity in antiquity, but he seems to have theorized that change is the fundamental principle of the universe, which operates by a continual process of opposites turning into each other. Empedocles (ca. 490–430), a Greek living in Sicily, created a simplified version of this idea: he suggested that the world works by a combination of love and strife, so that the four elements—air, earth, fire, and water—are constantly being conjoined and separated from one another. Anaxagoras (500–428 B.C.E.) came up with another variant on this idea, suggesting that the parts of the universe are in a constant process of separation and mixture, controlled by an underlying principle of intelligence, or mind. A little later in the fifth century B.C.E., the Greek atomists would develop the (startlingly modern) idea that the basic building blocks of matter are not fire, water, air, or earth but atoms and empty space (the void).

It is difficult to tell how shocking all these new theories were in the Greek world. There are stories about Anaxagoras being tried for impiety, but these are late and unreliable. Many Greeks in the sixth and fifth centuries B.C.E. seem to have been ready for a wide range of new speculations about the nature of the universe. Moreover, even the pre-Socratic speculators themselves seem often to have thought their new views were perfectly compatible with the old religious ideas about how the universe was made. Thales said that the world is made of water; but he also said, "Everything is full of gods."

1. All selections translated by Jonathan Barnes.

Thales[2]

Most of the first philosophers thought that principles in the form of matter were the only principles of all things. For they say that the element and first principle of the things that exist is that from which they all are and from which they first come into being and into which they are finally destroyed, its substance remaining and its properties changing. . . . There must be some nature—either one or more than one—from which the other things come into being, it being preserved. But as to the number and form of this sort of principle, they do not all agree. Thales, the founder of this kind of philosophy, says that it is water (that is why he declares that the earth rests on water). He perhaps came to acquire this belief from seeing that the nourishment of everything is moist and that heat itself comes from this and lives by this (for that from which anything comes into being is its first principle)—he came to his belief both for this reason and because the seeds of everything have a moist nature, and water is the natural principle of moist things.

Heraclitus[3]

Heraclitus of Ephesus is most clearly of this opinion [i.e. that everything will change into fire]. He holds that there is a world which is eternal and a world which is perishing, and he is aware that the created world is the former in a certain state. Now that he recognized that the world which is uniquely characterized by the totality of substance is eternal, is evident when he says:

> *The world, the same for all, neither any god nor any man made; but it was always and is and will be, fire ever-living, kindling in measures and being extinguished in measures.*

And that he believed it to be generated and destructible is indicated by the following words:

> *Turnings of fire: first, sea; of sea, half is earth, half lightning-flash.*

—He says in effect that, by reason and god which rule everything, fire is turned by way of air into moisture, the seed, as it were, of creation, which he calls sea; and from this, again, come earth and heaven and what they contain. He shows clearly in the following words that they are restored again and become fire:

> *Sea is dissolved and measured into the same proportion that existed at first.*

And the same holds for the other elements.

2. None of Thales's own writings survive. This passage is an account of his views, and those of the other "first philosophers," by the much later (fourth century B.C.E.) philosopher Aristotle.

3. Heraclitus's work survives only through quotations and citations by later writers. This passage was written by a prominent Christian writer from the second century C.E., Clement of Alexandria (ca. 150–215 C.E.). Since Clement lived some seven hundred years after Heraclitus, he had a very different perspective on theology and creation; but his testimony is valuable because he must have read Heraclitus's book—which is now lost. The lines in italics are apparently direct quotations from Heraclitus, while those in regular font summarize his views.

Empedocles[4]

I will tell a two-fold story. At one time they grew to be one alone
from being many, and at another they grew apart again to be
many from being one.
Double is the generation of mortal things, double their passing away:
one is born and destroyed by the congregation of everything,
the other is nurtured and flies apart as they grow apart again.
And these never cease their continual change,
now coming together by Love all into one,
now again all being carried apart by the hatred of Strife.
<Thus insofar as they have learned to become one from many>[5]
and again become many as the one grows apart,
to that extent they come into being and have no lasting life;
but insofar as they never cease their continual change,
to that extent they exist forever, unmoving in a circle.
But come, hear my words; for learning enlarges the mind.
As I said before when I revealed the limits of my words,
I will tell a two-fold story. At one time they grew to be one alone
from being many, and at another they grew apart again to be
many from being one—
fire and water and earth and the endless height of air,
and cursed Strife apart from them, balanced in every way,
and Love among them, equal in length and breadth.
Her you must regard with your mind: do not sit staring with your eyes.
She is thought to be innate also in the limbs of mortals,
by whom they think thoughts of love and perform deeds of union,
calling her Joy by name and Aphrodite,
whom no one has seen whirling among them—
no mortal man. Listen to the course of my argument, which does
not deceive:
these are all equal and of the same age,
but they hold different offices and each has its own character;
and in turn they come to power as time revolves.
And in addition to them nothing comes into being or ceases.

Anaxagoras[6]

Mind is something infinite and self-controlling, and it has been mixed with no thing but is alone itself by itself. For if it were not by itself but had been mixed with some other thing, it would share in all things, if it had been mixed with any. For in everything there is present a share of everything, as I have said earlier, and the things commingled with it would have prevented it from controlling anything in the way in which it does when it is actually alone by itself. For it is

4. This passage from Empedocles' poem "On Nature" is quoted by a philosophical writer from the fifth century C.E., Simplicius.

5. The angle brackets mean that this line may not belong in the original poem.

6. This passage is also quoted by Simplicius.

the finest of all things and the purest, and it possesses all knowledge about everything, and it has the greatest strength. And mind controls all those things, both great and small, which possess soul. And mind controlled the whole revolution, so that it revolved in the first place. And first it began to revolve in a small area, and it is revolving more widely, and it will revolve yet more widely. And mind recognizes all the things which are commingling and separating off and dissociating. And mind arranged everything—what was to be and what was and what now is and what will be—and also this revolution in which revolve the stars and the sun and the moon and the air and the ether which are separating off. But the revolution itself made them separate them off. And the dense is separating off from the rare, and the hot from the cold, and the bright from the dark, and the dry from the wet. And there are many shares of many things, but nothing completely separates off or dissociates one from another except mind. All mind, both great and small, is alike. Nothing else is alike, but each single thing is and was most patently those things of which it contains most.

LUCRETIUS

ca. 55 B.C.E.

The epic *On the Nature of Things,* by Lucretius (ca. 99–55 B.C.E.), is the only surviving work of an Epicurean Roman poet. Epicurus was a Greek philosopher who lived in the fourth and third centuries B.C.E. and whose philosophy emphasizes tranquility or peace of mind as the primary goal of human life. Epicureans believed that false beliefs—about the origins and nature of the universe and about death—and false fears about the gods are the primary sources of human anxiety. They were not atheists, but they denied that the gods played any part in the creation or direction of the universe; instead, the gods lived at the edge of the universe, in a state of perfect peace to which humans should aspire. Lucretius argues that the workings of the world, which most humans falsely ascribe to divine intervention, can all be explained in material terms; matter is composed of atoms, which are in a constant state of random motion, and this in itself is sufficient to explain the phenomena that we see around us. One of the most challenging aspects of Lucretius's work is the interplay between the scientific and the poetic, and between the materialist and the mythological. For instance, Lucretius denies that the gods direct the world, yet he begins his poem with a beautiful, moving description of how the goddess Venus controls every aspect of life on earth.

From On the Nature of Things[1]

From *Book I*

Mother of Romans, delight of gods and men,
Sweet Venus,[2] who under the wheeling signs of heaven
Rouse the ship-shouldering sea and the fruitful earth
And make them teem—for through you all that breathe
Are begotten, and rise to see the light of the sun;
From you, goddess, the winds flee, from you and your coming
Flee the storms of heaven; for you the artful earth
Sends up sweet flowers, for you the ocean laughs
And the calm skies shimmer in a bath of light.
And now, when the gates are wide for spring and its splendor
And the west wind, fostering life, blows strong and free,
Pricked in their hearts by your power, the birds of the air
Give the first sign, goddess, of you and your entering;
Then through the fertile fields the love-wild beasts
Frolic, and swim the rapids (so seized with your charm
They eagerly follow wherever you may lead);
Yes, across seas and mountains and hungering rivers
And the leaf-springing homes of the birds and the greening fields,
Into all hearts you strike your lure of love
That by desire they propagate their kinds.
And since it is you alone who govern the birth
And growth of things, since nothing without you
Can be glad or lovely or rise to the shores of light,
I ask you to befriend me as I try
To pen these verses *On the Nature of Things*
For my friend Memmius[3] whom you, goddess, have ever
Caused to excel, accomplished in all things.
All the more, goddess, grant them lasting grace!
In the meantime let the savage works of war
Rest easy, slumbering over land and sea.
For you alone can bless us mortal men
With quiet peace; Mars, potent of arms, holds sway
In battle, but surrenders at your bosom,
Vanquished by the eternal wound of love.
There, his chiseled neck thrown back, he gapes at you,
Goddess, and feeds his greedy eyes with love;
He reclines; his spirit lingers upon your lips.
Melting about him, goddess, as he rests
On your holy body, pour from your lips sweet nothings,
Seeking, renowned one, quiet peace for Rome.
For I cannot work with a clear mind while my country

1. Translated by Anthony M. Esolen.
2. Roman counterpart of the Greek goddess Aphrodite; goddess of sex and mother of Aeneas, founder of Rome. The opening of the poem is surprising, since Epicurean philosophers like Lucretius did not normally believe in the usual myths about the gods.
3. A Roman orator and apparently Lucretius's patron.

Suffers, nor can the illustrious scion of
The Memmian house neglect the common good.[4]

For by necessity the gods above
Enjoy eternity in highest peace,
Withdrawn and far removed from our affairs.
Free of all sorrow, free of peril, the gods
Thrive in their own works and need nothing from us,
Not won with virtuous deeds nor touched by rage.

Then withdraw from cares and apply your cunning mind
To hear the truth of reasoned theory,
That the verses I give you, arranged with diligent love,
You will not scorn before you understand.
I open for you by discussing the ultimate law
Of the gods and sky; I reveal the atoms, whence
Nature creates and feeds and grows all things
And into which she resolves them when they are spent;
"Matter," "engendering bodies," "the seeds of things"
Are other terms for atoms which I use
In setting forth their laws; and "first beginnings"—
For from these elements all the world is formed.

When before our eyes man's life lay groveling, prostrate,
Crushed to the dust under the burden of Religion
(Which thrust its head from heaven, its horrible face
Glowering over mankind born to die),
One man, a Greek, was the first mortal who dared
Oppose his eyes, the first to stand firm in defiance.[5]
Not the fables of gods, nor lightning, nor the menacing
Rumble of heaven could daunt him, but all the more
They whetted his keen mind with longing to be
First to smash open the tight-barred gates of Nature.
His vigor of mind prevailed, and he strode far
Beyond the fiery battlements of the world,
Raiding the fields of the unmeasured All.
Our victor returns with knowledge of what can arise,
What cannot, what law grants each thing its own
Deep-driven boundary stone and finite scope.
Religion now lies trampled beneath our feet,
And we are made gods by the victory.[6]

You hear these things, and I fear you'll think yourself
On the road to evil, learning the fundamentals
Of blasphemy. Not so! Too often Religion
Herself gives birth to evil and blasphemous deeds.

4. The poem must have been composed during one of the many Roman civil wars, which dominated the first century B.C.E.
5. The Greek was the philosopher Epicurus.
6. The translation here is a little loose; in fact, Lucretius would be reluctant to equate humans with gods. The original literally means "Victory makes us equal with the sky."

At Aulis, for instance:[7] the pride of the Greek people,
The chosen peers, defiled Diana's altar
With the shameful blood of the virgin Iphigenia.
As soon as they tressed her hair with the ritual fillet,
The tassels spilling neatly upon each cheek,
And she sensed her grieving father beside the altar
With the acolytes nearby, hiding the knife,
And countrymen weeping to look upon her—mute
With fear, she fell to her knees, she groped for the earth.
Poor girl, what good did it do her then, that she
Was the first to give the king the name of "father"?
Up to the altar the men escorted her, trembling;
Not so that when her solemn rites were finished
She might be cheered in the ringing wedding-hymn,
But filthily, at the marrying age, unblemished
Victim, she fell by her father's slaughter-stroke
To shove his fleet off on a *bon voyage!*
Such wickedness Religion can incite!

* * *

From *Book V*[8]

Just so, don't think that the holy seats of the gods
Are found in any region of the world.
Our minds can hardly see, remote from sense,
The slender substance of their deities.
As they ever elude the touch and the strike of our hands
They cannot touch a thing that we can touch.
A thing can't touch if it's not touchable.
Therefore their dwellings also must be different
From ours, and be as subtle as their bodies.
I'll prove this to you later, at some length.
Further, to say that for man's sake the gods
Wished to prepare this glorious world, and therefore
It's only right to praise their handiwork
And think it will be deathless and eternal—
Shocking, that what the gods in their timeless wisdom
Founded for mankind to outlast the ages
You should ever shake from its base by any force,
Pound it with words and topple it—Memmius, to
Invent such errors and paste them one to the next
Is stupid. What gain can our grateful hearts bestow
Upon the blessed immortal gods, that they
Might take one step to act on our behalf?

7. At Aulis, when the Greek ships gathered to sail against Troy, they found themselves becalmed. The priest Calchas said that Diana (Artemis in the Greek pantheon) was angry and could be appeased only if the Greek leader, Agamemnon, killed his daughter Iphigeneia.

8. In this much later passage, Lucretius explains why we should not accept the mythological stories about the gods and their creation of the world (like those found in Hesiod). He is not arguing that gods do not exist but, rather, that they do not intervene in human affairs.

What innovation after such long peace
Can lure them on to wish to change their lives?
Only someone whom the old order thwarted
Takes joy in a new one; but if nothing irksome
Has ever befallen you down the beautiful ages,
What could enkindle a love for novelty?
Their lives, I suppose, lay sunk in sorrow and darkness
Until there dawned the birthday of the world?
And what did it hurt, that *we* had not been made?
Now whoever's been born, he ought to want to stay
Alive, so long as pleasures keep their charm.
But for him who's never tasted the love of life—
Never been on the roster—what harm, in not being born?
The model, moreover, first planted in their minds
For the very idea of man and the birth of the world,
Where did they get it? How could they see what to make?
How could they ever find out about first-beginnings,
What those might make when you shuffle their order, if
Nature herself had given them no peek?
But many atoms jumbled in many ways,
Spurred on by blows through the endless stretch of time,
Are launched and driven along by their own weight
And come together and try all combinations,
Whatever their assemblies might create;
No wonder then, if into such arrangements
They happen also to fall, the tracks that would
Bring forth and still restore the universe.
But if I knew nothing of atoms, of what they were,
Still from the very ways of the heavens, from many
Other things I could name, I'd dare to assert
And prove that not for us and not by gods
Was this world made. There's too much wrong with it!
To start, what the vast sweep of the sky vaults over,
Mountains take up the lion's share and forests
Full of wild beasts, and sloughs and rocky cliffs
And the sea that holds the headlands far apart.
Worse, torrid heat and the constant fall of snow
Remove from mortals two-thirds of the earth.
And what's left to farm, Nature, through her own force,
Would choke with briars; man's strength must stand against it,
Inured to groan over the iron mattock,
To scratch a life by leaning hard at the plow.
The clods are rich, but the plow must turn them over,
Loosen and work them, prod them to give birth;
Crops won't spring up in the air all by themselves.
And now that our hard work has paid off in crops,
Breaking into leaf and flower over the fields,
The sun in the sky will scorch them in its rage
Or sudden storms will kill, or frost and ice,
Or the blasts of bullying winds will batter them down.
And the wild beasts that set your hairs to bristle,
Hostile to man, on the land, in the sea—why should

Nature create and feed them? Or why should the seasons
Bring pestilence? Why should early Death come stalking?
And then, a baby, tossed up like a mariner by
Fierce waves, lies naked on the beach, dumb, helpless
To save its life, when Nature has spilled it out
Of the clench of its mother's womb to the shores of light,
And fills the place with wailing—as is proper
For one whom so much suffering awaits.
But the various flocks and cattle and beasts grow up
And don't need rattles, or the kindly wet-nurse
Teasing with her sweet broken baby talk;
Don't need to change their clothes for the changing sky;
They need no weapons or high walls to guard
Their own, for the earth herself and artful Nature
Bring forth abundantly for all their needs.

First of all, since the stuff of earth and water,
And the soft breath of the air and the brilliant fire,
The four that make this universe,[9] are all
Composed of bodies that are born and die,
We must conclude the world is born, and dies.

For in fact, whatever we see whose parts and members
Are of a form to suffer birth and death,
Invariably these things must also die
And be born. Then since I see that the world's chief parts
And members are destroyed, and then reborn,
Surely the heavens and earth must also have
A time of origin and time of death.

Don't think that for my own sake in these questions
I've hustled it in as given that earth and fire
Die, and been sure of the death of water and air,
Claiming they'd all be born and grow again.
For starters, a good part of the earth, parched
By the relentless sun, stampeded under,
Is breathed forth in a wraith of floating dust
Which high winds scatter in the atmosphere.
And part of the soil is called to wash away
In storms, and the streams shave close and gnaw the rocks.
Besides, whatever the earth feeds and grows
Is restored to earth. And since she surely is
The womb of all things and their common grave,
Earth must dwindle, you see, and take on growth again.

9. It was commonly believed that the physical world is composed of four elements: earth, air, fire, and water.

Ancient Egyptian Literature

Ancient Egypt has one of the world's oldest literary traditions. The only others that can match its antiquity and longevity are those of ancient Mesopotamia, China, and India. Stretching over almost three millennia, from perhaps as early as 2700 B.C.E. to the common era, the texts that emerged from ancient Egypt display a remarkable range of themes, genres, and styles: biographical inscriptions honoring the dead from tombs, stone stelae, and statutes; hymns to the gods; accounts of travel adventures; laments of life and loss; wisdom texts advising future generations on how to live a good life in a flawed world; passionate love poetry; fantastic tales; and satirical fables.

For much of the Common Era, the literature of ancient Egypt was virtually unknown. Except for a few motifs and narratives that passed into Greek and from there into medieval European texts, the Egyptian literary tradition disappeared in the late fourth century C.E., and hieroglyphs, the "sacred engraved signs" of the Egyptian writing system, as the Greeks called them, could not be read. It was not until the nineteenth century that European scholars deciphered the forgotten language and gradually recovered Egypt's written heritage, including the rich body of its literature. We can now appreciate something of the variety, subtlety, and depth of that tradition and through it imagine the lives of kings and court officials, priests and scribes, merchants, and even peasants. Had the Egyptians set their writings down on durable clay tablets, as did their contemporaries in Mesopotamia, rather than on the fragile papyrus that they used, perhaps more works would have survived the ages. As it is, the fragments we know of and have been able to translate provide an exciting glimpse into one of the world's great civilizations.

THE ORAL AND WRITTEN IN EGYPTIAN LITERARY CULTURE

Egyptian texts were written in successive forms of the ancient Egyptian language, a member of the Afroasiatic-language family that was distantly related to ancient Semitic languages such as Hebrew and Akkadian. The classical form of the language is Middle Egyptian, written from about 2000 B.C.E. onward; although Middle Egyptian continued to be used as an elevated literary language, it was partly displaced by Late Egyptian (ca. 1300–900 B.C.E.), and later by Demotic (ca. 650 B.C.E.-third century C.E.). For most of its history, Egyptian was written in two main scripts: the more ceremonial and elaborate hieroglyphic script and the cursive form using ink on papyrus, called "hieratic" or "priestly writing" by the Greeks, which was used for everyday affairs and for religious texts.

Literacy was restricted to elites in ancient Egypt; perhaps as few as one in a hundred people could read and write. Thus, literature was not a medium for broad consumption by reading but was enjoyed mostly through oral delivery. Skillful speech was highly valued. The *Instruction of Ptahhotep*, a wisdom text, states that "perfect speech is more

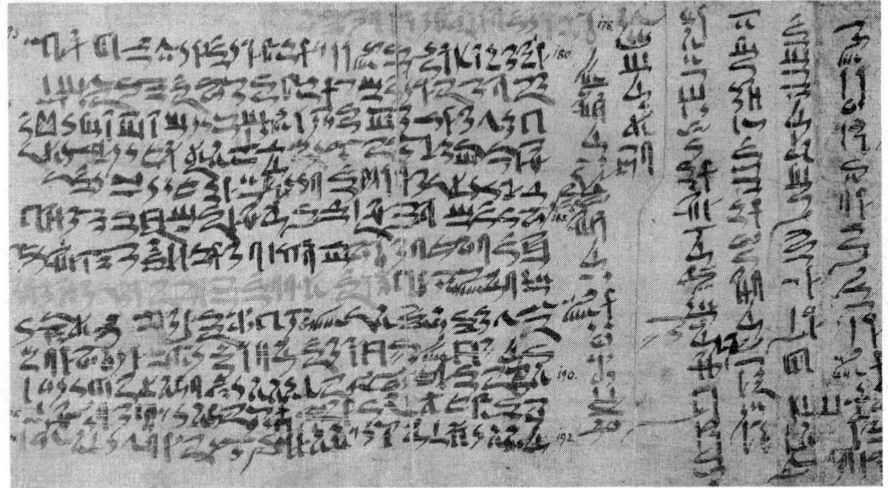

The Tale of Sinuhe in "hieratic" writing on papyrus.

hidden than malachite, yet it is found with the maidservants at the millstones." The frequent appearance of storytellers in texts shows that the Egyptians saw written compositions as part of a culture of oral performance. Their great pleasure in wordplay, alliteration, and repetition—features that come to the fore in oral recitation—is another indicator of the connection between writing and performance.

The earliest longer texts come from the Old Kingdom in the third millennium B.C.E. Inscriptions carved in the tombs of high-ranking officials praise the moral worth of their occupants and sometimes tell of memorable events in their lives. They are in metrical form and carefully crafted. Thousands of such texts survive from the three millennia of ancient Egyptian history, and they constitute the largest category of continuous composition surviving from ancient Egypt. Also from the Old Kingdom come the Pyramid Texts, such as the ***Cannibal Spell for King Unis,*** which were carved in the burial apartments of the kings and some queens from about 2325 B.C.E. onward.

THE CLASSICAL PERIODS OF EGYPTIAN LITERATURE

Kings of the Middle Kingdom (ca. 1940–1650 B.C.E.) expanded the use of writing and scribal schools. The first great period of Egyptian literature, which formed part of this development, saw the production of tales, wisdom texts, dialogues, and complaints. These genres employ complex imaginary settings and narrative frames such as cycles of stories. This fictional literature set the standard for later times, which looked back in awe to the Middle Kingdom, considering it the classical age of Egyptian literature. ***The Tale of Sinuhe***, a story of an ancient Egyptian's life abroad in Palestine and Syria and his triumphant return home, is the most elaborate example of these tales and features in our selections.

During the New Kingdom era (ca. 1500–1000 B.C.E.), motifs deriving from the Near East became more prominent in Egyptian literature, part of a larger cosmopolitanism that resulted from Egypt's active relations with other countries. A bold affirmation of this life and its pleasures appears in a new genre of the

New Kingdom, short poems performed at social gatherings, poems in praise of city life, and "harpist's songs," depicted as being performed by harpists, which meditate on the next life. In defiance of Egypt's traditional lavish tomb culture, some of these poems claim that constructing a monumental tomb with expensive grave goods is worthless and that one should instead enjoy this life on earth to the full. The passionate love poems featured in our selections appear only during the New Kingdom and are another expression of a forceful embracing of pleasures in this life.

THE LATE PERIOD (CA. 1000–30 B.C.E.)

The first millennium B.C.E. Egypt brought major upheavals to Egyptian society and literature. Egypt lost its imperial power and became the target of foreign invasions: as Nubians, Assyrians, Persians, and Alexander the Great's Macedonians swept through Egypt, ruling dynasties, the ethnic make-up of society, and religious beliefs and literary production changed drastically. Finally, in 30 B.C.E., Egypt lost its political independence; when Roman armies conquered the country, Queen Cleopatra, its last independent ruler, notoriously committed suicide by snakebite, and Egypt became a province of the Roman Empire.

Against this backdrop of foreign invasion and political instability, some literature of the Late Period carries more somber tones. For example, some autobiographical inscriptions now contain passages of intense grief. We can see this in our selections from the ***Stela of Taimhotep***, a remarkable composition in which the dead woman Taimhotep narrates her life and concludes with shattering lyrics lamenting the desolation that awaits us after death.

The new form of written Egyptian, Demotic, which first appeared around 650 B.C.E., was used for literary compositions into the third century C.E. Literature in the classical language, modeled on the style of the Middle and New Kingdoms, continued to be transmitted, while Demotic developed new themes and longer tales. In our selections, a brilliant example of the elaborate character of Late Period narratives is ***Setne Khamwas and Naneferkaptah***, a fantastic tale that involves magic, divine books that can kill, the obsessive search for ancient magical texts, grave robberies, and embarrassing dreams in the king's presence. In the Late Period, Egyptians could situate their fictional tales in many different earlier periods, and they took full advantage of this possibility.

Egypt is one of the world's great civilizations. Its culture faded during the third century C.E. and became overshadowed by the Hellenistic and Roman cultures that increasingly permeated Egypt's society. By that date, Egyptian literature had flourished for three millennia, three times longer than the most ancient European literary traditions today. With its fabulous age and rich record of innovation, Egypt's literature uniquely showcases the dynamics of change over time. It humbles us as we think about whether and how the world's literary traditions stand the test of time.

THE TALE OF SINUHE

nineteenth century B.C.E.

Popular and preserved in many copies, *The Tale of Sinuhe* is one of the most elaborate of all Middle Kingdom tales. Although it circulated in manuscript form as a text for reading aloud, it has the form of an autobiographical inscription that would have adorned the tomb of the speaker, the courtier Sinuhe. Sinuhe tells the remarkable story of his escape from home, trials and triumphs abroad, and glorious return. He flees from Egypt as a young man during the political crisis surrounding the royal succession in the early twelfth dynasty. When the dynasty's founder, King Amenemhat I (ca. 1940–1910 B.C.E.) dies, Sinuhe is accompanying the king's son Senwosret I on a military campaign. Fearing that he might become a victim of infighting, he deserts the army and settles in Palestine and Syria, where he spends his adult life making a successful career and living in prosperity. But, as he advances in years, his yearning to return to his homeland makes him accept a pardon from King Senwosret. After a dramatic encounter between the king and the former deserter, Sinuhe is accepted back into the Egyptian court, dies, and is buried in high honors. Sinuhe's story is a moving meditation on exile and home, life's patterns of adversity and success, royal mercy, and the nature and value of Egyptian identity. It speaks strongly to our world today, where so many people experience displacement, exile, and the challenges of conflicting identities.

The Tale of Sinuhe[1]

The Patrician and Count,[2]
Governor of the Sovereign's Domains in the Syrian lands,
the True Acquaintance of the King, whom he loves,
the Follower, Sinuhe says,
'I was a Follower who followed his lord,
a servant of the Royal Chambers[3]
and of the Patrician Lady,[4] the greatly praised,
the Queen of Senwosret in Khnemsut,
the Princess of Amenemhat in Qanefru,
Nefru, the blessed lady.

1. Translated by Richard B. Parkinson.
2. Sinuhe's first two titles attribute to him the highest standing among the Egyptian elite. The title "Governor" is otherwise unknown and probably fictitious. "Follower" is used for servants, including someone of high rank who serves royalty.
3. The private apartments of the king and his family.
4. The first element in the title sequence of Nefru, the queen of Senwosret I; "Khnemsut" is a name for that king's pyramid complex. The queen is said to be the daughter of King Amenemhat I; Qanefru is the name of his pyramid complex.

REGNAL YEAR 30, MONTH 3 OF THE INUNDATION SEASON, DAY 7:[5]
The God ascended to his horizon;
the Dual King Sehotepibre
mounted to heaven,
and was united with the sun,
the divine flesh mingling with its creator.
The Residence was in silence,[6]
hearts were in mourning,
the Great Portal was shut,
the entourage was bowed down,
and the patricians were in grief.

Now his Majesty had sent out an expedition to the Libyan land,[7]
with his eldest son at its head,
the Perfected God[8] Senwosret;
but now he was returning, having carried off Libyan captives
and all sorts of cattle without number.
The Friends of the Court[9]
sent to the western border
to inform the prince
of the affair which had happened in the Audience Hall.[1]

On the road the messengers found him.
They reached him at nightfall.
Not a moment did he wait;
the falcon flew off with his followers,[2]
without informing his expedition.
Now, when the royal children
accompanying him on this expedition were sent to,
one of them was summoned.
Now, when I was standing on duty,
I heard his voice as he spoke,
as I was a little way off.
My heart staggered, my arms spread out;
trembling fell on every limb.
I removed myself, leaping,

5. The date formula is written in red, both to mark a significant event and in imitation of administrative documents. The next five lines give a poetic narration of the death of Amenemhat I, in which he is taken up to heaven like a bird. "Dual King" is a title that evokes the two principal aspects of kingship. "Sehotepibre" is the throne name Amenemhat took on accession, in addition to the birth name that he retained.

6. The "Residence" is both the royal-palace complex and its surrounding town. The "Great Portal" is the principal entrance to the palace, which features again near the end of the tale. People are "bowed down" in a pose of mourning.

7. Probably an area near the Mediterranean coast to the west of the Nile delta.

8. A standard title of kings that indicates that they assumed the role of a junior god when they took the throne.

9. A formal title for members of a king's close entourage.

1. The official hall in which the king received visitors. The "affair" is the king's death, probably through assassination.

2. "Falcon" alludes to the description of Amenemhat flying up to heaven, while the mention of his entourage as "followers" alludes to Sinuhe's description of himself as a "Follower." Here, the king as falcon is a metaphor for swift travel, not for ascent to heaven.

to look for a hiding place.
I put myself between two bushes,
until the traveller had parted from the road.

I travelled southwards.[3]
I did not plan to reach this Residence,
expecting strife would happen;
I did not think to live after him.
I went across Lake Maaty in the region of the Sycomore.
I came to the Isle of Sneferu.
I passed a day on the edge of a field.
When it was daylight again, I made an early start.
I met a man standing in my way.
He saluted me, though I was afraid of him.
When it was supper-time,
I had arrived at Cattle-Quay.

I crossed in a rudderless barge[4]
blown by the west wind.
I passed east of Iaku,
above Lady of the Red Mountain.
I gave my feet a northwards path,
and I reached The Walls of the Ruler,
made to beat back the Syrians.
I crouched down in a bush
for fear of being seen by the watcher
on duty upon the wall.

I travelled in the night-time.[5]
When it was dawn I had reached Peten.
I alighted on an island of Kemur.
Thirst's attack overtook me,
and I was scorched, my throat parched.
I said, "This is the taste of death."
But I lifted up my heart, and gathered my limbs together,
as I heard the noise of cattle lowing, caught sight of Syrians,
and a leader of theirs, who had once been
in Egypt, recognized me.

Then he gave me water,
while he boiled milk for me.
I went with him to his tribe,
and what they did was good.

3. Sinuhe moves down the Nile delta to its apex, some way north of the royal residence and a suitable place to cross the Nile. The places named may be in the region of the great pyramids of Giza.

4. Boats would have their rudders removed to discourage theft. Metaphorically, the rudderless barge is a state that lacks leadership. After crossing the river, Sinuhe moves north along the eastern edge of the Nile delta to its northeast frontier fortifications.

5. Sinuhe has passed the wall and is in marshland just east of the border. He is found by nomads, who offer him standard desert hospitality.

Country gave me to country.
I set out for Byblos; I got to Qedem.[6]
I had spent half a year there,
when Amunenshi carried me off.
He was the ruler of upper Retjenu,
and he told me, "You'll be happy with me,
for you'll hear the speech of Egypt."
He said this, knowing my character
and having heard of my understanding,
and the Egyptians who were with him there
had vouched for me.

Then he said to me, "Why did you come here?
Has anything happened in the Residence?"
Then I said to him, "It's that the Dual King Sehotepibre
has gone to the horizon,
and how this all happened is unknown."
But I spoke in half-truths.[7]
"I have come from the expedition to the Libyan land:
it was reported to me, and my heart failed
and carried me off on the ways of flight.
I had not been talked of, and my face had not been spat upon;
I had heard no reproaches; my name had not been heard
in the herald's mouth.
I do not know what brought me to this country—it is like a
plan of God."
Then he said unto me, "So how is that land
without him—that worthy God,
fear of whom is throughout the countries
like Sekhmet's in a plague year?"[8]
I spoke thus to him, answering him,
"Indeed, his son has already entered the palace,[9]
and has taken up his father's inheritance.
Now, he is a God who is peerless,[1]
before whom no other exists.
He is a lord of understanding, excellent of plans, effective of orders;
coming and going are by his command.
He subjugates the countries.
His father stayed within his palace,
and he reported to him that what he had ordained was done.[2]

6. Byblos is a city on the Lebanon coast with which Egypt had longstanding relations. Qedem, which is a region rather than a specific place, is probably inland to the east. Upper Retjenu is perhaps in the same general area. The presence of Egyptians in Amunenshi's entourage implies that his polity is quite large.
7. This is the first of several passages in which Sinuhe explores his own motivation for his flight.
8. Sekhmet is the lioness goddess of disease, but also of healing.
9. Senwosret I had probably been co-regent with Amenemhat for ten years, a hitherto unprecedented arrangement that is perhaps glossed over here.
1. For the next forty lines, Sinuhe pronounces a seemingly standardized eulogy of the king as defender of Egypt and provider for his people.
2. Another likely allusion to the co-regency.

Now, he is a hero, active with his strong arm,
a champion without compare,
seen descending on barbarians, approaching the combat.
He curbs horns, weakens hands;
his foes cannot marshall troops.
He is vengeful, a smasher of foreheads;[3]
close to him no one can stand.
He is far-striding, destroying the fugitive;
there is no end for the man who shows him his back.
He is firm-hearted at the moment of forcing retreat.
He turns back again and again; he shows not his own back.
He is stout-hearted, seeing the masses;
he allows no rest around his heart.

He is bold, descending on Easterners;[4]
his joy is to plunder barbarians.
As soon as he takes up his shield, he tramples;
he needs no second blow to slay.
None can escape his arrow, none draw his bow.
As before the power of the Great One,
barbarians flee before him.
Having foreseen the end, he fights heedless of all else.

He is a lord of kindness, great of sweetness.
Through love he has conquered.
His city loves him more than its own members;
it rejoices at him more than at its God.
Men and women pass by, exulting at him.
He is a king, who conquered in the egg,
his eyes on it from birth.
He makes those born with him plentiful.
He is unique, God-given.
How joyful this land, since he has ruled!
He extends its borders.

He will conquer southern lands, without yet considering
northern countries.
He was begotten to strike Syrians, to trample Sand-farers.
Send to him, let him know your name,[5]
as a man far from his Majesty who enquires!
He will not fail to do good
for a country that will be loyal to him."

And he said unto me, "Well, Egypt is certainly happy,
knowing of his success.
But look, you are here,
and you will stay with me; I shall do you good."[6]

3. This evokes the icon of the king of Egypt smiting foreheads of enemies with a mace, which was known through its use on seals and other portable works of art.
4. These include Amunenshi, whom Sinuhe is addressing.
5. Sinuhe finally adjusts what he says in order to relate it to Amunenshi.
6. Amunenshi's reply deflates the rhetoric of Sinuhe's speech.

He placed me at the head of his children.
He joined me to his eldest daughter.
He had me make my choice of his country,
from the choicest of what was his,
on his border with another country.
It was a good land,
called Iaa.[7]
Figs were in it, and grapes;
its wine was more copious than its water;
great its honey, plentiful its moringa-oil,
with all kinds of fruit on its trees.
Barley was there, and emmer, and numberless were its
cattle of all kinds.[8]
Now, what came to me as a favourite was great.
He appointed me the ruler of a tribe
of the choicest of his country.

Provisions and strong drinks were made for me,
with wine as a daily supply, and cooked flesh,
and roast fowl, as well as wild game.
They would snare and lay it all out for me,
as well as the catch of my own hounds.
Many sweets were made for me,
with milk in every cooked dish.[9]

I spent many years there,[1]
and my children became heroes,
each man subjugating his tribe.
The messenger who went north and south to the Residence[2]
would tarry for me. I would make all men tarry.
I would give water to the thirsty,[3]
and I returned the wanderer to his path and rescued the robbed.
The Syrians who became so bold[4]
as to resist the countries' rulers—I countered their movements.

7. The name of this area is known from lists of foreign places dating from about four hundred years after the *Tale of Sinuhe,* but perhaps deriving from knowledge of the text. It is uncertain whether Iaa is an invented locality or a real one.
8. The landscape is described as settled and agricultural, but later allusions make it appear seminomadic. "Moringa-oil" is the standard culinary oil of ancient Egypt.
9. A probable piece of local color that has parallels in more recent Middle Eastern cuisine and likely relates to Jewish prohibitions against mixing milk and meat.
1. Sinuhe appears to stay about a generation in Iaa, but the tale's chronology is not very precise.
2. This alludes to diplomatic traffic and reminds the audience of the Egyptian speakers mentioned earlier in the text.
3. This is a standard good deed performed by members of the Egyptian elite; the next couple of actions are adjusted to the local context.
4. The "Syrians" are members of the numerous smaller local polities that are subordinate to "rulers." Sinuhe acts as general for Amunenshi ("This ruler of Retjenu," as the Syrian region was traditionally known), but the following passage gives him an almost royal role as a conqueror and defender of territory.

This ruler of Retjenu
would have me do many missions
as the commander of his army.
Every country for which I set out,
I made my attack on it,
and it was driven from its grasslands and wells;
I plundered its cattle and carried off its inhabitants,
and their food was taken away.
I killed the people in it with my strong arm, my bow,
my movements, and my excellent plans.

In his heart I attained high regard;
he loved me, knowing my valour.
He placed me at the head of his children, having seen the
strength of my arms.
A hero of Retjenu came
to provoke me in my tent;[5]
he was a peerless champion, who had subjugated all the land
He said he would fight with me, he planned to rob me,
and thought to plunder my cattle, on the advice of his tribe.
That ruler conferred with me;
I spoke thus, "I do not know him.[6]
So am I some ally of his, to walk around in his camp?
Or does this mean that I've opened his private quarters,
overturned his stockade?
It is resentment at seeing me do your missions.

How like am I to a bull of the roaming cattle in the midst
of another herd,
whom the bull of that little herd attacks,
whom that long-horned bull is charging!
Can an inferior ever be loved as a superior?
No barbarian can ever ally with a Delta man;[7]
what can establish the papyrus on the mountain?
Does that bull want to fight,
or does that champion bull want to sound a retreat
in terror of being equalled?

If he has the will to fight, let him speak his wish!
Does God not know what He has fated,
or does He know how it stands?"
When it was night I strung my bow and tried my arrows,[8]
sharpened my sword and polished my weapons.

5. The "hero of Retjenu" is a local strongman. Sinuhe is presented here as living in a nomadic encampment.
6. Sinuhe's elaborate speech here is modeled on public rhetoric. Its depiction of the fight for status compares human beings to cattle and suggests that Sinuhe has been wrongly accused of trying to get at the hero's women.
7. Barbarians, who are generally nomads, are especially incompatible with the sedentary delta inhabitants. In the converse case, "papyrus," the habitat of which is the marshland of the Nile delta, cannot grow on a mountain.
8. Having been challenged by the hero, Sinuhe prepares to fight him. The duel is a spectacle for the whole region, in which Sinuhe is perceived as the underdog.

When it was dawn, all Retjenu had come,
having incited its tribes and gathered its neighbouring
countries,
for it had planned this fight; and yet every breast burned for me,
the wives jabbered, and every heart was sore for me,
saying, "Is there another man mighty enough to fight him?"

Then his shield, his axe,
his armful of javelins fell to me:
after I had escaped his weapons and made them pass by me,
with his arrows spent in vain,
one after the other,
he approached me, and I shot him;
my arrow stuck in his neck,
he cried out, and fell on his face.
I felled him with his own axe,
and gave my war cry on his back,
while every Asiatic[9] was bellowing.
To Montu[1] I gave praises,
while his supporters mourned for him.
This ruler Amunenshi
took me into his arms.
Then I carried off his property and plundered his cattle.
What he planned to do to me, I did to him;
I seized what was in his tent, and stripped his camp.
With this I became great, and grew copious of wealth,
and grew plentiful of cattle.

For now God has acted so as to be gracious to one with
whom He was offended,[2]
whom He led astray to another country.
Today, He is satisfied.
A fugitive takes flight because of his surroundings;
but my reputation is in the Residence.
A creeping man creeps off because of hunger;
but I give bread to my neighbour.
A man leaves his land because of nakedness;
but I have bright linen, white linen.
A man runs off because of the lack of someone to send;
but I am plentiful of serfs.
Good is my house, spacious my dwelling place,
and memory of me is in the palace.
Whatever God fated this flight
—be gracious, and bring me home!
Surely You will let me see the place where my heart still stays!

9. An archaic term here for local Syrians.

1. The god of war, who guides kings in battle.

2. A renewed meditation on Sinuhe's motivation for flight, which leads here into a lyrical celebration of his success, followed at once by a sense of loss because he is abroad. This long passage is presented as something like a soliloquy.

What matters more than my being buried
in the land where I was born?
This is my prayer for help, that the good event befall,
that God give me grace!
May He act in this way, to make well the end of someone
whom He made helpless,
His heart sore for someone He compelled
to live in a foreign country!
Does this mean that He is so gracious today as to hear the
prayer of someone far off
who shall then turn from where he has roamed the earth
to the place from which he was carried away?
May the king of Egypt be gracious to me,[3]
that I may live on his grace!
May I greet the Mistress of the Land who is in his palace,
and hear her children's messages!
So shall my limbs grow young again, for now old age has fallen:
weakness has overtaken me,
my eyes are heavy, and my arms weak;
my legs have ceased to follow, and my heart is weary;
I am near to dying.
May they lead me to the cities of eternity![4]
May I follow the Lady of All,
and then she shall tell me that all is well with her children!
May she pass eternity above me![5]

Now the Majesty of the Dual King Kheperkare was told
about the state of affairs in which I was.
And his Majesty sent to me,
with bounty of royal giving,
to gladden the heart of this humble servant
like any ruler of a country,
and the royal children who were in his palace let me hear
their messages.[6]

Copy of the Decree Brought to this Humble Servant[7]
about his Being Brought Back to Egypt:
"Horus Living-of-Incarnations;
Two Ladies Living-of-Incarnations;

3. Sinuhe turns to thinking of the king and then of the queen mother, whom he used to serve.
4. The king and his family should provide for Sinuhe in death. In some periods kings donated monumental tombs to key members of the elite.
5. The queen mother, the "Lady of All," is assimilated to the sky goddess, Nut, who is in turn thought of as the lid of the coffin in which Sinuhe wishes to be laid to rest. In myth Nut is the ancestress of the king of Egypt.
6. The royal children should now be mature adults; here the tale condenses events.
7. The heading to the king's letter to Sinuhe is written in red to mark its significance. Royal communications are known as "decrees" rather than "letters." The full five-part titulary of Senwosret I as king and a line of good wishes follow the heading. The heading of the decree is then repeated in abbreviated form.

Golden Horus Living-of-Incarnations;
Dual King Kheperkare;
Son of Re Senwosret
—may he live for all time and eternity!
Royal Decree to the Follower Sinuhe:
Look, this decree of the king is brought to you
to inform you that your roving through countries,
going from Qedem to Retjenu,
country giving you to country,
was at the counsel of your own heart.[8]
What had you done, that you should be acted against?
You had not cursed, that your speech should be punished.
You had not spoken in the officials' council, that your utterances should be opposed.
This idea carried off your heart—
it was not in my heart against you.
This your Heaven, who is in my palace, endures
and flourishes in the kingship of the land
today as she did before,
and her children are in the Audience Hall.

You will store up the wealth given by them,
and live on their bounty.[9]
Return to Egypt!
And you will see the Residence where you grew up,
kiss the earth at the Great Portal,[1]
and join the Friends.
For today you have already begun to be old, have lost your virility,
and have in mind the day of burial,
the passing to blessedness.

A night vigil will be assigned to you, with holy oils[2]
and wrappings from the hands of Tayet.
A funeral procession will be made for you on the day of joining the earth,
with a mummy case of gold,
a mask of lapis lazuli,
a heaven over you,[3] and you placed in a hearse,
with oxen dragging you,
and singers going before you.
The dance of the Oblivious ones[4] will be done at the mouth of your tomb-chamber,

8. The king attributes responsibility for flight to Sinuhe himself. The next three lines are subtly different from Sinuhe's earlier statement to Amunenshi that no one had sought to accuse or pursue him.
9. This implies that the queen mother and royal children would provide the resources to maintain Sinuhe on his return.
1. The ceremonial entrance to the royal-palace complex, where both foreigners and Egyptians were expected to prostrate themselves and kiss the earth.
2. A brief allusion to mummification and attendant rituals. Tayet is the goddess of weaving.
3. A canopy placed over the mummy in its coffin for the funeral procession.
4. A dance known from tomb reliefs of the third millennium, and a mark of the highest status.

and the offering-invocation recited for you;
sacrifices will be made at the mouth of your offering-chapel,
and your pillars will be built of white stone
in the midst of the royal children's.
Your death will not happen in a foreign country;
Asiatics will not lay you to rest;
you will not be put in a ram's skin[5] when your coffin is made.
This is too long to be roaming the earth!
Think of your corpse—and return!"
As I stood in the middle of my tribe, this decree reached me.
It was read to me and I prostrated myself,
I touched the earth
and scattered it on my chest;
I roved round my camp, shouting and saying,
"How can this be done for a servant
whose heart led him astray to strange countries?
So good is the kindness which saves me from death!
Your spirit will let me make my end
with my limbs at home!"

Copy of the Reply to this Decree:
"The servant of the palace, Sinuhe says,
'Most happy welcome!
Concerning this flight which your humble servant[6] made in
his ignorance:
It is your spirit, Perfected God, Lord of the Two Lands,
which is loved by the Sungod, and favoured by Montu Lord
of Thebes;
Amun Lord of the Throne of the Two Lands,[7]
Sobek-Re, Horus, Hathor,
Atum and his company of Gods,
Sopdu-Neferbau-Semseru the eastern Horus,
the Lady of Imet—may she enfold your head!—
the divine Council upon the Flood,
Min-Horus in the midst of the countries,
Wereret Lady of Punt,
Nut, Haroeris-Re,
and all the Gods of the Homeland and the islands of the Sea—
may they give life and dominion to your nostrils,
endow you with their bounty,
and give you eternity without limit,

5. A typical burial for a nomad. From an Egyptian perspective, Syrians are nomads who have uncouth burial practices.
6. Letter writers term themselves "(humble) servants"; the king's decree and Sinuhe's reply are thus an exchange of letters.
7. Amun was the dynastic god of the twelfth dynasty. The other deities named are a group relating to Thebes followed by gods of the east, where Sinuhe is, and gods of foreign lands. Sopdu-Neferbau-Semseru is a form of an eastern Delta god that is otherwise unknown. The Lady of Imet is Wadjet, the serpent deity whose figure was worn as a protective emblem on the king's crown. Wereret is a form of Hathor, and Punt is a real but also semimythical land bordering the southern Red Sea.

all time without end!
May fear of you resound in lands and countries,
with the circuit of the sun curbed by you![8]
This is the prayer of a humble servant for his lord,
who saves from the West.
The lord of perception, perceiver of the people,[9]
perceives as the Majesty of the Court[1]
what your humble servant was afraid to say—
it is like an unrepeatably great matter.
O great God, equal of the Sungod in understanding
someone who willingly serves him!
Your humble servant is in the hand of him who enquires after him:
these things are placed at your disposal.
Your Majesty is Horus the conqueror;
your arms are mighty against all lands.
Now, may your Majesty command that he be made to bring
the Meki man from Qedem,[2]
the settler from out of Keshu,
and the Menus man from the lands of the Fenkhu.
They are rulers who are well known,
who live by love of you.
Without calling Retjenu to mind—it is yours, even like your hounds!

This flight which your humble servant made—
I had not planned it. It was not in my heart.[3]
I had not thought of it. I know not what parted me from
my place.
It was like the nature of a dream,
like a Delta man seeing himself in Elephantine,[4]
a man of the marshy lagoons in Southern Egypt.
I had no cause to be afraid; no one had run after me.
I had heard no reproaches; my name had not been heard in
the herald's mouth.
Only—that shuddering of my limbs,
my feet hastening,
my heart overmastering me,
the God who fated this flight dragging me away!
I was not presumptuous before,
for a man respects him who is acknowledged by his land,
and the Sungod has put respect for you throughout the land,

8. The sun encircles the known world, which the king of Egypt can claim to dominate.
9. The king's perception, which is comparable with that of the Sungod, is his most valuable quality for the elite, because through it he knows what they need.
1. The palace and the king's entourage are personified manifestations of the king himself.
2. Three local rulers are mentioned, from different parts of Syria. "Meki man" and "Menus man" are terms for rulers, following a usage known from Near Eastern texts of the same general period.
3. This is Sinuhe's final presentation of the reasons for his flight, adapted here to exalt the status of the king.
4. The southernmost town of Egypt, in a narrow stretch of land surrounded by desert. "Marshy lagoons" contrast strongly with the landscape of the south.

and terror of you in every country.
Whether I am at home,
whether I am in this place—
it is you who veils this horizon of mine.
The sun shines for love of you;[5]
the water of the river
is drunk when you wish;
the air of heaven
is breathed when you say.

Your humble servant will hand over to the chicks[6]
which your humble servant has begotten in this place.
A journey has been made for your humble servant!
May your Majesty do as you desire!
Men live on the breath of your giving:
may the Sungod, Horus, and Hathor love
these your noble nostrils,
which Montu Lord of Thebes desires
to live for all time!'"
I was allowed to spend a day in Iaa,
handing over my property to my children;
my eldest son was in charge of my tribe,
and all my property was his—
my servants, all my cattle,
my fruit, and all my orchard trees.
This humble servant then came southwards,
and I halted at the Ways of Horus.[7]
The commander there who was in charge of the garrison
sent a message to the Residence to inform them.

And his Majesty caused a worthy Overseer of the Peasants
 of the Royal Household to come,
accompanied by laden boats,
and bearing bounty of royal giving
for the Syrians who had come with me,
leading me to the Ways of Horus;
and I announced each one by his name.[8]
Every serving man was at his duty.
I set sail,
with kneading and brewing beside me,
until I reached the harbour of Itj-tawi.[9]

5. The section concludes with a brief lyrical passage evoking the idea that even foreigners depend on the king of Egypt for the air they breathe. This is taken up again in the next passage.
6. The family Sinuhe has raised in exile. The letter concludes with an abbreviated mention of the deities under whom Senwosret I rules.
7. The end of the route across North Sinai from Palestine, where a fortress marked the Egyptian frontier at the northeast corner of the Nile delta.
8. This passage presents the reception of a diplomatic mission. The Syrians have provided safe passage to Sinuhe; it is not stated whether they too continue by boat to the Residence.
9. The name of the twelfth-dynasty royal residence, perhaps near Lisht to the south of ancient Memphis.

When it was dawn, very early,[1]
they came and summoned me;
ten men coming,
ten men going,
ushering me to the palace.

I touched the ground between the sphinxes,[2]
as the royal children stood in the portal, receiving me;
and the Friends who usher to the Pillared Hall
were showing me the way to the Audience Hall.
I found his Majesty on the great throne
in the portal of electrum.[3]
Then I was stretched out prostrate,[4]
unconscious of myself in front of him,
while this God was addressing me amicably.
I was like a man seized in the dusk,
my soul had perished, my limbs failed,
my heart was not in my body.
I did not know life from death.

And his Majesty said to one of these Friends,
"Raise him up, let him speak to me!"
And his Majesty said, "Look, you have returned after
roaming foreign countries,
after flight has made its attack on you;
you are now elderly, and have reached old age.
Your burial is no small matter;
you will not be laid to rest by barbarians.
Act against yourself, act against yourself no more!
You did not speak when your name was announced—
are you afraid of punishment?"[5]
I answered this with the answer of a frightened man:
"What does my lord say to me, that I can answer?
For this is no disrespect towards God, but is a terror
which is in my body like that which created the fated flight.[6]
Look, I am in front of you, and life is yours;
may your Majesty do as he desires!"

And the royal children were ushered in,
and his Majesty said to the Queen,
"Look, Sinuhe has returned as an Asiatic,

1. In antiquity business probably followed the natural rhythm of the day. Here, the association with dawn also suggests a new beginning and integration with the king's role as manifestation of the Sungod on earth.
2. Protective sphinx statues would be set up beside the entrance gateway to the palace complex.
3. The king probably sits in a niche. Electrum is a white alloy of gold and silver; the area may either have been painted white or gilded with electrum.
4. Overawed, Sinuhe loses consciousness as he prostrates himself before the king. The following passage echoes Sinuhe's earlier sense of being near death when he left Egypt and was rescued by nomads.
5. The king acts the part of an angry god.
6. Sinuhe makes one last allusion to the motivation for his flight. In the next line he evokes the conception that a man's life depends on the king, who in turn receives it from the Sungod.

an offspring of the Syrians!"
She gave a very great cry,[7]
and the royal children shrieked as one.
And they said unto his Majesty,
"Is it really he,
sovereign, my lord?"
And his Majesty said, "It is really he."
Now they had brought with them their necklaces,[8]
their rattles and their sistra.
And they presented them to his Majesty:
"Your hands upon this beauty, enduring king,
these insignia of the Lady of Heaven!
May the Golden One give life to your nostrils,
the Lady of Stars enfold you!
South-crown fares north, North-crown south,[9]
joined and made one
in the words of your Majesty,
on whose brow the uraeus is placed!

You have delivered the poor from evil.
So may the Sungod, Lord of the Two Lands, be gracious to you!
Hail to you, as to the Lady of All!
Slacken your bow, withdraw your shaft![1]
Give breath to him who suffocates!
Give back the good we give on this good day—[2]
present us with North Wind's Son,[3]
the barbarian born in the Homeland!
Through fear of you he took flight,
through terror of you he left the land.
A face that has seen your face shall not pale!
An eye that has gazed at you shall not fear!"

And his Majesty said, "He shall not fear,
he shall not gibber in terror!
He will be a Friend among the officials,
and he will be appointed amongst the entourage.
Proceed to the Robing Chamber to attend on him!"

7. This evokes the role of goddesses in rituals, often acted by women, in which they ululate. The royal children's "shriek" is probably both childish and a reference to ritual shouting.
8. The text mentions three ritual instruments (one of them a necklace), used in the cult of the goddess Hathor, with whom the queen is identified. "Sistra" (singular *sistrum*) are a special type of metallic rattle. Hathor's role is to pacify the angry Sungod. The following song names Hathor as the "Golden One"; she is also the "Lady of Stars."
9. The two principal crowns of the king represent the halves of the country and are united in the double crown on the king's head. The "uraeus" is the fire-spitting protective snake that identifies the king and was alluded to earlier as the Lady of Imet.
1. The king takes on the role of the creator god Atum, who sometimes holds a bow and arrow.
2. The "good we give" is their ritual presentation of the emblems of Hathor.
3. A pun on the name of *Sinuhe* that refers to his exile in Syria, to the north of Egypt, while evoking the breeze that alleviates the heat in Egypt. Sinuhe's own name has occurred only twice in the text.

I went forth from the Audience Hall,
with the royal children giving me their hands.
And afterwards, we went through the Great Portal.[4]
I was appointed to the house of a prince,[5]
with costly things in it, with a bathroom in it
and divine images of the horizon,[6]
with treasures from the Treasury in it,
clothes of royal linen,
myrrh and kingly fine oil,
with officials whom the king loved in every room,
and every serving man at his duty.

The years were made to pass from my limbs;
I became clean-shaven, and my hair was combed.
A load was given back to the foreign country,[7]
and clothes back to the Sand-farers.
I was clad in fine linen;
I was anointed with fine oil.
I slept in a bed.
I returned the sand to those who are upon it
and the tree oil to those smeared with it.

I was given the house of a Governor,
such as belongs to a Friend.
Many craftsmen were building it,
all its trees were freshly planted.
Meals were brought to me from the palace,[8]
three and four times a day,
as well as what the royal children gave,
without making a moment's ceasing.
A pyramid of stone was built for me,[9]
in the midst of the pyramids.
The masons who construct the pyramid measured out its foundations;
the draughtsman drew in it;
the overseer of sculptors carved in it;
the overseer of the works which are in the burial grounds busied himself with it.
All the equipment to be put in a tomb shaft—

4. Sinuhe and the royal children leave the palace complex after his audience with the king.
5. This is the first specific mention of a male child of the king. The description of his house is probably close to that of a palace.
6. It is not clear what this line refers to. The "horizon" is the place of sunrise, also a euphemism for the tomb. Perhaps houses belonging to the royal family had wall paintings. Only kingly buildings would have had images of deities.
7. The dirt from Syria is washed off Sinuhe. A couple of variants of this idea follow. "Tree oil" is seen as inferior and foreign.
8. Dependence on central kitchens appears to have been common in the ancient world. Sinuhe does not seem to receive a household of his own servants.
9. No pyramid of a nonroyal person is known from this period. Either the word for pyramid is used with a broader meaning or the description is hyperbolic.

its share of these things was made.
I was given funerary priests;[1]
a funerary demesne was made for me,
with fields in it and a garden in its proper place,
as is done for a Chief Friend.
My image was overlaid with gold,[2]
and its kilt with electrum.
It is his Majesty who has caused this to be done.
There is no other lowly man for whom the like was done.
I was in the favours of the king's giving,
until the day of landing came.'[3]

So it ends, from start to finish,[4]
as found in writing.

1. Sinuhe receives an endowment to support and continue his mortuary cult after death and burial. At the same time, the "garden" implies that this is a place of delight to which his spirit could return from the next world.
2. No gilded statue of a nonroyal person is known; gilding seems to have been reserved for the gods and the king. This is another instance of likely hyperbole, as is implied by the next two lines. As he dies and is buried, Sinuhe's status becomes higher even than that of a normal member of the elite.
3. A euphemism for death. Since most travel in Egypt was by boat, one "landed" on the other side after death.
4. A short note by the copyist, known as a colophon, written in red at the end of the text.

EGYPTIAN LOVE POEMS[1]

ca. 1300–1100 B.C.E.

Although love poetry must have existed in oral form in earlier periods, love poems only survive on papyri, potsherds, and flakes of limestone from the later part of the New Kingdom. Looking at the women musicians and nearly nude girls singing and dancing in the paintings on tomb walls, we can imagine that love songs were performed with music and dance at banquets. Composed in rather informal, at times graphic language, similar texts were also used in the cult of goddesses and in praise of royal women. Egyptian love poetry shows striking parallels with love poetry of other Near Eastern traditions, such as the somewhat later Song of Songs in the **Hebrew Bible**.

The lovers in the poems are young and often not yet free from parental supervision. As a gesture of endearment, they address each other as "brother" and "sister," words that have a broad meaning in ancient Egyptian. Roughly half of the poems are spoken by the girl, and half by the boy. (A small group, not represented in this selection, gives the words of the garden tree in whose shade the girl and boy have a tryst.) Many poems imagine situations in which the lovers might meet and make themselves attractive to each other: by

1. All selections translated by Michael V. Fox.

going into the water to retrieve a fish—an erotic symbol—the girl, for example, can make her dress transparent and expose her charms. Many of the poems brim with imagery of the pleasures of desire and sex, but some also remind us how fleeting love can be: in one poem the girl worries, after the lovers have spent the night together, that the boy is now more interested in breakfast than in staying with her.

The Beginning of the Song That Diverts the Heart

(*Girl*)
How beautiful is your beloved,[2]
  the one adored of your heart,
    when she has returned from the meadow!
My beloved, my darling,
  my heart longs for your love—
    all that you created!
I say to you:
  See what happened!
I came ready to trap birds,
  my snare in one hand,
my cage in the other,
  together with my mat.[3]
All the birds of the land Punt[4]
  have descended on Egypt,
    anointed with myrrh.
The first to come
  takes my bait.
Its fragrance comes from Punt,
  its claws full of balm.[5]
My heart desires you.
  Let us release it[6] together.
I am with you, I alone,
  to let you hear the sound of my call,[7]
    for my lovely myrrh-anointed one.
You are here with me,
  as I set the snare.
Going to the field is pleasant (indeed)
  for one who loves it.[8]

2. In the original, this is literally "your sister." *Sister* and *brother* are frequent terms of affection in the Egyptian love songs. The terms imply intimacy, not consanguinity.
3. Perhaps to be placed as a cover over the birdcage.
4. A region bordering on the southern Red Sea from which aromatics came, as well as an ideal location known as "God's Land."
5. Or "its claws are caught by the balm." (The Egyptian can be read as a double entendre.) Birds were sometimes trapped by pitch smeared on a tree.
6. "It" is the "bait" mentioned before. This probably refers to the fulfilment of sexual desire.
7. Fowlers imitated bird calls to lure birds to the trap.
8. Just what "it" refers to is vague, perhaps intentionally so. Is it bird trapping? Lovemaking?

[My god, my Lotus . . .]

(*Girl*)
My god, my lotus . . .[1]
The north wind blows . . .
        How pleasant it is to go to the river. . . .
My heart longs to go down
        to bathe before you,
that I may show you my beauty
        in a tunic of the finest royal linen,
drenched in fragrant oils,
        my hair plaited in reeds.
I'd go down to the water with you,
        and come out to you carrying a red fish,[2]
                which feels just right in my fingers.
I'd set it before you,
        while gazing at your beauty.
O my hero, my beloved,
        come and see me!

(*Boy*)
My beloved's love
        is over there, on the other side,
The river surrounds my body.[3]
        The flood waters are powerful in this season,
                and a crocodile waits on the sandbank.
Yet I went down to the water
        to wade through the flood,
                my heart brave in the channel.
I found the crocodile to be like a mouse,[4]
        and the surface of the water like dry land to my feet.
It is her love
        that makes me strong.
                She casts a water spell for me!
I see my heart's beloved
        standing right before me!

(*Boy*)
My beloved has come,
        my heart rejoices,
                my arms are open to embrace her.
My heart is as happy in its place
        as a fish in its pond.
O night, you are mine forever,
        since my lady came to me!

1. The lotus was the most important Egyptian flower, whose aroma was held to excite the senses. The "north wind" is the breeze that makes the heat bearable and brings the breath of life.
2. A tilapia, a well-known erotic symbol that was also used as an amulet made of red stone.
3. He has—at least in imagination—stepped into the Nile, braving its dangers to reach the girl on the other side.
4. This alludes to tales of magic in which a magician can turn a tiny figure into a crocodile and vice versa.

[I wish I were her Nubian maid]

(*Boy*)
I wish I were her Nubian maid,
her attendant in secret,
as she brings her a bowl of mandragoras.[1]
It is in her hand,
while she gives pleasure.
In other words:
she would grant me
the hue of her whole body.[2]

(*Boy*)
I wish I were the laundryman
of my beloved's clothes,
for even just a month!
I would be strengthened
by grasping the garments
that touch her body.
For I would be washing out the moringa oils[3]
that are in her kerchief.
Then I'd rub my body
with her castoff garments,
and she . . .
O how I would be in joy and delight,
my body vigorous!

(*Boy*)
I wish I were her little signet ring,
the keeper of her finger!
I would see her love[4]
each and every day,
And I would steal her heart.

[I passed close by his house]

Sixth Stanza[1]

(*Girl*)
I passed close by his house,
and found his door ajar.
My beloved was standing beside his mother,
and with him all his brothers and sisters.
Love of him captures the heart
of all who walk along the way—

1. The mandragora fruit was thought to be an aphrodisiac. It was also an erotic symbol, both for its flower and probably for its long taproot.
2. In the boy's fantasy, he is a maidservant in the girl's bedchamber. He would offer fruit while the girl gave him pleasure. That is to say, she would let him see her naked.
3. Moringa oil was the normal ancient Egyptian oil, and evidently could be perfumed.
4. Her capacity to inspire love.
1. This poem and the next are excerpted from a set of numbered stanzas.

a precious youth without peer,
        a lover excellent of character!
He gazed at me when I passed by,
        but I must exult alone.
How joyfully does my heart rejoice, my beloved,
        since I first saw you!
If only mother knew my heart
        she would go inside for a while.
                O Golden One,[2] put that in her heart!
Then I could hurry to my beloved
        and kiss him in front of everyone,
                and not be ashamed because of anyone.
I would be happy to have them see
        that you know me,
                and would hold festival to my Goddess.
My heart leaps up to go forth
        that I may gaze on my beloved.
How lovely it is to pass by![3]

[Seven whole days]

Seventh Stanza

(*Boy*)
Seven whole days[1] I have not seen my beloved.
Illness has invaded me,
        my limbs have grown heavy,
                and I barely sense my own body.
Should the master physicians come to me,
        their medicines could not ease my heart.
The lector priests[2] have no good treatment,
        because my illness cannot be diagnosed.
But if someone tells me, "Here she is!"—that will revive me.
        Her name—that is what will get me up.
The coming and going of her messengers—
        that's what will revive my heart.
More potent than any medicine is my beloved for me;
        more powerful than the *Physician's Manual.*
Her coming in from outside is my amulet.[3]
        If I see her, I'll become healthy.
If she but gives me a glance, my limbs will regain vigor.
        If she speaks, I'll grow strong.
If I hug her, she'll drive illness from me.
        But she has been gone for seven days.

2. Hathor, the goddess of love.
3. Each stanza in this seven-stanza song starts and ends by punning on a word. In Egyptian *six* and *pass by* sound alike.
1. The number seven is used because this is the seventh stanza. Ancient Egypt did not have a seven-day week.
2. Specialists in religious and magical texts. Here the term means "magicians."
3. *Amulet* also means "well-being," and both senses apply here.

[Am I not here with you?]

(*Girl*)
Am I not here with you?
Then why have you set your heart to leave?
Why don't you embrace me?
Has my deed come back upon me?
If you seek to caress my thighs.
Is it because you are thinking of food
that you would go away?
Or because you are a slave to your belly?
Is it because you care about clothes?
Well, I have a bedsheet!
Is it because you are hungry that you would leave?
Then take my breasts
that their gift may flow forth to you.
Better a day in the embrace of my beloved
than thousands on thousands anywhere else!

SETNE KHAMWAS AND NANEFERKAPTAH (SETNE 1)

ca. 250 B.C.E.

The protagonist of *Setne Khamwas and Naneferkaptah*, and of another relatively well-preserved tale from the Ptolemaic period (332–30 B.C.E.), is based on the legendary son of the famous ruler Ramses II (ca. 1279–1213 B.C.E.), who was high priest of the god Ptah of Memphis and restored many ancient monuments. The fictional character is a magician who spends time in the old tombs of the necropolis, and in that way is comparable with his historical model. He is both a warning to others that one's ambitions should not overreach what is proper for human beings and a figure of fun, because his misjudgments get him into ridiculous situations.

The magic at the core of the Setne Khamwas tales had been a theme of Egyptian stories for at least fifteen hundred years. Egyptian magicians and healers were famous throughout the ancient Near East, and several motifs in the Setne tales have parallels in other ancient literatures, showing that they belonged to a wider literary world of the Near East and the Ancient Mediterranean.

Setne Khamwas and Naneferkaptah is set in the time of Ramses II, a thousand years before the tale was composed, but that period is made into the frame for yet older events, narrated by the deceased Ahwere, a king's daughter who had married her own brother,

Naneferkaptah. Naneferkaptah had stolen the magic book of the god Thoth, and had paid for this misdeed with the lives of his wife and son, driving him to suicide. Setne narrowly succeeds in stealing the same book from the tomb of Naneferkaptah, but then thinks he is being driven to commit terrible crimes by the beautiful woman Tabubu, with whom he desires to have sex. He finally suffers deep humiliation before Ramses II himself, which leads Setne to accept his father's advice and replace the book in the tomb. The tale should be set against the reality that almost all ancient tombs that contained anything of value were robbed, often while or very soon after the corpse was buried. It invites its audience to reflect on the dangers of obsessions with the past and the supernatural and on the importance of accepting the limits of a human lifetime.

Setne Khamwas and Naneferkaptah[1]

The lost beginning may be reconstructed as follows:

Prince Khamwas, son of King Ramses II and high priest of Ptah at Memphis, was a very learned scribe and magician who spent his time in the study of ancient monuments and books. One day he was told of the existence of a book of magic written by the god Thoth himself and kept in the tomb of a prince named Naneferkaptah (Na-nefer-ka-ptah), who had lived in the distant past and was buried somewhere in the vast necropolis of Memphis. After a long search, Prince Khamwas, accompanied by his foster brother Inaros, found the tomb of Naneferkaptah and entered it. He saw the magic book, which radiated a strong light, and tried to seize it. But the spirits of Naneferkaptah and of his wife Ahwere rose up to defend their cherished possession.

Ahwere and her son Merib were not buried in this Memphite tomb but rather in distant Coptos, where they had lost their lives. But the spirit of Ahwere was with her husband at this critical moment, and she now stood before Prince Khamwas and told him how her husband had acquired the magic book and how they had all paid for it with their lives. She begins her story by relating that she and Naneferkaptah had been brother and sister and the only children of a Pharaoh named Mernebptah. They had loved each other very much and had wanted to marry. But Pharaoh wished to marry his son to the daughter of a general and his daughter to the son of a general. In her anguish Ahwere had asked the steward of Pharaoh's palace to plead with Pharaoh on her behalf. The steward had done so and Pharaoh had become silent and distressed. To the steward's question, why he was distressed, Pharaoh answered:

(Here begins the story on page 3 of the papyrus)

"It is you who distress me. If it so happens that I have only two children, is it right to marry the one to the other? I will marry Naneferkaptah to the daughter of a general, and I will marry Ahwere to the son of another general, so that our family may increase!"

When the time came for the banquet to be set before Pharaoh, they came for me and took me to the banquet. But my heart was very sad and I did not have my former looks. Pharaoh said to me: "Ahwere, was it you who sent to me with those foolish words. 'Let me marry [Naneferkaptah, my] elder [brother]'?"

1. Translated by Miriam Lichtheim.

I said to him: "Let me marry the son of a general, and let him marry the daughter of another general, so that our family may increase!" I laughed and Pharaoh laughed.[2]

[When the steward of the palace came] Pharaoh [said to him]: "Steward, let Ahwere be taken to the house of Naneferkaptah tonight, and let all sorts of beautiful things be taken with her."

I was taken as a wife to the house of Naneferkaptah [that night, and Pharaoh] sent me a present of silver and gold, and all Pharaoh's household sent me presents. Naneferkaptah made holiday with me, and he entertained all Pharaoh's household. He slept with me that night and found me [pleasing. He slept with] me again and again, and we loved each other.

When my time of purification came I made no more purification. It was reported to Pharaoh, and his heart was very happy. Pharaoh had many things taken [out of the treasury] and sent me presents of silver, gold, and royal linen, all very beautiful. When my time of bearing came, I bore this boy who is before you, who was named Merib. He was entered in the register of the House of Life.[3]

[It so happened that] my brother Naneferkaptah [had no] occupation on earth but walking on the desert of Memphis, reading the writings that were in the tombs of the Pharaohs and on the stelae of the scribes of the House of Life and the writings that were on [the other monuments, for his zeal] concerning writings was very great.

After this there was a procession in honor of Ptah,[4] and Naneferkaptah went into the temple to worship. As he was walking behind the procession, reading the writings on the shrines of the gods, [an old priest saw] him and laughed. Naneferkaptah said to him: "Why are you laughing at me?" He said: "I am not laughing at you. I am laughing because you are reading writings that have no [importance for anyone]. If you desire to read writings, come to me and I will have you taken to the place where that book is that Thoth wrote with his own hand, when he came down following the other gods.[5] Two spells are written in it. When you [recite the first spell you will] charm the sky, the earth, the netherworld, the mountains, and the waters. You will discover what all the birds of the sky and all the reptiles are saying. You will see the fish of the deep [though there are twenty-one divine cubits[6] of water] over [them]. When you recite the second spell, it will happen that, whether you are in the netherworld or in your form on earth, you will see Pre appearing in the sky with his Ennead, and the Moon in its form of rising."[7]

2. His laughter, which has parallels in tales of the world of the gods, signifies that he has been won over. His initial reluctance to let Ahwere marry her brother is part of a wider issue, because only kings could marry immediate kin, and such marriages are known from only a few periods.

3. An institution attached to temples where texts were copied and scribes were trained, some of them both in everyday handwritten scripts and in the hieroglyphic display script. Princes were typically literate, but the focus here is more on ability to use magical texts than on general literacy.

4. The principal god of Memphis, whose temple was at the center of the city.

5. Thoth is the god of wisdom and of writing and is strongly associated with magic. He "goes down following the gods" because he is the secretary of the sungod and his entourage as such follows behind them.

6. About thirty-five feet.

7. The West is the realm of the dead. *Pre* is the later form of the name of the sungod, Re. Ennead is the principal group of nine deities associated with the sungod.

[Naneferkaptah said to him]: "As he (the king) lives, tell me a good thing that you desire, so that I may do it for you, and you send me to the place where this book is!"

The priest said to Naneferkaptah: "If you wish to be sent [to the place where this book is] you must give me a hundred pieces of silver for my burial, and you must endow me with two priestly stipends tax free."

Naneferkaptah called a servant and had the hundred pieces of silver given to the priest. He added the two stipends and had [the priest] endowed with them [tax free].

The priest said to Naneferkaptah: "The book in question is in the middle of the water of Coptos[8] in a box of iron. In the box of iron is a box of [copper. In the box of copper is] a box of juniper wood. In the box of juniper wood is a box of ivory and ebony. In the box of ivory and ebony is a [box of silver. In the box of silver] is a box of gold, and in it is the book. [There are six miles of] serpents, scorpions, and all kinds of reptiles around the box in which the book is, and there is [an eternal serpent around] this same box."

When the priest had thus spoken to Naneferkaptah, he did not know where on earth he was.[9] He came out of the temple, he told [me everything that had happened to him]. He [said] to me: "I will go to Coptos, I will bring this book, hastening back to the north again." But I chided the priest, saying: "May Neith[1] curse you for having told him these [dreadful things! You have brought] me combat, you have brought me strife. The region of Thebes,[2] I now find it [abhorrent]." I did what I could with Naneferkaptah to prevent him from going to Coptos; he did not listen to me. He went to [Pharaoh and told] Pharaoh everything that the priest had said to him.

Pharaoh said to him: "What is that [you want]?" He said to him: "Let the ship of Pharaoh be given to me with its equipment. I will take Ahwere [and her boy Merib] to the south with me. I will bring this book without delay."

The ship of Pharaoh was given [him] with its equipment. We boarded it, we set sail, we arrived [at Coptos]. It [was announced] to the priests of Isis of Coptos and the chief priest of Isis. They came down to meet us, hastening to meet Naneferkaptah, and their wives came down to meet me. [We went up from the shore and went into] the temple of Isis and Harpocrates.[3] Naneferkaptah sent for an ox, a goose, and wine. He made burnt offering and libation before Isis of Coptos and Harpocrates. We were taken to a very beautiful house [filled with all good things].

Naneferkaptah spent four days making holiday with the priests of Isis of Coptos, and the wives of the priests of Isis made holiday with me. When the morning of our fifth day came. Naneferkaptah had [much] pure [wax brought] to him. He made a boat filled with its rowers and sailors. He recited a spell to them, he made

8. This appears in later sections to be reached up the Nile. If it is a stretch of water near Coptos, it would have to be a small lake. Otherwise it might be the Red Sea, several days' journey from Coptos through the eastern desert of Egypt.

9. He was dazzled by what the priest said. The same idiom is used later when Setne encounters an exceedingly beautiful woman.

1. Neith is a major goddess of the area of Memphis and of the Nile delta.

2. The southern part of Upper Egypt. Coptos is a little to the north of Thebes. Ahwere knows that Naneferkaptah's mission can bring no good, and her dislike of Thebes—an attitude typical of people from the area of Memphis—is prescient.

3. Harpocrates was Horus's name as a child god, son of Osiris and Isis.

them live, he gave them breath, he put them on the water. He filled the ship of Pharaoh with sand, [he tied it to the other boat]. He [went] on board, and I sat above the water of Coptos, saying: "I shall learn what happens to him."

He said to the rowers: "Row me to the place where that book is!" [They rowed him by night] as by day. In three days he reached it. He cast sand before him, and a gap formed in the river. He found six miles of serpents, scorpions, and all kinds of reptiles around [the place where the book was]. He found an eternal serpent around this same box. He recited a spell to the six miles of serpents, scorpions, and all kinds of reptiles that were around the box, and did not let them come up. [He went to the place where] the eternal serpent was. He fought it and killed it. It came to life again and resumed its shape. He [fought it again, a second time, and killed it; it came to life again. He [fought it again, a third] time, cut it in two pieces, and put sand between one piece and the other.[4] [It died] and no longer resumed its shape.

Naneferkaptah went to the place where the box was. [He found it was a box of] iron. He opened it and found a box of copper. He opened it and found a box of juniper wood. He opened it and found a box of ivory and ebony. [He opened it and found a box of] silver. He opened it and found a box of gold. He opened it and found the book in it. He brought the book up out of the box of gold.

He recited a spell from it; [he charmed the sky, the earth, the netherworld, the] mountains, the waters. He discovered what all the birds of the sky and the fish of the deep and the beasts of the desert were saying. He recited another spell; he saw [Pre appearing in the sky with his Ennead], and the Moon rising, and the stars in their forms. He saw the fish of the deep, though there were twenty-one divine cubits of water over them. He recited a spell to the [water; he made it resume its form].

[He went on] board, he said to the rowers: "Row me back to the place [I came] from." They rowed him by night as by day. He reached me at the place where I was; [he found me sitting] above the water of Coptos, not having drunk nor eaten, not having done anything on earth, and looking like a person who has reached the Good House.[5]

I said to Naneferkaptah: ["Welcome back! Let me] see this book for which we have taken these [great] pains!" He put the book into my hand. I recited one spell from it; I charmed the sky, the earth, the netherworld, the mountains, the waters. I discovered what all the birds of the sky and the fish of the deep and the beasts were saying. I recited another spell; I saw Pre appearing in the sky with his Ennead. I saw the Moon rising, and all the stars of the sky in their forms. I saw the fish of the deep, though there were twenty-one divine cubits of water over them.

As I could not write[6]—I mean, compared with Naneferkaptah, my brother, who was a good scribe and very wise man—he had a sheet of new papyrus brought to him. He wrote on it every word that was in the book before him. He soaked it in beer, he dissolved it in water. When he knew it had dissolved, he drank it and knew what had been in it.[7]

4. This was a standard way of magically stopping a snake from coming back to life.
5. The embalmers' workshop. Naneferkaptah appears as if dead from his exertions.
6. Ahwere is not literate, but simply having the magic manuscript in her hands makes her able to read it and use its formulas.
7. By drinking the ashes of the inscribed papyrus, Naneferkaptah assimilates its contents.

We returned to Coptos the same day and made holiday before Isis of Coptos and Harpocrates. We went on board, we traveled north, we reached a point six miles north of Coptos.

Now Thoth had found out everything that had happened to Naneferkaptah regarding the book, and Thoth hastened to report it to Pre, saying: "Learn of my right and my case against Naneferkaptah, the son of Pharaoh Mernebptah![8] He went to my storehouse; he plundered it; he seized my box with my document. He killed my guardian who was watching over it!"[9] He was told: "He is yours together with every person belonging to him." They sent a divine power from heaven, saying: "Do not allow Naneferkaptah and any person belonging to him to get to Memphis safely!"

At a certain moment the boy Merib came out from under the awning of Pharaoh's ship, fell into the water, and drowned. All the people on board cried out. Naneferkaptah came out from his tent, recited a spell to him, and made him rise up, though there were twenty-one divine cubits of water over him. He recited a spell to him and made him relate to him everything that had happened to him, and the nature of the accusation that Thoth had made before Pre.[1]

We returned to Coptos with him. We had him taken to the Good House. We had him tended, we had him embalmed like a prince and important person. We laid him to rest in his coffin in the desert of Coptos. Naneferkaptah, my brother, said: "Let us go north, let us not delay, lest Pharaoh hear the things that have happened to us and his heart become sad because of them." We went on board, we went north without delay.

Six miles north of Coptos, at the place where the boy Merib had fallen into the river, I came out from under the awning of Pharaoh's ship, fell into the river, and drowned. All the people on board cried out and told Naneferkaptah. He came out from the tent of Pharaoh's ship, recited a spell to me, and made me rise up, though there were twenty-one divine cubits of water over me. He had me brought up, recited a spell to me, and made me relate to him everything that had happened to me, and the nature of the accusation that Thoth had made before Pre.

He returned to Coptos with me. He had me taken to the Good House. He had me tended, he had me embalmed in the manner of a prince and very important person. He laid me to rest in the tomb in which the boy Merib was resting. He went on board, he went north without delay.

Six miles north of Coptos, at the place where we had fallen into the river, he spoke to his heart saying: "Could I go to Coptos and dwell there also? If I go to Memphis now and Pharaoh asks me about his children, what shall I say to him? Can I say to him, 'I took your children to the region of Thebes; I killed them and stayed alive, and I have come to Memphis yet alive'?"

He sent for a scarf of royal linen belonging to him, and made it into a bandage; he bound the book, placed it on his body, and made it fast. Naneferkaptah came out from under the awning of Pharaoh's ship, fell into the water, and drowned. All the people on board cried out, saying: "Great woe, sad woe! Will he return, the good scribe, the learned man whose like has not been?"

8. A form of the name of Merneptah, the successor of Ramses II and a brother of the historical Setne Khamwas.
9. The snake that protected the chest with the papyrus.
1. Merib had learned of Thoth's complaint, presumably after he had drowned.

Pharaoh's ship sailed north, no man on earth knowing where Naneferkaptah was. They reached Memphis and sent word to Pharaoh. Pharaoh came down to meet Pharaoh's ship; he wore mourning and all the people of Memphis wore mourning, including the priests of Ptah, the chief priest of Ptah, the council, and all Pharaoh's household. Then they saw Naneferkaptah holding on to the rudders of Pharaoh's ship through his craft of a good scribe. They brought him up and saw the book on his body.

Pharaoh said: "Let this book that is on his body be hidden."[2] Then said the council of Pharaoh and the priests of Ptah and the chief priest of Ptah to Pharaoh: "Our great lord—O may he have the lifetime of Pre—Naneferkaptah was a good scribe and a very learned man!" Pharaoh had them give him entry into the Good House on the sixteenth day, wrapping on the thirty-fifth, burial on the seventieth day. And they laid him to rest in his coffin in his resting place.

These are the evil things that befell us on account of this book of which you say, "Let it be given to me." You have no claim to it, whereas our lives on earth were taken on account of it!

Setne takes the book

Setne said to Ahwere: "Let me have this book that I see between you and Naneferkaptah, or else I will take it by force!" Naneferkaptah rose from the bier and said: "Are you Setne, to whom this woman has told these dire things and you have not accepted them? The said book, will you be able to seize it through the power of a good scribe, or through skill in playing draughts with me? Let the two of us play draughts for it!" Said Setne, "I am ready."

They put before them the game board with its pieces, and they both played. Naneferkaptah won one game from Setne. He recited a spell to him, struck his head with the game-box that was before him, and made him sink into the ground as far as his legs. He did the same with the second game. He won it from Setne, and made him sink into the ground as far as his phallus. He did the same with the third game, and made him sink into the ground as far as his ears. After this Setne was in great straits at the hands of Naneferkaptah.

Setne called to his foster-brother Inaros, saying: "Hasten up to the earth and tell Pharaoh everything that has happened to me; and bring the amulets of my father Ptah[3] and my books of sorcery." He hastened up to the earth and told Pharaoh everything that had happened to Setne. Pharaoh said: "Take him the amulets of his father Ptah and his books of sorcery." Inaros hastened down into the tomb. He put the amulets on the body of Setne, and he jumped up in that very moment. Setne stretched out his hand for the book and seized it. Then, as Setne came up from the tomb, light went before him, darkness went behind him, and Ahwere wept after him, saying: "Hail, O darkness! Farewell, O light! Everything that was in the tomb has departed!" Naneferkaptah said to Ahwere: "Let your heart not grieve. I will make him bring this book back here, with a forked stick in his hand and a lighted brazier on his head!"[4]

2. The scroll and Naneferkaptah's skill as a magician have enabled his drowned body to become attached to the yacht's rudders and be transported underwater to Memphis. He knew that he would not escape drowning.

3. Ptah is Setne's "father" because Setne is high priest of Ptah, like the son of Ramses II after whom his character is modeled.

4. This image, which occurs again later, is modeled on the hieroglyph for a defeated enemy or on pictures of the dead being punished in the next world. In either case, Setne will have failed very visibly.

Setne came up from the tomb and made it fast behind him, as it had been. Setne went before Pharaoh and related to him the things that had happened to him on account of the book. Pharaoh said to Setne: "Take this book back to the tomb of Naneferkaptah like a wise man, or else he will make you take it back with a forked stick in your hand and a lighted brazier on your head." Setne did not listen to him. Then Setne had no occupation on earth but to unroll the book and read from it to everyone.

Setne and Tabubu

After this it happened one day that Setne was strolling in the forecourt of the temple of Ptah. Then he saw [a woman] who was very beautiful, there being no other woman like her in appearance. She was beautiful and wore many golden jewels, and maid servants walked behind her as well as two men servants belonging to her household. The moment Setne saw her, he did not know where on earth he was. He called his man servant, saying: "Hasten to the place where this woman is, and find out what her position is." The man servant hastened to the place where the woman was. He called to the maid servant who was following her and asked her, saying, "What woman is this?" She told him: "It is Tabubu, the daughter of the prophet of Bastet, mistress of Ankhtawi.[5] She has come here to worship Ptah, the great god."

The servant returned to Setne and related to him every word she had said to him. Setne said to the servant: "Go, say to the maid. 'It is Setne Khamwas, the son of Pharaoh Usermare,[6] who has sent me to say, "I will give you ten pieces of gold—spend an hour with me. Or do you have a complaint of wrongdoing? I will have it settled for you. I will have you taken to a hidden place where no one on earth shall find you." ' "[7]

The servant returned to the place where Tabubu was. He called her maid and told her. She cried out as if what he said was an insult. Tabubu said to the servant: "Stop talking to this foolish maid; come and speak with me." The servant hastened to where Tabubu was and said to her: "I will give you ten pieces of gold; spend an hour with Setne Khamwas, the son of Pharaoh Usermare. If you have a complaint of wrongdoing, he will have it settled for you. He will take you to a hidden place where no one on earth shall find you."

Tabubu said: "Go, tell Setne, 'I am of priestly rank, I am not a low person. If you desire to do what you wish with me, you must come to Bubastis, to my house. It is furnished with everything, and you shall do what you wish with me, without anyone on earth finding me and without my acting like a low woman of the street.' "

The servant returned to Setne and told him everything she had said to him. He said, "That suits (me)!" Everyone around Setne was indignant.

Setne had a boat brought to him. He went on board and hastened to Bubastis. When he came to the west of the suburb he found a very lofty house that

5. Bastet was one of the goddesses of Memphis. Prophets were high-ranking priests. The temple of Bastet was in a northwestern quarter of the city named Ankhtawi.

6. The throne name of Ramses II.

7. Setne says he will pay Tabubu for sex and, should she object and accuse him, he will go ahead and rape her.

had a wall around it, a garden on its north, and a seat at its door. Setne asked, "Whose house is this?" They told him, "It is the house of Tabubu." Setne went inside the wall. While he turned his face to the storehouse in the garden they announced him to Tabubu. She came down, took Setne's hand, and said to him: "By the welfare of the house of the prophet of Bastet, mistress of Ankhtawi, which you have reached, it will please me greatly if you will take the trouble to come up with me."

Setne walked up the stairs of the house with Tabubu. He found the upper story of the house swept and adorned, its floor adorned with real lapis-lazuli and real turquoise. Many couches were in it, spread with royal linen, and many golden cups were on the table. A golden cup was filled with wine and put into Setne's hand. She said to him, "May it please you to eat something. He said to her, "I could not do that." Incense was put on the brazier; ointment was brought to him of the kind provided for Pharaoh. Setne made holiday with Tabubu, never having seen anyone like her.

Setne said to Tabubu: "Let us accomplish what we have come here for." She said to him: "You will return to your house in which you live. I am of priestly rank; I am not a low person. If you desire to do what you wish with me you must make for me a deed of maintenance and of compensation in money for everything, all goods belonging to you." He said to her: "Send for the school-teacher." He was brought at once. He made for her a deed of maintenance and of compensation in money for everything, all goods belonging to him.

At this moment one came to announce to Setne, "Your children are below." He said, "Let them be brought up." Tabubu rose and put on a garment of royal linen. Setne saw all her limbs through it, and his desire became even greater than it had been before. Setne said: "Tabubu, let me accomplish what I have come here for!" She said to him: "You will return to your house in which you live. I am of priestly rank: I am not a low person. If you desire to do what you wish with me, you must make your children subscribe to my deed. Do not leave them to contend with my children over your property." He had his children brought and made them subscribe to the deed.

Setne said to Tabubu: "Let me accomplish what I have come for!" She said to him: "You will return to your house in which you live. I am of priestly rank; I am not a low person. If you desire to do what you wish with me, you must have your children killed. Do not leave them to contend with my children over your property." Setne said: "Let the abomination that came into your head be done to them." She had his children killed before him. She had them thrown down from the window to the dogs and cats. They ate their flesh, and he heard them as he drank with Tabubu.

Setne said to Tabubu: "Let us accomplish what we have come here for! All the things that you have said, I have done them all for you." She said to him: "Come now to this storehouse." Setne went to the storehouse. He lay down on a couch of ivory and ebony, his wish about to be fulfilled. Tabubu lay down beside Setne. He stretched out his hand to touch her, and she opened her mouth wide in a loud cry. Setne awoke in a state of great heat, his phallus in a[8] [. . .] and there were no clothes on him at all.

8. The text is corrupted here.

At this moment Setne saw a noble person borne in a litter, with many men running beside him, and he had the likeness of Pharaoh. Setne was about to rise but could not rise for shame because he had no clothes on. Pharaoh said: "Setne, what is this state that you are in?" He said: "It is Naneferkaptah who has done it all to me!" Pharaoh said: "Go to Memphis; your children want you; they stand in their rank before Pharaoh." Setne said to Pharaoh: "My great lord—O may he have the lifetime of Pre—how can I go to Memphis with no clothes on me at all?" Pharaoh called to a servant who was standing by and made him give clothes to Setne. Pharaoh said: "Setne, go to Memphis; your children are alive; they stand in their rank before Pharaoh."

Setne returns the book

When Setne came to Memphis he embraced his children, for he found them alive. Pharaoh said to Setne: "Was it a state of drunkenness you were in before?" Setne related everything that had happened with Tabubu and Naneferkaptah. Pharaoh said: "Setne, I did what I could with you before, saying, 'They will kill you if you do not take this book back to the place you took it from.' You have not listened to me until now. Take this book back to Naneferkaptah, with a forked stick in your hand and a lighted brazier on your head."

When Setne came out from before Pharaoh, there was a forked stick in his hand and a lighted brazier on his head. He went down into the tomb in which Naneferkaptah was. Ahwere said to him: "Setne, it is the great god Ptah who has brought you back safely." Naneferkaptah laughed, saying, "It is what I told you before." Setne greeted Naneferkaptah, and he found one could say that Pre was in the whole tomb.[9] Ahwere and Naneferkaptah greeted Setne warmly.

Setne said: "Naneferkaptah, is there any matter which is shameful?" Naneferkaptah said: "Setne, you know that Ahwere and her son Merib are in Coptos; here in this tomb they are through the craft of a good scribe.[1] Let it be asked of you to undertake the task of going to Coptos and [bringing them] here."

When Setne had come up from the tomb, he went before Pharaoh and related to Pharaoh everything that Naneferkaptah had said to him. Pharaoh said: "Setne, go to Coptos, bring Ahwere and her son Merib." He said to Pharaoh: "Let the ship of Pharaoh and its equipment be given to me."

The ship of Pharaoh and its equipment were given to him. He went on board, he set sail, he reached Coptos without delay. It was announced to the priests of Isis of Coptos, and the chief priest of Isis. They came down to meet him, they conducted him to the shore.

He went up from it, he went into the temple of Isis of Coptos and Harpocrates. He sent for an ox, a goose, and wine, and made burnt offering and libation before Isis of Coptos and Harpocrates. He went to the desert of Coptos with

9. The return of the scroll has filled the tomb with light.

1. Scribes were the traditional magicians.

the priests of Isis and the chief priest of Isis. They spent three days and three nights searching in all the tombs on the desert of Coptos, turning over the stelae of the scribes of the House of Life, and reading the inscriptions on them. They did not find the resting place in which Ahwere and her son were.

When Naneferkaptah found that they did not find the resting place of Ahwere and her son Merib, he rose up as an old man, a very aged priest, and came to meet Setne. When Setne saw him he said to the old man: "You have the appearance of a man of great age. Do you know the resting place in which Ahwere and her son Merib are?" The old man said to Setne: "My great-grandfather said to my grandfather, 'The resting place of Ahwere and her son Merib is at the south corner of the house of the [chief of police].'"

Setne said to the old man: "Perhaps there is some wrong that the chief of police did to you, on account of which you are trying to have his house torn down?" The old man said to Setne: "Have a watch set over me, and let the house of the chief of police be demolished. If they do not find Ahwere and her son Merib under the south corner of his house, let punishment be done to me."

They set a watch over the old man, and they found the resting place of Ahwere and her son Merib under the south corner of the house of the chief of police. Setne let the two noble persons[2] enter into Pharaoh's ship. He had the house of the chief of police built as it had been before. Naneferkaptah let Setne learn the fact that it was he who had come to Coptos, to let them find the resting place in which Ahwere and her son Merib were. Setne went on board Pharaoh's ship. He went north and without delay he reached Memphis with all the people who were with him. When it was announced before Pharaoh, he came down to meet the ship of Pharaoh. He let the noble persons enter into the tomb in which Naneferkaptah was. He had it closed over them all together.

Colophon

This is the complete text, a tale of Setne Khamwas and Naneferkaptah, and his wife Ahwere and her son Merib. It was copied by __________ in year 15, first month of winter.[3]

2. *Noble* is an ancient word that came to mean "mummy" in later periods. The mummies of Ahwere and Merib are carried in solemn procession onto the ship.

3. The text was copied during the Ptolemaic Period (a Hellenistic dynasty established in Egypt by generals of Alexander the Great) under King Ptolemy II, III, or IV, whose years 15 correspond to 271, 232, and 207 B.C.E., respectively.

STELA OF TAIMHOTEP

42 B.C.E.

This stela, which has been known since the beginnings of Egyptology in the early nineteenth century, tells the life story of Taimhotep, the second wife of Psherenptah, the high priest of the ancient capital Memphis, near modern Cairo. Taimhotep died in 42 B.C.E., and her husband followed her at the end of the next year. They belonged to a large priestly family that was prominent for more than two centuries. One of the few known inscriptions that tell of women's lives, Taimhotep's biography is composed in elaborately phrased Classical Egyptian, displaying an extraordinary command of a form of the language that had been current almost two thousand years earlier. The first two thirds (omitted from the selection here) speak about her traditional role as a woman, which was essentially to bear a male heir for her husband, whose titles and achievements fill much of the text. The last part starts with her death and continues with a remarkable group of poems pronounced from the beyond, depicting the next world as a terrible place and centering on Taimhotep's desperate yearning for water, a pressing concern for those buried in desert tombs. These poems were probably sung during funeral ceremonies as a dramatic outpouring of grief.

Stela of Taimhotep[1]

Year 10, month 2 of Emergence,[2] day 16
was the day on which I died.

There placed me my husband[3]—the priest of Ptah,
priest of Osiris, lord of Rosetau,
priest of the Dual King, Lord of the Two Lands,
Ptolemy, true of voice,[4]
keeper of secrets in the house of Ptah,
keeper of secrets in sky, earth, and underworld,
keeper of secrets in Rosetau,
keeper of secrets in Rutiset,[5]
chief controller of craftsmen, Psherenptah—in the West.
He performed for me all the rites for an effective mummy.
He buried me in a perfect burial.
He deposited my corpse in his tomb in the area of Rutiset.

1. Translated and with footnotes by John Baines.
2. The middle season of the three in the ancient Egyptian calendar. This date computes to 15 February 42 B.C.E. Taimhotep died at the age of thirty, not particularly young in the ancient context.
3. Psherenptah performed the funeral rituals for Taimhotep in person. "Rosetau" is a traditional name for a necropolis, particularly that of Memphis. Psherenptah's priesthood of Osiris, the god of the dead, was the relevant one for the funeral among the many he held.
4. Psherenptah was also priest of the mortuary cult of Ptolemy XII Neos Dionysos (known as Auletes [80–51 B.C.E.]). The culturally Greek ruler Ptolemy, whose capital was Alexandria, bears traditional Egyptian kingly titles.
5. Rutiset is the most ancient and hallowed area of the necropolis of Memphis, modern North Saqqara.

The stela of Taimhotep.

Oh my brother,[6] my husband,
my companion, great controller of craftsmen:
may your heart not tire in drinking and eating,
drunkenness and sexual pleasure.
Spend a perfect day and follow your heart[7] all the time.
Do not place care in your heart.

Years taken upon earth are good.
As for the West, it is a land of sleeping in darkness.[8]
It is dire to dwell in for those who are there.
Those who sleep in their cloth wrappings,[9]
they do not awaken to see their kin.
They do not see their fathers and their mothers;
their hearts miss their wives and their children.

The water of life that is for everyone therein, it is thirst before me;[1]
it comes to the one who is upon earth, but it is thirst for me.
Water is beside me,
but I do not know the place where it is,
since I came to this wadi.[2]

6. A term of endearment between spouses. Taimhotep is speaking to Psherenptah from the next world.

7. A traditional phrase meaning "do what you want."

8. The dead are supposed to be reborn to dwell in light. Taimhotep denies this.

9. Mummies were wrapped in multiple layers of cloth. Rituals performed on the mummy were supposed to enable the deceased to leave the mummy and move freely. Here the effectiveness of the ritual is denied.

1. Taimhotep can see water but cannot reach it.

2. The tomb is located in a dry depression in the desert.

Give me the water that is gone
so that I may say to myself: "my body is not far from water."[3]
Set my face to the north wind,
at the edge of the water.
Perhaps then my heart will be assuaged in its suffering.

As for death, "Come" is his name:[4]
everyone whom he summons, they come to him at once,
their hearts terror-struck in fear of him.
No one looks toward him among gods and humans;
the great ones among them like the small.

His finger is not repulsed from anyone he wishes to touch.
He snatches the son from his mother,
while the old man wanders in his path.
All the fearful plead before him;[5]
he does not turn his face to them; he does not come to the
one who beseeches him.
He does not listen to the one who extols him;
he does not look at the one who gives to him
gifts of all sorts.

Oh all who reach this desert place,[6] be fearful for me,
burn incense for me on the flame,
make libations at every festival of the West.

The scribe, one who makes live,[7] wise man,
keeper of secrets in the house of gold and in Tjenenet,[8]
the priest Harimhotep,
son of the priest Khaihap, true of voice,
born of Herankh.

3. Taimhotep imagines the effect of receiving a libation in the next world—a theme to which she returns—while also evoking an ideal location where there is both water and the coveted north wind, which brings cool air and makes the heat bearable. Scenes where the deceased receive libations by pools are common in the decoration of tombs and stelae.
4. Death is imagined as a malicious demon. This idea is known also from images.
5. Death is like a god who would hear prayers, but he does not heed them.
6. People were expected to visit the tombs of their relatives and might also perform offering formulas at other tombs. Taimhotep addresses passersby in the necropolis. Making libations is the core ritual act that will guarantee water to the deceased.
7. This is a title of a sculptor. The last lines identify the person who made the stela and perhaps composed its text. He was a kinsman of Taimhotep.
8. The "house of gold" was a treasury and craft workshop attached to temples. Tjenenet was an ancient temple in Memphis.

THE EPIC OF GILGAMESH

ca. 1900–250 B.C.E.

The Epic of Gilgamesh is the greatest work of ancient Mesopotamia and one of the earliest pieces of world literature. The story of its main protagonist, King Gilgamesh, and his quest for immortality touches on the most fundamental questions of what it means to be human: death and friendship, nature and civilization, power and violence, travel adventures and homecoming, love and sexuality. Because of the appeal of its central hero and his struggle with the meaning of culture in the face of human mortality, the epic spread throughout the ancient Near East and was translated into various regional languages during the second millennium B.C.E. As far as we know, no other literary work of the ancient world spread so widely across cultures and languages. And yet, after a long period of popularity, *Gilgamesh* was forgotten, seemingly for good: after circulating in various versions for many centuries, it vanished from human memory for over two thousand years. Its rediscovery by archeologists in the nineteenth century was a sensation and allows us to read a story that for many centuries was known to many cultures and people throughout the Near East but has come down to us today only by chance on brittle clay tablets.

KING GILGAMESH AND HIS STORY

Gilgamesh was thought to be a priest-king of the city-state of Uruk in Southern Mesopotamia, the lands around the rivers Euphrates and Tigris in modern-day Iraq. He probably ruled around 2700 B.C.E. and was remembered for the building of Uruk's monumental city walls, which were ten kilometers long and fitted with nine hundred towers; portions of these walls are still visible today. We will never know for sure how the historical king compares to the epic hero Gilgamesh. But soon after his death, he was venerated as a great king and judge of the Underworld. In the epic he appears as "two-thirds divine and one-third human," the offspring of Ninsun, a goddess in the shape of a wild cow, and of a human father named Lugalbanda. By some accounts, *Gilgamesh* means "the offspring is a hero," or, according to another etymology, "the old man is still a young man."

Gilgamesh was not written by one specific author but evolved gradually over the long span of a millennium. The earliest story of Gilgamesh appears around 2100 B.C.E. in a cycle of poems in the Sumerian language. Sumerian is the earliest Mesopotamian language. It is written in "cuneiform" script—wedge-shaped characters incised in clay or stone—and has no connection to any other known language. About six hundred years after Gilgamesh's death, kings of the third dynasty of Ur, another Mesopotamian city-state, claimed descent from the legendary king of Uruk and enjoyed hearing of the great deeds of Gilgamesh at court; the earliest cycle of Gilgamesh poems was written for these rulers. As in the later epic, in the Sumerian cycle of poems Gilgamesh is a powerful king and an awe-inspiring warrior. Gilgamesh's shattering realization that he will die and can attain immortality only by making a name for himself appears already in this earliest version of the Gilgamesh story, where he exclaims:

> I have peered over the city wall,
> I have seen the corpses floating in the river's water.
> So too it will come to pass for me, so it will happen to me . . .
> Since no man can avoid life's end,
> I would enter the mountain land and set up my name.

The Sumerian poetry cycle became the basis for the old version of *Gilgamesh,* written in Babylonian, a variant of the Akkadian language—a transnational written language that was widely used throughout the Ancient Near East. The traditional Babylonian epic version of *Gilgamesh,* which adapted the Sumerian poems into a connected narrative, circulated for more than fifteen hundred years. It was read widely from Mesopotamia to Syria, the Levant, and Anatolia and was translated into non-Mesopotamian languages such as Hittite, the language of an empire that controlled Turkey and Northern Syria in the latter half of the second millennium B.C.E.

The definitive revision of the epic is attributed to a Babylonian priest and scholar named Sin-leqi-unninni. He lived around 1200 B.C.E., and by his time King Gilgamesh had been dead for about fifteen hundred years. He carefully selected elements from the older traditions, inserted new plot elements, and added a preface to the epic. His version, included here in translation, is divided into eleven chapters recorded on eleven clay tablets. New fragments of *Gilgamesh* continue to surface from archaeological excavations; some pieces are still missing, and some passages are fragmentary and barely legible, but thanks to the painstaking work of scholars of Ancient Mesopotamia we can today read an extended, gripping narrative.

THE WORLD'S OLDEST EPIC HERO

The Gilgamesh of the epic is an awe-inspiring, sparkling hero, but at first also the epitome of a bad ruler: arrogant, oppressive, and brutal. As the epic begins, the people of Uruk complain to the Sumerian gods about Gilgamesh's overbearing behavior, and so the gods create the wild man Enkidu to confront Gilgamesh. While Gilgamesh is a mixture of human and divine, Enkidu is a blend of human and wild animal, though godlike in his own way. He is raised by beasts in the wilderness and eats what they eat. When he breaks hunters' traps for the sake of his animal companions he becomes a threat to human society and Gilgamesh decides to tame him with the attractions of urban life and civilization: for seven days Enkidu makes love to a harlot (prostitute), sent out for the purpose, and at her urging he takes a cleansing bath and accepts clothing and a first meal of basic human foodstuff, bread, and beer. Shamhat, the prostitute, leads him to the city of Uruk. Although he and Gilgamesh are at first bent on competing with each other, they quickly develop a deep bond of friendship.

Their friendship established, Gilgamesh proposes to Enkidu the first of their epic adventures: to travel to the great Cedar Forest and slay the giant Humbaba, who guards the forest for the harsh god Enlil. With the blessing of the sun god Shamash they succeed, and they cut down some magnificent trees that they float down the Euphrates River to Mesopotamia. But their violent act has its consequence: the dying giant curses them and Enlil is enraged. Their second adventure leads to a yet more ambiguous success, which will set in motion the tragic end of their friendship. Gilgamesh, cleansed from battle and radiant in victory, attracts the desire of Ishtar, goddess of love and warfare. Instead of politely

This modern impression of an ancient cylinder seal shows a bearded hero, kneeling and raising an outstretched lion above his head.

resisting her advances, Gilgamesh makes the fatal error of chiding her for her fickle passions and known cruelty toward her lovers, and heaps insults on the goddess. Scandalized by Gilgamesh's accusations, she unleashes the Bull of Heaven against the two friends, and it wreaks havoc in Uruk. After the heroic duo kills the Bull of Heaven, a council of the gods convenes to avoid further disaster. The gods decide that Gilgamesh and Enkidu have gone too far; one of them must die. The lot falls to Enkidu, because Gilgamesh is the king.

Enkidu's death brings Gilgamesh face to face with mortality. He mourns for Enkidu bitterly for seven days and nights and only when a worm creeps out of the corpse's nose does he accept that his friend is dead. Terrified that he too will die, Gilgamesh forsakes the civilized world to find the one human being known to have achieved immortality: Utanapishtim, survivor of the Great Flood. Like Enkidu in his days as a wild man, Gilgamesh roams the steppe, disheveled and clad in a lion-skin, and sets out on a quest to ask Utanapishtim for the secret of eternal life. He braves monsters, runs along the sun's path under the earth at night, encounters a mysterious woman who keeps a tavern at the edge of the world, passes a garden of jeweled trees, crosses the waters of death, and finally arrives at the doorstep of Utanapishtim and his wife. Utanapishtim's dramatic account of their experience and survival of the flood resembles the biblical story of Noah and the Great Flood in Genesis. At his wife's request, Utanapishtim gives Gilgamesh the chance to attain immortality by eating a magic plant, but he is afraid to try it and a serpent steals the magic plant and gains the power of immortality for itself. In the end Gilgamesh returns to Uruk, empty-handed. Although in the final moments of the epic he proudly surveys the mighty city walls of his making, he is a profoundly changed man.

AN ANCIENT EPIC

The word *epic* is originally Greek and refers to a long poem narrating important historical or cosmic events in elevated language and involving a panoramic sweep of action and a cast of protagonists who straddle the human and divine worlds. Some epics, like **Homer's *Iliad*,** tell of the foundation or destruction of civilizations or cities, featuring noisy battle scenes, in which the heroes can prove their strength, wisdom, and understanding of the workings of the divine order. Other epics, like **Homer's *Odyssey*,** focus on the travels and adventures of a central protagonist. Greek epics usually invoke the Muses, goddesses in charge of the arts and a poet's inspiration and inform the poets of past events and the world of the gods. They often include long speeches, in which protagonists remember past events or justify future actions. And they rely heavily on the repetition of lines with variation and on a rhetoric of parallels and contrasts. Scholars of Homeric epic have argued that repetition and formulaic expression helped the bards to remember and recite extensive storylines and point to the poems' oral and performative roots.

Gilgamesh shares a few fundamental features with Greek epic. True, there was no concept in Mesopotamia corresponding to the Western literary genre "epic," and *Gilgamesh* has no equivalent to the strict hexameter of Greek epic. A verse line in *Gilgamesh* is not defined by a fixed number of syllables or stresses but varies in length, which can only be inferred by context, such as patterns of parallelism. Still, in contrast to the literary works of other civilizations of the ancient world that had no epic, like China and East Asia, *Gilgamesh* can be considered part of a larger Near Eastern and Mediterranean epic tradition. Although *Gilgamesh* was only translated into cuneiform languages and never directly entered the epic repertoire of alphabet languages like Greek, it shared with the Greek tradition a number of classically epic motifs. In Achilles' mourning for his friend Patroclus (in Homer's *Iliad*) we can recognize Gilgamesh's desperation at the loss of Enkidu. Just as Gilgamesh finally returns to Uruk after challenging adventures, Odysseus (in Homer's *Odyssey*) returns to Ithaca from the Trojan War in the guise of a destitute stranger after performing dangerous feats. In *Gilgamesh* and Greek epics, scenes featuring councils of the gods who decide the fate of their heroes reflect religious beliefs about the intersection between human limitations and divine powers but are also astute plot devices that sharpen the profile of the heroes and their ways of confronting divine antagonism. We can see a parallel to the wiliness of the Greek gods and their personal preferences in the opposition of Shamash and Enlil, in particular in Enlil's argument that Enkidu should be sacrificed and Gilgamesh spared.

In contrast to the orally rooted Homeric epic, *Gilgamesh* was from the outset conceived as a literary work. With its elevated style, geometrically parallel phrases, and moments of complex word play, *Gilgamesh* was addressed to the sophisticated ears and minds of scholars and members of the royal court. We know that it was used in Babylonian schools to teach literature. This hypothesis is further supported when we look at the nuanced use of speech registers in the epic's portrayal of its protagonists. Utanapishtim speaks in an obscure archaic style that befits a sage from before the Great Flood, and he has a solemn way of rolling and doubling his consonants. The goddess Ishtar appears in an unfavorable light, talking like a low-class streetwalker. In contrast, Shamhat, the prostitute who brings Enkidu to the city, speaks with unexpected eloquence and distinction.

Shamhat is a thought-provoking example of the several powerful female protagonists in *Gilgamesh*. Much of what Gilgamesh accomplishes is ultimately due to women: his mother's pleas with the sun god Shamash allow him to kill Humbaba; the wife of the scorpion monster persuades her husband to give Gilgamesh entrance to the tunnel leading to the jeweled garden; and the mysterious woman he finds at the end of the world, the tavern keeper Siduri, helps him find Utanapishtim, whose wife persuades her husband to give Gilgamesh the plant of rejuvenation. In some of Gilgamesh's encounters there are touches of wit and parody. It is stunning to find this blend of epic grandeur and comic sobriety in the world's earliest epic. Part of the epic's subtlety is invisible today, because we know so much less about the historical and literary context of *Gilgamesh* than we know about the context of Greek epic. Still, the glimpses we get show the sophistication of the early Mesopotamian states and the art of literary narrative they developed.

Like Mesopotamian civilization and its cuneiform writing system, *Gilgamesh* eventually disappeared. In the seventh century B.C.E., when an invading force of ancient Iranian people called Medians sacked Nineveh, one of the capitals of the Assyrian Empire, copies of the epic written on clay tablets, which had been preserved in the palace library of Ashurbanipal, the last great Assyrian king (reigned 668–627 B.C.E.), vanished in the destruction. Although the epic did not disappear completely and still circulated until the third century B.C.E., it was only rediscovered in the 1850s, when an English explorer, Austen Henry Layard, dug up thousands of tablets from the site at Nineveh. They were later deciphered at the British Museum in London, and when the young curator George Smith made the stunning discovery that this epic contained a version of the biblical story of the flood, which had hitherto been considered unique to the book of Genesis, this challenged conceptions about the origin of biblical narrative. *Gilgamesh* was suddenly propelled into the canon of world literature.

The Epic of Gilgamesh took shape many centuries before the Greeks and Hebrews learned how to write, and it circulated in the Near East and Levant long before the book of Genesis and the Homeric epics took shape. The rediscovery of the names of the gods and humans who people the epic and of the history of the cities and lands in which they lived is a gradual, ongoing process. And the meaning of the epic itself is tantalizingly ambiguous. Has Gilgamesh succeeded or failed in his quest? What makes us human? Can civilization bring immortality? Whatever we decide to believe, the story of Gilgamesh and his companion Enkidu, of their quest for fame and immortality, speaks to contemporary readers with an urgency and immediacy that makes us forget just how ancient it is.

The Epic of Gilgamesh[1]

Tablet I

He who saw the wellspring, the foundations of the land,
Who knew the ways, was wise in all things,
Gilgamesh, who saw the wellspring, the foundations of the land,
He knew the ways, was wise in all things,
He it was who inspected holy places everywhere,

1. Translated by and with footnotes adapted from Benjamin R. Foster.

Full understanding of it all he gained,
He saw what was secret and revealed what was hidden,
He brought back tidings from before the flood,
From a distant journey came home, weary, at peace,
Engraved all his hardships on a monument of stone,
He built the walls of ramparted Uruk,[2]
The lustrous treasury of hallowed Eanna!
See its upper wall, whose facing gleams like copper,
Gaze at the lower course, which nothing will equal,
Mount the stone stairway, there from days of old,
Approach Eanna, the dwelling of Ishtar,
Which no future king, no human being will equal.
Go up, pace out the walls of Uruk,
Study the foundation terrace and examine the brickwork.
Is not its masonry of kiln-fired brick?
And did not seven masters lay its foundations?
One square mile of city, one square mile of gardens,
One square mile of clay pits, a half square mile of Ishtar's dwelling,
Three and a half square miles is the measure of Uruk!
Search out the foundation box of copper,
Release its lock of bronze,
Raise the lid upon its hidden contents,
Take up and read from the lapis tablet
Of him, Gilgamesh, who underwent many hardships.
Surpassing all kings, for his stature renowned,
Heroic offspring of Uruk, a charging wild bull,
He leads the way in the vanguard,
He marches at the rear, defender of his comrades.
Mighty floodwall, protector of his troops,
Furious flood-wave smashing walls of stone,
Wild calf of Lugalbanda, Gilgamesh is perfect in strength,
Suckling of the sublime wild cow, the woman Ninsun,[3]
Towering Gilgamesh is uncannily perfect.
Opening passes in the mountains,
Digging wells at the highlands' verge,
Traversing the ocean, the vast sea, to the sun's rising,
Exploring the furthest reaches of the earth,
Seeking everywhere for eternal life,
Reaching in his might Utanapishtim the Distant One,
Restorer of holy places that the deluge had destroyed,
Founder of rites for the teeming peoples,
Who could be his like for kingly virtue?
And who, like Gilgamesh, can proclaim, "I am king!"
Gilgamesh was singled out from the day of his birth,
Two-thirds of him was divine, one-third of him was human!

2. City-state ruled by King Gilgamesh. It was the largest city of Mesopotamia at the time and among its important temples featured Eanna, a sanctuary for the goddess of love and warfare, Ishtar.

3. Lugalbanda, Gilgamesh's father, was an earlier king of Uruk. His mother was Ninsun, a goddess called "the wild cow."

The Lady of Birth drew his body's image,
The God of Wisdom brought his stature to perfection.

He was perfection in height,
Ideally handsome

In the enclosure of Uruk he strode back and forth,
Lording it like a wild bull, his head thrust high.
The onslaught of his weapons had no equal.
His teammates stood forth by his game stick,
He was harrying the young men of Uruk beyond reason.
Gilgamesh would leave no son to his father,
Day and night he would rampage fiercely.
This was the shepherd of ramparted Uruk,
This was the people's shepherd,
Bold, superb, accomplished, and mature!
Gilgamesh would leave no girl to her mother!
The warrior's daughter, the young man's spouse,
Goddesses kept hearing their plaints.
The gods of heaven, the lords who command,
Said to Anu:[4]

> You created this headstrong wild bull in ramparted Uruk,
> The onslaught of his weapons has no equal.
> His teammates stand forth by his game stick,
> He is harrying the young men of Uruk beyond reason.
> Gilgamesh leaves no son to his father!
> Day and night he rampages fiercely.
> This is the shepherd of ramparted Uruk,
> This is the people's shepherd,
> Bold, superb, accomplished, and mature!
> Gilgamesh leaves no girl to her mother!

The warrior's daughter, the young man's spouse,
Anu kept hearing their plaints.

[*Anu speaks.*]

> Let them summon Aruru,[5] the great one,
> She created the boundless human race.
> Let her create a partner for Gilgamesh, mighty in strength,
> Let them contend with each other, that Uruk may have peace.

They summoned the birth goddess, Aruru:

> You, Aruru, created the boundless human race,
> Now, create what Anu commanded,

4. The sky god who is supreme in the pantheon but remote from human affairs. Uruk was known for its temples for Anu and Ishtar.
5. Goddess of birth.

To his stormy heart, let that one be equal,
Let them contend with each other, that Uruk may have peace.

When Aruru heard this,
She conceived within her what Anu commanded.
Aruru wet her hands,
She pinched off clay, she tossed it upon the steppe,
She created valiant Enkidu in the steppe,
Offspring of potter's clay, with the force of the hero Ninurta.[6]
Shaggy with hair was his whole body,
He was made lush with head hair, like a woman,
The locks of his hair grew thick as a grainfield.
He knew neither people nor inhabited land,
He dressed as animals do.
He fed on grass with gazelles,
With beasts he jostled at the water hole,
With wildlife he drank his fill of water.

A hunter, a trapping-man,
Encountered him at the edge of the water hole.
One day, a second, and a third he encountered him at the edge of the water hole.
When he saw him, the hunter stood stock-still with terror,
As for Enkidu, he went home with his beasts.
Aghast, struck dumb,
His heart in a turmoil, his face drawn,
With woe in his vitals,
His face like a traveler's from afar,
The hunter made ready to speak, saying to his father:

My father, there is a certain fellow who has come from the uplands,
He is the mightiest in the land, strength is his,
Like the force of heaven, so mighty is his strength.
He constantly ranges over the uplands,
Constantly feeding on grass with beasts,
Constantly making his way to the edge of the water hole.
I am too frightened to approach him.
He has filled in the pits I dug,
He has torn out my traps I set,
He has helped the beasts, wildlife of the steppe, slip from my hands,
He will not let me work the steppe.

His father made ready to speak, saying to the hunter:

My son, in Uruk dwells Gilgamesh,
There is no one more mighty than he.
Like the force of heaven, so mighty is his strength.

6. A god of agriculture and war. Son of Enlil.

> Take the road, set off towards Uruk,
> Tell Gilgamesh of the mightiness-man.
> He will give you Shamhat the harlot, take her with you,
> Let her prevail over him, instead of a mighty man.
> When the wild beasts draw near the water hole,
> Let her strip off her clothing, laying bare her charms.
> When he sees her, he will approach her.
> His beasts that grew up with him on the steppe will deny him.

Giving heed to the advice of his father,
The hunter went forth.
He took the road, set off towards Uruk,
To the king, Gilgamesh, he said these words:

> There is a certain fellow who has come from the uplands,
> He is mightiest in the land, strength is his,
> Like the force of heaven, so mighty is his strength.
> He constantly ranges over the uplands,
> Constantly feeding on grass with his beasts,
> Constantly making his way to the edge of the water hole.
> I am too frightened to approach him.
> He has filled in the pits I dug,
> He has torn out my traps I set,
> He has helped the beasts, wildlife of the steppe, slip
> from my hands,
> He will not allow me to work the steppe.

Gilgamesh said to him, to the hunter:

> Go, hunter, take with you Shamhat the harlot,
> When the wild beasts draw near the water hole,
> Let her strip off her clothing, laying bare her charms.
> When he sees her, he will approach her,
> His beasts that grew up with him on the steppe will deny him.

Forth went the hunter, taking with him Shamhat the harlot,
They took the road, going straight on their way.
On the third day they arrived at the appointed place.
Hunter and harlot sat down to wait.
One day, a second day, they sat by the edge of the water hole,
The beasts came to the water hole to drink,
The wildlife came to drink their fill of water.
But as for him, Enkidu, born in the uplands,
Who feeds on grass with gazelles,
Who drinks at the water hole with beasts,
Who, with wildlife, drinks his fill of water,
Shamhat looked upon him, a human-man,
A barbarous fellow from the midst of the steppe:

> There he is, Shamhat, open your embrace,
> Open your embrace, let him take your charms!

Be not bashful, take his vitality!
When he sees you, he will approach you,
Toss aside your clothing, let him lie upon you,
Treat him, a human, to woman's work!
His wild beasts that grew up with him will deny him,
As in his ardor he caresses you!

Shamhat loosened her garments,
She exposed her loins, he took her charms.
She was not bashful, she took his vitality.
She tossed aside her clothing and he lay upon her,
She treated him, a human, to woman's work,
As in his ardor he caressed her.
Six days, seven nights was Enkidu aroused, flowing into Shamhat.
After he had his fill of her delights,
He set off towards his beasts.
When they saw him, Enkidu, the gazelles shied off,
The wild beasts of the steppe shunned his person.
Enkidu had spent himself, his body was limp,
His knees stood still, while his beasts went away.
Enkidu was too slow, he could not run as before,
But he had gained reason and expanded his understanding.

He returned, he sat at the harlot's feet,
The harlot gazed upon his face,
While he listened to what the harlot was saying.
The harlot said to him, to Enkidu:

You are handsome, Enkidu, you are become like a god,
Why roam the steppe with wild beasts?
Come, let me lead you to ramparted Uruk,
To the holy temple, abode of Anu and Ishtar,
The place of Gilgamesh, who is perfect in strength,
And so, like a wild bull, he lords it over the young men.

As she was speaking to him, her words found favor,
He was yearning for one to know his heart, a friend.
Enkidu said to her, to the harlot:

Come, Shamhat, escort me
To the lustrous hallowed temple, abode of Anu and Ishtar,
The place of Gilgamesh, who is perfect in strength,
And so, like a wild bull, he lords it over the young men.
I myself will challenge him, I will speak out boldly,
I will raise a cry in Uruk: I am the mighty one!
I am come forward to alter destinies!
He who was born in the steppe is mighty, strength is his!

[*Shamhat speaks.*]

Come then, let him see your face,
I will show you Gilgamesh, where he is I know full well.

Come then, Enkidu, to ramparted Uruk,
Where fellows are resplendent in holiday clothing,
Where every day is set for celebration,
Where harps and drums are played.
And the harlots too, they are fairest of form,
Rich in beauty, full of delights,
Even the great gods are kept from sleeping at night!
Enkidu, you who have not learned to live,
Oh, let me show you Gilgamesh, the joy-woe man.
Look at him, gaze upon his face,
He is radiant with virility, manly vigor is his,
The whole of his body is seductively gorgeous.
Mightier strength has he than you,
Never resting by day or night.
O Enkidu, renounce your audacity!
Gilgamesh is beloved of Shamash,
Anu, Enlil, and Ea broadened his wisdom.[7]
Ere you come down from the uplands,
Gilgamesh will dream of you in Uruk.

[*The scene shifts to Uruk.*]

Gilgamesh went to relate the dreams, saying to his mother:

Mother, I had a dream last night:
There were stars of heaven around me,
Like the force of heaven, something kept falling upon me!
I tried to carry it but it was too strong for me,
I tried to move it but I could not budge it.
The whole of Uruk was standing by it,
The people formed a crowd around it,
A throng was jostling towards it,
Young men were mobbed around it,
Infantile, they were groveling before it!
[I fell in love with it], like a woman I caressed it,
I carried it off and laid it down before you,
Then you were making it my partner.

The mother of Gilgamesh, knowing and wise,
Who understands everything, said to her son,
Ninsun the wild cow, knowing and wise,
Who understands everything, said to Gilgamesh:

The stars of heaven around you,
Like the force of heaven, what kept falling upon you,
Your trying to move it but not being able to budge it,
Your laying it down before me,
Then my making it your partner,
Your falling in love with it, your caressing it like a woman,

7. Shamash was god of the sun and of oracles, overseeing matters of justice and right dealing; Enlil was supreme god on earth; Ea, a god of wisdom and magic, is known for his beneficence to the human race.

Means there will come to you a strong one,
A companion who rescues a friend.
He will be mighty in the land, strength will be his,
Like the force of heaven, so mighty will be his strength.
You will fall in love with him and caress him like a woman.
He will be mighty and rescue you, time and again.

He had a second dream,
He arose and went before the goddess, his mother,
Gilgamesh said to her, to his mother:

Mother, I had a second dream.
An axe was thrown down in a street of ramparted Uruk,
They were crowding around it,
The whole of Uruk was standing by it,
The people formed a crowd around it,
A throng was jostling towards it.
I carried it off and laid it down before you,
I fell in love with it, like a woman I caressed it,
Then you were making it my partner.

The mother of Gilgamesh, knowing and wise,
Who understands everything, said to her son,
Ninsun the wild cow, knowing and wise,
Who understands everything, said to Gilgamesh:

My son, the axe you saw is a man.
Your loving it like a woman and caressing it,
And my making it your partner
Means there will come to you a strong one,
A companion who rescues a friend,
He will be mighty in the land, strength will be his,
Like the strength of heaven, so mighty will be his strength.

Gilgamesh said to her, to his mother:

Let this befall according to the command of the great
counselor Enlil,
I want a friend for my own counselor,
For my own counselor do I want a friend!

Even while he was having his dreams,
Shamhat was telling the dreams of Gilgamesh to Enkidu,
Each was drawn by love to the other.

Tablet II

While Enkidu was seated before her,
Each was drawn by love to the other.
Enkidu forgot the steppe where he was born,
For six days, seven nights Enkidu was aroused and flowed
into Shamhat.

The harlot said to him, to Enkidu:

> You are handsome, Enkidu, you are become like a god,
> Why roam the steppe with wild beasts?
> Come, let me lead you to ramparted Uruk,
> To the holy temple, abode of Anu,
> Let me lead you to ramparted Uruk,
> To hallowed Eanna, abode of Ishtar,
> The place of Gilgamesh, who is perfect in strength,
> And so, like a wild bull, he lords it over the people.
> You are just like him,
> You will love him like your own self.
> Come away from this desolation, bereft even of shepherds.

He heard what she said, accepted her words,
He was yearning for one to know his heart, a friend.
The counsel of Shamhat touched his heart.
She took off her clothing, with one piece she dressed him,
The second she herself put on.
Clasping his hand, like a guardian deity she led him,
To the shepherds' huts, where a sheepfold was,
The shepherds crowded around him,
They murmured their opinions among themselves:

> This fellow, how like Gilgamesh in stature,
> In stature tall, proud as a battlement.
> No doubt he was born in the steppe,
> Like the force of heaven, mighty is his strength.

They set bread before him,
They set beer before him.
He looked uncertainly, then stared,
Enkidu did not know to eat bread,
Nor had he ever learned to drink beer!
The harlot made ready to speak, saying to Enkidu:

> Eat the bread, Enkidu, the staff of life,
> Drink the beer, the custom of the land.

Enkidu ate the bread until he was sated,
He drank seven juglets of the beer.
His mood became relaxed, he was singing joyously,
He felt lighthearted and his features glowed.
He treated his hairy body with water,
He anointed himself with oil, turned into a man,
He put on clothing, became like a warrior.
He took his weapon, hunted lions,
The shepherds lay down to rest at night.
He slew wolves, defeated lions,
The herdsmen, the great gods, lay down to sleep.
Enkidu was their watchman, a wakeful man,
He was tall.

He was making love with Shamhat.
He lifted his eyes, he saw a man.
He said to the harlot:

> Shamhat, bring that man here!
> Why has he come?
> I will ask him to account for himself.

The harlot summoned the man,
He came over, Enkidu said to him:

> Fellow, where are you rushing?
> What is this, your burdensome errand?

The man made ready to speak, said to Enkidu:

> They have invited me to a wedding,
> Is it not people's custom to get married?
> I have heaped high on the festival tray
> The fancy dishes for the wedding.
> People's veils are open for the taking.
> For Gilgamesh, king of ramparted Uruk,
> People's veils are open for the taking!
> He mates with the lawful wife,
> He first, the groom after.
> By divine decree pronounced,
> From the cutting of his umbilical cord, she is his due.[8]

At the man's account, his face went pale.

Enkidu was walking in front, with Shamhat behind him.

When he entered the street of ramparted Uruk,
A multitude crowded around him.
He stood there in the street of ramparted Uruk,
With the people crowding around him.
They said about him:

> He is like Gilgamesh in build,
> Though shorter in stature, he is stronger of frame.
> This man, where he was born,
> Ate the springtime grass,
> He must have nursed on the milk of wild beasts.

The whole of Uruk was standing beside him,
The people formed a crowd around him,
A throng was jostling towards him,
Young men were mobbed around him,
Infantile, they groveled before him.

In Uruk at this time sacrifices were underway,
Young men were celebrating.

8. This means that by his birthright Gilgamesh can take brides on their wedding nights, then leave them to their husbands.

The hero stood ready for the upright young man,
For Gilgamesh, as for a god, the partner was ready.
For the goddess of lovemaking, the bed was made,
Gilgamesh was to join with the girl that night.

Enkidu approached him,
They met in the public street.
Enkidu blocked the door to the wedding with his foot,
Not allowing Gilgamesh to enter.
They grappled each other, holding fast like wrestlers,
They shattered the doorpost, the wall shook.
Gilgamesh and Enkidu grappled each other,
Holding fast like wrestlers,
They shattered the doorpost, the wall shook!
They grappled each other at the door to the wedding,
They fought in the street, the public square.
It was Gilgamesh who knelt for the pin, his foot on the ground.
His fury abated, he turned away.
After he turned away,
Enkidu said to him, to Gilgamesh:

> As one unique did your mother bear you,
> The wild cow of the ramparts, Ninsun,
> Exalted you above the most valorous of men!
> Enlil has granted you kingship over the people.

They kissed each other and made friends.

[*Gilgamesh speaks.*]

> Enkidu has neither father nor mother,
> His hair was growing freely
> He was born in the steppe.

Enkidu stood still, listening to what he said,
He shuddered and sat down.
Tears filled his eyes,
He was listless, his strength turned to weakness.
They clasped each other,
They joined hands.

Gilgamesh made ready to speak,
Saying to Enkidu:

> Why are your eyes full of tears,
> Why are you listless, your strength turned to weakness?

Enkidu said to him, to Gilgamesh:

> Cries of sorrow, my friend, have cramped my muscles,
> Woe has entered my heart.

Gilgamesh made ready to speak,
Saying to Enkidu:

There dwells in the forest the fierce monster Humbaba,
You and I shall kill him
And wipe out something evil from the land.

Enkidu made ready to speak,
Saying to Gilgamesh:

My friend, I knew that country
When I roamed with the wild beasts.
The forest is sixty double leagues in every direction,
Who can go into it?
Humbaba's cry is the roar of a deluge,
His maw is fire, his breath is death.
Why do you want to do this?
The haunt of Humbaba is a hopeless quest.

Gilgamesh made ready to speak,
Saying to Enkidu:

I must go up the mountain forest,
I must cut a cedar tree
That cedar must be big enough
To make whirlwinds when it falls.

Enkidu made ready to speak,
Saying to Gilgamesh:

How shall the likes of us go to the forest of cedars, my friend?
In order to safeguard the forest of cedars,
Enlil has appointed him to terrify the people,
Enlil has destined him seven fearsome glories.[9]
That journey is not to be undertaken,
That creature is not to be looked upon.
The guardian of [. . .], the forest of cedars,
Humbaba's cry is the roar of a deluge,
His maw is fire, his breath is death.
He can hear rustling in the forest for sixty double leagues.
Who can go into his forest?
Adad is first and Humbaba is second.
Who, even among the gods, could attack him?
In order to safeguard the forest of cedars,
Enlil has appointed him to terrify the people,
Enlil has destined him seven fearsome glories.
Besides, whosoever enters his forest is struck down by disease.

9. It was believed that divine beings were surrounded by an awe-inspiring radiance. In the older versions of *Gilgamesh*, this radiance was considered removable, like garments or jewelry.

Gilgamesh made ready to speak,
Saying to Enkidu:

> Why, my friend, do you raise such unworthy objections?
> Who, my friend, can go up to heaven?
> The gods dwell forever in the sun,
> People's days are numbered,
> Whatever they attempt is a puff of air.
> Here you are, even you, afraid of death,
> What has become of your bravery's might?
> I will go before you,
> You can call out to me, "Go on, be not afraid!"
> If I fall on the way, I'll establish my name:
> "Gilgamesh, who joined battle with fierce Humbaba" they'll say.

You were born and grew up on the steppe,
When a lion sprang at you, you knew what to do.
Young men fled before you

You speak unworthily,
How you pule! You make me ill.
I must set my hand to cutting a cedar tree,
I must establish eternal fame.
Come, my friend, let's both be off to the foundry,
Let them cast axes such as we'll need.

Off they went to the craftsmen,
The craftsmen, seated around, discussed the matter.
They cast great axes,
Axe blades weighing 180 pounds each they cast.
They cast great daggers,
Their blades were 120 pounds each,
The cross guards of their handles thirty pounds each.
They carried daggers worked with thirty pounds of gold,
Gilgamesh and Enkidu bore ten times sixty pounds each.

Gilgamesh spoke to the elders of ramparted Uruk:

> Hear me, O elders of ramparted Uruk,
> The one of whom they speak
> I, Gilgamesh, would see!
> The one whose name resounds across the whole world,
> I will hunt him down in the forest of cedars.
> I will make the land hear
> How mighty is the scion of Uruk.
> I will set my hand to cutting a cedar,
> An eternal name I will make for myself!

The elders of ramparted Uruk arose,
They responded to Gilgamesh with their advice:

> You are young, Gilgamesh, your feelings carry you away,
> You are ignorant of what you speak, flightiness has taken you,
> You do not know what you are attempting.
> We have heard of Humbaba, his features are grotesque,
> Who is there who could face his weaponry?
> He can hear rustling in the forest for sixty double leagues.
> Who can go into it?
> Humbaba's cry is the roar of a deluge,
> His maw is fire, his breath is death.
> Adad is first and Humbaba is second.
> Who, even among the gods, could attack him?
> In order to safeguard the forest of cedars,
> Enlil has appointed him to terrify the people,
> Enlil has destined him seven fearsome glories.
> Besides, whosoever enters his forest is struck down by disease.

When Gilgamesh heard the speech of his counselors,
He looked at his friend and laughed:

> Now then, my friend, do you say the same?:
> "I am afraid to die"?

Tablet III

The elders spoke to him, saying to Gilgamesh:

> Come back safely to Uruk's haven,
> Trust not, Gilgamesh, in your strength alone,
> Let your eyes see all, make your blow strike home.
> He who goes in front saves his companion,
> He who knows the path protects his friend.
> Let Enkidu walk before you,
> He knows the way to the forest of cedars,
> He has seen battle, been exposed to combat.
> Enkidu will protect his friend, safeguard his companion,
> Let him return, to be a grave husband.[1]
> We in our assembly entrust the king to you,
> On your return, entrust the king again to us.

Gilgamesh made ready to speak,
Saying to Enkidu:

> Come, my friend, let us go to the sublime temple,
> To go before Ninsun, the great queen.
> Ninsun the wise, who is versed in all knowledge,
> Will send us on our way with good advice.

1. "Grave husband" plays on the words for "bride" and "interment" (grave); the phrase seems to portend Enkidu's death.

Clasping each other, hand in hand,
Gilgamesh and Enkidu went to the sublime temple,
To go before Ninsun, the great queen.
Gilgamesh came forward and entered before her:

O Ninsun, I have taken on a noble quest,
I travel a distant road, to where Humbaba is,
To face a battle unknown,
To mount a campaign unknown.
Give me your blessing, that I may go on my journey,
That I may indeed see your face safely again,
That I may indeed reenter joyfully the gate of ramparted Uruk,
That I may indeed return to hold the festival for the new year,
That I may indeed celebrate the festival for the new year twice over.
May that festival be held in my presence, the fanfare sound!
May their drums resound before you!

Ninsun the wild cow heard them out with sadness,
The speeches of Gilgamesh, her son, and Enkidu.
Ninsun entered the bathhouse seven times,
She bathed herself in water with tamarisk and soapwort.[2]
She put on a garment as beseemed her body,
She put on an ornament as beseemed her breast,
She set [. . .] and donned her tiara.
She climbed the stairs, mounted to the roof terrace,
She set up an incense offering to Shamash.
She made the offering, to Shamash she raised her hands in prayer:

Why did you endow my son Gilgamesh with a restless heart?
Now you have moved him to travel
A distant road, to where Humbaba is,
To face a battle unknown,
To mount an expedition unknown.
Until he goes and returns,
Until he reaches the forest of cedars,
Until he has slain fierce Humbaba,
And wipes out from the land the evil thing you hate,
In the day, when you traverse the sky,
May Aya, your bride, not fear to remind you,
"Entrust him to the watchmen of the night."

While Gilgamesh journeys to the forest of cedars,
May the days be long, may the nights be short,
May his loins be girded, his arms strong!
At night, let him make a camp for sleeping,
Let him make a shelter to fall asleep in.
May Aya,[3] your bride, not fear to remind you,

2. A medicinal plant used in cleansing and magic.
3. Goddess of dawn and wife of Shamash, the sun god, often called upon in prayers to intercede with her husband.

When Gilgamesh, Enkidu, and Humbaba meet,
Raise up for his sake, O Shamash, great winds against Humbaba,
South wind, north wind, east wind, west wind, moaning wind,
Blasting wind, lashing wind, contrary wind, dust storm,
Demon wind, freezing wind, storm wind, whirlwind:
Raise up thirteen winds to blot out Humbaba's face,
So he cannot charge forward, cannot retreat,
Then let Gilgamesh's weapons defeat Humbaba.
As soon as your own [radiance] flares forth,
At that very moment heed the man who reveres you.
May your swift mules [. . .] you,
A comfortable seat, a bed is laid for you,
May the gods, your brethren, serve you your favorite foods,
May Aya, the great bride, dab your face with the fringe of her
spotless garment.

Ninsun the wild cow made a second plea to Shamash:

O Shamash, will not Gilgamesh [. . .] the gods for you?
Will he not share heaven with you?
Will he not share tiara and scepter with the moon?
Will he not act in wisdom with Ea in the depths?
Will he not rule the human race with Irnina?[4]
Will he not dwell with Ningishzida[5] in the Land of No Return?

[*Ninsun apparently inducts Enkidu into the staff of her temple.*]

After Ninsun the wild cow had made her plea,
Ninsun the wild cow, knowing and wise, who understands everything,
She extinguished the incense, [she came down from the roof terrace],
She summoned Enkidu to impart her message:

Mighty Enkidu, though you are no issue of my womb,
Your little ones shall be among the devotees of Gilgamesh,
The priestesses, votaries, cult women of the temple.

She placed a token around Enkidu's neck:

As the priestesses take in a foundling,
And the daughters of the gods bring up an adopted child,
I herewith take Enkidu, as my adopted son,
may Gilgamesh treat him well.

His dignitaries stood by, wishing him well,
In a crowd, the young men of Uruk ran along behind him,

4. Another name for Ishtar and a local form of the goddess.

5. Literally "Lord of the Upright Tree," a netherworld deity.

While his dignitaries made obeisance to him:

Come back safely to Uruk's haven!
Trust not, Gilgamesh, in your strength alone,
Let your eyes see all, make your blow strike home.
He who goes in front saves his companion,
He who knows the path protects his friend.
Let Enkidu walk before you,
He knows the way to the forest of cedars.
He has seen battle, been exposed to combat.
Enkidu will protect his friend, safeguard his companion,
Let him return, to be a grave husband.
We in our assembly entrust the king to you,
On your return, entrust the king again to us.

The elders hailed him,
Counseled Gilgamesh for the journey:

Trust not, Gilgamesh, in your own strength,
Let your vision be clear, take care of yourself.
Let Enkidu go ahead of you,
He has seen the road, has traveled the way.
He knows the ways into the forest
And all the tricks of Humbaba.
He who goes first safeguards his companion,
His vision is clear, he protects himself.
May Shamash help you to your goal,
May he disclose to you what your words propose,
May he open for you the barred road,
Make straight the pathway to your tread,
Make straight the upland to your feet.
May nightfall bring you good tidings,
May Lugalbanda stand by you in your cause.
In a trice accomplish what you desire,
Wash your feet in the river of Humbaba whom you seek.
When you stop for the night, dig a well,
May there always be pure water in your waterskin.[6]
You should libate cool water to Shamash
And be mindful of Lugalbanda.

Tablet IV

At twenty double leagues they took a bite to eat,
At thirty double leagues they made their camp,
Fifty double leagues they went in a single day,
A journey of a month and a half in three days.
They approached Mount Lebanon.
Towards sunset they dug a well,
Filled their waterskin with water.

6. Travelers carried drinking water in leather bags.

Gilgamesh went up onto the mountain,
He poured out flour for an offering, saying.

O mountain, bring me a propitious dream!

Enkidu made Gilgamesh a shelter for receiving dreams,
A gust was blowing, he fastened the door.
He had him lie down in a circle of flour,
And spreading out like a net, Enkidu lay down in the doorway.
Gilgamesh sat there, chin on his knee.
Sleep, which usually steals over people, fell upon him.
In the middle of the night he awoke,
Got up and said to his friend:

My friend, did you not call me? Why am I awake?
Did you not touch me? Why am I disturbed?
Did a god not pass by? Why does my flesh tingle?
My friend, I had a dream,
And the dream I had was very disturbing.

The one born in the steppe,
Enkidu explained the dream to his friend:

My friend, your dream is favorable,
The dream is very precious as an omen.
My friend, the mountain you saw is Humbaba,
We will catch Humbaba and kill him,
Then we will throw down his corpse on the field of battle.
Further, at dawn the word of Shamash will be in our favor.

At twenty double leagues they took a bite to eat,
At thirty double leagues they made their camp,
Fifty double leagues they went in a single day,
A journey of a month and a half in three days.
They approached Mount Lebanon.
Towards sunset they dug a well,
They filled their waterskin with water.
Gilgamesh went up onto the mountain,
He poured out flour for an offering, saying:

O mountain, bring me a propitious dream!

Enkidu made Gilgamesh a shelter for receiving dreams,
A gust was blowing, he fastened the door.
He had him lie down in a circle of flour,
And spreading out like a net, Enkidu lay down in the doorway.
Gilgamesh sat there, chin on his knee.
Sleep, which usually steals over people, fell upon him.
In the middle of the night he awoke,

Got up and said to his friend:

> My friend, did you not call me? Why am I awake?
> Did you not touch me? Why am I disturbed?
> Did a god not pass by? Why does my flesh tingle?
> My friend, I had a second dream,
> And the dream I had was very disturbing.
> A mountain was in my dream, an enemy.
> It threw me down, pinning my feet,
> A fearsome glare grew ever more intense.
> A certain young man, handsomest in the world, truly handsome he was,
> He pulled me out from the base of the mountain,
> He gave me water to drink and eased my fear,
> He set my feet on the ground again.

The one born in the steppe,
Enkidu explained the dream to his friend:

> My friend, your dream is favorable,
> The dream is very precious as an omen.
> My friend, we will go [. . .]
> The strange thing was Humbaba,
> Was not the mountain, the strange thing, Humbaba?
> Come then, banish your fear.

At twenty double leagues they took a bite to eat,
At thirty double leagues they made their camp,
Fifty double leagues they went in a single day,
A journey of a month and a half in three days.
They approached Mount Lebanon.
Towards sunset they dug a well,
They filled their waterskin with water.
Gilgamesh went up onto the mountain,
He poured out flour as an offering, saying:

> O mountain, bring me a propitious dream!

Enkidu made Gilgamesh a shelter for receiving dreams,
A gust was blowing, he fastened the door.
He had him lie down in a circle of flour,
And spreading out like a net, Enkidu lay down in the doorway.
Gilgamesh sat there, chin on his knee.
Sleep, which usually steals over people, fell upon him.
In the middle of the night he awoke,
Got up and said to his friend:

> My friend, did you not call me? Why am I awake?
> Did you not touch me? Why am I disturbed?
> Did a god not pass by? Why does my flesh tingle?
> My friend, I had a third dream,
> And the dream I had was very disturbing.

The heavens cried out, the earth was thundering,
Daylight faded, darkness fell,
Lightning flashed, fire shot up,
The flames burgeoned, spewing death.
Then the glow was dimmed, the fire was extinguished,
The burning coals that were falling turned to ashes.
You who were born in the steppe, let us discuss it.

Enkidu [explained], helped him accept his dream,
Saying to Gilgamesh:

[*Enkidu's explanation is mostly lost, but perhaps it was that the volcanolike explosion was Humbaba, who flared up, then died.*]

Humbaba, like a god [. . .]
[. . .] the light flaring [. . .]
We will be victorious over him.
Humbaba aroused our fury
we will prevail over him.
Further, at dawn the word of Shamash will be in our favor.

At twenty double leagues they took a bite to eat,
A thirty double leagues they made their camp.
Fifty double leagues they went in a single day,
A journey of a month and a half in three days.
They approached Mount Lebanon.[7]
Towards sunset they dug a well,
They filled their waterskin with water.
Gilgamesh went up onto the mountain,
He poured out flour as an offering, saying:

O mountain, bring me a propitious dream!

Enkidu made Gilgamesh a shelter for receiving dreams,
A gust was blowing, he fastened the door.
He had him lie down in a circle of flour,
And spreading out like a net, Enkidu lay down in the doorway.
Gilgamesh sat there, chin on his knee.
Sleep, which usually steals over people, fell upon him.
In the middle of the night he awoke,

My friend, did you not call me? Why am I awake?
Did you not touch me? Why am I disturbed?
Did a god not pass by? Why does my flesh tingle?
My friend, I had a [fourth] dream,
The dream I had was very disturbing.
My friend, I saw a fourth dream,
More terrible than the other three.

7. Mountain ranges along the Mediterranean coast of present-day Lebanon.

I saw the lion-headed monster-bird Anzu[8] in the sky.
He began to descend upon us, like a cloud.
He was terrifying, his appearance was horrible!
His maw was fire, his breath death.

[*Enkidu explains the fourth dream.*]

The lion-headed monster-bird Anzu who descended upon us, like a cloud,
Who was terrifying, whose appearance was horrible,
Whose maw was fire, whose breath was death,
Whose dreadful aura frightens you.
The young man you saw was mighty Shamash

[*It is not clear how many dreams there were in all though one version refers to five. A poorly preserved manuscript of an old version includes the following dream that could be inserted here, as portions of it are fulfilled in Tablet VI.*]

I was grasping a wild bull of the steppe!
As it bellowed, it split the earth,
It raised clouds of dust, blotting out the sky.
I crouched down before it,
It seized my hands, pinioned my arms.
Someone pulled me out
He stroked my cheeks, he gave me to drink from his waterskin.

[*Enkidu explains the dream.*]

It is the god, my friend, to whom we go,
The wild bull was no enemy at all,
The wild bull you saw is Shamash, the protector,
He will take our hands in need.
The one who gave you water to drink from his waterskin
Is your god who proclaims your glory, Lugalbanda.
We should rely on one another,
We will accomplish together a deed unheard of in the land.

[*Something has happened to discourage Gilgamesh, perhaps an unfavorable oracle. Shamash comes to their aid with timely advice, just before they hear Humbaba's cry.*]

[Before Shamash his tears flowed down]:

Remember, stand by me, hear [my prayer],
Gilgamesh, scion of [ramparted Uruk]!

8. Monstrous bird with the head of a lion. He appears in a mythological story, where he steals power from the god Enlil but is defeated in battle by Enlil's son Ninurta.

Shamash heard what he said,
From afar a warning voice called to him from the sky:

Hurry, confront him, do not let him go off into the forest,
Do not let him enter the thicket!
He has not donned all of his seven fearsome glories,
One he has on, six he has left off!

They charged forward like wild bulls.
He let out a single bloodcurdling cry,
The guardian of the forest shrieked aloud,
Humbaba was roaring like thunder.

Gilgamesh made ready to speak,
Said to Enkidu:

Humbaba [. . .]
We cannot confront him separately.

Gilgamesh spoke to him, said to Enkidu:

My friend, why do we raise such unworthy objections?
Have we not crossed all the mountains?
The end of the quest is before us.
My friend knows battle,
You rubbed on herbs, you did not fear death,
Your battle cry should be dinning like a drum!
Let the paralysis leave your arm, let weakness quit your knees,
Take my hand, my friend, let us walk on together!
Your heart should be urging you to battle.
Forget about death,
He who marches first, protects himself,
Let him keep his comrade safe!
Those two will have established fame down through the ages.

The pair reached the edge of the forest,
They stopped their talk and stood there.

Tablet V

They stood at the edge of the forest,
They gazed at the height of the cedars,
They gazed at the way into the forest.
Where Humbaba would walk, a path was made,
Straight were the ways and easy the going.
They saw the cedar mountain, dwelling of the gods, sacred to the goddess Irnina.
On the slopes of that mountain, the cedar bears its abundance,
Agreeable is its shade, full of pleasures.
The undergrowth is tangled, the [thicket] interwoven.

[*In older versions, they begin to cut trees and Humbaba hears the noise. In the standard version, they meet Humbaba first.*]

Humbaba made ready to speak, saying to Gilgamesh:

> How well-advised they are, the fool Gilgamesh and the yokelman!
> Why have you come here to me?
> Come now, Enkidu, small-fry, who does not know his father,
> Spawn of a turtle or tortoise, who sucked no mother's milk!
> I used to see you when you were younger but would not go near you.
> Had I killed the likes of you, would I have filled my belly?
> you have brought Gilgamesh before me,
> you stand there, a barbarian foe!
> I should cut off your head, Gilgamesh, throat and neck,
> I should let cawing buzzard, screaming eagle, and vulture feed
> on your flesh.

Gilgamesh made ready to speak, saying to Enkidu:

> My friend, Humbaba's features have grown more grotesque,
> We strode up like heroes to vanquish him.

Enkidu made ready to speak, saying to Gilgamesh:

> Why, my friend, do you raise such unworthy objections?
> How you pule! You make me ill.
> Now, my friend, this has dragged on long enough.
> The time has come to pour the copper into the mold.
> Will you take another hour to blow the bellows,
> An hour more to let it cool?
> To launch the flood weapon, to wield the lash,
> Retreat not a foot, you must not turn back,
> Let your eyes see all, let your blow strike home!

[*In the combat with Humbaba, the rift valley of Lebanon is formed by their circling feet.*]

He struck the ground to confront him.
At their heels the earth split apart,
As they circled, the ranges of Lebanon were sundered!
The white clouds turned black,
Death rained down like fog upon them.
Shamash raised the great winds against Humbaba,
South wind, north wind, east wind, west wind, moaning wind,
Blasting wind, lashing wind, contrary wind, dust storm,
Demon wind, freezing wind, storm wind, whirlwind:
The thirteen winds blotted out Humbaba's face,
He could not charge forward, he could not retreat.
Then Gilgamesh's weapons defeated Humbaba.

Humbaba begged for life, saying to Gilgamesh:

You were once a child, Gilgamesh, you had a mother who bore you,
You are the offspring of Ninsun the wild cow.
You grew up to fulfill the oracle of Shamash, lord of the mountain:
"Gilgamesh, scion of Uruk, is to be king."

O Gilgamesh, spare my life!
Let me dwell here for you [as your . . .],
Say however many trees you [require . . .],
For you I will guard the myrtle wood [. . .].

Enkidu made ready to speak, saying to Gilgamesh:

My friend! Do not listen to what Humbaba says,
Do not heed his entreaties!

[*Humbaba is speaking to Enkidu.*]

You know the lore of my forest,
And you understand all I have to say.
I might have lifted you up, dangled you from a twig at the entrance to my forest,
I might have let cawing buzzard, screaming eagle, and vulture feed on your flesh.
Now then, Enkidu, mercy is up to you,
Tell Gilgamesh to spare my life!

Enkidu made ready to speak, saying to Gilgamesh:

My friend! Humbaba is guardian of the forest of cedars,
Finish him off for the kill, put him out of existence.
Humbaba is guardian of the forest of cedars,
Finish him off for the kill, put him out of existence,
Before Enlil the foremost one hears of this!
The great gods will become angry with us,
Enlil in Nippur, Shamash in Larsa.[9]
Establish your reputation for all time:
"Gilgamesh, who slew Humbaba."

May the pair of them never reach old age!
May Gilgamesh and Enkidu come across no graver friend to bank on![1]

9. Nippur and Larsa are cities in Babylonia with important temples to Enlil and Shamash, respectively.

1. This is one of the elaborate, sometimes obscure wordplays in *Gilgamesh*. In Humbaba's curse, *cross* sounds like *friend* and *bank* echoes *grave,* so that the giant's words can mean either "May they not cross water safely to the opposite bank" or "May they not find a friend to rely on."

[*An old version contains the following exchange between Gilgamesh and Enkidu concerning the seven fearsome glories of Humbaba.*]

Gilgamesh said to Enkidu:

> Now, my friend, let us go on to victory!
> The glories will be lost in the confusion,
> The glories will be lost and the brightness will [. . .].

Enkidu said to him, to Gilgamesh:

> My friend, catch the bird and where will its chicks go?
> Let us search out the glories later,
> They will run around in the grass like chicks.
> Strike him again, then kill his retinue.

[*Gilgamesh kills Humbaba. In some versions he has to strike multiple blows before the monster falls.*]

Gilgamesh heeded his friend's command,
He raised the axe at his side,
He drew the sword at his belt.
Gilgamesh struck him on the neck,
Enkidu, his friend, [. . .].
They pulled out [. . .] as far as the lungs,
He tore out the [. . .],
He forced the head into a cauldron.
[. . .] in abundance fell on the mountain,
He struck him, Humbaba the guardian, down to the ground.
His blood [. . .]
For two leagues the cedars [. . .].
He killed the glories with him.
He slew the monster, guardian of the forest,
At whose cry the mountains of Lebanon trembled,
At whose cry all the mountains quaked.
He slew the monster, guardian of the forest,
He trampled on the broken [. . .],
He struck down the seven glories.
The battle net [. . .], the sword weighing eight times sixty pounds,
He took the weight of ten times sixty pounds upon him,
He forced his way into the forest,
He opened the secret dwelling of the supreme gods.
Gilgamesh cut down the trees,
Enkidu chose the timbers.
Enkidu made ready to speak, said to Gilgamesh:

> You killed the guardian by your strength,
> Who else could cut through this forest of trees?
> My friend, we have felled the lofty cedar,
> Whose crown once pierced the sky.
> I will make a door six times twelve cubits high, two times twelve cubits wide,

One cubit shall be its thickness,
Its hinge pole, ferrule, and pivot box shall be unique.[2]
Let no stranger approach it, may only a god go through.
Let the Euphrates bring it to Nippur,
Nippur, the sanctuary of Enlil.
May Enlil be delighted with you,
May Enlil rejoice over it!

They lashed together a raft
Enkidu embarked
And Gilgamesh [. . .] the head of Humbaba.

Tablet VI

He washed his matted locks, cleaned his head strap,
He shook his hair down over his shoulders.
He threw off his filthy clothes, he put on clean ones,
Wrapping himself in a cloak, he tied on his sash,
Gilgamesh put on his kingly diadem.
The princess Ishtar coveted Gilgamesh's beauty:

Come, Gilgamesh, you shall be my bridegroom!
Give, oh give me of your lusciousness!
You shall be my husband and I shall be your wife.
I will ready for you a chariot of lapis and gold,
With golden wheels and fittings of gemstones,
You shall harness storm demons as if they were giant mules.
Enter our house amidst fragrance of cedar,
When you enter our house,
The splendid exotic doorsill shall do you homage,
Kings, nobles, and princes shall kneel before you,
They shall bring you gifts of mountain and lowland as tribute.
Your goats shall bear triplets, your ewes twins,
Your pack-laden donkey shall overtake the mule,
Your horses shall run proud before the wagon,
Your ox in the yoke shall have none to compare!

Gilgamesh made ready to speak,
Saying to the princess Ishtar:
What shall I give you if I take you to wife?
Shall I give you a headdress for your person, or clothing?
Shall I give you bread or drink?
Shall I give you food, worthy of divinity?
Shall I give you drink, worthy of queenship?
What would I get if I marry you?
You are a brazier that goes out when it freezes,
A flimsy door that keeps out neither wind nor draught,

2. Mesopotamian doors did not use hinges but were made of a panel attached to a post. It was this post, or "hinge pole," that rotated when the door was opened or closed, sometimes on a piece of metal, or "ferrule," at the bottom. The top of the post was cased or enclosed so the hinge pole would not slip off its pivot point.

A palace that crushes a warrior,
A mouse that gnaws through its housing,
Tar that smears its bearer,
Waterskin that soaks its bearer,
Weak stone that undermines a wall,
Battering ram that destroys the wall for an enemy,
Shoe that pinches its wearer!
Which of your lovers lasted forever?
Which of your heroes went up to heaven?
Come, I call you to account for your lovers:
He who had jugs of cream on his shoulders and [. . .] on his arm,
For Dumuzi,[3] your girlhood lover,
You ordained year after year of weeping.
You fell in love with the brightly colored roller bird,
Then you struck him and broke his wing.
In the woods he sits crying "My-wing!"
You fell in love with the lion, perfect in strength,
Then you dug for him ambush pits, seven times seven.
You fell in love with the wild stallion, eager for the fray,
Whip, goad, and lash you ordained for him,
Seven double leagues of galloping you ordained for him,
You ordained that he muddy his water when he drinks,
You ordained perpetual weeping for his mother, divine Silili.
You fell in love with the shepherd, keeper of herds,
Who always set out cakes baked in embers for you,
Slaughtered kids for you every day.
You struck him and turned him into a wolf,
His own shepherd boys harry him off,
And his own hounds snap at his heels!
You fell in love with Ishullanu,[4] your father's gardener,
Who always brought you baskets of dates,
Who daily made your table splendid.
You wanted him, so you sidled up to him:
"My Ishullanu, let's have a taste of your vigor!
Bring out your member, touch our sweet spot!"
Ishullanu said to you,
"Me? What do you want of me?
Hath my mother not baked? Have I not eaten?
Shall what I taste for food be insults and curses?
In the cold, is my cover to be the touch of a reed?"
When you heard what he said,
You struck him and turned him into a scarecrow,
You left him stuck in his own garden patch,
His well sweep goes up no longer, his bucket does not descend.
As for me, now that you've fallen in love with me, you will treat me
like them!

3. Shepherd god. He was a youthful lover of Ishtar, who let him be taken to the netherworld when she had to provide a substitute for herself.

4. According to a Sumerian myth, Ishtar seduced a gardener named Ishullanu whom she then sought to kill.

When Ishtar heard this,
Ishtar was furious and went up to heaven,
Ishtar went sobbing before Anu, her father,
Before Antum, her mother, her tears flowed down:

Father, Gilgamesh has said outrageous things about me,
Gilgamesh's been spouting insults about me,
Insults and curses against me!

Anu made ready to speak,
Saying to the princess Ishtar:

Well now, did you not provoke the king, Gilgamesh,
And so Gilgamesh spouted insults about you,
Insults and curses against you?

Ishtar made ready to speak,
Saying to Anu, her father:

Well then, Father, pretty please, the Bull of Heaven,
So I can kill Gilgamesh on his home ground.
If you don't give me the Bull of Heaven,
I'll strike [. . .] to its foundation,
I'll raise up the dead to devour the living,
The dead shall outnumber the living!

Anu made ready to speak,
Saying to the princess Ishtar:

If you insist on the Bull of Heaven from me,
Let the widow of Uruk gather seven years of chaff,
Let the farmer of Uruk raise seven years of hay.

Ishtar made ready to speak,
Saying to Anu, her father:

The widow of Uruk has gathered seven years of chaff,
The farmer of Uruk has raised seven years of hay.
With the Bull of Heaven's fury I will kill him!

When Anu heard what Ishtar said,
He placed the lead rope of the Bull of Heaven in her hand,
Ishtar led the Bull of Heaven away.

When it reached Uruk,
It dried up the groves, reedbeds, and marshes,
It went down to the river, it lowered the river by seven cubits.
At the bull's snort, a pit opened up,
One hundred young men of Uruk fell into it.
At its second snort, a pit opened up,
Two hundred young men of Uruk fell into it.

At its third snort, a pit opened up,
Enkidu fell into it, up to his middle.
Enkidu jumped out and seized the bull by its horns,
The bull spewed its foam in his face,
Swished dung at him with the tuft of its tail.
Enkidu made ready to speak,
Saying to Gilgamesh:

> I have seen, my friend, the strength of the Bull of Heaven,
> So knowing its strength, I know how to deal with it.
> I will get around the strength of the Bull of Heaven,
> I will circle behind the Bull of Heaven,
> I will grab it by the tuft of its tail,
> I will set my feet on its [. . .],
> Then you, like a strong, skillful slaughterer,
> Thrust your dagger between neck, horn, and tendon!

Enkidu circled behind the Bull of Heaven,
He grabbed it by the tuft of its tail,
He set his feet on its [. . .],
And Gilgamesh, like a strong, skillful slaughterer,
Thrust his dagger between neck, horn, and tendon!

After they had killed the Bull of Heaven,
They ripped out its heart and set it before Shamash.
They stepped back and prostrated themselves before Shamash,
Then the two comrades sat down beside each other.
Ishtar went up on the wall of ramparted Uruk,
She writhed in grief, she let out a wail:

> That bully Gilgamesh who demeaned me, he's killed the Bull of Heaven!

When Enkidu heard what Ishtar said,
He tore off the bull's haunch and flung it at her:

> If I could vanquish you, I'd turn you to this,
> I'd drape the guts beside you!

Ishtar convened the cult women, prostitutes, harlots,
She set up a lament over the haunch of the bull.

Gilgamesh summoned all the expert craftsmen,
The craftsmen marveled at the massiveness of its horns,
They were molded from thirty pounds each of lapis blue,
Their outer shell was two thumbs thick!
Six times three hundred quarts of oil, the capacity of both,
He donated to anoint the statue of his god, Lugalbanda.
He brought them inside and hung them up in his master bedroom.

They washed their hands in the Euphrates,
Clasping each other, they came away,

Paraded through the streets of Uruk.
The people of Uruk crowded to look upon them.
Gilgamesh made a speech
To the servant-women of his palace:

> Who is the handsomest of young men?
> Who is the most glorious of males?
> Gilgamesh is the handsomest of young men!
> Gilgamesh is the most glorious of males!
> She at whom we flung the haunch in our passion,
> Ishtar, she has no one in the street to satisfy her,

Gilgamesh held a celebration in his palace.
The young men slept stretched out on the couch of night.
While Enkidu slept, he had a dream.

Tablet VII

My friend, why were the great gods in council?

Enkidu raised,
spoke to the door as if it were human:[5]

> O bosky door, insensate,
> Which lends an ear that is not there,
> I sought your wood for twenty double leagues,
> Till I beheld a lofty cedar
> No rival had your tree in the forest.
> Six times twelve cubits was your height, two times twelve cubits was your width,
> One cubit was your thickness,
> Your hinge pole, ferrule, and pivot box were unique.
> I made you, I brought you to Nippur, I set you up.
> Had I known, O door, how you would requite me,
> And that this your goodness towards me [. . .],
> I would have raised my axe, I would have chopped you down,
> I would have floated you as a raft to the temple of Shamash,
> I would have set up the lion-headed monster-bird Anzu at its gate,
> Because Shamash heard my plea
> He gave me the weapon to kill Humbaba.
> Now then, O door, it was I who made you, it was I who set you up.
> I will tear you out!
> May a king who shall arise after me despise you,
> May he alter my inscription and put on his own![6]

5. Because there is a gap in the text, it is unclear why Enkidu curses the door so violently. Since it is made of cedar wood from the forest, it might embody the adventure that results in Enkidu's death.

6. These concluding words of Enkidu's curse of the cedar door parody traditional Mesopotamian inscriptions affixed to monuments, which called the wrath of the gods upon anyone who damaged, removed, or usurped the monument.

He tore out his hair, threw away his clothing.

When he heard out this speech, swiftly, quickly his tears flowed down,
When Gilgamesh heard out Enkidu's speech, swiftly, quickly, his tears
flowed down.

Gilgamesh made ready to speak, saying to Enkidu:

My friend, you are rational but you say strange things,
Why, my friend, does your heart speak strange things?
The dream is a most precious omen, though very frightening,
Your lips are buzzing like flies.
Though frightening, the dream is a precious omen.
The gods left mourning for the living,
The dream left mourning for the living,
The dream left woe for the living!
Now I shall go pray to the great gods,
I will be assiduous to my own god, I will pray to yours,
To Anu, father of the gods,
To Enlil, counselor of the gods,
I will make your image of gold beyond measure.
You can pay no silver, no gold can you [. . .],
What Enlil commanded is not like the [. . .] of the gods,
What he commanded, he will not retract.
The verdict he has scrivened, he will not reverse nor erase.
People often die before their time.

At the first glimmer of dawn,
Enkidu lifted his head, weeping before Shamash,
Before the sun's fiery glare, his tears flowed down:

I have turned to you, O Shamash, on account of the precious days
of my life,
As for that hunter, the entrapping-man,
Who did not let me get as much life as my friend,
May that hunter not get enough to make him a living.
Make his profit loss, cut down his take,
May his income, his portion evaporate before you,
Any wildlife that enters his traps, make it go out the window!

When he had cursed the hunter to his heart's content,
He resolved to curse the harlot Shamhat:

Come, Shamhat, I will ordain you a destiny,
A destiny that will never end, forever and ever!
I will lay on you the greatest of all curses,
Swiftly, inexorably, may my curse come upon you.
May you never make a home that you can enjoy,
May you never caress a child of your own,
May you never be received among decent women.
May beer sludge impregnate your lap,
May the drunkard bespatter your best clothes with vomit.

May your swain prefer beauties,
May he pinch you like potter's clay.
May you get no alabaster,
May no table to be proud of be set in your house.
May the nook you enjoy be a doorstep,
May the public crossroads be your dwelling,
May vacant lots be your sleeping place,
May the shade of a wall be your place of business.
May brambles and thorns flay your feet,
May toper and sober slap your cheek.[7]
May riffraff of the street shove each other in your brothel,
May there be a brawl there.
When you stroll with your cronies, may they catcall after you.
May the builder not keep your roof in repair,
May the screech owl roost in the ruins of your home.
May a feast never be held where you live.

May your purple finery be expropriated,
May filthy underwear be what you are given,
Because you diminished me, an innocent,
Yes me, an innocent, you wronged me in my steppe.

When Shamash heard what he said,
From afar a warning voice called to him from the sky:

O Enkidu, why curse Shamhat the harlot,
Who fed you bread, fit for a god,
Who poured you beer, fit for a king,
Who dressed you in a noble garment,
And gave you handsome Gilgamesh for a comrade?
Now then, Gilgamesh is your friend and blood brother!
Won't he lay you down in the ultimate resting place?
In a perfect resting place he will surely lay you down!
He will settle you in peaceful rest in that dwelling sinister,
Rulers of the netherworld will do you homage.
He will have the people of Uruk shed bitter tears for you,
He will make the pleasure-loving people burdened down for you,
And, as for him, after your death, he will let his hair grow matted,
He will put on a lion skin and roam the steppe.

When Enkidu heard the speech of the valiant Shamash,
His raging heart was calmed,
his fury was calmed:

Come, Shamhat, I will ordain you a destiny,
My mouth that cursed you, let it bless you instead.
May governors and dignitaries fall in love with you,
May the man one double league away slap his thighs in excitement,
May the man two double leagues away let down his hair.

7. That is, may anyone hit her, drunk or not.

May the subordinate not hold back from you, but open his trousers,
May he give you obsidian, lapis, and gold,
May ear bangles be your gift.
To the man whose wealth is secure, whose granaries are full,
May Ishtar of the gods introduce you,
For your sake may the wife and mother of seven be abandoned.

Enkidu was sick at heart,
He lay there lonely.
He told his friend what weighed on his mind:

My friend, what a dream I had last night!
Heaven cried out, earth made reply,
I was standing between them.
There was a certain man, his face was somber,
His face was like that of the lion-headed monster-bird Anzu,
His hands were the paws of a lion,
His fingernails were the talons of an eagle.
He seized me by the hair, he was too strong for me,
I hit him but he sprang back like a swing rope,
He hit me and capsized me like a raft.
Like a wild bull he trampled me,
"Save me, my friend!"—but you did not save me!
He trussed my limbs like a bird's.
Holding me fast, he took me down to the house of shadows,
  the dwelling of hell,
To the house whence none who enters comes forth,
On the road from which there is no way back,
To the house whose dwellers are deprived of light,
Where dust is their fare and their food is clay.
They are dressed like birds in feather garments,
Yea, they shall see no daylight, for they abide in darkness.
Dust lies thick on the door and bolt,
When I entered that house of dust,
I saw crowns in a heap,
There dwelt the kings, the crowned heads who once ruled the land,
Who always set out roast meat for Anu and Enlil,
Who always set out baked offerings, libated cool water from
  waterskins.
In that house of dust I entered,
Dwelt high priests and acolytes,
Dwelt reciters of spells and ecstatics,[8]
Dwelt the anointers of the great gods,
Dwelt old King Etana[9] and the god of the beasts,
Dwelt the queen of the netherworld, Ereshkigal.[1]

8. Reciters of spells were learned scholars, while prophets, or "ecstatics," were people who spoke in a trance without having studied their words. Ecstatics were sometimes social outcasts or people without education.

9. Ancient king who was said to have flown up to heaven on an eagle to find a plant that would help him and his wife have a child.

1. Queen of the netherworld and jealous sister of the goddess Ishtar.

Belet-seri,[2] scribe of the netherworld, was kneeling before her,
She was holding a tablet and reading to her,
She lifted her head, she looked at me:
"Who brought this man?"
I who went with you through all hardships,
Remember me, my friend, do not forget what I have undergone!
My friend had a dream needing no interpretation.

The day he had the dream, his strength ran out.
Enkidu lay there one day, a second day he was ill,
Enkidu lay in his bed, his illness grew worse.
A third day, a fourth day, Enkidu's illness grew worse.
A fifth, a sixth, a seventh,
An eighth, a ninth, a tenth day,
Enkidu's illness grew worse.
An eleventh, a twelfth day,
Enkidu lay in his bed.
He called for Gilgamesh, roused him with his cry:

My friend laid on me the greatest curse of all!
I feared the battle but will die in my bed,
My friend, he who falls quickly in battle is glorious.

[*Enkidu dies.*]

Tablet VIII

At the first glimmer of dawn,
Gilgamesh lamented his friend:

Enkidu, my friend, your mother the gazelle,
Your father the wild ass brought you into the world,
Onagers raised you on their milk,
And the wild beasts taught you all the grazing places.
The pathways, O Enkidu, to the forest of cedars,
May they weep for you, without falling silent, night and day.
May the elders of the teeming city, ramparted Uruk, weep for you,
May the crowd who blessed our departure weep for you.
May the heights of highland and mountain weep for you,
May the lowlands wail like your mother.
May the forest of balsam and cedar weep for you,
Which we slashed in our fury.
May bear, hyena, panther, leopard, deer, jackal,
Lion, wild bull, gazelle, ibex, the beasts and creatures of the steppe, weep for you.[3]
May the sacred Ulaya River[4] weep for you, along whose banks we once strode erect,
May the holy Euphrates weep for you,
Whose waters we libated from waterskins.

2. Literally "Lady of the Steppe," scribe and bookkeeper in the netherworld.
3. This refers to an episode that does not appear in the extant portions of the epic.
4. Karun River in the southwest of modern Iran.

May the young men of ramparted Uruk weep for you,
Who watched us slay the Bull of Heaven in combat.
May the plowman weep for you at his plow,
Who extolled your name in the sweet song of harvest home.
May they weep for you, of the teeming city of Uruk,
Who exalted your name at the first [. . .].
May the shepherd and herdsman weep for you,
Who held the milk and buttermilk to your mouth,
May the nurse weep for you,
Who treated your rashes with butter.
May the harlot weep for you,
Who massaged you with sweet-smelling oil.
Like brothers may they weep for you,
Like sisters may they tear out their hair for your sake.
Enkidu, as your father, your mother,
I weep for you bitterly.

Hear me, O young men, listen to me,
Hear me, O elders of Uruk, listen to me!
I mourn my friend Enkidu,
I howl as bitterly as a professional keener.
Oh for the axe at my side, oh for the safeguard by my hand,
Oh for the sword at my belt, oh for the shield before me,
Oh for my best garment, oh for the raiment that pleased me most!
An ill wind rose against me and snatched it away!
O my friend, swift wild donkey, mountain onager, panther of the steppe,
O Enkidu my friend, swift wild donkey, mountain onager, panther
of the steppe!
You who stood by me when we climbed the mountain,
Seized and slew the Bull of Heaven,
Felled Humbaba who dwelt in the forest of cedar,
What now is this sleep that has seized you?
Come back to me! You hear me not.

But, as for him, he did not raise his head.
He touched his heart but it was not beating.
Then he covered his friend's face, like a bride's.
He hovered round him like an eagle,
Like a lioness whose cubs are in a pitfall,
He paced to and fro, back and forth,
Tearing out and hurling away the locks of his hair,
Ripping off and throwing away his fine clothes like something foul.

At the first glimmer of dawn,
Gilgamesh sent out a proclamation to the land:

Hear ye, blacksmith, lapidary,[5] metalworker, goldsmith, jeweler!
Make an image of my friend,
Such as no one ever made of his friend!

5. Gem carver.

I will lay you down in the ultimate resting place,
In a perfect resting place I will surely lay you down.
I will settle you in peaceful rest in that dwelling sinister,
Rulers of the netherworld will do you homage.
I will have the people of Uruk shed bitter tears for you,
I will make the pleasure-loving people burdened down for you,
And, as for me, now that you are dead, I will let my hair grow matted,
I will put on a lion skin and roam the steppe!

He slaughtered fatted cattle and sheep, heaped them high for his friend,
They carried off all the meat for the rulers of the netherworld.
He displayed in the open for Ishtar, the great queen,
Saying: "May Ishtar, the great queen, accept this,
May she welcome my friend and walk at his side."

He displayed in the open for Ninshuluhha,[6] housekeeper of the netherworld,
Saying: "May Ninshuluhha, housekeeper of the crowded netherworld, accept this,
May she welcome my friend and walk at his side.
May she intercede on behalf of my friend, lest he lose courage."
The obsidian knife with lapis fitting,
The sharpening stone pure-whetted with Euphrates water,
He displayed in the open for Bibbu, meat carver of the netherworld,
Saying: "May Bibbu, meat carver of the crowded netherworld, accept this,
Welcome my friend and walk at his side."

Tablet IX

Gilgamesh was weeping bitterly for Enkidu, his friend,
As he roamed the steppe:

Shall I not die too? Am I not like Enkidu?
Oh woe has entered my vitals!
I have grown afraid of death, so I roam the steppe.
Having come this far, I will go on swiftly
Towards Utanapishtim,[7] son of Ubar-Tutu.
I have reached mountain passes at night.
I saw lions, I felt afraid,
I looked up to pray to the moon,
To the moon, beacon of the gods, my prayers went forth:
"Keep me safe!"

6. A netherworld deity in charge of ritual washing.
7. Akkadian name for the sage who, together with his wife, survived the Great Flood and became immortal. He resembles the biblical Noah and his name literally means "He Found Life." He is called "Ziusudra" in Sumerian and "Ullu" in Hittite.

[At night] he lay down, then awoke from a dream.
He rejoiced to be alive.
He raised the axe at his side,
He drew the sword from his belt,
He dropped among them like an arrow,
He struck the lions, scattered, and killed them.

[*Gilgamesh approaches the scorpion monsters who guard the gateway to the sun's passage through the mountains.*]

The twin peaks are called Mashum.
When he arrived at the twin peaks called Mashum,
Which daily watch over the rising and setting of the sun,
Whose peaks thrust upward to the vault of heaven,
Whose flanks reach downward to hell,
Where scorpion monsters guard its gateway,
Whose appearance is dreadful, whose venom is death,
Their fear-inspiring radiance spreads over the mountains,
They watch over the sun at its rising and setting,
When Gilgamesh saw their fearsomeness and terror,
He covered his face.
He took hold of himself and approached them.

The scorpion monster called to his wife:

> This one who has come to us, his body is flesh of a god!

The wife of the scorpion monster answered him:

> Two-thirds of him is divine, one-third is human.

The scorpion monster, the male one, called out,
To Gilgamesh, scion of the gods, he said these words:

> Who are you who have come this long way?

[*The scorpion monster apparently warns Gilgamesh that he has only twelve hours to get through the sun's tunnel before the sun enters it at nightfall.*]

The scorpion monster made ready to speak, spoke to him,
Said to Gilgamesh, [scion of the gods]:

> Go, Gilgamesh!

He opened to him the gateway of the mountain,
Gilgamesh entered the mountain.
He heeded the words of the scorpion monster,
He set out on the way of the sun.

When he had gone one double hour,
Dense was the darkness, no light was there,
It would not let him look behind him.
When he had gone two double hours,
Dense was the darkness, no light was there,
It would not let him look behind him.
When he had gone three double hours,
Dense was the darkness, no light was there,
It would not let him look behind him.
When he had gone four double hours,
Dense was the darkness, no light was there,
It would not let him look behind him.
When he had gone five double hours,
Dense was the darkness, no light was there,
It would not let him look behind him.
When he had gone six double hours,
Dense was the darkness, no light was there,
It would not let him look behind him.
When he had gone seven double hours,
Dense was the darkness, there was no light,
It would not let him look behind him.
When he had gone eight double hours, he rushed ahead,
Dense was the darkness, there was no light,
It would not let him look behind him.
When he had gone nine double hours, he felt the north wind,
Dense was the darkness, there was no light,
It would not let him look behind him.
When he had gone ten double hours,
The time for the sun's entry was drawing near.
When he had gone eleven double hours, just one double hour was left,
When he had gone twelve double hours, he came out ahead of the sun!
He had run twelve double hours, bright light still reigned!
He went forward, seeing the trees of the gods.
The carnelian bore its fruit,
Like bunches of grapes dangling, lovely to see,
The lapis bore foliage,
Fruit it bore, a delight to behold.

[*The fragmentary lines that remain continue the description of the wonderful grove.*]

Tablet X

[*Gilgamesh approaches the tavern of Siduri, a female tavern keeper who lives at the end of the earth. This interesting personage is unknown outside this poem, nor is it clear who her clientele might be in such a remote spot.*]

Siduri[8] the tavern keeper, who dwells at the edge of the sea,
For her was wrought the cuprack,[9] for her the brewing vat of gold,
Gilgamesh made his way towards her,
He was clad in a skin,
He had flesh of gods in his body.
Woe was in his vitals,
His face was like a traveler's from afar.
The tavern keeper eyed him from a distance,
Speaking to herself, she said these words,
She debated with herself:

> This no doubt is a slaughterer of wild bulls!
> Why would he make straight for my door?

At the sight of him the tavern keeper barred her door,
She barred her door and mounted to the roof terrace.
But he, Gilgamesh, put his ear to the door,
He lifted his chin.

Gilgamesh said to her, to the tavern keeper:

> Tavern keeper, when you saw me why did you bar your door,
> Bar your door and mount to the roof terrace?
> I will strike down your door, I will shatter your doorbolt,

Gilgamesh said to her, to the tavern keeper:

> I am Gilgamesh, who killed the guardian,
> Who seized and killed the bull that came down from heaven,
> Who felled Humbaba who dwelt in the forest of cedars,
> Who killed lions at the mountain passes.

The tavern keeper said to him, to Gilgamesh:

> If you are indeed Gilgamesh, who killed the guardian,
> Who felled Humbaba who dwelt in the forest of cedars,
> Who killed lions at the mountain passes,
> Who seized and killed the bull that came down from heaven,
> Why are your cheeks emaciated, your face cast down,
> Your heart wretched, your features wasted,
> Woe in your vitals,
> Your face like a traveler's from afar,

8. Literally "Maiden" in Hurrian, a language of northern Syria and northern Mesopotamia that was not related to Sumerian or Akkadian.

9. Some Mesopotamian drinking cups were conical, with pointed bottoms, so they were set on a wooden rack to hold them up.

Your features weathered by cold and sun,
Why are you clad in a lion skin, roaming the steppe?

Gilgamesh said to her, to the tavern keeper:

My cheeks would not be emaciated, nor my face cast down,
Nor my heart wretched nor my features wasted,
Nor would there be woe in my vitals,
Nor would my face be like a traveler's from afar,
Nor would my features be weathered by cold and sun,
Nor would I be clad in a lion skin, roaming the steppe,
But for my friend, swift wild donkey, mountain onager, panther
  of the steppe,
But for Enkidu, swift wild donkey, mountain onager, panther
  of the steppe,
My friend whom I so loved, who went with me through every hardship,
Enkidu, whom I so loved, who went with me through every hardship,
The fate of mankind has overtaken him.
Six days and seven nights I wept for him,
I would not give him up for burial,
Until a worm fell out of his nose.
I was frightened.
I have grown afraid of death, so I roam the steppe,
My friend's case weighs heavy upon me.
A distant road I roam over the steppe,
My friend Enkidu's case weighs heavy upon me!
A distant road I roam over the steppe,
How can I be silent? How can I hold my peace?
My friend whom I loved is turned into clay,
Enkidu, my friend whom I loved, is turned into clay!
Shall I too not lie down like him,
And never get up forever and ever?

[*An old version adds the following episode.*]

After his death I could find no life,
Back and forth I prowled like a bandit in the steppe.
Now that I have seen your face, tavern keeper,
May I not see that death I constantly fear!

The tavern keeper said to him, to Gilgamesh:

Gilgamesh, wherefore do you wander?
The eternal life you are seeking you shall not find.
When the gods created mankind,
They established death for mankind,
And withheld eternal life for themselves.
As for you, Gilgamesh, let your stomach be full,
Always be happy, night and day.
Make every day a delight,
Night and day play and dance.
Your clothes should be clean,

Your head should be washed,
You should bathe in water,
Look proudly on the little one holding your hand,
Let your mate be always blissful in your loins,
This, then, is the work of mankind.

Gilgamesh said to her, to the tavern keeper:

What are you saying, tavern keeper?
I am heartsick for my friend.
What are you saying, tavern keeper?
I am heartsick for Enkidu!

[*The standard version resumes.*]

Gilgamesh said to her, to the tavern keeper:

Now then, tavern keeper, what is the way to Utanapishtim?
What are its signs? Give them to me.
Give, oh give me its signs!
If need be, I'll cross the sea,
If not, I'll roam the steppe.

The tavern keeper said to him, to Gilgamesh:

Gilgamesh, there has never been a place to cross,
There has been no one from the dawn of time who could ever cross this sea.
The valiant Shamash alone can cross this sea,
Save for the sun, who could cross this sea?
The crossing is perilous, highly perilous the course,
And midway lie the waters of death, whose surface is impassable.
Suppose, Gilgamesh, you do cross the sea,
When you reach the waters of death, what will you do?
Yet, Gilgamesh, there is Ur-Shanabi,[1] Utanapishtim's boatman,
He has the Stone Charms with him as he trims pine trees in the forest.
Go, show yourself to him,
If possible, cross with him, if not, then turn back.

[*Gilgamesh advances and without preamble attacks Ur-Shanabi and smashes the Stone Charms.*]

When Gilgamesh heard this,
He raised the axe at his side,
He drew the sword at his belt,
He crept forward, went down towards them,
Like an arrow he dropped among them,
His battle cry resounded in the forest.
When Ur-Shanabi saw the shining [. . .],
He raised his axe, he trembled before him,

1. Servant of Utanapishtim, ferryman who crosses the ocean and the waters of death.

But he, for his part, struck his head [. . .] Gilgamesh,
He seized his arm [. . .] his chest.
And the Stone Charms, the protection . . . of the boat,
Without which no one crosses the waters of death,
He smashed them and threw them into the broad sea,
Into the channel he threw them, his own hands foiled him,
He smashed them and threw them into the channel!

Gilgamesh said to him, to Ur-Shanabi:

> Now then, Ur-Shanabi, what is the way to Utanapishtim?
> What are its signs? Give them to me,
> Give, oh give me its signs!
> If need be, I'll cross the sea,
> If not, I'll roam the steppe.

Ur-Shanabi said to him, to Gilgamesh:

> Your own hands have foiled you, Gilgamesh,
> You have smashed the Stone Charms, you have thrown them into the channel.

[*An old version has the following here.*]

> The Stone Charms, Gilgamesh, are what carry me,
> Lest I touch the waters of death.
> In your fury you have smashed them,
> The Stone Charms, they are what I had with me to make the crossing!
>
> Gilgamesh, raise the axe in your hand,
> Go down into the forest, cut twice sixty poles each five times twelve cubits long,
> Dress them, set on handguards,
> Bring them to me.

When Gilgamesh heard this,
He raised the axe at his side,
He drew the sword at his belt,
He went down into the forest, cut twice sixty poles each five times twelve cubits long,
He dressed them, set on handguards,
He brought them to him.
Gilgamesh and Ur-Shanabi embarked in the boat,
They launched the boat, they embarked upon it.
A journey of a month and a half they made in three days!
Ur-Shanabi reached the waters of death,
Ur-Shanabi said to him, to Gilgamesh:

> Stand back, Gilgamesh! Take the first pole,
> Your hand must not touch the waters of death,
> Take the second, the third, the fourth pole, Gilgamesh,
> Take the fifth, sixth, and seventh pole, Gilgamesh,

Take the eighth, ninth, and tenth pole, Gilgamesh,
Take the eleventh and twelfth pole, Gilgamesh.

With twice sixty Gilgamesh had used up the poles.
Then he, for his part, took off his belt,
Gilgamesh tore off his clothes from his body,
Held high his arms for a mast.
Utanapishtim was watching him from a distance,
Speaking to himself, he said these words,
He debated to himself:

Why have the Stone Charms, belonging to the boat, been smashed,
And one not its master embarked thereon?
He who comes here is no man of mine.

[*In the fragmentary lines that follow, Gilgamesh lands at Utanapishtim's wharf and questions him.*]

Utanapishtim said to him, to Gilgamesh:

Why are your cheeks emaciated, your face cast down,
Your heart wretched, your features wasted,
Woe in your vitals,
Your face like a traveler's from afar,
Your features weathered by cold and sun,
Why are you clad in a lion skin, roaming the steppe?

Gilgamesh said to him, to Utanapishtim:

My cheeks would not be emaciated, nor my face cast down,
Nor my heart wretched, nor my features wasted,
Nor would there be woe in my vitals,
Nor would my face be like a traveler's from afar,
Nor would my features be weathered by cold and sun,
Nor would I be clad in a lion skin, roaming the steppe,

But for my friend, swift wild donkey, mountain onager, panther of the steppe,
But for Enkidu, my friend, swift wild donkey, mountain onager, panther of the steppe,
He who stood by me as we ascended the mountain,
Seized and killed the bull that came down from heaven,
Felled Humbaba who dwelt in the forest of cedars,
Killed lions at the mountain passes,
My friend whom I so loved, who went with me through every hardship,
Enkidu, whom I so loved, who went with me through every hardship,
The fate of mankind has overtaken him.
Six days and seven nights I wept for him,
I would not give him up for burial,
Until a worm fell out of his nose.
I was frightened.
I have grown afraid of death, so I roam the steppe,

My friend's case weighs heavy upon me.
A distant road I roam over the steppe,
My friend Enkidu's case weighs heavy upon me!
A distant path I roam over the steppe,
How can I be silent? How can I hold my peace?
My friend whom I loved is turned into clay,
Enkidu, my friend whom I loved, is turned into clay!
Shall I too not lie down like him,
And never get up, forever and ever?

Gilgamesh said to him, to Utanapishtim:

So it is to go find Utanapishtim, whom they call the "Distant One,"
I traversed all lands,
I came over, one after another, wearisome mountains,
Then I crossed, one after another, all the seas.
Too little sweet sleep has smoothed my countenance,
I have worn myself out in sleeplessness,
My muscles ache for misery,
What have I gained for my trials?
I had not reached the tavern keeper when my clothes were worn out,
I killed bear, hyena, lion, panther, leopard, deer, ibex, wild beasts
of the steepe,
I ate their meat, I [. . .] their skins.
Let them close behind me the doors of woe,
Let them seal them with pitch and tar.

Utanapishtim said to him, to Gilgamesh:

Why, O Gilgamesh, did you prolong woe,
You who are formed of the flesh of gods and mankind,
You for whom the gods acted like fathers and mothers?
When was it, Gilgamesh, you [. . .] to a fool?

You strive ceaselessly, what do you gain?
When you wear out your strength in ceaseless striving,
When you torture your limbs with pain,
You hasten the distant end of your days.
Mankind, whose descendants are snapped off like reeds in a canebrake!
The handsome young man, the lovely young woman, death [. . .]
No one sees death,
No one sees the face of death,
No one hears the voice of death,
But cruel death cuts off mankind.
Do we build a house forever?
Do we make a home forever?
Do brothers divide an inheritance forever?
Do disputes prevail in the land forever?
Do rivers rise in flood forever?
Dragonflies drift downstream on a river,
Their faces staring at the sun,

Then, suddenly, there is nothing.
The sleeper and the dead, how alike they are!
They limn not death's image,
No one dead has ever greeted a human in this world.
The supreme gods, the great gods, being convened,
Mammetum, she who creates destinies, ordaining destinies with them,
They established death and life,
They did not reveal the time of death.

Tablet XI

Gilgamesh said to him, to Utanapishtim the Distant One:

As I look upon you, Utanapishtim,
Your limbs are not different, you are just as I am.
Indeed, you are not different at all, you are just as I am!
Yet your heart is drained of battle spirit,
You lie flat on your back, your arm idle.
You then, how did you join the ranks of the gods and find eternal life?

Utanapishtim said to him, to Gilgamesh:

I will reveal to you, O Gilgamesh, a secret matter,
And a mystery of the gods I will tell you.
The city Shuruppak,[2] a city you yourself have knowledge of,
Which once was set on the bank of the Euphrates,
That aforesaid city was ancient and gods once were within it.
The great gods resolved to send the deluge,
Their father Anu was sworn,
The counselor the valiant Enlil,
Their throne-bearer Ninurta,
Their canal-officer Ennugi,[3]
Their leader Ea was sworn with them.
He repeated their plans to the reed fence:
"Reed fence, reed fence, wall, wall!
Listen, O reed fence! Pay attention, O wall!
O Man of Shuruppak, son of Ubar-Tutu,
Wreck house, build boat,
Forsake possessions and seek life,
Belongings reject and life save!
Take aboard the boat seed of all living things.
The boat you shall build,
Let her dimensions be measured out:
Let her width and length be equal,
Roof her over like the watery depths."
I understood full well, I said to Ea, my lord:
"Your command, my lord, exactly as you said it,
I shall faithfully execute.
What shall I answer the city, the populace, and the elders?"

2. City in Babylonia reputed to antedate the flood, long abandoned at the time the epic was written.
3. Minor deity in charge of water courses.

Ea made ready to speak,
Saying to me, his servant:
"So, you shall speak to them thus:
'No doubt Enlil dislikes me,
I shall not dwell in your city.
I shall not set my foot on the dry land of Enlil,
I shall descend to the watery depths and dwell with my lord Ea.
Upon you he shall shower down in abundance,
A windfall of birds, a surprise of fishes,
He shall pour upon you a harvest of riches,
In the morning cakes in spates,
In the evening grains in rains.'"

At the first glimmer of dawn,
The land was assembling at the gate of Atrahasis:[4]
The carpenter carried his axe,
The reed cutter carried his stone,
The old men brought cordage,
The young men ran around,
The wealthy carried the pitch,
The poor brought what was needed.
In five days I had planked her hull:
One full acre was her deck space,
Ten dozen cubits, the height of each of her sides,
Ten dozen cubits square, her outer dimensions.[5]
I laid out her structure, I planned her design:
I decked her in six,
I divided her in seven,
Her interior I divided in nine.
I drove the water plugs into her,
I saw to the spars and laid in what was needful.
Thrice thirty-six hundred measures of pitch I poured in the oven,
Thrice thirty-six hundred measures of tar I poured out inside her.
Thrice thirty-six hundred measures basket-bearers brought aboard for oil,
Not counting the thirty-six hundred measures of oil that the offering consumed,
And the twice thirty-six hundred measures of oil that the boatbuilders made off with.
For the builders I slaughtered bullocks,
I killed sheep upon sheep every day,
Beer, ale, oil, and wine
I gave out to the workers like river water,
They made a feast as on New Year's Day,
I dispensed ointment with my own hand.

4. Literally "Super-wise," another Akkadian name of the immortal flood hero Utanapishtim.
5. The proportions of the boat suggest standard measures of both ship building and the construction of ziggurats, pyramidal temple towers.

By the setting of Shamash,[6] the ship was completed.
Since boarding was very difficult,
They brought up gangplanks, fore and aft,
They came up her sides two-thirds of her height.
Whatever I had I loaded upon her:
What silver I had I loaded upon her,
What gold I had I loaded upon her,
What living creatures I had I loaded upon her,
I sent up on board all my family and kin,
Beasts of the steppe, wild animals of the steppe, all types of skilled craftsmen I sent up on board.
Shamash set for me the appointed time:
"In the morning, cakes in spates,
In the evening, grains in rains,
Go into your boat and caulk the door!"
That appointed time arrived,
In the morning cakes in spates,
In the evening grains in rains,
I gazed upon the face of the storm,
The weather was dreadful to behold!
I went into the boat and caulked the door.
To the caulker of the boat, to Puzur-Amurri the boatman,
I gave over the edifice, with all it contained.

At the first glimmer of dawn,
A black cloud rose above the horizon.
Inside it Adad[7] was thundering,
While the destroying gods Shullat and Hanish[8] went in front,
Moving as an advance force over hill and plain.
Errakal[9] tore out the mooring posts of the world,
Ninurta[1] came and made the dikes overflow.
The supreme gods held torches aloft,
Setting the land ablaze with their glow.
Adad's awesome power passed over the heavens,
Whatever was light was turned into darkness.
He flooded the land, he smashed it like a clay pot!
For one day the storm wind blew,
Swiftly it blew, the flood came forth,
It passed over the people like a battle,
No one could see the one next to him,

6. The references to Shamash here and below suggest that in some now lost version of this story, Shamash, the god of justice, rather than Ea, the god of wisdom, warned Utanapishtim of the flood and told him how much time he had to build his ship. This substitution of one god for the other might be due to Shamash's role in the epic as protector of Gilgamesh. In the oldest account of the Babylonian story of the flood, Ea sets a timing device, apparently a water clock, to inform Utanapishtim of the time left before the onset of the deluge.
7. God of thunder.
8. Gods of destructive storms.
9. God of death.
1. God of war.

The people could not recognize one another in the downpour.
The gods became frightened of the deluge,
They shrank back, went up to Anu's highest heaven.
The gods cowered like dogs, crouching outside.
Ishtar screamed like a woman in childbirth,
And sweet-voiced Belet-ili[2] wailed aloud:
"Would that day had come to naught,
When I spoke up for evil in the assembly of the gods!
How could I have spoken up for evil in the assembly of the gods,
And spoken up for battle to destroy my people?
It was I myself who brought my people into the world,
Now, like a school of fish, they choke up the sea!"
The supreme gods were weeping with her,
The gods sat where they were, weeping,
Their lips were parched, taking on a crust.
Six days and seven nights
The wind continued, the deluge and windstorm leveled the land.
When the seventh day arrived,
The windstorm and deluge left off their battle,
Which had struggled, like a woman in labor.
The sea grew calm, the tempest stilled, the deluge ceased.

I looked at the weather, stillness reigned,
And the whole human race had turned into clay.
The landscape was flat as a rooftop.
I opened the hatch, sunlight fell upon my face.
Falling to my knees, I sat down weeping,
Tears running down my face.
I looked at the edges of the world, the borders of the sea,
At twelve times sixty double leagues the periphery emerged.
The boat had come to rest on Mount Nimush,[3]
Mount Nimush held the boat fast, not letting it move.
One day, a second day Mount Nimush held the boat fast, not letting it move.
A third day, a fourth day Mount Nimush held the boat fast, not letting it move.
A fifth day, a sixth day Mount Nimush held the boat fast, not letting it move.

When the seventh day arrived,
I brought out a dove and set it free.
The dove went off and returned,
No landing place came to its view, so it turned back.
I brought out a swallow and set it free,
The swallow went off and returned,
No landing place came to its view, so it turned back.
I brought out a raven and set it free,

2. A goddess of birth, who in one version of the flood story was said to have collaborated with the god Ea in creating the human race.

3. High peak sometimes identified with Pir Omar Gudrun in Kurdistan. Landing place of the ark in the Gilgamesh epic.

The raven went off and saw the ebbing of the waters.
It ate, preened, left droppings, did not turn back.
I released all to the four directions,
I brought out an offering and offered it to the four directions.
I set up an incense offering on the summit of the mountain,
I arranged seven and seven cult vessels,
I heaped reeds, cedar, and myrtle in their bowls.
The gods smelled the savor,
The gods smelled the sweet savor,
The gods crowded round the sacrificer like flies.

As soon as Belet-ili arrived,
She held up the great fly-ornaments that Anu had made
  in his ardor:
"O gods, these shall be my lapis necklace, lest I forget,
I shall be mindful of these days and not forget, not ever!
The gods should come to the incense offering,
But Enlil should not come to the incense offering,
For he, irrationally, brought on the flood,
And marked my people for destruction!"
As soon as Enlil arrived,
He saw the boat, Enlil flew into a rage,
He was filled with fury at the gods:
"Who came through alive? No man was to survive destruction!"
Ninurta made ready to speak,
Said to the valiant Enlil:
"Who but Ea could contrive such a thing?
For Ea alone knows every artifice."

Ea made ready to speak,
Said to the valiant Enlil:
"You, O valiant one, are the wisest of the gods,
How could you, irrationally, have brought on the flood?
Punish the wrongdoer for his wrongdoing,
Punish the transgressor for his transgression,
But be lenient, lest he be cut off,
Bear with him, lest he [. . .].
Instead of your bringing on a flood,
Let the lion rise up to diminish the human race!
Instead of your bringing on a flood,
Let the wolf rise up to diminish the human race!
Instead of your bringing on a flood,
Let famine rise up to wreak havoc in the land!
Instead of your bringing on a flood,
Let pestilence rise up to wreak havoc in the land!
It was not I who disclosed the secret of the great gods,
I made Atrahasis have a dream and so he heard the secret
  of the gods.
Now then, make some plan for him."
Then Enlil came up into the boat,

Leading me by the hand, he brought me up too.
He brought my wife up and had her kneel beside me.
He touched our brows, stood between us to bless us:
"Hitherto Utanapishtim has been a human being,
Now Utanapishtim and his wife shall become like us gods.
Utanapishtim shall dwell far distant at the source of the rivers."
Thus it was that they took me far distant and had me dwell at the source of the rivers.
Now then, who will convene the gods for your sake,
That you may find the eternal life you seek?
Come, come, try not to sleep for six days and seven nights.

As he sat there on his haunches,
Sleep was swirling over him like a mist.
Utanapishtim said to her, to his wife:

Behold this fellow who seeks eternal life!
Sleep swirls over him like a mist.

[*Utanapishtim's wife, taking pity on Gilgamesh, urges her husband to awaken him and let him go home*].

His wife said to him, to Utanapishtim the Distant One:

Do touch him that the man may wake up,
That he may return safe on the way whence he came,
That through the gate he came forth he may return to his land.

Utanapishtim said to her, to his wife:

Since the human race is duplicitous, he'll endeavor to dupe you.
Come, come, bake his daily loaves, put them one after another by his head,
Then mark the wall for each day he has slept.

She baked his daily loaves for him, put them one after another by his head,
Then dated the wall for each day he slept.
The first loaf was dried hard,
The second was leathery, the third soggy,
The crust of the fourth turned white,
The fifth was gray with mold, the sixth was fresh,
The seventh was still on the coals when he touched him, the man woke up.

Gilgamesh said to him, to Utanapishtim the Distant One:

Scarcely had sleep stolen over me,
When straightaway you touched me and roused me.

Utanapishtim said to him, to Gilgamesh:

Up with you, Gilgamesh, count your daily loaves,
That the days you have slept may be known to you.

The first loaf is dried hard,
The second is leathery, the third soggy,
The crust of the fourth has turned white,
The fifth is gray with mold,
The sixth is fresh,
The seventh was still in the coals when I touched you and
you woke up.

Gilgamesh said to him, to Utanapishtim the Distant One:

What then should I do, Utanapishtim, whither should I go,
Now that the Bereaver has seized my flesh?
Death lurks in my bedchamber,
And wherever I turn, there is death!

Utanapishtim said to him, to Ur-Shanabi the boatman:

Ur-Shanabi, may the harbor offer you no haven,
May the crossing point reject you,
Be banished from the shore you shuttled to.
The man you brought here,
His body is matted with filthy hair,
Hides have marred the beauty of his flesh.
Take him away, Ur-Shanabi, bring him to the washing place.
Have him wash out his filthy hair with water, clean as snow,
Have him throw away his hides, let the sea carry them off,
Let his body be rinsed clean.
Let his headband be new,
Have him put on raiment worthy of him.
Until he reaches his city,
Until he completes his journey,
Let his garments stay spotless, fresh and new.

Ur-Shanabi took him away and brought him to the washing place.
He washed out his filthy hair with water, clean as snow,
He threw away his hides, the sea carried them off,
His body was rinsed clean.
He renewed his headband,
He put on raiment worthy of him.
Until he reached his city,
Until he completed his journey,
His garments would stay spotless, fresh and new.

Gilgamesh and Ur-Shanabi embarked on the boat,
They launched the boat, they embarked upon it.
His wife said to him, to Utanapishtim the Distant One:

Gilgamesh has come here, spent with exertion,
What will you give him for his homeward journey?

At that he, Gilgamesh, lifted the pole,
Bringing the boat back by the shore.

Utanapishtim said to him, to Gilgamesh:

Gilgamesh, you have come here, spent with exertion,
What shall I give you for your homeward journey?
I will reveal to you, O Gilgamesh, a secret matter,
And a mystery of the gods I will tell you.
There is a certain plant, its stem is like a thornbush,
Its thorns, like the wild rose, will prick [your hand].
If you can secure this plant, [. . .]

No sooner had Gilgamesh heard this,
He opened a shaft, flung away his tools.
He tied heavy stones to his feet,
They pulled him down into the watery depths.
He took the plant though it pricked his hand.
He cut the heavy stones from his feet,
The sea cast him up on his home shore.

Gilgamesh said to him, to Ur-Shanabi the boatman:

Ur-Shanabi, this plant is cure for heartache,
Whereby a man will regain his stamina.
I will take it to ramparted Uruk,
I will have an old man eat some and so test the plant.
His name shall be "Old Man Has Become Young-Again-Man."
I myself will eat it and so return to my carefree youth.

At twenty double leagues they took a bite to eat,
At thirty double leagues they made their camp.

Gilgamesh saw a pond whose water was cool,
He went down into it to bathe in the water.
A snake caught the scent of the plant,
Stealthily it came up and carried the plant away,
On its way back it shed its skin.

Thereupon Gilgamesh sat down weeping,
His tears flowed down his face,
He said to Ur-Shanabi the boatman:

For whom, Ur-Shanabi, have my hands been toiling?
For whom has my heart's blood been poured out?
For myself I have obtained no benefit,
I have done a good deed for a reptile!
Now, floodwaters rise against me for twenty double leagues,
When I opened the shaft, I flung away the tools.
How shall I find my bearings?
I have come much too far to go back, and I abandoned the boat on the shore.

At twenty double leagues they took a bite to eat,
At thirty double leagues they made their camp.

When they arrived in ramparted Uruk,
Gilgamesh said to him, to Ur-Shanabi the boatman:

Go up, Ur-Shanabi, pace out the walls of Uruk.
Study the foundation terrace and examine the brickwork.
Is not its masonry of kiln-fired brick?
And did not seven masters lay its foundations?
One square mile of city, one square mile of gardens,
One square mile of clay pits, a half square mile of Ishtar's dwelling,
Three and a half square miles is the measure of Uruk!

THE HEBREW BIBLE

ca. 1000–300 B.C.E.

The sacred writings of the ancient Hebrew people are arguably the world's most influential texts. They have remained the sacred text of Judaism and have inspired two other major world religions: Christianity and Islam. Because these texts have been so influential in human affairs, and have become central to so many people's core religious beliefs, they are not often read in the same way as "literary" texts. But studying the books of the Hebrew Bible as literature—paying close attention to their narrative techniques, their imagery, characterization, and point of view—is not incompatible with religious faith. Close reading enriches our understanding and appreciation of these texts as supremely important cultural and historical documents, for readers of any religious background or belief.

The Hebrew Bible encompasses a rich variety of texts from different periods, composed in both poetry and prose. One of the obvious differences between the Bible and most works of "literature"—such as **Aeschylus's** ***Agamemnon*** or **Virgil's** ***Aeneid***—is that no single human hand composed the whole Bible, or even the whole of Genesis or Job. Traditionally, Moses is thought to have been the author of the first five books of the Bible and also, according to some traditions, the book of Job. But modern Bible scholars agree that these books, in their current form, must have been woven together from several different earlier sources. This theory explains the otherwise puzzling fact that there are often odd contradictions and repetitions in the narrative. For example, God tells Noah to take two of every kind of animal into the ark; but a little later, the Lord tells Noah to take seven pairs of each animal. The simplest explanation for this kind of discrepancy is that the text we have is a collage built of several earlier narratives, put together, or "redacted," into a single master story. Many scholars believe that it is possible to distinguish between the different original strands, each of which has its distinct stylistic features and perspectives on the narrative. For instance, one strand of the text is identified by the name that it uses for God, *YHWH* (a personal name for the Hebrew god: in English, *Jehovah*, and hence the strand is called *J*); in another strand (dubbed *E*), God is called *Elohim* (which comes from the standard Semitic term for any god, *el*).

The various sources have been put together with great skill, and the result is a text of extraordinary literary, philosophical, and theological richness. The lengthiest selections included here are abridged versions of the books of Genesis and Job. Perhaps the most important element running through the two is a complex ethical concern with how human suffering and prosperity come about and what role God plays in shaping human lives. The books resist easy answers to these questions. We might expect that God would simply punish wrongdoers and reward the righteous; and indeed, he does punish Adam and Eve for their disobedience. But often the relation between human behavior and divine favor is shown to be deeply mysterious. God favors Abel over Cain, blesses Noah and Abraham over all other humans, seems to pay more attention to Isaac than Ishmael, favors Jacob over Esau and Joseph over his brothers, and blesses the Hebrew people over all other inhabitants of the Middle East; but in none of these cases are we given an explanation, let alone a moral justification. Moreover, God allows even his favorites, such as Jacob, Joseph, and Job, to suffer terrible hardship before restoring them to prosperity. The book of Job brings this issue explicitly to the forefront. God's ways are mysterious, and instead of reinforcing a simple moral (like "Be good and God will bless you"), the Bible constantly undercuts it. But throughout these texts, we see that God's power is the major force in all of human history. It is no accident that the book of Genesis—unlike other ancient creation stories—begins not with earth, sky, and sea but with God himself, the originator of everything.

GENESIS

The first book of the Bible takes its name from the Greek word for "origin" or "birth"—*genesis*. The book tells a story of how the world, and the human race, came into existence; how humans first disobeyed God; and how God began to establish a special relationship with a series of chosen men and their families: Noah, Abraham, Isaac, Jacob, and Joseph. The book was probably redacted in the fifth century B.C.E., a period when the people of Judah were in exile in Babylon. One can understand Genesis in this context, as an attempt to consolidate Jewish identity in the midst of an alien culture.

The first section (chapters 1–11) recounts "creation history"—God's creation of the world and of humankind, and the development of early human society. Human beings occupy center stage in this account of the world's origin, as they do not in, for example, Mesopotamian and Greek creation stories. This early age is marked especially by God's anger at humanity, from his expulsion of Adam and Eve from Eden to his destruction of the Tower of Babel, which scatters human beings and divides their single language into many languages. God's decision to destroy humanity is presented as a reversal of the original act of creation. The flood mixes together again the waters that were separated on the second day of creation, and it destroys almost all the different kinds of animals created on the fifth and sixth days, together with almost all humans.

But not quite all animals and humans are destroyed. Noah and his family, and the animals taken onto the ark, are spared, because Noah has found favor in God's eyes; Noah's various wives and the chosen animals, it seems, have attracted no particular divine attention but benefit by association with Noah. This dramatic demonstration of God's power and willingness to favor certain members of the human race while destroying others leads to a new beginning. The second part of Genesis (chapters 12–50) moves from humanity in general to the stories of four men and their families: Abraham and his wife, Sarah; Isaac and his wife, Rebekah; Jacob and his wives, Leah and Rachel; and Joseph and his brothers. The transition is marked by God's first declaration of his commitment to the people of Israel. When he tells Noah's descendant Abram (who will be renamed Abraham) to leave his home in Mesopotamia, he declares, "I will make you a great nation and I will bless you and make your name great, and you shall be a blessing." Showing him the land of Canaan, he promises, "To your seed I will give this land." This positive covenant builds on the merely negative promise God has already made to humanity in general: that he will never again destroy the world by flood (chapter 9). Now there is a purpose in history: other peoples will be blessed through the people of Israel, who are chosen for a particularly close relationship with God.

Many complications arise that seem to threaten the fulfillment of the covenant—and add narrative excitement to the story. God has promised "this land" to Abraham's children, but repeatedly, Abraham's descendants—Jacob, and later Joseph and his brothers—must leave the land of their fathers, deferring the hope of a settled home in the promised land. The pattern of exile from home recurs again and again in the book of Genesis and recalls the expulsion of Adam and Eve from the Garden of Eden, while the strife between family members, especially brothers, and the theme of the triumph of a younger brother over an elder, constantly recall the story of Cain and Abel. Repeatedly, we see God's covenant fulfilled in unexpected ways, revealing his power and his surpassing of merely human expectations.

God himself can be seen as the most vivid and complex character of the book of Genesis. He, like the humans made in his image, enjoys an evening stroll through a cool garden; he is willing to scheme and make deals; he has his particular friends and his favorites; and he is capable of emotions: pleasure, hope, anger, and regret. But the human characters in this book, both men and women, are also strikingly vivid. They are people of intense feelings, and their relationships with one another, their loves, hatreds, fears, and desires, are evoked in compelling detail.

It is worthwhile to pay close attention to the way the text brings people's feelings, characters, and motivations to life, in just a few simple words. We often seem to be invited to ponder several possible layers of meaning in what people say, as when Abraham loads up Isaac with wood for the fire, takes the cleaver in his hand, and leads him into the mountain. Isaac says simply, "Father!" Is he scared? Does he know what his father plans to do? Does the word fill Abraham himself with guilt and horror? Or is he unshaking in his resolve to obey? A world of family conflict is opened up in the text's simple observations. "And Isaac loved Esau for the game that he brought him, but Rebekah loved Jacob" and "The LORD regarded Abel and his offering but He did not regard Cain and his offering." Reasons for these preferences seem to exist, but they are often deeply hidden.

The tale of Jacob, who is renamed "Israel," is central to this text and forms one of its most gripping story lines. Jacob and Esau are twins who fight each other even in the womb: as shown in Robert Crumb's memorable image, Jacob emerges already grabbing hold of his brother's heel—a detail reminiscent of the everlasting "enmity" between humanity and the serpent, which bites the heels of the children of Adam. As they grow older, the brothers grow ever more different: Esau is a wild, hairy man, while Jacob, the mother's boy, the clever one, likes to stay home. Jacob plays a pair of tricks on his brother, first duping him out of his birthright and then robbing him of his dying father's blessing. Understandably enough, Esau wants to kill him. And yet when Jacob travels away from home, he is granted a vision from God, who promises him protection, the inheritance of the land, and blessing for himself and for his "seed." Why, we may wonder, does God prefer the trickster Jacob over the loyal, filial Esau? Is he rewarded for his brains, which he certainly has in abundance? Or for his unstoppable drive to get ahead, evident even from the womb? Or is it his capacity to love, shown in his relationships with his mother, his favorite wife, and his favorite sons? Is it his willingness to engage directly with God and God's messengers, as when he wrestles with the angel all night and emerges declaring, "I have seen God face to face"? Whatever we decide, it is striking that Jacob, or "Israel," the father of the Jewish people, is presented in such fascinatingly unidealized terms. He is a fully human, rounded, and believable character.

Joseph, the firstborn of Jacob's favorite wife, Rachel, is a very different but equally fascinating character. Whereas Jacob's intelligence is practical, focused on the present—combining an acute ability to judge other people with a keen eye for how to protect and promote himself—Joseph is a dreamer, whose mind can read symbols and look to the future. He has a sense of his own great destiny, confirmed by his dreams, which represent him as the first of all his race. Dreams occupy an interesting middle ground in this story, between internal and external worlds: on the one hand, Joseph's dreams are a clue to his state of mind, his hopes for greatness; on the other, his dreams are a sign of the fact that God has favored him and will set him above his brothers. Like later prophets, Joseph suffers many tribulations. As Pharaoh dream interpreter, Joseph becomes a prototype for the later priests and prophets of Israel: he can discern divine purpose in the signs that remain mysterious to ordinary humans. Joseph's story forms a bridge to the book of Exodus, in which the Hebrew people will need long-term faith in God and in their destiny to survive the years of exile.

Like the ***Odyssey***, the book of Genesis is about the search for a homeland, a special place of belonging—although here the quest belongs not to a single man but to a whole people. As in the *Odyssey*, hospitality plays an essential part in the value structure of the text. It is often through human hospitality that God's plan can succeed. Abraham, sitting by his tent flap in the alien land of Mamre, passes a test of his hospitality with flying colors when he offers a lavish feast to the "three men" who turn out to be messengers of the Lord. We see the descendants of Abraham negotiate their relationships with the various other peoples who inhabit the area that God seems to have promised as their inheritance. At the same time, they must try to avoid total assimilation: Isaac insists, for example, that Jacob must not "take a wife from the daughters of Canaan"; in terms of culture, worship, and "seed," the people must remain distinct. Circumcision, which God enjoins on Abraham and his family, marks this male line off from its neighbors. But the story of Joseph illustrates the advantages of at

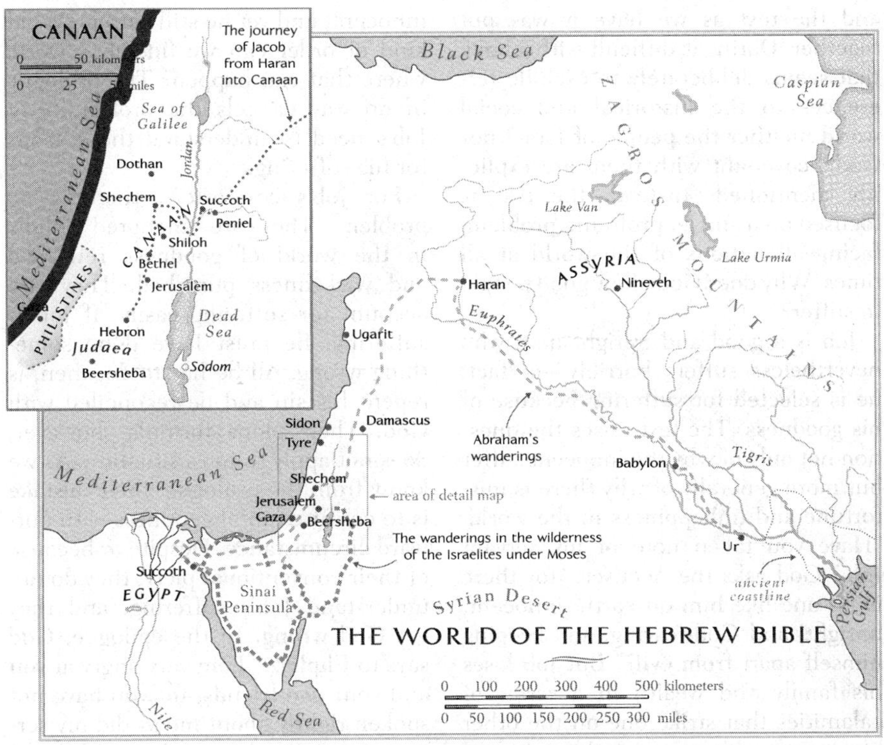

least partial assimilation. Joseph dresses as an Egyptian, marries an Egyptian woman, and has children by her, even as he remembers his family, his father, and the land of his birth; it is, indeed, through his power in the land of Egypt, and his willingness to serve Pharoah, that Joseph manages to save his family and preserve the future of Israel.

EXODUS

After the death of Joseph, the Hebrew people remain in Egypt and multiply, and the Egyptians become increasingly hostile toward this alien population. Moses, along with his brother Aaron, is chosen by God as the savior of the people, the man who will lead them out of slavery and exile and back to their homeland in Canaan. They escape from Egypt, crossing the waters of the Red Sea, which miraculously part to let them through and then wash back to drown Pharaoh and his army. In the wilderness, Moses goes to hear the word of God at the top of Mount Sinai, and the Ten Commandments are revealed to him: ten rules of ethical and religious conduct, to be carved on stone tablets, that will form the basis for the new law of the Hebrew people and their covenant with God.

JOB

The book of Job draws on an ancient folk tale about God and his Accuser (the Hebrew term is "Satan") testing a just man, who finally passes their test. But the biblical story makes this motif into the prose frame for an extraordinary poem recounting Job's conversations with his friends and with God. Perhaps sometime around the fifth century B.C.E., the poem was composed and the text as we have it was put together. Dating is difficult with a book that seems deliberately to exclude references to the historical and social world: neither the people of Israel nor God's covenant with them are explicitly mentioned. Instead, the text is focused on a single, profound problem, facing all nations of the world at all times. Why does God allow good people to suffer?

Job is a good and upright man who nevertheless suffers horribly—in fact, he is selected for suffering because of his goodness. The text raises the question not only of why the innocent suffer but more generally of why there is misfortune and unhappiness in the world. "Have you taken note of my servant Job," God asks the Accuser, "for there is no one like him on earth: innocent, upright, and God-fearing, and keeping himself apart from evil?" But Job loses his family and wealth in a series of calamities that strike one on the other like hammer blows and is then plagued with a horrible disease. In a series of magnificent speeches, he expresses his sense of his own innocence and demands one thing: to understand the reason for his suffering.

From the beginning, we can see a little farther into the problem than Job. In the prologue, the Accuser challenges God's praise of Job by pointing out that Job's goodness has never been tested; it is easy to be righteous in prosperity. Because we see that Job's afflictions originate in a test, we know that there is a reason for his suffering, but we may not find it a valid reason and may feel that Job is the object of sport for higher powers. If so, what we know from the prologue only makes the problem of innocent suffering worse. Alternatively, we can see God's wager as a sign of his respect for Job and his willingness to trust humanity to make good choices and remain faithful no matter what. But the fact remains that Job is innocent, and yet he still suffers. What kind of order can we find in a world where that can happen? The prologue in no way cancels the profundity of Job's need to understand the reasons for his suffering.

For Job's comforters, there is no problem. They are anchored solidly in the world of goodness rewarded and wickedness punished. They can account for suffering easily. If Job is suffering, he must have done something wrong. All he has to do, then, is repent his sin and be reconciled with God. Their pious formula, however, does not apply to Job's situation. As we know from the prologue, their mistake is to confuse moral goodness with outward circumstance. Despite or because of their conventional piety, they do not understand Job's suffering, and they get God wrong. In the epilogue, God says to Eliphaz, "I am very angry at you and your two friends, for you have not spoken rightly about me as did my servant Job." Job has spoken rightly by insisting on his innocence and not reducing God's ways to a formula. He also avoids identifying goodness with his fortune in life; unlike his friends, Job acknowledges that good people sometimes suffer dreadfully, and he is appalled by it. But he fulfills God's expectations because he does not curse or in any way repudiate him. Instead, Job wants God to meet him face to face. But he is mistaken to think that he and God can meet on such equal terms and that he merits an explanation. In the end, God does speak to him, but only to pose a series of wonderful but entirely unanswerable questions, such as "Where were you when I founded the earth?" There is no reciprocal conversation; Job simply, briefly, acknowledges his error and recognizes the vast, incommensurable greatness of God.

The text culminates in God's magnificent speech from the storm, which ranges over all of creation and its animal life. The contrast with the account of creation in the first chapter of Genesis, which puts human beings at the center, is dramatic. Here there are beasts whose might far surpasses that of humans, who seem just a part of the created world, and the poetry of this speech conveys the awe and mystery that are attributes of God. The book of Job does not explain innocent suffering, but it does leave us with a sense of what we cannot understand.

PSALMS

The book of Psalms is a collection of 150 poems or hymns. Traditionally, King David was imagined as the author, though modern scholars believe that the various poems come from different time periods, some from before Jerusalem was besieged and finally destroyed by the Babylonians (in 587 B.C.E.), while others (such as "By the Rivers of Babylon") were clearly composed afterward, at a time when the Hebrew people were exiled to the city of their conquerors. Most were composed to be used in worship, and they range in theme and mood, from hymns of praise or joyful thanksgiving to desperate songs of lament expressing the sorrows of a people in exile or the bitterness of a person unjustly wronged. The rich, vivid imagery of the Psalms—especially in the language of the King James translation, used here—has had an essential influence on the development of literature in English.

A NOTE ON THE TRANSLATION

Except for the Psalms, presented in the King James version, the biblical text given here is from the recent modern translations by Robert Alter. Alter's language is mostly contemporary, but he is conscious of the need to be faithful to the poetic rhythms of the original—both in the verse of the book of Job and in the rhythmical prose of Genesis (which includes short passages of verse). Far more than other translators, Alter preserves the simple syntax and verbal repetitions of the Hebrew—for instance, by repeating *and* no less than twenty times in the first eight verses of Genesis. The lack of subordination is an essential feature of the text's style, as are other kinds of word order that Alter tries to imitate in English, like emphatic inversion (God says, "To your seed I will give" rather than "I will give to your seed"). The Bible tells its complex story in a surprisingly small number of words, and nouns may take on greater power through their repetition in a number of different contexts: it is worthwhile to trace, for example, the use of *hand* or *house* or *brother* throughout the book of Genesis. Alter does not manage to retain every repetition or verbal effect of the Hebrew, but the translation comes close to mirroring the Bible's combination of simple, colloquial vocabulary (with occasional uses of archaic or peculiar phrasing) and vivid concrete metaphor. Alter uses *seed*, for example, to reflect the Hebrew imagery, instead of changing it to *children* or *offspring* (as the New Revised Standard Version does).

We also include one chapter of Robert Crumb's graphic-novel version of Genesis. This too uses the Alter translation but brings it to life with striking black-and-white illustrations of the characters and events. The chosen chapter includes one of the genealogical sections, which form an essential element in the Genesis narrative but often make for slow going for modern readers; Crumb's pictures transform the names into a memorable lineup of personalities. His version of the scene in which Jacob tricks Esau out of his birthright is a gripping realization of this emotionally charged story. Reading even a little of Crumb's version is a good reminder of what we may risk forgetting: that the Hebrew Bible is—for all its theological and philosophical profundity—a very entertaining book.

Genesis 1–4[1]

[*From Creation to the Murder of Abel*]

1. When God began to create heaven and earth, and the earth then was welter and waste[2] and darkness over the deep and God's breath[3] hovering over the waters, God said, "Let there be light." And there was light. And God saw the light, that it was good, and God divided the light from the darkness. And God called the light Day, and the darkness He called Night. And it was evening and it was morning, first day. And God said, "Let there be a vault in the midst of the waters, and let it divide water from water."[4] And God made the vault and it divided the water beneath the vault from the water above the vault, and so it was. And God called the vault Heavens, and it was evening and it was morning, second day. And God said, "Let the waters under the heavens be gathered in one place so that the dry land will appear," and so it was. And God called the dry land Earth and the gathering of waters He called Seas, and God saw that it was good. And God said, "Let the earth grow grass, plants yielding seed of each kind and trees bearing fruit of each kind, that has its seed within it upon the earth." And so it was. And the earth put forth grass, plants yielding seed, and trees bearing fruit of each kind, and God saw that it was good. And it was evening and it was morning, third day. And God said, "Let there be lights in the vault of the heavens to divide the day from the night, and they shall be signs for the fixed times and for days and years, and they shall be lights in the vault of the heavens to light up the earth." And so it was. And God made the two great lights, the great light for dominion of day and the small light for dominion of night, and the stars. And God placed them in the vault of the heavens to light up the earth and to have dominion over day and night and to divide the light from the darkness. And God saw that it was good. And it was evening and it was morning, fourth day. And God said, "Let the waters swarm with the swarm of living creatures and let fowl fly over the earth across the vault of the heavens." And God created the great sea monsters and every living creature that crawls, which the water had swarmed forth of each kind, and the winged fowl of each kind, and God saw that it was good. And God blessed them, saying, "Be fruitful and multiply and fill the water in the seas and let the fowl multiply in the earth." And it was evening and it was morning, fifth day. And God said, "Let the earth bring forth living creatures of each kind, cattle and crawling things and wild beasts of each kind. And so it was. And God made wild beasts of each kind and cattle of every kind and all crawling things on the ground of each kind, and God saw that it was good. And God said, "Let us make a human

1. Excerpts from Genesis are translated by Robert Alter. The notes are indebted to Alter's annotations.

2. The translator combines a rare English word (*welter*, meaning chaos, or the turmoil of rolling waves) with *waste* to render a phrase that is very rare in the Hebrew, *tohu wabohu*.

3. The Hebrew word for "breath," *ruah*, may also mean "spirit."

4. The water below the vault, or sky, is the ocean; the water above the vault is the rain.

in our image,[5] by our likeness, to hold sway over the fish of the sea and the fowl of the heavens and the cattle and the wild beasts and all the crawling things that crawl upon the earth.

And God created the human in his image,
in the image of God He created him,
male and female He created them.[6]

And God blessed them, and God said to them, "Be fruitful and multiply and fill the earth and conquer it, and hold sway over the fish of the sea and the fowl of the heavens and every beast that crawls upon the earth." And God said, "Look, I have given you every seed-bearing plant on the face of all the earth and every tree that has fruit bearing seed, yours they will be for food. And to all the beasts of the earth and to all the fowl of the heavens and to all that crawls on the earth, which has the breath of life within it, the green plants for food." And so it was. And God saw all that He had done, and, look, it was very good. And it was evening and it was morning, the sixth day.

2.[7] Then the heavens and the earth were completed, and all their array. And God completed on the seventh day the task He had done, and He ceased on the seventh day from all the task He had done. And God blessed the seventh day and hallowed it, for on it He had ceased from all His task that He had created to do. This is the tale of the heavens and the earth when they were created.

On the day the LORD God made earth and heavens, no shrub of the field being yet on the earth and no plant of the field yet sprouted, for the LORD God had not caused rain to fall on the earth and there was no human to till the soil, and wetness would well from the earth to water all the surface of the soil, then the LORD God fashioned the human, humus from the soil,[8] and blew into his nostrils the breath of life, and the human became a living creature. And the LORD God planted a garden in Eden, to the east, and He placed there the human He had fashioned. And the LORD God caused to sprout from the soil every tree lovely to look at and good for food, and the tree of life was in the midst of the garden, and the tree of knowledge, good and evil. Now a river runs out of Eden to water the garden and from there splits off into four streams. The name of the first is Pishon, the one that winds through the whole land of Havilah, where there is gold. And the gold of that land is goodly, bdellium[9] is there, and lapis lazuli. And the name of the second river is Gihon, the one that winds through all the land of Cush. And the name of the third river is Tigris, the one that goes to the east of Ashur. And the fourth river is Euphrates. And the LORD God took the human and set him down in the garden of Eden to till it and watch it. And the LORD God commanded the human, saying, "From

5. The Hebrew word for "human" is *'adam*, which also means "dust"; it is not the first man's name, but the noun denoting all humanity. It does not necessarily imply that the human is male.

6. Here and elsewhere in the translation, the indentation marks a shift into a brief passage of verse in the translation, reflecting a shift in the original.

7. This is the beginning of a different account of the Creation, which does not agree in all respects with the first.

8. There is a pun in the Hebrew on *'adam*, "human," and *'adamah*, "humus" or "soil."

9. A fragrant tree.

every fruit of the garden you may surely eat. But from the tree of knowledge, good and evil, you shall not eat, for on the day you eat from it, you are doomed to die." And the LORD God said, "It is not good for the human to be alone, I shall make him a sustainer beside him." And the LORD God fashioned from the soil each beast of the field and each fowl of the heavens and brought each to the human to see what he would call it, and whatever the human called a living creature, that was its name. And the human called names to all the cattle and to the fowl of the heavens and to all the beasts of the field, but for the human no sustainer beside him was found. And the LORD God cast a deep slumber on the human, and he slept, and He took one of his ribs and closed over the flesh where it had been, and the LORD God built the rib He had taken from the human into a woman and He brought her to the human. And the human said:

"This one at last, bone of my bones
and flesh of my flesh,
This one shall be called Woman,
for from man was this one taken."[1]

Therefore does a man leave his father and his mother and cling to his wife and they become one flesh. And the two of them were naked, the human and his woman, and they were not ashamed.

3. Now the serpent was most cunning of all the beasts of the field that the LORD God had made. And he said to the woman, "Though God said, you shall not eat from any tree of the garden—" And the woman said to the serpent, "From the fruit of the garden's trees we may eat, but from the fruit of the tree in the midst of the garden God has said, 'You shall not eat from it and you shall not touch it, lest you die.'" And the serpent said to the woman, "You shall not be doomed to die. For God knows that on the day you eat of it your eyes will be opened and you will become as gods knowing good and evil." And the woman saw that the tree was good for eating and that it was lust to the eyes and the tree was lovely to look at, and she took of its fruit and ate, and she also gave to her man, and he ate. And the eyes of the two were opened, and they knew they were naked, and they sewed fig leaves and made themselves loincloths.

And they heard the sound of the LORD God walking about in the garden in the evening breeze, and the human and his woman hid from the LORD God in the midst of the trees of the garden. And the LORD God called to the human and said to him, "Where are you?" And he said, "I heard Your sound in the garden and I was afraid, for I was naked, and I hid." And He said, "Who told you that you were naked? From the tree I commanded you not to eat have you eaten?" And the human said, "The woman whom you gave by me, she gave me from the tree, and I ate." And the LORD God said to the woman, "What is this you have done?" And the woman said, "The serpent beguiled me and I ate." And the LORD God said to the serpent, "Because you have done this,

1. "Man" is *ish* in Hebrew; "woman" is *ishshah*.

Cursed be you
  of all cattle and all beasts of the field.
On your belly shall you go
  and dust shall you eat all the days of your life.
Enmity will I set between you and the woman,
  between your seed and hers.
He will boot your head
  and you will bite his heel."[2]

To the woman He said,

"I will terribly sharpen your birth pangs,
  in pain shall you bear children.
And for your man shall be your longing,
  and he shall rule over you."

And to the human He said, "Because you listened to the voice of your wife and ate from the tree that I commanded you. 'You shall not eat from it,'

Cursed be the soil for your sake,
  with pangs shall you eat from it all the days of your life.
Thorn and thistle shall it sprout for you
  and you shall eat the plants of the field.
By the sweat of your brow shall you eat bread
  till you return to the soil,
    for from there were you taken,
for dust you are
  and to dust shall you return."

And the human called his woman's name Eve, for she was the mother of all that lives.[3] And the LORD God made skin coats for the human and his woman, and He clothed them. And the LORD God said, "Now that the human has become like one of us, knowing good and evil, he may reach out and take as well from the tree of life and live forever." And the LORD God sent him from the garden of Eden to till the soil from which he had been taken. And He drove out the human and set up east of the garden of Eden the cherubim and the flame of the whirling sword to guard the way to the tree of life.

4. And the human knew Eve his woman and she conceived and bore Cain, and she said, "I have got me a man with the LORD." And she bore as well his brother, Abel, and Abel became a herder of sheep while Cain was a tiller of the soil. And it happened in the course of time that Cain brought from the fruit of the soil an offering to the LORD. And Abel too had brought from the choice firstlings of his flock, and the LORD regarded Abel and his offering but He did not regard Cain and his offering, and Cain was very incensed, and his face fell. And the LORD said to Cain,

difference in gifts

2. "Boot . . . bite" represents a pun in Hebrew: the word for trampling, or "booting," is repeated to refer to the snake's reaction; it may refer to the snake's hiss just before it bites.

3. The name *Hawah*, Eve, is similar to the verbal root *hayah*, "to live."

"Why are you incensed,
  and why is your face fallen?
For whether you offer well,
  or whether you do not,
at the tent flap sin crouches
  and for you is its longing
    but you will rule over it."[4]

And Cain said to Abel his brother, "Let us go out to the field." And when they were in the field, Cain rose against Abel his brother and killed him. And the LORD said to Cain, "Where is Abel your brother?" And he said, "I do not know. Am I my brother's keeper?" And He said, "What have you done? Listen! your brother's blood cries out to me from the soil. And so, cursed shall you be by the soil that gaped with its mouth to take your brother's blood from your hand. If you till the soil, it will no longer give you its strength. A restless wanderer shall you be on the earth." And Cain said to the LORD, "My punishment is too great to bear. Now that You have driven me this day from the soil and I must hide from Your presence, I shall be a restless wanderer on the earth and whoever finds me will kill me." And the LORD said to him, "Therefore whoever kills Cain shall suffer sevenfold vengeance." And the LORD set a mark upon Cain so that whoever found him would not slay him.

And Cain went out from the LORD's presence and dwelled in the land of Nod east of Eden. And Cain knew his wife and she conceived and bore Enoch. Then he became the builder of a city and called the name of the city, like his son's name, Enoch. And Irad was born to Enoch,[5] and Irad begot Mehujael and Mehujael begot Methusael and Methusael begot Lamech. And Lamech took him two wives, the name of the one was Adah and the name of the other was Zillah. And Adah bore Jabal: he was the first of tent dwellers with livestock. And his brother's name was Jubal: he was the first of all who play on the lyre and pipe. As for Zillah, she bore Tubal-Cain, who forged every tool of copper and iron. And the sister of Tubal-Cain was Naamah. And Lamech said to his wives,

"Adah and Zillah, O hearken my voice,
  You wives of Lamech, give ear to my speech.
For a man have I slain for my wound,
  a boy for my bruising.
For sevenfold Cain is avenged,
  and Lamech seventy and seven."

And Adam again knew his wife and she bore a son and called his name Seth, as to say, "God has granted me[6] other seed in place of Abel, for Cain has killed him." As for Seth, to him, too, a son was born, and he called his name Enosh. It was then that the name of the LORD was first invoked.

4. Obscure; it seems to mean something like "Sin shall be eager for you, but you must master it."
5. This is the first of many lists of genealogies in the book of Genesis. Genealogy is one of the major ways in which the text evokes and orders historical time and creates a connection between past and present.
6. The pun in Hebrew is between the name *Shet* and the verb *shat*, "granted."

Genesis 6–9

[*Noah and the Flood*]

6. And it happened as humankind began to multiply over the earth and daughters were born to them, that the sons of God saw that the daughters of man were comely, and they took themselves wives howsoever they chose.[7] And the LORD said, "My breath shall not abide in the human forever, for he is but flesh. Let his days be a hundred and twenty years."

The Nephilim[8] were then on the earth, and afterward as well, the sons of God having come to bed with the daughters of man who bore them children: they are the heroes of yore, the men of renown.

And the LORD saw that the evil of the human creature was great on the earth and that every scheme of his heart's devising was only perpetually evil. And the LORD regretted having made the human on earth and was grieved to the heart. And the LORD said, "I will wipe out the human race I created from the face of the earth, from human to cattle to crawling thing to the fowl of the heavens, for I regret that I have made them." But Noah found favor in the eyes of the LORD. This is the lineage of Noah—Noah was a righteous man, he was blameless in his time, Noah walked with God—and Noah begot three sons, Shem and Ham and Japheth. And the earth was corrupt before God and the earth was filled with outrage. And God saw the earth and, look, it was corrupt, for all flesh had corrupted its ways on the earth. And God said to Noah, "The end of all flesh is come before me, for the earth is filled with outrage by them, and I am now about to destroy them, with the earth. Make yourself an ark of cypress wood, with cells you shall make the ark, and caulk it inside and out with pitch. This is how you shall make it: three hundred cubits, the ark's length; fifty cubits, its width; thirty cubits, its height. Make a skylight in the ark, within a cubit of the top you shall finish it, and put an entrance in the ark on one side. With lower and middle and upper decks you shall make it. As for me, I am about to bring the Flood, water upon the earth, to destroy all flesh that has within it the breath of life from under the heavens, everything on the earth shall perish. And I will set up my covenant with you, and you shall enter the ark, you and your sons and your wife and the wives of your sons, with you. And from all that lives, from all flesh, two of each thing you shall bring to the ark to keep alive with you, male and female they shall be. From the fowl of each kind and from the cattle of each kind and from all that crawls on the earth of each kind, two of each thing shall come to you to be kept alive. As for you, take you from every food that is eaten and store it by you, to serve for you and for them as food." And this Noah did; as all that God commanded him, so he did.

7. And the LORD said to Noah, "Come into the ark, you and all your household, for it is you I have seen righteous before Me in this generation. Of every clean animal take you seven pairs, each with its mate, and of every animal that is not

7. The passage is based on archaic myths (perhaps from an old Hittite tradition) about male gods ("the sons of God") having sex with mortal women. The allusion seems cryptic, perhaps because the monotheistic writer is avoiding explicit discussion of multiple semidivine or divine figures, although the idea of such beings would have been familiar to the ancient reader.

8. This appears to mean "the fallen ones."

clean, one pair, each with its mate.[9] Of the fowl of the heavens as well seven pairs, male and female, to keep seed alive over all the earth. For in seven days' time I will make it rain on the earth forty days and forty nights and I will wipe out from the face of the earth all existing things that I have made." And Noah did all that the LORD commanded him.

Noah was six hundred years old when the Flood came, water over the earth. And Noah and his sons and his wife and his sons' wives came into the ark because of the waters of the Flood. Of the clean animals and of the animals that were not clean and of the fowl and of all that crawls upon the ground two each came to Noah into the ark, male and female, as God had commanded Noah. And it happened after seven days, that the waters of the Flood were over the earth. In the six hundredth year of Noah's life, in the second month, on the seventeenth day of the month, on that day,

All the wellsprings of the great deep burst
and the casements of the heavens were opened.

And the rain was over the earth forty days and forty nights. That very day, Noah and Shem and Ham and Japheth, the sons of Noah, and Noah's wife, and the three wives of his sons together with them, came into the ark, they as well as beasts of each kind and cattle of each kind and each kind of crawling thing that crawls on the earth and each kind of bird, each winged thing. They came to Noah into the ark, two by two of all flesh that has the breath of life within it. And those that came in, male and female of all flesh they came, as God had commanded him, and the LORD shut him in. And the Flood was forty days over the earth, and the waters multiplied and bore the ark upward and it rose above the earth. And the waters surged and multiplied mightily over the earth, and the ark went on the surface of the water. And the waters surged most mightily over the earth, and all the high mountains under the heavens were covered. Fifteen cubits above them the waters surged as the mountains were covered. And all flesh that stirs on the earth perished, the fowl and the cattle and the beasts and all swarming things that swarm upon the earth, and all humankind. All that had the quickening breath of life in its nostrils, of all that was on dry land, died. And He wiped out all existing things from the face of the earth, from humans to cattle to crawling things to the fowl of the heavens, they were wiped out from the earth. And Noah alone remained, and those with him in the ark. And the waters surged over the earth one hundred and fifty days.

8. And God remembered Noah and all the beasts and all the cattle that were with him in the ark. And God sent a wind over the earth and the waters subsided. And the wellsprings of the deep were dammed up, and the casements of the heavens, the rain from the heavens held back. And the waters receded from the earth little by little, and the waters ebbed. At the end of a hundred and fifty days the ark came to rest, on the seventeenth day of the seventh month, on the

9. "Clean" and "not clean" refer to the categories of animals that might or might not be sacrificed; it does not refer to dietary restrictions, which came later in the tradition. There is clearly a discrepancy in the narratives here, between the previous chapter's specification of "two of each thing" and this chapter's requirement of "seven pairs."

mountains of Ararat. The waters continued to ebb, until the tenth month, on the first day of the tenth month, the mountaintops appeared. And it happened, at the end of forty days, that Noah opened the window of the ark he had made. And he sent out the raven and it went forth to and fro until the waters should dry up from the earth. And he sent out the dove to see whether the waters had abated from the surface of the ground. But the dove found no resting place for its foot and it returned to him to the ark, for the waters were over all the earth. And he reached out and took it and brought it back to him into the ark. Then he waited another seven days and again sent the dove out from the ark. And the dove came back to him at eventide and, look, a plucked olive leaf was in its bill, and Noah knew that the waters had abated from the earth. Then he waited still another seven days and sent out the dove, and it did not return to him again. And it happened in the six hundred and first year, in the first month, on the first day of the month, the waters dried up from the earth, and Noah took off the covering of the ark and he saw and, look, the surface of the ground was dry. And in the second month, on the twenty-seventh day of the month, the earth was completely dry. And God spoke to Noah, saying, "Go out of the ark, you and your wife and your sons and your sons' wives, with you. All the animals that are with you of all flesh, fowl and cattle and every crawling thing that crawls on the earth, take out with you, and let them swarm through the earth and be fruitful and multiply on the earth." And Noah went out, his sons and his wife and his sons' wives with him. Every beast, every crawling thing, and every fowl, everything that stirs on the earth, by their families, came out of the ark. And Noah built an altar to the LORD and he took from every clean cattle and every clean fowl and offered burnt offerings on the altar. And the LORD smelled the fragrant odor and the LORD said in His heart, "I will not again damn the soil on humankind's score. For the devisings of the human heart are evil from youth. And I will not again strike down all living things as I did. As long as all the days of the earth—

seedtime and harvest
and cold and heat
and summer and winter
and day and night
shall not cease."

9. And God blessed Noah and his sons and He said to them, "Be fruitful and multiply and fill the earth. And the dread and fear of you shall be upon all the beasts of the field and all the fowl of the heavens, in all that crawls on the ground and in all the fish of the sea. In your hand they are given. All stirring things that are alive, yours shall be for food, like the green plants, I have given all to you. But flesh with its lifeblood still in it you shall not eat. And just so, your lifeblood I will requite, from every beast I will requite it, and from humankind, from every man's brother. I will requite human life.

He who sheds human blood
by humans his blood shall be shed,[1]

1. There is wordplay in the original, between *'adam*, "human," and *dam*, "blood."

for in the image of God
He made humankind.
As for you, be fruitful and multiply,
swarm through the earth, and hold sway over it."

And God said to Noah and to his sons with him, "And I, I am about to establish My covenant with you and with your seed after you, and with every living creature that is with you, the fowl and the cattle and every beast of the earth with you, all that have come out of the ark, every beast of the earth. And I will establish My covenant with you, that never again shall all flesh be cut off by the waters of the Flood, and never again shall there be a Flood to destroy the earth." And God said, "This is the sign of the covenant that I set between Me and you and every living creature that is with you, for everlasting generations: My bow I have set in the clouds to be a sign of the covenant between Me and the earth, and so, when I send clouds over the earth, the bow will appear in the cloud. Then I will remember My covenant, between Me and you and every living creature of all flesh, and the waters will no more become a Flood to destroy all flesh. And the bow shall be in the cloud and I will see it, to remember the everlasting covenant between God and all living creatures, all flesh that is on the earth." And God said to Noah, "This is the sign of the covenant I have established between Me and all flesh that is on the earth."

And the sons of Noah who came out from the ark were Shem and Ham and Japheth, and Ham was the father of Canaan. These three were the sons of Noah, and from these the whole earth spread out. And Noah, a man of the soil, was the first to plant a vineyard. And he drank of the wine and became drunk, and exposed himself within his tent. And Ham the father of Canaan saw his father's nakedness and told his two brothers outside. And Shem and Japheth took a cloak and put it over both their shoulders and walked backward and covered their father's nakedness, their faces turned backward so they did not see their father's nakedness. And Noah woke from his wine and he knew what his youngest son had done to him.[2] And he said,

"Cursed be Canaan,
the lowliest slave shall he be
to his brothers."[3]

And he said,

"Blessed be the Lord
the God of Shem,
unto them shall Canaan be slave.

2. The text leaves it unclear what Ham has done. Perhaps simply seeing his father naked is breaking a taboo.

3. An obvious purpose of this story is to justify the idea that the Israelites, rather than the Canaanites, ought to control the land of Canaan—an important issue in later Israelite history. After antiquity, Noah's three sons were often believed to have been the ancestors of the three supposed racial groups in the world: Japheth was the ancestor of European and Asian peoples, Shem was the ancestor of the Semitic races, and Ham was the ancestor of Africans. This interpretation goes well beyond the text itself and has often been motivated, implicitly or explicitly, by racism.

May God enlarge Japheth,
may he dwell in the tents of Shem,
unto them shall Canaan be slave."

And Noah lived after the Flood three hundred and fifty years. And all the days of Noah were nine hundred and fifty years. Then he died.

From Genesis 11

[*The Tower of Babel*]

11. And all the earth was one language, one set of words. And it happened as they journeyed from the east that they found a valley in the land of Shinar and settled there. And they said to each other, "Come, let us bake bricks and burn them hard." And the brick served them as stone, and bitumen served them as mortar. And they said, "Come, let us build us a city and a tower with its top in the heavens, that we may make us a name, lest we be scattered over all the earth." And the LORD came down to see the city and the tower that the human creatures had built. And the LORD said, "As one people with one language for all, if this is what they have begun to do, now nothing they plot to do will elude them. Come, let us go down and baffle their language there so that they will not understand each other's language." And the LORD scattered them from there over all the earth and they left off building the city. Therefore it is called Babel, for there the LORD made the language of all the earth babble.[4] And from there the LORD scattered them over all the earth.

* * *

From Genesis 12, 17, 18

[*God's Promise to Abraham*]

12. And the LORD said to Abram,[5] "Go forth from your land and your birthplace and your father's house to the land I will show you. And I will make you a great nation and I will bless you and make your name great, and you shall be a blessing. And I will bless those who bless you, and those who damn you I will curse, and all the clans of the earth through you shall be blessed." And Abram went forth as the LORD had spoken to him and Lot went forth with him, Abram being seventy-five years old when he left Haran. And Abram took

4. The pun in Hebrew is between *balal*, "to mix" or "to confuse," and the Akkadian place name *Babel* (or *Babylon*), which probably originally meant "gate of heaven." The "tower" is presumably a ziggurat, the type of tall building surrounding temple complexes in many ancient Mesopotamian cultures.

5. Ten generations and hundreds of years have passed since the time of Noah. Abram is a descendant of Noah's son Shem.

Sarai his wife and Lot his nephew and all the goods they had gotten and the folk they had bought in Haran,[6] and they set out on the way to the land of Canaan, and they came to the land of Canaan. And Abram crossed through the land to the site of Shechem, to the Terebinth of Moreh. The Canaanite was then in the land. And the LORD appeared to Abram and said, "To your seed I will give this land." And he built an altar there to the LORD who had appeared to him.

* * *

17. And Abram was ninety-nine years old, and the LORD appeared to Abram and said to him, "I am El Shaddai.[7] Walk in My presence and be blameless, and I will grant My covenant between Me and you and I will multiply you very greatly." And Abram flung himself on his face, and God spoke to him, saying, "As for Me, this is My covenant with you: you shall be father to a multitude of nations. And no longer shall your name be called Abram but your name shall be Abraham, for I have made you father to a multitude of nations.[8] And I will make you most abundantly fruitful and turn you into nations, and kings shall come forth from you. And I will establish My covenant between Me and you and your seed after you through their generations as an everlasting covenant to be God to you and to your seed after you. And I will give unto you and your seed after you the land in which you sojourn, the whole land of Canaan, as an everlasting holding, and I will be their God."

And God said to Abraham, "As for you, you shall keep My commandment, you and your seed after you through their generations."

* * *

18. And the LORD appeared to him in the Terebinths of Mamre[9] when he was sitting by the tent flap in the heat of the day. And he raised his eyes and saw, and, look, three men were standing before him. He saw, and he ran toward them from the tent flap and bowed to the ground. And he said, "My lord, if I have found favor in your eyes, please do not go on past your servant. Let a little water be fetched and bathe your feet and stretch out under the tree, and let me fetch a morsel of bread, and refresh yourselves. Then you may go on, for have you not come by your servant?" And they said, "Do as you have spoken." And Abraham hurried to the tent to Sarah and he said, "Hurry! Knead three *seahs* of choice semolina flour and make loaves."[1] And to the herd Abraham ran and fetched a tender and goodly calf and gave it to the lad, who

6. Slaves. Slavery was a common institution in the ancient Near East. The slave girl Hagar will play an important part in the story, since she is the mother of Abram's first son, Ishmael.

7. *El* means God; the meaning of *Shaddai* is obscure.

8. The names *Abram* and *Abraham* both mean "exalted father." Abram and Sarai (later Sarah) have to change their names, not to gain titles with new meaning but as a sign of taking on their new roles as instruments of God's purpose.

9. Terebinths are small trees that produce turpentine; the word used here is sometimes interpreted to mean "oak trees." Mamre was the site of a cult shrine to the major Canaanite sky god.

1. A *seah* is a dry measure equal to about thirty cups; three *seahs* is almost five gallons—a lot of food for three people.

hurried to prepare it. And he fetched curds and milk and the calf that had been prepared and he set these before them, he standing over them under the tree, and they ate. And they said to him, "Where is Sarah your wife?" And he said, "There, in the tent." And he said, "I will surely return to you at this very season and, look, a son shall Sarah your wife have," and Sarah was listening at the tent flap, which was behind him. And Abraham and Sarah were old, advanced in years, Sarah no longer had her woman's flow. And Sarah laughed inwardly, saying, "After being shriveled, shall I have pleasure, and my husband is old?" And the LORD said to Abraham, "Why is it that Sarah laughed, saying, 'Shall I really give birth, old as I am?' Is anything beyond the LORD? In due time I will return to you, at this very season, and Sarah shall have a son." And Sarah dissembled, saying, "I did not laugh," for she was afraid. And He said, "Yes, you did laugh."

* * *

From Genesis 21, 22

[*Abraham and Isaac*]

21. And the LORD singled out Sarah as He had said, and the LORD did for Sarah as He had spoken. And Sarah conceived and bore a son to Abraham in his old age at the set time that God had spoken to him. And Abraham called the name of his son who was born to him, whom Sarah bore him, Isaac.[2] And Abraham circumcised Isaac his son when he was eight days old, as God had charged him. And Abraham was a hundred years old when Isaac his son was born to him. And Sarah said,

"Laughter has God made me,
  Whoever hears will laugh at me."

* * *

22. And it happened after these things that God tested Abraham. And He said to him, "Abraham!" and he said, "Here I am." And He said, "Take, pray, your son, your only one, whom you love, Isaac, and go forth to the land of Moriah and offer him up as a burnt offering on one of the mountains which I shall say to you." And Abraham rose early in the morning and saddled his donkey and took his two lads with him, and Isaac his son, and he split wood for the offering, and rose and went to the place that God had said to him. On the third day Abraham raised his eyes and saw the place from afar. And Abraham said to his lads, "Sit you here with the donkey and let me and the lad walk ahead and let us worship and return to you." And Abraham took the wood for the offering and put it on Isaac his son and he took in his hand the

2. "He who laughs."

fire and the cleaver, and the two of them went together. And Isaac said to Abraham his father, "Father!" and he said, "Here I am, my son." And he said, "Here is the fire and the wood but where is the sheep for the offering?" And Abraham said, "God will see to the sheep for the offering, my son." And the two of them went together. And they came to the place that God had said to him, and Abraham built there an altar and laid out the wood and bound Isaac his son and placed him on the altar on top of the wood. And Abraham reached out his hand and took the cleaver to slaughter his son. And the LORD's messenger called out to him from the heavens and said, "Abraham, Abraham!" and he said, "Here I am." And he said, "Do not reach out your hand against the lad, and do nothing to him, for now I know that you fear God and you have not held back your son, your only one, from Me." And Abraham raised his eyes and saw and, look, a ram was caught in the thicket by its horns, and Abraham went and took the ram and offered him up as a burnt offering instead of his son. And Abraham called the name of that place YHWH-Yireh, as is said to this day, "On the mount of the LORD there is sight."[3] And the LORD's messenger called out to Abraham once again from the heavens, and He said, "By My own Self I swear, declares the LORD, that because you have done this thing and have not held back your son, your only one, I will greatly bless you and will greatly multiply your seed, as the stars in the heavens and as the sand on the shore of the sea, and your seed shall take hold of its enemies' gate. And all the nations of the earth will be blessed through your seed because you have listened to my voice." And Abraham returned to his lads, and they rose and went together to Beersheba, and Abraham dwelled in Beersheba.

* * *

Genesis 25

[*Esau Spurns His Birthright*]

We give chapter 25 of Genesis in the graphic-novel version by Robert Crumb. The words are based on Robert Alter's translation. Readers are invited to think about how the extra visual material contributes to the text and how these pictures might change one's interpretation of the Bible. We have chosen this chapter partly because it includes one of the many genealogies in Genesis, which are an essential feature of the Hebrew Bible's narrative method but hard for modern readers to appreciate; they are made vivid by Crumb's pictures. Moreover, Crumb's powerful depiction of Rebekah's conversation with the Lord is a good reminder of how important the female characters (the Matriarchs) are in this narrative. The chapter also marks the beginning of the story of Jacob and Esau; illustrations emphasize the textual, visual distinction between the hairy, wild hunter Esau and the smooth-skinned, smooth-talking Jacob.

3. The place name means "The Lord (Yaweh) sees" or "The Lord is seen."

Chapter 25

AND ABRAHAM TOOK ANOTHER WIFE, AND HER NAME WAS KETURAH. AND SHE BORE HIM ZIMRAN AND JOKSHAN AND MEDAN AND MIDIAN AND ISHBAK AND SHUAH.

AND JOKSHAN BEGOT SHEBA AND DEDAN. AND THE SONS OF DEDAN WERE THE ASHURIM AND THE LETUSHIM AND THE LEUM-MIM. AND THE SONS OF MIDIAN WERE EPHAH AND EPHER AND ENOCH AND ABIDA AND ELDAAH. ALL THESE WERE THE DESCEND-ANTS OF KETURAH.

AND ABRAHAM GAVE EVERYTHING HE HAD TO ISAAC. AND TO THE SONS OF HIS CONCUBINES ABRAHAM GAVE GIFTS WHILE HE WAS STILL ALIVE, AND SENT THEM AWAY FROM ISAAC, HIS SON, EASTWARD, TO THE LAND OF THE EAST.

AND THESE ARE THE DAYS OF THE YEARS OF THE LIFE OF ABRAHAM, WHICH HE LIVED: 175 YEARS. AND ABRAHAM BREATHED HIS LAST AND DIED AT A RIPE OLD AGE, OLD AND SATED WITH YEARS, AND HE WAS GATHERED TO HIS KINFOLK.

AND ISAAC AND ISHMAEL, HIS SONS, BURIED HIM IN THE MACHPELAH CAVE IN THE FIELD OF EPHRON, SON OF ZOHAR THE HITTITE, WHICH FACES MAMRE, THE FIELD THAT ABRAHAM HAD BOUGHT FROM THE HITTITES. THERE ABRAHAM WAS BURIED, WITH SARAH, HIS WIFE.

AND IT CAME TO PASS AFTER THE DEATH OF ABRAHAM THAT GOD BLESSED HIS SON ISAAC, AND ISAAC SETTLED NEAR BEER-LAHAI-ROI.

AND THIS IS THE LINEAGE OF ISHMAEL, SON OF ABRAHAM WHOM HAGAR, THE EGYPTIAN, SARAH'S SLAVE-GIRL, BORE TO ABRAHAM. AND THESE ARE THE NAMES OF THE SONS OF ISHMAEL ACCORDING TO THEIR LINEAGE...

NEBAIOTH, THE FIRSTBORN OF ISHMAEL...

AND KEDAR...

AND ADBEEL...

AND MIBSAM...

AND MISHMA...

AND DUMA...

AND MASSA...

AND TEMA...

THESE ARE THE SONS OF ISHMAEL, AND THESE ARE THEIR NAMES, BY THEIR TOWNS AND BY THEIR STRONGHOLDS, TWELVE CHIEFTAINS ACCORDING TO THEIR CLANS.

AND THESE ARE THE YEARS OF THE LIFE OF ISHMAEL: 137 YEARS. AND HE BREATHED HIS LAST AND DIED AND HE WAS GATHERED TO HIS KINFOLK. AND THEY RANGED FROM HAVILAH TO SHUR, WHICH FACES EGYPT, AND TILL YOU COME TO ASSHUR.

IN THE FACE OF ALL HIS KIN HE WENT DOWN.

AND THIS IS THE LINEAGE OF ISAAC, SON OF ABRAHAM. ABRAHAM BEGOT ISAAC. AND ISAAC WAS FORTY YEARS OLD WHEN HE TOOK AS WIFE REBEKAH, DAUGHTER OF BETHUEL THE ARAMEAN FROM PADDAN-ARAM, SISTER OF LABAN THE ARAMEAN. AND ISAAC PLEADED WITH THE LORD ON BEHALF OF HIS WIFE, FOR SHE WAS BARREN.

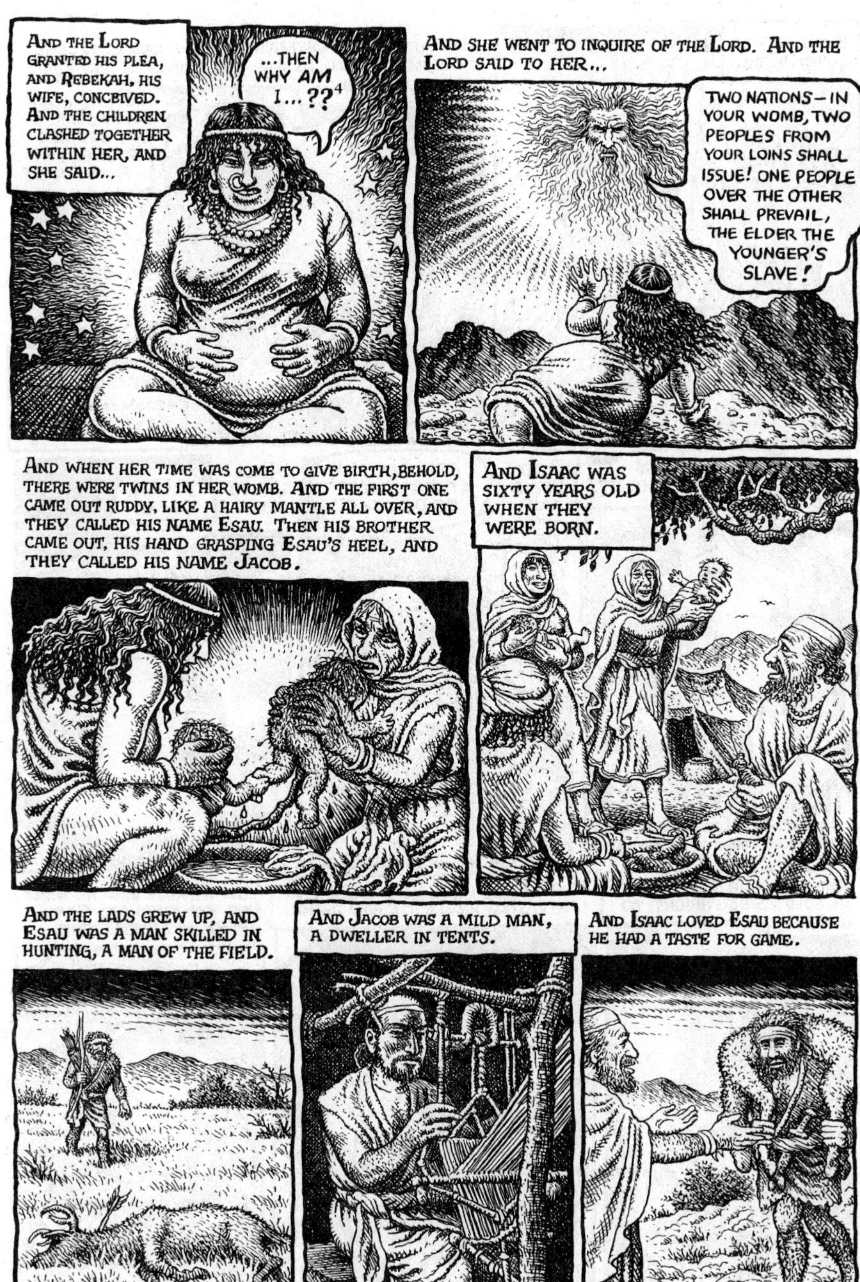

4. Rebekah's question is terse and open to interpretation. It may be elliptical (perhaps "Why am I . . . even having these babies?"), or it may imply, "Why me?"

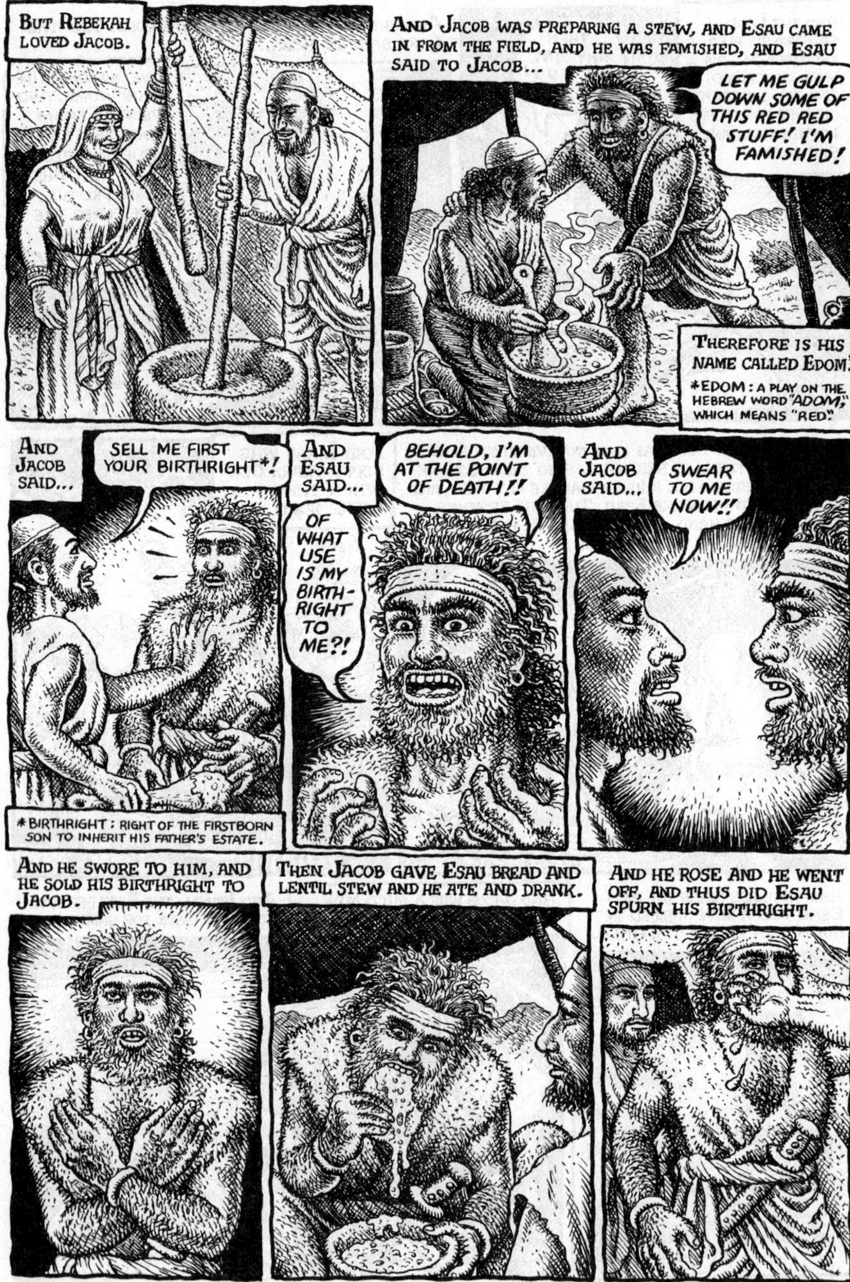
But Rebekah loved Jacob.
And Jacob was preparing a stew, and Esau came in from the field, and he was famished, and Esau said to Jacob...
Let me gulp down some of this red red stuff! I'm famished!
Therefore is his name called Edom.*
*Edom: a play on the Hebrew word "adom," which means "red."
And Jacob said...
Sell me first your birthright*!
*Birthright: right of the firstborn son to inherit his father's estate.
And Esau said...
Behold, I'm at the point of death!!
Of what use is my birthright to me?!
And Jacob said...
Swear to me now!!
And he swore to him, and he sold his birthright to Jacob.
Then Jacob gave Esau bread and lentil stew and he ate and drank.
And he rose and he went off, and thus did Esau spurn his birthright.

Genesis 27

[*Jacob and Esau*]

27. And it happened when Isaac was old, that his eyes grew too bleary to see, and he called to Esau his elder son and said to him, "My son!" and he said, "Here I am." And he said, "Look, I have grown old; I know not how soon I shall die. So now, take up, pray, your gear, your quiver and your bow, and go out to the field, and hunt me some game, and make me a dish of the kind that I love and bring it to me that I may eat, so that I may solemnly bless you before I die." And Rebekah was listening as Isaac spoke to Esau his son, and Esau went off to the field to hunt game to bring.

And Rebekah said to Jacob her son, "Look, I have heard your father speaking to Esau your brother, saying, 'Bring me some game and make me a dish that I may eat, and I shall bless you in the LORD's presence before I die.' So now, my son, listen to my voice, to what I command you. Go, pray, to the flock, and fetch me from there two choice kids that I may make them into a dish for your father of the kind he loves. And you shall bring it to your father and he shall eat, so that he may bless you before he dies." And Jacob said to Rebekah his mother, "Look, Esau my brother is a hairy man and I am a smooth-skinned man. What if my father feels me and I seem a cheat to him and bring on myself a curse and not a blessing?" And his mother said, "Upon me your curse, my son. Just listen to my voice and go, fetch them for me." And he went and he fetched and he brought to his mother, and his mother made a dish of the kind his father loved. And Rebekah took the garments of Esau her elder son, the finery that was with her in the house, and put them on Jacob her younger son, and the skins of the kids she put on his hands and on the smooth part of his neck. And she placed the dish, and the bread she had made, in the hand of Jacob her son. And he came to his father and said, "Father!" And he said, "Here I am. Who are you, my son?" And Jacob said to his father, "I am Esau your firstborn. I have done as you have spoken to me. Rise, pray, sit up, and eat of my game so that you may solemnly bless me." And Isaac said to his son, "How is it you found it this soon, my son?" And he said, "Because the LORD your God gave me good luck." And Isaac said to Jacob, "Come close, pray, that I may feel you, my son, whether you are my son Esau or not." And Jacob came close to Isaac his father and he felt him and he said, "The voice is the voice of Jacob and the hands are Esau's hands." But he did not recognize him for his hands were, like Esau's hands, hairy, and he blessed him. And he said, "Are you my son Esau?" And he said, "I am." And he said, "Serve me, that I may eat of the game of my son, so that I may solemnly bless you." And he served him and he ate, and he brought him wine and he drank. And Isaac his father said to him, "Come close, pray, and kiss me, my son." And he came close and kissed him, and he smelled his garments and he blessed him and he said, "See, the smell of my son is like the smell of the field that the LORD has blessed.

May God grant you
  from the dew of the heavens and the fat of the earth,
    and abundance of grain and drink.
May peoples serve you,
  and nations bow before you.

Be overlord to your brothers,
  may your mother's sons bow before you.
Those who curse you be cursed,
  and those who bless you, blessed."

And it happened as soon as Isaac finished blessing Jacob, and Jacob barely had left the presence of Isaac his father, that Esau his brother came back from the hunt. And he, too, made a dish and brought it to his father and he said to his father, "Let my father rise and eat of the game of his son so that you may solemnly bless me." And his father Isaac said, "Who are you?" And he said, "I am your son, your firstborn, Esau." And Isaac was seized with a very great trembling and he said, "Who is it, then, who caught game and brought it to me and I ate everything before you came and blessed him? Now blessed he stays." When Esau heard his father's words, he cried out with a great and very bitter outcry and he said to his father, "Bless me, too, Father!" And he said, "Your brother has come in deceit and has taken your blessing." And he said,

"Was his name called Jacob
  that he should trip me now twice by the heels?
My birthright he took,
  and look, now, he's taken my blessing."

And he said, "Have you not kept back a blessing for me?"

And Isaac answered and said to Esau, "Look, I made him overlord to you, and all his brothers I gave him as slaves, and with grain and wine I endowed him. For you, then, what can I do, my son?" And Esau said to his father, "Do you have but one blessing, my father? Bless me, too, Father." And Esau raised his voice and he wept. And Isaac his father answered and said to him,

"Look, from the fat of the earth be your dwelling
  and from the dew of the heavens above.
By your sword shall you live
  and your brother shall you serve.
And when you rebel
  you shall break off his yoke from your neck."

And Esau seethed with resentment against Jacob over the blessing his father had blessed him, and Esau said in his heart, "As soon as the time for mourning my father comes round, I will kill Jacob my brother." And Rebekah was told the words of Esau her elder son, and she sent and summoned Jacob her younger son and said to him, "Look, Esau your brother is consoling himself with the idea he will kill you. So now, my son, listen to my voice, and rise, flee to my brother Laban in Haran, and you may stay with him a while until your brother's wrath subsides, until your brother's rage against you subsides and he forgets what you did to him, and I shall send and fetch you from there. Why should I be bereft of you both on one day?" And Rebekah said to Isaac, "I loathe my life because of the Hittite women! If Jacob takes a wife from Hittite women like these, from the native girls, what good to me is life?"

From Genesis 28

[*Jacob's Dream*]

28. * * * And Jacob left Beersheba and set out for Haran. And he came upon a certain place and stopped there for the night, for the sun had set, and he took one of the stones of the place and put it at his head and he lay down in that place, and he dreamed, and, look, a ramp was set against the ground with its top reaching the heavens, and, look, messengers of God were going up and coming down it. And, look, the LORD was poised over him and He said, "I, the LORD, am the God of Abraham your father and the God of Isaac. The land on which you lie, to you I will give it and to your seed. And your seed shall be like the dust of the earth and you shall burst forth to the west and the east and the north and the south, and all the clans of the earth shall be blessed through you, and through your seed. And, look, I am with you and I will guard you wherever you go, and I will bring you back to this land, for I will not leave you until I have done that which I have spoken to you." And Jacob awoke from his sleep and he said, "Indeed, the LORD is in this place, and I did not know." And he was afraid and he said,

"How fearsome is this place!
This can be but the house of God,
and this is the gate of the heavens."

And Jacob rose early in the morning and took the stone he had put at his head, and he set it as a pillar and poured oil over its top. And he called the name of that place Bethel, though the name of the town before had been Luz. And Jacob made a vow, saying, "If the LORD God be with me and guard me on this way that I am going and give me bread to eat and clothing to wear, and I return safely to my father's house, then the LORD will be my God. And this stone that I set as a pillar will be a house of God, and everything that You give me I will surely tithe it to You."

From Genesis 29

[*Rachel and Leah*]

29. And Jacob lifted his feet and went on to the land of the Easterners. And he saw and, look, there was a well in the field, and, look, three flocks of sheep were lying beside it, for from that well they would water the flocks, and the stone was big on the mouth of the well. And when all the flocks were gathered there, they would roll the stone from the mouth of the well and would water the sheep and put back the stone in its place on the mouth of the well. And Jacob said to them, "My brothers, where are you from?" And they said, "We are from Haran." And he said to them, "Do you know Laban son of Nahor?" And they said, "We know him." And he said to them, "Is he well?" And they said, "He is well, and, look, Rachel his daughter is coming with the sheep." And he said, "Look, the day is still long. It is not time to gather in the herd. Water the sheep and take them to graze." And they said, "We cannot until all the flocks have gathered and the stone is rolled from the mouth of the well and we water the sheep." He was still speaking with them when Rachel came with her father's sheep, for she was a shepherdess. And it happened when Jacob saw Rachel daughter of Laban his mother's brother and the sheep of Laban his mother's brother that he stepped forward and rolled the stone from the mouth of the well and watered the sheep of Laban his mother's brother. And Jacob kissed Rachel and lifted his voice and wept. And Jacob told Rachel that he was her father's kin, and that he was Rebekah's son, and she ran and told her father. And it happened, when Laban heard the report of Jacob his sister's son, he ran toward him and embraced him and kissed him and brought him to his house. And he recounted to Laban all these things. And Laban said to him, "Indeed, you are my bone and my flesh."

And he stayed with him a month's time, and Laban said to Jacob, "Because you are my kin, should you serve me for nothing? Tell me what your wages should be." And Laban had two daughters. The name of the elder was Leah and the name of the younger Rachel. And Leah's eyes were tender, but Rachel was comely in features and comely to look at, and Jacob loved Rachel. And he said, "I will serve seven years for Rachel your younger daughter." And Laban said, "Better I should give her to you than give her to another man. Stay with me." And Jacob served seven years for Rachel, and they seemed in his eyes but a few days in his love for her. And Jacob said to Laban, "Give me my wife, for my time is done, and let me come to bed with her." And Laban gathered all the men of the place and made a feast. And when evening came, he took Leah his daughter and brought her to Jacob, and he came to bed with her. And Laban gave Zilpah his slavegirl to Leah his daughter as her slavegirl. And when morning came, look, she was Leah. And he said to Laban, "What is this you have done to me? Was it not for Rachel that I served you, and why have you deceived me?" And Laban said, "It is not done thus in our place, to give the younger girl before the firstborn. Finish out the bridal week of this one and we shall give you the other as well for the service you render me for still another seven years." And so Jacob did. And when he finished out the bridal week of the one, he gave him Rachel his daughter as wife. And Laban gave to Rachel his daughter Bilhah his slavegirl as her slavegirl. And he came to bed with Rachel, too, and, indeed, loved Rachel more than Leah, and he served him still another seven years.

* * *

From Genesis 31

[*Jacob's Flight Back to Canaan*]

31. And he[5] heard the words of Laban's sons, saying, "Jacob has taken everything of our father's, and from what belonged to our father he has made all this wealth." And Jacob saw Laban's face and, look, it was not disposed toward him

5. Jacob.

as in time past. And the LORD said to Jacob, "Return to the land of your fathers and to your birthplace and I will be with you."

* * *

From Genesis 32

[*Jacob Is Renamed Israel*]

32. * * * And he rose on that night and took his two wives and his two slavegirls and his eleven boys and he crossed over the Jabbok ford. And he took them and brought them across the stream, and he brought across all that he had. And Jacob was left alone, and a man wrestled with him until the break of dawn. And he saw that he had not won out against him and he touched his hip-socket and Jacob's hip-socket was wrenched as he wrestled with him. And he said, "Let me go, for dawn is breaking." And he said, "I will not let you go unless you bless me." And he said to him, "What is your name?" And he said, "Jacob." And he said, "Not Jacob shall your name hence be said, but Israel, for you have striven with God and men, and won out." And Jacob asked and said, "Tell your name, pray." And he said, "Why should you ask my name?" and there he blessed him. And Jacob called the name of the place Peniel, meaning, "I have seen God face to face and I came out alive." And the sun rose upon him as he passed Penuel[6] and he was limping on his hip. Therefore the children of Israel do not eat the sinew of the thigh which is by the hip-socket to this day, for he had touched Jacob's hip-socket at the sinew of the thigh.

From Genesis 33

[*Jacob and Esau Reconciled*]

33. And Jacob raised his eyes and saw and, look, Esau was coming, and with him were four hundred men. And he divided the children between Leah and Rachel, and between the two slavegirls. And he placed the slavegirls and their children first, and Leah and her children after them, and Rachel and Joseph[7] last. And he passed before them and bowed to the ground seven times until he drew near his brother. And Esau ran to meet him and embraced him and fell upon his neck and kissed him, and they wept. And he raised his eyes and saw the women and the children and he said, "Who are these with you?" And he said, "The children with whom God has favored your servant." And the slavegirls drew near, they and their children, and they bowed down. And Leah, too, and her children drew near, and they bowed down, and then Joseph and Rachel drew near and bowed down. And he said, "What do you mean by all this camp I have met?" And he said, "To find favor in the eyes of my lord." And Esau said, "I have much, my brother. Keep what you have." And Jacob said,

6. "Penuel" is an alternate spelling of "Peniel." It is not clear why the text uses both.

7. Joseph is the first-born son of Rachel and Jacob.

"O, no, pray, if I have found favor in your eyes, take this tribute from my hand, for have I not seen your face as one might see God's face, and you received me in kindness? Pray, take my blessing that has been brought you, for God has favored me and I have everything." And he pressed him, and he took it.

* * *

Genesis 37, 39–45

[*The Story of Joseph*]

37. And Jacob dwelled in the land of his father's sojournings, in the land of Canaan. This is the lineage of Jacob—Joseph, seventeen years old, was tending the flock with his brothers, assisting the sons of Bilhah and the sons of Zilpah, the wives of his father. And Joseph brought ill report of them to their father. And Israel loved Joseph more than all his sons, for he was the child of his old age, and he made him an ornamented tunic.[8] And his brothers saw it was he their father loved more than all his brothers, and they hated him and could not speak a kind word to him. And Joseph dreamed a dream and told it to his brothers and they hated him all the more. And he said to them, "Listen, pray, to this dream that I dreamed. And, look, we were binding sheaves in the field, and, look, my sheaf arose and actually stood up, and, look, your sheaves drew round and bowed to my sheaf." And his brothers said to him, "Do you mean to reign over us, do you mean to rule us?" And they hated him all the more, for his dreams and for his words. And he dreamed yet another dream and recounted it to his brothers, and he said, "Look, I dreamed a dream again, and, look, the sun and the moon and eleven stars were bowing to me." And he recounted it to his father and to his brothers, and his father rebuked him and said to him, "What is this dream that you have dreamed? Shall we really come, I and your mother and your brothers, to bow before you to the ground?" And his brothers were jealous of him, while his father kept the thing in mind.

And his brothers went to graze their father's flock at Shechem. And Israel said to Joseph, "You know, your brothers are pasturing at Shechem. Come, let me send you to them," and he said to him, "Here I am." And he said to him, "Go, pray, to see how your brothers fare, and how the flock fares, and bring me back word." And he sent him from the valley of Hebron and he came to Shechem. And a man found him and, look, he was wandering in the field, and the man asked him, saying, "What is it you seek?" And he said, "My brothers I seek. Tell me, pray, where are they pasturing?" And the man said, "They have journeyed on from here, for I heard them say, 'Let us go to Dothan.'" And Joseph went after his brothers and found them at Dothan. And they saw him from afar before he drew near them and they plotted against him to put him to death. And they said to each other, "Here comes that dream-master! And so now, let us kill him and fling him into one of the pits and we can say, a vicious beast has devoured him, and we shall see what will come of his dreams." And Reuben heard and came to his rescue and said, "We must not take his life."

8. Sometimes translated as a "coat of many colors," but the text does not actually mention color. It is probably a fancy garment with appliqués sewn on.

And Reuben said to them, "Shed no blood! Fling him into this pit in the wilderness and do not raise a hand against him"—that he might rescue him from their hands to bring him back to his father. And it happened when Joseph came to his brothers that they stripped Joseph of his tunic, the ornamented tunic that he had on him. And they took him and flung him into the pit, and the pit was empty, there was no water in it. And they sat down to eat bread, and they raised their eyes and saw and, look, a caravan of Ishmaelites was coming from Gilead, their camels bearing gum and balm and ladanum[9] on their way to take down to Egypt. And Judah said to his brothers, "What gain is there if we kill our brother and cover up his blood? Come, let us sell him to the Ishmaelites and our hand will not be against him, for he is our brother, our own flesh." And his brothers agreed. And Midianite merchantmen passed by and pulled Joseph up out of the pit and sold Joseph to the Ishmaelites for twenty pieces of silver, and they brought Joseph to Egypt.[1] And Reuben came back to the pit and, look, Joseph was not in the pit, and he rent his garments, and he came back to his brothers, and he said, "The boy is gone, and I, where can I turn?" And they took Joseph's tunic and slaughtered a kid and dipped the tunic in the blood, and they sent the ornamented tunic and had it brought to their father, and they said, "This we found. Recognize, pray, is it your son's tunic or not?" And he recognized it, and he said, "It is my son's tunic.

A vicious beast has devoured him,
Joseph is torn to shreds!"

And Jacob rent his clothes and put sackcloth round his waist and mourned for his son many days. And all his sons and all his daughters rose to console him and he refused to be consoled and he said, "Rather I will go down to my son in Sheol mourning,"[2] and his father keened for him.

But the Midianites had sold him into Egypt to Potiphar, Pharaoh's courtier, the high chamberlain.

39. And Joseph was brought down to Egypt, and Potiphar, courtier of Pharaoh, the high chamberlain, an Egyptian man, bought him from the hands of the Ishmaelites who had brought him down there. And the LORD was with Joseph and he was a successful man, and he was in the house of his Egyptian master. And his master saw that the LORD was with him, and all that he did the LORD made succeed in his hand, and Joseph found favor in his eyes and he ministered to him, and he put him in charge of his house, and all that he had he placed in his hands. And it happened from the time he put him in charge of his house and of all he had, that the LORD had blessed the Egyptian's house for Joseph's sake and the LORD's blessing was on all that he had in house and field. And he left all that he had in Joseph's hands, and he gave no thought to anything with him there save the bread he ate. And Joseph was comely in features and comely to look at.

9. A type of resin used in perfume and medicine.

1. The text here combines two different stories: that Joseph's brothers took him out of the pit and sold him to the Ishmaelites and that Midianite merchants found him and sold him. The second version seems to be part of an attempt to retell the story in a way that exonerates Reuben.

2. Sheol is the land of the dead.

And it happened after these things that his master's wife raised her eyes to Joseph and said, "Lie with me." And he refused. And he said to his master's wife, "Look, my master has given no thought with me here to what is in the house, and all that he has he has placed in my hands. He is not greater in this house than I, and he has held back nothing from me except you, as you are his wife, and how could I do this great evil and give offense to God?" And so she spoke to Joseph day after day, and he would not listen to her, to lie by her, to be with her. And it happened, on one such day, that he came into the house to perform his task, and there was no man of the men of the house there in the house. And she seized him by his garment, saying, "Lie with me." And he left his garment in her hand and he fled and went out. And so, when she saw that he had left his garment in her hand and fled outside, she called out to the people of the house and said to them, saying, "See, he has brought us a Hebrew man to play with us. He came into me to lie with me and I called out in a loud voice, and so, when he heard me raise my voice and call out, he left his garment by me and fled and went out." And she laid out his garment by her until his master returned to his house. And she spoke to him things of this sort, saying, "The Hebrew slave came into me, whom you brought us, to play with me. And so, when I raised my voice and called out, he left his garment by me and fled outside." And it happened, when his master heard his wife's words which she spoke to him, saying, "Things of this sort your slave has done to me," he became incensed. And Joseph's master took him and placed him in the prison-house, the place where the king's prisoners were held.

And he was there in the prison-house, and God was with Joseph and extended kindness to him, and granted him favor in the eyes of the prison-house warden. And the prison-house warden placed in Joseph's hands all the prisoners who were in the prison-house, and all that they were to do there, it was he who did it. The prison-house warden had to see to nothing that was in his hands, as the LORD was with him, and whatever he did, the LORD made succeed.

40. And it happened after these things that the cupbearer of the king of Egypt and his baker gave offense to their lord, the king of Egypt. And Pharaoh was furious with his two courtiers, the chief cupbearer and the chief baker. And he put them under guard in the house of the high chamberlain, the prison-house, the place where Joseph was held. And the high chamberlain assigned Joseph to them and he ministered to them, and they stayed a good while under guard.

And the two of them dreamed a dream, each his own dream, on a single night, each a dream with its own solution—the cupbearer and the baker to the king of Egypt who were held in the prison-house. And Joseph came to them in the morning and saw them and, look, they were frowning. And he asked Pharaoh's courtiers who were with him under guard in his lord's house, saying, "Why are your faces downcast today?" And they said to him, "We dreamed a dream and there is no one to solve it." And Joseph said to them, "Are not solutions from God? Pray, recount them to me." And the chief cupbearer recounted his dream to Joseph and said to him, "In my dream—and look, a vine was before me. And on the vine were three tendrils, and as it was budding, its blossom shot up, its clusters ripened to grapes. And Pharaoh's cup was in my hand. And I took the grapes and crushed them into Pharaoh's cup and I placed the cup in Pharaoh's palm." And Joseph said, "This is its solution. The three tendrils are three days.

Three days hence Pharaoh will lift up your head and restore you to your place, and you will put Pharaoh's cup in his hand, as you used to do when you were his cupbearer. But if you remember I was with you once it goes well for you, do me the kindness, pray, to mention me to Pharaoh and bring me out of this house. For indeed I was stolen from the land of the Hebrews, and here, too, I have done nothing that I should have been put in the pit." And the chief baker saw that he had solved well, and he said to Joseph, "I, too, in my dream—and look, there were three openwork baskets on my head, and in the topmost were all sorts of food for Pharaoh, baker's ware, and birds were eating from the basket over my head." And Joseph answered and said, "This is its solution. The three baskets are three days. Three days hence Pharaoh will lift up your head from upon you and impale you on a pole and the birds will eat your flesh from upon you."

And it happened on the third day, Pharaoh's birthday, that he made a feast for all his servants, and he lifted up the head of the chief cupbearer and the head of the chief baker in the midst of his servants. And he restored the chief cupbearer to his cupbearing, and he put the cup in Pharaoh's hand; and the chief baker he impaled—just as Joseph had solved it for them. But the chief cupbearer did not remember Joseph, no, he forgot him.

41. And it happened at the end of two full years that Pharaoh dreamed, and, look, he was standing by the Nile. And, look, out of the Nile came up seven cows, fair to look at and fat in flesh, and they grazed in the rushes. And, look, another seven cows came up after them out of the Nile, foul to look at and meager in flesh, and stood by the cows on the bank of the Nile. And the foul-looking meager-fleshed cows ate up the seven fair-looking fat cows, and Pharaoh awoke. And he slept and dreamed a second time, and, look, seven ears of grain came up on a single stalk, fat and goodly. And, look, seven meager ears, blasted by the east wind, sprouted after them. And the meager ears swallowed the seven fat and full ears, and Pharaoh awoke, and, look, it was a dream. And it happened in the morning that his heart pounded, and he sent and called in all the soothsayers of Egypt and all its wise men, and Pharaoh recounted to them his dreams, but none could solve them for Pharaoh. And the chief cupbearer spoke to Pharaoh, saying, "My offenses I recall today. Pharaoh had been furious with his servants and he placed me under guard in the house of the high chamberlain—me and the chief baker. And we dreamed a dream on the same night, he and I, each of us dreamed a dream with its own solution. And there with us was a Hebrew lad, a slave of the high chamberlain, and we recounted to him and he solved our dreams, each of us according to his dream he solved it. And it happened just as he had solved it for us, so it came about—me he restored to my post and him he impaled."

And Pharaoh sent and called for Joseph, and they hurried him from the pit, and he shaved and changed his garments and came before Pharaoh. And Pharaoh said to Joseph, "I dreamed a dream and none can solve it, and I have heard about you that you can understand a dream to solve it." And Joseph answered Pharaoh, saying, "Not I! God will answer for Pharaoh's well-being." And Pharaoh spoke to Joseph: "In my dream, here I was standing on the bank of the Nile, and, look, out of the Nile came up seven cows fat in flesh and fair in feature, and they grazed in the rushes. And, look, another seven cows came up after them, gaunt and very foul-featured and meager in flesh, I had not seen their like in all the land of Egypt for foulness. And the meager, foul cows ate up the first seven fat cows, and they were taken into their bellies and you could not tell that they had come into their bellies, for their looks were as foul as before, and I woke. And I saw in my dream, and, look, seven ears of grain came up on a single stalk, full and goodly. And, look, seven shriveled, meager ears, blasted by the east wind, sprouted after them. And the meager ears swallowed the seven goodly ears, and I spoke to my soothsayers and none could tell me the meaning." And Joseph said to Pharaoh, "Pharaoh's dream is one. What God is about to do He has told Pharaoh. The seven goodly cows are seven years, and the seven ears of grain are seven years. The dream is one. And the seven meager and foul cows who came up after them are seven years, and the seven meager ears of grain, blasted by the east wind, will be seven years of famine. It is just as I said to Pharaoh: what God is about to do He has shown Pharaoh. Look, seven years are coming of great plenty through all the land of Egypt. And seven years of famine will arise after them and all the plenty will be forgotten in the land of Egypt, and the famine will ravage the land, and you will not be able to tell there was plenty in the land because of that famine afterward, for it will be very grave. And the repeating of the dream to Pharaoh two times, this means that the thing has been fixed by God and God is hastening to do it. And so, let Pharaoh look out for a discerning, wise man and set him over the land of Egypt. Let Pharaoh do this: appoint overseers for the land and muster the land of Egypt in the seven years of plenty. And let them collect all the food of these good years that are coming and let them pile up grain under Pharaoh's hand, food in the cities, to keep under guard. And the food will be a reserve for the land for the seven years of famine which will be in the land of Egypt, that the land may not perish in the famine." And the thing seemed good in Pharaoh's eyes and in the eyes of his servants. And Pharaoh said to his servants, "Could we find a man like him, in whom is the spirit of God?" And Pharaoh said to Joseph, "After God has made known to you all this, there is none as discerning and wise as you. You shall be over my house, and by your lips all my folk shall be guided. By the throne alone shall I be greater than you." And Pharaoh said to Joseph, "See, I have set you over all the land of Egypt." And Pharaoh took off his ring from his hand and put it on Joseph's hand and had him clothed in fine linen clothes and placed the golden collar round his neck. And he had him ride in the chariot of his viceroy, and they called out before him *Abrekh*,[3] setting him over all the land of Egypt. And Pharaoh said to Joseph, "I am Pharaoh! Without you no man shall raise hand or foot in all the land of Egypt." And Pharaoh called Joseph's name Zaphenath-Paneah, and he gave him Asenath daughter of Potiphera, priest of On, as wife, and Joseph went out over the land of Egypt.

And Joseph was thirty years old when he stood before Pharaoh king of Egypt, and Joseph went out from Pharaoh's presence and passed through all the land of Egypt. And the land in the seven years of plenty made gatherings. And he collected all the food of the seven years that were in the land of Egypt and he placed food in the cities, the food from the fields round each city he placed within it. And Joseph piled up grain like the sand of the sea, very much, until he ceased counting, for it was beyond count.

And to Joseph two sons were born before the coming of the year of famine, whom Asenath daughter of Potiphera priest of On bore him. And Joseph called

3. Evidently an Egyptian word, perhaps meaning "Make way!"

the name of the firstborn Manasseh, meaning, God has released me from all the debt of my hardship, and of all my father's house. And the name of the second he called Ephraim, meaning, God has made me fruitful in the land of my affliction.

And the seven years of the plenty that had been in the land of Egypt came to an end. And the seven years of famine began to come, as Joseph had said, and there was famine in all the lands, but in the land of Egypt there was bread. And all the land of Egypt was hungry and the people cried out to Pharaoh for bread, and Pharaoh said to all of Egypt, "Go to Joseph. What he says to you, you must do." And the famine was over all the land. And Joseph laid open whatever had grain within and sold provisions to Egypt. And the famine grew harsh in the land of Egypt. And all the earth came to Egypt, to Joseph, to get provisions, for the famine had grown harsh in all the earth.

42. And Jacob saw that there were provisions in Egypt, and Jacob said to his sons, "Why are you fearful?" And he said, "Look, I have heard that there are provisions in Egypt. Go down there, and get us provisions from there that we may live and not die." And the ten brothers of Joseph went down to buy grain from Egypt. But Benjamin, Joseph's brother, Jacob did not send with his brothers, for he thought, Lest harm befall him.

And the sons of Israel came to buy provisions among those who came, for there was famine in the land of Canaan. As for Joseph, he was the regent of the land, he was the provider to all the people of the land. And Joseph's brothers came and bowed down to him, their faces to the ground. And Joseph saw his brothers and recognized them, and he played the stranger to them and spoke harshly to them, and said to them, "Where have you come from?" And they said, "From the land of Canaan, to buy food." And Joseph recognized his brothers but they did not recognize him. And Joseph remembered the dreams he had dreamed about them, and he said to them, "You are spies! To see the land's nakedness you have come." And they said to him, "No, my lord, for your servants have come to buy food. We are all the sons of one man. We are honest. Your servants would never be spies." And he said to them, "No! For the land's nakedness you have come to see." And they said, "Twelve brothers your servants are, we are the sons of one man in the land of Canaan, and, look, the youngest is now with our father, and one is no more." And Joseph said to them, "That's just what I told you, you are spies. In this shall you be tested—by Pharaoh! You shall not leave this place unless your youngest brother comes here. Send one of you to bring your brother, and as for the rest of you, you will be detained, and your words will be tested as to whether the truth is with you, and if not, by Pharaoh, you must be spies!" And he put them under guard for three days. And Joseph said to them on the third day, "Do this and live, for I fear God. If you are honest, let one of your brothers be detained in this very guardhouse, and the rest of you go forth and bring back provisions to stave off the famine in your homes. And your youngest brother you shall bring to me, that your words may be confirmed and you need not die." And so they did. And they said each to his brother, "Alas, we are guilty for our brother, whose mortal distress we saw when he pleaded with us and we did not listen. That is why this distress has overtaken us." Then Reuben spoke out to them in these words: "Didn't I say to you 'Do not sin against the boy,' and you would not listen? And now, look, his blood is requited." And they did not know that Joseph understood, for there was an interpreter between them. And he turned away from them and wept and returned to them and spoke to them, and he took Simeon from them and placed him in fetters before their eyes.

And Joseph gave orders to fill their baggage with grain and to put back their silver into each one's pack and to give them supplies for the way, and so he did for them. And they loaded their provisions on their donkeys and they set out from there. Then one of them opened his pack to give provender to his donkey at the encampment, and he saw his silver and, look, it was in the mouth of his bag. And he said to his brothers, "My silver has been put back and, look it's actually in my bag." And they were dumbfounded and trembled each before his brother, saying, "What is this that God has done to us?" And they came to Jacob their father, to the land of Canaan, and they told him all that had befallen them, saying, "The man who is lord of the land spoke harshly to us and made us out to be spies in the land. And we said to him, 'We are honest. We would never be spies. Twelve brothers we are, the sons of our father. One is no more and the youngest is now with our father in the land of Canaan.' And the man who is lord of the land said to us, 'By this shall I know if you are honest: one of your brothers leave with me and provisions against the famine in your homes take, and go. And bring your youngest brother to me that I may know you are not spies but are honest. I shall give you back your brother and you can trade in the land.'" And just as they were emptying their packs, look, each one's bundle of silver was in his pack. And they saw their bundles, both they and their father, and were afraid. And Jacob their father said to them, "Me you have bereaved. Joseph is no more and Simeon is no more, and Benjamin you would take! It is I who bear it all." And Reuben spoke to his father, saying, "My two sons you may put to death if I do not bring him back to you. Place him in my hands and I will return him to you." And he said, "My son shall not go down with you, for his brother is dead, and he alone remains, and should harm befall him on the way you are going, you would bring down my gray head in sorrow to Sheol."

43. And the famine grew grave in the land. And it happened when they had eaten up the provisions they had brought from Egypt, that their father said to them, "Go back, buy us some food." And Judah said to him, saying, "The man firmly warned us, saying, 'You shall not see my face unless your brother is with you.' If you are going to send our brother with us, we may go down and buy you food, but if you are not going to send him, we will not go down, for the man said to us, 'You shall not see my face unless your brother is with you.'" And Israel said, "Why have you done me this harm to tell the man you had another brother?" And they said, "The man firmly asked us about ourselves and our kindred, saying, 'Is your father still living? Do you have a brother?' And we told him, in response to these words. Could we know he would say, 'Bring down your brother?'" And Judah said to Israel his father, "Send the lad with me, and let us rise and go, that we may live and not die, neither we, nor you, nor our little ones. I will be his pledge, from my hand you may seek him: if I do not bring him to you and set him before you, I will bear the blame to you for all time. For had we not tarried, by now we could have come back twice." And Israel their father said to them, "If it must be so, do this: take of the best yield of the land in your baggage and bring down to the man as tribute some balm and some honey, gum and ladanum, pistachio nuts and almonds. And double the silver take in your hand, and the silver that was put back in the mouths of your bags bring back in your hand. Perhaps it was a mistake. And your brother take, and rise and go back to the man. And may El Shaddai grant you mercy before the man, that he discharge to you your other brother, and Benjamin. As for me, if I must be bereaved, I will be bereaved."

And the men took this tribute and double the silver they took in their hand, and Benjamin, and they rose and went down to Egypt and stood in Joseph's presence. And Joseph saw Benjamin with them and he said to the one who was over his house, "Bring the men into the house, and slaughter an animal and prepare it, for with me the men shall eat at noon." And the man did as Joseph had said, and the man brought the men to Joseph's house. And the men were afraid at being brought to Joseph's house, and they said, "Because of the silver put back in our bags the first time we've been brought, in order to fall upon us, to attack us, and to take us as slaves, and our donkeys." And they approached the man who was over Joseph's house, and they spoke to him by the entrance of the house. And they said, "Please, my lord, we indeed came down the first time to buy food, and it happened when we came to the encampment that we opened our bags and, look, each man's silver was in the mouth of his bag, our silver in full weight, and we have brought it back in our hand, and we have brought down more silver to buy food. We do not know who put our silver in our bags." And he said, "All is well with you, do not fear. Your God and the God of your father has placed treasure for you in your bags. Your silver has come to me."[4] And he brought Simeon out to them. And the man brought the men into Joseph's house, and he gave them water and they bathed their feet, and he gave provender to their donkeys. And they prepared the tribute against Joseph's arrival at noon, for they had heard that there they would eat bread. And Joseph came into the house, and they brought him the tribute that was in their hand, into the house, and they bowed down to him to the ground. And he asked how they were, and he said, "Is all well with your aged father of whom you spoke? Is he still alive?" And they said, "All is well with your servant, our father. He is still alive." And they did obeisance and bowed down. And he raised his eyes and saw Benjamin his brother, his mother's son, and he said, "Is this your youngest brother of whom you spoke to me?" And he said, "God be gracious to you, my son." And Joseph hurried out, for his feelings for his brother overwhelmed him and he wanted to weep, and he went into the chamber and wept there. And he bathed his face and came out and held himself in check and said, "Serve bread." And they served him and them separately and the Egyptians that were eating with him separately, for the Egyptians would not eat bread with the Hebrews, as it was abhorrent to Egypt. And they were seated before him, the firstborn according to his birthright, the youngest according to his youth, and the men marveled to each other. And he had portions passed to them from before him, and Benjamin's portion was five times more than the portion of all the rest, and they drank, and they got drunk with him.

44. And he charged the one who was over his house, saying, "Fill the men's bags with as much food as they can carry, and put each man's silver in the mouth of his bag. And my goblet, the silver goblet, put in the mouth of the bag

4. I.e., "I have been paid."

of the youngest, with the silver for his provisions." And he did as Joseph had spoken. The morning had just brightened when the men were sent off, they and their donkeys. They had come out of the city, they were not far off, when Joseph said to the one who was over his house, "Rise, pursue the men, and when you overtake them, say to them, 'Why have you paid back evil for good? Is not this the one from which my lord drinks, and in which he always divines?[5] You have wrought evil in what you did.'" And he overtook them and spoke to them these words. And they said to him, "Why should our lord speak words like these? Far be it from your servants to do such a thing! Why, the silver we found in the mouth of our bags we brought back to you from the land of Canaan. How then could we steal from your master's house silver or gold? He of your servants with whom it be found shall die, and, what's more, we shall become slaves to our lord." And he said, "Even so, as by your words, let it be: he with whom it be found shall become a slave to me, and you shall be clear." And they hurried and each man set down his bag on the ground and each opened his bag. And he searched, beginning with the oldest and ending with the youngest, and he found the goblet in Benjamin's bag. And they rent their garments, and each loaded his donkey and they returned to the city.

And Judah with his brothers came into Joseph's house, for he was still there, and they threw themselves before him to the ground. And Joseph said to them, "What is this deed you have done? Did you not know that a man like me would surely divine?" And Judah said, "What shall we say to my lord? What shall we speak and how shall we prove ourselves right? God has found out your servants' crime. Here we are, slaves to my lord, both we and the one in whose hand the goblet was found." And he said, "Far be it from me to do this! The man in whose hand the goblet was found, he shall become my slave, and you, go up in peace to your father." And Judah approached him and said, "Please, my lord, let your servant speak a word in my lord's hearing and let your wrath not flare against your servant, for you are like Pharaoh. My lord had asked his servants, saying, 'Do you have a father or brother?' And we said to my lord, 'We have an aged father and a young child of his old age, and his brother being dead, he alone is left of his mother, and his father loves him.' And you said to your servants, 'Bring him down to me, that I may set my eyes on him.' And we said to my lord, 'The lad cannot leave his father. Should he leave his father, he would die.' And you said to your servants, 'If your youngest brother does not come down with you, you shall not see my face again.' And it happened when we went up to your servant, my father, that we told him the words of my lord. And our father said, 'Go back, buy us some food.' And we said, 'We cannot go down. If our youngest brother is with us, we shall go down. For we cannot see the face of the man if our youngest brother is not with us.' And your servant, our father, said to us, 'You know that two did my wife bear me. And one went out from me and I thought, O, he's been torn to shreds, and I have not seen him since. And should you take this one, too, from my presence and harm befall him, you would bring down my gray head in evil to Sheol.' And so, should I come to your servant, my father, and the lad be not with us, for his life is bound to the lad's, when he saw the lad was not with us, he would die, and your servants would bring down the gray head of your servant, our father, in sorrow to Sheol. For your servant became pledge for the lad to my father, saying, 'If I do

5. Predicts the future from the appearance of liquid in the cup.

not bring him to you, I will bear the blame to my father for all time.' And so, let your servant, pray, stay instead of the lad as a slave to my lord, and let the lad go up with his brothers. For how shall I go up to my father, if the lad be not with us? Let me see not the evil that would find out my father!"

45. And Joseph could no longer hold himself in check before all who stood attendance upon him, and he cried, "Clear out everyone around me!" And no man stood with him when Joseph made himself known to his brothers. And he wept aloud and the Egyptians heard and the house of Pharaoh heard. And Joseph said to his brothers, "I am Joseph. Is my father still alive?" But his brothers could not answer him, for they were dismayed before him. And Joseph said to his brothers, "Come close to me, pray," and they came close, and he said, "I am Joseph your brother whom you sold into Egypt. And now, do not be pained and do not be incensed with yourselves that you sold me down here, because for sustenance God has sent me before you. Two years now there has been famine in the heart of the land, and there are yet five years without plowing and harvest. And God has sent me before you to make you a remnant on earth[6] and to preserve life, for you to be a great surviving group. And so, it is not you who sent me here but God, and He has made me father to Pharaoh and lord to all his house and ruler over all the land of Egypt. Hurry and go up to my father and say to him, 'Thus says your son Joseph: God has made me lord to all Egypt. Come down to me, do not delay. And you shall dwell in the land of Goshen[7] and shall be close to me, you and your sons and the sons of your sons and your flocks and your cattle and all that is yours. And I will sustain you there, for yet five years of famine remain—lest you lose all, you and your household and all that is yours.' And, look, your own eyes can see, and the eyes of my brother Benjamin, that it is my very mouth that speaks to you. And you must tell my father all my glory in Egypt and all that you have seen, and hurry and bring down my father here." And he fell upon the neck of his brother Benjamin and he wept, and Benjamin wept on his neck. And he kissed all his brothers and wept over them. And after that, his brothers spoke with him.

And the news was heard in the house of Pharaoh, saying, "Joseph's brothers have come." And it was good in Pharaoh's eyes and in his servants' eyes. And Pharaoh said to Joseph, "Say to your brothers: 'This now do. Load up your beasts and go, return to the land of Canaan. And take your father and your households and come back to me, that I may give you the best of the land of Egypt, and you shall live off the fat of the land.' And you, charge them: 'This now do. Take you from the land of Egypt wagons for your little ones and for your wives, and convey your father, and come. And regret not your belongings, for the best of all the land of Egypt is yours.'"

And so the sons of Israel did, and Joseph gave them wagons, as Pharaoh had ordered, and he gave them supplies for the journey. To all of them, each one, he gave changes of garments, and to Benjamin he gave three hundred pieces of silver and five changes of garments. And to his father he sent as follows: ten donkeys conveying from the best of Egypt, and ten she-asses conveying grain and bread and food for his father for the journey. And he sent off his brothers and they went, and he said to them, "Do not be perturbed on the journey."

6. I.e., "to ensure a posterity for you." 7. The Nile delta.

And they went up from Egypt and they came to the land of Canaan to Jacob their father. And they told him, saying, "Joseph is still alive," and that he was ruler in all the land of Egypt. And his heart stopped, for he did not believe them. And they spoke to him all the words of Joseph that he had spoken to them, and he saw the wagons that Joseph had sent to convey him, and the spirit of Jacob their father revived. And Israel said, "Enough! Joseph my son is still alive. Let me go see him before I die."

From Genesis 46, 47

[*Jacob Travels to Egypt*]

46. And Israel journeyed onward, with all that was his, and he came to Beersheba, and he offered sacrifices to the God of his father Isaac. And God said to Israel through visions of the night, "Jacob, Jacob," and he said, "Here I am." And He said, "I am the god, God of your father. Fear not to go down to Egypt, for a great nation I will make you there. I Myself will go down with you to Egypt and I Myself will surely bring you back up as well, and Joseph shall lay his hand on your eyes." And Jacob arose from Beersheba, and the sons of Israel conveyed Jacob their father and their little ones and their wives in the wagons Pharaoh had sent to convey him. And they took their cattle and their substance that they had got in the land of Canaan and they came to Egypt, Jacob and all his seed with him. His sons, and the sons of his sons with him, his daughters and the daughters of his sons, and all his seed, he brought with him to Egypt.

* * *

And Joseph harnessed his chariot and went up to meet Israel his father in Goshen, and appeared before him and fell on his neck, and he wept on his neck a long while. And Israel said to Joseph, "I may die now, after seeing your face, for you are still alive."

* * *

47. * * * And Joseph settled his father and his brothers and gave them a holding in the land of Egypt in the best of the land, in the land of Rameses, as Pharaoh had commanded. And Joseph sustained his father and his brothers and all his father's household with bread, down to the mouths of the little ones.

* * *

From Genesis 50

[*The Death of Joseph*]

50. * * * And Joseph dwelled in Egypt, he and his father's household, and Joseph lived a hundred and ten years. And Joseph saw the third generation of sons from Ephraim, and the sons, as well, of Machir son of Manasseh were born on Joseph's knees. And Joseph said to his brothers, "I am about to die, and God will surely single you out and take you up from this land to the land He promised to Isaac and to Jacob." And Joseph made the sons of Israel swear, saying, "When God indeed singles you out, you shall take up my bones from this place." And Joseph died, a hundred and ten years old, and they embalmed him and he was put in a coffin in Egypt.

From Exodus 19–20[1]

[*Moses Receives the Law*]

19. On the third new moon of the Israelites' going out from Egypt, on this day did they come to the Wilderness of Sinai. And they journeyed onward from Rephidim and they came to the Wilderness of Sinai, and Israel camped there over against the mountain. And Moses had gone up to God, and the LORD called out to him from the mountain, saying, "Thus shall you say to the house of Jacob, and shall you tell to the Israelites: 'You yourselves saw what I did to Egypt, and I bore you on the wings of eagles[2] and I brought you to Me. And now, if you will truly heed My voice and keep My covenant, you will become for Me a treasure among all the peoples, for Mine is all the earth. And as for you, you will become for Me a kingdom of priests and a holy nation.' These are the words that you shall speak to the Israelites."

And Moses came and he called to the elders of the people, and he set before them all these words that the LORD had charged him. And all the people answered together and said, "Everything that the LORD has spoken we shall do." And Moses brought back the people's words to the LORD. And the LORD said to Moses, "Look, I am about to come to you in the utmost cloud, so that the people may hear as I speak to you, and you as well they will trust for all time." And Moses told the people's words to the LORD. And the LORD said to Moses, "Go to the people and consecrate them today and tomorrow, and they shall wash their cloaks. And they shall ready themselves for the third day, for on the third day the LORD will come down before the eyes of all the people on Mount Sinai. And you shall set bounds for the people all around, saying, 'Watch yourselves not to go up on the mountain or to touch its edge. Whosoever touches the mountain is doomed to die. No hand shall touch him,[3] but He shall surely be stoned or be shot, whether beast or man, he shall not live. When the ram's horn blasts long, they[4] it is who will go up the mountain.'" And Moses came down from the mountain to the people, and he consecrated the people, and they washed their cloaks. And he said to the people, "Ready yourselves for three days. Do not go near a woman."[5] And it happened on the third day as it turned morning, that there was thunder and lightning and a heavy cloud on the mountain and the sound of the ram's horn, very strong, and

1. Translated by Robert Alter, to whose notes some of the following annotations are indebted.
2. A metaphor for salvation. "What I did unto the Egyptians" refers to the plagues that afflicted Egypt and to the destruction of the Egyptian army, as it pursued the departing Israelites, at the Red Sea.
3. Whoever violates the ban on touching the mountain will be impure and an outcast from the community. Therefore he has to be killed at a distance, with stones or arrows.
4. I.e., Moses and Aaron.
5. Sexual abstinence and the washing of clothes were methods of ritual purification.

all the people who were in the camp trembled. And Moses brought out the people toward God from the camp and they stationed themselves at the bottom of the mountain. And Mount Sinai was all in smoke because the LORD had come down on it in fire, and its smoke went up like the smoke from a kiln, and the whole mountain trembled greatly. And the sound of the ram's horn grew stronger and stronger. Moses would speak, and God would answer him with voice.[6] And the LORD came down on Mount Sinai, to the mountaintop, and the LORD called Moses to the mountaintop, and Moses went up. And the LORD said to Moses, "Go down, warn the people, lest they break through to the LORD to see and many of them perish. And the priests, too, who come near to the LORD, shall consecrate themselves,[7] lest the LORD burst forth against them." And Moses said to the Lord, "The people will not be able to come up to Mount Sinai, for You Yourself warned us, saying, 'Set bounds to the mountain and consecrate it.'" And the LORD said to him, "Go down, and you shall come up, you and Aaron[8] with you, and the priests and the people shall not break through to go up to the LORD, lest He burst forth against them." And Moses went down to the people and said it to them.

20. And God spoke all these words, saying: "I am the LORD your God Who brought you out of the land of Egypt, out of the house of slaves. You[9] shall have no other gods beside Me. You shall make you no carved likeness and no image of what is in the heavens above or what is on the earth below or what is in the waters beneath the earth. You shall not bow to them and you shall not worship them, for I am the LORD your God, a jealous god, reckoning the crime of fathers with sons, with the third generation and with the fourth, for My foes and doing kindness to the thousandth generation for My friends and for those who keep My commands. You shall not take the name of the LORD your God in vain, for the LORD will not acquit whosoever takes His name in vain. Remember the sabbath day to hallow it. Six days you shall work and you shall do your tasks, but the seventh day is a sabbath to the LORD your God. You shall do no task, you and your son and your daughter, your male slave and your slavegirl and your beast and your sojourner who is within your gates. For six days did the LORD make the heavens and the earth, the sea and all that is in it, and He rested on the seventh day. Therefore did the LORD bless the sabbath day and hallow it. Honor your father and your mother, so that your days may be long on the soil that the LORD your God has given you. You shall not murder. You shall not commit adultery. You shall not steal. You shall not bear false witness against your fellow man. You shall not covet your fellow man's wife, or his male slave, or his slavegirl, or his ox, or his donkey, or anything that your fellow man has."

And all the people were seeing the thunder and the flashes and the sound of the ram's horn and the mountain in smoke, and the people saw and they drew back and stood at a distance. And they said to Moses, "Speak you with us that we may hear, and let not God speak with us lest we die." And Moses said to the

6. I.e., with words.

7. I.e., they are to purify themselves and remain at the bottom of the mountain as the rest of the people do.

8. Moses' closest companion and in an early tradition his brother; Aaron was Israel's first High Priest.

9. Here and throughout this passage, the Hebrew text uses the singular of "you" (formulations of law elsewhere in the Hebrew Bible use the plural). The commandments are thus addressed to each person individually.

people, "Do not fear, for in order to test you God has come and in order that His fear be upon you, so that you do not offend." And the people stood at a distance, and Moses drew near the thick cloud where God was.

* * *

From Job[1]

1. A man there was in the land of Uz[2] Job, his name. And the man was blameless and upright and feared God and shunned evil. And seven sons were born to him, and three daughters. And his flocks came to seven thousand sheep and three thousand camels and five hundred yokes of cattle and five hundred she-asses and a great abundance of slaves. And that man was greater than all the dwellers of the East. And his sons would go and hold a feast, in each one's house on his set day, and they would call to their sisters to eat and drink with them. And it happened when the days of the feast came round, that Job would send and consecrate them and rise early in the morning and offer up burnt offerings according to the number of them all. For Job thought, Perhaps my sons have offended and cursed God in their hearts. Thus would Job do at all times.

And one day, the sons of God[3] came to stand in attendance before the LORD, and the Adversary,[4] too, came among them. And the LORD said to the Adversary, "From where do you come?" And the Adversary answered the LORD and said, "From roaming the earth and walking about in it." And the LORD said to the Adversary, "Have you paid heed to my servant Job, for there is none like him on earth, a blameless and upright man, who fears God and shuns evil?" And the Adversary answered the LORD and said, "Does Job fear God for nothing? Have You not hedged him about and his household and all that he has all around? The work of his hands You have blessed, and his flocks have spread over the land. And yet, reach out Your hand, pray, and strike all he has. Will he not curse You to Your face? And the LORD said to the Adversary, "Look, all that he has is in your hands. Only against him do not reach out your hand." And the Adversary went out from before the LORD's presence.

And one day, his sons and his daughters were eating and drinking wine in the house of their brother, the firstborn. And a messenger came to Job and said, "The cattle were plowing and the she-asses grazing by them, and Sabeans fell upon them and took them, and the lads they struck down by the edge of the sword, and I alone escaped to tell you." This one was still speaking when another came and said, "God's fire fell from the heavens and burned among the sheep and the lads and consumed them, and I alone escaped to tell you." This one was still speaking when another came and said, "Chaldaeans set out in three bands and pounced upon the camels and took them, and the lads they struck down by the edge of the sword." This one was still speaking when another came and said,

1. Translated by Robert Alter, to whom some of the following notes are indebted.
2. *'Uts* (Uz) means "counsel," or "advice," so the story takes place in an unreal, fabulous landscape: the Land of Counsel.
3. This phrase reflects a premonotheistic idea of a family or council of gods.
4. "The Adversary," or "the satan" (*hasatan* in the original), means a person, thing, or set of circumstances that is an obstacle to someone. It does not mean "devil"; the modern connotations of evil are absent from the original word, and clearly this "satan" is part of God's court.

"Your sons and your daughters were eating and drinking wine in the house of their brother, the firstborn. And, look, a great wind came from beyond the wilderness and struck the four corners of the house, and it fell on the young people, and they died. And I alone escaped to tell you." And Job rose and tore his garment and shaved his head and fell to the earth and bowed down.[5] And he said,

"Naked I came out from my mother's womb,
  and naked shall I return there.
The LORD has given and the LORD has taken.
  May the LORD's name be blessed."

With all this, Job did not offend, nor did he put blame on God.

2. And one day, the sons of God came to stand in attendance before the LORD, and the Adversary, too, came among them to stand in attendance before the LORD. And the LORD said to the Adversary, "From whence do you come?" And the Adversary answered the LORD and said, "From roaming the earth and walking about in it." And the LORD said to the Adversary, "Have you paid heed to My servant Job, for there is none like him on earth, a blameless and upright man, who fears God and shuns evil and still clings to his innocence, and you incited Me against him to destroy him for nothing." And the Adversary answered the LORD and said, "Skin for skin![6] A man will give all he has for his own life. Yet, reach out, pray, your hand and strike his bone and his flesh. Will he not curse You to Your face?" And the LORD said to the Adversary, "Here he is in your hands. Only preserve his life." And the Adversary went out from before the LORD's presence. And he struck Job with a grievous burning rash from the soles of his feet to the crown of his head. And he took a potsherd to scrape himself with, and he was sitting among the ashes. And his wife said to him, "Do you still cling to your innocence? Curse God and die." And he said to her, "You speak as one of the base women would speak. Shall we accept good from God, too, and evil we shall not accept?" With all this, Job did not offend with his lips.

And Job's three companions heard of all this harm that had come upon him, and they came, each from his place—Eliphaz the Temanite and Bildad the Shuhite and Zophar the Naamathite, and they agreed to meet to grieve with him and to comfort him. And they lifted up their eyes from afar and did not recognize him, and they lifted up their voices and wept, and each tore his garment, and they tossed dust on their heads toward the heavens. And they sat with him on the ground seven days and seven nights, and none spoke a word to him, for they saw that the pain was very great.

3. Afterward, Job opened his mouth and cursed his day. And Job spoke up and he said:

Annul the day that I was born
  and the night that said, "A man is conceived."
That day, let it be darkness.
  Let God above not seek it out,

5. Gestures of mourning.
6. An obscure proverb, perhaps meaning that Job will truly suffer only once pain touches his own skin.

nor brightness shine upon it.
Let darkness, death's shadow, foul it,
let a cloud-mass rest upon it,
let day-gloom dismay it.
That night, let murk overtake it.
Let it not join in the days of the year,
let it not enter the number of months.
Oh, let that night be barren,
let it have no song of joy.
Let the day-cursers hex it,
those ready to rouse Leviathan.[7]
Let its twilight stars go dark.
Let it hope for day in vain,
and let it not see the eyelids of dawn.
For it did not shut the belly's doors
to hide wretchedness from my eyes.
Why did I not die from the womb,
from the belly come out, breathe my last?
Why did knees welcome me,
and why breasts, that I should suck?
For now I would lie and be still,
would sleep and know repose
with kings and the councilors of earth,
who build ruins for themselves,
or with princes, possessors of gold,
who fill their houses with silver.
Or like a buried stillbirth I'd be,
like babes who never saw light.
There the wicked cease their troubling,
and there the weary repose.
All together the prisoners are tranquil,
they hear not the taskmaster's voice.
The small and the great are there,
and the slave is free of his master.
Why give light to the wretched
and life to the deeply embittered,
who wait for death in vain,
dig for it more than for treasure,
who rejoice at the tomb,
are glad when they find the grave?
—To a man whose way is hidden,
and God has hedged him about.
For before my bread my moaning comes,
and my roar pours out like water.
For I feared a thing—it befell me,
what I dreaded came upon me.
I was not quiet, I was not still,
I had no repose, and trouble came.

7. Leviathan is a sea monster, representing chaos in Canaanite mythology. The "day-cursers" are magicians.

4. And Eliphaz spoke out and he said:

If speech were tried against you, could you stand it?
  Yet who can hold back words?
Look, you reproved many,
  and slack hands you strengthened.
The stumbler your words lifted up,
  and bended knees you bolstered.
But now it comes to you and you cannot stand it,
  it reaches you and you are dismayed.
Is not your reverence your safety,
  your hope—your blameless ways?
Recall, pray: what innocent man has died,
  and where were the upright demolished?
As I have seen, those who plow mischief,
  those who plant wretchedness, reap it.
Through God's breath they die,
  before his nostrils' breathing they vanish.
The lion's roar, the maned beast's sound—
  and the young lions' teeth are smashed.
The king of beasts dies with no prey,
  the whelps of the lion are scattered.
And to me came a word in secret,
  and my ear caught a tag-end of it,
in musings from nighttime's visions
  when slumber falls upon men.
Fear called to me, and trembling,
  and all my limbs it gripped with fear.
And a spirit passed over my face,
  made the hair on my flesh stand on end.
It halted, its look unfamiliar,
  an image before my eyes,
    stillness, and a sound did I hear:
Can a mortal be cleared before God,
  can a man be made pure by his Maker?
Why, His servants He does not trust,
  His agents He charges with blame.
All the more so, the clay-house dwellers,
  whose foundation is in the dust,
    who are crushed more quickly than moths.
From morning to eve they are shattered,
  unawares they are lost forever.
Should their life-thread be broken within them,
  they die, and without any wisdom.

5. Call out, pray: will any answer you,
  and to whom of the angels will you turn?
For anger kills a fool,
  and the simple, envy slays.
I have seen a fool striking root—
  all at once his abode I saw cursed.

His children are distant from rescue
  and are crushed in the gate—none will save.
Whose harvest the hungry eat
  and from among thorns they take it away,
    and the thirsty pant for their wealth.
For crime does not spring from the dust,
  nor from the soil does wretchedness sprout.
But man is to wretchedness born
  like sparks flying upward.
Yet I search for El[8]
  and to God I make my case,
Who does great things without limit
  wonders beyond all number,
Who brings rain down on the earth
  and sends water over the fields.
Who raises the lowly on high—
  the downcast are lifted in rescue.
Thwarts the designs of the cunning,
  and their hands do not perform wisely.
He entraps the wise in their cunning,
  and the crooked's counsel proves hasty.
By day they encounter darkness,
  as in night they go groping at noon.
He rescues the simple from the sword,
  and from the hand of the strong, the impoverished,
and the indigent then has hope,
  and wickedness clamps its mouth shut.
Why, happy the man whom God corrects.
  Shaddai's reproof do not spurn!
For He causes pain and binds the wound,
  He deals blows but His hands will heal.
In six straits He will save you,
  and in seven harm will not touch you.
In famine He redeems you from death,
  and in battle from the sword.
From the scourge of the tongue you are hidden,
  and you shall fear not assault when it comes.
At assault and starvation you laugh,
  and the beasts of the earth you fear not.
With the stones of the field is your pact,
  the beasts of the field leagued with you.
And you shall know that your tent is peaceful,
  probe your home and find nothing amiss.
And you shall know that your seed is abundant,
  your offspring like the grass of the earth.
You shall come to the grave in vigor,
  as grain-shocks mount in their season.
Look, this we have searched, it is so.
  Hear it, and you—you should know.

8. God.

6. And Job spoke out and he said:

Could my anguish but be weighed,
  and my disaster on the scales be borne,
they would be heavier now than the sand of the sea.
  Thus my words are choked back.
For Shaddai's arrows are in me—
  their venom my spirit drinks.
    The terrors of God beset me.
Does the wild ass bray over his grass,
  the ox bellow over his feed?[9]
Is tasteless food eaten unsalted,
  does the oozing of mallows have savor?[1]
My throat refuses to touch them.
  They resemble my sickening flesh.
If only my wish were fulfilled,
  and my hope God might grant.
If God would deign to crush me,
  loose His hand and tear me apart.
And this still would be my comfort,
  I shrink back in pangs—he spares not.
    Yet I withhold not the Holy One's words.
What is my strength, that I should hope,
  and what my end that I should endure?
Is my strength the strength of stones,
  is my flesh made of bronze?
Indeed, there is no help within me,
  and prudence is driven from me.
The blighted man's friend owes him kindness,
  though the fear of Shaddai he forsake.
My brothers betrayed like a wadi,[2]
  like the channel of brooks that run dry.
They are dark from the ice,
  snow heaped on them.
When they warm, they are gone,
  in the heat they melt from their place.
The paths that they go on are winding,
  they mount in the void and are lost.
The caravans of Tema looked out,[3]
  the convoys of Sheba awaited.
Disappointed in what they had trusted,
  they reached it and their hopes were dashed.
For now you are His.
  You see panic and you fear.

9. Rhetorical questions. The idea is that animals do not complain when fed appropriately, and, by analogy, humans do not complain unless they are truly suffering.

1. The tasteless food may be literal (Job cannot eat because he is too upset), or metaphorical.

2. A desert ravine, which is full of water only in the rainy season; when summer comes, it runs dry.

3. For water, continuing the image of the dried-up *wadi*.

Did I say, Give for me,
  and with your wealth pay a ransom for me,
and free me from the hands of the foe,
  from the oppressors' hands redeem me?
Instruct me—as for me, I'll keep silent,
  and let me know where I went wrong.
How forceful are honest words.
  Yet what rebuke is the rebuke by you?
Do you mean to rebuke with words,
  treat the speech of the desperate as wind?
Even for the orphan you cast lots,
  and haggle for your companion.
And now, deign to turn toward me.
  To your face I will surely not lie.
Relent, pray, let there be no injustice.
  Relent. I am yet in the right.
Is there injustice on my tongue?
  Does my palate not taste disasters?

7. Does not man have fixed service on earth,
  and like a hired worker's his days?
Like a slave he pants for shade,
  like a hired worker he waits for his pay.
Thus I was heir to futile moons,
  and wretched nights were allotted to me.
Lying down, I thought, When shall I rise?—
  Each evening, I was sated with tossing till dawn.
My flesh was clothed with worms and earth-clods,
  my skin rippled with running sores.
My days are swifter than the weaver's shuttle.
  They snap off without any hope.
Recall that my life is a breath.
  Not again will my eyes see good.
The eye of who sees me will not make me out.
  Your eyes are on me—I am gone.
A cloud vanishes and goes off.
  Thus, who goes down to Sheol[4] will not come up.
He will not return to his home.
  His place will not know him again.
As for me, I will not restrain my mouth.
  I would lament with my spirit in straits
    I would speak when my being is bitter.
Am I Yamm[5] or am I the Sea Beast,
  that You should put a watch upon me?
When I thought my couch would console me,
  that my bed would bear my lament,
You panicked me in dreams

4. The land of the dead.
5. Yamm is the sea god in Canaanite mythology, also known as Leviathan; he was subdued by Baal, the weather god, whom Job here associates with his own God.

and in visions you struck me with terror.
And my throat would have chosen choking,
my bones—death.
I am sickened—I won't live forever.
Let me be, for my days are mere breath.
What is man that You make him great
and that You pay heed to him?
You single him out every morning,
every moment examine him.
How long till You turn away from me?
You don't let me go while I swallow my spit.[6]
What is my offense that I have done to You,
O Watcher of man?
Why did You make me Your target,
and I became a burden to You?
And why do You not pardon my crime
and let my sin pass away?
For soon I shall lie in the dust.
You will seek me, and I shall be gone.

8. And Bildad the Shuhite spoke out and he said,

How long will you jabber such things?—
the words of your mouth, one huge wind.
Would God pervert justice,
would Shaddai pervert what is right?
If your children offended Him,
He dispatched them because of their crime.
If you yourself sought out God,
and pleaded to Shaddai,
if you were honest and pure,
by now He would rouse Himself for you,
and would make your righteous home whole.
Then your beginning would seem a trifle
and your latter day very grand.
For ask, pray, generations of old,
take in what their fathers found out.
For we are but yesterday, unknowing,
for our days are a shadow on earth.
Will they not teach you and say to you,
and from their heart bring out words?
Will papyrus sprout with no marsh,
reeds grow grand without water?
Still in its blossom, not yet plucked,
before any grass it will wither.
Thus is the end of all who forget God,
and the hope of the tainted is lost.
Whose faith is mere cobweb,
a spider's house his trust.

6. I.e., not even for a second.

He leans on his house and it will not stand,
he grasps it and it does not endure.
—He is moist in the sun,
and his tendrils push out in his garden.
Round a knoll his roots twist,
on a stone house they take hold.
If his place should uproot him
and deny him—"I never saw you,"
why, this is his joyous way,
from another soil he will spring.
Look, God will not spurn the blameless,
nor hold the hand of evildoers.
He will yet fill your mouth with laughter
and your lips with a shout of joy.
Your foes will be clothed in disgrace,
and the tent of the wicked gone.

9. And Job spoke out and he said

Of course, I knew it was so:
how can man be right before God?
Should a person bring grievance against Him,
He will not answer one of a thousand.
Wise in mind, staunch in strength,
who can argue with Him and come out whole?
He uproots mountains and they know not,
overturns them in His wrath.
He makes earth shake in its setting,
and its pillars shudder.
He bids the sun not to rise,
and the stars He seals up tight.
He stretches the heavens alone
and tramples the crests of the sea.
He makes the Bear and Orion,
the Pleiades and the South Wind's chambers.
He performs great things without limit
and wonders without number.
Look, He passes over me and I do not see,
slips by me and I cannot grasp Him.
Look, He seizes—who can resist Him?
Who can tell him, "What do You do?"
God will not relent his fury.
Beneath him Rahab's[7] minions stoop.
And yet, as for me, I would answer Him,
would choose my words with Him.
Though in the right, I can't make my plea.
I would have to entreat my own judge.
Should I call out and He answer me,
I would not trust Him to heed my voice

7. Another name for the sea monster (Baal, or Leviathan).

Who for a hair would crush me
  and make my wounds many for nought.
He does not allow me to catch my breath
  as He sates me with bitterness.
If it's strength—He is staunch,
  and if it's justice—who can arraign Him?
Though in the right, my mouth will convict me,
  I am blameless, yet He makes me crooked.
I am blameless—I know not myself,
  I loathe my life.
It's all the same, and so I thought:
  the blameless and the wicked He destroys.
If a scourge causes death in an instant,
  He mocks the innocent's plight.
The earth is given in the wicked man's hand,
  the face of its judges He veils.
    If not He—then who else?
And my days are swifter than a courier.
  They have fled and have never seen good,
slipped away like reed ships,
  like an eagle swooping on prey.
If I said, I would forget my lament.
  I would leave my grim mood and be gladdened,
I was in terror of all my suffering.
  I knew You would not acquit me.
I will be guilty.
  Why should I toil in vain?
Should I bathe in snow,
  make my palms pure with lye,
You would yet plunge me into a pit,
  and my robes would defile me.
For He is not a man like me that I might answer Him,
  that we might come together in court.
Would there were an arbiter between us,
  who could lay his hand on us both,
who could take from me His rod,
  and His terror would not confound me.
I would speak, and I will not fear Him,
  for that is not the way I am.

10. My whole being loathes my life.
Let me give vent to my lament.
    Let me speak when my being is bitter.
I shall say to God: Do not convict me.
  Inform me why You accuse me.
Is it good for You to oppress,
  to spurn Your own palms' labor,
    and on the council of the wicked to shine?
Do You have the eyes of mortal flesh,
  do You see as man would see?
Are Your days like a mortal's days,

Your years like the years of a man,
that You should search out my crime
and inquire for my offense?
You surely know I am not guilty,
but there is none who saves from Your hand.
Your hands fashioned me and made me,
and then You turn round and destroy me!
Recall, pray, that like clay You worked me,
and to the dust You will make me return.
Why, You poured me out like milk
and like cheese You curdled me.
With skin and flesh You clothed me,
with bones and sinews entwined me.
Life and kindness you gave me,
and Your precepts my spirit kept.
Yet these did You hide in Your heart;
I knew that this was with You:
If I offended, You kept watch upon me
and of my crime would not acquit me.
If I was guilty, alas for me,
and though innocent, I could not raise my head,
sated with shame and surfeited with disgrace.
Like a triumphant lion You hunt me,
over again wondrously smite me.
You summon new witnesses against me
and swell up your anger toward me—
vanishings and hard service are mine.
And why from the womb did You take me?
I'd breathe my last, no eye would have seen me.
As though I had not been, I would be.
From belly to grave I'd be carried.
My days are but few—let me be.
Turn away that I may have some gladness
before I go, never more to return,
to the land of dark and death's shadow,
the land of gloom, thickest murk,
death's shadow and disorder,
where it shines thickest murk.

11. And Zophar the Naamathite spoke out and he said:
Shall a swarm of words be unanswered,
and should a smooth talker be in the right?
Your lies may silence folk,
you mock and no one protests.
And you say: my teaching is spotless,
and I am pure in your eyes.
Yet, if only God would speak,
and He would open His lips against you,
would tell you wisdom's secrets,
for prudence is double-edged.
And know, God leaves some of your crime forgotten.

Can you find what God has probed,
can you find Shaddai's last end?
Higher than heaven, what can you do,
deeper than Sheol, what can you know?
Longer than earth is its measure,
and broader than the sea.
Should He slip away or confine or assemble,
who can resist Him?
For He knows the empty folk,
He sees wrongdoing and surely takes note.
And a hollow man will get a wise heart
when a wild ass is born a man.
If you yourself readied your heart
and spread out your palms to Him,
if there is wrongdoing in your hands, remove it,
let no mischief dwell in your tents.
For then you will raise your face unstained,
you will be steadfast and will not fear.
For you will forget wretchedness,
like water gone off, recall it.
And life will rise higher than noon,
will soar, will be like the morning.
And you will trust, for there is hope,
will search, and lie secure.
You will stretch out, and none make you tremble,
and many pay court to you.
And the eyes of the wicked will pine,
escape will be lost to them,
and their hope—a last gasp of breath.

12. And Job spoke up and he said:
Oh yes, you are the people,
and with you wisdom will die!
But I, too, have a mind like you,
I am no less than you,
and who does not know such things?
A laughing-stock to his friend I am,
who calls to his God and is answered,
a laughing-stock of the blameless just man.
The smug man's thought scorns disaster,
readied for those who stumble.
The tents of despoilers are tranquil,
provokers of God are secure,
whom God has led by the hand.
Yet ask of the beasts, they will teach you,
the fowl of the heavens will tell you,
or speak to the earth, it will teach you,
the fish of the sea will inform you.
Who has not known in all these
that the LORD's hand has done this?
In Whose hand is the breath of each living thing,

and the spirit of all human flesh.
Does not the ear make out words,
the palate taste food?
In the aged is wisdom,
and in length of days understanding.
With Him are wisdom and strength,
He possesses counsel and understanding.
Why, He destroys and there is no rebuilding,
closes in on a man, leaves no opening.
Why, He holds back the waters and they dry up,
sends them forth and they turn the earth over.
With Him is power and prudence,
His the duped and the duper.
He leads counselors astray
and judges He drives to madness.
He undoes the sash of kings
and binds a loincloth round their waist.
He leads priests astray,
the mighty He misleads.
He takes away speech from the trustworthy,
and sense from the elders He takes,
He pours forth scorn on princes,
and the belt of the nobles He slackens,
lays bare depths from the darkness
and brings out to light death's shadow,
raises nations high and destroys them,
flattens nations and leads them away,
stuns the minds of the people's leaders,
makes them wander in trackless wastes—
they grope in darkness without light,
He makes them wander like drunken men.

13. Why, my eye has seen all,
my ear has heard and understood.
As you know, I, too, know.
I am no less than you.
Yet I would speak to Shaddai,
and I want to dispute with God.
And yet, you plaster lies,[8]
you are all quack-healers.
Would that you fell silent,
and this would be your wisdom.
Hear, pray, my dispute,
and to my lips' pleas listen closely.
Would you speak crookedness of God,
and of Him would you speak false things?
Would you be partial on His behalf,
would you plead the case of God?
Would it be good that He probed you,
as one mocks a man would you mock Him?

8. An idiom also found in the Psalms; the idea is that the truth is "plastered over" with lies.

He shall surely dispute with you
   if in secret you are partial.
Will not His majesty strike you with terror,
   and His fear fall upon you?
Your pronouncements are maxims of ash,
   your word-piles, piles of clay.
Be silent before me—I would speak,
   no matter what befalls me.
Why should I bear my flesh in my teeth,
   and my life-breath place in my palm?
Look, He slays me, I have no hope.
   Yet my ways I'll dispute to His face.
Even that becomes my rescue,
   for no tainted man comes before Him.
Hear, O hear my word
   and my utterance in your ear.
Look, pray, I have laid out my case,
   I know that I am in the right.
Who would make a plea against me?
   I would be silent then, breathe my last.
Just two things do not do to me,
   then would I not hide from Your presence.
Take Your palm away from me,
   and let Your dread not strike me with terror.
Call and I will reply,
   or I will speak, and answer me.
How many crimes and offenses have I?
   My offense and my wrong, inform me.
Why do You hide Your face,
   and count me Your enemy?
Would You harry a driven leaf,
   and a dry straw would You chase,
that You should write bitter things against me,
   make me heir to the crimes of my youth?
And You put my feet in stocks,
   watch after all my paths,
      on the soles of my feet make a mark.[9]

And man wears away like rot,
   like a garment eaten by moths.

14. Man born of woman,
   scant of days and sated with trouble,
like a blossom he comes forth and withers,
   and flees like a shadow—he will not stay.
Even on such You cast Your eye,
   and me You bring in judgment with You?
[Who can make the impure pure?

9. Probably a reference to branding or tattooing done to mark out a criminal.

No one.][1]
Oh, his days are decreed,
the number of his months are with You,
his limits You fixed that he cannot pass.
Turn away from him that he may cease,
until he serves out his day like a hired man.
For a tree has hope:
though cut down, it can still be removed,
and its shoots will not cease.
Though its root grow old in the ground
and its stock die in the dust,
from the scent of water it flowers,
and puts forth branches like a sapling.
But a strong man dies defeated,
man breathes his last, and where is he?
Water runs out from a lake,
and a river is parched and dries up,
but a man lies down and will not arise,
till the sky is no more he will not awake
and will not rouse from his sleep.
Would that You hid me in Sheol,
concealed me till Your anger passed,
set me a limit and recalled me.
If a man dies will he live?
All my hard service days I shall hope
until my vanishing comes.
Call out and I shall answer you,
for the work of Your hand You should yearn.
For then You would count my steps,
You would not keep watch over my offense.
My crime would be sealed in a packet,
You would plaster over my guilt.
And yet, a falling mountain crumbles,
a rock is ripped from its place.
Water wears away stones,
its surge sweeps up the dust of the earth,
and the hope of man You destroy.
You overwhelm him forever, and he goes off,
You change his face and send him away.
If his sons grow great, he will not know.
And should they dwindle, he will not notice them.
But the flesh upon him will ache,
his own being will mourn for him.

* * *

29. And Job again took up his theme and he said:
Would that I were as in moons of yore,
as the days when God watched over me,

1. This verse is bracketed because it is metrically too short; many scholars think it does not belong in the text.

when He shined his lamp over my head,
  by its light I walked in darkness,
as I was in the days of my prime—
  God an intimate of my tent,
when Shaddai still was with me,
  all around me my lads;
when my feet bathed in curds
  and the rock poured out streams of oil,
when I went out to the city's gate,
  in the square I secured my seat.[2]
Lads saw me and took cover,
  the aged arose, stood up.
Noblemen held back their words,
  their palm they put to their mouth.
The voice of the princes was muffled,
  their tongue to their palate stuck.
When the ear heard, it affirmed me,
  and the eye saw and acclaimed me.
For I would free the poor who cried out,
  the orphan with no one to help him.
The perishing man's blessing would reach me,
  and the widow's heart I made sing.
Righteousness I donned and it clothed me,
  like a cloak and a headdress, my justice.
Eyes I became for the blind,
  and legs for the lame I was.
A father I was for the impoverished,
  a stranger's cause I took up.
And I cracked the wrongdoer's jaws,
  from his teeth I would wrench the prey.
And I thought: In my nest I shall breathe my last,
  and my days will abound like the sand.
My root will be open to water,
  and dew in my branches abide,
My glory renewed within me,
  and my bow ever fresh in my hand.
To me they would listen awaiting
  and fall silent at my advice.
At my speech they would say nothing further,
  and upon them my word would drop.
They waited for me as for rain,
  and gaped open their mouths as for showers.
I laughed to them—they scarcely trusted—
  but my face's light they did not dim.
I chose their way and sat as chief,
  I dwelled like a king in his brigade
    when he comforts the mourning.

2. The square just inside the city gate was the town's meeting place; having a seat there would be a sign of status.

30. And now mere striplings laugh at me
  whose fathers I spurned
    to put with the dogs of my flock.
The strength of their hands—what use to me?
  From them the vigor has gone:
In want and starvation bereft
  they flee to desert land,
    the darkness of desolate dunes,
plucking saltwort from the bush,
  the roots of broomwood their bread.
From within they are banished—
  people shout over them as at thieves.
In river ravines they encamp,
  holes in the dust and crags.
Among bushes they bray,
  beneath thornplants they huddle.
Vile creatures and nameless, too,
  they are struck from the land.
And now I become their taunt,
  I become their mocking word.
They despised me, were distant to me,
  and from my face they did not spare their spit.
For my bowstring they loosed and abused me,
  cast off restraint toward me.
On the right, raw youths stand up,
  they make me run off
    and pave against me their roadways of ruin.
They shatter my path,
  my disaster devise,
    and none helps me against them.
Like a wide water-burst they come,
  in the shape of a tempest they tumble.
Terror rolls over me,
  pursues my path like the wind,
    and my rescue like a cloud passes on.
And now my life spills out,
  days of affliction seize me.
At night my limbs are pierced,
  and my sinews know no rest.
With great power He seizes my garment,
  grabs hold of me at the collar.
He hurls me into the muck,
  and I become like dust and ashes.
I scream to You and You do not answer,
  I stand still and You do not observe me.
You become a cruel one toward me,
  with the might of Your hand You hound me.
You bear me up, on the wind make me straddle,
  break me apart in a storm.
For I know You'll return me to death,
  the meetinghouse of all living things.

But one would not reach out against the afflicted
if in his disaster he screamed.
Have I not wept for the bleak-fated man,
sorrowed for the impoverished?
For I hoped for good and evil came.
I expected light and darkness fell.
My innards seethed and would not be still,
days of affliction greeted me.
In gloom did I walk, with no sun,
I rose in assembly and I screamed.
Brother I was to the jackals,
companion to ostriches.[3]
My skin turned black upon me,
my limbs were scorched by drought.
And my lyre has turned into mourning,
my flute, a keening sound.

31. A pact I sealed with my eyes—
I will not gaze on a virgin.
And what is the share from God above,
the portion from Shaddai in the heights?
Is there not ruin for the wrongdoer,
and estrangement for those who do evil?
Does He not see my way,
and all my steps count?
Have I walked in a lie,
has my foot hurried to deceit?
Let Him weigh me on fair scales,
that God know my blamelessness.
If my stride has strayed from the way,
and my heart gone after my eyes,
or the least thing stuck to my palms,
let me sow and another shall eat,
my offspring torn up by the roots.
If my heart was seduced by a woman,
and at the door of my friend I lurked,
let my wife grind for another
and upon her let others crouch.[4]
For that is lewdness,
and that is a grave crime.
For it is fire that consumes to Perdition,
and in all my yield eats the roots.
If I spurned the case of my slave
or my slavegirl, in their brief against me,
what would I do when God stands up,
and when He assays it, what would I answer?
Why, my Maker made him in the belly,
and formed him in the selfsame womb.

3. Known for their loud, mournful cries.
4. The "grinding" and "crouching" are implicit metaphors for sex.

Did I hold back the poor from his desire
  or make the eyes of the widow pine?
Did I eat my bread alone,
  and an orphan not eat from it?
For from my youth like a father I raised him,
  and from my mother's womb I led him.
If I saw a man failing, ungarbed,
  and no garment for the impoverished,
did his loins not then bless me,
  and from my sheep's shearing was he not warmed?
If I raised my hand against an orphan,
  when I saw my advantage in the gate,
let my shoulder fall out of its socket
  and my arm break off from its shaft.
For ruin from God is my fear,
  and His presence I cannot withstand.
If I made gold my bulwark,
  and fine gold I called my trust,
if I rejoiced that my wealth was great
  and that abundance my hand had found,
if I saw light when it gleamed
  and the moon gliding grand,
and my heart was seduced in secret,
  and my hand caressed my mouth,
this, too, would be a grave crime,
  for I would have denied God above.[5]
If I rejoiced at my foe's disaster,
  and exulted when harm found him out—
yet I did not let my mouth offend
  to seek out his life in an oath.
Did the men of my tent ever say,
  "Would that we were never sated of his flesh"?
The sojourner did not sleep outside.
  My doors to the wayfarer I opened.
Did I hide like Adam my wrongdoings,
  to bury within me my crime,
that I should fear the teeming crowd,
  and the scorn of clans terrify me,
    fall silent and keep within doors?
Would that I had someone to hear me out.
  Here's my mark—let Shaddai answer me,
    and let my accuser indict his writ.
I would bear it upon my shoulder,
  bind it as a crown upon me.
The number of my steps I would tell Him,
  like a prince I would approach him.
If my soil has cried out against me,
  and together its furrows wept,

5. Apparently refers to idolatrous worship of the sun and moon.

if I ate its yield without payment,
  and drove its owners to despair,
instead of wheat let nettles grow,
  and instead of barley, stinkweed.

Here end the words of Job.

* * *

38. And the LORD answered Job from the whirlwind and He said:
Who is this who darkens counsel
  in words without knowledge?
Gird, pray, your loins like a man,
  that I may ask you, and you can inform Me.
Where were you when I founded earth?
  Tell, if you know understanding.
Who fixed its measures, do you know,
  or who stretched a line upon it?
In what were its sockets sunk,
  or who laid its cornerstone,
when the morning stars sang together,
  and all the sons of God shouted for joy?
Who hedged the sea in with doors,
  when it gushed forth from the womb,
when I made cloud its clothing,
  and thick mist its swaddling bands?
I made breakers upon it My limit,
  and set a bolt with double doors.
And I said, "Thus far come, no further,
  here halt the surge of your waves."
Have you ever commanded the morning,
  appointed the dawn to its place,
to seize the earth's corners,
  that the wicked be shaken from it?
It turns like sealing clay,
  takes color like a garment,
and their light is withdrawn from the wicked,
  and the upraised arm is broken.
Have you come into the springs of the sea,
  in the bottommost deep walked about?
Have the gates of death been laid bare to you,
  and the gates of death's shadow have you seen?
Did you take in the breadth of the earth?
  Tell, if you know it all.
Where is the way that light dwells,
  and darkness, where is its place,
that you might take it to its home
  and understand the paths to its house?
You know, for were you born then,
  and the number of your days is great!
Have you come into the storehouse of snow,
  the storehouse of hail have you seen,

which I keep for a time of strife,
for a day of battle and war?
By what way does the west wind fan out,
the east wind whip over the earth?
Who split a channel for the torrent,
and a way for the thunderstorm,
to rain on a land without man,
wilderness bare of humankind,
to sate the desolate dunes
and make the grass sprout there?
Does the rain have a father,
or who begot the drops of dew?
From whose belly did the ice come forth,
to the frost of the heavens who gave birth?
Water congeals like stone,
and the face of the deep locks hard.
Can you tie the bands of the Pleiades,
or loose Orion's reins?
Can you bring constellations out in their season,
lead the Great Bear and her cubs?
Do you know the laws of the heavens,
can you fix their rule on earth?
Can you lift your voice to the cloud,
that the water-spate cover you?
Can you send lightning bolts on their way,
and they will say to you, "Here we are!"?
Who placed in the hidden parts wisdom,
or who gave the mind understanding?
Who counted the skies in wisdom,
and the jars of the heavens who tilted,
when the dust melts to a mass,
and the clods cling fast together?
Can you hunt prey for the lion,
fill the king of beast's appetite,
when it crouches in its den,
lies in ambush in the covert?
Who readies the raven's prey
when its young cry out to God
and stray deprived of food?

39. Do you know the mountain goats' birth-time,
do you mark the calving of the gazelles?
Do you number the months till they come to term
and know their birthing time?
They crouch, burst forth with their babes,
their young they push out to the world.
Their offspring batten, grow big in the wild,
they go out and do not return.
Who set the wild ass free,
and the onager's reins who loosed,

whose home I made in the steppes,
  his dwelling-place flats of salt?
He scoffs at the bustling city,
  the driver's shouts he does not hear.
He roams mountains for his forage,
  and every green thing he seeks.
Will the wild ox want to serve you,
  pass the night at your feeding trough?
Bind the wild ox with cord for the furrow,
  will he harrow the valleys behind you?
Can you rely on him with his great power
  and leave your labor to him?
Can you trust him to bring back your seed,
  gather grain on your threshing floor?
The ostrich's wing joyously beats.
  Is the pinion, the plume like the stork's?
For she leaves her eggs on the ground,
  and in the dust she lets them warm.
And she forgets that a foot can crush them,
  and a beast of the field stomp on them—
harsh, abandons her young to a stranger,
  in vain her labor, without fear.
For God made her forgetful of wisdom,
  and He did not allot her insight.
Now on the height she races,
  she scoffs at the horse and its rider.
Do you give might to the horse,
  do you clothe his neck with a mane?
Do you make his roar like locusts—
  his splendid snort is terror.
He churns up the valley exulting,
  in power goes out to the clash of arms.
He scoffs at fear and is undaunted,
  turns not back before the sword.
Over him rattles the quiver,
  the blade, the javelin, and the spear.
With clamor and clatter he swallows the ground,
  and ignores the trumpet's sound.
At the trumpet he says, "Aha,"
  and from afar he scents the fray,
    the thunder of captains, the shouts.
Does the hawk soar by your wisdom,
  spread his wings to fly away south?
By your word does the eagle mount
  and set his nest on high?
On the crag he dwells and beds down,
  on the crest of the crag his stronghold.
From there he seeks out food,
  from afar his eyes look down.
His chicks lap up blood,
  where the slain are, there he is.

40. And the LORD answered Job and He said:
Will he who disputes with Shaddai be reproved?
  Who argues with God, let him answer!
And Job answered the LORD and he said:
Look, I am worthless. What can I say back to You?
  My hand I put over my mouth.
Once have I spoken and I will not answer,
  twice, and will not go on.
And the LORD answered Job from the whirlwind and He said:
Gird, pray, your loins like a man.
  Let me ask you, and you will inform Me.
Will you indeed overthrow My case,
  hold Me guilty, so you can be right?
If you have an arm like God's,
  and with a voice like His you can thunder,
put on, pray, pride and preeminence,
  and grandeur and glory don.
Let loose your utmost wrath,
  see every proud man, bring him low.
See every proud man, make him kneel,
  tramp on the wicked where they are.
Bury them in the dust together,
  shut them up in the grave.
And I on my part shall acclaim you,
  for your right hand triumphs for you.
Look, pray: Behemoth[6] whom I made with you,
  grass like cattle he eats.
Look, pray: the power in his loins,
  the virile strength in his belly's muscles.
He makes his tail stand like a cedar,
  his balls' sinews twine together.
His bones are bars of bronze,
  his limbs like iron rods.
He is the first of the ways of God.
  Let his Maker draw near him with His sword!
For the mountains offer their yield to him,
  every beast of the field plays there.
Underneath the lotus he lies,
  in the covert of reeds and marsh.
The lotus hedges him, shades him,
  the brook willows stand around him.
Look, he swallows a river at his ease,
  untroubled while Jordan pours into his mouth.
Could one take him with one's eyes,
with barbs pierce his nose?

6. The Hebrew word *behemot* simply means "beasts"; the description suggests a mythologized version of the hippopotamus, an animal the poet had presumably never seen.

Could you draw Leviathan[7] with a hook,
and with a cord press down his tongue?
Could you put a lead-line in his nose,
and with a fish-hook pierce his cheek?
Would he urgently entreat you,
would he speak to you gentle words?
Would he seal a pact with you,
that you take him as lifelong slave?
Could you play with him like a bird,
and leash him for your young women?
Could hucksters haggle over him,
divide him among the traders?
Could you fill his skin with darts,
and a fisherman's net with his head?
Just put your hand upon him—
you will no more recall how to battle.

41. Look, all hope of him is dashed,
at his mere sight one is cast down.
No fierce one could arouse him,
and who before him could stand up?
Who could go before Me in this I'd reward,
under all the heavens he would be mine.
I would not keep silent about him,
about his heroic acts and surpassing grace.
Who can uncover his outer garb,
come into his double mail?
Who can pry open the doors of his face?
All around his teeth is terror.
His back is rows of shields,
closed with the tightest seal.
Each touches against the next,
no breath can come between them.
Each sticks fast to the next,
locked together, they will not part.
His sneezes shoot out light,
and his eyes are like the eyelids of dawn.
Firebrands leap from his mouth,
sparks of fire fly into the air.
From his nostrils smoke comes out,
like a boiling vat on brushwood.
His breath kindles coals,
and flame comes out of his mouth.
Strength abides in his neck,
and before him power dances.
The folds of his flesh cling together;
hard-cast, he will not totter.
His heart is cast hard as stone,

7. The mythical Canaanite sea monster, here associated with the crocodile.

cast hard as a nether millstone.[8]
When he rears up, the gods are frightened,[9]
when he crashes down, they cringe.
Who overtakes him with sword, it will not avail,
nor spear nor dart nor lance.
Iron he deems as straw,
and bronze as rotten wood.
No arrow can make him flee,
slingstones for him turn to straw.
Missiles are deemed as straw,
and he mocks the javelin's clatter.
Beneath him, jagged shards,
he draws a harrow over the mud.
He makes the deep boil like a pot,
turns sea to an ointment pan.
Behind him glistens a wake,
he makes the deep seem hoary.
He has no match on earth,
made as he is without fear.
All that is lofty he can see.
He is king over all proud beasts.

42. And Job answered the LORD and he said:
I know You can do anything,
and no devising is beyond You.
"Who is this obscuring counsel without knowledge?"[1]
Therefore I told but did not understand,
wonders beyond me that I did not know.
"Hear, pray, and I will speak
Let me ask you, that you may inform me."
By the ear's rumor I heard of You,
and now my eye has seen You.
Therefore do I recant,
And I repent in dust and ashes.

And it happened after the LORD had spoken these words to Job, that the LORD said to Eliphaz the Temanite: "My wrath has flared against you and your two companions because you have not spoken rightly of Me as did My servant Job. And now, take for yourselves seven bulls and seven rams and go to My servant Job, and offer a burnt-offering for yourselves, and Job My servant will pray on your behalf. To him only I shall show favor, not to do a vile thing to you, for you have not spoken rightly of Me as did my servant Job. And Eliphaz the Temanite and Bildad the Shuhite and Zophar the Naamathite went out and did according to all that the LORD had spoken to them, and the LORD showed favor to Job. And the LORD restored Job's fortunes when he prayed for

8. Flour was ground between two stones; the bottom one would have to be particularly hard, to withstand the pressure.

9. "Gods" = a sign that the text is not monotheistic. Job believes that his Lord is the best and strongest but not the only god.

1. I.e., giving advice in ignorance of the facts. The line is a quotation of the Lord's words to Job.

his companions, and the LORD increased twofold all that Job had. And all his male and female kinfolk and all who had known him before came and broke bread with him in his house and grieved with him and comforted him for all the harm that the LORD had brought on him. And each of them gave him one kesitah[2] and one golden ring. And the LORD blessed Job's latter days more than his former days, and he had fourteen thousand sheep and six thousand camels and a thousand yoke of oxen and a thousand she-asses. And he had seven sons and three daughters. And he called the name of the first one Dove and the name of the second Cinnamon and the name of the third Horn of Eye-shade.[3] And there were no women in the land so beautiful as Job's daughters. And their father gave them an estate among their brothers. And Job lived a hundred and forty years after this, and he saw his children and his children's children, four generations. And Job died, aged and sated in years.

Psalm 8[1]

1. O Lord our Lord, how excellent is thy name in all the earth! who hast set thy glory above the heavens.
2. Out of the mouth of babes and sucklings hast thou ordained strength because of thine enemies, that thou mightest still the enemy and the avenger.
3. When I consider thy heavens, the work of thy fingers, the moon and the stars, which thou hast ordained;
4. What is man, that thou art mindful of him? and the son of man, that thou visitest him?
5. For thou hast made him a little lower than the angels, and hast crowned him with glory and honour.
6. Thou madest him to have dominion over the works of thy hands; thou hast put all things under his feet:
7. All sheep and oxen, yea, and the beasts of the field;
8. The fowl of the air, and the fish of the sea, and whatsoever passeth through the paths of the seas.
9. O Lord our Lord, how excellent is thy name in all the earth!

Psalm 19

1. The heavens declare the glory of God; and the firmament sheweth his handywork.
2. Day unto day uttereth speech, and night unto night sheweth knowledge.
3. There is no speech nor language, where their voice is not heard.
4. Their line is gone out through all the earth, and their words to the end of the world. In them hath he set a tabernacle for the sun,

2. A valuable coin.
3. A substance used for eye makeup.

1. The text of the Psalms is that of the King James version.

5. Which is as a bridegroom coming out of his chamber, and rejoiceth as a strong man to run a race.

6. His going forth is from the end of the heaven, and his circuit unto the ends of it: and there is nothing hid from the heat thereof.

7. The law of the Lord is perfect, converting the soul: the testimony of the Lord is sure, making wise the simple.

8. The statutes of the Lord are right, rejoicing the heart: the commandment of the Lord is pure, enlightening the eyes.

9. The fear of the Lord is clean, enduring for ever: the judgments of the Lord are true and righteous altogether.

10. More to be desired are they than gold, yea, than much fine gold: sweeter also than honey and the honeycomb.

11. Moreover by them is thy servant warned: and in keeping of them there is great reward.

12. Who can understand his errors? cleanse thou me from secret faults.

13. Keep back thy servant also from presumptuous sins; let them not have dominion over me: then shall I be upright, and I shall be innocent from the great transgression.

14. Let the words of my mouth, and the meditation of my heart, be acceptable in thy sight, O Lord, my strength, and my redeemer.

Psalm 23

1. The Lord is my shepherd; I shall not want.

2. He maketh me to lie down in green pastures: he leadeth me beside the still waters.

3. He restoreth my soul: he leadeth me in the paths of righteousness for his name's sake.

4. Yea, though I walk through the valley of the shadow of death, I will fear no evil: for thou art with me; thy rod and thy staff they comfort me.

5. Thou preparest a table before me in the presence of mine enemies: thou anointest my head with oil; my cup runneth over.

6. Surely goodness and mercy shall follow me all the days of my life: and I will dwell in the house of the Lord for ever.

Psalm 104

1. Bless the Lord, O my soul. O Lord my God, thou art very great; thou art clothed with honour and majesty.

2. Who coverest thyself with light as with a garment: who stretchest out the heavens like a curtain:

3. Who layeth the beams of his chambers in the waters: who maketh the clouds his chariot: who walketh upon the wings of the wind:

4. Who maketh his angels spirits; his ministers a flaming fire:

5. Who laid the foundations of the earth, that it should not be removed for ever.

6. Thou coveredst it with the deep as with a garment: the waters stood above the mountains.

7. At thy rebuke they fled; at the voice of thy thunder they hasted away.

8. They go up by the mountains; they go down by the valleys unto the place which thou hast founded for them.

9. Thou hast set a bound that they may not pass over; that they turn not again to cover the earth.

10. He sendeth the springs into the valleys, which run among the hills.

11. They give drink to every beast of the field: the wild asses quench their thirst.

12. By them shall the fowls of the heaven have their habitation, which sing among the branches.

13. He watereth the hills from his chambers: the earth is satisfied with the fruit of thy works.

14. He causeth the grass to grow for the cattle, and herb for the service of man: that he may bring forth food out of the earth;

15. And wine that maketh glad the heart of man, and oil to make his face to shine, and bread which strengtheneth man's heart.

16. The trees of the Lord are full of sap; the cedars of Lebanon, which he hath planted;

17. Where the birds make their nests: as for the stork, the fir trees are her house.

18. The high hills are a refuge for the wild goats; and the rocks for the conies.

19. He appointed the moon for seasons: the sun knoweth his going down.

20. Thou makest darkness, and it is night: wherein all the beasts of the forest do creep forth.

21. The young lions roar after their prey, and seek their meat from God.

22. The sun ariseth, they gather themselves together, and lay them down in their dens.

23. Man goeth forth unto his work and to his labour until the evening.

24. O Lord, how manifold are thy works! in wisdom hast thou made them all: the earth is full of thy riches.

25. So is this great and wide sea, wherein are things creeping innumerable, both small and great beasts.

26. There go the ships: there is that leviathan, whom thou hast made to play therein.

27. These wait all upon thee; that thou mayest give them their meat in due season.

28. That thou givest them they gather: thou openest thine hand, they are filled with good.

29. Thou hidest thy face, they are troubled: thou takest away their breath, they die, and return to their dust.

30. Thou sendest forth thy spirit, they are created: and thou renewest the face of the earth.

31. The glory of the Lord shall endure for ever: the Lord shall rejoice in his works.

32. He looketh on the earth, and it trembleth: he toucheth the hills, and they smoke.

33. I will sing unto the Lord as long as I live: I will sing praise to my God while I have my being.
34. My meditation of him shall be sweet: I will be glad in the Lord.
35. Let the sinners be consumed out of the earth, and let the wicked be no more. Bless thou the Lord, O my soul. Praise ye the Lord.

Psalm 137

1. By the rivers of Babylon,[1] there we sat down, yea, we wept, when we remembered Zion.
2. We hanged our harps upon the willows in the midst thereof.
3. For there they that carried us away captive required of us a song; and they that wasted us required of us mirth, saying, Sing us one of the songs of Zion.
4. How shall we sing the Lord's song in a strange land?
5. If I forget thee, O Jerusalem, let my right hand forget her cunning.
6. If I do not remember thee, let my tongue cleave to the roof of my mouth; if I prefer not Jerusalem above my chief joy.
7. Remember, O Lord, the children of Edom[2] in the day of Jerusalem; who said, Rase it, rase it, even to the foundation thereof.
8. O daughter of Babylon, who art to be destroyed; happy shall he be, that rewardeth thee as thou hast served us.
9. Happy shall he be, that taketh and dasheth thy little ones against the stones.

1. On the Euphrates River. Jerusalem was captured and sacked by the Babylonians in 586 B.C.E. The Hebrews were taken away into captivity in Babylon.
2. The Edomites helped the Babylonians capture Jerusalem.

HOMER

eighth century B.C.E.

The *Iliad* and the *Odyssey* tell the story of the clash of two great civilizations, and the effects of war on both the winners and the losers. Both poems are about the Trojan War, a mythical conflict between a coalition of Greeks and the inhabitants of Troy, a city in Asia Minor. These are the earliest works of Greek literature, composed almost three thousand years before our time. Yet they are rich and sophisticated in their narrative techniques, and they provide extraordinarily vivid portrayals of people, social relationships, and feelings, especially our incompatible desires for honor and violence, and for peace and a home.

HISTORICAL CONTEXTS

On the Greek island of Crete is an enormous palace, dominated by monumental arches adorned with fierce lions, built by the earliest Greek-speaking people: the Myceneans, who probably inspired the Trojan legends. About 2000 B.C.E., they began building big, fortified cities around central palaces in the south of Greece. The Myceneans had a form of writing—not an alphabet but a "syllabary" (in which a symbol corresponds to each syllable, not to each letter)—as well as a centralized, tightly controlled economy and sophisticated artistic and architectural traditions. The metal they used for weapons, armor, and tools was predominantly bronze, and their time is therefore known as the Bronze Age.

After dominating the region for around six hundred years, Mycenean civilization came to an end in around 1200 B.C.E. Archaeological investigations suggest that the great cities were burnt or destroyed around this time, perhaps by invasion or war. The next few hundred years are known as the Dark Ages of Greece: people seem to have been less wealthy, and the cultural knowledge of the Myceneans, including the knowledge of writing, was lost.

Greeks of this time spoke many different dialects and lived in small towns and villages scattered across a wide area. They did not regain their knowledge of reading or writing until an alphabet, invented by a trading people called the Phoenicians, was adopted in the eighth century B.C.E.

One might think that an illiterate society could have nothing like "literature," a word based on the Latin for "letters" (*litterae*). In the centuries of Greek illiteracy, however, there developed a thriving tradition of oral poetry, especially on the Ionian coast, in modern-day Turkey. Travelling bards told tales of the lost age of heroes who fought with bronze, and of the great cities besieged and destroyed by war. The Homeric poems make use of folk memories of a real conflict or conflicts between the Mycenean Greeks and inhabitants of one or more cities in Asia Minor. The world of Homer is neither historical in a modern sense, nor purely fictional. Through poetry, the Greeks of the Dark Ages created and preserved their own past.

Oral poets in ancient Greece used a traditional form (a six-part line called hexameter), fitting their own riffs into the rhythm, with musical accompaniment. They also relied on common themes, traditional stories, traditional characters, traditional adjectives (such as "swift Achilles" or "black ships"), phrases that fit the rhythm of the line, and even whole scenes that follow a set pattern, such as the way a warrior gets dressed or the way that meals are prepared. Fluent poetic ad-libbing is very difficult; these techniques gave each performer a structure, so that stories and lines did not have to be generated entirely on the spot. We know that the tradition of this type of composition must have gone back hundreds of years, because the *Iliad* and the *Odyssey* include details that would have been anachronistic by the time these poems were written down, such as the use of bronze weapons: by the eighth century, soldiers fought with iron. Details from different periods are jumbled together, so that even in the eighth century B.C.E. the heroic, mythic world of the Homeric poems must have seemed quite distinct from everyday reality. In addition, the poems mix different Greek dialects, the speech of many different areas in the Greek-speaking world, into a language unlike anything anyone ever spoke.

It is hard to understand the relation between the heroic poetry composed and sung by illiterate bards in archaic Greece, and the written texts of the *Odyssey* and the *Iliad*. The question is made all the more difficult because the poems are far longer than most instances of oral poetic performance, including that of the oral poets living in the former Yugoslavia, who were studied by classicists in the twentieth century as the closest living analogy to ancient Greek bards. Good bards may be able to keep going for an hour or two: in the Homeric poems themselves, there are accounts of singers performing for a while after dinner. But a complete performance of either of these poems would have lasted at least twenty hours. This is much too long for an audience to sit through in an evening. It would also have been difficult for any poet, even a genius, to compose at this length without the use of writing. Perhaps, then, these poems are the work of an oral poet, or poets, who became literate. Or perhaps they represent a collaboration between one or more oral poets, and a scribe. In any case, soon after the Greeks developed their alphabet, they found a way to preserve their oral tradition in two monumental written poems.

These works make use of tradition in strikingly original ways, creating just two coherent stories out of the mass of legends that surrounded the Trojan War. They are long poems about heroes, a genre that later came to be called "epic"—from the Greek for "story" or "word." Throughout the ancient world, for hundreds of years to come, everybody knew the *Iliad* and the *Odyssey*. The poems were performed out loud, illustrated in paintings on vases or on walls, read, learned by heart, remembered, reworked, and imitated by everyone in the Greek and Roman worlds, from the Athenian tragedians to the Roman poet **Virgil**.

THE *ILIAD*

The title *Iliad* suggests a work about the Trojan War, since *Ilias* is another name for Troy. Greek readers or listeners would have been familiar with the background myths. Paris, a prince of Troy, son of King Priam, had to judge which of three goddesses should be awarded a golden apple: Athena, goddess of wisdom; Hera, the queen of the gods—a representative of power; or Aphrodite, goddess of sexual desire. He chose Aphrodite, and as his reward she gave him the most beautiful woman in the world, Helen of Sparta, as his wife. Unfortunately, Helen already had a husband: Menelaus, brother of the powerful general Agamemnon. When

Paris took Helen with him back to Troy from Mycenae, Agamemnon and Menelaus mustered a great army, a coalition drawn from many Greek cities, including the great heroes Achilles, the fastest runner and best fighter, and Odysseus, the cleverest of the Greeks. So began a war that lasted ten years, until Odysseus finally found a stratagem to enter the city walls of Troy. He built a wooden horse, filled it with Greek armed men, and tricked the Trojans into taking the horse into the city. The Greek soldiers leaped from the horse and killed the male inhabitants, captured the women, and razed the city to the ground.

Surprisingly, none of these events play any part in the main narrative of the *Iliad*, which begins when the war is already in its tenth year and ends before the capture of the city. Moreover, the central focus is not on the conflict between Greeks and Trojans, but on a conflict among the Greek commanders. The first word of the *Iliad* is "Rage," and the rage of Achilles—first against his comrade Agamemnon, and only later against the enemy Trojans—is the central subject of the poem. In Greek, the word used is *menis*, a term otherwise applied only to the wrath of the gods. Achilles' rage is an extraordinary thing, which sets him apart from the rest of humanity—Greeks and Trojans. The poem tells how Achilles, the greatest Greek hero and the son of a goddess, becomes alienated from his society, how his rage against the Greeks shifts into an inhuman aggression against the Trojans, and how he is at last willing to return to the human world.

The *Iliad* is about war, honor, and aggression. There are moments of graphic violence, when we are told exactly where the point of a spear or sword penetrates vulnerable human flesh: as when Achilles' friend Patroclus throws his spear at another warrior, Sarpedon, and catches him "just below the rib cage / where it protects the beating heart"; or when Hector rams his spear into Patroclus, "into the pit of his belly and all the way through"; or when Achilles' spear "pierced the soft neck but did not slit the windpipe." The precise anatomical detail reminds us of how vulnerable these warriors are, because they have mortal bodies—in contrast to the gods, who may participate in battle but can never die.

The plot deals with the exchange or ransoming of human bodies. Achilles' anger at Agamemnon is roused by a quarrel about who owns Briseis, a girl Achilles has seized as a prize of war but whom Agamemnon takes as recompense for the loss of his own girl, Chryseis. The story also hinges on the ownership of dead male bodies: the corpses, in turn, of Sarpedon, Patroclus, and Hector. War seems to produce its own kind of economy, a system of exchange: a live girl for a dead warrior, one life for another, or death for undying fame.

The *Iliad* is a violent poem, and, on one level, the violence simply contributes to the entertainment: it is exciting to hear or read about slaughter. But it would be a mistake to see the *Iliad* as pure military propaganda. At times, the poem brings out the terrible pity of war: the city of Troy will be ruined, the people killed or enslaved, and the poet looks back with regret to "the days of peace, before the Greeks came." Some similes compare the violence on the battlefield to the events of the world of peace, where people can plough the fields, build homes, and watch their sheep. But these similes may suggest that violence and the threat of pain and death are facts of life: even when people are at peace, there is murder, and lions or wolves leap into the fold to kill the sheep.

Within the narrow world of the battlefield, Homer's vividly imagined characters have choices to make. They cannot choose, like gods, to avoid death; but they can choose how they will die. The poem itself acknowledges that the exchange of honor for death may seem inadequate. After Agamemnon has treated him dishonorably, Achilles begins to question the whole heroic code, and its system of trading death for glory: "Nothing is worth my life," he declares, since prizes of honor can always be replaced but "a man's life cannot be won back." Unlike the other fighters, Achilles knows for sure—thanks to the goddess Thetis, his mother—that staying at Troy will mean his death. But all the warriors of the *Iliad* are conscious that in fighting they risk their own deaths. Achilles' choices—to fight and die soon, in this war, or go home and live a little longer—are therefore a starker version of the decision faced by all these warriors.

Fascinatingly, the *Iliad* makes the Trojans as fully human as the Greeks. The Trojan hero, Hector, seems to many readers the most likeable character in the poem, fighting not for honor or vengeance but to protect his wife and their infant son. One of the most touching moments comes as Hector says goodbye to his tearful wife before going into battle; a deep tenderness connects Hector and his family—in contrast to the more shallow associations of the Greeks with their female prisoners of war. As Hector reaches down to kiss his son, the child screams, frightened at seeing his father in his helmet. The parents laugh together, and Hector takes off the helmet so the baby will not be scared as he swings him in his arms. The moment is both heartwarming and chilling, since we know—and his wife knows—that this devoted father will never see his son again; the baby is right to be frightened, since he will soon be swung headlong from the city walls by the victorious Greeks.

The *Iliad* culminates in an astonishing encounter, between Priam, king of Troy, and Achilles, who has killed his son Hector. Priam goes to plead with Achilles to return his son's body, and the two enemies end up sitting together, each weeping for those they have lost. The experience of grief is common to all humans, even those who kill each other in war. The major contrast drawn by the *Iliad* is not between Greek and Trojan, but between the humans and the immortal gods. The gods play an important role in the action of the poem, sometimes intervening to cause or prevent a hero's death or dishonor. We are told at

Achilles (left) slays Hector. From a red-figured volute-krater (a large ceramic wine decanter), ca. 500–480 B.C.E.

the beginning that there is a connection between all the deaths caused by Achilles' rage and the will of Zeus: the whole action of the poem happened "as Zeus' will was done." But the presence of the gods does not turn the human characters into puppets, controlled only by the gods or by fate. Human characters are never forced by gods to act out of character. Rather, human action and divine action work together, and the gods provide a way of talking about the elements of human experience that are otherwise incomprehensible.

Moreover, the presence of the gods—like the similes—makes us particularly aware of what is distinctive about human life in war. In the world of the gods, there are conflicts about hierarchy, just as there are on earth: sometimes the lesser gods refuse to recognize the authority of Zeus, just as some Greek chieftains sometimes refuse to bow to Agamemnon. But on Olympus, all quarrels end in laughter and drinking, not death. The most important fact about all the warriors in the *Iliad* is that they die. Moreover, before death humans have to face grief, dishonor, loss, and pain—things that play little or no part in any god's life. Achilles in his rage refuses to accept the horror of loss: loss of honor, and the loss of his dearest friend, Patroclus. His rage can end, and he can eat again, only when he realizes that all humans, even the greatest warriors, have to have "hearts of iron," the ability to endure unendurable loss and keep on living. The *Iliad* provides a bleak but inspiring account of human suffering as a kind of power, which the gods themselves cannot achieve.

THE *ODYSSEY*

The *Odyssey*, which is included in its entirety in this anthology, has a special place in the study of world literature, since it deals explicitly with the relationship between the kind of people we know and those who are strange to us. It is about a journey that spans most of the world as it was known to Greeks at the time, and deals with issues that any student of world literature must confront, including the place of literature and memory in the formation of cultural identity. The poem shows us, in depth and in detail, the complex relationships between one westerner, a Greek man, and the other cultures that he encounters—not in war, but in the course of a long journey, where the worst enemies may lie inside his own household. The poem tells the story of Odysseus's homecoming from Troy, tracing his reclamation of a household from which he has been absent for the past twenty years. It is a gripping and varied tale, which includes fantasy and magic but also focuses on domestic details and on the human need for a family and a home.

The *Odyssey* is set after the *Iliad*, and was probably produced a little later, since it seems deliberately to avoid repeating anything that had been included in the *Iliad*, and fills in many important details that had been absent from the earlier poem—including allusions to the actual fall of Troy, and its aftermath. The *Odyssey* creates a different but complementary vision of the Trojan War, showing how the Greeks faced further danger in the long voyage back to Greece, and in their return to homes from which they had been absent for many years.

In the Greek original, the first word of the *Odyssey*—our first clue to the poem's subject—is *andra* ("man"). One man, Odysseus himself, is the center of the poem, in a way that no single hero, not even Achilles, is the center of the *Iliad*. The journey from war to peace requires different skills from those needed on the battlefield, and through the figure of Odysseus the poem shows us what those skills might be. He has strength and physical courage, but he also has brains: "the cunning hero" is the cleverest of those who fought at Troy. He is famously adaptable, a "man of many turns," able to deal with any eventuality, no matter how difficult or unexpected. He has psychological strength, an ability both to endure and to inflict pain without flinching; more than once, the poem connects the name *Odysseus* with the Greek word for "to be angry" or "hate" (*odyssomai*): Odysseus is the man hated by the god Poseidon. He has the patience and self-restraint required to bide his time until the moment comes for him to reveal himself to his household. Most of all, he has the will to go home, and to restore his home to its proper order. It is no accident that Odysseus's favorite weapon is not the sword or the spear but the bow, which shoots from a distance at the target of his choice.

"Man" is also the subject of the *Odyssey* in a broader sense, because the poem has a particular interest in the diversity of cultures and ways of life. The *Iliad* is set almost exclusively on the battlefield of Troy, and focused on the relationships between the aristocratic male warriors. By contrast, the *Odyssey* shows us a multitude of distinct worlds and cultures, including non-human cultures. Odysseus spends years on the luxurious island of the nymph Calypso; he encounters the sweet-singing Sirens, the monster Scylla, and the Lotus-eaters; and he disembarks on the island of the sun, with its tempting, delicious cows, and of the witch Circe, who can turn men to pigs. He is almost killed on the island of the shepherd-giants, the Cyclopes, and he is welcomed in the magical land of Phaeacia, where fruits flourish all season long, and where he meets the king, the queen, and the princess, Nausicaa, who is out to do laundry and play ball with her girlfriends, while day-dreaming about her future husband. The many cultures of the poem include both the exotic and the ordinary.

Even in the Greek world, we are given glimpses of several distinct ways of life. The rich land of Sparta, ruled by Menelaus and his recovered wife, the beautiful, sophisticated Helen, with her fancy embroidery and her narcotics, contrasts with the poor island of Ithaca, Odysseus's homeland, which is too stony to raise horses or plentiful crops. In Ithaca, we see the lives of women as well as men; of old Laertes, Odysseus's father, as well as his insecure young son, Telemachus; and of the poor as well as the rich—including the old nurse who washes Odysseus and the pig-keeper, Eumaeus, who gives him shelter. In showing multiple encounters between the Greek hero and people who are very different from him, the Homeric poem invites us to think about how we ought to behave toward people who are not the same as ourselves.

The *Odyssey* is particularly concerned with the laws of hospitality, which in Greek is *xenia*—a word that covers the whole relationship between guests and hosts, and between strangers and those who take them in. Hospitality is the fundamental criterion for civilized society in this poem. Cultures may vary in other respects, but any good society will accommodate the wandering guest. Odysseus encounters many strange peoples in the course of his wanderings. Some, like the goddess Calypso, are almost too welcoming: she invites him into her home and her bed, and keeps him there even when he longs to go home. Odysseus acknowledges that Calypso is far more beautiful than his own wife and that her island is more lush than his own stony home; but, movingly, he still wants to go back. This poem deals with the fundamental desire we feel for our own people and our own place, not because they are better than any other, but simply because they are ours. Similarly,

Odysseus rejects the possibility of starting his life over in the hospitable land of the Phaeacians. The monstrous one-eyed Cyclops, Polyphemus, is a grotesque counterpart to the good Phaeacian hosts: instead of welcoming and feeding his guests, the Cyclops wants to eat them for dinner. This encounter is a reminder of how distinctive, and unheroic, are the skills Odysseus needs to survive the journey home. Heroes in battle, in the *Iliad*, are always concerned that their names be remembered in times to come. But Odysseus defeats Polyphemus—whose name suggests "Much-named"—by denying his own name, calling himself "Noman." The journey home has to trump even Odysseus's heroic identity.

At times, Odysseus's own men seem to transgress the laws of hospitality, as when they kill the cattle of the Sun, which they have been expressly forbidden to touch. We see further variations on the theme of hospitality in the visits that Odysseus's son, Telemachus, pays to his father's friends. The account in the first four books of Telemachus' activities—short journeys to visit uncles, cousins, and kinsmen in the surrounding neighborhood—may seem oddly inconsequential, and even unheroic. But a great deal of the *Odyssey*'s attraction lies in the way it values the little details of human relationships and human feelings over grand tales of honor and killing in war.

Hospitality is tested most severely when Odysseus arrives back as a stranger in his own home. The suitors have seized control of his house and are abusing his unwitting hospitality, in his absence, by courting his wife, devouring his food and drink, and ruining his property. There are repeated references in the *Odyssey* to the nightmare double of Odysseus's return: the homecoming of Agamemnon, who came back from Troy only to be killed in his bath by his wife, Clytemnestra, and her lover, Aegisthus. Zeus, the king of the gods, insists at the beginning of the poem that Aegisthus is hated by the gods, and he praises Agamemnon's son, Orestes, who avenges his father's death by killing the adulterous murderer.

First-time readers may be surprised that the wanderings of Odysseus, across the sea from Troy back to his stony Greek homeland, Ithaca, occupy only a short part of the whole poem. In the second half of the poem, beginning at book 13, Odysseus is back home in Ithaca. But his journey is only half complete. He arrives home as a stranger, disguised as a poor beggar. The act of homecoming seems to require several stages, beyond merely reaching a geographic location. Odysseus comes up with multiple tales to explain his presence in Ithaca; he uses his many disguises to test the loyalty of those he meets—and, as in the encounter with Polyphemus, he must show enormous self-control in his willingness to suppress his identity, at least temporarily. Throughout the poem, Odysseus has a particularly close affinity with poets and storytellers; he himself narrates his wanderings to the Phaeacians, and, once back on Ithaca, he tells a series of false stories about who he is and where he comes from. Controlling and multiplying stories is one of the most important ways in which Odysseus is a "man of many turns," able to see the multiplicity of the world and constantly to redefine his own place in it.

In the course of his homecoming, Odysseus passes a series of tests, and gets tests of his own. He must show his mastery of weapons (such as the strongbow) and his knowledge of the people who make up his household. Odysseus has to win the peace by reconnecting with each loyal member of his home: his servants, his son, his father, and—most memorably—his wife, Penelope. He tests her loyalty by refusing to reveal himself to

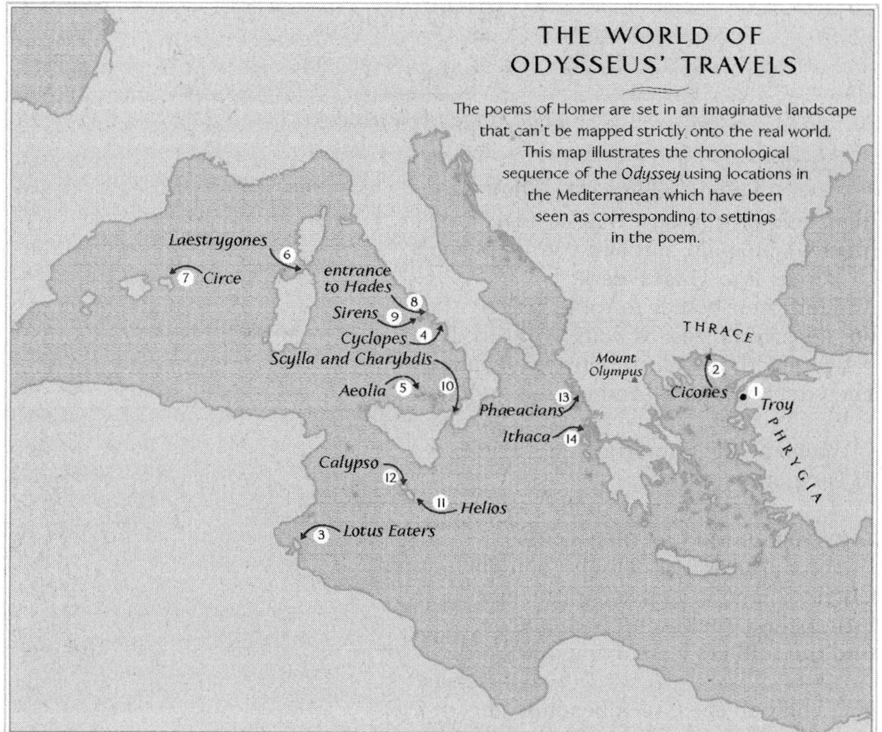

her right away. But she shows herself a perfect match for her trickster husband, putting him to yet another test. When it is bedtime, she asks the servant to bring out the bed—the bed that, as only Odysseus himself could know, is formed from a tree growing right through the house; if Odysseus were an imposter, he would think the bed could be moved. The immovable bed is, of course, an image for the permanence of Penelope and Odysseus's marriage. When they talk in the bed that night after sex, a simile suggests that now, at last, both Odysseus and Penelope have come home; he, weeping, and she, clinging to him, are like sailors saved from drowning, "glad / To be alive and set foot on dry land." The image first seems to apply to Odysseus, and then to Penelope—a shift that suggests the dynamic intimacy between husband and wife.

The *Odyssey* has elements we associate with many other types of literature: romance, folklore, heroism, mystery, travellers' tales, magic, military exploits, and family drama. It is a text that can be enjoyed on any number of levels: as a feminized version of epic—a heroic story focused not on men fighting wars, but a journey home; as a love story; as a fantasy about fathers, sons, and patriarchy; as an account of Greek identity; as a work of primitive anthropology; as a meditation on cultural difference; as a morality tale; or as a pilgrim's progress. As the first word indicates, this is a poem about "man": about humanity. An extraordinarily rich work, as multilayered and intelligent as its hero, the *Odyssey* is enjoyable on first reading, and worth rereading over and over again.

From The Iliad[1]

BOOK I

[*The Rage of Achilles*]

Rage:
Sing; Goddess,[2] Achilles' rage,
Black and murderous, that cost the Greeks
Incalculable pain, pitched countless souls
Of heroes into Hades' dark,
And left their bodies to rot as feasts
For dogs and birds, as Zeus' will was done.
Begin with the clash between Agamemnon—
The Greek warlord—and godlike Achilles.

Which of the immortals set these two
At each other's throats?
Apollo,
Zeus' son and Leto's, offended
By the warlord. Agamemnon had dishonored
Chryses,[3] Apollo's priest, so the god
Struck the Greek camp with plague,
And the soldiers were dying of it.
Chryses
Had come to the Greek beachhead camp
Hauling a fortune for his daughter's ransom.
Displaying Apollo's sacral ribbons
On a golden staff, he made a formal plea
To the entire Greek army, but especially
The commanders, Atreus' two sons:

"Sons of Atreus and Greek heroes all:
May the gods on Olympus grant you plunder
Of Priam's city[4] and a safe return home.
But give me my daughter back and accept
This ransom out of respect for Zeus' son,
Lord Apollo, who deals death from afar."

A murmur rippled through the ranks:
"Respect the priest and take the ransom."
But Agamemnon was not pleased
And dismissed Chryses with a rough speech:

"Don't let me ever catch you, old man, by these ships again,
Skulking around now or sneaking back later.

1. Translated by Stanley Lombardo.

2. The Muse, inspiration for epic poetry.

3. Chryses is from the town of Chryse near Troy. The Greeks had captured his daughter when they sacked Thebes (see below) and had given her to Agamemnon as his share of the booty.

4. Troy; Priam is its king. Olympus is the mountain in northern Greece that was supposed to be the home of the gods.

The god's staff and ribbons won't save you next time.
The girl is mine, and she'll be an old woman in Argos[5]
Before I let her go, working the loom in my house
And coming to my bed, far from her homeland.
Now clear out of here before you make me angry!"

The old man was afraid and did as he was told.
He walked in silence along the whispering surf line,
And when he had gone some distance the priest
Prayed to Lord Apollo, son of silken-haired Leto:

"Hear me, Silverbow, Protector of Chryse,
Lord of Holy Cilia, Master of Tenedos,[6]
And Sminthian[7] God of Plague!
If ever I've built a temple that pleased you
Or burnt fat thighbones of bulls and goats[8]—
   Grant me this prayer:
Let the Danaans[9] pay for my tears with your arrows!"

Apollo heard his prayer and descended Olympus' crags
Pulsing with fury, bow slung over one shoulder,
The arrows rattling in their case on his back
As the angry god moved like night down the mountain.

He settled near the ships and let loose an arrow.
Reverberation from his silver bow hung in the air.
He picked off the pack animals first, and the lean hounds,
But then aimed his needle-tipped arrows at the men
And shot until the death-fires crowded the beach.

Nine days the god's arrows rained death on the camp.
On the tenth day Achilles called an assembly.
Hera,[1] the white-armed goddess, planted the thought in him
Because she cared for the Greeks and it pained her
To see them dying. When the troops had all mustered,
Up stood the great runner Achilles, and said:

"Well, Agamemnon, it looks as if we'd better give up
And sail home—assuming any of us are left alive—
If we have to fight both the war and this plague.
But why not consult some prophet or priest
Or a dream interpreter, since dreams too come from Zeus,
Who could tell us why Apollo is so angry,

5. Agamemnon's home in the northeastern Peloponnesus, the southern part of mainland Greece.
6. An island off the Trojan coast. Like Chryse, Cilla is a town near Troy.
7. A cult epithet of Apollo, probably a reference to his role as the destroyer of field mice (the Greek *sminthos* means "mouse").
8. In sacrifice to Apollo.
9. The Greeks. Homer also calls them Achaeans and Argives.
1. Sister and wife of Zeus; she was hostile to the Trojans and therefore favored the Greeks.

If it's for a vow or a sacrifice he holds us at fault.
Maybe he'd be willing to lift this plague from us
If he savored the smoke from lambs and prime goats."

Achilles had his say and sat down. Then up rose
Calchas, son of Thestor, bird-reader supreme,
Who knew what is, what will be, and what has been.
He had guided the Greek ships to Troy
Through the prophetic power Apollo
Had given him, and he spoke out now:

"Achilles, beloved of Zeus, you want me to tell you
About the rage of Lord Apollo, the Arch-Destroyer.
And I will tell you. But you have to promise me and swear
You will support me and protect me in word and deed.
I have a feeling I might offend a person of some authority
Among the Greeks, and you know how it is when a king
Is angry with an underling. He might swallow his temper
For a day, but he holds it in his heart until later
And it all comes out. Will you guarantee my security?"

Achilles, the great runner, responded:

"Don't worry. Prophesy to the best of your knowledge.
I swear by Apollo, to whom you pray when you reveal
The gods' secrets to the Greeks, Calchas, that while I live
And look upon this earth, no one will lay a hand
On you here beside these hollow ships, no, not even
Agamemnon, who boasts he is the best of the Achaeans."

And Calchas, the perfect prophet, taking courage:

"The god finds no fault with vow or sacrifice.
It is for his priest, whom Agamemnon dishonored
And would not allow to ransom his daughter,
That Apollo deals and will deal death from afar.
He will not lift this foul plague from the Greeks
Until we return the dancing-eyed girl to her father
Unransomed, unbought, and make formal sacrifice
On Chryse. Only then might we appease the god."

He finished speaking and sat down. Then up rose
Atreus' son, the warlord Agamemnon,
Furious, anger like twin black thunderheads seething
In his lungs, and his eyes flickered with fire
As he looked Calchas up and down, and said:

"You damn soothsayer!
You've never given me a good omen yet.
You take some kind of perverse pleasure in prophesying
Doom, don't you? Not a single favorable omen ever!

Nothing good ever happens! And now you stand here
Uttering oracles before the Greeks, telling us
That your great ballistic god is giving us all this trouble
Because I was unwilling to accept the ransom
For Chryses' daughter but preferred instead to keep her
In my tent! And why shouldn't I? I like her better than
My wife Clytemnestra. She's no worse than her
When it comes to looks, body, mind, or ability.
Still, I'll give her back, if that's what's best.
I don't want to see the army destroyed like this.
But I want another prize ready for me right away.
I'm not going to be the only Greek without a prize,
It wouldn't be right. And you all see where mine is going."

And Achilles, strong, swift, and godlike:

"And where do you think, son of Atreus,
You greedy glory-hound, the magnanimous Greeks
Are going to get another prize for you?
Do you think we have some kind of stockpile in reserve?
Every town in the area has been sacked and the stuff all divided.
You want the men to count it all back and redistribute it?
All right, you give the girl back to the god. The army
Will repay you three and four times over—when and if
Zeus allows us to rip Troy down to its foundations."

The warlord Agamemnon responded:

"You may be a good man in a fight, Achilles,
And look like a god, but don't try to put one over on me—
It won't work. So while you have your prize,
You want me to sit tight and do without?
Give the girl back, just like that? Now maybe
If the army, in a generous spirit, voted me
Some suitable prize of their own choice, something fair—
But if it doesn't, I'll just go take something myself,
Your prize perhaps, or Ajax's, or Odysseus',[2]
And whoever she belongs to, it'll stick in his throat.

But we can think about that later.
Right now we launch
A black ship on the bright salt water, get a crew aboard,
Load on a hundred bulls, and have Chryseis[3] board her too,
My girl with her lovely cheeks. And we'll want a good man
For captain, Ajax or Idomeneus[4] or godlike Odysseus—

2. Ajax, son of Telamon, was the bravest of the Greeks after Achilles, Odysseus the most crafty of the Greeks.

3. Daughter of Chryses.

4. King of Crete and a prominent leader on the Greek side.

Or maybe you, son of Peleus, our most formidable hero—
To offer sacrifice and appease the Arch-Destroyer for us."

Achilles looked him up and down and said:

"You shameless, profiteering excuse for a commander!
How are you going to get any Greek warrior
To follow you into battle again? You know,
I don't have any quarrel with the Trojans,
They didn't do anything to *me* to make me
Come over here and fight, didn't run off *my* cattle or horses
Or ruin *my* farmland back home in Phthia,[5] not with all
The shadowy mountains and moaning seas between.
It's for *you*, dogface, for your precious pleasure—
And Menelaus'[6] honor—that we came here,
A fact you don't have the decency even to mention!
And now you're threatening to take away the prize
That I sweated for and the Greeks gave me.
I never get a prize equal to yours when the army
Captures one of the Trojan strongholds.
No, I do all the dirty work with my own hands,
And when the battle's over and we divide the loot
You get the lion's share and I go back to the ships
With some pitiful little thing, so worn out from fighting
I don't have the strength left even to complain.
Well, I'm going back to Phthia now. Far better
To head home with my curved ships than stay here,
Unhonored myself and piling up a fortune for you."

The warlord Agamemnon responded:

"Go ahead and desert, if that's what you want!
I'm not going to beg you to stay. There are plenty of others
Who will honor me, not least of all Zeus the Counselor.
To me, you're the most hateful king under heaven,
A born troublemaker. You actually *like* fighting and war.
If you're all that strong, it's just a gift from some god.
So why don't you go home with your ships and lord it over
Your precious Myrmidons.[7] I couldn't care less about you
Or your famous temper. But I'll tell you this:
Since Phoebus Apollo is taking away my Chryseis,
Whom I'm sending back aboard ship with my friends,
I'm coming to your hut and taking Briseis,[8]
Your own beautiful prize, so that you will see just how much
Stronger I am than you, and the next person will wince
At the thought of opposing me as an equal."

5. Achilles' home in northern Greece.
6. Agamemnon's brother. The aim of the expedition against Troy was to recover his wife, Helen, who had run off with Paris, a son of Priam.
7. The contingent led by Achilles.
8. A captive woman who had been awarded to Achilles.

Achilles' chest was a rough knot of pain
Twisting around his heart: should he
Draw the sharp sword that hung by his thigh,
Scatter the ranks and gut Agamemnon,
Or control his temper, repress his rage?
He was mulling it over, inching the great sword
From its sheath, when out of the blue
Athena[9] came, sent by the white-armed goddess
Hera, who loved and watched over both men.
She stood behind Achilles and grabbed his sandy hair,
Visible only to him: not another soul saw her.
Awestruck, Achilles turned around, recognizing
Pallas Athena at once—it was her eyes—
And words flew from his mouth like winging birds:

"Daughter of Zeus! Why have you come here?
To see Agamemnon's arrogance, no doubt.
I'll tell you where I place my bets, Goddess:
Sudden death for this outrageous behavior."

Athena's eyes glared through the sea's salt haze.

"I came to see if I could check this temper of yours,
Sent from heaven by the white-armed goddess
Hera, who loves and watches over both of you men.
Now come on, drop this quarrel, don't draw your sword.
Tell him off instead. And I'll tell you,
Achilles, how things will be: You're going to get
Three times as many magnificent gifts
Because of his arrogance. Just listen to us and be patient."

Achilles, the great runner, responded:

"When you two speak, Goddess, a man has to listen
No matter how angry. It's better that way.
Obey the gods and they hear you when you pray."

With that he ground his heavy hand
Onto the silver hilt and pushed the great sword
Back into its sheath. Athena's speech
Had been well-timed. She was on her way
To Olympus by now, to the halls of Zeus

9. A goddess, daughter of Zeus, and a patron of human ingenuity and resourcefulness, whether exemplified by handicrafts (such as carpentry or weaving) or cunning in dealing with others. One of her epithets is Pallas. Like Hera, she sided with the Greeks in the war.

And the other immortals, while Achilles
Tore into Agamemnon again:

"You bloated drunk,
With a dog's eyes and a rabbit's heart!
You've never had the guts to buckle on armor in battle
Or come out with the best fighting Greeks
On any campaign! Afraid to look Death in the eye,
Agamemnon? It's far more profitable
To hang back in the army's rear—isn't it?—
Confiscating prizes from any Greek who talks back
And bleeding your people dry. There's not a real man
Under your command, or this latest atrocity
Would be your last, son of Atreus.
Now get this straight. I swear a formal oath:
By this scepter,[1] which will never sprout leaf
Or branch again since it was cut from its stock
In the mountains, which will bloom no more
Now that bronze has pared off leaf and bark,
And which now the sons of the Greeks hold in their hands
At council, upholding Zeus' laws—
By this scepter I swear:
When every last Greek desperately misses Achilles,
Your remorse won't do any good then,
When Hector[2] the man-killer swats you down like flies.
And you will eat your heart out
Because you failed to honor the best Greek of all."

Those were his words, and he slammed the scepter,
Studded with gold, to the ground and sat down.

Opposite him, Agamemnon fumed.
Then Nestor
Stood up, sweet-worded Nestor, the orator from Pylos[3]
With a voice high-toned and liquid as honey.
He had seen two generations of men pass away
In sandy Pylos and was now king in the third.
He was full of good will in the speech he made:

"It's a sad day for Greece, a sad day.
Priam and Priam's sons would be happy indeed,
And the rest of the Trojans too, glad in their hearts,
If they learned all this about you two fighting,
Our two best men in council and in battle.
Now you listen to me, both of you. You are both

1. A wooden staff that symbolized authority. It was handed by a herald to whichever leader rose to speak in an assembly as a sign of his authority to speak.

2. Son of Priam; he was the foremost warrior among the Trojans.

3. A territory on the western shore of the Peloponnesus.

Younger than I am, and I've associated with men
Better than you, and they didn't treat me lightly.
I've never seen men like those, and never will,
The likes of Peirithous and Dryas, a shepherd to his people,
Caineus and Exadius and godlike Polyphemus,
And Aegeus' son, Theseus,[4] who could have passed for a god,
The strongest men who ever lived on earth, the strongest,
And they fought with the strongest, with wild things
From the mountains, and beat the daylights out of them.
I was their companion, although I came from Pylos,
From the ends of the earth—they sent for me themselves.
And I held my own fighting with them. You couldn't find
A mortal on earth who could fight with them now.
And when I talked in council, they took my advice.
So should you two now: taking advice is a good thing.
   Agamemnon, for all your nobility, don't take his girl.
Leave her be: the army originally gave her to him as a prize.
Nor should you, son of Peleus, want to lock horns with a king.
A scepter-holding king has honor beyond the rest of men,
Power and glory given by Zeus himself.
You are stronger, and it is a goddess[5] who bore you.
But he is more powerful, since he rules over more.
Son of Atreus, cease your anger. And I appeal
Personally to Achilles to control his temper, since he is,
For all Greeks, a mighty bulwark in this evil war."

And Agamemnon, the warlord:

"Yes, old man, everything you've said is absolutely right.
But this man wants to be ahead of everyone else,
He wants to rule everyone, give orders to everyone,
Lord it over everyone, and he's not going to get away with it.
If the gods eternal made him a spearman, does that mean
They gave him permission to be insolent as well?"

And Achilles, breaking in on him:

"Ha, and think of the names people would call me
If I bowed and scraped every time you opened your mouth.
Try that on somebody else, but not on me.
I'll tell you this, and you can stick it in your gut:
I'm not going to put up a fight on account of the girl.

4. Heroes of an earlier generation. Except for the Athenian Theseus, these are the Lapiths from Thessaly in northern Greece. At the wedding of Peirithous, the mountain-dwelling centaurs (half human, half horse) got drunk and tried to rape the women who were present. The Lapiths killed them after a fierce fight.

5. The sea nymph Thetis, who was married to the mortal Peleus (Achilles' father). She later left him and went to live with her father, Nereus, in the depths of the Aegean Sea.

You, all of you, gave her and you can all take her back.
But anything else of mine in my black sailing ship
You keep your goddamn hands off, you hear?
Try it. Let everybody here see how fast
Your black blood boils up around my spear."

So it was a stand-off, their battle of words,
And the assembly beside the Greek ships dissolved.
Achilles went back to the huts by his ships
With Patroclus[6] and his men. Agamemnon had a fast ship
Hauled down to the sea, picked twenty oarsmen,
Loaded on a hundred bulls due to the god, and had Chryses' daughter,
His fair-cheeked girl, go aboard also. Odysseus captained,
And when they were all on board, the ship headed out to sea.

Onshore, Agamemnon ordered a purification.
The troops scrubbed down and poured the filth
Into the sea. Then they sacrificed to Apollo
Oxen and goats by the hundreds on the barren shore.
The smoky savor swirled up to the sky.

That was the order of the day. But Agamemnon
Did not forget his spiteful threat against Achilles.
He summoned Talthybius and Eurybates,
Faithful retainers who served as his heralds:

"Go to the hut of Achilles, son of Peleus;
Bring back the girl, fair-cheeked Briseis.
If he won't give her up, I'll come myself
With my men and take her—and freeze his heart cold."

It was not the sort of mission a herald would relish.
The pair trailed along the barren seashore
Until they came to the Myrmidons' ships and encampment.
They found Achilles sitting outside his hut
Beside his black ship. He was not glad to see them.
They stood respectfully silent, in awe of this king,
And it was Achilles who was moved to address them first:

"Welcome, heralds, the gods' messengers and men's.
Come closer. You're not to blame, Agamemnon is,
Who sent you here for the girl, Briseis.
Patroclus,
Bring the girl out and give her to these gentlemen.
You two are witnesses before the blessed gods,
Before mortal men and that hard-hearted king,
If ever I'm needed to protect the others
From being hacked to bits. His mind is murky with anger,

6. Achilles' closest friend.

And he doesn't have the sense to look ahead and behind
To see how the Greeks might defend their ships."

Thus Achilles.
Patroclus obeyed his beloved friend
And brought Briseis, cheeks flushed, out of the tent
And gave her to the heralds, who led her away.
She went unwillingly.
Then Achilles, in tears,
Withdrew from his friends and sat down far away
On the foaming white seashore, staring out
At the endless sea. Stretching out his hands,
He prayed over and over to his beloved mother:

"Mother, since you bore me for a short life only,
Olympian Zeus was supposed to grant me honor.
Well, he hasn't given me any at all. Agamemnon
Has taken away my prize and dishonored me."

His voice, choked with tears, was heard by his mother
As she sat in the sea-depths beside her old father.
She rose up from the white-capped sea like a mist,
And settling herself beside her weeping child
She stroked him with her hand and talked to him:

"Why are you crying, son? What's wrong?
Don't keep it inside. Tell me so we'll both know."

And Achilles, with a deep groan:

"You already know. Why do I have to tell you?
We went after Thebes, Eëtion's[7] sacred town,
Sacked it and brought the plunder back here.
The army divided everything up and chose
For Agamemnon fair-cheeked Chryseis.
Then her father, Chryses, a priest of Apollo,
Came to our army's ships on the beachhead,
Hauling a fortune for his daughter's ransom.
He displayed Apollo's sacral ribbons
On a golden staff and made a formal plea
To the entire Greek army, but especially
The commanders, Atreus' two sons.
You could hear the troops murmuring,
'Respect the priest and take the ransom.'
But Agamemnon wouldn't hear of it
And dismissed Chryses with a rough speech.
The old man went back angry, and Apollo
Heard his beloved priest's prayer.

7. Eëtion was king of the Cilicians in Asia Minor and father of Hector's wife, Andromache. "Thebes" (or Thebe): the Cilicians' capital city, not the Greek or Egyptian city of the same name.

He hit the Greeks hard, and the troops
Were falling over dead, the god's arrows
Raining down all through the Greek camp.
A prophet told us the Arch-Destroyer's will,
And I demanded the god be appeased.
Agamemnon got angry, stood up
And threatened me, and made good his threat.
The high command sent the girl on a fast ship
Back to Chryse with gifts for Apollo,
And heralds led away my girl, Briseis,
Whom the army had given to me.
Now you have to help me, if you can.
  Go to Olympus
And call in the debt that Zeus owes you.
I remember often hearing you tell
In my father's house how you alone managed,
Of all the immortals, to save Zeus' neck
When the other Olympians wanted to bind him—
Hera and Poseidon[8] and Pallas Athena.
You came and loosened him from his chains,
And you lured to Olympus' summit the giant
With a hundred hands whom the gods call
Briareus but men call Aegaeon, stronger
Even than his own father Uranus,[9] and he
Sat hulking in front of cloud-black Zeus,
Proud of his prowess, and scared all the gods
Who were trying to put the son of Cronus in chains.
  Remind Zeus of this, sit holding his knees,
See if he is willing to help the Trojans
Hem the Greeks in between the fleet and the sea.
Once they start being killed, the Greeks may
Appreciate Agamemnon for what he is,
And the wide-ruling son of Atreus will see
What a fool he's been because he did not honor
The best of all the fighting Achaeans."

And Thetis, now weeping herself:

"O my poor child. I bore you for sorrow,
Nursed you for grief. Why? You should be
Spending your time here by your ships
Happily and untroubled by tears,
Since life is short for you, all too brief.
Now you're destined for both an early death
And misery beyond compare. It was for this
I gave birth to you in your father's palace
Under an evil star.
                I'll go to snow-bound Olympus

8. Brother of Zeus and god of the sea.
9. The Sky, husband of Earth and the first divine ruler. He was overthrown by his son Cronus, who in turn was overthrown by his son Zeus.

And tell all this to the Lord of Lightning.
I hope he listens. You stay here, though,
Beside your ships and let the Greeks feel
Your spite; withdraw completely from the war.
Zeus left yesterday for the River Ocean
On his way to a feast with the Ethiopians.[1]
All the gods went with him. He'll return
To Olympus twelve days from now,
And I'll go then to his bronze threshold
And plead with him. I think I'll persuade him."

And she left him there, angry and heartsick
At being forced to give up the silken-waisted girl.

Meanwhile, Odysseus was putting in
At Chryse with his sacred cargo on board.
When they were well within the deepwater harbor
They furled the sail and stowed it in the ship's hold,
Slackened the forestays and lowered the mast,
Working quickly, then rowed her to a mooring, where
They dropped anchor and made the stern cables fast.
The crew disembarked on the seabeach
And unloaded the bulls for Apollo the Archer.
Then Chryses' daughter stepped off the seagoing vessel,
And Odysseus led her to an altar
And placed her in her father's hands, saying:

"Chryses, King Agamemnon has sent me here
To return your child and offer to Phoebus
Formal sacrifice on behalf of the Greeks.
So may we appease Lord Apollo, and may he
Lift the afflictions he has sent upon us."

Chryses received his daughter tenderly.

Moving quickly, they lined the hundred oxen
Round the massive altar, a glorious offering,
Washed their hands and sprinkled on the victims
Sacrificial barley. On behalf of the Greeks
Chryses lifted his hands and prayed aloud:

"Hear me, Silverbow, Protector of Chryse,
Lord of Holy Cilla, Master of Tenedos,
As once before you heard my prayer,
Did me honor, and smote the Greeks mightily,
So now also grant me this prayer:
Lift the plague
From the Greeks and save them from death."

1. A people believed to live at the extreme edges of the world. Ocean was thought of as a river that encircled the earth.

Thus the old priest, and Apollo heard him.

After the prayers and the strewing of barley
They slaughtered and flayed the oxen,
Jointed the thighbones and wrapped them
In a layer of fat with cuts of meat on top.
The old man roasted them over charcoal
And doused them with wine. Younger men
Stood by with five-tined forks in their hands.
When the thigh pieces were charred and they had
Tasted the tripe, they cut the rest into strips,
Skewered it on spits and roasted it skillfully.
When they were done and the feast was ready,
Feast they did, and no one lacked an equal share.
When they had all had enough to eat and drink,
The young men topped off mixing bowls with wine
And served it in goblets to all the guests.
All day long these young Greeks propitiated
The god with dancing, singing to Apollo
A paean[2] as they danced, and the god was pleased.
When the sun went down and darkness came on,
They went to sleep by the ship's stern-cables.

Dawn came early, a palmetto of rose,
Time to make sail for the wide beachhead camp.
They set up mast and spread the white canvas,
And the following wind, sent by Apollo,
Boomed in the mainsail. An indigo wave
Hissed off the bow as the ship surged on,
Leaving a wake as she held on course through the billows.
When they reached the beachhead they hauled the black ship
High on the sand and jammed in the long chocks;
Then the crew scattered to their own huts and ships.

All this time Achilles, the son of Peleus in the line of Zeus,[3]
Nursed his anger, the great runner idle by his fleet's fast hulls.
He was not to be seen in council, that arena for glory,
Nor in combat. He sat tight in camp consumed with grief,
His great heart yearning for the battle cry and war.

Twelve days went by. Dawn.
The gods returned to Olympus,
Zeus at their head.
Thetis did not forget
Her son's requests. She rose from the sea
And up through the air to the great sky
And found Cronus' wide-seeing son
Sitting in isolation on the highest peak
Of the rugged Olympic massif.

2. A song of praise to Apollo.

3. Peleus was the son of Aeacus, son of Zeus.

She settled beside him, and touched his knees
With her left hand, his beard with her right,[4]
And made her plea to the Lord of Sky:

"Father Zeus, if I have ever helped you
In word or deed among the immortals,
   Grant me this prayer:
Honor my son, doomed to die young
And yet dishonored by King Agamemnon,
Who stole his prize, a personal affront.
Do justice by him, Lord of Olympus.
Give the Trojans the upper hand until the Greeks
Grant my son the honor he deserves."

Zeus made no reply but sat a long time
In silence, clouds scudding around him.
Thetis held fast to his knees and asked again:

"Give me a clear yes or no. Either nod in assent
Or refuse me. Why should you care if I know
How negligible a goddess I am in your eyes."

This provoked a troubled, gloomy response:

"This is disastrous. You're going to force me
Into conflict with Hera. I can just hear her now,
Cursing me and bawling me out. As it is,
She already accuses me of favoring the Trojans.
Please go back the way you came. Maybe
Hera won't notice. I'll take care of this.
And so you can have some peace of mind,
I'll say yes to you by nodding my head,
The ultimate pledge. Unambiguous,
Irreversible, and absolutely fulfilled,
Whatever I say yes to with a nod of my head."

And the Son of Cronus nodded. Black brows
Lowered, a glory of hair cascaded down from the Lord's
Immortal head, and the holy mountain trembled.

   Their conference over, the two parted. The goddess
Dove into the deep sea from Olympus' snow-glare
And Zeus went to his home. The gods all
Rose from their seats at their father's entrance. Not one
Dared watch him enter without standing to greet him.
And so the god entered and took his high seat.
                                                            But Hera
Had noticed his private conversation with Thetis,

4. She takes on the posture of the suppliant, which physically emphasizes the desperation and urgency of her request. Zeus was, above all other gods, the protector of suppliants.

The silver-footed daughter of the Old Man of the Sea,
And flew at him with cutting words:

"Who was that you were scheming with just now?
You just love devising secret plots behind my back,
Don't you? You can't bear to tell me what you're thinking,
Or you don't dare. Never have and never will."

The Father of Gods and Men answered:

"Hera, don't hope to know all my secret thoughts.
It would strain your mind even though you are my wife.
What it is proper to hear, no one, human or divine,
Will hear before you. But what I wish to conceive
Apart from the other gods, don't pry into that."

And Lady Hera, with her oxen eyes wide:

"Oh my. The awesome son of Cronus has spoken.
Pry? You know that I never pry. And you always
Cheerfully volunteer—whatever information you please.
It's just that I have this feeling that somehow
The silver-footed daughter of the Old Man of the Sea
May have won you over. She *was* sitting beside you
Up there in the mists, and she did touch your knees.
And I'm pretty sure that you agreed to honor Achilles
And destroy Greeks by the thousands beside their ships."

And Zeus, the master of cloud and storm:

"You witch! Your intuitions are always right.
But what does it get you? Nothing, except that
I like you less than ever. And so you're worse off.
If it's as you think it is, it's my business, not yours.
So sit down and shut up and do as I say.
You see these hands? All the gods on Olympus
Won't be able to help you if I ever lay them on you."

Hera lost her nerve when she heard this.
She sat down in silence, fear cramping her heart,
And gloom settled over the gods in Zeus' hall.
Hephaestus,[5] the master artisan, broke the silence,
Out of concern for his ivory-armed mother:

"This is terrible; it's going to ruin us all.
If you two quarrel like this over mortals
It's bound to affect us gods. There'll be no more
Pleasure in our feasts if we let things turn ugly.
Mother, please, I don't have to tell you,

5. The lame god of fire and the patron of craftspeople, especially metalworkers.

You have to be pleasant to our father Zeus
So he won't be angry and ruin our feast.
If the Lord of Lightning wants to blast us from our seats,
He can—that's how much stronger he is.
So apologize to him with silken-soft words,
And the Olympian in turn will be gracious to us."

He whisked up a two-handled cup, offered it
To his dear mother, and said to her:

"I know it's hard, mother, but you have to endure it.
I don't want to see you getting beat up, and me
Unable to help you. The Olympian can be rough.
Once before when I tried to rescue you
He flipped me by my foot off our balcony.
I fell all day and came down when the sun did
On the island of Lemnos[6] scarcely alive.
The Sintians had to nurse me back to health."

By the time he finished, the ivory-armed goddess
Was smiling at her son. She accepted the cup from him.
Then the lame god turned serving boy, siphoning nectar[7]
From the mixing bowl and pouring the sweet liquor
For all of the gods, who couldn't stop laughing
At the sight of Hephaestus hustling through the halls.

And so all day long until the sun went down
They feasted to their hearts' content,
Apollo playing beautiful melodies on the lyre,
The Muses singing responsively in lovely voices.
And when the last gleams of sunset had faded,
They turned in for the night, each to a house
Built by Hephaestus, the renowned master craftsman,
The burly blacksmith with the soul of an artist.
And the Lord of Lightning, Olympian Zeus, went to his bed,
The bed he always slept in when sweet sleep overcame him.
He climbed in and slept, next to golden-throned Hera.

Summary The Greeks, in spite of Achilles' withdrawal, continued to fight. They did not suffer excessively from Achilles' absence; on the contrary, they pressed the Trojans so hard that Hector, the Trojan leader, after rallying his men, returned to the city to urge the Trojans to offer special prayers and sacrifices to the gods.

6. An island in the Aegean Sea, inhabited by the Sintians.

7. The drink of the gods.

FROM BOOK VI

[*Hector Returns to Troy*]

And Hector left, helmet collecting light
Above the black-hide shield whose rim tapped
His ankles and neck with each step he took.

Then Glaucus, son of Hippolochus,
Met Diomedes[8] in no-man's-land.
Both were eager to fight, but first Tydeus' son
Made his voice heard above the battle noise:

"And which mortal hero are you? I've never seen you
Out here before on the fields of glory,
And now here you are ahead of everyone,
Ready to face my spear. Pretty bold.
I feel sorry for your parents. Of course,
You may be an immortal, down from heaven.
Far be it from me to fight an immortal god.
Not even mighty Lycurgus[9] lived long
After he tangled with the immortals,
Driving the nurses of Dionysus[1]
Down over the Mountain of Nysa
And making them drop their wands
As he beat them with an ox-goad. Dionysus
Was terrified and plunged into the sea,
Where Thetis received him into her bosom,
Trembling with fear at the human's threats.
Then the gods, who live easy, grew angry
With Lycurgus, and the Son of Cronus
Made him go blind, and he did not live long,
Hated as he was by the immortal gods.
No, I wouldn't want to fight an immortal.
But if you are human, and shed blood,
Step right up for a quick end to your life."

And Glaucus, Hippolochus' son:

"Great son of Tydeus, why ask about my lineage?
Human generations are like leaves in their seasons.
The wind blows them to the ground, but the tree
Sprouts new ones when spring comes again.
Men too. Their generations come and go.
But if you really do want to hear my story,
You're welcome to listen. Many men know it.
Ephyra,[2] in the heart of Argive horse country,

8. One of the foremost Greek leaders, son of Tydeus. "Glaucus": a Trojan ally, from Lycia in Asia Minor.
9. King of Thrace, a half-wild region along the north shore of the Aegean Sea.
1. God of the vine.
2. An old name for Corinth, a city in the northeast Peloponnesus.

Was home to Sisyphus, the shrewdest man alive,
Sisyphus son of Aeolus. He had a son, Glaucus,
Who was the father of faultless Bellerophon,
A man of grace and courage by gift of the gods.
But Proetus, whom Zeus had made king of Argos,
Came to hate Bellerophon
And drove him out. It happened this way.
Proetus' wife, the beautiful Anteia,
Was madly in love with Bellerophon
And wanted to have him in her bed.
But she couldn't persuade him, not at all,
Because he was so virtuous and wise.
So she made up lies and spoke to the king:
'Either die yourself, Proetus, or kill Bellerophon.
He wanted to sleep with me against my will.'
The king was furious when he heard her say this.
He did not kill him—he had scruples about that—
But he sent him to Lycia with a folding tablet
On which he had scratched many evil signs,
And told him to give it to Anteia's father,
To get him killed. So off he went to Lycia,
With an immortal escort, and when he reached
The river Xanthus,[3] the king there welcomed him
And honored him with entertainment
For nine solid days, killing an ox each day.
But when the tenth dawn spread her rosy light,
He questioned him and asked to see the tokens
He brought from Proetus, his daughter's husband.
And when he saw the evil tokens from Proetus,
He ordered him, first, to kill the Chimaera,
A raging monster, divine, inhuman—
A lion in the front, a serpent in the rear,
In the middle a goat—and breathing fire.
Bellerophon killed her, trusting signs from the gods.
Next he had to fight the glorious Solymi,
The hardest battle, he said, he ever fought,
And, third, the Amazons, women the peers of men.
As he journeyed back the king wove another wile.
He chose the best men in all wide Lycia
And laid an ambush. Not one returned home;
Blameless Bellerophon killed them all.
When the king realized his guest had divine blood,
He kept him there and gave him his daughter
And half of all his royal honor. Moreover,
The Lycians cut out for him a superb
Tract of land, plow-land and orchard.
His wife, the princess, bore him three children,
Isander, Hippolochus, and Laodameia.
Zeus in his wisdom slept with Laodameia,

3. A river in Lycia.

And she bore him the godlike warrior Sarpedon.
But even Bellerophon lost the gods' favor
And went wandering alone over the Aleian plain.
His son Isander was slain by Ares
As he fought against the glorious Solymi,
And his daughter was killed by Artemis
Of the golden reins. But Hippolochus
Bore me, and I am proud he is my father.
He sent me to Troy with strict instructions
To be the best ever, better than all the rest,
And not to bring shame on the race of my fathers,
The noblest men in Ephyra and Lycia.
This, I am proud to say, is my lineage."

Diomedes grinned when he heard all this.
He planted his spear in the bounteous earth
And spoke gently to the Lycian prince:

"We have old ties of hospitality!
My grandfather Oeneus long ago
Entertained Bellerophon in his halls
For twenty days, and they gave each other
Gifts of friendship.[4] Oeneus gave
A belt bright with scarlet, and Bellerophon
A golden cup, which I left at home.
I don't remember my father Tydeus,
Since I was very small when he left for Thebes
In the war that killed so many Achaeans.[5]
But that makes me your friend and you my guest
If ever you come to Argos, as you are my friend
And I your guest whenever I travel to Lycia.
So we can't cross spears with each other
Even in the thick of battle. There are enough
Trojans and allies for me to kill, whomever
A god gives me and I can run down myself.
And enough Greeks for you to kill as you can.
And let's exchange armor, so everyone will know
That we are friends from our fathers' days."

With this said, they vaulted from their chariots,
Clasped hands, and pledged their friendship.
But Zeus took away Glaucus' good sense,
For he exchanged his golden armor for bronze,
The worth of one hundred oxen for nine.
When Hector reached the oak tree by the Western Gate,

4. It was customary for guest-friends to exchange gifts.

5. Tydeus was one of the seven heroes who attacked Thebes. They were led by Oedipus's son Polynices, who was attempting to dislodge his brother, Eteocles, from the kingship. The brothers killed each other, and the rest of the seven also perished. Diomedes, along with the sons of the other champions, later sacked Thebes.

Trojan wives and daughters ran up to him,
Asking about their children, their brothers,
Their kinsmen, their husbands. He told them all,
Each woman in turn, to pray to the gods.
Sorrow clung to their heads like mist.

Then he came to Priam's palace, a beautiful
Building made of polished stone with a central courtyard
Flanked by porticoes, upon which opened fifty
Adjoining rooms, where Priam's sons
Slept with their wives. Across the court
A suite of twelve more bedrooms housed
His modest daughters and their husbands.
It was here that Hector's mother[6] met him,
A gracious woman, with Laodice,
Her most beautiful daughter, in tow.
Hecuba took his hand in hers and said:

"Hector, my son, why have you left the war
And come here? Are those abominable Greeks
Wearing you down in the fighting outside,
And does your heart lead you to our acropolis
To stretch your hands upward to Zeus?
But stay here while I get you
Some honey-sweet wine, so you can pour a libation
To Father Zeus first and the other immortals,
Then enjoy some yourself, if you will drink.
Wine greatly bolsters a weary man's spirits,
And you are weary from defending your kinsmen."

Sunlight shimmered on great Hector's helmet.

"Mother, don't offer me any wine.
It would drain the power out of my limbs.
I have too much reverence to pour a libation
With unwashed hands to Zeus almighty,
Or to pray to Cronion[7] in the black cloudbanks
Spattered with blood and the filth of battle.
But you must go to the War Goddess's[8] temple
To make sacrifice with a band of old women.
Choose the largest and loveliest robe in the house,
The one that is dearest of all to you,
And place it on the knees of braided Athena.
And promise twelve heifers to her in her temple,
Unblemished yearlings, if she will pity
The town of Troy, its wives, and its children,
And if she will keep from holy Ilion[9]
Wild Diomedes, who's raging with his spear.

6. Hecuba.
7. The son of Cronus (i.e., Zeus).
8. Athena's.
9. Another name for Troy.

Go then to the temple of Athena the War Goddess,
And I will go over to summon Paris,[1]
If he will listen to what I have to say.
I wish the earth would gape open beneath him.
Olympian Zeus has bred him as a curse
To Troy, to Priam, and all Priam's children.
If I could see him dead and gone to Hades,
I think my heart might be eased of its sorrow."

Thus Hector. Hecuba went to the great hall
And called to her handmaidens, and they
Gathered together the city's old women.
She went herself to a fragrant storeroom
Which held her robes, the exquisite work
Of Sidonian[2] women whom godlike Paris
Brought from Phoenicia when he sailed the sea
On the voyage he made for high-born Helen.
Hecuba chose the robe that lay at the bottom,
The most beautiful of all, woven of starlight,
And bore it away as a gift for Athena.
A stream of old women followed behind.

They came to the temple of Pallas Athena
On the city's high rock, and the doors were opened
By fair-checked Theano, daughter of Cisseus
And wife of Antenor, breaker of horses.
The Trojans had made her Athena's priestess.
With ritual cries they all lifted their hands
To Pallas Athena. Theano took the robe
And laid it on the knees of the rich-haired goddess,
Then prayed in supplication to Zeus' daughter:

"Lady Athena who defends our city,
Brightest of goddesses, hear our prayer.
Break now the spear of Diomedes
And grant that he fall before the Western Gate,
That we may now offer twelve heifers in this temple,
Unblemished yearlings. Only do thou pity
The town of Troy, its wives and its children."

But Pallas Athena denied her prayer.

While they prayed to great Zeus' daughter,
Hector came to Paris' beautiful house,
Which he had built himself with the aid
Of the best craftsmen in all wide Troy:
Sleeping quarters, a hall, and a central courtyard

1. Hector's brother, whose seduction and abduction of Helen, the wife of Menelaus, caused the war.

2. From the Phoenician city Sidon, on the coast of what is now Lebanon.

Near to Priam's and Hector's on the city's high rock.
Hector entered, Zeus' light upon him,
A spear sixteen feet long cradled in his hand,
The bronze point gleaming, and the ferrule gold.
He found Paris in the bedroom, busy with his weapons,
Fondling his curved bow, his fine shield, and breastplate.
Helen of Argos sat with her household women
Directing their exquisite handicraft.

Hector meant to shame Paris and provoke him:[3]

"This is a fine time to be nursing your anger,
You idiot! We're dying out there defending the walls.
It's because of you the city is in this hellish war.
If you saw someone else holding back from combat
You'd pick a fight with him yourself. Now get up
Before the whole city goes up in flames!"

And Paris, handsome as a god:

"That's no more than just, Hector,
But listen now to what I have to say.
It's not out of anger or spite toward the Trojans
I've been here in my room. I only wanted
To recover from my pain. My wife was just now
Encouraging me to get up and fight,
And that seems the better thing to do.
Victory takes turns with men. Wait for me
While I put on my armor, or go on ahead—
I'm pretty sure I'll catch up with you."

To which Hector said nothing.

But Helen said to him softly:
"Brother-in-law
Of a scheming, cold-blooded bitch,
I wish that on the day my mother bore me
A windstorm had swept me away to a mountain
Or into the waves of the restless sea,
Swept me away before all this could happen.
But since the gods have ordained these evils,
Why couldn't I be the wife of a better man,
One sensitive at least to repeated reproaches?
Paris has never had an ounce of good sense
And never will. He'll pay for it someday.
But come inside and sit down on this chair,

3. In book 3, Paris fought with Menelaus in single combat to settle the war. He was about to lose when Aphrodite spirited him off to his house in Troy, where she then persuaded Helen to join him. In book 4, fighting broke out again when the Trojan archer Pandarus, on Athena's advice, wounded Menelaus.

Dear brother-in-law. You bear such a burden
For my wanton ways and Paris' witlessness.
Zeus has placed this evil fate on us so that
In time to come poets will sing of us."

And Hector, in his burnished helmet:

"Don't ask me to sit, Helen, even though
You love me. You will never persuade me.
My heart is out there with our fighting men.
They already feel my absence from battle.
Just get Paris moving, and have him hurry
So he can catch up with me while I'm still
Inside the city. I'm going to my house now
To see my family, my wife and my boy. I don't know
Whether I'll ever be back to see them again, or if
The gods will destroy me at the hands of the Greeks."

And Hector turned and left. He came to his house
But did not find white-armed Andromache there.
She had taken the child and a robed attendant
And stood on the tower, lamenting and weeping—
His blameless wife. When Hector didn't find her inside,
He paused on his way out and called to the servants:

"Can any of you women tell me exactly
Where Andromache went when she left the house?
To one of my sisters or one of my brothers' wives?
Or to the temple of Athena along with the other
Trojan women to beseech the dread goddess?"

The spry old housekeeper answered him:

"Hector, if you want the exact truth, she didn't go
To any of your sisters, or any of your brothers' wives,
Or to the temple of Athena along with the other
Trojan women to beseech the dread goddess.
She went to Ilion's great tower, because she heard
The Trojans were pressed and the Greeks were strong.
She ran off to the wall like a madwoman,
And the nurse went with her, carrying the child."

Thus the housekeeper, but Hector was gone,
Retracing his steps through the stone and tile streets
Of the great city, until he came to the Western Gate.
He was passing through it out onto the plain
When his wife came running up to meet him,
His beautiful wife, Andromache,
A gracious woman, daughter of great Eëtion,
Eëtion, who lived in the forests of Plakos
And ruled the Cilicians from Thebes-under-Plakos—

His daughter was wed to bronze-helmeted Hector.
She came up to him now, and the nurse with her
Held to her bosom their baby boy,
Hector's beloved son, beautiful as starlight,
Whom Hector had named Scamandrius[4]
But everyone else called Astyanax, Lord of the City,
For Hector alone could save Ilion now.
He looked at his son and smiled in silence.
Andromache stood close to him, shedding tears,
Clinging to his arm as she spoke these words:

"Possessed is what you are, Hector. Your courage
Is going to kill you, and you have no feeling left
For your little boy or for me, the luckless woman
Who will soon be your widow. It won't be long
Before the whole Greek army swarms and kills you.
And when they do, it will be better for me
To sink into the earth. When I lose you, Hector,
There will be nothing left, no one to turn to,
Only pain. My father and mother are dead.
Achilles killed my father when he destroyed
Our city, Thebes with its high gates,
But had too much respect to despoil his body.
He burned it instead with all his armor
And heaped up a barrow. And the spirit women[5]
Came down from the mountain, daughters
Of the storm god, and planted elm trees around it.
I had seven brothers once in that great house.
All seven went down to Hades on a single day,
Cut down by Achilles in one blinding sprint
Through their shambling cattle and silver sheep.
Mother, who was queen in the forests of Plakos,
He took back as prisoner, with all her possessions,
Then released her for a fortune in ransom.
She died in our house, shot by Artemis'[6] arrows.
Hector, you are my father, you are my mother,
You are my brother and my blossoming husband.
But show some pity and stay here by the tower,
Don't make your child an orphan, your wife a widow.
Station your men here by the fig tree, where the city
Is weakest because the wall can be scaled.
Three times their elite have tried an attack here
Rallying around Ajax or glorious Idomeneus
Or Atreus' sons or mighty Diomedes,
Whether someone in on the prophecy told them
Or they are driven here by something in their heart."

4. After the Trojan river Scamander.
5. Mountain nymphs.
6. Artemis is the virgin goddess of the hunt, dispenser of natural and painless death to women.

And great Hector, helmet shining, answered her:

"Yes, Andromache, I worry about all this myself,
But my shame before the Trojans and their wives,
With their long robes trailing, would be too terrible
If I hung back from battle like a coward.
And my heart won't let me. I have learned to be
One of the best, to fight in Troy's first ranks,
Defending my father's honor and my own.
Deep in my heart I know too well
There will come a day when holy Ilion will perish,
And Priam and the people under Priam's ash spear.
But the pain I will feel for the Trojans then,
For Hecuba herself and for Priam king,
For my many fine brothers who will have by then
Fallen in the dust behind enemy lines—
All that pain is nothing to what I will feel
For you, when some bronze-armored Greek
Leads you away in tears, on your first day of slavery.
And you will work some other woman's loom
In Argos or carry water from a Spartan spring,
All against your will, under great duress.
And someone, seeing you crying, will say,
'That is the wife of Hector, the best of all
The Trojans when they fought around Ilion.'
Someday someone will say that, renewing your pain
At having lost such a man to fight off the day
Of your enslavement. But may I be dead
And the earth heaped up above me
Before I hear your cry as you are dragged away."

With these words, resplendent Hector
Reached for his child, who shrank back screaming
Into his nurse's bosom, terrified of his father's
Bronze-encased face and the horsehair plume
He saw nodding down from the helmet's crest.
This forced a laugh from his father and mother,
And Hector removed the helmet from his head
And set it on the ground all shimmering with light.
Then he kissed his dear son and swung him up gently
And said a prayer to Zeus and the other immortals:

"Zeus and all gods: grant that this my son
Become, as I am, foremost among Trojans,
Brave and strong, and ruling Ilion with might.
And may men say he is far better than his father
When he returns from war, bearing bloody spoils,
Having killed his man. And may his mother rejoice."

And he put his son in the arms of his wife,
And she enfolded him in her fragrant bosom

Laughing through her tears. Hector pitied her
And stroked her with his hand and said to her:

"You worry too much about me, Andromache.
No one is going to send me to Hades before my time,
And no man has ever escaped his fate, rich or poor,
Coward or hero, once born into this world.
Go back to the house now and take care of your work,
The loom and the shuttle, and tell the servants
To get on with their jobs. War is the work of men,
Of all the Trojan men, and mine especially."

With these words, Hector picked up
His plumed helmet, and his wife went back home,
Turning around often, her cheeks flowered with tears.
When she came to the house of man-slaying Hector,
She found a throng of servants inside,
And raised among these women the ritual lament.
And so they mourned for Hector in his house
Although he was still alive, for they did not think
He would ever again come back from the war,
Or escape the murderous hands of the Greeks.

Paris meanwhile
Did not dally long in his high halls.
He put on his magnificent bronze-inlaid gear
And sprinted with assurance out through the city.

Picture a horse that has fed on barley in his stall
Breaking his halter and galloping across the plain,
Making for his accustomed swim in the river,
A glorious animal, head held high, mane streaming
Like wind on his shoulders. Sure of his splendor
He prances by the horse-runs and the mares in pasture.

That was how Paris, son of Priam, came down
From the high rock of Pergamum,[7]
Gleaming like amber and laughing in his armor,
And his feet were fast.
He caught up quickly
With Hector just as he turned from the spot
Where he'd talked with his wife, and called out:

"Well, dear brother, have I delayed you too much?
Am I not here in time, just as you asked?"

Hector turned, his helmet flashing light:

7. The citadel of Troy.

"I don't understand you, Paris.
No one could slight your work in battle.
You're a strong fighter, but you slack off—
You don't have the will. It breaks my heart
To hear what the Trojans say about you.
It's on your account they have all this trouble.
Come on, let's go. We can settle this later,
If Zeus ever allows us to offer in our halls
The wine bowl of freedom to the gods above,
After we drive these bronze-kneed[8] Greeks from Troy."

Summary The Trojans rallied successfully and went over to the offensive. They drove the Greeks back to the light fortifications they had built around their beached ships. The Trojans lit their watchfires on the plain, ready to deliver the attack in the morning.

FROM BOOK VIII

[*The Tide of Battle Turns*]

But the Trojans had great notions that night,
Sitting on the bridge of war by their watchfires.

Stars: crowds of them in the sky, sharp
In the moonglow when the wind falls
And all the cliffs and hills and peaks
Stand out and the air shears down
From heaven, and all the stars are visible
And the watching shepherd smiles.

So the bonfires between the Greek ships
And the banks of the Xanthus,[9] burning
On the plain before Ilion.
And fifty men
Warmed their hands by the flames of each fire.

And the horses champed white barley,
Standing by their chariots, waiting for Dawn
To take her seat on brocaded cushions.

BOOK IX

[*The Embassy to Achilles*]

So the Trojans kept watch. But Panic,
Fear's sister, had wrapped her icy fingers
Around the Greeks, and all their best
Were stricken with unendurable grief.

8. I.e., with bronze greaves (the shin protectors of Homeric warriors).

9. One of the rivers of the Trojan plain.

When two winds rise on the swarming deep,
Boreas and Zephyr,[1] blowing from Thrace
In a sudden squall, the startled black waves
Will crest and tangle the surf with seaweed.

The Greeks felt like that, pummeled and torn.

Agamemnon's heart was bruised with pain
As he went around to the clear-toned criers
Ordering them to call each man to assembly,
But not to shout. He pitched in himself.
It was a dispirited assembly. Agamemnon
Stood up, weeping, his face like a sheer cliff
With dark springwater washing down the stone.
Groaning heavily he addressed the troops:
"Friends, Argive commanders and counsellors:
Great Zeus, son of Cronus,
Is a hard god, friends. He's kept me in the dark
After all his promises, all his nods my way
That I'd raze Ilion's walls before sailing home.
It was all a lie, and I see now that his orders
Are for me to return to Argos in disgrace,
And this after all the armies I've destroyed.
I have no doubt that this is the high will
Of the god who has toppled so many cities
And will in the future, all glory to his power.
So this is my command for the entire army:
Clear out with our ships and head for home.
There's no hope we will take Troy's tall town."

He spoke, and they were all stunned to silence,
The silence of an army too grieved to speak,
Until at last Diomedes' voice boomed out:

"I'm going to oppose you if you talk foolishness—
As is my right in assembly, lord. Keep your temper.
First of all, you insulted me, saying in public
I was unwarlike and weak.[2] Every Greek here,
Young and old alike, knows all about this.
The son of crooked Cronus split the difference
When he gave you gifts. He gave you a scepter
And honor with it, but he didn't give you
Strength to stand in battle, which is real power.
Are you out of your mind? Do you really think
The sons of the Achaeans are unwarlike and weak?
If you yourself are anxious to go home,
Then go. You know the way. Your ships are here
Right by the sea, and a whole fleet will follow you

1. The north and west winds, respectively.
2. This insult was voiced during Agamemnon's review of his forces before the battle (book 4).

Back to Mycenae.[3] But many a long-haired Achaean
Will stay, too, until we conquer Troy. And if they won't—
Well, let them all sail back to their own native land.
The two of us, Sthenelus[4] and I, will fight on
Until we take Ilion. We came here with Zeus."

He spoke, and all the Greeks cheered
The speech of Diomedes, breaker of horses.
Then up stood Nestor, the old charioteer:

"Son of Tydeus, you are our mainstay in battle
And the best of your age in council as well.
No Greek will find fault with your speech
Or contradict it. But it is not the whole story.
You are still young. You might be my son,
My youngest. Yet you have given prudent advice
To the Argive kings, since you have spoken aright.
But I, who am privileged to be your senior,
Will speak to all points. Nor will anyone
Scorn my words, not even King Agamemnon.
Only outlaws and exiles favor civil strife.
For the present, however, let us yield to night
And have our dinner. Guards should be posted
Outside the wall along the trench. I leave
This assignment to the younger men. But you,
Son of Atreus, take charge. You are King.
Serve the elders a feast. It is not unseemly.
Your huts are filled with wine which our ships
Transport daily over the sea from Thrace.
You have the means to entertain us and the men.
Then choose the best counsel your assembled guests
Can offer. The Achaeans are in great need
Of good counsel. The enemies' campfires
Are close to our ships. Can this gladden any heart?
This night will either destroy the army or save it."

They all heard him out and did as he said.
The guard details got their gear and filed out
On the double under their commanders:
Thrasymedes, Nestor's son; Ascalaphus
And Ialmenus, sons of Ares; Meriones,
Aphareus, and Diphyrus; and Creion,
The son of Lycomedes. Each of these seven
Had a hundred men under his command.
Spears in hand, they took up their positions
In a long line between the wall and the trench,[5]
Where they lit fires and prepared their supper.

3. The city near Argos that Agamemnon ruled.
4. Diomedes' companion.
5. In book 7, the Greeks built this wall and dug the trench in front of it to protect their ships, which were threatened by the Trojans.

Agamemnon meanwhile gathered the elders
Into his hut and served them a hearty meal.
They helped themselves to the dishes before them,
And when they had enough of food and drink,
The first to spin out his plan for them was Nestor,
Whose advice had always seemed best before,
And who spoke with their best interests at heart:

"Son of Atreus, most glorious lord,
I begin and end with you, since you are
King of a great people, with authority
To rule and right of judgment from Zeus.
It is yours to speak as well as to listen,
And to stand behind others whenever they speak
To our good. The final word is yours.
But I will speak as seems best to me.
No one will have a better idea
Than I have now, nor has anyone ever,
From the time, divine prince, you wrested away
The girl Briseis from Achilles' shelter,
Defying his anger and my opposition.
I tried to dissuade you, but you gave in
To your pride and dishonored a great man
Whom the immortals esteem. You took his prize
And keep it still. But it is not too late. Even now
We must think of how to win him back
With appeasing gifts and soothing words."

And the warlord Agamemnon responded:

"Yes, old man, you were right on the mark
When you said I was mad. I will not deny it.
Zeus' favor multiplies a man's worth,
As it has here, and the army has suffered for it.
But since I did succumb to a fit of madness,
I want to make substantial amends.
I hereby announce my reparations:
Seven unfired tripods,[6] ten gold bars,
Twenty burnished cauldrons, a dozen horses—
Solid, prizewinning racehorses
Who have won me a small fortune—
And seven women who do impeccable work,
Surpassingly beautiful women from Lesbos[7]
I chose for myself when Achilles captured the town.
And with them will be the woman I took,
Briseus's daughter, and I will solemnly swear
I never went to her bed and lay with her
Or did what is natural between women and men.

6. Three-footed kettles; such metal equipment was rare and highly valued.

7. A large island off the coast of present-day Turkey.

All this he may have at once. And if it happens
That the gods allow us to sack Priam's city,
He may when the Greeks are dividing the spoils
Load a ship to the brim with gold and bronze,
And choose for himself the twenty Trojan women
Who are next in beauty to Argive Helen.
And if we return to the rich land of Argos,
He will marry my daughter, and I will honor him
As I do Orestes,[8] who is being reared in luxury.
I have three daughters in my fortress palace,
Chrysothemis, Laodice, and Iphianassa.
He may lead whichever he likes as his bride
Back to Peleus' house, without paying anything,
And I will give her a dowry richer than any
A father has ever given his daughter.
And I will give him seven populous cities,
Cardamyle, Enope, grassy Hire,
Sacred Pherae, Antheia with its meadowlands,
Beautiful Aepeia, and Pedasus, wine country.
They are all near the sea, on sandy Pylos' frontier,
And cattlemen live there, rich in herds and flocks,
Who will pay him tribute as if he were a god
And fulfill the shining decrees of his scepter.
I will do all this if he will give up his grudge.
And he should. Only Hades cannot be appeased,
Which is why of all gods mortals hate him most.
And he should submit to me, inasmuch as I
Am more of a king and can claim to be elder."

And then spoke Nestor, the Gerenian rider:

"Son of Atreus, most glorious Agamemnon,
Your gifts for Achilles are beyond reproach.
But come, we must dispatch envoys
As soon as possible to Achilles' tent,
And I see before me who should volunteer.
Phoenix,[9] dear to Zeus, should lead the way,
Followed by Ajax and brilliant Odysseus.
Odius and Eurybates can attend them as heralds.
Now bring water for our hands and observe silence,
That we may beseech Zeus to have mercy on us."

Nestor spoke, and his speech pleased them all.
Heralds poured water over their hands,
And then youths filled bowls to the brim with drink
And served it all around, first tipping the cups.
Having made their libations and drunk their fill,
They went out in a body from Agamemnon's hut.

8. Agamemnon's son.

9. He is especially suited for this embassy because he was tutor to the young Achilles.

Gerenian Nestor filled their ears with advice,
Glancing at each, but especially at Odysseus,
On how to persuade Peleus' peerless son.

They went in tandem along the seething shore,
Praying over and over to the god in the surf[1]
For an easy time in convincing Achilles.
They came to the Myrmidons' ships and huts
And found him plucking clear notes on a lyre—
A beautiful instrument with a silver bridge
He had taken when he ransacked Eëtion's[2] town—
Accompanying himself as he sang the glories
Of heroes in war. He was alone with Patroclus,
Who sat in silence waiting for him to finish.
His visitors came forward, Odysseus first,
And stood before him. Surprised, Achilles
Rose from his chair still holding his lyre.
Patroclus, when he saw them, also rose,
And Achilles, swift and sure, received them:

"Welcome. Things must be bad to bring you here,
The Greeks I love best, even in my rage."

With these words Achilles led them in
And had them sit on couches and rugs
Dyed purple, and he called to Patroclus:

"A larger bowl, son of Menoetius,
And stronger wine, and cups all around.
My dearest friends are beneath my roof."

Patroclus obliged his beloved companion.
Then he cast a carving block down in the firelight
And set on it a sheep's back and a goat's,
And a hog chine too, marbled with fat.
Automedon[3] held the meat while Achilles
Carved it carefully and spitted the pieces.
Patroclus, godlike in the fire's glare,
Fed the blaze. When the flames died down
He laid the spits over the scattered embers,
Resting them on stones, and sprinkled the morsels
With holy salt. When the meat was roasted
He laid it on platters and set out bread
In exquisite baskets. Achilles served the meat,
Then sat down by the wall opposite Odysseus
And asked Patroclus to offer sacrifice.
After he threw the offerings[4] in the fire,
They helped themselves to the meal before them,

1. Poseidon, god of the sea.
2. Eëtion is Andromache's father. In book 6, she recalls his death at Achilles' hands.
3. Achilles' charioteer.
4. The portion of meat reserved for the gods.

And when they had enough of food and drink,
Ajax nodded to Phoenix. Odysseus saw this,
And filling a cup he lifted it to Achilles:

"To your health, Achilles, for a generous feast.
There is no shortage in Agamemnon's hut,
Or now here in yours, of satisfying food.
But the pleasures of the table are not on our minds.
We fear the worst. It is doubtful
That we can save the ships without your strength.
The Trojans and their allies are encamped
Close to the wall that surrounds our black ships
And are betting that we can't keep them
From breaking through. They may be right.
Zeus has been encouraging them with signs,
Lightning on the right. Hector trusts this—
And his own strength—and has been raging
Recklessly, like a man possessed.
He is praying for dawn to come early
So he can fulfill his threat to lop the horns
From the ships' sterns, burn the hulls to ash,
And slaughter the Achaeans dazed in the smoke.
This is my great fear, that the gods make good
Hector's threats, dooming us to die in Troy
Far from the fields of home. Up with you, then,
If you intend at all, even at this late hour,
To save our army from these howling Trojans.
Think of yourself, of the regret you will feel
For harm that will prove irreparable.
This is the last chance to save your countrymen.
Is it not true, my friend, that your father Peleus
Told you as he sent you off with Agamemnon:
'My son, as for strength, Hera and Athena
Will bless you if they wish, but it is up to you
To control your proud spirit. A friendly heart
Is far better. Steer clear of scheming strife,
So that Greeks young and old will honor you.'
You have forgotten what the old man said,
But you can still let go of your anger, right now.
Agamemnon is offering you worthy gifts
If you will give up your grudge. Hear me
While I list the gifts he proposed in his hut:
Seven unfired tripods, ten gold bars,
Twenty burnished cauldrons, a dozen horses—
Solid, prizewinning racehorses
Who have won him a small fortune—
And seven women who do impeccable work,
Surpassingly beautiful women from Lesbos
He chose for himself when you captured the town.
And with them will be the woman he took from you,
Briseus' daughter, and he will solemnly swear

He never went to her bed and lay with her
Or did what is natural between women and men.
All this you may have at once. And if it happens
That the gods allow us to sack Priam's city,
You may when the Greeks are dividing the spoils
Load a ship to the brim with gold and bronze,
And choose for yourself the twenty Trojan women
Who are next in beauty to Argive Helen.
And if we return to the rich land of Argos,
You would marry his daughter, and he would honor you
As he does Orestes, who is being reared in luxury.
He has three daughters in his fortress palace,
Chrysothemis, Laodice, and Iphianassa.
You may lead whichever you like as your bride
Back to Peleus' house, without paying anything,
And he would give her a dowry richer than any
A father has ever given his daughter.
And he will give you seven populous cities,
Cardamyle, Enope, grassy Hire,
Sacred Pherae, Antheia with its meadowlands,
Beautiful Aepeia, and Pedasus, wine country.
They are all near the sea, on sandy Pylos' frontier,
And cattlemen live there, rich in herds and flocks,
Who will pay you tribute as if you were a god
And fulfill the shining decrees of your scepter.
All this he will do if you give up your grudge.
But if Agamemnon is too hateful to you,
Himself and his gifts, think of all the others
Suffering up and down the line, and of the glory
You will win from them. They will honor you
Like a god.
And don't forget Hector.
You just might get him now. He's coming in close,
Deluded into thinking that he has no match
In the Greek army that has landed on his beach."

And Achilles, strong, swift, and godlike:

"Son of Laertes in the line of Zeus,
Odysseus the strategist—I can see
That I have no choice but to speak my mind
And tell you exactly how things are going to be.
Either that or sit through endless sessions
Of people whining at me. I hate like hell
The man who says one thing and thinks another.
So this is how I see it.
I cannot imagine Agamemnon,
Or any other Greek, persuading me,
Not after the thanks I got for fighting this war,
Going up against the enemy day after day.
It doesn't matter if you stay in camp or fight—

In the end, everybody comes out the same.
Coward and hero get the same reward:
You die whether you slack off or work.
And what do I have for all my suffering,
Constantly putting my life on the line?
Like a bird who feeds her chicks
Whatever she finds, and goes without herself,
That's what I've been like, lying awake
Through sleepless nights, in battle for days
Soaked in blood, fighting men for their wives.
I've raided twelve cities with our ships
And eleven on foot in the fertile Troad,
Looted them all, brought back heirlooms
By the ton, and handed it all over
To Atreus' son, who hung back in camp
Raking it in and distributing damn little.
What the others did get they at least got to keep.
They all have their prizes, everyone but me—
I'm the only Greek from whom he took something back.
He should be happy with the woman he has.
Why do the Greeks have to fight the Trojans?
Why did Agamemnon lead the army to Troy
If not for the sake of fair-haired Helen?
Do you have to be descended from Atreus
To love your mate? Every decent, sane man
Loves his woman and cares for her, as I did,
Loved her from my heart. It doesn't matter
That I won her with my spear. He took her,
Took her right out of my hands, cheated me,
And now he thinks he's going to win me back?
He can forget it. I know how things stand.
It's up to you, Odysseus, and the other kings
To find a way to keep the fire from the ships.
He's been pretty busy without me, hasn't he,
Building a wall, digging a moat around it,
Pounding in stakes for a palisade.
None of that stuff will hold Hector back.
When I used to fight for the Greeks,
Hector wouldn't come out farther from his wall
Than the oak tree by the Western Gate.
He waited for me there once, and barely escaped.
Now that I don't want to fight him anymore,
I will sacrifice to Zeus and all gods tomorrow,
Load my ships, and launch them on the sea.
Take a look if you want, if you give a damn,
And you'll see my fleet on the Hellespont
In the early light, my men rowing hard.
With good weather from the sea god,
I'll reach Phthia after a three-day sail.
I left a lot behind when I hauled myself here,
And I'll bring back more, gold and bronze,

Silken-waisted women, grey iron—
Everything except the prize of honor
The warlord Agamemnon gave me
And in his insulting arrogance took back.
So report back to him everything I say,
And report it publicly—get the Greeks angry,
In case the shameless bastard still thinks
He can steal us blind. He doesn't dare
Show his dogface here. Fine. I don't want
To have anything to do with him either.
He cheated me, wronged me. Never again.
He's had it. He can go to hell in peace,
The half-wit that Zeus has made him.
His gifts? His gifts mean nothing to me.
Not even if he offered me ten or twenty times
His present gross worth and added to it
All the trade Orchomenus[5] does in a year,
All the wealth laid up in Egyptian Thebes,
The wealthiest city in all the world,
Where they drive two hundred teams of horses
Out through each of its hundred gates.
Not even if Agamemnon gave me gifts
As numberless as grains of sand or dust,
Would he persuade me or touch my heart—
Not until he's paid in full for all my grief.
His daughter? I would not marry
The daughter of Agamemnon son of Atreus
If she were as lovely as golden Aphrodite
Or could weave like owl-eyed Athena.
Let him choose some other Achaean
More to his lordly taste. If the gods
Preserve me and I get home safe
Peleus will find me a wife himself.
There are many Greek girls in Hellas[6] and Phthia,
Daughters of chieftains who rule the cities.
I can have my pick of any of them.
I've always wanted to take a wife there,
A woman to have and to hold, someone with whom
I can enjoy all the goods old Peleus has won.
Nothing is worth my life, not all the riches
They say Troy held before the Greeks came,
Not all the wealth in Phoebus Apollo's
Marble shrine up in craggy Pytho.[7]
Cattle and flocks are there for the taking;
You can always get tripods and chestnut horses.
But a man's life cannot be won back

5. A city in central Greece, northwest of Thebes; it was one of the most important Greek cities from the Bronze Age onward.

6. Although Hellas later became the name for all of Greece, in Homer it refers to a region next to Achilles' home district of Phthia. Both are in northern Greece.

7. Apollo's oracular shrine at Delphi. Its wealth consisted of offerings made to the god by grateful worshippers.

Once his breath has passed beyond his clenched teeth.
My mother Thetis, a moving silver grace,
Tells me two fates sweep me on to my death.
If I stay here and fight, I'll never return home,
But my glory will be undying forever.
If I return home to my dear fatherland
My glory is lost but my life will be long,
And death that ends all will not catch me soon.
As for the rest of you, I would advise you too
To sail back home, since there's no chance now
Of storming Ilion's height. Zeus has stretched
His hand above her, making her people bold.
What's left for you now is to go back to the council
And announce my message. It's up to them
To come up with another plan to save the ships
And the army with them, since this one,
Based on appeasing my anger, won't work.
Phoenix can spend the night here. Tomorrow
He sails with me on our voyage home,
If he wants to, that is. I won't force him to come."

He spoke, and they were hushed in silence,
Shocked by his speech and his stark refusal.
Finally the old horseman Phoenix spoke,
Bursting into tears. He felt the ships were lost.
"If you have set your mind on going home,
Achilles, and will do nothing to save the ships
From being burnt, if your heart is that angry,
How could I stay here without you, my boy,
All by myself? Peleus sent me with you
On that day you left Phthia to go to Agamemnon,
A child still, knowing nothing of warfare
Or assemblies where men distinguish themselves.
He sent me to you to teach you this—
To be a speaker of words and a doer of deeds.
I could not bear to be left behind now
Apart from you, child, not even if a god
Promised to smooth my wrinkles and make me
As young and strong as I was when I first left
The land of Hellas and its beautiful women.
I was running away from a quarrel with Amyntor,
My father, who was angry with me
Over his concubine, a fair-haired woman
Whom he loved as much as he scorned his wife,
My mother. She implored me constantly
To make love to his concubine so that this woman
Would learn to hate the old man. I did as she asked.
My father found out and cursed me roundly,
Calling on the Furies[8] to ensure that never

8. Avenging spirits, particularly concerned with crimes committed by kin against kin.

Would a child of mine sit on his knees.
The gods answered his prayers, Underworld Zeus
And dread Persephone.[9] I decided to kill him
With a sharp sword, but some god calmed me down—
Putting in my mind what people would say,
The names they would call me—so that in fact
I would not be known as a parricide.
From then on I could not bear to linger
In my father's house, although my friends
And my family tried to get me to stay,
Entreating me, slaughtering sheep and cattle,
Roasting whole pigs on spits, and drinking
Jar after jar of the old man's wine.
For nine solid days they kept watch on me,
Working in shifts, staying up all night.
The fires stayed lit, one under the portico
Of the main courtyard, one on the porch
In front of my bedroom door. On the tenth night,
When it got dark, I broke through the latches
And vaulted over the courtyard fence,
Eluding the watchmen and servant women.
I was on the run through wide Hellas
And made it to Phthia's black soil, her flocks,
And to Lord Peleus. He welcomed me kindly
And loved me as a father loves his only son,
A grown son who will inherit great wealth.
He made me rich and settled me on the border,
Where I lived as king of the Dolopians.
I made you what you are, my godlike Achilles,
And loved you from my heart. You wouldn't eat,
Whether it was at a feast or a meal in the house,
Unless I set you on my lap and cut your food up
And fed it to you and held the wine to your lips.
Many a time you wet the tunic on my chest,
Burping up wine when you were colicky.
I went through a lot for you, because I knew
The gods would never let me have a child
Of my own. No, I tried to make you my child,
Achilles, so you would save me from ruin.
But you have to master your proud spirit.
It's not right for you to have a pitiless heart.
Even the gods can bend. Superior as they are
In honor, power, and every excellence,
They can be turned aside from wrath
When humans who have transgressed
Supplicate them with incense and prayers,
With libations and savor of sacrifice.
Yes, for Prayers are daughters of great Zeus.

9. Wife of Hades (the "Underworld Zeus").

Lame and wrinkled and with eyes averted,
They are careful to follow in Folly's footsteps,
But Folly is strong and fleet, and outruns them all,
Beating them everywhere and plaguing humans,
Who are cured by the Prayers when they come behind.
Revere the daughters of Zeus when they come,
And they will bless you and hear your cry.
Reject them and refuse them stubbornly,
And they will ask Zeus, Cronus' son, to have
Folly plague you,[1] so you will pay in pain.
No, Achilles, grant these daughters of Zeus
The respect that bends all upright men's minds.
If the son of Atreus were not offering gifts
And promising more, if he were still raging mad,
I would not ask you to shrug off your grudge
And help the Greeks, no matter how sore their need.
But he is offering gifts and promising more,
And he has sent to you a delegation
Of the best men in the army, your dearest friends.
Don't scorn their words or their mission here.
  No one could blame you for being angry before.
We all know stories about heroes of old,
How they were furiously angry, but later on
Were won over with gifts or appeased with words.
I remember a very old story like this, and since
We are all friends here, I will tell it to you now.
  The Curetes were fighting the Aetolians
In a bloody war around Calydon town.[2]
The Aetolians were defending their city
And the Curetes meant to burn it down.
This was all because gold-throned Artemis
Had cursed the Curetes,[3] angry that Oeneus
Had not offered her his orchard's first fruits.
The other gods feasted on bulls by the hundred,
But Oeneus forgot somehow or other
Only the sacrifice to great Zeus' daughter.
So the Archer Goddess, angry at heart,
Roused a savage boar, with gleaming white tusks,
And sent him to destroy Oeneus' orchard.
The boar did a good job, uprooting trees
And littering the ground with apples and blossoms.
But Oeneus' son, Meleager, killed it
After getting up a party of hunters and hounds
From many towns: it took more than a few men
To kill this huge boar, and not before

1. A serious curse, since the Greek word for "folly" can also mean "destruction."
2. A city in northwestern Greece. The Curetes and Aetolians were the local tribes, once allied but at odds in this story.
3. The Greek says, ambiguously, "had cursed them." Possibly Artemis cursed both Aetolians and Curetes, since Oeneus was king of the Aetolian city Calydon.

It set many a hunter on the funeral pyre.
But the goddess caused a bitter argument
About the boar's head and shaggy hide
Between the Curetes and Aetolians.
They went to war. While Meleager still fought
The Curetes had the worst of it
And could not remain outside Calydon's wall.[4]
But when wrath swelled Meleager's heart,
As it swells even the hearts of the wise,
And his anger rose against Althaea his mother,
He lay in bed with his wife, Cleopatra,
Child of Marpessa and the warrior Idas.
Idas once took up his bow against Apollo
To win lissome Marpessa. Her parents
Called the girl Halcyone back then
Because her mother wept like a halcyon,
The bird of sorrows, because the Archer God,
Phoebus Apollo, had stolen her daughter.
Meleager nursed his anger at Cleopatra's side,
Furious because his mother had cursed him,
Cursed him to the gods for murdering his uncle,[5]
Her brother, that is, and she beat the earth,
The nurturing earth, with her hands, and called
Upon Hades and Persephone the dread,
As she knelt and wet her bosom with tears,
To bring death to her son. And the Fury
Who walks in darkness heard her
From the pit of Erebus,[6] and her heart was iron.
Soon the enemy was heard at the walls again,
Battering the gates. The Aetolian elders
Sent the city's high priests to pray to Meleager
To come out and defend them, offering him
Fifty acres of Calydon's richest land
Wherever he chose, half in vineyard,
Half in clear plowland, to be cut from the plain.
And the old horseman Oeneus shook his doors,
Standing on the threshold of his gabled room,
And recited a litany of prayers to his son,
As did his sisters and his queenly mother.
He refused them all, and refused his friends,
His very best friends and boon companions.
No one could move his heart or persuade him
Until the Curetes, having scaled the walls
Were burning the city and beating down

4. The Greek text says only "the wall"—probably not Calydon's wall, since the Curetes should be attacking that city. It may be the wall of Pleuron, the Curetes' city. Or, as one commentator has suggested, the wall could be one built by the besieging Curetes around their encampment outside Calydon, as the Greeks have done at Troy.

5. In the course of the battles Meleager had killed one of his mother's brothers.

6. The underworld.

His bedroom door. Then his wife wailed
And listed for him all the woes that befall
A captured people—the men killed,
The town itself burnt, the women and children
Led into slavery. This roused his spirit.
He clapped on armor and went out to fight.
And so he saved the Aetolians from doom
Of his own accord, and they paid him none
Of those lovely gifts, savior or not.
Don't be like that. Don't think that way,
And don't let your spirit turn that way.
The ships will be harder to save when they're burning.
Come while there are gifts, while the Achaeans
Will still honor you as if you were a god.
But if you go into battle without any gifts,
Your honor will be less, save us or not."

And strong, swift-footed Achilles answered:

"I don't need that kind of honor, Phoenix.
My honor comes from Zeus, and I will have it
Among these beaked ships as long as my breath
Still remains and my knees still move.
Now listen to this. You're listening? Good.
Don't try to confuse me with your pleading
On Agamemnon's behalf. If you're his friend
You're no longer mine, although I love you.
Hate him because I hate him. It's as simple as that.
You're like a second father to me. Stay here,
Be king with me and share half the honor.
These others can take my message. Lie down
And spend the night on a soft couch. At daybreak
We will decide whether to set sail or stay."
And he made a silent nod to Patroclus
To spread a thick bed for Phoenix. It was time
For the others to think about leaving. Big Ajax,
Telamon's godlike son, said as much:

"Son of Laertes in the line of Zeus,
Resourceful Odysseus—it's time we go.
I do not think we will accomplish
What we were sent here to do. Our job now
Is to report this news quickly, bad as it is.
They will be waiting to hear. Achilles
Has made his great heart savage.
He is a cruel man, and has no regard
For the love that his friends honored him with,
Beyond anyone else who camps with the ships.
Pitiless. A man accepts compensation
For a murdered brother, a dead son.
The killer goes on living in the same town

After paying blood money, and the bereaved
Restrains his proud spirit and broken heart
Because he has received payment. But you,
The gods have replaced your heart
With flint and malice, because of one girl,
One single girl, while we are offering you
Seven of the finest women to be found
And many other gifts. Show some generosity
And some respect. We have come under your roof,
We few out of the entire army, trying hard
To be the friends you care for most of all."

And Achilles, the great runner, answered him:

"Ajax, son of Telamon in the line of Zeus,
Everything you say is after my own heart.
But I swell with rage when I think of how
The son of Atreus treated me like dirt
In public, as if I were some worthless tramp.
Now go, and take back this message:
I won't lift a finger in this bloody war
Until Priam's illustrious son Hector
Comes to the Myrmidons' ships and huts
Killing Greeks as he goes and torching the fleet.
But when he comes to my hut and my black ship
I think Hector will stop, for all his battle lust."

He spoke. They poured their libations
And headed for the ships, Odysseus leading.
Patroclus ordered a bed made ready
For Phoenix, and the old man lay down
On fleeces and rugs covered with linen
And waited for bright dawn. Achilles slept
In an inner alcove, and by his side
Lay a woman he had brought from Lesbos
With high, lovely cheekbones, Diomede her name,
Phorbas' daughter. Patroclus lay down
In the opposite corner, and with him lay Iphis,
A silken girl Achilles had given him
When he took steep Scyrus, Enyeus' city.

By now Odysseus and Ajax
Were in Agamemnon's quarters,
Surrounded by officers drinking their health
From gold cups and shouting questions.
Agamemnon, the warlord, had priority:

"Odysseus, pride of the Achaeans, tell me,
Is he willing to repel the enemy fire
And save the ships, or does he refuse,
His great heart still in the grip of wrath?"

Odysseus, who endured all, answered:

"Son of Atreus, most glorious Agamemnon,
Far from quenching his wrath, Achilles
Is filled with even more. He spurns you
And your gifts, and suggests that you
Think of a way to save the ships and the army.
He himself threatens, at dawn's first light,
To get his own ships onto the water,
And he said he would advise the others as well
To sail for home, since there is no chance now
You will storm Ilion's height. Zeus has stretched
His hand above her, making her people bold.
This is what he said, as these men here
Who came with me will tell you, Ajax
And the two heralds, prudent men both.
Phoenix will spend the night there. Tomorrow
He sails with Achilles on his voyage home,
If he wants to. He will not be forced to go."

They were stunned by the force of his words
And fell silent for a long time, hushed in grief,
Until at last Diomedes said in his booming voice:

"Son of Atreus, glorious Agamemnon,
You should never have pleaded with him
Or offered all those gifts. Achilles
Was arrogant enough without your help.
Let him do what he wants, stay here
Or get the hell out. He'll fight later, all right,
When he is ready or a god tells him to.
Now I want everyone to do as I say.
Enjoy some food and wine to keep up
Your strength, and then get some sleep.

When the rosy light first streaks the sky
Get your troops and horses into formation
Before the ships. Fight in the front yourselves."

The warlords assented, taken aback
By the authority of Diomedes' speech.
Each man poured libation and went to his hut,
Where he lay down and took the gift of sleep.

Summary After Achilles' refusal, the situation of the Greeks worsened rapidly. Agamemnon, Diomedes, and Odysseus were all wounded. The Trojans breached the stockade and fought beside the ships. Patroclus tried to bring Achilles to the aid of the Greeks, but the most he could obtain was permission for himself to fight, clad in Achilles' armor, at the head of the Myrmidons.

FROM BOOK XVI

[*Patroclus Fights and Dies*]

Sarpedon[7] saw his comrades running
With their tunics flapping loose around their waists
And being swatted down like flies by Patroclus.
He called out, appealing to their sense of shame:

"Why this sudden burst of speed, Lycian heroes?
Slow down a little, while I make the acquaintance
Of this nuisance of a Greek[8] who seems by now
To have hamstrung half the Trojan army."

And he stepped down from his chariot in his bronze
As Patroclus, seeing him, stepped down from his.

High above a cliff vultures are screaming
In the air as they savage each other's craws
With their hooked beaks and talons.

And higher still,
Zeus watched with pity as the two heroes closed
And said to his wife Hera, who is his sister too:

"Fate has it that Sarpedon, whom I love more
Than any man, is to be killed by Patroclus.
Shall I take him out of battle while he still lives
And set him down in the rich land of Lycia,
Or shall I let him die under Patroclus' hands?"

And Hera, his lady, her eyes soft and wide:

"Son of Cronus, what a thing to say!
A mortal man, whose fate has long been fixed,
And you want to save him from rattling death?
Do it. But don't expect all of us to approve.
Listen to me. If you send Sarpedon home alive,
You will have to expect other gods to do the same
And save their own sons—and there are many of them
In this war around Priam's great city.
Think of the resentment you will create.
But if you love him and are filled with grief,
Let him fall in battle at Patroclus' hands,
And when his soul and life have left him,
Send Sleep[9] and Death to bear him away

7. King of Lycia in Asia Minor, son of Zeus and a mortal woman; he is a Trojan ally (for his genealogy, see his cousin Glaucus's account in his speech to Diomedes in book 6, lines 155–217.

8. He is referring to Patroclus, who has returned to the battle wearing Achilles' armor.

9. The brother of Death, according to the Greeks.

To Lycia, where his people will give him burial
With mound and stone, as befits the dead."

The Father of Gods and Men agreed
Reluctantly, but shed drops of blood as rain
Upon the earth in honor of his own dear son
Whom Patroclus was about to kill
On Ilion's rich soil, far from his native land.

When they were close, Patroclus cast, and hit
Not Prince Sarpedon, but his lieutenant
Thrasymelus, a good man—a hard throw
Into the pit of his belly. He collapsed in a heap.
Sarpedon countered and missed. His bright spear
Sliced instead through the right shoulder
Of Pedasus,[1] who gave one pained, rasping whinny,
Then fell in the dust. His spirit fluttered off.
With the trace horse down, the remaining two
Struggled in the creaking yoke, tangling the reins.
Automedon[2] remedied this by drawing his sword
And cutting loose the trace horse. The other two
Righted themselves and pulled hard at the reins,
And the two warriors closed again in mortal combat.
Sarpedon cast again. Another miss. The spearpoint
Glinted as it sailed over Patroclus' left shoulder
Without touching him at all. Patroclus came back,
Leaning into his throw, and the bronze point
Caught Sarpedon just below the rib cage
Where it protects the beating heart. Sarpedon fell

As a tree falls, oak, or poplar, or spreading pine,
When carpenters cut it down in the forest
With their bright axes, to be the beam of a ship,

And he lay before his horses and chariot,
Groaning heavily and clawing the bloody dust,

Like some tawny, spirited bull a lion has killed
In the middle of the shambling herd, groaning
As it dies beneath the predator's jaws.

Thus beneath Patroclus the Lycian commander
Struggled in death. And he called his friend:

"Glaucus, it's time to show what you're made of
And be the warrior you've always been,
Heart set on evil war—if you're fast enough.

1. The third (or "trace") horse that ran alongside the pair pulling Patroclus's chariot to help it maneuver. The other two horses are immortal, given by the gods to Achilles' father Peleus. In the next lines, they shy away from contact with death.

2. Achilles' charioteer, whom Patroclus has borrowed, along with Achilles' chariot and armor.

Hurry, rally our best to fight for my body,
All the Lycian leaders. Shame on you,
Glaucus, until your dying day, if the Greeks
Strip my body bare beside their ships.
Be strong and keep the others going."

The end came as he spoke, and death settled
On his nostrils and eyes. Patroclus put his heel
On Sarpedon's chest and pulled out his spear.
The lungs came out with it, and Sarpedon's life.
The Myrmidons steadied his snorting horses.
They did not want to leave their master's chariot.

Glaucus could hardly bear to hear Sarpedon's voice,
He was so grieved that he could not save him.
He pressed his arm with his hand. His wound
Tormented him, the wound he got when Teucer
Shot him with an arrow as he attacked the wall.[3]
He prayed to Apollo, lord of bright distances:

"Hear me, O Lord, wherever you are
In Lycia or Troy, for everywhere you hear
Men in their grief, and grief has come to me.
I am wounded, Lord, my arm is on fire,
And the blood can't be staunched. My shoulder
Is so sore I cannot hold a steady spear
And fight the enemy. Sarpedon is dead,
My Lord, and Zeus will not save his own son.
Heal my wound and deaden my pain,[4]
And give me the strength to call the Lycians
And urge them on to fight, and do battle myself
About the body of my fallen comrade."

Thus Glaucus' prayer, and Apollo heard him.
He stilled his pain and staunched the dark blood
That flowed from his wound. Glaucus felt
The god's strength pulsing through him,
Glad that his prayers were so quickly answered.
He rounded up the Lycian leaders
And urged them to fight for Sarpedon's body,
Then went with long strides to the Trojans,
To Polydamas, Agenor, Aeneas,
And then saw Hector's bronze-strapped face,
Went up to him and said levelly:

"Hector, you have abandoned your allies.
We have been putting our lives on the line for you

3. The wall erected by the Greeks to protect their ships and breached by the Trojans. "Teucer": an archer on the Greek side, half-brother of Ajax.

4. Apollo, who inflicted the plague in book 1, is also the god of healing.

Far from our homes and loved ones,
And you don't care enough to lend us aid.
Sarpedon is down, our great warlord,
Whose word in Lycia was Lycia's law,
Killed by Patroclus under Ares' prodding.
Show some pride and fight for his body,
Or the Myrmidons will strip off the armor
And defile his corpse, in recompense
For all the Greeks we have killed by the ships."

This was almost too much for the Trojans.
Sarpedon, though a foreigner, had been
A mainstay of their city, the leader
Of a large force and its best fighter.
Hector led them straight at the Greeks, "For Sarpedon!"
And Patroclus, seeing them coming,
Urged on the already eager two Ajaxes:[5]

"Let me see you push these Trojans back
With everything you've ever had and more.
Sarpedon is down, first to breach our wall.
He's ours, to carve up his body and strip
The armor off. And all his little saviors
Are ours to massacre with cold bronze."

They heard this as if hearing their own words.
The lines on both sides hardened to steel.
Then Trojans and Lycians, Myrmidons and Greeks
Began fighting for the corpse, howling and cursing
As they threw themselves into the grinding battle.
And Zeus stretched hellish night over the armies
So they might do their lethal work over his son.

The Trojans at first pushed back the Greeks
When Epeigeus was hit, Agacles' son.
This man was far from the worst of the Myrmidons.
He once lived in Boudeum, but having killed
A cousin of his, came as a suppliant
To Peleus and silver-footed Thetis,
Who sent him with Achilles to fight at Troy.
He had his hand on the corpse when Hector
Brought down a stone on his head, splitting his skull
In two inside his heavy helmet. He collapsed
On Sarpedon's body, and death drifted over him.
Patroclus ached for his friend and swooped
Into the front like a hawk after sparrows—

5. Of the two Greek warriors with this name, the son of Telamon was among the most outstanding fighters at Troy; the less distinguished son of Oïleus still played a prominent role in battle (and, according to poetry outside the *Iliad*, in the sack of Troy). They are sometimes found fighting together.

Yes, my Patroclus—and they scattered like birds
Before your anger for your fallen comrade.
Sthenelaos, Ithaemenes' beloved son,
Never knew what hit him. The stone Patroclus threw
Severed the tendons at the nape of his neck.
The Trojan champions, including Hector,
Now withdrew, about as far as a javelin flies
When a man who knows how throws it hard
In competition or in mortal combat.

The Greeks pressed after them, and Glaucus,
The Lycian commander now, wheeled around
And killed Bathycles, a native of Hellas
And the wealthiest of the Myrmidons.
He was just catching up with Glaucus
When the Lycian suddenly pivoted on his heel
And put his spear straight into Bathycles' chest.
He fell hard, and the Greeks winced.
A good man was down, much to the pleasure
Of the Trojans, who thronged around his body.

But the Greeks took the offensive again,
And Meriones[6] killed Laogonus,
A priest of Idaean[7] Zeus who was himself
Honored as a god. Meriones thrust hard
Into his jaw, just beneath the ear,
And he was dead, in the hated dark.
Aeneas launched his spear at Meriones,
Hoping to hit him as he advanced
Under cover of his shield, but Meriones
Saw the spear coming and ducked forward,
Leaving it to punch into the ground and stand there
Quivering, as if Ares had twanged it
So it could spend its fury. Aeneas fumed:

"That would have been your last dance,[8] Meriones,
Your last dance, if only my spear had hit you!"

And Meriones, himself famed for his spear:

"Do you think you can kill everyone
Who comes up against you, Aeneas,
And defends himself? You're mortal stuff too.
If I got a solid hit on you with my spear
You'd be down in no time, for all your strength.
You'd give me the glory, and your life to Hades."
Patroclus would have none of this, and yelled:

6. A warrior from Crete on the Greek side.
7. Of Ida, a high mountain near Troy where Zeus had a cult (and from which he watches the fighting on the plain).
8. In Homer, dancing is the opposite of warfare.

"Cut the chatter, Meriones. You're a good man,
But don't think the Trojans arc going to retreat
From the corpse because you make fun of them.
Use hands in war, words in council.
Save your big speeches; we've got fighting to do."

And he moved ahead, with Meriones,
Who himself moved like a god, in his wake.

Woodcutters are working in a distant valley,
But the sound of their axes, and of trees falling,
Can be heard for miles around in the mountains.

The plain of Troy thrummed with the sound
Of bronze and hide stretched into shields,
And of swords and spears knifing into these.
Sarpedon's body was indistinguishable
From the blood and grime and splintered spears
That littered his body from head to foot.

But if you have ever seen how flies
Cluster about the brimming milk pails
On a dairy farm in early summer,

You will have some idea of the throng
Around Sarpedon's corpse.
And not once did Zeus
Avert his luminous eyes from the combatants.
All this time he looked down at them and pondered
When Patroclus should die, whether
Shining Hector should kill him then and there
In the conflict over godlike Sarpedon
And strip the armor from his body, or whether
He should live to destroy even more Trojans.
And as he pondered it seemed preferable
That Achilles' splendid surrogate should once more
Drive the Trojans and bronze-helmed Hector
Back to the city, and take many lives.
And Hector felt it, felt his blood turn milky,
And mounted his chariot, calling to the others
To begin the retreat, that Zeus' scales were tipping.
Not even the Lycians stayed, not with Sarpedon
Lying at the bottom of a pile of bodies
That had fallen upon him in this node of war.

The Greek stripped at last the glowing bronze
From Sarpedon's shoulders, and Patroclus gave it
To some of his comrades to take back to the ships.

Then Zeus turned to Apollo and said:

"Sun God, take our Sarpedon out of range.
Cleanse his wounds of all the clotted blood,
And wash him in the river far away
And anoint him with our holy chrism
And wrap the body in a deathless shroud
And give him over to be taken swiftly
By Sleep and Death to Lycia,
Where his people shall give him burial
With mound and stone, as befits the dead."

And Apollo went down from Ida
Into the howling dust of war,
And cleansed Sarpedon's wounds of all the blood,
And washed him in the river far away
And anointed him with holy chrism
And wrapped the body in a deathless shroud
And gave him over to be taken swiftly
By Sleep and Death to Lycia.

Patroclus called to his horses and charioteer
And pressed on after the Trojans and Lycians,
Forgetting everything Achilles had said[9]
And mindless of the black fates gathering above.
Even then you might have escaped them,
Patroclus, but Zeus' mind is stronger than men's,
And Zeus now put fury in your heart.

Do you remember it, Patroclus, all the Trojans
You killed as the gods called you to your death?
Adrastus was first, then Autonous, and Echeclus,
Perimas, son of Megas, Epistor, Melanippus,
Elasus, Mulius, and last, Pylartes,
And it would have been more, but the others ran,
Back to Troy, which would have fallen that day
By Patroclus' hands.

But Phoebus Apollo
Had taken his stand on top of Troy's wall.

Three times Patroclus
Reached the parapet, and three times
Apollo's fingers flicked against the human's shield
And pushed him off. But when he came back
A fourth time, like a spirit from beyond,
Apollo's voice split the daylight in two:

"Get back, Patroclus, back where you belong.
Troy is fated to fall, but not to you,

9. In sending Patroclus into battle, Achilles told him only to chase the Trojans from the Greek ships and not to pursue them all the way back to Troy.

Nor even to Achilles, a better man by far."

And Patroclus was off, putting distance
Between himself and that wrathful voice.

Hector had halted his horses at the Western Gate
And was deciding whether to drive back into battle
Or call for a retreat to within the walls.
While he pondered this, Phoebus Apollo
Came up to him in the guise of Asius.
This man was Hector's uncle on his mother's side,
And Apollo looked just like him as he spoke:

"Why are you out of action, Hector? It's not right.
If I were as much stronger than you as I am weaker,
You'd pay dearly for withdrawing from battle.
Get in that chariot and go after Patroclus.
Who knows? Apollo may give you the glory."

Hector commanded Cebriones, his charioteer,
To whip the horses into battle. Apollo melted
Into the throng, a god into the toil of men.
The Greeks felt a sudden chill,
While Hector and the Trojans felt their spirits lift.
Hector was not interested in the other Greeks.
He drove through them and straight for Patroclus,
Who leapt down from his own chariot
With a spear in one hand and in the other
A jagged piece of granite he had scooped up
And now cupped in his palm. He got set,
And without more than a moment of awe
For who his opponent was, hurled the stone.
The throw was not wasted. He hit Hector's
Charioteer, Cebriones, Priam's bastard son,
As he stood there holding the reins. The sharp stone
Caught him right in the forehead, smashing
His brows together and shattering the skull
So that his eyeballs spurted out and dropped
Into the dirt before his feet. He flipped backward
From the chariot like a diver, and his soul
Dribbled away from his bones. And you,
Patroclus, you, my horseman, mocked him:

"What a spring the man has! Nice dive!
Think of the oysters he could come up with
If he were out at sea, jumping off the boat
In all sorts of weather, to judge by the dive
He just took from his chariot onto the plain."

And with that he rushed at the fallen warrior

Like a lion who has been wounded in the chest
As he ravages a farmstead, and his own valor
Destroys him.

Yes, Patroclus, that is how you leapt
Upon Cebriones.
Hector vaulted from his chariot,
And the two of them fought over Cebriones

Like a pair of lions fighting over a slain deer
In the high mountains, both of them ravenous,
Both high of heart,

very much like these two
Human heroes hacking at each other with bronze.
Hector held Cebriones' head and would not let go.
Patroclus had hold of a foot, and around them
Greeks and Trojans squared off and fought.

Winds sometimes rise in a deep mountain wood
From different directions, and the trees—
Beech, ash, and cornelian cherry—
Batter each other with their long, tapered branches,
And you can hear the sound from a long way off,
The unnerving splintering of hardwood limbs.

The Trojans and Greeks collided in battle,
And neither side thought of yielding ground.

Around Cebriones many spears were stuck,
Many arrows flew singing from the string,
And many stones thudded onto the shields
Of men fighting around him. But there he lay
In the whirling dust, one of the great,
Forgetful of his horsemanship.

While the sun still straddled heaven's meridian,
Soldiers on both sides were hit and fell.
But when the sun moved down the sky and men
All over earth were unyoking their oxen,
The Greeks' success exceeded their destiny.
They pulled Cebriones from the Trojan lines
And out of range, and stripped his armor.

And then Patroclus unleashed himself.

Three times he charged into the Trojan ranks
With the raw power of Ares, yelling coldly,
And on each charge he killed nine men.
But when you made your fourth, demonic charge,

Then—did you feel it, Patroclus?—out of the mist,
Your death coming to meet you. It was
Apollo, whom you did not see in the thick of battle,
Standing behind you, and the flat of his hand
Found the space between your shoulder blades.
The sky's blue disk went spinning in your eyes
As Achilles' helmet rang beneath the horses' hooves,
And rolled in the dust—no, that couldn't be right[1]—
Those handsome horsehair plumes grimed with blood,
The gods would never let that happen to the helmet
That had protected the head and graceful brow
Of divine Achilles. But the gods did
Let it happen, and Zeus would now give the helmet
To Hector, whose own death was not far off.

Nothing was left of Patroclus' heavy battle spear
But splintered wood, his tasselled shield and baldric
Fell to the ground, and Apollo, Prince of the Sky,
Split loose his breastplate. And he stood there, naked,
Astounded, his silvery limbs floating away,
Until one of the Trojans slipped up behind him
And put his spear through, a boy named Euphorbus,
The best his age with a spear, mounted or on foot.
He had already distinguished himself in this war
By knocking twenty warriors out of their cars
The first time he went out for chariot lessons.
It was this boy who took his chance at you,
Patroclus, but instead of finishing you off,
He pulled his spear out and ran back where he belonged,
Unwilling to face even an unarmed Patroclus,
Who staggered back toward his comrades, still alive,
But overcome by the god's stroke, and the spear.

Hector was watching this, and when he saw
Patroclus withdrawing with a wound, he muscled
His way through to him and rammed his spearhead
Into the pit of his belly and all the way through.
Patroclus fell heavily. You could hear the Greeks wince.

A boar does not wear out easily, but a lion
Will overpower it when the two face off
Over a trickling spring up in the mountains
They both want to drink from. The boar
Pants hard, but the lion comes out on top.

So too did Hector, whose spear was draining the life
From Menoetius' son, who had himself killed many.

1. Because it was divinely made, part of the armor given by the gods to Peleus on his marriage to Thetis.

His words beat down on Patroclus like dark wings:

"So, Patroclus, you thought you could ransack my city
And ship our women back to Greece to be your slaves.
You little fool. They are defended by me,
By Hector, by my horses and my spear. I am the one,
Troy's best, who keeps their doom at bay. But you,
Patroclus, the vultures will eat you
On this very spot. Your marvelous Achilles
Has done you no good at all. I can just see it,
Him sitting in his tent and telling you as you left:
'Don't bother coming back to the ships,
Patroclus, until you have ripped Hector's heart out
Through his bloody shirt. That's what he said,
Isn't it? And you were stupid enough to listen."

And Patroclus, barely able to shake the words out:

"Brag while you can, Hector. Zeus and Apollo
Have given you an easy victory this time.
If they hadn't knocked off my armor,
I could have made mincemeat of twenty like you.
It was Fate, and Leto's son, who killed me.
Of men, Euphorbus. You came in third at best.
And one more thing for you to think over.
You're not going to live long. I see Death
Standing at your shoulder, and you going down
Under the hands of Peleus' perfect son."

Death's veil covered him as he said these things;
And his soul, bound for Hades, fluttered out
Resentfully, forsaking manhood's bloom.
He was dead when Hector said to him:

"Why prophesy my death, Patroclus?
Who knows? Achilles, son of Thetis,
May go down first under my spear."

And propping his heel against the body,
He extracted his bronze spear and took off
After Automedon. But Automedon was gone,
Pulled by immortal horses, the splendid gifts
The gods once gave to Peleus.

Summary Hector stripped Achilles' divine armor from Patroclus's corpse. A fierce fight for the body itself ended in partial success for the Greeks; they took Patroclus's body but had to retreat to their camp, with the Trojans at their heels.

BOOK XVIII

[*The Shield of Achilles*]

The fight went on, like wildfire burning.
Antilochus,[2] running hard like a herald,
Found Achilles close to his upswept hulls,
His great heart brooding with premonitions
Of what had indeed already happened.
"This looks bad,
All these Greeks with their hair in the wind
Stampeding off the plain and back to the ships.
God forbid that what my mother told me
Has now come true, that while I'm still alive
Trojan hands would steal the sunlight
From the best of all the Myrmidons.
Patroclus, Menoetius' brave son, is dead.
Damn him! I told him only to repel
The enemy fire from our ships,
And not to take on Hector in a fight."

Antilochus was in tears when he reached him
And delivered his unendurable message:

"Son of wise Peleus, this is painful news
For you to hear, and I wish it were not true.
Patroclus is down, and they are fighting
For his naked corpse. Hector has the armor."

A mist of black grief enveloped Achilles.
He scooped up fistfuls of sunburnt dust
And poured it on his head, fouling
His beautiful face. Black ash grimed
His fine-spun cloak as he stretched his huge body
Out in the dust and lay there,
Tearing out his hair with his hands.
The women, whom Achilles and Patroclus
Had taken in raids, ran shrieking out of the tent
To be with Achilles, and they beat their breasts
Until their knees gave out beneath them.
Antilochus, sobbing himself, stayed with Achilles
And held his hands—he was groaning
From the depths of his soul—for fear
He would lay open his own throat with steel.

The sound of Achilles' grief stung the air.

Down in the water his mother heard him,
Sitting in the sea depths beside her old father,
And she began to wail.

2. A son of Nestor. He has been sent to tell Achilles that Patroclus is dead.

And the saltwater women
Gathered around her, all the deep-sea Nereids,
Glaucē and Thaleia and Cymodocē,
Neseia and Speio, Thoē and ox-eyed Haliē,
Cymothoē, Actaeē, and Limnoeira,
Melitē and Iaera, Amphithoē and Agauē,
Doris, Panopē, and milk-white Galateia,
Nemertes, Apseudes, and Callianassa,
Clymenē, Ianeira, Ianassa, and Maera,
Oreithyia and Amatheia, hair streaming behind her,
And all of the other deep-sea Nereids.
They filled the silver, shimmering cave,
And they all beat their breasts.

Thetis led the lament:

"Hear me, sisters, hear the pain in my heart.
I gave birth to a son, and that is my sorrow,
My perfect son, the best of heroes.
He grew like a sapling, and I nursed him
As I would a plant on the hill in my garden,
And I sent him to Ilion on a sailing ship
To fight the Trojans. And now I will never
Welcome him home again to Peleus' house.
As long as he lives and sees the sunlight
He will be in pain, and I cannot help him.
But I'll go now to see and hear my dear son,
Since he is suffering while he waits out the war."

She left the cave, and they went with her,
Weeping, and around them a wave
Broke through the sea, and they came to Troy.
They emerged on the beach where the Myrmidons' ships
Formed an encampment around Achilles.
He was groaning deeply, and his mother
Stood next to him and held her son's head.
Her lamentation hung sharp in the air,
And then she spoke in low, sorrowful tones:

"Child, why are you crying? What pain
Has come to your heart? Speak, don't hide it.
Zeus has granted your prayer. The Greeks
Have all been beaten back to their ships
And suffered horribly. They can't do without you."

Achilles answered her:

"Mother, Zeus may have done all this for me,
But how can I rejoice? My friend is dead,
Patroclus, my dearest friend of all. I loved him,
And I killed him. And the armor—

Hector cut him down and took off his body
The heavy, splendid armor, beautiful to see,
That the gods gave to Peleus as a gift
On the day they put you to bed with a mortal.
You should have stayed with the saltwater women,
And Peleus should have married a mortal.
But now—it was all so you would suffer pain
For your ravaged son. You will never again
Welcome me home, since I no longer have the will
To remain alive among men, not unless Hector
Loses his life on the point of my spear
And pays for despoiling Menoetius' son."

And Thetis, in tears, said to him:

"I won't have you with me for long, my child,
If you say such things. Hector's death means yours."

From under a great weight, Achilles answered:

"Then let me die now. I was no help
To him when he was killed out there. He died
Far from home, and he needed me to protect him.
But now, since I'm not going home, and wasn't
A light for Patroclus or any of the rest
Of my friends who have been beaten by Hector,
But just squatted by my ships, a dead weight on the earth . . .
I stand alone in the whole Greek army
When it comes to war—though some do speak better.
I wish all strife could stop, among gods
And among men, and anger too—it sends
Sensible men into fits of temper,
It drips down our throats sweeter than honey
And mushrooms up in our bellies like smoke.
Yes, the warlord Agamemnon angered me.
But we'll let that be, no matter how it hurts,
And conquer our pride, because we must.
But I'm going now to find the man who destroyed
My beloved—Hector.
As for my own fate,
I'll accept it whenever it pleases Zeus
And the other immortal gods to send it.
Not even Heracles[3] could escape his doom.
He was dearest of all to Lord Zeus, but fate
And Hera's hard anger destroyed him.
If it is true that I have a fate like his, then I too
Will lie down in death.
But now to win glory

3. The greatest of Greek heroes, the son of Zeus by a mortal woman; pursued by the jealousy of Hera, he was forced to undertake twelve great labors and finally died in agony from the effects of a poisoned garment.

And make some Trojan woman or deep-breasted
Dardanian[4] matron wipe the tears
From her soft cheeks, make her sob and groan.
Let them feel how long I've been out of the war.
Don't try, out of love, to stop me. I won't listen."

And Thetis, her feet silver on the sand:

"Yes, child. It's not wrong to save your friends
When they are beaten to the brink of death.
But your beautiful armor is in the hands of the Trojans,
The mirrored bronze. Hector himself
Has it on his shoulders. He glories in it.
Not for long, though. I see his death is near.
But you, don't dive into the red dust of war
Until with your own eyes you see me returning.
Tomorrow I will come with the rising sun
Bearing beautiful armor from Lord Hephaestus."

Thetis spoke, turned away
From her son, and said to her saltwater sisters:

"Sink now into the sea's wide lap
And go down to our old father's house
And tell him all this. I am on my way
Up to Olympus to visit Hephaestus,
The glorious smith, to see if for my sake
He will give my son glorious armor."

As she spoke they dove into the waves,
And the silver-footed goddess was gone
Off to Olympus to fetch arms for her child.

And while her feet carried her off to Olympus,
Hector yelled, a yell so bloodcurdling and loud
It stampeded the Greeks all the way back
To their ships beached on the Hellespont's shore.
They could not pull the body of Patroclus
Out of javelin range, and soon Hector,
With his horses and men, stood over it again.
Three times Priam's resplendent son
Took hold of the corpse's heels and tried
To drag it off, bawling commands to his men.
Three times the two Ajaxes put their heads down,
Charged, and beat him back. Unshaken, Hector
Sidestepped, cut ahead, or held his ground
With a shout, but never yielded an inch.

It was like shepherds against a starving lion,
Helpless to beat it back from a carcass,

4. Trojan.

The two Ajaxes unable to rout
The son of Priam from Patroclus' corpse.
And Hector would have, to his eternal glory,
Dragged the body off, had not Iris[5] stormed
Down from Olympus with a message for Achilles,
Unbeknownst to Zeus and the other gods.
Hera had sent her, and this was her message:

"Rise, son of Peleus, most formidable of men.
Rescue Patroclus, for whom a terrible battle
Is pitched by the ships, men killing each other,
Some fighting to save the dead man's body,
The Trojans trying to drag it back
To windy Ilion. Hector's mind especially
Is bent on this. He means to impale the head
On Troy's palisade after he strips off its skin.
And you just lie there? Think of Patroclus
Becoming a ragbone for Trojan dogs. Shame
To your dying day if his corpse is defiled."

The shining sprinter Achilles answered her:

"Iris, which god sent you here?"

And Iris, whose feet are wind, responded:

"None other than Hera, Zeus' glorious wife.
But Zeus on high does not know this, nor do
Any of the immortals on snow-capped Olympus."

And Achilles, the great runner:

"How can I go to war? They have my armor.
And my mother told me not to arm myself
Until with my own eyes I see her come back
With fine weapons from Hephaestus.
I don't know any other armor that would fit,
Unless maybe the shield of Telamonian Ajax.[6]
But he's out there in the front ranks, I hope,
Fighting with his spear over Patroclus dead."

Windfoot Iris responded:

"We know very well that they have your armor.
Just go to the trench and let the Trojans see you.
One look will be enough. The Trojans will back off
Out of fear of you, and this will give the Greeks

5. Goddess of the rainbow and the usual messenger of the gods in the *Iliad*.
6. The son of Telemon, the more famous of the two heroes named Ajax. His distinctive attribute in the *Iliad* is a huge shield that covers his whole body.

Some breathing space, what little there is in war."

Iris spoke and was gone. And Achilles,
Whom the gods loved, rose. Around
His mighty shoulders Athena threw
Her tasselled aegis,[7] and the shining goddess
Haloed his head with a golden cloud
That shot flames from its incandescent glow.

Smoke is rising through the pure upper air
From a besieged city on a distant island.
Its soldiers have fought hard all day,
But at sunset they light innumerable fires
So that their neighbors in other cities
Might see the glare reflected off the sky
And sail to their help as allies in war.

So too the radiance that flared
From Achilles' head and up to the sky.
He went to the trench—away from the wall
And the other Greeks, out of respect
For his mother's tense command. Standing there,
He yelled, and behind him Pallas Athena
Amplified his voice, and shock waves
Reverberated through the Trojan ranks.

You have heard the piercing sound of horns
When squadrons come to destroy a city.

The Greek's voice was like that,
Speaking bronze that made each Trojan heart
Wince with pain.
And the combed horses
Shied from their chariots, eyes wide with fear,
And their drivers went numb when they saw
The fire above Achilles' head
Burned into the sky by the Grey-Eyed One.[8]
Three times Achilles shouted from the trench;
Three times the Trojans and their confederates
Staggered and reeled, twelve of their best
Lost in the crush of chariots and spears.
But the Greeks were glad to pull Patroclus' body
Out of range and placed it on a litter. His comrades
Gathered around, weeping, and with them Achilles,
Shedding hot tears when he saw his loyal friend
Stretched out on the litter, cut with sharp bronze.
He had sent him off to war with horses and chariot,

7. A tasseled garment or piece of armor that belonged to Zeus but was often carried by Athena in poetry and art. It induced panic when shaken at an enemy.

8. Athena.

But he never welcomed him back home again.

And now the ox-eyed Lady Hera
Sent the tireless, reluctant sun
Under the horizon into Ocean's streams,
Its last rays touching the departing Greeks with gold.
It had been a day of brutal warfare.

After the Trojans withdrew from battle,
They unhitched their horses from the chariots
And held an assembly before thinking of supper.
They remained on their feet, too agitated to sit,
Terrified, in fact, that Achilles,
After a long absence, was back.
Polydamas was the first to speak, prudent
Son of Panthous, the only Trojan who looked
Both ahead and behind.[9] This man was born
The same night as Hector, and was his comrade,
As good with words as Hector was with a spear.
He had their best interests at heart when he spoke:
"Take a good look around, my friends. My advice
Is to return to the city and not wait for daylight
On the plain by the ships. We are far from our wall.
As long as this man raged against Agamemnon,
The Greeks were easier to fight against.
I too was glad when I spent the night by the ships,
Hoping we would capture their upswept hulls.
That hope has given way to a terrible fear
Of Peleus' swift son. He is a violent man
And will not be content to fight on the plain
Where Greeks and Trojans engage in combat.
It is for our city he will fight, and our wives.
We must go back. Trust me, this is how it will be:
Night is holding him back now, immortal night.
But if he finds us here tomorrow
When he comes out in his armor in daylight,
Then you will know what Achilles is,
And you will be glad to be back in sacred Ilion—
If you make it back, and are not one
Of the many Trojans the dogs and vultures
Will feast upon. I hope I'm not within earshot.
But if we trust my words, as much as it may gall,
We will camp tonight in the marketplace, where
The city is protected by its towers, walls,
And high gates closed with bolted, polished doors.
At dawn we take our positions on the wall
In full armor, and so much the worse for him
If he wants to come out from the ships and fight us
For our wall. He will go back to the ships

9. I.e., he was a prophet; he knew the past and foresaw the future.

After he has had enough of parading
His high-necked prancers in front of the city.
He will not have the will to force his way in.
Dogs will eat him before he takes our town."

And Hector, glaring at him under his helmet:

"Polydamas, I don't like this talk
About a retreat and holing up in the city.
Aren't you sick of being penned inside our walls?
People everywhere used to talk about how rich
Priam's city was, all the gold, all the bronze.
Now the great houses are empty, their heirlooms
Sold away to Phrygia, to Maeonia,[1] since Zeus
Has turned wrathful. But now—when the great god,
Son of Cronus, has vouchsafed me the glory
Of hemming the Greeks in beside the sea—
Now is no time for you to talk like a fool.
Not a Trojan here will listen. I won't let them.
  Now hear this! All troops will mess tonight
With guards posted and on general alert.
If any of you are worried about your effects,
You can hand them over for distribution!
Better our men should have them than the Greeks.
At first light we strap on our armor
And start fighting hard by the ships.
If Achilles really has risen up again
And wants to come out, he'll find it tough going,
For I will be there. I, for one,
Am not retreating. Maybe he'll win, maybe I will.
The War God doesn't care which one he kills."

Thus Hector, and the Trojans cheered,
The fools, their wits dulled by Pallas Athena.
Hector's poor counsel won all the applause,
And not a man praised Polydamas' good sense.
Then the troops started supper.

But the Greeks
Mourned Patroclus the whole night through.
Achilles began the incessant lamentation,
Laying his man-slaying hands on Patroclus' chest
And groaning over and over like a bearded lion

Whose cubs some deer hunter has smuggled out
Of the dense woods. When the lion returns,
It tracks the human from valley to valley,
Growling low the whole time. Sometimes it finds him.

1. Countries in Asia Minor allied with Troy.

Achilles' deep voice sounded among the Myrmidons:

"It was all for nothing, what I said that day
When I tried to hearten the hero Menoetius,
Telling him I would bring his glorious son
Home to Opoeis[2] with his share of the spoils
After I had sacked Ilion. Zeus does not fulfill
A man's every thought. We two are fated
To redden the selfsame earth with our blood,
Right here in Troy. I will never return home
To be welcomed by my old father, Peleus,
Or Thetis, my mother. The earth here will hold me.
And since I will pass under the earth after you,
Patroclus, I will not bury you until
I have brought here the armor and head of Hector,
Who killed you, great soul. And I will cut
The throats of twelve Trojan princes
Before your pyre in my wrath. Until then,
You will lie here beside our upswept hulls
Just as you are, and round about you
Deep-bosomed Trojan and Dardanian women
Will lament you day and night, weeping,
Women we won with blood, sweat and tears,
Women we cut through rich cities to get."

With that, he ordered his companions
To put a great cauldron on the fire,
So they could wash the gore
From Patroclus' body without further delay.
They put a cauldron used for heating baths
Over a blazing fire and poured in the water,
Then stoked the fire with extra wood.
The flames licked the cauldron's belly
And the water grew warm. When it was boiling
In the glowing bronze, they washed the body,
Anointed it with rich olive oil,
And filled the wounds with a seasoned ointment.
Then they laid him on his bed, covered him
From head to foot with a soft linen cloth,
And spread a white mantle above it.
Then the whole night through the Myrmidons
Stood with Achilles, mourning Patroclus.

Zeus said to Hera, his wife and sister:

"So you have had your way, my ox-eyed lady.
You have roused Achilles, swift of foot. Truly,
The long-haired Greeks must be from your womb."

2. An ancient city near the eastern coast of the central Greek mainland and home of Menoetius, father of Patroclus.

And the ox-eyed lady Hera replied:

"Awesome son of Cronus, what a thing to say!
Even a mortal man, without my wisdom,
Will succeed in his efforts for another man.
How then was I—the highest of goddesses
Both by my own birth and by marriage to you,
The lord and ruler of all the immortals—
Not to cobble up evil for Troy in my wrath?"

While they spoke to each other this way,
Thetis' silver feet took her to Hephaestus' house,
A mansion the lame god had built himself
Out of starlight and bronze, and beyond all time.
She found him at his bellows, glazed with sweat
As he hurried to complete his latest project,
Twenty cauldrons on tripods to line his hall,
With golden wheels at the base of each tripod
So they could move by themselves to the gods' parties
And return to his house—a wonder to see.
They were almost done. The intricate handles
Still had to be attached. He was getting these ready,
Forging the rivets with inspired artistry,
When the silver-footed goddess came up to him.
And Charis,[3] Hephaestus' wife, lovely
In her shimmering veil, saw her, and running up,
She clasped her hand and said to her:

"My dear Thetis, so grave in your long robe,
What brings you here now? You almost never visit.
Do come inside so I can offer you something."

And the shining goddess led her along
And had her sit down in a graceful
Silver-studded chair with a footstool.
Then she called to Hephaestus, and said:

"Hephaestus, come here.
Thetis needs you for something."

And the renowned smith called back:

"Thetis? Then the dread goddess I revere
Is inside. She saved me when I lay suffering
From my long fall, after my shameless mother
Threw me out, wanting to hide my infirmity.
And I really would have suffered, had not Thetis
And Eurynome, a daughter of Ocean Stream,
Taken me into their bosom. I stayed with them

3. Literally, "Grace" or "Beauty."

Nine years, forging all kinds of jewelry,
Brooches and bracelets and necklaces and pins,
In their hollow cave, while the Ocean's tides,
Murmuring with foam, flowed endlessly around.
No one knew I was there, neither god nor mortal,
Except my rescuers, Eurynome and Thetis.
Now the goddess has come to our house.
I owe her my life and would repay her in full.
Set out our finest for her, Charis,
While I put away my bellows and tools."

He spoke and raised his panting bulk
Up from his anvil, limping along quickly
On his spindly shanks. He set the bellows
Away from the fire, gathered up the tools
He had been using, and put them away
In a silver chest. Then he took a sponge
And wiped his face and hands, his thick neck,
And his shaggy chest. He put on a tunic,
Grabbed a stout staff, and as he went out
Limping, attendants rushed up to support him,
Attendants made of gold who looked like real girls,
With a mind within, and a voice, and strength,
And knowledge of crafts from the immortal gods.
These busily moved to support their lord,
And he came hobbling up to where Thetis was,
Sat himself down on a polished chair,
And clasping her hand in his, he said:

"My dear Thetis, so grave in your long robe,
What brings you here now? You almost never visit.
Tell me what you have in mind, and I will do it
If it is anything that is at all possible to do."

And Thetis, shedding tears as she spoke:

"Hephaestus, is there a goddess on Olympus
Who has suffered as I have? Zeus son of Cronus
Has given me suffering beyond all the others.
Of all the saltwater women he singled me out
To be subject to a man, Aeacus' son Peleus.
I endured a man's bed, much against my will.
He lies in his halls forspent with old age,
But I have other griefs now. He gave me a son
To bear and to rear, the finest of heroes.
He grew like a sapling, and I nursed him
As I would nurse a plant in my hillside garden,
And I sent him to Ilion on a sailing ship
To fight the Trojans. And now I will never
Welcome him home again to Peleus' house.
As long as he lives and sees the sunlight

He will be in pain, and I cannot help him.
The girl that the army chose as his prize
Lord Agamemnon took out of his arms.
He was wasting his heart out of grief for her,
But now the Trojans have penned the Greeks
In their beachhead camp, and the Argive elders
Have petitioned him with a long list of gifts.
He refused to beat off the enemy himself,
But he let Patroclus wear his armor,
And sent him into battle with many men.
All day long they fought by the Scaean Gates
And would have sacked the city that very day,
But after Menoetius' valiant son
Had done much harm, Apollo killed him
In the front ranks and gave Hector the glory.
So I have come to your knees, to see if you
Will give my son, doomed to die young,
A shield and helmet, a fine set of greaves,
And a corselet too. His old armor was lost
When the Trojans killed his faithful companion,
And now he lies on the ground in anguish."

And the renowned smith answered her:

"Take heart, Thetis, and do not be distressed.
I only regret I do not have the power
To hide your son from death when it comes.
But armor he will have, forged to a wonder,
And its terrible beauty will be a marvel to men."

Hephaestus left her there and went to his bellows,
Turned them toward the fire and ordered them to work.
And the bellows, all twenty, blew on the crucibles,
Blasting out waves of heat in whatever direction
Hephaestus wanted as he hustled here and there
Around his forge and the work progressed.
He cast durable bronze onto the fire, and tin,
Precious gold and silver. Then he positioned
His enormous anvil up on its block
And grasped his mighty hammer
In one hand, and in the other his tongs.

He made a shield first, heavy and huge,
Every inch of it intricately designed.
He threw a triple rim around it, glittering
Like lightning, and he made the strap silver.
The shield itself was five layers thick, and he
Crafted its surface with all of his genius.

On it he made the earth, the sky, the sea,
The unwearied sun, and the moon near full,

And all the signs that garland the sky,
Pleiades, Hyades, mighty Orion,
And the Bear[4] they also call the Wagon,
Which pivots in place and looks back at Orion
And alone is aloof from the wash of Ocean.

On it he made two cities, peopled
And beautiful. Weddings in one, festivals,
Brides led from their rooms by torchlight
Up through the town, bridal song rising,
Young men reeling in dance to the tune
Of lyres and flutes, and the women
Standing in their doorways admiring them.
There was a crowd in the market-place
And a quarrel arising between two men
Over blood money for a murder,
One claiming the right to make restitution,
The other refusing to accept any terms.
They were heading for an arbitrator
And the people were shouting, taking sides,
But heralds restrained them. The elders sat
On polished stone seats in the sacred circle
And held in their hands the staves of heralds.
The pair rushed up and pleaded their cases,
And between them lay two ingots of gold
For whoever spoke straightest in judgment.

Around the other city two armies
Of glittering soldiery were encamped.
Their leaders were at odds—should they
Move in for the kill or settle for a division
Of all the lovely wealth the citadel held fast?
The citizens wouldn't surrender, and armed
For an ambush. Their wives and little children
Were stationed on the wall, and with the old men
Held it against attack. The citizens moved out,
Led by Ares and Pallas Athena,
Both of them gold, and their clothing was gold,
Beautiful and larger than life in their armor, as befits
Gods in their glory, and all the people were smaller.
They came to a position perfect for an ambush,
A spot on the river where stock came to water,
And took their places, concealed by fiery bronze.
Farther up they had two lookouts posted
Waiting to sight shambling cattle and sheep,
Which soon came along, trailed by two herdsmen
Playing their panpipes, completely unsuspecting.
When the townsmen lying in ambush saw this

4. Ursa Major, or the Big Dipper, which never descends below the horizon (i.e., into Ocean). The Pleiades, Hyades, and Orion are all clusters of stars or constellations. Orion was a giant hunter of Greek mythology.

They ran up, cut off the herds of cattle and fleecy
Silver sheep, and killed the two herdsmen.
When the armies sitting in council got wind
Of the ruckus with the cattle, they mounted
Their high-stepping horses and galloped to the scene.
They took their stand and fought along the river banks,
Throwing bronze-tipped javelins against each other.
Among them were Hate and Din and the Angel of Death,
Holding a man just wounded, another unwounded,
And dragging one dead by his heels from the fray,
And the cloak on her shoulders was red with human blood.
They swayed in battle and fought like living men,
And each side salvaged the bodies of their dead.

On it he put a soft field, rich farmland
Wide and thrice-tilled, with many plowmen
Driving their teams up and down rows.
Whenever they came to the end of the field
And turned, a man would run up and hand them
A cup of sweet wine. Then they turned again
Back up the furrow pushing on through deep soil
To reach the other end. The field was black
Behind them, just as if plowed, and yet
It was gold, all gold, forged to a wonder.

On it he put land sectioned off for a king,
Where reapers with sharp sickles were working.
Cut grain lay deep where it fell in the furrow,
And binders made sheaves bound with straw bands.
Three sheaf-binders stood by, and behind them children
Gathered up armfuls and kept passing them on.
The king stood in silence near the line of reapers,
Holding his staff, and his heart was happy.
Under an oaktree nearby heralds were busy
Preparing a feast from an ox they had slaughtered
In sacrifice, and women were sprinkling it
With abundant white barley for the reapers' dinner.

On it he put a vineyard loaded with grapes,
Beautiful in gold. The clusters were dark,
And the vines were set everywhere on silver poles.
Around he inlaid a blue enamel ditch
And a fence of tin. A solitary path led to it,
And vintagers filed along it to harvest the grapes.
Girls, all grown up, and light-hearted boys
Carried the honey-sweet fruit in wicker baskets.
Among them a boy picked out on a lyre
A beguiling tune and sang the Linos song[5]

5. I.e., a dirge for Linos, a fabled musician. It may originally have been associated in Near Eastern cult with the annual "death" of vegetation.

In a low, light voice, and the harvesters
    Skipped in time and shouted the refrain.

On it he made a herd of straight-horn cattle.
The cows were wrought of gold and tin
And rushed out mooing from the farmyard dung
To a pasture by the banks of a roaring river,
Making their way through swaying reeds.
Four golden herdsmen tended the cattle,
And nine nimble dogs followed along.
Two terrifying lions at the front of the herd
Were pulling down an ox. Its long bellows alerted
The dogs and the lads, who were running on up,
But the two lions had ripped the bull's hide apart
And were gulping down the guts and black blood.
The shepherds kept trying to set on the dogs,
But they shied away from biting the lions
    And stood there barking just out of harm's way.

On it the renowned lame god made a pasture
In a lovely valley, wide, with silvery sheep in it,
    And stables, roofed huts, and stone animal pens.

On it the renowned lame god embellished
A dancing ground, like the one Daedalus
Made for ringleted Ariadne[6] in wide Cnossus.
Young men and girls in the prime of their beauty
Were dancing there, hands clasped around wrists.
The girls wore delicate linens, and the men
Finespun tunics glistening softly with oil.
Flowers crowned the girls' heads, and the men
Had golden knives hung from silver straps.
They ran on feet that knew how to run
With the greatest ease, like a potter's wheel
When he stoops to cup it in the palms of his hands
And gives it a spin to see how it runs. Then they
Would run in lines that weaved in and out.
A large crowd stood round the beguiling dance,
Enjoying themselves, and two acrobats
    Somersaulted among them on cue to the music.

On it he put the great strength of the River Ocean,
Lapping the outermost rim of the massive shield.

And when he had wrought the shield, huge and heavy,
He made a breastplate gleaming brighter than fire

6. Daughter of Minos, king of Crete. Daedalus was the prototypical craftsman who built the labyrinth to house the Minotaur and who escaped from Crete on wings with his son Icarus. Cnossus was the site of Minos's great palace.

And a durable helmet that fit close at the temples,
Lovely and intricate, and crested with gold.
And he wrought leg-armor out of pliant tin.
And when the renowned lame god had finished this gear,
He set it down before Achilles' mother,
And she took off like a hawk from snow-capped Olympus,
Carrying armor through the sky like summer lightning.

Summary Achilles finally accepted gifts of restitution from Agamemnon, as he had refused to do earlier. His return to the fighting brought terror to the Trojans and turned the battle into a rout in which Achilles killed every Trojan that crossed his path. As he pursued Agenor, Apollo tricked him by rescuing his intended victim (he spirited him away in a mist) and assumed Agenor's shape to lead Achilles away from the walls of Troy. The Trojans took refuge in the city, all except Hector.

BOOK XXII

[*The Death of Hector*]

Everywhere you looked in Troy, exhausted
Soldiers, glazed with sweat like winded deer,
Leaned on the walls, cooling down
And slaking their thirst.
Outside, the Greeks
Formed up close to the wall, locking their shields.
In the dead air between the Greeks
And Troy's Western Gate, Destiny
Had Hector pinned, waiting for death.

Then Apollo called back to Achilles:

"Son of Peleus, you're fast on your feet,
But you'll never catch me, man chasing god.
Or are you too raging mad to notice
I'm a god? Don't you care about fighting
The Trojans anymore? You've chased them back
Into their town, but now you've veered off here.
You'll never kill me. You don't hold my doom."

And the shining sprinter, Achilles:

"That was a dirty trick, Apollo,
Turning me away from the wall like that!
I could have ground half of Troy face down
In the dirt! Now you've robbed me
Of my glory and saved them easily
Because you have no retribution to fear.
I swear, I'd make you pay if I could!"

His mind opened to the clear space before him,
And he was off toward the town, moving

Like a thoroughbred stretching it out
Over the plain for the final sprint home—

Achilles, lifting his knees as he lengthened his stride.

Priam saw him first, with his old man's eyes,
A single point of light on Troy's dusty plain.

Sirius[7] *rises late in the dark, liquid sky*
On summer nights, star of stars,
Orion's Dog they call it, brightest
Of all, but an evil portent, bringing heat
And fevers to suffering humanity.

Achilles' bronze gleamed like this as he ran.

And the old man groaned, and beat his head
With his hands, and stretched out his arms
To his beloved son, Hector, who had
Taken his stand before the Western Gate,
Determined to meet Achilles in combat.

Priam's voice cracked as he pleaded:

"Hector, my boy, you can't face Achilles
Alone like that, without any support—
You'll go down in a minute. He's too much
For you, son, he won't stop at anything!
O, if only the gods loved him as I do:
Vultures and dogs would be gnawing his corpse.
Then some grief might pass from my heart.
So many fine sons he's taken from me,
Killed or sold them as slaves in the islands.
Two of them now, Lycaon and Polydorus,
I can't see with the Trojans safe in town,
Laothoë's boys.[8] If the Greeks have them
We'll ransom them with the gold and silver
Old Altes gave us.[9] But if they're dead
And gone down to Hades, there will be grief
For myself and the mother who bore them.
The rest of the people won't mourn so much
Unless *you* go down at Achilles' hands.
So come inside the wall, my boy.
Live to save the men and women of Troy.
Don't just hand Achilles the glory
And throw your life away. Show some pity for me

7. The Dog Star, the brightest star in the constellation Canis Major. In Greece it rises in late summer, the hottest time of the year.
8. Laothoë was one of Priam's wives. Achilles killed Polydorus and Lycaon in the fighting outside the city (books 20 and 21).
9. The dowry of Laothoë, Altes' daughter.

Before I go out of my mind with grief
And Zeus finally destroys me in my old age,
After I have seen all the horrors of war—
My sons butchered, my daughters dragged off,
Raped, bedchambers plundered, infants
Dashed to the ground in this terrible war,
My sons' wives abused by murderous Greeks.
And one day some Greek soldier will stick me
With cold bronze and draw the life from my limbs,
And the dogs that I fed at my table,
My watchdogs, will drag me outside and eat
My flesh raw, crouched in my doorway, lapping
My blood.
When a young man is killed in war,
Even though his body is slashed with bronze,
He lies there beautiful in death, noble.
But when the dogs maraud an old man's head,
Griming his white hair and beard and private parts,
There's no human fate more pitiable."

And the old man pulled the white hair from his head,
But did not persuade Hector.
His mother then,
Wailing, sobbing, laid open her bosom
And holding out a breast spoke through her tears:

"Hector, my child, if ever I've soothed you
With this breast, remember it now, son, and
Have pity on me. Don't pit yourself
Against that madman. Come inside the wall.
If Achilles kills you I will never
Get to mourn you laid out on a bier, O
My sweet blossom, nor will Andromache,
Your beautiful wife, but far from us both
Dogs will eat your body by the Greek ships."

So the two of them pleaded with their son,
But did not persuade him or touch his heart.
Hector held his ground as Achilles' bulk
Loomed larger. He waited as a snake waits,

Tense and coiled
As a man approaches
Its lair in the mountains,
Venom in its fangs
And poison in its heart,
Glittering eyes
Glaring from the rocks:

So Hector waited, leaning his polished shield
Against one of the towers in Troy's bulging wall,

But his heart was troubled with brooding thoughts:

"Now what? If I take cover inside,
Polydamas will be the first to reproach me.
He begged me to lead the Trojans back
To the city on that black night when Achilles rose.
But I wouldn't listen, and now I've destroyed
Half the army through my recklessness.
I can't face the Trojan men and women now,
Can't bear to hear some lesser man say,
'Hector trusted his strength and lost the army.'
That's what they'll say. I'll be much better off
Facing Achilles, either killing him
Or dying honorably before the city.
  But what if I lay down all my weapons,
Bossed shield, heavy helmet, prop my spear
Against the wall, and go meet Achilles,
Promise him we'll surrender Helen
And everything Paris brought back with her
In his ships' holds to Troy—that was the beginning
Of this war—give all of it back
To the sons of Atreus and divide
Everything else in the town with the Greeks,
And swear a great oath not to hold
Anything back, but share it all equally,
All the treasure in Troy's citadel.
  But why am I talking to myself like this?
I can't go out there unarmed. Achilles
Will cut me down in cold blood if I take off
My armor and go out to meet him
Naked like a woman. This is no time
For talking, the way a boy and a girl
Whisper to each other from oak tree or rock,
A boy and a girl with all their sweet talk.
Better to lock up in mortal combat
As soon as possible and see to whom
God on Olympus grants the victory."

Thus spoke Hector.
                    And Achilles closed in
Like the helmeted God of War himself,
The ash-wood spear above his right shoulder
Rocking in the light that played from his bronze
In gleams of fire and the rising sun.
And when Hector saw it he lost his nerve,
Panicked, and ran, leaving the gates behind,
With Achilles on his tail, confident in his speed.

  You have seen a falcon
  In a long, smooth dive
  Attack a fluttering dove
  Far below in the hills.

The falcon screams,
Swoops, and plunges
In its lust for prey.

So Achilles swooped and Hector trembled
In the shadow of Troy's wall.
Running hard,
They passed Lookout Rock and the windy fig tree,
Following the loop of the wagon road.
They came to the wellsprings of eddying
Scamander,[1] two beautiful pools, one
Boiling hot with steam rising up,
The other flowing cold even in summer,
Cold as freezing sleet, cold as tundra snow.
There were broad basins there, lined with stone,
Where the Trojan women used to wash their silky clothes
In the days of peace, before the Greeks came.

They ran by these springs, pursuer and pursued—
A great man out front, a far greater behind—
And they ran all out. This was not a race
For such a prize as athletes compete for,
An oxhide or animal for sacrifice, but a race
For the lifeblood of Hector, breaker of horses.

But champion horses wheeling round the course,
Hooves flying, pouring it on in a race for a prize—
A woman or tripod—at a hero's funeral games

Will give you some idea of how these heroes looked
As they circled Priam's town three times running
While all the gods looked on.

Zeus, the gods' father and ours, spoke:

"I do not like what I see, a man close
To my heart chased down around Troy's wall.
Hector has burned many an ox's thigh
To me, both on Ida's peaks and in the city's
High holy places, and now Achilles
Is running him down around Priam's town.
Think you now, gods, and take counsel whether
We should save him from death or deliver him
Into Achilles' hands, good man though he be."

The grey-eyed goddess Athena answered:

"O Father,
You may be the Lord of Lightning and the Dark Cloud,

1. One of the two rivers in the plain of Troy.

But what a thing to say, to save a mortal man,
With his fate already fixed, from rattling death!
Do it. But don't expect us all to approve."

Zeus loomed like a thunderhead, but answered gently:

"There, there, daughter, my heart wasn't in it.
I did not mean to displease you, my child. Go now,
Do what you have in mind without delay."

Athena had been longing for action
And at his word shot down from Olympus,

As Achilles bore down on Hector.

A hunting hound starts a fawn in the hills,
Follows it through brakes and hollows,
And if it hides in a thicket, circles,
Picks up the trail, and renews the chase.

No more could Hector elude Achilles.
Every time Hector surged for the Western Gate
Under the massive towers, hoping for
Trojan archers to give him some cover,
Achilles cut him off and turned him back
Toward the plain, keeping the inside track.

Running in a dream, you can't catch up,
You can't catch up and you can't get away.

No more could Achilles catch Hector
Or Hector escape.
And how could Hector
Have ever escaped death's black birds
If Apollo had not stood by his side
This one last time and put life in his knees?
Achilles shook his head at his soldiers:
He would not allow anyone to shoot
At Hector and win glory with a hit,
Leaving him only to finish him off.

But when they reached the springs the fourth time,
Father Zeus stretched out his golden scales
And placed on them two agonizing deaths,
One for Achilles and one for Hector.
When he held the beam, Hector's doom sank down
Toward Hades. And Phoebus Apollo left him.

By now the grey-eyed goddess Athena
Was at Achilles' side, and her words flew fast:

"There's nothing but glory on the beachhead
For us now, my splendid Achilles,
Once we take Hector out of action, and
There's no way he can escape us now,
Not even if my brother Apollo has a fit
And rolls on the ground before the Almighty.
You stay here and catch your breath while I go
To persuade the man to put up a fight."

Welcome words for Achilles. He rested,
Leaning on his heavy ash and bronze spear,
While the goddess made her way to Hector,
The spitting image of Deïphobus.[2]
And her voice sounded like his as she said:

"Achilles is pushing you hard, brother,
In this long footrace around Priam's town.
Why don't we stand here and give him a fight?"

Hector's helmet flashed as he turned and said:

"Deïphobus, you've always been my favorite
Brother, and again you've shown me why,
Having the courage to come out for me,
Leaving the safety of the wall, while all
Priam's other sons are cowering inside."

And Athena, her eyes as grey as winter moons:

"Mother and father begged me by my knees
To stay inside, and so did all my friends.
That's how frightened they are, Hector. But I
Could not bear the pain in my heart, brother.
Now let's get tough and fight and not spare
Any spears. Either Achilles kills us both
And drags our blood-soaked gear to the ships,
Or he goes down with your spear in his guts."

That's how Athena led him on, with guile.
And when the two heroes faced each other,
Great Hector, helmet shining, spoke first:

"I'm not running any more, Achilles.
Three times around the city was enough.
I've got my nerve back. It's me or you now.
But first we should swear a solemn oath.
With all the gods as witnesses, I swear:
If Zeus gives me the victory over you,

2. Hector's brother.

I will not dishonor your corpse, only
Strip the armor and give the body back
To the Greeks. Promise you'll do the same."

And Achilles, fixing his eyes on him:

"Don't try to cut any deals with me, Hector.
Do lions make peace treaties with men?
Do wolves and lambs agree to get along?
No, they hate each other to the core,
And that's how it is between you and me,
No talk of agreements until one of us
Falls and gluts Ares with his blood.
By God, you'd better remember everything
You ever knew about fighting with spears.
But you're as good as dead. Pallas Athena
And my spear will make you pay in a lump
For the agony you've caused by killing my friends."

With that he pumped his spear arm and let fly.
Hector saw the long flare the javelin made, and ducked.
The bronze point sheared the air over his head
And rammed into the earth. But Athena
Pulled it out and gave it back to Achilles
Without Hector noticing. And Hector,
Prince of Troy, taunted Achilles:

"Ha! You missed! Godlike Achilles! It looks like
You didn't have my number after all.
You said you did, but you were just trying
To scare me with big words and empty talk.
Did you think I'd run and you'd plant a spear
In my back? It'll take a direct hit in my chest,
Coming right at you, that and a god's help too.
Now see if you can dodge this piece of bronze.
Swallow it whole! The war will be much easier
On the Trojans with you dead and gone."

And Hector let his heavy javelin fly,
A good throw, too, hitting Achilles' shield
Dead center, but it only rebounded away.
Angry that his throw was wasted, Hector
Fumbled about for a moment, reaching
For another spear. He shouted to Deïphobus,
But Deïphobus was nowhere in sight.
It was then that Hector knew in his heart
What had happened, and said to himself:

"I hear the gods calling me to my death.
I thought I had a good man here with me,
Deïphobus, but he's still on the wall.

Athena tricked me. Death is closing in
And there's no escape. Zeus and Apollo
Must have chosen this long ago, even though
They used to be on my side. My fate is here,
But I will not perish without some great deed
That future generations will remember."

And he drew the sharp broadsword that hung
By his side and gathered himself for a charge.

A high-flying eagle dives
Through ebony clouds down
To the sun-scutched[3] plain to claw
A lamb or a quivering hare

Thus Hector's charge, and the light
That played from his blade's honed edge.

Opposite him, Achilles exploded forward, fury
Incarnate behind the curve of his shield,
A glory of metalwork, and the plumes
Nodded and rippled on his helmet's crest,
Thick golden horsehair set by Hephaestus,
And his spearpoint glinted like the Evening Star

In the gloom of night
Star of perfect splendor,

A gleam in the air as Achilles poised
His spear with murderous aim at Hector,
Eyes boring into the beautiful skin,
Searching for the weak spot. Hector's body
Was encased in the glowing bronze armor
He had stripped from the fallen Patroclus,
But where the collarbones join at the neck
The gullet offered swift and certain death.
It was there Achilles drove his spear through
As Hector charged. The heavy bronze apex
Pierced the soft neck but did not slit the windpipe,
So that Hector could speak still.

He fell back in the dust.

And Achilles exulted:

"So you thought you could get away with it
Didn't you, Hector? Killing Patroclus
And ripping off his armor, *my* armor,
Thinking I was too far away to matter.

3. Sun-beaten.

You fool. His avenger was far greater—
And far closer—than you could imagine,
Biding his time back in our beachhead camp.
And now I have laid you out on the ground.
Dogs and birds are going to draw out your guts
While the Greeks give Patroclus burial."

And Hector, barely able to shake the words out:

"I beg you, Achilles, by your own soul
And by your parents, do not
Allow the dogs to mutilate my body
By the Greek ships. Accept the gold and bronze
Ransom my father and mother will give you
And send my body back home to be burned
In honor by the Trojans and their wives."

And Achilles, fixing him with a stare:

"Don't whine to me about my parents,
You dog! I wish my stomach would let me
Cut off your flesh in strips and eat it raw
For what you've done to me. There is no one
And no way to keep the clogs off your head,
Not even if they bring ten or twenty
Ransoms, pile them up here and promise more,
Not even if Dardanian Priam weighs your body
Out in gold, not even then will your mother
Ever get to mourn you laid out on a bier.
No, dogs and birds will eat every last scrap."

Helmet shining, Hector spoke his last words:

"So this is Achilles. There was no way
To persuade you. Your heart is a lump
Of iron. But the gods will not forget this,
And I will have my vengeance on that day
When Paris and Apollo destroy you
In the long shadow of Troy's Western Gate."

Death's veil covered him as he said these things,
And his soul, bound for Hades, fluttered out
Resentfully, forsaking manhood's bloom.

He was dead when Achilles spoke to him:

"Die and be done with it. As for my fate,
I'll accept it whenever Zeus sends it."

And he drew the bronze spear out of the corpse,
Laid it aside, then stripped off the blood-stained armor.
The other Greeks crowded around

And could not help but admire Hector's
Beautiful body, but still they stood there
Stabbing their spears into him, smirking.

"Hector's a lot softer to the touch now
Than he was when he was burning our ships,"

One of them would say, pulling out his spear.

After Achilles had stripped the body
He rose like a god and addressed the Greeks:

"Friends, Argive commanders and councillors,
The gods have granted us this man's defeat,
Who did us more harm than all the rest
Put together. What do you say we try
Laying a close siege on the city now
So we can see what the Trojans intend—
Whether they will give up the citadel
With Hector dead, or resolve to fight on?
  But what am I thinking of? Patroclus' body
Still lies by the ships, unmourned, unburied,
Patroclus, whom I will never forget
As long as I am among the living,
Until I rise no more; and even if
In Hades the dead do not remember,
Even there I will remember my dear friend.
  Now let us chant the victory paean, sons
Of the Achaeans, and march back to our ships
With this hero in tow. The power and the glory
Are ours. We have killed great Hector,
Whom all the Trojans honored as a god."

But it was shame and defilement Achilles
Had in mind for Hector. He pierced the tendons
Above the heels and cinched them with leather thongs
To his chariot, letting Hector's head drag.
He mounted, hoisted up the prize armor,
And whipped his team to a willing gallop
Across the plain. A cloud of dust rose
Where Hector was hauled, and the long black hair
Fanned out from his head, so beautiful once,
As it trailed in the dust. In this way Zeus
Delivered Hector into his enemies' hands
To be defiled in his own native land.

Watching this from the wall, Hector's mother
Tore off her shining veil and screamed,
And his old father groaned pitifully,
And all through town the people were convulsed
With lamentation, as if Troy itself,
The whole towering city, were in flames.

They were barely able to restrain
The old man, frantic to run through the gates,
Imploring them all, rolling in the dung,
And finally making this desperate appeal:

"Please let me go, alone, to the Greek ships.
I don't care if you're worried. I want to see
If that monster will respect my age, pity me
For the sake of his own father, Peleus,
Who is about my age, old Peleus
Who bore him and bred him to be a curse
For the Trojans, but he's caused me more pain
Than anyone, so many of my sons,
Beautiful boys, he's killed. I miss them all,
But I miss Hector more than all of them.
My grief for him will lay me in the earth.
Hector! You should have died in my arms, son!
Then we could have satisfied our sorrow,
Mourning and weeping, your mother and I."

The townsmen moaned as Priam was speaking.
Then Hecuba raised the women's lament:

"Hector, my son, I am desolate!
How can I live with suffering like this,
With you dead? You were the only comfort
I had, day and night, wherever you were
In the town, and you were the only hope
For Troy's men and women. They honored you
As a god when you were alive, Hector.
Now death and doom have overtaken you."

And all this time Andromache had heard
Nothing about Hector—news had not reached her
That her husband was caught outside the walls.
She was working the loom in an alcove
Of the great hall, embroidering flowers
Into a purple cloak, and had just called
To her serving women, ordering them
To put a large cauldron on the fire, so
A steaming bath would be ready for Hector
When he came home from battle. Poor woman,
She had little idea how far from warm baths
Hector was, undone by the Grey-Eyed One
And delivered into the hands of the Greeks.

Then she heard the lamentation from the tower.

She trembled, and the shuttle fell
To the floor. Again she called her women:

"Two of you come with me. I must see
What has happened. That was Hecuba's voice.
My heart is in my throat, my knees are like ice.
Something terrible has happened to one
Of Priam's sons. O God, I'm afraid
Achilles has cut off my brave Hector
Alone on the plain outside the city
And has put an end to my husband's
Cruel courage. Hector never held back
Safe in the ranks; he always charged ahead,
Second to no one in fighting spirit."

With these words on her lips Andromache
Ran outdoors like a madwoman, heart racing,
Her two waiting-women following behind.
She reached the tower, pushed through the crowd,
And looking out from the wall saw her husband
As the horses dragged him disdainfully
Away from the city to the hollow Greek ships.

Black night swept over her eyes.
She reeled backward, gasping, and her veil
And glittering headbands flew off,
And the diadem golden Aphrodite
Gave her on that day when tall-helmed Hector
Led her from her father's house in marriage.
And now her womenfolk were around her,
Hector's sisters and his brother's wives,
Holding her as she raved madly for death,
Until she caught her breath and her distraught
Spirit returned to her breast. She moaned then
And, surrounded by Trojan women, spoke:

"Hector, you and I have come to the grief
We were both born for, you in Priam's Troy
And I in Thebes in the house of Eëtion
Who raised me there beneath wooded Plakos
Under an evil star. Better never to have been born.
And now you are going to Hades' dark world,
Underground, leaving me in sorrow,
A widow in the halls, with an infant,
The son you and I bore but cannot bless.
You can't help him now you are dead, Hector,
And he can never help you. Even if
He lives through this unbearable war,
There's nothing left for him in life but pain
And deprivation, all his property
Lost to others. An orphan has no friends.
He hangs his head, his cheeks are wet with tears.
He has to beg from his dead father's friends,
Tugging on one man's cloak, another's tunic,

And if they pity him he gets to sip
From someone's cup, just enough to moisten
His lips but not enough to quench his thirst.
Or a child with both parents still alive
Will push him away from a feast, taunting him,
'Go away, your father doesn't eat with us.'
And the boy will go to his widowed mother
In tears, Astyanax, who used to sit
In his father's lap and eat nothing, but
Mutton and marrow. When he got sleepy
And tired of playing he would take a nap
In a soft bed nestled in his nurse's arms
His dreaming head filled with blossoming joy.
But now he'll suffer, now he's lost his father.
The Trojans called him Astyanax
Because you alone were Troy's defender,
You alone protected their walls and gates.
Now you lie by the curved prows of the ships,
Far from your parents. The dogs will glut
On your naked body, and shiny maggots
Will eat what's left.
Your clothes are stored away,
Beautiful, fine clothes made by women's hands—
I'll burn them all now in a blazing fire.
They're no use to you, you'll never lie
On the pyre in them. Burning them will be
Your glory before Trojan men and women."

And the women's moans came in over her lament.

Summary Achilles buried Patroclus, and the Greeks celebrated the dead hero's fame with athletic games, for which Achilles gave the prizes.

BOOK XXIV

[*Achilles and Priam*]

The funeral games were over.
The troops dispersed and went to their ships,
Where they turned their attention to supper
And a good night's sleep. But sleep
That masters all had no hold on Achilles.
Tears wet his face as he remembered his friend.
He tossed and turned, yearning for Patroclus,
For his manhood and his noble heart,
And all they had done together, the shared pain,
The battles fought, the hard times at sea.
Thinking on all this, he would weep softly,
Lying now on his side, now on his back,
And now face down. Then he would rise
To his feet and wander in a daze along the shore.
Dawn never escaped him. As soon as she appeared

Over the sea and the dunes, he would hitch
Horses to his chariot and drag Hector behind.
When he had hauled him three times around
Patroclus' tomb, he would rest again in his hut,
Leaving Hector stretched face down in the dust.
But Apollo kept Hector's flesh undefiled,
Pitying the man even in death. He kept him
Wrapped in his golden aegis, so that Achilles
Would not scour the skin as he dragged him.

So Achilles defiled Hector in his rage.
The gods, looking on, pitied Hector,
And urged Hermes to steal the body,
A plan that pleased all but Hera,
Poseidon, and the Grey-Eyed One,
Who were steady in their hatred
For sacred Ilion and Priam's people
Ever since Paris in his blindness
Offended these two goddesses
And honored the one who fed his fatal lust.[4]

Twelve days went by. Dawn.
Phoebus Apollo addressed the immortals:

"How callous can you get? Has Hector
Never burned for you thighs of bulls and goats?
Of course he has. But now you cannot
Bring yourselves to save even his bare corpse
For his wife to look upon, and his mother,
And child, and Priam, and his people, who would
Burn him in fire and perform his funeral rites.
No, it's the dread Achilles that you prefer.
His twisted mind is set on what he wants,
As savage as a lion bristling with pride,
Attacking men's flocks to make himself a feast.
Achilles has lost all pity and has no shame left.
Shame sometimes hurts men, but it helps them too.
A man may lose someone dearer than Achilles has,
A brother from the same womb, or a son,
But when he has wept and mourned, he lets go.
The Fates have given men an enduring heart.
But this man? After he kills Hector,
He ties him behind his chariot
And drags him around his dear friend's tomb.
Does this make him a better or nobler man?
He should fear our wrath, good as he may be,
For he defiles the dumb earth in his rage."

4. Aphrodite, whom Paris judged more beautiful than Athena and Hera because he found the bribe that she offered him—Helen—the most attractive.

This provoked an angry response from Hera:

"What you say might be true, Silverbow,
If we valued Achilles and Hector equally.
But Hector is mortal and suckled at a woman's breast,
While Achilles is born of a goddess whom I
Nourished and reared myself, and gave to a man,
Peleus, beloved of the gods, to be his wife.
All of you gods came to her wedding,
And you too were at the feast, lyre in hand,
Our forever faithless and fair-weather friend."

And Zeus, who masses the thunderheads:

"Calm down, Hera, and don't be so indignant.
Their honor will not be the same. But Hector
Was dearest to the gods of all in Ilion,
At least to me. He never failed to offer
A pleasing sacrifice. My altar never lacked
Libation or burnt savor, our worship due.
But we will not allow his body to be stolen—
Achilles would notice in any case. His mother
Visits him continually night and day.
But I would have one of you summon Thetis
So that I might have a word with her. Achilles
Must agree to let Priam ransom Hector."

Thus spoke Zeus,
And Iris stormed down to deliver his message.
Midway between Samos[5] and rocky Imbros,
She dove into the dark sea. The water moaned
As it closed above her, and she sank into the deep

Like a lead sinker on a line
That takes a hook of sharpened horn
Down to deal death to nibbling fish.

She found Thetis in a cave's hollow, surrounded
By her saltwater women and wailing
The fate of her faultless son, who would die
On Trojan soil, far from his homeland.
Iris, whose feet are like wind, stood near her:

"Rise, Thetis. Zeus in his wisdom commands you."

And the silver-footed goddess answered her:

"Why would the great god want me? I am ashamed
To mingle with the immortals, distraught as I am.
But I will go, and he will not speak in vain."

5. I.e., Samothrace. It and Imbros are islands in the northeast Aegean Sea.

And she veiled her brightness in a shawl.
Of midnight blue and set out with Iris before her.
The sea parted around them in waves.
They stepped forth on the beach
And sped up the sky, and found themselves
Before the face of Zeus. Around him
Were seated all the gods, blessed, eternal.
Thetis sat next to him, and Athena gave place.
Hera put in her hand a fine golden cup
And said some comforting words. Thetis drank
And handed the cup back. Then Zeus,
The father of gods and men, began to speak:

"You have come to Olympus, Thetis,
For all your incurable sorrow. I know.
Even so, I will tell you why I have called you.
For nine days the gods have argued
About Hector's corpse and about Achilles.
Some want Hermes to steal the body away,
But I accord Achilles the honor in this, hoping
To retain your friendship along with your respect.
Go quickly now and tell your son our will.
The gods are indignant, and I, above all,
Am angry that in his heart's fury
He holds Hector by the beaked ships
And will not give him up. He may perhaps fear me
And so release the body. Meanwhile,
I will send Iris to great-souled Priam
To have him ransom his son, going to the ships
With gifts that will warm Achilles' heart."

Zeus had spoken, and the silver-footed goddess
Streaked down from the peaks of Olympus
And came to her son's hut. She found him there
Lost in grief. His friends were all around,
Busily preparing their morning meal,
For which a great, shaggy ram had been slaughtered.
Settling herself beside her weeping child,
She stroked him with her hand and talked to him:

"My son, how long will you let this grief
Eat at your heart, mindless of food and rest?
It would be good to make love to a woman.
It hurts me to say it, but you will not live
Much longer. Death and Doom are beside you.
Listen now, I have a message from Zeus.
The gods are indignant, and he, above all,
Is angry that in your heart's fury
You hold Hector by these beaked ships
And will not give him up. Come now,
Release the body and take ransom for the dead."

And Achilles, swift of foot, answered her:

"So be it. Let them ransom the dead,
If the god on Olympus wills it so."

So mother and son spoke many words
To each other, with the Greek ships all around.

Meanwhile, Zeus dispatched Iris to Troy:

"Up now, swift Iris, leave Olympus
For sacred Ilion and tell Priam
He must go to the Greek ships to ransom his son
With gifts that will soften Achilles' heart.
Alone he must go, with only one attendant,
An elder, to drive the mule cart and bear the man
Slain by Achilles back to the city.
He need have no fear. We will send
As his guide and escort Hermes himself,
Who will lead him all the way to Achilles.
And when he is inside Achilles' hut,
Achilles will not kill him, but will protect him
From all the rest, for he is not a fool,
Nor hardened, nor past awe for the gods.[6]
He will in kindness spare a suppliant."

Iris stormed down to deliver this message.
She came to the house of Priam and found there
Mourning and lamentation. Priam's sons
Sat in the courtyard around their father,
Fouling their clothes with tears. The old man,
Wrapped in his mantle, sat like graven stone.
His head and neck were covered with dung
He had rolled in and scraped up with his hands.
His daughters and sons' wives were wailing
Throughout the house, remembering their men,
So many and fine, dead by Greek hands.
Zeus' messenger stood near Priam,
Who trembled all over as she whispered:

"Courage, Priam, son of Dardanus,
And have no fear. I have come to you
Not to announce evil, but good.
I am a messenger from Zeus, who
Cares for you greatly and pities you.
You must go to the Greek ships to ransom Hector
With gifts that will soften Achilles' heart.
You must go alone, with only one attendant,
An elder, to drive the mule cart and bear the man

6. Suppliants were under the protection of the gods, especially of Zeus.

Slain by Achilles back to the city.
You need have no fear. We will send
As your guide and escort Hermes himself,
Who will lead you all the way to Achilles.
And when you are inside Achilles' hut,
Achilles will not kill you, but will protect you
From all the rest, for he is not a fool,
Nor hardened, nor past awe for the gods.
He will in kindness spare a suppliant."

Iris spoke and was gone, a blur in the air.
Priam ordered his sons to ready the mule cart
And fasten onto it the wicker trunk.
He himself went down to a high-vaulted chamber,
Fragrant with cedar, that glittered with jewels.
And he called to Hecuba, his wife, and said:

"A messenger has come from Olympian Zeus.
I am to go to the ships to ransom our son
And bring gifts that will soften Achilles' heart.
What do you make of this, Lady? For myself,
I have a strange compulsion to go over there,
Into the wide camp of the Achaean ships."

Her first response was a shrill cry, and then:

"This is madness. Where is the wisdom
You were once respected for at home and abroad?
How can you want to go to the Greek ships alone
And look into the eyes of the man who has killed
So many of your fine sons? Your heart is iron.
If he catches you, or even sees you,
He will not pity you or respect you,
Savage and faithless as he is. No, we must mourn
From afar, sitting in our hall. This is how Fate
Spun her stern thread[7] for him in my womb,
That he would glut lean hounds far from his parents,
With that violent man close by. I could rip
His liver bleeding from his guts and eat it whole.
That would be at least some vengeance
For my son. He was no coward, but died
Protecting the men and women of Troy
Without a thought of shelter or flight."

And the old man, godlike Priam:

"Don't hold me back when I want to go,
And don't be a bird of ill omen
In my halls. You will not persuade me!

7. Fate or the Fates were often pictured as spinning the thread of a person's life.

If anyone else on earth told me to do this,
A seer, diviner, or priest, we would
Set it aside and count it false.
But I heard the goddess myself and saw her face.
I will go, and her word will not be in vain.
If I am fated to die by the Achaean ships,
It must be so. Let Achilles cut me down
As soon as I have taken my son in my arms
And have satisfied my desire for grief."

He began to lift up the lids of chests
And took out a dozen beautiful robes,
A dozen single-fold cloaks, as many rugs,
And added as many white mantles and tunics.
He weighed and brought out ten talents of gold,
Two glowing tripods and four cauldrons with them,
And an exquisite cup, a state gift from the Thracians
And a great treasure. The old man spared nothing
In his house, not even this, in his passion
To ransom his son. Once out in the portico,
He drove off the men there with bitter words:

"Get out, you sorry excuses for Trojans!
Don't you have enough grief at home that you
Have to come here and plague me? Isn't it enough
That Zeus has given me the pain and sorrow
Of losing my finest son? You'll feel it yourselves
Soon enough. With him dead you'll be much easier
For the Greeks to pick off. But may I be dead and gone
Before I see my city plundered and destroyed."

And he waded through them, scattering them
With his staff. Then he called to his sons
In a harsh voice—Helenus and Paris,
Agathon, Pammon, Antiphonus, Polites,
Deïphobus, Hippothous, and noble Dius—
These nine, and shouted at them:

"Come here, you miserable brats. I wish
All of you had been killed by the ships
Instead of Hector. I have no luck at all.
I have fathered the best sons in all wide Troy,
And not one, not one I say, is left. Not Mestor,
Godlike Mestor, not Troilus, the charioteer,
Not Hector, who was like a god among men,
Like the son of a god, not of a mortal.
Ares killed them, and now all I have left
Are these petty delinquents, pretty boys, and cheats,
These dancers, toe-tapping champions,
Renowned throughout the neighborhood for filching goats!
Now will you please get the wagon ready
And load all this on, so I can leave?"

They cringed under their father's rebuke
And brought out the smooth-rolling wagon,
A beauty, just joinered,[8] and clamped on
The wicker trunk. They took the mule yoke
Down from its peg, a knobbed boxwood yoke
Fitted with guide rings, and the yoke-band with it,
A rope fifteen feet long. They set the yoke with care
Upon the upturned end of the polished pole,
Placing the ring on the thole-pin, and lashed it
Tight to the knob with three turns each way,
Then tied the ends to the hitch under the hook.
This done, they brought from the treasure chamber
The lavish ransom for Hector's head and heaped it
On the hand-rubbed wagon. Then they yoked the mules,
Strong-hooved animals that pull in harness,
Splendid gifts of the Mysians[9] to Priam.
And for Priam they yoked to a chariot horses
Reared by the king's hand at their polished stall.

So Priam and his herald, their minds racing,
Were having their rigs yoked in the high palace
When Hecuba approached them sorrowfully.
She held in her right hand a golden cup
Of honeyed wine for them to pour libation
Before they went. Standing by the horses she said:

"Here, pour libation to Father Zeus, and pray
For your safe return from the enemy camp,
Since you are set on going there against my will.
Pray to Cronion, the Dark Cloud of Ida,
Who watches over the whole land of Troy,
And ask for an omen, that swiftest of birds
That is his messenger, the king of birds,
To appear on the right before your own eyes,
Something to trust in as you go to the ships.
But if Zeus will not grant his own messenger,
I would not advise or encourage you
To go to the ships, however eager you are."

And Priam, with grave dignity:

"I will not disregard your advice, my wife.
It is good to lift hands to Zeus for mercy."
And he nodded to the handmaid to pour
Pure water over his hands, and she came up
With basin and pitcher. Hands washed,
He took the cup from his wife and prayed,
Standing in the middle of the courtyard
And pouring out wine as he looked up to heaven:

8. I.e., new-made.

9. A people of central Asia Minor.

"Father Zeus, who rules from Ida,
Most glorious, most great,
Send me to Achilles welcome and pitied.
And send me an omen, that swiftest of birds
That is your messenger, the king of birds,
To appear on the right before my own eyes,
That I may trust it as I go to the ships."

Zeus heard his prayer and sent an eagle,
The surest omen in the sky, a dusky hunter
Men call the dark eagle, a bird as large
As a doorway, with a wingspan as wide
As the folding doors to a vaulted chamber
In a rich man's house. It flashed on the right
As it soared through the city, and when they saw it
Their mood brightened.

Hurrying now, the old man
Stepped into his chariot and drove off
From the gateway and echoing portico.
In front of him the mules pulled the wagon
With Idaeus at the reins. Priam
Kept urging his horses with the lash
As they drove quickly through the city.
His kinsmen trailed behind, all of them
Wailing as if he were going to his death.
When they had gone down from the city
And onto the plain, his sons and sons-in-law
Turned back to Troy. But Zeus saw them
As they entered the plain, and he pitied
The old man, and said to his son, Hermes:

"Hermes, there's nothing you like more
Than being a companion to men,[1] and you do obey—
When you have a mind to. So go now
And lead Priam to the Achaean ships, unseen
And unnoticed, until he comes to Achilles."

Thus Zeus, and the quicksilver courier complied,
Lacing on his feet the beautiful sandals,
Immortal and golden, that carry him over
Landscape and seascape in a rush of wind.
And he took the wand he uses to charm
Mortal eyes asleep and make sleepers awake.
Holding this wand, the tough quicksilver god
Flew down to Troy on the Hellespont,
And walked off as a young prince whose beard
Was just darkening, youth at its loveliest.

1. Among his many functions, Hermes is an escort to travelers (in particular, he guides the souls of the dead to the underworld). He is also a trickster and will put the guards at the Greek wall to sleep so that Priam can pass through.

Priam and Idaeus had just driven past
The barrow of Ilus[2] and had halted
The mules and horses in the river to drink.
By now it was dusk. Idaeus looked up
And was aware of Hermes close by.
He turned to Priam and said:

"Beware, son of Dardanus, there's someone here,
And if we're not careful we'll be cut to bits.
Should we escape in the chariot
Or clasp his knees and see if he will pity us?"

But the old man's mind had melted with fear.
The hair bristled on his gnarled limbs,
And he stood frozen with fear. But the Helper came up
And took the old man's hand and said to him:

"Sir, where are you driving your horses and mules
At this hour of the night, when all else is asleep?
Don't you fear the fury of the Achaeans,
Your ruthless enemies, who are close at hand?
If one of them should see you bearing such treasure
Through the black night, what would you do?
You are not young, sir, and your companion is old,
Unable to defend you if someone starts a fight.
But I will do you no harm and will protect you
From others. You remind me of my own dear father."

And the old man, godlike Priam, answered:

"Yes, dear son, it is just as you say.
But some god has stretched out his hand
And sent an auspicious wayfarer to meet me.
You have an impressive build, good looks,
And intelligence. Blessed are your parents."

And the Guide, limned in silver light:

"A very good way to put it, old sir.
But tell me this now, and tell me the truth:
Are you taking all of this valuable treasure
For safekeeping abroad or are you
All forsaking sacred Ilion in fear?
You have lost such a great warrior, the noblest,
Your son. He never let up against the Achaeans."

And the old man, godlike Priam, answered:

"Who are you, and from what parents born,
That you speak so well about my ill-fated son?"

2. Priam's grandfather. The tomb was a landmark on the Trojan plain.

And Hermes, limned in silver, answered:

"Ah, a test! And a question about Hector.
I have often seen him win glory in battle
He would drive the Argives back to their ships
And carve them to pieces with his bronze blade.
And we stood there and marvelled, for Achilles,
Angry with Agamemnon, would not let us fight.
I am his comrade in arms, from the same ship,
A Myrmidon. My father is Polyctor,
A wealthy man, and about as old as you.
He has six other sons, seven, counting me.
We cast lots, and I was chosen to come here.
Now I have come out to the plain from the ships
Because at dawn the Achaeans
Will lay siege to the city. They are restless,
And their lords cannot restrain them from battle."

And the old man, godlike Priam, answered him:

"If you really are one of Achilles' men,
Tell me this, and I want the whole truth.
Is my son still by the ships, or has Achilles
Cut him up by now and thrown him to the dogs?"

And Hermes, limned in silver light:

"Not yet, old sir. The dogs and birds have not
Devoured him. He lies beside Achilles' ship
Amid the huts just as he was at first. This is now
The twelfth day he has been lying there,
But his flesh has not decayed at all, nor is it
Consumed by worms that eat the battle-slain.
Achilles does drag him around his dear friend's tomb,
And ruthlessly, every morning at dawn,
But he stays unmarred. You would marvel, if you came,
To see him lie as fresh as dew, washed clean of blood,
And uncorrupted. All the wounds he had are closed,
And there were many who drove their bronze in him.
This is how the blessed gods care for your son,
Corpse though he be, for he was dear to their hearts."

And the old man was glad, and answered:

"Yes, my boy. It is good to offer
The immortals their due. If ever
There was anyone in my house
Who never forgot the Olympian gods,
It was my son. And so now they have
Remembered him, even in death.
But come, accept from me this fine cup,
And give me safe escort with the gods

Until I come to the hut of Peleus' son."

And Hermes, glimmering in the dark:

"Ah, an old man testing a young one.
But you will not get me to take gifts from you
Without Achilles' knowledge. I respect him
And fear him too much to defraud him.
I shudder to think of the consequences.
But I would escort you all the way to Argos,
With attentive care, by ship or on foot,
And no one would fight you for scorn of your escort."

And he leapt onto the chariot,
Took the reins and whip, and breathed
Great power into the horses and mules.
When they came to the palisade and trench
Surrounding the ships, the guards were at supper.
Hermes sprinkled them with drowsiness,
Then opened the gates, pushed back the bars,
And led in Priam and the cart piled with ransom.
They came to the hut of the son of Peleus
That the Myrmidons had built for their lord.
They built it high, out of hewn fir beams,
And roofed it with thatch reaped from the meadows.
Around it they made him a great courtyard
With thick-set staves. A single bar of fir
Held the gate shut. It took three men
To drive this bar home and three to pull it back,
But Achilles could work it easily alone.
Hermes opened the gate for Priam
And brought in the gifts for Peleus' swift son.
As he stepped to the ground he said:

"I am one of the immortals, old sir—the god
Hermes. My father sent me to escort you here.
I will go back now and not come before
Achilles' eyes. It would be offensive
For a god to greet a mortal face to face.
You go in, though, and clasp the knees
Of the son of Peleus, and entreat him
By his father and rich-haired mother
And by his son, so you will stir his soul."

And with that Hermes left and returned
To high Olympus. Priam jumped down
And left Idaeus to hold the horses and mules.
The old man went straight to the house
Where Achilles, dear to Zeus, sat and waited.

He found him inside. His companions sat
Apart from him, and a solitary pair,
Automedon and Alcimus, warriors both,

Were busy at his side. He had just finished
His evening meal. The table was still set up.
Great Priam entered unnoticed. He stood
Close to Achilles, and touching his knees,
He kissed the dread and murderous hands
That had killed so many of his sons.

Passion sometimes blinds a man so completely
That he kills one of his own countrymen.
In exile, he comes into a wealthy house,
And everyone stares at him with wonder.

So Achilles stared in wonder at Priam.
Was he a god?
And the others there stared
And wondered and looked at each other.
But Priam spoke, a prayer of entreaty:

"Remember your father, godlike Achilles.
He and I both are on the doorstep
Of old age. He may well be now
Surrounded by enemies wearing him down
And have no one to protect him from harm.
But then he hears that you are still alive
And his heart rejoices, and he hopes all his days
To see his dear son come back from Troy.
But what is left for me? I had the finest sons
In all wide Troy, and not one of them is left.
Fifty I had when the Greeks came over,
Nineteen out of one belly, and the rest
The women in my house bore to me.
It doesn't matter how many they were,
The god of war has cut them down at the knees.
And the only one who could save the city
You've just now killed as he fought for his country,
My Hector. It is for him I have come to the Greek ships,
To get him back from you. I've brought
A fortune in ransom. Respect the gods, Achilles.
Think of your own father, and pity me.
I am more pitiable. I have borne what no man
Who has walked this earth has ever yet borne.
I have kissed the hand of the man who killed my son."

He spoke, and sorrow for his own father
Welled up in Achilles. He took Priam's hand
And gently pushed the old man away.
The two of them remembered. Priam,
Huddled in grief at Achilles' feet, cried
And moaned softly for his man-slaying Hector.
And Achilles cried for his father and

For Patroclus. The sound filled the room.

When Achilles had his fill of grief
And the aching sorrow left his heart,
He rose from his chair and lifted the old man
By his hand, pitying his white hair and beard.
And his words enfolded him like wings:

"Ah, the suffering you've had, and the courage.
To come here alone to the Greek ships
And meet my eye, the man who slaughtered
Your many fine sons! You have a heart of iron.
But come, sit on this chair. Let our pain
Lie at rest a while, no matter how much we hurt.
There's nothing to be gained from cold grief.
Yes, the gods have woven pain into mortal lives,
While they are free from care.
Two jars
Sit at the doorstep of Zeus, filled with gifts
That he gives, one full of good things,
The other of evil. If Zeus gives a man
A mixture from both jars, sometimes
Life is good for him, sometimes not.
But if all he gives you is from the jar of woe,
You become a pariah, and hunger drives you
Over the bright earth, dishonored by gods and men.
Now take Peleus. The gods gave him splendid gifts
From the day he was born. He was the happiest
And richest man on earth, king of the Myrmidons,
And although he was a mortal, the gods gave him
An immortal goddess to be his wife.
But even to Peleus the god gave some evil:
He would not leave offspring to succeed him in power,
Just one child, all out of season. I can't be with him
To take care of him now that he's old, since I'm far
From my fatherland, squatting here in Troy,
Tormenting you and your children. And you, old sir,
We hear that you were prosperous once.
From Lesbos down south clear over to Phrygia
And up to the Hellespont's boundary,
No one could match you in wealth or in sons.
But then the gods have brought you trouble,
This constant fighting and killing around your town.
You must endure this grief and not constantly grieve.
You will not gain anything by torturing yourself
Over the good son you lost, not bring him back.
Sooner you will suffer some other sorrow."

And Priam, old and godlike, answered him:

"Don't sit me in a chair, prince, while Hector
Lies uncared for in your hut. Deliver him now
So I can see him with my own eyes, and you—
Take all this ransom we bring, take pleasure in it,
And go back home to your own fatherland,
Since you've taken this first step and allowed me
To live and see the light of day."

Achilles glowered at him and said:

"Don't provoke me, old man. It's my own decision
To release Hector to you. A messenger came to me
From Zeus—my own natural mother,
Daughter of the old sea god. And I know you,
Priam, inside out. You don't fool me one bit.
Some god escorted you to the Greek ships.
No mortal would have dared come into our camp,
Not even your best young hero. He couldn't have
Gotten past the guards or muscled open the gate.
So just stop stirring up grief in my heart,
Or I might not let you out of here alive, old man—
Suppliant though you are—and sin against Zeus."

The old man was afraid and did as he was told.

The son of Peleus leapt out the door like a lion,
Followed by Automedon and Alcimus, whom Achilles
Honored most now that Patroclus was dead.
They unyoked the horses and mules, and led
The old man's herald inside and seated him on a chair.
Then they unloaded from the strong-wheeled cart
The endless ransom that was Hector's blood price,
Leaving behind two robes and a fine-spun tunic
For the body to he wrapped in and brought inside.
Achilles called the women and ordered them
To wash the body well and anoint it with oil,
Removing it first for fear that Priam might see his son
And in his grief be unable to control his anger
At the sight of his child, and that this would arouse
Achilles' passion and he would kill the old man
And so sin against the commandments of Zeus.

After the female slaves had bathed Hector's body
And anointed it with olive, they wrapped it 'round
With a beautiful robe and tunic, and Achilles himself
Lifted him up and placed him on a pallet
And with his friends raised it onto the polished cart.
Then he groaned and called out to Patroclus:

"Don't be angry with me, dear friend, if somehow
You find out, even in Hades, that I have released
Hector to his father. He paid a handsome price,

And I will share it with you, as much as is right."

Achilles reentered his hut and sat down again
In his ornately decorated chair
Across the room from Priam, and said to him:

"Your son is released, sir, as you ordered.
He is lying on a pallet. At dawn's first light
You will go see him yourself.
Now let's think about supper.
Even Niobe[3] remembered to eat
Although her twelve children were dead in her house,
Six daughters and six sturdy sons.
Apollo killed them with his silver bow,
And Artemis, showering arrows, angry with Niobe
Because she compared herself to beautiful Leto.
Leto, she said, had borne only two, while she
Had borne many. Well, these two killed them all.
Nine days they lay in their gore, with no one
To bury them, because Zeus had turned
The people to stone. On the tenth day
The gods buried them. But Niobe remembered
She had to eat, exhausted from weeping.
Now she is one of the rocks in the lonely hills
Somewhere in Sipylos, a place they say is haunted
By nymphs who dance on the Achelous' banks,
And although she is stone she broods on the sorrows
The gods gave her.[4]
Well, so should we, old sir,
Remember to eat. You can mourn your son later
When you bring him to Troy. You owe him many tears."

A moment later Achilles was up and had slain
A silvery sheep. His companions flayed it
And prepared it for a meal, sliced it, spitted it,
Roasted the morsels and drew them off the spits.
Automedon set out bread in exquisite baskets
While Achilles served the meat. They helped themselves
And satisfied their desire for food and drink.
Then Priam, son of Dardanus, gazed for a while
At Achilles, so big, so much like one of the gods,
And Achilles returned his gaze, admiring
Priam's face, his words echoing in his mind.
When they had their fill of gazing at each other,
Priam, old and godlike, broke the silence:

3. Wife of Amphion, one of the two founders of the great Greek city of Thebes.

4. The legend of Niobe being turned into stone is thought to have had its origin in a rock face of Mount Sipylus (in Asia Minor) that resembled a woman who wept inconsolably for the loss of her children. The Achelous River runs near Mount Sipylus.

"Show me to my bed now, prince, and quickly,
So that at long last I can have the pleasure of sleep.
My eyes have not closed since my son lost his life
Under your hands. I have done nothing but groan
And brood over my countless sorrows,
Rolling in the dung of my courtyard stables.
Finally I have tasted food and let flaming wine
Pass down my throat. I had eaten nothing till now."

Achilles ordered his companions and women
To set bedsteads on the porch and pad them
With fine, dyed rugs, spread blankets on top,
And cover them over with fleecy cloaks.
The women went out with torches in their hands
And quickly made up two beds. And Achilles,
The great sprinter, said in a bitter tone:

"You will have to sleep outside, dear Priam.
One of the Achaean counselors may come in,
As they always do, to sit and talk with me,
As well they should. If one of them saw you here
In the dead of night, he would tell Agamemnon,
And that would delay releasing the body.
But tell me this, as precisely as you can.
How many days do you need for the funeral?
I will wait that long and hold back the army."

And the old man, godlike Priam, answered:

"If you really want me to bury my Hector,
Then you could do this for me, Achilles.
You know how we are penned in the city,
Far from any timber, and the Trojans are afraid.
We would mourn him for nine days in our halls,
And bury him on the tenth, and feast the people.
On the eleventh we would heap a barrow over him,
And on the twelfth day fight, if fight we must."

And Achilles, strong, swift, and godlike:

"You will have your armistice."

And he clasped the old man's wrist
So he would not be afraid.
And so they slept,
Priam and his herald, in the covered courtyard,
Each with a wealth of thoughts in his breast.
But Achilles slept inside his well-built hut,
And by his side lay lovely Briseis.

Gods and heroes slept the night through,
Wrapped in soft slumber. Only Hermes

Lay awake in the dark, pondering how
To spirit King Priam away from the ships
And elude the strong watchmen at the camp's gates.
He hovered above Priam's head and spoke:

"Well, old man, you seem to think it's safe
To sleep on and on in the enemy camp
Since Achilles spared you. Think what it cost you
To ransom your son. Your own life will cost
Three times that much to the sons you have left
If Agamemnon and the Greeks know you are here."

Suddenly the old man was afraid. He woke up the herald.
Hermes harnessed the horses and mules
And drove them through the camp. No one noticed.
And when they reached the ford of the Xanthus,
The beautiful, swirling river that Zeus begot,
Hermes left for the long peaks of Olympus.

Dawn spread her saffron light over earth,
And they drove the horses into the city
With great lamentation. The mules pulled the corpse.
No one in Troy, man or woman, saw them before
Cassandra, who stood like golden Aphrodite
On Pergamon's height. Looking out she saw
Her dear father standing in the chariot
With the herald, and then she saw Hector
Lying on the stretcher in the mule cart.
And her cry went out through all the city:

"Come look upon Hector, Trojan men and women,
If ever you rejoiced when he came home alive
From battle, a joy to the city and all its people."

She spoke. And there was not a man or woman
Left in the city, for an unbearable sorrow
Had come upon them. They met Priam by the gates
As he brought the body through, and in the front
Hector's dear wife and queenly mother threw themselves
On the rolling cart and pulled out their hair
As they clasped his head amid the grieving crowd.
They would have mourned Hector outside the gates
All the long day until the sun went down,
Had not the old man spoken from his chariot:

"Let the mules come through. Later you will have
Your fill of grieving, after I have brought him home."

He spoke, and the crowd made way for the cart.
And they brought him home and laid him
On a corded bed, and set around him singers
To lead the dirge and chant the death song.

They chanted the dirge, and the women with them.
White-armed Andromache led the lamentation
As she cradled the head of her man-slaying Hector:

"You have died young, husband, and left me
A widow in the halls. Our son is still an infant,
Doomed when we bore him. I do not think
He will ever reach manhood. No, this city
Will topple and fall first. You were its savior,
And now you are lost. All the solemn wives
And children you guarded will go off soon
In the hollow ships, and I will go with them.
And you, my son, you will either come with me
And do menial labor for a cruel master,
Or some Greek will lead you by the hand
And throw you from the tower, a hideous death,[5]
Angry because Hector killed his brother,
Or his father, or son. Many, many Greeks
Fell in battle under Hector's hands.
Your father was never gentle in combat.
And so all the townspeople mourn for him,
And you have caused your parents unspeakable
Sorrow, Hector, and left me endless pain.
You did not stretch your hand out to me
As you lay dying in bed, nor did you whisper
A final word I could remember as I weep
All the days and nights of my life."

The women's moans washed over her lament,
And from the sobbing came Hecuba's voice:

"Hector, my heart, dearest of all my children,
The gods loved you when you were alive for me,
And they have cared for you also in death.
My other children Achilles sold as slaves
When he captured them, shipped them overseas
To Samos, Imbros, and barren Lemnos.
After he took your life with tapered bronze
He dragged you around Patroclus' tomb, his friend
Whom you killed, but still could not bring him back.
And now you lie here for me as fresh as dew,
Although you have been slain, like one whom Apollo
Has killed softly with his silver arrows."

The third woman to lament was Helen.
"Oh, Hector, you were the dearest to me by far
Of all my husband's brothers. Yes, Paris
Is my husband, the godlike prince

5. Astyanax was, in fact, hurled from Troy's walls after the city fell.

Who led me to Troy. I should have died first.
This is now the twentieth year
Since I went away and left my home,
And I have never had an unkind word from you.
If anyone in the house ever taunted me,
Any of my husband's brothers or sisters,
Or his mother—my father-in-law was kind always—
You would draw them aside and calm them
With your gentle heart and gentle words.
And so I weep for you and for myself,
And my heart is heavy, because there is no one left
In all wide Troy who will pity me
Or be my friend. Everyone shudders at me."

And the people's moan came in over her voice.

Then the old man, Priam, spoke to his people:

"Men of Troy, start bringing wood to the city,
And have no fear of an Argive ambush.
When Achilles sent me from the black ships,
He gave his word he would not trouble us
Until the twelfth day should dawn."

He spoke, and they yoked oxen and mules
To wagons, and gathered outside the city.
For nine days they hauled in loads of timber.
When the tenth dawn showed her mortal light,
They brought out their brave Hector
And all in tears lifted the body high
Onto the bier, and threw on the fire.

Light blossomed like roses in the eastern sky.

The people gathered around Hector's pyre,
And when all of Troy was assembled there
They drowned the last flames with glinting wine.
Hector's brothers and friends collected
His white bones, their cheeks flowered with tears.
They wrapped the bones in soft purple robes
And placed them in a golden casket, and laid it
In the hollow of the grave, and heaped above it
A mantle of stones. They built the tomb
Quickly, with lookouts posted all around
In case the Greeks should attack early.
When the tomb was built, they all returned
To the city and assembled for a glorious feast
In the house of Priam, Zeus' cherished king.

That was the funeral of Hector, breaker of horses.

The Odyssey[1]

BOOK I

Speak, Memory—[2]
Of the cunning hero,[3]
The wanderer, blown off course time and again
After he plundered Troy's sacred heights.
Speak
Of all the cities he saw, the minds he grasped,
The suffering deep in his heart at sea
As he struggled to survive and bring his men home
But could not save them, hard as he tried—
The fools—destroyed by their own recklessness
When they ate the oxen of Hyperion the Sun,[4]
And that god snuffed out their day of return.

Of these things,

Speak, Immortal One,[5]
And tell the tale once more in our time.

By now, all the others who had fought at Troy—
At least those who had survived the war and the sea—
Were safely back home. Only Odysseus
Still longed to return to his home and his wife.
The nymph Calypso,[6] a powerful goddess—
And beautiful—was clinging to him
In her caverns and yearned to possess him.
The seasons rolled by, and the year came
In which the gods spun the thread
For Odysseus to return home to Ithaca,
Though not even there did his troubles end,
Even with his dear ones around him.
All the gods pitied him, except Poseidon,[7]
Who stormed against the godlike hero
Until he finally reached his own native land.

But Poseidon was away now, among the Ethiopians,
Those burnished people at the ends of the earth—
Some near the sunset, some near the sunrise—
To receive a grand sacrifice of rams and bulls.

1. Translated by Stanley Lombardo.
2. In the original, the first word is *andra* (man)—translated here as "hero"—and the first words rendered literally are "Man to me sing, Muse." Lombardo emphasizes the theme of memory, an important one in the poem, and reminds us that memory is, in Greek myth, the mother of the Muses.
3. Odysseus, who is not named until several lines later.
4. Hyperion was, in Greek mythology, a Titan, one of the generation of gods that preceded the Olympians. He was associated with the sun. The story of how Odysseus's men ate the cattle of the sun will be told in book 12.
5. The Muse.
6. Goddess, daughter of the Titan Atlas, who holds up the sky; her name connotes "hiding" or "secrecy."
7. God of the sea, brother of Zeus.

There he sat, enjoying the feast.
The other gods
Were assembled in the halls of Olympian Zeus,[8]
And the Father of Gods and Men was speaking.
He couldn't stop thinking about Aegisthus,
Whom Agamemnon's son, Orestes, had killed:[9]

"Mortals! They are always blaming the gods
For their troubles, when their own witlessness
Causes them more than they were destined for!
Take Aegisthus now. He marries Agamemnon's
Lawful wife and murders the man on his return
Knowing it meant disaster—because we did warn him,
Sent our messenger, quicksilver Hermes,[1]
To tell him not to kill the man and marry his wife,
Or Agamemnon's son, Orestes, would pay him back
When he came of age and wanted his inheritance.
Hermes told him all that, but his good advice
Meant nothing to Aegisthus. Now he's paid in full."

Athena[2] glared at him with her owl-grey eyes:

"Yes, O our Father who art most high—
That man got the death he richly deserved,
And so perish all who would do the same.
But it's Odysseus I'm worried about,
That discerning, ill-fated man. He's suffered
So long, separated from his dear ones,
On an island that lies in the center of the sea,
A wooded isle that is home to a goddess,
The daughter of Atlas, whose dread mind knows
All the depths of the sea and who supports
The tall pillars that keep earth and heaven apart.
His daughter detains the poor man in his grief,
Sweet-talking him constantly, trying to charm him
Into forgetting Ithaca. But Odysseus,
Longing to see even the smoke curling up
From his land, simply wants to die. And yet you
Never think of him, Olympian. Didn't Odysseus
Please you with sacrifices beside the Greek ships
At Troy? Why is Odysseus so odious,[3] Zeus?"

Zeus in his thunderhead had an answer for her:

8. King of the gods.

9. Agamemnon was the leader of the Greek armies in the Trojan War. In his ten-year absence, his wife, Clytemnestra, took a lover, Aegisthus; when Agamemnon returned from the war, Aegisthus and Clytemnestra killed him in his bath. Orestes, Agamemnon's son, avenged his father by killing his killers. Other versions of the myth, including that of Aeschylus (in his *Oresteia* plays), make Clytemnestra more important in the story than Aegisthus; perhaps deliberately, she is not named here.

1. Messenger god.

2. Goddess of wisdom, who favors Odysseus.

3. There is a pun on Odysseus's name in the original Greek.

"Quite a little speech you've let slip through your teeth,
Daughter. How could I forget godlike Odysseus?
No other mortal has a mind like his, or offers
Sacrifice like him to the deathless gods in heaven.
But Poseidon is stiff and cold with anger
Because Odysseus blinded his son, the Cyclops
Polyphemus, the strongest of all the Cyclopes,
Nearly a god. The nymph Thoösa bore him,
Daughter of Phorcys, lord of the barren brine,
After mating with Poseidon in a scalloped sea-cave.[4]
The Earthshaker[5] has been after Odysseus
Ever since, not killing him, but keeping him away
From his native land. But come now,
Let's all put our heads together and find a way
To bring Odysseus home. Poseidon will have to
Put aside his anger. He can't hold out alone
Against the will of all the immortals."

And Athena, the owl-eyed goddess, replied:

"Father Zeus, whose power is supreme,
If the blessed gods really do want
Odysseus to return to his home,
We should send Hermes, our quicksilver herald,
To the island of Ogygia without delay
To tell that nymph of our firm resolve
That long-suffering Odysseus gets to go home.
I myself will go to Ithaca
To put some spirit into his son—
Have him call an assembly of the long-haired Greeks
And rebuke the whole lot of his mother's suitors.
They have been butchering his flocks and herds.
I'll escort him to Sparta and the sands of Pylos
So he can make inquiries about his father's return
And win for himself a name among men."

Athena spoke, and she bound on her feet
The beautiful sandals, golden, immortal,
That carry her over landscape and seascape
On a puff of wind. And she took the spear,
Bronze-tipped and massive, that the Daughter uses
To level battalions of heroes in her wrath.
She shot down from the peaks of Olympus
To Ithaca, where she stood on the threshold
Of Odysseus' outer porch. Holding her spear,
She looked like Mentes,[6] the Taphian captain,
And her eyes rested on the arrogant suitors.

4. The Cyclopes are one-eyed giants. Phorcys is a minor sea god.
5. The Earthshaker is Poseidon, who had power over earthquakes.
6. Friend of Odysseus.

They were playing dice in the courtyard,
Enjoying themselves, seated on the hides of oxen
They themselves had slaughtered. They were attended
By heralds and servants, some of whom were busy
Blending water and wine in large mixing bowls,
Others wiping down the tables with sponges
And dishing out enormous servings of meat.

Telemachus spotted her first.
He was sitting with the suitors, nursing
His heart's sorrow, picturing in his mind
His noble father, imagining he had returned
And scattered the suitors, and that he himself,
Telemachus, was respected at last.
Such were his reveries as he sat with the suitors.
And then he saw Athena.
He went straight to the porch,
Indignant that a guest had been made to wait so long.
Going up to her he grasped her right hand in his
And took her spear, and his words had wings:

"Greetings, stranger. You are welcome here.
After you've had dinner, you can tell us what you need."

Telemachus spoke, and Pallas Athena
Followed him into the high-roofed hall.
When they were inside he placed her spear
In a polished rack beside a great column
Where the spears of Odysseus stood in a row.
Then he covered a beautifully wrought chair
With a linen cloth and had her sit on it
With a stool under her feet. He drew up
An intricately painted bench for himself
And arranged their seats apart from the suitors
So that his guest would not lose his appetite
In their noisy and uncouth company—
And so he could inquire about his absent father.
A maid poured water from a silver pitcher
Into a golden basin for them to wash their hands
And then set up a polished table nearby.
Another serving woman, grave and dignified,
Set out bread and generous helpings
From the other dishes she had. A carver set down
Cuts of meat by the platter and golden cups.
Then a herald came by and poured them wine.

Now the suitors swaggered in. They sat down
In rows on benches and chairs. Heralds
Poured water over their hands, maidservants
Brought around bread in baskets, and young men
Filled mixing bowls to the brim with wine.

The suitors helped themselves to all this plenty,
And when they had their fill of food and drink,
They turned their attention to the other delights,
Dancing and song, that round out a feast.
A herald handed a beautiful zither
To Phemius, who sang for the suitors,
Though against his will. Sweeping the strings
He struck up a song. And Telemachus,
Putting his head close to Pallas Athena's
So the others wouldn't hear, said this to her:

"Please don't take offense if I speak my mind.
It's easy for them to enjoy the harper's song,
Since they are eating another man's stores
Without paying anything—the stores of a man
Whose white bones lie rotting in the rain
On some distant shore, or still churn in the waves.
If they ever saw him make landing on Ithaca
They would pray for more foot speed
Instead of more gold or fancy clothes.
But he's met a bad end, and it's no comfort to us
When some traveler tells us he's on his way home.
The day has long passed when he's coming home.
But tell me this, and tell me the truth:
Who are you, and where do you come from?
Who are your parents? What kind of ship
Brought you here? How did your sailors
Guide you to Ithaca, and how large is your crew?
I don't imagine you came here on foot.
And tell me this, too. I'd like to know,
Is this your first visit here, or are you
An old friend of my father's, one of the many
Who have come to our house over the years?"

Athena's seagrey eyes glinted as she said:

"I'll tell you nothing but the unvarnished truth.
I am Mentes, son of Anchialus, and proud of it.
I am also captain of the seafaring Taphians.
I just pulled in with my ship and my crew,
Sailing the deep purple to foreign ports.
We're on our way to Cyprus with a cargo of iron
To trade for copper. My ship is standing
Offshore of wild country away from the city,
In Rheithron harbor under Neion's woods.
You and I have ties of hospitality,
Just as our fathers did, from a long way back.
Go and ask old Laertes.[7] They say he never
Comes to town any more, lives out in the country,

7. Odysseus's father.

A hard life with just an old woman to help him.
She gets him his food and drink when he comes in
From the fields, all worn out from trudging across
The ridge of his vineyard plot.
I have come
Because they say your father has returned,
But now I see the gods have knocked him off course.
He's not dead, though, not godlike Odysseus,
No way in the world. No, he's alive all right.
It's the sea keeps him back, detained on some island
In the middle of the sea, held captive by savages.
And now I will prophesy for you, as the gods
Put it in my heart and as I think it will be,
Though I am no soothsayer or reader of birds.
Odysseus will not be gone much longer
From his native land, not even if iron chains
Hold him. He knows every trick there is
And will think of some way to come home.
But now tell me this, and I want the truth:
Tall as you are, are you Odysseus' son?
You bear a striking resemblance to him,
Especially in the head and those beautiful eyes.
We used to spend quite a bit of time together
Before he sailed for Troy with the Argive fleet.
Since then, we haven't seen each other at all."

Telemachus took a deep breath and said:

"You want the truth, and I will give it to you.
My mother says that Odysseus is my father.
I don't know this myself. No one witnesses
His own begetting. If I had my way, I'd be the son
Of a man fortunate enough to grow old at home.
But it's the man with the most dismal fate of all
They say I was born from—since you want to know."

Athena's seagrey eyes glinted as she said:

"Well, the gods have made sure your family name
Will go on, since Penelope has borne a son like you.
But there is one other thing I want you to tell me.
What kind of a party is this? What's the occasion?
Some kind of banquet? A wedding feast?
It's no neighborly potluck, that's for sure,
The way this rowdy crowd is carrying on
All through the house. Any decent man
Would be outraged if he saw this behavior."

Telemachus breathed in the salt air and said:

"Since you ask me these questions as my guest—
This, no doubt, was once a perfect house,

Wealthy and fine, when its master was still home.
But the gods frowned and changed all that
When they whisked him off the face of the earth.
I wouldn't grieve for him so much if he were dead,
Gone down with his comrades in the town of Troy,
Or died in his friends' arms after winding up the war.
The entire Greek army would have buried him then,
And great honor would have passed on to his son.
But now the whirlwinds have snatched him away
Without a trace. He's vanished, gone, and left me
Pain and sorrow. And he's not the only cause
I have to grieve. The gods have given me other trials.
All of the nobles who rule the islands—
Doulichium, Samê, wooded Zacynthus—
And all those with power on rocky Ithaca
Are courting my mother and ruining our house.
She refuses to make a marriage she hates
But can't stop it either. They are eating us
Out of house and home, and will kill me someday."

And Pallas Athena, with a flash of anger:

"Damn them! You really do need Odysseus back.
Just let him lay his hands on these mangy dogs!
If only he would come through that door now
With a helmet and shield and a pair of spears,
Just as he was when I saw him first,
Drinking and enjoying himself in our house
On his way back from Ephyre. Odysseus
Had sailed there to ask Mermerus' son, Ilus,
For some deadly poison for his arrowheads.
Ilus, out of fear of the gods' anger,
Would not give him any, but my father
Gave him some, because he loved him dearly.
That's the Odysseus I want the suitors to meet.
They wouldn't live long enough to get married!
But it's on the knees of the gods now
Whether he comes home and pays them back
Right here in his halls, or doesn't.
So it's up to you
To find a way to drive them out of your house.
Now pay attention and listen to what I'm saying.
Tomorrow you call an assembly and make a speech
To these heroes, with the gods as witnesses.
The suitors you order to scatter, each to his own.
Your mother—if in her heart she wants to marry—
Goes back to her powerful father's house.
Her kinfolk and he can arrange the marriage,
And the large dowry that should go with his daughter.
And my advice for you, if you will take it,
Is to launch your best ship, with twenty oarsmen,

And go make inquiries about your long-absent father.
Someone may tell you something, or you may hear
A rumor from Zeus, which is how news travels best.
Sail to Pylos first and ask godly Nestor,
Then go over to Sparta and red-haired Menelaus.[8]
He was the last home of all the bronzeclad Greeks.
If you hear your father's alive and on his way home,
You can grit your teeth and hold out one more year.
If you hear he's dead, among the living no more,
Then come home yourself to your ancestral land,
Build him a barrow and celebrate the funeral
Your father deserves. Then marry off your mother.
After you've done all that, think up some way
To kill the suitors in your house either openly
Or by setting a trap. You've got to stop
Acting like a child. You've outgrown that now.
Haven't you heard how Orestes won glory
Throughout the world when he killed Aegisthus,
The shrewd traitor who murdered his father?
You have to be aggressive, strong—look at how big
And well-built you are—so you will leave a good name.
Well, I'm off to my ship and my men,
Who are no doubt wondering what's taking me so long.
You've got a job to do. Remember what I said."

And Telemachus, in his clear-headed way:

"My dear guest, you speak to me as kindly
As a father to his son. I will not forget your words.
I know you're anxious to leave, but please stay
So you can bathe and relax before returning
To your ship, taking with you a costly gift,
Something quite fine, a keepsake from me,
The sort of thing a host gives to his guest."

And Athena, her eyes grey as saltwater:

"No, I really do want to get on with my journey.
Whatever gift you feel moved to make,
Give it to me on my way back home,
Yes, something quite fine. It will get you as good."

With these words the Grey-eyed One was gone,
Flown up and away like a seabird. And as she went
She put courage in Telemachus' heart
And made him think of his father even more than before.
Telemachus' mind soared. He knew it had been a god,
And like a god himself he rejoined the suitors.

8. Brother of Agamemnon, husband of Helen, whose abduction by Paris caused the Trojan War.

They were sitting hushed in silence, listening
To the great harper as he sang the tale
Of the hard journeys home that Pallas Athena
Ordained for the Greeks on their way back from Troy.

His song drifted upstairs, and Penelope,
Wise daughter of Icarius, took it all in.
She came down the steep stairs of her house—
Not alone, two maids trailed behind—
And when she had come among the suitors
She stood shawled in light by a column
That supported the roof of the great house,
Hiding her cheeks behind her silky veils,
Grave handmaidens standing on either side.
And she wept as she addressed the brilliant harper:

"Phemius, you know many other songs
To soothe human sorrows, songs of the exploits
Of gods and men. Sing one of those
To your enraptured audience as they sit
Sipping their wine. But stop singing this one,
This painful song that always tears at my heart.
I am already sorrowful, constantly grieving
For my husband, remembering him, a man
Renowned in Argos and throughout all Hellas."

And Telemachus said to her coolly:

"Mother, why begrudge our singer
Entertaining us as he thinks best?
Singers are not responsible; Zeus is,
Who gives what he wants to every man on earth.
No one can blame Phemius for singing the doom
Of the Danaans:[9] it's always the newest song
An audience praises most. For yourself,
You'll just have to endure it and listen.
Odysseus was not the only man at Troy
Who didn't come home. Many others perished.
You should go back upstairs and take care of your work,
Spinning and weaving, and have the maids do theirs.
Speaking is for men, for all men, but for me
Especially, since I am the master of this house."

Penelope was stunned and turned to go,
Her son's masterful words pressed to her heart.
She went up the stairs to her room with her women
And wept for Odysseus, her beloved husband,
Until grey-eyed Athena cast sleep on her eyelids.

9. Danaans are Greeks. Homer does not use a general term for the Greeks, instead referring to three Greek tribes: Danaans, Argives, and Achaeans.

All through the shadowy halls the suitors
Broke into an uproar, each of them praying
To lie in bed with her. Telemachus cut them short:

"Suitors of my mother—you arrogant pigs—
For now, we're at a feast. No shouting, please!
There's nothing finer than hearing
A singer like this, with a voice like a god's.
But in the morning we will sit in the meeting ground,
So that I can tell all of you in broad daylight
To get out of my house. Fix yourselves feasts
In each others' houses, use up your own stockpiles.
But if it seems better and more profitable
For one man to be eaten out of house and home
Without compensation—then eat away!
For my part, I will pray to the gods eternal
That Zeus grant me requital: Death for you
Here in my house. With no compensation."

Thus Telemachus. And they all bit their lips
And marveled at how boldly he had spoken to them.
Then Antinous, son of Eupeithes, replied:

"Well, Telemachus, it seems the gods, no less,
Are teaching you how to be a bold public speaker.
May the son of Cronus[1] never make you king
Here on Ithaca, even if it is your birthright."

And Telemachus, taking in a breath:

"It may make you angry, Antinous,
But I'll tell you something. I wouldn't mind a bit
If Zeus granted me this—if he made me king.
You think this is the worst fate a man can have?
It's not so bad to be king. Your house grows rich,
And you're held in great honor yourself. But,
There are many other lords on seawashed Ithaca,
Young and old, and any one of them
Could get to be king, now that Odysseus is dead.
But I will be master of my own house
And of the servants that Odysseus left me."

Then Eurymachus, Polybus' son, responded:

"It's on the knees of the gods, Telemachus,
Which man of Greece will rule this island.
But you keep your property and rule your house,
And may no man ever come to wrest them away
From you by force, not while men live in Ithaca.
But I want to ask you, sir, about your visitor.

1. Zeus.

Where did he come from, what port
Does he call home, where are his ancestral fields?
Did he bring news of your father's coming
Or was he here on business of his own?
He sure up and left in a hurry, wouldn't stay
To be known. Yet by his looks he was no tramp."

And Telemachus, with a sharp response:

"Eurymachus, my father is not coming home.
I no longer trust any news that may come,
Or any prophecy my mother may have gotten
From a seer she has summoned up to the house.
My guest was a friend of my father's from Taphos.
He says he is Mentes, son of Anchialus
And captain of the seafaring Taphians."

Thus Telemachus. But in his heart he knew
It was an immortal goddess.

And now
The young men plunged into their entertainment,
Singing and dancing until the twilight hour.
They were still at it when the evening grew dark,
Then one by one went to their own houses to rest.

Telemachus' room was off the beautiful courtyard,
Built high and with a surrounding view.
There he went to his bed, his mind teeming,
And with him, bearing blazing torches,
Went true-hearted Eurycleia, daughter of Ops
And Peisenor's grandaughter. Long ago,
Laertes had bought her for a small fortune
When she was still a girl. He paid twenty oxen
And honored her in his house as he honored
His wedded wife, but he never slept with her
Because he would rather avoid his wife's wrath.
Of all the women, she loved Telemachus the most
And had nursed him as a baby. Now she bore
The blazing torches as Telemachus opened
The doors to his room and sat on his bed.
He pulled off his soft tunic and laid it
In the hands of the wise old woman, and she
Folded it and smoothed it and hung it on a peg
Beside the corded bed. Then she left the room,
Pulled the door shut by its silver handle,
And drew the bolt home with the strap.

There Telemachus
Lay wrapped in a fleece all the night through,
Pondering the journey Athena had shown him.

BOOK II

Dawn's pale rose fingers brushed across the sky,
And Odysseus' son got out of bed and dressed.
He slung his sharp sword around his shoulder,
Then tied oiled leather sandals onto his feet,
And walked out of the bedroom like a god.
Wasting no time, he ordered the heralds
To call an assembly. The heralds' cries
Rang out through the town, and the men
Gathered quickly, their long hair streaming.
Telemachus strode along carrying a spear
And accompanied by two lean hounds.
Athena shed a silver grace upon him,
And everyone marveled at him as he entered.
The elders made way as he took his father's seat.

First to speak was the hero Aegyptius,
A man bowed with age and wise beyond telling.
His son, Antiphus, had gone off to Troy
In the ships with Odysseus (and was killed
In the cave of the Cyclops, who made of him
His last savage meal). Of three remaining sons,
One, Eurynomus, ran with the suitors,
And the other two kept their father's farm.
But Aegyptius couldn't stop mourning the one that was lost
And was weeping for him as he spoke out now:

"Hear me now, men of Ithaca.
We have never once held assembly or sat
In council since Odysseus left.
Who has called us together today?
Which of the young men, or of the elders,
Has such urgent business as this?
Has he had news of the army's return,
Some early report he wants to tell us about?
Or is there some other public matter
He wants to address? He's a fine man
In my eyes, and may Zeus bless him."

Telemachus was glad to hear these words,
And he rose from his seat, eager to speak.
There he stood, in the midst of the assembly,
And the herald Peisenor, a wise counselor,
Placed the staff in the hands of Odysseus' son.
In his speech he addressed old Aegyptius first:

"You won't have to look very far to find out
Who called this assembly. I called it myself.
No, I have not had news of the army's return,
Any early report I could tell you about.

Nor is there any other public matter
I want to address. It's a private matter,
My own need. Trouble has come to my house
In two forms. First, I have lost my noble father.
He was your king once, and like a father
To all of you, gentle and kind. And now,
There is even greater trouble, far greater,
Which will destroy my house and home.
Suitors have latched on to my mother,
Against her will, and they are the sons
Of the noblest men here. They shrink
From going to her father Icarius' house
So that he could arrange his daughter's dowry
And give her away to the man he likes best.
Instead, they gather at our house day after day,
Slaughtering our oxen and sheep and fat goats,
Living high and drinking wine recklessly.
We've lost almost everything, because
We don't have Odysseus to protect our house.
We can't defend ourselves. If it came to a fight
We would only show how pathetic we are.
Not that I wouldn't defend myself
If I had the power. Things have gone too far.
The ruin of my house has become a public disgrace.
You should all be indignant, and feel shame
Before your neighbors, and fear the wrath
Of the gods, who may yet turn against you.
I beg you by Olympian Zeus and by Themis,[2]
Who calls and dismisses assemblies of men,
Stop this, my friends, and let me be alone
In my grief—unless my father, Odysseus,
Was your enemy and did you some harm
And now you are paying me back in malice
By urging these suitors on. Better for me
If you yourselves, Ithacans all,
Were to eat up my treasures and flocks.
Then I might get restitution someday.
I'd go through the town and bend people's ears
And ask for our goods until they were all given back.
But there is nothing I can do now. There's no cure
For what you are making me suffer now."

He spoke in anger, bursting into tears
As he threw the scepter onto the ground.
The crowd was motionless with pity. No one
Had the heart to respond to him harshly,
Except Antinous, who now said:

"Well, the big speaker, the mighty orator.
You've got some nerve, Telemachus,

2. Goddess whose name means "right" or "justice."

Laying the blame on us. It's not the suitors
Who are at fault, but your own mother,
Who knows more tricks than any woman alive.
It's been three years now, almost four,
Since she's been toying with our affections.
She encourages each man, leading us on,
Sending messages. But her mind is set elsewhere.
Here's just one of the tricks she devised:
She set up a great loom in the main hall
And started weaving a sizeable fabric
With a very fine thread, and she said to us:

'Young men—my suitors, since Odysseus is dead—
Eager as you are to marry me, you must wait
Until I finish this robe—it would be a shame
To waste my spinning—a shroud for the hero
Laertes, when death's doom lays him low.
I fear the Achaean women would reproach me
If he should lie in death shroudless for all his wealth.'

"We were persuaded by this appeal to our honor.
Every day she would weave at the great loom,
And every night she would unweave by torchlight.
She fooled us for three years with her craft.
But in the fourth year, as the seasons rolled by,
And the moons waned, and the days dragged on,
One of her women who knew all about it
Told us, and we caught her unweaving
The gloried shroud. Then we forced her to finish it.
Now here is the suitors' answer to you,
And let every Achaean hear it as well:
Send your mother away with orders to marry
Whichever man her father likes best.
But if she goes on like this much longer,
Torturing us with all she knows and has,
All the gifts Athena has given her,
Her talent for handiwork, her good sense,
Her cleverness—all of which go far beyond
That of any of the heroines of old,
Tyro or Alcmene or garlanded Mycene,
Not one of whom had a mind like Penelope's,
Even though now she is not thinking straight—
We will continue to eat you out of house and home
For as long as she holds to this way of thinking
Which the immortal gods have put in her breast.
She is building quite a reputation for herself,
But at your expense. As for us, we're staying put
Until she chooses one of the Achaeans to marry."

Telemachus, drawing a deep breath, responded:

"Antinous, I cannot throw out of my house

The mother who bore me and raised me.
As for my father, he may be alive or dead
But he is not here. It would not be fair
If I had to pay a great price to Icarius,
As I would if I sent my mother back to him
On my own initiative. And the spirits would send me
Other evils, for my mother would curse me
As she left the house, and call on the Furies.[3]
And men all over would hold me at fault.
So I will never tell my mother to leave.
As for you, if you don't like it,
If this offends your sense of fairness,
Get out of my house! Fix yourselves feasts
In each others' houses, use up your own stockpiles.
But if it seems better and more profitable
For one man to be eaten out of house and home
Without compensation—then eat away!
But I will pray to the gods eternal
That Zeus grant me requital: Death for you
Here in my house. With no compensation."

Telemachus spoke, and Zeus in answer
Sent forth two eagles from a mountain peak.
They drifted lazily for a while on the wind,
Side by side, with wings outstretched.
But when they were directly above the assembly
With its hub-bub of voices, they wheeled about
And beat their wings hard, looking down
On the heads of all with death in their eyes.
Then they savaged each others' craws
With their talons and veered off to the east
Across the city and over the houses
Of the men below. Everyone was amazed,
And they all wondered what these birds portended.
Then the old hero Halitherses stepped forth,
Mastor's son, the best man of his time
In reading bird flight and uttering oracles.
He was full of good will in the speech that he made.
"Hear me men of Ithaca, and I mean
The suitors especially, since a great tide of woe
Is rising to engulf them. Odysseus
Shall not be away from his home much longer.
Even now he is near, sowing death for the suitors,
One and all, grim for them and grim for many others
Who dwell on Ithaca. But let us take thought now
Of how to make an end of this. Or better,
Let the suitors themselves make an end.
I am no inexperienced prophet,
But one who knows well, and I declare

3. Spirits of vengeance.

That everything is coming true for that man,
Just as I told him when he left for Troy:
That after bitter pain and loss of all comrades
He would finally reach home after twenty years
Unknown to anyone. Now it is all coming true."

Eurymachus, Polybus' son, answered him:

"Get out of here, old man. Go home and prophesy
For your own children—you don't want them to get hurt.
I'm a better prophet than you when it comes to this.
There are lots of birds under the sun, flying
All over the place, and not all of them are omens.
As for Odysseus, he died a long way from here,
And you should have died with him.
Then you wouldn't spout so many prophecies,
Or be egging Telemachus on in his anger,
Hoping he'll give you a gift to take home.
I'll tell you this, and I guarantee it'll be done:
If you, with all your experience and lore,
Talk a younger man into getting angry,
First, we'll go harder on him, and second,
We'll slap you with a fine so big
It'll make you choke when you have to pay it.
And this is my advice to Telemachus:
Send your mother back to her father's house
And have them prepare a wedding feast
And all the gifts that go with a beloved daughter.
Until then, the sons of the Achaeans will not stop
Their bitter courtship. One thing's for sure,
We fear no man, no, not even Telemachus
With all his big talk. We don't give a damn
For your prophecies, old man, and when they don't
Come true, you'll be more despised than ever.
And you, Telemachus, your inheritance
Is going down the drain and will never be restored
As long as your mother puts off this marriage.
After all, we wait here patiently day after day
Competing for her, and do not go after
Other women who might make us good wives."

And Telemachus, keeping his wits about him:

"I'm done pleading with you, Eurymachus,
And all the rest of you suitors. I've had my say.
Now the gods know all this, and so do the Achaeans.
All I want now is a fast ship and twenty men
Who will crew for me as I sail here and there.
I'm going to Sparta and to sandy Pylos
For news of my father, who has been long gone.
Someone may tell me something, or I may hear

A rumor from Zeus, which is how news travels best.
If I hear my father's alive and on his way home,
I can grit my teeth and hold out one more year.
If I hear he's dead, among the living no more,
I'll come home myself to my ancestral land,
Build him a barrow and celebrate the funeral
My father deserves. Then I'll marry off my mother."

He spoke and sat down. Then up rose Mentor,
An old friend of Odysseus. It was him,
Old Mentor, that Odysseus had put in charge
Of all his house when he left with the ships.
He spoke out now with good will to all:

"Hear me now, men of Ithaca.
Kings might as well no longer be gentle and kind
Or understand the correct order of things.
They might as well be tyrannical butchers
For all that any of Odysseus' people
Remember him, a godly king as kind as a father.
I have no quarrel with the suitors. True,
They are violent and malicious men,
But at least they are risking their own lives
In devouring the house of Odysseus,
Who, they say, will never return.
It is the rest of the people I am angry with.
You all sit here in silence and say nothing,
Not a word of rebuke to make the suitors quit,
Although you easily outnumber them."

Leocritus, Evenor's son, answered him:

"What kind of thing is that to say, Mentor,
You stubborn old fool, telling us to stop?
And do you think that even with superior numbers
People are going to fight us over a dinner?
Even if Odysseus, your Ithacan hero himself
Showed up, all hot to throw the suitors
Out of his house—well, let's just say
His wife wouldn't be too happy to see him,
No matter how much she missed him, that's how ugly
His death would be. No, you're way off the mark.
Now let's everybody scatter and go home.
Mentor and Halitherses can outfit Telemachus.
They're old friends of his father. But I think
He'll be getting his news sitting here in Ithaca
For a long time to come. He's not going anywhere."

With those words the brief assembly was over.
Everyone returned to their homes, but the suitors
Went off to the house of godlike Odysseus.

Telemachus, though, went down to the shore,
Washed his hands in the surf, and prayed to Athena:

"Hear me, god of yesterday. You came to our house
And commanded me to sail the misty sea
In search of news of my long-absent father.
Now the townspeople are blocking all that,
Especially the suitors, those arrogant bastards."

He prayed, and Athena was with him,
Looking just like Mentor and with Mentor's voice.
Her words flew to Telemachus on wings:

"You won't turn out to be a fool or a coward,
Telemachus, not if any of Odysseus' spirit
Has been instilled in you. Now there was a man
Who made sure of his words and deeds! Don't worry,
You'll make this journey, and it won't be in vain.
If you're really Odysseus' and Penelope's son,
You'll finish whatever you set your mind to.
You know, few sons turn out to be like their fathers;
Most turn out worse, a few better.
No, you don't have it in you to be a fool or a coward,
And you've got something of Odysseus' brains,
So there's reason to think you'll finish this job.
Never mind, then, about the suitors' schemes.
They're mad, not an ounce of sense or justice in them,
And they have no idea of the dark death
Closing in on them, doomed all to die on a single day.
As for you, the journey you have your heart set on
Won't be delayed. I myself, your father's old comrade,
Will equip a fast ship and sail along with you.
You get the provisions and stow them aboard,
Wine in jars and barley meal in tight skins,
Food that will stick to men's ribs. I'll go through town
And round up a volunteer crew. There are plenty of ships
In Ithaca, old and new. I'll scout out the best one,
Get her rigged, and launch her onto the open sea."

Thus Athena, daughter of Zeus.

And Telemachus, the voice of the goddess
Ringing in his ears, went on to his house
With a troubled heart. There he found
The haughty suitors, flaying goats
And singeing swine in the courtyard.
Antinous came up to him with a laugh
And clasped his hand and said to him:

"Ah, Telemachus, the dauntless orator,
That's the spirit! No hard feelings now!

Let's just eat and drink as we always have.
The townspeople will provide you with everything—
A ship, a crew—to speed you on to sacred Pylos
In your search for news of your noble father."

And Telemachus, drawing in his breath:

"Antinous, there is no way I can relax
Or enjoy myself with you arrogant bastards.
Isn't it bad enough that you have eaten through
Much of my wealth while I was still a child?
Now that I'm grown, and hear things from others,
And get angrier and angrier at what I see and hear,
I'm going to do my best to nail you to the wall,
Either by going to Pylos or staying here in this land.
But I am going, and I'll make the journey count,
Even though I have to sail in another man's ship
And can't captain my own, which I'm sure suits you fine."

And he withdrew his hand from Antinous'.
The suitors, busy with preparing the feast,
Jeered at him as they swaggered through the hall:

"Hey, everybody! Telemachus is planning to murder us!
He'll bring reinforcements from sandy Pylos,
Or even from Sparta. He's really serious.
Or he'll go to Ephyre and get deadly poisons
To put in our wine-bowl and kill us all."

And another would sneer:

"Who knows?
If he goes off wandering in a hollow ship,
He may die as Odysseus did, far from his friends.
That would mean more work for us, dividing
All his possessions and giving his house
Over to his mother—and the man she marries."

That's how their talk went. But Telemachus
Went down to his father's treasure chamber,
A large room where there lay gold and bronze
Piled to the ceiling. And there were clothes in chests,
Fragrant olive oil, and great jars of wine,
Old and sweet, an undiluted, heavenly drink,
Ranged in rows along the wall, ready for Odysseus
Should he ever return after all his suffering.
The close-fitting, double doors were locked,
And the room was watched day and night
By a wise old stewardess, Eurycleia,
Daughter of Ops, son of Peisenor. Telemachus
Had summoned her and now spoke to her there:

"Nurse, siphon me off some wine in jars,
The sweetest, mellowest wine we have
After what you are holding in reserve
For Odysseus, that unlucky man,
Should he ever return from the jaws of death.
Fill twelve jars and fit them with lids,
And pour some barley meal into well-sewn skins.
I'll need twenty quarts of ground barley meal.
But don't let anyone know. Just have all this
Ready to go. I'll pick it up this evening
After my mother has gone to bed upstairs.
I'm off to Sparta and to sandy Pylos
To see if I can get some news of my father."

He spoke, and Eurycleia gave a shrill cry.
She sobbed as her words went out to him:

"Ah, where did you get this idea, child?
Why would you want to travel abroad, you,
A beloved only son? Zeus-born Odysseus
Perished far from home, in a strange land.
These men, as soon as you are gone, will plot
To have you killed by treachery, and then divide
All these things among themselves. No, stay here
With what is yours. There is no need for you
To wander and suffer on the barren sea."

And Telemachus, in his cool-headed way:

"Don't worry, nurse. There is a god
Behind all this. But swear you won't say
Anything to my mother for a dozen days or so,
Or until she misses me herself or has heard
That I am gone. I don't want her crying."

And the old woman swore to the gods
That she would say nothing. That done,
She drew the wine for him in jars
And poured the barley meal into skins,
While Telemachus went back to join the suitors.

Owl-eyed Athena saw what to do next.
Assuming the form of Telemachus,
She went through the town recruiting sailors,
Telling them to gather by the ship at dusk.
Then she asked Noemon, Phronius' son,
For a fast ship, and he cheerfully agreed.

When the sun set and shadows hung everywhere,
She drew the swift ship down to the sea,
Put in all the gear a benched sailing ship needs,

And then moored it at the harbor's mouth. The crew
Gathered around, and the goddess encouraged each man.

Then she moved on, making her way
To the house of godlike Odysseus. There
She shed sweet sleep on the suitors
And made their minds wander in their wine
And knocked the cups from their hands. Eyelids heavy,
They stumbled to their feet and one by one
Staggered through the city home and to bed.

Athena's eyes flashed in the dark.
She looked like Mentor now, and in his voice
She called Telemachus out from the hall:

"Telemachus, your crew is ready with the oars
And waiting for you. It's time to set forth."

Pallas Athena led the way quickly,
And the man followed in the deity's footsteps.
They came down to the ship and the sea
And found the crew standing on the beach,
Their hair blowing in the offshore breeze.
And Telemachus, feeling his father's blood:

"This way, men! We have provisions to haul.
Everything's ready at my house. My mother
Knows nothing of all this, nor do any
Of the women, except for one I told."

He led the way, and they brought the provisions
Down to the ship and stowed them below.
Athena went aboard, followed by Telemachus,
And they sat side by side on the stern of the ship
As the men untied the cables and then came aboard
To sit at their benches. The Grey-eyed One[4]
Put the wind at their backs, a strong gust from the West
That came in chanting over the wine-dark water.
Telemachus called to the crew to rig the sail.
Falling to, they raised the fir mast,
Set it in its socket, braced it with forestays
And hauled up the white sail. The wind
Bellied the canvas, and an indigo wave
Hissed off the bow as the ship sped on.
When they had made all the tackle secure
In their swift black ship, they set out bowls
Brimming with wine, and poured libations
To the immortal gods, most of all
To the daughter of Zeus with seagrey eyes.

The ship bore through the night and into the dawn.

4. Athena.

BOOK III

The sun rose from the still, beautiful water
Into the bronze sky, to shine upon the gods
And upon men who die on the life-giving earth.

The ship came to Pylos, Nestor's great city.
Onshore, black bulls were being sacrificed
To the blue-maned Lord of the Sea.[5]
Nine companies of five hundred men
Were each assigned nine bulls for sacrifice.
They had just tasted the innards and were burning
The thigh pieces for the god when the ship
Pulled in to shore. The crew furled the sail,
Moored the vessel and disembarked.
Telemachus stepped off the ship behind Athena,
And the goddess, eyes glinting, said to him:

"There's no need to feel embarrassed, Telemachus,
Not at all. This is why you have sailed the sea—
To get news of your father, to find out his fate
And where the earth conceals him. Come on, now,
Go straight up to Nestor. Let's see what he knows.
Ask him yourself, so he'll tell you the truth.
Not that he would lie. He's very wise."

And Telemachus, taking in a breath:

"How should I go up to him, Mentor,
And what should I say? I'm not used
To making clever speeches. And besides,
A young man just doesn't question an elder."

Athena's eyes glinted in the morning light:

"You'll come up with some things yourself, Telemachus,
And a god will suggest others. I do not think
You were born and bred without the gods' good will."

Thus Pallas Athena. She led the way quickly,
And the man followed in the deity's footsteps.
They came to the great company of Pylians
And there found Nestor sitting with his sons.
All around him were men preparing for the feast,
Skewering meat on spits and roasting it.
But when they saw the new arrivals, they all
Crowded around, clasping their hands in welcome
And inviting them to sit down. Nestor's son
Peisistratus was first, taking them both by the hand
And having them sit down at the feast

5. Poseidon.

On soft fleeces spread on the sandy beach
Beside his father and Thrasymedes his brother.
Then he gave them servings of the inner organs
And poured wine into a golden cup. Passing it on
To Pallas Athena, he spoke directly to her,
The daughter of Zeus, who wields the aegis:

"Pray now, stranger, to Lord Poseidon,
For it is his feast you have happened upon.
When you have poured libations and have said
The ritual prayers, pass the cup of sweet wine
On to your friend, so that he too may pour,
Since I have no doubt he also prays to the gods.
All men have need of the immortal gods.
But he is younger than you, about my age,
So to you I will give the golden cup first."

He spoke, and handed her the cup of sweet wine,
And Athena rejoiced at his respect for custom
In handing her the golden cup first.
Without hesitation she prayed to Poseidon:

"Hear me, Poseidon who laps all the earth,
And do not refuse to fulfill my prayer.
Bring renown to Nestor first, and his sons,
And grant your grace to all the men of Pylos
In return for this glorious sacrifice.
And grant also to Telemachus and to me
A safe return home, having accomplished
All that we came for in our swift black ship."

Thus Athena's prayer, which she herself granted.
Then she gave Telemachus the beautiful cup,
And Odysseus' true son prayed the same way.

The meat was roasted now. They drew it
Off the spits and served it up for the feast.
When they had eaten and drunk all that they wanted,
Nestor, the Gerenian horseman, spoke:

"It is seemlier to ask our guests who they are
Now that they have enjoyed some food with us.
Who are you, strangers? Where do you sail from?
Are you on some business, or are you adventurers
Wandering the seas, risking your own lives
And bringing trouble to men in foreign lands?"

Telemachus felt a sudden surge of courage,
Implanted in his heart by Athena herself
So that he would inquire about his absent father
And win for himself a name among men:

"Nestor, son of Neleus, glory of the Achaeans,
You ask where we are from, and I will tell you.
We have come from Ithaca, under Mount Neion,
But my business is my own, not the Ithacans'.
I come for news of my father, any news at all
About noble Odysseus, who once, they say,
Fought beside you and sacked the city of Troy.
We have heard where each of the other heroes
Who fought the Trojans met his bitter end.
But Zeus has placed Odysseus' death
Beyond hope of knowing. No one can say
Exactly where Odysseus died,
Whether it was on land, overcome by enemies,
Or on the deep sea in Amphtrite's[6] waves.
And so I am at your knees, to see if you
Can tell me how my father met his end,
Whether you saw it with your own eyes,
Or heard about it from someone else,
Some wanderer. He was born to sorrow,
More than any man on earth. And do not,
Out of pity, spare me the truth, but tell me
Whatever you have seen, whatever you know.
I beseech you, if my father, noble Odysseus,
Ever fulfilled a promise he made to you
In the land of Troy, where the Achaeans suffered,
Remember it now, and tell me the truth."

And Nestor, the Gerenian horseman, answered:

"Ah, my friend, you bring to my mind
The sorrow we bravely endured in that land,
Heroes all and the sons of heroes—
Everything we suffered on the misty sea,
Looting and plundering wherever Achilles led,
And all of our battles around Priam's great city,
Where our best were killed. There lies
Ajax, dear to Ares, there great Achilles,
There Patroclus, like a god in council,
There my own dear son, Antilochus,
Strong and swift, a peerless warrior.
And there were many more losses we suffered.
No mortal man could recount them all.
Even if you stayed for five or six years
And wanted to hear the whole tale of woe,
You would return home weary before the end.
For nine years we devised all sorts of strategies
To bring Troy down—which the son of Cronus[7]

6. Amphtrite is a sea goddess.

7. Zeus.

Scarcely brought to pass. In that effort
No man could match Odysseus for cunning.
Your father was the master of all strategies—
If indeed you are his son. I am amazed
As I look upon you. The way you speak
Is very much like him. One would not think
A younger man could speak so appropriately.
Now all that time Odysseus and I
Never disagreed in assembly or council.
We had one heart, and with our wisdom
We advised the Argives on the best course to take.
But when we had sacked Priam's tall town,
Zeus planned in his heart a bitter journey home
For the Greeks—who were not all prudent or just,
Which is why the wrath of the Grey-eyed One
Brought many of them to an evil end.
She caused a quarrel between Atreus' two sons,
Agamemnon and Menelaus. It happened this way:
These two called an assembly of the entire army
In a reckless manner, toward sunset
And all out of order. We had all been drinking.
They made their speeches, and announced their purpose
In assembling the troops. Menelaus wanted
The entire army to set their sights homeward,
To begin shipping out on the open sea,
But this was not at all to Agamemnon's liking.
He wanted to delay their departure
And offer formal sacrifice to appease
The wrath of Athena—the fool,
He had no idea she would never relent.
The minds of the eternal ones are not quickly turned.
So these two stood there exchanging insults,
And the soldiers rose up with one huge roar
And took sides. We spent that night
Nursing our resentment against each other,
For Zeus was bringing on our doom.
At dawn some of us hauled our ships
To the bright water and loaded on board
Our goods and our softly belted women.
Half of the army held back, remaining
With King Agamemnon, son of Atreus,
But half of us embarked and launched our ships,
Which pulled away swiftly, for some god
Had made the teeming water smooth as glass.
We pulled in to Tenedos and offered sacrifice,
Eager to reach home, but Zeus held firm
Against our immediate return and stirred up
Still more dissension. Some now turned back
Their curved ships, following Odysseus,
A wise leader with a flexible mind,
Out of respect for Lord Agamemnon.

But I fled on with all my ships,
For I knew that Zeus had evil in mind.
Diomedes also got his men out then,
And Menelaus brought up the rear.
He caught up with us in Lesbos
As we were debating the long journey ahead,
Whether we should sail above rugged Chios
And on to Psyria, keeping Chios on our left,
Or go below Chios past windy Mimas.
We asked the god to give us a sign
And he showed us one, telling us
To cut through the sea straight to Euboea,
The sooner to get ourselves out of danger.
A shrill wind rose up and started to blow,
And the ships flew over the teeming brine.
We put in at Geraestus that night,
And, with all that water behind us,
We sacrificed many bulls to Poseidon.
On the fourth day Diomedes made Argos,
But I held on toward Pylos, and the wind
Did not die down once since it began to blow.

"And so I came home, dear child, knowing nothing
Of who survived and who was lost.
But what I have heard sitting here in my halls
You too shall hear, as is only right.
The Myrmidons, they say, made it safely home,
Led by the son of great-souled Achilles;
Philoctetes too; and Idomeneus
Brought back to Crete all of his men
Who survived the war; he lost none at sea.
Of Agamemnon you have already heard,
Far off though you be, how he came home
And how Aegisthus plotted his grisly death
And then paid for it in a horrible way.
How good it is for a son to be left
When a man dies! Agamemnon's son
Avenged his death, killing his murderer,
The treacherous Aegisthus. You too, my friend—
For I see that you are handsome and tall—
Should be brave and strong, and win a name for yourself."

And Telemachus, in his clear-headed way:

"Nestor, son of Neleus, glory of the Achaeans,
Truly, Orestes was a son who took vengeance,
And the Achaeans will spread his fame
To future generations. I wish the gods
Would clothe me in such strength, that I
Might take vengeance on the suitors
For their transgressions against me.

They are violent and malicious men.
But the gods have spun into the web of my life
No such happiness for me or my father,
And so I will simply have to endure."

Nestor, the Gerenian horseman, answered:

"Now that you've mentioned it, I recall hearing
That a crowd of suitors for your mother's hand,
Uninvited by you, are causing you trouble.
Why do you put up with this? Has some god
Turned the townspeople against you?
Who knows but that Odysseus may come some day,
Alone or with an army, and make them pay in blood.
Ah, if only grey-eyed Athena chose to love you
The way she did glorious Odysseus
In the land of Troy! I have never seen
A god show love so openly
As Athena did to him. You could see her
Standing at his side! If she would choose
To love you like that and take care of you,
Some of those suitors might forget about marriage!"

And Telemachus answered him:

"I do not think, sir, this will ever happen.
The very thought amazes me. It is too much
To hope for, even if the gods willed it."

Then Athena, eyes flashing, put in:

"Telemachus, what a thing to say!
It is easy for a god to bring a man safely home,
Even from far away. And speaking for myself,
I would rather suffer on my homeward journey
Than be killed at my hearth, as Agamemnon was—
By the treachery of Aegisthus and of his own wife.
But even the gods cannot ward off death,
The great leveler, from a man they love,
Not when destiny comes to lay him low."

And Telemachus answered him:

"Mentor, let us speak of this no longer,
For all our grief. He cannot return.
The gods have already devised his death.
But now I have another question for Nestor,
Steeped as he is in knowledge and wisdom.
He has been king for three generations
And has the look of an immortal god.
Nestor, son of Neleus, tell me this:

How was Agamemnon, son of Atreus, slain?
Where was Menelaus? How could Aegisthus
Dare to plot the murder of a king, a man
Far more powerful than he himself was?
Was Menelaus not in Argos, and did his absence
Encourage Aegisthus to commit the murder?"

And Nestor, the Gerenian horseman:

"Well then, my child, I will tell you all.
You yourself have guessed what would have happened
If Atreus' son, red-haired Menelaus,
Had come back from Troy and found Aegisthus
Still alive in his halls. His dead body
Would never have been buried in earth;
Dogs and birds would have ripped it apart
As it lay on the plain far from the city,
Nor would any Greek woman have wept for him,
So monstrous was the crime he planned and committed.
While we toiled and sweated over there in Troy,
He relaxed in a corner of bluegrass Argos
Sweet-talking the wife of Agamemnon,
Noble Clytemnestra. At first she refused
The whole sordid affair. She had good sense,
And with her was a singer whom Agamemnon,
When he left for Troy, had strictly ordered
To guard his wife. But when the gods doomed her
To be undone, Aegisthus took the singer of tales
To a desert island and left him there
For the dogs and birds. And he led her off,
Just as willing as he was, to his own house.
Many an ox's thigh he burned on the altars,
Many an offering he made of tapestries and gold
When he accomplished the great deed
He had never hoped in his heart to achieve.
        Menelaus and I were sailing then
On our way back from Troy, the best of friends.
But when we came to holy Sunium,
The cape of Athens, Phoebus Apollo
Shot Menelaus' pilot with his arrows,
Killing him softly as he held the tiller
Of the speeding ship—Phrontis his name,
The best rough-weather pilot in all the world.
So Menelaus stopped, eager though he was
To press on, and gave his comrade a funeral.
When he got his ships on the deep purple again
He made good time to Malea's steep height,
But then Zeus put trouble in his way, shearing
Blasts of shrill winds down from the sky,
And the waves swelled to the size of mountains.
Then he split the fleet into two, bringing some

To the part of Crete where the Cydonians live,
Near the Iardanus river. There is a smooth cliff
Sheer to the misty sea on the border of Gortyn,
Where the Southwest Wind drives huge waves
Against the headland on the left, toward Phaestus.
The only breakwater is a small rock offshore.
So, some of the fleet came there. The men
Barely escaped with their lives, but the ships
Were broken to pieces against the reef.
Five other black ships, though, were blown
All the way to Egypt, and Menelaus
Wandered up and down that coast with his ships,
A stranger in a strange land, amassing
A fortune in gold and goods. Aegisthus,
Meanwhile, was working his evil at home.
Having killed the son of Atreus
And subdued the people, he reigned
For seven years in gold-crusted Mycenae.
In the eighth year, though, he met his doom
In the person of Orestes, come back from Athens.
Orestes killed his father's murderer,
The treacherous Aegisthus, and, having killed him,
Invited all the Argives to a funeral feast
For his hateful mother and her craven lover.
On that very day Menelaus arrived,
Bearing all the treasure his ships could hold.
 So don't you wander long from home, my friend,
Leaving your wealth behind, and in your house
Insolent men who might divide up your goods
While you are gone on a useless journey.
Still, I think you should visit Menelaus,
For he has just lately returned from abroad,
From a country no one would hope to return to
Once a storm has driven him off course
Into a sea so wide that not even migrating birds
Make the trip more than once a year,
So great is that sea and so terrible.
 So then,
Go off now with your ship and your crew.
Or if you would rather travel by land,
We have chariots and horses at your disposal.
My sons are at your service, ready to guide you
To gleaming Lacedaemon, where Menelaus lives.
Beseech him yourself, so he'll tell you the truth.
Not that he would lie. He's very wise."

The sun set on his words, and darkness came on.
Athena's eyes flashed grey as she said:

"You have told the tale well, old man.
But come, cut the tongues and mix the wine
So we can pour libations to Poseidon

And the other gods, and then think of sleep.
It is late. Twilight has faded to dark,
And it is not right to linger at feasts of the gods."

Thus Zeus' daughter, and they did as she said.
Heralds poured water over their hands
And youths filled bowls to the brim with drink
And served it to all, first pouring into each cup
A few drops for libation. They cut the tongues,
Threw them on the fire, and standing up in turn
Poured libations upon them. Having done so,
And having drunk to their heart's content,
Athena and godlike Telemachus
Both started to head for their hollow ship,
But Nestor prevailed upon them to stay:

"God forbid you should go to your ship—
As if I were poor and didn't have enough
Cloaks and blankets for myself and my guests
To sleep softly upon! I have plenty of cloaks and blankets,
And Odysseus' son shall never lie down
On the deck of a ship while I am alive,
Or any child of mine is left in the halls
To entertain strangers who come to my house."

And Athena, her eyes flecked with dark gold:

"Well spoken, old friend, and Telemachus
Would do well to accept your invitation.
It is better that way. So he will go with you
To sleep in your house, but I will go back
To the black ship and have a word with the crew
To raise their spirits. I am the only
Older man among them. They are all youngsters,
Telemachus' age, and sail with us as friends.
I will spend this night down there by the ship,
But at dawn I am off to the Cauconians
To collect an old debt, and not a small one at that.
But send this young man on his way
In a chariot, and send your son with him,
And the fastest, strongest horses you have."

Thus Athena, her eyes flashing in the dark,
And as she left they saw only a vulture
Beating its long, dusky wings.
                                        Their jaws dropped
And the old man could scarcely believe his eyes.
He grabbed Telemachus' hand and said to him:

"If you have gods as escorts when you are so young,
I do not think you will turn out badly at all!
This was no other of the Olympian gods

But the daughter of Zeus, Tritogeneia,[8]
Most glorious Athena, who also honored
Your noble father among the Argive forces.
Be gracious, Lady, and grant me renown—
Me, my sons, and my venerable wife.
And in return I will sacrifice to you
A yearling heifer, broad of brow and unbroken,
Which no man has ever led beneath the yoke.
And I will plate her horns with gold for sacrifice."

Thus Nestor, and Pallas Athena heard his prayer.
Then the old Gerenian horseman led his sons
And daughters' husbands to his beautiful palace,
Where they sat down in rows on benches and chairs.
The housekeeper opened a jar of wine
Eleven years old. The old man mixed a bowl
Of this sweet wine, and as he poured libations
He prayed over and over to Pallas Athena,
Daughter of Zeus who holds the aegis.

When they had all poured libations
And drunk wine to their hearts' content,
They went home to their houses to take their rest.
But Nestor told Telemachus to sleep
Under the echoing portico on a corded bed
Next to Peisistratus, a good man with a spear
And the only of Nestor's sons still unmarried.
Nestor himself slept in an inner room
With his wife, the lady of the house, beside him.

As soon as Dawn appeared in the sky
Nestor, the Gerenian horseman, rose
And went to sit on the polished stones
Outside his high doors, the white stones,
Glistening with oil, upon which of old
Neleus would sit, like a god in counsel.
Neleus had met his fate long ago
And gone down to Hades' undergloom,
And now upon these stones in his turn
Sat Nestor of Gerenia, holding a scepter.
His sons came out and gathered about him,
Echephron and Stratius and Perseus,
Aretus and godlike Thrasymedes,
And as the sixth, the hero Peisistratus.
And they brought godlike Telemachus
And had him sit beside Gerenian Nestor,
Who then spoke:

8. This title for Athena seems to mean "third-born."

"Quickly now, my sons,
That I may propitiate Athena,
Who came to me at the feast of the god
As clear as day. One of you go to the plain
For a heifer, and have the cowherd
Drive her here speedily. Let another go
To the black ship of great-hearted Telemachus
And bring his crew, leaving only two behind.
And someone go fetch the goldsmith Laerces
To plate the horns of the heifer with gold.
The rest of you stay here, and have the serving women
Prepare a feast throughout our glorious halls,
And bring seats, plenty of logs, and fresh water."

Thus Nestor, and they all set to work. The heifer
Came from the plain, and from the sailing ship
Came Telemachus' crew. The smith came
With the tools of his trade, a bronze hammer,
An anvil, and a pair of well-made tongs
With which he wrought gold. And Athena came
To accept the sacrifice.
Nestor, the old charioteer,
Gave the smith gold, and the smith worked it
And leafed it around the heifer's horns
To make the goddess rejoice at the offering.
Stratius and Echephron led the heifer up
By the horns, and Aretus came from the chamber
Carrying water for their hands in a basin
Embossed with flowers. In his other hand he held
A basket of barley. Thrasymedes stood by
With a sharp axe to strike down the heifer,
And Perseus held the blood-bowl. Nestor began
The washing of hands and sprinkling of barley,
Praying hard to Athena as he cut the first hairs
From the victim's head and threw them on the fire.
These rites done, high-hearted Thrasymedes
Came up and struck. When the axe severed
The sinews of the neck, and the heifer collapsed,
The women raised the ritual cry, Nestor's daughters,
The wives of his sons, and his august wife,
Eurydice, eldest of Clymenus' daughters.
Then the men raised the heifer's head from the ground
And held it for Peisistratus to cut the throat.
When the black blood had flowed out, and the life
Left the bones, they butchered the heifer,
Jointing the thigh pieces in ritual order
And covering them with a double layer of fat
And with bits cut raw from the rest of the carcass.
These the old man burned on split logs
And poured bright wine over them. At his side
Were young men holding five-tined forks.

When the thigh pieces were burned and the innards tasted,
They carved up the rest, skewered the pieces,
And roasted them holding the spits in their hands.

Meanwhile, Telemachus was being bathed
By Polycaste, Nestor's youngest daughter.
When this lovely girl had bathed him, rubbed him with oil,
And thrown on his shoulders a tunic and cloak,
Telemachus came forth like an immortal god
And took his seat beside Nestor, shepherd of the people.

When they had roasted the meat and drawn it
Off the spits, they sat down and feasted,
Waited upon by worthy men who poured their wine
Into golden cups. When they had enough
To eat and drink, Gerenian Nestor spoke:

"My sons, yoke the combed horses to the chariot
So that Telemachus may begin his journey."

He spoke, and they did as he said,
Quickly yoking the horses. The housekeeper
Placed in the chariot bread and wine
And the sort of fare kings and lords eat.
Telemachus mounted the beautiful chariot,
And Peisistratus, Nestor's son,
Stepped in beside him and took the reins.
He flicked the lash and the horses took off,
Eating up the plain and leaving behind them
The high rock of Pylos. All day long
They jostled the yoke that held them together.

As the sun set and the world grew dark
They came to Pherae and pulled up at the house
Of Diocles, son of Ortilochus,
Himself a son of the river Alpheus.
There they spent the night, and Diocles
Gave them the hospitality due to guests.

When Dawn brushed the pale sky with rose,
They yoked the horses, stepped up into
The inlaid chariot and drove out through the gate
And echoing portico. Peisistratus
Flicked the lash and the horses took off.
When they reached the level, wheat-bearing plains
They kept pushing on—so strong were their horses—
Until the sun set and the world grew dark.

BOOK IV

They came to the hollows of Lacedaemon[9]
And drove to Menelaus' palace,
Which they found filled with guests. Menelaus
Was hosting a double wedding party
For his son and his daughter. He was sending her
To wed the son of Achilles, as he had promised
Long ago in Troy, and now the gods
Were bringing the marriage to pass.
He was sending her off with horses and chariots
For her journey to the city of the Myrmidons,
Over whom her husband-to-be was lord.
For his son he was bringing a bride
From Sparta, the daughter of Alector.
This son, Megapenthes, was born from a slave woman,
For the gods had made Helen barren
After the birth of her daughter Hermione,
Who had the beauty of golden Aphrodite.
So Menelaus' kinsfolk and neighbors
Were feasting in the great hall. A bard
Was singing and playing the lyre,
And two tumblers whirled among the guests
And led them in the dancing.
Telemachus
And Nestor's son halted their horses
At the gate, and Eteoneus,
Menelaus' right-hand man, came out and saw them
And went through the hall to bring the news
To the shepherd of the people. He stood
At Menelaus' shoulder and his words flew fast:

"Two strangers have arrived, Lord Menelaus,
Two men in the line of Zeus by their looks.
Should we unyoke their horses, or should we
Send them elsewhere for hospitality?"

And red-haired Menelaus, greatly displeased:

"It's not like you to talk nonsense like this,
Eteoneus. How many times have you and I
Enjoyed the hospitality of others,
Hoping that Zeus would someday put an end
To our hard traveling? Unyoke their horses
And bring our new guests in to the feast."

He spoke, and Eteoneus hurried through the halls,
Calling other attendants to come along with him.
They unyoked the sweating horses and tied them
At the stalls, where they threw before them
A mixture of spelt and white barley. They leaned

9. Sparta.

The chariot against the gleaming entrance walls
And led the men into the palace. Their eyes
Went wide as they looked around the mansion
Of this sky-bred king, for a light as of the sun
Or the moon played over the high-roofed home
Of glorious Menelaus. When they had taken it all in,
They went into the polished tubs. When the maids
Had bathed them and rubbed them down with oil,
And clothed them in tunics and fleecy cloaks,
They sat down on chairs beside Menelaus.
A maid poured water from a golden pitcher
Into a silver basin for them to wash their hands
And then set up a polished table nearby.
Another serving woman, grave and dignified,
Set out bread and served generous helpings
From the other dishes she had; a carver set down
Cuts of meat by the platter and golden cups;
And a herald came by and poured them wine.
Then red-haired Menelaus said in greeting:

"Enjoy yourselves and eat. After supper
We will ask who you are—your bloodlines
Have not been lost in you. You belong
To the race of men who are sceptered kings,
Bred from Zeus. You're not just anybody."

And he set before them the prime cut of roast beef
That had been served to him as a mark of honor.
They helped themselves to the feast before them,
And when they had enough of food and drink,
Telemachus spoke to Nestor's son, holding
His head close so the others wouldn't hear:

"Do you see all this, Peisistratus, my friend,
These echoing halls flashing with bronze,
With gold, amber, silver, and ivory?
This must be what the court of Olympian Zeus
Looks like. This is unimaginable wealth!"

Menelaus, the red-haired king, overheard him,
And, speaking to both of them, had this to say:

"No mortal man could challenge Zeus, my boys.
His halls and possessions are everlasting.
My wealth may be matched by another man's
Or maybe not. For it is true I brought home
Shiploads after wandering for eight hard years.
Cyprus, Phoenicia, Egypt—I went all over,
Came to the Ethiopians, the Sidonians,
The Erembi, even to Libya,
Where the lambs have horns soon after they're born.

The ewes give birth three times a year there,
And neither shepherd nor lord ever runs short
Of cheese, meat or milk; the flocks are milked year round.
While I wandered through those lands amassing wealth
My brother was murdered, caught off guard
By treachery and the guile of his accursed wife.
So I do not enjoy being lord of this wealth.
You may have heard of all this from your fathers,
Whoever they may be, for I suffered greatly
And saw my house ruined, with all its treasures.
I would gladly live with a third of my wealth
And have those men back who perished in Troy
Far from the bluegrass pastures of Argos. And yet,
Though I weep for them often in my halls,
Easing my heart, I do not grieve constantly—
A man can get too much of chill grief.
I miss them all, but there is one man I miss
More than all the others. When I think of him
I don't want to sleep or eat, for no one
In the entire Greek army worked as hard
As Odysseus, and all he ever got for it
Was pain and sorrow, and I cannot forget
My sorrow for him. He has been gone so long,
And we do not know whether he is alive or dead.
Old Laertes must mourn for him, Penelope too,
And Telemachus, who was an infant when he left."

His words roused in Telemachus the desire
To weep for his father. Hot tears
Fell from his eyes when he heard his father's name,
And he pulled his purple cloak over his face.
Seeing this, Menelaus wondered
Whether he should allow Telemachus
To bring up his father himself, or whether
He should draw him out with pointed questions.

While Menelaus pondered this,
Helen came from her fragrant bedroom
Like gold-spindled Artemis. Adraste,
Her attendant, drew up a beautiful chair for her,
And Alcippe brought her a soft wool rug.
Another maid, Phylo, brought a silver basket—
A gift from Alcandre, wife of Polybus,
Who lived in Thebes, the city in Egypt
That has the wealthiest houses in the world.
Polybus had given Menelaus two silver baths,
Two tripods, and ten bars of gold.
And his wife, Alcandre, gave to Helen
Beautiful gifts of her own—a golden spindle
And a silver basket with gold-rimmed wheels.
This basket Phylo now placed beside her,

Filled with fine-spun yarn, and across it
Was laid the spindle, twirled with violet wool.
Helen sat upon the chair, a footstool
Under her feet, and questioned her husband:

"Do we know, Menelaus, who our guests
Claim to be? Shall I speak my mind or not?
My heart urges me to speak. I have never seen
Such a resemblance between any two people,
Man or woman, as between this man
And Odysseus' son—as I imagine him now—
Telemachus, who was a newborn baby
When for my sake, shameless thing that I was,
The Greeks came to Troy with war in their hearts."

And Menelaus, the red-haired king:

"Now that you mention it, I see
The resemblance myself—the feet, the hands,
The way he looks at you, that head of hair.
And just now when I was talking about Odysseus,
Saying how much he went through for my sake,
Tears welled up in his eyes, bitter tears,
And he covered his face with his purple cloak."

At this Nestor's son Peisistratus spoke up:

"Menelaus, son of Atreus, Zeus-bred king,
This is indeed, as you say, Odysseus' son.
But he is prudent and would not think it proper,
When he just got here, to make a big speech
Before you—whose voice delights us as a god's.
Nestor of Gerenia sent me with him as a guide,
For he was eager to see you, hoping that
You could suggest something he could do or say.
A son has many problems to face at home
When his father is gone and there is no one else
To help him. So it is now with Telemachus,
Whose father is gone, and there is no one else
Among the people to keep him from harm."

And Menelaus, the red-haired king:

"What's this? Here in my house, the son
Of my dear friend who did so much for me!
I used to think that if he came back
I would give him a welcome no other Greek
Could ever hope to have—if Olympian Zeus
Had brought us both home from over the sea
In our swift ships. I would have given him
A city of his own in Argos, built him a house,

Brought him over from Ithaca with his goods,
His son and all of his people—a whole city
Cleared out just for him! We would have been together,
Enjoying each other's company, and nothing
Would have parted us until death's black cloud
Finally enfolded us. But I suppose Zeus himself
Begrudged us this, for Odysseus alone,
That unlucky man, was never brought home."

His words aroused in all of them
A longing for lamentation. Argive Helen,
A child of Zeus, wept; Telemachus wept;
And Menelaus wept, the son of Atreus.
Nor could Nestor's son keep his eyes dry,
For he remembered Antilochus,
His flawless brother, who had been killed
By Memnon, Dawn's resplendent son,
And this memory gave wings to his words:

"Son of Atreus, old Nestor used to say,
Whenever we talked about things like this,
That no one could match your understanding.
So please understand me when I say
That I do not enjoy weeping after supper—
And it will be dawn before we know it.
Not that I think it's wrong to lament the dead.
This is all we can do—cut our hair
And shed some tears. I lost someone myself
At Troy, my brother, not the least hero there.
You probably knew him. I am too young
Ever to have seen him, but men say Antilochus
Could run and fight as well as any man alive."

And Menelaus, the red-haired king:

"No one could have put that better, my friend,
Not even someone much older. Your speech,
Wise and clear, shows the sort of father you have.
It's easy to spot a man for whom Zeus
Has spun out happiness in marriage and children,
As he has done for Nestor throughout his life.
And now he has reached a sleek old age in his halls,
And his sons are wise and fight with the best.
So we will stop this weeping, and once more
Think of supper. Let the servants pour water
Over our hands. Telemachus and I will have
Much to say to each other come morning."

So he spoke, and Asphalion,
Menelaus' attendant, poured water
Over their hands, and they reached out

For all the good cheer spread out before them.

But Helen, child of Zeus, had other ideas.
She threw a drug into the wine bowl
They were drinking from, a drug
That stilled all pain, quieted all anger
And brought forgetfulness of every ill.
Whoever drank wine laced with this drug
Would not be sad or shed a tear that day,
Not even if his own father and mother
Should lie there dead, or if someone killed
His brother, or son, before his eyes.
Helen had gotten this potent, cunning drug
From Polydamna, the wife of Thon,
A woman in Egypt, where the land
Proliferates with all sorts of drugs,
Many beneficial, many poisonous.
Men there know more about medicines
Than any other people on earth,
For they are of the race of Paeeon, the Healer.
When she had slipped the drug into the wine,
Helen ordered another round to be poured,
And then she turned to the company and said:

"Menelaus, son of Atreus in the line of Zeus,
And you sons of noble fathers, it is true
That Zeus gives easy lives to some of us
And hard lives to others—he can do anything, after all—
But you should sit now in the hall and feast
And entertain yourselves by telling stories.
I'll start you off. I couldn't begin to tell you
All that Odysseus endured and accomplished,
But listen to what that hero did once
In the land of Troy, where the Achaeans suffered.
First, he beat himself up—gave himself some nasty bruises—
Then put on a cheap cloak so he looked like a slave,
And in this disguise he entered the wide streets
Of the enemy city. He looked like a beggar,
Far from what he was back in the Greek camp,
And fooled everyone when he entered Troy.
I alone recognized him in his disguise
And questioned him, but he cleverly put me off.
It was only after I had bathed him
And rubbed him down with oil and clothed him
And had sworn a great oath not to tell the Trojans
Who he really was until he got back to the ships,
That he told me, at last, what the Achaeans planned.
He killed many Trojans before he left
And arrived back at camp with much to report.
The other women in Troy wailed aloud,
But I was glad inside, for my heart had turned

Homeward, and I rued the infatuation
Aphrodite gave me when she led me away
From my native land, leaving my dear child,
My bridal chamber, and my husband,
A man who lacked nothing in wisdom or looks."
And Menelaus, the red-haired king:

"A very good story, my wife, and well told.
By now I have come to know the minds
Of many heroes, and have traveled far and wide,
But I have never laid eyes on anyone
Who had an enduring heart like Odysseus.
Listen to what he did in the wooden horse,
Where all we Argive chiefs sat waiting
To bring slaughter and death to the Trojans.
You came there then, with godlike Deiphobus.
Some god who favored the Trojans
Must have lured you on. Three times you circled
Our hollow hiding place, feeling it
With your hands, and you called out the names
Of all the Argive leaders, making your voice
Sound like each of our wives' in turn.
Diomedes and I, sitting in the middle
With Odysseus, heard you calling
And couldn't take it. We were frantic
To come out, or answer you from inside,
But Odysseus held us back and stopped us.
Then everyone else stayed quiet also,
Except for Anticlus, who wanted to answer you,
But Odysseus saved us all by clamping
His strong hands over Anticlus' mouth
And holding them there until Athena led you off."

Then Telemachus said in his clear-headed way:

"Menelaus, son of Atreus in the line of Zeus,
It is all the more unbearable then, isn't it?
My father may have had a heart of iron,
But it didn't do him any good in the end.
Please send us to bed now. It is time
We rested and enjoyed some sweet sleep."

He spoke, and Helen of Argos told her maids
To place beds on the porch and spread upon them
Beautiful purple blankets and fleecy cloaks.
The maids went out of the hall with torches
And made up the beds, and a herald
Led the guests out to them. So they slept there
On the palace porch, the hero Telemachus
And Nestor's glorious son. But Menelaus slept
In the innermost chamber of that high house

Next to Helen, Zeus' brightness upon her.

Dawn brushed her pale rose fingers across the sky,
And Menelaus got out of bed and dressed.
He slung his sharp sword around his shoulder,
Tied oiled leather sandals onto his feet,
And walked out of the bedroom like a god.
Then he sat down next to Telemachus and said:

"Tell me, Telemachus, what has brought you here
To gleaming Sparta over the sea's broad back?
Public business or private? Tell me the truth."

Telemachus took a deep breath and said:

"Menelaus, son of Atreus in the line of Zeus,
I came to see if you could tell me anything
About my father. My land is in ruin.
I'm being eaten out of house and home
By hostile men who constantly throng my halls
Slaughtering my sheep and horned cattle
In their arrogant courtship of my mother.
And so I am at your knees. Tell me
How my father, Odysseus, met his end,
Whether you saw it with your own eyes,
Or heard about it from someone else,
Some wanderer. He was born to sorrow,
More than any man on earth. And do not,
Out of pity, spare me the truth, but tell me
Whatever you have seen, whatever you know.
I beseech you, if my father, noble Odysseus,
Ever fulfilled a promise he made to you
In the land of Troy, where the Achaeans suffered,
Remember it now, and tell me the truth."
And Menelaus, deeply troubled by this:

"Those dogs! Those puny weaklings,
Wanting to sleep in the bed of a hero!
A doe might as well bed her suckling fawns
In the lair of a lion, leaving them there
In the bush and then going off over the hills
Looking for grassy fields. When the lion
Comes back, the fawns die an ugly death.
That's the kind of death these men will die
When Odysseus comes back. O Father Zeus,
And Athena and Apollo, bring Odysseus back
With the strength he showed in Lesbos once
When he wrestled a match with Philomeleides
And threw him hard, making all of us cheer—
That's the Odysseus I want the suitors to meet!
They'd get married all right—to bitter death.

But, as to what you ask me about,
I will not stray from the point or deceive you.
No, I will tell you all that the infallible
Old Man of the Sea told me, and hide nothing.
I was in Egypt, held up by the gods
Because I failed to offer them sacrifice.
The gods never allow us to forget them.
There is an island in the whitecapped sea
Just north of Egypt. Men call it Pharos,
And it lies one hard day's sailing offshore.
There is a good harbor there where ships
Take on fresh water before heading out to sea.
The gods kept me stuck in that harbor
For twenty days. A good sailing breeze
Never rose up, and all my supplies
Would have been exhausted, and my crew spent,
Had not one of the gods taken pity on me
And saved me. This was Eidothea,
Daughter of Proteus, the Old Man of the Sea.
Somehow I had moved her heart. She met me
As I wandered alone, apart from my crew,
Who roamed the island continually, fishing
With bent hooks, their bellies cramped with hunger.
She came close to me and spoke:

'Are you completely out of your mind, stranger,
Or do you actually like suffering like this?
You've been marooned on this island a long time
With no end in sight, and your crew's fading fast.'

"She spoke like this, and I answered her:

'I tell you, goddess—whichever goddess you are—
That I am not stranded here of my own free will.
I must have offended one of the immortals.
But you tell me—for gods know everything—
Which of the immortals is pinning me down here
And won't let me go. And tell me how
I can sail back home over the teeming sea.'

"And the shining goddess answered me:

'Well, all right, stranger, since you ask.
This is the haunt of an unerring immortal,
Egyptian Proteus, the Old Man of the Sea,
Who serves Poseidon and knows all the deeps.
They say he's my father. If you can
Somehow catch him in ambush here,
He will tell you the route, and the distance too,
Of your journey home over the teeming sea.
And he will tell you, prince, if you so wish,

What has been done in your house for better or worse
While you have been gone on your long campaign.'

"So she spoke, and I answered her:

'Show me yourself how to ambush
The old god, or he may give me the slip.
It's hard for a mortal to master a god.'

"And the shining goddess answered me:

'I'll tell you exactly what you need to know.
When the sun is at high noon, the unerring
Old Man of the Sea comes from the salt water,
Hidden in dark ripples the West Wind stirs up,
And then lies down to sleep in the scalloped caves.
All around him seals, the brine-spirit's brood,
Sleep in a herd. They come out of the grey water
With breath as fetid as the depths of the sea.
I will lead you there at break of day
And lay you in a row, you and three comrades
Chosen by you as the best on your ship.
Now I'll tell you all the old man's wiles.
First, he will go over the seals and count them,
And when he has counted them off by fives,
He will lie down like a shepherd among them.
As soon as you see him lying down to rest,
Screw up your courage to the sticking point
And pin him down, no matter how he struggles
And tries to escape. He will try everything,
And turn into everything that moves on the earth,
And into water also, and a burning flame.
Just hang on and grip him all the more tightly.
When he finally speaks to you of his own free will
In the shape you saw him in when he lay down to rest,
Then ease off, hero, and let the old man go,
And ask him which of the gods is angry with you,
And how you can sail home over the teeming sea.'

"And with that she slipped into the surging sea.
I headed for my ships where they stood on the sand
And brooded on many things as I went.
When I had come down to the ships and the sea,
We made supper, and when night came on,
We lay down to take our rest on the beach.
When dawn came, a palmetto of rose,
I went along the shore of the open sea
Praying over and over to the immortal gods,
Taking with me the three of my crew
I trusted the most for any adventure.

"The goddess, meanwhile, dove underwater

And now came back with the skins of four seals,
All newly flayed. She was out to trick her father.
She scooped out hiding places for us in the sand
And sat waiting as we cautiously drew near.
Then she had us lie down in a row, and threw
A seal skin over each of us. It would have been
A gruesome ambush—the stench of the seals
Was unbearable—but the goddess saved us
By putting ambrosia under each man's nose,
Drowning out the stench with its immortal fragrance.
So we waited patiently all morning long,
And then the seals came from the water in throngs.
They lay down in rows along the seashore,
And at noon the Old One came from the sea.
He found the fat seals and went over the herd,
Counting them up. He counted us first,
Never suspecting any kind of trick,
And then he lay down. We rushed him
With a shout and got our hands on him,
And the Old One didn't forget his wiles,
Turning first into a bearded lion,
Then a serpent, a leopard, and a huge boar.
He even turned into flowing water,
And into a high, leafy tree. But we
Held on, gritting our teeth, and at last
The wily Old One grew weary, and said to me:

'Which god have you plotted with, son of Atreus,
To catch me off-guard? What do you want?'

"He spoke, and I answered him:

'You know, old man—don't try to put me off—
How long I have been stuck on this island
With no end in sight. I'm losing heart.
Just tell me this—you gods know everything—
Which of the immortals has marooned me here?
How can I sail home over the teeming sea?'

"When I said this, he answered:

'You should have offered noble sacrifice to Zeus
And the other gods before embarking
If you wanted a speedy journey home
Over the deep purple sea. It is not your fate
To come home to your friends and native land
Until you go once more to the waters of the Aegyptus,
The sky-fed river, and offer holy hecatombs[1]
To the immortal gods who hold high heaven.
Only then will they grant the journey you desire.'

1. A sacrifice of a hundred cattle.

"When he said this my spirit was crushed.
It was a long, hard pull over the misty deep
Back to the Aegyptus. Still, I answered:

'I will do all these things, just as you say.
But tell me this, and tell me the truth:
Did all the Achaeans make it home in their ships,
All those whom Nestor and I left at Troy?
Or did any die on shipboard, or in their friends' arms,
After winding up the war?'

"To which Proteus said:

'Why, son of Atreus, ask me about this?
You don't need to know. Nor do I think
You will be free from tears once you have heard it.
Many were killed in the war. You were there
And know who they were. Many, too, survived.
On the homeward journey two heroes died.
Another still lives, perhaps, held back by the sea.

'Ajax went down among his long-oared ships.
Poseidon had driven him onto Gyrae's rocks
But saved him from the sea. He would have escaped,
Despite Athena's hatred, but he lost his wits
And boasted loudly that he had survived the deep
In spite of the gods. Poseidon heard this boast,
And with his trident he struck Gyrae's rock
And broke it asunder. One part held firm,
But the other part, upon which Ajax sat
In his blind arrogance, fell into the gulf
And took Ajax with it. And so he perished,
His lungs full of saltwater.
Your brother, though,
Outran the fates in his hollow ships,
With the help of Hera. But when he was nearing
Malea's heights, a stormwind caught him
And carried him groaning over the teeming sea
To the frontier of the land where Thyestes once lived
And after him Thyestes' son, Aegisthus.[2]
Then the gods gave him a following wind
And safe passage homeward. Agamemnon
Rejoiced to set foot on his ancestral land.
He fell to the ground and kissed the good earth
And hot tears of joy streamed from his eyes,
So glad was he to see his homeland again.
But from a high lookout a watchman saw him.
Aegisthus had treacherously posted him there

2. Thyestes was the brother of Atreus, father of Agamemnon and Menelaus.

And promised a reward of two bars of gold.
He had been keeping watch for a year by then
So that Agamemnon would not slip by unseen
And unleash his might, and now he reported
His news to Aegisthus, who acted quickly
And set a trap. He chose his twenty best men
And had them wait in ambush. Opposite them,
On the hall's farther side, he had a feast prepared,
And then he drove off in his chariot,
Brooding darkly, to invite Agamemnon.
So he brought Agamemnon up to the palace
Unaware of his doom and slaughtered him
The way an ox is slaughtered at the stall.
None of Agamemnon's men was left alive,
Nor any of Aegisthus'. All were slain in the hall.'

"Proteus spoke, and my heart was shattered.
I wept and wept as I sat on the sand, losing
All desire to live and see the light of the sun.
When I could not weep or flail about any more,
The unerring Old Man of the Sea addressed me:
'Weep no more, son of Atreus. We gain nothing
By such prolonged bouts of grief. Instead,
Go as quickly as you can to your native land.
Either Aegisthus will still be alive, or
Orestes may have beat you to it and killed him,
And you may happen to arrive during his funeral.'

"These words warmed my heart, although
I was still in shock. Then I asked him:

'I know now what became of these two,
But who is the third man, the one who's alive,
But held back by the sea, or perhaps is dead.
I want to hear about him, despite my grief.'

"Proteus answered me without hesitation:

'It is Laertes' son, whose home is in Ithaca.
I saw him on an island, shedding salt tears,
In the halls of Calypso, who keeps him there
Against his will. He has no way to get home
To his native land. He has no ships left,
No crew to row him over the sea's broad back.
As for you, Menelaus, Zeus' cherished king,
You are not destined to die and to meet your fate
In bluegrass Argos. The immortals will take you
To the ends of the earth and the Elysian Fields,
Where Rhadamanthus lives and life is easiest.
No snow, nor storm, nor heavy rain comes there,
But a sighing wind from the West always blows

Off the Ocean, a cooling breeze for men.
For Helen is your wife, and in the gods' eyes
You are the son-in-law of great Zeus himself.'[3]

"And with that he dove into the surging sea.
I went back to the ships with my godlike companions
And brooded on many things as I went.
When we had come down to the ships and the sea,
And had made supper, immortal night came on,
And we lay down to take our rest on the beach.
When dawn came with palmettoes of rose,
We hauled our ships down to the shining water,
And set up the masts and sails in the hulls.
The crews came aboard, and sitting in rows
They beat the sea white with their churning oars.
And so I sailed back to the rain-fed Aegyptus,
Moored my ships, and offered perfect sacrifice.
When I had appeased the everlasting gods
I heaped up a barrow for Agamemnon
So that his memory would not fade. Only then
Did I set sail for home, and the gods gave me
A following wind that brought me back swiftly.
Well, now, I want you to stay in my halls
Until eleven or twelve days have passed,
And then I will give you a royal send-off
And these splendid gifts: three horses
And a polished chariot, and a beautiful cup,
So that you can pour libations to the deathless gods
And remember me all the days of your life."

Telemachus answered in his clear-headed way:

"Son of Atreus, do not keep me here long.
I could spend a year in your house
And never miss my home or my parents.
That's how much I enjoy listening to you
And hearing your tales. But even now
My crew is getting restless back in Pylos
And you are keeping me long here.
As for gifts,
Give me whatever treasure you will,
But I will not take horses to Ithaca.
They are better off here for you to enjoy,
For you rule a wide plain, with lotus
Everywhere, and galingale, and wheat and spelt,
And heavy ears of white barley. But Ithaca
Has no broad horse-runs or meadowlands at all.
Its pasture is for goats, and more lovely
Than horse pasture. None of the islands

3. Helen was the daughter of Zeus, who made love to Leda in the guise of a swan.

That slope to the sea has rich meadows, or is good
For driving horses, and Ithaca least of all."

And Menelaus, who could make his voice
Carry in battle, said to Telemachus:

"You are of good blood, my boy, to talk like that!
All right, I will change my gifts, as I easily can.
Of all the gifts that lie stored in my house
I will give you the most beautiful—
And the most valuable—a well-wrought bowl,
Solid silver, with the lip finished in gold,
The work of Hephaestus. The hero Phaedimus,
King of the Sidonians, gave it to me
When I stayed at his house on my way home.
Now I want you to take it home with you."

And while they talked to each other,
The banqueters came to their lord's palace,
Driving sheep with them and bringing wine,
And bread that their veiled wives had sent with them.
And so they were busy with the feast in Menelaus' halls.

Meanwhile, back in Ithaca,
The suitors were entertaining themselves
In front of Odysseus' palace again,
Throwing the javelin and discus
On the level terrace, arrogant as ever.
Antinous and Eurymachus, who were
Their natural leaders, were sitting there,
And Noemon, son of Phronius,
Came up to them and asked Antinous:

"Antinous, do we have any idea
When Telemachus will return from Pylos?
He's gone off with a ship of mine,
And I need her to cross over to Elis,
Where I have twelve brood mares
And ten mules still at the teat. I would like
To drive one of them off and break him in."
When he said this, Antinous and Eurymachus
Just looked at each other. They had no idea
Telemachus had gone to Neleian Pylos.
They thought he was somewhere out in the field
With the sheep flocks, or off with the swineherd.
Antinous questioned Noemon closely:

"Tell me exactly when Telemachus left
And who went with him, a hand-picked crew
From the island, or his own fieldhands and slaves?
He could have done it either way. And tell me this,

So I'll have it right. Did he force you to give him
The ship, or were you just doing him a favor?"

And Noemon answered him:

"I gave it freely. What else could I do,
When a man like that, with all his troubles,
Asks me? It would be hard to refuse him.
Those who went with him are the best in town,
After ourselves, and when they boarded
I noticed Mentor going on board, too,
As their leader, either Mentor or a god
Who looked just like him. I wonder about this,
Because I saw Mentor here yesterday morning,
After he had set sail for sandy Pylos."

With that, Noemon left for his father's house.
Antinous and Eurymachus were furious.
They made the suitors stop their games
And had them sit down. Antinous
Addressed them. His black heart was seething
With anger, and his eyes burned like fire:

"Unbelievable! Telemachus has some nerve,
Pulling off this voyage. We never thought
We'd see it happen, and the boy is up and gone,
Just like that, with all of us against it,
Launching a ship and picking the best crew around.
He's going to start giving us trouble soon.
May Zeus cripple him before he reaches manhood!
All right, now, give me a ship and twenty men
So I can lie in ambush and watch for him
As he comes through the strait between Ithaca
And rocky Samos. He'll be sorry
He ever made this voyage in search of his father."

They all praised his speech and urged him on.
Then they stood up and went to Odysseus' palace.

It did not take Penelope long to find out
The suitors' dark intentions. The herald,
Medon, was the one who brought her word.
He had overheard the suitors talking
As he stood outside the courtyard
Where they were weaving their plots, and now
He went through the hall to tell Penelope.
As he crossed the threshold, she asked him:

"Medon, why have the suitors sent you here?
To tell the handmaids of divine Odysseus

To drop everything and prepare a feast for them?
May this be their last courtship, their last party,
Oh, may this latest feast be their last of all!
Do you hear me, you thronging leeches
Who are eating away Telemachus' property?
You surely weren't listening to your fathers
When you were children, or you would have heard
What kind of man Odysseus was to them,
How he never wronged anyone in word or deed,
How he was fair to everyone, unlike
Most sceptered kings, who all have their favorites.
He never lost his temper with any man at all.
But your vile deeds and hearts are plain to see,
And there is no gratitude for kindness past."

Then Medon, the tactful herald:

"If only this were the greatest evil, Lady,
But there is a greater and more grievous.
The suitors are planning—and may Zeus
Never bring their plans to pass—to kill Telemachus
On his way back home. He went to sandy Pylos
And gleaming Lacedaemon for news of his father."

When Medon said these things, Penelope felt
That her heart had been unstrung. Her eyes
Filled with tears, and she was unable to speak
For a long time. Finally she said to the herald:

"Medon, why is my son gone? There was no need
For him to board any sea-going ships,
Which men use to cross the wide water
As they use horses on land. Why did he go?
So that not even his name would be left among men?"

And Medon, the tactful herald:

"I do not know whether a god urged him on,
Or his own heart moved him to go to Pylos
To learn either of his father's return
Or of the manner in which he met his fate."

So saying, Medon went into Odysseus' house.
Pain washed over Penelope and seeped
Into her bones. She could not bring herself
To sit down in one of the many chairs
That were there in the house, but sat curled
On the worn threshold of her bedroom
And wept. Around her the women of the house
Moaned softly, the old and the young,

And Penelope spoke to them through her tears:

"Hear me, my friends, for the god on Olympus
Has given me pain beyond all other women
Of my generation. I have lost a fine husband
With a heart like a lion, the glory of the Danaans,
The pride of all Hellas, a man of many virtues.
And now the winds have ripped my beloved son
From my house. I never even heard him leave.
You were cruel, each of you, not to think
Of getting me from bed, for you must have known
He was going aboard that hollow black ship.
If I had known he was setting out on this journey,
He would have stayed here, despite his willfulness,
Or else he would have left me dead in our halls.
Quick now, someone go get old Dolios,
The servant whom my father gave me
Before I left home and who now tends my orchards.
He should sit with Laertes and tell him all this.
Laertes may be able to weave some plan
And complain to the people about these men
Who want to destroy his and Odysseus' line."

And her beloved nurse, Eurycleia, said:

"Child, you can spare me or stab me
With a sword, but I will not hide what I know.
I was in on all this. I got his provisions,
Bread and sweet wine. He made me swear
Not to tell you until twelve days had passed
Or until you missed him yourself or heard
He had gone. He didn't want you crying.
Now take a bath and put on some clean clothes.
Then go upstairs with the serving women
And pray to Athena, daughter of Zeus.
No matter what, she can save your son from death.
But do not trouble the old man. He has
Troubles enough. Yet I do not think
The line of Laertes, son of Arcesius,
Is entirely hated by the blessed gods.
There may still be someone in that line to own
This high hall and all the rich fields around."

So the old nurse soothed Penelope's grief
And kept her eyes dry. Penelope bathed
And put on clean clothes. Then she went upstairs
With the serving women, put barley for strewing
In a basket, and prayed to Athena:
"Hear me, Mystic Daughter of Zeus.
If ever in these halls my cunning Odysseus
Burned fat thighbones of bulls or sheep for you,

Remember it now and save my beloved son.
Protect him from the arrogant suitors' violence."

Penelope voiced this prayer, and Athena heard it,
While down in the shadowy halls below
These same suitors were talking noisily,
Making crude comments such as these:

"So while the lady upstairs gets ready to marry
One of her suitors, she has no idea
That her suitors are arranging to murder her son!"

But they had no idea of what was being arranged.
Antinous had some words for all of them:

"Are you crazy? Stow that kind of talk,
Or someone may report it to those inside.
We're going to do what we said we would
Under cover of silence. We're all in this together."

And he picked out the twenty best men there.
They went down to the shore of the sea
And hauled a fast ship out onto the water.
They set up mast and sail in that black ship
And fit the oars into the leather thole-straps,
All in due order. Then they unfurled the white sails.
Their attendants brought all their gear aboard,
And they moored the ship where she would catch
The evening breeze. Then they disembarked,
Ate their dinner, and waited for twilight.

Penelope lay in her room upstairs.
She would not touch any food or drink
But only lay there worrying about her son,
Wondering whether he would escape from death
Or be killed by the insolent suitors.

Surrounded by men, a lion broods and then panics
When they begin to tighten their crafty ring.

So too Penelope, until sleep drifted over her,
And she sank back with all her body relaxed.

Athena's eyes were flashing in the dark.
She made a phantom in the form of a woman,
Iphthime, daughter of great Icarius,
Now wed to Eumelus, whose home was in Pherae.
She sent the phantom into Odysseus' house
To stop Penelope's weeping and sobbing.
It drifted into her room through the keyhole
And stood above her head, and spoke to her:

"Asleep, Penelope, and broken-hearted?
The blessed gods are unwilling that you
Should weep and be sad, for your son will return.
He has not offended the gods at all."

And Penelope, slumbering sweetly
At the gate of dreams, answered her:

"Why have you come here, sister? You live
Far away and have seldom come before.
You tell me to stop grieving, tell me to rest
From the sorrows that plague my mind and heart.
Long ago now I lost my fine husband,
A lion-hearted man, the glory of the Danaans,
The pride of Hellas, a man of many virtues.
And now my beloved son has gone away
In a hollow ship, a mere child, who knows nothing
Of the world of men. I grieve for him even more
Than for my husband. I am trembling with fear
That he will get hurt, either among the people
He has gone off to visit, or on the open sea.
For his many enemies are plotting against him
And mean to kill him before he gets home."

The glimmering phantom answered her:

"Take heart, and don't be so afraid. The guide
Who goes with him is one many men pray for
To stand at their side, a powerful ally—
Pallas Athena. And she pities you in your grief,
For it is she who sent me to tell you this."

And Penelope, in her circumspect way:

"If you are truly a god and have heard a god's voice,
Tell me also of that man of many sorrows,
Whether he still lives and sees the light of the sun,
Or whether he is dead and in Hades' dark world."

The glimmering phantom answered her:

"No, I will not speak of him, whether he be
Alive or dead. Empty words are ill spoken."

And the phantom slipped through the keyhole
And became a sigh in the air. Penelope
Started up from sleep, and her heart was warmed
By the clear dream that had come in the soft black night.

By now the suitors had embarked and set sail,
Their hearts set on murdering Telemachus.
There is a rocky island out in the sea,

Midway between Ithaca and rugged Samos.
Asteris is its name, not very big,
But it has a harbor with outlets on either side
Where a ship can lie. There the suitors waited.

BOOK V

Dawn reluctantly
Left Tithonus[4] in her rose-shadowed bed,
Then shook the morning into flakes of fire.

Light flooded the halls of Olympus
Where Zeus, high Lord of Thunder,
Sat with the other gods, listening to Athena
Reel off the tale of Odysseus' woes.
It galled her that he was still in Calypso's cave:

"Zeus, my father—and all you blessed immortals—
Kings might as well no longer be gentle and kind
Or understand the correct order of things.
They might as well be tyrannical butchers
For all that any of Odysseus' people
Remember him, a godly king as kind as a father.
No, he's still languishing on that island, detained
Against his will by that nymph Calypso,
No way in the world for him to get back to his land.
His ships are all lost, he has no crew left
To row him across the sea's crawling back.
And now the islanders are plotting to kill his son
As he heads back home. He went for news of his father
To sandy Pylos and white-bricked Sparta."

Storm Cloud Zeus had an answer for her:

"Quite a little speech you've let slip through your teeth,
Daughter. But wasn't this exactly your plan
So that Odysseus would make them pay for it later?
You know how to get Telemachus
Back to Ithaca and out of harm's way
With his mother's suitors sailing in a step behind."

Zeus turned then to his son Hermes and said:

"Hermes, you've been our messenger before.
Go tell that ringleted nymph it is my will
To let that patient man Odysseus go home.
Not with an escort, mind you, human or divine,
But on a rickety raft—tribulation at sea—

4. Dawn's lover, a mortal man whom she made immortal (though not ageless) and brought to live with her in the sky.

Until on the twentieth day he comes to Schería
In the land of the Phaeacians, our distant relatives,
Who will treat Odysseus as if he were a god
And take him on a ship to his own native land
With gifts of bronze and clothing and gold,
More than he ever would have taken back from Troy
Had he come home safely with his share of the loot.
That's how he's destined to see his dear ones again
And return to his high-gabled Ithacan home."

Thus Zeus, and the quicksilver messenger
Laced on his feet the beautiful sandals,
Golden, immortal, that carry him over
Landscape and seascape on a puff of wind.
And he picked up the wand he uses to charm
Mortal eyes to sleep and make sleepers awake.

Holding this wand the tough quicksilver god
Took off, bounded onto Pieria
And dove through the ether down to the sea,

Skimming the waves like a cormorant,
The bird that patrols the saltwater billows
Hunting for fish, seaspume on its plumage,

Hermes flying low and planing the whitecaps.

When he finally arrived at the distant island
He stepped from the violet-tinctured sea
On to dry land and proceeded to the cavern
Where Calypso lived. She was at home.
A fire blazed on the hearth, and the smell
Of split cedar and arbor vitae[5] burning
Spread like incense across the whole island.
She was seated inside, singing in a lovely voice
As she wove at her loom with a golden shuttle.
Around her cave the woodland was in bloom,
Alder and poplar and fragrant cypress.
Long-winged birds nested in the leaves,
Horned owls and larks and slender-throated shorebirds
That screech like crows over the bright saltwater.
Tendrils of ivy curled around the cave's mouth,
The glossy green vine clustered with berries.
Four separate springs flowed with clear water, criss-
Crossing channels as they meandered through meadows
Lush with parsley and blossoming violets.
It was enough to make even a visiting god
Enraptured at the sight. Quicksilver Hermes

5. An evergreen, whose name means "tree of life."

Took it all in, then turned and entered
The vast cave.
Calypso knew him at sight.
The immortals have ways of recognizing each other,
Even those whose homes are in outlying districts.
But Hermes didn't find the great hero inside.
Odysseus was sitting on the shore,
As ever those days, honing his heart's sorrow,
Staring out to sea with hollow, salt-rimmed eyes.

Calypso, sleek and haloed, questioned Hermes
Politely, as she seated him on a lacquered chair:

"My dear Hermes, to what do I owe
The honor of this unexpected visit? Tell me
What you want, and I'll oblige you if I can."

The goddess spoke, and then set a table
With ambrosia and mixed a bowl of rosy nectar.[6]
The quicksilver messenger ate and drank his fill,
Then settled back from dinner with heart content
And made the speech she was waiting for:

"You ask me, goddess to god, why I have come.
Well, I'll tell you exactly why. Remember, you asked.
Zeus ordered me to come here; I didn't want to.
Who would want to cross this endless stretch
Of deserted sea? Not a single city in sight
Where you can get a decent sacrifice from men.
But you know how it is: Zeus has the aegis,
And none of us gods can oppose his will.
He says you have here the most woebegone hero
Of the whole lot who fought around Priam's city
For nine years, sacked it in the tenth, and started home.
But on the way back they offended Athena,[7]
And she swamped them with hurricane winds and waves.
His entire crew was wiped out, and he
Drifted along until he was washed up here.
Anyway, Zeus wants you to send him back home. Now.
The man's not fated to rot here far from his friends.
It's his destiny to see his dear ones again
And return to his high-gabled Ithacan home."

He finished, and the nymph's aura stiffened.
Words flew from her mouth like screaming hawks:

6. Magic food of the gods.

7. This passage is unusual in ascribing the deaths of Odysseus's companions to Athena, not Poseidon. In most versions of the myth, the Greeks offended Athena during the sack of the city, by various war crimes including the rape of the prophetess Cassandra by the Greek hero Ajax, in Athena's temple.

"You gods are the most jealous bastards in the universe—
Persecuting any goddess who ever openly takes
A mortal lover to her bed and sleeps with him.
When Dawn caressed Orion[8] with her rosy fingers,
You celestial layabouts gave her nothing but trouble
Until Artemis finally shot him on Ortygia—
Gold-throned, holy, gentle-shafted assault goddess!
When Demeter followed her heart and unbound
Her hair for Iasion and made love to him
In a late-summer field, Zeus was there taking notes
And executed the man with a cobalt lightning blast.[9]
And now you gods are after me for having a man.
Well, I was the one who saved his life, unprying him
From the spar he came floating here on, sole survivor
Of the wreck Zeus made of his streamlined ship,
Slivering it with lightning on the wine-dark sea.
I loved him, I took care of him, I even told him
I'd make him immortal and ageless all of his days.
But you said it, Hermes: Zeus has the aegis
And none of us gods can oppose his will.
So all right, he can go, if it's an order from above,
Off on the sterile sea. How I don't know.
I don't have any oared ships or crewmen
To row him across the sea's broad back.
But I'll help him. I'll do everything I can.
To get him back safely to his own native land."

The quicksilver messenger had one last thing to say:

"Well send him off now and watch out for Zeus' temper.
Cross him and he'll really be rough on you later."

With that the tough quicksilver god made his exit.

Calypso composed herself and went to Odysseus,
Zeus' message still ringing in her ears.
She found him sitting where the breakers rolled in.
His eyes were perpetually wet with tears now,
His life draining away in homesickness.
The nymph had long since ceased to please.
He still slept with her at night in her cavern,
An unwilling lover mated to her eager embrace.
Days he spent sitting on the rocks by the breakers,
Staring out to sea with hollow, salt-rimmed eyes.
She stood close to him and started to speak:

"You poor man. You can stop grieving now
And pining away. I'm sending you home.
Look, here's a bronze axe. Cut some long timbers

8. Orion was a human hunter with whom Dawn fell in love; the huntress goddess, Artemis, shot and killed him.

9. Demeter, goddess of the harvest, fell in love with Iasion (and in some versions had two sons by him); Zeus killed him with a thunderbolt.

And make yourself a raft fitted with topdecks,
Something that will get you across the sea's misty spaces.

I'll stock it with fresh water, food and red wine—
Hearty provisions that will stave off hunger—and
I'll clothe you well and send you a following wind
To bring you home safely to your own native land,
If such is the will of the gods of high heaven,
Whose minds and powers are stronger than mine."

Odysseus' eyes shone with weariness. He stiffened,
And shot back at her words fletched like arrows:

"I don't know what kind of send-off you have in mind,
Goddess, telling me to cross all that open sea on a raft,
Painful, hard sailing. Some well-rigged vessels
Never make it across with a stiff wind from Zeus.
You're not going to catch me setting foot on any raft
Unless you agree to swear a solemn oath
That you're not planning some new trouble for me."

Calypso's smile was like a shower of light.
She touched him gently, and teased him a little:

"Blasphemous, that's what you are—but nobody's fool!
How do you manage to say things like that?
All right. I swear by Earth and Heaven above
And the subterranean water of Styx[1]—the greatest
Oath and the most awesome a god can swear—
That I'm not planning more trouble for you, Odysseus.
I'll put my mind to work for you as hard as I would
For myself, if ever I were in such a fix.
My heart is in the right place, Odysseus,
Nor is it a cold lump of iron in my breast."

With that the haloed goddess walked briskly away
And the man followed in the deity's footsteps.
The two forms, human and divine, came to the cave
And he sat down in the chair which moments before
Hermes had vacated, and the nymph set out for him
Food and drink such as mortal men eat.
She took a seat opposite godlike Odysseus
And her maids served her ambrosia and nectar.
They helped themselves to as much as they wanted,
And when they had their fill of food and drink
Calypso spoke, an immortal radiance upon her:
"Son of Laertes in the line of Zeus, my wily Odysseus,
Do you really want to go home to your beloved country
Right away? Now? Well, you still have my blessings.

1. River of the underworld.

But if you had any idea of all the pain
You're destined to suffer before getting home,
You'd stay here with me, deathless—
Think of it, Odysseus!—no matter how much
You missed your wife and wanted to see her again.
You spend all your daylight hours yearning for her.
I don't mind saying she's not my equal
In beauty, no matter how you measure it.
Mortal beauty cannot compare with immortal."

Odysseus, always thinking, answered her this way:

"Goddess and mistress, don't be angry with me.
I know very well that Penelope,
For all her virtues, would pale beside you.
She's only human, and you are a goddess,
Eternally young. Still, I want to go back.
My heart aches for the day I return to my home.
If some god hits me hard as I sail the deep purple,
I'll weather it like the sea-bitten veteran I am.
God knows I've suffered and had my share of sorrows
In war and at sea. I can take more if I have to."

The sun set on his words, and the shadows darkened.
They went to a room deep in the cave, where they made
Sweet love and lay side by side through the night.

Dawn came early, touching the sky with rose.

Odysseus put on a shirt and cloak,
And the nymph slipped on a long silver robe
Shimmering in the light, cinched it at the waist
With a golden belt and put a veil on her head.
What to do about sending Odysseus off?
She handed him an axe, bronze, both edges honed.
The olive-wood haft felt good in his palms.
She gave him a sharp adze, too, then led the way
To the island's far side where the trees grew tall,
Alder and poplar and silver fir, sky-topping trees
Long-seasoned and dry that would keep him afloat.
Calypso showed him where the trees grew tall
Then went back home, a glimmer in the woods,
While Odysseus cut timber.
                                        Working fast,
He felled twenty trees, cut them to length,
Smoothed them skillfully and trued them to the line.
The glimmer returned—Calypso with an auger—
And he drilled the beams through, fit them up close
And hammered them together with joiners and pegs.
About the size of a deck a master shipwright
Chisels into shape for a broad-bowed freighter
Was the size Odysseus made his wide raft.

He fit upright ribs close-set in the decking
And finished them with long facing planks.
He built a mast and fit in a yardarm,
And he made a rudder to steer her by.
Then he wove a wicker-work barrier
To keep off the waves, plaiting it thick.
Calypso brought him a large piece of cloth
To make into a sail, and he fashioned that, too.
He rigged up braces and halyards and lines,
Then levered his craft down to the glittering sea.

Day four, and the job was finished.
Day five, and Calypso saw him off her island,
After she had bathed him and dressed him
In fragrant clothes. She filled up a skin
With wine that ran black, another large one
With water, and tucked into a duffel
A generous supply of hearty provisions.
And she put a breeze at his back, gentle and warm.

Odysseus' heart sang as he spread sail to the wind,
And he steered with the rudder, a master mariner
Aboard his craft. Sleep never fell on his eyelids
As he watched the Pleiades and slow-setting Boötes
And the Bear (also known as the Wagon)
That pivots in place and chases Orion
And alone is aloof from the wash of Ocean.[2]
Calypso, the glimmering goddess, had told him
To sail with the stars of the Bear on his left.
Seventeen days he sailed the deep water,
And on the eighteenth day the shadowy mountains
Of the Phaeacians' land loomed on the horizon,
To his eyes like a shield on the misty sea.

And Poseidon saw him.
From the far Solymi Mountains
The Lord of Earthquake, returning from Ethiopia,
Saw him, an image in his mind bobbing on the sea.
Angrier than ever, he shook his head
And cursed to himself:

"Damn it all, the gods
Must have changed their minds about Odysseus
While I was away with the Ethiopians.
He's close to Phaeacia, where he's destined to escape
The great ring of sorrow that has closed around him.
But I'll bet I can still blow some trouble his way."

He gathered the clouds, and gripping his trident
He stirred the sea. And he raised all the blasts

2. The constellation Ursa Major remains above the horizon.

Of every wind in the world and covered with clouds
Land and sea together. Night rose in the sky.
The winds blew hard from every direction,
And lightning-charged Boreas[3] rolled in a big wave.
Odysseus felt his knees and heart weaken.
Hunched over, he spoke to his own great soul:

"Now I'm in for it.
I'm afraid that Calypso was right on target
When she said I would have my fill of sorrow
On the open sea before I ever got home.
It's all coming true. Look at these clouds
Zeus is piling like flowers around the sky's rim,
And he's roughened the sea, and every wind
In the world is howling around me.
Three times, four times luckier than I
Were the Greeks who died on Troy's wide plain!
If only I had gone down on that day
When the air was whistling with Trojan spears
In the desperate fight for Achilles' dead body.
I would have had burial then, honored by the army.
As it is I am doomed to a wretched death at sea."

His words weren't out before a huge cresting wave
Crashed on his raft and shivered its timbers.
He was pitched clear of the deck. The rudder flew
From his hands, the mast cracked in two
Under the force of the hurricane winds,
And the yardarm and sail hove into the sea.
He was under a long time, unable to surface
From the heaving swell of the monstrous wave,
Weighed down by the clothes Calypso had given him.
At last he came up, spitting out saltwater,
Seabrine gurgling from his nostrils and mouth.
For all his distress, though, he remembered his raft,
Lunged through the waves, caught hold of it
And huddled down in its center shrinking from death.

An enormous wave rode the raft into cross-currents.

The North Wind in autumn sweeps through a field
Rippling with thistles and swirls them around.

So the winds swirled the raft all over the sea,
South Wind colliding at times with the North,
East Wind shearing away from the West.

And the White Goddess saw him, Cadmus' daughter
Ino,[4] once a human girl with slim, beautiful ankles

3. The North Wind.

4. Human girl transformed into a sea nymph.

Who had won divine honors in the saltwater gulfs.
She pitied Odysseus his wandering, his pain,
And rose from the water like a flashing gull,
Perched on his raft, and said this to him:
"Poor man. Why are you so odious to Poseidon,
Odysseus,[5] that he sows all this grief for you?
But he'll not destroy you, for all of his fury.
Now do as I say—you're in no way to refuse:
Take off those clothes and abandon your raft
To the winds' will. Swim for your life
To the Phaeacians' land, your destined safe harbor.
Here, wrap this veil tightly around your chest.
It's immortally charmed: Fear no harm or death.
But when with your hands you touch solid land
Untie it and throw it into the deep blue sea
Clear of the shore so it can come back to me."

With these words the goddess gave him the veil
And slipped back into the heavy seas
Like a silver gull. The black water swallowed her.
Godlike Odysseus brooded on his trials
And spoke these words to his own great soul:

"Not this. Not another treacherous god
Scheming against me, ordering me to abandon my raft.
I will not obey. I've seen with my own eyes
How far that land is where she says I'll be saved.
I'll play it the way that seems best to me.
As long as the timbers are still holding together
I'll hang on and gut it out right here where I am.
When and if a wave shatters my raft to pieces,
Then I'll swim for it. What else can I do?"

As he churned these thoughts in the pit of his stomach
Poseidon Earthshaker raised up a great wave—
An arching, cavernous, sensational tsunami—
And brought it crashing down on him.

As storm winds blast into a pile of dry chaff
And scatter the stuff all over the place,

So the long beams of Odysseus' raft were scattered.
He went with one beam and rode it like a stallion,
Stripping off the clothes Calypso had given him
And wrapping the White Goddess' veil round his chest.
Then he dove into the sea and started to swim
A furious breaststroke. The Lord of Earthquake saw him
And said to himself with a slow toss of his head:

5. There is a pun on Odysseus's name in the Greek, similar to "odious . . . Odysseus."

"That's right. Thrash around in misery on the open sea
Until you come to human society again.
I hope that not even then will you escape from evil."

With these words he whipped his sleek-coated horses
And headed for his fabulous palace on Aegae.

But Zeus' daughter Athena had other ideas.
She barricaded all the winds but one
And ordered them to rest and fall asleep.
Boreas, though, she sent cracking through the waves,
A tailwind for Odysseus until he was safe on Phaeacia,
And had beaten off the dark birds of death.

Two nights and two days the solid, mitered waves
Swept him on, annihilation all his heart could foresee.
But when Dawn combed her hair in the third day's light,
The wind died down and there fell
A breathless calm. Riding a swell
He peered out and saw land nearby.

You know how precious a father's life is
To children who have seen him through a long disease,
Gripped by a malevolent spirit and melting away,
But then released from suffering in a spasm of joy.

The land and woods were that welcome a sight
To Odysseus. He kicked hard for the shoreline,
But when he was as close as a shout would carry
He heard the thud of waves on the rocks,
Thundering surf that pounded the headland
And bellowed eerily. The sea churned with foam.
There were no harbors for ships, no inlets or bays,
Only jutting cliffs and rocks and barnacled crags.
Odysseus' heart sank and his knees grew weak.
With a heavy sigh he spoke to his own great soul:

"Ah, Zeus has let me see land I never hoped to see
And I've cut my way to the end of this gulf,
But there's no way to get out of the grey saltwater.
Only sharp rocks ahead, laced by the breakers,
And beyond them slick stone rising up sheer
Right out of deep water, no place for a foothold,
No way to stand up and wade out of trouble.
If I try to get out here a wave might smash me
Against the stone cliff. Some mooring that would be!
If I swim around farther and try to find
A shelving shore or an inlet from the sea,
I'm afraid that a squall will take me back out
Groaning deeply on the teeming dark water,
Or some monster will attack me out of the deep

From the swarming brood of great Amphtrite.
I know how odious I am to the Earthshaker."

As these thoughts welled up from the pit of his stomach
A breaker bore him onto the rugged coast.
He would have been cut to ribbons and his bones crushed
But grey-eyed Athena inspired him.
Slammed onto a rock he grabbed it with both hands
And held on groaning until the breaker rolled by.
He had no sooner ducked it when the backwash hit him
And towed him far out into open water again.

It was just like an octopus pulled out of its hole
With pebbles stuck to its tentacles,

Odysseus' strong hands clinging to the rocks
Until the skin was ripped off. The wave
Pulled him under, and he would have died
Then and there. But Athena was with him.
He surfaced again: the wave spat him up landwards,
And he swam along parallel to the coast, scanning it
For a shelving beach, an inlet from the sea,
And when he swam into the current of a river delta
He knew he had come to the perfect spot,
Lined with smooth rocks and sheltered from the wind.
He felt the flowing of the rivergod, and he prayed:

"Hear me, Riverlord, whoever you are
And however men pray to you:
I am a fugitive from the sea
And Poseidon's persecution,
A wandering mortal, pitiful
To the gods, I come to you,
To your water and your knees.
I have suffered much, O Lord,
Lord, hear my prayer."

At these words the god stopped his current,
Made his waters calm and harbored the man
In his river's shallows. Odysseus crawled out
On hands and knees. The sea had broken his spirit.
His whole body was swollen, and saltwater trickled
From his nose and mouth. Breath gone, voice gone,
He lay scarcely alive, drained and exhausted.
When he could breathe again and his spirit returned
He unbound the goddess' veil from his body
And threw it into the sea-melding river
Where it rode the crest of a wave down the current
And into Ino's own hands. He turned away from the river,
Sank into a bed of rushes, and kissed the good earth.
Huddled over he spoke to his own great soul:

"What am I in for now? How will this end?
If I keep watch all night here by the river
I'm afraid a hard frost—or even a gentle dew—
Will do me in, as weak as I am.
The wind blows cold from a river toward dawn.
But if I climb the bank to the dark woods up there
And fall asleep in a thicket, even if I survive
Fatigue and cold and get some sweet sleep,
I'm afraid I'll fall prey to some prowling beast."

He thought it over and decided it was better
To go to the woods. They were near the water
On an open rise. He found two olive trees there,
One wild, one planted, their growth intertwined,
Proof against blasts of the wild, wet wind,
The sun unable to needle light through,
Impervious to rain, so thickly they grew
Into one tangle of shadows. Odysseus burrowed
Under their branches and scraped out a bed.
He found a mass of leaves there, enough to keep warm
Two or three men on the worst winter day.
The sight of these leaves was a joy to Odysseus,
And the godlike survivor lay down in their midst
And covered himself up.

A solitary man
Who lives on the edge of the wilderness
And has no neighbors, will hide a charred log
Deep in the black embers and so keep alive
The fire's seed and not have to rekindle it
From who knows where.

So Odysseus buried
Himself in the leaves. And Athena sprinkled
His eyes with sleep for quickest release
From pain and fatigue.
And she closed his eyelids.

BOOK VI

So Odysseus slept, the godlike survivor
Overwhelmed with fatigue.
But the goddess Athena
Went off to the land of the Phaeacians,
A people who had once lived in Hypereia,
Near to the Cyclopes, a race of savages
Who marauded their land constantly. One day
Great Nausithous led his people
Off to Schería, a remote island,
Where he walled off a city, built houses
And shrines, and parceled out fields.
After he died and went to the world below,
Alcinous ruled, wise in the gods' ways.

Owl-eyed Athena now came to his house
To devise a passage home for Odysseus.
She entered a richly decorated bedroom
Where a girl as lovely as a goddess was sleeping,
Nausicaa, daughter of noble Alcinous.
Two maids, blessed with the beauty of Graces,
Slept on either side of the closed, polished doors.
Athena rushed in like a breath of wind,
Stood over Nausicaa's head, and spoke to her
In the guise of her friend, the daughter
Of the famed mariner Dymas. Assuming
This girl's form, the owl-eyed goddess spoke:

"Nausicaa, how could your mother have raised
Such a careless child? Your silky clothes
Are lying here soiled, and your wedding is near!
You'll have to dress yourself and your party well,
If you want the people to speak highly of you
And make your mother and father glad.
We'll wash these clothes at the break of dawn.
I'll go with you and help so you'll get it done quickly.
You're not going to be a virgin for long, you know!
All the best young men in Phaeacia are eager
To marry you—as well they should be.
Wake up now, and at dawn's first blush
Ask your father if he will hitch up the mulecart
To carry all these sashes and robes and things.
It'll be much more pleasant than going on foot.
The laundry pools are a long way from town."

The grey-eyed goddess spoke and was gone,
Off to Olympus, which they say is forever
The unmoving abode of the gods, unshaken
By winds, never soaked by rain, and where the snow
Never drifts, but the brilliant sky stretches
Cloudless away, and brightness streams through the air.
There, where the gods are happy all the world's days,
Went the Grey-eyed One after speaking to the girl.

Dawn came throned in light, and woke Nausicaa,
Who wondered at the dream as it faded away.
She went through the house to tell her parents,
Her dear father and mother. She found them within,
Her mother sitting by the hearth with her women,
Spinning sea-blue yarn. Her father she met
As he headed for the door accompanied by elders
On his way to a council the nobles had called.
She stood very close to her father and said:

"Daddy, would you please hitch up a wagon for me—
A high one that rolls well—so I can go to the river
And wash our good clothes that are all dirty now.

You yourself should wear clean clothes
When you sit among the first men in council.
And you have five sons who live in the palace,
Two married and three still bachelors.
They always want freshly washed clothes
To wear to the dances. This has been on my mind."

She was too embarrassed to mention marriage
To her father, but he understood and said:

"Of course you can have the mules, child,
And anything else. Go on. The servants will rig up
A high, smooth-rolling wagon fitted with a trunk."

He called the servants, and they got busy
Rolling out a wagon and hitching up mules.
Nausicaa brought out a pile of laundry
And loaded it into the polished cart,
While her mother packed a picnic basket
With all sorts of food and filled a goatskin with wine.
The girl put these up on the cart, along with
A golden flask of oil her mother gave her
For herself and her maids to rub on their skin.
She took the lash and the glossy reins
And had the mules giddyup. They jangled along
At a steady pace, pulling the clothes and the girl,
While the other girls, her maids, ran alongside.

They came to the beautiful, running river
And the laundry pools, where the clear water
Flowed through strongly enough to clean
Even the dirtiest clothes. They unhitched the mules
And shooed them out along the swirling river's edge
To munch the sweet clover. Then they unloaded
The clothes, brought them down to the water,
And trod them in the trenches, working fast
And making a game of it. When the clothes were washed
They spread them out neatly on the shore of the sea
Where the waves scoured the pebbled beach clean.
Then they bathed themselves and rubbed rich olive oil
Onto their skin, and had a picnic on the river's banks
While they waited for the sun to dry the clothes.
When the princess and her maids had enough to eat
They began to play with a ball, their hair streaming free.

Artemis sometimes roams the mountains—
Immense Taygetus, or Erymanthus—
Showering arrows upon boars or fleet antelope,
And with her play the daughters of Zeus
Who range the wild woods—and Leto is glad
That her daughter towers above them all
With her shining brow, though they are beautiful all—

So the unwed princess among her attendants.

But when she was about to fold the clothes,
Yoke the mules, and head back home,
The Grey-eyed One sprung her plan:
Odysseus would wake up, see the lovely girl,
And she would lead him to the Phaeacians' city.
The princess threw the ball to one of the girls,
But it sailed wide into deep, swirling water.
The girls screamed, and Odysseus awoke.
Sitting up, he tried to puzzle it out:

"What kind of land have I come to now?
Are the natives wild and lawless savages,
Or godfearing men who welcome strangers?
That sounded like girls screaming, or the cry
Of the spirit women who hold the high peaks,
The river wells, and the grassy meadows.
Can it be I am close to human voices?
I'll go have a look and see for myself."

With that Odysseus emerged from the bushes.
He broke off a leafy branch from the undergrowth
And held it before him to cover himself.

A weathered mountain lion steps into a clearing,
Confident in his strength, eyes glowing.
The wind and rain have let up, and he's hunting
Cattle, sheep, or wild deer, but is hungry enough
To jump the stone walls of the animal pens.

So Odysseus advanced upon these ringleted girls,
Naked as he was. What choice did he have?
He was a frightening sight, disfigured with brine,
And the girls fluttered off to the jutting beaches.
Only Alcinous' daughter stayed. Athena
Put courage in her heart and stopped her trembling.
She held her ground, and Odysseus wondered
How to approach this beautiful girl. Should he
Fall at her knees, or keep his distance
And ask her with honeyed words to show him
The way to the city and give him some clothes?
He thought it over and decided it was better
To keep his distance and not take the chance
Of offending the girl by touching her knees.
So he started this soft and winning speech:

"I implore you, Lady: Are you a goddess
Or mortal? If you are one of heaven's divinities
I think you are most like great Zeus' daughter
Artemis. You have her looks, her stature, her form.

If you are a mortal and live on this earth,
Thrice blest is your father, your queenly mother,
Thrice blest your brothers! Their hearts must always
Be warm with happiness when they look at you,
Just blossoming as you enter the dance.
And happiest of all will be the lucky man
Who takes you home with a cartload of gifts.
I've never seen anyone like you,
Man or woman. I look upon you with awe.
Once, on Delos, I saw something to compare—
A palm shoot springing up near Apollo's altar.
I had stopped there with the troops under my command
On what would prove to be a perilous campaign.
I marveled long and hard when I saw that tree,
For nothing like it had ever grown from the earth.
And I marvel now, Lady, and I am afraid
To touch your knees. Yet my pain is great.
Yesterday, after twenty days, I pulled myself out
Of the wine-dark sea. All that time, wind and wave
Bore me away from Ogygia Island,
And now some spirit has cast me up here
To suffer something new. I do not think
My trials will end soon. The gods have much more
In store for me before that ever happens.
Pity me, mistress. After all my hardships
It is to you I have come first. I don't know
A soul who lives here, not a single one.
Show me the way to town, and give me
A rag to throw over myself, some piece of cloth
You may have brought along to bundle the clothes.
And for yourself, may the gods grant you
Your heart's desire, a husband and a home,
And the blessing of a harmonious life.
For nothing is greater or finer than this,
When a man and woman live together
With one heart and mind, bringing joy
To their friends and grief to their foes."

And white-armed Nausicaa answered him:

"Stranger, you do not seem to be a bad man
Or a fool. Zeus himself, the Olympian god,
Sends happiness to good men and bad men both,
To each as he wills. To you he has given these troubles,
Which you have no choice but to bear. But now,
Since you have come to our country,
You shall not lack clothing, nor anything needed
By a sore-tried suppliant who presents himself.
I will show you where the city is and tell you
That the people here are called Phaeacians.
This is their country, and I am the daughter
Of great-hearted Alcinous, the Phaeacians' lord."

Then the princess called to the ringleted girls:

"Stop this now. Running away at the sight of a man!
Do you think he is part of an enemy invasion?
There is no man on earth, nor will there ever be,
Slippery enough to invade Phaeacia,
For we are very dear to the immortal gods,
And we live far out in the surging sea,
At the world's frontier, out of all human contact.
This poor man comes here as a wanderer,
And we must take care of him now. All strangers,
All beggars, are under the protection of Zeus,
And even small gifts are welcome. So let's feed
This stranger, give him something to drink,
And bathe him in the river, out of the wind."

The girls stopped, turned, and urged each other on.
They took Odysseus to a sheltered spot,
As Nausicaa, Alcinous' daughter, had ordered.
They set down a mantle and a tunic,
Gave him a golden flask of olive oil,
And told him to wash in the river.
Then sunlit Odysseus said to them:

"Stay off a ways there, girls, and let me
Wash the brine off my shoulders myself
And rub myself down. It's been a long time
Since my skin has felt oil. But I don't want
To wash in front of you. I'd be ashamed
To come out naked in front of young girls."

The girls went off and talked with Nausicaa,
And Odysseus rinsed off with river water
All the brine that caked his shoulders and back,
And he scrubbed the salty scurf from his scalp.
He finished his bath, rubbed himself down with oil,
And put on the clothes the maiden had given him.
Then Athena, born from Zeus, made him look
Taller and more muscled, and made his hair
Tumble down his head like hyacinth flowers.

Imagine a craftsman overlaying silver
With pure gold. He has learned his art
From Pallas Athena and Lord Hephaestus,
And creates works of breathtaking beauty.

So Athena herself made Odysseus' head and shoulders
Shimmer with grace. He walked down the beach
And sat on the sand. The princess was dazzled,
And she said to her white-armed serving girls:

"Listen, this man hasn't come to Phaeacia
Against the will of the Olympian gods.
Before, he was a terrible sight, but now,
He's like one of the gods who live in the sky.
If only such a man would be called my husband,
Living here, and content to stay here.
Well, go on, give him something to eat and drink."

They were only too glad to do what she said.
They served Odysseus food and drink,
And the long-suffering man ate and drank
Ravenously. It had been a long fast.

Nausicaa had other things on her mind.
She folded the clothes and loaded the wagon,
Hitched up the mules and climbed aboard.
Then she called to Odysseus and said:

"Get ready now, stranger, to go to the city,
So I can show you the way to my father's house,
Where I promise you will meet the best of the Phaeacians.
Now this is what you must do—and I think you understand:
As long as we're going through countryside and farms,
Keep up with my handmaidens behind the wagon.
Just jog along with them. I'll lead the way,
And we'll soon come to the city. It has a high wall
Around it, and a harbor on each side.
The isthmus gets narrow, and the upswept hulls
Are drawn up to the road. Every citizen
Has his own private slip. The market's there, too,
Surrounding Poseidon's beautiful temple
And bounded by stones set deep in the earth.
There men are always busy with their ships' tackle,
With cables and sails, and with planing their oars.
Phaeacians don't care for quivers and bows
But for oars and masts and streamlined ships
In which they love to cross the grey, salt sea.
It's their rude remarks I would rather avoid.
There are some insolent louts in this town,
And I can just hear one of them saying:
'Well, who's this tall, handsome stranger trailing along
Behind Nausicaa? Where'd she pick him up?
She'll probably marry him, some shipwreck she's taken in
From parts unknown. He's sure not local.
Maybe a god has come to answer her prayers,
Dropped out of the sky for her to have and to hold.
It's just as well she's found herself a husband
From somewhere else, since she turns up her nose
At the many fine Phaeacians who woo her.'
That's what they'll say, and it will count against me.
I myself would blame anyone who acted like this,

A girl who, with her father and mother to tell her better,
Kept the company of men before her wedding day.
No, stranger, be quick to understand me,
So that you can win from my father an escort home,
And soon at that.
Close by the road you will find
A grove of Athena, beautiful poplars
Surrounded by a meadow. A spring flows through it.
Right there is my father's estate and vineyard,
About as far from the city as a shout would carry.
Sit down there and wait for a while, until
We reach the city and arrive at my house.
When you think we've had enough time to get there,
Go into the city and ask any Phaeacian
For the house of my father, Lord Alcinous.
It's very easy to spot, and any child
Can lead you there. There's no other house
In all Phaeacia built like the house
Of the hero Alcinous. Once you're safely within
The courtyard, go quickly though the hall
Until you come to my mother. She'll be sitting
By the hearth in the firelight, spinning
Sea-blue yarn—a sight worth seeing—
As she leans against a column, her maids behind her.
Right beside her my father sits on his throne,
Sipping his wine like an immortal god.
Pass him by and throw your arms
Around my mother's knees, if you want to see
Your homeland soon, however far it may be.
If she smiles upon you, there is hope that you will
Return to your home and see your loved ones again."

And she smacked the mules with the shining lash.
They trotted on smartly, leaving the river behind.
She drove so that Odysseus and the girls
Could keep up, and used the lash with care.
The sun had set when they reached the grove
Sacred to Athena. Odysseus sat down there
And said this prayer to great Zeus' daughter:

"Hear me, mystic child of the Storm God,[6]
O hear me now, as you heard me not
When I was shattered by the Earthshaker's blows.
Grant that I come to Phaeacia pitied and loved."

Thus his prayer, and Pallas Athena heard it
But did not appear to him face to face, not yet,
Out of respect for her uncle,[7] who would rage against
Godlike Odysseus until he reached home.

6. Zeus.

7. Poseidon.

BOOK VII

While Odysseus was praying in the grove,
The strong mules bore Nausicaa to the city.
She pulled up at the gate of her father's palace,
And her brothers, men like gods, crowded around,
Unhitched the mules, and took the clothes inside.
Nausicaa went to her bedroom, where Eurymedusa,
Her waiting-woman, kindled a fire for her.
Eurymedusa had come from Apeire
In the curved ships, long ago, and had been chosen
From the spoils of war for Alcinous,
Who ruled the Phaeacians as if he were a god.
It was this old woman who had reared
White-armed Nausicaa in the palace
And who now prepared her supper on the fire.

As Odysseus started out for the city,
Athena enveloped him in magic mist,
So that none of the Phaeacians he might meet
Along the way would challenge him
And ask him who he was.
He was about to enter
The lovely city when the Grey-eyed One
Came up to him. She looked like a young girl
Carrying a pitcher, standing there before him,
And godlike Odysseus questioned her:

"My child, I wonder if you could guide me
To the house of Alcinous, the man
Who is lord of this people? I am a traveler
From a far land, a stranger in need,
And I know no one in this city."

Athena's eyes flashed in the blue sealight:

"Well of course, grandad, I'll show you
Where Alcinous lives. His house is close to ours.
Come on, I'll lead the way. But you'll have to be quiet.
Don't look at anyone or ask any questions.
The people here aren't very tolerant of strangers
Or very welcoming. All they trust are their ships,
In which they cross the great ocean, because
Poseidon lets them. Their ships are very fast,
Fast as a flying bird, or even a thought."

Thus Pallas Athena, and she led the way
Quickly, while Odysseus followed
In the goddess' footsteps. None of the Phaeacians
Noticed him as he moved through their city,
For the dread goddess, her hair done up in braids,
Would not allow them, shedding around him

A magical mist that made him invisible.
She had a soft spot in her heart for the hero.

Odysseus marveled at the harbors
And the shapely ships, at the meeting grounds
And the long walls capped with palisades.
When they came to the king's palace,
The Grey-eyed One was the first to speak:

"Here you are, grandad, the house you asked for.
You will find the lords feasting at a banquet.
Go inside and don't be afraid of anything.
Things turn out better for a man who is bold,
Especially if he's a stranger from a distant land.
The first person you'll meet is the queen. Arete
Is her name, and she's from the same line
As King Alcinous. It goes like this:
First Nausithous was born from Poseidon
And Periboea, a most beautiful woman,
The youngest daughter of Eurymedon,
Who once was king of the arrogant Giants.
He brought destruction down on his reckless people
And on himself. Well, anyway, Poseidon
Lay with Periboea and she bore a son,
Nausithous, who ruled the Phaeacians.
Nausithous fathered Rhexenor and Alcinous.
Rhexenor had just got married when Apollo
Shot him with his silver bow in his hall.
He didn't leave a son, but did leave a daughter,
Only one, Arete. Alcinous married her
And honored her as no other woman on earth
Is honored, of all the women who keep house
For their husbands—that's how she is honored,
From the heart, and always has been,
Both by her children and by Alcinous himself
As by the people, who look to her as a goddess
And greet her as one when she goes through the city.
She understands everything, and has sound judgment
And settles quarrels with a generous heart.
If she likes you, there is a very good chance
You will get to see your dear ones again
And the high-roofed hall in your own native land."

Thus the goddess with the seagrey eyes,
And then she was off over the desolate water,
Leaving lovely Schería. She came to Marathon
And the wide streets of Athens, and she disappeared
Into the great house of Erechtheus.

But Odysseus
Went to the glorious palace of Alcinous.

There he stood, heart pounding as he took it all in
Before crossing the bronze threshold. Gleams
As of the sun or the moon played over the high roof
Of Alcinous' house. The bronze walls, surmounted
With a blue enamel frieze, stretched from the threshold
To the inner hall. The outer doors were golden,
And silver doorposts were set in the bronze threshold.
The lintel was silver and the door handle gold.
Flanking the door were two gold and silver dogs
Made by Hephaestus[8] with all his art
To guard the palace, and they were immortal
And ageless. Inside, seats were built flush to the walls
On either side, stretching from the threshold
To the inner hall, and upon them were flung
Robes of a fine, soft weave, the craft of women.
The Phaeacian leaders would sit on these seats
Eating and drinking, and they lacked for nothing.
Golden statues of young men stood on pedestals
Holding torches to light the night for banqueters.
There were fifty slave women scattered through the house,
Some grinding yellow grain on the millstone,
Others weaving cloth or twirling yarn on spindles
As they sat, fluttering like so many leaves on a poplar,
And the finely woven fabric glistened with oil.
For just as the Phaeacian men outstrip all others
In sailing ships on the sea, so too are the women
Skilled above all others in working the loom.
Athena has given them a deep understanding
Of beautiful handiwork.
Outside the courtyard,
Just beyond the doors, are four acres, of orchard
Surrounded by a hedge. The trees there grow tall,
Blossoming pear trees and pomegranates,
Apple trees with bright, shiny fruit, sweet figs
And luxuriant olives. The fruit of these trees
Never perishes nor fails, summer or winter—
It lasts year round, and the West Wind's breath
Continually ripens apple after apple, pear upon pear,
Fig after fig, and one bunch of grapes after another.
The fruitful vineyard is planted there, too.
One warm, level spot is for drying grapes
In the sun; elsewhere, some grapes are being gathered
And others trod upon. In front, the unripe clusters
Are losing their bloom, and others are turning purple.
By the last row of vines are trim garden plots
With rich blooms of all sorts throughout the year.
Two separate springs flow through the orchard,
One of them meandering throughout the garden,
While the other flows under the courtyard threshold,

8. God of fire and metalworking.

And from this spring the townspeople draw their water.

Odysseus stood and gazed at all of the blessings
The gods had lavished on the house of Alcinous.
When he had taken it all in, he passed quickly
Over the threshold and entered the house.
There he found the Phaeacian nobles
Tipping their cups in honor of Hermes,
To whom they poured libations last of all
When they thought it was time to take their rest.
Odysseus, the godlike survivor, went through the hall
In the heavy mist Athena had wrapped him in,
Until he came to Arete and Lord Alcinous.
There he threw his arms around Arete's knees,
And the magical mist melted away at that moment.
They were all hushed to silence, marveling
At the sight of Odysseus, who now made his prayer:

"Arete, daughter of godlike Rhexenor,
To your husband and to your knees I come
In great distress, and to these banqueters also—
May the gods grant prosperity to them
In this life, and may each of them hand down
Their wealth and honor to their children after them.
Grant me but this: a speedy passage home,
For I have suffered long, far from my people."

And with that he sat down in the ashes
By the fireside. The hall fell silent.
Finally Echeneus, a Phaeacian elder,
Wise in the old ways and the ways of words,
Spoke out with good will among them:

"Alcinous, this will not do at all. It is not proper
That a guest sit in the ashes on the hearth.
We are all holding back, waiting on your word.
Come, help the stranger up and have him sit
Upon a silver-studded chair. And bid the heralds
Mix wine, so we may pour libations also to Zeus,
Lord of Thunder, who walks beside suppliants.
And let the housekeeper bring out food for our guest."

When the sacred King Alcinous heard this,
He took the hand of Odysseus, the cunning hero,
And raised him from the fireside and had him sit
On a polished chair from which he asked his son
Laodamas to rise, for he was Alcinous'
Best beloved son, and sat at his right hand.
A maid poured water from a golden pitcher
Into a silver basin for him to wash his hands
And then set up a polished table nearby.

Another serving woman, grave and dignified,
Set out bread and generous helpings
From the other dishes she had. So Odysseus,
Who had endured much, ate and drank.
And the sacred King Alcinous spoke to the herald:

"Pontonous, mix the bowl and serve wine
To all, so we may pour libations also to Zeus,
Lord of Thunder, who walks beside suppliants."

Pontonous mixed the mellow wine
And served it to all, pouring out first
Drops for libation, which they all tipped out.
When they had drunk to their heart's content,
Alcinous addressed them and said:

"Hear me, Phaeacian lords and counselors,
So I may speak to you what is in my heart.
Now that you have feasted, go home to your rest.
In the morning we will invite more of the elders
And entertain the stranger in our halls
And offer fine sacrifices to the gods.
Then we will think of how to convey our guest
To his own native land, so he may come home
Speedily and with joy, be it ever so far.
Nor shall he suffer any harm or misfortune
Before he sets foot upon his own land. Thereafter,
He shall suffer whatever fate
The Spinners[9] spun for him when he was born.
But if he is one of the immortals
Come down from heaven, then the gods
Have changed their ways. Always before this,
Whenever we offered sacrifice to them,
They appeared to us in their own bright forms,
And they sat with us and shared the feast.
Even when one of us meets them on the road
They do not conceal themselves, for we are kin,
Just like the Cyclopes and savage Giants."

Odysseus, always thinking, answered him:

"Don't worry about that, Alcinous. I am not like
The immortals, either in build or looks.
I am completely human. Better to liken me
To the most woebegone man you ever knew.
That's who I'd compare myself to.
I could tell you much more, a long tale
Of the suffering I've had by the will of the gods,
But all I want now is to be allowed to eat,

9. The Fates, who spin the threads of human lives.

Despite my grief. There is nothing more shameless
Than this belly of ours, which forces a man
To pay attention to it, no matter how many
Troubles he has, how much pain is in his heart.
I have pain in my heart, but my belly always
Makes me eat and drink and forget my troubles,
Pestering me to keep it filled. So then,
Please do move quickly at break of day
To set me ashore on my own native land,
Even though it be after all my suffering.
I'd die gladly once I've seen my home again,
My household servants and my high-roofed hall."

They praised him, and urged that the stranger
Be sped on his way. He had said all the right things.
Then, when they had poured libations and drunk
To their heart's content, they went home to rest.
Odysseus was left behind in the hall
Sitting beside Arete and godlike Alcinous.
The serving women cleared away the dishes,
And then white-armed Arete broke the silence.
She had recognized the mantle and tunic
As soon as she saw them, for she had made
These beautiful clothes herself, with her handmaids,
And when she spoke her words flew on wings:

"Stranger, I myself will ask you this first.
Who are you, and where do you come from?
And who gave you these clothes? Did you not say
That you came here wandering over the sea?"

And Odysseus, never at a loss for words:

"It would be hard, my lady, to tell the tale
Of all my troubles, since the heavenly gods
Have given me many. But I will tell you what
You ask me about.
There is an island,
Ogygia, that lies far off in the sea.
Atlas' daughter lives there, guileful Calypso,
Her hair rich as sea-foam, a dread goddess.
No one, mortal or divine, ever visits her.
It was my bad luck to be led to her hearth
By some mysterious force, all alone,
Washed up there after Zeus shattered my ship,
Slivering it with lightning on the wine-dark sea.
My whole crew went down in that wreck,
But I hung on to the curved keel of my ship,
Adrift for nine days. The tenth black night
Brought me to the island of Ogygia
And the awesome goddess. She took me in,

Gave me food, and said she would make me
Immortal and ageless for all of my days.
But she never touched my heart. I spent
Seven years with Calypso. The immortal clothes
She gave me were always wet with my tears.
Then, when the eighth year came around, she told me
I could go, either because of some message from Zeus,
Or because she herself had changed her mind.
She sent me off on a sturdy raft, well stocked
With bread and wine, and she clothed me well,
And put a breeze at my back, gentle and warm.
Seventeen days I sailed the deep water,
And on the eighteenth day the shadowy mountains
Of your land appeared, and my heart was glad.
But my luck turned sour, and I was soon engulfed
In suffering sent by the Earthshaker Poseidon.
He stirred up the winds, blocking my course,
And roused up huge seas that left me groaning
And unable to stay with my raft, which was
Shattered to pieces by the hurricane winds.
I swam my way through all that saltwater
Until wind and wave brought me here to your coast.
But if I had tried to come ashore, the pounding surf
Would have smashed me to bits on the beetling crags.
I swam back out and then along the coast
Until I came to a river, the perfect spot,
Lined with smooth stones and sheltered from the wind.
I staggered out, exhausted. Night was coming on.
I climbed the river bank and lay down to sleep
In the bushes, covering myself with dry leaves.
Some god shed upon me boundless slumber,
And I slept in the leaves, my heart troubled—
Slept through the night, through dawn and high noon,
And did not wake until the sun was going down.
When I awoke I saw your daughter's handmaids
Playing on the shore, and saw your daughter
Like a goddess among them. It was she
I supplicated, and she understood
Everything perfectly. You would not expect
Anyone so young to act with such grace,
For the young are thoughtless. She gave me bread
And bright red wine, bathed me in the river
And gave me these clothes.
As much as it pains me
To recall it, all I have told you is true."

And Alcinous responded:

"Stranger,
My daughter was out of line in not bringing you
Here to our house along with her handmaids,
Since you went to her first as a suppliant."

And Odysseus, with his usual presence of mind:

"Do not rebuke your blameless daughter for this,
My lord. She did tell me to follow along
With the girls, but I refused out of fear and shame,
Thinking your heart might cloud over with anger.
People everywhere, I have found, have tempers."

Alcinous answered him:

"Stranger,
My heart is not like that, to grow angry
Without cause. Better to give all things their due.
I would wish, by Zeus, by Athena and Apollo,
That you, being the kind of man you are—
My kind of man—would marry my daughter
And stay here and be called my son. I would
Give you a house filled with possessions
If you chose to remain, but no Phaeacian
Will ever keep you here against your will—
And may such a thing never please Father Zeus.
As for your send-off, so you can be sure of it,
It will be tomorrow. You will lie down and sleep
While they row you over the calm water
Until you come to your home, or wherever you will,
Even if it is much farther away than Euboea,
Which our sailors say is the farthest of lands.
They went there once when they took Rhadamanthus
To visit Tityus, the son of Earth.[1]
They made the round trip in a single day
Without even trying. But you will see for yourself
How good our ships and rowers are."

Odysseus, the godlike survivor, was glad,
And he spoke in prayer:

"Father Zeus,
Let Alcinous accomplish all that he says.
May his fame never fade over all the earth,
And may I reach at last my own native land."

So they spoke, and white-armed Arete told her maids
To place a bed on the porch and spread upon it
Beautiful purple blankets and fleecy cloaks.
The maids went out of the hall with torches
And made up the bed. Then they called to Odysseus:

"You may lie down, stranger. Your bed is made."

These were welcome words, and Odysseus,
Who had suffered much, fell asleep on the bed

1. Rhadamanthus was a just king; Tityus was a giant, son of Gaia (Earth).

Under the echoing portico. But Alcinous lay down
In the innermost chamber of that lofty house,
And his lady shared his bed and slept beside him.

BOOK VIII

Dawn spread her roselight over the sky,
And Alcinous awoke in all his sacred might,
As did Zeus-born Odysseus, sacker of cities.
Alcinous led the way to the Phaeacian assembly,
Which was built near the harbor. The Phaeacians
Filed in and sat on the polished stones
Close by each other, and Pallas Athena,
Disguised as Alcinous' herald, went through the city
To lay the groundwork for Odysseus' trip home,
Going up to each man and saying to him:

"Gather round, Phaeacian leaders and counselors,
And go to the assembly to learn of the stranger
Who has just arrived at Alcinous' palace,
Driven over the sea, a man like a god."

This got their attention, and the seats
In the assembly filled up quickly with men
Who marveled at the sight of Laertes' son,
For Athena poured on his shoulders and head
A shimmering grace and made him taller
And more heavily muscled, so that he would be
Welcomed by the Phaeacians as a man to respect,
And so he would be able to accomplish the feats
The Phaeacians would use to test his mettle.
When the men were all gathered, Alcinous spoke:

"Hear me, Phaeacian lords and counselors,
So I may speak what is in my heart.
This stranger has come to my house
In his wanderings. I don't know who he is,
Or if he has come from the east or the west.
He asks for passage home, and asks us to set
A firm time for departure. Let us speed him
On his way, as we have always done.
No one has ever come to my house
And languished here long for lack of transport.
Haul a black ship, then, onto the bright saltwater
For her maiden voyage. And pick two and fifty
Of the best young sailors in all the land.
When you have lashed the oars well at the benches,
Disembark and hurry to my house. We have a feast
To prepare, and I will provide well for all!
Those are my orders for the younger men.
But you others, all the sceptered kings,

Come to my palace and help me entertain
The stranger in the hall. Let no one refuse.
And summon the godlike singer of tales,
Demodocus. For the god has given him,
Beyond all others, song that delights
However his heart urges him to sing."

So saying, he led the way, followed
By the sceptered kings. A herald went
For the godlike singer, and two and fifty
Chosen young sailors went, as he ordered,
Down to the shore of the barren sea.
There they hauled a ship out onto the water.
They set up mast and sail in that swift, black ship,
Fit the oars into the leather thole-straps,
All in due order, and then unfurled the white sails.
They moored the ship where her sails would catch
The evening breeze, and then went their way
To the great palace of wise Alcinous.
The porticoes, courtyards, and rooms were filled
With crowds of men both young and old.
Alcinous sacrificed for them a dozen sheep,
Eight white-tusked boars, and two shambling oxen,
Which they flayed and dressed for the feast.
Then the herald came up leading Demodocus.
The Muse loved this man, but gave him
Good and evil both, snuffing out the light
Of his eyes as she opened his heart to sweet song.
Pontonous, the herald, had the bard sit
Among the banqueters on a silver-studded chair
Propped against a column, and he hung the clear-toned lyre
On a peg above Demodocus' head
And showed him how to reach it with his hands.
He set up a table and basket beside the bard
And a cup of wine ready at hand.
They all reached out to the feast before them,
And when they had satisfied their appetites,
The Muse moved the bard to sing of heroes.
The piece that he sang was already famed
Throughout the world—the quarrel
Odysseus once had with Achilles,
Going head to head at a feast of the gods
With violent words, and Agamemnon,
The warlord, rejoiced that these two,
The best of the Greeks, were at each other's throats.
For long ago, when he crossed the stone threshold
In sacred Pytho to consult the oracle,
Apollo had prophesied that this would happen.[2]
That was in the days when the great tide of woe

2. Pytho is Delphi, home to an oracle of Apollo, god of prophecy.

Was rolling in upon Trojans and Greeks alike
Through the will of great Zeus.
This was the song
The renowned bard sang. But Odysseus
Pulled his great purple cloak over his head
And hid his handsome face. He was ashamed
To let the Phaeacians see his tears falling down.
Whenever the singer paused, Odysseus
Would wipe away his tears, pick up his great cup
And pour libations to the gods. But when the singer
Started again, urged on by the Phaeacian lords,
Who delighted in his words, Odysseus
Would cover his head again and moan.
He managed to conceal his tears from everyone
Except Alcinous, who sat at his elbow
And could not help but hear his heavy sighs.
Alcinous acted quickly and said to his guests:

"Hear me, Phaeacian nobles and lords.
We have had enough of feasting now,
And of the lyre that complements a feast.
We should go outdoors for some contests now,
All the athletic events, so that this stranger
Can tell his friends back home how good we are
In boxing, wrestling, jumping, and footraces."

And with that he led them outdoors. The herald
Hung the clear-toned lyre on its peg
And led Demodocus by the hand
Out of the hall and along the road
The nobles had gone down to see the games.
They made their way to the assembly grounds,
And huge crowds trailed along, thousands
Past counting.
Then up rose the young heroes.
Up rose Acroneus and Ocyalus and Elatreus;
Nauteus, Prymneus, Anchialus, and Eretmeus;
Ponteus, Proreus, Thoön, and Anabesineus;
Amphialus, Polyneus' son and Tecton's grandson;
And Euryalus, a match for the War God
And son of Naubolus. He was the handsomest
Of the Phaeacians, after peerless Laodamas.
And up rose the three sons of Alcinous,
Laodamas, Halius, and godlike Clytoneus.

The first contest was a footrace. The course
Stretched out before them from the starting post,
And they were off, raising dust from the plain
As they sped along. No one could keep up
With Clytoneus, who extended his lead
To the length of a furrow a mule-team plows.

That's how far ahead he was when he reached the crowd,
Leaving the rest of the field far behind.
Wrestling was next, and in this painful sport
Euryalus outdid the other young princes.
The best jumper proved to be Amphialus;
Elatreus took the discus throw; and Laodamas,
Alcinous' son, outboxed all comers.
Everyone had enjoyed the games, and then
Alcinous' son Laodamas said to his friends:

"Come on, now. We should ask the stranger
Whether he is skilled in any sport. His build
Is impressive enough, his thighs and calves,
His arms and stout neck. This man is strong!
He's still got what it takes, but he has been broken
By many hardships. Nothing's worse than the sea
To get a man out of shape, no matter how strong he is."

And Euryalus answered him:

"Well spoken, Laodamas. Go ahead
And challenge him yourself, in public."

When Laodamas heard this, he strode out
Front and center and spoke to Odysseus:

"You should come forward, too, as our guest,
And try your hand at one of the sports,
If you are skilled in any. I'm sure you are,
For there is no greater glory a man can win in life
Than the glory he wins with his hands and feet.
So shrug off your cares and give it a try.
It won't delay your journey. Your ship
Is already launched and the crew is ready."

Odysseus, always thinking, answered him this way:

"Laodamas, why do you provoke me like this?
I have more serious things on my mind
Than track and field. I've had my share of suffering,
And paid my dues. Now I sit in the middle
Of your assembly, longing to return home,
A suppliant before your king and all the people."

Then Euryalus taunted him to his face:

"You know, stranger, I've seen a lot of sportsmen,
And you don't look like one to me at all.
You look more like the captain of a merchant ship,
Plying the seas with a crew of hired hands

And keeping a sharp eye on his cargo,
Greedy for profit. No, you're no athlete."

Odysseus stared the man down and said:

"That's an ugly thing to say, stranger,
And it makes you look like a reckless fool.
The sad truth is that the gods don't give anyone
All their gifts, whether it's looks, intelligence,
Or eloquence. One man might not have good looks,
But the gods crown his words with beauty,
And men look at him with delight. He speaks
With unfaltering grace and sweet modesty,
And stands out in any crowd. When he walks
Through town, men look upon him as a god.
Another man might look like an immortal,
But his words are not crowned with beauty.
That's how it is with you. Your looks
Are outstanding. Not even a god
Could improve them. But your mind is crippled.
And now you've got my blood pumping
With your rude remarks. I'm no novice in sports,
As you suggest. No, I was one of the best,
When I could trust my youth and my hands.
Now I'm slowed down by my aches and pains
And the suffering I've had in war and at sea.
Even so, even with all I've been through,
I'll give your games a try. Your words
Cut deep, and now you've got me going."

He jumped up, cloak still on, and grabbed a discus
Larger than the others, thicker and much heavier
Than the one the Phaeacians used for competition.
Winding up, he let it fly, and the stone,
Launched with incredible force from his hand,
Hummed as it flew. The Phaeacians ducked
As the discus zoomed overhead and finally landed
Far beyond the other marks. Pallas Athena,
Who looked like a man now, marked the spot
Where it came down, and she called out to him:

"Even a blind man could find your mark, stranger,
For it's not all mixed up with the others
But way out front. You can be confident
No Phaeacian will come close to this throw."

Odysseus cheered up at this, glad to see
A loyal supporter out on the field.
In a lighter mood now, he spoke to the Phaeacians:

"Match that if you can, boys. In a minute
I'll get another one out just as far or farther.

And if anyone else has the urge to try me,
Step right up—I'm angry now—
I don't care if it's boxing, wrestling,
Or even running. Come one, come all—
Except Laodamas, who is my host.
Only a fool would challenge the man
Who gives him hospitality in a distant land.
He would only wind up hurting himself.
But I wouldn't turn down anyone else,
Or take any of you lightly. I only want
To see what you're made of, and to test myself.
I'm not weak in any athletic event,
And I really know how to handle a bow.
I'm always the first to hit my man
In the enemy lines, no matter how many archers
Are standing with me and getting off shots.
Only Philoctetes, of all the Greeks,
Outshot me at Troy. No one else came close,
Nor could any man now alive on this earth.
I do not compare myself to the men of old,
To Heracles, or Oechalian Eurytus,
Who tried to outshoot the immortal gods.
Eurytus died young, killed by Apollo,
Who was angry that he had challenged him
To a contest with the bow.
As for the spear,
I can throw it farther than you can shoot an arrow.
It's only in running that I fear some Phaeacian
May beat me to the line. I've taken a pounding
Out in the waves, and didn't come here aboard
A well-stocked ship, so my legs are still shaky."

He spoke, and they were all stunned to silence.
Only Alcinous was able to answer:

"Your words, stranger, are not ungracious.
You want only to demonstrate your prowess,
Angry that this man stood up at the games
And taunted you in a way no one ever would
Who knew in his heart how to speak fitly.
But now listen to my words, so that one day,
As you sit feasting with your wife and children,
You may tell another hero what you remember
Of the Phaeacians' skill in the feats that Zeus
Established as ours in our forefathers' days.
For we are not flawless boxers or wrestlers,
But we are swift of foot, and the best sailors,
And we love feasts and the lyre and dancing,
Fresh clothes, warm baths, and soft beds.
Up now, let the best dancers in Phaeacia dance,
So that the stranger can tell his friends back home

How superior we are in seamanship,
In fleetness of foot, in dancing, and in song.
Someone go get Demodocus his lyre,
Which is lying somewhere in the palace halls."

Thus godlike Alcinous, and the herald left
To get the hollow lyre from the king's palace.
Then up rose the officials, nine in all,
Who were in charge of the games. They marked out
A wide dancing ring and made the ground level.
The herald returned with the lyre, and Demodocus
Moved to the middle of the dancing ring,
Surrounded by boys in the bloom of youth,
Accomplished dancers all. Their feet struck the floor
Of the sacred ring, and as Odysseus watched
He marveled at how their feet flashed in the air.

Then Demodocus swept the strings of his lyre
And began his song. He sang of the passion
Between Ares and gold-crowned Aphrodite,
How they first made love in Hephaestus' house,
Sneaking around, and how the War God Ares
Showered her with gifts and shamed the bed
Of her husband, Hephaestus. But it wasn't long
Before Hephaestus found out. Helios told him
That he had seen them lying together in love.[3]
When Hephaestus heard this heart-wrenching news
He went to his forge, brooding on his wrongs,
And set the great anvil up on its block
And hammered out a set of unbreakable bonds,
Bonds that couldn't loosen, bonds meant to stay put.
When he had wrought this snare, furious with Ares,
He went to his bedroom and spread the bonds
All around the bedposts, and hung many also
From the high roofbeams, as fine as cobwebs,
So fine not even the gods could see them.
When he had spread this cunning snare
All around the bed, he pretended to leave
On a trip to Lemnos, his favorite city.
Ares wasn't blind, and when he saw Hephaestus
On his way out, he headed for the house
Of the glorious smith, itching to make love
To the Cytherean goddess.[4] She had been visiting
Her father, Zeus, and was just sitting down
When Ares came in, took her hand, and said:

3. Aphrodite, the goddess of sex, was married to the god Hephaestus, but had an affair with Ares, god of war; Helios, the sun god, who sees whatever the sun sees, revealed the truth.

4. Aphrodite.

"Let's go to bed, my love, and lie down together.
Hephaestus has left town, off to Lemnos no doubt
To visit the barbarous Sintians."

This suggestion appealed to the goddess,
And they climbed into bed. They were settling in
When the chains Hephaestus had cunningly wrought
Fell all around them. They couldn't move an inch,
Couldn't lift a finger, and by the time it sank in
That there was no escape, there was Hephaestus,
Gimpy-legged and glorious, coming in the door.
He had turned back on his way to Lemnos
As soon as Helios, his spy, gave him the word.
He stood in the doorway, seething with anger,
And with an ear-splitting yell called to the gods:

"Father Zeus and all you blessed gods eternal,
Come see something that is as ridiculous
As it is unendurable, how Aphrodite,
Daughter of Zeus, scorns me for being lame
And loves that marauder Ares instead
Because he is handsome and well-knit, whereas I
Was born misshapen, which is no one's fault
But my parents', who should have never begotten me!
Come take a look at how these two
Have climbed into my bed to make love and lie
In each other's arms. It kills me to see it!
But I don't think they will want to lie like this
Much longer, no matter how loving they are.
No, they won't want to sleep together for long,
But they're staying put in my little snare
Until her father returns all of the gifts
I gave him to marry this bitch-faced girl,
His beautiful, yes, but faithless daughter."

Thus Hephaestus, and the gods gathered
At his bronze threshold.
Poseidon came,
The God of Earthquake, and Hermes the Guide,
And the Archer Apollo. The goddesses
All stayed home, out of modesty; but the gods
Stood in the doorway and laughed uncontrollably
When they saw Hephaestus' cunning and craft.
One of them would look at another and snigger:

"Crime doesn't pay."
"The slow catches the swift.
Slow as he is, old Gimpy caught Ares,
The fastest god on Olympus."
"Ares has to pay the fine for adultery."

That was the general drift of their jibes.
And then Apollo turned to Hermes and said:

"Tell me, Hermes, would you be willing
To be pinched in chains if it meant you could lie
Side by side with golden Aphrodite?"

And the quicksilver messenger shot back:

"I tell you what, Apollo. Tie me up
With three times as many unbreakable chains,
And get all the gods and goddesses, too,
To come here and look, if it means I can sleep
Side by side with golden Aphrodite."

The gods roared with laughter, except Poseidon
Who did not think it was funny. He kept
Pleading that Ares should be released,
And his words winged their way to Hephaestus:

"Let him go, and I will ensure he will pay you
Fair compensation before all the gods."

And the renowned god, lame in both legs:

"Do not ask me to do this, Poseidon.
Worthless is the surety assured for the worthless.
How could I ever hold you to your promise
If Ares slipped out of the bonds and the debt?"

Poseidon the Earthshaker did not back off:

"Hephaestus, if Ares gets free and disappears
Without paying the debt, I will pay it myself."

And the renowned god, lame in both legs:

"I cannot refuse you. It wouldn't be right."

And with that the strong smith undid the bonds,
And the two of them, free at last from their crimp,
Shot out of there, Ares to Thrace,
And Aphrodite, who loves laughter and smiles,
To Paphos on Cyprus, and her precinct there
With its smoking altar. There the Graces
Bathed her and rubbed her with the ambrosial oil
That glistens on the skin of the immortal gods.
And then they dressed her in beautiful clothes,
A wonder to see.

This was the song

The renowned bard sang, and Odysseus
Was glad as he listened, as were the Phaeacians,
Men who are famed for their long-oared ships.

Then Alcinous had Halius and Laodamas
Dance alone, for no one could match them.
They picked up a beautiful iridescent ball,
The work of Polybus. One of them
Would lean backward and toss it high
Toward the shadowy clouds, and the other
Would leap and catch it and shoot it back up
Before his feet ever touched ground again.
When they had tried their skill with upward throws
They started to dance on the bounteous earth,
Tossing the ball constantly back and forth.
The others beat time as they stood on the field,
And thunderous applause rose from the crowd.

Then Odysseus said to Alcinous:

"Lord Alcinous, you said that your dancers
Are the best in the world, and your words
Have proved true. I am in awe before them."
So he spoke, and the sacred king was glad.
He turned to his sea-loving people and said:

"Hear me Phaeacian lords and counselors.
Our guest seems in my eyes to be a man
Of the highest discernment. Come, then,
Let us give him a gift that befits a guest.
Twelve honored kings are lords in Phaeacia,
And I myself am the thirteenth king.
Let each of you twelve bring here now
A fresh cloak and tunic and a bar of fine gold.
Let us get these all together at once,
So that our guest may have these gifts in hand
And be glad at heart when he goes to supper.
And let Euryalus apologize and give him a gift,
For what he said to our guest was in no way proper."

The lords all approved of what Alcinous said,
And each sent a herald to fetch the gifts.
Then Euryalus in turn answered Alcinous:

"Lord Alcinous, renowned above all men,
I will indeed apologize to our guest, as you bid.
And I will give him this sword, all bronze
And with a silver hilt. It comes with a scabbard
Of newly sawn ivory, and will be worth much to him."

And he put the silver-studded sword
Into Odysseus' hands and said to him:

"Revered stranger and guest, if any word
Has been harshly spoken, may the winds
Snatch it away. And may the gods grant
That you see your wife and come to your homeland,
For you have suffered long apart from your people."

And Odysseus, whose thoughts were many:

"And you, my friend, be well, and may the gods
Grant you happiness. And may you never miss
This sword you have given me to make amends."

He spoke, and slung the silver-studded sword
Around one shoulder.
The sun went down,
And the gifts were ready to be presented.
The heralds brought them into the palace
And Alcinous' sons set them down
Before their mother. They were beautiful gifts.
Alcinous, the sacred king, led the way
And the lords entered and sat on their thrones.
Then Alcinous in his might addressed Arete:

"Bring out the finest chest you have, my wife,
And place in it a newly washed cloak and tunic.
And heat water for our guest in a bronze cauldron,
So that when he has bathed and seen the gifts
The Phaeacians have brought all neatly stowed,
He will enjoy the feast and the words of the song.
And I will give him this beautiful cup,
Pure gold, to remember me by all of his days
As he pours wine to Zeus and to the other gods."

He spoke, and Arete signaled her women
To set a cauldron on the fire instantly.
They filled the cauldron with water for a bath,
Set kindling beneath it and lit the fire.
The flames licked the belly of the cauldron
And the water grew warm.
Arete meanwhile
Brought out a handsome chest for the stranger
And placed within it the beautiful gifts,
The clothes and the gold which the nobles gave.
And she herself placed in it a cloak
And beautiful tunic. And she said to Odysseus:

"There is the lid. Tie it down with a knot
As a precaution against someone robbing you

On your way back, when you are lying asleep
On your journey home in the swift, black ship."

When Odysseus, who had borne much, heard this,
He tied the lid down quickly with a cunning knot
He had learned from Circe. Then the housekeeper came
To tell him it was time to go and bathe. The warm bath
Was a welcome sight to Odysseus. He had not been
Cared for like this since leaving Calypso,
Who had treated him as if he were a god.

When the women had bathed him, rubbed him with oil,
And clothed him in a beautiful tunic and cloak,
Odysseus strode from the bath and was on his way
To join the men drinking wine.
Nausicaa,
Beautiful as only the gods could make her,
Stood by the doorpost of the great hall.
Her eyes went wide when she saw Odysseus,
And her words beat their way to him on wings:

"Farewell, stranger, and remember me
In your own native land. I saved your life."

And Odysseus, whose thoughts ran deep:

"Nausicaa, daughter of great Alcinous,
So may Zeus, Hera's thundering lord,
Grant that I see my homeland again.
There I will pray to you, as to a god,
All of my days. I owe you my life."

And he took his seat next to Lord Alcinous.
They were serving food and mixing the wine
When the herald came up leading the bard,
Honored Demodocus, and seated him on a chair
Propped against a tall pillar in the middle of the hall.
Odysseus, with great presence of mind,
Cut off part of a huge chine of roast pork
Glistening with fat, and said to the herald:

"Herald, take this cut of meat to Demodocus
For him to eat. And I will greet him
Despite my grief. Bards are revered
By all men upon earth, for the Muse
Loves them well and has taught them the songways."

The herald brought the cut of meat to Demodocus
And placed it in his hands, much to the bard's delight.
Then everyone reached out to the feast before them,
And when they had eaten and drunk to their hearts' content,
Odysseus spoke to Demodocus:

"I don't know whether it was the Muse
Who taught you, or Apollo himself,[5]
But I praise you to the skies, Demodocus.
When you sing about the fate of the Greeks
Who fought at Troy, you have it right,
All that they did and suffered, all they endured.
It's as if you had been there yourself,
Or heard a first-hand account. But now,
Switch to the building of the wooden horse
Which Epeius made with Athena's help,
The horse which Odysseus led up to Troy
As a trap, filled with men who would
Destroy great Ilion.[6] If you tell me this story
Just as it happened, I will tell the whole world
That some god must have opened his heart
And given to you the divine gift of song."

So he spoke, and the bard, moved by the god,
Began to sing. He made them see it happen,
How the Greeks set fire to their huts on the beach
And were sailing away, while Odysseus
And the picked men with him sat in the horse,
Which the Trojans had dragged into their city.
There the horse stood, and the Trojans sat around it
And could not decide what they should do.
There were three ways of thinking:
Hack open the timbers with pitiless bronze,
Or throw it from the heights to the rocks below,
Or let it stand as an offering to appease the gods.
The last was what would happen, for it was fated
That the city would perish once it enclosed
The great wooden horse, in which now sat
The Greek heroes who would spill Troy's blood.
The song went on. The Greeks poured out
Of their hollow ambush and sacked the city.
He sang how one hero here and another there
Ravaged tall Troy, but how Odysseus went,
Like the War God himself, with Menelaus
To the house of Deiphobus, and there, he said,
Odysseus fought his most daring battle
And won with the help of Pallas Athena.

This was his song. And Odysseus wept. Tears
Welled up in his eyes and flowed down his cheeks.

A woman wails as she throws herself upon
Her husband's body. He has fallen in battle
Before the town walls, fighting to the last
To defend his city and protect his children.

5. God associated with poetry, who carried the lyre.
6. Troy.

As she sees him dying and gasping for breath
She clings to him and shrieks, while behind her
Soldiers prod their spears into her shoulders and back,
And as they lead her away into slavery
Her tear-drenched face is a mask of pain.

So too Odysseus, pitiful in his grief.
He managed to conceal his tears from everyone
Except Alcinous, who sat at his elbow
And could not help but hear his heavy sighs.
Alcinous acted quickly and said to his guests:

"Hear me, Phaeacian counselors and lords—
Demodocus should stop playing his lyre.
His song is not pleasing to everyone here.
Ever since dinner began and the divine bard
Rose up to sing, our guest has not ceased
From lamentation. He is overcome with grief.
Let the lyre stop. It is better if we all,
Host and guest alike, can enjoy the feast.
All that we are doing we are doing on behalf
Of the revered stranger, providing him
With passage home and gifts of friendship.
A stranger and suppliant is as dear as a brother
To anyone with even an ounce of good sense.
So there is no need, stranger, for you to withhold
What I am about to ask for, no need to be crafty
Or think of gain. Better to speak the plain truth.
Tell me your name, the one you were known by
To your mother and father and your people back home.
No one is nameless, rich man or poor.
Parents give names to all of their children
When they are born. And tell me your country,
Your city, and your land, so that our ships
May take you there, finding their way by their wits.
For Phaeacian ships do not have pilots,
Nor steering oars, as other ships have.
They know on their own their passengers' thoughts,
And know all the cities and rich fields in the world,
And they cross the great gulfs with the greatest speed,
Hidden in mist and fog, with never a fear
Of damage or shipwreck.
                                        But I remember hearing
My father, Nausithous, say how Poseidon
Was angry with us because we always give
Safe passage to men. He said that one day
Poseidon would smite a Phaeacian ship
As it sailed back home over the misty sea,
And would encircle our city within a mountain.
The old man used to say that, and either the god
Will bring it to pass or not, as suits his pleasure.
But tell me this, and tell me the truth.

Where have you wandered, to what lands?
Tell me about the people and cities you saw,
Which ones are cruel and without right and wrong,
And which are godfearing and kind to strangers.
And tell me why you weep and grieve at heart
When you hear the fate of the Greeks and Trojans.
This was the gods' doing. They spun that fate
So that in later times it would turn into song.
Did some kinsman of yours die at Troy,
A good, loyal man, your daughter's husband
Or your wife's father, someone near and dear,
Or perhaps even a relative by blood?
Or was it a comrade, tried and true?
A friend like that is no less than a brother."

BOOK IX

And Odysseus, his great mind teeming:

"My Lord Alcinous, what could be finer
Than listening to a singer of tales
Such as Demodocus, with a voice like a god's?
Nothing we do is sweeter than this—
A cheerful gathering of all the people
Sitting side by side throughout the halls,
Feasting and listening to a singer of tales,
The tables filled with food and drink,
The server drawing wine from the bowl
And bringing it around to fill our cups.
For me, this is the finest thing in the world.
But you have a mind to draw out of me
My pain and sorrow, and make me feel it again.
Where should I begin, where end my story?
Heaven has sent me many tribulations.
I will tell you my name first, so that you, too,
Will know who I am, and when I escape
The day of my doom, I will always be
Your friend and host, though my home is far.
I am Odysseus, great Laertes' son,
Known for my cunning throughout the world,
And my fame reaches even to heaven.
My native land is Ithaca, a sunlit island
With a forested peak called Neriton,
Visible for miles. Many other islands
Lie close around her—Doulichion, Samê,
And wooded Zacynthus—off toward the sunrise,
But Ithaca lies low on the evening horizon,
A rugged place, a good nurse of men.
No sight is sweeter to me than Ithaca. Yes,
Calypso, the beautiful goddess, kept me
In her caverns, yearning to possess me;

And Circe, the witch of Aeaea, held me
In her halls and yearned to possess me;
But they could not persuade me or touch my heart.
Nothing is sweeter than your own country
And your own parents, not even living in a rich house—
Not if it's far from family and home.
But let me tell you of the hard journey homeward
Zeus sent me on when I sailed from Troy.

From Ilion the wind took me to the Cicones
In Ismaros. I pillaged the town and killed the men.
The women and treasure that we took out
I divided as fairly as I could among all hands
And then gave the command to pull out fast.
That was my order, but the fools wouldn't listen.
They drank a lot of wine and slaughtered
A lot of sheep and cattle on the shore.
Some of the town's survivors got away inland
And called their kinsmen. There were more of them,
And they were braver, too, men who knew how to fight
From chariots and on foot. They came on as thick
As leaves and flowers in spring, attacking
At dawn. We were out of luck, cursed by Zeus
To suffer heavy losses. The battle-lines formed
Along our beached ships, and bronze spears
Sliced through the air. As long as the day's heat
Climbed toward noon, we held our ground
Against superior numbers. But when the sun
Dipped down, the Cicones beat us down, too.
We lost six fighting men from each of our ships.
The rest of us cheated destiny and death.

We sailed on in shock, glad to get out alive
But grieving for our lost comrades.
I wouldn't let the ships get under way
Until someone had called out three times
For each mate who had fallen on the battlefield.
And then Zeus hit us with a norther,
A freak hurricane. The clouds blotted out
Land and sea, and night climbed up the sky.
The ships pitched ahead. When their sails
Began to shred in the gale-force winds,
We lowered them and stowed them aboard,
Fearing the worst, and rowed hard for the mainland.
We lay offshore two miserable days and nights.
When Dawn combed her hair in the third day's light,
We set up the masts, hoisted the white sails,
And took our seats. The wind and the helmsmen
Steered the ships, and I would have made it home
Unscathed, but as I was rounding Cape Malea
The waves, the current, and wind from the North
Drove me off course past Cythera Island.

Nine days of bad winds blew us across
The teeming seas. On the tenth day we came
To the land of the Lotus-Eaters.
We went ashore,
And the crews lost no time in drawing water
And preparing a meal beside their ships.
After they had filled up on food and drink,
I sent out a team—two picked men and a herald—
To reconnoiter and sound out the locals.
They headed out and made contact with the Lotus-Eaters,
Who meant no harm but did give my men
Some lotus to eat. Whoever ate that sweet fruit
Lost the will to report back, preferring instead
To stay there, munching lotus, oblivious of home.
I hauled them back wailing to the ships,
Bound them under the benches, then ordered
All hands to board their ships on the double
Before anyone else tasted the lotus.
They were aboard in no time and at their benches,
Churning the sea white with their oars.

We sailed on, our morale sinking,
And we came to the land of the Cyclopes,
Lawless savages who leave everything
Up to the gods. These people neither plow nor plant,
But everything grows for them unsown:
Wheat, barley, and vines that bear
Clusters of grapes, watered by rain from Zeus.
They have no assemblies or laws but live
In high mountain caves, ruling their own
Children and wives and ignoring each other.

A fertile island slants across the harbor's mouth,
Neither very close nor far from the Cyclopes' shore.
It's well-wooded and populated with innumerable
Wild goats, uninhibited by human traffic.
Not even hunters go there, tramping through the woods
And roughing it on the mountainsides.
It pastures no flocks, has no tilled fields—
Unplowed, unsown, virgin forever, bereft
Of men, all it does is support those bleating goats.
The Cyclopes do not sail and have no craftsmen
To build them benched, red-prowed ships
That could supply all their wants, crossing the sea
To other cities, visiting each other as other men do.
These same craftsmen would have made this island
Into a good settlement. It's not a bad place at all
And would bear everything in season. Meadows
Lie by the seashore, lush and soft,
Where vines would thrive. It has level plowland
With deep, rich soil that would produce bumper crops

Season after season. The harbor's good, too,
No need for moorings, anchor-stones, or tying up.
Just beach your ship until the wind is right
And you're ready to sail. At the harbor's head
A spring flows clear and bright from a cave
Surrounded by poplars.
                                    There we sailed in,
Some god guiding us through the murky night.
We couldn't see a thing. A thick fog
Enveloped the ships, and the moon
Wasn't shining in the cloud-covered sky.
None of us could see the island, or the long waves
Rolling toward the shore, until we ran our ships
Onto the sandy beach. Then we lowered sail,
Disembarked, and fell asleep on the sand.

Dawn came early, with palmettoes of rose,
And we explored the island, marveling at it.
The spirit-women, daughters of Zeus,
Roused the mountain goats so that my men
Could have a meal. We ran to the ships,
Got our javelins and bows, formed three groups
And started to shoot. The god let us bag our game,
Nine goats for each of the twelve ships,
Except for my ship, which got ten.

So all day long until the sun went down
We feasted on meat and sweet wine.
The ships had not yet run out of the dark red
Each crew had taken aboard in large jars
When we ransacked the Cicones' sacred city.
And we looked across at the Cyclopes' land.
We could see the smoke from their fires
And hear their voices, and their sheep and goats.
When the sun set, and darkness came on
We went to sleep on the shore of the sea.
As soon as dawn brightened in the rosy sky,
I assembled all the crews and spoke to them:

'The rest of you will stay here while I go
With my ship and crew on reconnaissance.
I want to find out what those men are like,
Wild savages with no sense of right or wrong
Or hospitable folk who fear the gods.'

With that, I boarded ship and ordered my crew
To get on deck and cast off. They took their places
And were soon whitening the sea with their oars.
As we pulled in over the short stretch of water,
There on the shoreline we saw a high cave
Overhung with laurels. It was a place
Where many sheep and goats were penned at night.

Around it was a yard fenced in by stones
Set deep in the earth, and by tall pines and crowned oaks.
This was the lair of a huge creature, a man
Who pastured his flocks off by himself,
And lived apart from others and knew no law.
He was a freak of nature, not like men who eat bread,
But like a lone wooded crag high in the mountains.

I ordered part of my crew to stay with the ship
And counted off the twelve best to go with me.
I took along a goatskin filled with red wine,
A sweet vintage I had gotten from Maron,
Apollo's priest on Ismaros, when I spared both him
And his wife and child out of respect for the god.
He lived in a grove of Phoebus Apollo
And gave me splendid gifts: seven bars of gold,
A solid-silver bowl, and twelve jars of wine,
Sweet and pure, a drink for the gods.
Hardly anyone in his house, none of the servants,
Knew about this wine—just Maron, his wife,
And a single housekeeper. Whenever he drank
This sweet dark red wine, he would fill one goblet
And pour it into twenty parts of water,
And the bouquet that spread from the mixing bowl
Was so fragrant no one could hold back from drinking.
I had a large skin of this wine, a sack
Of provisions—and a strong premonition
That we had a rendezvous with a man of great might,
A savage with no notion of right and wrong.

We got to the cave quickly. He was out,
Tending his flocks in the rich pastureland.
We went inside and had a good look around.
There were crates stuffed with cheese, and pens
Crammed with lambs and kids—firstlings,
Middlings, and newborns in separate sections.
The vessels he used for milking—pails and bowls
Of good workmanship—were brimming with whey.
My men thought we should make off with some cheese
And then come back for the lambs and kids,
Load them on board, and sail away on the sea.
But I wouldn't listen. It would have been far better
If I had! But I wanted to see him, and see
If he would give me a gift of hospitality.
When he did come he was not a welcome sight.

We lit a fire and offered sacrifice
And helped ourselves to some of the cheese.
Then we sat and waited in the cave
Until he came back, herding his flocks.
He carried a huge load of dry wood

To make a fire for his supper and heaved it down
With a crash inside the cave. We were terrified
And scurried back into a corner.
He drove his fat flocks into the wide cavern,
At least those that he milked, leaving the males—
The rams and the goats—outside in the yard.
Then he lifted up a great doorstone,
A huge slab of rock, and set it in place.
Two sturdy wagons—twenty sturdy wagons—
Couldn't pry it from the ground—that's how big
The stone was he set in the doorway. Then,
He sat down and milked the ewes and bleating goats,
All in good order, and put the sucklings
Beneath their mothers. Half of the white milk
He curdled and scooped into wicker baskets,
The other half he let stand in the pails
So he could drink it later for his supper.
He worked quickly to finish his chores,
And as he was lighting the fire he saw us and said:

'Who are you strangers? Sailing the seas, huh?
Where from, and what for? Pirates, probably,
Roaming around causing people trouble.'

He spoke, and it hit us like a punch in the gut—
His booming voice and the sheer size of the monster—
But even so I found the words to answer him:
'We are Greeks, blown off course by every wind
In the world on our way home from Troy, traveling
Sea routes we never meant to, by Zeus' will no doubt.
We are proud to be the men of Agamemnon,
Son of Atreus, the greatest name under heaven,
Conquerer of Troy, destroyer of armies.
Now we are here, suppliants at your knees,
Hoping you will be generous to us
And give us the gifts that are due to strangers.
Respect the gods, sir. We are your suppliants,
And Zeus avenges strangers and suppliants,
Zeus, god of strangers, who walks at their side.'

He answered me from his pitiless heart:

'You're dumb, stranger, or from far away,
If you ask me to fear the gods. Cyclopes
Don't care about Zeus or his aegis
Or the blessed gods, since we are much stronger.
I wouldn't spare you or your men
Out of fear of Zeus. I would spare them only
If I myself wanted to. But tell me,
Where did you leave your ship? Far
Down the coast, or close? I'd like to know.'

Nice try, but I knew all the tricks and said:

'My ship? Poseidon smashed it to pieces
Against the rocks at the border of your land.
He pushed her in close and the wind did the rest.
These men and I escaped by the skin of our teeth.'

This brought no response from his pitiless heart
But a sudden assault upon my men. His hands
Reached out, seized two of them, and smashed them
To the ground like puppies. Their brains spattered out
And oozed into the dirt. He tore them limb from limb
To make his supper, gulping them down
Like a mountain lion, leaving nothing behind—
Guts, flesh, or marrowy bones.
Crying out, we lifted our hands to Zeus
At this outrage, bewildered and helpless.
When the Cyclops had filled his huge belly
With human flesh, he washed it down with milk,
Then stretched out in his cave among his flocks.
I crept up close and was thinking about
Drawing my sharp sword and driving it home
Into his chest where the lungs hide the liver.
I was feeling for the spot when another thought
Checked my hand: we would die to a man in that cave,
Unable to budge the enormous stone
He had set in place to block the entrance. And so,
Groaning through the night, we waited for dawn.

As soon as dawn came, streaking the sky red,
He rekindled the fire and milked his flocks,
All in good order, placing the sucklings
Beneath their mothers. His chores done,
He seized two of my men and made his meal.
After he had fed he drove his flocks out,
Easily lifting the great stone, which he then set
Back in place as lightly as if he were setting
A lid upon a quiver. And then, with loud whistling,
The Cyclops turned his fat flocks toward the mountain,
And I was left there, brooding on how
I might make him pay and win glory from Athena.

This was the best plan I could come up with:
Beside one of the sheep pens lay a huge pole
Of green olive which the Cyclops had cut
To use as a walking stick when dry. Looking at it
We guessed it was about as large as the mast
Of a black ship, a twenty-oared, broad-beamed
Freighter that crosses the wide gulfs.
That's how long and thick it looked. I cut off

About a fathom's length from this pole
And handed it over to my men. They scraped it
And made it smooth, and I sharpened the tip
And took it over to the fire and hardened it.
Then I hid it, setting it carefully in the dung
That lay in piles all around the cave.
And I told my men to draw straws to decide
Which of them would have to share the risk with me—
Lift that stake and grind it in his eye
While he was asleep. They drew straws and came up with
The very men I myself would have chosen.
There were four of them, and I made five.

At evening he came, herding his fleecy sheep.
He drove them straight into the cave, drove in
All his flocks in fact. Maybe he had some
Foreboding, or maybe some god told him to.
Then he lifted the doorstone and set it in place,
And sat down to milk the goats and bleating ewes,
All in good order, setting the sucklings
Beneath their mothers. His chores done,
Again he seized two of my men and made his meal.
Then I went up to the Cyclops and spoke to him,
Holding an ivy-wood bowl filled with dark wine.

'Cyclops, have some wine, now that you have eaten
Your human flesh, so you can see what kind of drink
Was in our ship's hold. I was bringing it to you
As an offering, hoping you would pity me
And help me get home. But you are a raving
Maniac! How do you expect any other man
Ever to visit you after acting like this?'

He took the bowl and drank it off, relishing
Every last, sweet drop. And he asked me for more:

'Be a pal and give me another drink. And tell me
Your name, so I can give you a gift you'll like.
Wine grapes grow in the Cyclopes' land, too.
Rain from the sky makes them grow from the earth.
But this—this is straight ambrosia and nectar.'

So I gave him some more of the ruby-red wine.
Three times the fool drained the bowl dry,
And when the wine had begun to work on his mind,
I spoke these sweet words to him:

'Cyclops,
You ask me my name, my glorious name,
And I will tell it to you. Remember now,

To give me the gift just as you promised.
Noman is my name. They call me Noman[7]—
My mother, my father, and all my friends, too.'

He answered me from his pitiless heart:

'Noman I will eat last after his friends.
Friends first, him last. That's my gift to you.'

He listed as he spoke and then fell flat on his back,
His thick neck bent sideways. He was sound asleep,
Belching out wine and bits of human flesh
In his drunken stupor. I swung into action,
Thrusting the stake deep in the embers,
Heating it up, and all the while talking to my men
To keep up their morale. When the olivewood stake
Was about to catch fire, green though it was,
And was really glowing, I took it out
And brought it right up to him. My men
Stood around me, and some god inspired us.
My men lifted up the olivewood stake
And drove the sharp point right into his eye,
While I, putting my weight behind it, spun it around
The way a man bores a ship's beam with a drill,
Leaning down on it while other men beneath him
Keep it spinning and spinning with a leather strap.
That's how we twirled the fiery-pointed stake
In the Cyclops' eye. The blood formed a whirlpool
Around its searing tip. His lids and brow
Were all singed by the heat from the burning eyeball
And its roots crackled in the fire and hissed
Like an axe-head or adze a smith dips into water
When he wants to temper the iron—that's how his eye
Sizzled and hissed around the olivewood stake.
He screamed, and the rock walls rang with his voice.
We shrank back in terror while he wrenched
The blood-grimed stake from his eye and flung it
Away from him, blundering about and shouting
To the other Cyclopes, who lived around him
In caverns among the windswept crags.
They heard his cry and gathered from all sides
Around his cave and asked him what ailed him:

'Polyphemus, why are you hollering so much
And keeping us up the whole blessed night?
Is some man stealing your flocks from you,
Or killing you, maybe, by some kind of trick?'

And Polyphemus shouted out to them:

7. In Greek, "Noman"—*oudeis*—sounds a little like *Odysseus*.

'Noman is killing me by some kind of trick!'

They sent their words winging back to him:

'If no man is hurting you, then your sickness
Comes from Zeus and can't be helped.
You should pray to your father, Lord Poseidon.'

They left then, and I laughed in my heart
At how my phony name had fooled them so well.
Cyclops meanwhile was groaning in agony.
Groping around, he removed the doorstone
And sat in the entrance with his hands spread out
To catch anyone who went out with the sheep—
As if I could be so stupid. I thought it over,
Trying to come up with the best plan I could
To get us all out from the jaws of death.
I wove all sorts of wiles, as a man will
When his life is on the line. My best idea
Had to do with the sheep that were there, big,
Thick-fleeced beauties with wool dark as violets.
Working silently, I bound them together
With willow branches the Cyclops slept on.
I bound them in threes. Each middle sheep
Carried a man underneath, protected by
The two on either side: three sheep to a man.
As for me, there was a ram, the best in the flock.
I grabbed his back and curled up beneath
His shaggy belly. There I lay, hands twined
Into the marvelous wool, hanging on for dear life.
And so, muffling our groans, we waited for dawn.

When the first streaks of red appeared in the sky,
The rams started to bolt toward the pasture.
The unmilked females were bleating in the pens,
Their udders bursting. Their master,
Worn out with pain, felt along the backs
Of all of the sheep as they walked by, the fool,
Unaware of the men under their fleecy chests.
The great ram headed for the entrance last,
Heavy with wool—and with me thinking hard.
Running his hands over the ram, Polyphemus said:

'My poor ram, why are you leaving the cave
Last of all? You've never lagged behind before.
You were always the first to reach the soft grass
With your big steps, first to reach the river,
First to want to go back to the yard
At evening. Now you're last of all. Are you sad
About your master's eye? A bad man blinded me,
Him and his nasty friends, getting me drunk,
Noman—but he's not out of trouble yet!

If only you understood and could talk,
You could tell me where he's hiding. I would
Smash him to bits and spatter his brains
All over the cave. Then I would find some relief
From the pain this no-good Noman has caused me.'

He spoke, and sent the ram off through the door.
When we had gone a little way from the cave,
I first untangled myself from the ram
And then untied my men. Then, moving quickly,
We drove those fat, long-shanked sheep
Down to the ship, keeping an eye on our rear.
We were a welcome sight to the rest of the crew,
But when they started to mourn the men we had lost
I forbade it with an upward nod of my head,
Signaling each man like that and ordering them
To get those fleecy sheep aboard instead,
On the double, and get the ship out to sea.
Before you knew it they were on their benches
Beating the sea to white froth with their oars.
When we were offshore but still within earshot,
I called out to the Cyclops, just to rub it in:

'So, Cyclops, it turns out it wasn't a coward
Whose men you murdered and ate in your cave,
You savage! But you got yours in the end,
Didn't you? You had the gall to eat the guests
In your own house, and Zeus made you pay for it.'

He was even angrier when he heard this.
Breaking off the peak of a huge crag
He threw it toward our ship, and it carried
To just in front of our dark prow. The sea
Billowed up where the rock came down,
And the backwash pushed us to the mainland again,
Like a flood tide setting us down at the shore.
I grabbed a long pole and shoved us off,
Nodding to the crew to fall on the oars
And get us out of there. They leaned into it,
And when we were twice as far out to sea as before
I called to the Cyclops again, with my men
Hanging all over me and begging me not to:

'Don't do it, man! The rock that hit the water
Pushed us in and we thought we were done for.
If he hears any sound from us, he'll heave
Half a cliff at us and crush the ship and our skulls
With one throw. You know he has the range.'

They tried, but didn't persuade my hero's heart—
I was really angry—and I called back to him:

'Cyclops, if anyone, any mortal man,
Asks you how you got your eye put out,
Tell him that Odysseus the marauder did it,
Son of Laertes, whose home is on Ithaca.'

He groaned, and had this to say in response:

'Oh no! Now it's coming to me, the old prophecy.
There was a seer here once, a tall handsome man,
Telemos Eurymides. He prophesied well
All his life to the Cyclopes. He told me
That all this would happen some day,
That I would lose my sight at Odysseus' hands.
I always expected a great hero
Would come here, strong as can be.
Now this puny, little, good-for-nothing runt
Has put my eye out—because he got me drunk.
But come here, Odysseus, so I can give you a gift,
And ask Poseidon to help you on your way.
I'm his son, you know. He claims he's my father.
He will heal me, if he wants. But none
Of the other gods will, and no mortal man will.'

He spoke, and I shouted back to him:

'I wish I were as sure of ripping out your lungs
And sending you to Hell as I am dead certain
That not even the Earthshaker will heal your eye.'

I had my say, and he prayed to Poseidon,
Stretching his arms out to starry heaven:

'Hear me, Poseidon, blue-maned Earth-Holder,
If you are the father you claim to be.
Grant that Odysseus, son of Laertes,
May never reach his home on Ithaca.
But if he is fated to see his family again,
And return to his home and own native land,
May he come late, having lost all companions,
In another's ship, and find trouble at home.'

He prayed, and the blue-maned sea-god heard him.
Then he broke off an even larger chunk of rock,
Pivoted, and threw it with incredible force.
It came down just behind our dark-hulled ship,
Barely missing the end of the rudder. The sea
Billowed up where the rock hit the water,
And the wave pushed us forward all the way
To the island where our other ships waited
Clustered on the shore, ringed by our comrades
Sitting on the sand, anxious for our return.

We beached the ship and unloaded the Cyclops' sheep,
Which I divided up as fairly as I could
Among all hands. The veterans gave me the great ram,
And I sacrificed it on the shore of the sea
To Zeus in the dark clouds, who rules over all.
I burnt the thigh pieces, but the god did not accept
My sacrifice, brooding over how to destroy
All my benched ships and my trusty crews.

So all the long day until the sun went down
We sat feasting on meat and drinking sweet wine.
When the sun set and darkness came on
We lay down and slept on the shore of the sea.
Early in the morning, when the sky was streaked red,
I roused my men and ordered the crews
To get on deck and cast off. They took their places
And were soon whitening the sea with their oars.

We sailed on in shock, glad to get away alive
But grieving for the comrades we had lost."

BOOK X

"We came next to the island of Aeolia,
Home of Aeolus, son of Hippotas,
Dear to the immortals. Aeolia
Is a floating island surrounded by a wall
Of indestructible bronze set on sheer stone.
Aeolus' twelve children live there with him,
Six daughters and six manly sons.
He married his daughters off to his boys,
And they all sit with their father and mother
Continually feasting on abundant good cheer
Spread out before them. Every day
The house is filled with steamy savor
And the courtyard resounds. Every night
The men sleep next to their high-born wives
On blankets strewn on their corded beds.
We came to their city and their fine palace,
And for a full month he entertained me.
He questioned me in great detail about Troy,
The Greek fleet, and the Greeks' return home.
I told him everything, from beginning to end.
And when I, in turn, asked if I might leave
And requested him to send me on my way,
He did not refuse, and this was his send-off:
He gave me a bag made of the hide of an ox
Nine years old, which he had skinned himself,
And in this bag he bound the wild winds' ways,
For Zeus had made him keeper of the winds,
To still or to rouse whichever he will.

He tied this bag down in the hold of my ship
With a bright silver cord, so that not a puff
Could escape. But he let the West Wind out
To blow my ships along and carry us home.
It was not to be. Our own folly undid us.

For nine days and nights we sailed on.
On the tenth day we raised land, our own
Native fields, and got so close we saw men
Tending their fires. Then sleep crept up on me,
Exhausted from minding the sail the whole time
By myself. I wouldn't let any of my crew
Spell me, because I wanted to make good time.
As soon as I fell asleep, the men started to talk,
Saying I was bringing home for myself
Silver and gold as gifts from great Aeolus.
You can imagine the sort of things they said:

'This guy gets everything wherever he goes.
First, he's freighting home his loot from Troy,
Beautiful stuff, while we, who made the same trip,
Are coming home empty-handed. And now
Aeolus has lavished these gifts upon him.
Let's have a quick look, and see what's here,
How much gold and silver is stuffed in this bag.'

All malicious nonsense, but it won out in the end,
And they opened the bag. The winds rushed out
And bore them far out to sea, weeping
As their native land faded on the horizon.
When I woke up and saw what had happened
I thought long and hard about whether I should
Just go over the side and end it all in the sea
Or endure in silence and remain among the living.
In the end I decided to bear it and live.
I wrapped my head in my cloak and lay down on the deck
While an evil wind carried the ships
Back to Aeolia. My comrades groaned.

We went ashore and drew water
And the men took a meal beside the swift ships.
When we had tasted food and drink
I took a herald and one man
And went to Aeolus' glorious palace.
I found him feasting with his wife and children,
And when we came in and sat on the threshold
They were amazed and questioned me:

'What happened, Odysseus? What evil spirit
Abused you? Surely we sent you off

With all you needed to get back home
Or anywhere else your heart desired.'

I answered them from the depths of my sorrow:

'My evil crew ruined me, that and stubborn sleep.
But make it right, friends, for you have the power.'

I made my voice soft and tried to persuade them,
But they were silent. And then their father said:

'Begone from this island instantly!
You are the most cursed of all living things.
It would go against all that is right
For me to help or send on his way
A man so despised by the blessed gods.
Begone! You are cursed by heaven!'

And with that he sent me from his house,
Groaning heavily. We sailed on from there
With grief in our hearts. Because of our folly
There was no breeze to push us along,
And our morale sank because the rowing was hard.
We sailed on for six solid days and nights,
And on the seventh we came to Lamus,
The lofty city of Telepylus
In the land of the Laestrygonians,
Where a herdsman driving in his flocks at dusk
Calls to another driving his out at dawn.
A man could earn a double wage there
If he never slept, one by herding cattle
And another by pasturing white sheep,
For night and day make one twilight there.
The harbor we came to is a glorious place,
Surrounded by sheer cliffs. Headlands
Jut out on either side to form a narrow mouth,
And there all the others steered in their ships
And moored them close together in the bay.
No wave, large or small, ever rocks a boat
In that silvery calm. I alone moored my black ship
Outside the harbor, tying her up
On the rocks that lie on the border of the land.
Then I climbed to a rugged lookout point
And surveyed the scene. There was no sign
Of plowed fields, only smoke rising up from the land.

I sent out a team—two picked men and a herald—
To reconnoiter and find out who lived there.
They went ashore and followed a smooth road
Used by wagons to bring wood from the mountains
Down to the city. In front of the city
They met a girl drawing water. Her father

Was named Antiphates, and she had come down
To the flowing spring Artacia,
From which they carried water to the town.
When my men came up to her and asked her
Who the people there were and who was their king,
She showed them her father's high-roofed house.
They entered the house and found his wife inside,
A woman, to their horror, as huge as a mountain top.
At once she called her husband, Antiphates,
Who meant business when he came. He seized
One of my men and made him into dinner.
The other two got out of there and back to the ships,
But Antiphates had raised a cry throughout the city,
And when they heard it, the Laestrygonians
Came up on all sides, thousands of them,
Not like men but like the Sons of the Earth,
The Giants.[8] They pelted us from the cliffs
With rocks too large for a man to lift.
The sounds that came from the ships were sickening,
Sounds of men dying and boats being crushed.
The Laestrygonians speared the bodies like fish,
And carried them back for their ghastly meal.
While this was happening I drew my sword
And cut the cables of my dark-prowed ship,
Barking out orders for the crew to start rowing
And get us out of there. They rowed for their lives,
Ripping the sea, and my ship sped joyfully
Out and away from the beetling rocks,
But all of the others were destroyed as they lay.

We sailed on in shock, glad to get out alive
But grieving for the comrades we'd lost.
And we came to Aeaea, the island that is home
To Circe, a dread goddess with richly coiled hair
And a human voice. She is the sister
Of dark-hearted Aeetes, and they are both sprung
From Helios and Perse, daughter of Ocean.[9]
Some god guided us into a harbor
And we put in to shore without a sound.
We disembarked and lay there for two days and two nights,
Eating our hearts out with wearines and grief.
But when Dawn combed her hair in the third day's light,
I took my sword and spear and went up
From the ship to open ground, hoping to see
Plowed fields, and to hear human voices.
So I climbed to a rugged lookout point
And surveyed the scene. What I saw was smoke

8. The Giants were children of Earth, fertilized by the blood of Uranus after his castration.
9. Perse is one of the many daughters of Ocean; Aeetes was the cruel king of Colchis, owner of the Golden Fleece and father of Medea.

Rising up from Circe's house. It curled up high
Through the thick brush and woods, and I wondered
Whether I should go and have a closer look.
I decided it was better to go back to the ship
And give my crew their meal, and then
Send out a party to reconnoiter.
I was on my way back and close to the ship
When some god took pity on me,
Walking there alone, and sent a great antlered stag
Right into my path. He was on his way
Down to the river from his pasture in the woods,
Thirsty and hot from the sun beating down,
And as he came out I got him right on the spine
In the middle of his back. The bronze spear bored
All the way through, and he fell in the dust
With a groan, and his spirit flew away.
Planting my foot on him, I drew the bronze spear
Out of the wound and laid it down on the ground.
Then I pulled up a bunch of willow shoots
And twisted them together to make a rope
About a fathom long. I used this to tie
The stag's feet together so I could carry him
Across my back, leaning on my spear
As I went back to the ship. There was no way
An animal that large could be held on one shoulder.
I flung him down by the ship and roused my men,
Going up to each in turn and saying to them:

'We're not going down to Hades, my friends,
Before our time. As long as there is still
Food and drink in our ship, at least
We don't have to starve to death.'

When they heard this, they drew their cloaks
From their faces, and marveled at the size
Of the stag lying on the barren seashore.
When they had seen enough, they washed their hands
And prepared a glorious feast. So all day long
Until the sun went down we sat there feasting
On all that meat, washing it down with wine.
When the sun set and darkness came on,
We lay down to sleep on the shore of the sea.

When Dawn brushed the eastern sky with rose,
I called my men together and spoke to them:

'Listen to me, men. It's been hard going.
We don't know east from west right now,
But we have to see if we have any good ideas left.
We may not. I climbed up to a lookout point.
We're on an island, ringed by the endless sea.

The land lies low, and I was able to see
Smoke rising up through the brushy woods.'

This was too much for them. They remembered
What Antiphates, the Laestrygonian, had done,
And how the Cyclops had eaten their comrades.
They wailed and cried, but it did them no good.
I counted off the crew into two companies
And appointed a leader for each. Eurylochus
Headed up one group and I took the other,
And then we shook lots in a bronze helmet.
Out jumped the lot of Eurylochus, brave heart,
And so off he went, with twenty-two men,
All in tears, leaving us behind in no better mood.

They went through the woods and found Circe's house
In an upland clearing. It was built of polished stone
And surrounded by mountain lions and wolves,
Creatures Circe had drugged and bewitched.
These beasts did not attack my men, but stood
On their hind legs and wagged their long tails,
Like dogs fawning on their master who always brings
Treats for them when he comes home from a feast.
So these clawed beasts were fawning around my men,
Who were terrified all the same by the huge animals.
While they stood like this in the gateway
They could hear Circe inside, singing in a lovely voice
As she moved about weaving a great tapestry,
The unfading handiwork of an immortal goddess,
Finely woven, shimmering with grace and light.
Polites, a natural leader, and of all the crew
The one I loved and trusted most, spoke up then:

'Someone inside is weaving a great web,
And singing so beautifully the floor thrums with the sound.
Whether it's a goddess or a woman, let's call her out now.'

And so they called to her, and she came out
And flung open the bright doors and invited them in.
They all filed in naively behind her,
Except Eurylochus, who suspected a trap.
When she had led them in and seated them
She brewed up a potion of Pramnian wine
With cheese, barley, and pale honey stirred in,
And she laced this potion with insidious drugs
That would make them forget their own native land.
When they had eaten and drunk, she struck them
With her wand and herded them into the sties outside.
Grunting, their bodies covered with bristles,
They looked just like pigs, but their minds were intact.
Once in the pens, they squealed with dismay,

And Circe threw them acorns and berries—
The usual fare for wallowing swine.

Eurylochus at once came back to the ship
To tell us of our comrades' unseemly fate,
But, hard as he tried, he could not speak a word.
The man was in shock. His eyes welled with tears,
And his mind was filled with images of horror.
Finally, under our impatient questioning,
He told us how his men had been undone:

'We went through the woods, as you told us to,
Glorious Odysseus, and found a beautiful house
In an upland clearing, built of polished stone.
Someone inside was working a great loom
And singing in a high, clear voice, some goddess
Or a woman, and they called out to her,
And she came out and opened the bright doors
And invited them in, and they naively
Filed in behind her. But I stayed outside,
Suspecting a trap. And they all disappeared,
Not one came back. I sat and watched
For a long, long time, and not one came back.'

He spoke, and I threw my silver-studded sword
Around my shoulders, slung on my bow,
And ordered Eurylochus to retrace his steps
And lead me back there. But he grabbed me by the knees
And pleaded with me, wailing miserably:
'Don't force me to go back there. Leave me here,
Because I know that you will never come back yourself
Or bring back the others. Let's just get out of here
With those that are left. We might still make it.'

Those were his words, and I answered him:

'All right, Eurylochus, you stay here by the ship.
Get yourself something to eat and drink.
I'm going, though. We're in a really tight spot.'

And so I went up from the ship and the sea
Into the sacred woods. I was closing in
On Circe's house, with all its bewitchment,
When I was met by Hermes. He had a golden wand
And looked like a young man, a hint of a moustache
Above his lip—youth at its most charming.
He clasped my hand and said to me:

'Where are you off to now, unlucky man,
Alone, and in rough, uncharted terrain?

Those men of yours are up in Circe's house,
Penned like pigs into crowded little sties.
And you've come to free them? I don't think so.
You'll never return; you'll have to stay there, too.
Oh well, I will keep you out of harm's way.
Take this herb with you when you go to Circe,
And it will protect you from her deadly tricks.
She'll mix a potion and spike it with drugs,
But she won't be able to cast her spell
Because you'll have a charm that works just as well—
The one I'll give you—and you'll be forewarned.
When Circe strikes you with her magic wand,
Draw your sharp sword from beside your thigh
And rush at her with murder in your eye.
She'll be afraid and invite you to bed.
Don't turn her down—that's how you'll get
Your comrades freed and yourself well loved.
But first make her swear by the gods above
She will not unsex you when you are nude,
Or drain you of your manly fortitude.'

So saying, Hermes gave me the herb,
Pulling it out of the ground, and showed it to me.
It was black at the root, with a milk-white flower.
Moly, the gods call it, hard for mortal men to dig up,
But the gods can do anything. Hermes rose
Through the wooded island and up to Olympus,
And I went on to Circe's house, brooding darkly
On many things. I stood at the gates
Of the beautiful goddess' house and gave a shout.
She heard me call and came out at once,
Opening the bright doors and inviting me in.
I followed her inside, my heart pounding.
She seated me on a beautiful chair
Of finely wrought silver, and prepared me a drink
In a golden cup, and with evil in her heart
She laced it with drugs. She gave me the cup
And I drank it off, but it did not bewitch me.
So she struck me with her wand and said:

'Off to the sty, with the rest of your friends.'

At this, I drew the sharp sword that hung by my thigh
And lunged at Circe as if I meant to kill her.
The goddess shrieked and, running beneath my blade,
Grabbed my knees and said to me wailing:

'Who are you, and where do you come from?
What is your city and who are your parents?
I am amazed that you drank this potion
And are not bewitched. No other man

Has ever resisted this drug once it's past his lips.
But you have a mind that cannot be beguiled.
You must be Odysseus, the man of many wiles,
Who Quicksilver Hermes always said would come here
In his swift black ship on his way home from Troy.
Well then, sheath your sword and let's
Climb into my bed and tangle in love there,
So we may come to trust each other.'

She spoke, and I answered her:

'Circe, how can you ask me to be gentle to you
After you've turned my men into swine?
And now you have me here and want to trick me
Into going to bed with you, so that you can
Unman me when I am naked. No, Goddess,
I'm not getting into any bed with you
Unless you agree first to swear a solemn oath
That you're not planning some new trouble for me.'

Those were my words, and she swore an oath at once
Not to do me any harm, and when she finished
I climbed into Circe's beautiful bed.

Meanwhile, her serving women were busy,
Four maidens who did all the housework,
Spirit women born of the springs and groves
And of the sacred rivers that flow to the sea.
One of them brought rugs with a purple sheen
And strewed them over chairs lined with fresh linen.
Another drew silver tables up to the chairs
And set golden baskets upon them. The third
Mixed honey-hearted wine in a silver bowl
And set out golden cups. The fourth
Filled a cauldron with water and lit a great fire
Beneath it, and when the water was boiling
In the glowing bronze, she set me in a tub
And bathed me, mixing in water from the cauldron
Until it was just how I liked it, and pouring it over
My head and shoulders until she washed from my limbs
The weariness that had consumed my soul.
When she had bathed me and rubbed me
With rich olive oil, and had thrown about me
A beautiful cloak and tunic, she led me to the hall
And had me sit on a silver-studded chair,
Richly wrought and with a matching footstool.
A maid poured water from a silver pitcher
Over a golden basin for me to wash my hands
And then set up a polished table nearby.
And the housekeeper, grave and dignified,
Set out bread and generous helpings
From all the dishes she had. She told me to eat,

But nothing appealed. I sat there with other thoughts
Occupying my mind, and my mood was dark.
When Circe noticed I was just sitting there,
Depressed, and not reaching out for food,
She came up to me and spoke winged words:

'Why are you just sitting there, Odysseus,
Eating your heart out and not touching your food?
Are you afraid of some other trick? You need not be.
I have already sworn I will do you no harm.'

So she spoke, and I answered her:

'Circe, how could anyone bring himself—
Any decent man—to taste food and drink
Before seeing his comrades free?
If you really want me to eat and drink,
Set my men free and let me see them.'

So I spoke, and Circe went outside
Holding her wand and opened the sty
And drove them out. They looked like swine
Nine or ten years old. They stood there before her
And she went through them and smeared each one
With another drug. The bristles they had grown
After Circe had given them the poisonous drug
All fell away, and they became men again,
Younger than before, taller and far handsomer.
They knew me, and they clung to my hands,
And the house rang with their passionate sobbing.
The goddess herself was moved to pity.

Then she came to my side and said:

'Son of Laertes in the line of Zeus,
My wily Odysseus, go to your ship now
Down by the sea and haul it ashore.
Then stow all the tackle and gear in caves
And come back here with the rest of your crew.'

So she spoke, and persuaded my heart.
I went to the shore and found my crew there
Wailing and crying beside our sailing ship.
When they saw me they were like farmyard calves
Around a herd of cows returning to the yard.
The calves bolt from their pens and run friskily
Around their mothers, lowing and mooing.
That's how my men thronged around me
When they saw me coming. It was as if
They had come home to their rugged Ithaca,
And wailing miserably they said so to me:

'With you back, Zeus-born, it is just as if
We had returned to our native Ithaca.
But tell us what happened to the rest of the crew.'

So they spoke, and I answered them gently:

'First let's haul our ship onto dry land
And then stow all the tackle and gear in caves.
Then I want all of you to come along with me
So you can see your shipmates in Circe's house,
Eating and drinking all they could ever want.'

They heard what I said and quickly agreed.
Eurylochus, though, tried to hold them back,
Speaking to them these winged words:

'Why do you want to do this to yourselves,
Go down to Circe's house? She will turn all of you
Into pigs, wolves, lions, and make you guard her house.
Remember what the Cyclops did when our shipmates
Went into his lair? It was this reckless Odysseus
Who led them there. It was his fault they died.'

When Eurylochus said that, I considered
Drawing my long sword from where it hung
By my thigh and lopping off his head,
Close kinsman though he was by marriage.
But my crew talked me out of it, saying things like:

'By your leave, let's station this man here
To guard the ship. As for the rest of us,
Lead us on to the sacred house of Circe.'

And so the whole crew went up from the sea,
And Eurylochus did not stay behind with the ship
But went with us, in mortal fear of my temper.

Meanwhile, back in Circe's house, the goddess
Had my men bathed, rubbed down with oil,
And clothed in tunics and fleecy cloaks.
We found them feasting well in her halls.
When they recognized each other, they wept openly
And their cries echoed throughout Circe's house.
Then the shining goddess stood near me and said:

'Lament no more. I myself know
All that you have suffered on the teeming sea
And the losses on land at your enemies' hands.
Now you must eat, drink wine, and restore the spirit
You had when you left your own native land,

Your rugged Ithaca. You are skin and bones now
And hollow inside. All you can think of
Is your hard wandering, no joy in your heart,
For you have, indeed, suffered many woes.'

She spoke, and I took her words to heart.
So we sat there day after day for a year,
Feasting on abundant meat and sweet wine.
But when a year had passed, and the seasons turned,
And the moons waned and the long days were done,
My trusty crew called me out and said:

'Good god, man, at long last remember your home,
If it is heaven's will for you to be saved
And return to your house and your own native land.'

They spoke, and I saw what they meant.
So all that long day until the sun went down
We sat feasting on meat and sweet red wine.
When the sun set and darkness came on,
My men lay down to sleep in the shadowy hall,
But I went up to Circe's beautiful bed
And touching her knees I beseeched the goddess:

'Circe, fulfill now the promise you made
To send me home. I am eager to be gone
And so are my men, who are wearing me out
Sitting around whining and complaining
Whenever you happen not to be present.'

So I spoke, and the shining goddess answered:

'Son of Laertes in the line of Zeus,
My wily Odysseus—you need not stay
Here in my house any longer than you wish.
But there is another journey you must make first—
To the house of Hades and dread Persephone,[1]
To consult the ghost of Theban Tiresias,
The blind prophet, whose mind is still strong.
To him alone Persephone has granted
Intelligence even after his death.
The rest of the dead are flitting shadows.'

This broke my spirit. I sat on the bed
And wept. I had no will to live, nor did I care
If I ever saw the sunlight again.
But when I had my fill of weeping and writhing,
I looked at the goddess and said:

1. Hades is god of the underworld. Persephone is his wife.

‘And who will guide me on this journey, Circe?
No man has ever sailed his black ship to Hades.’

And the goddess, shining, answered at once:

‘Son of Laertes in th
My wily Odysseus—
A pilot to guide your
Spread the white sail
The North Wind’s br
But when your ship c
You will see a shelvin
Tall poplars and willo
Beach your ship there
And go yourself to the
There into Acheron fl
And Cocytus, a branc
And there is a rock wh
Flow into one. At that
And do as I say.
Dig an
And around it pour lib
First with milk and ho
And a third time with v
And pray to the loomin
Vowing sacrifice on Ithaca, a barren heifer,
The herd’s finest, and rich gifts on the altar,
And to Tiresias alone a great black ram.
After these supplications to the spirits,
Slaughter a ram and a black ewe, turning their heads
Toward Erebus,[2] yourself turning backward
And leaning toward the streams of the river.
Then many ghosts of the dead will come forth.
Call to your men to flay the slaughtered sheep
And burn them as a sacrifice to the gods below,
To mighty Hades and dread Persephone.
You yourself draw your sharp sword and sit there,
Keeping the feeble death-heads from the blood
Until you have questioned Tiresias.
Then, and quickly, the great seer will come.
He will tell you the route and how long it will take
For you to reach home over the teeming deep.’

Dawn rose in gold as she finished speaking.
Circe gave me a cloak and tunic to wear
And the nymph slipped on a long silver robe
Shimmering in the light, cinched it at the waist
With a golden belt and put a veil on her head.
I went through the halls and roused my men,
Going up to each with words soft and sweet:

2. The underworld.

'Time to get up! No more sleeping late.
We're on our way. Lady Circe has told me all.'

So I spoke, and persuaded their heroes' hearts.
But not even from Circe's house could I lead my men
Unscathed. One of the crew, Elpenor, the youngest,
Not much of a warrior nor all that smart,
Had gone off to sleep apart from his shipmates,
Seeking the cool air on Circe's roof
Because he was heavy with wine.
He heard the noise of his shipmates moving around
And sprang up suddenly, forgetting to go
To the long ladder that led down from the roof.
He fell headfirst, his neck snapped at the spine,
And his soul went down to the house of Hades.

As my men were heading out I spoke to them:

'You think, no doubt, that you are going home,
But Circe has plotted another course for us,
To the house of Hades and dread Persephone,
To consult the ghost of Theban Tiresias.'

This broke their hearts. They sat down
Right where they were and wept and tore their hair,
But no good came of their lamentation.

While we were on our way to our swift ship
On the shore of the sea, weeping and crying,
Circe had gone ahead and tethered a ram and a black ewe
By our tarred ship. She had passed us by
Without our ever noticing. Who could see
A god on the move against the god's will?"

BOOK XI

"When we reached our black ship
We hauled her onto the bright saltwater,
Set up the mast and sail, loaded on
The sheep, and boarded her ourselves,
Heartsick and weeping openly by now.
The dark prow cut through the waves
And a following wind bellied the canvas,
A good sailing breeze sent by Circe,
The dread goddess with a human voice.
We lashed everything down and sat tight,
Leaving the ship to the wind and helmsman.
All day long she surged on with taut sail;
Then the sun set, and the sea grew dark.

The ship took us to the deep, outermost Ocean
And the land of the Cimmerians, a people

Shrouded in mist. The sun never shines there,
Never climbs the starry sky to beam down at them,
Nor bathes them in the glow of its last golden rays;
Their wretched sky is always racked with night's gloom.
We beached our ship there, unloaded the sheep,
And went along the stream of Ocean
Until we came to the place spoken of by Circe.

There Perimedes and Eurylochus held the victims
While I dug an ell-square pit with my sword,
And poured libation to all the dead,
First with milk and honey, then with sweet wine,
And a third time with water. Then I sprinkled
White barley and prayed to the looming dead,
Vowing sacrifice on Ithaca—a barren heifer,
The herd's finest, and rich gifts on the altar,
And to Tiresias alone a great black ram.
After these supplications to the spirits,
I cut the sheeps' throats over the pit,
And the dark blood pooled there.
Then out of Erebus
The souls of the dead gathered, the ghosts
Of brides and youths and worn-out old men
And soft young girls with hearts new to sorrow,
And many men wounded with bronze spears,
Killed in battle, bearing blood-stained arms.
They drifted up to the pit from all sides
With an eerie cry, and pale fear seized me.
I called to my men to flay the slaughtered sheep
And burn them as a sacrifice to the gods,
To mighty Hades and dread Persephone.
Myself, I drew my sharp sword and sat,
Keeping the feeble death-heads from the blood
Until I had questioned Tiresias.

First to come was the ghost of Elpenor,
Whose body still lay in Circe's hall,
Unmourned, unburied, since we'd been hard pressed.
I wept when I saw him, and with pity in my heart
Spoke to him these feathered words:

'Elpenor, how did you get to the undergloom
Before me, on foot, outstripping our black ship?'

I spoke, and he moaned in answer:

'Bad luck and too much wine undid me.
I fell asleep on Circe's roof. Coming down
I missed my step on the long ladder
And fell headfirst. My neck snapped

At the spine and my ghost went down to Hades.
Now I beg you—by those we left behind,
By your wife and the father who reared you,
And by Telemachus, your only son,
Whom you left alone in your halls—
When you put the gloom of Hades behind you
And beach your ship on the Isle of Aeaea,
As I know you will, remember me, my lord.
Do not leave me unburied, unmourned,
When you sail for home, or I might become
A cause of the gods' anger against you.
Burn me with my armor, such as I have,
Heap me a barrow on the grey sea's shore,
In memory of a man whose luck ran out.
Do this for me, and fix in the mound the oar
I rowed with my shipmates while I was alive.'

Thus Elpenor, and I answered him:

'Pitiful spirit, I will do this for you.'

Such were the sad words we exchanged
Sitting by the pit, I on one side holding my sword
Over the blood, my comrade's ghost on the other.

Then came the ghost of my dead mother,
Anticleia, daughter of the hero Autolycus.
She was alive when I left for sacred Ilion.
I wept when I saw her, and pitied her,
But even in my grief I would not allow her
To come near the blood until I had questioned Tiresias.

And then he came, the ghost of Theban Tiresias,
Bearing a golden staff. He knew me and said:

'Odysseus, son of Laertes, master of wiles,
Why have you come, leaving the sunlight
To see the dead and this joyless place?
Move off from the pit and take away your sword,
So I may drink the blood and speak truth to you.'

I drew back and slid my silver-studded sword
Into its sheath. After he had drunk the dark blood
The flawless seer rose and said to me:

'You seek a homecoming sweet as honey,
Shining Odysseus, but a god will make it bitter,
For I do not think you will elude the Earthshaker,
Who has laid up wrath in his heart against you,
Furious because you blinded his son. Still,

You just might get home, though not without pain,
You and your men, if you curb your own spirit,
And theirs, too, when you beach your ship
On Thrinacia. You will be marooned on that island
In the violet sea, and find there the cattle
Of Helios the Sun, and his sheep, too, grazing.
Leave these unharmed, keep your mind on your homecoming,
And you may still reach Ithaca, though not without pain.
But if you harm them, I foretell doom for you,
Your ship, and your crew. And even if you
Yourself escape, you will come home late
And badly, having lost all companions
And in another's ship. And you shall find
Trouble in your house, arrogant men
Devouring your wealth and courting your wife.
Yet vengeance will be yours, and when you have slain
The suitors in your hall, by ruse or by sword,
Then you must go off again, carrying a broad-bladed oar,
Until you come to men who know nothing of the sea,
Who eat their food unsalted, and have never seen
Red-prowed ships or oars that wing them along.
And I will tell you a sure sign that you have found them,
One you cannot miss. When you meet another traveler
Who thinks you are carrying a winnowing fan,
Then you must fix your oar in the earth
And offer sacrifice to Lord Poseidon,
A ram, a bull, and a boar in its prime.
Then return to your home and offer
Perfect sacrifice to the immortal gods
Who hold high heaven, to each in turn.
And death will come to you off the sea,
A death so gentle, and carry you off
When you are worn out in sleek old age,
Your people prosperous all around you.
All this will come true for you as I have told.'

Thus Tiresias. And I answered him:

'All that, Tiresias, is as the gods have spun it.
But tell me this: I see here the ghost
Of my dead mother, sitting in silence
Beside the blood, and she cannot bring herself
To look her son in the eye or speak to him.
How can she recognize me for who I am?'

And Tiresias, the Theban prophet:

'This is easy to tell you. Whoever of the dead
You let come to the blood will speak truly to you.
Whoever you deny will go back again.'

With that, the ghost of Lord Tiresias
Went back into Hades, his soothsaying done.

But I stayed where I was until my mother
Came up and drank the dark blood. At once
She knew me, and her words reached me on wings:

'My child, how did you come to the undergloom
While you are still alive? It is hard for the living
To reach these shores. There are many rivers to cross,
Great bodies of water, nightmarish streams,
And Ocean itself, which cannot be crossed on foot
But only in a well-built ship. Are you still wandering
On your way back from Troy, a long time at sea
With your ship and your men? Have you not yet come
To Ithaca, or seen your wife in your halls?'

So she spoke, and I answered her:

'Mother, I came here because I had to,
To consult the ghost of the prophet Tiresias.
I have not yet come to the coast of Achaea
Or set foot on my own land. I have had nothing
But hard travels from the day I set sail
With Lord Agamemnon to go to Ilion,
Famed for its horses, to fight the Trojans.
But tell me truly, how did you die?
Was it a long illness, or did Artemis
Shoot you suddenly with her gentle arrows?
And tell me about my father and my son,
Whom I left behind. Does the honor I had
Still remain with them, or has it passed
To some other man, and do they all say
I will never return? And what about my wife?
What has she decided, what does she think?
Is she still with my son, keeping things safe?
Or has someone already married her,
Whoever is now the best of the Achaeans?'[3]

So I spoke, and my mother answered at once:

'Oh, yes indeed, she remains in your halls,
Her heart enduring the bitter days and nights.
But the honor that was yours has not passed
To any man. Telemachus holds your lands
Unchallenged, and shares in the feasts
To which all men invite him as the island's lawgiver.
Your father, though, stays out in the fields
And does not come to the city. He has no bed
Piled with bright rugs and soft coverlets
But sleeps in the house where the slaves sleep,
In the ashes by the fire, and wears poor clothes.
In summer and autumn his vineyard's slope

3. Greeks.

Is strewn with beds of leaves on the ground,
Where he lies in his sorrow, nursing his grief,
Longing for your return. His old age is hard.
I died from the same grief. The keen-eyed goddess
Did not shoot me at home with her gentle shafts,
Nor did any long illness waste my body away.
No, it was longing for you, my glorious Odysseus,
For your gentle heart and your gentle ways,
That robbed me of my honey-sweet life.'
So she spoke, and my heart yearned
To embrace the ghost of my dead mother.
Three times I rushed forward to hug her,
And three times she drifted out of my arms
Like a shadow or a dream. The pain
That pierced my heart grew ever sharper,
And my words rose to my mother on wings:

'Mother, why do you slip away when I try
To embrace you? Even though we are in Hades,
Why can't we throw our arms around each other
And console ourselves with chill lamentation?
Are you a phantom sent by Persephone
To make me groan even more in my grief?'

And my mother answered me at once:

'O my child, most ill-fated of men,
It is not that Persephone is deceiving you.
This is the way it is with mortals.
When we die, the sinews no longer hold
Flesh and bones together. The fire destroys these
As soon as the spirit leaves the white bones,
And the ghost flutters off and is gone like a dream.
Hurry now to the light, and remember these things,
So that later you may tell them all to your wife.'

That was the drift of our talk.

Then the women came,
Sent by Persephone, all those who had been
The wives and daughters of the heroes of old.
They flocked together around the dark blood,
But I wanted to question them one at a time.
The best way I could think of to question them
Was to draw the sharp sword from beside my thigh,
And keep them from drinking the blood all at once.
They came up in procession then, and one by one
They declared their birth, and I questioned them all.
The first one I saw was highborn Tyro,
Who said she was born of flawless Salmoneus

And was wed to Cretheus, a son of Aeolus.
She fell in love with a river, divine Enipeus,
The most beautiful of all the rivers on earth,
And she used to play in his lovely streams.
But the Earthshaker took Enipeus' form
And lay with her in the swirling eddies
Near the river's mouth. And an indigo wave,
Towering like a mountain, arched over them
And hid the god and the mortal woman from view.
He unbound the sash that had kept her virgin
And shed sleep upon her. And when the god
Had finished his lovemaking, he took her hand
And called her name softly and said to her:

'Be happy in this love, woman. As the year turns
You will bear glorious children, for a god's embrace
Is never barren. Raise them and care for them.
Now go to your house and say nothing of this,
But I am Poseidon, who makes the earth tremble.'

With that he plunged into the surging sea.
And Tyro conceived and bore Pelias and Neleus,
Who served great Zeus as strong heroes both,
Pelias with his flocks in Iolcus' grasslands,
And Neleus down in sandy Pylos.
She bore other children to Cretheus: Aeson,
Pheres, and the charioteer Amythaon.

Then I saw Antiope, daughter of Asopus,
Who boasted she had slept in the arms of Zeus
And bore two sons, Amphion and Zethus,
Who founded seven-gated Thebes and built its walls,
Since they could not live in the wide land of Thebes
Without walls and towers, mighty though they were.

Next I saw Alcmene, Amphitryon's wife,
Who bore Heracles, the lionhearted battler,
After lying in Zeus' almighty embrace.
And I saw Megara, too, wife of Heracles,
The hero whose strength never wore out.

I saw Oedipus' mother, beautiful Epicaste,
Who unwittingly did a monstrous deed,
Marrying her son, who had killed his father.
The gods soon brought these things to light;
Yet, for all his misery, Oedipus still ruled
In lovely Thebes, by the gods' dark designs.
But Epicaste, overcome by her grief,
Hung a deadly noose from the ceiling rafters
And went down to implacable Hades' realm,

Leaving behind for her son all of the sorrows
A mother's avenging spirits can cause.[4]

And then I saw Chloris, the great beauty
Whom Neleus wedded after courting her
With myriad gifts. She was the youngest daughter
Of Amphion, king of Minyan Orchomenus.
As queen of Pylos, she bore glorious children,
Nestor, Chromius, and lordly Periclymenus,
And magnificent Pero, a wonder to men.
Everyone wanted to marry her, but Neleus
Would only give her to the man who could drive
The cattle of mighty Iphicles to Pylos,
Spiral-horned, broad-browed, stubborn cattle,
Difficult to drive. Only Melampus,
The flawless seer, rose to the challenge,
But he was shackled by Fate. Country herdsmen
Put him in chains, and months went by
And the seasons passed and the year turned
Before he was freed by mighty Iphicles,
After he had told him all of his oracles,
And so the will of Zeus was fulfilled.

I saw Leda also, wife of Tyndareus,
Who bore to him two stout-hearted sons,
Castor the horseman and the boxer Polydeuces.
They are under the teeming earth though alive,
And have honor from Zeus in the world below,
Living and dying on alternate days.
Such is the honor they have won from the gods.

After her I saw Iphimedeia,
Aloeus' wife. She made love to Poseidon
And bore two sons, who did not live long,
Godlike Otus and famed Ephialtes,
The tallest men ever reared upon earth
And the handsomest after gloried Orion.
At nine years old they measured nine cubits
Across the chest, and were nine fathoms tall.
They threatened to wage a furious war
Against the immortal Olympian gods,
And were bent on piling Ossa on Olympus,
And forested Pelion on top of Ossa
And so reach the sky. And they would have done it,
But the son of Zeus and fair-haired Leto
Destroyed them both before the down blossomed
Upon their cheeks and their beards had come in.

And I saw Phaedra and Procnis
And lovely Ariadne, whom Theseus once

4. This passage gives a version of the myth different from that of Sophocles' play, in which Oedipus's mother is called Jocasta.

Tried to bring from Crete to sacred Athens
But had no joy of her. Artemis first
Shot her on Dia, the seagirt island,
After Dionysus told her he saw her there.[5]

And I saw Maera and Clymene
And hateful Eriphyle, who valued gold
More than her husband's life.[6]
But I could not tell you
All the wives and daughters of heroes I saw.
It would take all night. And it is time
To sleep now, either aboard ship with the crew
Or here in this house. My journey home
Is up to you, and to the immortal gods."

He paused, and they sat hushed in silence,
Spellbound throughout the shadowy hall.
And then white-armed Arete began to speak:

"Well, Phaeacians, does this man impress you
With his looks, stature, and well-balanced mind?
He is my guest, moreover, though each of you
Shares in that honor. Do not send him off, then,
Too hastily, and do not stint your gifts
To one in such need. You have many treasures
Stored in your halls by grace of the gods."

Then the old hero Echeneus spoke up:

"Friends, the words of our wise queen
Are not wide of the mark. Give them heed.
But upon Alcinous depend both word and deed."

And Alcinous answered:

"Arete's word will stand, as long as I live
And rule the Phaeacians who love the oar.
But let our guest, though he longs to go home,
Endure until tomorrow, until I have time
To make our gift complete. We all have a stake
In getting him home, but mine is greatest,
For mine is the power throughout the land."

And Odysseus, who missed nothing:

5. In other versions of the myth, Ariadne was abandoned by Theseus on the island of Naxos and rescued by Dionysus, god of wine.

6. Bribed with the necklace of Harmonia, she persuaded her husband, Amphrarus, to join the attack on Thebes, although she knew he would die.

"Lord Alcinous, most renowned of men,
You could ask me to stay for even a year
While you arranged a send-off with glorious gifts,
And I would assent. Better far to return
With a fuller hand to my own native land.
I would be more respected and loved by all
Who saw me come back to Ithaca."

Alcinous answered him:

"Odysseus, we do not take you
For the sort of liar and cheat the dark earth breeds
Among men everywhere, telling tall tales
No man could ever test for himself.
Your words have outward grace and wisdom within,
And you have told your tale with the skill of a bard—
All that the Greeks and you yourself have suffered.
But tell me this, as accurately as you can:
Did you see any of your godlike comrades
Who went with you to Troy and met their fate there?
The night is young—and magical. It is not yet time
To sleep in the hall. Tell me these wonders.
Sit in our hall and tell us of your woes
For as long as you can bear. I could listen until dawn."

And Odysseus, his mind teeming:

"Lord Alcinous, most glorious of men,
There is a time for words and a time for sleep.
But if you still yearn to listen, I will not refuse
To tell you of other things more pitiable still,
The woes of my comrades who died after the war,
Who escaped the Trojans and their battle-cry
But died on their return through a woman's evil.

When holy Persephone had scattered
The women's ghosts, there came the ghost
Of Agamemnon, son of Atreus,
Distraught with grief. Around him were gathered
Those who died with him in Aegisthus' house.
He knew me as soon as he drank the dark blood.
He cried out shrilly, tears welling in his eyes,
And he stretched out his hands, trying to touch me,
But he no longer had anything left of the strength
He had in the old days in those muscled limbs.
I wept when I saw him, and with pity in my heart
I spoke to him these winged words:

'Son of Atreus, king of men, most glorious
Agamemnon—what death laid you low?
Did Poseidon sink your fleet at sea,
After hitting you hard with hurricane winds?
Or were you killed by enemy forces on land,

As you raided their cattle and flocks of sheep
Or fought to capture their city and women?'

And Agamemnon answered at once:

'Son of Laertes in the line of Zeus,
My crafty Odysseus—No,
Poseidon did not sink my fleet at sea
After hitting us hard with hurricane winds,
Nor was I killed by enemy forces on land.
Aegisthus was the cause of my death.
He killed me with the help of my cursed wife
After inviting me to a feast in his house,
Slaughtered me like a bull at a manger.
So I died a most pitiable death,
And all around me my men were killed
Relentlessly, like white-tusked swine
For a wedding banquet or dinner party
In the house of a rich and powerful man.
You have seen many men cut down, both
In single combat and in the crush of battle,
But your heart would have grieved
As never before at the sight of us lying
Around the wine-bowl and the laden tables
In that great hall. The floor steamed with blood.
But the most piteous cry I ever heard
Came from Cassandra, Priam's daughter.[7]
She had her arms around me down on the floor
When Clytemnestra ran her through from behind.
I lifted my hands and beat the ground
As I lay dying with a sword in my chest,
But that bitch, my wife, turned her back on me
And would not shut my eyes or close my lips
As I was going down to Death. Nothing
Is more grim or more shameless than a woman
Who sets her mind on such an unspeakable act
As killing her own husband. I was sure
I would be welcomed home by my children
And all my household, but she, with her mind set
On stark horror, has shamed not only herself
But all women to come, even the rare good one.'

Thus Agamemnon, and I responded:

'Ah, how broad-browed Zeus has persecuted
The house of Atreus from the beginning,
Through the will of women. Many of us died
For Helen's sake, and Clytemnestra
Set a snare for you while you were far away.'[8]

7. Cassandra, who had the gift of prophecy from Apollo, was brought back from Troy as a prize of war by Agamemnon.

8. Helen and Clytemnestra were sisters.

And Agamemnon answered me at once:

'So don't go easy on your own wife either,
Or tell her everything you know.
Tell her some things, but keep some hidden.
But your wife will not bring about your death,
Odysseus. Icarius' daughter,
Your wise Penelope, is far too prudent.
She was newly wed when we went to war.
We left her with a baby boy still at the breast,
Who must by now be counted as a man,
And prosperous. His father will see him
When he comes, and he will embrace his father,
As is only right. But my wife did not let me
Even fill my eyes with the sight of my son.
She killed me before I could do even that.
But let me tell you something, Odysseus:
Beach your ship secretly when you come home.
Women just can't be trusted any more.
And one more thing. Tell me truthfully
If you've heard anything about my son
And where he is living, perhaps in Orchomenus,
Or in sandy Pylos, or with Menelaus in Sparta.
For Orestes has not yet perished from the earth.'

So he spoke, and I answered him:

'Son of Atreus, why ask me this?
I have no idea whether he is alive or dead,
And it is not good to speak words empty as wind.'

Such were the sad words we had for each other
As we stood there weeping, heavy with grief.

Then came the ghost of Achilles,[9] son of Peleus,
And those of Patroclus and peerless Antilochus
And Ajax,[1] who surpassed all the Danaans,
Except Achilles, in looks and build.
Aeacus' incomparable grandson, Achilles, knew me,
And when he spoke his words had wings:

'Son of Laertes in the line of Zeus,
Odysseus, you hard rover, not even you
Can ever top this, this bold foray
Into Hades, home of the witless dead
And the dim phantoms of men outworn.'

So he spoke, and I answered him:

9. Best of the Greek heroes, prominent character in the *Iliad*.

1. Strong Greek hero known for defensive fighting.

'Achilles, by far the mightiest of the Achaeans,
I have come here to consult Tiresias,
To see if he has any advice for me
On how I might get back to rugged Ithaca.
I've had nothing but trouble, and have not yet set foot
On my native land. But no man, Achilles,
Has ever been as blessed as you, or ever will be.
While you were alive the army honored you
Like a god, and now that you are here
You rule the dead with might. You should not
Lament your death at all, Achilles.'

I spoke, and he answered me at once:

'Don't try to sell me on death, Odysseus.
I'd rather be a hired hand back up on earth,
Slaving away for some poor dirt farmer,
Than lord it over all these withered dead.
But tell me about that boy of mine.
Did he come to the war and take his place
As one of the best? Or did he stay away?
And what about Peleus? What have you heard?
Is he still respected among the Myrmidons,
Or do they dishonor him in Phthia and Hellas,
Crippled by old age in hand and foot?
And I'm not there for him up in the sunlight
With the strength I had in wide Troy once
When I killed Ilion's best and saved the army.
Just let me come with that kind of strength
To my father's house, even for an hour,
And wrap my hands around his enemies' throats.
They would learn what it means to face my temper.'

Thus Achilles, and I answered him:

'I have heard nothing of flawless Peleus,
But as for your son, Neoptolemus,
I'll tell you all I know, just as you ask.
I brought him over from Scyros myself,
In a fine vessel, to join the Greek army
At Troy, and every time we held council there,
He was always the first to speak, and his words
Were never off the mark. Godlike Nestor and I
Alone surpassed him. And every time we fought
On Troy's plain, he never held back in the ranks
But charged ahead to the front, yielding
To no one, and he killed many in combat.
I could not begin to name them all,
All the men he killed when he fought for us,
But what a hero he dismantled in Telephus' son,

Eurypylus, dispatching him and a crowd
Of his Ceteian compatriots. Eurypylus
Came to Troy because Priam bribed his mother.
After Memnon, I've never seen a handsomer man.
And then, too, when all our best climbed
Into the wooden horse Epeius made,
And I was in command and controlled the trapdoor,
All the other Danaan leaders and counselors
Were wiping away tears from their eyes
And their legs shook beneath them, but I never saw
Neoptolemus blanch or wipe away a tear.
No, he just sat there handling his sword hilt
And heavy bronze spear, and all he wanted
Was to get out of there and give the Trojans hell.
And after we had sacked Priam's steep city,
He boarded his ship with his share of the loot
And more for valor. And not a scratch on him.
He never took a hit from a spear or sword
In close combat, where wounds are common.
When Ares rages anyone can be hit.'

So I spoke, and the ghost of swift-footed Achilles
Went off with huge strides through the fields of asphodel,
Filled with joy at his son's preeminence.

The other ghosts crowded around in sorrow,
And each asked about those who were dear to him.
Only the ghost of Telamonian Ajax
Stood apart, still furious with me
Because I had defeated him in the contest at Troy
To decide who would get Achilles' armor.
His goddess mother had put it up as a prize,
And the judges were the sons of the Trojans
And Pallas Athena. I wish I had never won.
That contest buried Ajax, that brave heart,
The best of the Danaans in looks and deeds,
After the incomparable son of Peleus.
I tried to win him over with words like these:

'Ajax, son of flawless Telamon,
Are you to be angry with me even in death
Over that accursed armor? The gods
Must have meant it to be the ruin of the Greeks.
We lost a tower of strength to that armor.
We mourn your loss as we mourn the loss
Of Achilles himself. Zeus alone
Is to blame. He persecuted the Greeks
Terribly, and he brought you to your doom.
No, come back, Lord Ajax, and listen!
Control your wrath and rein in your proud spirit.'

I spoke, but he said nothing. He went his way
To Erebus, to join the other souls of the dead.
He might yet have spoken to me there, or I
Might yet have spoken to him, but my heart
Yearned to see the other ghosts of the dead.

There I saw Minos,[2] Zeus' glorious son,
Scepter in hand, judging the dead
As he sat in the wide-gated house of Hades;
And the dead sat, too, and asked him for judgments.

And then Orion[3] loomed up before me,
Driving over the fields of asphodel
The beasts he had slain in the lonely hills,
In his hands a bronze club, forever unbroken.

And I saw Tityos, a son of glorious Earth,
Lying on the ground, stretched over nine acres,
And two vultures sat on either side of him
And tore at his liver, plunging their beaks
Deep into his guts, and he could not beat them off.
For Tityos had raped Leto, a consort of Zeus,
As she went to Pytho through lovely Panopeus.

And I saw Tantalus there in his agony,
Standing in a pool with water up to his chin.
He was mad with thirst, but unable to drink,
For every time the old man bent over
The water would drain away and vanish,
Dried up by some god, and only black mud
Would be left at his feet. Above him dangled
Treetop fruits, pears and pomegranates,
Shiny apples, sweet figs, and luscious olives.
But whenever Tantalus reached up for them,
The wind tossed them high to the shadowy clouds.

And I saw Sisyphus there in his agony,
Pushing a monstrous stone with his hands.
Digging in hard, he would manage to shove it
To the crest of a hill, but just as he was about
To heave it over the top, the shameless stone
Would teeter back and bound down to the plain.
Then he would strain every muscle to push it back up,
Sweat pouring from his limbs and dusty head.

And then mighty Heracles loomed up before me—
His phantom that is, for Heracles himself

2. Son of Zeus and Europa; he became judge of the dead.

3. Famous hunter.

Feasts with the gods and has as his wife
Beautiful Hebe,[4] daughter of great Zeus
And gold-sandaled Hera. As he moved
A clamor arose from the dead around him,
As if they were birds flying off in terror.
He looked like midnight itself. He held his bow
With an arrow on the string, and he glared around him
As if he were always about to shoot. His belt,
A baldric of gold crossing his chest,
Was stark horror, a phantasmagoria
Of Bears, and wild Boars, and green-eyed Lions,
Of Battles, and Bloodshed, Murder and Mayhem.
May this be its maker's only masterpiece,
And may there never again be another like it.
Heracles recognized me at once,
And his words beat down on me like dark wings:

'Son of Laertes in the line of Zeus,
Crafty Odysseus—poor man, do you too
Drag out a wretched destiny
Such as I once bore under the rays of the sun?
I was a son of Zeus and grandson of Cronus,
But I had immeasurable suffering,
Enslaved to a man who was far less than I
And who laid upon me difficult labors.[5]
Once he even sent me here, to fetch
The Hound of Hell,[6] for he could devise
No harder task for me than this. That hound
I carried out of the house of Hades,
With Hermes and grey-eyed Athena as guides.'

And Heracles went back into the house of Hades.
But I stayed where I was, in case any more
Of the heroes of yesteryear might yet come forth.
And I would have seen some of them—
Heroes I longed to meet, Theseus and Peirithous,[7]
Glorious sons of the gods—but before I could,
The nations of the dead came thronging up
With an eerie cry, and I turned pale with fear
That Persephone would send from Hades' depths
The pale head of that monster, the Gorgon.[8]

4. Hebe means "youth."
5. Eurystheus, at the behest of the goddess Hera, laid the labors on Heracles, whom she resented as an illegitimate son of her husband, Zeus.
6. Cerberus, guard dog of the underworld.
7. A son of Poseidon, Theseus was a mythic king of Athens and killer of the Minotaur. Peirithous was his best friend, a son of Zeus; together they went to the underworld, hoping to abduct Persephone.
8. Female monster whose gaze turns onlookers to stone.

I went to the ship at once and called to my men
To get aboard and untie the stern cables.
They boarded quickly and sat at their benches.
The current bore the ship down the River Ocean.
We rowed at first, and then caught a good tailwind."

BOOK XII

"Our ship left the River Ocean
And came to the swell of the open sea
And the Island of Aeaea,
Where Dawn has her dancing grounds
And the Sun his risings. We beached our ship
On the sand, disembarked, and fell asleep
On the shore, waiting for daybreak.

Light blossomed like roses in the eastern sky,
And I sent some men to the house of Circe
To bring back the body of Elpenor.
We cut wood quickly, and on the headland's point
We held a funeral, shedding warm tears.
When the body was burned, and the armor with it,
We heaped up a mound, dragged a stone onto it,
And on the tomb's very top we planted his oar.

While we were busy with these things,
Circe, aware that we had come back
From the Underworld, put on her finest clothes
And came to see us. Her serving women
Brought meat, bread, and bright red wine,
And the goddess shone with light as she spoke:

'So you went down alive to Hades' house.
Most men die only once, but you twice.
Come, though, eat and drink wine
The whole day through. You sail at dawn.
I will tell you everything on your route,
So that you will not come to grief
In some web of evil on land or sea.'

She spoke, and our proud hearts consented.
All day long until the sun went down
We sat feasting on meat and good red wine.
When the sun set and darkness came on
My men went to sleep beside the ship's stern-cables.
But Circe took me by the hand and had me sit
Away from my men. And she lay down beside me
And asked me about everything. I told her all
Just as it happened, and then the goddess spoke:

'So all that is done. But now listen
To what I will tell you. One day a god

Will remind you of it. First, you will come
To the Sirens, who bewitch all men
Who come near. Anyone who approaches
Unaware and hears their voice will never again
Be welcomed home by wife and children
Dancing with joy at his return—
Not after the Sirens bewitch him with song.
They loll in a meadow, and around them are piled
The bones of shriveled and moldering bodies.
Row past them, first kneading sweet wax
And smearing it into the ears of your crew
So they cannot hear. But if you yourself
Have a mind to listen, have them bind you
Hand and foot upright in the mast-step
And tie the ends of the rope to the mast.
Then you can enjoy the song of the Sirens.
If you command your crew and plead with them
To release you, they should tie you up tighter.
After your men have rowed past the Sirens,
I will not prescribe which of two ways to go.
You yourself must decide. I will tell you both.

'One route takes you past beetling crags
Pounded by blue-eyed Amphitrítê's seas.
The blessed gods call these the Wandering Rocks.
Not even birds can wing their way through.
Even the doves that bring ambrosia to Zeus
Crash and perish on that slick stone,
And the Father has to replenish their numbers.
Ships never get through. Whenever one tries,
The sea is awash with timbers and bodies
Blasted by the waves and the fiery winds.
Only one ship has ever passed through,
The famous Argo as she sailed from Aeetes,
And even she would have been hurled onto those crags
Had not Hera loved Jason and sent his ship through.[9]

'On the other route there are two rocks.
One stabs its peak into the sky
And is ringed by a dark blue cloud. This cloud
Never melts, and the air is never clear
During summer or autumn. No mortal man
Could ever scale this rock, not even if he had
Twenty hands and feet. The stone is as smooth
As if it were polished. Halfway up the cliff
Is a misty cave facing the western gloom.
It is there you will sail your hollow ship

9. The Greek hero Jason went in the world's first ship, the *Argo*, to get the Golden Fleece from Aeetes, king of Colchis; the goddess Hera helped him get home.

If you listen to me, glorious Odysseus.
The strongest archer could not shoot an arrow
Up from his ship all the way to the cave,
Which is the lair of Scylla. She barks and yelps
Like a young puppy, but she is a monster,
An evil monster that not even a god
Would be glad to see. She has—listen to this—
Twelve gangly legs and six very long necks,
And on each neck is perched a bloodcurdling head,
Each with three rows of close-set teeth
Full of black death. Up to her middle
She is concealed in the cave, but her heads dangle
Into the abyss, and she fishes by the rock
For dolphins and seals or other large creatures
That the moaning sea breeds in multitudes.
No crew can boast to have sailed past Scylla
Unscathed. With each head she carries off a man,
Snatching him out of his dark-prowed vessel.

'The other rock, as you will see, Odysseus,
Lies lower—the two are close enough
That you could shoot an arrow across—
And on this rock is a large, leafy fig tree.
Beneath this tree the divine Charybdis
Sucks down the black water. Three times a day
She belches it out and three times a day
She sucks it down horribly. Don't be there
When she sucks it down. No one could save you,
Not even Poseidon, who makes the earth tremble.
No, stay close to Scylla's rock, and push hard.
Better to mourn six than the whole crew at once.'

Thus Circe. And I, in a panic:

'I beg you, goddess, tell me, is there
Any way I can escape from Charybdis
And still protect my men from the other?'

And the goddess, in a nimbus of light:

'There you go again, always the hero.
Won't you yield even to the immortals?
She's not mortal, she's an immortal evil,
Dread, dire, ferocious, unfightable.
There is no defense. It's flight, not fight.
If you pause so much as to put on a helmet
She'll attack again with just as many heads
And kill just as many men as before.

Just row past as hard as you can. And call upon
Crataiïs, the mother who bore her as a plague to men.
She will stop her from attacking a second time.

'Then you will come to Thrinacia,
An island that pastures the cattle of the Sun,
Seven herds of cattle and seven flocks of sheep,
Fifty in each. They are immortal.
They bear no young and they never die off,
And their shepherds are goddesses,
Nymphs with gorgeous hair, Phaethusa
And Lampetiê, whom gleaming Neaera
Bore to Helios, Hyperion the Sun.[1]
When she had borne them and reared them
She sent them to Thrinacia, to live far away
And keep their father's spiral-horned cattle.
If you leave these unharmed and keep your mind
On your journey, you might yet struggle home
To Ithaca. But if you harm them, I foretell
Disaster for your ship and crew, and even if you
Escape yourself, you shall come home late
And badly, having lost all your companions.'

Dawn rose in gold as she finished speaking,
And light played about her as she disappeared
Up the island.
I went to the ship
And got my men going. They loosened
The stern cables and were soon in their benches,
Beating the water white with their oars.
A following wind rose in the wake
Of our dark-prowed ship, a sailor's breeze
Sent by Circe, that dread, beautiful goddess.
We tied down the tackling and sat tight,
Letting the wind and the helmsman take over.

Then I made a heavy-hearted speech to my men:

'Friends, it is not right that one or two alone
Should know what the goddess Circe foretold.
Better we should all know, live or die.
We may still beat death and get out of this alive.
First, she told us to avoid the eerie voices
Of the Sirens and sail past their soft meadows.
She ordered me alone to listen. Bind me
Hand and foot upright in the mast-step
And tie the ends of the rope to the mast.
If I command you and plead with you
To release me, just tie me up tighter.'

1. Helios and Hyperion are both sun gods, here confused.

Those were my instructions to the crew.

Meanwhile, our good ship was closing fast
On the Sirens' island, when the breeze we'd had
Tailed off, and we were becalmed—not a breath

Of wind left—some spirit lulled the waves.
My men got up and furled the sails,
Stowed them in the ship's hold, then sat down
At their oars and whitened the water with pine.
Myself, I got out a wheel of wax, cut it up
With my sharp knife, and kneaded the pieces
Until they were soft and warm, a quick job
With Lord Helios glaring down from above.
Then I went down the rows and smeared the wax
Into all my men's ears. They in turn bound me
Hand and foot upright to the mast,
Tied the ends of the rope to the mast, and then
Sat down and beat the sea white with their oars.
We were about as far away as a shout would carry,
Surging ahead, when the Sirens saw our ship
Looming closer, and their song pierced the air:

'Come hither, Odysseus,
  glory of the Achaeans,
Stop your ship
  so you can hear our voices.
No one has ever sailed
  his black ship past here
Without listening to the honeyed
  sound from our lips.
He journeys on delighted
  and knows more than before.
For we know everything
  that the Greeks and Trojans
Suffered in wide Troy
  by the will of the gods.
We know all that happens
  on the teeming earth.'

They made their beautiful voices carry,
And my heart yearned to listen. I ordered my men
To untie me, signaling with my brows,
But they just leaned on their oars and rowed on.
Perimedes and Eurylochus jumped up,
Looped more rope around me, and pulled tight.
When we had rowed past, and the Sirens' song
Had faded on the waves, only then did my crew
Take the wax from their ears and untie me.

We had no sooner left the island when I saw
The spray from an enormous wave

And heard its booming. The oars flew
From my men's frightened hands
And shirred in the waves, stopping the ship
Dead in the water. I went down the rows
And tried to boost the crew's morale:

'Come on, men, this isn't the first time
We've run into trouble. This can't be worse
Than when the Cyclops with his brute strength
Had us penned in his cave. We got out
By my courage and fast thinking. One day
We'll look back on this. Now let's do as I say,
Every man of you! Stay on your benches
And beat the deep surf with your oars!
Zeus may yet deliver us from death.
Helmsman, here's my command to you,
And make sure you remember it, since
You're steering this vessel: Keep the ship
Away from this heavy surf. Hug the cliff,
Or before you know it she'll swerve
To starboard and you'll send us all down.'

I spoke, they obeyed. But I didn't mention
Scylla. There was nothing we could do about that,
And I didn't want the crew to freeze up,
Stop rowing, and huddle together in the hold.
Then I forgot Circe's stern warning
Not to arm myself no matter what happened.
I strapped on my bronze, grabbed two long spears
And went to the foredeck, where I thought
Scylla would first show herself from the cliff.
But I couldn't see her anywhere, and my eyes
Grew weary scanning the misty rock face.

We sailed on up the narrow channel, wailing,
Scylla on one side, Charybdis on the other
Sucking down saltwater. When she belched it up
She seethed and bubbled like a boiling cauldron
And the spray would reach the tops of the cliffs.
When she sucked it down you could see her
Churning within, and the rock bellowed
And roared, and you could see the sea floor
Black with sand. My men were pale with fear.
While we looked at her, staring death in the eyes,
Scylla seized six of my men from our ship,
The six strongest hands aboard. Turning my eyes
To the deck and my crew, I saw above me
Their hands and feet as they were raised aloft.
They cried down to me, calling me by name
That one last time in their agony.

You know
How a fisherman on a jutting rock
Casts his bait with his long pole. The horned hook
Sinks into the sea, and when he catches a fish
He pulls it writhing and squirming out of the water.
Writhing like that my men were drawn up the cliff.
And Scylla devoured them at her door, as they shrieked
And stretched their hands down to me
In their awful struggle. Of all the things
That I have borne while I scoured the seas,
I have seen nothing more pitiable.

When we had fled Charybdis, the rocks,
And Scylla, we came to the perfect island
Of Hyperion the Sun, where his herds ranged
And his flocks browsed. While our black ship
Was still out at sea I could hear the bleating
Of the sheep and the lowing of the cattle
As they were being penned, and I remembered
The words of the blind seer, Theban Tiresias,
And of Circe, who gave me strict warnings
To shun the island of the warmth-giving Sun.
And so I spoke to my crew with heavy heart:

'Hear my words, men, for all your pain.
So I can tell you Tiresias' prophecies
And Circe's, too, who gave me strict warnings
To shun the island of the warmth-giving Sun,
For there she said was our gravest peril.
No, row our black ship clear of this island.'

This broke their spirits, and at once
Eurylochus answered me spitefully:

'You're a hard man, Odysseus, stronger
Than other men, and you never wear out,
A real iron-man, who won't allow his crew,
Dead tired from rowing and lack of sleep,
To set foot on shore, where we might make
A meal we could enjoy. No, you just order us
To wander on through the swift darkness
Over the misty deep, and be driven away
From the island. It is at night that winds rise
That wreck ships. How could we survive
If we were hit by a South Wind or a West,
Which sink ships no matter what the great gods want?
No, let's give in to black night now
And make our supper. We'll stay by the ship,
Board her in the morning, and put out to sea.'

Thus Eurylochus, and the others agreed.
I knew then that some god had it in for us,
And my words had wings:

'Eurylochus,
It's all of you against me alone. All right,
But swear me a great oath, every last man:
If we find any cattle or sheep on this island,
No man will kill a single cow or sheep
In his recklessness, but will be content
To eat the food immortal Circe gave us.'

They swore they would do just as I said,
And when they had finished the words of the oath,
We moored our ship in a hollow harbor
Near a sweet-water spring. The crew disembarked
And skillfully prepared their supper.
When they had their fill of food and drink,
They fell to weeping, remembering how Scylla
Had snatched their shipmates and devoured them.
Sweet sleep came upon them as they wept.
Past midnight, when the stars had wheeled around,
Zeus gathered the clouds and roused a great wind
Against us, an ungodly tempest that shrouded
Land and sea and blotted out the night sky.
At the first blush of Dawn we hauled our ship up
And made her fast in a cave where you could see
The nymphs' beautiful seats and dancing places.
Then I called my men together and spoke to them:

'Friends, there is food and drink in the ship.
Let's play it safe and keep our hands
Off those cattle, which belong to Helios,
A dread god who hears and sees all.'

So I spoke, and their proud hearts consented.

Then for a full month the South Wind blew,
And no other wind but the East and the South.
As long as my men had grain and red wine
They didn't touch the cattle—life was still worth living.
But when all the rations from the ship were gone,
They had to roam around in search of game—
Hunting for birds and whatever they could catch
With fishing hooks. Hunger gnawed at their bellies.

I went off by myself up the island
To pray to the gods to show me the way.
When I had put some distance between myself
And the crew, and found a spot
Sheltered from the wind, I washed my hands

And prayed to the gods, but all they did
Was close my eyelids in sleep.

Meanwhile,
Eurylochus was giving bad advice to the crew:

'Listen to me, shipmates, despite your distress.
All forms of death are hateful, but to die
Of hunger is the most wretched way to go.
What are we waiting for? Let's drive off
The prime beef in that herd and offer sacrifice
To the gods of broad heaven. If we ever
Return to Ithaca, we will build a rich temple
To Hyperion the Sun, and deposit there
Many fine treasures. If he becomes angry
Over his cattle and gets the other gods' consent
To destroy our ship, well, I would rather
Gulp down saltwater and die once and for all
Than waste away slowly on a desert island.'

Thus Eurylochus, and the others agreed.
In no time they had driven off the best
Of Helios' cattle, pretty, spiral-horned cows
That were grazing close to our dark-prowed ship.
They surrounded these cows and offered prayers
To the gods, plucking off tender leaves
From a high-crowned oak in lieu of white barley,
Of which there was none aboard our benched ship.
They said their prayers, cut the cows' throats,
Flayed the animals and carved out the thigh joints,
Wrapped these in a double layer of fat
And laid all the raw bits upon them.
They had no wine to pour over the sacrifice
And so used water as they roasted the entrails.
When the thighs were burned and the innards tasted,
They carved up the rest and skewered it on spits.

That's when I awoke, bolting upright.
I started down to the shore, and as I got near the ship
The aroma of sizzling fat drifted up to me.
I groaned and cried out to the undying gods:

'Father Zeus, and you other immortals,
You lulled me to sleep—and to my ruin—
While my men committed this monstrous crime!'

Lampetiê rushed in her long robes to Helios
And told him that we had killed his cattle.
Furious, the Sun God addressed the immortals:

'Father Zeus, and you other gods eternal,
Punish Odysseus' companions, who have insolently
Killed the cattle I took delight in seeing
Whenever I ascended the starry heaven
And whenever I turned back from heaven to earth.
If they don't pay just atonement for the cows
I will sink into Hades and shine on the dead.'

And Zeus, who masses the clouds, said:

'Helios, you go on shining among the gods
And for mortal men on the grain-giving earth.
I will soon strike their ship with sterling lightning
And shatter it to bits on the wine-purple sea.'

All this I heard from rich-haired Calypso,
Who said she heard it from Hermes the Guide.

When I reached the ship I chewed out my men,
Giving each one an earful. But there was nothing
We could do. The cattle were already dead.
Then the gods showed some portents
Directed at my men. The hides crawled,
And the meat, both roasted and raw,
Mooed on the spits, like cattle lowing.

Each day for six days my men slaughtered oxen
From Helios' herd and gorged on the meat.
But when Zeus brought the seventh day,
The wind tailed off from gale force.
We boarded ship at once and put out to sea
As soon as we had rigged the mast and sail.
When we left the island behind, there was
No other land in sight, only sea and sky.
Then Zeus put a black cloud over our ship
And the sea grew dark beneath it. She ran on
A little while, and then the howling West Wind
Blew in with hurricane force. It snapped
Both forestays, and the mast fell backward
Into the bilge with all of its tackle.
On its way down the mast struck the helmsman
And crushed his skull. He fell from the stern
Like a diver, and his proud soul left his bones.
In the same instant, Zeus thundered
And struck the ship with a lightning bolt.
She shivered from stem to stern and was filled
With sulfurous smoke. My men went overboard,
Bobbing in the waves like sea crows
Around the black ship, their day of return
Snuffed out by the Sun God.
I kept pacing the deck until the sea surge

Tore the sides from the keel. The waves
Drove the bare keel on and snapped the mast
From its socket; the leather backstay
Was still attached, and I used this to lash
The keel to the mast. Perched on these timbers
I was swept along by deathly winds.

Then the West Wind died down,
And, to my horror, the South Wind rose.
All that way, back to the whirlpool,
I was swept along the whole night through
And at dawn reached Scylla's cliff
And dread Charybdis. She was sucking down
Seawater, and I leapt up
To the tall fig tree, grabbed hold of it
And hung on like a bat. I could not
Plant my feet or get myself set on the tree
Because its roots spread far below
And its branches were high overhead,
Long, thick limbs that shaded Charybdis.
I just grit my teeth and hung on
Until she spat out the mast and keel again.
It seemed like forever. Finally,
About the hour a man who has spent the day
Judging quarrels that young men bring to him
Rises from the marketplace and goes to dinner,
My ship's timbers surfaced again from Charybdis.
I let go with my hands and feet
And hit the water hard beyond the spars.
Once aboard, I rowed away with my hands.
As for Scylla, Zeus never let her see me,
Or I would have been wiped out completely.

I floated on for nine days. On the tenth night
The gods brought me to Ogygia
And to Calypso, the dread, beautiful goddess,
Who loved me and took care of me.
But I have told that tale only yesterday,
Here in your hall, to yourself and your wife,
And I wouldn't bore you by telling it again."

BOOK XIII

Odysseus finished his story,
And they were all spellbound, hushed
To silence throughout the shadowy hall,
Until Alcinous found his voice and said:

"Odysseus, now that you have come to my house,
High-roofed and founded on bronze, I do not think

You will be blown off course again
Before reaching home.
Hear now my command,
All who drink the glowing wine of Elders
Daily in my halls and hear the harper sing:
Clothes for our guest lie in a polished sea-chest,
Along with richly wrought gold and all the other gifts
The Phaeacian lords have brought to the palace.
But now each man of us gives him a cauldron, too.
We will recoup ourselves later with a general tax.
It is hard to make such generous gifts alone."

They were all pleased with what Alcinous said.
Each man went to his own house to sleep,
And when Dawn's rosy fingers appeared in the sky
They hurried to the ship with their gifts of bronze.
Alcinous, the sacred king himself, went on board
And stowed them away beneath the benches
Where they would not hinder the rowers' efforts.
Then they all went back to feast in the palace.

In their honor Alcinous sacrificed an ox
To Zeus, the Dark Cloud, who rules over all.
They roasted the haunches and feasted gloriously
While the godlike harper, honored Demodocus,
Sang in their midst.
But Odysseus
Kept turning his head toward the shining sun,
Urging it down the sky. He longed to set forth.

A man who has been in the fields all day
With his wooden plow and wine-faced oxen
Longs for supper and welcomes the sunset
That sends him homeward with weary knees.

So welcome to Odysseus was the evening sun.
As soon as it set he addressed the Phaeacians,
Alcinous especially, and his words had wings:

"Lord Alcinous, I bid you and your people
To pour libation and send me safely on my way.
And I bid you farewell. All is now here
That my heart has desired—passage home
And cherished gifts that the gods in heaven
Have blessed me with. When I reach home
May I find my wife and loved ones unharmed.
May you enjoy your wife and children here,

May the gods send you everything good,
And may harm never come to your island people."

They all cheered this speech, and demanded
That the stranger and guest be given passage home.
Alcinous then nodded to his herald:

"Pontonous, mix a bowl of wine and serve
Cups to all, that we may pray to Lord Zeus
And send our guest to his own native land."

Thus the King, and Pontonous mixed
The mellow-hearted wine and served it to all.
Still seated, they tipped their cups to the gods
Who possess wide heaven. Then Odysseus
Stood up and placed a two-handled cup
In Arete's hands, and his words rose on wings:

"Be well, my queen, all of your days, until age
And death come to you, as they come to all.
I am leaving now. But you, Lady—enjoy this house,
Your children, your people, and Lord Alcinous."

And godlike Odysseus stepped over the threshold.
Alcinous sent a herald along
To guide him to the shore and the swift ship there,
And Arete sent serving women with him,
One carrying a cloak and laundered shirt,
And another to bring the strong sea-chest.
A third brought along bread and red wine.
They came down to the sea, and the ship's crew
Stowed all these things away in the hold,
The food and drink, too. Then they spread out
A rug and a linen sheet on the stern deck
For Odysseus to sleep upon undisturbed.
He climbed on board and lay down in silence
While they took their places upon the benches
And untied the cable from the anchor stone.
As soon as they dipped their oars in the sea,
A deep sleep fell on his eyelids, a sleep
Sound, and sweet, and very much like death.

And as four yoked stallions spring all together
Beneath the lash, leaping high,
And then eat up the dusty road on the plain,

So lifted the keel of that ship, and in her wake
An indigo wave hissed and roiled

As she ran straight ahead. Not even a falcon,
Lord of the skies, could have matched her pace,
So light her course as she cut through the waves,
Bearing a man with a mind like the gods',
A man who had suffered deep in his heart,
Enduring men's wars and the bitter sea—
But now he slept, his sorrows forgotten.

The sea turned silver
Under the star that precedes the dawn,
And the great ship pulled up to Ithaca.

Phorcys,[2] the Old Man of the Sea,
Has a harbor there. Two fingers of rock
Curl out from the island, steep to seaward
But sloping down to the bay they protect
From hurricane winds and high waves outside.
Inside, ships can ride without anchor
In the still water offshore.
At the harbor's head a slender-leaved olive
Stands near a cave glimmering through the mist
And sacred to the nymphs called Naiades.[3]
Inside are bowls and jars of stone
Where bees store honey, and long stone looms
Where the nymphs weave shrouds as dark as the sea.
Waters flow there forever, and there are two doors,
One toward the North Wind, by which humans
Go down, the other toward the South Wind,
A door for the gods. No men enter there:
It is the Way of Immortals.

The Phaeacians
Had been here before. In they rowed,
And with such force that their ship was propelled
Half of its length onto the shelving shore.
The crew disembarked, lifting Odysseus
Out of the ship—sheet, carpet, and all—
And laying him down, sound asleep, on the sand.
Then they hauled from the ship all of the goods
The Phaeacian lords had given him
As he was going home—all thanks to Athena.
They piled these together near the bole of the olive,
Away from the path, fearing that someone
Might come along before Odysseus awoke
And rob him blind.

Then the Phaeacians went home.
But the Earthshaker did not forget the threats
He had leveled against Odysseus,
And he asked Zeus what he intended to do:

2. A sea god.

3. Sea nymphs.

"I lose face among the gods, Zeus,
When I'm not respected by mortal men—
The Phaeacians yet, my own flesh and blood!
I swore that Odysseus would have to suffer
Before getting home—I didn't say
He would never get home, because you had already
Agreed that he would—and now they've brought him
Over the sea while he napped on their ship,
And set him down in Ithaca, and given him
Gifts of bronze and clothing and gold,
More than he ever would have taken out of Troy
Had he come home safely with his share of the loot."

And Zeus, clouds scudding around him:

"What a thing for you to say—you, the Temblor![4]
Dishonored by the gods? It would be hard for us
To sling insults at our eldest and best.
And if some over-confident hero fails
To pay you respect, you can always pay him back.
Do as you please, and as your heart desires."

And Poseidon, the Lord of Earthquake:

"I would do just that, Dark Cloud,
But I like to keep an eye on your temper.
I want to smash that beautiful Phaeacian ship
As it sails for home over the misty sea,
Smash it, so that they will stop this nonsense
Once and for all, giving men safe passage!
And I'll hem their city in with a mountain."

And Zeus, from out of his nimbus of cloud:

"Well, now, this is what I would do:
Wait until all of the people in the city see her
Pulling in to port, and then turn her to stone,
Stone shaped like a ship, a marvel for all men.
And then hem their city in with a mountain."

When he heard this, the Lord of Earthquake
Went to Schería, where the Phaeacians live,
And waited. The great seafaring ship
Was closing in fast when Poseidon slapped it
With the flat of his hand and turned it to stone
Rooted in the seafloor. Then the god was gone.

4. A "temblor" is an earth tremor.

The Phaeacians, men who understood the sea,
Kept turning to each other, saying things like:

"Who did that?"
"Stopped her dead in the water
When she was at top speed, pulling in home."

"She was in plain view, from stem to stern!"

Winged words,
But they had no idea what had happened.

Then Alcinous spoke to his people:

"Alas for the prophecy of old that I heard
From my father. He said that Poseidon
Would be angry with us for giving safe passage
And that one day he would wreck a beautiful ship
As it sailed for home over the misty sea.
And he would hem our city in with a mountain.
What the old man said is all coming true.
Now hear what I have to say. Let us all agree
Never again to provide safe escort
To any man who comes to our city.
And we will sacrifice twelve chosen bulls
To Lord Poseidon, so may he pity us
And not enclose our town with a mountain."

Trembling with fear they prepared the bulls,
And soon all the Phaeacian leaders and lords
Were standing around Poseidon's altar
Saying their prayers.

Odysseus, meanwhile,
Awoke from sleep in his ancestral land—
And did not recognize it. He had been gone so long,
And Pallas Athena had spread haze all around.
The goddess wanted to explain things to him,
And to disguise him, so that his wife and dear ones
Would not know who he was until he had made
The arrogant suitors pay for their outrage.
So everything on Ithaca now looked different
To its lord—the winding trails, the harbors,
The towering rocks and the trees. Odysseus
Sprang to his feet and gazed at his homeland.
He groaned, smacked his thighs with his hands,
And in a voice choked with tears, said:

"What land have I come to now? Who knows
What kind of people live here—lawless savages,

Or godfearing men who take kindly to strangers?
Where am I going to take all these things? Where
Am I going to go myself? I should have stayed
With the Phaeacians until I could go on from there
To some other powerful king who would have
Entertained me and sent me off homeward bound.
Now I don't even know where to put this stuff.
I can't leave it here as easy pickings for a thief.
Those Phaeacian lords were not as wise
As they seemed, nor as just, bringing me here
To this strange land. They said they would bring me
To Ithaca's shore, but that's not what they've done.
May Zeus pay them back, Zeus, god of suppliants,
Who spots transgressors and punishes them.
Well, I'd better count my goods and go over them.
Those sailors may have made off with some in their ship."

And he set about counting the hammered tripods,
The cauldrons, the gold, the finely woven clothes.
Nothing was missing. It was his homeland he missed
As he paced along the whispering surf-line,
Utterly forlorn.
                    And then Athena was beside him
In the form of a young man out herding sheep.
She had the delicate features of a prince,
A fine-spun mantle folded over her shoulders,
Sandals on her glistening feet, a spear in her hand.
Odysseus' spirits soared when he saw her,
And he turned to her with these words on his lips:

"Friend—you are the first person I've met here—
I wish you well. Now don't turn on me.
Help me keep these things safe, and keep me safe,
I beg you at your knees as if you were a god.
And tell me this, so I will know:
What land is this, who are the people here?
Is this an island, or a rocky arm
Of the mainland shore stretching out to sea?"

Athena's eyes glinted with azure light:

"Where in the world do you come from, stranger,
That you have to ask what land this is?
It's not exactly nameless! Men from all over
Know this land, sailing in from the sunrise
And from far beyond the evening horizon.
It's got rough terrain, not for driving horses,
But it's not at all poor even without wide open spaces.
There's abundant grain here, and wine-grapes,
Good rainfalls, and rich, heavy dews.
Good pasture, too, for goats and for cattle,

And all sorts of timber, and year-round springs.
That's why Ithaca is a name heard even in Troy,
Which they say is far from any Greek land."

And Odysseus, who had borne much,
Felt joy at hearing his homeland described
By Pallas Athena, Zeus' own daughter.
His words flew out as if on wings—
But he did not speak the truth. He checked that impulse,
And, jockeying for an advantage, made up this story:

"I've heard of Ithaca, of course—even in Crete,
Far over the sea, and now I've just come ashore
With my belongings here. I left as much
To my sons back home. I've been on the run
Since killing a man, Orsilochus,
Idomeneus' son, the great sprinter.
No one in all Crete could match his speed.
He wanted to rob me of all of the loot
I took out of Troy—stuff I had sweated for
In hand-to-hand combat in the war overseas—
Because I wouldn't serve under his father at Troy
But led my own unit instead. I ambushed him
With one of my men, got him with a spear
As he came back from the fields. It was night,
Pitch-black. No one saw us, and I got away
With a clean kill with sharp bronze. Then,
I found a ship, Phoenician, and made it
Worth the crew's while to take me to Pylos,
Or Elis maybe, where the Epeans are in power.
Well, the wind pushed us back from those shores—
It wasn't their fault, they didn't want to cheat me—
And we were driven here in the middle of the night
And rowed like hell into the harbor. Didn't even
Think of chow, though we sure could have used some,
Just got off the boat and lay down, all of us.
I slept like a baby, dead to the world,
And they unloaded my stuff from the ship's hold
And set it down next to me where I lay on the sand.
Then off they went to Sidonia, the big city,
And I was left here, stranded, just aching inside."

Athena smiled at him, her eyes blue as the sea,
And her hand brushed his cheek. She was now
A tall, beautiful woman, with an exquisite touch
For handiwork, and her words had wings:

"Only a master thief, a real con artist,
Could match your tricks—even a god

Might come up short. You wily bastard,
You cunning, elusive, habitual liar!
Even in your own land you weren't about
To give up the stories and sly deceits
That are so much a part of you.
Never mind about that though. Here we are,
The two shrewdest minds in the universe,
You far and away the best man on earth
In plotting strategies, and I famed among gods
For my clever schemes. Not even you
Recognized Pallas Athena, Zeus' daughter,
I who stand by you in all your troubles
And who made you dear to all the Phaeacians.
And now I've come here, ready to weave
A plan with you, and to hide the goods
The Phaeacians gave you—which was my idea—
And to tell you what you still have to endure
In your own house. And you do have to endure,
And not tell anyone, man or woman,
That you have come home from your wanderings.
No, you must suffer in silence, and take a beating."

And Odysseus, his mind teeming:

"It would be hard for the most discerning man alive
To see through all your disguises, Goddess.
I know this, though: you were always kind to me
When the army fought at Troy.
But after we plundered Priam's steep city,
And boarded our ships, and a god scattered us,
I didn't see you then, didn't sense your presence
Aboard my ship or feel you there to help me.
No, and I suffered in my wanderings
Until the gods released me from my troubles.
It wasn't until I was on Phaeacia
That you comforted me—and led me to the city.
Now I beg you, by your Father—I don't believe
I've come to sunlit Ithaca, but to some other land.
I think you're just giving me a hard time,
And trying to put one over on me. Tell me
If I've really come to my own native land."

And Athena, her eyes glinting blue:

"Ah, that mind of yours! That's why
I can't leave you when you're down and out:
Because you're so intelligent and self-possessed.
Any other man come home from hard travels
Would rush to his house to see his children and wife.
But you don't even want to hear how they are
Until you test your wife, who,

As a matter of fact, just sits in the house,
Weeping away the lonely days and nights.
I never lost faith, though. I always knew in my heart
You'd make it home, all your companions lost,
But I couldn't bring myself to fight my uncle,
Poseidon, who had it in for you,
Angry because you blinded his son.[5]
And now, so you will believe, I will show you
Ithaca from the ground up: There is the harbor
Of Phorcys, the Old Man of the Sea, and here,
At its head, is the slender-leaved olive tree
Standing near a cave that glimmers in the mist
And is sacred to the nymphs called Naiades.
Under that cavern's arched roof you sacrificed
Many a perfect victim to the nymphs.
And there stands Mount Neriton, mantled in forest."

As she spoke, the goddess dispelled the mist.
The ground appeared, and Odysseus,
The godlike survivor, felt his mind soar
At the sight of his land. He kissed the good earth,
And with his palms to the sun, Odysseus prayed:

"Nymphs, Naiades, daughters of Zeus![6]
I never thought I would see you again.
Take pleasure in my whispered prayers
And we will give you gifts as before,
If Zeus' great daughter Athena
Allows me to live and my son to reach manhood."

And Athena, her eyes glinting blue:

"You don't have to worry about that.
Right now, let's stow these things in a nook
Of the enchanted cave, where they'll be safe for you.
Then we can talk about a happy ending."

With that, the goddess entered the shadowy cave
And searched out its recesses while Odysseus
Brought everything closer—the gold, the bronze,
The well-made clothes the Phaeacians had given him.
And Zeus' own daughter stored them away
And blocked the entrance to the cave with a stone.
Then, sitting at the base of the sacred olive,
The two plotted death for the insolent suitors.
Athena began their discussion this way:

5. Polyphemus the Cyclops.

6. The Naiades were sometimes presented as daughters of Poseidon.

"Son of Laertes in the line of Zeus,[7]
Odysseus, the master tactician—consider how
You're going to get your hands on the shameless suitors,
Who for three years now have taken over your house,
Proposing to your wife and giving her gifts.
She pines constantly for your return,
But she strings them along, makes little promises,
Sends messages—while her intentions are otherwise."

And Odysseus, his mind teeming:

"Ah, I'd be heading for the same pitiful death
That Agamemnon met in his house
If you hadn't told me all this, Goddess.
Weave a plan so I can pay them back!
And stand by me yourself, give me the spirit I had
When we ripped down Troy's shining towers!
With you at my side, your eyes glinting
And your mind fixed on battle—I would take on
Three hundred men if your power were with me."

And Athena, eyes reflecting the blue sea-light:

"Oh, I'll be there all right, and I'll keep my eye on you
When we get down to business. And I think
More than one of these suitors destroying your home
Will spatter the ground with their blood and brains.
Now let's see about disguising you. First,
I'll shrivel the skin on your gnarly limbs,
And wither that tawny hair. A piece of sail-cloth
Will make a nice, ugly cloak. Then
We'll make those beautiful eyes bleary and dim.
You'll look disgusting to all the suitors, as well as to
The wife and child you left behind in your halls.
But you should go first to your swineherd.
He may only tend your pigs, but he's devoted to you,
And he loves your son and Penelope.
You'll find him with the swine. They are feeding
By Raven's Rock and Arethusa's spring,
Gorging on acorns and drinking black water,
Which fattens swine up nicely. Stay with him,
Sit with him a while and ask him about everything,
While I go to Lacedaemon, land of lovely women,
To summon Telemachus. Your son, Odysseus,
Went to Menelaus' house in Sparta
Hoping for news that you are still alive."

7. The word *diogenes*, "in the line of Zeus," is often used vaguely of monarchs, not necessarily implying genealogical descent.

And Odysseus, his mind teeming:

"You knew. Why didn't you tell him?
So he could suffer too, roving barren seas
While my wife's suitors eat him out of house and home?"

Athena answered, her eyes glinting blue:

"You needn't worry too much about him.
I accompanied him in person. I wanted him
To make a name for himself by traveling there.
He's not exactly laboring as he takes his ease
In Menelaus' luxurious palace.
Sure, these young louts have laid an ambush for him
In a ship out at sea, meaning to kill him
Before he reaches home. But I don't think they will.
These suitors who have been destroying your home
Will be six feet under before that'll ever happen."

So saying, Athena touched him with a wand.
She shriveled the flesh on his gnarled limbs,
And withered his tawny hair. She wrinkled the skin
All over his body so he looked like an old man,
And she made his beautiful eyes bleary and dim.
Then she turned his clothes into tattered rags,
Dirty and smoke-grimed, and cast about him
A great deerskin cloak with the fur worn off.
And she gave him a staff and a ratty pouch
All full of holes, slung by a twisted cord.

Having laid their plans, they went their own ways,
The goddess off to Sparta to fetch Telemachus.

BOOK XIV

Odysseus went up from the harbor
Along a rough path until he reached a high,
Wooded area where Athena had told him
He would find the noble swineherd. This man
Cared for his master's property
Better than any other slave Odysseus had.

He found him sitting in front of his house,
Which had a high-fenced yard with a view all around.
It was a fine, spacious yard, built by the herdsman
For his absent master's swine. Neither Penelope
Nor old Laertes knew anything of it.
He had built it with huge stones coped with thorns
And wedged on the outside with close-set stakes
Of split, black heart-oak. Inside the yard
He had made twelve sties, one next to the other,

As beds for the swine, and in each were penned
Fifty wallowing swine—breeding females.
The boars slept outside, and were far scarcer,
Their numbers depleted by the godlike suitors
Who feasted on them. The swineherd was always
Sending the best of all the fatted hogs.
There were three hundred and sixty in all.

Close by,
The dogs slept, four of them, wild as beasts,
Reared by the swineherd, who was a man
Who could have commanded a platoon in war.
At the moment, he was fitting sandals to his feet,
Cutting the tanned leather to size.
The other herdsman had gone off with the swine,
One here, one there, one to drive a boar to town
So that the insolent suitors could sacrifice it
And satisfy their hunger for meat.

Suddenly,
The baying hounds caught sight of Odysseus
And rushed at him barking and snarling.
Odysseus, remembering his tricks, sat down
And let the staff fall from his hand. Even so,
He would have been mauled on his own farmstead,
But the swineherd was hot on the dogs' heels,
Dropping the leather as he ran through the gate
And calling aloud to the dogs. He scattered them
With a shower of stones, and then addressed
The man who was his master, saying:

"Another moment, old man, and the dogs
Would have ripped you open, and it's me
You would have blamed for it, as if the gods
Haven't given me enough grief already.
It's for my master, a man like a god, I grieve
As I stay out here raising fat hogs
For other men to eat, while he wanders hungry
In some foreign land, if he's still alive, that is,
And still sees the sunlight. But come with me.
Let's go to my hut, old man, so that you,
When you have had your fill of food and wine,
Can tell me your story—where you are from,
And all the suffering you have endured."

So the godlike swineherd led him into his hut.
Once inside, he had him sit down on a pile
Of thick brushwood over which he spread
The skin of a shaggy wild goat, a large, thick hide
On which he usually slept. Odysseus was glad

That he welcomed him like this, and said so:

"May Zeus and all the gods bless you, stranger,
For welcoming me with such an open heart."

And you answered him, Eumaeus, my swineherd:

"It would not be right for me to show less respect
Even to someone less worthy than you.
All strangers and beggars come from Zeus,
And our gifts to them are welcome though small,
Since this is how it is with slaves, always fearful
Of the masters over them, especially
Young masters. Yes, and the gods have blocked
The return of the master who would have treated me
With kindness, given me possessions of my own,
A house, some land, and a wife courted by many,
The things a kind master gives to his servant
Whose long, hard work a god has made prosper,
As the work I have done has come to prosper.
My master would have rewarded me richly for this,
Had he grown old here. But he's gone, perished—
As I wish Helen and all her clan had perished,
Since she has unstrung the knees of many heroes.
Yes, he too went to Ilion, land of fine horses,
To fight the Trojans on Agamemnon's account."

So saying, he tucked his tunic up in his belt
And went to the sties where the swine were penned.
He picked out two and slaughtered them both,
Singed them, butchered them, and put them on spits.
When he had roasted everything, he brought it out
Hot on the spits and served it to Odysseus,
Sprinkling the pork with white barley meal.
Then he mixed sweet wine in an ivy-wood bowl,
Sat down across from Odysseus, and said:

"Eat now, stranger, such food as slaves eat,
Young porkers. The fatted hogs the suitors eat,
Men who have no fear of the gods, and feel no pity.
The blessed ones do not love wickedness
But honor justice and repay righteousness!
Even men who wage war in a foreign land
And sail for home with their ships filled with loot—
Even men like that fear the wrath of the gods.
But these men here must know something,
Must have heard from a god that my master is dead,
Since they are so unwilling to conduct their courtship
In a way that is just, or to return to their homes.
They just lounge about squandering our goods,
Sparing nothing in their insolence.

Every day and night they slaughter our animals—
Not just one or two, either—and waste our wine.
At least my master's holdings are huge. No hero,
Either on the dark mainland or Ithaca itself,
Has nearly as much. Twenty men together
Could not match his wealth. Let me count it for you.
Twelve herds of cattle over on the mainland,
And as many flocks of sheep, droves of swine,
And spreading herds of goats—all of them pastured
By his own herdsmen or hired foreigners.
And more herds of goats, eleven in all,
Range our island's coasts. Good men watch them,
And every day each of these men drives up
The best fatted goat in all of his flock
For the suitors to eat. Myself, I keep these swine,
And always pick out the best to send to them."

As he spoke, Odysseus was silently
Eating his pork and drinking wine—
And chewing on how to punish the suitors.
When he had satisfied his appetite for food,
The swineherd filled for him the drinking bowl
He ordinarily used himself and gave it to him
Brimming with wine. Odysseus gladly took it,
And his words flew on wings to the swineherd:

"Well, who was it, my friend, who bought you?
Who is this rich and powerful man?
You said he died fighting on Agamemnon's account.
Tell me his name. I might recognize it.
Zeus only knows who I might have met
And have some news of. I've wandered far."
And the swineherd, a leader of men:

"Old man, no wanderer who came with news of him
Could ever convince his wife and son. Besides,
All a needy vagabond ever does is tell lies.
He has no interest at all in telling the truth.
Whenever a wanderer comes to Ithaca,
He goes to my mistress with a cock and bull story.
She receives him kindly and questions him closely,
And tears fall from her eyes and she weeps and cries
The way a woman will whose husband dies abroad.
And you'd make up a story, too, old man,
In an instant, if you thought you could get
A cloak and tunic out of it.
But by now,
Dogs and birds have torn the flesh from his bones,
And his soul has crawled off. Or deep in the sea
Fish have picked his bones clean, and they now lie
On a shore somewhere, wrapped in deep sand.

No, he's dead and gone, and there is nothing left
For his dear ones but grief, and for me especially,
For never again will I find a master so mild,
However far I go, even if I go home again
To my mother and father, where I was born
And where they reared me. Yet,
As much as I miss them and miss my homeland,
I miss Odysseus more. There, I said his name.
I would rather not say his name when he is not here,
For he loved me greatly and cared for me. Instead,
I call him my brother, though he is not here."

Odysseus, who had borne much, replied:

"Well, my friend, since you refuse to believe,
And since you insist he will never come home,
I'll not just say it, but will solemnly swear
That Odysseus will come back. As for a reward
For bringing this news, give it to me
When he does return—a tunic and cloak—
And not a moment before. Until that man
Is actually here, I will accept nothing,
However great my need. I hate like hell
A man who caves in to his poverty
And tells a batch of lies.
I swear by Zeus,
Above all gods, and by this hospitable table,
And the hearth of flawless Odysseus himself—
That everything will happen just as I say:
Before this month is out Odysseus will come,
In the dark of the moon, before the new crescent.
He shall return, and take vengeance upon
All those who dishonor his wife and his son."

And you answered him, Eumaeus, my swineherd:

"I'll never be paying you any reward,
Nor will Odysseus ever come home.
Now let's just drink quietly and think about
Other things. Don't remind me of all this.
I feel such pain and grief in my heart
Whenever anyone mentions my master.
We'll just let your oath be. May Odysseus
Come back, as I desire, and as Penelope does,
And the old man Laertes, and godlike Telemachus,
Odysseus' son. And now he weighs on my mind,
Telemachus. The gods made him grow
Like a sapling, and I thought he would be a match
For his father, a splendid man to look at.
Then one of the immortals, or maybe a man,
Knocked the sense out of him, and he left
For sacred Pylos, trying to track down his father.

And now the suitors are ambushing him
As he sails for home, so that the line
Of godlike Arceisius may come to an end
On Ithaca, and leave no name behind.
But there's nothing we can do, whether he's caught
Or escapes with a helping hand from Zeus.
But tell me, old man, about your own troubles,
And tell me this, so that I can be sure of it.
Who are you, and where do you come from?
Where is your city, and where are your parents?
On what kind of ship did you come, and how
Did sailors bring you to Ithaca? Who were they?
I don't suppose you walked all the way here."

And Odysseus, his mind teeming:

"I will tell you all of this, down to the last detail.
If you and I could only have food and sweet wine
For the duration, feasting on and on quietly
Here in your hut, leaving the work to others—
It would easily take me a full year, and even then
I would not finish my heart's tale of sorrows,
All that I have endured by the will of the gods.
I was born in Crete, son of a wealthy man
Who had many other sons born to his lawful wife.
My own mother was a concubine,
But my father, Castor, son of Hylax,
Treated me like one of his true-born sons.
He was honored as a god by the Cretans
For his wealth, prosperity, and glorious sons.
But death carried him away to Hades,
And his sons parceled out his estate
Among themselves, leaving me just a small share,
And a house to live in. But I was able to marry
A wife from a propertied family
Because of my real worth. I was no weakling,
And I held my own in battle. All that's gone now,
But I think you can judge the grain from the stubble.
I'm overwhelmed now with aches and pains,
But back then Athena and Ares
Gave me the power to crush men in war.
When I set an ambush, lying in wait
With hand-picked men to give the enemy hell,
I never got nervous, never saw death looming.
I was the first to jump out and kill whoever
Gave way before me and started to run.
I was good in war. But fieldwork
Was not to my taste, nor caring for a household
Where children are reared. Oared ships are what I liked,
And war, polished spears, and arrows,
All the grim things that make most people shudder.
I suppose I liked what a god put in my heart—

One man's meat is another man's poison.
Before the Greeks ever set foot in Troy,
I had already led nine expeditions,
Amphibious assaults against foreign cities.
I made a lot in those wars. I would cull
The loot I liked best and get even more
When the rest was divided later by lot.
So my house grew rich, and I became
One of the most feared and respected men in Crete.
But when thundering Zeus opened the war
That unstrung the knees of many heroes,
I was urged to go with glorious Idomeneus
And lead our ships to Troy. I could not refuse.
The people's voice had to be heard. Nine years
We Greeks waged war, and in the tenth
We sacked Priam's city and sailed for home
In our ships, and a god scattered the fleet.
But Zeus had more trouble in store for me.
I stayed home for only a month, enjoying
My children, my wife, and all my possessions.
Then I felt an urge to voyage to Egypt
With my godlike companions. I fitted out
Nine ships with care. It didn't take long
For my men to gather, and when they had,
I feasted them for six days, giving them
All the animals they needed for sacrifice—
Enough for the gods and for their own banquets.
On the seventh day we set sail from Crete
Under a fresh North Wind and ran on as easily
As if we were in a current. My ships sailed
Without any mishap, free of disease,
Guided by the wind and the pilot's hand.
On the fifth day I moored my ships
In the river Nile, and you can be sure I ordered
My trusty mates to stand by and guard them
While I sent out scouts to look around.
But the crews got restless and cocky
And started pillaging the Egyptian countryside,
Carrying off the women and children
And killing the men. The cry came to the city,
And at daybreak troops answered the call.
The whole plain was filled with infantry,
War chariots, and the glint of bronze.
Thundering Zeus threw my men into a panic,
And not one had the courage to stand and fight
Against odds like that. It was bad.
They killed many of us outright with bronze
And led the rest to their city to work as slaves.
But Zeus put an idea into my mind.
I'm sorry I took it. It would have been better
If I had died in Egypt, met my fate there—

So much more suffering was waiting for me.
I took off my helmet, dropped my shield,
Let the spear fall from my hands, and walked straight
To the king's chariot. I clasped his knees
And kissed them. It worked. He pitied me,
Took me in his chariot, and drove me weeping
To his own home, warding off all the spears
That were aimed at me by the angry mob,
For he respected Zeus, god of strangers,
Indignant and wrathful above all other gods.
    Seven years I stayed there, amassing wealth,
For all the Egyptians gave me gifts.
When the eighth year rolled around, there came
A man from Phoenicia, avaracious and sly,
And a general scoundrel. He persuaded me
To go off with him to his house in Phoenicia,
And I stayed with him there for one full year,
After which he took me in a seafaring ship
Bound for Libya, pretending we were taking
A cargo there, when his real intent
Was to sell me there for an enormous price.
I suspected treachery but had to go aboard.
The ship ran on under a fresh North Wind,
Staying above Crete in a mid-sea course.
Then Zeus devised the crew's utter destruction.
    When we left Crete behind, there was
No other land in sight, only sea and sky.
Then Zeus put a black cloud over our ship.
The sea grew dark beneath it, and Zeus thundered
And struck the ship with a lightning bolt.
She shivered from stem to stern and was filled
With sulfurous smoke. The men went overboard,
Bobbing in the waves like sea crows
Around the black ship, their day of return
Snuffed out by the god. As for me,
Zeus himself, in the midst of my distress,
Put into my hands the surging mast
Of the dark-prowed ship. That saved my life.
I clung to the mast as the terrible winds
Bore me along. I was out there nine days,
And on the tenth black night a great wave
Rolled me ashore in the Thesprotians' land.
The Thesprotian king, the hero Pheidon,
Took me in. There was no talk of ransom,
For his son had found me, overcome
With cold and fatigue, and raised me up
By the hand, and led me to his father's palace,
Where he gave me a tunic and cloak to wear.
    It was there I learned of Odysseus.
The king said he had been his guest there
On his way back to his native land. He showed me

All the treasure Odysseus had amassed,
Bronze, gold, and wrought iron, enough to feed
His children's children for ten generations,
All stored there for him in the halls of the king.
Odysseus, he said, had gone to Dodona
To consult the oak-tree oracle of Zeus[8]
And ask how he should return to Ithaca—
Openly or in secret—after being gone so long.
And he swore to me, as he poured libations
There in his house, that a ship was launched,
And a crew standing by, to take him home.
But he sent me off first, since a Thesprotian ship
Happened to be leaving for Dulichium,
Where I wanted to go. He told that crew
To escort me to King Acastus there.
Somehow the crew turned against me,
And I was destined for even more pain.
When the ship left land, it wasn't long before
They hatched a plot to sell me as a slave.
They stripped off my clothes, the tunic and cloak,
And made me wear the rags you see on me now.
At evening they reached the coast of Ithaca.
They tied me up in the ship and went ashore
And got busy with their supper there on the beach.
The gods themselves must have untied my bonds,
They came off so easily, and wrapping my head
In the rags I wore, I slid down the smooth plank
Into the sea. I started to swim a breast stroke
And was soon out of the water and away from them.
I went upland a ways and found a leafy thicket
And huddled up in it. They looked all over,
Moaning and groaning, but couldn't see any profit
In continuing their search, and so they went back aboard
Their hollow ship. The gods kept me under cover—
Easy for them—and guided me to the farmstead
Of a wise man. It seems I'm still destined to live."

And you answered him, Eumaeus, my swineherd:

"You poor, wandering wretch. You've wrung my heart
With all the particulars of your suffering.
But the part of your story about Odysseus
Just isn't right, and I'm not buying it.
Why should a man in such a fix as you are
Want to lie like that? I know all about
The return of my master—how the gods spited him
In not letting him die among the Trojans
Or in his friends' arms after he had wound up the war.

8. Oracle in Epirus, in northwestern Greece. Here, priests and priestesses interpreted the rustling of leaves, to determine the will of the gods.

The entire Greek army would have buried him then,
And great honor would have passed on to his son.
As it is, the whirlwinds have snatched him away.
Myself, I live out here with the swine. I never go
Into the city, unless Penelope asks me to
When news comes to her from somewhere.
Then everyone sits around the visitor
And questions him, both those who miss
Their absent lord, and those who enjoy
Devouring his goods without recompense.
But I don't ask anything, not since the time
An Aetolian fooled me with his phony story.
He had killed a man and was wandering the earth.
He came to my house, and I welcomed him.
He said he had seen Odysseus in Crete
At Idomeneus' house, repairing some of his ships
That storms had battered. And he said he would be back
By summer or harvest, bringing with him
Piles of treasure and his godlike companions.
And now, you woeful old man, since some god
Has steered you my way, don't you try
To charm me or win me over with lies.
It's not for that I'll show you respect or kindness,
But for fear of Zeus, and out of pity for you."

And Odysseus, his mind teeming:

"You have a heart that just won't believe.
Not even my oath was enough to convince you.
Let's make a bet, with the gods on Olympus
As witnesses. If your master comes back,
You give me a cloak and tunic to wear
And get me to Dulichium, where I want to be.
But if he doesn't come back as I say he will,
Have your slaves jump me and throw me off a cliff,
So that the next beggar will think twice before lying."

And the noble, godlike swineherd answered:

"And that would earn me a fine reputation,
Now and forever, wouldn't it, stranger?
First I welcome you into my hut, and then
I take you outside and end your sweet life.
And afterwards I'll pray to Zeus, son of Cronus,
With a clear conscience!
It's time for supper.
I hope my men come back soon
So we can make a tasty meal here in the hut."

As they were speaking, the herders came up
Driving the swine. They put the sows in the sties

Where they always slept, and an amazing racket
Rose from the animals as they were being penned.
The swineherd called to the workers and said:

"Bring the best boar we have so I can slaughter him
For the stranger here, and for us, too.
We have worked long and hard with these tuskers
While others eat up our labor free of charge."

With that, he started to split wood with an axe
While they brought in a five-year-old fatted boar
And set him down by the hearth. The swineherd
Did not forget the immortals—he had a good mind for this—
Casting into the fire as a first offering
Bristles from the head of the white-tusked boar
And praying that Odysseus would return to his home.
Then he came down hard with a piece of split oak
And the boar's spirit left him. They cut his throat,
Singed him, and then butchered him quickly.
The swineherd cut off, as more first offerings,
Bits of raw flesh from each part of the animal,
Then wrapped them in fat, sprinkled them with barley,
And then threw them into the fire. The rest
They cut up and roasted with care on spits.
When it was done, they pulled the roast pork from the spits
And piled it on platters. The swineherd carved,
For he had a good sense of fairness,
And he divided the meat into seven portions.
He set aside one for the Nymphs and for Hermes,
Saying a prayer, and served the rest to the men,
Honoring Odysseus with the long chine
Of the white-tusked boar, and so pleasing his master.
And Odysseus, always thinking, said:

"Eumaeus, may you be as dear to Father Zeus
As you are to me, for so honoring a man like me."

And you answered him, Eumaeus, my swineherd:

"Eat, my strange guest, and enjoy what we have.
God gives us one thing and holds another back,
Just as he pleases, for he can do all things."

He spoke, and sacrificed the first offerings
To the eternal gods, and poured libations
Of sparkling wine. Then he handed the cup
To Odysseus, sacker of cities, and took his seat.
The bread was served by Mesaulius,
Whom the swineherd had bought all on his own
While his master was gone, without the help of his mistress
Or of old Laertes, buying him

From the Taphians with his own resources.
They reached for the good cheer spread before them,
And when they had enough of food and drink,
Mesaulius took away the leftovers, and they all
Longed for rest, their stomachs full of bread and meat.

The evening sky was foreboding and moonless,
And a damp West Wind was starting to blow.
It began to rain, and it would rain all night.
Odysseus spoke, testing the swineherd,
Seeing if he would take off his own cloak
And give it to him, or tell one of his men
To do so, since he cared for him deeply:

"Hear me now, Eumaeus, and the rest of you men,
While I boast a little. It must be the wine
Befuddling me, which gets even sensible men
Singing and laughing and up to dance,
And sometimes to say things better left unsaid.
But I've cut loose now and won't hide anything.
Oh, to be young again and with the strength I had
When we went out on ambush under Troy's wall.
Our leaders were Odysseus and Menelaus,
And I was third in command, at their request.
When we had come up close to the steep city wall,
We took our places on the perimeter
Down in the brush and reeds of the swampland,
Lying there crouched beneath our shields.
The North Wind swooped down, and night came on
Foul and bitter cold. Snow drifted down
And covered us like frost, and ice rimmed our shields.
Everyone else had on cloaks and tunics
And slept peacefully, their shields on their shoulders.
But I had stupidly left my cloak behind at camp,
Because I didn't think it would be cold that night,
And had come out with only my shield and belt.
During the third watch, when the stars had turned
In their wheeling course, I nudged Odysseus,
Who was lying next to me, and he heard me say,
'Son of Laertes in the line of Zeus,
Wily Odysseus—listen, I'm about dead over here;
This cold is killing me. I don't have a cloak.
Some god talked me into coming out here
With only a tunic, and now there's no going back.'
He put his mind to work and came up with a plan.
That's how he was; he could think up things
As well as he could fight. He whispered to me,
'Be quiet now, or one of our men will hear you.'
Then he propped his head up on an elbow and said,
'Listen, men. I had a dream from the gods.
We've come too far from the ships. We need someone

To request Agamemnon, commander-in-chief,
To send out more troops from our beach-head camp.'
He had no sooner spoken than Thoas
Was on his feet. He flung aside his purple cloak
And sprinted off to the ships, and wrapped in that cloak
I lay down gladly until Dawn shone with gold.
Oh, to be young again and still have my strength!
Then one of the swineherds would give me a cloak,
Both out of kindness and out of respect for a man.
But now they scorn me because I am dressed in rags."

And you answered him, Eumaeus, my swineherd:

"There's nothing wrong with your story, old man,
And nothing you've said is out of line
Or unprofitable. So you won't go without.
You'll have clothing, yes, and everything else
A suppliant in need ought to receive—
At least for tonight. But in the morning
You'll have to shake out those old rags of yours.
We don't have extra tunics or cloaks
Around here. Each man has only one.
But when Odysseus' son comes, he himself
Will give you a cloak and tunic to wear,
And will send you wherever your heart desires."

So saying, the swineherd sprang to his feet
And started to make up a bed for Odysseus
Near the fire, spreading it with goatskins and fleeces.
There Odysseus lay down, and Eumaeus
Threw over him a large, heavy cloak
That he kept as a spare for stormy weather.

So there Odysseus slept, with the young men
All around him. But not the swineherd.
He would not settle for a bed inside,
Away from the boars. He got himself ready
To go sleep outdoors, and Odysseus was glad
That he took such good care of the property
Of his absent master. First, Eumaeus
Slung his sharp sword over his sturdy shoulders
And put on a thick cloak to keep out the wind.
Then picking up the fleece of a large, fatted goat,
And grabbing a javelin to ward off dogs and men,
He went out to sleep with the white-tusked boars
Under a hollow rock, out of the cold North Wind.

BOOK XV

Pallas Athena now went to wide Lacedaemon
To tell Odysseus' son it was time to return.
She found Telemachus and Nestor's noble son

On the porch of Menelaus' palace.
Nestor's son was sleeping, but Telemachus
Had been lying awake all through the night
Thinking about his father. Athena,
Her eyes flashing in the dark, said to him:

"Telemachus, you've been away too long.
Think of the wealth you left behind at home
And all those insolent men ready to devour it.
Your journey will have been for nothing.
Hurry, now, and rouse Menelaus
To send you on your way, so you can find
Your blameless mother still at home.
Her father and brothers are pressuring her
To marry Eurymachus, because of all the suitors
He gives the best presents, and now has
Stepped up his wooing. You have to watch out
She doesn't carry off all your treasure.
You know what a woman's heart is like.
She wants to enrich the house of the one who weds her,
Never mind about her former children
And the husband she once loved. Once he's dead,
She doesn't give any of them a thought.
No, you go, and put all your possessions
In the keeping of the best maidservant in the house,
Until the gods show you your honored bride.
And one more thing for you to keep in mind.
The suitors' ringleaders have set up an ambush
In the strait between Ithaca and rocky Samos.
They mean to kill you before you make it home.
I don't think they will. Those mooching suitors
Will be in their graves before they can get at you.
But keep your ship out away from the islands,
And sail by night as well. One of the gods
Who watches over you will put a wind at your back.
When you make landfall on Ithaca,
Send your crew with the ship on to the city,
But you go first to the swineherd's hut;
He has a soft spot in his heart for you.
Spend the night there and tell him to go
Into the city and bring word to Penelope
That you are safe and have come back from Pylos."

And with that she was off to high Olympus.

Telemachus awoke and woke up Peisistratus
With a nudge of his heel, saying to him:

"Wake up, Peisistratus. Get your horses
And yoke them up so we can get on the road."
Nestor's son Peisistraus answered:

"Telemachus, there's no way we can drive
In the dark, no matter how eager we are
To get on the road. Besides, it'll be light soon,
And we should wait until Menelaus comes out
And sets gifts on the chariot and sends us off
With a farewell speech. A guest remembers
A host's hospitality for as long as he lives."

He spoke, and Dawn rose up splashed with gold.
Menelaus, who had just gotten out of bed
With Helen, was coming toward them,
And when Telemachus saw him
The young hero quickly threw on his silky tunic,
Flung a cloak on his shoulders, and went out,
The true son of godlike Odysseus.
When he reached Menelaus he said to him:

"Menelaus, son of Atreus in the line of Zeus,
Send me back home to my own native land,
For my heart is now eager to return to my home."

And Menelaus, famed for his war cry:

"Telemachus, far be it from me to detain you here
When you yearn to go home. I no more approve
Of a host who is too welcoming than of one
Who is too cold. Due measure in all things.
It is just as wrong to rush a guest's departure
When he doesn't want to go, as it is
To hold him back when he is ready to leave.
Make a guest welcome for as long as he stays
And send him off whenever he wants to go.
But do stay until I can bring some gifts out
And load them onto your chariot, fine gifts,
As you will see. And I will order the women
To prepare you a meal from our well-stocked larder.
It's a double honor, and sensible, too,
For the traveler to eat before setting forth
Over the boundless earth. And if you wish to go
All through Hellas and into the heart of Argos,
I myself will go with you. I'll yoke up horses
And give you a tour of the cities of men,
And no one will send us away empty-handed.
Everyone will give us at least one thing,
A fine bronze tripod or perhaps a cauldron,
A team of mules or a golden cup."

And Telemachus, in his cool-headed way:

"Menelaus, son of Atreus in the line of Zeus,
I would rather go straight home. I did not leave
Anyone behind to watch my possessions.

I'm afraid that in my search for my godlike father
I may perish myself, or that some precious thing
May be lost from my house while I am away."

When he heard this, Menelaus at once
Ordered his wife and her serving women
To prepare a meal from their well-stocked larder.
Then Eteoneus, just risen from bed,
Came up—his house was nearby—and Menelaus
Had him kindle a fire and roast some of the meat.
While he was doing this, Menelaus himself
Went down to his scented treasure chamber
Accompanied by Helen and Megapenthes.
When they came to where the treasure was stored
The son of Atreus took a two-handled cup
And had his son Megapenthes bring a mixing bowl
Of solid silver. But Helen went to the chests
That held her robes, the richly embroidered robes
She herself had made. And this beautiful woman,
Helen of Argos, lifted out the robe
That had the finest embroideries, an ample robe
That shone like starlight beneath all the rest.
Then they went back through the house and came
To Telemachus, to whom Menelaus said:

"Telemachus, may Zeus, Hera's thundering lord,
Bring you to your home, just as you desire.
Of all the gifts that lie stored in my house
I will give you the most beautiful—
And the most valuable—a well-wrought bowl,
Solid silver, with the lip finished in gold,
Made by Hephaestus. The hero Phaedimus,
King of the Sidonians, gave it to me
When I stayed at his house on my way home.
Now I want you to take it home with you."

And the son of Atreus placed the double-handled goblet
In Telemachus' hands. Then strong Megapenthes
Brought the gleaming silver mixing bowl over
And set it before him. And Helen, lovely in her bones,
Came up with the robe and said to him:

"I, too, give you a gift, dear child, this robe,
A memento from the hands of Helen,
For your bride to wear on your wedding day.
Until then let it lie in your mother's keeping.
And my wish for you is that you come with joy
To your native land and your ancestral home."

She put the robe in his hands, and he received it
With gratitude. Then Peisistratus put all of the gifts

Into the chariot's trunk and looked at them a while
With wonder in his heart.
Menelaus now
Led them into the house, and the two sat down.
A maid poured water from a silver pitcher
Over a golden basin for them to wash their hands
And then set up a polished table nearby.
Another serving woman, grave and dignified,
Set out bread and generous helpings
From the other dishes she had. Boethus' son
Carved the meat nearby and divided it up,
And the son of Menelaus poured the wine.
They reached out to all the good cheer before them,
And when they had their fill of food and drink,
Telemachus and glorious Nestor's son
Yoked the horses, mounted the inlaid chariot,
And drove through the gate and echoing portico.
And the son of Atreus, red-haired Menelaus,
Went after them, holding in his right hand
A golden cup filled with honey-hearted wine
So they could pour libations before setting out.
He stood before the horses, lifted the cup, and said:

"Farewell, young men, and bring my greetings
To Nestor, the old commander. He was to me
Kind as a father when we Greeks fought at Troy."

And Telemachus, in his clear-headed way:

"We will tell him all these things, just as you say,
Zeus-born, when we come to his land,
As surely as I wish I would find Odysseus home,
So I could tell him how good you have been to me
During my visit with you, and tell him how
I come home myself with many a treasure."

As he spoke, a bird flew by on his right,
An eagle, clutching in his talons a silvery goose,
A large, tame fowl from the yard. Men and women
Ran after it shouting. The eagle got closer,
Then veered off to the right in front of the horses.
This lifted everyone's spirits. Nestor's son
Peisistratus was the first one to speak:

"Zeus-born Menelaus, what does this mean?
Is it a sign for us two, or for yourself?"

Menelaus, the warlord, was thinking this over,
Looking for the right way to interpret the sign,
When long-robed Helen took the words from his mouth:

"I will prophesy as the immortals prompt me
And as I see it myself. Just as this eagle
Came from the mountain, where he was born and bred,
And snatched up the goose bred in the house,
So shall Odysseus, after long, hard travels,
Return to his home, and take vengeance.
Or he is already at home and is even now
Sowing the seeds of the suitors' destruction."

And Telemachus, in his spirited way:

"May Hera's thundering lord[9] grant it,
And I will pray to you as to a god."

He flicked the lash and the horses took off
Through the city and out to the plain. All day long
They jostled the yoke that held them together.

As the sun set and the world grew dark,
They came to Pherae and pulled up at the house
Of Diocles, son of Ortilochus,
Himself a son of the river Alpheus.
There they spent the night, and Diocles
Gave them the hospitality due to guests.

When Dawn brushed the pale sky with rose,
They yoked the horses, stepped up into
The inlaid chariot and drove out through the gate
And echoing portico. Peisistratus
Flicked the lash and the horses took off.
Soon after they reached the high rock of Pylos,
And Telemachus had a word with Nestor's son:

"I wonder if you could do me a favor,
Peisistratus? You and I go back a long way
Because of our fathers' friendship. Moreover,
We're the same age, and this journey together
Will cement our friendship. This is what I want:
Do not drive me farther than my ship.
Drop me off there. I'm afraid the old man
Will keep me in his house against my will.
He means well, but I really have to get home."

Nestor's son thought it over, trying to decide
How he could rightfully do Telemachus this favor.
He made up his mind and turned off to the sea
And the ship there. He stowed the beautiful gifts
From Menelaus—the clothes and the gold—

9. Zeus, husband of Hera, god of thunder.

In the ship's stern and urged his friend on,
Speaking to him words that had wings:

"Get yourself and your crew aboard quickly,
Before I reach home and tell the old man.
If there's one thing I'm sure of it's this:
Once he has you in his house he won't let you go,
And he'll come here to get you himself
If he has to, and he won't go home empty-handed.
No matter what, he's going to be angry."

And he drove his horses back to the city
With their beautiful manes flowing in the wind
And quickly reached his father's palace.

Meanwhile, Telemachus was urging on his crew:

"Put all the gear in order on this black ship, men,
And let's go aboard and get under way."

They carried out his orders and were soon
All on board and sitting on their benches.

Telemachus was busy with all of this,
And was offering sacrifice to Athena
By the ship's stern, when there came up to him
A traveler from a distant land. He was in exile
From Argos, because he had killed a man,
And he was a seer. He traced his descent
From Melampus, who had lived in Pylos
In the old days as one of its wealthiest men
But left for other parts, fleeing great Neleus,
That most lordly man, who had seized his wealth
And kept it from him for one full year.
Melampus lay imprisoned in Phylacus' house
And suffered terribly because of Neleus' daughter
And the delusion which the goddess Erinys[1]
Had laid upon him. He escaped, however,
And drove off the lowing cattle from Phylace
To Pylos, and got even with godlike Neleus,
And brought Neleus' daughter home
To be his brother's wife. He himself then left
For the horse country of Argos, his destiny being
To live there and rule over many Argives.
There he took a wife and built a lofty house
And fathered two strong sons. These sons
Were Mantius and Antiphates, and one of them,
Antiphates, sired great-hearted Oicles,
And Oicles was the father of Amphiarus,
Whom Zeus and Apollo showered with love.
But he did not reach the threshold of old age,

1. A Fury, divine spirit of vengeance, who could make her victims crazy.

Dying in Thebes because of a woman's gifts.
Melampus' other son, Mantius,
Sired Polypheides and Clytius.
Clytius, because he was so beautiful,
Was snatched away by gold-stitched Dawn
To live with the immortals. And Apollo
Made Polypheides a seer, a high-hearted man
And the best of men after Amphiaraus was dead.
Eventually, he quarreled with his father
And moved to Hyperesia, and was the prophet there.

It was his son, Theoclymenus by name,
Who now came up to Telemachus
As he was pouring libations by his black ship
And spoke to him these winged words:

"Friend, since I find you making sacrifice here,
I implore you by your sacrifice and by your god,
Then by your own life and the lives of your crew—
Tell me truly what I ask and do not hide it.
Who are you, and where are you from?
Where is your city, and where do your parents live?"

Telemachus answered in his clear-headed way:

"Well then, stranger, I will tell you exactly.
I was born in Ithaca, and my father is Odysseus—
If he ever existed. But he has met a grim fate.
So I have taken my comrades and a black ship
In search of news of my long-absent father."

And godlike Theoclymenus answered:

"I, too, have left my country, because
I killed a man, one of my own clan.
He has many brothers and kinsmen left
In bluegrass Argos, powerful men,
And I am on the run to escape a black fate
At their hands. It seems I am doomed to be
A wanderer. Take me on your ship, please,
Since I have taken refuge with you now.
Don't let them kill me. I think they are coming."

And Telemachus, in his cool-headed way:

"I won't push you away if you want to come.
Welcome aboard, and share whatever we have."

With that he relieved him of his bronze spear
And slid it onto the deck of the ship.
They went aboard. Telemachus sat down

In the stern, Theoclymenus beside him.
The sailors untied the stern cables
And Telemachus called out orders to them
To take hold of the tackling. They fell to,
Raising the firwood mast and setting it
Into its socket. They made it fast with forestays
And hauled up the white sail with rawhide ropes.
And Athena, her eyes flashing with sea-light,
Gave them a tailwind that ripped through the sky,
Speeding the ship across the bright salt sea.
Krouni and Chalcis, with its beautiful streams,
Passed by quickly, and then the sun went down
And the seaways grew dark. The ship surged on
With Zeus' wind behind it, on to Pheae
And past limewhite Elis, where the Epeans rule.
Then Telemachus steered her out again
To the swiftly passing islands, wondering whether
He would dodge death or be caught by the suitors.

Meanwhile, Odysseus and the noble swineherd
Were having supper with the others in the hut.
When they had satisfied their appetite
For food and drink, Odysseus spoke among them,
Testing Eumaeus to see whether he would
Still take care of him there on the farmstead
Or send him off to the city:

"Listen now, Eumaeus, and you other men, too.
In the morning I'm off to beg in the city,
I don't want to eat you out of house and home.
So tell me what I need to know, and give me a guide
Who can lead me there. Once in the city
I can knock about on my own, as I must,
Hoping for a cup of water and a loaf of bread.
And I might go up to Odysseus' house
And bring some news to Penelope.
I might make the rounds of the insolent suitors
And see if they will give me some dinner
From all the good food they have. I might even
Start waiting on them, doing whatever they need.
I'll tell you something now. Thanks to Hermes,
The Guide, who lends grace and glory
To all that men do, when it comes to serving
No one can touch me, in splitting firewood,
Building a fire, roasting meat and carving it,
Or in pouring wine, or in any of the things
Lesser men do when they wait on nobles."

And the swineherd, greatly troubled, responded:

"Where did you get such a notion, stranger?
You must want to die, if you really intend

To go in there with that mob of suitors,
Whose arrogance reaches the iron heavens.
Their serving men are not at all like you.
They're young, well dressed in tunics and cloaks,
Handsome and sleek. The tables are polished
And piled high with bread, meat, and wine.
Stay here. You're not bothering anyone,
Not me nor any other man who is here.
But when Odysseus' son comes, he himself
Will give you a cloak and tunic to wear,
And will send you wherever your heart desires."

And the enduring, godlike Odysseus answered:

"Eumaeus, may you be as dear to father Zeus
As you are to me, for you have given me a rest
From wandering the world in grief and pain.
Nothing is harder on a man than homelessness.
But when it comes to feeding his belly, a man will endure
Whatever hardship and sorrows he must.
But now, since you are keeping me here
A while, and asking me to wait for Telemachus,
Tell me about noble Odysseus' mother,
And his father, whom he left behind
On the brink of old age when he went to Troy.
Are they still alive and under the sun,
Or are they dead now and in Hades' gloom?"

The noble swineherd made this response:

"I will tell you, stranger, since you ask.
Laertes is still alive, but prays constantly
That his life will dwindle away in his halls.
He grieves terribly for his missing son
And for his own lady, his wedded wife.
He took her death hard, and it delivered him
To an unripe old age. She herself died
Of grief for her son, a miserable death
That I would wish on no one dear to me.
For as long as she lived, hard as it was for her,
I always enjoyed seeing how she was,
Asking about her health, for she herself
Had brought me up with long-robed Ctimene,
Her youngest child. I was brought up with her,
Almost as if I were one of the family.
When we reached that lovely time of our youth,
They sent her to Samê, sent her off to be married,
And got themselves countless gifts in exchange.
As for me, my lady clothed me in a cloak and tunic,
Very fine ones, and gave me sandals for my feet,
And sent me off to the fields. But in her heart
She loved me more than that. I do without now,

But the blessed gods make my work prosper.
I stay busy with it, and it gives me enough
To eat and drink and give some to beggars.
From my mistress now I get nothing pleasant,
Word or deed. Trouble has come to the house—
These overbearing men. But servants still need
To speak to their mistress face to face,
Hear all the gossip, eat and drink,
And afterward take something back to the fields,
The sort of thing that warms a servant's heart."

Odysseus, his mind teeming, responded:

"You must have been awfully young, Eumaeus,
When you were forced to travel so far away
From your parents and home. How did it happen?
Did your parents live in a broad-wayed city
That was ransacked in war? Or were you alone
Out in the fields with your cattle and sheep
When raiders grabbed you and took you in their ship
And sold you for a good price to your master here?"

Then the swineherd Eumaeus told his story:

"Well, stranger, since you're curious about this,
Sit back and relax and drink your wine.
These nights are ungodly long. There's time to sleep
And to enjoy stories both. You shouldn't lie down
Too early. Too much sleep can leave a man tired.
If any of the rest of you would like,
You can go sleep outside. Just eat something
At daybreak and go out with our master's swine.
We two are going to stay here in the hut,
Eating and drinking and swapping stories
About each others' hard times. Past sorrows
Can comfort a man, especially one
Who has suffered much and wandered far.
But on to what you asked me about.
There is an island called Syria—
You may have heard of it—above Ortygia
And off toward the setting of the summer sun.
It doesn't have many people, but it's good land,
Rich in flocks and herds, full of grapes and wheat.
There's never any famine, and no disease.
When folks grow old, Apollo and Artemis
Come to town with their silver bows
And shoot them dead with their gentle arrows.
There are two cities that take up the island,
And my father Ctesius, son of Ormenus,
Ruled over both, a man like a god.
One day some Phoenician traders arrived,

Greedy men, with a shipload of baubles.
In my father's house was a Phoenician woman,
Tall and beautiful and skilled at crafts.
One of the craggy Phoenicians seduced her
As she was washing her clothes, lying with her
In their hollow ship—the sort of thing
That will gull the mind of any woman.
Afterward, he asked her who she was
And where she came from. She promptly pointed
To the high roof of my father's house:

'I am proud to say I am from bronze-rich Sidon
And am a daughter of Arybas, a wealthy man.
But Taphian pirates abducted me
As I came from the fields, and brought me here
And sold me to the master of that house over there,
Who paid a small fortune for me.'

"The man who had lain with her in secret said:

'Would you like to return with us to your home
And see your high-roofed house, and your parents, too?
They are still alive and said to be rich.'

"And the Phoenician woman responded:

'Perhaps, if you sailors will swear an oath
That you will bring me home without harming me.'

"When they had sworn the oath, the woman said:

'Be quiet now, and if any of you sees me
In the street or at the well, don't speak to me,
Or someone may tell the old king in the palace
And he might suspect something and lock me up
In painful bonds and sentence you to death.
Don't forget this. Just sell all your merchandise,
And as soon as your ship is laden with goods,
Send a messenger to me up in the palace.
I'll bring whatever gold I can lay my hands on.
And there's something else I can put up for my passage.
I'm the nurse of one of my master's children,
A clever boy who always tags along with me.
I'll bring him on board. He'll get a good price
In whatever foreign land you sell him off.'

"And with that she went off to the beautiful palace.
The Phoenicians stayed in our land for a full year
And filled their ship through all the trade they did.
When their ship was loaded for their voyage home,
They sent a messenger to tip off the woman.

A cunning man came to my father's house
With a golden necklace strung with amber.
While the women in the hall, and my noble mother,
Were looking it over and offering a price,
The man nodded to the woman in silence,
Nodded and went back to his hollow ship.
She took me by the hand and led me outside,
Stopping on the porch to scoop up three
Of the golden goblets left on the tables
By retainers of my father who had banqueted there
And then gone off to debate in the council.
She tucked these goblets into her bosom
And bore them off. I innocently followed.
The sun went down and the streets grew dark.
We hurried on to the glimmering harbor
Where the Phoenician ship was moored.
They had us board, and the ship set sail
Over the water with a following wind.
We sailed on for six solid days and nights,
But when Zeus put a seventh day in the sky,
Artemis came with her showering arrows
And shot the woman. She fell with a thud
Into the hold, like a tern plunging down.
They threw her overboard for the seals and fish,
And there I was, with a broken heart.
The wind and the waves bore the ship along
To Ithaca, where Laertes bought me.
And that was how I first saw this land."

Then Zeus-bred Odysseus said to him:

"Eumaeus, your story, with its tale
Of your painful ordeal, has touched my heart.
But in your case Zeus has set some good
Alongside the evil, since after all your suffering
You wound up at the house of a kindly man
Who gives you food and drink and treats you well.
You have a good life. But as for me, I came here
While wandering around from city to city."

They spoke to one another in this way
And then lay down to sleep, but not for long,
For Dawn soon rose in the blossoming sky.

Telemachus and his crew were now near to shore
And furling the sails in the early light.
They struck the mast quickly and rowed the ship
Up to her mooring. They threw out the anchor-stones,
Made the stern cables fast, and then disembarked
Onto the beach, where they prepared their meal
And mixed the glinting wine. After they had eaten,

Telemachus, clear-headed as ever, spoke to them:
"You men row the black ship to the town
While I go visit the fields and the herdsmen.
Around dusk, after I've looked over my lands,
I'll come to the city, and tomorrow morning
I'll set before you, as wages for your journey,
An excellent feast of meat and fine wine."

Then godlike Theoclymenus put in:

"And where shall I go, dear child? To whose house,
Of all those who are lords in rocky Ithaca?
Or should I go straight to yours and your mother's house?"

And Telemachus, in his clear-headed way:

"Ordinarily I would say go to our house,
For it has everything needed for hospitality.
But it wouldn't work out for you right now
Since I'll be away, and my mother won't see you.
She doesn't appear often before the suitors
But weaves at her loom in an upper chamber.
I'll tell you, though, whom you can go to:
Eurymachus, son of Polybus, whom now
The Ithacans look to as if he were a god.
He's the best man and is the most eager
To marry my mother and take over
My father's position. Only Olympian Zeus,
High in the air, knows if their doom will come
Crashing down on them before any wedding day."

As he spoke a bird flew by on the right,
A hawk, swift herald of Apollo, clutching
A dove in his talons, plucking her as he flew
And shedding her feathers down to the ground
Between the ship and Telemachus himself.
Theoclymenus called him aside
And, clasping his hand, said to him:

"Telemachus, that bird did not fly by on our right
Without a god sending it. I knew when I saw it
That it was a bird of omen. Your lineage
Is Ithaca's most royal. You will rule forever."

And Telemachus, clear-headed and calm:

"Would that what you say come true, stranger.
Then you would have from me such gifts
That whoever met you would call you blessed."

Then he said to Peiraeus, his trusted companion:

"Peiraeus, you have always come through for me,
And you went with me to Pylos. So now,
I ask you to show this stranger hospitality
In your house. Take good care of him until I come."

And Peiraeus, a spearman in his own right, said:

"Telemachus, no matter how long you stay out here,
I'll take care of him and give him my hospitality."

Then Peiraeus boarded the ship and gave the order
For the crew to board and untie the stern cables.
They were soon at their places. Telemachus, though,
Put on his fine sandals, took his bronze-tipped spear
From the ship's deck, and stood by as the crew
Untied the cables and shoved off.
Then Odysseus' son
Stepped out with swift strides until he reached
The farmstead where his countless swine were kept
By a servant whose heart was loyal and true.

BOOK XVI

Meanwhile, in the hut, Odysseus
And the noble swineherd had kindled a fire
And were making breakfast in the early light.
They had already sent the herdsmen out
With the droves of swine.
The dogs fawned
Around Telemachus and did not bark at him
As he approached. Odysseus noticed
The dogs fawning and heard footsteps.
His words flew fast to Eumaeus:

"Eumaeus, one of your men must be coming,
Or at least someone you know. The dogs aren't barking
And are fawning around him. I can hear his footsteps."

His words weren't out when his own son
Stood in the doorway. Up jumped the swineherd
In amazement, and from his hands fell the vessels
He was using to mix the wine. He went
To greet his master, kissing his head
And his shining eyes and both his hands.

And as a loving father embraces his own son
Come back from a distant land after ten long years,
His only son, greatly beloved and much sorrowed for—

So did the noble swineherd clasp Telemachus
And kiss him all over—he had escaped from death—
And sobbing he spoke to him these winged words:

"You have come, Telemachus, sweet light!
I thought I would never see you again
After you left in your ship for Pylos. But come in,
Dear child, let me feast my eyes on you
Here in my house, come back from abroad!
You don't visit the farm often, or us herdsmen,
But stay in town. It must do your heart good
To look at that weeviling crowd of suitors."

And Telemachus, in his clear-headed way:

"Have it your way, Papa. But it's for your sake I've come,
To see you with my own eyes, and to hear from you
Whether my mother is still in our house,
Or someone else has married her by now,
And Odysseus' bed, with no one to sleep in it,
Has become a nest of spider webs."

The swineherd answered him:

"Yes, she's in your house, waiting and waiting
With an enduring heart, poor soul,
Weeping away the lonely days and nights."

He spoke, and took the young man's spear.
Telemachus went in, and as he crossed
The stone threshold, Odysseus stood up
To offer him his seat, but Telemachus,
From across the room, checked him and said:

"Keep your seat, stranger. We'll find another one
Around the place. Eumaeus here can do that."

He spoke, and Odysseus sat down again.
The swineherd piled up some green brushwood
And covered it with a fleece, and upon this
The true son of Odysseus sat down.
Then the swineherd set out platters of roast meat—
Leftovers from yesterday's meal—
And hurried around heaping up bread in baskets
And mixing sweet wine in an ivy-wood bowl.
Then he sat down opposite godlike Odysseus,
And they helped themselves to the fare before them.
When they had enough to eat and drink,
Telemachus spoke to the godlike swineherd:

"Where did this stranger come from, Papa?
What kind of sailors brought him to Ithaca?
I don't suppose he walked to our island."

And you answered, Eumaeus, my swineherd:

"I'll tell you everything plainly, child.
He says he was born somewhere in Crete
And that it has been his lot to be a roamer
And wander from city to city. But now
He has run away from a Thesprotian ship
And come to my farmstead. I put him in your hands.
Do as you wish. He declares he is your suppliant."

And Telemachus, wise beyond his years:

"This makes my heart ache, Eumaeus.
How can I welcome this guest in my house?
I am still young, and I don't have the confidence
To defend myself if someone picks a fight.
As for my mother, her heart is torn.
She can't decide whether to stay here with me
And keep the house, honoring her husband's bed
And the voice of the people, or to go away
With whichever man among her suitors
Is the best of the Achaeans, and offers the most gifts.
But as to our guest—now that he's come to your house,
I will give him a tunic and cloak, fine clothes,
And a two-edged sword, and sandals for his feet,
And passage to wherever his heart desires.
Or keep him here if you wish, at your farmstead
And take care of him. I'll send the clothes
And all of his food, so it won't be a hardship
For you or your men. What I won't allow
Is for him to come up there among the suitors.
They are far too reckless and arrogant,
And I fear they will make fun of him, mock him,
And it would be hard for me to take that.
But what could I do? One man, however powerful,
Can't do much against superior numbers."

Then Odysseus, who had borne much, said:

"My friend—surely it is right for me to speak up—
It breaks my heart to hear you talk about
The suitors acting like this in your house
And going against the will of a man as great as you.
It is against your will, isn't it? What happened?
Do the people up and down the land all hate you?
Has a god turned them against you? Or do you blame
Your brothers, whom a man has to rely upon

In a fight, especially if a big fight comes up?
I wish I were as vigorous as I am angry,
Or were a son of flawless Odysseus, or Odysseus himself!
Then I would put my neck on the chopping block
If I did not give them hell when I came into
The halls of Odysseus, son of Laertes!
But if they overwhelmed me with superior numbers,
I would rather be dead, killed in my own halls,
Than have to keep watching these disgraceful deeds,
Strangers mistreated, men dragging the women
Through the beautiful halls, wine spilled,
Bread wasted, and all with no end in sight."

Telemachus answered in his clear-headed way:

"Well, stranger, I'll tell you the whole story.
It's not that the people have turned against me,
Nor do I have any brothers to blame. Zeus
Has made our family run in a single line.
Laertes was the only son of Arcesius,
And Laertes had only one son, Odysseus,
Who only had me, a son he never knew.
And so now our house is filled with enemies,
All of the nobles who rule the islands—
Dulichium, Samê, wooded Zacynthus—
And all of those with power on rocky Ithaca
Are courting my mother and ruining our house.
She neither refuses to make a marriage she hates
Or is able to stop it. They are eating us
Out of house and home, and will come after me soon.
But all of this rests on the knees of the gods.
Eumaeus, go tell Penelope right away
That I'm safe and back from Pylos.
I'll wait for you here. Tell only her
And don't let any of the suitors find out.
Many of them are plotting against me."

And you answered him, Eumaeus, my swineherd:

"I follow you, Telemachus, I understand.
But tell me this. Should I go the same way
To Laertes also, and tell him the news?
Poor man, for a while he still oversaw the fields,
Although he was grieving greatly for Odysseus,
And would eat and drink with the slaves in the house
Whenever he had a notion. But now, since the very day
You sailed to Pylos, they say he hasn't been
Eating or drinking as before, or overseeing the fields.
He just sits and groans, weeping his heart out,
And the flesh is wasting away from his bones."

And Telemachus, in his clear-headed way:

"That's hard, but we will let him be, despite our pain.
If mortals could have all their wishes granted,
We would choose first the day of my father's return.
No, just deliver your message and come back,
And don't go traipsing all through the countryside
Looking for Laertes. But tell my mother
To send the housekeeper as soon as she can,
Secretly. She could bring the old man the message."

So the swineherd got going. He tied on his sandals
And was off to the city.
The swineherd's departure
Was not unnoticed by Athena. She approached
The farmstead in the likeness of a woman,
Beautiful, tall, and accomplished in handiwork,
And stood in the doorway of Eumaeus' hut,
Showing herself to Odysseus. Telemachus
Did not see her before him or notice her presence,
For the gods are not visible to everyone.
But Odysseus saw her, and the dogs did, too,
And they did not bark, but slunk away whining
To the other side of the farmstead. The goddess
Lifted her brows, and Odysseus understood.
He went out of the hut, past the courtyard's great wall,
And stood before her. Athena said to him:

"Son of Laertes in the line of Zeus,
Tell your son now and do not keep him in the dark,
So that you two can plan the suitors' destruction
And then go into town. As for myself,
I will not be gone long. No, I am eager for battle."

With this, she touched him with her golden wand.
A fresh tunic and cloak replaced his rags,
And he was taller and younger, his skin tanned,
His jawline firm, and his beard glossy black.
Having worked her magic, the goddess left,
And Odysseus went back into the hut.
His son was astounded. Shaken and flustered,
He turned away his eyes for fear it was a god,
And words fell from his lips in nervous flurries:

"You look different, stranger, than you did before,
And your clothes are different, and your complexion.
You must be a god, one of the immortals
Who hold high heaven. Be gracious to us
So we can offer you acceptable sacrifice
And finely wrought gold. And spare us, please."

And godlike Odysseus, who had borne much:

"I am no god. Why liken me to the deathless ones?
No, I am your father, on whose account you have suffered
Many pains and endured the violence of men."

Saying this, he kissed his son, and let his tears
Fall to the ground. He had held them in until now.
But Telemachus could not believe
That this was his father, and he blurted out:

"You cannot be my father Odysseus.
You must be some spirit, enchanting me
Only to increase my grief and pain later.
No mortal man could figure out how to do this
All on his own. Only a god could so easily
Transform someone from old to young.
A while ago you were old and shabbily dressed,
And now you are like the gods who hold high heaven."

And Odysseus, from his mind's teeming depths:

"Telemachus, it does not become you to be so amazed
That your father is here in this house. You can be sure
That no other Odysseus will ever come.
But I am here, just as you see, home at last
After twenty years of suffering and wandering.
So you will know, this is Athena's doing.
She can make me look like whatever she wants:
A beggar sometimes, and sometimes a young man
Wearing fine clothes. It's easy for the gods
To glorify a man or to make him look poor."

He spoke, and sat down. And Telemachus
Threw his arms around his wonderful father
And wept. And a longing arose in both of them
To weep and lament, and their shrill cries
Crowded the air

like the cries of birds—
Sea-eagles or taloned vultures—
Whose young chicks rough farmers have stolen
Out of their nests before they were fledged.

Their tears were that piteous. And the sun,
Its light fading, would have set on their weeping,
Had not Telemachus suddenly said to his father:

"What ship brought you here, Father,
And where did the crew say they were from?
I don't suppose you came here on foot."

And Odysseus, the godlike survivor:

"I'll tell you the truth about this, son.
The Phaeacians brought me, famed sailors
Who give passage to all who come their way.
They brought me over the sea as I slept
In their swift ship, and set me ashore on Ithaca
With donations of bronze and clothing and gold,
Splendid treasures that are now stored in caves
By grace of the gods. I have come here now
At Athena's suggestion. You and I must plan
How to kill our enemies. List them for me now
So I can know who they are, and how many,
And so I can weigh the odds and decide whether
You and I can go up against them alone
Or whether we have to enlist some allies."

Telemachus took a deep breath and said:

"Father, look now, I know your great reputation,
How you can handle a spear and what a strategist you are,
But this is too much for me. Two men
Simply cannot fight against such superior numbers
And superior force. There are not just ten suitors,
Or twice that, but many times more. Here's the count:
From Dulichium there are fifty-two—
The pick of their young men—and six attendants.
From Samê there are twenty-four,
From Zacynthus there are twenty,
And from Ithaca itself, twelve, all the noblest,
And with them are Medon the herald,
The divine bard, and two attendants who carve.
If we go up against all of them in the hall,
I fear your vengeance will be bitter indeed.
Please try to think of someone to help us,
Someone who would gladly be our ally."

And Odysseus, who had borne much:

"I'll tell you who will help. Do you think
That Athena and her father, Zeus,
Would be help enough? Or should I think of more?"

Telemachus answered in his clear-headed way:

"You're talking about two excellent allies,
Although they do sit a little high in the clouds
And have to rule the whole world and the gods as well."

And Odysseus, who had borne much:

"Those two won't hold back from battle for long.
They'll be here, all right, when the fighting starts
Between the suitors and us in my high-roofed halls.

For now, go at daybreak up to the house,
And keep company with these insolent hangers-on.
The swineherd will lead me to the city later
Looking like an old, broken-down beggar.
If they treat me badly in the house,
Just endure it. Even if they drag me
Through the door by my feet, or throw things at me,
Just bear it patiently. Try to dissuade them,
Try to talk them out of their folly, sure,
But they won't listen to you at all,
Because their day of reckoning is near.
And here's something else for you to keep in mind:
When Athena in her wisdom prompts me,
I'll give you a signal. When you see me nod,
Take all the weapons that are in the hall
Into the lofted storeroom and stow them there.
When the suitors miss them and ask you
Where they are, set their minds at ease, saying:
'Oh, I have stored them out of the smoke.
They're nothing like they were when Odysseus
Went off to Troy, but are all grimed with soot.
Also, a god put this thought into my head,
That when you men are drinking, you might
Start quarreling and someone could get hurt,
Which would ruin your feasting and courting.
Steel has a way of drawing a man to it.'
But leave behind a couple of swords for us,
And two spears and oxhide shields—leave them
Where we can get to them in a hurry.
Pallas Athena and Zeus in his cunning
Will keep the suitors in a daze for a while.
    And one more thing before you go.
If you are really my son and have my blood
In your veins, don't let anyone know
That Odysseus is at home—not Laertes,
Not the swineherd, not anyone in the house,
Not even Penelope. You and I by ourselves
Will figure out which way the women are leaning.
We'll test more than one of the servants, too,
And see who respects us and fears us,
And who cares nothing about either one of us
And fails to honor you. You're a man now."

And Odysseus' resplendent son answered:

"You'll soon see what I'm made of, Father,
And I don't think you'll find me lacking.
But I'm not sure your plan will work
To our advantage. Think about it.
It'll take forever for you to make the rounds
Testing each man, while back in the house
The high-handed suitors are having a good time

Eating their way through everything we own.
I agree you should find out which of the women
Dishonor you, and which are innocent.
But as for testing the men in the fields,
Let's do that afterward, if indeed you know
Something from Zeus, who holds the aegis."

While these two were speaking to each other,
The sturdy ship that brought Telemachus
And his crew from Pylos was pulling in
To Ithaca. They sailed into the deep harbor
And hauled the black ship up onto the shore.
Porters in high spirits relieved them of their gear
And carried the beautiful gifts to Clytius' house.
They sent a herald ahead to Odysseus' palace
To tell Penelope that Telemachus
Was out in the country and had ordered the ship
To sail on to the city so that she, the queen,
Would not fall to weeping with worry.
So it happened that the swineherd and herald
Met while they were bringing the same message
To Odysseus' wife. When they reached the palace,
The herald spoke out in the women's presence:

"As of now, Lady, your son has returned."

But the swineherd went up to Penelope
And told her all that her son had asked him to.
His message delivered, he left the hall
And went through the courtyard and back to his swine.

This was bad news for the suitors.
They filed out of the hall and past the great wall
Of the courtyard and sat down before the gates.
Eurymachus, Polybus' son, was first to speak:

"Damn it! Telemachus has some nerve,
Pulling off this voyage. We never thought
We'd see it happen. Well, let's get a tarred ship
Out on the water, the best we have, and a crew
To man the oars and tell our men out at sea
To get back here as soon as they can."

He was still speaking when Amphinomus,
Turning around, saw a ship in the harbor,
Sails being furled, the crew with oars in their hands.
He chuckled softly and said to his companions:

"Well, so much for a message. Here they are.
Either some god told them, or they spotted
Telemachus' ship sailing by but couldn't catch her."

They trooped down to the shore and made quick work
Of hauling the black ship onto the beach.
Attendants relieved the crew of their gear,
And the whole company went off to the assembly.
They wouldn't allow anyone else, young or old,
To sit with them. Antinous rose to speak:

"Just look at how the gods have saved this man!
Day after day watchmen sat on the windy heights,
Relieving each other until the sun went down.
And we never spent the night on the shore
But were out at sea all night, waiting for dawn,
Waiting for Telemachus, out for his blood—
And now some god has delivered him home.
We'll have to find a way to do him in here.
We can't let him slip through our hands again.
As long as Telemachus is still alive
I don't like our odds in what we're trying to do.
He's shrewd and he's smart, and the people
Aren't on our side at all any more.
We have to act before he calls an assembly.
I don't think he's going to let things slide.
He's going to be angry, and he'll stand up
And tell everyone how we plotted his death
But could not catch him. They won't approve
When they hear of our crimes, and there's a danger
They'll do something to us, drive us out
Of our land, and we'll wind up in exile.
No, we have to beat him to it, jump him
Out in the fields away from the city,
Or on the road. We'll keep all his possessions,
Dividing them fairly among us. His house, though,
We'll give to his mother and whoever weds her.
But if you don't like this plan, if you'd rather
He stay alive and keep his ancestral wealth,
We shouldn't keep gathering here any more
And devouring all this pleasant fare.
Each man will have to court her from his own house,
Sending her gifts and trying to win her hand,
And she will marry the man who offers the most
And comes to her as her fated husband."

He spoke, and they all sat there in silence
Until Amphinomus stood up to speak.
Son of Nisus and grandson of Aretias,
He led the suitors who came from Dulichium,
With its grassy meadows and rich wheatfields.
Penelope liked him, for the way he spoke
And the good sense he showed, and now
He spoke to the suitors with good will to all:

"Friends, I would not willingly choose to kill
Telemachus. It is a serious matter to murder
Someone of royal stock. We should first consult
The will of the gods. If great Zeus ordains it,
I will kill him myself, and urge on others.
But if the gods are against it, I urge you to stop."

Amphinomus' speech carried the day. The suitors
Stood up and went back to Odysseus' house,
Entered and sat on their polished chairs.

Penelope now had a notion to come out
Among her overbearing, insolent suitors.
She had learned of the plot to kill her son
In his own house—the herald Medon told her
After he overheard the suitors talking—
And so the beautiful lady came
Into the hall with her serving women.
When she had come among the suitors
She stood shawled in light by a column
That supported the roof of the great house.
Hiding her cheeks behind her silken veils,
She spoke these harsh words to Antinous:

"Antinous, you are a haughty and evil man.
They say you are the best of your generation
In all of Ithaca in counsel and in speech,
But you don't measure up to your reputation.
You must be mad. Plotting Telemachus' death!
Don't you care at all that your father was once
A suppliant here? Zeus witnesses this,
And it is unholy for suppliants and hosts
To harm each other. Or haven't you heard
Of the time your father came to this house
As a fugitive? The people were angry with him
Because he had joined up with the Taphian pirates
And harassed our allies, the Thesprotians.
The citizens wanted to beat him to death
And gobble up his large and pleasant estate,
But they were held in check by Odysseus.
It is his house that you are now gobbling up
Without atonement, his wife you are wooing,
His son you are trying to kill—and as for me,
You are causing me unspeakable distress.
Stop it, I tell you, and tell the others to stop."

Then Eurymachus, son of Polybus, answered:

"Penelope, Icarius' wise daughter,
Cheer up. Don't be so upset by all this.
There's not a man alive, nor will there ever be,

Who will lay hands on your son, Telemachus,
While I still breathe and look upon this earth.
Anyone who tries, I give you my solemn assurance,
Will spill his black blood around the point of my spear.
No, I, too, often sat on Odysseus' knees,
And the great hero would put roast meat in my hands
And make me sip red wine. And so Telemachus
Is the dearest of all men to me, and I guarantee
He need have no fear of death—from the suitors,
That is. From the gods there is no avoiding it."

A heart-warming speech, but he was still planning
To kill her son.
Penelope went upstairs
To her softly lit rooms and wept for Odysseus,
Her beloved husband, until grey-eyed Athena
Cast sweet sleep upon the woman's eyelids.

Evening fell, and the swineherd came back
To Odysseus and his son, who had slaughtered
A yearling boar and were busy making supper.
Athena drew near to Odysseus and tapped him
With her wand, making him into an old man again,
Clothed in rags. She was afraid the swineherd
Would recognize him and, unable to keep the secret,
Go bring the news to Penelope.

Telemachus looked up and said to the swineherd:

"You're back, Eumaeus. What news from town?
Have the suitors returned from their ambush,
Or are they still looking for me to sail past?"

And you answered him, Eumaeus, my swineherd:

"It wasn't my business to nose around town
Asking about that, and I wanted to come back
As soon as I had delivered my message.
On the way in, though, I met up with a herald
Sent by your shipmates. He was fast
And got there first to tell your mother the news.
I know one more thing, for I saw it myself.
I was above the city, by the hill of Hermes,
On my way back, when I saw a sailing ship
Pull into our harbor. She had a large crew
And was loaded with shields and bladed spears.
I thought it was them, but I don't really know."

Telemachus smiled, feeling his ancestors' blood,
And glanced at Odysseus, avoiding the swineherd's eye.
When they had finished preparing the meal,

They fell to feasting. There was plenty for everyone,
And when they all had enough of food and drink,
Their minds turned toward rest, and they took the gift of sleep.

BOOK XVII

When Dawn brushed the early sky with rose
Odysseus' son bound on his beautiful sandals
And hefted his spear. He was in a hurry
To get to the city, and he said to his swineherd:

"I'm off to the town, Eumaeus. My mother
Won't stop crying until she sees me again,
In person. But this is what I want you to do.
Take this down-and-out stranger into the city
So that he can beg for food. Whoever wants to
Can give him some bread and a cup of water.
There's no way I can worry about everyone,
I have too much on my mind. If the stranger
Gets upset about this, it's just too bad.
I'm the sort of person who likes to talk straight."

And Odysseus, his mind teeming, said:

"Friend, don't think I'm eager myself
To be left behind here. For a beggar like me,
It's better to beg for food in the town
Than out in the fields, and whoever wants to
Can give me something. I'm past the age
Where I can stay on a farm and have to do
Everything some foreman tells me.
You go on. This man here will lead me to town
As soon as I have warmed myself by the fire
And the sun is higher. These clothes I'm wearing
Are not so good, and the morning frost
Might do me in. You say the city is pretty far."

Thus Odysseus, and Telemachus strode quickly
Out of the farmstead, sowing death for the suitors
With every step he took.
When he came to the house
He leaned his spear against a tall pillar
And went in over the stone threshold.
Eurycleia
Spotted him first, as she was spreading fleeces
Over finely wrought chairs. She burst into tears
And ran straight over to him. The other maids
Of Odysseus' household gathered around
And kissed his head and shoulders in welcome.

Then from her bedroom came wise Penelope,
Looking like Artemis[2] or golden Aphrodite.
She burst into tears and threw her arms around him
And kissed his head and both his shining eyes,
And through her sobs spoke these winged words:

"You have come, Telemachus, sweet light!
I thought I would never see you again
After you left in your ship for Pylos—
Behind my back—for news of your father.
But tell me, what did you find out about him?"

Telemachus answered her coolly:

"Don't make me weep, mother, or get me
All worked up. I barely escaped with my life.
Now bathe yourself and put on clean clothes,
Then go to your bedroom upstairs with your maids
And vow formal sacrifice to the immortal gods
In the hope that Zeus will grant us vengeance.
I'm going to town so I can invite to our house
A stranger who came here with me from Pylos.
I sent him on ahead with some of my crew,
And I told Peiraeus to take him home
And show him hospitality until I arrived."

Penelope's response to this died on her lips.
She bathed, and dressed herself in clean clothes,
And vowed sacrifices to the immortal gods,
Praying that Zeus would grant them vengeance some day.

Telemachus went out through the hall
Holding a spear, two lean hounds at his side.
Athena shed a silver grace upon him,
And everyone marveled at him as he passed.
The haughty suitors crowded around him,
Fine words on their lips, and evil in their hearts.
Telemachus slipped away from the throng
And went to sit down over to one side
With Mentor, Antiphus, and Halitherses,
Old friends of his father. They wanted to know
Everything Telemachus had done. And then
Peiraeus came up, leading the stranger, Theoclymenus,
Up through the city to where the men were gathered.
Telemachus did not keep his back to him long
But went up to the stranger, who was his guest.
It was Peiraeus who spoke first, saying:

2. Artemis, goddess of hunting, was associated with chastity and the moon.

"Telemachus, get some women over to my house,
So I can send you the gifts Menelaus gave you."

And Telemachus, in his clear-headed way:

"Peiraeus, we don't know how things will turn out.
Should the suitors treacherously kill me at home
And divide among them my family's wealth,
I would rather that you keep all these gifts
And enjoy them, rather than any of that crowd.
But if I manage to sow the seeds of their death,
I'll be glad to have all of it back from you then."

Saying that, Telemachus led the stranger,
Who had endured much in life, to his house.
They went inside and laid their cloaks on chairs,
And then went into the polished tubs and bathed.
When the maids had bathed them and rubbed them
With oil, and flung upon them fleecy cloaks and tunics,
They came out of the baths and sat down on chairs.
A maid poured water from a golden pitcher
Into a silver basin for them to wash their hands
And then set up a polished table nearby.
Another serving woman, grave and dignified,
Set out bread and generous helpings
From the other dishes she had.
Penelope
Sat opposite her son by the doorpost of the hall,
Leaning back on a chair and spinning fine yarn.
The two men reached for the good cheer before them,
And when they had their fill of food and drink,
Penelope was the first to speak:

"Telemachus,
I think I will go now to my room upstairs
And lie down on my bed, which has become for me
A sorrowful bed, ever wet with my tears
Since the day Odysseus left for Troy
With the sons of Atreus. You do not have the heart
To tell me, before the suitors come in,
Whatever you have heard about your father's return."

And Telemachus, in his clear-headed way:

"Rest assured I will tell you now, mother.
We went to Pylos, and Nestor, the king there,
Took me into his house. He welcomed me
As a father might welcome his long-lost son,
And he put me up with his own glorious sons.
But he said he had heard nothing from anyone
About whether Odysseus was dead or alive.

He sent me in a chariot to visit Menelaus,
Atreus' son, and there I saw Helen,
For whose sake the Greek and Trojan armies
Suffered so much, by the will of the gods.
Then Menelaus asked me why I had come
To gleaming Lacedaemon. I told him why,
And this is exactly what he told me then:
'Those dogs! Those puny weaklings,
Wanting to sleep in the bed of a hero!
A doe might as well bed her suckling fawns
In the lair of a lion, leaving them there
In the bush and then going off over the hills
Looking for grassy fields. When the lion
Comes back, the fawns die an ugly death.
That's the kind of death these men will die
When Odysseus comes back. O Father Zeus,
And Athena and Apollo, bring Odysseus back
With the strength he showed in Lesbos once
When he wrestled a match with Philomeleides
And threw him hard, making all of us cheer—
That's the Odysseus I want the suitors to meet!
They'd get married all right—to bitter death.
But, as to what you ask me about,
I will not stray from the point or deceive you.
No, I will tell you all that the infallible
Old Man of the Sea told me, and hide nothing.
He said he saw him on an island, miserable,
In the halls of Calypso, who keeps him there
Against his will. He has no way to get home
To his native land. He has no ships left,
No crew to row him over the sea's broad back.'
Those were the words of Menelaus, Atreus' son,
The great spearman. When I finished up there,
I set out for home, and a fair wind from the gods
Brought me back quickly to my native land."

So he spoke, and his words wrung her heart.
Then Theoclymenus made his voice heard:

"Revered lady, wife of Laertes' son, Odysseus,
Menelaus is in the dark about all this, but now
Hear what I have to say, for I will prophesy
Unerringly to you and conceal nothing.
With Zeus above all gods as my witness,
I swear, by this table of hospitality,
And by Odysseus' hearth, to which I have come,
That this same Odysseus, mark my words,
Is at this moment in his own native land,
Sitting still or on the move, learning of this evil,
And he is sowing evil for all the suitors.
Such is the bird of omen I saw

From the ship, and I cried it out to Telemachus."

And Penelope, calm and circumspect:

"Ah, stranger, may your words come true.
Then you would know my kindness, and my gifts
Would make you blessed in all men's eyes."
While they spoke to each other in this way,
The suitors were entertaining themselves
In front of Odysseus' palace again,
Throwing the javelin and discus
On the level terrace, arrogant as ever.
When it was time for dinner, and the flocks
Were coming in from the fields, Medon,
Who was the suitors' favorite herald
And was always at their feasts, called out:

"Young men, now that you have enjoyed yourselves
On the field, come inside so we can prepare a feast.
Dinner at dinnertime is not a bad thing at all."

It didn't take much to persuade them. Up they rose
And filed into the stately house. They laid their cloaks
On the chairs, and some of them got busy
Slaughtering great sheep and plump goats,
Fattened hogs, too, and a heifer of the herd.

While they were making their dinner, Odysseus
And the noble swineherd were getting ready
To go up from the fields to the city.
The swineherd started off by saying:

"Well, stranger, since you're eager to go
To the city today, as my master ordered—
Although for my part I'd rather have you here
To mind the farm, but I do respect him
And fear him, and I certainly don't want
A tongue-lashing from him, which could go hard—
Anyway, we'd better get going. It's late
In the day, and it'll be colder toward evening."

And Odysseus, his mind teeming:

"No need to tell me that. I understand.
Let's go. You lead the way, all the way.
But, if you have one cut, give me a staff
To lean on. You said the trail was slippery."

He spoke, and threw around his shoulders
His ratty pouch, full of holes and slung
By a twisted cord. Eumaeus gave him a staff

That suited him, and the two of them set out.
The dogs and the herdsmen stayed behind
To guard the farmstead. And so the swineherd
Led his master to the city, looking like
An old, broken-down beggar, leaning
On a staff and dressed in miserable rags.

They were well along the rugged path
And near to the city when they came to a spring
Where the townspeople got their water.
This beautiful fountain had been made
By Ithacus, and Neritus, and Polyctor.
A grove of poplars encircled it
And the cold water flowed from the rock above,
On top of which was built an altar to the nymphs,
Where all wayfarers made offerings.
There
Melanthius, son of Dolius, met them
As he was driving his she-goats, the best
In the herds, into town for the suitors' dinner.
Two herdsmen trailed along behind him.
When he saw Eumaeus and his companion,
He greeted them with language so ugly
It made Odysseus' blood boil to hear it:

"Well, look at this, trash dragging along trash.
Birds of a feather, as usual. Where
Are you taking this walking pile of shit,
You miserable hog-tender, this diseased beggar
Who will slobber all over our feasts?
How many doorposts has he rubbed with his shoulders,
Begging for scraps? You think he's ever gotten
A proper present, a cauldron or sword? Ha!
Give him to me and I'll have him sweep out the pens
And carry loads of shoots for the goats to eat,
Put some muscle on his thigh by drinking whey.
I'll bet he's never done a hard day's work in his life.
No, he prefers to beg his way through town
For food to stuff into his bottomless belly.
I'll tell you this, though, and you can count on it.
If he comes to the palace of godlike Odysseus,
He'll be pelted with footstools aimed at his head.
If he's lucky they'll only splinter on his ribs."

And as he passed Odysseus, the fool kicked him
On the hip, trying to shove him off the path.
Odysseus absorbed the blow without even quivering—
Only stood there and tried to decide whether
To jump the man and knock him dead with his staff
Or lift him by the ears and smash his head to the ground.
In the end, he controlled himself and just took it.

But the swineherd looked the man in the eye
And told him off, and lifted his hands in prayer:

"Nymphs of the spring, daughters of Zeus,
If Odysseus ever honored you by burning
Thigh bones of lambs and kids wrapped in rich fat,
Grant me this prayer:
May my master come back,
May some god guide him back!
Then,
He would scatter all that puffery of yours,
All the airs you put on strutting around town
While bad herdsmen destroy all the flocks."
Melanthius, the goatherd, came back with this:

"Listen to the dog talk, with his big, bad notions.
I'm going to take him off in a black ship someday
Far from Ithaca, and sell him for a fortune.
You want my prayer? May Apollo with his silver bow
Strike Telemachus dead today in his halls,
Or may the suitors kill him, as surely as Odysseus
Is lost for good in some faraway land."

He left them with that. They walked on slowly,
While the goatherd pushed ahead and came quickly
To the palace. He went right in and sat down
Among the suitors, opposite Eurymachus,
Whom he liked best of all. The servers
Set out for him a helping of meat,
And the grave housekeeper brought him bread.

Odysseus and the swineherd came up to the house
And halted. The sound of the hollow lyre
Drifted out to them, for Phemius
Was sweeping the strings as he began his song.
Odysseus took the swineherd's hand and said:

"Eumaeus, this beautiful house must be Odysseus'.
It would stand out anywhere. Look at all the rooms
And stories, and the court built with wall and coping,
And the well-fenced double gates. No one could scorn it.
And I can tell there are many men feasting inside
From the savor of meat wafting out from it,
And the sound of the lyre, which rounds out a feast."

And you answered him, swineherd Eumaeus:

"You don't miss a thing, do you? Well,
Let's figure out what we should do here.
Either you go in first and mingle with the suitors,
While I wait here; or you wait here,

If you'd rather, and I'll go in before you.
But don't wait long, or someone might see you
And either throw something at you or smack you.
Think it over. What would you like to do?"

And Odysseus, the godlike survivor:

"I understand. You don't have to prompt me.
You go in before me, and I'll wait here.
I've had things thrown at me before,
And I have an enduring heart, Eumaeus.
God knows I've had my share of suffering
In war and at sea. I can take more if I have to.
But no one can hide a hungry belly.
It's our worst enemy. It's why we launch ships
To bring war to men across the barren sea."

And as they talked, a dog that was lying there
Lifted his head and pricked up his ears.
This was Argus, whom Odysseus himself
Had patiently bred—but never got to enjoy—
Before he left for Ilion. The young men
Used to set him after wild goats, deer, and hare.
Now, his master gone, he lay neglected
In the dung of mules and cattle outside the doors,
A deep pile where Odysseus' farmhands
Would go for manure to spread on his fields.
There lay the hound Argus, infested with lice.
And now, when he sensed Odysseus was near,
He wagged his tail and dropped both ears
But could not drag himself nearer his master.
Odysseus wiped away a tear, turning his head
So Eumaeus wouldn't notice, and asked him:

"Eumaeus, isn't it strange that this dog
Is lying in the dung? He's a beautiful animal,
But I wonder if he has speed to match his looks,
Or if he's like the table dogs men keep for show."

And you answered him, Eumaeus, my swineherd:

"Ah yes, this dog belonged to a man who has died
Far from home. He was quite an animal once.
If he were now as he was when Odysseus
Left for Troy, you would be amazed
At his speed and strength. There's nothing
In the deep woods that dog couldn't catch,
And what a nose he had for tracking!
But he's fallen on hard times, now his master
Has died abroad. These feckless women
Don't take care of him. Servants never do right

When their masters aren't on top of them.
Zeus takes away half a man's worth
The day he loses his freedom."

So saying,
Eumaeus entered the great house
And the hall filled with the insolent suitors.
But the shadow of death descended upon Argus,
Once he had seen Odysseus after twenty years.

Godlike Telemachus spotted the swineherd first
Striding through the hall, and with a nod of his head
Signaled him to join him. Eumaeus looked around
And took a stool that lay near, one that the carver
Ordinarily sat on when he sliced meat for the suitors
Dining in the hall. Eumaeus took this stool
And placed it at Telemachus' table, opposite him,
And sat down. A herald came and served him
A portion of meat, and bread from the basket.

Soon after, Odysseus came in, looking like
An old, broken-down beggar, leaning
On a staff and dressed in miserable rags.
He sat down on the ashwood threshold
Just inside the doors, leaning back
On the cypress doorpost, a post planed and trued
By some skillful carpenter in days gone by.
Telemachus called the swineherd over
And taking a whole loaf from the beautiful basket
And all the meat his hands could hold, said to him:

"Take this over to the stranger, and tell him
To go around and beg from each of the suitors.
Shame is no good companion for a man in need."

Thus Telemachus. The swineherd nodded,
And going over to Odysseus, said to him:

"Telemachus gives you this, and he tells you
To go around and beg from each of the suitors.
Shame, he says, is not good for a beggar."

And Odysseus, his mind teeming:

"Lord Zeus, may Telemachus be blessed among men
And may he have all that his heart desires."

And he took the food in both his hands
And set it down at his feet on his beggar's pouch.
Odysseus ate as long as the bard sang in the hall.

When the song came to an end, and the suitors
Began to be noisy and boisterous, Athena
Drew near to him and prompted him
To go among the suitors and beg for crusts
And so learn which of them were decent men
And which were scoundrels—not that the goddess had
The slightest intention of sparing any of them.

Odysseus made his rounds from right to left,
Stretching his hands out to every side,
As if he had been a beggar all his life.
They all pitied him and gave him something,
And they wondered out loud who he was
And where he had come from. To which questions
Melanthius, the goatherd, volunteered:

"Hear me, suitors of our noble queen.
As to this stranger, I have seen him before.
The swineherd brought him here, but who he is
I have no idea, or where he claims he was born."
At this, Antinous tore into the swineherd:

"Swineherd! Why did you bring this man to town?
Don't we have enough tramps around here without him,
This nuisance of a beggar who will foul our feast?
I suppose you don't care that these men are eating away
Your master's wealth, or you wouldn't have invited him."

The swineherd Eumaeus came back with this:

"You may be a fine gentleman, Antinous,
But that's an ugly thing to say. Who, indeed,
Ever goes out of his way to invite a stranger
From abroad, unless it's a prophet, or healer,
Or a builder, or a singer of tales—someone like that,
A master of his craft who benefits everyone.
Men like that get invited everywhere on earth.
But who would burden himself with a beggar?
You're just plain mean, the meanest of the suitors
To Odysseus' servants, and especially to me.
But I don't care, as long as my lady Penelope
Lives in the hall, and godlike Telemachus."

To which Telemachus responded coolly:

"Quiet! Don't waste your words on this man.
Antinous is nasty like that—provoking people
With harsh words and egging them on."

And then he had these fletched words for Antinous:

"Why, Antinous, you're just like a father to me,
Kindly advising me to kick this stranger out.
God forbid that should ever happen. No,
Go ahead and give him something. I want you to.
Don't worry about my mother or anyone else
In this house, when it comes to giving things away.
But the truth is that you're just being selfish
And would rather eat more yourself than give any away."

And Antinous answered him:

"What a high and mighty speech, Telemachus!
Look now, if only everyone gave him what I will,
It would be months before he darkened your door."

As he spoke he grabbed the stool upon which
He propped his shining feet whenever he dined
And brandished it beneath the table.
But all the rest gave the beggar something
And filled his pouch with bread and meat.
And Odysseus would have had his taste of the suitors
Free of charge, but on his way back to the threshold
He stopped by Antinous' place and said:

"Give me something, friend. You don't look like
You are the poorest man here—far from it—
But the most well off. You look like a king.
So you should give me more than the others.
If you did, I'd sing your praises all over the earth.
I, too, once had a house of my own, a rich man
In a wealthy house, and I gave freely and often
To any and everyone who wandered by.
I had slaves, too, more than I could count,
And everything I needed to live the good life.
But Zeus smashed it all to pieces one day—
Who knows why?—when he sent me out
With roving pirates all the way to Egypt
So I could meet my doom.
I moored my ships
In the river Nile, and you can be sure I ordered
My trusty mates to stand by and guard them
While I sent out scouts to look around.
Then the crews got cocky and overconfident
And started pillaging the Egyptian countryside,
Carrying off the women and children
And killing the men. The cry came to the city,
And at daybreak troops answered the call.
The whole plain was filled with infantry,
War chariots, and the glint of bronze.
Thundering Zeus threw my men into a panic,

And not one had the courage to stand and fight
Against odds like that. It was bad.
They killed many of us outright with bronze
And led the rest to their city to work as slaves.
But they gave me to a friend of theirs, from Cyprus,
To take me back there and give me to Dmetor,
Son of Iasus, who ruled Cyprus with an iron hand.
From there I came here, with all my hard luck."

Antinous had this to say in reply:

"What god has brought this plague in here?
Get off to the side, away from me,
Or I'll show you Egypt and Cyprus,
You pushy panhandler! You don't know your place.
You make your rounds and everyone
Hands things out recklessly. And why shouldn't they?
It's easy to be generous with someone else's wealth."

Odysseus took a step back and answered him:

"It's too bad your mind doesn't match your good looks.
You wouldn't give a suppliant even a pinch of salt
If you had to give it from your own cupboard.
Here you sit at another man's table
And you can't bear to give me a piece of bread
From the huge pile that's right by your hand."

This made Antinous even angrier,
And he shot back with a dark scowl:

"That does it. I'm not going to let you just
Breeze out of here if you're going to insult me."

As he spoke he grabbed the footstool and threw it,
Hitting Odysseus under his right shoulderblade.
Odysseus stood there as solid as a rock
And didn't even blink. He only shook his head
In silence, and brooded darkly.
Then he went back to the threshold and sat down
With his pouch bulging and spoke to the suitors:

"Hear me, suitors of our glorious queen,
So I can speak my mind. No one regrets
Being hit while fighting for his own possessions,
His cattle or sheep. But Antinous struck me
Because of my belly, that vile growling beast
That gives us so much trouble. If there are gods
For beggars, or avenging spirits,
May death come to Antinous before marriage does."

Antinous, son of Eupeithes, answered:

"Just sit still and eat, stranger—or get the hell out.
Keep talking like this and some of the young men here
Will haul you by the feet all through the house
And strip the skin right off your back."

Thus Antinous. But the other suitors
Turned on him, one of them saying:

"That was foul, Antinous, hitting a poor beggar.
You're done for if he turns out to be a god
Come down from heaven, the way they do,
Disguised as strangers from abroad or whatever,
Going around to different cities
And seeing who's lawless and who lives by the rules."

Antinous paid no attention to this.
Telemachus took it hard that his father was struck
But he kept it inside. Not a tear
Fell from his eye. He only shook his head
In silence, and brooded darkly.

When Penelope, sitting with her maids,
Heard the stranger had been struck, she said:

"So may you be struck by the Archer God."

And Eurynome, the housekeeper, said to her:

"If our prayers were answered, not one of these men
Would live to see Dawn take her seat in the sky."

Penelope answered in her circumspect way:

"They're all hateful, nurse, for their evil designs,
But Antinous is like black death itself.
Some poor stranger makes his rounds through the house
Begging alms from the men because he is in need,
And all the others fill his pouch with gifts,
But Antinous throws a footstool at him
And hits him in the back beneath his shoulder."

Thus Penelope, sitting with her women,
While noble Odysseus ate his dinner.
Then she called the swineherd to her and said:

"Noble Eumaeus, tell the stranger to come here
So that I can greet him and ask him if perhaps
He has heard anything about Odysseus
Or seen him with his own eyes. By his looks
He is a man who has wandered the world."

And you, my swineherd, answered her:

"I wish the men would keep quiet, Lady,
For his speech could charm your very soul.
Three nights I had him with me, and three days
I kept him in my hut, for it was to me he first came
When he jumped ship—but he still did not finish
The long story of all his hard times.
It was just as when men gaze at a bard
Who sings to them songs learned from the gods,
Bittersweet songs, and they could listen forever—
That's how he charmed me when he sat in my house.
He says he's an ancestral friend of Odysseus,
And that he comes from Crete, the land of Minos.[3]
It was from Crete he came here, on a hard journey
That gets ever harder as he wanders on
Like a rolling stone. He insists he has news
That Odysseus is near, over in Thesprotia,
Alive and well, and bringing many treasures home."

And Penelope, calm and circumspect:

"Go call him here, so he can tell me face to face.
As for these men, let them play their games outside
Or here in the house. They're in a good mood,
As well they might be, their own possessions
Lying safe at home, their bread and sweet wine
Feeding only their servants, while they themselves
Mob our house day after day, slaughtering
All our oxen, our sheep and fat goats,
Partying and recklessly drinking our wine,
Ruining everything. For there is no man here
Like Odysseus to protect this house.
But if Odysseus should ever come home,
He and his son would make them pay for this outrage."

Just as she finished, Telemachus sneezed,
A loud sneeze that rang through the halls.
Penelope laughed and said to Eumaeus:

"Go ahead and call the stranger for me!
Didn't you see my son sneeze at my words?
That means death will surely come to the suitors,
One and all. Not a single man will escape.
And one more thing—what do you think of this?
If I find that he speaks everything truly,
I'll clothe him in a handsome tunic and cloak."

3. Legendary king of Crete.

The swineherd took this all in. He went over
To Odysseus, and his words flew fast:

"Penelope, Telemachus' mother,
Wants to see you. Her heart urges her,
For all her pain, to ask you about her husband.
If she finds that you speak everything truly,
She will give you a handsome tunic and cloak,
Which you really do need. As for your belly,
You'll still have to fill it by public begging."

And Odysseus, who had borne much:

"Eumaeus, I will soon be telling the whole truth
To Penelope, Icarius' wise daughter.
For I know Odysseus very well,
And he and I have been through much the same grief.
But I'm leery of this mob of rough suitors,
Whose arrogance grates on the sky's iron dome.
Just now as I was making my way through the hall,
Not doing any harm to anyone, this man
Struck me—hard—and neither Telemachus
Nor anyone else did anything to stop him.
So please ask Penelope, for all her eagerness,
To wait in the hall until the sun goes down.
Then she can ask me about her husband's return.
And she can seat me nearer the fire. These clothes
I have on are not very good, as you should know,
For it was to you first I came as a suppliant."

When he heard this the swineherd went off,
And when he crossed the threshold Penelope said:

"You're not bringing him with you, Eumaeus.
What does he mean by this? Does he fear someone
More than he should, or is there something else here
That makes him hang back? A shy beggar's a poor one."

And you answered her, Eumaeus, my swineherd:

"What he says is right, as anyone would agree,
About avoiding the violence of arrogant men.
He asks you to wait until the sun goes down.
And it would be far seemlier for you too, Lady,
If you and the stranger had your talk in private."

Penelope answered in her circumspect way:

"Our guest is no fool. He sees what could happen.
These men are bent on senseless violence,
More than any mortal men I can imagine."

Thus Penelope, and the godlike swineherd,
Having said his piece to her, went off
Into the throng of suitors. He found Telemachus,
And with his head close to him so no one could hear,
He spoke to him these feathered words:

"I am going off now, dear Telemachus,
To guard the swine and all—
Your livelihood and mine. You take charge
Of everything here. Take care of yourself,
First and foremost, and be on the lookout
So you don't get hurt. Many of these men
Are up to no good. May Zeus destroy them
Utterly, before any harm can come to us."

And Telemachus, in his cool-headed way:

"Amen to that. Go after supper. But at dawn
Come back with your best boars for sacrifice.
Everything here is up to me, and the gods."

So the swineherd sat down again on a polished chair.
When he had eaten and drunk to his heart's content,
He went off to his swine, leaving the courts and hall
Full of banqueters. They were singing and dancing
And having a good time, for it was evening now.

BOOK XVIII

And now there came the town beggar
Making his rounds, known throughout Ithaca
For his greedy belly and endless bouts
Of eating and drinking. He had no real strength
Or fighting power—just plenty of bulk.
Arnaeus was the name his mother had given him,
But the young men all called him Irus
Because he was always running errands for someone.[4]
He had a mind to drive Odysseus out of his own house
And started in on him with words like this:

"Out of the doorway, geezer, before I throw you out
On your ear! Don't you see all these people
Winking at me to give you the bum's rush?
I wouldn't want to stoop so low, but if you don't
Get out now, I may have to lay hands on you."

Odysseus gave him a measured look and said:

4. The name *Irus* recalls Iris, the messenger goddess who runs errands for the other gods.

"What's wrong with you? I'm not doing
Or saying anything to bother you. I don't mind
If someone gives you a handout, even a large one.
This doorway is big enough for both of us.
There's no need for you to be jealous of others.
Now look, you're a vagrant, just like I am.
Prosperity is up to the gods. But if I were you,
I'd be careful about challenging me with your fists.
I might get angry, and old man though I am,
I just might haul off and bust you in the mouth.
I'd have more peace and quiet tomorrow.
I don't think you'd come back a second time
To the hall of Laertes' son, Odysseus."

This got Irus angry, and he answered:

"Listen to the mangy glutton run on,
Like an old kitchen woman! I'll fix him good—
Hit him with a left and then a right until
I knock his teeth out onto the ground,
The way we'd do a pig caught eating the crops.
Put 'em up, and everybody will see how we fight.
How are you going to stand up to a younger man?"

That's how they goaded each other on
There on the great polished threshold.
Antinous took this in and said with a laugh:

"How about this, friends? We haven't had
This much fun in a long time. Thank God
For a little entertainment! The stranger and Irus
Are getting into a fight. Let's have them square off!"

They all jumped up laughing and crowded around
The two tattered beggars. And Antinous said:

"Listen, proud suitors, to my proposal.
We've got these goat paunches on the fire,
Stuffed with fat and blood, ready for supper.
Whichever of the two wins and proves himself
The better man, gets the stuffed paunch of his choice.
Furthermore, he dines with us in perpetuity
And to the exclusion of all other beggars."

Everyone approved of Antinous' speech.
Then Odysseus, who knew all the moves, said:

"Friends, there's no way a broken-down old man
Can fight with a younger. Still, my belly,
That troublemaker, urges me on. So,
I'll just have to get beat up. But all of you,
Swear me an oath that no one, favoring Irus,
Will foul me and beat me for him."

They all swore that they wouldn't hit him,
And then Telemachus, feeling his power, said:

"Stranger, if you have the heart for this fight,
Don't worry about the onlookers. If anyone
Strikes you, he will have to fight us all.
I guarantee this as your host, and I am joined
By Antinous and Eurymachus,
Lords and men of discernment both."

Everyone praised this speech.
Then Odysseus
Tied his rags around his waist, revealing
His sculpted thighs, his broad shoulders,
His muscular chest and arms. Athena
Stood near the hero, magnifying his build.
The suitors' jaws dropped open.
They looked at each other and said things like:

"Irus is history."
"Brought it on himself, too."
"Will you look at the thigh on that old man!"

So they spoke. Irus' heart was in his throat,
But some servants tucked up his clothes anyway
And dragged him out, his rolls of fat quivering.
Antinous laid into him, saying:

"You big slob. You'll be sorry
You were ever born, if you try to duck
This woebegone, broken-down old man.
I'm going to give it to you straight now.
If he gets the better of you and beats you,
I'm going to throw you on a black ship
And send you to the mainland to King Echetus,
The maimer,[5] who will slice off your nose and ears
With cold bronze, and tear out your balls
And give them raw to the dogs to eat."

This made Irus tremble even more.
They shoved him out into the middle,
And both men put up their fists. Odysseus,
The wily veteran, thought it over.
Should he knock the man stone cold dead,
Or ease up on the punch and just lay him out flat?
Better to go easy and just flatten him, he thought,
So that the crowd won't get suspicious.
The fighters stood tall, circling each other,

5. King in mainland Greece, with a reputation for cruelty.

And as Irus aimed a punch at his right shoulder,
Odysseus caught him just beneath the ear,
Crushing his jawbone. Blood ran from his mouth,
And he fell in the dust snorting like an ox
And gnashing his teeth, his heels kicking the ground.
The suitors lifted their hands and died
With laughter. Odysseus took Irus by one fat foot
And dragged him out through the doorway
All the way to the court and the portico's gates.
He propped him up against the courtyard's wall,
Stuck his staff in his hand, and said to him:

"Sit there now and scare off the pigs and dogs,
And stop lording it over the other beggars,
You sorry bastard, or things could get worse."

And he slung his old pouch over one shoulder,
Walked back to the threshold, and sat down.
The suitors went inside, laughing and joking,
And one of them came up to Odysseus and said:

"May Zeus and the other gods grant you, stranger,
Whatever your heart most dearly desires,
Since you have ended this glutton's begging career.
We'll ship him off to Echetus the maimer!"

Odysseus took heart at these auspicious words.
Antinous set before him the huge paunch
Stuffed with fat and blood, and Amphinomus
Served him a couple of loaves from the basket,
Toasted him with a golden cup, and said:

"Hail to the revered stranger. May good fortune
Come to you, though you have only bad luck now."

And Odysseus, from his mind's teeming depths:

"Amphinomus, you come across as a sensible man,
Just as your father was. I have heard of him,
Nisus of Dulichium, a good man, and wealthy,
Known far and wide. They say you are his son,
And you seem soft-spoken, a good man yourself.
So I'll tell you something you should take to heart.
Of all the things that breathe and move upon it,
Earth nurtures nothing feebler than man.
While the gods favor him and his step is quick,
He thinks he will never have to suffer in life.
Then when the blessed ones bring evil his way,
He bears it in sorrow with an enduring heart.
Our outlook changes with the kind of day
Zeus our Father decides to give us.
I, too, once got used to prosperity,
And I did many foolish things in my pride,

Trusting my father and brothers would save me.
So I know a man should never be an outlaw,
But keep in peace the gifts heaven gives him.
Just look at what the suitors are doing now,
Wasting the wealth and dishonoring the wife
Of a man who, I tell you, will not be gone long
From his family and friends and his native land.
He's very close. Better for you if some god
Leads you away from here and takes you home
Before you meet him upon his return.
Once he's under this roof, I do not think
The suitors will escape without blood being spilled."

He spoke, poured a libation, drank the sweet wine,
And then gave the cup back to Amphinomus,
Who went away through the hall with his head bowed
And his heart heavy with a sense of foreboding.
He would not escape death, though. Pallas Athena
Had him pinned, and he would be killed outright
By a spear from the hand of Telemachus.

And now the Grey-eyed One put into the heart
Of Penelope, Icarius' wise daughter,
A notion to show herself to the suitors.
All of a sudden she wanted to make their blood pound—
And to make herself more worthy than ever
In the eyes of her son, and of her husband.
With a whimsical laugh she said to the housekeeper:

"Eurynome, my heart longs, though it never has before,
To show myself to the suitors, hateful as they are.
And I would like to say something to my son,
Something that might help him—he should not
Continually keep the company of the suitors,
Overbearing men who speak politely to his face
And plan all the while to hurt him later."

And the housekeeper Eurynome said:

"Yes indeed, child, everything you said is right.
Go on then, and speak your mind to your son
And don't hide anything—after you have bathed,
That is, and dabbed your cheeks with ointment.
Don't go like this, bleary-eyed from crying.
All this grieving only makes you look worse.
Your son is that age, you know. You prayed your heart out
For the gods to let you see him as a bearded man."

And Penelope, in her circumspect way:

"Eurynome, don't try, even though you love me,
To talk me into bathing and putting on makeup.

Any beauty I had the Olympian gods destroyed
On the day my husband left in the hollow ships.
But go tell Autonoë and Hippodameia
To come stand by my side when I enter the hall.
It would be shameful for me to go alone among men."

She spoke, and the old housekeeper went off
To tell the two women Penelope wanted them.

Athena's eyes glinted. She had another idea.
First, she made Penelope so sweetly drowsy
That she leaned back, her whole body limp,
And went to sleep right there on her couch.
Then the shimmering goddess went to work on her,
So that all the men would gape in wonder.
First she cleansed her lovely face, using
The pure, distilled Beauty that Aphrodite
Anoints herself with when she goes garlanded
Into the beguiling dance of the Graces.[6]
Then she made her look taller, and filled out her figure,
And made her skin whiter than polished ivory.
Her work done, the goddess glimmered away.
Just then, some of the women came by,
Talking noisily, and Penelope woke up.
She rubbed her cheeks with her hands and said:

"What a soft, sweet sleep! If only Artemis
Would send as soft a death to me at once
So I would no longer waste away in sorrow,
Longing for my dear husband's winning ways.
He was in all ways the very best of men."

She spoke. Light from the upper rooms
Flooded the stairs as Penelope came down,
Not alone, two maids trailed behind—
And when she had come among the suitors
She stood in her glory beside a column
That supported the roof of the great house,
Hiding her cheeks behind her silken veils,
Grave handmaidens standing on either side.
The suitors' knees grew weak when they saw her.
They were spellbound, in love, and each man prayed
That he would lie beside her in bed. But,

It was to her son, Telemachus, that she spoke:

"Telemachus, what can you be thinking of?
You were intelligent even as a child,

6. Three goddesses, associated with beauty, joy, and good feelings.

But now that you have reached manhood—
So handsome and tall that any stranger
Who happened to see you would be able to tell
You're a rich man's son—you're not thinking straight,
Not any more. Just look at what has happened
Here in these halls! How would you like it
If our guest, sitting as he is in our house,
Were to be treated roughly and come to harm?
It would be a disgrace, and the shame would be yours."

And Telemachus, in his clear-headed way:

"I don't blame you for being angry, Mother,
But I'm aware of all this myself. I know
Everything that is going on here, good and bad.
I used to think as a child, but not any more.
But I can't think clearly with all these men
Sitting around driving me to distraction.
They don't mean me any good, and I have
No one to help me. But I can tell you this,
That the fight between the stranger and Irus
Did not go the way the suitors wanted.
Our guest proved to be the better man.
O Father Zeus, and Athena and Apollo,
If only the suitors were beaten like that,
Their limbs unstrung, nodding their heads,
Some in the courtyard and some in the hall,
Just as Irus now sits by the gate,
Lolling his head as if he were drunk,
Unable to stand up or get himself home,
Wherever that is, because his limbs are like putty."

Thus mother and son. Then Eurymachus
Addressed Penelope, saying to her:

"Daughter of Icarius, wise Penelope,
If all the Greeks throughout the mainland
Could see you now, even more suitors
Would be here tomorrow, feasting in your hall,
For you are far and away the most beautiful
And most intelligent woman in the world."

And wise Penelope answered him:

"Eurymachus, the gods destroyed my beauty
On the day when the Argives sailed for Ilion
And with them went my husband, Odysseus.
If he were to come back and be part of my life,
My fame would be greater and more resplendent.
But now I grieve, so many sorrows

Has some spirit visited upon me.
And this much is true: when Odysseus left
He clasped my right hand in his and said to me:
'I do not think, my wife, that all the Greeks
Will return from Ilion safe and sound.
They say the Trojans are real warriors,
Spearmen and bowmen, and they drive chariots,
Which can turn the tide in any battle.
So I do not know whether the god of war
Will send me back or if I'll go down
There in Troy. So everything here is in your hands.
Take care of my father and of my mother
As you do now, or even more, when I am gone.
But when you see our son a bearded man,
Marry whom you will, and leave this house.'
So he spoke, and it's all coming true.
There will come a night when a hateful marriage
Will darken my bed, cursed as I am, my happiness
Destroyed by Zeus. And I have more heartache.
This isn't the way suitors usually behave
When men compete for the hand of a lady,
A woman of some worth, a rich man's daughter.
They bring cattle, and fat sheep,
To feast the bride's friends, and they give her
Glorious gifts. They do not devour
Another's livelihood without recompense."

She spoke, and Odysseus, the godlike survivor,
Smiled inwardly to see how she extracted gifts
From the suitors, weaving a spell upon them
With her words, while her mind was set elsewhere.

Then Antinous, Eupeithes' son, said to her:

"Daughter of Icarius, wise Penelope,
As far as gifts go, take whatever any man
Wishes to give. It's not good to refuse gifts.
But as for us, we're not going back to our lands
Or anywhere else until you marry
Whoever proves to be the best of the Achaeans."

Everyone approved of what Antinous said,
And each man sent a herald to fetch his gifts.
Antinous' man brought a beautiful robe,
All embroidered. It had twelve golden brooches,
Each of them fitted with hooked clasps.
Eurymachus' man came back right away
With an intricately crafted golden chain
Strung with amber and bright as the sun.

Eurydamas' attendants brought a pair of earrings,
Three elegant teardrops gleaming from each.
From the house of Peisander, Polyctor's son,
There came a necklace of exquisite beauty.
And so it went, each man bringing
One lovely gift after another.

And Penelope,
A moving silver grace, went up to her chamber,
Her women behind her bearing the beautiful gifts.

The suitors turned to amusing themselves
With dance and song until evening fell.
When twilight shaded their merrymaking
They set up three braziers in the great hall
To give them light. They stoked these with kindling,
Seasoned and dry and newly split with the axe.
They set torches between the braziers,
And the household women set about lighting them.
Zeus-bred Odysseus, always thinking,
Went up to these women and had a word with them:

"Maidservants of Odysseus, your long-absent lord,
Go off now to where your revered queen is sitting
And do your spinning, or card wool, by her side.
Sit with her and keep her company. Cheer her up.
I'll take care of keeping the torches lit
For these men. Even if they stay up until dawn
They won't outlast me. I can put up with a lot."

The women looked at each other and laughed.
Then Melantho, fair-cheeked and sassy,
Had some ugly words for him. This Melantho
Was born to Dolius, but Penelope
Had reared her as her very own child,
Spoiling her with toys and whatever she wanted.
Even so she had no feeling for Penelope
But loved Eurymachus and slept with him.
And now she lit into Odysseus:

"You must be out of your mind, you old wreck,
Unwilling to go to the blacksmith's to sleep
Or anywhere else. You just blabber on here,
Bold as can be, with all these real men around,
Feeling no fear. Are you drunk, or are you
Always like this, with all your blather?
Pleased with yourself, aren't you, because you beat that bum,
Irus? Someone a lot better than Irus
Might stand up to you soon and pound you
Bloody with his fists as he drives you outside."

Odysseus shot her a dark look and growled:

"Just let me tell Telemachus what you are saying,
You bitch. He'll cut you to ribbons on the spot."

His words scattered the women, sending them
Flying through the hall in terror, convinced
That he meant what he said.
Odysseus
Took his stand by the torches, keeping them lit
And watching all the men. But his heart seethed
With other business, soon to be finished.

Now Athena was not about to let the suitors
Abstain from insults. She wanted pain
To sink deeper into Odysseus' bones.
And so Eurymachus began to jeer
At him for his friends' entertainment:

"Hear me, suitors of our glorious queen,
While I speak my mind. It is not without
The will of the gods that this man has come
To Odysseus' palace. We get a nice glow
Of torchlight from him—from his head,
That is, since it doesn't have a hair on it!"

And then speaking directly to Odysseus,
Destroyer of cities, Eurymachus said:

"I wonder if you'd like to be a hired hand,
Stranger. Should I hire you to work
On one of my outlying farms gathering fieldstones
And planting tall trees? Oh, I'll pay you.
I'll keep you fed the year round out there,
Give you some clothes and sandals to wear.
But you've never done a hard day's work
In your life, preferring to beg your way through town
For food to stuff into your bottomless belly."

And Odysseus, his mind teeming:

"Eurymachus, I wish we could have a contest
Working in the fields during the summertime,
When the days are long, just you and I
Out in a hayfield with long, curved scythes,
And plenty of grass so we could test our work,
Fasting until late evening.
Or how about this?
We could each drive oxen, the best there are,
Big and tawny, both well fed with grass,
The same age, yoked the same way, tireless animals—
And each with four acres of rich soil to plow.

Then you'd see if I could cut a straight furrow
Clear to the end.
And it would be even better
If Zeus brought war upon us from somewhere,
Today, right now, and I had a shield, two spears,
And a bronze helmet that fit close to my temples.
Then you would see me out in the front ranks,
And you wouldn't stand here jeering at me
Because of my belly. But you are insufferable,
And you have a hard heart. No doubt you think
You are some great man, a tough guy,
Because you hang out with puny weaklings.
If Odysseus came back home, these doors,
Wide as they are, would be far too narrow
For you to squeeze through as you made for daylight."

This made Eurymachus all the more furious.
Scowling at Odysseus he said to him:

"You won't get away with this kind of talk,
Bold as can be with all these real men around,
Feeling no fear. Are you drunk, or are you
Always like this, with all your blather?
Are you all pumped up because you beat that bum, Irus?"

And he grabbed a footstool, but Odysseus,
Wary of the man, sat down at the knees
Of Amphinomus, the suitor from Dulichium,
And Eurymachus' missile struck a cupbearer
On the right hand. The wine jug he held
Clattered to the ground, and the man groaned
And fell backward into the dust.
The suitors
Were in an uproar throughout the shadowy hall.
One man would glance at his neighbor and say:

"Better if the stranger had never made it here;
Then he couldn't have brought us all this trouble.
Here we are, brawling about beggars. Our feasts
Will be ruined if we let things turn ugly."

Then Telemachus made his voice heard:

"You are all raving now. Your drunken guzzling
Is beginning to show, or some god
Is stirring you up. But now that you have feasted,
Go home and get some rest—whenever you're ready,
Of course. I'm not driving anyone away."

He spoke, and they all bit their lips and marveled
At Telemachus for speaking so boldly.
Then Amphinomus addressed the suitors:

"Friends, no man should be angry at a thing
Fairly spoken, or respond by arguing.
Do not mistreat this stranger any longer,
Or any of godlike Odysseus' household.
Now let the cupbearer start us off
So we can pour libation and go home to rest.
This stranger we will leave in Odysseus' halls—
Where he landed—and in Telemachus' keeping."

Amphinomus' words pleased everyone,
And a bowl was mixed by his herald, Mulius.
He served a cup to each man in turn,
And they poured libations to the blessed gods
And drank sweet wine to their hearts' content.
Then they all went home and took their rest.

BOOK XIX

So Odysseus was left alone in the hall,
Planning death for the suitors with Athena's aid.
He spoke winged words to Telemachus:

"Telemachus, get all the weapons out of the hall.
When the suitors miss them and ask you
Where they are, set their minds at ease, saying:
'Oh, I have stored them out of the smoke.
They're nothing like they were when Odysseus
Went off to Troy, but are all grimed with soot.
Also, a god put this thought into my head,
That when you men are drinking, you might
Start quarreling and someone could get hurt,
Which would ruin your feasting and courting.
Steel has a way of drawing a man to it."

Thus Odysseus. Telemachus nodded,
And calling Eurycleia he said to her:

"Nurse, shut the women inside their rooms
While I put my father's weapons away,
The beautiful weapons left out in the hall
And dulled by the smoke since he went off to war.
I was just a child then. But now I want
To store them away, safe from the smoke."

And Eurycleia, his old nurse, said:

"Yes, child, you are right
To care for the house and guard its wealth.
But who will fetch a light and carry it for you,
Since you won't let any of the women do it?"

Telemachus coolly answered her:

"This stranger here. I won't let anyone
Who gets rations be idle, even a traveler
From a distant land."

Telemachus' words sank in,
And the nurse locked the doors of the great hall.
Odysseus and his illustrious son sprang up
And began storing away the helmets, bossed shields,
And honed spears. And before them Pallas Athena,
Bearing a golden lamp, made a beautiful light.
Telemachus suddenly blurted out to his father:

"Father, this is a miracle I'm seeing!
The walls of the house, the lovely panels,
The beams of fir, and the high columns
Are glowing like fire. Some god is inside,
One of the gods from the open sky."

Odysseus, his mind teeming, replied:

"Hush. Don't be too curious about this.
This is the way of the gods who hold high heaven.
Go get some rest. I'll remain behind here
And draw out the maids—and your mother,
Who in her grief will ask many questions."

And Telemachus went out through the hall
By the light of blazing torches. He came
To his room, lay down, and waited for dawn.
Odysseus again was alone in the hall,
Planning death for the suitors with Athena's aid.

Penelope, wary and thoughtful,
Now came from her bedroom, and she was like
Artemis or golden Aphrodite.
They set a chair for her by the fire
Where she always sat, a chair inlaid
With spiraling ivory and silver
Which the craftsman Icmalius had made long ago.
It had a footstool attached, covered now
With a thick fleece.

Penelope sat down,
Taking everything in. White-armed maids
Came out from the women's quarters
And started to take away all of the food,
Clearing the tables and picking up the cups
From which the men had been drinking.
They emptied the braziers, scattering the embers

Onto the floor, and then stocked them up
With loads of fresh wood for warmth and light.

Then Melantho started in on Odysseus again:

"Are we going to have to put up with you all night,
Roaming though the house and spying on the women?
Go on outside and be glad you had supper,
Or you'll soon stagger out struck with a torch."

And Odysseus answered from his teeming mind:

"What's wrong with you, woman? Are you mean to me
Because I'm dirty and dressed in rags
And beg through the land? I do it because I have to.
That's how it is with beggars and vagabonds.
You know, I too once lived in a house in a city,
A rich man in a wealthy house, and I often gave
Gifts to wanderers, whatever they needed.
I had servants, too, countless servants,
And plenty of everything else a man needs
To live the good life and be considered wealthy.
But Zeus crushed me. Who knows why?
So be careful, woman. Someday you may lose
That glowing beauty that makes you stand out now.
Or your mistress may become fed up with you.
Or Odysseus may come. We can still hope for that.
But even if, as seems likely, he is dead
And will never return, his son, Telemachus,
Is now very much like him, by Apollo's grace,
And if any of the women are behaving loosely
It won't get by him. He's no longer a child."

None of this was lost on Penelope,
And she scolded the maidservant, saying:

"Your outrageous conduct does not escape me,
Shameless whore that you are, and it will be
On your own head. You knew very well,
For you heard me say it, that I intended
To question the stranger here in my halls
About my husband; for I am sick with worry."

Then to Eurynome, the housekeeper, she said:

"Bring a chair here with a fleece upon it
So that the stranger can sit down and tell his tale
And listen to me. I have many questions for him."

So Eurynome brought up a polished chair
And threw a fleece over it, and upon it sat

Odysseus, patient and godlike.
Penelope, watchful, began with a question:

"First, stranger, let me ask you this:
Who are you and where are you from?"

Odysseus, his mind teeming, answered her:

"Lady, no one on earth could find fault with you,
For your fame reaches the heavens above,
Just like the fame of a blameless king,
A godfearing man who rules over thousands
Of valiant men, upholding justice.
His rich, black land bears barley and wheat,
The trees are laden with fruit, the flocks
Are always with young, and the sea teems with fish—
Because he rules well, and so his people prosper.
Ask me, therefore, about anything else,
But not about my birth or my native land.
That would fill my heart with painful memories.
I have many sorrows, and it wouldn't be right
To sit here weeping in another's house,
Nor is it good to be constantly grieving.
I don't want one of your maids, or you yourself,
To be upset with me and say I am awash with tears
Because the wine has gone to my head."

And Penelope, watching, answered him:

"Stranger, the gods destroyed my beauty
On the day when the Argives sailed for Ilion
And with them went my husband, Odysseus.
If he were to come back and be part of my life,
My fame would be greater and more resplendent so.
But now I ache, so many sorrows
Has some spirit showered upon me.
All of the nobles who rule the islands—
Dulichium, Samê, wooded Zacynthus—
And all those with power on rocky Ithaca
Are courting me and ruining this house.
So I pay no attention to strangers
Or to suppliants or public heralds. No,
I just waste away with longing for Odysseus.
My suitors press on, and I weave my wiles.
First some god breathed into me the thought
Of setting up a great loom in the main hall,
And I started weaving a vast fabric
With a very fine thread, and I said to them:

'Young men—my suitors, since Odysseus is dead—
Eager as you are to marry me, you must wait

Until I finish this robe—it would be a shame
To waste my spinning—a shroud for the hero
Laertes, when death's doom lays him low.
I fear the Achaean women would reproach me
If he should lie in death shroudless for all his wealth.'

"So I spoke, and their proud hearts consented.
Every day I would weave at the great loom,
And every night unweave the web by torchlight.
I fooled them for three years with my craft.
But in the fourth year, as the seasons rolled by,
And the moons waned, and the days dragged on,
My shameless and headstrong serving women
Betrayed me. The men barged in and caught me at it,
And a howl went up. So I was forced to finish the shroud.
Now I can't escape the marriage. I'm at my wit's end.
My parents are pressing me to marry,
And my son agonizes over the fact
That these men are devouring his inheritance.
He is a man now, and able to preside
Over a household to which Zeus grants honor.
But tell me of your birth, for you are not sprung,
As the saying goes, from stock or stone."

And Odysseus, from his mind's teeming depths:

"Honored wife of Laertes' son, Odysseus,
Will you never stop asking about my lineage?
All right, I will tell you, but bear in mind
You are only adding to the sorrows I have.
For so it is when a man has been away from home
As long as I have, wandering from city to city
And bearing hardships. Still, I will tell you.
Crete is an island that lies in the middle
Of the wine-dark sea, a fine, rich land
With ninety cities swarming with people
Who speak many different languages.
There are Achaeans there, and native Cretans,
Cydonians, Pelasgians, and three tribes of Dorians.
One of the cities is great Cnossus,
Where Minos ruled and every nine years
Conversed with great Zeus. He was the father
Of my father, the great hero Deucalion.[7]
Deucalion had another son, Idomeneus,
Who sailed his beaked ships to Ilion
Following the sons of Atreus.[8] I was the younger,
And he the better man. My name is Aethon.

7. Every nine years, Minos, king of Crete, was instructed on how to rule by his father, Zeus. Deucalion, his son, succeeded him as king.
8. Agamemnon and Menelaus.

It was in Crete that I saw Odysseus
And gave him gifts of hospitality.
He had been blown off course rounding Malea
On his way to Troy. He put in at Amnisus,
Where the cave of Eileithyia[9] is found.
That is a difficult harbor, and he barely escaped
The teeth of the storm. He went up to the city
And asked for Idomeneus, claiming to be
An old and honored friend. But Idomeneus' ships
Had left for Troy ten days before, so I
Took him in and entertained him well,
Drawing on the ample supplies in the house.
I gathered his men and distributed to them
Barley meal, wine, and bulls for sacrifice
From the public supplies, to keep them happy.
They stayed for twelve days. A norther so strong
You could barely stand upright in it
Had them corraled—some evil spirit had roused it.
On the thirteenth day the wind dropped, and they left."

All lies, but he made them seem like the truth,
And as she listened, her face melted with tears.

Snow deposited high in the mountains by the wild West Wind
Slowly melts under the East Wind's breath,
And as it melts the rivers rise in their channels.

So her lovely cheeks coursed with tears as she wept
For her husband, who was sitting before her.
Odysseus pitied her tears in his heart,
But his eyes were as steady between their lids
As if they were made of horn or iron
As he concealed his own tears through guile.
When Penelope had cried herself out,
She spoke to him again, saying:

"Now I feel I must test you, stranger,
To see if you really did entertain my husband
And his godlike companions, as you say you did.
Tell me what sort of clothes he wore, and tell me
What he was like, and what his men were like."

And Odysseus, from his mind's teeming depths:

"Lady, it is difficult for me to speak
After we've been apart for so long. It has been
Twenty years since he left my country.
But I have an image of him in my mind.
Odysseus wore a fleecy purple cloak,
Folded over, and it had a brooch

9. Goddess associated with childbirth.

With a double clasp, fashioned of gold,
And on the front was an intricate design:
A hound holding in his forepaws a dappled fawn
That writhed to get free. Everyone marveled
At how, though it was all made of gold,
The hound had his eye fixed on the fawn
As he was strangling it, and the fawn
Twisted and struggled to get to its feet.
And I remember the tunic he wore,
Glistening like onionskin, soft and shiny
And with a sheen like sunlight. There were
Quite a few women who admired it.
But remember, now, I do not know
Whether Odysseus wore this at home,
Or whether one of his men gave it to him
When he boarded ship, or someone else,
For Odysseus was a man with many friends.
He had few equals among the Achaeans.
I, too, gave him gifts—a bronze sword,
A beautiful purple cloak, and a fringed tunic,
And I gave him a ceremonious send-off
In his benched ship. And one more thing:
He had a herald, a little older than he was,
And I will tell you what he looked like.
He was slope-shouldered, with dark skin
And curly hair. His name was Eurybates,
And Odysseus held him in higher esteem
Than his other men, because they thought alike."

These words stirred up Penelope's grief.
She recognized the unmistakeable tokens
Odysseus was giving her. She wept again,
And then composed herself and said to him:

"You may have been pitied before, stranger,
But now you will be loved and honored
Here in my halls. I gave him those clothes.
I folded them, brought them from the storeroom,
And pinned on the gleaming brooch,
To delight him. But I will never welcome him
Home again, and so the fates were dark
When Odysseus left in his hollow ship
For Ilion, that curse of a city."

And Odysseus, from his mind's teeming depths:

"Revered wife of Laertes' son, Odysseus,
Do not mar your fair skin with tears any more,
Or melt your heart with weeping for your husband.
Not that I blame you. Any woman weeps
When she has lost her husband, a man with whom
She has made love and whose children she has borne—

And the husband you've lost is Odysseus,
Who they say is like the immortal gods.
Stop weeping, though, and listen to my words,
For what I am about to tell you is true.
I have lately heard of Odysseus' return,
That he is near, in the rich land of Thesprotia,
Still alive. And he is bringing home treasures,
Seeking gifts, and getting them, throughout the land.
But he lost his trusty crew and his hollow ship
On the wine-dark sea. As he was sailing out
From the island of Thrinacia, Zeus and Helios
Hit him hard because his companions had killed
The cattle of the Sun. His men went under,
But he rode his ship's keel until the waves
Washed him ashore in the land of the Phaeacians,
Whose race is closely akin to the gods'.
They treated him as if he were a god,
Gave him many gifts, and were more than willing
To escort him home. And he would have been here
By now, but he thought it more profitable
To gather wealth by roaming the land.
No one is as good as Odysseus
At finding ways to gain an advantage.
I had all this from Pheidon, the Thesprotian king.
And he swore to me, as he poured libations
There in his house, that a ship was already launched,
And a crew standing by, to take him home.
He sent me off first, since a Thesprotian ship
Happened to be leaving for Dulichium,
But before I left, Pheidon showed me
All the treasure Odysseus had amassed,
Bronze, gold, and wrought iron, enough to feed
His children's children for ten generations,
All stored there for him in the halls of the king.
Odysseus, he said, had gone to Dodona
To consult the oak-tree oracle of Zeus
And ask how he should return to Ithaca—
Openly or in secret—after being gone so long.
So he is safe, and will come soon.
He is very near, and will not be away long
From his dear ones and his native land.
I will swear to this. Now Zeus on high
Be my witness, and this hospitable table,
And the hearth of flawless Odysseus himself—
That everything will happen just as I say:
Before this month is out Odysseus will come,
In the dark of the moon, before the new crescent."

And Penelope, watching him carefully:

"Ah, stranger, may your words come true.
Then you would know my kindness, and my gifts

Would make you blessed in all men's eyes.
But I know in my heart that Odysseus
Will never come home, and that you will never
Find passage elsewhere, since there is not now
Any master in the house like Odysseus—
If he ever existed—to send honored guests
Safely on their way, or to welcome them.
But still, wash our guest's feet, maidens,
And prepare a bed for him. Set up a frame
And cover it with cloaks and lustrous blankets
To keep him cozy and warm. When golden Dawn
Shows her first light, bathe him and anoint him,
So he can sit side by side with Telemachus
And share in the feast here in the hall.
And anyone who causes this man any pain
Will regret it sorely and will accomplish nothing
Here in this house, however angry he gets.
For how would you ever find out, stranger,
Whether or not I surpass all other women
In presence of mind, if you sit down to dinner
Squalid and disheveled here in my hall?
Our lives are short. A hard-hearted man
Is cursed while he lives and reviled in death.
But a good-hearted man has his fame spread
Far and wide by the guests he has honored,
And men speak well of him all over the earth."

And Odysseus, his mind teeming, answered her:

"Revered wife of Odysseus, Laertes' son,
I lost all interest in cloaks and blankets
On the day I left the snowy mountains of Crete
In my long-oared ship. I will lie down tonight,
As I have through many a sleepless night,
On a poor bed, waiting for golden-throned Dawn.
Nor do I have any taste for foot-baths,
And none of the serving women here in your hall
Will touch my feet, unless there is some old,
Trustworthy woman who has suffered as I have.
I would not mind if she touched my feet."

And Penelope, watching him carefully:

"Of all the travelers who have come to my house,
None, dear guest, have been as thoughtful as you
And none as welcome, so wise are your words.
I do have an old and trustworthy woman here,
Who nursed and raised my ill-starred husband,
Taking him in her arms the day he was born.
She will wash your feet, frail as she is.
Eurycleia, rise and wash your master's—that is,

Wash the feet of this man who is your master's age.
Odysseus' feet and hands are no doubt like his now,
For men age quickly when life is hard."

At this, the old woman hid her face in her hands.
Shedding warm tears, she spoke through her sobs:

"My lost child, I can do nothing for you.
Zeus must have hated you above all other men,
Although you were always godfearing. No one
Burned more offerings to the Lord of Lightning,
So many fat thighbones, bulls by the hundreds,
With prayers that you reach a sleek old age
And raise your glorious son. And now the god has
Deprived you alone of your day of return.
And I suppose, stranger, women mocked him, too,
When he came to some man's gloried house
In a distant land, just as these cheeky bitches
All mock you here. It is to avoid their insults
That you will not allow them to wash your feet.
But Penelope, Icarius' wise daughter,
Has asked me to do it, and I will,
For her sake and for yours,
For my heart is throbbing with sorrow.
But listen now to what I have to say.
Many road-weary strangers have come here,
But I have never seen such a resemblance
As that between you and Odysseus,
In looks, voice—even the shape of your feet."

And Odysseus, from his mind's teeming depths:

"Oh, everyone who has seen us both says that,
Old woman, that we are very much alike,
Just as you yourself have noticed."

And the old woman took the shining basin
She used for washing feet, poured
Cold water into it, and then added the hot.
Odysseus, waiting, suddenly sat down at the hearth
And turned away toward the shadows. The scar!
It flashed through his mind that his old nurse
Would notice his scar as soon as she touched him,
And then everything would be out in the open.
She drew near and started to wash her master,
And knew at once the scar from the wound
He had gotten long ago from a boar's white tusk
When he had gone to Parnassus to visit Autolycus,
His mother's father, who was the best man on earth
At thieving and lying, skills he had learned

From Hermes.[1] He had won the god's favor
With choice burnt offerings of lambs and kids.

Autolycus had visited Ithaca once
When his grandson was still a newborn baby.
After he finished supper, Eurycleia
Put the child in his lap and said to him:

"Autolycus, now name the child
Of your own dear child. He has been much prayed for."

Then Autolycus made this response:

"Daughter and son-in-law of mine,
Give this child the name I now tell you.
I come here as one who is odious,[2] yes,
Hateful to many for the pain I have caused
All over the land. Let this child, therefore,
Go by the name of Odysseus.
For my part, when he is grown up
And comes to the great house of his mother's kin
In Parnassus, where my possessions lie,
I will give him a share and send him home happy."

In due time, Odysseus came to get these gifts
From Autolycus. His grandfather
And his uncles all welcomed him warmly,
And Amphithea, his mother's mother,
Embraced Odysseus and kissed his head
And beautiful eyes. Autolycus told his sons
To prepare a meal, and they obeyed at once,
Leading in a bull, five years old,
Which they flayed, dressed, and butchered.
They skewered the meat, roasted it skillfully,
And then served out portions to everyone.
All day long until the sun went down
They feasted to their hearts' content.
But when the sun set and darkness came on
They went to bed and slept through the night.
When Dawn brushed the early sky with rose,
They went out to hunt—Autolycus' sons
Running their hounds—and with them went
Godlike Odysseus. They climbed the steep wooded slopes
Of Mount Parnassus and soon reached
The windy hollows. The sun was up now,
Rising from the damasked waters of Ocean
And just striking the fields, when the beaters came
Into a glade. The dogs were out front,

1. Trickster and messenger god.
2. Again, the pun on Odysseus's name is in the Greek.

Tracking the scent, and behind the dogs
Came Autolycus' sons and noble Odysseus,
His brandished spear casting a long shadow.
Nearby, a great boar was lying in his lair,
A thicket that was proof against the wild wet wind
And could not be pierced by the rays of the sun,
So dense it was. Dead leaves lay deep
Upon the ground there. The sound of men and dogs
Pressing on through the leaves reached the boar's ears,
And he charged out from his lair, back bristling
And his eyes spitting fire. He stood at bay
Right before them, and Odysseus rushed him,
Holding his spear high, eager to thrust.
The boar was too quick. Slashing in,
He got Odysseus in the thigh, right above the knee,
His white tusk tearing a long gash in the muscle
Just shy of the bone. Even so, Odysseus
Did not miss his mark, angling his spear
Into the boar's right shoulder. The gleaming point
Went all the way through, and with a loud grunt
The boar went down and gasped out his life.
Autolycus' sons took care of the carcass
And tended the wound of the flawless Odysseus,
Skillfully binding it and staunching the blood
By chanting a spell. Then they quickly returned
To their father's house. When Odysseus
Had regained his strength, Autolycus and his sons
Gave him glorious gifts and sent him home happy,
Home to Ithaca. His mother and father
Rejoiced at his return and asked him all about
How he got his scar; and he told them the story
Of how a boar had gashed him with his white tusk
As he hunted on Parnassus with Autolycus' sons.

This was the scar the old woman recognized
When the palm of her hand ran over it
As she held his leg. She let the leg fall,
And his foot clanged against the bronze basin,
Tipping it over and spilling the water
All over the floor. Eurycleia's heart
Trembled with mingled joy and grief,
Tears filled her eyes, and her voice
Was choked as she reached out
And touched Odysseus' chin and said:

"You are Odysseus, dear child. I did not know you
Until I laid my hands on my master's body."

She spoke, and turned her eyes toward Penelope,
Wanting to show her that her husband was home.
But Penelope could not return her gaze

Or understand her meaning, for Athena
Had diverted her mind. Odysseus reached
For the old woman's throat, seized it in his right hand
And drawing her closer with his other, he said:

"Do you want to destroy me? You yourself
Nursed me at your own breast, and now
After twenty hard years I've come back home.
Now that some god has let you in on the secret,
You keep it to yourself, you hear? If you don't,
I'll tell you this, and I swear I'll do it:
If, with heaven's help, I subdue the suitors,
I will not spare you—even if you are my nurse—
When I kill the other women in the hall."

And Eurycleia, the wise old woman:

"How can you say that, my child? You know
What I'm made of. You know I won't break.
I'll be as steady as solid stone or iron.
And I'll tell you this, and you remember it:
If, with heaven's help, you subdue the proud suitors,
I'll list for you all the women in the house,
Those who dishonor you and those who are true."

And Odysseus, his mind teeming:

"Nurse, you don't have to tell me about them.
I'll keep an eye out and get to know each one.
Don't say a thing. Just leave it up to the gods."

At this, the old woman went off for more water
To wash his feet, since it had all been spilled.
When she had washed him and rubbed on oil,
Odysseus pulled his chair close to the fire again
To keep warm, and hid the scar with his rags.

Penelope now resumed their talk:

"There's one more thing I want to ask you about,
And then it will be time to get some sleep—
At least for those to whom sweet sleep comes
Despite their cares. But some god has given me
Immeasurable sorrow. By day
I console myself with lamentation
And see to my work and that of my women.
But at night, when sleep takes hold of others,
I lie in bed, smothered by my own anxiety,

Mourning restlessly, my heart racing.
Just as the daughter of Pandareus,
The pale nightingale, sings sweetly

In the greening of spring, perched in the leaves,
And trills out her song of lament for her son,
Her beloved Itylus, whom she killed unwittingly,
Itylus, the son of Zethus her lord[3]—
So too my heart is torn with dismay.
Should I stay here with my son
And keep everything safe and just as it is,
My goods, my slaves, my high-gabled house,
Honoring my husband's bed and public opinion—
Or should I go with whoever is best
Of all my suitors, and gives me gifts past counting?
And then there's my son. While he was young
And not yet mature, he kept me from leaving
My husband's house and marrying another.
But now that he's grown and come into manhood,
He begs me to leave, worried because
These Achaean men are devouring his goods.
  But listen now to a dream I had
And tell me what it means. In my dream
I have twenty geese at home. I love to watch them
Come out of the water and eat grains of wheat.
But a huge eagle with a hooked beak comes
Down from the mountain and breaks their necks,
Killing them all. They lie strewn through the hall
While he rides the wind up to the bright sky.
I weep and wail, still in my dream,
And Achaean ladies gather around me
As I grieve because the eagle killed my geese.
Then the eagle comes back and perches upon
A jutting roofbeam and speaks to me
In a human voice, telling me not to cry:

'Take heart, daughter of famed Icarius.
This is no dream, but a true vision
That you can trust. The geese are the suitors,
And I, who was once an eagle, am now
Your husband come back, and I will deal out doom,
A grisly death for all of the suitors.'

"So he spoke, and I woke up refreshed.
Looking around I saw the geese in the house,
Feeding on wheat by the trough, as before."

And Odysseus, his mind teeming:

"Lady, there is no way to give this dream
Another slant. Odysseus himself has shown you
How he will finish this business. The suitors' doom
Is clear. Not one will escape death's black birds."

3. Zethus's wife envied her sister-in-law, Niobe, who had six sons to her one. She wanted to kill one of Niobe's children, but ended up killing her own son, Itylus, by mistake, in a fit of madness. Zeus changed her into a nightingale.

And Penelope, in her circumspect way:

"Stranger, you should know that dreams
Are hard to interpret, and don't always come true.
There are two gates for dreams to drift through,
One made of horn and the other of ivory.
Dreams that pass through the gate of ivory
Are deceptive dreams and will not come true,
But when someone has a dream that has passed
Through the gate of polished horn, that dream
Will come true. My strange dream, though,
Did not come from there. If it had,
It would have been welcome to me and my child.
One more thing, and, please, take it to heart.
Dawn is coming, the accursed dawn of the day
Which will sever me from the house of Odysseus.
I will announce a contest. Odysseus
Used to line up axes inside his hall,
Twelve of them, like the curved chocks
That prop up a ship when it is being built,
And he would stand far off and send an arrow
Whizzing through them all. I will propose
This contest to my suitors, and whoever
Can bend that bow and slip the string on its notch
And shoot an arrow through all twelve axes,
With him will I go, leaving behind this house
I was married in, this beautiful, prosperous house,
Which I will remember always, even in my dreams."

And Odysseus, from the depths of his teeming mind:

"Revered wife of Laertes' son, Odysseus,
Do not put off this contest any longer,
For Odysseus will be here, with all his cunning,
Handling that polished bow, before these men
Could ever string it and shoot through the iron."

Then Penelope, still watching him:

"If you were willing, stranger, to sit here
Beside me in my halls and give me joy,
Sleep would never settle upon my eyes.
But we cannot always be sleepless,
For every thing there is a season, and a time
For all we do on the life-giving earth.
I will go now to my room upstairs
And lie on my bed, which has become
A sorrowful bed, wet with my tears
Since the day Odysseus left
For Ilion, that accursed city.
I will lie there, but you can lie here

In the hall. Spread some blankets on the floor,
Or have the maids make up a bed for you."

Saying this, Penelope went upstairs
To her softly lit room, not alone,
For her women went up with her.
Once in her room she wept for Odysseus,
Her beloved husband, wept until Athena
Let sweet sleep settle upon her eyelids.

BOOK XX

Odysseus lay down to sleep
On the outer porch. He spread out
An uncured oxhide, and on top of that
He layered fleeces from the many sheep
That were always being slaughtered
There in his house. Eurynome
Covered him with a cloak, and there he lay,
Sleepless, his mind racing with thoughts
Of how to punish the suitors.
And then the women
Came from the house, on their way,
As usual, to sleep with the suitors,
Laughing with each other and giggling.
Odysseus felt his chest tighten. He brooded
For a long time over what he should do—
Rush out and kill every last one of them,
Or let them sleep with the arrogant bastards
This one last time. He growled under his breath

The way a dog standing over her pups growls
When she sees a stranger and digs in to fight—

So Odysseus growled at their iniquity,
But he slapped his chest hard and scolded his heart:

"Endure, my heart. You endured worse than this
On that day when the invincible Cyclops
Ate our comrades. You bore it until your cunning
Got you out of the cave where you thought you would die."

In this way Odysseus scolded his heart,
And his heart in obedience beat steady and strong.
But the great hero himself tossed and turned.

It was like a man roasting a paunch
Stuffed with fat and blood over a fire.

He can't wait for it to be done
And so keeps turning it over and over—

Odysseus tossing and turning as he pondered how
To get his hands on the shameless suitors,
One man against many.
And then Athena came
Down from the sky, and stood above his head
In the form of a woman, and spoke to him:

"Why are you sleepless, most ill-fated of men?
This is your house, and in this house are your wife
And child, a son any father would hope for."

And Odysseus, his mind teeming:

"Yes, Goddess, all that you say is true,
But my heart is brooding over this—
How to get my hands on the shameless suitors,
Alone as I am, against the whole pack of them.
And worse, even if I were to kill them
By your will and the will of Zeus, how
Would I get out of it? Think about that."

And Athena, eyes flashing in the dark:

"Let it go, Odysseus. Some people trust
Their puny human friends more than you trust me.
And here I am, a goddess, protecting you
In all your trials. To put it plainly,
Even if there were fifty squadrons of armed men
All around us, doing their mortal best to kill us,
You would still be able to run off their cattle!
Now get some sleep. Staying up all night
Will only sap your strength. All your troubles,
Odysseus, will soon be over."
Athena spoke
And shed sleep on his eyelids, and then
She was off to Olympus, a being of light.

While Odysseus slept, his cares melting away
Under the spell of sleep, his wife awoke,
And she wept as she sat upon her soft bed.
When her heart had its fill of weeping,
The godlike woman prayed to Artemis:

"Artemis, mighty daughter of Zeus—please,
Shoot an arrow into my breast and take my life
This very moment. This is my wish,
Or that a storm wind snatch me away
And bear me off over the gloomy passes

And cast me down at the mouth of Ocean,
As winds once bore off Pandareus' daughters.
The gods had slain their parents, and they were left
Orphans in their halls. Aphrodite fed them
Cheese, sweet honey, and mellow wine;
Hera made them wise and beautiful
Beyond all women; holy Artemis made them tall;
And Athena taught them glorious handiwork.
But while Aphrodite was off to high Olympus
To arrange their marriages, on her way to Zeus,
The high lord of thunder, who knows all,
All the good and bad fortune of mortal men—
The storm spirits snatched the girls away
And gave them as slaves to the hateful Furies.
So may the Olympians blot me out,
Or Artemis, in her tall headdress, shoot me,
That I may pass beneath the hateful earth
With Odysseus in my mind's eye, never
To gratify the heart of a lesser man.
Grief is endurable when one weeps by day
But can sleep at night. Sleep makes us forget
All things, both the good and the bad,
Once it enshrouds our eyelids. But some spirit
Keeps sending me bad dreams. This very night
There slept with me again someone who looked
Just like Odysseus when he left with the army,
And my heart was glad, because I did not think
It was a dream, but the waking truth at last."

She spoke, and Dawn came, seated on gold.
Odysseus heard Penelope's voice as she wept
And in that moment between sleep and waking
He felt in his heart that she knew him already
And was standing beside his head.
He picked up
The cloak and fleeces on which he had slept
And put them on a chair in the hall. Then he took
The oxhide outside and set it down, and,
Lifting his palms to the sky, he prayed to Zeus:

"Father Zeus, if it was the gods' will
To bring me home over land and sea
After afflicting me, show me a sign.
Let someone of those stirring inside the house
Speak for me a word of good omen,
And send me a sign also from the open sky."

Zeus in his wisdom heard his prayer
And thundered from snow-capped Olympus
High above the clouds. Odysseus was glad.
And a woman uttered a word of omen

As she ground at a mill nearby in the house.
Twelve women in all worked the mills there,
Grinding barley and wheat into flour,
The marrow of men. The other women,
Their wheat ground, were sleeping now,
But she, the weakest of them, was still at it.
Stopping her mill, she spoke these words:

"Father Zeus, lord of gods and men.
That was a loud thunderclap out of a clear sky!
You must be showing someone a sign.
Will you answer an old woman's prayer?
Let this be the last and final day
The suitors feast in Odysseus' hall.
I've broken my back grinding their grain.
Let this meal be their last."

Odysseus smiled at this omen, and at the thunder
From Zeus. He would have his vengeance.

The other women were up now, huddled together
As they kindled the day's fire on the hearth.
Telemachus rose from bed, a godlike man,
And got dressed. He slung his sharp sword
Around one shoulder, tied fine leather sandals
Onto his supple feet, and, spear in hand,
Went to the threshold and spoke to Eurycleia:

"Dear nurse, have you looked after our guest;
Given him a bed and food, or is he lying uncared for?
That's my mother's style, wise as she is,
Honoring one man outrageously
And sending a better man away neglected."

And Eurycleia, with all her wits about her:

"Don't blame her, child, when she is blameless.
He sat and drank wine as long as he wanted,
But he said he wasn't hungry. She asked him.
When he got tired and wanted to sleep,
She told the women to make up a bed,
But he, like many who are down on their luck,
Wouldn't sleep on a bed, or under blankets.
He lay on an undressed oxhide and some fleeces
Out on the porch, and we threw a cloak over him."

Thus Eurycleia, and Telemachus went out,
Spear in hand and two hounds at his heels,
To join the other men in the public square.
Then Eurycleia, Peisenor's granddaughter,
A noble woman, called to her maids:

"Some of you get busy and sweep the hall
And sprinkle it, and put the purple coverlets
On the good chairs. And we'll need some others,
To sponge down the tables, and wash the bowls
And goblets. The rest of you go down
And fetch water from the spring, quickly.
The suitors will be here early today.
It's a feast day, a holiday for everyone."

She spoke, and they did as she said. Twenty
Went down to the spring with its dark water,
And the rest did their house work skillfully.

Then in came the town's serving men. They started
Splitting logs, doing a good job of it. The women
Came back from the spring, and behind them
Came the swineherd, driving three prime boars,
The herd's finest. He let them feed in the courtyard
And then turned to Odysseus with a pleasant manner:

"Stranger, are you getting any more respect yet,
Or are they still insulting you in the hall?"

And Odysseus, his mind teeming:

"Eumaeus, it is outrageous the way these men
Carry on in another man's house. May the gods
Punish them! They have no sense of shame."

After this exchange, Melanthius came up,
The goatherd, leading the best she-goats
From all the herds for the suitors' feast.
Two herdsmen followed him. He tethered the goats
In the echoing portico, and then taunted Odysseus:

"Are you still here, pestering everyone?
Why don't you get the hell outside?
You and I are going to have to settle this
With our fists. I don't like your way of begging.
There are other feasts you can go to, you know."

Odysseus made no response, but sat
Shaking his head and brooding darkly.

And then a third herdsman came, Philoetius,
Driving for the suitors a barren heifer
And fat she-goats. This livestock had been brought over,
Along with Philoetius, by ferrymen
Who ply the straits with all sorts of passengers.
He tethered the animals in the echoing portico
And then went up to the swineherd and asked:

"Who's the new arrival, swineherd?
Where does he say he comes from,
And who are his parents and kinsmen?
Poor guy! He looks like some kind of king,
But the gods can make it tough
For wanderers, even if they're royalty."

He spoke, then came up to Odysseus,
Stretched out his right hand, and said:

"Welcome, stranger, and may good luck
Come your way, hard as things are for you now.
Father Zeus, no god curses us worse than you!
You have no pity for men. You beget them,
Then plunge them into misery and pain.
Stranger, I broke into a sweat when I saw you,
And my eyes are full of tears. You remind me
Of Odysseus. He too is clothed in rags like this,
I suppose, and is a wanderer like you,
If he is still alive, that is, and still sees the sunlight.
But if he is already dead and has gone to Hades,
Then I weep for noble Odysseus.
He put me in charge of his cattle when I was a boy
In the land of the Cephallenians, and now
Those cattle are past counting. No breed
Ever flourished like that for any mortal man.
But now other men order me to drive them
So they can eat them, with no regard at all
For the son in the house, or the gods' wrath.
No, they're hot to divide among themselves
All the property of our long-absent master.
As for myself, I go around and around in my heart,
Trying to decide. It would be very bad of me,
While my master's son still lives, to go off
To some other place with my cattle,
To a foreign land. But it is worse still
To stay here and suffer, in charge of herds
Handed over to others. I would have fled
Long ago, believe me, to some powerful lord,
Because things here are no longer bearable,
Except that I still imagine, still have some hope
That my unfortunate master will someday return
And scatter the suitors out of this house."

And Odysseus, his great mind teeming:

"You're a good man, cowherd, and smart,
And I see that you understand things,
So I will say something and seal it with an oath.
With Zeus and all the gods above as witnesses,
And by Odysseus' hearth, and this table

Of hospitality to which I have come,
I swear that while you are here, Odysseus
Will come home, and you will see, if you wish,
The death of the suitors, who lord it over this hall."

To which the cowherd responded:

"May Zeus bring what you say to pass, stranger.
Then you would see what these hands can do."

And Eumaeus, too, prayed to all the gods
That wise Odysseus might return to his home.

So went their talk.
The suitors, meanwhile,
Were laying plans for Telemachus' death,
But as they talked a bird appeared on their left,
A high-flying eagle with a dove in its talons.
This prompted Amphinomus to say to them:

"This plan of ours isn't going to work, friends—
Killing Telemachus. We might as well just eat."

The suitors all agreed with Amphinomus.
Going into the house of godlike Odysseus,
They laid their cloaks on chairs and got busy
Slaughtering big sheep and plump goats
And fatted swine, and the herd's prize heifer.
They roasted the entrails, served them, and mixed wine
In the bowls. The swineherd passed out the cups,
Philoetius handed out bread from a beautiful basket,
And Melanthius poured for them. They reached out
To all the tasty dishes spread before them.

Telemachus, pressing his advantage,
Showed Odysseus to a seat
Inside the great hall by the stone threshold,
Giving him a shabby stool beside a little table.
He served him a portion of the entrails
And a cup of wine, and he said to him:

"Sit here among these heroes and sip your wine.
I myself will protect you from their insults
And keep their hands from you. This house
Is not a public inn, but the palace of Odysseus,
Who inherited it to pass on to me.
So, all you suitors, control yourselves.
I don't want any fights breaking out here."

They bit their lips at this and wondered
At Telemachus. It had been a bold speech.
Then Antinous, Eupeithes' son, said:

"Hard as it is, we'd better listen to him, men.
Telemachus really means business now.
If Zeus had allowed it, we'd have shut his mouth
By now, here in these halls, fine speaker or not."

But Telemachus paid no attention to Antinous.

Meanwhile, down in the town, heralds
Were leading a sacrifice of one hundred bulls
Through the streets, and Achaean men,
Their long hair flowing, were gathering
In a shady grove sacred to Apollo,
The god whose arrows strike from afar.[4]

In Odysseus' palace they were now drawing
The roasted meat from the spits and dividing it up
For a glorious feast. The servers set out
A portion for Odysseus equal to the others,
This at the command of Telemachus,
Godlike Odysseus' own true son.

But Athena was not about to let the suitors
Abstain from insults. She wanted the pain
To sink deeper into Odysseus' bones.
There was a particularly arrogant suitor
From the island of Samê—Ctessipus by name.
This man, relying on his enormous wealth,
Courted the wife of the long-absent Odysseus.
He spoke now among the insolent crowd:

"Hear me, suitors. I have something to say.
The stranger here has been served a portion
Equal to ours. This is all as it should be.
It would not be right to deprive any guest
Telemachus entertains here in these halls.
So I'd like to give him a gift myself,
A little gratuity he might want to pass on
To the bath woman or one of the other slaves
Who live in the house of godlike Odysseus."

So saying, he picked up an ox's hoof
From a basket and threw it hard. Odysseus
Snapped his head aside and dodged it,
Smiling to himself, a grim and bitter smile.
The ox's hoof crashed into the solid wall,

And Telemachus tore into Ctessipus:

"You're damned lucky you missed him,
Ctessipus—or rather that he dodged your throw—

4. Apollo carries a bow; his arrows can bring plague.

Or I would have rammed my spear into your gut,
And your father would have been busy
With your funeral instead of making plans for a wedding.
No more of this ugliness in my house—from anyone!
I understand now what's going on around here,
The good and the bad. I was a child before.
But we still have to put up with all this,
Seeing the sheep slaughtered, the wine drunk,
The bread—one man can't stop many.
You don't have to be hostile to me,
But if you are determined to cut me down,
Well, I'd rather be killed in cold blood
Than have to watch this disgusting behavior—
Guests mistreated and men dragging the women
Shamefully through these beautiful halls."

Dead silence reigned in those beautiful halls
Until Agelaus, son of Damastor, said:

"Friends, no one should get angry at a speech
Justly spoken, or respond to it harshly.
We should stop mistreating the stranger
And all of the servants in Odysseus' house.
But I would like to offer to Telemachus,
And to his mother, some friendly advice,
And I hope that it gets through to both of them.
As long as you still held hope in your hearts
That Odysseus would find his way back home,
No one could blame you for waiting for him
And restraining the suitors—clearly the better course
Had he ever come back and returned to his home.
But now it is clear he will never return.
Sit down with your mother and tell her this.
Tell her to marry the best of her suitors,
Whoever that is, whoever gives her the most.
Then you can enjoy what your father has left you,
And she can keep another man's house."

Telemachus answered in his cool-headed way:

"I swear by Zeus and by my poor father,
Who has either perished far from Ithaca
Or is wandering still, that I do not, Agelaus,
Delay my mother's marriage. On the contrary,
I encourage her to marry the man of her choice,
And I offer her a dowry of gifts past counting.
But it would be shameful for me to order her to leave—
May the gods forbid it—against her own will."

Thus Telemachus. And Pallas Athena
Touched the suitors' minds with hysteria.

They couldn't stop laughing, and as they laughed
It seemed to them that their jaws were not theirs,
And the meat that they ate was dabbled with blood.
Tears filled their eyes, and their hearts raced.
Then the seer Theoclymenus spoke among them:

"Wretches, what wicked thing is this that you suffer?
You are shrouded in night from top to toe,
Lamentation flares, your cheeks melt with tears,
And the walls of the house are spattered with blood.
The porch and the court are crowded with ghosts
Streaming down to the undergloom. The sun is gone
From heaven, and an evil mist spreads over the land."

Thus the seer, and they just giggled at him.
Eurymachus was the first to actually speak:

"This newly arrived stranger has lost his mind!
Quick, get him outside, since he thinks it's night in here."

To which the seer Theoclymenus replied:

"I don't need any escorts, Eurymachus.
I have eyes, ears, and my own two feet,
And a mind in good working order.
I'll leave under my own power, for I can see
Evil coming upon you, inescapable evil
For every last one of you who in your blind pride
Do violence to the house of Odysseus."

And with that he left the great hall
And went to Peiraeus, who took him in gladly.
The suitors stood there smirking at each other
And tried to provoke Telemachus
By ridiculing his guests with comments like these:

"Hey, Telemachus, you don't have much luck
With the kind of guests you keep around.
You've got this filthy vagabond here
Who always wants a handout of bread and wine
And can't help out with anything, a useless load.
Then this other one posing as a prophet.
If you ask me we ought to throw them on a ship
And send them off to the Sicilians.
At least then you would turn a little profit."

So went their talk. But Telemachus ignored them,
Watching his father in silence, waiting for the moment
When he would lay his hands on the shameless suitors.

By now Penelope, Icarius' wise daughter,
Had set her chair across from the suitors

And heard the words of each man in the hall.
During all their laughter they had been busy
Preparing their dinner, a tasty meal
For which they had slaughtered many animals.
But no meal could be more graceless than the one
A goddess and a hero would serve to them soon.
After all, they started the whole ugly business.

BOOK XXI

Owl-eyed Athena now prompted Penelope
To set before the suitors Odysseus' bow
And the grey iron, implements of the contest
And of their death.
Penelope climbed
The steep stairs to her bedroom and picked up
A beautiful bronze key with an ivory handle
And went with her maids to a remote storeroom
Where her husband's treasures lay—bronze, gold,
And wrought iron. And there lay the curved bow
And the quiver, still loaded with arrows,
Gifts which a friend of Odysseus had given him
When they met in Lacedaemon long ago.
This was Iphitus, Eurytus' son, a godlike man.
They had met in Messene, in the house of Ortilochus.
Odysseus had come to collect a debt
The Messenians owed him: three hundred sheep
They had taken from Ithaca in a sea raid,
And the shepherds with them. Odysseus
Had come to get them back, a long journey
For a young man, sent by his father and elders.
Iphitus had come to search for twelve mares
He had lost, along with the mules they were nursing.
These mares turned out to be the death of Iphitus
When he came to the house of Heracles,
Zeus' tough-hearted son, who killed him,
Guest though he was, without any regard
For the gods' wrath or the table they had shared—
Killed the man and kept the strong-hoofed mares.[5]
It was while looking for these mares that Iphitus
Met Odysseus and gave him the bow
Which old Eurytus had carried and left to his son.
Odysseus gave him a sword and spear
To mark the beginning of their friendship
But before they had a chance to entertain each other
Zeus' son killed Iphitus, son of Eurytus,
A man like the gods. Odysseus did not take
The bow with him on his black ship to Troy.
It lay at home as a memento of his friend,
And Odysseus carried it only on Ithaca.

5. Heracles killed Iphitus in a dispute over the mares of Iphitus's father, Eurytus.

Penelope came to the storeroom
And stepped onto the oak threshold
Which a carpenter in the old days had planed,
Leveled, and then fitted with doorposts
And polished doors. Lovely in the half-light,
She quickly loosened the thong from the hook,
Drove home the key and shot back the bolts.
The doors bellowed like a bull in a meadow
And flew open before her. Stepping through,
She climbed onto a high platform that held chests
Filled with fragrant clothes. She reached up
And took the bow, case and all, from its peg,
Then sat down and laid the gleaming case on her knees
Her eyes welling with tears. Then she opened the case
And took out her husband's bow. When she had her fill
Of weeping, she went back to the hall
And the lordly suitors, bearing in her hands
The curved bow and the quiver loaded
With whining arrows. Two maidservants
Walked beside her, carrying a wicker chest
Filled with the bronze and iron gear her husband
Once used for this contest. When the beautiful woman
Reached the crowded hall, she stood
In the doorway flanked by her maidservants.
Then, covering her face with her shining veil,
Penelope spoke to her suitors:

"Hear me, proud suitors. You have used this house
For an eternity now—to eat and drink
In its master's absence, nor could you offer
Any excuse except your lust to marry me.
Well, your prize is here, and this is the contest.
I set before you the great bow of godlike Odysseus.
Whoever bends this bow and slips the string on its notch
And shoots an arrow through all twelve axes,
With him will I go, leaving behind this house
I was married in, this beautiful, prosperous house,
Which I will remember always, even in my dreams."

Penelope said this, and then ordered Eumaeus
To set out for the suitors the bow and grey iron.
All in tears, Eumaeus took them and laid them down,
And the cowherd wept, too, when he saw
His master's bow. Antinous scoffed at them both:

"You stupid yokels! You can't see farther than your own noses.
What a pair! Disturbing the lady with your bawling.
She's sad enough already because she's lost her husband.
Either sit here in silence or go outside to weep,
And leave the bow behind for us suitors. This contest
Will separate the men from the boys. It won't be easy

To string that polished bow. There is no man here
Such as Odysseus was. I know. I saw him myself
And remember him well, though I was still a child."

So Antinous said, hoping in his heart
That he would string the bow first and shoot an arrow
Through the iron. But the only arrow
He would touch first would be the one shot
Into his throat from the hands of Odysseus,
The man he himself was dishonoring
While inciting his comrades to do the same.

And then Telemachus, with a sigh of disgust:

"Look at me! Zeus must have robbed me of my wits.
My dear mother declares, for all her good sense,
That she will marry another and abandon this house,
And all I do is laugh and think it is funny.
Well, come on, you suitors, here's your prize,
A woman the likes of whom does not exist
In all Achaea, or in sacred Pylos,
Nowhere in Argos or in Mycenae,
Or on Ithaca itself or on the dark mainland.
You all know this. Why should I praise my mother?
Let's get going. Don't start making excuses
To put off stringing the bow. We'll see what happens.
And I might give that bow a try myself.
If I string it and shoot an arrow through the axeheads,
It won't bother me so much that my honored mother
Is leaving this house and going off with another,
Because I would at least be left here as someone
Capable of matching his father's prowess."

With that he took off his scarlet cloak, stood up,
And unstrapped his sword from his shoulders.
Then he went to work setting up the axeheads,
First digging a long trench true to the line
To hold them in a row, and then tamping the earth
Around each one. Everyone was amazed
That he made such a neat job of it
When he had never seen it done before.
Then he went and took his stance on the threshold
And began to try the bow. Three times
He made it quiver as he strained to string it,
And three times he eased off, although in his heart
He yearned to draw that bow and shoot an arrow
Through the iron axeheads. And on his fourth try
He would have succeeded in muscling the string
Onto its notch, but Odysseus reined him in,
Signaling him to stop with an upward nod.
So Telemachus said for all to hear:

"I guess I'm going to be a weakling forever!
Or else I'm still too young and don't have the strength
To defend myself against an enemy.
But come on, all of you who are stronger than me—
Give the bow a try and let's settle this contest."

And he set the bow aside, propping it against
The polished, jointed door, and leaning the arrow
Against the beautiful latch. Then Telemachus
Sat down on the chair from which he had risen.

Antinous, Eupeithes' son, then said:

"All right. We go in order from left to right,
Starting from where the wine gets poured."

Everyone agreed with Antinous' idea.
First up was their soothsayer, Leodes,
Oenops' son. He always sat in the corner
By the wine-bowl, and he was the only one
Who loathed the way the suitors behaved.
He now carried the bow and the arrow
Onto the threshold, took his stance,
And tried to bend the bow and string it,
But his tender, unworn hands gave out,
And he said for all the suitors to hear:

"Friends, I'm not the man to string this bow.
Someone else can take it. I foresee it will rob
Many a young hero of the breath of life.
And that will be just as well, since it is far better
To die than live on and fall short of the goal
We gather here for, with high hopes day after day.
You might hope in your heart—you might yearn—
To marry Penelope, the wife of Odysseus,
But after you've tried this bow and seen what it's like,
Go woo some other Achaean woman
And try to win her with your gifts. And Penelope
Should just marry the highest bidder,
The man who is fated to be her husband."

And he set the bow aside, propping it against
The polished, jointed door, and leaning the arrow
Against the beautiful latch. Then
He sat down on the chair from which he had risen.
And Antinous heaped contempt upon him:

"What kind of thing is that to say, Leodes?
I'm not going to stand here and listen to this.
You think this bow is going rob some young heroes
Of life, just because you can't string it?

The truth is your mother didn't bear a son
Strong enough to shoot arrows from bows.
But there are others who will string it soon enough."

Then Antinous called to Melanthius, the goatherd:

"Get over here and start a fire, Melanthius,
And set by it a bench with a fleece over it,
And bring out a tub of lard from the pantry,
So we can grease the bow, and warm it up.
Then maybe we can finish this contest."

He spoke, and Melanthius quickly rekindled the fire
And placed by it a bench covered with a fleece
And brought out from the pantry a tub of lard
With which the young men limbered up the bow—
But they still didn't have the strength to string it.

Only Antinous and godlike Eurymachus,
The suitors' ringleaders—and their strongest—
Were still left in the contest.

Meanwhile,
Two other men had risen and left the hall—
The cowherd and swineherd—and Odysseus himself
Went out, too. When the three of them
Were outside the gates, Odysseus said softly:

"Cowherd and swineherd, I've been wondering
If I should tell you what I'm about to tell you now.
Let me ask you this. What would you do
If Odysseus suddenly showed up here
Out of the blue, just like that?
Would you side with the suitors or Odysseus?
Tell me how you stand."

And the cattle herder answered him:

"Father Zeus, if only this would come true!
Let him come back. Let some god guide him.
Then you would see what these hands could do."

And Eumaeus prayed likewise to all the gods
That Odysseus would return.

When Odysseus
Was sure of both these men, he spoke to them again:

"I am back, right here in front of you.
After twenty hard years I have returned to my home.
I know that only you two of all my slaves

Truly want me back. I have heard
None of the others pray for my return.
So this is my promise to you. If a god
Beats these proud suitors down for me,
I will give you each a wife, property,
And a house built near mine. You two shall be
Friends to me and brothers to Telemachus.
And look, so you can be sure of who I am,
Here's a clear sign, that scar from the wound
I got from a boar's tusk when I went long ago
To Parnassus with the sons of Autolycus."

And he pulled his rags aside from the scar.
When the two men had examined it carefully,
They threw their arms around Odysseus and wept,
And kept kissing his head and shoulders in welcome.
Odysseus kissed their heads and hands,
And the sun would have gone down on their weeping,
Had not Odysseus stopped them, saying:

"No more weeping and wailing now. Someone might come
Out of the hall and see us and tell those inside.
We'll go back in now—not together, one at a time.
I'll go first, and then you. And here's what to watch for.
None of the suitors will allow the bow and quiver
To be given to me. It'll be up to you, Eumaeus,
To bring the bow over and place it in my hands.
Then tell the women to lock the doors to their hall,
And if they hear the sound of men groaning
Or being struck, tell them not to rush out
But to sit still and do their work in silence.
Philoetius, I want you to bar the courtyard gate
And secure it quickly with a piece of rope."

With this, Odysseus entered his great hall
And sat down on the chair from which he had risen.
Then the two herdsmen entered separately.

Eurymachus was turning the bow
Over and over in his hands, warming it
On this side and that by the fire, but even so
He was unable to string it. His pride hurt,
Shoulders sagging, he groaned and then swore:

"Damn it! It's not just myself I'm sorry for,
But for all of us—and not for the marriage either.
That hurts, but there are plenty of other women,
Some here in Ithaca, some in other cities.
No, it's that we fall so short of Odysseus'
Godlike strength. We can't even string his bow!
We'll be laughed at for generations to come!"

Antinous, son of Eupeithes, answered him:

"That'll never happen, Eurymachus,
And you know it. Now look, today is a holiday
Throughout the land, a sacred feast
In honor of Apollo, the Archer God.
This is no time to be bending bows.
So just set it quietly aside for now.
As for the axes, why don't we leave them
Just as they are? No one is going to come
Into Odysseus' hall and steal those axes.
Now let's have the cupbearer start us off
So we can forget about the bow
And pour libations. Come morning,
We'll have Melanthius bring along
The best she-goats in all the herds,
So we can lay prime thigh-pieces
On the altar of Apollo, the Archer God,
And then finish this business with the bow."

Antinous' proposal carried the day.
The heralds poured water over everyone's hands,
And boys filled the mixing bowls up to the brim
And served out the wine, first pouring
A few drops into each cup for libation.
When they had poured out their libations
And drunk as much as they wanted, Odysseus
Spoke among them, his heart full of cunning:

"Hear me, suitors of the glorious queen—
And I address Eurymachus most of all,
And godlike Antinous, since his speech
Was right on the mark when he said that for now
You should stop the contest and leave everything
Up to the gods. Tomorrow the Archer God
Will give the victory to whomever he chooses.
But come, let me have the polished bow.
I want to see, here in this hall with you,
If my grip is still strong, and if I still have
Any power left in these gnarled arms of mine,
Or if my hard traveling has sapped all my strength."

They seethed with anger when they heard this,
Afraid that he would string the polished bow,
And Antinous addressed him contemptuously:

"You don't have an ounce of sense in you,
You miserable tramp. Isn't it enough
That we let you hang around with us,
Undisturbed, with a full share of the feast?
You even get to listen to what we say,

Which no other stranger, much less beggar, can do.
It's wine that's screwing you up, as it does
Anyone who guzzles it down. It was wine
That deluded the great centaur, Eurytion,
In the hall of Peirithous, the Lapith hero.
Eurytion got blind-drunk and in his madness
Did a terrible thing in Peirithous' house.
The enraged Lapiths sliced off his nose and ears
And dragged him outside, and Eurytion
Went off in a stupor, mutilated and muddled.
Men and centaurs have been at odds ever since.[6]
Eurytion hurt himself because he got drunk.
And you're going to get hurt, too, I predict,
Hurt badly, if you string the bow. No one
In all the land will show you any kindness.
We'll send you off in a black ship to Echetus,
Who maims them all. You'll never get out alive.
So just be quiet and keep on drinking,
And don't challenge men who are younger than you."

It was Penelope who answered Antinous:

"It is not good, or just, Antinous,
To cheat any of Telemachus' guests
Who come to this house. Do you think
That if this stranger proves strong enough
To string Odysseus' bow, he will then
Lead me to his home and make me his wife?
I can't imagine that he harbors this hope.
So do not ruin your feast on that account.
The very idea is preposterous."

Eurymachus responded to this:

"Daughter of Icarius, wise Penelope,
Of course it's preposterous that this man
Would marry you. That's not what we're worried about.
But we are embarrassed at what men—and women—will say:
'A bunch of weaklings were wooing the wife
Of a man they couldn't touch—they couldn't even string
His polished bow. Then along came a vagrant
Who strung it easily and shot through the iron.'
That's what they'll say, to our lasting shame."

And Penelope, her eyes narrowing:

"Eurymachus, men who gobble up
The house of a prince cannot expect
To have a good reputation anywhere.
So there isn't any point in bringing up honor.

6. The Lapiths were a legendary people of Thessaly; they fought with the Centaurs at the wedding of Peirithous.

This stranger is a very well-built man
And says he is the son of a noble father.
So give him the bow and let us see what happens.
And here is my promise to all of you.
If Apollo gives this man the glory
And he strings the bow, I will clothe him
In a fine cloak and tunic, and give him
A javelin to ward off dogs and men,
And a double-edged sword, and sandals
For his feet, and I will give him passage
To wherever his heart desires."

This time it was Telemachus who answered:

"As for the bow, Mother, no man alive
Has a stronger claim than I do to give it
To whomever I want, or to deny it—
No, none of the lords on rocky Ithaca
Nor on the islands over toward Elis,
None of them could force his will upon me,
Not even if I wanted to give this bow
Outright, case and arrows and all,
As a gift to the stranger.
Go to your rooms,
Mother, and take care of your work,
Spinning and weaving, and have the maids do theirs.
This bow is men's business, and my business
Especially, since I am the master of this house."

Penelope was stunned and turned to go,
Her son's masterful words pressed to her heart.
She went up the stairs to her room with her women
And wept for Odysseus, her beloved husband,
Until grey-eyed Athena cast sleep on her eyelids.

Downstairs, the noble swineherd was carrying
The curved bow across the hall. The suitors
Were in an uproar, and one of them called out:

"Where do you think you're going with that bow,
You miserable swineherd? You're out of line.
Go back to your pigsties, where your own dogs
Will wolf you down—a nice, lonely death—
If Apollo and the other gods smile upon us."

Afraid, the swineherd stopped in his tracks
And set the bow down. Men were yelling at him
All through the hall, and now Telemachus weighed in:

"Keep going with the bow. You'll regret it
If you try to obey everyone. I may be
Younger than you, but I'll chase you back

Into the country with a shower of stones.
I am stronger than you. I wish I were as strong
When it came to the suitors. I'd throw more than one
Out of here in a sorry state. They're all up to no good."

This got the suitors laughing hilariously
At Telemachus. The tension in the room eased,
And the swineherd carried the bow
Across to Odysseus and put it in his hands.
Then he called Eurycleia aside and said:

"Telemachus says you should lock the doors to the hall,
And if the women hear the sound of men groaning
Or being struck, tell them not to rush out
But to sit still and do their work in silence."

Eumaeus' words sank in, and Eurycleia
Locked the doors to the crowded hall.

Meanwhile, Philoetius left without a word
And barred the gates to the fenced courtyard.
Beside the portico there lay a ship's hawser
Made of papyrus. Philoetius used this
To secure the gates, and then he went back in,
Sat down on the chair from which he had risen,
And kept his eyes on Odysseus.

He was handling the bow, turning it over and over
And testing its flex to make sure that worms
Had not eaten the horn in its master's absence.
The suitors glanced at each other
And started to make sarcastic remarks:

"Ha! A real connoisseur, an expert in bows!"

"He must have one just like it in a case at home."

"Or plans to make one just like it, to judge by the way
The masterful tramp keeps turning it in his hands."

"May he have as much success in life
As he'll have in trying to string that bow."

Thus the suitors, while Odysseus, deep in thought,
Was looking over his bow. And then, effortlessly,

Like a musician stretching a string
Over a new peg on his lyre, and making
The twisted sheep-gut fast at either end,

Odysseus strung the great bow. Lifting it up,
He plucked the string, and it sang beautifully
Under his touch, with a note like a swallow's.
The suitors were aghast. The color drained
From their faces, and Zeus thundered loud,
Showing his portents and cheering the heart
Of the long-enduring, godlike Odysseus.
One arrow lay bare on the table. The rest,
Which the suitors were about to taste,
Were still in the quiver. Odysseus picked up
The arrow from the table and laid it upon
The bridge of the bow, and, still in his chair,
Drew the bowstring and the notched arrow back.
He took aim and let fly, and the bronze-tipped arrow
Passed clean through the holes of all twelve axeheads
From first to last. And he said to Telemachus:

"Well, Telemachus, the guest in your hall
Has not disgraced you. I did not miss my target,
Nor did I take all day in stringing the bow.
I still have my strength, and I'm not as the suitors
Make me out to be in their taunts and jeers.
But now it is time to cook these men's supper,
While it is still light outside, and after that,
We'll need some entertainment—music and song—
The finishing touches for a perfect banquet."

He spoke, and lowered his brows. Telemachus,
The true son of godlike Odysseus, slung on
His sharp sword, seized his spear, and gleaming in bronze
Took his place by his father's side.

BOOK XXII

And now Odysseus' cunning was revealed.
He stripped off his rags and leapt with his bow
To the great threshold. Spreading the arrows
Out before his feet, he spoke to the suitors:

"Now that we've separated the men from the boys,
I'll see if I can hit a mark that no man
Has ever hit. Apollo grant me glory!"

As he spoke he took aim at Antinous,
Who at that moment was lifting to his lips
A golden cup—a fine, two-eared golden goblet—
And was just about to sip the wine. Bloodshed
Was the farthest thing from his mind.
They were at a banquet. Who would think
That one man, however strong, would take them all on
And so ensure his own death? Odysseus

Took dead aim at Antinous' throat and shot,
And the arrow punched all the way through
The soft neck tissue. Antinous fell to one side,
The cup dropped from his hands, and a jet
Of dark blood spurted from his nostrils.
He kicked the table as he went down,
Spilling the food on the floor, and the bread
And roast meat were fouled in the dust.
The crowd
Burst into an uproar when they saw
Antinous go down. They jumped from their seats
And ran in a panic through the hall,
Scanning the walls for weapons—
A spear, a shield. But there were none to be had.
Odysseus listened to their angry jeers:

"You think you can shoot at men, you tramp?"

"That's your last contest—you're as good as dead!"

"You've killed the best young man in Ithaca!"

"Vultures will eat you on this very spot!"

They all assumed he had not shot to kill,
And had no idea how tightly the net
Had been drawn around them. Odysseus
Scowled at the whole lot of them, and said:

"You dogs! You thought I would never
Come home from Troy. So you wasted my house,
Forced the women to sleep with you,
And while I was still alive you courted my wife
Without any fear of the gods in high heaven
Or of any retribution from the world of men.
Now the net has been drawn tight around you."

At these words the color drained from their faces,
And they all looked around for a way to escape.
Only Eurymachus had anything to say:

"If you are really Odysseus of Ithaca,
Then what you say is just. The citizens
Have done many foolish things in this house
And many in the fields. But the man to blame
Lies here dead, Antinous. He started it all,
Not so much because he wanted a marriage
Or needed one, but for another purpose,
Which Zeus did not fulfill: he wanted to be king
In Ithaca, and to kill your son in ambush.
Now he's been killed, and he deserved it.

But spare your people. We will pay you back
For all we have eaten and drunk in your house.
We will make a collection; each man will put in
The worth of twenty oxen; we will make restitution
In bronze and gold until your heart is soothed.
Until then no one could blame you for being angry."

Odysseus fixed him with a stare and said:

"Eurymachus, not even if all of you
Gave me your entire family fortunes,
All that you have and ever will have,
Would I stay my hands from killing.
You courted my wife, and you will pay in full.
Your only choice now is to fight like men
Or run for it. Who knows, one or two of you
Might live to see another day. But I doubt it."

Their blood turned milky when they heard this.
Eurymachus now turned to them and said:

"Friends, this man is not going to stop at anything.
He's got his arrows and bow, and he'll shoot
From the threshold until he's killed us all.
We've got to fight back. Draw your swords
And use the tables as shields. If we charge him
In a mass and push him from the doorway
We can get reinforcements from town in no time.
Then this man will have shot his last shot."

With that, he drew his honed bronze sword
And charged Odysseus with an ear-splitting cry.
Odysseus in the same instant let loose an arrow
That entered his chest just beside the nipple
And spiked down to his liver. The sword fell
From Eurymachus' hand. He spun around
And fell on a table, knocking off dishes and cups,
And rolled to the ground, his forehead banging
Up and down against it and his feet kicking a chair
In his death throes, until the world went dark.
Amphinomus went for Odysseus next,
Rushing at him with his sword drawn,
Hoping to drive him away from the door.
Telemachus got the jump on him, though,
Driving a bronze-tipped spear into his back
Square between his shoulder blades
And through to his chest. He fell with a thud,
His forehead hammering into the ground.
Telemachus sprang back, leaving the spear
Right where it was, stuck in Amphinomus,

Fearing that if he tried to pull it out
Someone would rush him and cut him down
As he bent over the corpse. So he ran over
To his father's side, and his words flew fast:

"I'll bring you a shield, Father, two spears
And a bronze helmet—I'll find one that fits.
When I come back I'll arm myself
And the cowherd and swineherd. Better armed than not."

And Odysseus, the great tactician:

"Bring me what you can while I still have arrows
Or these men might drive me away from the door."

And Telemachus was off to the room
Where the weapons were stored. He took
Four shields, eight spears, and four bronze helmets
With thick horsehair plumes and brought them
Quickly to his father. Telemachus armed himself,
The two servants did likewise, and the three of them
Took their stand alongside the cunning warrior,
Odysseus. As long as the arrows held out
He kept picking off the suitors one by one,
And they fell thick as flies. But when the master archer
Ran out of arrows, he leaned the bow
Against the doorpost of the entrance hall
And slung a four-ply shield over his shoulder,
Put on his head a well-wrought helmet
With a plume that made his every nod a threat,
And took two spears tipped with heavy bronze.

Built into the higher wall of the main hall
Was a back door reached by a short flight of stairs
And leading to a passage closed by double doors.
Odysseus posted the swineherd at this doorway,
Which could be attacked by only one man at a time.
It was just then that Agelaus called to the suitors:

"Let's one of us get up to the back door
And get word to the town. Act quickly
And this man will have shot his last."

But the goatherd Melanthius answered him:

"That won't work, Agelaus.
The door outside is too near the courtyard—
An easy shot from where he is standing—
And the passageway is dangerously narrow.
One good man could hold it against all of us.
Look, let me bring you weapons and armor

From the storeroom. That has to be where
Odysseus and his son have laid them away."

So saying, Melanthius clambered up
To Odysseus' storerooms. There he picked out
Twelve shields and as many spears and helmets
And brought them out quickly to give to the suitors.
Odysseus' heart sank, and his knees grew weak
When he saw the suitors putting on armor
And brandishing spears. This wasn't going to be easy.
His words flew out to Telemachus:

"One of the women in the halls must be
Waging war against us—unless it's Melanthius."

And Telemachus, cool-headed under fire:

"No, it's my fault, Father, and no one else's.
I must have left the storeroom door open,
And one of them spotted it.
Eumaeus!
Go close the door to the storeroom,
And see whether one of the women is behind this,
Or Melanthius, son of Dolius, as I suspect."

As they were speaking, Melanthius the goatherd
Was making another trip to the storeroom
For more weapons. The swineherd spotted him
And was quick to point him out to Odysseus:

"There he goes, my lord Odysseus—
The sneak—just as we thought, on his way
To the storeroom! Tell me what to do.
Kill him if I prove to be the better man,
Or bring him to you, so he can pay in full
For all the wrongs he has done here in your house?"

Odysseus brought his mind to bear on this:

"Telemachus and I will keep the suitors busy
In the hall here. Don't worry about that.
Tie him up. Bend his arms and legs behind him
And lash them to a board strapped onto his back.
Then hoist him up to the rafters in the storeroom
And leave him there to twist in the wind."

This was just what Eumaeus and the cowherd
Wanted to hear. Off they went to the storeroom,
Unseen by Melanthius, who was inside
Rooting around for armor and weapons.
They lay in wait on either side of the door,

And when Melanthius crossed the threshold,
Carrying a beautiful helmet in one hand
And in the other a broad old shield,
Flecked with rust—a shield the hero Laertes
Had carried in his youth but that had long since
Been laid aside with its straps unstitched—
Eumaeus and the cowherd Philoetius
Jumped him and dragged him by the hair
Back into the storeroom. They threw him
Hard to the ground, knocking the wind out of him,
And tied his hands and feet behind his back,
Making it hurt, as Odysseus had ordered.
Then they attached a rope to his body
And hoisted him up along the tall pillar
Until he was up by the rafters, and you,
Swineherd Eumaeus, you mocked him:

"Now you'll really be on watch, Melanthius,
The whole night through, lying on a feather bed—
Just your style—and you're sure to see
The early dawn come up from Ocean's streams,
Couched in gold, at the hour when you drive your goats
Up to the hall to make a feast for the suitors."

So Melanthius was left there, racked with pain,
While Eumaeus and the cowherd put on their armor,
Closed the polished door, and rejoined Odysseus,
The cunning warrior. So they took their stand
There on the threshold, breathing fury,
Four of them against the many who stood in the hall.

And then Athena was with them, Zeus' daughter
Looking just like Mentor and assuming his voice.
Odysseus, glad to see her, spoke these words:

"Mentor, old friend, help me out here.
Remember all the favors I've done for you.
We go back a long way, you and I."

He figured it was Athena, the soldier's goddess.
On the other side, the suitors yelled and shouted,
Agelaus' voice rising to rebuke Athena:

"You there, Mentor, don't let Odysseus
Talk you into helping him and fighting us.
This is the way I see it turning out.
When we have killed these men, father and son,
We'll kill you next for what you mean to do
In this hall. You'll pay with your life.
And when we've taken care of all five of you,
We'll take everything you have, Mentor,

Everything in your house and in your fields,
And add it to Odysseus' property.
We won't let your sons stay in your house
Or let your daughters or even your wife
Go about freely in the town of Ithaca."

This made Athena all the more angry,
And she turned on Odysseus and snapped at him:

"I can't believe, Odysseus, that you,
Of all people, have lost the guts you had
When you fought the Trojans for nine long years
To get Helen back, killing so many in combat
And coming up with the plan that took wide Troy.[7]
How is it that now, when you've come home,
You get all teary-eyed about showing your strength
To this pack of suitors? Get over here
Next to me and see what I can do. I'll show you
What sort of man Mentor, son of Alcimus, is,
And how he repays favors in the heat of battle."

Athena spoke these words, but she did not yet
Give Odysseus the strength to turn the tide.
She was still testing him, and his glorious son,
To see what they were made of. As for herself,
The goddess flew up to the roofbeam
Of the smoky hall, just like a swallow.

The suitors were now rallied by Agelaus
And by Damastor, Eurynomus, and Amphimedon,
As well as by Demoptolemus and Peisander,
Son of Polyctor, and the warrior Polybus.
These were the best of the suitors lucky enough
To still be fighting for their lives. The rest
Had been laid low by the showers of arrows.
Agelaus now made this speech to them:

"He's had it now. Mentor's abandoned him
After all that hot air, and the four of them
Are left alone at the outer doors.
All right, now. Don't throw your spears all at once.
You six go first, and hope that Zeus allows
Odysseus to be hit and gives us the glory.
The others won't matter once he goes down."

They took his advice and gave it their best,
But Athena made their shots all come to nothing,
One man hitting the doorpost, another the door,
Another's bronze-tipped ash spear sticking

7. The Trojan Horse.

Into the wall. Odysseus and his men
Weren't even nicked, and the great hero said to them:

"It's our turn now. I say we throw our spears
Right into the crowd. These bastards mean to kill us
On top of everything else they've done to wrong me."

He spoke, and they all threw their sharp spears
With deadly aim. Odysseus hit Demoptolemus;
Telemachus got Euryades; the swineherd, Elatus;
And the cattle herder took out Peisander.
They all bit the dirt at the same moment,
And the suitors retreated to the back of the hall,
Allowing Odysseus and his men to run out
And pull their spears from the dead men's bodies.

The suitors rallied for another volley,
Throwing their sharp spears with all they had.
This time Athena made most of them miss,
One man hitting the doorpost, another the door,
Another's bronze-tipped ash spear sticking
Into the wall. But Amphimedon's spear
Grazed Telemachus' wrist, breaking the skin,
And Ctessipus' spear clipped Eumaeus' shoulder
As it sailed over his shield and kept on going
Until it hit the ground. Then Odysseus and his men
Got off another round into the throng,
Odysseus, sacker of cities, hitting Eurydamas;
Telemachus getting Amphimedon; the swineherd, Polybus;
And lastly the cattle herder striking Ctessipus
Square in the chest. And he crowed over him:

"Always picking a fight, just like your father.
Well, you can stop all your big talk now.
We'll let the gods have the last word this time.
Take this spear as your host's gift, fair exchange
For the hoof you threw at godlike Odysseus
When he made his rounds begging in the hall."

Thus the herder of the spiral-horned cattle.

Odysseus, meanwhile, had skewered Damastor's son
With a hard spear-thrust in hand-to-hand fighting,
And Telemachus killed Leocritus, Evenor's son,
Piercing him in the groin and driving his bronze spear
All the way through. Leocritus pitched forward,
His forehead slamming onto the ground.

Only then
Did Athena hold up her overpowering aegis
From her high perch, and the minds of the suitors
Shriveled with fear, and they fled through the hall

Like a herd of cattle that an iridescent gadfly
Goads along on a warm spring afternoon,

With Odysseus and his men after them

Like vultures with crooked talons and hooked beaks
Descending from the mountains upon a flock
Of smaller birds, who fly low under the clouds
And over the plain. The vultures swoop down
To pick them off; the smaller birds cannot escape,
And men thrill to see the chase in the sky.

Odysseus and his cohorts were clubbing the suitors
Right and left all through the hall; horrible groans
Rose from their lips as their heads were smashed in,
And the floor of the great hall smoked with blood.
It was then that Leodes, the soothsayer, rushed forward,
Clasped Odysseus' knees, and begged for his life:

"By your knees, Odysseus, respect me
And pity me. I swear I have never said or done
Anything wrong to any woman in your house.
I tried to stop the suitors when they did such things,
But they wouldn't listen, wouldn't keep their hands clean,
And now they've paid a cruel price for their sins.
And I, their soothsayer, who have done no wrong,
Will be laid low with them. That's the gratitude I get."

Odysseus scowled down at the man and said:

"If you are really their soothsayer, as you boast you are,
How many times must you have prayed in the halls
That my sweet homecoming would never come,
And that you would be the one my wife would go off with
And bear children to! You're a dead man."

As he spoke his strong hand reached for a sword
That lay nearby—a sword Agelaus had dropped
When he was killed. The soothsayer was struck
Full in the neck. His lips were still forming words
When his lopped head rolled in the dust.

All this while the bard, Phemius, was busy
Trying not to be killed. This man, Terpes' son,
Sang for the suitors under compulsion.
He stood now with his pure-toned lyre
Near the high back door, trying to decide
Whether he should slip out from the hall
And crouch at the altar of Zeus of the Courtyard—
The great altar on which Laertes and Odysseus
Had burned many an ox's thigh—
Or whether he should rush forward

And supplicate Odysseus by his knees.
Better to fall at the man's knees, he thought.
So he laid the hollow lyre on the ground
Between the wine-bowl and silver-studded chair
And ran up to Odysseus and clasped his knees.
His words flew up to Odysseus like birds:

"By your knees, Odysseus, respect me
And pity me. You will regret it someday
If you kill a bard—me—who sings for gods and men.
I am self-taught, and a god has planted in my heart
All sorts of songs and stories, and I can sing to you
As to a god. So don't be too eager
To slit my throat. Telemachus will tell you
That I didn't come to your house by choice
To entertain the suitors at their feasts.
There were too many of them; they made me come."

Telemachus heard him and said to his father:

"He's innocent; don't kill him.
And let's spare the herald, Medon,
Who used to take care of me when I was a child,
If Philoetius hasn't already killed him—
Or the swineherd—or if he didn't run into you
As you were charging through the house."

Medon heard what Telemachus said.
He was under a chair, wrapped in an oxhide,
Cowering from death. Now he jumped up,
Stripped off the oxhide, ran to Telemachus
And fell at his knees. His words rose on wings:

"I'm here, Telemachus! Hold back, and ask your father
To hold back too, or he might kill me with cold bronze,
Strong as he is and as mad as he is at the suitors,
Who ate away his house and paid you no honor."

Odysseus smiled at this and said to him:

"Don't worry, he's saved you. Now you know,
And you can tell the world, how much better
Good deeds are than evil. Go outside, now,
You and the singer, and sit in the yard
Away from the slaughter, until I finish
Everything I have to do inside the house."

So he spoke, and the two went out of the hall
And sat down by the altar of great Zeus,
Wide-eyed and expecting death at any moment.
Odysseus, too, had his eyes wide open,
Looking all through his house to see if anyone
Was still alive and hiding from death.

But everyone he saw lay in the blood and dust,
The whole lot of them,

like fish that fishermen
Have drawn up in nets from the grey sea
Onto the curved shore. They lie all in heaps
On the sand beach, longing for the salt waves,
And the blazing sun drains their life away.

So too the suitors, lying in heaps.

Then Odysseus called to Telemachus:

"Go call the nurse Eurycleia for me.
I want to tell her something."

So Telemachus went
To Eurycleia's room, rattled the door, and called:

"Get up and come out here, old woman—you
Who are in charge of all our women servants.
Come on. My father has something to say to you."

Eurycleia's response died on her lips.
She opened the doors to the great hall,
Came out, and followed Telemachus
To where Odysseus, spattered with blood and grime
Stood among the bodies of the slain.

A lion that has just fed upon an ox in a field
Has his chest and cheeks smeared with blood,
And his face is terrible to look upon.

So too Odysseus,
Smeared with gore from head to foot.

When Eurycleia
Saw all the corpses and the pools of blood,
She lifted her head to cry out in triumph—
But Odysseus stopped her cold,
Reining her in with these words:

"Rejoice in your heart, but do not cry aloud.
It is unholy to gloat over the slain. These men
Have been destroyed by divine destiny
And their own recklessness. They honored no one,
Rich or poor, high or low, who came to them.
And so by their folly they have brought upon themselves
An ugly fate.

Now tell me, which of the women
Dishonor me and which are innocent?"

And Eurycleia, the loyal nurse:

"Yes indeed, child, I will tell you all.
There are fifty women in your house,
Servants we have taught to do their work,
To card wool and bear all the drudgery.
Of these, twelve have shamed this house
And respect neither me nor Penelope herself.
Telemachus has only now become a man,
And his mother has not allowed him
To direct the women servants.
May I go now
To the upstairs room and tell your wife?
Some god has wrapped her up in sleep."

Odysseus, his mind teeming, answered her:

"Don't wake her yet. First bring those women
Who have acted so disgracefully."

While the old woman went out through the hall
To tell the women the news—and to summon twelve—
Odysseus called Telemachus and the two herdsmen
And spoke to them words fletched like arrows:

"Start carrying out the bodies,
And have the women help you.
Then sponge down
All of the beautiful tables and chairs.
When you have set the whole house in order,
Take the women outside between the round house
And the courtyard fence. Slash them with swords
Until they have forgotten their secret lovemaking
With the suitors. Then finish them off."

Thus Odysseus, and the women came in,
Huddled together and shedding salt tears.
First they carried out the dead bodies
And set them down under the courtyard's portico,
Propping them against each other. Odysseus himself
Kept them at it. Then he had them sponge down
All of the beautiful tables and chairs.
Telemachus, the swineherd, and the cowherd
Scraped the floor with hoes, and the women
Carried out the scrapings and threw them away.
When they had set the whole house in order,
They took the women out between the round house
And the courtyard fence, penning them in
With no way to escape. And Telemachus,
In his cool-headed way, said to the others:

"I won't allow a clean death for these women—
The suitors' sluts—who have heaped reproaches
Upon my own head and upon my mother's."

He spoke, and tied the cable of a dark-prowed ship
To a great pillar and pulled it about the round house,
Stretching it high so their feet couldn't touch the ground.

Long-winged thrushes, or doves, making their way
To their roosts, fall into a snare set in a thicket,
And the bed that receives them is far from welcome.

So too these women, their heads hanging in a row,
The cable looped around each of their necks.
It was a most piteous death. Their feet fluttered
For a little while, but not for long.

Then they brought Melanthius outside,
And in their fury they sliced off
His nose and ears with cold bronze
And pulled his genitals out by the root—
Raw meat for the dogs—and chopped off
His hands and feet.

This done,
They washed their own hands and feet
And went back into their master's great hall.

Then Odysseus said to Eurycleia:

"Bring me sulfur, old woman, and fire,
So that I can fumigate the hall.
And go tell Penelope to come down here,
And all of the women in the house as well."

And Eurycleia, the faithful nurse:

"As you say, child. But first let me bring you
A tunic and a cloak for you to put on.
You should not be standing here like this
With rags on your body. It's not right."

Odysseus, his mind teeming, answered her:

"First make a fire for me here in the hall."

He spoke, and Eurycleia did as she was told.
She brought fire and sulfur, and Odysseus
Purified his house, the halls and the courtyard.

Then the old nurse went through Odysseus'
Beautiful house, telling the women the news.

They came from their hall with torches in their hands
And thronged around Odysseus and embraced him.
And as they kissed his head and shoulders and hands
He felt a sudden, sweet urge to weep,
For in his heart he knew them all.

BOOK XXIII

The old woman laughed as she went upstairs
To tell her mistress that her husband was home.
She ran up the steps, lifting her knees high,
And, bending over Penelope, she said:

"Wake up, dear child, so you can see for yourself
What you have yearned for day in and day out.
Odysseus has come home, after all this time,
And has killed those men who tried to marry you
And who ravaged your house and bullied your son."

And Penelope, alert now and wary:

"Dear nurse, the gods have driven you crazy.
The gods can make even the wise mad,
Just as they often make the foolish wise.
Now they have wrecked your usually sound mind.
Why do you mock me and my sorrowful heart,
Waking me from sleep to tell me this nonsense—
And such a sweet sleep. It sealed my eyelids.
I haven't slept like that since the day Odysseus
Left for Ilion—that accursed city.
Now go back down to the hall.
If any of the others had told me this
And wakened me from sleep, I would have
Sent her back with something to be sorry about!
You can thank your old age for this at least."

And Eurycleia, the loyal nurse:

"I am not mocking you, child. Odysseus
Really is here. He's come home, just as I say.
He's the stranger they all insulted in the great hall.
Telemachus has known all along, but had
The self-control to hide his father's plans
Until he could pay the arrogant bastards back."

Penelope felt a sudden pang of joy. She leapt
From her bed and flung her arms around the old woman,
And with tears in her eyes she said to her:

"Dear nurse, if it is true, if he really has
Come back to his house, tell me how

He laid his hands on the shameless suitors,
One man alone against all of that mob."

Eurycleia answered her:

"I didn't see and didn't ask. I only heard the groaning
Of men being killed. We women sat
In the far corner of our quarters, trembling,
With the good solid doors bolted shut
Until your son came from the hall to call me,
Telemachus. His father had sent him to call me.
And there he was, Odysseus, standing
In a sea of dead bodies, all piled
On top of each other on the hard-packed floor.
It would have warmed your heart to see him,
Spattered with blood and filth like a lion.
And now the bodies are all gathered together
At the gates, and he is purifying the house
With sulfur, and has built a great fire,
And has sent me to call you. Come with me now
So that both your hearts can be happy again.
You have suffered so much, but now
Your long desire has been fulfilled.
He has come himself, alive, to his own hearth,
And has found you and his son in the hall.
As for the suitors, who did him wrong,
He's taken his revenge on every last man."

And Penelope, ever cautious:

"Dear nurse, don't gloat over them yet.
You know how welcome the sight of him
Would be to us all, and especially to me
And the son he and I bore. But this story
Can't be true, not the way you tell it.
One of the immortals must have killed the suitors,
Angry at their arrogance and evil deeds.
They respected no man, good or bad,
So their blind folly has killed them. But Odysseus
Is lost, lost to us here, and gone forever."

And Eurycleia, the faithful nurse:

"Child, how can you say this? Your husband
Is here at his own fireside, and yet you are sure
He will never come home! Always on guard!
But here's something else, clear proof:
The scar he got from the tusk of that boar.
I noticed it when I was washing his feet
And wanted to tell you, but he shrewdly clamped
His hand on my mouth and wouldn't let me speak.

Just come with me, and I will stake my life on it.
If I am lying you can torture me to death."

Still wary, Penelope replied:

"Dear nurse, it is hard for you to comprehend
The ways of the eternal gods, wise as you are.
Still, let us go to my son, so that I may see
The suitors dead and the man who killed them."

And Penelope descended the stairs, her heart
In turmoil. Should she hold back and question
Her husband? Or should she go up to him,
Embrace him, and kiss his hands and head?
She entered the hall, crossing the stone threshold,
And sat opposite Odysseus, in the firelight
Beside the farther wall. He sat by a column,
Looking down, waiting to see if his incomparable wife
Would say anything to him when she saw him.
She sat a long time in silence, wondering.
She would look at his face and see her husband,
But then fail to know him in his dirty rags.
Telemachus couldn't take it any more:

"Mother, how can you be so hard,
Holding back like that? Why don't you sit
Next to father and talk to him, ask him things?
No other woman would have the heart
To stand off from her husband who has come back
After twenty hard years to his country and home.
But your heart is always colder than stone."

And Penelope, cautious as ever:

"My child, I am lost in wonder
And unable to speak or ask a question
Or look him in the eyes. If he really is
Odysseus come home, the two of us
Will be sure of each other, very sure.
There are secrets between us no one else knows."

Odysseus, who had borne much, smiled,
And his words flew to his son on wings:

"Telemachus, let your mother test me
In our hall. She will soon see more clearly.
Now, because I am dirty and wearing rags,
She is not ready to acknowledge who I am.
But you and I have to devise a plan.
When someone kills just one man,
Even a man who has few to avenge him,

He goes into exile, leaving country and kin.
Well, we have killed a city of young men,
The flower of Ithaca. Think about that."

And Telemachus, in his clear-headed way:

"You should think about it, Father. They say
No man alive can match you for cunning.
We'll follow you for all we are worth,
And I don't think we'll fail for lack of courage."

And Odysseus, the master strategist:

"Well, this is what I think we should do.
First, bathe yourselves and put on clean tunics
And tell the women to choose their clothes well.
Then have the singer pick up his lyre
And lead everyone in a lively dance tune,
Loud and clear. Anyone who hears the sound,
A passerby or neighbor, will think it's a wedding,
And so word of the suitors' killing won't spread
Down through the town before we can reach
Our woodland farm. Once there we'll see
What kind of luck the Olympian[8] gives us."

They did as he said. The men bathed
And put on tunics, and the women dressed up.
The godlike singer, sweeping his hollow lyre,
Put a song in their hearts and made their feet move,
And the great hall resounded under the tread
Of men and silken-waisted women dancing.
And people outside would hear it and say:

"Well, someone has finally married the queen,
Fickle woman. Couldn't bear to keep the house
For her true husband until he came back."

But they had no idea how things actually stood.

Odysseus, meanwhile, was being bathed
By the housekeeper, Eurynome. She
Rubbed him with olive oil and threw about him
A beautiful cloak and tunic. And Athena
Shed beauty upon him, and made him look
Taller and more muscled, and made his hair
Tumble down his head like hyacinth flowers.

Imagine a craftsman overlaying silver
With pure gold. He has learned his art

8. Zeus.

From Pallas Athena and Lord Hephaestus,[9]
And creates works of breathtaking beauty.

So Athena herself made his head and shoulders
Shimmer with grace. He came from the bath
Like a god, and sat down on the chair again
Opposite his wife, and spoke to her and said:

"You're a mysterious woman.
The gods
Have given to you, more than to any
Other woman, an unyielding heart.
No other woman would be able to endure
Standing off from her husband, come back
After twenty hard years to his country and home.
Nurse, make up a bed for me so I can lie down
Alone, since her heart is a cold lump of iron."

And Penelope, cautious and wary:

"You're a mysterious man.
I am not being proud
Or scornful, nor am I bewildered—not at all.
I know very well what you looked like
When you left Ithaca on your long-oared ship.
Nurse, bring the bed out from the master bedroom,
The bedstead he made himself, and spread it for him
With fleeces and blankets and silky coverlets."

She was testing her husband.
Odysseus
Could bear no more, and he cried out to his wife:

"By God, woman, now you've cut deep.
Who moved my bed? It would be hard
For anyone, no matter how skilled, to move it.
A god could come down and move it easily,
But not a man alive, however young and strong,
Could ever pry it up. There's something telling
About how that bed's built, and no one else
Built it but me.
There was an olive tree
Growing on the site, long-leaved and full,
Its trunk thick as a post. I built my bedroom
Around that tree, and when I had finished
The masonry walls and done the roofing
And set in the jointed, close-fitting doors,
I lopped off all of the olive's branches,
Trimmed the trunk from the root on up,

9. Athena and Hephaestus are both associated with crafts.

And rounded it and trued it with an adze until
I had myself a bedpost. I bored it with an auger,
And starting from this I framed up the whole bed,
Inlaying it with gold and silver and ivory
And stretching across it oxhide thongs dyed purple.
So there's our secret. But I do not know, woman,
Whether my bed is still firmly in place, or if
Some other man has cut through the olive's trunk."

At this, Penelope finally let go.
Odysseus had shown he knew their old secret.
In tears, she ran straight to him, threw her arms
Around him, kissed his face, and said:

"Don't be angry with me, Odysseus. You,
Of all men, know how the world goes.
It is the gods who gave us sorrow, the gods
Who begrudged us a life together, enjoying
Our youth and arriving side by side
To the threshold of old age. Don't hold it against me
That when I first saw you I didn't welcome you
As I do now. My heart has been cold with fear
That an imposter would come and deceive me.
There are many who scheme for ill-gotten gains.
Not even Helen, daughter of Zeus,
Would have slept with a foreigner had she known
The Greeks would go to war to bring her back home.
It was a god who drove her to that dreadful act,
Or she never would have thought of doing what she did,
The horror that brought suffering to us as well.
But now, since you have confirmed the secret
Of our marriage bed, which no one has ever seen—
Only you and I and a single servant, Actor's daughter,
Whom my father gave me before I ever came here
And who kept the doors of our bridal chamber—
You have persuaded even my stubborn heart."

This brought tears from deep within him,
And as he wept he clung to his beloved wife.

Land is a welcome sight to men swimming
For their lives, after Poseidon has smashed their ship
In heavy seas. Only a few of them escape
And make it to shore. They come out
Of the grey water crusted with brine, glad
To be alive and set foot on dry land.

So welcome a sight was her husband to her.
She would not loosen her white arms from his neck,
And rose-fingered Dawn would have risen
On their weeping, had not Athena stepped in

And held back the long night at the end of its course
And stopped gold-stitched Dawn at Ocean's shores
From yoking the horses that bring light to men,
Lampus and Phaethon, the colts of Dawn.

Then Odysseus said to his wife:

"We have not yet come to the end of our trials.
There is still a long, hard task for me to complete,
As the spirit of Tiresias foretold to me
On the day I went down to the house of Hades
To ask him about my companions' return
And my own. But come to bed now,
And we'll close our eyes in the pleasure of sleep."

And Penelope calmly answered him:

"Your bed is ready for you whenever
You want it, now that the gods have brought you
Home to your family and native land.
But since you've brought it up, tell me
About this trial. I'll learn about it soon enough,
And it won't be any worse to hear it now."

And Odysseus, his mind teeming:

"You are a mystery to me. Why do you insist
I tell you now? Well, here's the whole story.
It's not a tale you will enjoy, and I have no joy
In telling it.
Tiresias told me that I must go
To city after city carrying a broad-bladed oar,
Until I come to men who know nothing of the sea,
Who eat their food unsalted, and have never seen
Red-prowed ships or the oars that wing them along.
And he told me that I would know I had found them
When I met another traveler who thought
The oar I was carrying was a winnowing fan.[1]
Then I must fix my oar in the earth
And offer sacrifice to Lord Poseidon,
A ram, a bull, and a boar in its prime.
Then at last I am to come home and offer
Grand sacrifice to the immortal gods
Who hold high heaven, to each in turn.
And death shall come to me from the sea,
As gentle as this touch, and take me off
When I am worn out in sleek old age,
With my people prosperous around me.
All this Tiresias said would come true."

1. I.e., the traveler will not recognize an oar, because he will never have seen the sea.

Then Penelope, watching him, answered:

"If the gods are going to grant you a happy old age,
There is hope your troubles will someday be over."

While they spoke to one another,
Eurynome and the nurse made the bed
By torchlight, spreading it with soft coverlets.
Then the old nurse went to her room to lie down,
And Eurynome, who kept the bedroom,
Led the couple to their bed, lighting the way.
When she had led them in, she withdrew,
And they went with joy to their bed
And to their rituals of old.

Telemachus and his men
Stopped dancing, stopped the women's dance,
And lay down to sleep in the shadowy halls.

After Odysseus and Penelope
Had made sweet love, they took turns
Telling stories to each other. She told him
All that she had to endure as the fair lady
In the palace, looking upon the loathsome throng
Of suitors, who used her as an excuse
To kill many cattle, whole flocks of sheep,
And to empty the cellar of much of its wine.
Odysseus told her of all the suffering
He had brought upon others, and of all the pain
He endured himself. She loved listening to him
And did not fall asleep until he had told the whole tale.

He began with how he overcame the Cicones
And then came to the land of the Lotus-Eaters,
And all that the Cyclops did, and how he
Paid him back for eating his comrades.
Then how he came to Aeolus,
Who welcomed him and sent him on his way,
But since it was not his destiny to return home then,
The stormwinds grabbed him and swept him off
Groaning deeply over the teeming saltwater.
Then how he came to the Laestrygonians,
Who destroyed his ships and all their crews,
Leaving him with only one black-tarred hull.
Then all of Circe's tricks and wiles,
And how he sailed to the dank house of Hades
To consult the spirit of Theban Tiresias
And saw his old comrades there
And his aged mother who nursed him as a child.
Then how he heard the Sirens' eternal song,
And came to the Clashing Rocks,

And dread Charybdis and Scylla,
Whom no man had ever escaped before.
Then how his crew killed the cattle of the Sun,
And how Zeus, the high lord of thunder,
Slivered his ship with lightning, and all his men
Went down, and he alone survived.
And he told her how he came to Ogygia,
The island of the nymph Calypso,
Who kept him there in her scalloped caves,
Yearning for him to be her husband,
And how she took care of him, and promised
To make him immortal and ageless all his days
But did not persuade the heart in his breast.
Then how he crawled out of the sea in Phaeacia,
And how the Phaeacians honored him like a god
And sent him on a ship to his own native land
With gifts of bronze and clothing and gold.

He told the story all the way through,
And then sleep, which slackens our bodies,
Fell upon him and released him from care.

The Grey-eyed One knew what to do next.
When she felt that Odysseus was satisfied
With sleep and with lying next to his wife,
She roused the slumbering, golden Dawn,
Who climbed from Ocean with light for the world.
Odysseus got up from his rose-shadowed bed
And turned to Penelope with these instructions:

"My wife, we've had our fill of trials now,
You here, weeping over all the troubles
My absence caused, and I, bound by Zeus
To suffer far from the home I yearned for.
Now that we have both come to the bed
We have long desired, you must take charge
Of all that is mine in the house, while I
See to replenishing the flocks and herds
The insolent suitors have depleted.
I'll get some back on raids, some as tribute,
Until the pens are full again. But now,
I want you to know I am going to our farm
To see my father, who has suffered terribly
On my account. You don't need me to tell you
That when the sun rises the news will spread
That I have killed the suitors in our hall. So,
Go upstairs with your women and sit quietly.
Don't look outside or speak to anyone."

Odysseus spoke and put on his beautiful armor.
He woke Telemachus, and the cowherd

And swineherd, and had them arm also.
They strapped on their bronze, opened the doors
And went out, Odysseus leading the way.
It was light by now, but Athena hid them
In darkness, and spirited them out of the city.

BOOK XXIV

Hermes, meanwhile, was calling forth
The ghosts of the suitors. He held the wand
He uses to charm mortal eyes to sleep
And make sleepers awake; and with this beautiful,
Golden wand he marshaled the ghosts,
Who followed along squeaking and gibbering.

Bats deep inside an eerie cave
Flit and gibber when one of them falls
From the cluster clinging to the rock overhead.

So too these ghosts, as Hermes led them
Down the cold, dank ways, past
The streams of Ocean, past the White Rock,
Past the Gates of the Sun and the Land of Dreams,
Until they came to the Meadow of Asphodel,
Where the spirits of the dead dwell, phantoms
Of men outworn.

Here was the ghost of Achilles,
And those of Patroclus, of flawless Antilochus,
And of Ajax, the best of the Achaeans
After Achilles, Peleus' incomparable son.
These ghosts gathered around Achilles
And were joined by the ghost of Agamemnon,
Son of Atreus, grieving, he himself surrounded
By the ghosts of those who had died with him
And met their fate in the house of Aegisthus.
The son of Peleus was the first to greet him:

"Son of Atreus, we believed that you of all heroes
Were dear to thundering Zeus your whole life through,
For you were the lord of the great army at Troy,
Where we Greeks endured a bitter campaign.
But you too had an early rendezvous with death,
Which no man can escape once he is born.
How much better to have died at Troy
With all the honor you commanded there!
The entire Greek army would have raised you a tomb,
And you would have won glory for your son as well.
As it was, you were doomed to a most pitiable death."

And the ghost of Agamemnon answered:

"Godlike Achilles, you did have the good fortune
To die in Troy, far from Argos. Around you fell
Some of the best Greeks and Trojans of their time,
Fighting for your body, as you lay there
In the howling dust of war, one of the great,
Your horsemanship forgotten. We fought all day
And would never have stopped, had not Zeus
Halted us with a great storm. Then we bore your body
Back to the ships and laid it on a bier, and cleansed
Your beautiful flesh with warm water and ointments,
And the men shed many hot tears and cut their hair.
Then your mother[2] heard, and she came from the sea
With her saltwater women, and an eerie cry
Rose over the deep. The troops panicked,
And they would have run for the ships, had not
A man who was wise in the old ways stopped them,
Nestor, whose counsel had prevailed before.
Full of concern, he called out to the troops:

'Argives and Achaeans, halt! This is no time to flee.
It is his mother, with her immortal nymphs,
Come from the sea to mourn her dead son.'

"When he said that the troops settled down.
Then the daughters of the Old Man of the Sea
Stood all around you and wailed piteously,
And they dressed you in immortal clothing.
And the Muses, all nine, chanted the dirge,
Singing responsively in beautiful voices.
You couldn't have seen a dry eye in the army,
So poignant was the song of the Muses.
For seventeen days we mourned you like that,
Men and gods together. On the eighteenth day
We gave you to the fire, slaughtering sheep
And horned cattle around you. You were burned
In the clothing of the gods, with rich unguents
And sweet honey, and many Greek heroes
Paraded in arms around your burning pyre,
Both infantry and charioteers,
And the sound of their marching rose to heaven.
When the fire had consumed you,
We gathered your white bones at dawn, Achilles,
And laid them in unmixed wine and unguents.
Your mother had given us a golden urn,
A gift of Dionysus, she said, made by Hephaestus.
In this urn lie your white bones, Achilles,
Mingled with those of the dead Patroclus.
Just apart lie the bones of Antilochus
Whom you honored most after Patroclus died.

2. Thetis, a sea goddess.

Over them all we spearmen of the great army
Heaped an immense and perfect barrow
On a headland beside the broad Hellespont
So that it might be seen from far out at sea
By men now and men to come.
Your mother, Thetis,
Had collected beautiful prizes from the gods
And now set them down in the middle of the field
To honor the best of the Achaean athletes.
You have been to many heroes' funeral games
Where young men contend for prizes,
But you would have marveled at the sight
Of the beautiful prizes silver-footed Thetis
Set out for you. You were very dear to the gods.
Not even in death have you lost your name,
Achilles, nor your honor among men.
But what did I get for winding up the war?
Zeus worked out for me a ghastly death
At the hands of Aegisthus and my murderous wife."

As these two heroes talked with each other,
Quicksilver Hermes was leading down
The ghosts of the suitors killed by Odysseus.
When Hermes and these ghosts drew near,
The two heroes were amazed and went up to see
Who they were. The ghost of Agamemnon
Recognized one of them, Amphimedon,
Who had been his host in Ithaca, and called out:

"Amphimedon! Why have you come down
Beneath the dark earth, you and your company,
All men of rank, all the same age? It's as if
Someone had hand-picked the city's best men.
Did Poseidon sink your ships and drown you
In the wind-whipped waves? Was it that, or
Did an enemy destroy you on land
As you cut off their cattle and flocks of sheep—
Or as they fought for their city and women?
Tell me. Remember who is asking—
An old friend of your house. I came there
With godlike Menelaus to urge Odysseus
To sail with the fleet to Ilion. A full month
That journey to Ithaca took us—hard work
Persuading Odysseus, destroyer of cities."

The ghost of Amphimedon responded:

"Son of Atreus, most glorious Agamemnon,
I remember all that, just as you tell it,
And I will tell you exactly what happened to us,

And how it ended in our bitter death.
We were courting the wife of Odysseus,
Long gone by then. She loathed the thought
Of remarrying, but she wouldn't give us a yes or no.
Her mind was bent on death and darkness for us.
Here is one of the tricks she dreamed up:
She set up a loom in the hall and started weaving—
A huge, fine-threaded piece—and then came out and said:

'Young men—my suitors, since Odysseus is dead—
Eager as you are to marry me, you must wait
Until I finish this robe—it would be a shame
To waste my spinning—a shroud for the hero
Laertes, when death's doom lays him low.
I fear the Achaean women would reproach me
If he should lie shroudless for all his wealth.'

"We went along with this appeal to our honor.
Every day she would weave at the great loom,
And every night she would unweave by torchlight.
She fooled us for three years with her craft.
But in the fourth year, as the seasons rolled by,
And the moons waned, and the days dragged on,
One of her women who knew all about it
Told us, and we caught her unweaving
The gloried shroud. Then we forced her to finish it.
When it was done she washed it and showed it to us,
And it shone like the sun or the moon.
It was then
That some evil spirit brought Odysseus
From who knows where to the border of his land,
Where the swineherd lived. Odysseus' son
Put in from Pylos in his black ship and joined him.
These two, after they had plotted an ugly death
For the suitors, came up to the town, first Telemachus
And then later Odysseus, led by the swineherd,
Who brought his master wearing tattered clothes,
Looking for all the world like a miserable old beggar,
Leaning on a staff, his rags hanging off him.
None of us could know who he was, not even
The older men, when he showed up like that.
We threw things at him and gave him a hard time.
He just took it, pelted and taunted in his own house,
Until, prompted by Zeus, he and Telemachus
Removed all the weapons from the hall
And locked them away in a storeroom.
Then he showed all his cunning. He told his wife
To set before the suitors his bow and grey iron—
Implements for a contest, and for our ill-fated death.
None of us were able to string that bow.
We couldn't even come close. When it came

Around to Odysseus, we cried out and objected,
'Don't give the bow to that beggar,
No matter what he says!' Telemachus alone
Urged him on and encouraged him to take it.
And he did. The great Odysseus
Took the bow, strung it easily, and shot an arrow
Straight through the iron. Then he stood on the threshold,
Poured the arrows out, and glaring around him
He shot Lord Antinous. And then he shot others,
With perfect aim, and we fell thick and fast.
You could see that some god was helping them,
The way they raged through the hall, cutting us down
Right and left; and you could hear
The hideous groans of men as their heads
Were bashed in. The floor smoked with blood.
That's how we died, Agamemnon. Our bodies
Still lie uncared for in Odysseus' halls.
Word has not yet reached our friends and family,
Who could wash the black blood from our wounds
And lay us out with wailing, as is due the dead."

And the ghost of Agamemnon responded:

"Well done, Odysseus, Laertes' wily son!
You won a wife of great character
In Icarius' daughter. What a mind she has,
A woman beyond reproach! How well Penelope
Kept in her heart her husband, Odysseus.
And so her virtue's fame will never perish,
And the gods will make among men on earth
A song of praise for steadfast Penelope.
But Tyndareus' daughter[3] was evil to the core,
Killing her own husband, and her song will be
A song of scorn, bringing ill-repute
To all women, even the virtuous."

That was the drift of their talk as they stood
In the Dark Lord's halls deep under the earth.

Odysseus and the others went from the town
And made good time getting down to Laertes'
Well-kept fields. The old man had worked hard
Reclaiming the land from the wilderness.
His farmhouse was there with a row of huts around it
Where the field hands ate and rested and slept.
These were his slaves, and they did as he wished.
There was an old Sicilian woman, too,
Who took good care of the old man out in the country.

3. Clytemnestra.

Odysseus had a word with the herdsmen and his son:

"Go into the farmhouse and make yourselves busy.
Sacrifice the best pig and roast it for dinner.
I am going to test my father. Will he recognize me?
Will he know who I am after all these years?"

He disarmed and gave his weapons to the herdsmen.
They hurried off indoors, leaving Odysseus
To search through the rows of fruit trees and vines.
He did not find Dolius, or any of his sons
Anywhere in the orchard. Old Dolius had taken them
To gather fieldstones for a garden wall.
But he found his father, alone, on a well-banked plot,
Spading a plant. He had on an old, dirty shirt,
Mended and patched, and leather leggings
Pieced together as protection from scratches.
He wore gloves because of the bushes, and on his head
He had a goatskin cap, crowning his sorrow.
Odysseus, who had borne much, saw him like this,
Worn with age and a grieving heart,
And wept as he watched from a pear tree's shade.
He thought it over. Should he just throw his arms
Around his father, kiss him and tell him all he had done,
And how he'd returned to his homeland again—
Or should he question him and feel him out first?
Better that way, he thought, to feel him out first
With a few pointed remarks. With this in mind,
Godlike Odysseus walked up to his father,
Who kept his head down and went on digging.
His illustrious son stood close by him and said:

"Well, old-timer, you certainly know how to garden.
There's not a plant, a fig tree, a vine or an olive,
Not a pear tree or leek in this whole garden untended.
But if I may say so without getting you angry,
You don't take such good care of yourself. Old age
Is hard, yes. But unwashed, scruffy and dressed in rags?
It can't be that your lord is too lax to care for you,
And anyway there's nothing in your build or looks
To suggest you're a slave. You look more like a king,
The sort of man who after he has bathed and eaten
Sleeps on a soft bed, as is only right for elders.
Come on now and give me a straight answer.
Whose slave are you? Whose orchard is this?
And tell me this, too, so that I can be sure:
Is this really Ithaca I've come to, as I was told
By that man I ran into on my way over here?
He wasn't very polite, couldn't be bothered
To tell me what I wanted, or even to hear me out.
I've been trying to find out about an old friend

I entertained at my house once, whether he's still alive
Or is dead by now and gone down to Hades.
So I'll ask you, if you'll give me your attention.
I was host to a man once back in my own country,
A man who means more to me than anyone else
Who has ever visited my home from abroad.
He claimed his family was from Ithaca, and he said
His father was Laertes, son of Arcesius.
I took him into my home, and entertained him
In a style befitting the wealth in my house,
And gave him suitable gifts to seal our friendship:
Seven ingots of fine gold, a silver mixing bowl
Embossed with flowers, twelve cloaks, as many
Carpets, mantles and tunics, and his choice of four
Beautiful women superbly trained in handicrafts."

A tear wet his father's cheek as he answered:

"You've come to the land you're looking for, stranger,
But it's in the hands of haughty and violent men.
You've given all those generous gifts in vain.
If you were to find him alive here in Ithaca
He would send you off with the beautiful gifts
And fine hospitality you deserve as his friend.
But tell me this now, and tell me the truth:
How many years has it been since you hosted
Your ill-fated guest, my son—if I ever had a son?
Born for sorrow he was, and now far from home,
Far from his loved ones, his bones are picked clean
By fish undersea; or on some wild shore
His body is feeding the scavenging birds,
Unburied, unmourned by his mother and me,
Who brought him into this world. Nor has his wife,
Penelope, patient and wise, who brought him so much,
Lamented her husband on a funeral bier
Or closed his eyelids, as is due the dead.
And tell me this, too, so that I will know.
Who are you?
What city are you from? Who are your parents?
And where have you moored the sailing ship
That brought you and your crew of heroes here?
Or did you come as a passenger on another's ship
That put you ashore and went on its way?"

And Odysseus, his great mind teeming:

"I'll tell you everything point by point.
I come from Alybas and have my home there.
I'm the son of Apheidas and Polypemon's grandson.
My name is Eperitus. Some storm spirit drove me
Off course from Sicily and, as luck had it, here.

My ship stands off wild country far from the town.
As for Odysseus, it's been five years now
Since he left my land, ill-fated maybe,
But the birds were good when he sailed out—
On the right. This cheered me as I sent him off,
And he was cheered, too, our hearts full of hope
We would meet again and exchange splendid gifts."

A black mist of pain shrouded Laertes.
He scooped up fistfuls of shimmering dust
And groaned as he poured it upon his grey head.
This wrung Odysseus' heart, and bitter longing
Stung his nostrils as he watched his father.
With a bound he embraced him, kissed him and said:

"I'm the one that you miss, Father, right here,
Back in my homeland after twenty years.
But don't cry now. Hold back your tears.
I'm telling you, we really have to hurry.
I've killed the suitors in our house and avenged
All of the wrongs that have grieved your heart."

But Laertes' voice rang out in answer:

"If you are really Odysseus and my son come back,
Give me a sign, a clear sign I can trust."

And Odysseus, the master strategist:

"First, here's the scar I got on Parnassus
From that boar's bright tusk. Mother and you
Had sent me to my grandfather Autolycus
To collect some presents he had promised me
When he had visited us here. And let me count off
All of the trees in the orchard rows
You gave me one day when I was still a boy.
You gave me thirteen pear trees, ten apple trees,
Forty fig trees, and fifty vine rows
That ripened one by one as the season went on
With heavy clusters of all sorts of grapes."

He spoke, and the old man's knees went slack
As he recognized the signs Odysseus showed him.
He threw his arms around his beloved son
And gasped for breath. And godly Odysseus,
Who had borne much, embraced him.
When he had caught his breath and his spirit returned,
Laertes' voice rang out to the sky:

"Father Zeus, there are still gods on high Olympus,
If the suitors have really paid the price!

But now I have a terrible fear
That all of Ithaca will be upon us soon,
And word will have gone out to Cephallenia, too."

And Odysseus, his mind teeming:

"We don't have to worry about that right now.
Let's go to the cottage near the orchard.
I sent Telemachus there, and the cowherd
And swineherd, to prepare a meal for us."

And they went together to the house
With its comfortable rooms and found
Telemachus and the two herdsmen there
Carving huge roasts and mixing wine.
While they were busy with these tasks,
The old Sicilian woman bathed great Laertes
In his own house and rubbed him down
With olive oil and threw about his shoulders
A handsome cloak. And Athena came
And made the shepherd of the people
Taller than before and added muscle to his frame.
When he came from the bath, his son marveled
At his deathless, godlike appearance,
And his words rose to his father on wings:

"Father, surely one of the gods eternal
Has made you larger, and more handsome, too."

And Laertes, feeling the magic, answered him:

"I wish by Zeus and Athena and Apollo
That I could have stood at your side yesterday
In our house, armor on my shoulders,
As the man I was when I took Nericus,
The mainland town, commanding the Cephallenians!
I would have beaten the daylights out of them
There in our halls, and made your heart proud."

While they were talking, the others
Had finished preparing the meal.
They all sat down on benches and chairs
And were just serving themselves food
When old Dolius came in with his sons,
Weary from their work in the fields.
Their mother, the old Sicilian woman,
Had gone out to call them. It was she
Who made their meals and took care
Of Dolius, now that old age had set in.
When they saw Odysseus, and realized

Who he was, they stood there dumbfounded.
Odysseus spoke to them gently and said:

"Old man, sit down to dinner, and all of you,
You can stop being amazed. Hungry as we are,
We've been waiting a long time for you."

He spoke, and Dolius ran up to him
With arms outstretched, and clasped
Odysseus' hand and kissed him on the wrist.
Trembling with excitement, the old man said:

"My dear Odysseus, you have come back home.
We missed you so much but never hoped
To see you again. The gods themselves
Have brought you back. Welcome, welcome,
And may the gods grant you happiness.
But tell me this—I have to know—
Does Penelope know that you have returned,
Or should we send her a messenger?"

And Odysseus, his mind teeming:

"She knows, old man. You don't have to worry."

He spoke, and Dolius sat down in a polished chair.
His sons then gathered around glorious Odysseus
And greeted him and clasped his hands
And then sat down in order next to their father.

While they were busy with their meal,
Rumor, that swift messenger, flew
All through the city, telling everyone
About the grim fate the suitors had met.
Before long a crowd had gathered
Outside Odysseus' palace, and the sound
Of their lamentation hung in the air.
They carried their dead out of the hall
And buried them. Those from other cities
They put aboard ships to be brought home by sea.
Then they all went to the meeting place,
Sad at heart. When they were assembled,
Eupeithes rose and spoke among them,
Upon his heart an unbearable grief
For his son Antinous, the first man
Whom Odysseus killed. Weeping for him
He addressed the assembly and said:

"My friends, it is truly monstrous—
What this man has done to our city.

First, he sailed off with many of our finest men
And lost the ships and every man aboard.
Now he has come back and killed many others,
By far the best of the Cephallenians.
We must act now, before he runs off to Pylos
Or takes refuge with the Epean lords of Elis.
We will be disgraced forever if we don't avenge
Our sons' and brothers' deaths, and if we don't,
I see no point in living. I'd rather be dead.
Let's move now, before they cross the sea!"

He wept as he spoke, and they all pitied him.
Then up came Medon and the godlike bard
From Odysseus' halls. They had just woken up
From a long sleep and now stood in the midst
Of the wondering crowd. Medon had this to say:

"Hear me, men of Ithaca. It was not without the will
Of the deathless gods that Odysseus managed this.
I myself saw one of the immortals
Close to Odysseus. He looked just like Mentor
But was a god, now appearing in front of Odysseus,
Urging him on, then raging through the hall
Terrifying the suitors, who fell thick and fast."

He spoke, and they all turned pale with fear.
Then the old hero Halitherses, son of Mastor,
Rose to speak. He alone looked ahead and behind,
And spoke with the best of intentions to them:

"Now hear what I have to say, men of Ithaca.
You have only yourselves to blame, my friends,
For what has happened. You would not obey me
Nor Mentor, shepherd of the people, when we told you
To make your sons stop their foolishness.
It was what your sons did that was truly monstrous,
Wasting the wealth and dishonoring the wife
Of a great man, who they said would never return.
Now listen to me and keep your peace. Some of you
Are asking for trouble—and you just might find it."

Less than half of them took his advice
And stayed in their seats. Most of them
Jumped up with a whoop and went with Eupeithes.
They rushed to get weapons, and when the mob
Had armed themselves in glowing bronze,
They put the city behind them, following Eupeithes,
Who in his folly thought he would avenge
His son's death, but met his own fate instead.
Eupeithes would never return home again.

Athena, meanwhile, was having a word with Zeus:

"Father of us all, Son of Cronus most high,
Tell me what is hidden in that mind of yours.
Will you let this grim struggle go on?
Or will you establish peace on Ithaca?"

And Zeus in his thunderhead responded:

"Why question me, Daughter? Wasn't this
Your plan, to have Odysseus pay them back
With a vengeance? Do as you will,
But I will tell you what would be fitting.
Now that Odysseus has paid the suitors back,
Let all parties swear a solemn oath,
That he will be king on Ithaca all of his days.
We, for our part, will have them forget
The killing of their sons and brothers.
Let them live in friendship as before,
And let peace and prosperity abound."

This was all Athena needed to hear,
And she streaked down from Olympus' peaks.

The meal was over. Seeing that his company
Had satisfied their hunger, Odysseus said:

"Someone should go out to see if they're coming."

One of Dolius' sons went to the doorway,
Looked out, and saw the mob closing in.
His words flew fast to Odysseus:

"They're almost here. We'd better arm quickly."

They jumped up and put on their gear,
Odysseus and his three men and Dolius' six sons.
Laertes and Dolius armed themselves, too,
Warriors in a pinch despite their white hair.
When they had strapped on their bronze
They opened the doors and headed out
Behind Odysseus.

Athena joined them,
Looking for all the world like Mentor,
And Odysseus was glad to see her. He turned
To his son Telemachus and said:

"Telemachus, now you will see firsthand
What it means to distinguish yourself in war.

Don't shame your ancestors. We have been
Strong and brave in every generation."

And Telemachus coolly answered him:

"The way I feel now, I don't think you'll see me
Shaming my ancestors, as you put it, Father."

Laertes was delighted with this and exclaimed:

"What a day, dear gods! My son and grandson
Going head to head to see who is best."

The Grey-eyed One stood next to him and said:

"Son of Arcesius, my dearest comrade,
Say a prayer to Zeus and his grey-eyed daughter,
And then cast your long-shadowed spear."

Pallas Athena breathed great strength into him,
And with a prayer to Zeus' grey-eyed daughter,
Laertes cast his long-shadowed spear
And hit Eupeithes square in the helmet.
Bronze bored through bronze, and Eupeithes
Thudded to the ground, his armor clattering.
Odysseus and his glorious son
Charged the front lines, thrusting hard
With their swords and spears. They would have killed
Every last man—not one would have gone home—
Had not Athena, daughter of the Storm Cloud,
Given voice to a cry that stopped them all cold:

"ITHACANS!
Lay down your arms now,
And go your ways with no more bloodshed."

Thus Athena, and they turned pale with fear.
The weapons dropped from their trembling hands
And fell to the ground as the goddess' voice
Sent shock waves through them. They turned
Back toward the city and ran for their lives.
With a roar, the great, long-suffering Odysseus
Gathered himself and swept after them

Like a soaring raptor.

At that moment
Zeus, Son of Cronus, hurled down
A flaming thunderbolt that landed at the feet
Of his owl-eyed daughter, who said:

"Son of Laertes in the line of Zeus,
Cunning Odysseus—restrain yourself.
End this quarrel and cease from fighting
Lest broad-browed Zeus frown upon you."

Thus Athena. The man obeyed and was glad,
And the goddess made both sides swear binding oaths—
Pallas Athena, daughter of the Storm Cloud,
Who looked like Mentor and spoke with his voice.

AESOP

ca. 620–564 B.C.E.

When people think of the literature of ancient Greece and Rome, they hardly ever think of folk tales. This may be partly because in the modern world, Aesop's fables are usually presented as children's literature—although nobody in antiquity saw them this way. Moreover, it is tempting to think of "classical literature" as a particularly elevated type of writing, represented primarily by ancient tragedy and epic. Aesop's fables, an enjoyable hodgepodge of funny anecdotes, proverbs, animal stories, and morality tales from the ancient Greco-Roman world, form no part of the usual canon. But this is, in itself, a good reason to read them. Aesop gives us a window into ancient culture different from that offered by **Homer** or **Sophocles.** These well-known but noncanonical stories also provoke us to reconsider our assumptions about what literature is.

Greek tradition gave the name *Aesop* to the originator of this genre and constructed a set of legends about his life. He had supposedly been a slave and was known for his ugliness and outspokenness. But there is no reason to believe that this has any historical accuracy. Rather, the stories about Aesop gave the Greeks and Romans a way of talking about the fable itself: it was, like its quasifictional inventor, lowly, down-to-earth, unpretentious, and fun.

The stories that appear here are based on a long oral and written tradition and come from a huge range of written sources. In particular, the Greek fable tradition seems to have important links with tales told in Egypt, India, and the Near East: the Indian text the *Pañcatantra*, and the tales about the Buddha called *jātakas*, seem to parallel some of the Greek Aesopic material. Additionally, Aesop's fables include references to animals that are not native to Greece, including the camel, the elephant, and the dung beetle. These connections are a useful reminder that Greek and Roman cultures were heavily influenced by those of their neighbors, and that people from different nations and communities shared stories with one another.

Whereas more-formal kinds of literature may remain fixed in their written form, fables live in the mouths of those who tell them. The ancient Greeks and Romans probably shared fables over dinner and drinks; fables were cited by poets, comedians, philosophers, orators, politicians, and historians throughout classical antiquity and into the Middle Ages. Many classical writers use or allude to fables, including the Greek comedian **Aristophanes**, the Roman poet **Horace**, and the later Roman novelist **Apuleius.** Fables are present from the beginnings of Greek literature, in the eighth century B.C.E.; the genre is prominent in the poetry of **Hesiod**, Homer's contemporary. The earliest Greek prose collection of fables was probably made around the third century B.C.E., although this has not survived. Many later prose and verse adaptations were made by other ancient writers, including the Roman poet Phaedrus; and new collections of Aesop, with additions from the oral tradition, continued to be made until the thirteenth century C.E. and beyond. Some of the most famous Aesopic fables appear for the first time in the work of medieval Christian monks. Thus, unlike, say, **Virgil's *Aeneid*,** Aesop's fables were not produced by a single author at a single point in time; instead, they were gathered at different times by many authors, from many long-forgotten storytellers.

Many of these stories have an explicit didactic purpose—much more so than most literature. Sometimes a moral is attached to the beginning or end of the fable; sometimes a character in the story points out its implication. Since fables are told and retold many times, their interpretation may change in different tellings. For instance, in "The Two Men, the Eagle, and the Fox," we get an explicit moral at the end—"we should give appropriate thanks to our benefactors"—that clearly contradicts the moral inside the story, in which the fox suggests that we should treat nasty people better than benefactors, since it is more important to get on these people's good side. More commonly, we find tensions between different fables—just as, in our own tradition, there are contradictions in proverbial wisdom: too many cooks spoil the broth, but many hands make light work. Such tensions illuminate areas of unconscious cultural disagreement.

But as a whole, the fables recommend a consistent set of values. "High" and "serious" kinds of literature, like tragedy and epic, allow us to identify, aspirationally, with people whose status is higher than our own; fables, by contrast, evoke characters who are lowly, and often not even human. They are aimed at ordinary people, not aristocrats, and often suggest the danger and folly of trying to change one's status in life, create revolution, or usurp the position of one's betters. The fable is usually a conservative genre that reinforces the status quo. These stories recommend honesty and integrity: many stories mock pretentious characters, whose boasts cannot be matched by real achievement or people whose words do not match reality; we all know what happened to the boy who cried wolf. They value kindness and gratitude—as in the famous story of the shepherd who pulls a thorn from a lion's paw—but also, perhaps most important, the kind of street smarts that enable a person to survive, in any circumstances. The cat's single ability, to climb a tree and escape the hounds, outweighs the fox's whole bag of tricks.

First-time readers of the fables may be surprised to discover that they are not all animal stories and that not all of them have explicit, or even implicit, morals. The various collections of Aesopic tales include all kinds of narratives lumped together. Some stories tell how the world came to be as it is—such as the tale of how the tortoise got its shell. Some feature plants or vegetables, or gods, or foolish humans rather than animals. Some are records of weird ancient beliefs about zoology—such as the claim that hyenas are hermaphrodites. Some seem to make no particular claim to moral teaching and function simply as jokes. The first fable included here, "Demades and the Athenians," is a good introduction to how the ancients may have seen the fable. The audience fails to listen when an orator tries to lecture about politics; but as soon as he begins a fable, the crowd is all ears. He launches into a story that sounds like any promising bar joke: "The goddess Demeter, a swallow, and an eel were walking together down the road." But the punch line, in this case, is that there is no punch line; the audience is robbed of its hope for a funny story. This is a fable against fables, but it is also a reminder of the main reason why they were so popular for so many centuries: fables give easy access to pure narrative pleasure. They can appeal to anybody, of any age, from any era.

From Fables[1]

Demades and the Athenians

The orator Demades[2] was trying to address his Athenian audience. When he failed to get their attention, he asked if he might tell them an Aesop's fable. The audience agreed, so Demades began his story. "The goddess Demeter,[3] a swallow, and an eel were walking together down the road. When they reached a river, the swallow flew up in the air and the eel jumped into the water." Demades then fell silent. The audience asked, "And what about the goddess Demeter?" "As for Demeter," Demades replied, "she is angry at all of you for preferring Aesop's fables to politics!"

So it is that foolish people disregard important business in favour of frivolities.

The Wolf, the Dog, and the Collar

A comfortably plump dog happened to run into a wolf. The wolf asked the dog where he had been finding enough food to get so big and fat. "It is a man," said the dog, "who gives me all this food to eat." The wolf then asked him, "And what about that bare spot there on your neck?" The dog replied, "My skin has been rubbed bare by the iron collar which my master forged and placed upon my neck." The wolf then jeered at the dog and said, "Keep your luxury to yourself then! I don't want anything to do with it, if my neck will have to chafe against a chain of iron!"

The Fox, the Lion, and the Footprints

A lion had grown old and weak. He pretended to be sick, which was just a ruse to make the other animals come and pay their respects so that he could eat them all up, one by one. The fox also came to see the lion, but she greeted him from outside the cave. The lion asked the fox why she didn't come in. The fox replied, "Because I see the tracks of those going in, but none coming out."

Other people's lives are lessons in how we can avoid danger: it is easy to enter the house of a powerful man, but once you are inside, it may already be too late to get out.

Jupiter and the Frogs

While the frogs were hopping about in the freedom of their pond they began shouting to Jupiter[4] that they wanted a king who could hold their dissolute habits in check. Jupiter laughed and bestowed on the frogs a small piece of wood which he dropped all of a sudden into their pond. As the wood splashed lightly into the water, it terrified the timid frogs. They plunged into the mud and hid there a long time until one frog happened to raise her head cautiously up out of the water. After studying the king, she summoned the other frogs.

1. Translated by Laura Gibbs.
2. An orator and politician from the 4th century B.C.E.
3. Demeter was a goddess associated with grain and harvest. She was worshipped in a secret cult known as the Eleusinian Mysteries.
4. Jupiter is the father and king of the Greek gods.

Putting aside their fear, the frogs all raced over and began jumping on the piece of wood, rudely making fun of it. When the frogs had showered their king with shame and scorn, they asked Jupiter to send them another one. Jupiter was angry that they had made fun of the king he had given them, so he sent them a water-snake, who killed the frogs one by one with her piercing sting. As the water-snake was happily eating her fill, the useless creatures ran away, speechless in their fright. They secretly sent a message to Jupiter through Mercury,[5] begging him to put a stop to the slaughter, but Jupiter replied, "Since you rejected what was good in order to get something bad, you had better put up with it—or else something even worse might happen!"

The Stomach and the Body[6]

Back when all the parts of the human body did not function in unison as is the case today, each member of the body had its own opinion and was able to speak. The various members were offended that everything won by their hard work and diligent efforts was delivered to the stomach while he simply sat there in their midst, fully at ease and just enjoying the delights that were brought to him. Finally, the members of the body revolted: the hands refused to bring food to the mouth, the mouth refused to take in any food, and the teeth refused to chew anything. In their angry effort to subdue the stomach with hunger, the various parts of the body and the whole body itself completely wasted away. As a result, they realized that the work done by the stomach was no small matter, and that the food he consumed was no more than what he gave back to all the parts of the body in the form of blood which allows us to flourish and thrive, since the stomach enriches the blood with digested food and then distributes it equally throughout the veins.

The Shepherd and the Lion[7]

While he was wandering in the fields, a lion got a thorn stuck in his paw. He immediately went to a shepherd, wagging his tail as he said, "Don't be afraid! I have come to ask your help; I'm not looking for food." The lion then lifted his paw and placed it in the man's lap. The shepherd pulled out the thorn from the lion's paw and the lion went back into the woods. Later on, the shepherd was falsely accused of a crime and at the next public games he was released from jail and thrown to the beasts. As the wild animals rushed upon him from all sides, the lion recognized that this was the same man who had healed him. Once again the lion raised his paw and placed it in the shepherd's lap. When the king understood what had happened, he commanded that the lion be spared and that the gentle shepherd be sent back home to his family.

When a man acts righteously, he can never be defeated by the punishments inflicted on him by his enemies.

5. Messenger god.
6. In this version, the story has no explicit moral. But in other versions—Plutarch's, for instance, which Shakespeare followed in *Coriolanus*—the story is used to justify the existence of aristocrats in society.
7. In another version of this story, the shepherd is called Androcles.

The Two Men, the Eagle, and the Fox

An eagle was once caught by a man who immediately clipped his wings and turned him loose in the house with the chickens. The eagle was utterly dejected and grief-stricken. Another man bought the eagle and restored the eagle's feathers. The eagle then soared on his outspread wings and seized a hare, which he promptly brought back as a gift for the man who had rescued him. A fox saw what the eagle was doing and shouted, "He's not the one who needs your attention! You should give the hare to the first man, so that if he ever catches you again, he won't deprive you of your wing feathers like the first time."

The fable shows that we should give appropriate thanks to our benefactors, while avoiding evil-doers.

The Fox and the Raven

A story about a fox and a raven which urges us not to trust anyone who is trying to deceive us.

The raven seized a piece of cheese and carried his spoils up to his perch high in a tree. A fox came up and walked in circles around the raven, planning a trick. "What is this?" cried the fox. "O raven, the elegant proportions of your body are remarkable, and you have a complexion that is worthy of the king of the birds! If only you had a voice to match, then you would be first among the fowl!" The fox said these things to trick the raven and the raven fell for it: he let out a great squawk and dropped his cheese. By thus showing off his voice, the raven let go of his spoils. The fox then grabbed the cheese and said, "O raven, you do have a voice, but no brains to go with it!"

If you follow your enemies' advice, you will get hurt.

The Ant and the Cricket

During the wintertime, an ant was living off the grain that he had stored up for himself during the summer. The cricket came to the ant and asked him to share some of his grain. The ant said to the cricket, "And what were you doing all summer long, since you weren't gathering grain to eat?" The cricket replied, "Because I was busy singing I didn't have time for the harvest." The ant laughed at the cricket's reply, and hid his heaps of grain deeper in the ground. "Since you sang like a fool in the summer," said the ant, "you had better be prepared to dance the winter away!"

This fable depicts lazy, careless people who indulge in foolish pastimes, and therefore lose out.

The Boy Who Cried "Wolf"

There was a boy tending the sheep who would continually go up to the embankment and shout, "Help, there's a wolf!" The farmers would all come running only to find out that what the boy said was not true. Then one day there really was a wolf, but when the boy shouted they didn't believe him and no one came to his aid. The whole flock was eaten by the wolf.

The story shows that this is how liars are rewarded: even if they tell the truth, no one believes them.

The Fox and the Stork

Do no harm—and if someone does get hurt, then turn-about is fair play, as this fable cautions.

The fox is said to have started it by inviting the stork to dinner and serving a liquid broth on a marble slab which the hungry stork could not so much as taste. The stork, in turn, invited the fox to dinner and served a narrow-mouthed jug filled with crumbled food. The stork was able to thrust her beak inside and eat as much as she wanted, while her guest was tormented with hunger. As the fox was licking the neck of the jug in vain, the stork is supposed to have said, "When others follow your example, you have to grin and bear it."

The Dog in the Manger

People frequently begrudge something to others that they themselves cannot enjoy. Even though it does them no good, they won't let others have it. Listen to a fable about such an event.

There was a wicked dog lying in a manger full of hay. When the cattle came and wanted to eat, the dog barred their way, baring his teeth. The cattle said to the dog, "You are being very unfair by begrudging us something we need which is useless to you. Dogs don't eat hay, but you will not let us near it." The same thing happened when a dog was holding a bone in his mouth: the dog couldn't chew on the bone that way, but no other dog was able to chew on it either.

The fable shows that it is not easy to avoid envy: with some effort you can try to escape its effects, but it never goes away entirely.

The North Wind and the Sun

The Sun and the North Wind were quarrelling with each other as to which of the two of them would be able to make a man disrobe. The North Wind went first, blowing fiercely against the man. Yet as the man grew colder and colder, he only wrapped himself up more snugly in his cloak, clutching at it tightly so as to keep a firm grip no matter how hard the wind might be blowing. Thus the North Wind did the man no harm at all and failed to make him strip off his clothes. Next, the Sun began to shine upon the man so brightly that the very air of the day grew hotter and hotter. The man immediately took off his cloak and bundled it up on his shoulders.

The fable shows that to take a humble approach is always more effective and practical than making empty boasts.

The Sow and the Lioness

The story goes that a sow who had delivered a whole litter of piglets loudly accosted a lioness. "How many children do you breed?" asked the sow. "I breed only one," said the lioness, "but he is very well bred!"

The fable shows that a single man who is remarkable for physical strength and bravery and wisdom is mightier than many weak and foolish people.

The Fox and the Cat

Against lawyers and the like.

The fox ran into the cat and asked, "How many tricks and dodges do you know?" The cat replied, "Actually, I don't know more than one." The fox then asked the cat, "What trick is that?" The cat said, "When the dogs are chasing me, I know how to climb trees and escape." The cat then asked the fox, "And how many tricks do you know?" The fox said, "I know seventeen, and that gives me a full bag of tricks! Come with me, and I'll show you my tricks so that the dogs won't be able to catch you." The cat agreed and the two of them went off together. The hunters began to chase them with their dogs, and the cat said, "I hear the dogs; I'm scared." The fox replied, "Don't be afraid! I will give you a good lesson in how to get away." The dogs and the hunters drew nearer. "Well," said the cat, "I'm going to have to leave you now; I want to do my trick." And so the cat jumped up in the tree. The dogs let the cat go and chased the fox until they caught him: one of the dogs grabbed the fox by the leg, another grabbed his belly, another his back, another his head. The cat, who was sitting up high in the tree, shouted, "Fox! Fox! Open up your bag of tricks! Even so, I'm afraid all of them put together are not going to save you from the hands and teeth of those demons!"

The Tortoise and the Hare

The hare laughed at the tortoise's feet but the tortoise declared, "I will beat you in a race!" The hare replied, "Those are just words. Race with me, and you'll see! Who will mark out the track and serve as our umpire?" "The fox," replied the tortoise, "since she is honest and highly intelligent." When the time for the race had been decided upon, the tortoise did not delay, but immediately took off down the race-course. The hare, however, lay down to take a nap, confident in the speed of his feet. Then, when the hare eventually made his way to the finish line, he found that the tortoise had already won.

The story shows that many people have good natural abilities which are ruined by idleness; on the other hand, sobriety, zeal, and perseverance can prevail over indolence.

The Fisherman and the Fish

A fisherman was pulling in the net which he had just cast and, as luck would have it, the net was filled with all kinds of sea creatures. The little fish escaped to the bottom of the net and slipped out through its many holes, but the big fish was caught and lay stretched out flat aboard the boat.

To be small is a way to stay safe and avoid problems, whereas you rarely see a man with a big reputation who is able to keep out of danger.

The Mice, the Cat, and the Bell

There were once some mice who held a meeting about how to defend themselves from the cat. A certain wise mouse said, "A bell should be tied around the neck of the cat so that we would be able to hear him wherever he goes and have advance warning of his attacks." They all agreed with this proposal. A mouse then asked, "Who will tie the bell around the cat's neck?" One mouse answered, "Not me, that's for sure!" Another answered: "Not me either! I wouldn't so much as go near that cat for anything in the world!"

The Fox and the Grapes

Driven by hunger, a fox tried to reach some grapes hanging high on the vine. Although she leaped with all her strength, she couldn't manage to reach the grapes. As she went away, the fox remarked, "Oh, you aren't even ripe yet! I don't need any sour grapes."

People who speak disparagingly of things that they cannot attain would do well to apply this instructive little story to their own lives.

The Beauty Contest of the Animals[8]

Zeus had decided to award prizes to the most beautiful animal babies, so he inspected each and every one of them in order to reach a decision. The monkey also participated, claiming to be the mother of a very beautiful baby: a naked, snub-nosed little monkey whom she cradled in her arms. When the gods took a look at that monkey they all started to laugh, but his mother insisted, "The winner is for Zeus to decide! But in my eyes this one is the most beautiful of all."

The Dog, the Meat, and the Reflection

A dog seized some meat from the butcher shop and ran away with it until he came to a river. When the dog was crossing the river, he saw the reflection of the meat in the water, and it seemed much larger than the meat he was carrying. He dropped his own piece of meat in order to try to snatch at the reflection. When the reflection disappeared, the dog went to grab the meat he had dropped but he was not able to find it anywhere, since a passing raven had immediately snatched the meat and gobbled it up. The dog lamented his sorry condition and said, "Woe is me! I foolishly abandoned what I had in order to grab hold of a phantom, and thus I ended up losing both that phantom and what I had to begin with."

This fable is about greedy people who grasp at more than they need.

The Shepherd and the Sea

There was a shepherd tending his flocks in a place beside the sea. When he saw that the sea was calm and mild, he decided that he wanted to make a

8. A moral is attached to some versions of this story, probably a later addition: "Each person thinks his own child is beautiful."

voyage. He sold his flocks and bought some dates which he loaded onto a ship. He then set sail, but a fierce storm blew up and capsized the ship. The shepherd lost everything and barely managed to get to shore. Later on, when the sea had grown calm once again, the shepherd saw a man on the beach praising the sea for her tranquillity. The shepherd remarked, "That's just because she's after your dates!"

The Wolf in Sheep's Clothing

You can get into trouble by wearing a disguise.

A wolf once decided to change his nature by changing his appearance, and thus get plenty to eat. He put on a sheepskin and accompanied the flock to the pasture. The shepherd was fooled by the disguise. When night fell, the shepherd shut up the wolf in the fold with the rest of the sheep, and as the fence was placed across the entrance, the sheepfold was securely closed off. But when the shepherd wanted a sheep for his supper, he took his knife and killed . . . the wolf.

Someone who wears a disguise often loses his life and finds that his performance occasions a major catastrophe.

The Crow, the Eagle, and the Feathers

A fable against people who boast that they have something they do not.

There was a crow who saw that she was ugly and black, so she complained to the eagle. The eagle told her to borrow some feathers from her fellow birds. The crow did as the eagle suggested, taking feathers from the tail of the peacock, from the wings of the dove, and so on and so forth, appropriating the other birds' feathers. When the crow decided that she was sufficiently well dressed, she began to laugh at the other birds and yell at them. The other birds then went and complained to the eagle about the boastful crow. The eagle replied, "Let every bird take back her feathers, and thus humiliate the crow." This is what they did, and so the crow was left ugly and naked.

The Black Man in the River[9]

Someone saw a black man from India washing himself in a river and said to him, "You better keep still and not stir up the mud in the water, or you are never going to turn that body of yours white!"

This fable shows that nothing in this world can change its nature.

The Two Hyenas

They say that the hyena has a double nature: for a period of time the hyena is male, and then later on she is female. The story goes that when a male hyena

9. The Greek word in the original translated as "black man," *aethiops*, literally means "with sun-burned face"; it was used in antiquity for any dark-skinned person, from Africa or India, although it is the etymological root for *Ethiopia*.

was treating a female badly, she said to him, "Listen here: remember how things used to be, and don't forget that I will be a male hyena the next time around!"

The fable is a lesson for someone who is temporarily in a position of authority: people who have been judged in the past can later on be in a position to judge their former teachers.

Aesop and His Ugly Mistress

Aesop was once the slave of an ugly woman who wasted entire days adorning herself with make-up, but even with all her fancy clothes and pearls and silver and gold she still could not find anyone who would so much as touch her. "Might I say a few words?" asked Aesop. "Go ahead," she replied. "I think that you could achieve all your hopes and dreams," said Aesop, "if only you would put aside this finery." "Do you really find me so much more attractive when I'm just my sweet little old self?" she asked. "Quite the opposite," said Aesop, "but if you stopped giving your jewellery away, you could give your bedsprings a break." "I'm going to break every bone in your body!" she answered back, and ordered them to beat the indiscreet slave with whips. Shortly thereafter, a thief stole one of the mistress's silver bracelets. When she was told that the bracelet was nowhere to be found, the mistress was enraged and summoned all the slaves, threatening them with painful punishments if they didn't tell the truth. "Threaten the others," said Aesop, "but you aren't going to fool me, my mistress: it's because I told the truth just now that you had me whipped and beaten!"

The Daughter and the Hired Mourners[1]

There was a rich man who had two daughters, but one of his daughters died. He hired some women to do the mounring and they let loose a whole chorus of weeping. The other daughter remarked to her mother, "We are surely wretched women if we cannot come up with a lament for our own loss, while these women, who are not even members of the family, beat their breasts and grieve so deeply." The mother replied, "Don't be surprised, my child: they do it for the money!"

The Donkey, the Dog, and the Letter

A donkey and a dog were journeying together when they found a sealed letter on the ground. The donkey took the letter, broke the seals, and opened it. The donkey then began to read the letter aloud, while the dog sat there listening. The letter happened to be about food, that is, about barley and straw and hay. As the donkey was reading, the dog grew impatient, and finally he said to the donkey, "You can skip that part, my dear; perhaps further down you will find some information about meat and bones." The donkey scanned the rest of the letter but he didn't find what the dog was looking for. The dog then said to the donkey, "Throw it back on the ground; it has nothing to offer!"

The story shows that different people are interested in different things.

1. It was normal practice in antiquity to pay professional mourners to wail at funerals.

The City Mouse and the Country Mouse

A city mouse once happened to pay a visit to the house of a country mouse where he was served a humble meal of acorns. The city mouse finished his business in the country, and by means of insistent invitations he persuaded the country mouse to come pay him a visit. The city mouse then brought the country mouse into a room that was overflowing with food. As they were feasting on various delicacies, a butler opened the door. The city mouse quickly concealed himself in a familiar mouse-hole, but the poor country mouse was not acquainted with the house and frantically scurried around the floorboards, frightened out of his wits. When the butler had taken what he needed, he closed the door behind him. The city mouse then urged the country mouse to sit back down to dinner. The country mouse refused and said, "How could I possibly do that? Oh, how scared I am! Do you think that the man is going to come back?" This was all that the terrified mouse was able to say. The city mouse insisted, "My dear fellow, you could never find such delicious food as this anywhere else in the world." "Acorns are enough for me," the country mouse maintained, "so long as I am secure in my freedom!"

It is better to live in self-sufficient poverty than to be tormented by the worries of wealth.

The Man and the Golden Eggs

A man had a hen that laid a golden egg for him each and every day. The man was not satisfied with this daily profit, and instead he foolishly grasped for more. Expecting to find a treasure inside, the man slaughtered the hen. When he found that the hen did not have a treasure inside her after all, he remarked to himself, "While chasing after hopes of a treasure, I lost the profit I held in my hands!"

The fable shows that people often grasp for more than they need and thus lose the little they have.

Mercury and the Two Women

Mercury was once the guest of two women who treated him in a cheap and tawdry manner. One of these women was the mother of an infant still in his cradle, while the other woman was a prostitute. In order to return the women's hospitality as they deserved, Mercury paused on the threshold of their door as he was leaving and said, "You are gazing upon a god: I am prepared to give you right now whatever it is you want." The mother beseeched the god to allow her to see her son with a beard as soon as possible, while the prostitute wanted the power to attract anything she touched. Mercury flew away and the women went back inside, where they found the baby with a beard, wailing and screaming. This made the prostitute laugh so hard that her nose filled with snot (as sometimes happens), but when she touched her hand to her nose, the nose followed her hand until it reached all the way down to the floor. In this way the woman who had laughed at someone else ended up being laughed at herself.[2]

2. One version has this moral: "Do not ask for more than you deserve."

The Old Man and His Sons

Among the folk of days gone by, there was a very elderly gentleman who had many sons. When he was about to reach the end of his life, the old man asked his sons to bring to him a bundle of slender rods, if there happened to be some lying about. One of his sons came and brought the bundle to his father. "Now try, with all your might, my sons, to break these rods that have been bound together." They were not able to do so. The father then said, "Now try to break them one by one." Each rod was easily broken. "O my sons," he said, "if you are all of the same mind, then no one can do you any harm, no matter how great his power. But if your intentions differ from one another, then what happened to the single rods is what will happen to each of you!"[3]

The Monkey and Her Two Children

The monkey gives birth to two babies, but after giving birth she does not mother them equally. She comforts one of them with cruel embraces, choking him with her unfortunate affection; meanwhile, she casts the other child away as superfluous and unimportant. This is the one who goes off into the wilds and is able to survive.

The same thing can be said about certain people: in such cases, it is better to be their enemy than their friend.

The Vegetables and the Weeds

Somebody saw a gardener irrigating his vegetables and said to him, "How is it that wild plants, without having been planted and without having been cultivated, spring up each season, while the plants that you yourself plant in the garden frequently wither from lack of water?" The gardener replied, "The wild plants are cared for by divine providence, which is sufficient in and of itself, while our own plants must depend for their care on human hands."

This story shows that a mother's nurturing is stronger than a stepmother's attentions.

Zeus and the Tortoise

Zeus invited all the animals to his wedding. The tortoise alone was absent, and Zeus did not know why, so he asked the tortoise her reason for not having come to the feast. The tortoise said, "Be it ever so humble, there's no place like home."[4] Zeus got angry at the tortoise and ordered her to carry her house with her wherever she went.

The fable shows that people often prefer to live simply at home than to live lavishly at someone else's house.

3. A moral to this story reads: "Brotherly love is humanity's greatest good; even the lowly are exalted by it."

4. Literally, "Home is dear, home is best"—a Greek proverb.

Prometheus[5] *and the Tears*

This is also something that Aesop said. The clay which Prometheus used when he fashioned man was not mixed with water but with tears. Therefore, one should not try to dispense entirely with tears, since they are inevitable.

5. Prometheus was one of the Titans (divine beings who preceded the Olympian gods). According to Greek mythology, he was a friend to early humanity; sometimes, as here, he is represented as having created humankind out of clay.

SAPPHO

born ca. 630 B.C.E.

Sappho is the only ancient Greek female author whose work survives at all. She was an enormously talented poet, much admired in antiquity; a later poet called her the tenth Muse. In the third century B.C.E., scholars at the great library in Alexandria arranged her poems in nine books, of which the first contained more than a thousand lines. But what we have now are pitiful remnants: one (or possibly two) complete short poems, and a collection of quotations from her work by ancient writers, supplemented by bits and pieces written on ancient scraps of papyrus found in excavations in Egypt. Yet these fragments fully justify the enthusiasm of the ancient critics; Sappho's poems (insofar as we can guess at their nature from the fragments) give us the most vivid evocation of the joys and sorrows of desire in all Greek literature.

About Sappho's life we know almost nothing. She was born about 630 B.C.E. on the fertile island of Lesbos, off the coast of Asia Minor, and spent most of her life there. Her poems suggest that she was married and had a daughter—although we should never assume that Sappho's "I" implies autobiography. It is difficult to find any evidence to answer the questions that we most want to ask. Were these poems performed for women only, or for mixed audiences? Was it common for women to compose poetry on ancient Lesbos? How did Sappho's work win acceptance in the male-dominated world of ancient Greece? We simply do not know. We also know frustratingly little about ancient attitudes toward female same-sex relationships. In the nineteenth century, Sappho's poems were the inspiration for the coinage of the modern term *lesbian.* But no equivalent term was used in the ancient world. Sappho's poems evoke a world in which girls lived an intense communal life of their own, enjoying activities and festivals in which only women took part, in which they were fully engaged with one another. Beyond the evidence of the poems themselves, however, little remains to put these works into historical context.

What we do know, and what we must always bear in mind while reading these poems, is that they were composed not to be read on papyrus or in a book but to be performed by a group of dancing, singing women and girls (a "chorus"), to the accompaniment of musical instruments. Other poets of the period composed in the choral genre, including Alcaeus, a male contemporary who was also from Lesbos. The ancient Greek equivalent of the short, nonnarrative literary form we refer to as lyric poetry was literally "lyric": it was sung to the lyre or kithara, ancestors of the modern guitar. It is not really poetry but the lyrics to songs, whose music is lost. These songs evoke many vivid actions, emotions, and images, which were presumably dramatized by the dancers, who might well, for example, have acted out the swift journey of Aphrodite's chariot in poem 1 ["Deathless Aphrodite of the spangled mind"], "whipping their wings down the sky."

Sappho's poems were produced almost two hundred years after the Homeric epics, and we can read them as offering a response, and perhaps a challenge, to the (mostly masculine) world of epic. The ***Iliad*** concentrates on the battlefield, where men fight and die, while the ***Odyssey*** shows us the struggles of a male warrior to rebuild his homeland in the aftermath of war. By contrast, Sappho's poems focus on women more than men, and on feelings more than actions. Like **Homer**, Sappho often refers to the physical world in vivid detail (the stars, the trees, the flowers, the sunlight), as well as to the Olympian gods, and to mythology. But she interprets these topics very differently. In poem 44, she uses the characters of the *Iliad* but concentrates on the marriage of Hector and Andromache rather than the war. Aphrodite, goddess of love and sex, seems more important to Sappho than Zeus, the father of the gods. Poem 16 offers another reinterpretation of the Trojan War, as a story not about men fighting but about a woman in love: "(Helen) / left her fine husband / behind and went sailing to Troy." Sappho emphasizes beauty and personal choices, and suggests that love matters more than armies, and more even than home, family, parents, or children.

But Sappho's vision of love is anything but sentimental. Many of these poems evoke intense negative emotions: alienation, jealousy, and rage. In poem 31, for example, the speaker describes her overwhelming feelings as she watches the woman she loves talking to a man: she trembles, her heart races, she feels close to death. The precise clinical detail of the narrator, as she observes herself, adds to the vividness of this account of emotional breakdown. Sappho is able to describe feelings both from the outside and from the inside, and painfully evokes a sense of distance, from the beloved and from herself: "I don't know what to do / two states of mind in me," she says in a fragment (51). In the last poem included here, the speaker is suffering from a different kind of alienation: watching young girls dance and sing, she stands aside, unable to participate, and bitterly regrets the loss of her own youth.

Sappho repeatedly invokes the goddess associated with sexual desire: Aphrodite. It may be tempting to read Aphrodite as simply a personification of the speaker's own desires. But Sappho presents her as a real and terrifying force in the universe, who may afflict the speaker with all the "sweet-bitter" agony of love, and who may also be invoked—as in poem 1—to serve her rage and aggression, acting as Sappho's own military "ally" in her desire to inflict pain on the girl who has hurt her.

Some passages of Sappho, including the famous account of jealousy, poem 31, were preserved through quotation by other ancient writers. But many of these poems survived only on scraps of papyrus, mostly dug up from the trash-heaps of the ancient Egyptian city of Oxyrhynchus. It is exciting that we have even this much Sappho: much of our present text was discovered as late as the nineteenth century; the final poem in the selection here was found in 2004 in the papier-mâché-type wrapping used on an Egyptian mummy. Most of the papyrus finds are torn and crumpled, so that words and whole lines are often missing from the poems. Some of these gaps can be filled in from our knowledge of Sappho's dialect and the strict meter in which she wrote. In poem 16, for instance, at the end of the third stanza and the beginning of the fourth, the mutilated papyrus tells us that someone or something led Helen astray, and there are traces of a word that seems to have described Helen. The name *Cypris* (the "Cyprian One," the love goddess Aphrodite) and phrases that mean "against her will" or "as soon as she saw him [Paris]" would fit the spaces and the meter. Uncertain as these supplements are, they could help determine our understanding of the poem. Rather than give possibly misleading reconstructions here and in similar cases, the translator, Anne Carson, has marked gaps in the text with square brackets, so that the reader can decide what Sappho might have meant. As you read, also bear in mind that the translator determined the layout on the page, including line breaks and brackets. The final poem is translated by Martin West, in a somewhat different style.

Poem 1[1]

Deathless Aphrodite of the spangled mind,[2]
child of Zeus, who twists lures, I beg you
do not break with hard pains,
        O lady, my heart

but come here if ever before
you caught my voice far off
and listening left your father's
        golden house and came,

yoking your car. And fine birds brought you,
quick sparrows[3] over the black earth
whipping their wings down the sky
        through midair—

they arrived. But you, O blessed one,
smiled in your deathless face

1. All selections except the last are translated by Anne Carson.
2. Or "of the spangled throne"; the manuscripts preserve both readings (in the Greek there is a single letter's difference between them). The word translated here as "spangled" usually refers to a surface shimmering with bright contrasting colors. The reader should choose whether to imagine a goddess seated in splendor on a highly wrought throne or a love goddess whose mind is shifting and fickle.
3. Aphrodite's sacred birds.

and asked what (now again) I have suffered and why
(now again) I am calling out

and what I want to happen most of all
in my crazy heart. Whom should I persuade (now again)
to lead you back into her love? Who, O
Sappho, is wronging you?

For if she flees, soon she will pursue.
If she refuses gifts, rather will she give them.
If she does not love, soon she will love
even unwilling.

Come to me now: loose me from hard
care and all my heart longs
to accomplish, accomplish. You
be my ally.

Poem 16

Some men say an army of horse and some men say an army on foot
and some men say an army of ships is the most beautiful thing
on the black earth. But I say it is
what you love.

Easy to make this understood by all.
For she who overcame everyone
in beauty (Helen)[4]
left her fine husband

behind and went sailing to Troy.
Not for her children nor her dear parents
had she a thought, no—
][5] led her astray

] for
] lightly
] reminded me now of Anaktoria[6]
who is gone.
I would rather see her lovely step
and the motion of light on her face

4. Helen, wife of Menelaus, who left her husband for Paris of Troy—the start of the Trojan War.
5. Square brackets indicate where the papyrus on which the poem is preserved is torn and words or whole lines are missing.
6. Presumably a girlfriend; nothing is known about her. The name may connote "princess" (since *anax* means "leader" or "king"). "Anaktoria" was also the name for the city of Miletus, a powerful community in Asia Minor, which became incorporated into the Lydian Empire.

than chariots of Lydians[7] or ranks
 of footsoldiers in arms.[8]

Poem 31

He seems to me equal to gods that man
whoever he is who opposite you
sits and listens close
 to your sweet speaking

and lovely laughing—oh it
puts the heart in my chest on wings
for when I look at you, even a moment, no speaking
 is left in me

no: tongue breaks and thin
fire is racing under skin
and in eyes no sight and drumming
 fills ears

and cold sweat holds me and shaking
grips me all, greener than grass
I am and dead—or almost
 I seem to me.

But all is to be dared, because even a person of poverty[9]

Poem 44[1]

Kypros[2]
herald came
Idaos[3] swift messenger
]
and of the rest of Asia imperishable fame.

7. A wealthy and powerful non-Greek people in Asia Minor, with whom Sappho, living on Lesbos just off the coast, shows herself familiar. A generation or so later, the Lydians would be absorbed into the expanding Persian Empire, but in Sappho's time they were near the height of their prosperity.
8. The poem may have ended here. The papyrus preserves scraps of three more stanzas that may have belonged either to this or to a different poem.
9. The quotation that is our only source for this poem breaks off here, although this looks like the beginning of a new stanza.
1. This poem is our only surviving example of Sappho's narrative poetry. It tells the story of the wedding of Hector and Andromache, characters famous in myth who are featured in the *Iliad*. Some scholars believe that this poem may have been performed at a real wedding.
2. The island of Cyprus ("Kypros") was one of the most important cult centers for the goddess Aphrodite. It is not clear how the island fits into this poem, whose beginning is lost.
3. Herald in Troy.

Hektor and his men are bringing a glancing girl
from holy Thebe and from onflowing Plakia—[4]
delicate Andromache on ships over the salt
sea. And many gold bracelets and purple
perfumed clothes, painted toys,
and silver cups innumerable and ivory.
So he spoke. And at once the dear father rose up.
And news went through the wide town to friends.
Then sons of Ilos[5] led mules beneath
fine-running carts and up climbed a whole crowd
of women and maidens with tapering ankles,
but separately the daughters of Priam [
And young men led horses under chariots [
]in great style
]charioteers
]

]like to gods
]holy all together
set out for Ilios[6]
and sweetflowing flute and kithara[7] were mingled
with the clip of castanets and piercingly then the maidens
sang a holy song and straight up the air went
amazing sound [
and everywhere in the roads was [
bowls and cups [
myrrh and cassia and frankincense were mingled.
And all the elder women shouted aloud
and all the men cried out a lovely song
calling on Paon[8] farshooting god of the lyre,
and they were singing a hymn for Hektor and Andromache
like to gods.

Fragment 48

you came and I was crazy for you
and you cooled my mind that burned with longing

Fragment 51

I don't know what to do
two states of mind in me

4. Homeland of Andromache, in central Greece.
5. The "sons of Ilos" are Trojans, since Ilos was the legendary founder of Troy (Ilium).
6. Troy.
7. A stringed instrument, similar to the lyre; perhaps this poem itself was sung to the kithara.
8. Apollo.

Fragment 55[9]

Dead you will lie and never memory of you
will there be nor desire into the aftertime—for you do not
share in the roses
of Pieria,[1] but invisible too in Hades' house[2]
you will go your way among dim shapes. Having been breathed out.

Poem 94

I simply want to be dead.
Weeping she left me

with many tears and said this:
Oh how badly things have turned out for us.
Sappho, I swear, against my will I leave you.

And I answered her:
Rejoice, go and
remember me. For you know how we cherished you.

But if not, I want
to remind you
]and beautiful times we had.

For many crowns of violets
and roses
]at my side you put on

and many woven garlands
made of flowers
around your soft throat.
And with sweet oil
costly
you anointed yourself

and on a soft bed
delicate
you would let loose your longing

and neither any[ ]nor any
holy place nor
was there from which we were absent

no grove[ ]no dance
]no sound
[

9. This passage was part of a longer poem, apparently addressed to a rich but untalented woman; it survives only in quotation.
1. Pieria is the birthplace of the Muses, according to Hesiod. Sappho suggests that those who are blessed with poetic talent are given the "roses / of Pieria."
2. Hades is the god of the dead.

Fragment 102

sweet mother I cannot work the loom
I am broken with longing for a boy by slender Aphrodite

Fragment 104A[3]

Evening
you gather back
all that dazzling dawn has put asunder:
you gather a lamb
gather a kid
gather a child to its mother

Fragment 105A[4]

as the sweetapple reddens on a high branch
high on the highest branch and the applepickers forgot—
no, not forgot: were unable to reach

Fragment 105B

like the hyacinth in the mountains that shepherd men
with their feet trample down and on the ground the purple
flower

Fragment 112

blest bridegroom, your marriage just as you prayed
has been accomplished
and you have the bride for whom you prayed
gracious your form and your eyes
as honey: desire is poured upon your lovely face
Aphrodite has honored you exceedingly

3. This may have been part of an epithalamium (wedding song); perhaps the poem went on to say that evening also brings the bride to her husband.
4. This and the next fragment may be from wedding songs. It may be the bride, who was virgin and inaccessible to men until marriage, who is compared to the sweet apple. The hyacinth could be a reference to virginity.

Fragment 130

Eros[5] the melter of limbs (now again) stirs me—
sweetbitter unmanageable creature who steals in

Poem 168B[6]

Moon has set
and Pleiades:[7] middle
night, the hour goes by,
alone I lie.[8]

The New Sappho[9]

(You for) the fragrant-bosomed (Muses') lovely gifts
(be zealous,) girls, (and the) clear melodious lyre:
(but my once tender) body old age now
(has seized;) my hair's turned (white) instead of dark;
my heart's grown heavy, my knees will not support me,
that once on a time were fleet for the dance as fawns.
This state I oft bemoan; but what's to do?
Not to grow old, being human, there's no way.
Tithonus[1] once, the tale was, rose-armed Dawn,
love-smitten, carried off to the world's end,
handsome and young then, yet in time gray age
o'ertook him, husband of immortal wife.

5. God of love.
6. It is not certain that this fragment is by Sappho.
7. A cluster of seven stars; in Greek mythology, they were originally seven nymphs.
8. In the Greek, the form of the word for "alone" shows that the speaker is female.
9. Translated by Martin West. In this poem, the round brackets enclose words conjectured by the translator.
1. The goddess Dawn fell in love with a Trojan called Tithonus and carried him off. She could make him immortal, but not immune to old age. In some versions of the myth, he turned into a cicada, whom the Greeks imagined as eternally singing—a kind of insect poet.

ANCIENT ATHENIAN DRAMA

Modern readers usually find Athenian drama easy to appreciate. Aristophanes' physical, earthy humor is still funny today, and his wild fantasies raise political and social questions that are still relevant in modern times. The tragedies of **Aeschylus, Sophocles,** and **Euripides** provide compelling stories about human relationships, whose absorbing, often violent or melodramatic plots invite us to think about profound issues, such as the nature of justice, the meaning of suffering, and clashes between family and state and between human and divine perspectives.

But the original performance contexts of Greek drama were radically different from anything modern readers and theatergoers have experienced. The city festivals of Athens, at which all new comedies and tragedies were first performed, involved a mixture of things we usually regard as wholly separate: politics, religion, music, poetry, serious drama, slapstick, open-air spectacles, and dance. For the combination of drama with song and dance, in a popular format performed for large audiences, our closest analogy might be the Broadway musical. Like Greek tragedy, shows such as *Beauty and the Beast* and *The Little Mermaid* update a traditional, mythic story for a contemporary audience. But Broadway shows usually take place indoors, and have no obvious connection to politics or religion. To get a sense of the strangeness of Athenian dramatic festivals, imagine a major public political event, like the inauguration of a new American president, combine it with a major religious gathering like an evangelical rally, a papal audience, or the Hajj to Mecca, then add to the mix the Cannes Film festival, a Veterans Day march, a Thanksgiving Day parade (with all the floats), and a grand open-air musical event like Woodstock. The resulting hybrid would be a modern equivalent of the two major Athenian religious occasions that included major dramatic performances: the Great Dionysia and the Lernaea. Both festivals included tragedy and comedy, although tragedy was more central to the Dionysia, while comedy played a larger role at the Lernaea.

Both festivals were held in honor of the god Dionysus, who was associated with alcohol, and, more generally, with overturning the rules and conventions of the normal, everyday world. Dionysus was a wild figure: he rode a chariot pulled by leopards, dressed in strange, effeminate clothing and an ivy crown, and was accompanied by ecstatic, crazy women (the Maenads) and hairy, permanently erect half-goat men called Satyrs. The Athenians knew him as an exotic, foreign god who originated somewhere in Asia Minor before being incorporated in the Olympian pantheon. We should remember the subversive, outsider status of this god when reading Athenian drama.

We know very little about the origins of tragedy or comedy. The word *comedy* seems to come from *komos*, a Greek word denoting a drunken procession. Aristotle tells us that *tragedy* (*tragoidia* in Greek) means "goat song," and suggests that the genre originated as part of a ritual in which a goat was sacrificed or offered as a prize. Sometime in the late sixth century B.C.E., rural celebrations in honor of Dionysus became an official, annual part of the urban festival calendar. Originally, the main entertainment was probably choruses of dancers, who sang hymns and competed for prizes; later, some form of tragedy and, later still, comedy were added to the program. Thespis, from whose name we get the term *thespian*—a character about whom we know next to nothing—is traditionally said to have invented tragedy in the year 534 B.C.E. He "stepped out of the Chorus," creating a part for a single actor who could talk back to the chorus. The invention of the individual actor, distinct from the group, was enormously important: it paved the way for the whole subsequent history of Western drama.

Tragedy was something new in the late sixth century, but contests of poetry in performance had long been a part of Athenian culture. At the largest city festival, the Panathenaia ("All-Athenian," in honor of the city's goddess, Athena), performers called rhapsodes recited parts of **Homer's *Iliad*** and ***Odyssey***; the best performers won prizes. The Homeric poems were an essential model for later drama. Aeschylus supposedly called his own work "slices from the feast of Homer." It was not merely the plots of Greek tragedy that were "Homeric," although like the *Iliad* and *Odyssey* many tragedies dealt with the heroes who fought in the Trojan War. Dramatists also learned from Homer how to create vivid dialogue and fast, exciting narrative, as well as sympathy for a range of different characters, Greek and foreigner alike.

This detail from the so-called Pronomos Vase, painted in the late fifth century B.C.E., depicts actors preparing for a satyr play.

Each year at the Great Dionysia, three tragic poets were chosen by the official city governor (the *archon*), to produce a tetralogy of plays for each day's entertainment. Performances began at dawn and included three tragedies, which might or might not concentrate on a linked set of stories, followed by a lighter play featuring satyrs (a "satyr play"). A rich Athenian citizen put up the money to pay for the costs of each day's performance, including purchase of costumes and masks, and training of the chorus members and actors. These producers prided themselves on their participation, and gloated if the performance they had financed won the competition: at least one backer tried to rig the results by making a night raid to destroy the gold crowns and costumes that had been ordered for his rival's chorus to wear. Before the dramatic performances began, the tribute paid to the city of Athens by

A contemporary photograph of the remains of the theater of Dionysus in Athens.

her allies was heaped up in the theater for all to see, and the orphans of Athenian men killed in war in the previous year marched in front of the audience, wearing armor provided at the expense of the city. Athenian drama itself can be seen as a comparable display, a demonstration to foreigners and to the Athenians themselves of the city's artistic and intellectual riches, as well as a meditation on its vulnerability.

The only complete works of Greek drama that have survived are a small selection of the tragedies of Aeschylus, Sophocles, and Euripides, and a few comedies by Aristophanes. But of course far more people composed plays in this period, some of which were probably excellent; there were other poets—such as Agathon, the tragedian who appears in **Plato's *Symposium***—who were awarded first prize in the competitions. We have just the names of most of these other dramatists, along with some titles and some tantalizing fragments.

Similarly, the scripts are all that survive of Greek drama, and wishful thinking leads one to imagine that what we have is the most important part: we tend to think of these plays simply as "literature," words on a page. But the words must have formed only a small part of the total effect of the original performances. Those sitting in the upper areas of the theater may well not have been able to hear everything, despite the good acoustics of the theater. The music, gestures, costumes, props, and visual effects may well have had a larger impact on most audience members than any individual detail of phrasing. Writing the script was also a tiny part of the work of a dramatist. The poet was also the director, composer, and choreographer of the plays he created; in the earliest days of drama, the poets were probably also actors in their own work. The prizes were not awarded for writing, but for the work of coaching the actors and dancers: the usual phrase to describe what a dramatist does is "to teach a chorus." In 425, when Aristophanes wrote his first play but had it directed by somebody else, the prize was awarded to the director, not the poet.

The theater of Dionysus, where the plays were performed, held at least 13,000 people, perhaps as many as 17,000—a number comparable to the

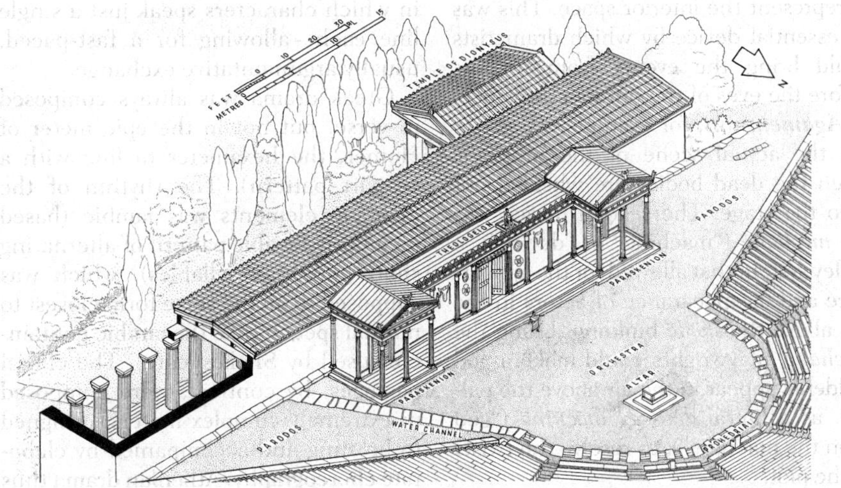

A reconstruction of the Dionysus theater by the theater and architectural scholar Richard Leacroft. An actor stands in the *orchēstra*, while another stands on the roof of the *skēnē*.

seating available in Madison Square Garden. This figure represents a high proportion of the male citizen body, estimated to have been about forty or sixty thousand people—although the total population of Athens, including women, children, foreigners, and slaves may have been ten times that large.

It is possible that a few women came to the theater in the fifth century; women were almost certainly in attendance by the fourth century. We do not know whether slaves were present. In any case, the majority of the audience consisted of male citizens. In the participatory democracy of fifth-century Athens, the whole citizen body was eligible to participate in policy making, and citizens were accustomed to meet together in public to determine military and domestic policy, at least once a month and usually more often. The structure of the dramatic festival was reminiscent of other political assemblies, where citizens sat to hear speeches on several sides of a case and made their decisions between competing sides.

The theater was an open-air venue, with seating in the round. The central space, called the *orchēstra* (which means "dancing area"), lay at the lowest point of the valley; on the slopes of the hill, spectators sat on wooden benches, surrounding the performance area on three sides. At one end of the *orchēstra* was a wooden platform or stage, with a wooden building on it (the *skēnē*), which could be used to represent whatever interior space was necessary for the play: a palace, a house, a cave, or any other type of structure. There were thus three possible ways for actors to come on and off stage: to the left or right of the stage, or through the doors of the building. Entrances and exits tend to be particularly important in Greek drama, because they took a long time; the audience would have been watching the characters make their way into the playing area before they actually reached the stage. When reading these plays, it is a good idea to pay particular attention to the moments when a new character comes on.

There were also two major structural devices that expanded the possibilities of the playing space. The *ekkuklēma* ("trolley" or "thing that rolls out") was a wooden platform on wheels, which could be trundled out from the central doors of the *skēnē*, and was conventionally used to represent the interior space. This was an essential device by which dramatists could bring the events from indoors before the eyes of the outdoor audience. In ***Agamemnon***, for example, we get to see the actual scene of the murders, when the dead bodies are wheeled out onto the stage. The second device was the *mēchanē* ("machine" or "device"), a pulley system that allowed for the appearance and disappearance of actors in the air, above the *skēnē* building. Using the *mēchanē*, playwrights could make a god suddenly appear in the air above the palace, as a literal *deus ex māchinā* ("god from the machine"), to resolve the twists of the plot.

All the actors who performed in Athenian drama were men—including those playing female parts. All actors wore masks. Tragedy and comedy both used a tiny number of actors for the speaking parts. In the first few decades of the century, there were only two actors; later, three actors were used. This meant that the same actors had to play multiple roles, appearing in different masks as the play required. The use of masks, as well as the open-air space, must have necessitated a very different style of acting from that of modern cinema, television, or stage. Facial expressions would have been invisible behind the mask, and were therefore irrelevant; instead, actors must have relied on gestures, body language, and a strongly projected voice.

The dialogue sections of ancient Athenian plays usually show two—occasionally three—characters in confrontation or discussion with one another. Dialogue may be free-flowing and apparently natural. But dramatists made use of two important dialogue techniques. One is the *agon* ("contest" or "struggle"), in which one character makes a long, sometimes legalistic speech, arguing a particular case, and a second character replies with another speech, putting the case against. The other is *stichomythia* ("line-speech"), in which characters speak just a single line each—allowing for a fast-paced, usually argumentative exchange.

Greek drama was always composed in verse, but not in the epic meter of Homer, the hexameter (a line with a six-part pattern). The rhythm of the dialogue elements was iambic (based on a fairly flexible pattern of alternating short and long syllables), which was supposed to be the verse form closest to normal speech (like the iambic pentameter used by Shakespeare). The choral passages, by contrast, were composed in extremely complex meters, designed to be sung and accompanied by elaborate choreography. Athenian drama thus combined two very different theatrical experiences, interspersing plot-driven, character-heavy dialogue with music, poetry, and dance.

The chorus was composed of twelve—later, fifteen—masked dancers, of whom only one, the "leader," had a speaking role. This group is used in different ways by the different dramatists, and varies radically from play to play. In comedy, the choruses are often nonhuman: Aristophanes, whose plays are frequently named for the chorus, created groups of frogs, birds, wasps, and clouds. The choruses of tragedy are usually more naturalistic; a notable exception is the divine, snake-haired Furies who form the chorus of Aeschylus's *Eumenides*.

The chorus is often a group of inhabitants of the place where the action occurs: it can be used to represent the voice of the ordinary person or the word on the street—although it does not always express the voice of common sense, and it frequently fails to get things right. Sometimes the chorus listens sympathetically to the main characters, acting as an internal audience and allowing for the revelation of inner thoughts that might otherwise be hard for the dramatist to bring out. Sometimes, on the other hand, the chorus is either neutral or positively hostile toward the main characters. Choruses can be characters themselves, with their own biases and preoccupations.

The choral songs and dances can allow the dramatist to put the events of the play in a broader perspective: the chorus may take us back in time, looking to earlier events in the same myth, or tracing parallels between this story and others; or it may reflect on the ethical, theological, and metaphysical implications of the events at hand. The poet may also use the chorus to provide a break from the main narrative, a switch to an entirely different mood or perspective. Choral songs can increase the dramatic tension or surprise, as when a cheerful, optimistic song is followed by disaster.

Mutilation and violent death, by murder or suicide, accident, fate, or the gods, are frequent events in Greek tragedy. The threat of violence—which may or may not be averted—provides a strong element in the interest of these plays. But compared to modern television drama or action movies, there is little visible horror. Dead bodies are often displayed onstage, but the actual killing usually takes place offstage. The messenger speech is therefore one of the most important conventions of Athenian drama. Long, vivid, blow-by-blow accounts of offstage disasters allow the audience to imagine and visualize events that the dramatist cannot or will not bring onstage.

Comic poets made up their own plots from scratch, and were able to create stories that combined reality, fantasy, and myth however they chose. Comic poets could depict caricatures of real people—famous politicians, fellow poets like Euripides, or the philosopher Socrates—mixing with made-up characters, as well as with gods and heroes (like Dionysus and Heracles) and personifications (like "The People"). Comedy often made direct references to recent events, and parodied, satirized, or directly attacked the behavior of real contemporary people.

The plots of Greek tragedy, by contrast, focus on a few traditional story patterns, set in the distant past and in non-Athenian city-states: Argos, Thebes, or Troy. But though tragedians used preexisting stories, they felt free, within reason, to shape the myths in their own way; for instance, Aeschylus, Sophocles, and Euripides created very different plays focused on the story of Electra, daughter of the murdered Agamemnon. Tragedy was often relevant in some way to contemporary concerns, but its political and social perspectives are never as explicit as those of comedy.

Since Greek tragedy and comedy were always performed at a religious festival, we might expect these dramas to be more obviously "religious" than they seem at first blush. Comedians often bring gods on stage, but they are not treated in a markedly reverent way: for instance, Dionysus in **Aristophanes' *Frogs*** is a craven coward with a flatulence problem. The power of the gods is usually a more serious issue in tragedy; but even here, modern readers may be surprised at how cruel and unreliable the Greek gods often seem to be. It is perhaps helpful to remember that Athenians of the fifth century—unlike most believers in modern monotheistic religions—saw no necessary connection between religion and morality. Gods are, by definition, immortal and powerful; they need not also be nice. Athenian drama was an act of service to the gods in general, and to Dionysus in particular, because it overturned the everyday world and explored the power of the imagination, showing—in Euripides' words—"how god makes possible the unexpected." By serving the gods, displaying the strange and surprising ways that divine forces operate on human lives, Athenian dramatists were also serving their audiences, creating dramas that were gripping, profound, and unpredictable: qualities that readers still appreciate in these works today.

AESCHYLUS
ca. 524–456 B.C.E.

Aeschylus is the earliest Greek dramatist whose work survives. His plays represent the first stage in the long history of later Western drama. But Aeschylean tragedy is by no means primitive or simple. Aeschylus was a dramatic innovator: his most important invention was the introduction of the second actor, which created the possibility of conflict between individuals (rather than simply between a single actor and the group of the chorus). This essential move caused him to be called the "creator of tragedy." His language, imagery, and stagecraft are highly sophisticated, his characters are complex and compelling, and his work invites deep meditation on relationships between myth and history, men and women, justice and suffering, language and meaning, human and divine.

LIFE AND TIMES

Aeschylus's life and work were closely tied up with the changing political situation of Greece in his time. He was born in the late sixth century, around 524 B.C.E., in the town of Eleusis, in Attica. The main city of the region was Athens, a major city-state (*polis*), which included the rural area outside the city, as well as the urban downtown. Aeschylus's life was dominated by the stratospheric cultural, political, economic, and military rise of Athens, where he lived and worked. During Aeschylus's lifetime, Athens changed its political system from tyranny to democracy, fought off foreign invaders against enormous odds, and grew to become the most powerful community in the contemporary Mediterranean world.

When Aeschylus was born, Athens was not yet a democratic state. From 541 to 510, the city was under one-man rule, dominated by a "tyrant" (a single, powerful ruler; the word in Greek does not necessarily carry negative connotations). In 510 B.C.E., after the last tyrant was ousted from power, Athens became one of the world's first democracies. From this time onward, the city was governed by a fifty-member council, which was elected by the votes of all citizens. The majority of the population—including women, slaves, and resident foreigners—were not citizens and did not get a vote. But the shift from tyranny to the new political system of democracy, which took place when Aeschylus was around fifteen years old, was an enormously significant one. Democracy created a sense of community and pride among Athenian citizens, which helped them band together with other Greek states against a major military threat: the invading Persian Empire.

Darius the Great, ruler of Persia, built up the largest empire the world had yet seen. He subdued many parts of the Greek world, and in 490 B.C.E. tried to defeat the remaining cities, in a fierce battle in the bay of Marathon near Athens. All Athenian men of fighting age, including Aeschylus and his brother, Cynegeirus, gathered in defense, and, despite being outnumbered at least two to one, the Athenians were the victors. Cynegeirus was fatally wounded when his arm was chopped off by an enemy battle-axe, but Aeschylus lived to tell the tale.

Ten years later, Darius's son Xerxes mustered the Persian forces again, and again invaded Attica. On land, the Greek forces, led by the Spartan general Leonidas and his three hundred men, were slaughtered at Thermopylae. But by sea, in the bay of Salamis, the Athenian navy—probably including Aeschylus—won a decisive victory, sinking hundreds of Persian ships and destroying Xerxes's hope of expanding his father's empire. The battle of Salamis was a turning point in the history of Athens, and arguably in the whole history of later Western culture. After this victory, Athens was free from foreign invasion and eventually became the dominant power in the Greek and Mediterranean worlds.

A few years after Salamis, in 472 B.C.E., Aeschylus produced *Persians*, which is our earliest surviving Greek tragedy. *Persians* focuses on the battle of Salamis, but told from the Persian point of view: it evokes the devastation of Xerxes, his army, his family, and his people as a result of the Greek victory. Aeschylus encourages his audience to sympathize with and weep for the defeated. But he also celebrates Greek victory, and frames it in explicitly ideological terms. Whereas the Persians are subject to the rule of the emperor and his family, the Greeks, led by democratic Athens, are fighting for freedom: they urge each other on with the inspiring cry "Forward, you sons of Hellas! Set your country free!" The trilogy that included *Persians* was awarded first prize at the Great Dionysia, and it established Aeschylus's reputation as the finest tragedian of his day.

Aeschylus was a successful and prolific artist, who composed some ninety tragedies. Many won first prize in the Great Dionysia. Unfortunately, only seven complete plays survive: *Persians, Seven against Thebes, Suppliant Women, Prometheus Bound* (whose authorship has been doubted by some modern scholars), and the three plays of the *Oresteia: Agamemnon, Libation Bearers,* and *Eumenides.*

Aristophanes' comedy ***Frogs***, which was first performed in 405 B.C.E.—some fifty years after Aeschylus's death—provides our most vivid evidence for the tragedian's contemporary reputation. The play features a competition, set in Hades (since both competitors are dead), between Aeschylus and **Euripides**, to decide who is the poet most likely to save the city in times of war. Aeschylus's style is presented as heavy, dignified, nonnaturalistic, and full of strange or archaic turns of phrase, which may be all but incomprehensible. At the same time, he inspires his audiences to feel proud of and fight for their city: anybody witnessing *Persians*, boasts Aeschylus, would be "smitten / with longing for victory over the enemy." But it would be a mistake to see Aeschylus as a simple propagandist. He draws our attention to deep-rooted moral, political, and religious conflicts.

Around 456 B.C.E., two years after the production of what contemporaries agreed was his masterpiece, the *Oresteia*, Aeschylus died in the Greek city of Gela in Sicily, supposedly killed by a falling tortoise. His four-line epitaph celebrates Aeschylus as a brave patriot, whose finest achievement was his military service on behalf of his country. The lines emphasize his participation in the battle of Marathon against the Persian invasion and make no mention of the fact that he also wrote plays:

> This tomb hides Aeschylus, son of
> Euphorion,
> the Athenian, who died in fruitful
> Gela.
> The sacred battlefield of Marathon
> could tell his famous courage,
> And the long-haired Mede, who
> knows it well.

THE WORK

Aeschylus's *Agamemnon* is the first play in a trilogy of three linked plays, the *Oresteia,* which was composed and first performed in the year 458 B.C.E. The *Oresteia* is the only complete trilogy we have from ancient Athens. It was clearly a great success: Aeschylus was awarded first prize by the competition judges, and subsequent works by Aeschylus's younger contemporaries, **Sophocles** and Euripides, often refer back to the *Oresteia*.

Agamemnon is the legendary king of Mycenae whose brother, Menelaus, husband of Helen, led the Greek forces in their war against Troy to get Helen back and avenge Menelaus's honor. As *Agamemnon* begins, the king himself is still absent from his home; he has not yet returned from the war. A chorus of twelve old men of Argos evokes the helplessness of those left at home, as they wait for news from the war. Then they take us back in time, recalling—in somewhat elliptical fashion—the most important event lying behind the events of the play: Agamemnon's killing of his own daughter, Iphigeneia. It is essential to keep this backstory in our minds as we read the rest of *Agamemnon*. After the abduction of Helen by Paris, the Greek fleet assembled at Aulis, ready to sail to Troy. But the ships were becalmed: no wind came. Calchas, the prophet, then told Agamemnon that he must sacrifice his daughter in order to bring wind to let the fleet sail to Troy. Agamemnon, we are told, had a moment of terrible indecision, but chose, in the end, to kill his own child rather than betray his fleet. The chorus gives us a tear-jerking account of her death: the beautiful young girl, who has often sung at her father's dinner parties, is gagged and slaughtered. The gods send the winds; the ships sail.

Iphigeneia's death is important because it anticipates many of the themes of the play. It is the first of a series of conflicts between a man and a woman, and between different models of justice. Loyalty to family seems irreconcilable with loyalty to the city, or the group. This first death of the Trojan War initiates a long series of killings of the innocent and the guilty at Troy, of enemies in battle, but also of one family member by another at home.

We may be able to guess that the evils of Aulis will lead to further evils back home in Argos; we may intuit, at least, that this story will not have a happy ending. But it is essential to Aeschylus's technique that the threat is oblique, hinted at by symbols and metaphors, and the actual outcome is not revealed until the final scene. Knowledge, in *Agamemnon,* comes slowly, and only at the cost of human suffering. The chorus declares that Zeus himself has established the principle that wisdom comes by suffering: *pathei mathos* (in Greek, *pathos*, suffering, rhymes with *mathos*, learning or wisdom). But the chorus's odes make us face hard questions about how the relationship between suffering and understanding works: whether pain makes people, or societies, better or whether suffering simply teaches us how to suffer. The will of the gods—the most important here being Zeus—remains dark to humans, who struggle to find a moral purpose in the universe.

The atmosphere of the play—mysterious and heavy with foreboding—is created largely through Aeschylus's manipulation of the audience's point of view, and especially through his use of the chorus. This chorus, much more than most Greek choruses, is put in the same position as the audience. Like us, it must watch and wait, and struggle to make sense of events as they unfold. Our identification with the chorus, and with the watchman who begins the play, is increased because the dramatic action of *Agamemnon* happens, as it were, in real time: the performance, like the play, would have begun at dawn.

As always in Greek tragedy, sections of dialogue between characters, and between the chorus and individual characters, alternate with choral sections in much more complex meters, when chorus members danced and sang in the central "dancing space" (*orchēstra*). In *Agamemnon*, the choral songs (or "odes") help put the main story into a larger causal pattern. They look back in time—for instance, to the killing of Iphigeneia and to the abduction of Helen by Paris—and they also search, apparently without much success, for a theological or moral pattern in the strange events they see.

The chorus plays a more central role in *Agamemnon* than in later Greek tragedies, such as ***Oedipus the King*** or ***Medea***. Instead of simply commenting on the actions and dialogue of the characters, the chorus is itself a main character in the play, even at times trying to intervene—as when its members put up their sticks to try to fight with Clytaemnestra's lover, Aegisthus. By the time he composed *Agamemnon*, Aeschylus had adopted Sophocles's new technique of using three actors, not just two (the model he had worked with earlier in his career); but he does so minimally and rarely uses even two actors at the same time. Most scenes in *Agamemnon* involve dialogue between the chorus and a single character. The central debate between Clytaemnestra and Agamemnon is thrown into sharp relief, because it is so rare in this play that characters speak to each other rather than to the chorus. There is a particular shock when Cassandra, the Trojan prophetess whom Agamemnon brings home as a concubine, finally speaks, because the audience may not have been expecting the third actor to have a speaking role at all.

When Cassandra does speak, it is in such densely metaphorical language that the chorus cannot understand what she is saying. Only gradually do her words begin to make a kind of sense, as the chorus realizes, too late, that terrible things are happening inside the palace. Cassandra's utterances in this extraordinary scene are an extreme example of the way that *Agamemnon* as a whole operates. Meaning is conveyed by imagery, and both the audience and the characters onstage struggle to make sense of the hints the gods provide.

Aeschylus also makes his images visible onstage. For instance, when Agamemnon arrives home victorious from Troy, riding a chariot piled high with spoils, the entrance of a chariot, decked out in battle regalia, thundering into the *orchēstra*, must have been a memorable spectacle—and a reminder of the display of real Athenian spoils and tribute that would have taken place a day or two earlier in the festival of Dionysus, in the same space. Clytaemnestra invites her husband to step down from his chariot and walk into the palace on a rich array of scarlet tapestries. Agamemnon is initially reluctant, reminding his wife that he is a Greek man, not a barbarian or a god, and ought not, therefore, to risk the anger of the gods by puffing himself up with excessive regal pomp, and by destroying this beautiful, valuable fabric with his trampling feet. But in a short, brilliantly condensed exchange that uses *stichomythia* (dialogue in which each character speaks only one line at a time), Clytaemnestra overcomes her husband's resistance and persuades him that he should indeed step on the cloths, crushing them as he takes the long walk from the middle of the *orchēstra*, up onto the stage, and inside the palace doors. Located at almost the exact midpoint of the play, this exchange marks its central turning point. This is the moment when Agamemnon changes from the triumphal conqueror of Troy to the victim in his own home, as he moves from the military space of his chariot down into the domestic space of the palace. The scene provides a visible enactment of several threads of imagery from the choral odes, looking both backward, to Aulis, and forward, to the later scenes of the play. The king who walks on blood-red cloths will bathe in real blood inside the house.

The house or palace—represented onstage by the *skēnē*, the wooden stage building at the back of the dancing area—is a particularly important and sinister place in *Agamemnon*; indeed, the most important events in the play are the entrances and exits from the palace. At the opening of the play, we see the watchman stationed on top of the *skēnē*, "like a dog." But his speech hints that, unlike most watchdogs, he has to look out for danger inside the house, even more than from outside. Hard times have come to Argos, and the palace is ruled by the sinister figure of a woman who "maneuvers like a man." In Athenian culture, upper-class women were kept closely inside the house; they rarely went out, except to attend funerals or religious ceremonies. The boldness with which Clytaemnestra repeatedly bursts out of the house—just as much as her strangely outspoken manner—is a sign that she does not behave in an appropriately feminine manner. At the climax of the play, Aeschylus even allows the audience to enter the palace, revealing the area that has—up to this point—been hidden. He uses a stage device called the *ekkuklēma*, the "wheel-out trolley," to move the contents of the *skēnē* out onto the stage, in a final revelation of the inside of that mysterious house.

This is the first play in a trilogy; the other two plays show how the cycle of violence and revenge can continue in future generations but can also be finally resolved, through civic justice, the rule of law, and the reassertion of patriarchal hierarchy. But *Agamemnon* is also a self-contained work, whose narrative moves from darkness to light, from ignorance to revelation, from Troy to Argos, and from male to female power, through a climactic conflict (in the tapestry scene), to a violent and horrifying denouement. *Agamemnon* has the gripping power of any good murder story. The play shows us, with terrible vividness, how one death can lead to another, and it invites us to wonder about divine purposes at work in human lives, and about whether the killings of war can ever come to a peaceful end.

Agamemnon[1]

Characters

WATCHMAN
CLYTAEMNESTRA
HERALD
AGAMEMNON
CASSANDRA
AEGISTHUS
CHORUS, *the Old Men of Argos and their* LEADER
Attendants of Clytaemnestra and of Agamemnon, bodyguard of Aegisthus

[TIME AND SCENE: *A night in the tenth and final autumn of the Trojan war. The house of Atreus in Argos. Before it, an altar stands unlit; a* WATCHMAN *on the high roofs fights to stay awake.*]

WATCHMAN Dear gods, set me free from all the pain,
the long watch I keep, one whole year awake . . .
propped on my arms, crouched on the roofs of Atreus
like a dog.
I know the stars by heart,
the armies of the night, and there in the lead
the ones that bring us snow or the crops of summer,
bring us all we have—
our great blazing kings of the sky,
I know them, when they rise and when they fall . . .
and now I watch for the light, the signal-fire[2]
breaking out of Troy, shouting Troy is taken.
So she commands, full of her high hopes.
That woman[3]—she maneuvers like a man.

And when I keep to my bed, soaked in dew,
and the thoughts go groping through the night
and the good dreams that used to guard my sleep . . .
not here, it's the old comrade, terror, at my neck.
I mustn't sleep, no—
[*Shaking himself awake.*]
Look alive, sentry.
And I try to pick out tunes, I hum a little,
a good cure for sleep, and the tears start,
I cry for the hard times come to the house,
no longer run like the great place of old.

Oh for a blessed end to all our pain,
some godsend burning through the dark—

1. Translated by Robert Fagles, who also wrote the list of characters and all stage directions (in italics). No ancient play has these.
2. I.e., the bonfire nearest to Argos, the last in a chain extending all the way to Troy, each one visible from the next when fired at night.
3. Clytaemnestra.

[*Light appears slowly in the east; he struggles to his feet and scans it.*]
I salute you!
You dawn of the darkness, you turn night to day—
I see the light at last.
They'll be dancing in the streets of Argos[4]
thanks to you, thanks to this new stroke of—
Aieeeeee!
There's your signal clear and true, my queen!
Rise up from bed—hurry, lift a cry of triumph
through the house, praise the gods for the beacon,
if they've taken Troy . . .
But there it burns,
fire all the way. I'm for the morning dances.
Master's luck is mine. A throw of the torch
has brought us triple-sixes[5]—we have won!
My move now—
[*Beginning to dance, then breaking off, lost in thought.*]
Just bring him home. My king,
I'll take your loving hand in mine and then . . .
the rest is silence. The ox is on my tongue.[6]
Aye, but the house and these old stones,
give them a voice and what a tale they'd tell.
And so would I, gladly . . .
I speak to those who know; to those who don't
my mind's a blank. I never say a word.

[*He climbs down from the roof and disappears into the palace through a side entrance. A* CHORUS, *the old men of Argos who have not learned the news of victory, enters and marches round the altar.*]

CHORUS Ten years gone, ten to the day
our great avenger went for Priam—
Menelaus[7] and lord Agamemnon,
two kings with the power of Zeus,
the twin throne, twin sceptre,
Atreus' sturdy yoke of sons
launched Greece in a thousand ships,
armadas cutting loose from the land,
armies massed for the cause, the rescue—

4. In Homer, Agamemnon, son of Atreus, is king of Mycenae. Later Greek poets, however, referred to his kingdom as Argos or Mycenae, perhaps because the Achaeans in Homer are sometimes called Argives. In 463 B.C.E., just five years before the production of the play, Argos had defeated Mycenae in battle and put an end to the city, displacing the inhabitants or selling them into slavery. Soon after, Argos and Athens entered into an alliance, aimed at Sparta. Since this alliance will be alluded to in the last play of the trilogy, it is important for Aeschylus to establish the un-Homeric location of the action right at the beginning.

5. The highest throw in the ancient Greek dice game.

6. A proverbial phrase for enforced silence.

7. Another son of Atreus, also a king of Argos and commander of the Greek expedition against Troy. Priam was the king of Troy. His son Paris abducted (or seduced) Menelaus's wife, Helen.

[*From within the palace* CLYTAEMNESTRA *raises a cry of triumph.*]
the heart within them screamed for all-out war!
Like vultures robbed of their young,
  the agony sends them frenzied,
soaring high from the nest, round and
round they wheel, they row their wings,
stroke upon churning thrashing stroke,
but all the labor, the bed of pain,
  the young are lost forever.
Yet someone hears on high—Apollo,
Pan or Zeus[8]—the piercing wail
these guests of heaven raise,
and drives at the outlaws, late
but true to revenge, a stabbing Fury![9]

[CLYTAEMNESTRA *appears at the doors and pauses with her entourage.*][1]
So towering Zeus the god of guests[2]
drives Atreus' sons at Paris,
all for a woman manned by many
the generations wrestle, knees
grinding the dust, the manhood drains,
the spear snaps in the first blood rites
  that marry Greece and Troy.
And now it goes as it goes
and where it ends is Fate.
And neither by singeing flesh
nor tipping cups of wine[3]
nor shedding burning tears can you
enchant away the rigid Fury.

[CLYTAEMNESTRA *lights the altar-fires.*]
We are the old, dishonoured ones,[4]
the broken husks of men.
Even then they cast us off,
the rescue mission left us here
to prop a child's strength upon a stick.
What if the new sap rises in his chest?

8. The movements of birds are regarded as prophetic signs. Apollo is mentioned perhaps as a prophetic god, Pan as a god of the wild places, Zeus because eagles and vultures were symbolic of his power.

9. This is the first mention of one of these avenging spirits, who will actually appear on stage as the chorus of the final play. Furies are called Erinyes in Greek.

1. There are no stage directions on the manuscript copies of the plays that have come down to us. Here the translator had the queen enter so that she will be visible on stage when the chorus addresses her by name in line 93. Other scholars, pointing out that in Greek tragedy characters who are offstage are often addressed, disagree, and bring Clytaemnestra on stage only at line 256.

2. Zeus was thought to be particularly interested in punishing those who violated the code of hospitality. Paris had been a guest in Menelaus's house.

3. Neither by burnt sacrifice nor by pouring libations.

4. The general sense of the passage is that only two classes of the male population are left in Argos: those who are too young to fight and those who, like the chorus, are too old.

He has no soldiery in him,
no more than we,
and we are aged past aging,
gloss of the leaf shriveled,
three legs at a time[5] we falter on.
Old men are children once again,
a dream that sways and wavers
into the hard light of day.
But you,
daughter of Leda, queen Clytaemnestra,
what now, what news, what message
drives you through the citadel
burning victims?[6] Look,
the city gods, the gods of Olympus,
gods of the earth and public markets—
all the altars blazing with your gifts!
Argos blazes! Torches
race the sunrise up her skies—
drugged by the lulling holy oils,
unadulterated,
run from the dark vaults of kings.
Tell us the news!
What you can, what is right—
Heal us, soothe our fears!
Now the darkness comes to the fore,
now the hope glows through your victims,
beating back this raw, relentless anguish
gnawing at the heart.

[CLYTAEMNESTRA *ignores them and pursues her rituals; they assemble for the opening chorus.*]

O but I still have power to sound the god's command at the roads
that launched the kings. The gods breathe power through my song,
my fighting strength, Persuasion grows with the years—
I sing how the flight of fury hurled the twin command,
one will that hurled young Greece
and winged the spear of vengeance straight for Troy!
The kings of birds to kings of the beaking prows, one black,
one with a blaze of silver
skimmed the palace spearhand right
and swooping lower, all could see,
plunged their claws in a hare, a mother
bursting with unborn young—the babies spilling,
quick spurts of blood—cut off the race just dashing into life!
Cry, cry for death, but good win out in glory in the end.

5. I.e., using a stick, or cane, to support them when they walk.

6. Clytaemnestra is sacrificing in thanksgiving for the news of Troy's fall; the chorus does not know that the news has come via the signal fires.

But the loyal seer of the armies studied Atreus' sons,
two sons with warring hearts—he saw two eagle-kings
devour the hare and spoke the things to come,[7]
"Years pass, and the long hunt nets the city of Priam,
the flocks beyond the walls,
a kingdom's life and soul—Fate stamps them out.
Just let no curse of the gods lour on us first,
shatter our giant armor
forged to strangle Troy. I see
pure Artemis bristle in pity—
yes, the flying hounds of the Father
slaughter for armies . . . their own victim . . . a woman
trembling young, all born to die—She[8] loathes the eagles' feast!"
Cry, cry for death, but good win out in glory in the end.
"Artemis, lovely Artemis, so kind
to the ravening lion's tender, helpless cubs,
the suckling young of beasts that stalk the wilds—
bring this sign for all its fortune,
all its brutal torment home to birth!
I beg you, Healing Apollo, soothe her before
her crosswinds hold us down and moor the ships too long,[9]
pressing us on to another victim . . .
nothing sacred, no
no feast to be eaten[1]
the architect of vengeance
[*Turning to the palace.*]
growing strong in the house
with no fear of the husband
here she waits
the terror raging back and back in the future
the stealth, the law of the hearth, the mother—
Memory womb of Fury child-avenging Fury!"
So as the eagles wheeled at the crossroads,

7. The seer Calchas identified the two eagles ("kings of birds") as symbolic of the two kings and their action as a symbolic prophecy of the destruction of Troy. The two eagles seized and tore a pregnant hare, which meant that the two kings would destroy Troy, thus killing not only the living Trojans but the Trojan generations yet unborn.

8. Artemis, a virgin goddess, patron of hunting, and protectress of wildlife, is angry that the eagles ("the flying hounds") have destroyed a pregnant animal. The prophet fears that she may turn her wrath against the kings whom the eagles represent. "A woman trembling young": just as the eagles kill the hare, the kings will kill Agamemnon's daughter Iphigenia. The Greek text refers only to the hare, but the translator has made the allusion clear.

9. Calchas foresees the future. Artemis will send unfavorable winds to prevent the sailing of the Greek expedition from Aulis, the port of embarkation. She will demand the sacrifice of Agamemnon's daughter Iphigenia as the price of the fleet's release. He prays that in spite of its bad aspects, the omen will be truly prophetic—that is, that the Achaeans will capture Troy. He goes on to anticipate and try to avert some of the evils it portends.

1. At an ordinary sacrifice the celebrants gave the gods their due portion and then feasted on the animal's flesh. The word *sacrifice* comes to have the connotation of "feast." There will be no feast at this sacrifice, since the victim will be a human being. The ominous phrase reminds us of a feast of human flesh that has already taken place, Thyestes' feasting on his own children through the trickery of his brother, Atreus.

Calchas clashed out the great good blessings mixed with doom
for the halls of kings, and singing with our fate
we cry, cry for death, but good win out in glory in the end.

Zeus, great nameless all in all,
if that name will gain his favor,
I will call him Zeus.[2]
I have no words to do him justice,
weighing all in the balance,
all I have is Zeus, Zeus—
lift this weight, this torment from my spirit,
cast it once for all.

He who was so mighty once,[3]
storming for the wars of heaven,
he has had his day.
And then his son[4] who came to power
met his match in the third fall
and he is gone. Zeus, Zeus—
raise your cries and sing him Zeus the Victor!
You will reach the truth:

Zeus has led us on to know,
the Helmsman lays it down as law
that we must suffer, suffer into truth.
We cannot sleep, and drop by drop at the heart
the pain of pain remembered comes again,
and we resist, but ripeness comes as well.
From the gods enthroned on the awesome rowing-bench[5]
there comes a violent love.

So it was that day the king,
the steersman at the helm of Greece,
would never blame a word the prophet said—
swept away by the wrenching winds of fortune
he conspired! Weatherbound we could not sail,
our stores exhausted, fighting strength hard-pressed,
and the squadrons rode in the shallows off Chalkis[6]
where the riptide crashes, drags,

2. It was important, in prayer, to address the divinity by his or her right name: here the chorus uses an inclusive formula—they call on Zeus by whatever name pleases him.
3. Uranus, father of Cronus and grandfather of Zeus, the first lord of heaven. This whole passage refers to a primitive legend that told how Uranus was violently supplanted by his son, Cronus, who was in his turn overthrown by his son, Zeus. This legend is made to bear new meaning by Aeschylus, for he suggests that it is not a meaningless series of acts of violence but a progression to the rule of Zeus, who stands for order and justice. Thus the law of human life that Zeus proclaims and administers—that wisdom comes through suffering—has its counterpart in the history of the establishment of the divine rule.
4. Cronus.
5. The bench of the ship where the helmsman sat.
6. The unruly water of the narrows between Aulis on the mainland and Chalkis on the island of Euboea.

and winds from the north pinned down our hulls at Aulis,
port of anguish . . . head winds starving,
sheets and the cables snapped
  and the men's minds strayed,
    the pride, the bloom of Greece
  was raked as time ground on,
ground down, and then the cure for the storm
and it was harsher—Calchas cried,
"My captains, Artemis must have blood!"—
  so harsh the sons of Atreus
    dashed their scepters on the rocks,
  could not hold back the tears,

and I still can hear the older warlord saying,
"Obey, obey, or a heavy doom will crush me!—
Oh but doom *will* crush me
  once I rend my child,
    the glory of my house—
  a father's hands are stained,
blood of a young girl streaks the altar.
Pain both ways and what is worse?
Desert the fleets, fail the alliance?
  No, but stop the winds with a virgin's blood,
    feed their lust, their fury?—feed their fury!—
  Law is law!—
            Let all go well."

And once he slipped his neck in the strap of Fate,
his spirit veering black, impure, unholy,
once he turned he stopped at nothing,
    seized with the frenzy
      blinding driving to outrage—
wretched frenzy, cause of all our grief!
Yes, he had the heart
    to sacrifice his daughter!—
  to bless the war that avenged a woman's loss,
    a bridal rite that sped the men-of-war.

"My father, father!"—she might pray to the winds;
no innocence moves her judges mad for war.
Her father called his henchmen on,
    on with a prayer,
      "Hoist her over the altar
like a yearling, give it all your strength!
She's fainting—lift her,
  sweep her robes around her,
but slip this strap in her gentle curving lips . . .
  here, gag her hard, a sound will curse the house"—

and the bridle chokes her voice . . . her saffron robes
pouring over the sand
her glance like arrows showering
wounding every murderer through with pity
clear as a picture, live,
she strains to call their names . . .
I remember often the days with father's guests
when over the feast her voice unbroken,
pure as the hymn her loving father
bearing third libations,[7] sang to Saving Zeus—
transfixed with joy, Atreus' offspring
throbbing out their love.

What comes next? I cannot see it, cannot say.
The strong techniques of Calchas do their work.[8]
But Justice turns the balance scales,
sees that we suffer
and we suffer and we learn.
And we will know the future when it comes.
Greet it too early, weep too soon.
It all comes clear in the light of day.
Let all go well today, well as she could want,
[*Turning to* CLYTAEMNESTRA.]
our midnight watch, our lone defender,
single-minded queen.

LEADER We've come,
Clytaemnestra. We respect your power.
Right it is to honor the warlord's woman
once he leaves the throne.
But why these fires?
Good news, or more good hopes? We're loyal,
we want to hear, but never blame your silence.

CLYTAEMNESTRA Let the new day shine, as the proverb says,
glorious from the womb of Mother Night.
[*Lost in prayer, then turning to the* CHORUS.]
You will hear a joy beyond your hopes.
Priam's citadel—the Greeks have taken Troy!

LEADER No, what do you mean? I can't believe it.

CLYTAEMNESTRA Troy is ours. Is that clear enough?

LEADER The joy of it,
stealing over me, calling up my tears—

CLYTAEMNESTRA Yes, your eyes expose your loyal hearts.

LEADER And you have proof?

7. Offerings of wine. At a banquet three libations were poured, the third and last to Zeus the savior; the last libation was accompanied by a hymn of praise.

8. This seems to refer to the sacrifice of Iphigenia. Some scholars take the Greek words to refer to the fulfillment of Calchas's prophecies.

CLYTAEMNESTRA I do,
I must. Unless the god is lying.
LEADER That,
or a phantom spirit sends you into raptures.
CLYTAEMNESTRA No one takes me in with visions—senseless dreams.
LEADER Or giddy rumor, you haven't indulged yourself—
CLYTAEMNESTRA You treat me like a child, you mock me?
LEADER Then when did they storm the city?
CLYTAEMNESTRA Last night, I say, the mother of this morning.
LEADER And who on earth could run the news so fast?
CLYTAEMNESTRA The god of fire—rushing fire from Ida![9]
And beacon to beacon rushed it on to me,
my couriers riding home the torch.
From Troy
to the bare rock of Lemnos, Hermes' Spur,[1]
and the Escort winged the great light west
to the Saving Father's face, Mount Athos[2] hurled it
third in the chain and leaping Ocean's back
the blaze went dancing on to ecstasy—pitch-pine
streaming gold like a new-born sun—and brought
the word in flame to Mount Makistos'[3] brow.
No time to waste, straining, fighting sleep,
that lookout heaved a torch glowing over
the murderous straits of Euripos to reach
Messapion's[4] watchmen craning for the signal.
Fire for word of fire! tense with the heather
withered gray, they stack it, set it ablaze—
the hot force of the beacon never flags,
it springs the Plain of Asôpos, rears
like a harvest moon to hit Kithairon's[5] crest
and drives new men to drive the fire on.
That relay pants for the far-flung torch,
they swell its strength outstripping my commands
and the light inflames the marsh, the Gorgon's Eye,[6]
it strikes the peak where the wild goats range[7]—
my laws, my fire whips that camp!
They spare nothing, eager to build its heat,
and a huge beard of flame overcomes the headland
beetling down the Saronic Gulf,[8] and flaring south
it brings the dawn to the Black Widow's[9] face—

9. The mountain range near Troy. The names that follow in this speech designate the places where beacon fires flashed the message of Troy's fall to Argos. The chain began at Ida.
1. Hermes' cliff is on the island of Lemnos (off the coast of Asia Minor).
2. On a rocky peninsula in northern Greece.
3. On the island of Euboea off the coast of central Greece.
4. A mountain on the mainland.
5. A mountain near Thebes.
6. Lake Gorgopis.
7. Mount Aegiplanctus on the Isthmus of Corinth.
8. The sea.
9. Mount Arachnaeus ("spider") in Argive territory. This is the fire seen by the watchman at the beginning of the play.

the watch that looms above your heads—and now
the true son of the burning flanks of Ida
crashes on the roofs of Atreus' sons!

And I ordained it all.
Torch to torch, running for their lives,
one long succession racing home my fire.
One,
first in the laps and last,[1] wins out in triumph.
There you have my proof, *my* burning sign, I tell you—
the power my lord passed on from Troy to me!

LEADER We'll thank the gods, my lady—first this story,
let me lose myself in the wonder of it all!
Tell it start to finish, tell us all.

CLYTAEMNESTRA The city's ours—in our hands this very day!
I can hear the cries in crossfire rock the walls.
Pour oil and wine in the same bowl,
what have you, friendship? A struggle to the end.
So with the victors and the victims—outcries,
you can hear them clashing like their fates.

They are kneeling by the bodies of the dead,
embracing men and brothers, infants over
the aged loins that gave them life, and sobbing,
as the yoke constricts their last free breath,
for every dear one lost.
And the others,
there, plunging breakneck through the night—
the labor of battle sets them down, ravenous;
to breakfast on the last remains of Troy.
Not by rank but the lots of chance they draw,
they lodge in the houses captured by the spear,
settling in so soon, released from the open sky,
the frost and dew. Lucky men, off guard at last,
they sleep away their first good night in years.

If only they are revering the city's gods,
the shrines of the gods who love the conquered land,
no plunderer will be plundered in return.
Just let no lust, no mad desire seize the armies[2]
to ravish what they must not touch—
overwhelmed by all they've won!
The run for home

1. The chain of beacons is compared to a relay race in which the runners carry torches; the last runner (who runs the final lap) comes in first to win.

2. The audience was familiar with the traditional account, according to which Agamemnon and his army failed signally to respect the gods and temples of Troy.

and safety waits, the swerve at the post,[3]
the final lap of the gruelling two-lap race.
And even if the men come back with no offense
to the gods, the avenging dead may never rest—
Oh let no new disaster strike! And here
you have it, what a woman has to say.
Let the best win out, clear to see.
A small desire but all that I could want.

LEADER Spoken like a man, my lady, loyal,
full of self-command. I've heard your sign
and now your vision.
[*Reaching towards her as she turns and re-enters the palace.*]
Now to praise the gods.
The joy is worth the labor.

CHORUS O Zeus my king and Night, dear Night,[4]
queen of the house who covers us with glories,[5]
you slung your net on the towers of Troy,
neither young nor strong could leap
the giant dredge net of slavery,
all-embracing ruin.
I adore you, iron Zeus of the guests
and your revenge—you drew your longbow
year by year to a taut full draw
till one bolt, not falling short
or arching over the stars,
could split the mark of Paris!

The sky stroke of god!—it is all Troy's to tell,
but even I can trace it to its cause:
god does as god decrees.
And still some say
that heaven would never stoop to punish men
who trample the lovely grace of things
untouchable. How wrong they are!
A curse burns bright on crime—
full-blown, the father's crimes will blossom,
burst into the son's.[6]
Let there be less suffering . . .
give us the sense to live on what we need.

3. Greek runners turned at a post and came back on a parallel track.
4. Troy fell to a night attack.
5. Probably the moon and stars; an obscure expression in the original.
6. The language throughout this passage is significantly general. The chorus refers to Paris, but everything it says is equally applicable to Agamemnon, who sacrificed his daughter for his ambitions. The original Greek is corrupt (that is, has been garbled in the handwritten tradition) but seems to proclaim the doctrine that the sins of the fathers are visited on the children. So Paris and Agamemnon pay for the misdeeds of their ancestors (as well as their own).

Bastions of wealth
are no defense for the man
who treads the grand altar of Justice
down and out of sight.

Persuasion, maddening child of Ruin
overpowers him—Ruin plans it all.
And the wound will smolder on,
there is no cure,
a terrible brilliance kindles on the night.
He is bad bronze scraped on a touchstone:
put to the test, the man goes black.[7]
Like the boy who chases
a bird on the wing, brands his city,
brings it down and prays,
but the gods are deaf
to the one who turns to crime, they tear him down.

So Paris learned:
he came to Atreus' house
and shamed the tables spread for guests,
he stole away the queen.

And she left her land *chaos*, clanging shields,
companions tramping, bronze prows, men in bronze,
and she came to Troy with a dowry, death,
strode through the gates
defiant in every stride,
as prophets of the house[8] looked on and wept,
"Oh the halls and the lords of war,
the bed and the fresh prints of love.
I *see* him, unavenging, unavenged,
the stun of his desolation is so clear—
he longs for the one who lies across the sea
until her phantom seems to sway the house.

Her curving images,
her beauty hurts her lord,
the eyes starve and the touch
of love is gone,

and radiant dreams are passing in the night,
the memories throb with sorrow, joy with pain . . .
it is pain to dream and see desires
slip through the arms,
a vision lost forever

7. Inferior bronze, adulterated with lead, turns black with use.

8. Menelaus's.

winging down the moving drifts of sleep."
So he grieves at the royal hearth
yet others' grief is worse, far worse.
All through Greece for those who flocked to war
they are holding back the anguish now,
you can feel it rising now in every house;
I tell you there is much to tear the heart.

They knew the men they sent,
but now in place of men
ashes and urns come back
to every hearth.[9]

War, War, the great gold-broker of corpses
holds the balance of the battle on his spear!
Home from the pyres he sends them,
home from Troy to the loved ones,
weighted with tears, the urns brimmed full,
the heroes return in gold-dust,[1]
dear, light ash for men; and they weep,
they praise them, "He had skill in the swordplay,"
"He went down so tall in the onslaught,"
"All for another's woman." So they mutter
in secret and the rancor steals
toward our staunch defenders, Atreus' sons.

And there they ring the walls, the young,
the lithe, the handsome hold the graves
they won in Troy; the enemy earth
rides over those who conquered.

The people's voice is heavy with hatred,
now the curses of the people must be paid,
and now I wait, I listen . . .
there—there is something breathing
under the night's shroud. God takes aim
at the ones who murder many;
the swarthy Furies stalk the man
gone rich beyond all rights—with a twist
of fortune grind him down, dissolve him
into the blurring dead—there is no help.
The reach for power can recoil,
the bolt of god can strike you at a glance.

9. This strikes a contemporary note. In Homer the fallen Achaeans are buried at Troy, but in Aeschylus's Athens the dead were cremated on the battlefield, and their ashes were brought home for burial.

1. I.e., in ashes. The war god is a broker who gives, in exchange for bodies, gold dust (the word used for *bodies* could mean living bodies or corpses).

Make me rich with no man's envy,
neither a raider of cities, no,
nor slave come face to face with life
overpowered by another.

[*Speaking singly.*]
—Fire comes and the news is good,
it races through the streets
but is it true? Who knows?
Or just another lie from heaven?
—Show us the man so childish, wonderstruck,
he's fired up with the first torch,
then when the message shifts
he's sick at heart.

—Just like a woman
to fill with thanks before the truth is clear.

—So gullible. Their stories spread like wildfire,
they fly fast and die faster;
rumors voiced by women come to nothing.

LEADER Soon we'll know her fires for what they are,
her relay race of torches hand-to-hand—
know if they're real or just a dream,
the hope of a morning here to take our senses.
I see a herald running from the beach
and a victor's spray of olive shades his eyes
and the dust he kicks, twin to the mud of Troy,
shows he has a voice—no kindling timber
on the cliffs, no signal-fires for him.
He can shout the news and give us joy,
or else . . . please, not that.
Bring it on,
good fuel to build the first good fires.
And if anyone calls down the worst on Argos
let him reap the rotten harvest of his mind.

[*The* HERALD *rushes in and kneels on the ground.*]

HERALD Good Greek earth, the soil of my fathers!
Ten years out, and a morning brings me back.
All hopes snapped but one—I'm home at last.
Never dreamed I'd die in Greece, assigned
the narrow plot I love the best.
And now
I salute the land, the light of the sun,
our high lord Zeus and the king of Pytho[2]—
no more arrows, master, raining on our heads!

2. Apollo.

At Scamander's banks we took our share,
your longbow brought us down like plague.[3]
Now come, deliver us, heal us—lord Apollo!
Gods of the market, here, take my salute.
And you, my Hermes,[4] Escort,
loving Herald, the herald's shield and prayer!—
And the shining dead[5] of the land who launched the armies,
warm us home . . . we're all the spear has left.

You halls of the kings, you roofs I cherish,
sacred seats—you gods that catch the sun,
if your glances ever shone on him in the old days,
greet him well—so many years are lost.
He comes, he brings us light in the darkness,
free for every comrade, Agamemnon lord of men.

Give him the royal welcome he deserves!
He hoisted the pickax of Zeus who brings revenge,
he dug Troy down, he worked her soil down,
the shrines of her gods and the high altars, gone!—
and the seed of her wide earth he ground to bits.
That's the yoke he claps on Troy. The king,
the son of Atreus comes. The man is blest,
the one man alive to merit such rewards.

Neither Paris nor Troy, partners to the end,
can say their work outweighs their wages now.
Convicted of rapine, stripped of all his spoils,
and his father's house and the land that gave it life—
he's scythed them to the roots. The sons of Priam
pay the price twice over.

LEADER Welcome home
from the wars, herald, long live your joy.

HERALD *Our* joy—
now I could die gladly. Say the word, dear gods.

LEADER Longing for your country left you raw?

HERALD The tears fill my eyes, for joy.

LEADER You too,
down the sweet disease that kills a man
with kindness . . .

HERALD Go on, I don't see what you—

LEADER Love
for the ones who love you—that's what took you.

3. Compare the opening scene of the *Iliad* (pp. 230–31), where Apollo punishes the Greeks with his arrows (a metaphor for plague).

4. The gods' messenger and patron deity of heralds.

5. The heroes of the past, who are buried in Argos and worshipped.

HERALD You mean
the land and the armies hungered for each other?
LEADER There were times I thought I'd faint with longing.
HERALD So anxious for the armies, why?
LEADER For years now,
only my silence kept me free from harm.
HERALD What,
with the kings gone did someone threaten you?
LEADER So much . . .
now as you say, it would be good to die.
HERALD True, we *have* done well.
Think back in the years and what have you?
A few runs of luck, a lot that's bad.
Who but a god can go through life unmarked?
A long, hard pull we had, if I would tell it all.
The iron rations, penned in the gangways
hock by jowl like sheep. Whatever miseries
break a man, our quota, every sunstarved day.

Then on the beaches it was worse. Dug in
under the enemy ramparts—deadly going.
Out of the sky, out of the marshy flats
the dews soaked us, turned the ruts we fought from
into gullies, made our gear, our scalps
crawl with lice.
And talk of the cold,
the sleet to freeze the gulls, and the big snows
come avalanching down from Ida. Oh but the heat,
the sea and the windless noons, the swells asleep,
dropped to a dead calm . . .

But why weep now?
It's over for us, over for them.
The dead can rest and never rise again;
no need to call their muster. We're alive,
do we have to go on raking up old wounds?
Good-by to all that. Glad I am to say it.

For us, the remains of the Greek contingents,
the good wins out, no pain can tip the scales,
not now. So shout this boast to the bright sun—
fitting it is—wing it over the seas and rolling earth:

"Once when an Argive expedition captured Troy
they hauled these spoils back to the gods of Greece,
they bolted them high across the temple doors,
the glory of the past!"
And hearing that,
men will applaud our city and our chiefs,

and Zeus will have the hero's share of fame—
he did the work.
That's all I have to say.

LEADER I'm convinced, glad that I was wrong.
Never too old to learn; it keeps me young.
[CLYTAEMNESTRA *enters with her women.*]
First the house and the queen, it's their affair,
but I can taste the riches.

CLYTAEMNESTRA I cried out long ago![6]—
for joy, when the first herald came burning
through the night and told the city's fall.
And there were some who smiled and said,
"A few fires persuade you Troy's in ashes.
Women, women, elated over nothing."

You made me seem deranged.
For all that I sacrificed—a woman's way,
you'll say—station to station on the walls
we lifted cries of triumph that resounded
in the temples of the gods. We lulled and blessed
the fires with myrrh and they consumed our victims.
[*Turning to the* HERALD.]
But enough. Why prolong the story?
From the king himself I'll gather all I need.
Now for the best way to welcome home
my lord, my good lord . . .
No time to lose!
What dawn can feast a woman's eyes like this?
I can see the light, the husband plucked from war
by the Saving God and open wide the gates.

Tell him that, and have him come with speed,
the people's darling—how they long for him.
And for his wife,
may he return and find her true at hall,
just as the day he left her, faithful to the last.
A watchdog gentle to him alone,
[*Glancing towards the palace.*]
savage
to those who cross his path. I have not changed.
The strains of time can never break our seal.
In love with a new lord, in ill repute I am
as practiced as I am in dyeing bronze.

That is my boast, teeming with the truth.
I am proud, a woman of my nobility—
I'd hurl it from the roofs!

6. As the watchman had told her to (line 30).

[*She turns sharply, enters the palace.*]

LEADER She speaks well, but it takes no seer to know
she only says what's right.

[*The* HERALD *attempts to leave; the* LEADER *takes him by the arm.*]

Wait, one thing.
Menelaus, is he home too, safe with the men?[7]
The power of the land—dear king.

HERALD I doubt that lies will help my friends,
in the lean months to come.

LEADER Help us somehow, tell the truth as well.
But when the two conflict it's hard to hide—
out with it.

HERALD He's lost, gone from the fleets![8]
He and his ship, it's true.

LEADER After you watched him
pull away from Troy? Or did some storm
attack you all and tear him off the line?

HERALD There,
like a marksman, the whole disaster cut to a word.

LEADER How do the escorts give him out—dead or alive?

HERALD No clear report. No one knows . . .
only the wheeling sun that heats the earth to life.

LEADER But then the storm—how did it reach the ships?
How did it end? Were the angry gods on hand?

HERALD This blessed day, ruin it with *them*?
Better to keep their trophies far apart.

When a runner comes, his face in tears,
saddled with what his city dreaded most,
the armies routed, two wounds in one,
one to the city, one to hearth and home . . .
our best men, droves of them, victims
herded from every house by the two-barb whip
that Ares[9] likes to crack,
that charioteer
who packs destruction shaft by shaft,
careening on with his brace of bloody mares—
When he comes in, I tell you, dragging that much pain,
wail your battle-hymn to the Furies, and high time!

But when he brings salvation home to a city
singing out her heart—
how can I mix the good with so much bad

7. The relevance of this question and the following speeches lies in the fact that Menelaus's absence makes Agamemnon's murder easier (his presence might have made it impossible) and in the fact that Menelaus is bringing Helen home.

8. For what happened to Menelaus, see *Odyssey* 4 (pp. 365 ff.).

9. The war god.

and blurt out this?—
"Storms swept the Greeks,
and not without the anger of the gods!"

Those enemies for ages, fire[1] and water,
sealed a pact and showed it to the world—
they crushed our wretched squadrons.
Night looming,
breakers lunging in for the kill
and the black gales come brawling out of the north—
ships ramming, prow into hooking prow, gored
by the rush-and-buck of hurricane pounding rain
by the cloudburst—
ships stampeding into the darkness,
lashed and spun by the savage shepherd's hand![2]

But when the sun comes up to light the skies
I see the Aegean heaving into a great bloom
of corpses . . . Greeks, the pick of a generation
scattered through the wrecks and broken spars.

But not us, not our ship, our hull untouched.
Someone stole us away or begged us off.
No mortal—a god, death grip on the tiller,
or lady luck herself, perched on the helm,
she pulled us through, she saved us. Aye,
we'll never battle the heavy surf at anchor,
never shipwreck up some rocky coast.

But once we cleared that sea-hell, not even
trusting luck in the cold light of day,
we battened on our troubles, they were fresh—
the armada punished, bludgeoned into nothing.

And now if one of them still has the breath
he's saying *we* are lost. Why not?
We say the same of him. Well,
here's to the best.
And Menelaus?
Look to it, he's come back, and yet . . .
if a shaft of the sun can track him down,
alive, and his eyes full of the old fire—
thanks to the strategies of Zeus, Zeus
would never tear the house out by the roots—
then there's hope our man will make it home.

1. Lightning.
2. The ships were scattered like sheep dispersed by a cruel shepherd.

You've heard it all. Now you have the truth.
[*Rushing out.*]

CHORUS Who—what power named the name[3] that drove your fate?—
what hidden brain could divine your future,
steer that word to the mark,
to the bride of spears,
the whirlpool churning armies,
Oh for all the world a Helen!
Hell at the prows, hell at the gates
hell on the men-of-war,
from her lair's sheer veils she drifted
launched by the giant western wind,
and the long tall waves of men in armor,
huntsmen[4] trailing the oar-blades' dying spoor
slipped into her moorings,
Simois'[5] mouth that chokes with foliage,
bayed for bloody strife,

for Troy's Blood Wedding Day—she drives her word,
her burning will to the birth, the Fury
late but true to the cause,
to the tables shamed
and Zeus who guards the hearth[6]—
the Fury makes the Trojans pay!
Shouting their hymns, hymns for the bride
hymns for the kinsmen doomed
to the wedding march of Fate.
Troy changed her tune in her late age,
and I think I hear the dirges mourning
"Paris, born and groomed for the bed of Fate!"
They mourn with their life breath,
they sing their last, the sons of Priam
born for bloody slaughter.

So a man once reared
a lion cub at hall, snatched
from the breast, still craving milk
in the first flush of life.
A captivating pet for the young,
and the old men adored it, pampered it
in their arms, day in, day out,
like an infant just born.
Its eyes on fire, little beggar,
fawning for its belly, slave to food.

3. Helen. The name contains the Greek root *hele-*, which means "destroy."
4. The Achaean army, which came after her.
5. A river in Troy.
6. I.e., protects the host and guest.

But it came of age
and the parent strain broke out
and it paid its breeders back.
Grateful it was, it went
through the flock to prepare a feast,
an illicit orgy—the house swam with blood,
one could resist that agony—
massacre vast and raw!
From god there came a priest of ruin,
adopted by the house to lend it warmth.

And the first sensation Helen brought to Troy . . .
call it a spirit
shimmer of winds dying
glory light as gold
shaft of the eyes dissolving, open bloom
that wounds the heart with love.
But veering wild in mid-flight
she whirled her wedding on to a stabbing end,
slashed at the sons of Priam—hearthmate, friend to the death,
sped by Zeus who speeds the guest,
a bride of tears, a Fury.

There's an ancient saying, old as man himself:
men's prosperity
never will die childless,
once full-grown it breeds.
Sprung from the great good fortune in the race
comes bloom on bloom of pain—
insatiable wealth. But not I,
I alone say this. Only the reckless act
can breed impiety, multiplying crime on crime,
while the house kept straight and just
is blessed with radiant children.[7]

But ancient Violence longs to breed,
new Violence comes
when its fatal hour comes, the demon comes
to take her toll—no war, no force, no prayer
can hinder the midnight Fury stamped
with parent Fury moving through the house.

But Justice shines in sooty hovels,[8]

7. These lines begin with the traditional Greek view that immoderate good fortune (or excellence of any kind beyond the average) is itself the cause of disaster. The chorus, however, rejects this view and states that only an act of evil produces evil consequences.
8. The homes of the poor.

loves the decent life.
From proud halls crusted with gilt by filthy hands
she turns her eyes to find the pure in spirit—
spurning the wealth stamped counterfeit with praise,
she steers all things toward their destined end.[9]

[AGAMEMNON *enters in his chariot, his plunder borne before him by his entourage; behind him, half hidden, stands* CASSANDRA. *The old men press toward him.*]

Come, my king, the scourge of Troy,
the true son of Atreus—
How to salute you, how to praise you
neither too high nor low, but hit
the note of praise that suits the hour?
So many prize some brave display,
they prefer some flaunt of honor
once they break the bounds.
When a man fails they share his grief,
but the pain can never cut them to the quick.
When a man succeeds they share his glory,
torturing their faces into smiles.
But the good shepherd knows his flock.
When the eyes seem to brim with love
and it is only unction,
he will know, better than we can know.
That day you marshaled the armies
all for Helen—no hiding it now—
I drew you in my mind in black;
you seemed a menace at the helm,
sending men to the grave
to bring her home, that hell on earth.
But now from the depths of trust and love
I say Well fought, well won—
the end is worth the labor!
Search, my king, and learn at last
who stayed at home and kept their faith
and who betrayed the city.[1]

AGAMEMNON First,
with justice I salute my Argos and my gods,
my accomplices who brought me home and won
my rights from Priam's Troy—the just gods.
No need to hear our pleas. Once for all
they consigned their lots to the urn of blood,[2]
they pitched on death for men, annihilation

9. Here the chorus admits, by implication, that the poor are less likely to commit evil acts.
1. The chorus tries to warn Agamemnon against flatterers and dissemblers, but he misses its drift.
2. In an Athenian law court there were two urns—one for acquittal, one for condemnation—into which the jurors dropped their pebbles. (The audience will see them on stage in the final play of the trilogy.)

for the city. Hope's hand, hovering
over the urn of mercy, left it empty.
Look for the smoke—it is the city's seamark,
building even now.
The storms of ruin live!
Her last dying breath, rising up from the ashes
sends us gales of incense rich in gold.

For that we must thank the gods with a sacrifice
our sons will long remember. For their mad outrage
of a queen we raped their city—we were right.
The beast of Argos, foals of the wild mare,[3]
thousands massed in armor rose on the night
the Pleiades went down,[4] and crashing through
their walls our bloody lion lapped its fill,
gorging on the blood of kings.
Our thanks to the gods,
long drawn out, but it is just the prelude.

[CLYTAEMNESTRA *approaches with her women; they are carrying dark red tapestries.* AGAMEMNON *turns to the* LEADER.]

And your concern, old man, is on my mind.
I hear you and agree, I will support you.
How rare, men with the character to praise
a friend's success without a trace of envy,
poison to the heart—it deals a double blow.
Your own losses weigh you down but then,
look at your neighbor's fortune and you weep.
Well I know. I understand society,
the fawning mirror of the proud.
My comrades . . .
they're shadows, I tell you, ghosts of men
who swore they'd die for me. Only Odysseus:
I dragged that man to the wars[5] but once in harness
he was a trace-horse,[6] he gave his all for me.
Dead or alive, no matter, I can praise him.

And now this cause involving men and gods.
We must summon the city for a trial,
found a national tribunal. Whatever's healthy,
shore it up with law and help it flourish.
Wherever something calls for drastic cures

3. The wooden horse, the stratagem with which the Greeks captured the city.
4. The setting of a group of stars in the constellation Taurus, late in the fall.
5. Feigning madness to escape going to Troy, Odysseus was tricked into demonstrating his sanity.
6. A third horse that ran beside the team that pulled a chariot; it lent help when special maneuvering was needed, particularly in making tight turns.

we make our noblest effort: amputate or wield
the healing iron, burn the cancer at the roots.

Now I go to my father's house—
I give the gods my right hand, my first salute.
The ones who sent me forth have brought me home.

[*He starts down from the chariot, looks at* CLYTAEMNESTRA, *stops, and offers up a prayer.*]

Victory, you have sped my way before,
now speed me to the last.

[CLYTAEMNESTRA *turns from the king to the* CHORUS.]

CLYTAEMNESTRA Old nobility of Argos
gathered here, I am not ashamed to tell you
how I love the man. I am older,
and the fear dies away . . . I am human.
Nothing I say was learned from others.
This is my life, my ordeal, long as the siege
he laid at Troy and more demanding.
First,
when a woman sits at home and the man is gone,
the loneliness is terrible,
unconscionable . . .
and the rumors spread and fester,
a runner comes with something dreadful,
close on his heels the next and his news worse,
and they shout it out and the whole house can hear;
and wounds—if he took one wound for each report
to penetrate these walls, he's gashed like a dragnet,
more, if he had only died . . .
for each death that swelled his record, he could boast
like a triple-bodied Geryon[7] risen from the grave,
"Three shrouds I dug from the earth, one for every body
that went down!"
The rumors broke like fever,
broke and then rose higher. There were times
they cut me down and eased my throat from the noose.
I wavered between the living and the dead.

[*Turning to* AGAMEMNON.]

And so
our child is gone, not standing by our side,
the bond of our dearest pledges, mine and yours;
by all rights our child should be here . . .
Orestes. You seem startled.
You needn't be. Our loyal brother-in-arms
will take good care of him, Strophios[8] the Phocian.

7. A monster (eventually killed by Heracles) who had three bodies and three heads.

8. King of Phocis, a mountainous region near Delphi. His son, Pylades, accompanies Orestes when he returns to avenge Agamemnon's death.

He warned from the start we court two griefs in one.
You risk all on the wars—and what if the people
rise up howling for the king, and anarchy
should dash our plans?
Men, it is their nature,
trampling on the fighter once he's down.
Our child is gone. That is my self-defense
and it is true.
For me, the tears that welled
like springs are dry. I have no tears to spare.
I'd watch till late at night, my eyes still burn,
I sobbed by the torch I lit for you alone.
[*Glancing towards the palace.*]
I never let it die . . . but in my dreams
the high thin wail of a gnat would rouse me,
piercing like a trumpet—I could see you
suffer more than all
the hours that slept with me could ever bear.

I endured it all. And now, free of grief,
I would salute that man the watchdog of the fold,
the mainroyal,[9] saying stay of the vessel,
rooted oak that thrusts the roof sky-high,
the father's one true heir.
Land at dawn to the shipwrecked past all hope,
light of the morning burning off the night of storm,
the cold clear spring to the parched horseman—
O the ecstasy, to flee the yoke of Fate!

It is right to use the titles he deserves.
Let envy keep her distance. We have suffered
long enough.
[*Reaching toward* AGAMEMNON.]
Come to me now, my dearest,
down from the car of war, but never set the foot
that stamped out Troy on earth again, my great one.

Women, why delay? You have your orders.
Pave his way with tapestries.[1]
[*They begin to spread the crimson tapestries between the king and the palace doors.*]
Quickly.
Let the red stream flow and bear him home
to the home he never hoped to see—Justice,
lead him in!
Leave all the rest to me.

9. Upper section of the mainmast.
1. To walk on those tapestries, wall hangings dyed with the expensive crimson, would be an act of extravagant pride.

The spirit within me never yields to sleep.
We will set things right, with the god's help.
We will do whatever Fate requires.

AGAMEMNON There
is Leda's daughter,[2] the keeper of my house.
And the speech to suit my absence, much too long.
But the praise that does us justice,
let it come from others, then we prize it.
This—
You treat me like a woman. Groveling, gaping up at me!
What am I, some barbarian[3] peacocking out of Asia?
Never cross my path with robes and draw the lightning.
Never—only the gods deserve the pomps of honor
and the stiff brocades of fame. To walk on them . . .
I am human, and it makes my pulses stir
with dread.
Give me the tributes of a man
and not a god, a little earth to walk on,
not this gorgeous work.
There is no need to sound my reputation.
I have a sense of right and wrong, what's more—
heaven's proudest gift. Call no man blest
until he ends his life in peace, fulfilled.
If I can live by what I say, I have no fear.

CLYTAEMNESTRA One thing more. Be true to your ideals and tell me—

AGAMEMNON True to my ideals? Once I violate them I am lost.

CLYTAEMNESTRA Would you have sworn this act to god in a time of terror?

AGAMEMNON Yes, if a prophet called for a last, drastic rite.

CLYTAEMNESTRA But Priam—can you see him if he had your success?

AGAMEMNON Striding on the tapestries of God, I see him now.

CLYTAEMNESTRA And *you* fear the reproach of common men?

AGAMEMNON The voice of the people—aye, they have enormous power.

CLYTAEMNESTRA Perhaps, but where's the glory without a little gall?

AGAMEMNON And where's the woman in all this lust for glory?

CLYTAEMNESTRA But the great victor—it becomes him to give way.

AGAMEMNON Victory in this . . . war of ours, it means so much to you?

CLYTAEMNESTRA O give way! The power is yours if you surrender all of
your own free will to me.

AGAMEMNON Enough.
If you are so determined—
[*Turning to the women, pointing to his boots.*]
Let someone help me off with these at least.
Old slaves, they've stood me well.
Hurry,
and while I tread his splendors dyed red in the sea,[4]

2. Clytaemnestra. Helen is also a daughter of Leda.

3. Foreigner, with negative connotations.

4. The dye was made from shellfish.

may no god watch and strike me down with envy
from on high. I feel such shame—
to tread the life of the house, a kingdom's worth
of silver in the weaving.

[*He steps down from the chariot to the tapestries and reveals* CASSANDRA, *dressed in the sacred regalia, the fillets, robes and scepter of Apollo.*]

Done is done.
Escort this stranger[5] in, be gentle.
Conquer with compassion. Then the gods
shine down upon you, gently. No one chooses
the yoke of slavery, not of one's free will—
and she least of all. The gift of the armies,
flower and pride of all the wealth we won,
she follows me from Troy.
And now,
since you have brought me down with your insistence,
just this once I enter my father's house,
trampling royal crimson as I go.

[*He takes his first steps and pauses.*]

CLYTAEMNESTRA There is the sea
and who will drain it dry? Precious as silver,
inexhaustible, ever-new, it breeds the more we reap it—
tides on tides of crimson dye our robes blood-red.
Our lives are based on wealth, my king,
the gods have seen to that.
Destitution, our house has never heard the word.
I would have sworn to tread on legacies of robes,
at one command from an oracle, deplete the house—
suffer the worst to bring that dear life back!

[*Encouraged,* AGAMEMNON *strides to the entrance.*]

When the root lives on, the new leaves come back,
spreading a dense shroud of shade across the house
to thwart the Dog Star's[6] fury. So you return
to the father's hearth, you bring us warmth in winter
like the sun—
And you are Zeus when Zeus
tramples the bitter virgin grape for new wine
and the welcome chill steals through the halls, at last
the master moves among the shadows of his house, fulfilled.

[AGAMEMNON *goes over the threshold; the women gather up the tapestries while* CLYTAEMNESTRA *prays.*]

Zeus, Zeus, master of all fullfillment, now fulfill our prayers—
speed our rites to their fulfillment once for all!

5. Cassandra, daughter of Priam, Agamemnon's share of the human booty from the sack of Troy. She was loved by Apollo, who gave her the gift of prophecy; but when she refused her love to the god, he saw to it that her prophecies, though true, would never be believed until it was too late.

6. Sirius; its appearance in the summer sky marked the beginning of the hot season (the "dog days" of summer).

[*She enters the palace, the doors close, the old men huddle in terror.*]

CHORUS Why, why does it rock me, never stops,
this terror beating down my heart,
this seer that sees it all—
it beats its wings, uncalled unpaid
thrust on the lungs
the mercenary song beats on and on
singing a prophet's strain—
and I can't throw it off
like dreams that make no sense,
and the strength drains
that filled the mind with trust,
and the years drift by and the driven sand
has buried the mooring lines
that churned when the armored squadrons cut for Troy . . .
and now I believe it, I can prove he's home,
my own clear eyes for witness—
Agamemnon!
Still it's chanting, beating deep so deep in the heart
this dirge of the Furies, oh dear god,
not fit for the lyre,[7] its own master
it kills our spirit
kills our hopes
and it's real, true, no fantasy—
stark terror whirls the brain
and the end is coming
Justice comes to birth—
I pray my fears prove false and fall
and die and never come to birth!
Even exultant health, well we know,
exceeds its limits,[8] comes so near disease
it can breach the wall between them.

Even a man's fate, held true on course,
in a blinding flash rams some hidden reef;
but if caution only casts the pick of the cargo—
one well-balanced cast—
the house will not go down, not outright;[9]
laboring under its wealth of grief
the ship of state rides on.

Yes, and the great green bounty of god,
sown in the furrows year by year and reaped each fall
can end the plague of famine.

7. A stringed instrument played on joyful occasions (hence "lyric" poetry).
8. Excess, even in blessings like health, is always dangerous.
9. These lines refer to a traditional Greek belief that the fortunate person could avert the envy of heaven by deliberately getting rid of some precious possession.

But a man's lifeblood
        is dark and mortal.
Once it wets the earth
what song can sing it back?
Not even the master-healer[1]
    who brought the dead to life—
Zeus stopped the man before he did more harm.

Oh, if only the gods had never forged
the chain that curbs our excess,
    one man's fate curbing the next man's fate,
my heart would outrace my song, I'd pour out all I feel—
            but no, I choke with anguish,
        mutter through the nights.
Never to ravel out a hope in time
and the brain is swarming, burning—

[CLYTAEMNESTRA *emerges from the palace and goes to* CASSANDRA, *impassive in the chariot.*]

CLYTAEMNESTRA Won't you come inside? I mean you, Cassandra.
Zeus in all his mercy wants you to share
some victory libations with the house.
The slaves are flocking. Come, lead them
up to the altar of the god who guards
our dearest treasures.
                Down from the chariot,
no time for pride. Why even Heracles,[2]
they say, was sold into bondage long ago,
he had to endure the bitter bread of slaves.
But if the yoke descends on you, be grateful
for a master born and reared in ancient wealth.
Those who reap a harvest past their hopes
are merciless to their slaves.
                    From us
you will receive what custom says is right.

[CASSANDRA *remains impassive.*]

LEADER It's *you* she is speaking to, it's all too clear.
You're caught in the nets of doom—obey
if you can obey, unless you cannot bear to.
CLYTAEMNESTRA Unless she's like a swallow, possessed
of her own barbaric song,[3] strange, dark.
I speak directly as I can—she must obey.
LEADER Go with her. Make the best of it, she's right.
Step down from the seat, obey her.

1. Asclepius, the mythical physician who was so skilled that he finally succeeded in restoring a dead man to life. Zeus struck him with a thunderbolt for going too far.

2. The Greek hero, famous for his twelve labors that rid the Earth of monsters, was at one time forced to be the slave to Omphale, an Eastern queen.

3. The comparison of foreign speech to the twittering of a swallow was a Greek commonplace.

CLYTAEMNESTRA Do it *now*—
I have no time to spend outside. Already
the victims crowd the hearth, the Navelstone,[4]
to bless this day of joy I never hoped to see!—
our victims waiting for the fire and the knife,
and you,
if you want to taste our mystic rites, come now.
If my words can't reach you—
[*Turning to the* LEADER.]
Give her a sign,
one of her exotic handsigns.

LEADER I think
the stranger needs an interpreter, someone clear.
She's like a wild creature, fresh caught.

CLYTAEMNESTRA She's mad,
her evil genius murmuring in her ears.
She comes from a *city* fresh caught.
She must learn to take the cutting bridle
before she foams her spirit off in blood—
and that's the last I waste on her contempt!
[*Wheeling, re-entering the palace. The* LEADER *turns to* CASSANDRA, *who remains transfixed.*]

LEADER Not I, I pity her. I will be gentle.
Come, poor thing. Leave the empty chariot—
Of your own free will try on the yoke of Fate.

CASSANDRA Aieeeeee! Earth—Mother—
Curse of the Earth—Apollo Apollo!

LEADER Why cry to Apollo?
He's not the god to call with sounds of mourning.

CASSANDRA Aieeeeee! Earth—Mother—
Rape of the Earth—Apollo Apollo!

LEADER Again, it's a bad omen.
She cries for the god who wants no part of grief.[5]
[CASSANDRA *steps from the chariot, looks slowly towards the rooftops of the palace.*]

CASSANDRA God of the long road,
Apollo *Apollo* my destroyer—
you destroy me once,[6] destroy me twice—

LEADER She's about to sense her own ordeal, I think.
Slave that she is, the god lives on inside her.

CASSANDRA God of the iron marches,
Apollo *Apollo* my destroyer—
where, where have you led[7] me now? what house—

4. An altar of Zeus Herkeios, guardian of the hearth, which was the religious center of the home.

5. Apollo (and the Olympian gods in general) was not invoked in mourning or lamentation.

6. The name *Apollo* suggests the Greek word *apollumi*, "destroy." He destroyed her the first time when he saw to it that no one would believe her prophecies. "God of the long road": Apollo Agyieus. This statue, a conical pillar, was set up outside the door of the house; no doubt there was one onstage.

7. The Greek word (a form of the verb *agō*) suggests the god's title Agyieus.

LEADER The house of Atreus and his sons. Really—
don't you know? It's true, see for yourself.
CASSANDRA No . . . the house that hates god,
an echoing womb of guilt, kinsmen
torturing kinsmen, severed heads,
slaughterhouse of heroes, soil streaming blood—
LEADER A keen hound, this stranger.
Trailing murder, and murder she will find.
CASSANDRA See, my witnesses—
I trust to them, to the babies
wailing, skewered on the sword,
their flesh charred, the father gorging on their parts[8]—
LEADER We'd heard your fame as a seer,
but no one looks for seers in Argos.
CASSANDRA Oh no, what horror, what new plot,[9]
new agony this?—
it's growing, massing, deep in the house,
a plot, a monstrous—*thing*
to crush the loved ones, no,
there is no cure, and rescue's far away[1] and—
LEADER I can't read these signs; I knew the first,
the city rings with them.
CASSANDRA You, you godforsaken—you'd do *this*?
The lord of your bed,
you bathe him . . . his body glistens, then—
how to tell the climax?—
comes so quickly, see,
hand over hand shoots out, hauling ropes—
then lunge!
LEADER Still lost. Her riddles, her dark words of god—
I'm groping, helpless.
CASSANDRA No no, look *there*!—
what's that? some net flung out of hell—
No, *she* is the snare,
the bedmate, deathmate, murder's strong right arm!
Let the insatiate discord in the race
rear up and shriek "Avenge the victim—stone them dead!"
LEADER What Fury is this? Why rouse it, lift its wailing
through the house? I hear you and lose hope.
CHORUS Drop by drop at the heart, the gold of life ebbs out.
We are the old soldiers . . . wounds will come
with the crushing sunset of our lives.
Death is close, and quick.
CASSANDRA Look out! *look out!*—
Ai, drag the great bull from the mate!—

8. The feast of Thyestes, who was tricked by his brother, Atreus, into eating his own children. The story is told by Aegisthus below (lines 1606–43).

9. Clytaemnestra's murder of Agamemnon.

1. A reference to Menelaus (distant in space) and Orestes (distant in time).

a thrash of robes, she traps him—
writhing—
black horn glints, twists—
she gores him through!
And now he buckles, look, the bath swirls red—
There's stealth and murder in the cauldron, do you hear?
LEADER I'm no judge, I've little skill with the oracles,
but even I know danger when I hear it.
CHORUS What good are the oracles to men? Words, more words,
and the hurt comes on us, endless words
and a seer's techniques have brought us
terror and the truth.
CASSANDRA The agony—O I am breaking!—Fate's so hard,
and the pain that floods my voice is mine alone.
Why have you brought me here, tormented as I am?
Why, unless to die with him, why else?
LEADER AND CHORUS Mad with the rapture—god speeds you on
to the song, the deathsong,
like the nightingale[2] that broods on sorrow,
mourns her son, her son,
her life inspired with grief for him,
she lilts and shrills, dark bird that lives for night.
CASSANDRA The nightingale—O for a song, a fate like hers!
The gods gave her a life of ease, swathed her in wings,
no tears, no wailing. The knife waits for me.
They'll splay me on the iron's double edge.
LEADER AND CHORUS Why?—what god hurls you on, stroke on stroke
to the long dying fall?
Why the horror clashing through your music,
terror struck to song?—
why the anguish, the wild dance?
Where do your words of god and grief begin?
CASSANDRA Ai, the wedding, wedding of Paris,
death to the loved ones. Oh Scamander,[3]
you nursed my father . . . once at your banks
I nursed and grew, and now at the banks
of Acheron,[4] the stream that carries sorrow,
it seems I'll chant my prophecies too soon.
LEADER AND CHORUS What are you saying? Wait, it's clear,
a child could see the truth, it wounds within,
Like a bloody fang it tears—
I hear your destiny—breaking sobs,
cries that stab the ears.

2. Philomela was raped by Tereus, the husband of her sister Procne. The two sisters avenged themselves by killing Tereus's son, Itys, and serving up his flesh to Tereus to eat. Procne was changed into a nightingale mourning for Itys (the name is an imitation of the sound of the nightingale's song).
3. A Trojan river.
4. One of the rivers of the underworld.

CASSANDRA Oh the grief, the grief of the city
ripped to oblivion. Oh the victims,
the flocks my father burned at the wall,
rich herds in flames . . . no cure for the doom
that took the city after all, and I,
her last ember, I go down with her.

LEADER AND CHORUS You cannot stop, your song goes on—
some spirit drops from the heights and treads you down
and the brutal strain grows—
your death-throes come and come and
I cannot see the end!

CASSANDRA Then off with the veils that hid the fresh young
bride[5]—
we will see the truth.
Flare up once more, my oracle! Clear and sharp
as the wind that blows toward the rising sun,
I can feel a deeper swell now, gathering head
to break at last and bring the dawn of grief.

No more riddles. I will teach you.
Come, bear witness, run and hunt with me.
We trail the old barbaric works of slaughter.

These roofs—look up—there is a dancing troupe
that never leaves. And they have their harmony
but it is harsh, their words are harsh, they drink
beyond the limit. Flushed on the blood of men
their spirit grows and none can turn away
their revel breeding in the veins—the Furies!
They cling to the house for life. They sing,
sing of the frenzy that began it all,
strain rising on strain, showering curses
on the man who tramples on his brother's bed.[6]

There. Have I hit the mark or not? Am I a fraud,
a fortune-teller babbling lies from door to door?
Swear how well I know the ancient crimes
that live within this house.

LEADER And if I did?
Would an oath bind the wounds and heal us?
But you amaze me. Bred across the sea,
your language strange, and still you sense the truth
as if you had been here.

CASSANDRA Apollo the Prophet
introduced me to his gift.

5. At this point, as the meter indicates, Cassandra changes from lyric song, the medium of emotion, to spoken iambic lines, the medium of rational discourse.

6. Thyestes, who seduced the wife of his brother, Atreus.

LEADER A *god*—and moved with love?
CASSANDRA I was ashamed to tell this once,
but now . . .
LEADER We spoil ourselves with scruples,
long as things go well.
CASSANDRA He came like a wrestler,
magnificent, took me down and breathed his fire
through me and—
LEADER You bore him a child?
CASSANDRA I yielded,
then at the climax I recoiled—I deceived Apollo!
LEADER But the god's skills—they seized you even then?
CASSANDRA Even then I told my people all the grief to come.
LEADER And Apollo's anger never touched you?—is it possible?
CASSANDRA Once I betrayed him I could never be believed.
LEADER We believe you. Your visions seem so true.
CASSANDRA Aieeeee!—
the pain, the terror! the birth-pang of the seer
who tells the truth—
it whirls me, oh,
the storm comes again, the crashing chords!
Look, you see them nestling at the threshold?
Young, young in the darkness like a dream,
like children really, yes, and their loved ones
brought them down . . .
their hands, they fill their hands
with their own flesh, they are serving it like food,
holding out their entrails . . . now it's clear,
I can see the armfuls of compassion, see the father
reach to taste and—
For so much suffering,
I tell you, someone plots revenge.
A lion[7] who lacks a lion's heart,
he sprawled at home in the royal lair
and set a trap for the lord on his return.
My lord . . . I must wear his yoke, I am his slave.
The lord of the men-of-war, he obliterated Troy—
he is so blind, so lost to that detestable hellhound
who pricks her ears and fawns and her tongue draws out
her glittering words of welcome—
No, he cannot see
the stroke that Fury's hiding, stealth, murder.
What outrage—the woman kills the man!
What to call
that . . . monster of Greece, and bring my quarry down?

7. Aegisthus.

Viper coiling back and forth?
Some sea-witch?—
Scylla[8] crouched in her rocky nest—nightmare of sailors?
Raging mother of death, storming deathless war against
the ones she loves!
And how she howled in triumph,
boundless outrage. Just as the tide of battle
broke her way, she seems to rejoice that he
is safe at home from war, saved for her.

Believe me if you will. What will it matter
if you won't? It comes when it comes,
and soon you'll see it face to face
and say the seer was all too true.
You will be moved with pity.

LEADER Thyestes' feast,
the children's flesh—that I know,
and the fear shudders through me. It's true,
real, no dark signs about it. I hear the rest
but it throws me off the scent.

CASSANDRA Agamemnon.
You will see him dead.

LEADER Peace, poor girl!
Put those words to sleep.

CASSANDRA No use,
the Healer[9] has no hand in this affair.

LEADER Not if it's true—but god forbid it is!

CASSANDRA You pray, and they close in to kill!

LEADER What man prepares this, this dreadful—

CASSANDRA Man?
You *are* lost, to every word I've said.

LEADER Yes—
I don't see who can bring the evil off.

CASSANDRA And yet I know my Greek, too well.

LEADER So does the Delphic oracle,[1]
but he's hard to understand.

CASSANDRA His *fire*!—
sears me, sweeps me again—the torture!
Apollo Lord of the Light, you burn,
you blind me—
Agony!
She is the lioness,
she rears on her hind legs, she beds with the wolf
when her lion king goes ranging—
she will kill me—

8. A human-eating sea monster (see *Odyssey* 12, pp. 467–77).
9. Apollo.
1. Apollo's oracle; its replies were celebrated for their obscurity and ambiguity.

Ai, the torture!
She is mixing her drugs,
adding a measure more of hate for me.
She gloats as she whets the sword for him.
He brought me home and we will pay in carnage.

Why mock yourself with these—trappings, the rod,
the god's wreath, his yoke around my throat?
Before I die I'll tread you—
[*Ripping off her regalia, stamping it into the ground.*]
Down, out,
die die die!
Now you're down. I've paid you back.
Look for another victim—I am free at last—
make her rich in all your curse and doom.
[*Staggering backwards as if wrestling with a spirit tearing at her robes.*]
See,
Apollo himself, his fiery hands—I feel him again,
he's stripping off my robes, the Seer's robes!
And after he looked down and saw me mocked,
even in these, his glories, mortified by friends
I loved, and they hated me, they were so blind
to their own demise—
I went from door to door,
I was wild with the god, I heard them call me
"Beggar! Wretch! Starve for bread in hell!"

And I endured it all, and now he will
extort me as his due. A seer for the Seer.
He brings me here to die like this,
not to serve at my father's altar. No,
the block is waiting. The cleaver steams
with my life blood, the first blood drawn
for the king's last rites.
[*Regaining her composure and moving to the altar.*]
We will die,
but not without some honor from the gods.
There will come another[2] to avenge us,
born to kill his mother, born
his father's champion. A wanderer, a fugitive
driven off his native land, he will come home
to cope the stones of hate that menace all he loves.
The gods have sworn a monumental oath: as his father lies
upon the ground he draws him home with power like a prayer.

Then why so pitiful, why so many tears?
I have seen my city faring as she fared,

2. Orestes.

and those who took her, judged by the gods,
faring as they fare. I must be brave.
It is my turn to die.
[*Approaching the doors.*]
I address you as the Gates of Death.
I pray it comes with one clear stroke,
no convulsions, the pulses ebbing out
in gentle death. I'll close my eyes and sleep.

LEADER So much pain, poor girl, and so much truth,
you've told so much. But if you *see* it coming,
clearly—how can you go to your own death,
like a beast to the altar driven on by god,
and hold your head so high?

CASSANDRA No escape, my friends,
not now.

LEADER But the last hour should be savored.

CASSANDRA My time has come. Little to gain from flight.

LEADER You're brave, believe me, full of gallant heart.

CASSANDRA Only the wretched go with praise like that.

LEADER But to go nobly lends a man some grace.

CASSANDRA My noble father—you and your noble children.
[*She nears the threshold and recoils, groaning in revulsion.*]

LEADER What now? what terror flings you back?
Why? Unless some horror in the brain—

CASSANDRA Murder.
The house breathes with murder—bloody shambles![3]

LEADER No, no, only the victims at the hearth.

CASSANDRA I know that odor. I smell the open grave.

LEADER But the Syrian myrrh,[4] it fills the halls with splendor,
can't you sense it?

CASSANDRA Well, I must go in now,
mourning Agamemnon's death and mine.
Enough of life!
[*Approaching the doors again and crying out.*]
Friends—I cried out,
not from fear like a bird fresh caught,
but that you will testify to *how* I died.
When the queen, woman for woman, dies for me,
and a man falls for the man who married grief.
That's all I ask, my friends. A stranger's gift
for one about to die.

LEADER Poor creature, you
and the end you see so clearly. I pity you.

CASSANDRA I'd like a few words more, a kind of dirge,
it is my own. I pray to the sun,

3. A slaughterhouse.
4. Incense burned at the sacrifice. Another interpretation of this line runs, "What you speak of (that is, the smell of the open grave) is no Syrian incense, giving splendor to the palace."

the last light I'll see,
that when the avengers cut the assassins down
they will avenge me too, a slave who died,
an easy conquest.
Oh men, your destiny.
When all is well a shadow can overturn it.
When trouble comes a stroke of the wet sponge,
and the picture's blotted out. And that,
I think that breaks the heart.

[*She goes through the doors.*]

CHORUS But the lust for power never dies—
men cannot have enough.
No one will lift a hand to send it
from his door, to give it warning,
"Power, never come again!"
Take this man: the gods in glory
gave him Priam's city to plunder,
brought him home in splendor like a god.
But now if he must pay for the blood
his fathers shed, and die for the deaths
he brought to pass, and bring more death
to avenge his dying, show us one
who boasts himself born free
of the raging angel, once he hears—

[*Cries break out within the palace.*]

AGAMEMNON Aagh!
Struck deep—the death-blow, deep—

LEADER Quiet. Cries,
but who? Someone's stabbed—

AGAMEMNON Aaagh, again . . .
second blow—struck home.

LEADER The work is done,
you can feel it. The king, and the great cries—
Close ranks now, find the right way out.

[*But the old men scatter, each speaks singly.*]

CHORUS —I say send out heralds, muster the guard,
they'll save the house.

—And I say rush in now,
catch them red-handed—butchery running on their blades.

—Right with you, do something—now or never!

—Look at them, beating the drum for insurrection.

—Yes,
we're wasting time. They rape the name of caution,
their hands will never sleep.

—Not a plan in sight.
Let men of action do the planning, too.

—I'm helpless. Who can raise the dead with words?

—What, drag out our lives? bow down to the tyrants,
the ruin of the house?

—Never, better to die
on your feet than live on your knees.

—Wait,
do we take the cries for signs, prophesy like seers
and give him up for dead?

—No more suspicions,
not another word till we have proof.

—Confusion
on all sides—one thing to do. See how it stands
with Agamemnon, once and for all we'll see—

[*He rushes at the doors. They open and reveal a silver cauldron that holds the body of* AGAMEMNON *shrouded in bloody robes, with the body of* CASSANDRA *to his left and* CLYTAEMNESTRA *standing to his right, sword in hand. She strides towards the* CHORUS.]

CLYTAEMNESTRA Words, endless words I've said to serve the moment—
Now it makes me proud to tell the truth.
How else to prepare a death for deadly men
who seem to love you? How to rig the nets
of pain so high no man can overleap them?

I brooded on this trial, this ancient blood feud
year by year. At last my hour came.
Here I stand and here I struck
and here my work is done.
I did it all. I don't deny it, no.
He had no way to flee or fight his destiny—

[*Unwinding the robes from* AGAMEMNON*'s body, spreading them before the altar where the old men cluster around them, unified as a chorus once again.*]

our never-ending, all embracing net, I cast it
wide for the royal haul, I coil him round and round
in the wealth, the robes of doom, and then I strike him
once, twice, and at each stroke he cries in agony—
he buckles at the knees and crashes here!
And when he's down I add the third, last blow,
to the Zeus who saves the dead beneath the ground

I send that third blow home in homage like a prayer.[5]

So he goes down, and the life is bursting out of him—
great sprays of blood, and the murderous shower
wounds me, dyes me black and I, I revel
like the Earth when the spring rains come down,
the blessed gifts of god, and the new green spear
splits the sheath and rips to birth in glory!

So it stands, elders of Argos gathered here.
Rejoice if you can rejoice—I glory.
And if I'd pour upon his body the libation
it deserves, what wine could match my words?
It is right and more than right. He flooded
the vessel of our proud house with misery,
with the vintage of the curse and now
he drains the dregs. My lord is home at last.

LEADER You appall me, you, your brazen words—
exulting over your fallen king.

CLYTAEMNESTRA And you,
you try me like some desperate woman.
My heart is steel, well you know. Praise me,
blame me as you choose. It's all one.
Here is Agamemnon, my husband made a corpse
by this right hand—a masterpiece of Justice.
Done is done.

CHORUS Woman!—what poison cropped from the soil
or strained from the heaving sea, what nursed you,
drove you insane? You brave the curse of Greece.
You have cut away and flung away and now
the people cast you off to exile,
broken with our hate.

CLYTAEMNESTRA And now you sentence me?—
you banish *me* from the city, curses breathing
down my neck? But *he*—
name one charge you brought against him then.
He thought no more of it than killing a beast,
and his flocks were rich, teeming in their fleece,
but he sacrificed his own child, our daughter,
the agony I labored into love,
to charm away the savage winds of Thrace.[6]

Didn't the law demand you banish him?—
hunt him from the land for all his guilt?
But now you witness what I've done

5. Like the third libation to Zeus (see p. 662, n. 7).

6. Winds from the North (at Aulis).

and you are ruthless judges.
Threaten away!
I'll meet you blow for blow. And if I fall
the throne is yours. If god decrees the reverse,
late as it is, old men, you'll learn your place.

CHORUS Mad with ambition,
shrilling pride!—some Fury
crazed with the carnage rages through your brain—
I can see the flecks of blood inflame your eyes!
But vengeance comes—you'll lose your loved ones,
stroke for painful stroke.

CLYTAEMNESTRA Then learn this, too, the power of my oaths.
By the child's Rights I brought to birth,
by Ruin, by Fury—the three gods to whom
I sacrificed this man—I swear my hopes
will never walk the halls of fear so long
as Aegisthus lights the fire on my hearth.
Loyal to me as always, no small shield
to buttress my defiance.
Here he lies.
He brutalized me. The darling of all
the golden girls[7] who spread the gates of Troy.
And here his spearprize . . . what wonders she beheld!—
the seer of Apollo shared my husband's bed,
his faithful mate who knelt at the rowing-benches,
worked by every hand.
They have their rewards.
He as you know. And she, the swan of the gods
who lived to sing her latest, dying song—
his lover lies beside him.
She brings a fresh, voluptuous relish to my bed!

CHORUS Oh quickly, let me die—
no bed of labor, no, no wasting illness . . .
bear me off in the sleep that never ends,
now that he has fallen,
now that our dearest shield lies battered—
Woman made him suffer,
woman struck him down.
Helen the wild, maddening Helen,
one for the many, the thousand lives
you murdered under Troy. Now you are crowned
with this consummate wreath, the blood
that lives in memory, glistens age to age.
Once in the halls she walked and she was war,
angel of war, angel of agony, lighting men to death.

7. In Greek *chrysēidōn*, which recalls the girl in the first book of the *Iliad* (1.119–22), Chryseis, whom Agamemnon said he preferred to Clytaemnestra.

CLYTAEMNESTRA Pray no more for death, broken
as you are. And never turn
your wrath on her, call her
the scourge of men, the one alone
who destroyed a myriad Greek lives—
Helen the grief that never heals.

CHORUS The *spirit*!—you who tread
the house and the twinborn sons of Tantalus[8]—
you empower the sisters, Fury's twins
whose power tears the heart!
Perched on the corpse your carrion raven
glories in her hymn,
her screaming hymn of pride.

CLYTAEMNESTRA Now you set your judgment straight,
you summon *him*! Three generations
feed the spirit in the race.
Deep in the veins he feeds our bloodlust—
aye, before the old wound dies
it ripens in another flow of blood.

CHORUS The great curse of the house, the spirit,
dead weight wrath—and you can praise it!
Praise the insatiate doom that feeds
relentless on our future and our sons.
Oh all through the will of Zeus,
the cause of all, the one who works it all.
What comes to birth that is not Zeus?
Our lives are pain, what part not come from god?

Oh, my king, my captain,
how to salute you, how to mourn you?
What can I say with all my warmth and love?
Here in the black widow's web you lie,
gasping out your life
in a sacrilegious death, dear god,
reduced to a slave's bed,
my king of men, yoked by stealth and Fate,
by the wife's hand that thrust the two-edged sword.

CLYTAEMNESTRA You claim the work is mine, call me
Agamemnon's wife—you are so wrong.
Fleshed in the wife of this dead man,
the spirit lives within me,
our savage ancient spirit of revenge.
In return for Atreus' brutal feast
he kills his perfect son—for every
murdered child, a crowning sacrifice.

8. Father of Pelops, grandfather of Atreus. "Sons": descendants—that is, Agamemnon and Menelaus.

CHORUS And *you*, innocent of his murder?
And who could swear to that? and how? . . .
and still an avenger could arise,
bred by the fathers' crimes, and lend a hand.
He wades in the blood of brothers,
stream on mounting stream—black war erupts
and where he strides revenge will stride,
clots will mass for the young who were devoured.

Oh my king, my captain,
how to salute you, how to mourn you?
What can I say with all my warmth and love?
Here in the black widow's web you lie,
gasping out your life
in a sacrilegious death, dear god,
reduced to a slave's bed,
my king of men, yoked by stealth and Fate,
by the wife's hand that thrust the two-edged sword.

CLYTAEMNESTRA No slave's death, I think—
no stealthier than the death he dealt
our house and the offspring of our loins,
Iphigeneia, girl of tears.
Act for act, wound for wound!
Never exult in Hades, swordsman,
here you are repaid. By the sword
you did your work and by the sword you die.

CHORUS The mind reels—where to turn?
All plans dashed, all hope! I cannot think . . .
the roofs are toppling, I dread the drumbeat thunder
the heavy rains of blood will crush the house
the first light rains are over—
Justice brings new acts of agony, yes,
on new grindstones Fate is grinding sharp the sword of Justice.

Earth, dear Earth,
if only you'd drawn me under
long before I saw him huddled
in the beaten silver bath.
Who will bury him, lift his dirge?
[*Turning to* CLYTAEMNESTRA.]
You, can you dare *this*?
To kill your lord with your own hand
then mourn his soul with tributes, terrible tributes—
do his enormous works a great dishonor.
This godlike man, this hero. Who at the grave
will sing his praises, pour the wine of tears?
Who will labor there with truth of heart?

CLYTAEMNESTRA This is no concern of yours.
The hand that bore and cut him down
will hand him down to Mother Earth.
This house will never mourn for him.
Only our daughter Iphigeneia,
by all rights, will rush to meet him
first at the churning straits,[9]
the ferry over tears—
she'll fling her arms around her father,
pierce him with her love.

CHORUS Each charge meets counter-charge.
one can judge between them. Justice.
The plunderer plundered, the killer pays the price.
The truth still holds while Zeus still holds the throne:
the one who acts must suffer—
that is law. Who, who can tear from the veins
the bad seed, the curse? The race is welded to its ruin.

CLYTAEMNESTRA At last you see the future and the truth!
But I will swear a pact with the spirit
born within us. I embrace his works,
cruel as they are but done at last,
if he will leave our house
in the future, bleed another line
with kinsmen murdering kinsmen.
Whatever he may ask. A few things
are all I need, once I have purged
our fury to destroy each other—
purged it from our halls.

[AEGISTHUS *has emerged from the palace with his bodyguard and stands triumphant over the body of* AGAMEMNON.]

AEGISTHUS O what a brilliant day
it is for vengeance! Now I can say once more
there are gods in heaven avenging men,
blazing down on all the crimes of earth.
Now at last I see this man brought down
in the Furies' tangling robes. It feasts my eyes—
he pays for the plot his father's hand contrived.

Atreus, this man's father, was king of Argos.
My father, Thyestes—let me make this clear—
Atreus' brother challenged him for the crown,
and Atreus drove him out of house and home
then lured him back, and home Thyestes came,
poor man, a suppliant to his own hearth,
to pray that Fate might save him.

9. The river of the underworld over which the dead were ferried.

So it did.
There was no dying, no staining our native ground
with *his* blood. Thyestes was the guest,
and this man's godless father—
[*Pointing to* AGAMEMNON.]
the zeal of the host outstripping a brother's love,
made my father a feast that seemed a feast for gods,
a love feast of his children's flesh.
He cuts
the extremities, feet and delicate hands
into small pieces, scatters them over the dish
and serves it to Thyestes throned on high.
He picks at the flesh he cannot recognize,
the soul of innocence eating the food of ruin—
look,
[*Pointing to the bodies at his feet.*]
that feeds upon the house! And then,
when he sees the monstrous thing he's done, he shrieks,
he reels back head first and vomits up that butchery,
tramples the feast—brings down the curse of Justice:
"Crash to ruin, all the race of Pleisthenes,[1] crash down!"

So you see him, down. And I, the weaver of Justice,
plotted out the kill. Atreus drove us into exile,
my struggling father and I, a babe-in-arms,
his last son, but I became a man
and Justice brought me home. I was abroad
but I reached out and seized my man,
link by link I clamped the fatal scheme
together. Now I could die gladly, even I—
now I see this monster in the nets of Justice.

LEADER Aegisthus, you revel in pain—you sicken me.
You say you killed the king in cold blood,
singlehanded planned his pitiful death?
I say there's no escape. In the hour of judgment,
trust to this, your head will meet the people's
rocks and curses.

AEGISTHUS You say! you slaves at the oars—
while the master of the benches cracks the whip?
You'll learn, in your late age, how much it hurts
to teach old bones their place. We have techniques—
chains and the pangs of hunger,
two effective teachers, excellent healers.
They can even cure old men of pride and gall.
Look—can't you see? The more you kick
against the pricks, the more you suffer.

1. A name sometimes inserted into the genealogy of the house of Tantalus.

LEADER You, pathetic—
the king had just returned from battle.
You waited out the war and fouled his lair,
you planned my great commander's fall.

AEGISTHUS Talk on—
you'll scream for every word, my little Orpheus.[2]
We'll see if the world comes dancing to your song,
your absurd barking—snarl your breath away!
I'll make you dance, I'll bring you all to heel.

LEADER *You* rule Argos? You who schemed his death
but cringed to cut him down with your own hand?

AEGISTHUS The treachery was the woman's work, clearly.
I was a marked man, his enemy for ages.
But I will use his riches, stop at nothing
to civilize his people. All but the rebel:
him I'll yoke and break—
no cornfed colt, running free in the traces.
Hunger, ruthless mate of the dark torture-chamber,
trains her eyes upon him till he drops!

LEADER Coward, why not kill the man yourself?
Why did the woman, the corruption of Greece
and the gods of Greece, have to bring him down?
Orestes—If he still sees the light of day,
bring him home, good Fates, home to kill
this pair at last. Our champion in slaughter!

AEGISTHUS Bent on insolence? Well, you'll learn, quickly.
At them, men—you have your work at hand!

[*His men draw swords; the old men take up their sticks.*]

LEADER At them, fist at the hilt, to the last man—

AEGISTHUS Fist at the hilt, I'm not afraid to die.

LEADER It's death you want and death you'll have—
we'll make that word your last.

[CLYTAEMNESTRA *moves between them, restraining* AEGISTHUS.]

CLYTAEMNESTRA No more, my dearest,
no more grief. We have too much to reap
right here, our mighty harvest of despair.
Our lives are based on pain. No bloodshed now.

Fathers of Argos, turn for home before you act
and suffer for it. What we did was destiny.
If we could end the suffering, how we would rejoice.
The spirit's brutal hoof has struck our heart.
And that is what a woman has to say.
Can you accept the truth?

[CLYTAEMNESTRA *turns to leave.*]

2. A mythical singer who charmed all nature with his music.

AEGISTHUS But these . . . mouths
that bloom in filth—spitting insults in my teeth.
You tempt your fates, you insubordinate dogs—
to hurl abuse at me, your master!
LEADER No Greek
worth his salt would grovel at your feet.
AEGISTHUS I—I'll stalk you all your days!
LEADER Not if the spirit brings Orestes home.
AEGISTHUS Exiles feed on hope—well I know.
LEADER More,
gorge yourself to bursting—soil justice, while you can.
AEGISTHUS I promise you, you'll pay, old fools—in good time, too!
LEADER Strut on your own dunghill, you cock beside your mate.
CLYTAEMNESTRA Let them howl—they're impotent. You and I have power now.
We will set the house in order once for all.
[*They enter the palace; the great doors close behind them; the old men disband and wander off.*]

SOPHOCLES

ca. 496–406 B.C.E.

The seven surviving plays of Sophocles are often considered the most perfect achievement of ancient Athens. They show us people—presented with psychological depth and subtlety—who stand apart from others, on the edges of their social groups. Sophocles invites us to ask what it means to be part of a family, part of a city, part of a team or an army, or part of the human race. Can we choose to embrace or reject our family, friends, and society, or do we have to accept the place to which we were born? Is it a gesture of heroism or folly to be an outsider? What should we do if forced to choose between our family and a wider social group? These thought-provoking and compelling dramas explore themes that are just as relevant today as they were in the fifth century B.C.E., and they provide the classic treatments of mythic figures, such as Oedipus and Antigone, who have been central to later Western culture.

LIFE AND TIMES

Sophocles was a generation younger than **Aeschylus**, and had an unusually long, successful, productive, and apparently happy life. He was born at the start of the fifth century, around 496 B.C.E. in the village of Colonus, which was a short distance north of Athens. His family was probably fairly wealthy—his father may have owned a workshop producing armor, a particularly saleable product at this time of war—and Sophocles seems to have been well educated. An essential element in Greek boys' education at this time was studying the Homeric poems, and Sophocles obviously learned this lesson well; in later times, he was called the "most Homeric" of the three surviving Athenian tragedians. He was a good-looking, charming boy and a talented dancer. In 480, when he was about fifteen or sixteen, he was chosen to lead a group of naked boys who danced in the victory celebrations for Athens' defeat of the Persian navy at Salamis. The beginning of his public career thus coincided with his city's period of greatest glory and international prestige.

Athens became the major power in the Mediterranean world in the middle decades of the fifth century, a period known as the golden or classical age. The most important political figure in the newly dominant city-state was Pericles, a statesman who was also Sophocles' personal friend and who particularly encouraged the arts. Pericles seems to have instituted various legal measures to enable the theater to flourish: for instance, rich citizens were obliged to provide funding for theater productions, and the less wealthy may have had their theater tickets subsidized.

The prosperity of Sophocles' city took a sharp turn for the worse around 431 B.C.E., when the poet would have been in his mid-sixties. The Peloponnesian War, between Athens and Sparta, began at that time and would last until after Sophocles' death. Soon after the outbreak of war, Sophocles' friend Pericles died in a terrible plague that afflicted the whole city. In the last decades of the century, the city became increasingly impoverished and demoralized by war.

Sophocles worked in the Athenian theater all his life. He made some important technical changes in the theater, including the introduction of scene painting, and the increase of the chorus members from twelve to fifteen. His most important innovation was bringing in a third actor (a "tritagonist"). This allowed for three-way dialogues, and a drama that concentrates on the complex interactions and relationships of individuals with one another. The chorus in Sophocles' dramas became far less central to the plot than it had been in Aeschylus; this is part of the reason why Sophocles' plays may seem more modern to twenty-first century readers and audiences.

Another quality that makes Sophocles particularly accessible to modern readers is his interest in realistic characterization. Sophocles' most memorable characters are intense, passionate, and often larger than life, but always fully human. They frequently adopt positions that seem extreme, but for which they have the best of motives. Sophocles' tragedies ask us to consider when and how it is right to compromise, and to measure the slim divide between concession and selling out. Clashes between stubborn heroism and the voice of moderation are found in all Sophocles' surviving plays.

Contemporaries gave Sophocles' talent its due. He won first prize at the Great Dionysia for the first time in 468, defeating his older rival, Aeschylus; he was still under thirty at the time. Sophocles would defeat Aeschylus several more times in the course of his career. His output was large: he composed over a hundred and twenty plays. The seven that survive include the three Theban plays, dealing with Oedipus and his family: *Oedipus the King*, *Antigone*, and *Oedipus at Colonus*. These were written at intervals of many years, and were never intended to be performed together. The other four surviving tragedies are: *Ajax*, about a strongman hero who is driven mad by Athena and about the consequences of his madness; *Trachiniae*, about Heracles' agonizing death at the hands of his jealous wife Deineira (who had thought the poison she gave him was a love potion); *Electra*, which focuses on the unending grief and rage of Agamemnon's daughter after her father's murder; and *Philoctetes*, about the Greek embassy to persuade an embittered, wounded hero to return to battle in Troy. The dating of most of these plays is uncertain, although we know *Philoctetes* is a late play, composed in 409 B.C.E. The judges at the Great Dionysia loved Sophocles' work: he won first prize over twenty times, and never came lower than second.

Sophocles seems to have been equally popular as a person, known for his mellow, easygoing temperament, his religious piety, and his appreciation for the beauty of adolescent boys. We are told that he had "so much charm of character that he was loved everywhere, by everyone." He was friendly with the prominent intellectuals of his day, including the world's first historian, **Herodotus.** He participated actively in the political activity of the city; he served under Pericles as a treasurer in 443 and 442, and was elected as a general under him in 441. After the Sicilian disaster in 413, in which Athens lost enormous numbers of men and ships, Sophocles—then in his eighties—was one of ten men elected to an emergency group formed for policy formation. Sophocles' participation in public life suggests that he was seen as a trustworthy and wise member of the community. Sophocles was married and had five sons, one of whom, Iophon, became a tragedian himself. He lived to advanced old age, and was over ninety when he died.

OEDIPUS THE KING

Many first-time readers of *Oedipus the King* will already know the shocking skeleton Oedipus eventually discovers: that he killed his father and married his mother, without knowing what he was doing. The mythical background to this play is familiar to readers today, and would have been well known, in its broad outlines, to Sophocles' original audience. This is a drama not of surprise, but of suspense: we watch Oedipus uncover the buried truth about himself and his parentage, of which he, unlike us, is ignorant. The mystery, which is gradually revealed to the spectators in the course of Sophocles' play, is not what the king has done, but how he will discover what he has done, and how he will respond to this terrible new knowledge.

The legend goes that Laios, son of Labdakos and king of Thebes, learned long ago from the Delphic oracle (sacred to Apollo) that his son would kill him. When Laius had a son, by his wife Jokasta, he gave the baby to a shepherd to be exposed on Mount Kithaeron. Exposure, a fairly common practice in the ancient world, involved leaving a baby out in some wild place, presumably to die; it allowed parents to dispose of unwanted children without incurring blood guilt. Laios increased the odds against the child's survival by piercing and binding his feet, so there was no chance he could crawl away. But the shepherd felt sorry for the boy and saved him. He was adopted by the childless king and queen of Corinth (Korinth), Polybos and Merope, and grew up believing himself to be their son.

One day another oracle warned Oedipus that he would kill his father and marry his mother. Oedipus fled Corinth and ran away, in the direction of Thebes, to avoid this fate. At a place where three paths crossed, he encountered his real father, Laios, without knowing who he was; they quarreled, and Oedipus killed Laios. When he reached Thebes, he found the city oppressed by a dreadful female monster, a Sphinx—part human, part lion, often also depicted in Greek art with the wings of an eagle and the tail of a snake. The Sphinx refused to let anybody into the city unless they could answer her riddle: "What walks on four legs in the morning, two legs at noon, and three legs in the evening?" She strangled and devoured all travelers who failed to answer the riddle. But Oedipus gave the right answer: "Man." (Human beings crawl on all fours in infancy, walk on two feet in adulthood, and use a cane in old age.) The Sphinx was defeated, and Oedipus was welcomed into the city as a savior. He married the newly widowed queen, Jokasta, and took over the throne.

When Sophocles' play begins, Oedipus has been ruling Thebes successfully for many years, and has four children by Jokasta, two sons and two daughters. But a new trouble is now afflicting the city. Plague has come to Thebes, and the dying inhabitants are searching for the reason why the gods are angry with the city.

The city of Athens suffered a terrible plague in 429 B.C.E., and the play may well have been composed and performed soon afterward—although the dating is uncertain and disputed. Sophocles certainly seems to invite comparisons between the real Athens and the mythical Thebes. Oedipus himself can be seen as a typical fifth-century Athenian: he is optimistic, irascible, self-confident, both pious and skeptical in his attitudes toward religion, and a committed believer in the power of human reason.

In his ***Poetics***, the philosopher **Aristotle** describes this play as the finest of all Greek tragedies. It includes two plot patterns that he thought were essential to good drama: a reversal of fortune (*peripeteia*), and a recognition (*anagnorisis*). Aristotle famously cites Oedipus as an example of someone whose fall into misfortune is the result not of bad deeds or evil character, but of some "mistake"—the Greek word is *hamartia*. Later critics applied the quite different concept of a "tragic flaw" to Oedipus, suggesting that we are supposed to see the disastrous events of the drama as somehow the king's own fault. An important consideration against this reading is that in *Oedipus at Colonus*, a later play about the last days of Oedipus, Sophocles makes his hero give a compelling self-defense: "How is my *nature* evil— / if all I did was to return a blow?" There is a clear distinction in Greek thought between moral culpability—which is attached to deliberate, conscious actions—and religious pollution, which may afflict even those who are morally innocent. Readers must decide for themselves how far they think Sophocles goes in presenting his Oedipus as a sympathetic or even admirable figure.

Another popular approach to the play has been to see it as a classic "tragedy of fate," in which a man is brought low by destiny or the gods. Here, we need to distinguish the myth—which can plausibly be seen as a story about the inevitable unfolding of divine will—from Sophocles' treatment of the myth in his play, which creates a more complex relationship between destiny and human action. Before Sophocles, Aeschylus had produced a trilogy that dealt with the family of Laius and Oedipus. This does not survive, but it is likely that it showed the gradual fulfillment of an inherited curse. In Sophocles' play, our attention is focused less on the original events and their causes (the killing of Laios and the marriage to Jokasta) than on the process by which Oedipus uncovers what he has done.

Sophocles multiplies the number of oracles and messengers in the story, and Apollo—the god associated with prophecy, poetry, and interpretation, as well as with light and the sun—presides over the complex unfolding of the truth. Oracles are only one of many types of riddling, ambiguous, or ambivalent language used in the play, which is concerned with all kinds of interpretation. Moments of dramatic irony, when the audience hears a meaning of which the speaker is unaware, are another important reminder that words may have more than one sense. For instance, Oedipus says, "Laios / had no luck fathering children," and vows to fight for him "as I would for my own father"—speaking more truly than he knows. The interplay between literal and metaphorical meanings forms another essential technique in the play. Sophocles creates a relationship between literal and metaphorical blindness, between the light of the sun and the light of insight, between Oedipus as "father" of his people and as real father to his own siblings, and between sickness as a physical affliction and as a metaphor for pollution.

The riddle of the Sphinx defines humanity by the number of feet we use at different points in our lives. Sophocles seems to suggest that the name *Oedipus* is closely associated with feet: it can be read either as "Know-Foot" (from the verb *oida,* "to know," and *pous*, "foot"—an appropriate name for the man who guessed the Sphinx's riddle), or as "Swell-Foot" (from the verb *oidao,* to swell—a reminder of the baby Oedipus's wounded feet). The first interpretation of his name makes Oedipus seem like an Everyman figure, a representative of all humanity: he is the one who truly understands the human condition. The second reminds us of the ways in which Oedipus is not like us: his feet mark the fact that he was cast out by his parents, rejected from his city, and that he has, unwittingly, done things that seem to make it impossible for him to be part of any human community.

Sigmund Freud famously claimed that the Oedipus myth represents a universal psychological phenomenon, the "Oedipus Complex," which involves the (supposed) desire of all boys to kill their fathers and marry their mothers. But Sophocles' Oedipus does not suffer from Freud's complex: his terrible actions are committed in total ignorance, not through an unconscious desire for patricide or sex with his mother. Another way to think of Sophocles' Oedipus is as a hero who, like Odysseus, struggles to find his way back home after many wanderings and an encounter with terrible monsters—but finds himself in a perverted version of the homecoming story, in which the arrival is not the end but the beginning of a nightmare.

A play whose secret you already know might seem unlikely to be interesting. But it is impossible to be bored by *Oedipus the King*. The plot races to its terrible conclusion with the twisting, breakneck pace of a thrilling murder mystery, while the contradictory figure of Oedipus himself—the blind rationalist, the polluted king, the killer of his father, the son and husband of Jokasta, the hunter and the hunted, the stranger in his own home—is a commanding presence, who dominates the stage even when he can no longer see.

ANTIGONE

Although funeral practices vary from one culture to another, reverence for the dead and the assumption that we have a responsibility to dispose of corpses in a proper fashion are essential features of all human societies. But Sophocles' *Antigone* explores a situation where the duty to honor and bury the dead seems to conflict with another deep human imperative: the need to create strong community bonds, and to make sharp distinctions between enemies and friends, especially in times of war.

The play was probably composed earlier than *Oedipus the King*, around 442 B.C.E. But it is set at a later point in the chronology of the myth. Oedipus has made his terrible discoveries, and is dead. His two sons, Eteokles and Polyneikes, have fought over the inheritance of the throne of Thebes. While Eteokles had control of Thebes, Polyneikes gathered an army, with the help of the king of Argos, and set siege to the walled city with its seven gates. The brothers eventually faced each other in single combat, and both were killed. *Antigone* begins in the aftermath of this conflict. Eteokles, defender of the city, has been buried with full honor, but the body of Polyneikes, as leader of the army that attacked Thebes, still lies outside the city walls. Kreon, brother of Oedipus's wife, Jokasta, has now assumed the throne, and has sent out an edict that the body of the traitor Polyneikes must be left unburied.

Several earlier epic narratives and dramas had dealt with the story of Thebes, including Aeschylus's *Seven against Thebes*, which concentrates on the terrible killing of one brother by the other. Sophocles' treatment of the myth was original in a number of important ways. Earlier versions had described Kreon's refusal to bury any of the Argive dead; he was eventually persuaded to do so by the king of Argos. But Sophocles concentrates not on a whole army of dead soldiers but on a single dead brother, and he sets Kreon in conflict not with a fellow king, but with the members of his own family: his son, Haimon, his wife, Eurydike, and his niece, Antigone—characters who were sketchy or nonexistent in earlier versions. Sophocles transforms a story about a clash between two cities into a drama concerned with conflicts between community and family, between man and woman, between young and old, between religious and secular duties, and between the rights of the living and those of the dead. The play shows us a series of oppositions, between values or themes (love and hate, city and family, living and dead) and between characters: Antigone and her sister, Ismene; Kreon and his son, Haimon; and, above all, Kreon and Antigone.

Antigone often seems to invite us to take sides on points of principle, and many readers find themselves siding more with Antigone than with Kreon. Antigone's decision to bury her brother, a lone woman standing up against the king, seems an obvious instance of "speaking truth to power." Modern readers usually like rebels. Antigone seems, in several scenes of the play, to stand for values we can all cheer for—love, loyalty, and eternal, divine truth—against mere political expediency. She declares, in one inspiring and famous speech, that she opposes Kreon's edict, because she chooses to obey the "unwritten and infallible laws" of the gods.

But the play shows us that there is more than one side even to such points of principle as the duty to bury the dead. Sophocles' characters are complex, and neither Antigone nor Kreon can be reduced to a single moral stance. Antigone talks about what she owes to "the dead," as if she was committed to the burial of all family members; but in at least one instance, she suggests that her actions are inspired specifically by her dead brother: if she had lost a husband or a child, they could be replaced, but "with my mother and father in Hades, / a new brother could never bloom for me." Antigone's devotion to Polyneikes is presented as strange and extreme, almost erotic—in contrast to the moderate position of her sister, Ismene. Antigone's identity as a woman is equally complex. Burying the dead was normally the province of women in Greek society. But Antigone also shows an obsessive preoccupation with the "masculine" values of her own honor and glory, which she refuses to share with anybody. She faces death with courage, and even eagerness; but our final glimpse of her is as a vulnerable young girl, full of regret at the life she will never live.

Kreon, an equally complex figure, is far more sympathetic than he might seem at first glance. It is a mistake to see him simply as an embodiment of civic, secular law rather than the rights of individuals and the family. Kreon presents himself, not Antigone, as the real defender of family life and of religion. He suggests that Zeus, as the sky god who protects families, will support his attempts to impose order both on his city and on the members of his household: "A man who keeps his own house in order / will be perceived as righteous by his city." His debate with his son, Haimon, reminds us that Antigone is not necessarily acting against the values of the city: Kreon, not Antigone, may be the one acting out of "self-will," against the community. Moreover, Kreon's actions are clearly motivated by his own anxieties about his authority, as a ruler, as a father, and as a man. "Never let a woman overwhelm a king," he declares. Similarly, he is shocked by the idea that his son might dare to correct his father. He acknowledges, too late, that his inflexibility has destroyed his home.

The most important theme in *Antigone* is love: both sexual love and love of family. These are represented by two different words in Greek: *eros*, sexual desire, and *philia*, the love that binds us to members of our family and our close friends. Sophocles explores the implications of a traditional Greek ethical rule, that you should "love your friends, and hate your enemies." The play invites us to consider what happens when family members become political enemies: do they remain friends, or not? Is love more important than any ideological or moral principle? Or can love itself be taken too far?

The translations printed here use versions of the names and places that are closer to the Greek, rather than the more usual Latin forms—for instance, Korinth, not Corinth; Jokasta, not Jocasta; Bakkhos, not Bacchus, and so on.

Oedipus the King[1]

Characters

DELEGATION OF THEBANS, *mostly young (silent)*
OEDIPUS, *King of Thebes*
PRIEST OF ZEUS
KREON, *Jokasta's brother*
CHORUS *of older Theban men*
LEADER *(of the Chorus)*
TIRESIAS, *blind prophet of Apollo*
Boy to lead Tiresias (silent)
JOKASTA, *Oedipus' wife*
Attendants and maids (silent)
MESSENGER *from Korinth*
HERDSMAN, *formerly of Laios' house*
SERVANT, *from Oedipus' house*
ANTIGONE *and* ISMENE, *Oedipus' daughters (silent)*

SCENE: *Before the Royal Palace in Thebes. The palace has an imposing central double door. Two altars stand near it; one is to Apollo. The delegation of Thebans enters carrying olive branches wound with wool strips.* * * * *Oedipus enters through the great doors.*[2]

1. Translated by Robert Bagg.
2. All stage directions (in italics), as well as the list of characters, are by the translator.

OEDIPUS My children—*you* are the fresh green life
old Kadmos[3] nurtures and protects.
But why are you surging at *me* like this—
with your wool-strung boughs[4]—while
the city is swollen with howls of pain,
reeking incense, and prayers sung
to the Healing God?[5] To have others
tell me these things wouldn't be right,
my sons. So I've come out myself.

My name is Oedipus—the famous—
as everyone calls me.
Tell me, old man,
yours is the natural voice for the rest,
what troubles you? You're terrified?
Looking for reassurance? Be certain
I'll give you all the help I can.
I'd be a hard man if an approach
like yours failed to rouse my pity.

PRIEST You rule our land Oedipus! You can see
who comes to your altars—how varied
we are in years: children too weak-winged
to fly far, others hunched with age,
a few priests—I am a priest of Zeus—
joined by the best of our young lads.
More of us wait with wool-strung boughs
in the markets, and at Athena's two temples.
Some, at the river shrine, are watching
ashes for the glow of prophecy.[6]
You can see our city going under,
too feeble to lift its head clear
of the angry murderous waves.
Plague blackens our flowering farmland,
sickens our cattle where they graze.
Our women in labor give birth to nothing.

A burning god rakes his fire through our town;
he hates us with fever, he empties
the House of Kadmos, enriching
black Hades[7] with our groans and tears.
We haven't come to beg at your hearth
because we think you're the gods' equal.
We've come because you are the best man
at handling trouble or confronting gods.

3. The mythical founder of the city of Thebes.
4. Representing their status as supplicants.
5. Apollo.
6. Divinators and priests told the future by looking at the burnt embers of sacrificed animals.
7. Land of the dead.

You came to Thebes, you freed us
from the tax we paid with our lives
to that rasping Singer.[8] You did it with no
help from us. We had nothing to teach you.

People say—they believe!—you had a god's
help when you restored life to our city.
Oedipus, we need *now* the great power
men everywhere know you possess.
Find some way to protect us—learn it
from a god's whisper, or a man's.
This much I know: guidance
from men proven right in the past
will meet a crisis with the surest force.
Act as our greatest man! Act
as you did when you first seized fame!
We believe your nerve saved us then.
Don't let us look back on your rule and say,
He lifted us once, but then let us down.
Put us firmly back on our feet,
so Thebes will never fall again.

You were a bird from god, you brought good luck
the day you rescued us. Be that man now!
If you want to rule us, it's better
to rule the living than a barren waste;
walled cities and ships are worthless—
when they've been emptied of people.

OEDIPUS I do pity you, children. Don't think I'm unaware.
I know what need brings you: this sickness
ravages all of you. Yet, sick as you are,
not one of you suffers a sickness like mine.
Yours is a private grief, you feel
only what touches you. But my heart grieves
for you, for myself, and for our city.
You've come to wake me to all this.
There was no need. I haven't been sleeping.
I have wept tears enough, for long enough;
my mind has raced down every twisting path.
And after careful thought, I've set in motion
the only cure I could find: I've sent Kreon,
my wife's brother, to Phoibos at Delphi,[9]

8. The Sphinx, the winged female monster that terrorized the city of Thebes until her riddle was finally answered by Oedipus. The riddle comes in various different versions and is never actually cited by Sophocles, but one common version goes, "What walks on four feet in the morning, two at noon, and three at night?" Oedipus answered, "Man," because humans crawl in infancy, walk on two feet as adults, and walk with a stick in old age.

9. Apollo, whose oracle was at Delphi.

to hear what action or what word of mine
will save this town. Already, counting the days,
I'm worried: what is Kreon doing?
He takes too long, more time than he needs.
But when he comes, I'd be the criminal—*not*
to do everything god shows me to do.

PRIEST Well-timed! The moment you spoke,
your men gave the sign: Kreon's arriving.

OEDIPUS O Lord Apollo
may the luck he brings save us! Luck so bright
we can see it—just as we see him now.

(KREON *enters from the countryside, wearing a laurel crown speckled with red.*[1])

PRIEST He must bring pleasing news. If not, why would
he wear a laurel crown dense with berries?

OEDIPUS We'll know very soon; he's within earshot.
Prince! Brother kinsman, son of Menoikeos!
What kind of answer have you brought from god?

KREON A good one. No matter how dire, if troubles
turn out well—everything will be fine.

OEDIPUS What did the god say? Nothing you've said
so far alarms or reassures me.

KREON Do you want me to speak in front of these men?
If so, I will. If not, let's go inside.

OEDIPUS Speak here, to all of us. I suffer
more for them than for my own life.

KREON Then I'll report what I heard from Apollo.
He made his meaning very clear.
He commands we drive out what corrupts us,
what sickens our city. We now harbor
something incurable. He says: purge it.

OEDIPUS Tell me the source of our trouble.
How do we cleanse ourselves?

KREON By banishing a man or killing him. It's blood—
kin murder—that brings this storm on our city.

OEDIPUS Who is the man god wants us to punish?

KREON As you know, King, our city was ruled once
by Laios, before you came to take the helm.

OEDIPUS I've heard as much. Though I never saw him.

KREON Well, Laios was murdered. Now god tells you
plainly: with your own hands punish
the very men whose hands killed Laios.

OEDIPUS Where do I find these men? How do I track
vague footprints from a bygone crime?

KREON The god said: here, in our own land.
What we look for we can capture;
what we ignore goes free.

1. A sign of good news.

OEDIPUS Was Laios killed at home? Or in the fields?
Or did they murder him on foreign ground?

KREON He told us his journey would take him
close to god. But he never came back.

OEDIPUS Did none of his troop see and report
what happened? Isn't there anyone
to question whose answers might help?

KREON All killed but a single terrified
survivor, able to tell us but one fact.

OEDIPUS What was it? One fact might lead to many,
if we had one small clue to give us hope.

KREON They had the bad luck, he said, to meet bandits
who struck them with a force many hands strong.
This wasn't the violence of one man only.

OEDIPUS What bandit would dare commit such a crime . . .
unless somebody here had hired him?

KREON That was our thought, but after Laios
died, we were mired in new
troubles—and no avenger came.

OEDIPUS But here was your kingship murdered!
What kind of trouble could have blocked your search?

KREON The Sphinx's song. So wily, so baffling!
She forced us to forget the dark past,
to confront what lay at our feet.

OEDIPUS Then I'll go back, start fresh,
and light up that darkness.
Apollo was exactly right, and so were you,
to turn our minds back to the murdered man.
It's time I joined your search for vengeance;
our country and the god deserve no less.
This won't be on behalf of distant kin—
I'll banish this plague for my own sake.
Laios' killer might one day come for me,
exacting vengeance with that same hand.
Defending the dead man serves *my* interest.
Rise, children, quick, up from the altar,
pick up those branches that appeal to god.
Someone go call the people of Kadmos here—
tell them I'm ready to do anything.
With god's help our good luck
is assured; without it we're doomed.

(*Exit* OEDIPUS, *into the palace.*)

PRIEST Stand up, children. He has proclaimed
himself the cure we came to find.
May god Apollo, who sent the oracle,
be our savior and end this plague!

(*The Theban suppliants leave; the* CHORUS *enters.*)

CHORUS What will you say to Thebes,
Voice from Zeus?[2] What sweet sounds
convey your will from golden Delphi
to our bright city?
We're at the breaking point,
our minds are wracked with dread.
Our wild cries reach out to you,
Healing God from Delos[3]—
in holy fear we ask: does your will
bring a new threat, or has an old doom
come round again as the years wheel by?
Say it, Great Voice,
you who answer us always,
speak as Hope's golden child.

Athena, immortal daughter of Zeus,
your help is the first we ask;
then Artemis your sister
who guards our land, throned
in the heart of our city.
And Apollo, whose arrows
strike from far off![4] Our three
defenders against death: come now!
Once before, when ruin threatened,
you drove the flames of fever from our city.
Come to us now!
The troubles I suffer are endless.
The plague attacks our troops;
I can think of no weapon
that will keep a man safe.
Our rich earth shrivels what it grows;
women in labor scream, but no
children are born to ease their pain.
One life after another flies—
you see them pass—
like birds driving their strong wings
faster than flash-fire
to the death god's western shore.

Our city dies as its people die
these countless deaths, her children
rot in the streets, unmourned,
spreading more death.

2. Apollo was the son of Zeus, and spoke for him.

3. Island of Apollo's birth.

4. Athena: warrior goddess, daughter of Zeus, associated with wisdom and technology. Artemis: sister of Apollo, a goddess associated with hunting, childbirth, and the moon, who protected the weak. Apollo: god associated with sunlight, poetry, prophecy, healing, and plague. His arrows could cause disease.

Young wives and gray mothers
wash to our altars, their cries
carry from all sides, sobbing
for help, each lost in her pain.
A hymn rings out to the Healer;
an oboe answers,
keening in a courtyard.
Against all this, Goddess,
golden child of Zeus,[5]
send us the bright shining
face of courage.

Force that raging killer, the god Ares,[6]
to turn his back and run from our land.
He wields no weapons of war to kill us,
but burning with his fever,
we shout in the hot blast of his charge.
Blow Ares to the vast sea-room
of Amphitritê, banish him
under a booming wind
to jagged harbors in the roiling
seas off Thrace.[7] If night
doesn't finish the god's black work,
the day will finish it.
Lightning lurks
in your fiery will,
O Zeus, our Father. Blast it
into the god who kills us.
Apollo, lord of the morning light,
draw back your taut, gold-twined
bowstring, fire the sure arrows
that rake our attackers and keep them at bay.

Artemis, bring your radiance
into battle on bright quick feet
down through the morning hills.
I call on the god whose hair
is bound with gold,
the god who gave us our name,
Bakkhos!—the wine-flushed—who answers
the maenads' cries,[8] running

5. Athena. The Healer is Apollo.
6. God of war, not elsewhere associated with plague.
7. Thrace was a place in the northeast of Greece, known for its savagery. Amphitrite is a sea goddess, consort of Poseidon.
8. Bakkhos is god of wine; the maenads (or bacchantes) are his female followers.

beside them! Bakkhos,
come here on fire,
pine-torch flaring.
Face with us the one god
all the gods hate: Ares!

(**OEDIPUS** *has entered while the* **CHORUS** *was singing.*)

OEDIPUS I heard your prayer. It will be answered
if you trust and obey my words:
pull hard with me, bear down on the one cure
that will stop this plague. Help
will come, the evils will be gone.
I hereby outlaw the killer
myself, by my own words, though I'm a stranger
both to the crime and to accounts of it.

But unless I can mesh some clue I hold
with something known of the killer, I will
be tracking him alone, on a cold trail.
Since I've come late to your ranks, Thebans,
and the crime is past history,
there are some things that you,
the sons of Kadmos, must tell me.

If any one of you knows how Laios,
son of Labdakos, died, he must
tell me all that he knows.
He should not be afraid to name
himself the guilty one: I swear
he'll suffer nothing worse than exile.
Or if you know of someone else—
a foreigner—who struck the blow, speak up.
I will reward you now, I will thank you always.
But if you know the killer and don't speak—
out of fear—to shield kin or yourself,
listen to what that silence will cost you.
I order everyone in my land,
where I hold power and sit as king:

don't let that man under your roof,
don't speak with him, no matter who he is.
Don't pray or sacrifice with him,
don't pour purifying water for him.
I say this to all my people:
drive him from your houses.
He is our sickness. He poisons us.
This the Pythian god[9] has shown me.

9. Apollo, whose priestess at Delphi was called the Pythia.

This knowledge makes me an ally—
of both the god and the dead king.
I pray god that the unseen killer,
whoever he is, and whether he killed
alone or had help, be cursed with a life
as evil as he is, a life
of utter human deprivation.
I pray this, too: if he's found at my hearth,
inside my house, and I know he's there,
may the curses I aimed at others punish me.
I charge you all—act on my words,
for my sake and the god's, for our dead land
stripped barren of its harvests,
abandoned by its gods.
Even if god had not forced the issue,
this crime should not have gone uncleansed.
You should have looked to it! The dead man
was not only noble, he was your king!
But as my luck would have it,
I have his power, his bed—a wife
who shares our seed. And had she borne
the children of us both, she might
have linked us closer still. But Laios
had no luck fathering children, and Fate
itself came down on his head.
These concerns make me fight for Laios
as I would for my own father.
I'll stop at nothing to trace his murder
back to the killer's hand.
I act in this for Labdakos and Polydoros,
for Kadmos and Agenor[1]—all our kings.
I warn those who would disobey me:
god make their fields harvest dust,
their women's bodies harvest death.
O you gods,
let them die from the plague that kills
us now, or die from something worse.
As for the rest of us, who are
the loyal sons of Kadmos:
may justice go with us,
the gods be always at our side.

CHORUS King, your curse forces me to speak.
None of us is the killer.
And none of us can point to him.
Apollo ordered us to search,
it's up to him to find the killer.

1. Kadmos, son of Agenor, was founder and first king of Thebes; Polydoros was his son, and Labdakos, son of Polydoros, Laios's father, was his grandson.

OEDIPUS So he must. But what man can force
the gods to act against their will?
LEADER May I suggest a second course of action?
OEDIPUS Don't stop at two. Not if you have more.
LEADER Tiresias[2] is the man whose power of seeing
shows him most nearly what Apollo sees.
If we put our questions to him, King,
he could give us the clearest answers.
OEDIPUS But I've seen to this already.
At Kreon's urging I've sent for him—twice now.
I find it strange that he still hasn't come.
LEADER There were rumors—too faint and old to be much help.
OEDIPUS What were they? I'll examine every word.
LEADER They say Laios was killed by some travelers.
OEDIPUS That's something even I have heard.
But the man who did it—no one sees him.
LEADER If fear has any hold on him
he won't linger in Thebes, not after
he hears threats of the kind you made.
OEDIPUS If murder didn't scare him, my words won't.
LEADER There's the man who will convict him:
god's prophet, led here at last.
God gave to him what he gave no one else:
the truth—it's living in his mind.

(*Enter* TIRESIAS, *led by a* BOY.)

OEDIPUS Tiresias, you are master of the hidden world.
You can read earth and sky, you know
what knowledge to reveal and what to hide.
Though your eyes can't see it,
your mind is well aware of the plague
that afflicts us. Against it, we have no
savior or defense but you, my Lord.
If you haven't heard it from messengers,
we now have Apollo's answer: to end
this plague we must root out Laios' killers.
Find them, then kill or banish them.
Help us do this. Don't begrudge us
what you divine from bird cries, show us
everything prophecy has shown you.
Save Thebes! Save yourself! Save me!
Wipe out what defiles us, keep
the poison of our king's murder
from poisoning the rest of us.
We're in your hands. The best use a man
makes of his powers is to help others.
TIRESIAS The most terrible knowledge is the kind
it pays no wise man to possess.

2. Prophet of Thebes.

I knew this, but I forgot it.
I should never have come here.

OEDIPUS What? You've come, but with no stomach for this?

TIRESIAS Let me go home. Your life will then
be easier to bear—and so will mine.

OEDIPUS It's neither lawful nor humane
to hold back god's crucial guidance
from the city that raised you.

TIRESIAS What you've said has made matters worse.
I won't let that happen to me.

OEDIPUS For god's sake, if you know something,
don't turn your back on us! We're on our knees.

TIRESIAS You don't understand! If I spoke
of my grief, then it would be yours.

OEDIPUS What did you say? You know and won't help?
You would betray us all and destroy Thebes?

TIRESIAS I'll cause no grief to you or me. Why ask
futile questions? You'll learn nothing.

OEDIPUS So the traitor won't answer.
You would enrage a rock.
Still won't speak?
Are you so thick-skinned nothing touches you?

TIRESIAS You blame your rage on *me*? When you
don't see how she embraces you,
this fury you live with?[3] No, you blame me.

OEDIPUS Who wouldn't be enraged? Your refusal
to speak dishonors the city.

TIRESIAS It will happen. My silence can't stop it.

OEDIPUS If it must happen, you should tell me now.

TIRESIAS I'd rather not. Rage at that, if you like,
with all the savage fury in your heart.

OEDIPUS That's right. I *am* angry enough to speak
my mind. I think you helped plot the murder.
Did everything but kill him with your own hands.
Had you eyes, though, I would have said
you alone were the killer.

TIRESIAS That's your truth? Now hear mine:
honor the curse your own mouth spoke.
From this day on, don't speak to me
or to your people here. You are the plague.
You poison your own land.

OEDIPUS So. The appalling charge has been at last
flushed out, into the open. What makes you
think you'll escape?

TIRESIAS I have escaped.
I foster truth, and truth guards me.

3. "Rage" or "fury" is a feminine noun (*orge*) in the original, reinforcing the veiled reference to the female inhabitant of the palace, Jokasta.

OEDIPUS Who taught you this truth? Not your prophet's trade.
TIRESIAS You did. By forcing me to speak.
OEDIPUS Speak what? Repeat it so I understand.
TIRESIAS You missed what I said the first time?
Are you provoking me to make it worse?
OEDIPUS I heard you. But you made no sense. Try again.
TIRESIAS You killed the man whose killer you now hunt.
OEDIPUS The second time is even more outrageous.
You'll wish you'd never said a word.
TIRESIAS Shall I feed your fury with more words?
OEDIPUS Use any words you like. They'll be wasted.
TIRESIAS I say: you have been living unaware
in the most hideous intimacy
with your nearest and most loving kin,
immersed in evil that you cannot see.
OEDIPUS You think you can blithely go on like this?
TIRESIAS I can, if truth has any strength.
OEDIPUS Oh, truth has strength, but you have none.
You have blind eyes, blind ears, and a blind brain.
TIRESIAS And you're a desperate fool—throwing taunts at me
that these men, very soon, will throw at you.
OEDIPUS You survive in the grip of black
unbroken night! You can't harm me
or any man who can see the sunlight.
TIRESIAS I'm not the one who will bring you down.
Apollo will do that. You're his concern.
OEDIPUS Did you make up these lies? Or was it Kreon?
TIRESIAS Kreon isn't your enemy. You are.
OEDIPUS Wealth and a king's power,
the skill that wins every time—
how much envy, what malice they provoke!
To rob me of power—power I didn't ask for,
but which this city thrust into my hands—
my oldest friend here, loyal Kreon, worked
quietly against me, aching to steal my throne.
He hired for the purpose this fortuneteller—
conniving bogus beggar-priest!—a man
who knows what he wants but cannot seize it,
being but a blind groper in his art.
Tell us now, when or where did you ever
prove you had the power of a seer?
Why—when the Sphinx who barked black songs
was hounding us—why didn't you speak up
and free the city? Her riddle wasn't the sort
just anyone who happened by could solve:
prophetic skill was needed. But the kind
you learned from birds or gods failed you. It took
Oedipus, the know-nothing, to silence her.
I needed no help from the birds;

I used my wits to find the answer.
I solved it—the same man for whom you plot
disgrace and exile, so you can
maneuver close to Kreon's throne.
But your scheme to rid Thebes of its plague
will destroy both you and the man who planned it.
Were you not so frail, I'd make you
suffer exactly what you planned for me.

LEADER He spoke in anger, Oedipus—but so
did you, if you'll hear what we think.
We don't need angry words. We need insight—
how best to carry out the god's commands.

TIRESIAS You may be king, but my right
to answer makes me your equal.
In this respect, I am as much
my own master as you are.
You do not own my life.
Apollo does. Nor am I
Kreon's man. Hear me out.
Since you have thrown my blindness at me
I will tell you what your eyes don't see:
what evil you are steeped in.
You don't see
where you live or who shares your house.
Do you know your parents?
You are their enemy
in this life and down there with the dead.
And soon their double curse—
your father's and your mother's—
will lash you out of Thebes
on terror-stricken feet.
Your eyes, which now see life,
will then see darkness.
Soon your shriek will burrow
in every cave, bellow
from every mountain outcrop on Kithairon,[4]
when what your marriage means strikes home,
when it shows you the house
that took you in. You sailed
a fair wind to a most foul harbor.
Evils you cannot guess
will bring you down to what you are.
To what your children are.
Go on, throw muck at Kreon,
and at the warning spoken through my mouth.
No man will ever be
ground into wretchedness as you will be.

4. Mountain range near Thebes, on which Oedipus was left to die as an infant.

OEDIPUS Should I wait for him to attack me more?
May you be damned. Go. Leave my house
now! Turn your back and go.

TIRESIAS I'm here only because you sent for me.

OEDIPUS Had I known you would talk nonsense,
I wouldn't have hurried to bring you here.

TIRESIAS I seem a fool to you, but the parents
who gave you birth thought I was wise.

OEDIPUS What parents? Hold on. Who was my father?

TIRESIAS Today you will be born. Into ruin.

OEDIPUS You've always got a murky riddle in your mouth.

TIRESIAS Don't you outsmart us all at solving riddles?

OEDIPUS Go ahead, mock what made me great.

TIRESIAS Your very luck is what destroyed you.

OEDIPUS If I could save the city, I wouldn't care.

TIRESIAS Then I'll leave you to that. Boy, guide me out.

OEDIPUS Yes, let him lead you home. Here, underfoot,
you're in the way. But when you're gone,
you'll give us no more grief.

TIRESIAS I'll go. But first I must finish
what you brought me to do—
your scowl can't frighten me.
The man you have been looking for,
the one your curses threaten, the man
you have condemned for Laios' death:
I say that man is here.
You think he's an immigrant,
but he will prove himself a Theban native,
though he'll find no joy in that news.
A blind man who still has eyes,
a beggar who's now rich, he'll jab
his stick, feeling the road to foreign lands.

(OEDIPUS *enters the palace.*)[5]

He'll soon be shown father and brother
to his own children, son and husband
to the mother who bore him—she took
his father's seed and his seed,
and he took his own father's life.
You go inside. Think through
everything I have said.
If I have lied, say of me, then—
I have failed as a prophet.

(*Exit* TIRESIAS.)

CHORUS What man provokes
the speaking rock of Delphi?

5. Like all the stage directions, this one is added by the translator. If Oedipus is still within earshot, it is hard to understand how he could fail to make sense of Tiresias's words.

This crime that sickens speech
is the work of *his* bloody hands.
Now his feet will need to outrace
a storm of wild horses, for
Apollo is running him down,
armed with bolts of fire.
He and the Fates close in,
dread gods who never miss.

From snowfields
high on Parnassos
the word blazes out to us all:
track down the man no one can see.
He takes cover in thick brush,
he charges up the mountain
bull-like to its rocks and caves,
going his bleak, hunted way,
struggling to escape the doom
Earth spoke from her sacred mouth.[6]
But that doom buzzes low,
never far from his ear.

Fear is what the man who reads birds[7]
makes us feel, fear we can't fight.
We can't accept what he says
but have no power to challenge him.
We thrash in doubt, we can't see
even the present clearly,
much less the future.
And we've heard of no feud
embittering the House
of Oedipus in Korinth[8]
against the House of Laios here,
no past trouble and none now,
no proof that would make us blacken
our king's fame, as he seeks
to avenge our royal house
for this murder not yet solved.

Zeus and Apollo make no mistakes
when they predict what people do.
But there is no way to tell
whether an earthbound prophet sees
more of the future than we can—

6. Delphi was supposed to be the center of Earth.
7. Ancient priests and seers tried to interpret the will of the gods by observing the flight patterns of birds.
8. The chorus still assumes that Oedipus comes from the house of Korinth (more usually spelled Corinth), the son of Polybos and Merope.

though in knowledge and skill
one person may surpass another.
But never, not till I see the charges
proved against him,
will I give credence
to a man who blames Oedipus.
All of us saw his brilliance
prevail when the wingèd virgin
Sphinx came at him: he passed the test
that won the people's love.
My heart can't find him guilty.

(KREON *enters.*)

KREON Citizens, I hear that King Oedipus
has made a fearful charge against me.
I'm here to prove it false.
If he thinks anything I've said or done
has made this crisis worse, or injured him,
then I have no more wish to live.
This is no minor charge.
It's the most deadly I could suffer,
if my city, my own people—you!—
believe I'm a traitor.

LEADER He could have spoken in a flash
of ill-considered anger.

KREON Did he say *I* persuaded the prophet to lie?

LEADER That's what he said. What he meant wasn't clear.

KREON When he announced my guilt—tell me,
how did his eyes look? Did he seem sane?

LEADER I can't say. I don't question what my rulers do.
Here he comes, now, out of the palace.

(OEDIPUS *enters.*)

OEDIPUS So? You come here? You have the nerve
to face me in my own house? When you're exposed
as its master's murderer?
Caught trying to steal my kingship?
In god's name, what weakness did you see
in me that led you to plot this?
Am I a coward or a fool?
Did you suppose I wouldn't notice
your subtle moves? Or not fight back?
Aren't you attempting something
downright stupid—to win absolute power
without partisans or even friends?
For that you'll need money—and a mob.

KREON Now you listen to me.
You've had your say, now hear mine.
Don't judge until you've heard me out.

OEDIPUS You speak shrewdly, but I'm a poor learner

from someone I know is my enemy.

KREON I'll prove you are mistaken to think that.

OEDIPUS How can you prove you're not a traitor?

KREON If you think mindless presumption
is a virtue, then you're not thinking straight.

OEDIPUS If you think attacking a kinsman
will bring you no harm, you must be mad.

KREON I'll grant that. Now, how have I attacked you?

OEDIPUS Did you, or did you not, urge me
to send for that venerated prophet?

KREON And I would still give you the same advice.

OEDIPUS How long ago did King Laios . . .

KREON Laios? Did what? Why speak of him?

OEDIPUS . . . die in that murderous attack?

KREON That was far back in the past.

OEDIPUS Did this seer practice his craft here, then?

KREON With the same skill and respect he has now.

OEDIPUS Back then, did he ever mention my name?

KREON Not in my hearing.

OEDIPUS Didn't you try to hunt down the killer?

KREON Of course we did. We found out nothing.

OEDIPUS Why didn't your expert seer accuse me then?

KREON I don't know. So I'd rather not say.

OEDIPUS There is one thing you can explain.

KREON What's that? I'm holding nothing back.

OEDIPUS Just this. If that seer hadn't conspired with you,
he would never have called me Laios' killer.

KREON If he said that, *you heard him*, I didn't.
I think you owe me some answers.

OEDIPUS Question me. I have no blood on my hands.

KREON Did you marry my sister?

OEDIPUS Do you expect me to deny that?

KREON You both have equal power in this country?

OEDIPUS I give her all she asks.

KREON Do I share power with you both as an equal?

OEDIPUS You shared our power and betrayed us with it.

KREON You're wrong. Think it through rationally, as I have.
Who would prefer the anxiety-filled
life of a king to one that lets him sleep at night—
if his share of power still equaled a king's?
Nothing in my nature hungers for power—
for me it's enough to enjoy a king's rights,
enough for any prudent man. All I want,
you give me—and it comes with no fear.
To be king would rob my life of its ease.
How could my share of power be more pleasant
than this painless pre-eminence, this ready
influence I have? I'm not so misguided
that I would crave honors that are burdens.

But as things stand, I'm greeted and wished well
on all sides. Those who want something from you
come to me, their best hope of gaining it.
Should I quit this good life for a worse one?
Treason never corrupts a healthy mind.
I have no love for such exploits.
Nor would I join someone who did.
Test me. Go to Delphi yourself.
Find out whether I brought back
the oracle's exact words. If you find
I plotted with that omen-reader, seize me
and kill me—not on your authority
alone, but on mine, for I'd vote my own death.
But don't convict me because of a wild thought
you can't prove, one that only you believe.
There's no justice in your reckless confusion
of bad men with good men, traitors with friends.
To cast off a true friend is like suicide—
killing what you love as much as your life.
Time will instruct you in these truths, for time
alone is the sure test of a just man—
but you can know a bad man in a day.

LEADER That's good advice, my lord—
for someone anxious not to fall.
Quick thinkers can stumble.

OEDIPUS When a conspirator moves
abruptly and in secret against me,
I must out-plot him and strike first.
If I pause and do nothing, he
will take charge, and I will have lost.

KREON What do you want? My banishment?

OEDIPUS No. It's your death I want.

KREON Then start by defining "betrayal" . . .

OEDIPUS You talk as though you don't believe me.

KREON How can I if you won't use reason?

OEDIPUS I reason in my own interest.

KREON You should reason in mine as well.

OEDIPUS In a traitor's interest?

KREON What if you're wrong?

OEDIPUS I still must rule.

KREON Not when you rule badly.

OEDIPUS Did you hear him, Thebes!

KREON Thebes isn't yours alone. It's mine as well!

LEADER My Lords, stop this. Here's Jokasta
leaving the palace—just in time
to calm you both. With her help, end your feud.

(*Enter* JOKASTA *from the palace.*)

JOKASTA Wretched men! Why are you out here

so reckless, yelling at each other?
Aren't you ashamed? With Thebes sick and dying
you two fight out some personal grievance?
Oedipus. Go inside. Kreon, go home.
Don't make us all miserable over nothing.

KREON Sister, it's worse than that. Oedipus
your husband threatens either to drive me
from my own country, or to have me killed.

OEDIPUS That's right. I caught him plotting to kill me,
Lady. False prophecy was his weapon.

KREON I ask the gods to sicken and destroy me
if I did anything you charge me with.

JOKASTA Believe what he says, Oedipus.
Accept the oath he just made to the gods.
Do it for my sake too, and for these men.

LEADER Give in to him, Lord, we beg you.
With all your mind and will.

OEDIPUS What do you want me to do?

LEADER Believe him. This man was never a fool.
Now he backs himself up with a great oath.

OEDIPUS You realize what you're asking?

LEADER I do.

OEDIPUS Then say it to me outright.

LEADER Groundless rumor shouldn't be used by you
to scorn a friend who swears his innocence.

OEDIPUS You know, when you ask this of me
you ask for my exile—or my death.

LEADER No! We ask neither. By the god
outshining all others, the Sun—
may I die the worst death possible, die
godless and friendless, if I want those things.
This dying land grinds pain into my soul—
grinds it the more if the bitterness
you two stir up adds to our misery.

OEDIPUS Then let him go, though it means my death
or my exile from here in disgrace.
What moves my pity are your words, not his.
He will be hated wherever he goes.

KREON You are as bitter when you yield
as you are savage in your rage.
But natures like your own
punish themselves the most—
which is the way it should be.

OEDIPUS Leave me alone. Go.

KREON I'll go. You can see nothing clearly.
But these men see that I'm right.

(KREON *goes off.*)

LEADER Lady, why the delay? Take him inside.

JOKASTA I will, when you tell me what happened.
LEADER They had words. One drew a false
conclusion; the other took offense.
JOKASTA Both sides were at fault?
LEADER Both sides.
JOKASTA What did they say?
LEADER Don't ask that. Our land needs no more trouble.
No more trouble! Let it go.
OEDIPUS I know you mean well when you try to calm me,
but do you realize where it will lead?
LEADER King, I have said this more than once.
I would be mad, I would lose my good sense,
if I lost faith in you—you
who put our dear country
back on course when you found her
wandering, crazed with suffering.
Steer us straight, once again,
with all your inspired luck.
JOKASTA In god's name, King, tell me, too.
What makes your rage so relentless?
OEDIPUS I'll tell you, for it's you I respect, not the men.
Kreon brought on my rage by plotting against me.
JOKASTA Go on. Explain what provoked the quarrel.
OEDIPUS He says I murdered Laios.
JOKASTA Does he know this himself? Or did someone tell him?
OEDIPUS Neither. He sent that crooked seer to make the charge
so he could keep his own mouth innocent.
JOKASTA Then you can clear yourself of all his charges.
Listen to me, for I can make you believe
no man, ever, has mastered prophecy.
This one incident will prove it.
A long time back, an oracle reached Laios—
I don't say Apollo himself sent it,
but the priests who interpret him did.
It said that Laios was destined to die
at the hands of a son born to him and me.
Yet, as rumor had it, foreign bandits
killed Laios at a place where three roads meet.

(OEDIPUS *reacts with sudden intensity to her words.*)

But the child was barely three days old
when Laios pinned its ankle joints together,
then had it left, by someone else's hands,
high up a mountain far from any roads.
That time Apollo failed to make Laios die
the way he feared—at the hands of his own son.
Doesn't that tell you how much sense
prophetic voices make of our lives?
You can forget them. When god wants

something to happen, he makes it happen.
And has no trouble showing what he's done.

OEDIPUS Just now, something you said made my heart race.
Something . . . I remember . . . wakes up terrified.

JOKASTA What fear made you turn toward me and say that?

OEDIPUS I thought you said, Laios was struck down
where three roads meet.

JOKASTA That's the story they told. It hasn't changed.

OEDIPUS Tell me, where did it happen?

JOKASTA In a place called Phokis, at the junction
where roads come in from Delphi and from Daulis.

OEDIPUS How long ago was it? When it happened?

JOKASTA We heard the news just before you came to power.

OEDIPUS O Zeus! What did you will me to do?

JOKASTA Oedipus, you look heartsick. What is it?

OEDIPUS Don't ask me yet. Describe Laios to me.
Was he a young man, almost in his prime?

JOKASTA He was tall, with some gray salting his hair.
He looked then not very different from you now.

OEDIPUS Like me? I'm finished! It was aimed at me,
that savage curse I hurled in ignorance.

JOKASTA What did you say, my Lord? Your face scares me.

OEDIPUS I'm desperately afraid the prophet sees.
Tell me one more thing. Then I'll be sure.

JOKASTA I'm so frightened I can hardly answer.

OEDIPUS Did Laios go with just a few armed men,
or the large troop one expects of a prince?

JOKASTA There were five only, one was a herald.
And there was a wagon, to carry Laios.

OEDIPUS Ah! I see it now. Who told you this, Lady?

JOKASTA Our slave. The one man who survived and came home.

OEDIPUS Is he by chance on call here, in our house?

JOKASTA No. When he returned and saw
that you had all dead Laios' power,
he touched my hand and begged me to send him
out to our farmlands and sheepfolds,
so he'd be far away and out of sight.
I sent him. He was deserving—though a slave—
of a much larger favor than he asked.

OEDIPUS Can you send for him right away?

JOKASTA Of course. But why do you need him?

OEDIPUS I'm afraid, Lady, I've said too much.
That's why I want to see him now.

JOKASTA I'll have him come. But don't I have the right
to know what so deeply disturbs you, Lord?

OEDIPUS So much of what I dreaded has come true.
I'll tell you everything I fear.
No one has more right than you do,
to know the risks to which I'm now exposed.

Polybos of Korinth was my father.
My mother was Merope, a Dorian.
I was the leading citizen, when Chance
struck me a sudden blow.
Alarming as it was, I took it
much too hard. At a banquet,
a man who had drunk too much wine
claimed I was not my father's son.
Seething, I said nothing. All that day
I barely held it in. But next morning
I questioned mother and father. Furious,
they took their anger out on the man
who shot the insult. They reassured me.
But the rumor still rankled, it hounded me.
So with no word to my parents,
I traveled to the Pythian oracle.
But the god would not honor me
with the knowledge I craved.
Instead,
his words flashed other things—
horrible, wretched things—at me:
I would be my mother's lover,
I would show the world children
no one could bear to look at, I
would murder the father whose seed I am.
When I heard that, and ever after,
I traced the road back to Korinth
only by looking at the stars. I fled
to somewhere I'd never see outrages
like those the god promised, happen to me.
But my flight carried me to just the place
where, you tell me, the king was killed.
Oh, woman, here is the truth. As I approached
the place where three roads joined,
a herald, a colt-drawn wagon, and a man
like the one you describe, met me head on.
The man out front and the old man himself
began to crowd me off the road.
The driver, who's forcing me aside,
I smash in anger.
The old man watches me,
he measures my approach, then leans out
lunging with his two-spiked goad
dead at my skull. He's more than repaid:
I hit him so fast with the staff
this hand holds, he's knocked back
rolling off the cart. Where he lies, face up.
Then I kill them all.

But if this stranger and Laios . . . were the same blood,
whose triumph could be worse than mine?
Is there a man alive the gods hate more?
Nobody, no Theban, no foreigner,
can take me to his home.
No one can speak with me.
They all must drive me out.
I am the man—no one else—
who laid this curse on myself.
I make love to his wife with hands
repulsive from her husband's blood.
Can't you see that I'm evil,
my whole nature, utter filth?
Look, I must be banished. I must
never set eyes on my people, never
set foot in my homeland, because . . .
I'll marry my own mother,
kill Polybos my father,
who brought me up and gave me birth.
If someone said things like these
must be the work of a savage god,
he'd be speaking the truth. O you
pure and majestic gods! Never,
never, let the day such things happen
arrive for me. Let me never see it.
Let me vanish from men's eyes
before that doom comes down on me.

LEADER What you say terrifies us, Lord. But don't lose hope
until you hear from the eyewitness.

OEDIPUS That is the one hope I have left—to wait
for this man to come in from the fields.

JOKASTA When he comes, what do you hope to hear?

OEDIPUS This: if his story matches yours,
I will have escaped disaster.

JOKASTA What did I say that would make such a difference?

OEDIPUS He told you Laios was killed by bandits.
If he still claims there were several,
then I cannot be the killer. One man
cannot be many. But if he says: one man,
braving the road alone, did it,
there's no more doubt.
The evidence will drag me down.

JOKASTA You can be sure that was the way
he first told it. How can he take it back?
The entire city heard him, not just me.
Even if now he changes his story,
Lord, he could never prove that Laios'
murder happened as the god predicted.

Apollo

said plainly: my son would kill Laios.
That poor doomed child had no chance
to kill his father, for he was killed first.
After that, no oracle ever
made me look right, then left, in fear.

OEDIPUS You've thought this out well. Still, you must
send for that herdsman. Don't neglect this.

JOKASTA I'll send for him now. But come inside.
Would I do anything to displease you?

(**OEDIPUS** *and* **JOKASTA** *enter the palace.*)

CHORUS Let it be my good luck
to win praise all my life
for respecting the sky-walking laws
born to stride
through the light-filled heavens.
Olympos
alone was their father,
no human mind could conceive them;
those laws
neither sleep nor forget—
a mighty god lives on in them
who does not age.
A violent will[9]
fathers the tyrant,
and violence, drunk
on wealth and power,
does him no good;
he scales the heights—
until he's thrown
down to his doom,
where quick feet are no use.
But there's another fighting spirit
I ask god never to destroy—
the kind that makes our city thrive.
That god will protect us
I will never cease to believe.

But if a man
speaks and acts with contempt—
flouts the law, sneers
at the stone gods in their shrines—
let a harsh death punish
his doomed indulgence.
Even as he wins he cheats,
he denies himself nothing,
his hand reaches for things

9. The Greek word here for "will" is *hubris*, which usually connotes "violence."

too sacred to be touched.
When crimes like these, which god hates,
are not punished—but *honored*—
what good man will think his own life
safe from god's arrows piercing his soul?
Why should I dance[1] to *this* holy song?

If prophecies don't show the way
to events all men can see,
I will no longer honor
the holy place untouchable:
Earth's navel at Delphi.[2]
I will not go to Olympia
nor the temple at Abai.[3]
You, Zeus who hold power, if Zeus
lord of all is really who you are,
look at what's happening here:
prophecies made to Laios fade,
men ignore them;
Apollo is nowhere
glorified with praise;
the gods lose force.

(JOKASTA *enters from the palace carrying a suppliant's branch and some smoldering incense. She approaches the altar of Apollo near the palace door.*)

JOKASTA Lords of my country, this thought
came to me: to visit the gods' shrines
with incense and a bough in my hands.
Oedipus lets alarms of every kind
inflame his mind. He won't let past
experience calm his present fears,
as a man of sense would.
He's at the mercy of everybody's
terrifying words. Since he won't listen to me,
Apollo—you're the nearest god—

(*Enter* MESSENGER *from the countryside.*)

I come praying for your good will. Look,
here is my branch. Cleanse us, cure our sickness.
When we see Oedipus distraught, we all shake,
as though sailing with a fearful helmsman.

MESSENGER Can you point out to me, strangers,
the house where King Oedipus lives? Better
yet, tell me if you know where he is now.

1. The Greek verb here, *choreuein*, connotes "dance in a chorus," linking the mythical drama to the real theatrical performance.
2. Delphi had a sacred stone, supposed to be the belly button of the earth.
3. Olympia was the site of a sanctuary of Zeus; Abai is a city in central Greece.

LEADER That's the house where he lives, stranger. He's inside.
This woman is his wife and mother . . . of his children.

MESSENGER I wish her joy, and the family joy
that comes when a marriage bears fruit.

JOKASTA And joy to you, stranger, for those kind words.
What have you to tell us? Or to ask?

MESSENGER Great news, Lady, for you and your mate.

JOKASTA What news? Who sent you to us?

MESSENGER I come from Korinth.
You'll rejoice at my news, I'm sure—
but it may also make you grieve.

JOKASTA What? How can it possibly do both?

MESSENGER They're going to make him king. So say
the people who live on the isthmus.[4]

JOKASTA Isn't old Polybos still in power?

MESSENGER No longer. Death has laid him in the tomb.

JOKASTA You're saying, old man, Polybos has died?

MESSENGER Kill me if that's not the truth.

(JOKASTA *speaks to a servant girl, who then runs inside.*)

JOKASTA Girl, run to your master with the news.
You oracles of the gods! Where are you now?
The man Oedipus feared he would kill,
the man he ran from, that man's dead.
Chance killed him. Not Oedipus. Chance!

(OEDIPUS *enters quickly from the palace.*)

OEDIPUS Darling Jokasta, my loving wife,
why did you ask me to come out?

JOKASTA Listen to what this man has to say.
See what it does to god's proud oracle.

OEDIPUS Where's he from? What's his news?

JOKASTA From Korinth. Your father isn't . . .
Polybos . . . is no more . . . he's dead.

OEDIPUS Say it, old man. I want to hear it from your mouth.

MESSENGER If plain fact is what you want first,
have no doubt he is dead and gone.

OEDIPUS Was it treason, or did disease bring him down?

MESSENGER A slight push tips an old man into stillness.

OEDIPUS Then some sickness killed him?

MESSENGER That, and the long years he had lived.

OEDIPUS Oh, yes, wife! Why should we scour Pythian smoke
or fear birds shrieking overhead?
If signs like these had been telling the truth
I would have killed my father. But he's dead.
He's safely in the ground. And here I am,
who didn't lift a spear. Or did he
die of longing for me? That might

4. Korinth was built on an isthmus.

have been what my killing him meant.
This time, Polybos' death has dragged
those worthless oracles with him to Hades.

JOKASTA Didn't I tell you that before?

OEDIPUS You did. But I was still driven by fear.

JOKASTA Don't let these things worry you anymore.

OEDIPUS Not worry that I'll share my mother's bed?

JOKASTA Why should a human being live in fear?
Chance rules our lives!
Who has any sure knowledge of the future?
It's best to take life as it comes.
This marriage with your mother—don't fear it.
In their very dreams, too, many men
have slept with their mothers.
Those who believe such things mean nothing
will have an easier time in life.

OEDIPUS A brave speech! I would like to believe it.
But how can I if my mother's still living?
While she lives, I will live in fear,
no matter how persuasive you are.

JOKASTA Your father's tomb shines a great light.

OEDIPUS On him, yes! But I fear her. She's alive.

MESSENGER What woman do you fear?

OEDIPUS I dread that oracle from the god, stranger.

MESSENGER Would it be wrong for someone else to know it?

OEDIPUS No, you may hear it. Apollo told me
I would become my mother's lover, that I
would have my father's blood on these hands.
Because of that, I haven't gone near Korinth.
So far, I've been very lucky—and yet,
there's no greater pleasure
than to look our parents in the eyes!

MESSENGER Did this oracle drive you into exile?

OEDIPUS I didn't want to kill my father, old man.

MESSENGER Then why haven't I put your fears to rest,
King? I came here hoping to be useful.

OEDIPUS I would give anything to be free of fear.

MESSENGER I confess I came partly for that reason—
to be rewarded when you've come back home.

OEDIPUS I will never live where my parents live.

MESSENGER My son, you can't possibly know what you're doing.

OEDIPUS Why is that, old man? In god's name, tell me.

MESSENGER Is it because of them you won't go home?

OEDIPUS I am afraid Apollo spoke the truth.

MESSENGER Afraid you'd do your parents unforgivable harm?

OEDIPUS Exactly that, old man. I am in constant fear.

MESSENGER Your fear is groundless. Do you understand?

OEDIPUS How can it be groundless if I'm their son?

MESSENGER But Polybos was no relation to you.

OEDIPUS What? Polybos was not my father?
MESSENGER No more than I am. Exactly the same.
OEDIPUS How the same? He fathered me and you didn't.
MESSENGER He didn't father you any more than I did.
OEDIPUS Why did he say, then, that I was his son?
MESSENGER He took you from my hands as a gift.
OEDIPUS He loved me so much—knowing I came from you?
MESSENGER He had no children. That moved him to love you.
OEDIPUS And you? Did you buy me? Or find me somewhere?
MESSENGER I found you in the wooded hollows of Kithairon.
OEDIPUS Why were you wandering way out there?
MESSENGER I had charge of the sheep grazing those slopes.
OEDIPUS A migrant hired to work our flocks?
MESSENGER I saved your life that day, my son.
OEDIPUS When you picked me up, what was wrong with me?
MESSENGER Your ankles know. Let them tell you.
OEDIPUS Ahh! Why do you bring up that ancient wound?
MESSENGER Your ankles had been pinned. I set you free.
OEDIPUS From birth I've carried the shame of those scars.
MESSENGER That was the luck that named you, Oedipus.[5]
OEDIPUS Did my mother or my father do this to me?
Speak the truth for god's sake.
MESSENGER I don't know. The man who gave you to me
will know.
OEDIPUS You took me from someone?
You didn't chance on me yourself?
MESSENGER I took you from another shepherd.
OEDIPUS Who was he? Tell me as plainly as you can.
MESSENGER He was known as someone who worked for Laios.
OEDIPUS The same Laios who was once king *here*?
MESSENGER The same. This man worked as his shepherd.
OEDIPUS Is he alive? Can I see him?
MESSENGER Someone from here could answer that better.
OEDIPUS Does anyone here know what has become
of this shepherd? Has anyone seen him
in town or in the fields? Speak up now.
The time has come to make everything known.
LEADER I believe he means that same herdsman
you've already sent for. Your wife
would be the best one to ask.
OEDIPUS Lady, do you
recall the man we sent for?
Is that the man he means?
JOKASTA Why ask about him? Don't listen to him.
Ignore his words. Forget he said them.

5. In Greek the name *Oedipus* suggests "Swollen Foot."

OEDIPUS With clues like these in my hands, how can I
fail to solve the mystery of my birth?
JOKASTA For god's sake, if you care about your life,
give up your search. Let my pain be enough!
OEDIPUS You'll be fine! What if my mother was born
from slaves—from three generations of slaves—
how could that make you lowborn?
JOKASTA Listen to me: I beg you. Don't do this.
OEDIPUS I cannot listen. I must have the truth.
JOKASTA I'm thinking only of what's best for you.
OEDIPUS *What's best for me* exasperates me now.
JOKASTA You poor child! Never find out who you are.
OEDIPUS Someone, bring me the herdsman. Let
that woman glory in her precious birth.
JOKASTA Oh you poor doomed child! That is the only name
I can call you now. None other, forever!

(JOKASTA *runs into the palace.*)

LEADER Why has she left like that, Oedipus,
driven off by a savage grief? I'm afraid
something horrendous will break this silence.
OEDIPUS Let it burst! My seed may well *be* common!
Even so, I still must know who I am.
The meanness of my birth may shame
her womanly pride. But since, in my
own eyes, I am the child of Luck—
she is the source of my well-being—
never will I be dishonored.
Luck is the mother who raised me; the months
are my brothers, who've seen me through
the low times in my life and the high ones.
Those are the powers that made me.
I could never betray them *now*—
by calling off the search
for the secret of my birth!
CHORUS By the gods of Olympos, if I have
a prophet's range of eye and mind—
tomorrow's moonlight
will shine on you, Kithairon.
Oedipus will honor you—
his native mountain,
his nurse, his mother. Nothing
will keep us from dancing
then, mountain joyful to our king!
We call out to Phoibos Apollo:
be the cause of our joy!

(CHORUS *turns toward* OEDIPUS.)

My son, who was your mother?
Which nymph bore you to Pan,[6]
the mountain rover?
Was it Apollo's bride
to whom you were born
in the grassy highlands?
Or did Hermes, Lord of Kyllene,
or Bakkhos of the mountain peaks,
take you—a sudden joy—
from nymphs of Helikon,
whose games he often shares?[7]

OEDIPUS Old men, if it's possible
to recognize a man I've never met,
I think I see the herdsman we've been waiting for.
Our fellow would be old, like the stranger approaching.
Those leading him are my own men.
But I expect you'll know him better.
Some of you will know him by sight.

(*Enter* HERDSMAN, *led by Oedipus' servants.*)

LEADER I do know him. He is from Laios' house,
a trustworthy shepherd if he ever had one.
OEDIPUS Korinthian, I'll ask you to speak first:
is this the man you mean?
MESSENGER You're looking at him.
OEDIPUS Now you, old man. Look at me.
Answer every question I ask you.
Did you once come from Laios' house?
HERDSMAN I did. I wasn't a bought slave,
I was born and raised in their house.
OEDIPUS What was your job? How did you spend your time?
HERDSMAN My life I have spent tending sheep.
OEDIPUS In what region did you normally work?
HERDSMAN Mainly Kithairon, and the country thereabouts.

(OEDIPUS *gestures toward the* MESSENGER.)

OEDIPUS That man. Do you recall ever seeing him?
HERDSMAN Recall how? Doing what? Which man?

(OEDIPUS *goes to the* MESSENGER *and puts*
his hand on him.)

OEDIPUS This man right here. Have you ever seen him before?
HERDSMAN Not that I recognize—not right away.
MESSENGER It's no wonder, master. His memory's faded,
but I'll revive it for him. I'm sure he knows me.
We worked the pastures on Kithairon together—

6. Pan was a woodland god, patron of shepherds.
7. Dionysos (Bakkhos), god of wine, like Pan and Hermes, haunted the wild places, woods, and mountains. Hermes was born on Mount Kyllene in Arcadia.

he with his two flocks, me with one—
for three whole grazing seasons, from early spring
until Arcturos[8] rose. When the weather turned cold
I'd drive my flocks home to their winter pens,
he'd drive his away to Laios' sheepfolds.
Do I describe what happened, old friend? Or don't I?

HERDSMAN That's the truth, but it was so long ago.

MESSENGER Do you remember giving me a boy
I was to raise as my own son?

HERDSMAN What? Why ask me that?

MESSENGER There, my friend, is the man who was that boy.

(*He nods toward* OEDIPUS.)

HERDSMAN Damn you! Shut up and say nothing.

OEDIPUS Don't attack him for his words, old man.
Yours beg to be punished far more than his.

HERDSMAN Tell me, royal master, what've I done wrong?

OEDIPUS You didn't answer him about the boy.

HERDSMAN He's trying to make something out of nothing.

OEDIPUS Speak of your own free will. Or under torture.

HERDSMAN Dear god! I'm an old man. Don't hurt me.

OEDIPUS One of you, bind his arms behind his back.

(SERVANTS *approach the* HERDSMAN *and*
start to seize his arms.)

HERDSMAN Why this, you doomed man? What else must you know?

OEDIPUS Did you give him the child, as he claims you did?

HERDSMAN I did. I wish that day I had died.

OEDIPUS You will die if you don't speak the truth.

HERDSMAN Answering you is what will get me killed.

OEDIPUS I think this man is deliberately stalling.

HERDSMAN No! I've said it once. I gave him the boy.

OEDIPUS Was the boy from your house? Or someone else's?

HERDSMAN Not from my house. Someone gave him to me.

OEDIPUS The person! Name him! From what house?

HERDSMAN Don't ask me that, master. For god's sake, don't.

OEDIPUS If I have to ask one more time, you'll die.

HERDSMAN He was a child from the house of Laios.

OEDIPUS A slave? Or a child born of Laios' blood?

HERDSMAN Help me! I am about to speak terrible words.

OEDIPUS And I to hear them. But hear them I must!

HERDSMAN The child was said to be Laios' own son.
Your lady in the house would know that best.

OEDIPUS *She* gave the child to you?

HERDSMAN She gave him, King.

OEDIPUS To do what?

HERDSMAN I was to let it die.

8. The main star in the constellation Boötes; its appearance in the sky, just before dawn, in September, signals the end of summer.

OEDIPUS Kill her own child?
HERDSMAN She feared prophecies.
OEDIPUS What prophecies?
HERDSMAN That this child would kill his father.
OEDIPUS Why, then, did you give him to this old man?
HERDSMAN Out of pity, master. I hoped this man
would take him back to his own land.
But that man saved him for this—
the worst grief of all. If the child
he speaks of is you, master, now you
know: your birth has doomed you.
OEDIPUS All! All! It all happened!
It was all true. O light! Let this
be the last time I look on you.
You see now what I am—
the child who must not be born!
I loved where I must not love!
I killed where I must not kill!

(OEDIPUS *runs into the palace.*)

CHORUS Men and women who live and die,
I set no value on your lives.
Which one of you ever, reaching
for blessedness that lasts,
finds more than what *seems* blest?
You live in that seeming
a while, then it vanishes.
Your fate teaches me this, Oedipus,
yours, you suffering man, the story
god spoke through you: never call
any man fortunate.

O Zeus, no man drew a bow like this man!
He shot his arrow home,
winning power, pleasure, wealth;
he killed the virgin Sphinx,
who sang the god's dark oracles;
her claws were hooked and sharp.
He fought off death in our land;
he towered against its threat.
Since those times I've called you my king,
honoring you mightily, my Oedipus,
who wielded the great might of Thebes.

But now—nobody's story
has the sorrow of yours,
O my so famous Oedipus—
the same great harbor

welcomed you
first as child, then as father
tumbling upon your bridal bed.
How could the furrows your father plowed, doomed
man, how could they suffer so long in silence?

Time, who sees all, caught you
living a life you never willed.
Time damns this marriage that is
no marriage, where the fathered child
fathered children himself.
O son of Laios, I wish
I'd never seen you! I fill my lungs,
I sing with all my power
the plain truth in my heart.
Once you gave me new breath,
O my Oedipus!—but now
you close my eyes in darkness.

(*Enter* SERVANT *from the palace.*)

SERVANT You've always been our land's most honored men.
If you still have a born Theban's love
for the House of Labdakos, you'll be crushed
by what you're about to see and hear.
No rivers could wash this house clean—
not the Danube, not the Rion—
it hides so much evil that now
is coming to light. What happened here
was not involuntary evil, it was willed.
The griefs that punish us the most
are those we've chosen for ourselves.

LEADER We already knew more than enough
to make us grieve. Do you have more to tell?

SERVANT It is the briefest news to say or hear.
Our royal lady Jokasta is dead.

LEADER That pitiable woman. How did she die?

SERVANT She killed herself. You will be spared the worst—
since you weren't there to see it.
But you will hear, exactly as I can
recall it, what that wretched woman suffered.
She came raging through the courtyard
straight for her marriage bed, the fists
of both her hands clenched in her hair.
Once in, she slammed the doors shut and called out
to Laios, so long dead; she remembered
his living sperm of long ago, who killed Laios,
while she lived on to breed with her son
more ruined children.

She grieved for the bed
she had loved in, giving birth
to all those doubled lives—
husband fathered by husband,
children sired by her child.
From this point on I don't know how she died—
Oedipus burst in shouting,
distracting us from her misery.
We looked on, stunned, as he plowed through us
raging, asking us for a spear,
asking for the wife who was no wife
but the same furrowed twice-mothering earth
from whom he and his children sprang.
He was frantic, yet some divine hand
drove him toward his wife—none of us near him did.
As though someone were guiding him, he lunged,
with a savage yell, at the double doors,
wrenching the bolts from their sockets.
He burst into the room. We saw her there:
the woman above us, hanging by the neck,
swaying there in a noose of tangled cords.
He saw. And bellowing in anguish
he reached up, loosening the noose that held her.
With the poor lifeless woman laid out on the ground
this, then, was the terror we saw: he pulled
the long pins of hammered gold clasping her gown,
held them up, and punched them into his eyes,
back through the sockets. He was screaming:
"Eyes, now you will not, no, never
see the evil I suffered, the evil I caused.
You will see blackness—where once
were lives you should never have lived to see,
yearned-for faces you so long failed to know."
While he howled out these tortured words—
not once, but many times—his raised hands
kept beating his eyes. The blood kept coming,
drenching his beard and cheeks. Not a few wet drops,
but a black storm of bloody hail lashing his face.

What this man and this woman did
broke so much evil loose! That evil joins
the whole of both their lives in grief.
The happiness they once knew was real,
but now that happiness is in ruins—
wailing, death, disgrace. Whatever misery
we have a name for, is here.

LEADER Has his grief eased at all?

SERVANT He shouts for someone to open the door bolts:

"Show this city its father-killer," he cries,
"Show it its mother . . ." He said the word, I can't.
He wants to banish himself from the land,
not doom this house any longer
by living here, under his own curse.
He's so weak, though, he needs to be helped.
No one could stand up under a sickness like his.
Look! The door bolts are sliding open.
You will witness a vision of such suffering
even those it revolts will pity.

(OEDIPUS *emerges from the slowly opening palace doors. He is blinded. * * * He moves with the aid of a servant.*)

LEADER Your pain is terrible to see,
pure, helpless anguish,
more moving than anything
my eyes have ever touched.
O man of pain,
where did your madness come from?
What god would go
to such inhuman lengths
to savage your defenseless life?

(*Moans.*)

I cannot look at you—
though there's so much
to ask you, so much to learn,
so much that holds my eyes—
so strong are the shivers of awe
you send through me.

OEDIPUS Ahhh! My life
screams in pain.
Where is my misery
taking me?
How far does my voice fly,
fluttering out there
on the wind?
O god, how far have you thrown me?

LEADER To a hard place. Hard to watch, hard to hear.

OEDIPUS Darkness buries me in her hate, takes me
in her black hold.
Unspeakable blackness.
It can't be fought off,
it keeps coming,
wafting evil all over me.
Ahhh!
Those goads piercing my eyes,
those crimes stabbing my mind,
strike through me—one deep wound.

LEADER It is no wonder you feel
nothing but pain now,
both in your mind and in your flesh.

OEDIPUS Ah friend, you're still here,
faithful to the blind man.
I know you are near me. Even
in my darkness I know your voice.

LEADER You terrify us. How could you
put out your eyes? What god drove you to it?

OEDIPUS It was Apollo who did this.
He made evil, consummate evil,
out of my life.
But the hand
that struck these eyes
was my hand.
I in my wretchedness
struck me, no one else did.
What good was left for my eyes to see?
Nothing in this world could I see now
with a glad heart.

LEADER That is so.

OEDIPUS Whom could I look at? Or love?
Whose greeting could I answer
with fondness, friends?
Take me quickly from this place.
I am the most ruined, the most cursed,
the most god-hated man who ever lived.

LEADER You're broken by what happened, broken
by what's happening in your own mind.
I wish you'd never learned the truth.

OEDIPUS May he die, the man
who found me in the pasture,
who unshackled my feet,
who saved me from that death for a worse life,
a life I cannot thank him for.
Had I died then, I would have caused
no great grief to my people and myself.

LEADER I wish he had let you die.

OEDIPUS I wouldn't have come home to kill my father,
no one could call me lover
of her from whose body I came.
I have no god now.
I'm son to a fouled mother,
I fathered children in the bed
where my father once gave me
deadly life. If ever an evil
rules all other evils
it is my evil, the life
god gave to Oedipus.

LEADER I wish I could say you acted wisely.
You would have been better off dead than blind.

OEDIPUS There was no better way than mine.
No more advice! If I had eyes, how could
they bear to look at my father in Hades?
Or at my devastated mother? Not even
hanging could right the wrongs I did them both.
You think I'd find the sight of my children
delightful, born to the life mine must live?
Never, ever, delightful to my eyes!
Nor this town, its wall, gates and towers;
nor the sacred images of our gods.
I severed myself from these joys when I
banished the vile killer—myself!—
totally wretched now, though I was raised
more splendidly than any Theban.
But now the gods have proven me
defiled, and of Laios' own blood.
And once I've brought such disgrace on myself,
how could I look calmly on my people?
I could not! If I could deafen my ears
I would. I'd deaden my whole body,
go blind and deaf to shut those evils out.
The silence in my mind would be sweet.
O Kithairon, why did you take me in?
Or once you had seized me, why didn't you
kill me instantly, leaving no trace of my birth?
O Polybos and Korinth, and that palace
they called the ancient home of my fathers!
I was their glorious boy growing up,
but under that fair skin
festered a hideous disease.
My vile self now shows its vile birth.
You,
three roads, and you, darkest ravine,
you, grove of oaks, you, narrow place
where three paths drank blood from my hands,
my fathering blood pouring into you:
Do you remember what I did while you watched?
And when I came here, what I did then?
O marriages! You marriages! You created us,
we sprang to life, then from that same seed
you burst fathers, brothers, sons,
kinsmen shedding kinsmen's blood,
brides and mothers and wives—the most loathsome
atrocities that strike mankind.
I must not name what should not be.
If you love the gods, hide me out there,
kill me, heave me into the sea,

anywhere you can't see me.
Come, take me. Don't shy away. Touch
this human derelict. Don't fear me, trust me.
No other man, only myself,
can be afflicted with my sorrows.

LEADER Here's Kreon. He's come when you need him,
to take action or to give you advice.
He is the only ruler we have left
to guard Thebes in your place.

OEDIPUS Can I say anything he'll listen to?
Why would he believe me?
I wronged him so deeply.
I proved myself so false to him.

(KREON *enters.*)

KREON I haven't come to mock you, Oedipus.
I won't dwell on the wrongs you did me.

(KREON *speaks to the attendants.*)

Men, even if you've no respect
for a fellow human being, show some
for the life-giving flame of the Sun god:
don't leave this stark defilement out here.
The earth, the holy rain, the light, can't bear it.

Quickly, take him back to the palace.
If these sorrows are shared
only among the family,
that will spare us further impiety.

OEDIPUS Thank god! I feared much worse from you.
Since you've shown me, a most vile man,
such noble kindness, I have one request.
For your sake, not for mine.

KREON What is it? Why do you ask me like that?

OEDIPUS Expel me quickly to some place
where no living person will find me.

KREON I would surely have done that. But first
I need to know what the god wants me to do.

OEDIPUS He's given his command already.
I killed my father. I am unholy. I must die.

KREON So the god said. But given
the crisis we're in, we had better
be absolutely sure before we act.

OEDIPUS You'd ask about a broken man like me?

KREON Surely, by now, you're willing to trust god.

OEDIPUS I am. But now I must ask for something
within your power. I beg you! Bury her
who's lying inside—as you think proper.
Give her the rites due your kinswoman.
As for me, don't condemn my father's city
to house me while I'm still alive.

Let me live out my life on Kithairon,
the very mountain—
the one I've made famous—
that my father and mother chose for my tomb.
Let me die there, as my parents decreed.
And yet, I know this much:
no sickness can kill me. Nothing can.
I was saved from that death
to face an extraordinary evil.
Let my fate take me now, where it will.

My children, Kreon. My sons.
They're grown now. They won't need your help.

They'll find a way to live anywhere.
But my poor wretched girls, who never
ate anywhere but at my table;
they've never lived apart from me.
I fed them with my own hands.
Care for them.
If you're willing, let me touch them now,
let me give in to my grief.
Grant it Kreon, from your great heart.
If I could touch them, I would
imagine them as my eyes once saw them.

(*The gentle sobbing of Oedipus' two daughters is heard offstage. Soon two small girls enter.*)

What's this?
O gods, are these my children sobbing?
Has Kreon pitied me?
Given me my own dear children?
Has he?

KREON I have. I brought them to you
because I knew how much joy,
as always, you would take in them.

OEDIPUS Bless this kindness of yours. Bless your luck.
May the gods guard you better than they did me.
Children, where are you? Come to me.
These are your brother's hands, hands
of the man who created you, hands that caused
my once bright eyes to go dark.
He, children, saw nothing, knew nothing,
he fathered you where his own life began,
where his own seed grew. Though I can't
see you, I can weep for you . . .

(OEDIPUS *takes his daughters in his arms.*)

when I think how bitter your lives will be.
I know the life that men will make you live.
What public gatherings, what festivals

could you attend? None! You would be sent home
in tears, without your share of holy joy.
When the time comes to marry, my daughters,
what man will risk the revulsion—
the infamy!—that will wound you
just as it wounded your parents?
What evil is missing? Your father killed
his father, he had children with the mother
who bore him, fathered you
at the source of his own life.
Those are the insults
you will face. Who will marry you?
No one, my children. You will grow old
unmarried, living a dried-up childless life.
Kreon, you're all the father they have now.
The parents who conceived them are both lost.
Keep these two girls from rootless wandering,
unmarried and helpless. They are your kin.
Don't bring them down to what I am.
Pity them. They are so young, and but for you,
alone. Touch my hand, kind man,
make that touch your promise.

(KREON *touches him.*)

Children, had you been old enough
to comprehend, I would have taught you more.
Now, all I can do is ask you to pray:
that you live only where you're welcomed;
that your lives be happier than mine was,
the father from whose seed you were born.

KREON Enough grief. Go inside now.
OEDIPUS Bitter words, which I must obey.
KREON Time runs out on all things.
OEDIPUS Grant my request before I go.
KREON Speak.
OEDIPUS Banish me from my homeland.
KREON Ask god to do that, not me.
OEDIPUS I am the man the gods hate most.
KREON Then you will have your wish.
OEDIPUS You consent?
KREON I never promise if I can't be sure.
OEDIPUS Then lead me inside.
KREON Come. Let go of your children now.
OEDIPUS Don't take them from me.
KREON Give up your power, too.
You won the power once, but you couldn't
keep it to the end of your life.

(KREON *leads* OEDIPUS *into the palace.*)

CHORUS Thebans, that man is the same Oedipus
whose great mind solved the famous riddle.
He was a most powerful man.
Which of us seeing his glory, his prestige,
did not wish his luck could be ours?
Now look at what wreckage the seas
of savage trouble have made of his life.
To know the truth of a man, wait
till you see his life end.
On that day, look at him.
Don't claim any man is god's friend
until he has passed through life
and crossed the border into death—
never having been god's victim.

(*All leave.*)

Antigone[1]

CHARACTERS

ANTIGONE, *daughter of Oedipus*
ISMENE, *daughter of Oedipus*
CHORUS *of Theban Elders*
LEADER (*of the Chorus*)
KREON, *King of Thebes, uncle of Antigone and Ismene*
GUARD
Kreon's Men (*silent*)
HAIMON, *son of Kreon*
TIRESIAS, *prophet of Thebes*
Lad (*silent*)
MESSENGER
EURYDIKE, *wife of Kreon*

SCENE: *Dawn in front of Kreon's palace in Thebes, the day after the battle in which the Theban defenders repelled an attack on the city by an Argive coalition that included the rebel Polyneikes, elder son of Oedipus. Polyneikes and his younger brother Eteokles, who has remained loyal to Thebes, have killed each other simultaneously in face-to-face combat at one of Thebes' seven gates. Kreon has suddenly seized the throne.* * * * *Antigone and Ismene enter through the central doors.*[2]

1. Translated by Robert Bagg.

2. All stage directions (in italics), as well as the list of characters, are by the translator.

ANTIGONE Ismene, love! My own kind! Born
like me from that same womb!
Can you think of one evil—
of all those Oedipus started—
that Zeus hasn't used our own lives
to finish? There's nothing—no pain
no shame, no terror, no humiliation!—
you and I haven't seen and shared.
Now there's this new command
our commander in chief[3]
imposes on the whole city—
do you know about it?
Have you heard? *You don't know*,
do you? It threatens our loved ones
as if they were our enemies!

ISMENE No word of our family has reached *me*,
Antigone, welcome or painful,
not since we sisters lost our brothers
in one day, when their hands struck
the double blow that killed them both.
And since the Argive army fled last night
I've heard nothing that could improve our luck—
or make it any worse.

ANTIGONE That's what I thought.
That's why I've brought you out past the gates—
where no one but you can hear what I say.

ISMENE What's wrong?
It's plain something you've heard makes you livid.

ANTIGONE It's Kreon. The way he's treated our brothers.
Hasn't he buried one with honor?
But he's shamed the other. Disgraced him!
Eteokles, they say, was laid to rest
according to law and custom.
The dead will respect him in Hades.
But Polyneikes' sorry body can't be touched.
The city is forbidden to mourn him or bury him
—no tomb, no tears. Convenient forage
for cruising birds to feast their fill.
That's the clear order our good general
gives you and me—yes, I said me!
They say he's coming here to proclaim it
in person to those who haven't heard it.
This is not something he takes lightly.
Violate any provision—the sentence is
you're stoned to death in your own city.

3. Kreon.

Now you know.
And soon you'll prove
how nobly born you really are.
Or did our family breed a coward?

ISMENE If that's the bind we're in, you poor thing,
what good can *I* do by yanking the knot
tighter—*or* by trying to pry it loose?

ANTIGONE Make up your mind. Will you join me?
Share the burden?

ISMENE At what risk? What are you asking?

ANTIGONE (*Raising up her hands.*)
Will you help these hands lift his body?

ISMENE You want to bury him? Break the law?

ANTIGONE I'm going to bury my brother—your brother!—
with or without your help. I won't betray him.

ISMENE You scare me, sister. Kreon's forbidden this.

ANTIGONE He's got *no right* to keep me from what's mine!

ISMENE He's mine too!
Just think what our father's
destruction meant for us both.
Because of those horrible deeds—
all self-inflicted, all self-detected
he died hated and notorious,[4]
his eyes battered into blindness
by his own hands. And then
his wife and mother—two roles -hanged herself
for one woman—disposed
of her life with a noose
of twisted rope. And now
our poor brothers die the same day
in a mutual act of kin murder!
Think how much worse
our own deaths will be—abandoned
as we are—if we defy the king's
proclamation and his power.
Remember, we're women. How
can we fight men. They're stronger.
We must accept these things—and worse to come.
I want the Spirits of the Dead

4. This play was written before *Oedipus the King* and *Oedipus at Colonus*. Each of the plays uses a different version of the myth. In *Oedipus at Colonus*, the king ends his life with redemption and triumph.

to understand this: I'm not free.
I must obey whoever's in charge.
It's crazy to attempt the impossible!

ANTIGONE Then I'll stop asking you! And if you change
your mind, I won't accept your help.
Go be the person you've chosen to be.
I'll bury Polyneikes myself. I'll do
what's honorable, and then I'll die.
I who love him will lie down
next to him who loves me—
my criminal conduct blameless!—
for I owe more to the dead, with whom
I will spend a much longer time,
than I will ever owe to the living.
Go ahead, please yourself—defy
laws the gods expect us to honor.

ISMENE I'm not insulting them! But how can I
defy the city? I don't have the strength.

ANTIGONE Then make that your excuse. I'll heal
with earth the body of the brother I love.

ISMENE I feel so sorry for you. And afraid.

ANTIGONE Don't waste your fear. Straighten out your own life.

ISMENE At least tell nobody what you're planning!
Say nothing about it. And neither will I.

ANTIGONE No! Go on, tell them all!
I will hate you much more for your silence—
if you don't shout it everywhere.

ISMENE You're burning to do what should stop you cold.

ANTIGONE One thing I do know: I'll please those who matter.

ISMENE *As if* you could! You love fights you can't win.

ANTIGONE When my strength is exhausted, I'll quit.

ISMENE Hopeless passion is wrong from the start.

ANTIGONE Say that again and I'll despise you.
So will the dead—and they'll hate you
far longer. But go! Let me and my
recklessness deal with this alone.
No matter what I suffer
I won't die dishonored.

(*Exit* ANTIGONE *toward open country;* ISMENE *calls out her next lines as her sister leaves, then she enters the palace through the great central doors.*)

ISMENE If you're determined, go ahead.
And know this much: you are a fool
to attempt this, but you're loved all
the more by the family you love.

(CHORUS *of Theban Elders enters singing.*)

CHORUS Morning sunlight, loveliest ever
to shine on seven-gated Thebes!

Day's golden eye, risen at last
over Dirke's[5] glittering waters!
You stampede the Argive!
Invading in full battle gear,
his white shield flashing, he's wrenched
by your sharp piercing bit
into headlong retreat!
This attacker who championed
quarrelsome Polyneikes
skimmed through our farmland—
a white-feathered Eagle[6]
screeching, horse-hair
flaring from the helmets
of well-armed troops.

He had circled our houses, threatening
all seven gates, his spearpoints
out for blood, but he was thrown back
before his jaws could swell
with our gore, before the Firegod's
incendiary pinetar
engulfed the towers ringing our walls.
He cannot withstand the harsh blare
of battle that roars up
around him—and our Dragon[7]
wrestles him down.

How Zeus hates a proud tongue![8]
And when this river of men
surged forward, with arrogance
loud as its flash of gold,
he struck—with his own lightning—
that firebrand shouting in triumph
from the battlements!
Free-falling from the mad
fury of his charge, torch
still in his hand,
he crashed to earth, the man
who'd turned on us the raving
blast of his loathsome words.
But threats stuck in his throat:
To each enemy soldier
Ares the brute wargod,[9]

5. A river in Thebes.
6. The eagle is the emblem of the white-shielded Argives.
7. The dragon symbolizes Thebes. According to myth, the Thebans were born from dragon's teeth, sown by Kadmos.
8. Zeus struck down with a lightning bolt the most arrogant of the Argive invaders, Capaneus.
9. Ares, god of war, was an ancestor of the Theban royalty and patron of Thebes.

our surging wheelhorse,
assigned a separate doom,
shattering every attack.

Now seven captains facing seven gates,
our captains matching theirs,
throw down their arms as trophies
for Zeus—all but the doomed pair[1]
born to one father, one mother—
who share even their death
when their twin spears drive home.

Victory is now ours!
Her name is pure glory,[2]
her joy resounds
through Thebes' own joy—Thebes
swarming with chariots!
Let us now banish
this war from our minds
and visit each god's temple,
singing all night long! May
Bakkhos,[3] the god whose dancing
rocks Thebes, be there to lead us!

(*Enter* KREON.)

LEADER Enter our new king,
Kreon, the son of Menoikeus,
who came to power
abruptly, when the gods changed our luck.
What plans does he turn over
in his mind—what will he ponder
with the Council of Elders
summoned in his new role?

KREON Men, we have just survived some rough weather.
Monstrous waves have battered our city,
but now the gods have steadied the waters.
I sent my servants to gather you here
because, of all my people, I know
your veneration for Laios' royal
power has never wavered. When Oedipus
ruled our city, and then was struck down, you
stood by his sons. Now both of them fall
together, killed in one lethal exchange.

1. Polyneikes and Eteokles. The victors in Greek battle set up the armor of one of the dead as a trophy, to mark their place of triumph.
2. *Nike* ("Victory") is a feminine noun in Greek. Nike was represented in art as a winged woman.
3. Bakkhos (Dionysos), god of wine and revelry, is associated with Thebes, since his mother, Semele, was a Theban princess.

Because each struck the other's deathblow, each
was defiled by his own brother's blood.
As nearest kin to the men killed,
I've taken power and assumed the throne.

You cannot measure a man's character,
policies, or his common sense—until
you see him in action, enforcing old laws
and making new ones. To me, there's nothing
worse than a man, while he's running a city,
who fails to act on sound advice—but fears
something so much his mouth clamps shut.
Nor have I any use for a man whose friend
means more to him than his country.
Believe me, Zeus, for you miss nothing,
I'll always speak out when I see Thebes choosing
destruction rather than deliverance.
I'll never think our country's enemy
can be my friend. Keep this in mind:
Our *country* is the ship that must keep us safe.
It's only on board her, among the men
who sail her upright, that we make true friends.

Such are the principles I will follow
to preserve Thebes' greatness. Akin to these
are my explicit orders concerning
Oedipus' sons: Eteokles, who died
fighting for our city, and who excelled
in combat, will be given the rituals
and burial proper to the noble dead.

But his brother—I mean Polyneikes, who
returned from exile utterly determined
to burn down his own city, incinerate
the gods we worship, revel in kinsmen's blood,
enslave everyone left alive—
as for him, it is now a crime for Thebans
to bury him or mourn him. Dogs and birds
will savage and outrage his corpse—
an ugly and a visible disgrace.
That is my thinking. And I will never
tolerate giving a bad man more respect
than a good one. Only those faithful to Thebes
will I honor—in this life and after death.

LEADER That is your pleasure, Kreon: Punish Thebes'
betrayers and reward her defenders.
You have all the authority you need
to discipline the living and the dead.

KREON Are you willing to help enforce this law?
LEADER Ask someone younger to shoulder that burden.
KREON But I've already posted men at the corpse.
LEADER Then what instructions do you have for me?
KREON Don't join the cause of those who break this law.
LEADER Who but a fool would want to die?
KREON Exactly. He'd be killed. But easy money
frequently kills those it deludes.

(*Enter* GUARD. *He tends to mime the actions he describes.*)

GUARD I didn't run here at such a breakneck
pace, King, that I'm winded. Pausing to think
stopped me, wheeled me around, headed me back
more than once. My mind kept yelling at me:
"Reckless fool—why go where you'll be punished?"
Then: "Lazy clod! Dawdling, are you? What if
Kreon hears this news from somebody else?—
you'll pay for it."
I made myself dizzy,
hurrying slowly, stretching out a short road.
I finally realized I had to come.
If I'm talking annihilation here,
I'll still say it, since I'm of the opinion
nothing but my own fate can cause me harm.
KREON What's making you so agitated?
GUARD I've got to explain my role in this matter.
I didn't do it, I didn't see who did.
So it wouldn't be right to punish me.
KREON You're obsessed with protecting yourself.
That's a nice fortified wall you've thrown up
around your news—which must be odd indeed.
GUARD You bet. And bad news must be broken slowly.
KREON Why not just tell it? Then you can vanish.
GUARD But I *am* telling you! That corpse—someone's
buried it and run off. They sprinkled thirsty
dust on it. Then did all the rituals.
KREON What are you saying? What man would dare do this?
GUARD I've no idea. No marks from a pickaxe,
no dirt thrown up by a shovel. The ground's
all hard and dry, unbroken—no wheel ruts.
Whoever did this left no trace.
When the man on dawn-watch showed it to us,
we all got a nasty surprise. The dead man
had dropped out of sight. He wasn't entombed,
but dusted over, as though someone had tried
to stave off defilement. There was no sign
dogs or wild animals had chewed the corpse.
Then we all started yelling rough words, threats,
blaming each other, every guard ready

to throw punches—nobody to stop us.
Every man under suspicion—but none
of us convicted. We all denied it—
swearing to god we'd handle red-hot iron
or walk through fire to back up our oaths.

After interrogation got us nowhere,
one man spoke up and made us hang our heads
toward the ground in terror. We couldn't do
what he said—or avoid trouble if we did.
He advised us to tell you what happened,
not try to hide it. That seemed our best move.
So we drew lots to choose the messenger.
I lost—I'm no happier to be here
than you are to see me. Don't I know that.
Nobody loves the man who brings bad news.

LEADER King, something has been bothering me: Suppose
this business was inspired by the gods?

KREON Stop! Before your words fill me with rage.
Now, besides sounding old, you sound senile.
How could anyone possibly believe
the gods protect this corpse? Did *they* cover
his nakedness to reward him for loyal
service—this man who came here to burn
their colonnaded temples and treasuries,
to wipe out their country and tear up its laws?
Do you think that the gods honor rebels?
They don't. But for a good while now
men who despise me have been muttering
under their breaths—my edict bruised their necks.
They were rebelling against a just yoke—
unlike you good citizens who support me.
I'm sure these malcontents bribed my sentries
to do what they did.
Mankind's most deadly
invention is money—it plunders cities,
encourages men to abandon their homes,
tempts honest people to do shameful things.
It instructs them in criminal practice,
drives them to act on every godless impulse.
By doing this for silver, these men have
guaranteed that, sooner or later,
they'll pay the price.
But you who worship Zeus—
since Zeus enforces his own will through mine—
be sure of this, it is my solemn oath:
If you don't find the man who carried out
this burial and drag him before me,
a quick trip to Hades won't be your fate.

You will all be strung up—and you'll hang
for a while, your insolence on display.
From then on, you may calculate exactly
how much profit to expect from your crimes.
More men are destroyed by ill-gotten wealth
than such "wealth" ever saved from destruction.

GUARD May I speak further? Or shall I just leave?

KREON Don't you realize that your words pain me?

GUARD Do your ears ache, or does the pain go deeper?

KREON Why does the source of my pain interest you?

GUARD I just sting your ears. The man
who did this stabs your gut.

KREON You've run off at the mouth since you were born.

GUARD Maybe so. But I had no part in this crime.

KREON I think you did. Sold your life for some silver.

GUARD It's a sad thing when a judge gets it wrong.

KREON You'll soon be on the wrong end of a judgment
yourself.
If you don't find the guilty one,
you'll find your greed buys you nothing but grief.

GUARD I hope he's caught, but Fate will decide that.
And you'll never see me coming back here.
Now that I have been spared—when everything
seemed so desperate—all I can think about
is how much gratitude I owe the gods.

(*Exit* GUARD *to open country;* KREON *enters his palace.*)

ELDERS Wonders[4] abound, but none
more astounding than man!
He crosses to the far side
of white seas, blown
by winter gales, sailing
below huge waves;
he wears Earth down—
our primal, eternal,
inexhaustible god—
his stallion-sired mules
plowing her soil
back and forth
year after year.

All breeds of carefree
bird, savage beast
and deep-sea creature,
ingenious man
snares in his woven nets;
he drives the mountain herds

4. The word for "wonders" (*ta deina*) can connote either "strange" or "terrible."

from wild lairs down to his folds;
he coaxes rough-maned horses
to thrust their necks through his yoke;
he tames the tireless mountain bull.

He has taught himself speech,
wind-quick thought,
and all the talents
that govern a city;
how to take shelter
from cold skies or pelting rain;
never baffled,
always resourceful,
he accepts every challenge;
but from Hades alone
has he found no way out—
though from hopeless disease
he has found a defense.

Exceeding all expectation,
his robust power to create
sometimes brings evil,
at other times, excellence.
When he follows the laws
Earth teaches him—
and Justice, which he's sworn
the gods he will enforce—
he soars with his city.
But reckless and corrupt,
a man will be driven
from his nation disgraced.

Let no man guilty of such things
share my hearth or invade my thoughts.

(*Enter* GUARD, *from countryside, leading* ANTIGONE.)

LEADER I'm stunned—what's this? A warning from the gods?
I know this girl. She is Antigone.
Don't we all recognize her?
Unlucky Oedipus was her father,
now her own luck runs out.
What's happening? You—under guard?
Are you a prisoner? Did you break
the king's law? Commit some thoughtless act?

GUARD There's your perpetrator. We caught her
burying the corpse. Where's Kreon?

(*Enter* KREON.)

LEADER Here he comes. Just in time.

KREON What makes my arrival so timely?

GUARD Sir, never promise something won't happen;
second thoughts can make your first one a lie.
I vowed I'd never come back here,
after you tongue-lashed me with those threats.
Then came a pleasure like no other,
because it's a total surprise, something
we hope for but can't believe will happen.
So I came back—though I swore I wouldn't—
to bring you the girl we caught sprinkling dust
on the dead body. No need to throw dice—
this time the good fortune was all mine.
Now she's all yours. Question and convict her—
do as you see fit. But I have the right
to go free of trouble once and for all.

KREON Your prisoner—where was she when captured?

GUARD Covering up the dead body. There you have it.

KREON Do you know what you just said? No mistake?

GUARD I saw her bury the man you said no one
could bury. How can I say it plainer?

KREON How did you see her? Was she caught in the act?

GUARD Here's what happened. We went back there
after those ugly threats of yours, to brush
the dirt off the body and strip it down
to its rotting flesh. Afterwards, we hunkered
upwind under some hills to spare us any stench
the body might have sent our way. Each man
kept alert, and kept his neighbor alert,
by raking him with outbursts of abuse
if he seemed to neglect his watch.
We kept at it until the round sun had climbed
the heavens and baked us in the noon heat.
Then, rising from the earth, a whirlwind
whipped up the dust, and terror filled the sky,
choking the grasslands, tearing leaves off trees,
churning up grit all around us.
Our eyes squeezed shut,
we waited out this god-sent pestilence.
After a bit the dust cleared, and we saw her
cry out in anguish, a piercing scream
like a bird homing to find her nest robbed.
When she saw the body stripped naked,
she wailed one more time, then yelled a string
of curses at those who'd done it. She scooped up
powdery dust and, from a graceful bronze
urn, poured out three cool swallows[5] for the dead.
Soon as we saw this, we moved into stop her.
She wasn't a bit shocked, when we charged her

5. She pours the dust as a "libation," a liquid sacrificial offering.

with the earlier crime, and now this one—
didn't deny a thing. That pleased,
but also troubled me. Escaping blame
oneself is always a relief; still, it hurts
to cause your own people grief. But all that
matters much less to me than my own safety.

KREON (*To* ANTIGONE.)

You! Don't stand there nodding your head.
Out with it! Admit this or deny it.

ANTIGONE I swear I did. And I don't deny it.

KREON (*To* GUARD.)

You are excused from this grim business.
You're now free to go anywhere you please.

(*Exit* GUARD. *To* ANTIGONE.)

Explain something to me without elaborating.
Were you aware of my decree forbidding this?

ANTIGONE Of course I knew. We all knew.

KREON And still you dared to violate the law?

ANTIGONE I did. It wasn't *Zeus* who issued me
this order. And Justice—who lives below—
was not involved. They'd never condone it!
I deny that your edicts—since *you*, a mere man,
imposed them—have the force to trample on
the gods' unwritten and infallible laws.
Their laws are not ephemeral, they weren't
made yesterday, and they will last forever.
No man knows how far back in time they go.
I'd never let any man's arrogance
bully me into breaking the gods' laws.
I'll die someday—how could I not know that?
I knew it without your proclamation.
If I do die young, that's an advantage,
for doesn't a person like me, who lives
besieged by trouble, escape by dying?
My own death isn't going to bother me,
but I would be devastated to see
my mother's son die and rot unburied.
I've no regrets for what I've done. And if you
consider my acts foolhardy, I say:
Look at the fool charging me with folly.

LEADER It's apparent this girl's nature is savage
like her father's. She hasn't got the sense
to back off when she gets into trouble.

KREON Stubborn spirits are the first to crack.
It's always the iron tool hardened by fire
that snaps and shatters. And headstrong horses
can be tamed by a small iron bit.
There's no excuse for a slave

to preen when her master's home.
This girl learned insolence long before
she broke this law. What's more, she keeps on
insulting us, and then gloats about it.
There is no doubt that if she emerges
victorious, and is never punished,
I am no man, *she* will be the man here.

I don't care if she is my sister's child,
a blood relative, closer than all those
who worship Zeus in my household,
she—and her sister—still must die.
I charge her sister too with conspiring
to bury Polyneikes. Bring her out.
I observed her inside just now,
screaming, hysterical, deranged.
Someone who intends to commit a crime
can lose control of a guilty conscience.
Her furtive treason gives itself away.

(*Two of Kreon's Men enter the palace.* KREON *turns to* ANTIGONE.)

But I also hate it when someone caught
red-handed tries to glorify her crime.

ANTIGONE Take me and kill me—is that your whole plan?
KREON That's it. When that's done I'll be satisfied.
ANTIGONE Then what stops you? Are you waiting for me
to accept what you've said? I never will.
And nothing I say will ever please you.
Yet, since you did mention glory, how
could I do anything more glorious
than build my own brother a tomb?
These men here would approve my actions—
if fear didn't seal their lips.
Tyranny
is fortunate in many ways: it can,
for instance, say and do anything it wants.
KREON These Thebans don't see it your way.
ANTIGONE But they do. To please you they bite their tongues.
KREON Aren't you ashamed not to follow their lead?
ANTIGONE Since when is it shameful to honor a brother?
KREON You had another brother who died fighting him?
ANTIGONE That's right. Born to the same mother and father.
KREON Then why do you honor Polyneikes
when doing so desecrates Eteokles?
ANTIGONE Eteokles wouldn't agree with you.
KREON Oh, but he would—because you've honored
treason as though it were patriotism.
ANTIGONE It was his *brother* who died, not his *slave*!

KREON That brother died ravaging our country!
Eteokles fell fighting to protect it.
ANTIGONE Hades will still expect his rituals.
KREON The brave deserve better than the vile.
ANTIGONE Who knows what matters to the dead?
KREON Not even death reconciles enemies.
ANTIGONE I made no enemies by being born!
I made my lifelong friends at birth.
KREON Then go down to them! Love your dead brothers!
While I'm alive, no woman governs me.

(*Enter* ISMENE, *led in by Kreon's Men.*)

LEADER Ismene's coming from the palace.
She cries the loving tears of a sister;
her eyes fill up, her flushed face darkens;
tears pour down her cheeks.
KREON Now you—a viper
who slithered through my house, quietly
drinking my blood! I never knew
I nurtured *two* insurrections,
both attacking my throne.
Go ahead,
confess your role in this burial
party. Or do you claim ignorance?
ISMENE I confess it—if she'll let me.
I accept my full share of the blame.
ANTIGONE Justice won't let you make that claim, sister!
You refused to help me. You took no part.
ISMENE You're leaving on a grim voyage. I'm not
ashamed to suffer with you the whole way.
ANTIGONE The dead in Hades know who buried him.
I don't want love that just shows up in words.
ISMENE You'll disgrace me, sister! Don't keep me
from honoring our dead! Let me come with you!
ANTIGONE Don't try to share my death! Don't try to claim
you helped me bury him! My death's enough.
ISMENE With you dead, why would I want to live?
ANTIGONE Ask Kreon that! You sprang to his defense.
ISMENE Why do you wound me? It does you no good.
ANTIGONE I'm sorry if my scorn for him hurts you.
ISMENE I can still help you. Tell me what to do.
ANTIGONE Go on living. I'd rather you survived.
ISMENE Then you want to exclude me from your fate?
ANTIGONE You made the choice to live. I chose to die.
ISMENE And I've told you how much I hate that choice.
ANTIGONE Some think you're right. *Others* think I am.
ISMENE Then aren't we both equally wrong?
ANTIGONE Gather your strength. Your life goes on. Long ago
I dedicated mine to the dead.

KREON One woman only now shows her madness—
the other's been out of her mind since birth.
ISMENE King, when you are shattered by grief
your native wit vanishes. It just goes.

KREON You surely lost your wits when you teamed up
with a criminal engaged in a crime.
ISMENE What would my life be like without her?
KREON You're living that life now. Hers is over.
ISMENE Then you're willing to kill your own son's bride?
KREON Oh yes. He'll find other fields to plow.
ISMENE No other woman would suit him so well.
KREON I want no pernicious wives for my son.
ANTIGONE Dearest Haimon! How your father hates you!
KREON Enough! No more talk about this marriage.
ISMENE You're going to rob your son of his bride?
KREON Hades will cancel their marriage for me.
LEADER Then you've made up your mind she will die?
KREON Both *my* mind and *your* mind. No more delay,
men, take them in. Make sure they behave
like women. Don't let either slip away.
Even the brave will try to run
when they see death closing in.

(*Kreon's Men take* ANTIGONE *and* ISMENE *inside.*)

ELDERS Lucky are those
whose lives
never taste evil!
For once the gods
attack a family,
their curse never relents.
It sickens life after life,
rising like a deep
sea swell, a darkness
boiling from below, driven
by the wild stormwinds
of Thrace that churn up
black sand from the sea floor—
the battered headlands
moan as the storm pounds in.

I see sorrows that struck
the dead Labdakids long ago
break over their children,
wave on wave of sorrows!
Each generation fails
to protect its own youth—
because a god always hacks
at their roots, draining
strength that could set them free.

Now the hope that brightened
over the last rootstock
alive in the house
of Oedipus, in its turn
is struck down—
by the blood-drenched dust
the death-gods demand,
by reckless talk,
by Furies[6] in the mind.

O Zeus,
what human arrogance
can rival your power?
Neither Sleep,
who beguiles us all,
nor the tireless, god-driven months
overcome it.
O Monarch
whom time cannot age—
you live in the magical
sunrays of Olympos!
One law of yours rules
our own and future time,
just as it ruled the past:
Nothing momentous man
achieves will go unpunished.

For Hope is a wanderer
who profits multitudes
but tempts just as many
with light-headed longings—
and a man's failure
dawns on him only
when blazing coals
scald his feet.

The man was wise
who said these words:
"Evil seems noble—
early and late—to minds
unbalanced by the gods,
but only for a moment
will such men
hold off catastrophe."

(*Enter* HAIMON.)

LEADER There's Haimon,
the youngest of your sons.
Does he come here enraged

6. Spirits of vengeance.

that you have sentenced Antigone,
the bride he's been promised,
or in shock that his hopes
for marriage have been crushed?

KREON We'll soon have an answer
better than any prophet's.
My son, now that you've heard
my formal condemnation
of your bride, have you come here
to attack your father?
Or will I be dear to you still,
no matter what I do?

HAIMON I'm yours, father. I respect your wisdom.
Show me the straight path, and I'll take it.
I couldn't value any marriage more
than the excellent guidance you give me.

KREON Son, that's exactly how you need to think:
Follow your father's orders in all things.
It's the reason men pray for loyal sons
to be born and raised in their houses—
so they can harm their father's enemies
and show his friends respect to match his own.
If a man produces worthless children,
what has he spawned? His grief, his rivals' glee.

Don't throw away your judgment, son,
for the pleasure this woman offers.
You'll feel her turn ice cold in your arms—
you'll feel her scorn in the bedroom. No wound
cuts deeper than poisonous love. So spit
this girl out like the enemy she is.
Let her find a mate in Hades.
I caught her in open defiance—
she alone in the whole city—and I will take
her life, just as I promised. I will not
show myself as a liar to my people.
It is useless for her to harp on the Zeus
of family life:[7] If I indulge my own
family in rebelliousness,
I must indulge it everywhere.

A man who keeps his own house in order
will be perceived as righteous by his city.
But if anyone steps out of line, breaks
our laws, thinks he can dictate to his king,
he shouldn't expect any praise from me.

7. Zeus was the defender of bonds between family members.

Citizens must obey men in office
appointed by the city, both in minor matters
and in the great questions of what is just—
even when they think an action unjust.
Obedient men lead ably and serve well.
Caught in a squall of spears, they hold their ground.
They make brave soldiers you can trust.
Insubordination is our worst crime.
It wrecks cities and empties homes. It breaks
and routs even allies who fight beside us.
Discipline is what saves the lives of all
good people who stay out of trouble.
And to make sure we enforce discipline—
never let a woman overwhelm a king.
Better to be driven from power, if it
comes to that, by a man. Then nobody
can say you were beaten by some female.

LEADER Unless the years have sapped my wits, King,
what you have just said was wisely said.

HAIMON Father, the gods instill reason in men.
It's the most valuable thing we possess.
I don't have the skill—nor do I want it—
to contradict all the things you have said.
Though someone else's perspective might help.
Look, it's not in your nature to notice
what people say—what they're condemning.
That harsh look on your face makes men afraid—
no one tells you what you'd rather not hear.
But I hear, unobserved, what people think.
Listen. Thebes aches for this girl. *No person*
ever, they're saying, *less deserved to die—*
no one's ever been so unjustly killed
for actions as magnificent as hers.
When her own brother died in that bloodbath
she kept him from lying out there unburied,
fair game for flesh-eating dogs and vultures.
Hasn't she earned, they ask, *golden honor*?
Those are the words they whisper in the shadows.

There's nothing I prize more, father,
than your welfare.
What makes a son prouder
than a father's thriving reputation?
Don't fathers feel the same about their sons?

Attitudes are like clothes; you can change them.
Don't think that what you say is always right.

Whoever thinks that he alone is wise,
that he's got a superior tongue and brain,
open him up and you'll find him a blank.
It's never shameful for even a wise man
to keep on learning new things all his life.
Be flexible, not rigid. Think of trees
caught in a raging winter torrent: those
that bend will survive with all their limbs
intact; those that resist are swept away.
Or take a captain who cleats his mainsheet
down hard, never easing off in a blow;
he'll capsize his ship and go right on sailing,
his rowing benches where his keel should be.
Step back from your anger, let yourself change.

If I, as a younger man, can offer
a thought, it's this: Yes, it would be better
if men were born with perfect understanding.
But things don't work that way. The best response
to worthy advice is to learn from it.

LEADER King, if he has said anything to ease
this crisis, you had better learn from it.
Haimon, you do the same. You both spoke well.
KREON So men my age should learn from one of yours?
HAIMON If I happen to be right, yes! Don't look
at my youth, look at what I've accomplished.
KREON What? Backing rebels makes you proud?
HAIMON I'm not about to condone wrongdoing.
KREON Hasn't *she* been attacked by that disease?
HAIMON Your fellow citizens would deny it.
KREON Shall Thebans dictate how I should govern?
HAIMON Listen to yourself: You talk like a boy.
KREON Should I yield to them—or rule Thebes myself?
HAIMON It's not a *city* if one man owns it.
KREON Don't we say men in power *own* their cities?
HAIMON You'd make a first-rate king of a wasteland.
KREON It seems this *boy* fights on the woman's side.
HAIMON Only if you're the woman. You're my concern.
KREON Then why do you make open war on me?
HAIMON What I attack is your abuse of power.
KREON Is protecting my interest an abuse?
HAIMON What is it you protect by scorning the gods?
KREON Look at yourself! A woman overpowers you.
HAIMON But no disgraceful impulse ever will.
KREON Your every word supports that woman.
HAIMON And you, and me, and the gods of this earth.
KREON You will not marry her while she's on this earth.
HAIMON Then she will die, and dead, kill someone else.
KREON You are brazen enough to threaten me?

HAIMON What threatens you is hearing what I think.
KREON Your mindless attack on me threatens you.
HAIMON I'd question your mind if you weren't my father.
KREON Stop your snide deference! You are her slave.
HAIMON You're talking at me, but you don't hear me.
KREON Really? By Olympos above, I hear you.
And I can assure you, you're going to
suffer the consequences of your attacks.

(KREON *speaks to his Men.*)

Bring out the odious creature. Let her
die at once in his presence. Let him watch,
this bridegroom, as she's killed beside him.

(*Two Men enter palace.*)

HAIMON Watch her die next to me? You think I'd do that?
Your eyes won't see my face, ever again.
Go on raving to friends who can stand you.

(*Exit* HAIMON.)

LEADER King, the young man's fury hurls him out.
Rage makes a man his age utterly reckless.
KREON Let him imagine he's superhuman.
He'll never save the lives of those two girls.
LEADER Then you intend to execute them both?
KREON Not the one with clean hands.
I think you're right about her.
LEADER The one you're going to kill—how will you do it?
KREON I will lead her along a deserted road,
and hide her, alive, in a hollow cave.
I'll leave her just enough food to evade
defilement—so the city won't be infected.[8]
She can pray there to Hades, the one god
whom she respects. Maybe he will spare her!
Though she's more likely to learn, in her last hours,
that she's thrown her life away on the dead.

(KREON *remains on stage during the next choral ode, presumably retiring into the background.*)

ELDERS Love, you win all
your battles!—raising
havoc with our herds,
dwelling all night
on a girl's soft cheeks,
cruising the oceans,
invading homes
deep in the wilds!
No god can outlast you,
no mortal outrun you.

8. Kreon imagines that if Antigone dies from starvation after the food runs out, the city will not incur "blood guilt" from her death.

And those you seize go mad.

You wrench even good men's minds
so far off course they crash in ruins.
Now you ignite hatred in men
of the same blood—but allure flashing
from the keen eyes of the bride
always wins, for Desire wields
all the power of ancient law:
Aphrodite[9] the implacable
plays cruel games with our lives.

(*Enter* ANTIGONE, *dressed in purple as a bride, guarded by Kreon's Men.*)

LEADER This sight also drives *me*
outside the law. I can't stop
my own tears flowing when I see
Antigone on her way
to the bridal chamber,
where we all lie down in death.

ANTIGONE Citizens of our fatherland, you see me
begin my last journey. I take one last look
at sunlight that I'll never see again.
Hades, who chills each one of us to sleep,
will guide me down to Acheron's[1] shore.
I'll go hearing no wedding hymn
to carry me to my bridal chamber, or songs
girls sing when flowers crown a bride's hair;
I'm going to marry the River of Pain.[2]

LEADER Don't praise and glory go with you
to the deep caverns of the dead?
You haven't been wasted by disease;
you've helped no sword earn its keep.
No, you have chosen of your own free will
to enter Hades while you're still alive.
No one else has ever done that.

ANTIGONE I once heard that a Phrygian stranger,
Niobe, the daughter of Tantalos,
died a hideous death on Mt. Sipylos.[3]
Living rock, like relentless ivy,
crushed her. Now, people say, she slowly
erodes; rain and snow
never leave her, they constantly
pour like tears from her eyes,

9. Goddess associated with sexual desire; she is the mother of Desire (*Eros*).
1. A river in the underworld.
2. Acheron.
3. Niobe, wife of Amphion (King of Thebes), boasted that she had more children than Leto, the mother of the twin gods Apollo and Artemis. In revenge, they killed all her children. Niobe fled to Phrygia and was turned into a rock on Mount Sipylos. A real rock formation there looks like a woman's face, and the snow melting down its surface resembles tears.

drenching the clefts of her body.
My death will be like hers,
when the god at last lets me sleep.

LEADER You forget, child, she was a goddess,[4]
with gods for parents, not a mortal
begotten by mortals like ourselves.
It's no small honor for a mere woman
to suffer so godlike a fate—in both
how she has lived, and the way she will die.

ANTIGONE Now I'm being laughed at!
In the name of our fathers' gods,
wait till I'm gone, don't mock me
while I stand here in plain sight—
all you rich citizens of this town!

At least I can trust you,
headwaters of the river
Dirke,[5] and you, holy
plains around Thebes, home
of our great chariot-fleet,
to bear me witness: Watch them
march me off to my strange tomb,
my heaped-up rock-bound prison,
without a friend to mourn me
or any law to protect me—

me, a miserable woman
with no home here on earth
and none down with the dead,
not quite alive, not yet a corpse.

LEADER You took the ultimate risk when you smashed
yourself against the throne of Justice.
But the stiff price you're paying, daughter,
is one you inherit from your father.

ANTIGONE You've touched my worst grief,
the fate of my father, which I
keep turning over in my mind.
We all were doomed, the whole
grand house of Labdakos,
by my mother's horrendous,
incestuous, coupling with her son.
From what kind of parents was I born?

I'm going to them now,
I'm dying unmarried.

4. Tantalus, Niobe's father, was (in some versions of the myth) a son of Zeus; her mother was also a goddess.

5. In Thebes.

And brother Polyneikes,
wasn't yours too a deadly
marriage?[6] And when you
were slaughtered, so was I.

LEADER Your pious conduct might deserve some praise,
but no assault on power will ever
be tolerated by him who wields it.
It was your own hot-headed
willfulness that destroyed you.

ANTIGONE No friends, no mourners, no wedding songs
go with me, they push me down a road
that runs through sadness;
they have prepared it for me, alone.
Soon I will lose sight of the sun's holy eye,
wretched, with no one to love me,
no one to grieve.

(KREON *moves forward, speaking first to* ANTIGONE, *then to his Men.*)

KREON You realize, don't you, that singing.
and wailing would go on forever
if they did the dying any good?

Hurry up now, take her away.
And when you've finished
enclosing her, just as I've ordered,
inside the cave's vault,
leave her there—absolutely
isolated—to decide whether
she wants to die at once, or go
on living in that black hole.
So we'll be pure as far as she's concerned.
In either case, today will be the last.
she'll ever spend above the ground.

ANTIGONE My tomb, my bridal bedroom, my home
dug from rock, where they'll keep me forever—
I'll join my family there, so many of us dead,
already welcomed by Persephone.[7]
I'll be the last to arrive, and the worst off,
going down with most of my life unlived.
I hope my coming will please my father,
comfort my mother, and bring joy
to you, brother, because I washed your dead
bodies, dressed you with my hands, and poured
blessèd offerings of drink on your graves.

6. Polyneikes married the daughter of Adrastus of Argos, to seal the alliance that enabled him to march against Thebes.

7. Queen of the underworld.

Now, because I honored your corpse,
Polyneikes, *this* is how I'm repaid!
I honored you as wise men would think right
But I wouldn't have taken that task on
had I been a mother who lost her child,
or if my husband were rotting out there.
For them, I would never defy my city.
You want to know what law lets me say this?
If my husband were dead, I could remarry.
A new husband could give me a new child.
But with my father and mother in Hades,
a new brother could never bloom for me.
That is the law that made me die for you,
Polyneikes. But Kreon says I'm wrong,
terribly wrong. And now I'm his captive,
he pulls me by the wrist to no bride's bed;
I won't hear bridal songs, or feel the joy
of married love, and I will have no share
in raising children. No, I will go grieving,
friendless, and alive to a hollow tomb.
Tell me, gods, which of *your* laws did I break?

I'm too far gone to expect your help.
But whose strength can I count on, when acts
of blessing are considered blasphemy?
If the gods are happy I'm sentenced to die
I hope one day I'll discover
what divine law I have broken.
But if my judges are at fault, I want *them*
to suffer the pain they inflict on me now.

LEADER She's still driven by raw gusts
raging through her mind.

KREON I have no patience with such outbursts.
And none for men who drag their feet.

ANTIGONE I think you're saying that my death is near.

KREON It will be carried out. Don't think otherwise.

ANTIGONE I leave you, Thebes, city of my fathers.
I leave you, ancient gods.[8] This very moment,
I'm being led away. They cannot wait!
Look at me, princely citizens of Thebes:
I'm the last daughter of the kings who ruled you.
Look at what's done to me, and by whom
it's done, to punish me for keeping faith.

(*Kreon's Men lead* ANTIGONE *offstage.*)

8. The Theban royal house was descended from the gods Ares and Aphrodite.

ELDERS Like you, lovely Danae[9] endured her loss
of heavenly sunlight
in a brass-bound cell—
a prison secret as a tomb.
Night and day she was watched.
Like yours, my daughter,
her family was a great one.
The seed of Zeus, which fell
on her as golden rain,
she treasured in her womb.
Fate is strange and powerful;
wealth cannot protect us,
nor can war, high city towers,
or storm-beaten black ships.

Impounded too, was Lycurgos,
short-tempered son of Dryas,
King of Edonia:[1] To pay
him back for insulting
defiance, Dionysos shut
him up in a rocky cell;
there his surging madness ebbed.
He learned too late how mad
he was to taunt this god
with derisive laughter:
When he tried to suppress
Bakkhanalian torches
and women fired by their god,
he angered the Muses
who love the oboe's song.

By waters off the Black Rocks,
a current joins two seas;
the Bosphoros' channel
follows the Thracian
coast of Salmydessos.
Ares from his nearby city
saw this wild assault—
the savage wife of Phineus
attacking his two sons:[2]

9. Daughter of Acrisius, king of Argos. It was prophesied that he would be killed by his daughter's son, so he shut his daughter up in a bronze tower, hoping she would never have a lover or son. But Zeus came to her in the form of a golden rain shower, and she had a son, Perseus, who did in the end accidentally kill his grandfather.

1. Thrace. Lycurgos opposed the introduction of Dionysiac religion into his kingdom and was imprisoned by Dionysos.

2. This stanza refers to a story that Cleopatra, daughter of the Athenian princess Orithyia, whom Boreas, the North Wind, carried off to his home in Thrace, was married to Phineus, the Thracian king, and bore him two sons. He later abandoned her and married Eidothea, who put out the eyes of Cleopatra's sons, while Ares, god of war, watched. The application of the story to Antigone's situation is unclear.

Her stab-wounds darkened
their vengeance-craving eyes,
burst with a pointed shuttle
gripped in her blood-drenched hands.

Broken spirits, they howled
in their pain—these sons
of a woman unhappy
in her marriage, this daughter
descended from the ancient
Erektheids.[3] Nursed in caves
among her father's stormwinds,
this daughter of the gods,
this child of Boreas,
rode swift horses over the mountains—
yet Fate broke her brutally, my child.

(*Enter* TIRESIAS *and the Lad who guides him.*)

TIRESIAS Theban lords, we walk here side by side,
one pair of eyes looking out for us both.
Blind men must travel with somebody's help.

KREON What news do you bring, old man Tiresias?

TIRESIAS I'll tell you. Then you must trust this prophet.

KREON I've never questioned the advice you've given.

TIRESIAS And it helped you keep Thebes on a straight course?

KREON I know your value. I learned it first-hand.

TIRESIAS Take care.
You're standing on the razor's edge of fate.

KREON What do you mean? That makes me shudder.

TIRESIAS You'll comprehend when you hear the warnings
issued by my art. When I took my seat
at my accustomed post of augury,
birds from everywhere fluttering nearby,
I heard a strange sound coming from their midst.
They screeched with such mindless ferocity,
any meaning their song possessed was drowned out.
I knew the birds were tearing at each other
with lethal talons; the hovering beats
of thrashing wings could have meant nothing else.
Alarmed, I lit a sacrificial fire,
but the god failed to keep his flames alive.
Then from charred thighbones came a rancid slime,
smoking and sputtering, oozing out
into the ashes; the gall-bladder burst open;
liquefying thighs slid free from the strips
of fat enfolding them.
But my attempt
at prophecy failed; the signs I had sought

3. Royal house of Athens.

never appeared—this I learned from my lad.
He's my guide, just as I'm the guide for others.

Kreon, your mind has sickened Thebes.
Our city's altars, and our city's braziers,
have been defiled, all of them, by dogs
and birds, with flesh torn from the wretched
corpse of Oedipus' fallen son.
Because of this, the gods will not accept
our prayers or the offerings of burnt meat
that come from our hands. No bird now sings
a clear omen—their keen cries have been garbled
by the taste of a slain man's thickened blood.
Think about these facts, son.
All men go wrong;
but when a man blunders, he won't be stripped
of his wits and his strength if he corrects
the error he's committed and then ends
his stubborn ways. Stubbornness, you well know,
will provoke charges of stupidity.

Respect the dead. Don't spear the fallen.
How much courage does it take
to kill a dead man?
Let me
help you. My counsel is sound and well meant.
No advice is sweeter than that from a wise
source who has only your interests at heart.

KREON Old man, like archers at target practice,
you all aim arrows at me. And now you
stoop to using prophecy against me.
For a long time I have been merchandise
sold far and wide by you omen-mongers.
Go, make your money, strike your deals, import
silver from Sardis, gold from India,
if it suits you. But you won't hide that corpse
under the earth! Never—even if Zeus'
own eagles fly scraps of flesh to his throne.

Defilement isn't something I fear—it won't
persuade me to order this burial.
I don't accept that men can defile gods.
But even the cleverest of mortals,
venerable Tiresias, will be brought
down hard, if, hoping to turn a profit,
they clothe ugly ideas in handsome words.
TIRESIAS Does any man grasp . . . does he realize . . .
KREON Realize . . . what? What point are you making?

TIRESIAS . . . that no possession is worth more than good sense?
KREON Just as its absence is our worst disease.
TIRESIAS But hasn't that disease infected you?
KREON I won't trade insults with you, prophet.
TIRESIAS You do when you call my prophecies false.
KREON Your profession has always loved money.
TIRESIAS And tyrants have a penchant for corruption.
KREON You know you're abusing a king in power?
TIRESIAS You hold power because I helped you save Thebes.
KREON You're a shrewd prophet. But you love to cause harm.
TIRESIAS You'll force me to say what's clenched in my heart.
KREON Say it. Unless you've been paid to say it.
TIRESIAS I don't think it will pay you to hear it.
KREON Get one thing straight: My conscience can't be bought.
TIRESIAS Then tell your conscience this: You will not live
for many circuits of the chariot sun
before you trade a child born from your loins
for all the corpses whose deaths you have caused.
You have thrown children from the sunlight
down to the shades of Hades, ruthlessly
housing a living person in a tomb,
while you detain here, among us, something
that belongs to the gods who live below
our world—the naked unwept corpse you've robbed
of the solemn grieving we owe our dead.
None of this should have been any concern
of yours—or of the Olympian gods—
but you have involved them in your outrage!
Therefore, avengers wait to ambush you—
the Furies sent by Hades and its gods
will punish you for the crimes I have named.

Do you think someone hired me to tell you this?

It won't be long before wailing breaks out
from the women and men in your own house.
And hatred against you will surge in all
the countries whose sons, in mangled pieces,
received their rites of burial
from dogs, wild beasts, or flapping birds
who have carried the stench of defilement
to the homelands and the hearths of the dead.

Since you've provoked me, these are the arrows
I have shot in anger, like a bowman,
straight at your heart—arrows you cannot dodge,
and whose pain you will feel.
Lad, take me home—
let this man turn his anger on younger

people. That might teach him to hold his tongue,
and to think more wisely than he does now.

(*Exit* TIRESIAS *led by the Lad.*)

LEADER This old man leaves stark prophecies behind.
Never once, while my hair has gone from black
to white, has this prophet told Thebes a lie.

KREON I'm well aware of that! It unnerves me.
Surrender would be devastating,
but if I stand firm, I could be destroyed.

LEADER What you need is some very clear advice,
son of Menoikeus.

KREON What must I do?
If you have such advice, give it to me.

LEADER Free the girl from her underground prison.
Build a tomb for the corpse you have let rot.

KREON That's your advice? I should surrender?

LEADER Yes, King. Do it now. For the gods
act quickly to abort human folly.

KREON I can hardly say this. But I'll give up
convictions I hold passionately—
and do what you ask. We can't fight
the raw power of destiny.

LEADER Then go!
Yourself. Delegate this to no one.

KREON I'll go just as I am. Move out, men. Now!
All of you, bring axes and run toward
that rising ground. You can see it from here.
Because I'm the one who has changed, I who
locked her away will go there to free her.
My heart is telling me we must obey
established law until the day we die.

(*Exit* KREON *and his Men toward open country.*)

ELDERS God with myriad names—
lustrous child
of Kadmos' daughter,
son of thundering Zeus—
you govern fabled Italy;
you preside at Eleusis,
secluded Valley of Demeter
that welcomes all pilgrims.[4]
O Bakkhos! Thebes
is your homeland,
mother-city of maenads[5]
on the quietly flowing

4. Kadmos's daughter is Semele, mother of Dionysos (Bakkhos). Eleusis, the site of a mystery cult to Demeter, goddess of the harvest, is near Athens.

5. Female worshippers of Dionysos.

Ismenos, where the dragon's
teeth were sown.[6]

Now you stand on the ridges rising
up the twin peaks of Parnassos.[7]
There through the wavering
smoke-haze your torches flare;
there walk your devotees,
the nymphs of Korykia,
beside Kastalia's fountains.
Thick-woven ivy on Nysa's sloping hills,
grape-clusters ripe on verdant shorelines
propel you here, while voices
of more than human power
sing "Evohoi!"[8]—your name divine
when the streets of Thebes
are your final destination.

By honoring Thebes
beyond all cities,
you honor your mother
whom the lightning killed.[9]
Now a plague
ravages our city. Come home
on healing footsteps—down
the slopes of Parnassos,
or over the howling channel.
Stars breathing their gentle fire
shine joy on you as they rise,
O master of nocturnal voices!
Take shape before our eyes, Bakkhos,
son of Zeus our king, let the Thyiads[1]
come with you, let them climb
the mad heights of frenzy
as you, Iakkhos,[2] the bountiful,
watch them
dance through the night.

(*Enter* MESSENGER.)

MESSENGER Neighbors, who live not far from the grand
old houses of Amphion and Kadmos,[3]
you can't trust anything in a person's life—
praiseworthy or shameful—never to change.

6. The population of Thebes was supposed to have grown from dragon's teeth, sown by Kadmos.
7. The two cliffs above Delphi, where Dionysos was thought to reside in the winter months.
8. A cry associated with Dionysiac ecstasy.
9. Semele was killed when she saw her lover, Zeus, god of lightning, in his full glory, which was too much for a human.
1. Maenads.
2. Alternative name for Dionysos.
3. Builder and founder of Thebes.

Fate lifts up—and fate cuts down—both the lucky
and the unlucky, day in and day out.
No prophet can tell us what happens next.
Kreon always seemed someone to envy,
to me at least. He saved from attack
the homeland where we sons of Kadmos live;
this won him absolute power. He was
the brilliant father of patrician children.
Now it has all slipped away. For when things
that give pleasure and meaning to our lives
desert a man, he's not a human being
any more—he becomes a breathing corpse.
Amass wealth if you can, show off your house;
display the panache of a great monarch.
But if joy disappears from your life
I wouldn't give the shadow cast by smoke
for all you possess. Only happiness matters.

LEADER Should our masters expect more grief? What's happened?

MESSENGER Death. And the killer is alive.

LEADER Name the murderer. Name the dead. Tell us.

MESSENGER Haimon is dead. The hand that killed him was his own . . .

LEADER . . . father's? Or do you mean he killed himself?

MESSENGER He killed himself. Raging at his killer father.

LEADER Tiresias, you spoke the truth.

MESSENGER You know the facts, now you must cope with them.

(*Enter* EURYDIKE.)

LEADER I see Eurydike, soon to be crushed,
approaching from inside the house.
She may have heard what's happened to her son.

EURYDIKE I heard all of you speaking as I came out—
on my way to offer prayers to Athena.
I happened to unlatch the gate,
to open it, when words of our disaster
carried to my ears. I fainted, terrified
and dumbstruck, in the arms of my servants.
Please tell me your news. Tell me all of it.
I'm someone who has lived through misfortune.

MESSENGER O my dear Queen, I will spare you nothing.
I'll tell you truthfully what I've just seen.
Why should I say something to soothe you
that will later prove me a liar?
Straight talk is always best.
I traveled with your husband to the far
edge of the plain where Polyneikes' corpse,
mangled by wild dogs, lay still uncared-for.

We prayed for mercy to the Goddess
of Roadways; and to Pluto, asking them

to restrain their anger.[4] We washed his remains
with purified water. Using boughs stripped
from nearby bushes, we burned what was left,
then mounded a tomb from his native earth.

After that we turned toward the girl's deadly
wedding cavern—with its bed of cold stone.
Still far off, we heard an enormous wail
coming from somewhere near the unhallowed
portico—so we turned back to tell Kreon.
As the king arrived, these incoherent
despairing shouts echoed all around him.
First he groaned, then he yelled out in raw pain,

"Am I a prophet? Will my worst fears come true?
Am I walking down the bitterest street
of my life? That's my son's voice greeting me!

"Move quickly, men, run through that narrow gap
where the stones have been pulled loose from the wall,
go where the cavern opens out. Tell me
the truth—is that Haimon's voice I'm hearing,
or have the gods played some trick on my ears?"

Following orders from our despondent
master, we stared in. At the tomb's far end
there she was, hanging by the neck, a noose
of finely woven linen holding her aloft.
He fell against her, arms hugging her waist,
grieving for the bride he'd lost to Hades,
for his father's acts, for his own doomed love.

When Kreon saw all this he stepped inside,
groaned horribly, and called out to his son:
"My desperate child! What have you done? What
did you think you were doing? When did the gods
destroy your reason? Come out of there, son.
I beg you."
His son then glared straight at him
with savage eyes, spat in his face, spoke not
one word in answer, but drew his two-edged sword.
His father leapt back, Haimon missed his thrust.
Then this raging youth—with no warning—turned
on himself, tensed his body to the sword,
and drove half its length deep into his side.

4. The Goddess of the Roadways is Hecate, associated with crossroads, ghosts, and witchcraft. Pluto is god of the underworld.

Still conscious, he clung to her with limp arms,
gasping for breath, spurts of his blood pulsing
onto her white cheek.
Then he lay there, his dead
body embracing hers, married at last,
poor man—not up here, but somewhere
in Hades—proving that of all mankind's
evils, thoughtless violence is the worst.

(*Exit* EURYDIKE.)

LEADER What do you make of that? She turns and leaves
without saying one word, brave or bitter.

MESSENGER I don't like it. I hope that having heard
the sorry way her son died, she won't grieve
for him in public. Maybe she's gone
to ask her maids to mourn him in the house.
This woman never loses her composure.

LEADER I'm not so sure. To me this strange silence
seems ominous as an outburst of grief.

MESSENGER I'll go in and find out.
She could have disguised the real
intent of her impassioned heart.
But I agree: Her silence is alarming.

(*Exit* MESSENGER *into the palace;* KREON *enters carrying the body of* HAIMON *wrapped in cloth; his Men follow, bringing a bier on which* KREON *will lay his son in due course.*)

LEADER Here comes our king, burdened
with a message all too clear:
This wasn't caused by anyone's vengeance—
may I say it?—but by his own father's blunders.

KREON Oh, what errors of the mind I have made!
Deadly, bull-headed blunders.
You all see it—the man
who murdered, and the son
who's dead. What I did
was blind and wrong!
You died so young, my son,
your death happened so fast!
Your life was cut short
not through your mad acts,
but through mine.

LEADER You saw the right course of action
but took it far too late.

KREON I've learned that lesson now—
in all its bitterness.
Sometime back, a god struck
my head an immense blow,
it drove me
to act in brutal ways,

ways that stamped out
all my happiness.
What burdens and what pain
men suffer and endure.

(*Enter* MESSENGER *from palace.*)

MESSENGER Master, your hands are full of sorrow,
you bear its full weight.
But other sorrows are in store—
you'll face them soon, inside your house.

KREON Can any new
calamity make
what's happened worse?

MESSENGER Your wife is dead—so much
a loving mother to your son,
poor woman, that she died
of wounds just now inflicted.

KREON Oh Hades, you are hard
to appease! We flood
your harbor, you want more.
Why are you trying
to destroy me?

(*Turning to Messenger.*)

What have you to tell me
this time?—you who bring
nothing but deadly news.
I was hardly alive, and now, my young friend,
you've come back to kill me again.
Son, what are you telling me?
What is this newest message

(*The palace doors open;* EURYDIKE'*s corpse is revealed.*)

that buries me? My wife is dead.
Slaughter after slaughter.

LEADER Now you see it. Your house no longer hides it.

KREON I see one more violent death. With what
else can fate punish me? I have
just held my dead son in my arms—
now I see another dear body.
Oh unhappy mother, oh my son.

MESSENGER There, at the altar, she pierced
herself with a sharp blade.
Her eyes went quietly dark
and she closed them.
She had first mourned aloud
the empty marriage bed
of her dead son Megareus.[5]

5. Another son of Kreon and Eurydike, killed during the siege of the city. Tiresias had prophesied that his death would save the city.

Then with her last breath
she cursed you, Kreon,
killer of your own son.

KREON Ahhh! That sends fear
surging through me.
Why hasn't someone
driven a two-edged
sword through my heart?
I'm a wretched coward,
awash with terror.

MESSENGER The woman whose corpse you see
condemns you for the deaths of her sons.

KREON Tell me how she did it.

MESSENGER She drove the blade below her liver,
so she could suffer the same wound
that killed Haimon, for whom she mourns.

KREON There's no one I can blame,
no other mortal.
I am the only one.

(KREON *looks at and touches the body of* HAIMON *as his Men assemble to escort him offstage.*)

I killed you, that's the reality.
Men, take me inside,
I'm less than nothing now.

LEADER You are doing what's right,
if any right can be found
among all these misfortunes.
It's best to say little
in the face of evil.

KREON Let it come, let it happen now—
let my own kindest fate
make this my final day on earth.
That would be kindness itself.
Let it happen, let it come.
Never let me see
tomorrow's dawn.

LEADER That's in the future. We
must deal with the present.
The future will be shaped
by those who control it.

KREON My deepest desires are in that prayer.

LEADER Stop your prayers.
No human being
evades calamity
once it has struck.

(KREON *puts his hand on* HAIMON*'s corpse.*)

KREON Take me from this place.
A foolish, impulsive man

who killed you, my son, mindlessly,
killed you as well, my wife.
I'm truly cursed! I don't know
where to rest my eyes,
or on whose shoulders
I can lean my weight.
My hands warp
all they touch;

(KREON, *still touching* HAIMON'*s corpse, looks toward* EURYDIKE'*s, then lifts his hand and moves off toward the palace.*)

and over there,
fate's avalanche
pounds my head.

LEADER Good sense is crucial
to human happiness.
Never fail to respect the gods,
for the huge claims of proud men
are always hugely punished—
by blows that, as the proud grow old,
pound wisdom through their minds.

(*All leave.*)

EURIPIDES

ca. 480–406 B.C.E.

LIFE AND TIMES

Euripides strikes many readers as the liveliest, funniest, and most provocative of the three great Athenian tragedians whose work survives. A younger contemporary of **Aeschylus** and **Sophocles**, Euripides lived through most of the cultural and political turmoil of the fifth century, and was seen as one of the most influential voices for the revolutionary new ideas that were developing in this period. Controversial in his own time for his use of colloquial language and his depictions of unheroic heroes, sexually promiscuous women, and cruel, violent gods, Euripides has lost none of his power to shock, provoke, amuse, and engage his audiences.

We know little of Euripides' personal life. He seems to have been married twice, and had three sons. He was a productive but only moderately successful tragedian: he wrote over ninety plays, but won first prize only four times. He specialized in unexpected plot twists and novel approaches to his mythological material: for instance, his play about Helen of Troy (*Helen*) makes her an entirely virtuous woman, who never ran off with Paris or committed adultery. There are many moments of humor in Euripides, far more so than in Aeschylus or Sophocles. At the same time, his vision is often very dark. His later plays about the Trojan War (such as *Hecuba* and *Trojan Women*) are easy to read as terrible indictments of the suffering caused to women, children, and families by the contemporary Peloponnesian War between Athens and Sparta.

He spent most of his life in Athens, but in his old age went to visit Macedon, where he died. It has often been suggested that he left Athens in outrage at the city's failure to appreciate him, but there is no evidence for this. Euripides was probably always popular with audiences, albeit less so with the judges of the dramatic competition, who perhaps felt an obligation to uphold civic ideals. Euripides continued to be widely read, quoted, and enjoyed for generations after his death.

Medea was first performed in the spring of 431 B.C.E., immediately before the outbreak of the Peloponnesian War. It was a time of prosperity for the city: the Greeks had defeated the Persians in the year of Euripides' birth, and now the Athenian Empire extended across the Mediterranean. Athens was full of pride in the political, artistic, and intellectual achievements of the citizens.

It was also a time of new, antitraditional ideas, brought by the Sophists, men from other societies who came to Athens to teach "cleverness" or "wisdom"—*sophia*. The Sophists were seen by some as a mark of Athens' progressive openness to new modes of thought, but by others as a dangerous influence, liable to corrupt the city's young men. The tragedies of Euripides were associated by the comic dramatist, Aristophanes, and probably many others, with the iconoclasm of the Sophists. The plays were clearly found shocking and controversial by contemporaries. Euripides uses traditional myths, but shifts attention away from the deeds of heroes toward domestic wrangling, and shows up moral and psychological weaknesses. Euripides was seen as a cynical realist about human nature: Sophocles said that while he showed people as they ought to be, Euripides showed them as they are.

Euripides put male heroes onstage in humiliated positions: they are bedraggled and dressed in rags, or are presented as obvious cowards, liars, or brutes. Euripides' outspoken, lustful or violent, though often sympathetic, women were found particularly outrageous by his contemporaries. Lower-class characters and slaves were prominent, and sympathetically portrayed. In religious terms, too, his plays were challenging and controversial: his characters often question the old Greek myths about the gods, and the gods themselves often seem arbitrary or cruel in their dealings with humanity. Euripides also included vivid and realistic descriptions of violence, as in the messenger speech of the *Medea*, a horrifying account of how the princess Creusa's hair was burned up by her golden crown, while her poisoned dress corroded her skin and finally ripped the flesh from her bones.

THE WORK

Medea, like almost all Greek tragedies, is based on a traditional story. According to myth, the hero Jason was told by his uncle, Pelias, that he could not claim his rightful inheritance, the throne of Iolcus, unless he could perform a seemingly impossible quest: cross the Black Sea to the distant barbarian land of Colchis, ruled by the savage king Aeetes, and bring back to Greece the Golden Fleece, which was guarded by a dragon. Jason assembled a group of the finest Greek heroes, and built the world's first ship—the *Argo*—to take them to Colchis. Once they arrived, King Aeetes set Jason the task of ploughing a field with a team of fire-breathing bulls. Luckily, the king's daughter, Medea, fell in love with Jason. She was skilled in magic, and enabled him to plough the field, lull the dragon to sleep, steal the fleece, and escape back to Greece, killing her own brother to distract the attention of their enraged Colchian pursuers. When they arrived in Iolcus, Pelias tried to go back on his word, and hang onto power. Medea got back at him by persuading Pelias' daughters that they could make their father immortal by boiling him alive—which was, of course, untrue. After the scandal was discovered, Jason and Medea were forced into exile. The couple had children, and eventually moved to Corinth. There, Jason decided to divorce Medea and marry a native Corinthian princess instead. With that, the action of *Medea* begins.

The most well-known part of the myth was the story of the quest of the Argonauts (sailors in the *Argo*) for the Golden Fleece. But Euripides focuses not on this heroic narrative but on its squalid aftermath, and he seems to have invented certain key aspects of the story. In previous versions, the children were either murdered by Creon's family or, according to another story, accidentally killed by Medea, when she tried to use magic to make them immortal. The shocking events at the end of this play would not have been anticipated by Euripides' audience.

Euripides' concentration on the domestic troubles in Corinth, rather than the heroic quest, allows him to present Jason in a disturbingly unheroic light: as a cad who struggles to muster unconvincing strategic and rhetorical arguments to justify his shabby treatment of his first wife. Although Jason tries to talk like a Sophist, it is Medea who is the real possessor of *sophia* in the play. The term *sophia* has negative and positive connotations: it can suggest deep understanding, but it can also imply mere cleverness. The play invites us to consider which character is the smartest: Jason, with his dodges and evasions, or Medea, with her unpredictable, cruel stratagems.

Medea is strongly marked as an outsider in three crucial ways: as a woman in a male-dominated world; as a foreigner or "barbarian" in a Greek city; and as a smart person surrounded by fools. On all these grounds, the play initially seems to invite us to side with Medea. She is obviously the wronged party in her relationship with Jason; and yet, even as she expresses her devastation at the betrayal, she never presents herself as a victim. Rather, she is fierce, "like a wild lion," and highly articulate in her analysis of her situation. She claims even the male values of military honor for herself and for all women, suggesting in one famous passage that women who undergo the pain and danger of childbirth are far braver than men who fight in war: "I'd rather take my stand behind / a shield three times than go through childbirth once." It is tempting to read these lines as proto-feminist, and to see Euripides, the clever poet, as sympathetic to his clever heroine, and as a defender of the rights and dignity of women and foreigners, before an audience of Athenian male citizens.

But as the play goes on, our vision of Medea is likely to change. We may begin to see her, not as strong and brave, but as scarily violent; not as wise, but as too clever by half. This is a disturbing play, which forces readers to revise their feelings several times. Is Medea smart and sensible in her defense of her honor and her rights, or is she driven crazy by the gods of passion? Or should we see her as an agent of the gods, imposing divine justice on oath-breaking humans? Is Euripides challenging or confirming Greek male prejudices against foreigners and women? Is he recommending new forms of wisdom, or warning against the false cleverness of upstarts and outsiders? And what does it say about the city of Athens, that it is the Athenian king,

Aegeus, who will welcome this terrifying figure into his community?

Thematically, the most important threads in the play include the opposition of order and chaos, and the idea of time, especially the reversal of time. The Nurse opens the play by wishing that history could be reversed: "I wish the Argo never had set sail," she declares: the play begins with a desire to undo the beginning. Medea is the granddaughter of a god, Helios, the Sun, which associates her closely with the regular passing of time, in the sun's rising and setting. Her violent revenge at the injustice done to her can be seen as an attempt to do the impossible: to undo, by violence, her life history ever since the sailing of the *Argo*, to regain her lost honor and go back to her old self, an unmarried princess. It can also be seen as an attempt at justice, a restoration of order out of chaos—but at a terrible cost, and in violation of all moderation and humanity.

Medea is an endlessly fascinating play that seems strikingly modern in its examination of family life, infidelity, failed sexual relationships, the experience of immigrants in a foreign land, and how it feels to be an oppressed or marginalized member of society. It also points to the fear, felt by many people both ancient and modern, that the apparently weaker members of a community, such as women and resident aliens, may be smarter than their masters, and may, if provoked enough, rise up to destroy their oppressors.

Medea[1]

Characters

NURSE, *of Medea*
TUTOR, *of Medea and Jason's children*
MEDEA
CHORUS, *women of Corinth*
CREON, *king of Corinth*
JASON
AEGEUS, *king of Athens*
MESSENGER
CHILDREN, *of Medea and Jason*

SCENE: *A normal house on a street in Corinth. The elderly* NURSE *steps out of its front door.*[2]

NURSE I wish the *Argo*[3] never had set sail,
had never flown to Colchis through the dark
Clashing Rocks;[4] I wish the pines had never
been felled along the hollows on the slopes
of Pelion, to fit their hands with oars—
those heroes who went off to seek the golden
pelt for Pelias. My mistress then,
Medea, never would have sailed away

1. Translated by Diane Arnson Svarlien.
2. The list of characters and all stage directions, in italics, are by Robin Mitchell-Boyask.
3. The first ship, constructed by Jason for his quest for the Golden Fleece.
4. Colchis, home of Medea, lay on the other side of the Black Sea, past the rocks near the mouth of the Bosphorus.

to reach the towers of Iolcus' land;[5]
the sight of Jason never would have stunned
her spirit with desire. She would have never
persuaded Pelias' daughters to kill their father,[6]
never had to come to this land—Corinth.[7]
Here she's lived in exile with her husband
and children, and Medea's presence pleased
the citizens. For her part, she complied
with Jason in all things. There is no greater
security than this in all the world:
when a wife does not oppose her husband.
But now, there's only hatred. What should be
most loved has been contaminated, stricken
since Jason has betrayed them—his own children,
and my lady, for a royal bed.
He's married into power: Creon's daughter.[8]
Poor Medea, mournful and dishonored,
shrieks at his broken oaths, the promise sealed
with his right hand (the greatest pledge there is)—
she calls the gods to witness just how well
Jason has repaid her. She won't touch food;
surrendering to pain, she melts away
her days in tears, ever since she learned
of this injustice. She won't raise her face;
her eyes are glued to the ground. Friends talk to her,
try to give her good advice; she listens
the way a rock does, or an ocean wave.
At most, she'll turn her pale neck aside,
sobbing to herself for her dear father,
her land, her home, and all that she betrayed
for Jason, who now holds her in dishonor.
This disaster made her realize:
a fatherland is no small thing to lose.
She hates her children, feels no joy in seeing them.
I'm afraid she might be plotting something.
Her mind is fierce, and she will not endure
ill treatment. I know her. I'm petrified
to think what thoughts she might be having now:
a sharpened knife-blade thrust right through the liver—
she could even strike the royal family, murder
the bridegroom too, make this disaster worse.
She's a terror. There's no way to be
her enemy and come out as the victor.

5. Thessaly, in Greece.

6. Pelias, Jason's uncle, reneged on a promise to give Jason the throne of Iolchus if he brought back the Golden Fleece. In revenge, Medea persuaded Pelias's daughters to boil him alive, in the belief that they would make him young again.

7. After the scandal of Pelias's murder, Jason and Medea had to go into exile, to Corinth.

8. Creon, king of Corinth, is not the same as the Kreon of Thebes in Sophocles' Theban plays.

Here come the children, resting from their games,
with no idea of their mother's troubles.
A child's mind is seldom filled with pain.

(*Enter the* TUTOR *from the house with the two children of* JASON *and* MEDEA.)

TUTOR Timeworn stalwart of my mistress' household,
why do you stand here by the gates, alone,
crying out your sorrows to yourself?
You've left Medea alone. Doesn't she need you?
NURSE Senior attendant to the sons of Jason,
decent servants feel their masters' griefs
in their own minds, when things fall out all wrong.
As for me, my pain was so intense
that a desire crept over me to come out here
and tell the earth and sky my mistress' troubles.
TUTOR Poor thing. Is she not done with weeping yet?
NURSE What blissful ignorance! She's barely started.
TUTOR The fool—if one may say such things of masters—
she doesn't even know the latest outrage.
NURSE What is it, old man? Don't begrudge me that.
TUTOR Nothing. I'm sorry that I spoke at all.
NURSE By your beard, don't hide this thing from *me*,
your fellow-servant. I can keep it quiet.
TUTOR As I approached the place where the old men
sit and play dice, beside the sacred spring
Peirene,[9] I heard someone say—he didn't
notice I was listening—that Creon,
the ruler of this land, intends to drive
these children and their mother out of Corinth.
I don't know if it's true. I hope it isn't.
NURSE Will Jason let his sons be so abused,
even if he's fighting with their mother?
TUTOR He has a new bride; he's forgotten them.
He's no friend to this household anymore.
NURSE We are destroyed, then. Before we've bailed our boat
from the first wave of sorrow, here's a new one.
TUTOR But please, don't tell your mistress. Keep it quiet.
It's not the time for her to know of this.
NURSE Children, do you hear the way your father
is treating you? I won't say, *May he die!*
—he is my master—but it's obvious
he's harming those whom he should love. He's guilty.
TUTOR Who isn't? Are you just now learning this,
that each man loves himself more than his neighbor?
If their father doesn't cherish them, because
he's more preoccupied with his own bed—

9. Spring in Corinth.

NURSE Go inside now, children. Everything
will be all right.

(*The* TUTOR *turns the children toward the house.*)

And you, keep them away—
don't let them near their mother when she's like this.
I've seen her: she looks fiercer than a bull;
she's giving them the eye, as if she means
to do something. Her rage will not let up,
I know, until she lashes out at someone.
May it be enemies she strikes, and not her loved ones!

(*In the following passage,* MEDEA *sings and the* NURSE *chants.*)

MEDEA (*From within the house, crying out in rage.*)

Aaaah!
Oh, horrible, horrible, all that I suffer,
my unhappy struggles. I wish I could die.

NURSE You see, this is it. Dear children, your mother
has stirred up her heart, she has stirred up her rage.
Hurry up now and get yourselves inside the house—
but don't get too close to her, don't let her see you:
her ways are too wild, her nature is hateful,
her mind is too willful.
Go in. Hurry up!

(*Exit the* TUTOR *and children into the house.*)

It's clear now, it's starting: a thunderhead rising,
swollen with groaning, and soon it will flash
as her spirit ignites it—then what will she do?
Her heart is so proud, there is no way to stop her;
her soul has been pierced by these sorrows.

MEDEA *Aaaah!*
The pain that I've suffered, I've suffered so much,
worth oceans of weeping. O children, accursed,
may you die—with your father! Your mother is hateful.
Go to hell, the whole household! Every last one.

NURSE Oh, lord. Here we go. What have *they* done—the children?
Their father's done wrong—why should you hate *them*?
Oh, children, my heart is so sore, I'm afraid
you will come to some harm.
Rulers are fierce
in their temperament; somehow, they will not be governed;
they like to have power, always, over others.
They're harsh, and they're stubborn. It's better to live
as an equal with equals. I never would want
to be grand and majestic—just let me grow old
in simple security. Even the *word*

"moderation" sounds good when you say it. For mortals
the middle is safest, in word and in deed.
Too much is too much, and there's always a danger
a god may get angry and ruin your household.

(*Enter the* CHORUS *of Corinthian women from the right, singing.*)

CHORUS *I heard someone's voice, I heard someone shout:*
the woman from Colchis: poor thing, so unhappy.
Is her grief still unsoftened? Old woman, please tell us—
I heard her lament through the gates of my hall.
Believe me, old woman, I take no delight
when this house is in pain. I have pledged it my friendship.

NURSE This house? It no longer exists. It's all gone.
He's taken up with his new royal marriage.
She's in her bedroom, my mistress, she's melting
her life all away, and her mind can't be eased
by a single kind word from a single dear friend.

MEDEA *Aaaah!*
May a fire-bolt from heaven come shoot through my skull!
What do I gain by being alive?
Oh, god. How I long for the comfort of death.
I hate this life. How I wish I could leave it.

[Strophe]

CHORUS Do you hear, O Zeus, O sunlight and earth,
this terrible song, the cry
of this unhappy bride?
Poor fool, what a dreadful longing,
this craving for final darkness.
You'll hasten your death. Why do it?
Don't pray for this ending.
If your husband reveres a new bed, a new bride,
don't sharpen your mind against him.
You'll have Zeus himself supporting
your case. Don't dissolve in weeping
for the sake of your bedmate.

MEDEA *Great goddess Themis and Artemis, holy one:*[1]
do you see what I suffer, although I have bound
my detestable husband with every great oath?
May I see him, along with his bride and the palace
scraped down to nothing, crushed into splinters.
He started it. He was the one with the nerve

1. Themis, whose name means "Right" or "Lawfulness," is a female Titan associated with order and keeping promises. Artemis is a goddess who protects virgins and women in childbirth.

to commit this injustice. Oh father, oh city,
I left you in horror—I killed my own brother.[2]

NURSE You hear what she says, and the gods that she prays to:
Themis, and Zeus, the enforcer of oaths?
There's no way my mistress's rage will die down
into anything small.

[Antistrophe]

CHORUS How I wish she'd come outside, let us see
her face, let her hear our words
and the sound of our voice.
If only she'd drop her anger,
unburden her burning spirit,
let go of this weight of madness.
I'll stand by our friendship.
Hurry up, bring her here, get her out, go inside,
and bring her to us. Go tell her
that we are her friends. Please hurry!
She's raging—the ones inside may
feel the sting of her sorrow.

NURSE I'll do as you ask, but I fear that my mistress
won't listen to me.
I will make the effort—what's one more attempt?
But her glare is as fierce as a bull's, let me tell you—
she's wild like a lion who's just given birth
whenever a servant tries telling her anything.

You wouldn't go wrong, you'd be right on the mark,
if you called them all half-wits, the people of old:
they made lovely songs for banquets and parties,
but no one took time to discover the music
that might do some good, the chords or the harmony
people could use to relieve all the hateful
pain and distress that leads to the downfall
of houses, the deaths and the dreadful misfortunes.
Let me tell you, there would be some gain in that—music
with the power to heal. When you're having a sumptuous
feast, what's the point of a voice raised in song?
Why bother with singing? The feast is enough
to make people happy. That's all that they need.

(*Exit the* NURSE *into the house.*)

2. After the theft of the Golden Fleece, Jason and Medea were pursued by the outraged Colchians. To slow them down, Medea killed her brother, Aspyrtus, and threw his body parts behind her.

CHORUS *I heard a wail, a clear cry of pain;*
she rails at the betrayer of her bed,
the bitter bridegroom.
For the injustice she suffers, she calls on the gods:
Themis of Zeus, protectress of oaths,
who brought her to Hellas,[3] *over the salt water dark as night,*
through the waves of Pontus' forbidding gate.[4]

(*Enter* MEDEA *from the house, attended by the* NURSE *and other female servants. Here spoken dialogue resumes.*)

MEDEA Women of Corinth, I have stepped outside
so you will not condemn me. Many people
act superior—I'm well aware of this.
Some keep it private; some are arrogant
in public view. Yet there are other people
who, just because they lead a quiet life,
are thought to be aloof. There is no justice
in human eyesight: people take one look
and hate a man, before they know his heart,
though no injustice has been done to them.
A foreigner must adapt to a new city,
certainly. Nor can I praise a citizen
who's willful, and who treats his fellow townsmen
harshly, out of narrow-mindedness.

My case is different. Unexpected trouble
has crushed my soul. It's over now; I take
no joy in life. My friends, I want to die.
My husband, who was everything to me—
how well I know it—is the worst of men.

Of all the living creatures with a soul
and mind, we women are the most pathetic.
First of all, we have to buy a husband:[5]
spend vast amounts of money, just to get
a master for our body—to add insult
to injury. And the stakes could not be higher:
will you get a decent husband, or a bad one?
If a woman leaves her husband, then she loses
her virtuous reputation. To refuse him
is just not possible. When a girl leaves home
and comes to live with new ways, different rules,
she has to be a prophet—learn somehow
the art of dealing smoothly with her bedmate.
If we do well, and if our husbands bear

3. Greece.
4. Pontus is the Black Sea; the "gate" is the Bosphorus.
5. In ancient Greece, the bride's family had to pay a dowry to the husband.

the yoke without discomfort or complaint,
our lives are admired. If not, it's best to die.
A man, when he gets fed up with the people
at home, can go elsewhere to ease his heart
—he has friends, companions his own age.
We must rely on just one single soul.
They say that we lead safe, untroubled lives
at home while they do battle with the spear.
They're wrong. I'd rather take my stand behind
a shield three times than go through childbirth once.

Still, my account is quite distinct from yours.
This is your city. You have your fathers' homes,
your lives bring joy and profit. You have friends.
But I have been deserted and outraged—
left without a city by my husband,
who stole me as his plunder from the land
of the barbarians. Here I have no mother,
no brother, no blood relative to help
unmoor me from this terrible disaster.
So, I will need to ask you one small favor.
If I should find some way, some strategy
to pay my husband back, bring him to justice,
keep silent. Most of the time, I know, a woman
is filled with fear. She's worthless in a battle
and flinches at the sight of steel. But when
she's faced with an injustice in the bedroom,
there is no other mind more murderous.

CHORUS I'll do as you ask. You're justified, Medea,
in paying your husband back. I'm not surprised
you grieve at your misfortunes.
Look! I see Creon,
the lord of this land, coming toward us now.
He has some new decision to announce.

(*Enter* CREON *from the right, with attendants.*)

CREON You with the grim face, fuming at your husband,
Medea, I hereby announce that you
must leave this land, an exile, taking with you
your two children. You must not delay.
This is my decision. I won't leave
until I've thrown you out, across the border.

MEDEA Oh, god. I'm crushed; I'm utterly destroyed.
My enemies, their sails unfurled, attack me
and there's no land in sight, there's no escape
from ruin. Although I suffer, I must ask:
Creon, why do you send me from this land?

CREON I'll speak plainly: I'm afraid of you.
You could hurt my daughter, even kill her.
Every indication points that way.

You're wise by nature, you know evil arts,
and you're upset because your husband's gone
away from your bedroom. I have heard reports
that you've made threats, that you've devised a plan
to harm the bride, her father, and the bridegroom.
I want to guard against that. I would rather
have you hate me, woman, here and now,
than treat you gently and regret it later.

MEDEA Oh, god.
Creon, this is not the first time: often
I've been injured by my reputation.
Any man who's sensible by nature
will set a limit on his children's schooling
to make sure that they never grow too wise.
The wise are seen as lazy, and they're envied
and hated. If you offer some new wisdom
to half-wits, they will only think you're useless.
And those who are considered experts hate you
when the city thinks you're cleverer than they are.
I myself have met with this reaction.
Since I am wise, some people envy me,
some think I'm idle, some the opposite,
and some feel threatened. Yet I'm not all that wise.

And you're afraid of me. What do you fear?
Don't worry, Creon. I don't have it in me
to do wrong to a man with royal power.
What injustice have you done to me?
Your spirit moved you, and you gave your daughter
as you saw fit. My husband is the one
I hate. You acted well, with wise restraint.
And now, I don't begrudge your happiness.
My best to all of you—celebrate the wedding.
Just let me stay here. I know when I'm beaten.
I'll yield to this injustice. I'll submit
in silence to those greater than myself.

CREON Your words are soothing, but I'm terrified
of what's in your mind. I trust you less than ever.
It's easier to guard against a woman
(or man, for that matter) with a fiery spirit
than one who's wise and silent. You must leave
at once—don't waste my time with talk. It's settled.
Since you are my enemy, and hate me,
no ruse of yours can keep you here among us.

(MEDEA *kneels before* CREON *and grasps his hand and knees in supplication.*)[6]

6. This was a conventional way of asking a favor.

MEDEA No, by your knees! By your new-married daughter!
CREON You're wasting words. There's no way you'll persuade me.
MEDEA You'll drive me out, with no reverence for my prayers?
CREON I care more for my family than for you.
MEDEA How clearly I recall my fatherland.
CREON Yes, that's what *I* love most—after my children.
MEDEA Oh, god—the harm Desire does to mortals!
CREON Depending on one's fortunes, I suppose.
MEDEA Zeus, do not forget who caused these troubles.
CREON Just leave, you fool. I'm tired of struggling with you.
MEDEA Struggles. Yes. I've had enough myself.
CREON My guards will force you out in just a moment.
MEDEA Oh please, not that! Creon, I entreat you!
CREON You intend to make a scene, I gather.
MEDEA I'll leave, don't worry. That's not what I'm asking.
CREON Why are you forcing me? Let go of my hand!
MEDEA Please, let me stay just one more day, that's all.
I need to make arrangements for my exile,
find safe asylum for my children, since
their father doesn't give them any thought.
Take pity on them. You yourself have children.
It's only right for you to treat them kindly.
If we go into exile, I'm not worried
about myself—I weep for their disaster.
CREON I haven't got a ruler's temperament;
reverence has often led me into ruin.
Woman, I realize this is all wrong,
but you shall have your wish. I warn you, though:
[if the sun god's lamp should find you and your children
still within our borders at first rising,]
it means your death. I've spoken; it's decided.
Stay for one day only, if you must.
You won't have time to do the things I fear.

(*Exit* CREON *and attendants to the right.* MEDEA *rises to her feet.*)

CHORUS Oh, god! This is horrible, unhappy woman,
the grief that you suffer. Where will you turn?
Where will you find shelter? What country, what home
will save you from sorrow? A god has engulfed you,
Medea—this wave is now breaking upon you,
there is no way out.
MEDEA Yes, things are all amiss. Who could deny it?
Believe me, though, that's not how it will end.
The newlyweds have everything at stake,
and struggles await the one who made this match.
Do you think I ever could have fawned
on him like that without some gain in mind,
some ruse? I never would have spoken to him,
or touched him with my hands. He's such an idiot.

He could have thrown me out, destroyed my plans;
instead he's granted me a single day
to turn three enemies to three dead bodies:
the father, and the bride, and my own husband.
I know so many pathways to their deaths,
I don't know which to turn to first, my friends.
Shall I set the bridal home on fire,
creeping silently into their bedroom?

There's just one threat. If I am apprehended
entering the house, my ruse discovered,
I'll be put to death; my enemies
will laugh at me. The best way is the most
direct, to use the skills I have by nature
and poison them, destroy them with my drugs.

Ah, well.

All right, they die. What city will receive me?
What host will offer me immunity,
what land will take me in and give me refuge?
There's no one. I must wait just long enough
to see if any sheltering tower appears.
Then I will kill in silence, by deceit.
But if I have no recourse from disaster,
I'll take the sword and kill them, even if
it means my death. I have the utmost nerve.
Now, by the goddess whom I most revere,
Hecate,[7] whom I choose as my accomplice,
who dwells within my inmost hearth, I swear:
no one can hurt my heart and then fare well.
I'll turn their marriage bitter, desolate—
they'll regret the match, regret my exile.

And now, spare nothing that is in your knowledge,
Medea: make your plan, prepare your ruse.
Do this dreadful thing. There is so much
at stake. Display your courage. Do you see
how you are suffering? Do not allow
these Sisyphean snakes[8] to laugh at you
on Jason's wedding day. Your father is noble;
your grandfather is Helios. You have
the knowledge, not to mention woman's nature:
for any kind of noble deed, we're helpless;
for malice, though, our wisdom is unmatched.

7. Goddess associated with the moon and with witchcraft.

8. Sisyphus, an earlier king of Corinth, was notorious for his treachery; the "Sisyphean snakes" are the Corinthians.

This painted limestone statue, discovered in Saqqara, Egypt, in 1850, depicts a scribe writing on a tablet. It dates from the third millennium B.C.E. Scribes were highly respected members of court in ancient literate societies; their work is the primary reason we have any sense of life in deep antiquity.

Clay tablets (right and top) and envelope (left) from central Turkey, dating from ca. 1850 B.C.E. These objects contain a letter, written in cuneiform, from someone named "Ashur-malik" to his brother "Ashur-idi" in which the former complains that his family has been left in Ashur without food, fuel, or clothing over the winter. The letter writer ran out of room on the large tablet and so had to continue his complaint on the little supplemental tablet.

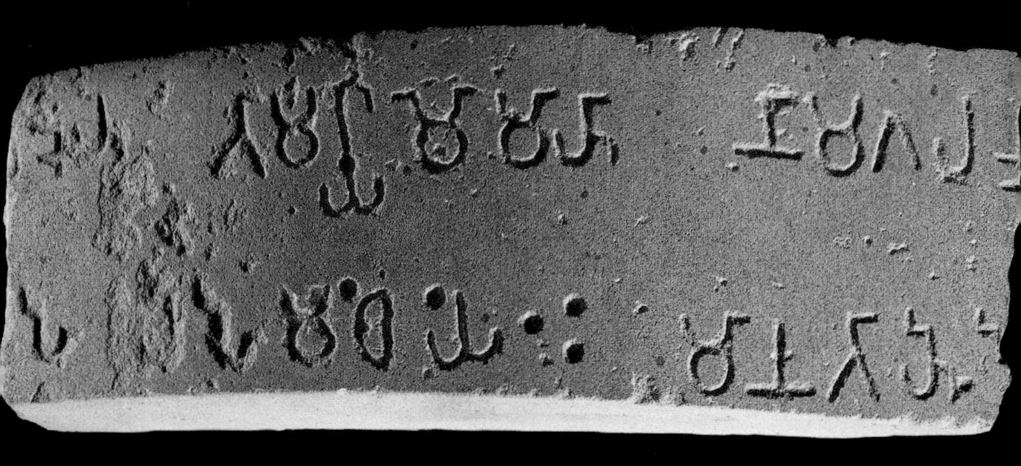

This fragment, part of the 'sixth pillar edict' of King Aśoka (third century B.C.E.), shows the Brahmi script used during the Mauryan Dynasty in northern India. The Brahmi script is the ancestral source of all modern Indian scripts.

XXI

CHORUS

[Strophe 1]

The streams of the holy rivers are flowing backward.
Everything runs in reverse—justice is upside down.
Men's minds are deceitful, and nothing is settled,
not even oaths that are sworn by the gods.
The tidings will change, and a virtuous reputation
will grace my name. The race of women will reap
honor, no longer the shame of disgraceful rumor.

[Antistrophe 1]

The songs of the poets of old will no longer linger
on my untrustworthiness. Women were never sent
the gift of divine inspiration by Phoebus
Apollo, lord of the elegant lyre,[9]
the master of music—or I could have sung my own song
against the race of men. The fullness of time
holds many tales: it can speak of both men and women.

[Strophe 2]

You sailed away from home and father,
driven insane in your heart; you traced a path
between the twin cliffs of Pontus.[1]
The land you live in is foreign.
Your bed is empty, your husband
gone. Poor woman, dishonored,
sent into exile.

[Antistrophe 2]

The Grace of oaths is gone, and Reverence
flies away into the sky, abandoning
great Hellas.[2] No father's dwelling
unmoors you now from this heartache.
Your bed now yields to another:
now a princess prevails,
greater than you are.

(*Enter* JASON *from the right.*)

JASON This is not the first time—I have often
observed that a fierce temper is an evil
that leaves you no recourse. You could have stayed
here in this land, you could have kept your home
by simply acquiescing in the plans
of those who are greater. You are now an exile
because of your own foolish words. To me
it makes no difference. You can keep on calling

9. Phoebus ("shining") Apollo is the god of the sun and of poetry, usually depicted with the lyre, a stringed instrument that was used to accompany poetic performance.

1. The path between the cliffs is Bosphorus.

2. Greece.

Jason the very worst of men. However,
the words you spoke against the royal family—
well, consider it a gain that nothing worse
than exile is your punishment. As for me,
I wanted you to stay. I always tried
to calm the king, to soothe his fuming rage.
But you, you idiot, would not let up
your words against the royal family. That's why
you are now an exile. All the same,
I won't let down my loved ones. I have come here
looking out for your best interests, woman,
so you won't be without the things you need
when you go into exile with the children.
You'll need money—banishment means hardship.
However much you hate me, I could never
wish you any harm.

MEDEA You are the worst!
You're loathsome—that's the worst word I can utter.
You're not a man. You've come here—most detested
by the gods, by me, by all mankind.
That isn't courage, when you have the nerve
to harm your friends, then look them in the face.
No, that's the worst affliction known to man:
shamelessness.
And yet, I'm glad you've come.
Speaking ill to you will ease my soul,
and listening will cause you pain. I'll start
at the beginning. First, I saved your life—
as every single man who sailed from Hellas
aboard the *Argo* knows—when you were sent
to yoke the fire-breathing bulls, and sow
the deadly crop.[3] I killed the dragon, too:
the sleepless one, who kept the Golden Fleece
enfolded in his convoluted coils;[4]
I was your light, the beacon of your safety.
For my part, I betrayed my home, my father,
and went with you to Pelion's slopes, Iolcus[5]
with more good will than wisdom—and I killed
Pelias, in the cruelest possible way:
at his own children's hands. I ruined their household.

And you—you *are* the very worst of men—
betrayed me, after all of that. You wanted
a new bed, even though I'd borne you children.

3. Jason was challenged by Medea's father, King Aeetes, to plough a field with a pair of fire-breathing bulls, and sow it with dragon's teeth, which would instantly grow into armed men. With Medea's help, he succeeded.

4. The Golden Fleece hung from a tree, round which coiled a fierce dragon; Medea succeeded in defeating the dragon.

5. Ancestral kingdom of Jason.

If you had still been childless, anyone
could understand your lust for this new marriage.

All trust in oaths is gone. What puzzles me
is whether you believe those gods (the ones
who heard you swear) no longer are in power,
or that the old commandments have been changed?
You realize full well you broke your oath.

Ah, my right hand, which you took so often,
clinging to my knees.[6] What was the point
of touching me? You are despicable.
My hopes have all gone wrong. Well, then! You're here:
I have a question for you, friend to friend.
(What good do I imagine it will do?
Still, I'll ask, since it makes you look worse.)
Where do I turn now? To my father's household
and fatherland, which I betrayed for you?
Or Pelias' poor daughters? Naturally
they'll welcome me—the one who killed their father!

Here is my situation. I've become
an enemy to my own family, those
whom I should love, and I have gone to war
with those whom I had no reason at all
to hurt, and all for your sake. In exchange,
you've made me the happiest girl in all of Hellas.
I have you, the perfect spouse, a marvel,
so trustworthy—though I must leave the country
friendless and deserted, taking with me
my friendless children! What a charming scandal
for a newlywed: your children roam
as beggars, with the one who saved your life.

Zeus! For brass disguised as gold, you sent us
reliable criteria to judge.
But when a man is base, how can we know?
Why is there no sign stamped upon his body?

CHORUS This anger is a terror, hard to heal,
when loved ones clash with loved ones in dispute.

JASON It seems that I must have a way with words
and, like a skillful captain, reef my sails
in order to escape this gale that blows
without a break—your endless, tired harangue.
The way I see it, woman (since you seem
to feel that I must owe you some huge favor),

6. Touching a person's right hand and knees was a way of asking for a favor, assuming the position of a supplicant. Medea is implying that Jason has failed to pay her back for the favors she did him.

it was Cypris,[7] no other god or mortal,
who saved me on my voyage. Yes, your mind
is subtle. But I must say—at the risk
of stirring up your envy and your grudges—
Eros[8] was the one who forced your hand:
his arrows, which are inescapable,[9]
compelled you to rescue me. But I won't put
too fine a point on that. You *did* support me.
You saved my life, in fact. However, you
received more than you gave, as I shall prove.
First of all, you live in Hellas now
instead of your barbarian land. With us,
you know what justice is, and civil law:
not mere brute force. And every single person
in Hellas knows that you are wise. You're famous.
You'd never have that kind of reputation
if you were living at the edge of nowhere.
As for me, I wouldn't wish for gold
or for a sweeter song than Orpheus'[1]
unless I had the fame to match my fortune.

Enough about my struggles—you're the one
who started this debate. As for my marriage
to the princess, which you hold against me,
I shall show you how I acted wisely
and with restraint, and with the greatest love
toward you and toward our children—Wait! Just listen!
When I moved here from Iolcus, bringing with me
disaster in abundance, with no recourse,
what more lucky windfall could I find
(exile that I was) than marrying
the king's own child? It's not that I despised
your bed—the thought that irritates you most—
nor was I mad with longing for a new bride,
or trying to compete with anyone—
to win the prize for having the most children.
I have enough—no reason to complain.
My motive was the best: so we'd live well
and not be poor. I know that everyone
avoids a needy friend. I wanted to raise
sons in a style that fits my family background,
give brothers to the ones I had with you,
and treat them all as equals. This would strengthen

7. Aphrodite, goddess of sex.
8. Cupid, god of sex—the son of Aphrodite.
9. Eros fires arrows that inspire desire.
1. Orpheus, son of the god Apollo and the muse Calliope, was a poet-singer with semimagical powers: even wild animals were fascinated by his songs. Orpheus was famously devoted to his wife, Eurydice; when she died, he traveled down to the underworld to try to rescue her.

the family, and I'd be blessed with fortune.
What do *you* need children for? For me, though,
it's good if I can use my future children
to benefit my present ones. Is that
bad planning? If you weren't so irritated
about your bed, you'd never say it was.
But you're a woman—and you're all the same!
If everything goes well between the sheets
you think you have it all. But let there be
some setback or disaster in the bedroom
and suddenly you go to war against
the things that you should value most. I mean it—
men should really have some other method
for getting children. The whole female race
should not exist. It's nothing but a nuisance.

CHORUS Jason, you've composed a lovely speech.
But I must say, though you may disagree:
you have betrayed your wife. You've been unjust.

MEDEA Now, this is where I differ from most people.
In my view, someone who is both unjust
and has a gift for speaking—such a man
incurs the greatest penalty. He uses
his tongue to cover up his unjust actions,
and this gives him the nerve to stop at nothing
no matter how outrageous. Yet he's not
all that wise. Take your case, for example.

Spare me this display of cleverness;
a single word will pin you to the mat.
If you weren't in the wrong, you would have told me
your marriage plans, not kept us in the dark—
your loved ones, your own family!

JASON Yes, of course
you would have been all for it! Even now
you can't control your rage against the marriage.

MEDEA That's not what you were thinking. You imagined
that for an older man, a barbarian wife
was lacking in prestige.

JASON No! Please believe me:
It wasn't for the woman's sake I married
into the king's family. As I have said,
I wanted to save you, and give our children
royal brothers, a safeguard for our household.

MEDEA May I not have a life that's blessed with fortune
so painful, or prosperity so irritating.

JASON Your prayer could be much wiser: don't consider
what's useful painful. When you have good fortune,
don't see it as a hardship.

MEDEA Go ahead—
you have somewhere to turn!—commit this outrage.
I am deserted, exiled from this land.
JASON You brought that on yourself. Don't blame another.
MEDEA Did I remarry? How did I betray you?
JASON You blasphemously cursed the royal family.
MEDEA And I'm a curse to your family as well.
JASON I won't discuss this with you any further.
If you'd like me to help you and the children
with money for your exile, then just say so.
I'm prepared to give with an open hand,
and make arrangements with my friends to show you
hospitality. They'll treat you well.
You'd be an idiot to refuse this offer.
You'll gain a lot by giving up your anger.
MEDEA I wouldn't stay with your friends, and I would never
accept a thing from you. Don't even offer.
There is no profit in a bad man's gift.
JASON All the same, I call the gods to witness:
I only want to help you and the children.
But you don't want what's good; you push away
your friends; you're willful. And you'll suffer for it.
MEDEA Get out of here. A craving for your new bride
has overcome you—you've been away so long.
Go, celebrate your wedding. It may be
(the gods will tell) a marriage you'll regret.
(*Exit* JASON *to the right.*)

CHORUS

[Strophe 1]

Desire, when it comes on too forcefully, never bestows
excellence, never makes anyone prestigious.
When she comes with just the right touch, there's no goddess
more gracious
than Cypris.
Mistress, never release from your golden bow
an inescapable arrow, smeared with desire
and aimed at my heart.

[Antistrophe 1]

Please, let me be cherished by Wisdom, be loved by Restraint,
loveliest gift of the gods. May dreadful Cypris
never stun my spirit with love for the bed of another
and bring on
anger, battles of words, endless fighting, strife.
Let her be shrewd in her judgment; let her revere
the bedroom at peace.

[Strophe 2]

O fatherland, O home, never allow
me to be without a city:
a grief without recourse, life that's hard to live through,
most distressing of all fates.
May I go to my death, my death
before I endure that; I'd rather face
my final day. There's no worse heartache
than to be cut off from your fatherland.

[Antistrophe 2]

We've seen it for ourselves; nobody else
gave me this tale to consider.
No city, no friend will treat you with compassion
in your dreadful suffering.
May he die, the ungracious man
who won't honor friends, who will not unlock
his mind to clear, calm thoughts of kindness.
I will never call such a man my friend.

(*Enter* AEGEUS *from the left.*)[2]

AEGEUS[3] Medea, I wish all the best to you.
There is no finer way to greet a friend.
MEDEA All the best to you, Aegeus, son
of wise Pandion. Where are you traveling from?
AEGEUS I've come from Phoebus' ancient oracle.[4]
MEDEA What brought you to the earth's prophetic navel?[5]
AEGEUS Seeking how I might beget a child.
MEDEA By the gods, are you still childless?
AEGEUS Still childless. Some god must be to blame.
MEDEA Do you have a wife, or do you sleep alone?
AEGEUS I'm married, and we share a marriage bed.
MEDEA Well, what did Phoebus say concerning children?
AEGEUS His words were too profound for human wisdom.
MEDEA May I hear the oracle? Is it permitted?
AEGEUS Yes, why not? This calls for a wise mind.
MEDEA Then tell me, if indeed it is permitted.
AEGEUS He said, "Don't loose the wineskin's hanging foot . . ."[6]
MEDEA Before you do what thing? Or reach what place?
AEGEUS Before returning to my paternal hearth.

2. This stage direction is a modern guess, though presumably the direction of Aegeus' entrance must differ from those of all previous entrances in the play—underscoring the unexpectedness of his arrival.
3. The king of Athens.
4. Delphi.
5. At Delphi was a stone that was supposedly the navel of the Earth.
6. Wine was sometimes stored in animal skins, the leg being used as a spigot for dispensing drinks. The imagery suggests both "Don't get drunk" and "Don't have sex."

MEDEA And why have you sailed here? What do you need?
AEGEUS There is a man named Pittheus, lord of Troezen . . .[7]
MEDEA Pelops' son.[8] They say he's very pious.
AEGEUS I want to bring this prophecy to him.
MEDEA Yes. He's wise, and well-versed in such things.
AEGEUS And most beloved of my war companions.
MEDEA Good luck to you. May you get what you desire.
AEGEUS But you—your eyes are melting. What's the matter?
MEDEA My husband is the very worst of men.
AEGEUS What are you saying? Why the low spirits? Tell me.
MEDEA Jason treats me unjustly. I've done him no harm.
AEGEUS What has he done? Explain to me more clearly.
MEDEA He has another wife, who takes my place.
AEGEUS No. He wouldn't dare. It's much too shameful.
MEDEA It's true. His former loved ones are dishonored.
AEGEUS Did he desire another? Or tire of you?
MEDEA Oh yes, he felt desire. We cannot trust him.
AEGEUS Let him go, if he's as bad as you say.
MEDEA He desired a royal marriage-bond.
AEGEUS Who's giving away the bride? Go on, continue.
MEDEA Creon, the ruler of this land of Corinth.
AEGEUS Woman, your pain is understandable.
MEDEA I am destroyed. And that's not all—I'm exiled.
AEGEUS By whom? This is new trouble on top of trouble.
MEDEA By Creon. He is driving me from Corinth.
AEGEUS And Jason is allowing it? Shame on him.
MEDEA He claims to be against it, but he'll manage
to endure it somehow.

(MEDEA *again assumes the supplicant position.*)

Listen, I entreat you;
by your beard and by your knees, I beg you:
Have pity on me; pity my misfortune.
Don't let me go deserted into exile;
receive me in your home and at your hearth.
If you do it, may the gods grant your desire
for children; may you die a prosperous man.
You don't know what a windfall you have found!
I'll cure your childlessness, make you a father.
I know the drugs required for such things.
AEGEUS For many reasons, woman, I am eager
to grant this favor to you: first, the gods;
and secondly, the children that you promise.
I'm at a total loss where that's concerned.
But this is how it is. When you arrive,

7. Pittheus will give his daughter Aethra to Aegeus, after getting him drunk; the Athenian hero Theseus will be conceived in this way.

8. Pelops, son of Tantalus, was served up as food to the gods by his father. The gods restored him to life, and he became the founder of the Peloponnese.

I'll treat you justly, try to shelter you.
However, you must know this in advance:
I'm not willing to escort you from this land.
If you can come to my house on your own,
I'll let you stay there—it will be your refuge.
I will not give you up to anyone.
But you must leave this land all by yourself.
My hosts here must have no complaint with me.

MEDEA So be it. But if I had some assurance
that I could trust you, I'd have all I need.

AEGEUS You don't believe me? Tell me, what's the problem?

MEDEA Oh, I believe you. But I have enemies:
Creon, and the house of Pelias.
If they come for me, and you're not bound
by any oath, then you might let them take me.
A promise in words only, never sworn
by any gods, might not be strong enough
to keep you from befriending them, from yielding
to their delegations. I'm completely helpless;
they have prosperity and royal power.

AEGEUS Your words show forethought. If you think it's best,
I'll do it without any hesitation.
In fact, this is the safest course for me:
I'll have a good excuse to turn away
your enemies. And things are settled well
for you, of course. I'll swear: just name the gods.

MEDEA Swear by the Earth we stand on, and by Helios—
my father's father[9]—and the whole race of gods.

AEGEUS To do or not do what? Just say the word.

MEDEA Never to expel me from your land yourself,
and never, as long as you live, to give me up
willingly to any enemy.

AEGEUS I swear by Earth, by Helios' sacred light,
by all the gods: I'll do just as you say.

MEDEA Fine. And if you don't? What would you suffer?

AEGEUS Whatever an unholy man deserves.

(MEDEA *rises.*)

MEDEA Fare well, then, on your voyage. This is good.
I'll find you in your city very soon,
once I've done my will, and had my way.

(*Exit* AEGEUS *to the left. The* CHORUS *address him as he leaves.*)

CHORUS May lord Hermes, the child of Maia,[1] escort you
and bring you back home. May you do as you please,
and have all you want. In my judgment, Aegeus,
you're a good, noble man.

9. Helios, the Sun, is father of Aeetes, king of Colchis, Medea's father.

1. Hermes, the messenger god, was the child of Zeus by the nymph Maia.

MEDEA O Zeus, and Zeus's Justice, and the light
of Helios, I now shall be the victor
over my enemies. My friends, I've set my foot
upon the path. My enemies will pay
what justice demands—I now have hope of this.
This man, when I was at my lowest point,
appeared, the perfect harbor for my plans.
When I reach Pallas' city,[2] I shall have
a steady place to tie my ship. And now
I'll tell you what my plans are. Hear my words;
they will not bring you pleasure. I will send
a servant to bring Jason here to see me.
When he comes, I'll soothe him with my words:
I'll say that I agree with him, that he
was right to marry into the royal family,
betraying me—well done, and well thought out!
"But let my children stay here!" I will plead—
not that I would leave them in this land
for my enemies to outrage—my own children.
No: this is my deceit, to kill the princess.
I'll send them to her, bearing gifts in hand
—a delicate robe, and a garland worked in gold.
If she takes these fine things and puts them on,
she, and anyone who touches her,
will die a painful death. Such are the drugs
with which I will smear them.
But enough of that.
Once that's done, the next thing I must do
chokes me with sorrow. I will kill the children—
my children. No one on this earth can save them.
I'll ruin Jason's household, then I'll leave
this land, I'll flee the slaughter of the children
I love so dearly. I will have the nerve
for this unholy deed. You see, my friends,
I will not let my enemies laugh at me.

Let it go. What do I gain by being alive?
I have no fatherland, no home, no place
to turn from troubles. The moment I went wrong
was when I left my father's house, persuaded
by the words of that Greek man. If the gods will help me,
he'll pay what justice demands. He'll never see
them alive again, the children that I bore him.
Nor will he ever father another child:
his new bride, evil woman, she must die
an evil death, extinguished by my drugs.
Let no one think that I'm a simpleton,

2. Athens, city of Athena (Pallas).

or weak, or idle—I am the opposite.
I treat my friends with kindness, and come down hard
on the heads of my enemies. This is the way to live,
the way to win a glorious reputation.

CHORUS Since you have brought this plan to us, and since
I want to help you, and since I support
the laws of mankind, I ask you not to do this.

MEDEA There is no other way. It's understandable
that you would say this—you're not the one who's suffered.

CHORUS Will you have the nerve to kill your children?

MEDEA Yes: to wound my husband the most deeply.

CHORUS And to make yourself the most miserable of women.

MEDEA Let it go. Let there be no more words
until it's done.

(*To her attendant.*)

You: go now, and bring Jason.
When I need to trust someone, I turn to you.
If you're a woman and mean well to your mistress,
do not speak of the things I have resolved.

(*Exit the attendant to the right.*)

CHORUS

[Strophe 1]

The children of Erechtheus[3] have always prospered,
descended from blessèd gods.
They graze, in their sacred stronghold, on glorious
wisdom,
with a delicate step through the clear and brilliant air.
They say that there
the nine Pierian Muses[4] once gave birth
to Harmony with golden hair.

[Antistrophe 1]

They sing that Cypris dipped her pitcher in the waters
of beautiful Cephisus;[5]
she sighed, and her breaths were fragrant
and temperate breezes.
With a garland of sweet-smelling roses in her hair
she sends Desires
to take their places alongside Wisdom's throne
and nurture excellence with her.

3. Athenians. Erechtheus was a legendary king of Athens.
4. The Muses are the daughters of Zeus and Mnemosyne (Memory). They inspire poetic and musical creation, and their birthplace is Pieria.
5. River in Athens.

[Strophe 2]

How can this city
of holy rivers,
receiver of friends and loved ones,
receive you—when you've murdered your own children,
most unholy woman—among them?
Just think of this deathblow aimed at the helpless,
think of the slaughter you'll have on your hands.
Oh no, by your knees, we beg you,
we beg you, with every plea
we can plead: do not kill your children.

[Antistrophe 2]

Where will you find it,
the awful courage?
The terrible nerve—how can you?
How can your hand, your heart, your mind go through with
this slaughter? How will you be able
to look at your children, keep your eyes steady,
see them beseech you, and not fall apart?
Your tears will not let you kill them;
your spirit, your nerve will fail:
you will not soak your hands in their blood.

(*Enter* JASON *from the right.*)

JASON I've come because you summoned me. Despite
the hate between us, I will hear you out.
What is it this time, woman? What do you want?
MEDEA Jason, I beg you, please forgive the things
I said. Your heart should be prepared, receptive
like a seed bed. We used to love each other.
It's only right for you to excuse my anger.
I've thought it over, and I blame myself.
Pathetic! Really, I must have been insane
to stand opposed to those who plan so well,
to be an enemy to those in power
and to my husband, who's done so well by me:
marrying the royal princess, to beget
brothers for my children. Isn't it time
to drop my angry spirit, since the gods
have been so bountiful? What's wrong with me?
Don't I have children? Aren't we exiles? Don't we
need whatever friendship we can get?
That's what I said to myself. I realize
that I've been foolish, that there is no point
to all my fuming rage. I give you credit
for wise restraint, for making this connection,
this marriage that's in all our interests. Now
I understand that you deserve my praise.

I was such a moron. I should have supported
your plans, I should have made arrangements with you,
I should have stood beside the bridal bed,
rejoiced in taking care of your new bride.

We women—oh, I won't say that we're bad,
but we are what we are. You shouldn't sink
down to our level, trading childish insults.
I ask for your indulgence. I admit
I wasn't thinking straight, but now my plans
are much improved where these things are concerned.

(MEDEA *turns toward the house to call the children.*)

Oh, children! Come out of the house, come here,
come out and greet your father, speak to him.
Come set aside, together with your mother,
the hatred that we felt toward one we love.

(*The* CHILDREN *come out from the house, escorted by the* TUTOR *and attendants.*)

We've made a treaty. My rage has gone away.
Take his right hand.
                                        Oh, god, my mind is filled
with bad things, hidden things. Oh, children, look—
your lovely arms, the way you stretch them out.
Will you look this way your whole long lives?
I think I'm going to cry. I'm filled with fear.
After all this time, I'm making up
my quarrel with your father. This tender sight
is washed with tears; my eyes are overflowing.

CHORUS In my eyes too fresh tears are welling up.
May this evil not go any further.

JASON Woman, I approve your new approach—
not that I blame you for the way you felt.
It's only right for a female to get angry
if her husband smuggles in another wife.
But this new change of heart is for the best.
After all this time, you've recognized
the winning plan. You're showing wise restraint.
And as for you, my children, you will see
your father is no fool. I have provided
for your security, if the gods will help me.
Yes, I believe that you will be the leaders
here in Corinth, with your future brothers.
Grow up strong and healthy. All the rest
your father, with the favor of the gods,
will take care of. I pray that I may see you
grown up and thriving, holding sway above
my enemies.

(JASON *turns to* MEDEA.)

You! Why have you turned
your face away, so pale? Why are fresh tears
pouring from your eyes? Why aren't you happy
to hear what I have had to say?

MEDEA It's nothing.
I was only thinking of the children.

JASON Don't worry now. I'll take good care of them.

MEDEA I'll do as you ask. I'll trust in what you say.
I'm female, that's all. Tears are in my nature.

JASON So—why go on? Why moan over the children?

MEDEA They're mine. And when you prayed that they would live,
pity crept over me. I wondered: would they?
As for the things you came here to discuss,
we've covered one. I'll move on to the next.
Since the royal family has seen fit
to exile me (and yes, I realize
it's for the best—I wouldn't want to stay
to inconvenience you, or this land's rulers,
who see me as an enemy of the family),
I will leave this land, go into exile,
but you must raise your children with your own hand:
ask Creon that they be exempt from exile.

JASON Though I may not persuade him, I must try.

MEDEA And ask your wife to ask her father: please
let the children be exempt from exile.

JASON Certainly. I think I will persuade her.

MEDEA No doubt, if she's a woman like all others.
And for this work, I'll lend you my support.
I'll send her gifts, much lovelier, I know,
than any living person has laid eyes on:
a delicate robe, and a garland worked in gold.
The children will bear them. Now, this very minute,
let one of the servants bring these fine things here.

(*An attendant goes into the house to carry out this request. She, or another servant, returns with the finery.*)

She will be blessed a thousandfold with fortune:
with you, an excellent man to share her bed,
and these possessions, these fine things that once
my father's father, Helios, passed down
to his descendants. Take these wedding gifts
in your arms, my children; go and give them
to the lucky bride, the royal princess.
These are gifts that no one could find fault with.

(*The attendant puts the gifts in the children's arms.*)

JASON You fool! Why let these things out of your hands?
Do you think the royal household needs more robes,
more gold? Hold onto these. Don't give them up.
If my wife thinks anything of me,
I'm sure that I mean more to her than wealth.

MEDEA Don't say that. Even the gods can be persuaded
by gifts. And gold is worth a thousand words.
She has the magic charm; the gods are helping
her right now: she's young, and she has power.
To save my children from exile, I'd give my life,
not merely gold. You, children, when you've entered
that wealthy house, must supplicate your father's
young wife, my mistress. You must plead with her
and ask her that you be exempt from exile.
Give her these fine things. That is essential:
she must receive these gifts with her own hands.
Go quickly now, and bring back to your mother
the good news she desires—that you've succeeded.

(*The children, bearing the gifts, leave with the* TUTOR *to the right.*)

CHORUS

[Strophe 1]

Now I no longer have hope that the children will live,
no longer. They walk to the slaughter already.
The bride will receive the crown of gold;
she'll receive her horrible ruin.
Upon her golden hair, with her very own hands,
she'll place the fine circlet of Hades.[6]

[Antistrophe 1]

She'll be persuaded; the grace and the heavenly gleam
will move her to try on the robe and the garland.
The bride will adorn herself for death,
for the shades below. She will fall
into this net; her death will be horrible. Ruin
will be inescapable, fated.

[Strophe 2]

And you, poor thing, bitter bridegroom, in-law to
royalty:
you don't know you're killing your children,
bringing hateful death to your bride.
How horrible: how unaware you are of your fate.

[Antistrophe 2]

I cry for your pain in turn, poor thing; you're a
mother, yet
you will slaughter them, your own children,
for the sake of your bridal bed,
the bed that your husband now shares with somebody else.

(*The* TUTOR *returns, at the right, from the palace with the children.*)

6. Death.

TUTOR Mistress, your children are released from exile.
The princess happily received the gifts
with her own hands. As far as she's concerned,
the children's case is settled; they're at peace.

Ah!
Why are you upset by your good fortune?
MEDEA Oh, god.
TUTOR Your cry is out of tune. This is good news!
MEDEA Oh god, oh god.
TUTOR Have I made some mistake?
Is what I've said bad news, and I don't know it?
MEDEA You've said what you have said. I don't blame you.
TUTOR So—why are you crying? Why are your eyes cast down?
MEDEA Old man, I am compelled. The gods and I
devised this strategy. What was I thinking?
TUTOR Don't worry now. Your children will bring you home.
MEDEA I'll send others home before that day.
TUTOR You're not the only woman who's lost her children.
We're mortals. We must bear disasters lightly.
MEDEA I'll do as you ask. Now, go inside the house
and see to the children's needs, as usual.

(*Exit* TUTOR *into the house.*)

Oh, children, children, you two have a city
and home, in which you'll live forever parted
from your mother. You'll leave poor me behind.
I'll travel to another land, an exile,
before I ever have the joy of seeing
you blessed with fortune—before your wedding days,
before I prepare your beds and hold the torches.[7]
My willfulness has cost me all this grief.
I raised you, children, but it was no use;
no use, the way I toiled, how much it hurt,
the pain of childbirth, piercing like a thorn.
And I had so much hope when you were born:
you'd tend to my old age, and when I died,
you'd wrap me in my shroud with your own hands:
an admirable fate for anyone.
That sweet thought has now been crushed. I'll be parted
from both of you, and I will spend my years
in sorrow and in pain. Your eyes no longer
will look upon your mother. You'll move on
to a different life.
Oh god, your eyes, the way
you look at me. Why do you smile, my children,
your very last smile? Aah, what will I do?
The heart goes out of me, women, when I look

7. Torches were an important feature of ancient weddings, which took place at night.

at my children's shining eyes. I couldn't do this.
Farewell to the plans I had before.
I'll take my children with me when I leave.
Why should I, just to cause their father pain,
feel twice the pain myself by harming them?
I will not do it. Farewell to my plans.
But wait—what's wrong with me? What do I want?
To allow my enemies to laugh at me?
To let them go unpunished?
What I need
is the nerve to do it. I was such a weakling,
to let a soothing word enter my mind.
Children, go inside the house.

(*The children start to go toward the house, but, as* MEDEA *continues to speak, they continue to watch and listen to her, delaying their entry inside.*)

Whoever
is not permitted to attend these rites,
my sacrifice, let that be his concern.
I won't hold back the force that's in my hand.

Aah!
Oh no, my spirit, please, not that! Don't do it.
Spare the children. Leave them alone, poor thing.
They'll live with me there. They will bring you joy.

By the avenging ones[8] who live below
in Hades, no, I will not leave my children
at the mercy of my enemies' outrage.
Anyway, the thing's already done.
She won't escape. The crown is on her head.
The royal bride's destroyed, wrapped in her robes.
I know it. Now, since I am setting foot
on a path that will break my heart, and sending them
on one more heartbreaking still, I want to speak
to my children.

(MEDEA *reaches toward her children; they come back to her.*)

Children, give me your right hands,
give them to your mother, let me kiss them.
Oh, how I love these hands, how I love these mouths,
the way the children stand, their noble faces!
May fortune bless you—in the other place.
Your father's taken all that once was here.
Oh, your sweet embrace, your tender skin,
your lovely breath, oh children.
Go now—go.

(*The children go inside.*)

8. The Furies.

I cannot look at them. Grief overwhelms me.
I know that I am working up my nerve
for overwhelming evil, yet my spirit
is stronger than my mind's deliberations:
this is the source of mortals' deepest grief.

CHORUS Quite often I've found myself venturing deeper
than women do normally into discussions
and subtle distinctions, and I would suggest
that we have our own Muse, who schools us in wisdom—
not every woman, but there are a few,
you'll find one among many, a woman who doesn't
stand entirely apart from the Muses.

Here's my opinion: the childless among us,
the ones who have never experienced parenthood,
have greater good fortune than those who have children.
They don't know—how could they?—if children
are pleasant
or hard and distressing. Their lack of experience
saves them from heartache.
But those who have children, a household's sweet
offshoot—
I see them consumed their whole lives with concern.
They fret from the start: are they raising them well?
And then: will they manage to leave them enough?
Then finally: all of this toil and heartache,
is it for children who'll turn out to be
worthless or decent? That much is unclear.

There's one final grief that I'll mention. Supposing
your children have grown up with plenty to live on,
they're healthy, they're decent—if fortune decrees it,
Death comes and spirits their bodies away
down to the Underworld. What is the point, then,
if the gods, adding on to the pains that we mortals
endure for the sake of our children, send death,
most distressing of all? Tell me, where does that leave us?

MEDEA My friends, I have been waiting for some time,
keeping watch to see where this will lead.
Look now: here comes one of Jason's men
breathing hard—he seems to be about
to tell us of some new and dreadful act.

(*Enter the* MESSENGER *from the right.*)

MESSENGER Medea, run away! Take any ship
or wagon that will carry you. Leave now!

MEDEA Why should I flee? What makes it necessary?

MESSENGER The royal princess and her father Creon
have just now died—the victims of your poison.

MEDEA This news is excellent. From this day forth
I'll count you as a friend and benefactor.
MESSENGER What are you saying? Are you sane at all,
or raving? You've attacked the royal hearth—
how can you rejoice, and not be frightened?
MEDEA I could tell my own side to this story.
But calm down, friend, and please describe to me
how they were destroyed. If you can say
that they died horribly, I'll feel twice the pleasure.
MESSENGER When we saw that your two boys had come
together with their father to the bride's house,
all of us—we servants who have felt
the pain of your misfortunes—were delighted;
the talk was that you'd settled your differences,
you and your husband. We embraced the boys,
kissing their hands, their golden hair. And I,
overjoyed as I was, accompanied
the children to the women's quarters. She—
the mistress we now honor in your place—
before she caught sight of your pair of boys
was gazing eagerly at Jason. Then
she saw the children, and she covered up
her eyes, as if the sight disgusted her,
and turned her pale cheek aside. Your husband
tried to cool down the girl's bad temper,
saying, "Don't be hateful toward your loved ones!
Please, calm your spirit, turn your head this way,
and love those whom your husband loves. Receive
these gifts, and ask your father, for my sake,
not to send these children into exile."
Well, when she saw the fine things, she gave in
to everything the man said. They had barely
set foot outside the door—your children and
their father—when she took the intricate
embroidered robe and wrapped it round her body,
and set the golden crown upon her curls,
and smiled at her bright image—her lifeless double—
in a mirror, as she arranged her hair.
She rose, and with a delicate step her lovely
white feet traversed the quarters. She rejoiced
beyond all measure in the gifts. Quite often
she extended her ankle, admiring the effect.

What happened next was terrible to see.
Her skin changed color, and her legs were shaking;
she reeled sideways, and she would have fallen
straight to the ground if she hadn't collapsed in
her chair.

Then one of her servants, an old woman,
thinking that the girl must be possessed
by Pan[9] or by some other god, cried out—
a shriek of awe and reverence—but when
she saw the white foam at her mouth, her eyes
popping out, the blood drained from her face,
she changed her cry to one of bitter mourning.
A maid ran off to get the princess' father;
another went to tell the bride's new husband
of her disaster. Everywhere the sound
of running footsteps echoed through the house.
And then, in less time than it takes a sprinter
to cover one leg of a stadium race,
the girl, whose eyes had been shut tight, awoke,
poor thing, and she let out a terrible groan,
for she was being assaulted on two fronts:
the golden garland resting on her head
sent forth a marvelous stream of all-consuming
fire, and the delicate robe, the gift
your children brought, was starting to corrode
the white flesh of that most unfortunate girl.
She jumped up, with flames all over her,
shaking her hair, tossing her head around,
trying to throw the crown off. But the gold
gripped tight, and every movement of her hair
caused the fire to blaze out twice as much.
Defeated by disaster, she fell down
onto the ground, unrecognizable
to anyone but a father. She had lost
the look her eyes had once had, and her face
had lost its beauty. Blood was dripping down,
mixed with fire, from the top of her head
and from her bones the flesh was peeling back
like resin, shorn by unseen jaws of poison,
terrible to see. We all were frightened
to touch the corpse. We'd seen what had just
happened.
But her poor father took us by surprise:
he ran into the room and threw himself—
not knowing any better—on her corpse.
He moaned, and wrapped her in his arms,
and kissed her,
crying, "Oh, my poor unhappy child,
what god dishonors you? What god destroys you?
Who has taken you away from me,

9. Woodland or countryside god, usually represented with goat legs, associated with violent divine possession and fear ("panic").

an old man who has one foot in the grave?
Let me die with you, child." When he was done
with his lament, he tried to straighten up
his aged body, but the delicate robe
clung to him as ivy clings to laurel,
and then a terrible wrestling match began.
He tried to flex his knee; she pulled him back.
If he used force, he tore the aged flesh
off of his bones. He finally gave up,
unlucky man; his soul slipped away
when he could fight no longer. There they lie,
two corpses, a daughter and her aged father,
side by side, a disaster that longs for tears.

About your situation, I am silent.
You realize what penalty awaits you.
About our mortal lives, I feel the way
I've often felt before: we are mere shadows.
I wouldn't hesitate to say that those
who seem so wise, who deal in subtleties—
they earn the prize for being the greatest fools.
For really, there is no man blessed with fortune.
One man might be luckier, more prosperous
than someone else, but no man's ever blessed.

(*Exit the* MESSENGER *to the right.*)

CHORUS On this day fortune has bestowed on Jason
much grief, it seems, as justice has demanded.
Poor thing, we pity you for this disaster,
daughter of Creon, you who have descended
to Hades' halls because of your marriage to Jason.
MEDEA My friends, it is decided: as soon as possible
I must kill my children and leave this land
before I give my enemies a chance
to slaughter them with a hand that's moved by
hatred.
They must die anyway, and since they must,
I will kill them. I'm the one who bore them.
Arm yourself, my heart. Why am I waiting
to do this terrible, necessary crime?
Unhappy hand, act now. Take up the sword,
just take it; approach the starting post of pain
to last a lifetime; do not weaken, don't
remember that you love your children dearly,
that you gave them life. For one short day
forget your children. Afterward, you'll grieve.
For even if you kill them, they were yours;
you loved them. I'm a woman cursed by fortune.

(MEDEA *enters the house.*)

CHORUS

[Strophe 1]

O Earth, O radiant beam
of Helios, look down and see her—
this woman, destroyer, before she can lay
her hand stained with blood,
her kin-killing hand
upon her own children
descended from you
the gods' golden race;
for such blood to spill
at the hands of a mortal
fills us with fear.
Light born from Zeus,
stop her, remove
this bloodstained Erinys;[1]
take her away
from this house cursed with vengeance.

[Antistrophe 1]

Your toil has all been in vain,
in vain, all the heartache of raising
your children, your dearest, O sorrowful one
who once left behind
the dark Clashing Rocks
most hostile to strangers.
What burden of rage
descended upon
your mind? Why does wild
slaughter follow on slaughter?
Blood-spatter, stain,
slaughter of kin,
murder within
the family brings grief
tuned to the crime
from the gods to the household.

CHILD (*From within the house.*)
Oh no!

CHORUS

[Strophe 2]

Do you hear the shouts, the shouts of her children?
Poor woman: she's cursed, undone by her fortune.

CHILD 1 Oh, how can I escape my mother's hand?

CHILD 2 Dear brother, I don't know. We are destroyed.

1. Fury.

CHORUS Shall I go inside?
I ought to prevent this,
the slaughter of children.
CHILD 1 Yes, come and stop her! That is what we need.
CHILD 2 We're trapped; we're caught! The sword is at our throats.
CHORUS Poor thing: after all
you were rock, you were iron:
to reap with your own hand
the crop that you bore;
to cut down your kin
with a fate-dealing hand.

[Antistrophe 2]

I've heard of just one, just one other woman
who dared to attack, to hurt her own children:

Ino, whom the gods once drove insane
and Zeus's wife sent wandering from her home.[2]

The poor woman leapt
to sea with her children:
an unholy slaughter.

She stepped down from a steep crag's rocky edge
and died with her two children in the waves.
What terrible deed
could surpass such an outrage?
O bed of their marriage,
O woman's desire:
such harm have you done,
so much pain have you caused.

(*Enter* JASON *from the right.*)

JASON Women, you who stand here near the house—
is she at home, Medea, the perpetrator
of all these terrors, or has she gone away?
Oh yes, she'll have to hide beneath the earth
or lift her body into the sky with wings
to escape the royal family's cry for justice.
Does she think she can murder this land's rulers
then simply flee this house, with no requital?
I'm worried about the children more than her—
the ones she's hurt will pay her back in kind.
I've come to save my children, save their lives.
The family might retaliate, might strike
the children for their mother's unholy slaughter.

2. Ino, a daughter of Cadmus, king of Thebes, was driven mad by Dionysos to participate—along with Cadmus's mother—in the dismemberment of her nephew, Pentheus. Later, she was married to King Athamas and, driven mad by Hera, she leapt into the sea with one or more of their sons.

CHORUS Poor man. Jason, if you realized
how bad it was, you wouldn't have said that.
JASON What is it? Does she want to kill *me* now?
CHORUS Your children are dead, killed by their mother's hand.
JASON What are you saying, women? You have destroyed me.
CHORUS Please understand: your children no longer exist.
JASON Where did she kill them? Inside the house, or outside?
CHORUS Open the gates; you'll see your children's slaughter.
JASON Servants, quick, open the door, unbar it;
undo the bolts, and let me see this double
evil: their dead bodies, and the one
whom I will bring to justice.

(MEDEA *appears above the roof in a flying chariot, with the bodies of the children.*)[3]

MEDEA Why are you trying
to pry those gates? Is it their corpses you seek,
and me, the perpetrator? Stop your struggle.
If you need something, ask me. Speak your mind.
But you will never touch us with your hand.
My father's father, Helios, gives me safety
from hostile hands. This chariot protects me.
JASON You hateful thing, O woman most detested
by the gods, by me, by all mankind—
you dared to strike your children with a sword,
children you bore yourself. You have destroyed me,
left me childless. And yet you live, you look
upon the sun and earth, you who had the nerve
to do this most unholy deed. I wish
you would die. I have more sense now than I had
the day I took you from your barbarian land
and brought you to a Greek home—you're a plague,
betrayer of your father and the land
that raised you. But the gods have sent the vengeance
that *you* deserve to crash down on *my* head.
You killed your brother right at home, then climbed
aboard the *Argo* with its lovely prow.
That's how your career began. You married
me, and bore me children. For the sake
of passion, of your bed, you have destroyed them.
No Greek woman would have had the nerve
to do this, but I married you instead:
a hateful bond. You ruined me. You're not
a woman; you're a lion, with a nature
more wild than Scylla's,[4] the Etruscan freak.
I couldn't wound you with ten thousand insults;
there's nothing you can't take. Get out of here,

3. The stage mechanism used in the original production would have been the *mechane*, a crane typically used for divine appearances in Athenian tragedy.
4. Scylla is the sea monster who threatens Odysseus and his men in the *Odyssey*.

you filth, you child-murderer. For me,
all that's left is tears for my misfortune.
I'll never have the joy of my bride's bed,
nor will I ever again speak to my children,
my children, whom I raised. And now I've lost them.

MEDEA I would have made a long speech in reply
to yours, if father Zeus were unaware
of what I've done for you, and how you've acted.
You dishonored my bed. There was no way
you could go on to lead a pleasant life,
to laugh at me—not you, and not the princess;
nor could Creon, who arranged your marriage,
exile me and walk away unpunished.
So go ahead, call me a lion, call me
a Scylla, skulking in her Etruscan cave.
I've done what I had to do. I've jabbed your heart.

JASON You feel the pain yourself. This hurts you, too.

MEDEA The pain is good, as long as you're not laughing.

JASON O children, you were cursed with an evil mother.

MEDEA O sons, you were destroyed by your father's sickness.

JASON *My* right hand is not the one that killed them.

MEDEA Your outrage, and your newfound bride, destroyed them.

JASON The bedroom was enough to make you kill?

MEDEA Does that pain mean so little to a woman?

JASON Yes,
to one with wise restraint. To you, it's everything.

MEDEA *They* exist no longer. That will sting you.

JASON They exist. They live to avenge your crime.

MEDEA The gods know who was first to cause this pain.

JASON Oh yes. They know your mind. They spit on it.

MEDEA Go on and hate me. I detest your voice.

JASON I feel the same. That makes it easy to leave you.

MEDEA What shall I do, then? I'd like nothing better.

JASON Let me bury their bodies. Let me grieve.

MEDEA Forget it. I will take them away myself
and bury them with this hand, in the precinct
sacred to Hera of the rocky heights.
No enemy will treat their graves with outrage.
To this land of Sisyphus[5] I bequeath
a holy festival, a ritual
to expiate in times to come this most
unholy slaughter.[6] I myself will go
to live together with Pandion's son
Aegeus, in Erechtheus's city.[7]

5. Corinth. Sisyphus was a notorious traitor, punished in the underworld for his deceitfulness by having to push a rock eternally up a hill, never managing to get it to the top without its rolling back down.

6. There really was a sacred cult to "Hera of the rocky heights" at Corinth.

7. Athens.

And you, an evil man, as you deserve,
will die an evil death, struck on the head
by a fragment of the *Argo*. You will see
how bitter was the outcome of my marriage.

(*Here the meter changes from spoken dialogue to chanted anapests.*)[8]

JASON May you be destroyed by the children's Erinys[9]
and bloodthirsty Justice!

MEDEA What spirit, what god
listens to you, you liar, you breaker
of oaths, you deceiver of guests?

JASON You are loathsome.
You murdered your children.

MEDEA Get out of here, go—
go bury your wife.

JASON I'm leaving, bereft
of my sons.

MEDEA Do you think that you're mourning them now?
Just wait till you're old.

JASON Oh, dearest children.

MEDEA To me, not to you.

JASON And yet you still did this?

MEDEA To make you feel pain.

JASON I wish I could hold them and kiss them, my children.

MEDEA You long for them now and you want to embrace them,
but you are the one who pushed them away.

JASON By the gods, let me touch the soft skin of my children.

MEDEA No. What's the point? You are wasting your words.

(*The chariot flies away with* MEDEA *and the bodies of the children.*)

JASON Zeus, do you hear how I'm driven away,
do you see what I suffer at her loathsome hands,
this lion, this child-killer!
With all my strength
I mourn for them now and I call on the gods
and spirits to witness that you killed my children
and now won't allow me to touch them or bury them.
I wish now that I'd never fathered them, only
to see them extinguished, to see what you've done.

(*Exit* JASON *to the right, accompanied by the* CHORUS.)

CHORUS Zeus on Olympus enforces all things;
the gods can accomplish what no one would hope for.
What we expect may not happen at all,
while the gods find a way, against all expectation,
to do what they want, however surprising.
And that is exactly how this case turned out.

8. This rhythm was often used for marching; it signals that the chorus and other characters will soon be leaving the theater.

9. Spirit of vengeance.

ARISTOPHANES

ca. 450–385 B.C.E.

Aristophanes is the only comic poet from fifth-century Athens whose writing has survived. His plays work on many levels: they combine the most basic kinds of humor (obscene sexual and scatalogical jokes, as well as physical comedy and farce) with sharp political and social satire, literary allusions and parodies, strange flights of fantasy (such as choruses of talking animals and topsy-turvy scenarios that turn the known world upside-down), and beautiful passages of poetry. His dramas, of which eleven survive complete, tell us a great deal about the attitudes of fifth-century Athenians, and are still funny today.

LIFE AND TIMES

We know little about Aristophanes' life, beyond the fact that he was a prolific comic dramatist. In the small city-state of Athens, he was personally acquainted with the leading writers, thinkers, and politicians of his day, including those whom he satirized in his plays. Aristophanes was fairly successful in his own lifetime: he won first prize in several of the dramatic competitions at which his work was performed.

Most of Aristophanes' work dates from the years of the Peloponnesian War (431–404 B.C.E.). The war, in fact, is one of his main comic targets, as are the political demagogues, and newfangled thinkers and writers, whom Aristophanes presents as responsible for the decline in traditional moral values. Figures who are mocked repeatedly in these plays include Socrates, who is presented as a sophist with dangerous ideas that may corrupt the young and bring down traditional democratic Athens; **Euripides**, the tragedian, who is shown as similarly corrupting in his depiction of loose women and blasphemous religious ideas; and Cleon, the demagogue, who supposedly misleads the common people and stirs them up for war. It is easy to see Aristophanes as a conservative or traditionalist throughout his career: someone who objected to the city's expensive military and imperial ambitions and spoke out against new ideas and styles of literature. But Aristophanes is also willing to mock the traditionalists and to suggest revolutionary ideas of his own. In Aristophanic comedy, the hero typically upsets the status quo to produce extraordinary results, including an ending in which dreams come true. For instance, in *Birds* (414 B.C.E.), two Athenians, tired of the war and taxes, go off to found a new city; they organize the birds, who cut off the smoke of sacrifice that the gods live on, and force Zeus to surrender the government of the universe to the birds. The audience may be left doubtful about how the crazy, utopian, or dystopian world of comic fantasy measures up against reality. How seriously can we take Aristophanes as a political writer? Were his plays meant to raise a laugh? Or were they designed to change the way Athenians thought, talked, and voted? These possibilities are not, of course, incompatible.

LYSISTRATA

Lysistrata has a particularly appealing premise: the women of Athens and Sparta decide to go on sex strike, to stop the Peloponnesian War. When the play was first performed (in 411 B.C.E.), the Athenian fleet had recently been destroyed in the Sicilian Expedition

(413 B.C.E.); many citizens lost their lives, while others were enslaved, and the economic as well as military consequences for the city were disastrous. Athenian victory now seemed unlikely, and public sentiment had begun to turn against the war. In this play the Athenian women, who have no political rights, seize the Acropolis, the repository of the city's treasury, and leave the men without sex or the money to carry on the war. They coordinate similar revolutions in all the Greek cities, including Sparta. The men are eventually "starved" into submission, and the Spartans come to Athens to end the war.

Aristophanes does not miss any of the comic possibilities inherent in his plot. Myrrhine's teasing game with her husband, Kinesias, for example, is classic theater, and the final appearance of the rigid Spartan ambassadors and their equally tense Athenian hosts is a visual and verbal climax of astonishing brilliance. But serious issues are also at stake. Lysistrata, whose name means "Dissolver of Armies," is a true heroine, presented in entirely positive terms; it is hard not to feel that she is right to try to stop the Peloponnesian War.

Lysistrata makes us ask serious questions, not just about this war, but about war in general. Why do the men insist on pursuing this "futile war," for which none of them can give a reasonable justification? To stop is "unthinkable," but nobody can explain why. Aristophanes suggests that the dirty secret of imperialism is that war and territorial aggression are a substitute for sex, and vice versa. The great expression of this diagnosis is the scene in which the Athenian and Spartan ambassadors divide up the naked body of Reconciliation, personified as a beautiful woman; they relate her various anatomical features to territories of Greece over which their cities were fighting. The concept is at once devastatingly accurate and, one could argue, an oversimplification. Such reductiveness is characteristic of comedy, which—in contrast to tragedy—offers us the reassurance that our craziest wishful fantasies can, somehow, come true.

The play raises similarly important questions about the social position of women. Ancient Athens was a particularly patriarchal society: elite women rarely left the house except for funerals or religious festivals, and women had no political rights—they were not citizens, and could not vote. *Lysistrata* seems to make the radical suggestion that things might go a lot better if women, not men, were in charge of the city. Lysistrata declares that "the women will deal with the war": it is too important a matter to be left to men, for women are its real victims. When asked what the women will do, she explains that they will treat politics just as they do wool in their household tasks: "Draw it apart with spindles—make some sense of it." The traditional tasks of women, including spinning and weaving, train one in the patient management of details, and this kind of skill, Lysistrata suggests, is precisely what is missing from the masculine headlong pursuit of war. Here and throughout the play, Aristophanes works with gender stereotypes, both inviting us to see the world through them and holding them up to good-natured ridicule. In her level-headed reasonableness and her common-sense commitment to peace, Lysistrata is the exception, not the norm. Most of the female characters in the play are obsessed with wine and sex. They are tricky and deceitful, always probing for men's weaknesses; they pose an obstacle to the conduct of serious political business. So men say, and the women in this play admit it. But trickery and deceit are here enlisted in the service of peace—in contrast to their destructive effects in, for example, Euripides' ***Medea***. It is difficult to know how seriously we should take the apparent proto-feminism of the play. Is Aristophanes really urging his male fellow citizens to let their wives take over the running of politics? Or is the idea of a government of women simply an argument ad absurdum: if men behave so crazily, could women do worse?

We do not know what the Athenians thought of the play. All we know is that they were not swayed by its serious undertone; the war continued for seven more exhausting years, until Athens's last fleet was defeated, the city laid open to the enemy, and the empire lost.

A NOTE ON THE TRANSLATION

The translation here is—appropriately—by a woman, the classical scholar Sarah Ruden. Ruden renders Aristophanes' verse into a regular English iambic line, a useful reminder that this play is poetry, not prose; she also brings out the liveliness and frequent colloquialisms of the language. Aristophanes uses a lot of slang, and his language and imagery are sometimes crude, deliberately dirty, or shocking: it is therefore justifiable to render his Greek into vivid, slangy, and sometimes obscene English. Those who do not want to encounter bad language ought to steer clear of this play.

Lysistrata[1]

CHARACTERS[2]

LYSISTRATA[3]
CALONICE
MYRRHINE
LAMPITO
MEN'S CHORUS LEADER
CHORUS OF OLD MEN
WOMEN'S CHORUS LEADER
CHORUS OF OLD WOMEN
COUNCILOR
OLD WOMEN #1, #2, AND #3
WOMEN #1, #2, AND #3
CINESIAS
CINESIAS' BABY
SPARTAN HERALD
UNITED CHORUS
UNITED CHORUS LEADER
SPARTAN AMBASSADOR
ATHENIAN AMBASSADORS #1 AND #2
ATHENIAN WOMEN
BOEOTIAN WOMAN
CORINTHIAN WOMAN
SPARTAN AND OTHER FOREIGN WOMEN
FEMALE SCYTHIAN GUARD
TWO SLAVES
FOUR MALE SCYTHIAN GUARDS
CINESIAS' SLAVE
ATHENIAN AMBASSADORS
SPARTAN AMBASSADORS
THE AMBASSADORS' SLAVES
RECONCILIATION
PIPER

SCENE: *A large rectangular stage behind a bare circular area with an altar in the middle. Two ramplike entrances to the circular area at the left and right. A stage building with up to three doors in front, and a hatch to allow actors onto the roof. Scene descriptions and stage directions occur nowhere in an ancient Greek dramatic text, but the context here suggests that the action begins on the lower slopes of the Acropolis or in an Athenian residential district. The action later moves to the outside of the Propylaea, or ceremonial gates leading to the top of the Acropolis, then probably to lower Athens again, and then to the outside of a banqueting hall. But the action should be considered continuous or nearly continuous: a Greek chorus remained the whole time after its entrance, and scene changes in an open-air theater with no curtain would have been sketchy.*

1. Translated by Sarah Ruden, to whose notes some of the annotations are indebted.
2. The list of characters and all stage directions (in italics) are by the translator.
3. The name of the heroine means "dissolver of armies."

(*Enter* LYSISTRATA, *a good-looking young matron.*)

LYSISTRATA If I'd invited them to hoot and prance
At Bacchic rites,[4] or at some sleazy shrine,
I would have had to crawl through tambourines
To get here. As it is, no woman's showed,
Except my neighbor Calonice.[5] Hi.

(*Enter* CALONICE, *a middle-aged matron.*)

CALONICE Hi, Lysistrata. Honey, what's gone wrong?
Don't spoil your pretty face with ratty snarls!
Your eyebrows look like bows to shoot me dead.

LYSISTRATA Oh, Calonice, this just burns me up.
Women are slacking off, can't make the grade.
Our husbands say we're cunning to the point
Of—well—depravity.

CALONICE Darn tootin' right!

LYSISTRATA But given word to meet me here today—
A vital matter needs our serious thought—
They're sleeping in.

CALONICE But sweetie, soon they'll come.
Sometimes it's quite a challenge sneaking out.
The husband might require some straightening up,
The maid a screech to get her out of bed,
The kid a bath, a nibble, or a nap.

LYSISTRATA But what I have to say means more than that
To women.

CALONICE Precious, what *is* eating you?
Why summon us in this mysterious way?
What is it? Is it . . . big?

LYSISTRATA Of course.

CALONICE And hard?

LYSISTRATA Count on it.

CALONICE Then how could they not have *come*?

LYSISTRATA Oh, shut your mouth. They *would* have flocked for that.
No, this thing I've gone through exhaustively;
I've worked it over, chewed it late at night.

CALONICE Pathetic if it needed that much help.

LYSISTRATA It's this pathetic: in the women's hands
Is the salvation of the whole of Greece.

CALONICE In women's hands? It's hanging by a thread.

LYSISTRATA We hold within our grasp the city's plight.
The Peloponnesians may be wiped out—

CALONICE By Zeus, that's best, as far as we're concerned—

LYSISTRATA And the Boeotians with them, root and branch[6]—

4. Festivities to honor Dionysos, god of wine; hence, a good occasion for drinking.

5. Her name means "lovely victory"; she talks in a slangy style in the original, and uses a lot of double entendres.

6. Peloponnesians and Boeotians were enemies of Athens during the Peloponnesian War.

CALONICE All of them, fine, except those gorgeous eels.[7]
LYSISTRATA I won't say Athens, since the omen's bad.
Imagine if I'd said it—shocking, huh?
If all the women come together here—
Boeotians, Peloponnesians, and the rest—
And us—together we can salvage Greece.
CALONICE What thoughtful thing could women ever do?
What vivid venture? We just sit decked out
In saffron gowns, makeup about this thick,
Cimberian lingerie[8] and platform shoes.
LYSISTRATA It's those that I intend to save our race:
Those dresses, and perfume, and rouge, and shoes,
And little see-through numbers that we wear.
CALONICE How's that?
LYSISTRATA The men surviving won't lift up
Their spears (against each other, anyway).
CALONICE By the Two Gods,[9] I've got a dress to dye!
LYSISTRATA Or shields—
CALONICE I've got a negligée to try!
LYSISTRATA Or knives—
CALONICE Ooh, ooh, and shoes! And shoes to buy!
LYSISTRATA So shouldn't all the other women come?
CALONICE Well, YES! With wings to boost them, hours ago!
LYSISTRATA It's such a bitch assembling Attica.[1]
You know they'd rather die than be on time.
Nobody even came here from the coast,
Or out of Salamis.
CALONICE I'm sure they got
Up on those mounts of theirs at break of day.
LYSISTRATA
I thought it would be only logical
For the Acharnians to start the crowd,[2]
But they're not here yet.
CALONICE Well, Theogenes' wife
Has raised her glass to us—any excuse.[3]
No, wait. Look thataway: here come a few.
LYSISTRATA And now a couple more.

(*Several women straggle in, among them* MYRRHINE, *a young and beautiful matron.*)

CALONICE Yuck, what a smell!
Where are they from?

7. Eels, a luxury import item in Athens, became unavailable in the war years.
8. Apparently an exotic type of garment.
9. Demeter, goddess of fertility and harvest, and her daughter, Persephone.
1. Athens was in Attica, a larger geographical area that functioned as a single political unit. The coast of Attica and the island of Salamis just off the coast were important strategic points in wartime.
2. The area of Acharnia was badly hit by Spartan invasions.
3. The reference is unclear.

LYSISTRATA The puke-bush swamp.[4]
CALONICE By Zeus,
It must be quite a place to raise a stink.
MYRRHINE Ooh, Lysistrata, are we very late?
Too mad to say?
LYSISTRATA Why should I not be mad?
This is important! Why not come on time?
MYRRHINE Well, it was dark—I couldn't find my thing[5]—
But say what's on your mind, now that we're here.
LYSISTRATA No, wait a little while. The other wives,
The Boeotians and the Peloponnesians,
Are on the way.
MYRRHINE All right, of course we'll wait.
Look over there, though—that's not Lampito?

(Enter LAMPITO, *a strapping woman in a distinct, more revealing costume. Several others in various foreign dress accompany her, including a Boeotian and a Corinthian Woman.)*

LYSISTRATA Darling Laconian,[6] Lampito, hail!
How I admire your gleaming gorgeousness,
Your radiant skin, your body sleek and plump.
I bet that you could choke a bull.
LAMPITO I could.
I'm in such shape I kick my own sweet ass.[7]
CALONICE *(Prodding curiously.)*
And what a brace of boobs. How bountiful!
LAMPITO What am I s'pposed to be? A pig for sale?
LYSISTRATA And what's this other young thing's origin?
LAMPITO Boeotia sent her as a delegate.
She's at your service.
MYRRHINE *(Peeking under woman's clothes.)*
Boeotian—sure enough:
Just look at what a broad and fertile plain.[8]
CALONICE *(Peeking likewise.)*
She's even pulled the weeds. Now *that* is class.
LYSISTRATA And what's the other girl?
LAMPITO Corinthian.
Hell, ain't she fine?
LYSISTRATA Damn right she's fine . . . from here,
And get another angle on her—wow!
LAMPITO We're like a women's army. Who put out
The word to assemble?
LYSISTRATA That was me.
LAMPITO How come?
Tell us what's going on.

4. Region called Anagyrus, notorious for its smelly bushes (*anagyrus*).
5. Literally, "little belt"—a garter belt?
6. Spartan. Spartan women went outside much more than Athenian women, and even exercised outside.
7. A Spartan dance involved this movement.
8. Pennyroyal, a common Boeotian plant, also meant "pubic hair."

CALONICE Yeah, honey, what?
What all-important burr is up your butt?
LYSISTRATA The time has come. But first you answer me
One weensy little thing.
CALONICE Okay. Just ask.
LYSISTRATA I know you all have husbands far from home
On active service. Don't you miss the men,
The fathers of your children, all this time?
CALONICE My husband's been away five months in Thrace.
Somebody's gotta watch the general.
MYRRHINE Mine's been in Pylos seven freaking months.
LAMPITO Once in a while, mine's back, but then he's off.
It's like that shield's a friggin' pair of wings.
LYSISTRATA And since the Milesians deserted us[9]
(Along with every scrap of lover here),
We've even lost those six-inch substitutes,
Those dinky dildos for emergencies.
If I could find a way to end this war,
Would you be willing partners?
CALONICE *I* sure would.
I'd sacrifice my nicest dress to buy
Some wine (and sacrifice the wine to me).
MYRRHINE I'd cut myself in two and donate half—
A flat slice like a bottom-feeding fish.
LAMPITO I'd hike clear up Mount Taygetus to see
If peace is flashin' somewhere way far off.
LYSISTRATA Fine. So. Here goes. You need to know the plan.
Yes, ladies. How we force the men to peace.
How are we going to do it? We must all
Hold off—
CALONICE From *what*?
LYSISTRATA You're positive you will?
CALONICE We'll do it! Even if it costs our lives.
LYSISTRATA From now on, no more penises for you.

(*The women begin to disperse.*)

Wait! You can't all just turn and walk away!
And what's this purse-lipped shaking of your heads?
You're turning pale—is that a tear I see?
Will you or not? You can't hold out on me!
CALONICE No, I don't think so. Let the war go on.
MYRRHINE Me? Not a chance in hell, so screw the war.
LYSISTRATA That's it, my piscine heroine? You said
Just now that you'd bisect yourself for peace.
CALONICE ANYTHING else for me. I'd walk through fire,
But do without a dick? Be serious!
There's nothing, Lysistrata, like a dick.

9. Miletus revolted from Athenian control in 412 B.C.E., the year before this play was performed. Apparently Miletus produced dildos.

LYSISTRATA (*Turning to* WOMAN #1.)
And you?
WOMAN #1
Me? Mmm, I'll take the fire, thanks.
LYSISTRATA Oh, gender fit for boning up the butt!
No wonder we're the stuff of tragedies:
Some guy, a bit of nookie, and a brat.[1]
(*To* LAMPITO.) But you, sweet foreigner, if you alone
Stand with me, then we still could save the day.
Give me your vote!
LAMPITO Shit, it's no easy thing
To lie in bed alone without no dong . . .
But count me in. Peace we just gotta have.
LYSISTRATA The only *woman* in this half-assed horde!
CALONICE Suppose we did—the thing you say we should—
Which gods forbid—what has that got to do
With peace?
LYSISTRATA A lot, I promise you. If we
Sit in our quarters, powdered daintily,
As good as nude in those imported slips,
And—just—slink by, with crotches nicely groomed,
The men will swell right up and want to boink,
But we won't let them near us, we'll refuse—
Trust me, they'll make a treaty at a dash.
LAMPITO You're right! You know how Menelaus saw
Helen's bazooms and threw his weapon down.[2]
CALONICE But what if they just shrug and walk away?
LYSISTRATA For them, there's just one place a dildo fits.[3]
CALONICE As if a fake is lots of fun for us.
Suppose they grab us, drag us into bed.
We'll have no choice.
LYSISTRATA Resist. Hang on the door.
CALONICE Suppose they beat us.
LYSISTRATA Yield a lousy lay.
They force a woman, and it's no more fun.
Plus, no more housework! They'll give up—you'll see
How fast. No husband's going to like to screw
Unless he knows his woman likes it too.
CALONICE If that's the thing you're set on, fine—okay.
LAMPITO We'll force the Spartan husbands into peace:
No cheating, quibbling, squabbling any more.
But what about them lowlifes in your town?
What'll you do so they don't run amok?
LYSISTRATA We'll handle things on our side. Don't you fret.
LAMPITO I will. You know that god of yours has got

1. Alludes to a lost tragedy by Sophocles in which the heroine gets pregnant by the god Poseidon.
2. Menelaus intended to kill Helen after he got her back from the Trojan War; but he was overwhelmed by her beauty, and could not do it.
3. An obscure line in the original.

An expense account for sails and all the rest.[4]
LYSISTRATA We've put aside that obstacle ourselves.
Today we occupy the citadel.
This is the mission of the senior squad.
While we confer here, they've gone up to fake
A sacrifice and storm the Acropolis.
LAMPITO You *are* a clever thang. Fine all around!
LYSISTRATA Let's quickly swear an oath, my friend, and set
Our concord up unbendable as bronze.
LAMPITO Give us whatever oath you wanna give.
LYSISTRATA So where's the guard? (I'm talking to you! Wake up!)

(*Enter Female Scythian Guard in an exotic uniform.*)[5]

Bring here your shield and set it upside down.

(*She obeys. The women pause.*)

Now where's the sacrifice?
CALONICE What can we find
To swear on, Lysistrata?
LYSISTRATA Aeschylus
Had people drain the blood of slaughtered sheep
Into a shield.[6]
CALONICE A shield? To swear for peace?
Excuse me, honey, but that can't be right.
LYSISTRATA What else, then?
CALONICE We could find a giant stud,
A pure white stallion, say, and hack him up.
LYSISTRATA What do you mean, a horse?[7]
CALONICE We need to swear
On *something*.
LYSISTRATA Listen up! I know the way:
A big black drinking bowl laid on its back;
A jar of Thasian to sacrifice;
An oath to mix no water with the wine.[8]
LAMPITO Shit sakes, I like that more than I can say.
LYSISTRATA Somebody bring a jar out, and a bowl.

(*The items are brought.*)

MYRRHINE Hey, sisters, that's some massive pottery!
CALONICE (*Snatching.*)
Just fondling it, you'd start to feel real good.
LYSISTRATA Put the bowl down and help me hold the beast.

(CALONICE *relinquishes her hold. All the women join in lifting the jar.*)

Holy Persuasion, and our Bowl for Pals,
Be gracious toward this women's sacrifice.

4. "That god" is Athena. On the Athenian Acropolis was the treasury of the Delian League, which financed Athens' war effort.
5. Foreign slaves generically known as Scythians were the main security force in Athens. In real life they were always male.
6. In his play *Seven against Thebes*.
7. Reference obscure.
8. Greeks usually drank wine mixed with water; unmixed wine was drunk rarely, and was seen as extremely intoxicating.

(LYSISTRATA *opens the jar. The women pour.*)

CALONICE Propitiously the gleaming blood spurts forth!
LAMPITO By Castor,[9] and it smells real pretty too.
MYRRHINE Girls, let me be the first to swear the oath.
CALONICE No way, by Aphrodite.[1] We'll draw lots.
LYSISTRATA Grip the bowl's rim, Lampito and the rest.

(*They obey.*)

One of you, speak for all, repeat my words,
Then everybody else confirm the oath.
Neither my boyfriend nor my wedded spouse—
CALONICE Neither my boyfriend nor my wedded spouse—
LYSISTRATA Shall touch me when inflated. Say it, girl!
CALONICE Shall touch me when inflated. Holy hell!
Knees—Lysistrata—wobbly. Gonna faint!
LYSISTRATA (*Sternly, ignoring this distress.*)
I shall stay home unhumped both night and day,
CALONICE I shall stay home unhumped both night and day,
LYSISTRATA While wearing makeup and a flashy dress,
CALONICE While wearing makeup and a flashy dress,
LYSISTRATA That I may give my man the scorching hots,
CALONICE That I may give my man the scorching hots,
LYSISTRATA But I will not consent to what he wants,
CALONICE But I will not consent to what he wants,
LYSISTRATA And if he forces me, against my will,
CALONICE And if he forces me, against my will,
LYSISTRATA Then I will sulk, I will not hump along;
CALONICE Then I will sulk, I will not hump along;
LYSISTRATA I will not point my slippers at the roof;
CALONICE I will not point my slippers at the roof;
LYSISTRATA Nor, like a lion knickknack, ass in air[2]—
CALONICE Nor, like a lion knickknack, ass in air—
LYSISTRATA Abiding by these vows, may I drink wine;
CALONICE Abiding by these vows, may I drink wine;
LYSISTRATA If I transgress, let water fill the bowl.
CALONICE If I transgress, let water fill the bowl.
LYSISTRATA Now do you all consent?
ALL By Zeus, we do.
LYSISTRATA I dedicate this bowl. (*She drinks heartily.*)
CALONICE Just drink your share!
We've got to work together, starting now.

(*All drink. A mass ululation is heard offstage.*)

LAMPITO Somebody's shouting.
LYSISTRATA As I said before:
It's our contingent on the citadel.

9. Castor and his twin, Pollux, were demigods, revered in Sparta.
1. Goddess of sex.
2. Ornamental lions were typically represented as if about to pounce, front legs low to the ground and hindquarters raised.

They've taken it already. Lampito,
You go arrange things back in Sparta. These

(*Indicates Spartan Women.*)

Will need to stay with us as hostages.
We'll join the rest of the Athenians
And help them heave the bars behind the doors.

CALONICE You think the men will find out right away
And all gang up on us?

LYSISTRATA The hell with them.
They can't make threats or fires fierce enough.
These doors stay shut. We only open them
On those exact conditions we've set down.

CALONICE So Aphrodite help us, we'll stay put,
Or not deserve the cherished title "Bitch."

(*All the women exit into stage building.*)

(*Enter a* CHORUS *of twelve Old Men, carrying logs, unlit torches, and pots of burning charcoal.*)

MEN'S CHORUS LEADER Draces, lead on, ignore your throbbing back
Under the fresh, green weight of olive trunks.

CHORUS OF OLD MEN A long life brings lots
That's surprising to see.
This, Strumodorus, is a new one on me.
At our expense
This pestilence
Festered at home indoors.
They've taken our citadel!
Athena's image as well!
They've barred the ceremonial gates, the whores!

MEN'S CHORUS LEADER Straight ahead is the fortress, Philurgus.
To pile up one pyre and set it afire
For all with a hand in this wicked affair
Can pass without debate or amendments
Or special pleading—well, first get Lycon's wife.[3]

CHORUS OF OLD MEN Demeter's my witness, this stunt isn't cute.
Like Cleomenes, these girls won't find it a hoot.
Cocky Spartan! He went away,
Dealt with efficiently, let's say,
His arms surrendered. He wore a crappy trace
Of the clothes that he came in.
He was blasted with famine,
With six hard years of beard and crud on his face.[4]

MEN'S CHORUS LEADER Fierce was the siege that we sat for the bastard,
Camping in seventeen ranks at the bulwark.
But the gods and Euripides both detest women.

3. Lycon was a politician whose wife had a reputation for promiscuity.
4. Parodic account of the brief seizure of the Athenian Acropolis by a Spartan king, Cleomenes, in 508 B.C.E.

I'll cram their impertinence straight back inside—
If I don't, take my Marathon monument down.[5]

CHORUS OF OLD MEN The cliff in the road
Where I haul my load
Is right before me, I have come so fast.
Too bad—no mule!
So much to pull.
Literally, this is a pain in the ass.
But I won't tire—
I'll puff the fire—
Won't get distracted—it's got to last!

(*They blow, recoil.*)

Oh shit, the smoke!
I'm going to choke!
From the basin where it slept,
Lord Hercules, how savagely it leapt,
Like a rabid bitch, to bite me in the eyes.
It's Lemnian, I think,
From the land where women stink.[6]
It reeks of everything that I despise.
Up to the heights!
Defend our rights!
The goddess needs us, don't you realize?

(*They blow, recoil.*)

Oh hell, the ash!
I'm going to crash!

MEN'S CHORUS LEADER Gods answer our prayers and the fire rears high.
Assignment The First: put the logs on the ground.
Here are some torches to ram in the brazier.
Rush then, and batter yourselves on the gates.
Call for surrender. A slit should spread open.
Otherwise, light the gates, smoke the broads out.
Put down your logs, men. (This smoke is a hassle!)
The generals in Samos are shirking the work.[7]

(*He heaves his wood down.*)

That's better—the load has stopped warping my back.
This bucket of coals has the task to provide
Me—hey, me first!—with a virulent torch.
Great goddess Victory, give me a prize[8]
For feminine insolence valiantly squished.

(*The men busy themselves with lighting torches.*)

(*A* CHORUS *of twelve Old Women enter from the opposite side, carrying water jars.*)

5. The battle of Marathon, in 490 B.C.E., was a heroic victory for Athens against a Persian invasion. To have participated, these men would have to be about a hundred years old.

6. When the women of the island of Lemnos neglected the rites of the goddess Aphrodite, she punished them with a foul odor.

7. The navy was based at Samos.

8. Athena Nike (Athena goddess of victory) had a temple to the right of the Propylaea (the gateway of the Acropolis).

WOMEN'S CHORUS LEADER Women, that bright thing in a murky cloud—
Is it a fire? Quick, let's get on the scene.
CHORUS OF OLD WOMEN Nicodice, hurry!
Calyce's getting lit!
Critylla's getting buffeted
By blazing winds
And old men full of shit.
Oh, dear! Oh, my! Am I too late?
I went at dawn to wrangle free this water.
I struggled through the crash and screech and slaughter—
Elbows flailing, jars askew—
Scurvy maids, slaves with tattoos—
In a panic raised this urn,
Downright manic to return
To keep my friends from getting singed.
I heard the news about unhinged
Codgers who, like lumberjacks,
Dumped their logs in ten-ton stacks
And launched the most
Outrageous boasts.
They said they'd make ashes of living profanity.
Help, Goddess, save women from such inhumanity,
And they will restore your dear nation to sanity.
That's why, O Golden-Helmeted One,
They dared to occupy your throne.
Oh, be their ally, Triton's daughter.[9]
Zap every spark out with this water.
Help us haul it to the top.
What these beasts are doing must stop!

(The women notice the men and their equipment.)

WOMEN'S CHORUS LEADER Wait! What can this be? They've been busy pricks.
Is this the work of conscientious citizens—or dicks?

(The men notice the women.)

MEN'S CHORUS LEADER We didn't reckon on this other swarm
Of women, rushing toward the gates to help.
WOMEN'S CHORUS LEADER What are you scared of? Do we seem a throng?
You're looking at just .01 percent.
MEN'S CHORUS LEADER Impossible to let them blather on!
We'd better whack them with this wood instead.
WOMEN'S CHORUS LEADER Girls, put your pitchers down, out of the way,
So if they lift a hand, we'll be prepared.
MEN'S CHORUS LEADER If somebody had done a proper job
Of slapping them, they'd keep their yappers shut.
WOMEN'S CHORUS LEADER Fine. Try it. Here's a cheek for you to smack.
And then I'll tear your balls off like a bitch.

9. The goddess with the golden helmet, Triton's daughter, is Athena.

MEN'S CHORUS LEADER Shut up! I'll pound you hollow if you don't.
WOMEN'S CHORUS LEADER Just put a fingertip on Stratyllis—
MEN'S CHORUS LEADER And if I pummel her? What will you do?
WOMEN'S CHORUS LEADER I'll gnaw your lungs and claw your entrails out.
MEN'S CHORUS LEADER Euripides is my authority
On women: "She's a creature lacking shame."[1]
WOMEN'S CHORUS LEADER Honey, we'd better lift these jars again.
MEN'S CHORUS LEADER What did you bring the water for, you scum?
WOMEN'S CHORUS LEADER And what's the fire for, you senile coots?
Fogies flambés?
MEN'S CHORUS LEADER A funeral for your friends!
WOMEN'S CHORUS LEADER We'll put the pyre out before it's lit.
MEN'S CHORUS LEADER *You'd* meddle with *my* fire?
WOMEN'S CHORUS LEADER As you'll see.
MEN'S CHORUS LEADER Maybe I ought to toast you with this torch.
WOMEN'S CHORUS LEADER Have you got soap? I've got the water here.
MEN'S CHORUS LEADER A bath, you rancid hag?
WOMEN'S CHORUS LEADER Get clean, get laid.
MEN'S CHORUS LEADER You hear what nerve—?
WOMEN'S CHORUS LEADER Why not? I'm not a slave.
MEN'S CHORUS LEADER I'll squelch that yelp.
WOMEN'S CHORUS LEADER You're not the judge of me!
MEN'S CHORUS LEADER Set fire to her hair!

(The men threaten with their torches.)

WOMEN'S CHORUS LEADER Help, River God!

(The women empty one set of pitchers over the men.)

MEN'S CHORUS LEADER Hell!
WOMEN'S CHORUS LEADER Oh, was that too hot?

(The women make use of auxiliary pitchers.)

MEN'S CHORUS LEADER Hot?! Stop it, slut!
WOMEN'S CHORUS LEADER I'm watering you so you'll grow nice and high.
MEN'S CHORUS LEADER I'm shivering and shaking myself dry.
WOMEN'S CHORUS LEADER But you've got fire to warm your footsies by.

(Enter COUNCILOR,[2] *accompanied by Two Slaves with crowbars, and Four Male Scythian Guards.)*

COUNCILOR These flaming women, spoiled with kettledrums,
And ritual howls, and this Adonis thing—
You hear them whoop it up—they're on the *roofs*[3]—
Exactly like in the Assembly once.
Demostratus—goddamn him—made the speech

1. Probably a quotation from a lost tragedy.
2. A board of ten councilors had recently taken over much of the city's administration, from the Council of the Five Hundred.
3. Refers to a ritual practice: during the festival of Adonis, women went to the rooftops to mourn for him. Adonis was a mythical boy beloved by the goddess Aphrodite and tragically killed while hunting.

That sent us into Sicily.[4] Just then
His dancing dame yelled, "Poor Adonis!" He
Moved that we try Zacynthus[5] for recruits.
Feeling no pain, the woman on the tiles
Burped, "Mourn Adonis!" And Demostratus
Blasted along, that psycho. This is what
Happens because of women on the loose.

MEN'S CHORUS LEADER No kidding. What about the women here?
They've even emptied pitchers on our heads,
Washed us against our will. Our cloaks are drenched.
You'd think that we were all incontinent.

COUNCILOR Briny Poseidon, that's what we deserve,
Conniving with our wives the way we do,
Drawing them diagrams for decadence—
Of course they sprout conspiracies like this.
We stride into a jeweler's and we say,
"Goldsmith, the necklace that you made my wife—
She was, uh, dancing—hard—the other night.
The prong—you know—got jiggled and fell out.
I have to sail to Salamis today,
But if you're free this evening, go around
And put that thing back in, and screw it tight."
Or at a leather workshop someone asks
A strapping, really well-equipped young man,
"Oh, Mister Shoemaker, you know my wife's
Little toe, and how tender it can get,
Rubbed by her sandal strap? Drop by at noon
And give her hole a jimmy and a stretch."
No wonder it's resulted in *this* mess.
I AM A COUNCILOR. It is my JOB
To find the wood for oars and PAY FOR IT.
And now these WOMEN shut the gates on me!
It's no good standing here. Those crowbars, quick!
I'll separate these women from their gall.

(*A slave is indecisive.*)

Hey, slack-jaw, move! What are you waiting for?
You're looking for a pub where you can hide?
Both of you, put these levers in the gates
From that side, and from here I'll stick mine in
And help you shove.

(LYSISTRATA *emerges from the stage building.*)

LYSISTRATA Right, you can shove those bars.
It doesn't take a tool to bring me out.
You don't need siege equipment here. Just brains.

4. In a disastrous naval expedition to Sicily, which set out in 415 B.C.E. (just before this play was produced), huge numbers of Athenian ships and men were lost. The full extent of the disaster was presumably still unknown, but Athenians at home probably feared bad news.

5. Island allied with Athens.

COUNCILOR Really, you walking poo? Where *is* that guard?
Grab her and tie her hands behind her back.

LYSISTRATA By Artemis, if that state property's
Fingertip touches me, I'll make him wail.

(Guard backs away.)

COUNCILOR You're scared of her? Grab her around the waist,
And you—look sharp and help him tie her hands.

*(*OLD WOMAN #1 *enters from door.)*

OLD WOMAN #1 Pandrosus[6] help me. Lay one cuticle
On her, and I shall beat you till you shit.

(The two guards slink off.)

COUNCILOR Such language! Where'd the other archer go?
Get this one first. Just hear that potty mouth!

*(*OLD WOMAN #2 *enters from door.)*

OLD WOMAN #2 By Phosphorus,[7] one hangnail grazes her,
And you'll be nursing eyes as black as tar.

(Third guard retreats.)

COUNCILOR What *is* this? Where's a guard? Get hold of her!
One little expedition's at an end.

*(*OLD WOMAN #3 *enters from door.)*

OLD WOMAN #3 Go near her, by Tauropolus,[8] and I
Will give you screaming lessons on your hair.

(Fourth guard makes himself scarce.)

COUNCILOR Now I'm in deep. I've got no archers left.
We can't let women have the final stomp!
Scythians, we must form a battle line
And march straight at them.

(Guards reluctantly gather together again from a distance.)

LYSISTRATA You'll find out, I swear,
That we've got four divisions tucked away,
Heavy-armed women itching for a fight.

COUNCILOR Attendants, twist their arms behind their backs.

(The guards advance.)

LYSISTRATA Thunder out, allied women, from the walls!
Sellers of garlic, gruel, and poppy seeds,
Greengrocers, bakers, landladies—attack!
Yank them and shove them! Sock them! Hammer them!
Insult, belittle them—get really coarse!

(A mob of women enters and descends on the guards with physical and verbal abuse.)

Fall back! To strip their dignity's enough.

6. Mythical Athenian princess.
7. Epithet of Artemis and Hecate, moon goddesses; it means "Bringer of Light."
8. The goddess Artemis.

(*The women retreat. The guards lie flattened and immobile.*)

COUNCILOR My bodyguard reduced to diddly-squat!

LYSISTRATA But what were you expecting? Facing troops?
Or herding slaves? Apparently you don't
Think we have guts.

COUNCILOR The female gut's quite deep:
I've seen the way that you perform in bars.

MEN'S CHORUS LEADER Hey you, our Councilor: you're wasting words
By arguing with wild things like a fool.
They didn't even let us get undressed,
But bathed us without benefit of soap.

WOMEN'S CHORUS LEADER Well, you, sir, think your fellow citizens
Are fit for bullying. You *want* black eyes?
Given the choice, I'd play a prim, demure
Young girl, disturbing no one by so much
As blinking. I'm a hornet when I'm roused.

CHORUS OF OLD MEN O, Zeus, what shall we do with these vermin?
We can't just take it. Let's examine
How it happened,
Why these women
Plotted to snatch the bouldered shrine,
Out of bounds, high in the air,
The Acropolis,
And make it theirs.

MEN'S CHORUS LEADER (*To* COUNCILOR.)
Challenge, refute! Whatever sounds right must be wrong!
If they shortchange us, it's the ultimate disgrace.

COUNCILOR Right. Question Number One: I am anxious to hear
Your motivation for barring the fortress doors.

LYSISTRATA Keeping the money here will starve the war to death.

COUNCILOR Money—and war? Huh?

LYSISTRATA There's a rats' nest in this town.
Pisander[9] and his public office-stalking ilk
Raised hell—it yielded marvelous chances to steal.
Who gives a hoot what they do now? The money's safe.

COUNCILOR And *your* plan is—?

LYSISTRATA You have to ask? It's *management*.

COUNCILOR Of public funds? By *you*?

LYSISTRATA And what's so strange in that?
You let us women do the budgeting at home.

COUNCILOR It's not the same at all!

LYSISTRATA Because—?

COUNCILOR You don't fight wars!

LYSISTRATA And you don't have to either.

9. Athenian politician.

COUNCILOR We're in jeopardy!
LYSISTRATA We'll save you.
COUNCILOR You?
LYSISTRATA Yeah, us.
COUNCILOR But that's unthinkable.
LYSISTRATA Think what you like.
COUNCILOR Unutterable.
LYSISTRATA No, uttered.
It doesn't matter how you feel.
COUNCILOR THIS ISN'T RIGHT!
LYSISTRATA Too bad.
COUNCILOR BUT I DON'T WANT IT!
LYSISTRATA Then you need it more.
COUNCILOR How can you meddle in the stern affairs of state?
LYSISTRATA Listen here—
COUNCILOR The hand may be quicker than the mouth.
LYSISTRATA Listen! And keep a grip on your hands.
COUNCILOR Can't manage.
I'm furious!
WOMAN #1 And what you're *going* to be is *sore*.
COUNCILOR No, *you'll* be sore, old buzzard! (*To* LYSISTRATA.) You, go on.
LYSISTRATA I will.
Throughout this futile war, we women held our peace.
Propriety (and husbands) permitted no peep
To escape our mouths. But we weren't exactly pleased.
We did hear how things were going. When you had passed
Some subnormally thought-out, doom-laden decree,
We'd say, aching, but on the surface simpering,
"What rider to the treaty did you decide on
Today at the Assembly?" "That's not your affair!
Shut up." And lo, I did shut up.
OLD WOMAN #1 *I* wouldn't have.
COUNCILOR We'd have clocked you if you didn't.
LYSISTRATA That's why I did.
Another day we'd ask, about some even more
Malignant move, "Do you *ever* think first, big boy?"
He'd glare, order me back to my wool and warn
That I could soon be wailing. "*Men* will see to the war."
COUNCILOR And right he was, by Zeus.
LYSISTRATA You worthless loser, why?
Because ineptitude's a shield against advice?
It got so you were yakking in the streets yourselves:
"We've got no *men* left in the country." "Yeah, no fake."
Hearing stuff like that, we decided women would
Muster and deliver Greece. Why piddle around?
We've got some useful things to tell you. If you stay
Quiet the way *we* always did, we'll set you straight.
COUNCILOR Insufferably presumptuous notion!
LYSISTRATA SHUT UP!!

COUNCILOR Shut up for you, abomination in a veil!
I'd sooner perish.
LYSISTRATA So you're hung up on the veil?

(*The* COUNCILOR *is mobbed and outfitted as a housewife.*)

Hang one on yourself. Try mine.
Drape it around your skull.
Sit on this chair. Don't whine!
OLD WOMAN #1 Hike up your skirt, card gobs of wool
Into a basket on the floor.
LYSISTRATA Look dumb. Chew gum.
The women will deal with the war.
WOMEN'S CHORUS LEADER Leave your pitchers, women, leap up.
Friends are struggling, we must keep up.

I will never tire of dancing.
Waking strength will move my feet.
I'll accept the worst ordeals.
What's so fine as to compete
With these women's sense and valor,
With their charm and civic zeal?

Grannies on the go, mommies with mucho macho,
The wind is behind your rage, so harden, advance!
LYSISTRATA If the Cyprian Goddess and sweet Eros breathe
Desire through us till our thighs and bosoms steam,
Thereby equipping men with feel-good weaponry,
The Greeks will rename us *Anti*-Battle-Axes![1]
COUNCILOR What are you going to do?
LYSISTRATA Well, first of all, we'll stop
Those kooks who go shopping in battle gear.
OLD WOMAN #1 Hell, yes!
LYSISTRATA They haul an armory among the pottery
And greens, and bash around—it's like some goddamn cult.
COUNCILOR They're dedicated men!
LYSISTRATA No, dedicated dweebs.
They heft their doughty Gorgon[2] shields and buy sardines.
OLD WOMAN #1 A captain, streaming-haired, aloft upon his steed,
Proffered a bronze hat to be shoveled full of soup.
A Thracian—just like Tereus![3]—clattered his shield
And downed forthwith the figs of the routed vendor.
COUNCILOR But there's a perfect pandemonium worldwide.
How would you cope?
LYSISTRATA Without a lot of strain.

1. The Cyprian Goddess is Aphrodite, goddess of sex; Eros is her son, "Desire." "Anti-Battle-Axes" is a direct translation of *Lysimaches*. Lysimache was a real woman, a priestess of Athena.
2. Monstrous female monster who turned onlookers to stone. Her image was common on shields.
3. A mythical Thracian king who raped his wife's sister; together, the women punished him by making him eat his children.

COUNCILOR What?! How?
LYSISTRATA Say that the wool's a mass of tangles. Take it thus,

(*Miming throughout.*)

Draw it apart with spindles—make some sense of it.
That's how we'll loosen up this war—if we're allowed.
Ambassadors are spindles—they can sort it out.
COUNCILOR Spindles and gobs of wool—it's just too fatuous.
We're in a crisis.
LYSISTRATA With a modicum of smarts,
You'd copy the administration of our wool.
COUNCILOR Do tell me how.
LYSISTRATA First, give the fleece a bath to dunk
Away the sheep dung. Spread your city on a bed
Next, and beat out all the layabouts and briars.
Then card out any clumps—you know, the cliques of chumps,
Magistracy-mongers.[4] Pluck their little heads off.
Comb what's left into a single goodwill basket.
Wad in your resident aliens and other
Nice foreigners, and don't leave out public debtors.
And heck, as for the city's scattered colonies,
I want you to construe them as neglected tufts,
Each on its lonesome. Gather them all together,
Bunch them up tight, and finally you'll have one
Big ball. Use it to weave the city something fine.
COUNCILOR Wads and rods and balls—the paradigm's atrocious!
What have you got to do with war?
LYSISTRATA You scrap of scum,
We fight it twice: it's we who give the hoplites life,
And then we send them off, for you—
COUNCILOR That spot is sore!
LYSISTRATA Us young and frisky females, who must seize the night,
War puts to bed beside ourselves. But screw us wives:
I ache for the girls turned crones and never married.
COUNCILOR Don't men get old?
LYSISTRATA You *know* it's nothing like the same!
Any decrepit veteran, no questions asked,
Can get a child-bride, but a woman's chance is zip
After her prime. She sits there maiming daisies—crap!
COUNCILOR As long as men can get it up—
LYSISTRATA Why don't you die and shut it up?

(*The women mob the* COUNCILOR *and dress and equip him as a corpse.*)

We've got a plot. Just buy a box.
And here's a wreath for you!
A honey-cake to bribe the dog—
OLD WOMAN #1 And holy ribbons, too—
OLD WOMAN #2 A coin to get you on the boat—

4. Oligarchic clubs.

LYSISTRATA That's all—it's time to rush off.
Charon's calling. Till he's full
He's not allowed to push off.[5]
COUNCILOR Such disrespect for my authority!
I'll march straight to the other councilors:
My person's an indictment of your deeds.

(*He exits with attendants.* LYSISTRATA *calls after him.*)

LYSISTRATA You're angry that we didn't lay you out?
Don't worry, sir. At dawn, two days from now,
We'll come and give you the traditional rites.

(*The women exit into the stage building.*)

MEN'S CHORUS LEADER Lovers of freedom, rouse yourselves from sleep!
Strip down, my friends, and take this problem on.

(*They remove their cloaks.*)

CHORUS OF OLD MEN I've got a whiff of larger plans at work—
The reign of terror that we thought was gone![6]
Suppose Laconians have gathered here
With someone—oooh, with Cleisthenes,[7] let's say—
To stir this goddamn plague of women up
And take my bare-essential jury pay.
MEN'S CHORUS LEADER Scandalous! Women scold us citizens
And blab about a war they've never seen:
"We'll RECONCILE you with LACONIANS."
Give me a wolf to pet—I'm just as keen.
"I'll hide my weapon under myrtle boughs."[8]
This plot against our precious liberty
I'll foil. On guard against a tyranny,
I'll march in armor while I shop and pose
Beside Aristogiton's statue—see!

(*Strikes a pose.*)

And here's a splendid opportunity
To bop this impious old troll's nose!

(*His fist is raised against the* WOMEN'S CHORUS LEADER.)

WOMEN'S CHORUS LEADER Your mother's going to think you're
someone else.
Ladies, lay down your wraps.

(*They do so.*)

CHORUS OF OLD WOMEN We're going to tell
The city several things it needs to know.
I owe it this. It brought me up so well:
At seven as a Mystery-Carrier;
A Grinder in the holy mill at ten;

5. Charon ferried the dead across the river to the underworld.
6. Refers to the time when Athens was ruled by tyrants, expelled in 510 B.C.E.
7. Effeminate politician.
8. Quotation from a song about two lovers, Harmodius and Aristogiton, who plotted to kill the tyrant Hippias.

Later, at Brauron, as a bright-robed Bear;
A comely, fig-decked Basket-Bearer then.[9]
WOMEN'S CHORUS LEADER That's why I'll serve my city with a chat.
So I'm a woman—why should you resent
That I come forward with the best advice?
I've done my share and more; it's men I've lent.
You wretched drool-bags, since the Persian Wars,
Just fritter our inheritance away,[1]
No taxes to replace the cash you spend.
You're going to ruin all of us someday.
You dare to gripe? Let out one vicious word,
I'll send this slipper bashing through your beard.

(*She removes a shoe and strikes a threatening pose with it.*)

CHORUS OF OLD MEN Isn't this too obnoxious to ignore?
It started bad—how nasty can it get?
Justice and Truth rely on those with balls.
MEN'S CHORUS LEADER Strip off your shirts, let women smell men's sweat,
Stride free of wrappings hampering a fight.

(*They comply.*)

CHORUS OF OLD MEN Remember how we manned Leipsydrion?[2]
Shake off these rags of age and grow fresh wings!
Swoop like the swift young eagles we were then!
MEN'S CHORUS LEADER We let these wrestlers get the slightest hold,
Their grasping handiwork will never end:
They'll build themselves some ships, become marines,
Like Artemisia[3] attacking men!
If they try horsemanship, you'd better cross
The cavalry off your list. A woman on
Her mount clings tight, however hard the ride.
She won't slip off: e.g., the Amazons
Battling in Micon's picture.[4] No, the stocks
Are where these girls belong, with sturdy locks!
CHORUS OF OLD WOMEN Give me a prod. You'll find out soon enough
My anger's like a savage, frothing boar.
You'll scream for neighbors' help: "I'm getting reamed!"
WOMEN'S CHORUS LEADER Quick, women, put your dresses on the floor.

(*They do so.*)

Let the men sniff the creature so annoyed—
CHORUS OF OLD WOMEN If she just hears bad words, she'll bite men gory,
Disqualifying them for civic tasks:
Cf. the beetle and the eagle story.[5]

9. Roles in religious rituals carried out by virgin girls. Fig necklaces symbolized fertility.
1. Athenian victory against the Persians had won the city wealth, in spoils; but the war against Sparta depleted the city treasury.
2. Attic town that played a part in the attempt to oust the tyrant Hippias from Athens in the 6th century B.C.E.
3. Queen who fought on the Persian side in the battle of Salamis, in 480 B.C.E.
4. Presumably Micon painted famous Amazon scenes.
5. In a fable, the beetle revenges herself on the eagle by rolling its eggs out of the nest. Here, the suggestion is presumably that the women will attack the men's testicles (their "eggs").

WOMEN'S CHORUS LEADER Phooey on you! Lampito's my defense,
Ismene, too (a well-connected girl).
Pass seven laws against me, I don't care—
Everyone hates you, in the whole known world!
I have a friend, the sweet Boeotian eel.
I wanted her to come, the other day,
To share my festive rites of Hecate.[6]
Her keepers told me, "No. Because *they* say."
Either you stop it or you'll learn a trick
You won't enjoy: to flip and break your neck.

(*It is several days later. Enter* LYSISTRATA, *visibly distressed.*)

WOMEN'S CHORUS LEADER Our queenly leader, chief conspirator,
Why come you forth in such a royal snit?
LYSISTRATA The dastard weakness of the female mind
Bids me to pace in fury and despair.
WOMEN'S CHORUS LEADER Alas, what say you?
LYSISTRATA Naught but plainest truth.
WOMEN'S CHORUS LEADER What dire news? Reveal it to your friends.
LYSISTRATA Shameful to speak, but heavy to withhold.
WOMEN'S CHORUS LEADER Hide not from me our sore calamity.
LYSISTRATA Well, in a word, our movement's getting fucked.
WOMEN'S CHORUS LEADER Zeus!
LYSISTRATA Why call on Zeus? Our nature's not *his* fault.
And anyway, it's me who can't enforce
Husband aversion. AWOL's spreading fast.
The other day I caught one near Pan's cave,
Making the hole a tunnel just her size.
A second sought civilian status by
Rappelling from a crane, another tried
To ride a sparrow down to You-Know-Who's.
I had to grab her hair and drag her back.
Trying for furloughs, they evoke a vast
Supply of fiction. Here's a sample now.

(*Stops* WOMAN #1, *who has entered from the stage building and is dashing off toward the side.*)

Where are *you* running to?
WOMAN #1 I'm going home.
I have to rescue my—Milesian wool
From—moths. They're going to shred it.
LYSISTRATA Moths, my ass!
Get back inside!
WOMAN #1 By the Two Gods,[7] I will.
I only need to spread it on the bed.
LYSISTRATA You'll do no spreading, 'cause you're staying put.
WOMAN #1 I sacrifice my *wool*?
LYSISTRATA Yes, for the cause.

6. Goddess of moonlight and witchcraft.

7. Demeter and Persephone.

(WOMAN #2 *enters in a tragic pose, scurrying away at the same time.*)

WOMAN #2 Pity me and my fine Amorgos flax,
At home, left on the stems!

LYSISTRATA Example B
Is skulking off to peel a pile of thread.
You, turn around!

WOMAN #2 (*Stopping reluctantly.*) I swear by Hecate,
I'll only stay to give it one good—shuck.[8]

LYSISTRATA No shucking way. If I give in to you,
There's going to be no end of applicants.

(WOMAN #3 *enters, clutching a protruding stomach.*)

WOMAN #3 Goddess of Childbirth, spare me for an hour!
This place is sacrosanct—I've got to leave![9]

LYSISTRATA What *is* this crap?

WOMAN #3 My baby's almost here!

LYSISTRATA Yesterday you weren't pregnant.

WOMAN #3 Now I am!
Please, Lysistrata, let me go. The nurse
Is waiting for me.

LYSISTRATA Sounds a lot like bull.

(*She feels the front of the woman's dress.*)

There's something hard here.

WOMAN #3 It's a baby boy.

LYSISTRATA By Aphrodite, not my guess at all.
It's hollow metal. Let me take a peek.

(*She dives under the woman's dress, emerges with a giant helmet.*)

You idiot, the holy helmet's here![1]
You're pregnant, huh?

WOMAN #3 By Zeus, I swear I am.

LYSISTRATA And what's this for?

WOMAN #3 If I were overcome
On the way home, I'd have a kind of nest.
It seems to work for doves, at any rate.

LYSISTRATA No kidding. If that's your excuse, then wait
Five days to have a party for this hat.[2]

WOMAN #3 But I can't even sleep here since I saw
The sacred snake.[3] You gotta let me go!

WOMAN #1 I won't survive, I've been awake so long.
These stupid honking owls won't take a rest.[4]

8. There is a double entendre in the original, because the same verb is used for "shucking," or separating flax from its fibers, and for pushing back the foreskin of the penis.
9. It was forbidden to give birth on sacred ground.
1. Probably Athena's helmet, from the statue in the Parthenon.
2. After the birth of a child, it was normal to wait five days, and then have a "family welcoming" party.
3. Believed to live in a rocky crevice on the Acropolis.
4. Owls were sacred to Athena.

LYSISTRATA Magical stuff—shut up about it, hey?
You want your men. You don't think they want you?
They're spending nasty nights outside your beds.
Dear ladies, just be patient for a bit,
And see our project through, clear to the end.
An oracle assures us that we'll win
If we're united. Here, I've got the text.
WOMAN #3 What does it say?
LYSISTRATA Be quiet and I'll read.

(*She takes out a scroll.*)

Swallows will come together, huddling close—
Fleeing hoopoes—renouncing phalluses[5]—
Bad things will end, when Zeus the Thunderer
Brings low the lofty—
WOMAN #3 Hmm, we'll be on top?
LYSISTRATA But if the bickering birds fly separate ways,
Leaving the sacred temple, it will show
That—swallows are the world's most shameless trash.
WOMAN #3 The sacred words are plain. Oh, help us, gods.
LYSISTRATA We won't give in to hassles, but persist.
Let's go inside. It would be a disgrace
To prove unworthy of the oracle.

(*The women exit into the stage building.*)

CHORUS OF OLD MEN When I was a boy, I heard a tale
I'd like to share with you.
There was a young man named Melanion.[6]
They told him to get married, and he said, "Pooh!"
He fled to the mountains, where he lived,
Hunting hares.
He had a great dog,
And he wove his own snares.
He never went home. His hatred
Continued burning bright.
And we hate women just as much,
Because we know what's right.
MEN'S CHORUS LEADER Give me a kiss, you hag.
WOMEN'S CHORUS LEADER Oh, yuck, that onion smell!
MEN'S CHORUS LEADER And now a hearty kick!

(*Crotch shows as he lifts leg.*)

WOMEN'S CHORUS LEADER Chain up your animal!
MEN'S CHORUS LEADER Myronides and Phormion[7] were formidably furred:
Their enemies took one look at them and ran.

5. The original includes a pun on the word for "coot," which also meant "penis."
6. The myth usually suggests that Melanion went to the wilderness to be with his beloved, Atalanta.
7. Athenian war heroes.

A nest of black hair in the crack at the back
Is the sign of a genuine man.

CHORUS OF OLD WOMEN It's our turn to tell you a tale.
(We don't like the Melanion one.)
Timon once lurked in the thorns,
A wild man, the Ghouls' foster son.[8]
He stayed away
Till his dying day,
Cursing mankind with venom.
He loathed all of you,
The same as we do,
But was always a sweetie to women.

WOMEN'S CHORUS LEADER Shall I bash your jaw?

MEN'S CHORUS LEADER I'll be so sore!

WOMEN'S CHORUS LEADER A kick at least.

(Her leg is lifted, threatening a view of crotch.)

MEN'S CHORUS LEADER Talk about beasts!

WOMEN'S CHORUS LEADER Fine, but I'm glad that mine
Doesn't run wild and free.
Though I'm not especially young,
I groom it tenderly.

(The choruses step back.)

(LYSISTRATA appears on the roof of the stage building.)

LYSISTRATA Whoopee! Get over here, you women, quick!

(Enter WOMAN #1, MYRRHINE, and several other women onto the roof.)

WOMAN #1 What is it? Tell me what you're squalling at.

LYSISTRATA A man—he's coming in a frenzied charge,
With Aphrodite's offering—of meat.
O Queen of Cyprus and of Cythera
And Paphos! (Yeah, bud, come *straight up* to us!)

WOMAN #1 Where is our mystery man?

LYSISTRATA By Chloe's shrine.[9]

WOMAN #1 No question—that thing's male. Who could he be?

LYSISTRATA All of you look. Does someone know him?

MYRRHINE Zeus!
I do. My husband—it's Cinesias.[1]

LYSISTRATA Your duty is to roast him on that spit.
You will, you won't, you might—just lead him on.
Remember, though: you swore on booze—no sex!

MYRRHINE Leave it to me.

LYSISTRATA But I'll stay here and pull
The opening stunts and get him all worked up
For you to play with. Go back in and hide.

8. Timon was a 5th-century B.C.E. Athenian known for hating everybody, men and women equally. No other source says he was "a sweetie to women."

9. Demeter Chloe: Demeter of the Green Shoots.

1. His name is cognate with the verb "to move," slang for "to fuck."

(*All the women but* LYSISTRATA *exit. Enter* CINESIAS, *with his* SLAVE, *who is carrying* CINESIAS' BABY. *A giant codpiece hangs from* CINESIAS' *waist.* LYSISTRATA *descends by ladder or through the stage building to meet* CINESIAS.)

CINESIAS I'm screwed—I mean I'm not! I'm stretched so tight
Skilled torture couldn't do a better job.
LYSISTRATA Who's gotten past the sentinels?
CINESIAS It's me.
LYSISTRATA A man?
CINESIAS Yeah, can't you see?
LYSISTRATA I see. Get lost.
CINESIAS Who's going to throw me out?
LYSISTRATA The lookout. Me.
CINESIAS I need Myrrhine. Call her for me—please.
LYSISTRATA Myrrhine? Huh? You need her? Who are you?
CINESIAS Her husband. I'm Cinesias from—
LYSISTRATA Hey!
I know *you*, or I've often heard your name.
All of us know it. You're quite famous here.
Your wife's mouth never takes a break from you.
She toasts you every time she has a snack—
Smooth eggs, or juicy apples—
CINESIAS Gods! O gods!
LYSISTRATA Just Aphrodite. When we mention men,
That wife of yours declares without delay:
"They're all a pile of crud compared to mine."
CINESIAS Call her, c'mon.
LYSISTRATA And what's it worth to you?
CINESIAS What have I got on me? Oh, right, there's *this*.
It's all I have, but you can take it and—
LYSISTRATA There, now. I'll call her down to you.
CINESIAS And fast.

(LYSISTRATA *exits into stage building.*)

There's nothing now in life to bring me joy.
She left the house! She left me on my own!
When I return at night, the whole place seems
So empty, and I ache. The food has got
No taste for me. All I can feel is dick.

(MYRRHINE *appears on the roof of the stage building, calling behind her.*)

MYRRHINE I love him, oh, I do! He won't accept
My yearning love. Don't make me go out there.
CINESIAS Myrrhine, I don't get it, baby doll.
Come down here.
MYRRHINE That event will not occur.
CINESIAS I call, Myrrhine, and you won't come down?
MYRRHINE What the hell for? Why are you bothering?
CINESIAS What *for*? To keep my prick from crushing me.

MYRRHINE See you around.
CINESIAS No—listen to your son.
(*To* BABY.) You little—call your Mama, or I'll—
BABY Waaah!
Mama! Mama! Mama!
CINESIAS What's wrong with you? No feeling for your child?
Six days he's gone without a bath or food.
MYRRHINE Poor baby. Daddy doesn't give a hoot.
CINESIAS Monster, at least come down and feed your whelp.
MYRRHINE Ah, motherhood! What choice do I have now?

(*She descends and approaches him.*)

CINESIAS (*Aside.*) Maybe my mind's just soggy, but she seems
Wonderfully young—her face has such allure.
And see that snippy way she struts along.
It's making me so horny I could croak.
MYRRHINE (*Taking* BABY.) My lovey-pie—too bad about your Dad.
Give Mommy kiss, my honey-dumpling-bun.
CINESIAS What are you up to here? What have they done
To lure you off? Why are you hurting me?
You're hurting too!

(*He reaches for her.*)

MYRRHINE Your hand can stop right there.
CINESIAS My stuff at home—it's your stuff too—is shot
Since you've been gone.
MYRRHINE My, my, that's too, *too* bad.
CINESIAS That nicest cloth of yours—the hens got in—
You ought to see it.
MYRRHINE Only if I cared.
CINESIAS And all this time we've ditched the rituals
Of Aphrodite. Aren't you coming back?
MYRRHINE Not me, by Zeus, unless you make a deal
To stop this war.
CINESIAS If that's the way we vote,
That's what we'll do.
MYRRHINE Then you trot off and vote,
And I'll trot home. For now, I've sworn to stay.
CINESIAS Then lie down here with me. It's been so long.
MYRRHINE No, not a chance—in spite of how I feel.
CINESIAS You love me? Honey, then why not lie down?
MYRRHINE Don't be ridiculous! The baby's here.
CINESIAS Right. Yeah. Okay. Boy, you can take it home.

(SLAVE *takes* BABY *back and exits.*)

There, do you see a baby anymore?
So if you'd just—
MYRRHINE You're crazy! Where's a spot
To do it here?
CINESIAS Uh, there's the grove of Pan.

MYRRHINE And how am I to purify myself?
CINESIAS No sweat. There's the Clepsydra[2] you can use.
MYRRHINE I swore an *oath*. And now I break my word?
CINESIAS Forget your oath. 'Cause that's my lookout, huh?
MYRRHINE I'll get a cot for us.
CINESIAS No, stay right here.
The ground is fine.
MYRRHINE Apollo help me, no!
Stretch till you twang, before I lay you there!

(*She exits.*)

CINESIAS There's no mistaking such a doting fuss.

(*She returns with a cot.*)

MYRRHINE Hurry, lie down. I'm going to get undressed.

(CINESIAS *lies down.*)

Now what—? I've got to drag a mattress out.
CINESIAS But I don't care!
MYRRHINE By Artemis, you can't
Think we could do it on the cords.
CINESIAS Kiss me.
MYRRHINE Okay.

(*She kisses him.*)

CINESIAS Fantastic. You come back real fast.

(*She exits, returns with a mattress, nudges* CINESIAS *off the cot, and places the mattress on it.*)

MYRRHINE Mattress. All right. Lie down.

(*She rearranges him.*)

I'll soon be nude!
Whoops! I forgot—something—a pillow, yes!
CINESIAS But I don't need one.
MYRRHINE That's too bad. I do.

(*She exits.*)

CINESIAS Oh, what an epic prank on my poor prick!

(*She returns with a pillow.*)

MYRRHINE Head up. (*She places the pillow under his head.*) I've got the whole collection now.
CINESIAS I'm sure you do. Come here, my cutie-sweet.
MYRRHINE Just let me get this bra off. One more time:
You wouldn't lead me on about the peace?
CINESIAS If I do that, Zeus strike me dead.
MYRRHINE A sheet!
CINESIAS By Zeus, forget the sheet! I want to screw!
MYRRHINE Don't worry, you'll get screwed. I'll be right back.

2. A spring on the Acropolis. Nobody could enter a sanctuary after sex unless they washed first.

(*She exits.*)

CINESIAS She's going to decorate until I die.

(*She enters with a sheet.*)

MYRRHINE Up just a little. (*She spreads the sheet under him.*)
CINESIAS (*Indicating penis.*) How is *this* for up?
MYRRHINE Do you want oil?
CINESIAS No! By Apollo! No!
MYRRHINE My, looks like you don't know what's good for you.

(*She exits.*)

CINESIAS Great Zeus in heaven, make the bottle spill!

(*She returns with oil bottle.*)

MYRRHINE Hold out your hand, take some, and spread it on.

(*He takes a sample.*)

CINESIAS Yuck, I don't like it. All I smell's delay.
It's got no nuance of MY WIFE and SEX.
MYRRHINE Well, shame on me! I brought the one from Rhodes.
CINESIAS No, never mind, it's perfect.
MYRRHINE You're a dork.

(*She exits.*)

CINESIAS Perfume's inventor ought to cram the stuff.

(*She enters, offers him a bottle.*)

MYRRHINE Take this.
CINESIAS I've *got* one that's about to crack!
Lie down, you tramp! Don't bring me anything!
MYRRHINE Okay, I'm lying down.

(*She perches on edge of bed.*)

I've only got
To get my shoes off. Honey, don't forget:
You're voting for a treaty.
CINESIAS I'll assess—

(*She dashes away and exits.*)

Shit! Shit!! She's gone. She rubbed me out and ran.
She plucked my cock, consigning me to dust.

Oh, woe! Whom shall I screw?[3]
The loveliest one is gone.
Who'll take this orphan on?
I need a pimp! Hey, you—
Go hire me a nanny for my dong.
CHORUS OF OLD MEN Misery, woe on woe!
Lo, I brim over with compassion:
You're foully swindled of your ration!

3. The language of this passage parodies tragedy.

Forsooth, your guts are going to blow!
How will your nuts remain
Intact? Will you not go insane?
Your manly parts are out of luck
Without their regular morning fuck.

CINESIAS Great Zeus, how dreadfully I twitch!

CHORUS OF OLD MEN That's from the world's most evil bitch.
She tortured you, the filthy cheat.

CHORUS OF OLD WOMEN No, no! She's absolutely sweet.

CHORUS OF OLD MEN She's a curse. She's a disease.

CINESIAS She is! O Zeus, please, please!
You know the way your whirlwind flips
And flings the brush piles that it whips?
And twists and loops them in a blur,
And dumps them down? Do that to her.
But when you let her touch the ground
She must land tidily around
My prong, okay? And right away?

(*Enter* SPARTAN HERALD, *bent over and holding his cloak out in front.* CINESIAS *has recovered enough of his composure to face him.*)

SPARTAN HERALD Where do you find the Elders in this town?
No, sorry, your—Directors?[4] I got news.

CINESIAS Are you a human being or a pole?[5]

SPARTAN HERALD By the Twin Gods, I've come official-like
From Sparta, 'cause we need to compromise.

CINESIAS Then please explain that pike beneath your clothes.

SPARTAN HERALD (*Dodging* CINESIAS' *eyes.*) I swear, it's nothing.

CINESIAS But you're turned away.
Your cloak is hiding something. Have you got
Some swelling from the ride?

SPARTAN HERALD (*Aside.*) His mind is gone.

CINESIAS Come on, you scamming bastard, it's a bone!

SPARTAN HERALD By Zeus, it ain't. Back off, you crazy fart.

CINESIAS What is it, then?

SPARTAN HERALD Uh, it's a Spartan staff.

CINESIAS (*Opening cloak.*) Then here's a Spartan staff that's just changed sides.
I know the whole thing. You can tell the truth
About what Lacedaemon's going through.

SPARTAN HERALD Well, us and our confederate states is stuck.
Stuck standing up. We need to *snatch*[6] a piece.

4. The Spartans had a Council of Elders; the Athenians were governed differently, by Directors (the *prytaneis*). The Spartan speaks in dialect, which would presumably have sounded a little boorish to Athenian ears: hence the translator's use of terms like "I got."

5. Reference to a Spartan fertility spirit with a huge phallus.

6. "We need to *snatch* a piece" is literally *Pellene*: apparently a pun on the name of a prostitute, and of a territory coveted by Sparta.

CINESIAS And who's the source of this catastrophe?
Pan?[7]

SPARTAN HERALD No, Lampito—I think it was her plan.
And then all over Sparta, when they heard,
The women thundered from the starting line—
There went our pussy in a cloud of dust.

CINESIAS How are you making out, then?

SPARTAN HERALD Hey, we're *not*.
The whole damn town's bent double like we's kicked.
Before we lay a finger on a twat,
The women say we gotta all wise up
And make a treaty with the other Greeks.

CINESIAS They got together and they plotted this,
All of the women. I can see it now.
Quick, have the Spartans send ambassadors,
Fully empowered to reach a settlement.
And on the evidence of this my dick
I'll make our Council choose some legates too.

SPARTAN HERALD I'm off. You got the whole thing figured out.

(*They exit.*)

MEN'S CHORUS LEADER To get on top of women—try a fire,
It's easier. A leopard's got more shame.

WOMEN'S CHORUS LEADER And knowing this, you won't give up this fight,
When you can always trust me as a friend?

MEN'S CHORUS LEADER Women revolt me. And it stays that way.

WOMEN'S CHORUS LEADER There's lots of time. But I can't bear to see
You standing garmentless. You look absurd.
I'll come and put this cloak back over you.

(*She drapes it around him.*)

MEN'S CHORUS LEADER By Zeus, you've done a thing that isn't vile.
I stripped when I was raging for a fight.

WOMEN'S CHORUS LEADER Now you're a man again, and not a clown.
If you were nice, I might have grabbed that beast
Still lodging in your eye, and plucked him out.

MEN'S CHORUS LEADER So that's what's galling me. Here, take my ring.
Gouge out the critter, let me see him. Gods,
All day he's masticated in that lair.

WOMEN'S CHORUS LEADER For sure, here goes. But what a grouchy guy.

(*Removes bug.*)

Oh, Zeus, I've never seen a gnat this big.
Just look. It's like some monster from the swamp.

7. The god Pan was associated with extreme emotional states ("panic") and with wildness.

MEN'S CHORUS LEADER You helped. That thing was excavating me . . .
And now it's gone. There's water in my eyes.
WOMEN'S CHORUS LEADER I'll wipe it off, though you've been quite a pain.

(*She wipes his face and kisses him.*)

And here's a kiss.
MEN'S CHORUS LEADER No—
WOMEN'S CHORUS LEADER It's not up to you!
MEN'S CHORUS LEADER Up your wazoo! You're born to flatter us!
The adage says it all: that women are
Abomination indispensable.
But let's make peace, and in the time to come
I'll neither dump on you nor take your crap.
Let's all line up and dance to celebrate.

(*The two choruses unite and address the audience.*)

UNITED CHORUS Gentlemen, I don't mean to call
A fellow citizen a snot or blot
Or anything like that at all.
No, *au contraire!* I'll be much more than fair!
Sufficient are the evils that you've got.
Man or woman, just tell me
If you'd like a bit—
Two thousand, or, say, three[8]—
I've got so much of it.
We'll even give you bags to haul it.
In peaceful times we won't recall it:
Just keep the goodies from our coffers.
Oops: we've forgotten what we offered.

We've just invited really swell
Carystians, from overseas.[9]
We're going to entertain them well,
With perfectly braised, tenderly glazed
Piglet served with purée of peas.
Spruce yourself up (don't leave out
The kids!) and come today.
March in, nothing to ask about,
And no one in the way.
Barge boldly to the doors.
Pretend the place is yours.
Don't even bother to knock—
It's going to be locked.

(*The* SPARTAN AMBASSADORS *approach, bent over, holding their cloaks out in front, trying to conceal massive erections. Slaves accompany them.*)

8. A substantial sum of money.

9. From a city in Euboea, allied with Athens.

UNITED CHORUS LEADER Here come the Spartan legates, beards a-drag—
In clothing that looks draped around a crate.
Laconian gentlemen, our best to you!
Tell us in what condition you've arrived.
SPARTAN AMBASSADOR This isn't gonna take a wordy talk.

(*Opens cloak.*)

A look-see for yourselves should do the trick.
UNITED CHORUS LEADER Oh, wow. The situation's pretty tense,
A crisis getting more and more inflamed.
SPARTAN AMBASSADOR It's crazy. Anyway, what's there to say?
We'll accept any kind of terms for peace.

(*Enter* ATHENIAN AMBASSADORS, *like the Spartans under obvious strain. Slaves accompany them also.*)

UNITED CHORUS LEADER These natives have a tic a lot like yours,
Of bending down like wrestlers, with a lot
Of room for something underneath their cloaks.
They have some hypertrophy of the groin.
ATHENIAN AMBASSADOR #1 (*To* UNITED CHORUS.) Where's Lysistrata?
Someone's got to know.

(*Pulls cloak aside to display contents, gestures toward Spartans.*)

We're here, they're here, but both are way up there.
UNITED CHORUS LEADER I seem to see a certain parallel
Between these two diseases—cramps at dawn?
ATHENIAN AMBASSADOR #1 Worse, we've arrived at wits' and gonads' end.
If we don't hurry and negotiate,
We'll have to make a date with Cleisthenes.[1]
UNITED CHORUS LEADER If I were you, I'd cover up those things.
What if a prankster with a chisel sees?[2]
ATHENIAN AMBASSADOR #1 That's good advice.

(*Covers himself.*)

SPARTAN AMBASSADOR By the Twin Gods, it is.
We better wrap these bigger duds around.

(*Covers himself likewise.*)

ATHENIAN AMBASSADOR #1 Greetings to you, dear Spartans. We've been stiffed.
SPARTAN AMBASSADOR And us, too, pal. Maybe the audience
Could see that we was playing with ourselves.
ATHENIAN AMBASSADOR #1 Let's get through our agenda double-quick.
What do you want?
SPARTAN AMBASSADOR We're the ambassadors.
We're here about a treaty.

1. An Athenian contemporary often satirized by Aristophanes for his effeminacy and willingness to be sodomized.
2. Refers to an infamous occasion in 415 B.C.E., when rioters broke the phalluses off many of the Herms in Athens. Herms were statues of Hermes, equipped with phalluses, that were placed for protection outside houses.

ATHENIAN AMBASSADOR #1 So are we.
But only Lysistrata's up to it.
Let's ask her. She can be the referee.
SPARTAN AMBASSADOR Lysis or Strata—anyone who can.

(*Enter* LYSISTRATA.)

ATHENIAN AMBASSADOR #1 It looks like there's no need for us to call.
She heard us. She's already coming out.
UNITED CHORUS LEADER You who've got by far the biggest balls of all,
Show you've got the greatest tact and gall of all!
Be high-class, low-class, sweet, self-righteous—everything.
Every last minister in Greece now stumbles
Under your spell, surrendering his grumbles.
LYSISTRATA It's not hard work. You only have to swoop
The moment when they're bursting for a deal.
But here's the test. Goddess of Deals, come out!

(RECONCILIATION, *an actor in a body stocking padded to look like a nude woman, enters.*)

To start with, take the Spartans by the hand—
And don't get rough, don't have it all your way;
Don't wreck it like our stupid husbands did.
Be gentle as a mother in her house—
But if he pulls his hand back, take his dong.
Lead the Athenians to center stage.
(Anything you can grab can be the leash.)
Laconian gentlemen, stand close to me,
And our guys here, and hear my reasons out.

(RECONCILIATION *has arranged the* ATHENIAN *and* SPARTAN AMBASSADORS *on either side of* LYSISTRATA.)

I am a woman, but I have a mind
That wasn't bad to start with, and I got
A first-class education listening
To Father and the elders year on year.
I now shall do what's right and give you hell
Together, for a single holy bowl
Sprinkles fraternal altars at the games:
Delphic, Pylaean, and Olympian.[3]
I could go on and on and on and on!
You see barbarian armies threatening,
But you destroy the towns and lives of Greeks.
That's quite a climax to my preface, huh?
ATHENIAN AMBASSADOR #1 What? This bald behemoth[4] is killing me.
LYSISTRATA Laconians, I'm turning now to you.
Don't you remember how a suppliant
From Sparta, Pericleidas, roosted here,

3. Delphi, Pylos, and Olympos are all sites of festival competitions in which different cities participated.
4. His monstrous penis.

Next to the altar, pale (his uniform
Bright red), and begged for troops. Messene and
Poseidon both at once had shaken you.
And Cimon took four thousand armored men
And made your territory safe again.[5]
After this gift from the Athenians,
You come and rip their land apart as thanks?

ATHENIAN AMBASSADOR #1 Right, Lysistrata! Bunch of criminals!

(SPARTAN AMBASSADOR *is enthralled by* RECONCILIATION.)

SPARTAN AMBASSADOR I guess we are—that's such a gorgeous ass.[6]

LYSISTRATA You think I'm going to spare my countrymen?

(*Turns to* ATHENIANS.)

Laconians once came to rescue you—
You only had the sheepskins on your backs.
The Spartans, marching out with you one day,
Erased large numbers of Thessalian goons.
A single ally made you Hippias-free:
Denuded of the rags of refugees,
And draped in your own polity again.[7]

SPARTAN AMBASSADOR (*Staring at* RECONCILIATION.)
I never seen a woman so first-rate.

ATHENIAN AMBASSADOR #1 (*Staring likewise.*)
I've never gazed on such a spiffy quim.

LYSISTRATA With these good deeds already on the tab,
Why squabble like a bunch of stupid jerks?
Be reconciled. There's nothing in the way.

(*In the following scene,* RECONCILIATION *serves as a map.*)

SPARTAN AMBASSADOR Okay, if we can have this little loop,
We're in.

ATHENIAN AMBASSADOR #1 What's that, my friend?

SPARTAN AMBASSADOR Pylos, I mean.
For years we've tried to get a finger in.[8]

ATHENIAN AMBASSADOR #1 Poseidon help me, *that* you will not do.

LYSISTRATA Let go.

ATHENIAN AMBASSADOR #1 But I've got uprisings to quell!

LYSISTRATA Just ask them for another piece instead.

ATHENIAN AMBASSADOR #1 Give me this thingy—this cute brushy bit,
And this deep gulf behind, which I'll explore—
And these nice legs of land: I want them too.

SPARTAN AMBASSADOR Buddy, you can't have every friggin' thing!

5. In 464 B.C.E., the Spartans were in political danger from a revolt by their serf population (the Helots of Messene), and simultaneously suffered an earthquake (supposedly caused by Poseidon). They asked Athens for help, and the general Cimon brought troops, but the Spartans became suspicious and sent him home without accepting any aid. The episode caused great affront in Athens.

6. Literally, "asshole." The Spartans were supposed to be obsessed with anal sex.

7. The Spartans helped the Athenians overthrow the tyranny of Hippias, in 510 B.C.E.

8. The city of Pylos was of great strategic importance. There is another pun here: *Pylos*, "Gate," can also refer to bodily orifices.

LYSISTRATA Hey! Make some compromise and part the legs.
ATHENIAN AMBASSADOR #1 I'm going to strip right down and start to plow.
SPARTAN AMBASSADOR I'm going to spread manure on my field.
LYSISTRATA And you can do it when you're reconciled.
If you're quite ready for a settlement,
Then scatter and confer with your allies.
ATHENIAN AMBASSADOR #1 Why bother? Situated in my prong,
They'll judge precisely as I do. They'll want
To screw—
SPARTAN AMBASSADOR And ours are just like yours, I swear—
ATHENIAN AMBASSADOR #1 And our Carystians especially.
LYSISTRATA You're both correct! While you're still abstinent,
We'll have the women on the citadel
Open their boxes for you.[9] You can feast
And then exchange your pledges of good faith.
Then each of you can take his wife and go
Straight home—
ATHENIAN AMBASSADOR #1 Finally. Let's not stand around.
SPARTAN AMBASSADOR Show me—
ATHENIAN AMBASSADOR #1 The fastest exit we can make.

(LYSISTRATA *and the* AMBASSADORS *exit together, leaving the slaves, who settle down outside the stage building.*)

UNITED CHORUS Embroidered throws to beat the cold,
Dresses and capes—none better, a
Big pile of jewelry, solid gold—
Send kids to take the stuff away,
For Basket-Bearing girls, et cetera.
"Help yourselves," I always say,
"To anything you find.
I don't seal up the jars or check
What money's left behind."
In fact, there's nothing left at all,
Unless I'm going blind.

Not enough bread,
But slaves to feed,
And hosts of hungry kids?
I've got plenty of baby-fine wheat
For every citizen in need.
This dust grows into strapping loaves to eat.
Come in—bring duffel bags and sacks!
My slave will stuff them full with any
Dry goods that you lack.
Too bad my dog will fuck you up.
He's waiting at the back.

(*Slaves sprawl sleepily in front of stage building. Thick-voiced* ATHENIAN AMBASSADOR #1 *pounds on the door from inside.*)

9. A double-entendre in the original.

ATHENIAN AMBASSADOR #1 Open!

(*Barges through, knocking slave in front of door out of the way.* AMBASSADOR *is garlanded, unsteady on his feet, and carrying a torch.*)

That's what you get for bein' there!

(*Begins kicking and pushing dazed slaves.*)

And you guys too—what if I take this torch
And carbonize you? (*To audience.*) What a dumb cliché.
I'm not going through with it. Okay! Calm down!
To make you happy I can play a boob.

(ATHENIAN AMBASSADOR #2, *similar in appearance, enters from same door.*)

ATHENIAN AMBASSADOR #2 I'll help. Two boobs beat one—like this one here.

(*Assaults slave.*)

Haul ass! Or you'll be howling for your hair.

ATHENIAN AMBASSADOR #1 Throw yourselves out! Our Spartan guests inside
Don't want to kick their way through piles of you.

(*Slaves flee.*)

ATHENIAN AMBASSADOR #2 I've never seen a party good as this.
Those Spartans sure are fun—now who'da thought?
And we're a damn sight smarter when we're drunk.

ATHENIAN AMBASSADOR #1 I tell ya, being sober's bad for us.
I'm gonna move that anyone we send
Anywhere to negotiate, get sloshed.
The trouble's been, we're sober when we go
To Sparta, so we're spoilers from the start.
What they *do* say, we're not prepared to hear.
And everything they *don't* say, we assume.
We've all got different versions in the end.
But now we're fine. Someone sang "Telamon"
When what we wanted was "Cleitagora":[1]
We slapped him on the back and told him, "Great!"

(*Slaves slink back onstage.*)

I can't believe those slaves are comin' back.
Get out! The whip is looking for you guys.

(*Slaves exit.* SPARTAN AMBASSADORS *enter, with a* PIPER.)

ATHENIAN AMBASSADOR #2 Already we've got Spartans walking through.

SPARTAN AMBASSADOR (*To* PIPER.) Hey, my best buddy, can we hear the pipes?
There's something good I got to dance and sing.
It's for our friends in Athens—and for us.

1. Drinking songs on mythological themes.

ATHENIAN AMBASSADOR #1 Zeus blast us if those pipes can't use a blast.
It's wonderful to watch you Spartans dance.

(*The* PIPER *strikes up a tune.*)

SPARTAN AMBASSADOR Memory, rouse, for my young sake,
The Muse who knows of both our nations:
How, godlike, the Athenians at Artemisium
Smashed the hulls of the Medes and were victorious,
While Leonidas led us Spartans
Fierce as boars sharpening their tusks;
Foam blossomed over our jaws,
Ran down our legs.
The Persians were as
Many as the sand grains.[2]
Huntress in the wilderness,
Come to us, O holy virgin,[3]
Bless our treaty,
Unite us forever.
May our friendship
Never be troubled.
May our bond turn us
From wily foxes into men.
Come, O come,
Maiden with your pack of hounds.

(*Enter* LYSISTRATA *with the* ATHENIAN *and* SPARTAN WOMEN.)

ATHENIAN AMBASSADOR #1 All but one thing is nicely put to bed.
Reclaim your wives, Laconians, and we
Will take our own. Each woman by her man,
And each man by his woman, celebrate,
Give thanks in joyful dances for the gods,
And vow to never go so wrong again.

(*The couples join the* UNITED CHORUS, *and all dance in pairs.*)

Bring on the dancers, invite the Graces,
Call Artemis and her twin, God of the joyous cry,
To lead the dance; and call the god of Nysa,
His eyes glittering, companion of the maenads;
And Zeus of the lightning bolt, and his blessed consort,
And all the spirits as witnesses
Forever mindful of gentle Peace,
Whom the goddess Cypris gave us.[4]

UNITED CHORUS Shout to the gods,
Leap up, rejoice.
A victory dance,
A holy song!

2. In 480 B.C.E., the Athenian navy fought the Persians off Artemisium, while three hundred Spartans, under King Leonidas, held the pass at Thermopylae.

3. The goddess Artemis.

4. The twin of Artemis is Apollo. The god of Nysa is Dionysos. Zeus's consort is Hera. Cypris is Aphrodite.

ATHENIAN AMBASSADOR #1 Add a new song to my new song.
SPARTAN AMBASSADOR Spartan Muse, come once more,
Leave your pretty Taygetus.
Help us hymn in fitting words Apollo in Amyclae,
And Athena of the Bronze House,
And the noble children of Tyndareos
Who play beside the Eurotas.[5]
Start off lightly
And jump up high.
Sing for Sparta,
Where thudding feet
Worship the gods.
The girls like colts
Leap by the river.
Their steps pound.
The dust rises.
They frisk and shake their hair
Like bacchants with their wands.
And Leda's daughter leads them,
Lovely, holy patroness of the chorus.[6]

Tie your hair back, let your footsteps fall
With the speed of a deer's, and clap your hands.
Our Goddess of the Bronze House has victory over all.

(*All exit, singing and dancing.*)

5. Athena had a bronze-plated temple in Sparta. The children of Tyndareos are Castor and Pollux, favorite heroes of Sparta. The Eurotas is the Spartan river.

6. Helen of Troy, who was originally from Sparta and was worshipped there as a goddess.

PLATO

429–347 B.C.E.

It is often said that all later Western philosophical writings are just "footnotes to Plato." Plato's dialogues have shaped how we think about politics, ethics, metaphysics, reason, education, truth, desire, God, and the soul. But Plato was not only a great thinker, but also a great writer. The brilliance of his literary achievement was recognized in antiquity. The ancient critical work *On the Sublime* imagines Plato challenging **Homer** to a wrestling match; he is the only later writer, the author suggests, whose work could possibly rival the ***Iliad*** and the ***Odyssey***. Plato's dialogues have the intellectual complexity of great philosophy, but also the comedy, pathos, and vivid evocations of people and places that we associate with great drama—or the novel.

LIFE AND TIMES

Plato came from a prominent and aristocratic Athenian family. In his youth, he was apparently interested mainly in poetry (we are told that he composed at least one tragedy), and in sports. *Plato* means "broad-shouldered" and is probably a nickname from his wrestling days; his real name was apparently Aristocles. But Plato's life was changed when, in his late teens or twenties, he encountered the most prominent of the Sophists ("wisdom teachers") in the city: Socrates.

Socrates is often seen as the world's first philosopher, but he wrote nothing. He must have been an extraordinary person, who inspired devotion in his followers—from all walks of Athenian society—as well as mistrust and controversy among those outside his intimate circle. Many of his acquaintances and students wrote dialogues featuring fictionalized portraits of the master. Plato and Xenophon are the only students of Socrates whose work survives in bulk, and they give us two very different versions of the ideal thinker, teacher, and moral hero. Xenophon's Socrates is a conventional teacher, who recommends common-sense principles and teaches in a fairly straightforward way: by telling people what to do and think. Plato's Socrates is a puzzling and fascinating figure, who claims not to be a teacher at all, and who works by questions, irony, and myth. It is difficult to know which of these literary characters comes closer to the historical Socrates. Plato's own depiction of Socrates varies enormously from one text to another. In some, Socrates professes total ignorance, and the result of all his questions is only to show that other people, too, have incomplete understanding of basic evaluative concepts, like courage, pleasure, and holiness. In others, Plato's Socrates makes far more substantive philosophical claims. Perhaps Plato modulated the character of Socrates depending on the setting or genre of each dialogue. In any case, none of the dialogues reflect the real Socrates with any degree of precision; all are the literary and philosophical creation of Plato.

What is certain is that the life and, still more, the death of Socrates had a profound impact on Athenian society in general, and on Plato in particular. In 399 B.C.E., when Plato would have been thirty, Socrates was put on trial for inventing new deities, failing to believe in the gods of the city, and "corrupting the youth"; none of these things were infractions of specific laws, but Socrates was probably charged under the general law against "impiety."

Five years before Socrates' trial, Athens had lost the Peloponnesian War. In the aftermath of the war, Athenian democratic government failed: many citizens blamed democracy for the bad decisions the city had made during the long years of war. In place of the rule of the people, a repressive dictatorial regime seized power, dominated by thirty Athenians of oligarchic sympathies. "The Thirty," as they came to be known, were overthrown eight months later, and a democratic constitution was reinstituted. Some members of the Thirty, as well as other prominent Athenians who had or were suspected of antidemocratic leanings, were associates of Socrates; one, Critias, was Plato's uncle. The trial may well have been part of the reaction against the Thirty, especially since one of his main accusers, Anytus, was a leader of the restored democracy. Socrates was declared guilty and condemned to death. The means of execution was drinking poison (hemlock). Plato tells us that he himself was sick, and could not be present at the moment of his beloved teacher's death. But he wrote in the *Phaedo* a fictional account of Socrates' brave end, surrounded by loving and intellectual followers, and maintaining his philosophical principles right up to the end.

After Socrates died, Plato became a writer, philosopher, and teacher. He featured Socrates as the principal speaker in philosophical dialogues that explored a variety of ethical and political problems; the *Republic*, an account of an ideal political and educational system, is the most famous. Plato's imagined city is not a democracy; indeed, democracy—the system under which Socrates was condemned—is roundly criticized as little better than tyranny, since, Plato's Socrates suggests here, it gives power to the ignorant many over the enlightened few. Ideally, this text suggests, rulers should become philosophers or philosophers, rulers: under such a system, it implies, a man like Socrates would not be a criminal condemned to death, but the leader he deserved to be.

Beyond writing, Plato made several attempts to educate his contemporaries, and change the societies around him. He founded the Academy (from which we get the modern term *academics*), which was the earliest prototype for the modern university, the first-ever philosophical school with a permanent location. The Academy remained active as a center of philosophical training and research until it was suppressed by the Roman emperor Justinian in 529 C.E. Plato also made three trips to Sicily, attempting to convert the tyrants of Syracuse into philosopher-kings. He failed; but, more important, he tried—despite the fact that the Sicilian court was hardly a safe environment for an interfering Athenian philosopher, and these trips could well have resulted in slavery or death. The attempt shows the depth of his commitment to trying to change the world and be, like his beloved Socrates, not only a zealous idealistic philosopher but also a brave and good man. He devoted the last thirteen years of his life to teaching and writing at his Academy, where he died and was buried.

THE *SYMPOSIUM*

The *Symposium* (which means "Drinking Party") is deservedly one of Plato's best-loved works. Its subject—sexual love, for which the Greek term is *Eros*—is of universal interest and appeal. This dialogue has a wide range of vivid characters, all based on real historical figures whom Plato knew. These include the soupy young tragic poet Agathon; the pompously scientific doctor Eryximachus; the hiccuping, fantastical comedian Aristophanes; the sexy, drunken playboy Alcibiades; and, above all, the extraordinary figure of Socrates himself. The setting, at a party, gives us a memorable image of what elite Athenian nightlife might have been like: men lounging together on sofas, drinking wine (diluted with water, in the Greek fashion), being entertained by scantily dressed flute girls, and enjoying conversation at all different levels—from highbrow philosophical and literary discussion to flirting, teasing, and drunken banter.

Plato probably wrote the *Symposium* between 384 and 379 B.C.E., some thirty years after the party that it describes. The historical setting is important, and we are made conscious of it from the beginning, by the introductory "frame." Some Platonic dialogues open with the words of the first main speaker. Here, however, we begin with a conversation that precedes the main conversation and explains how what we are about to read came to be told. A follower of Socrates, Apollodorus, is accosted in the street by a friend, who begs to be told about the famous party at the house of Agathon. Apollodorus explains that the party was not a recent event, but took place several years before: at the time of Agathon's first victory in the dramatic competition at the Great Dionysia (in 416 B.C.E.). Readers of the translation may well forget about the introductory frame as they read on; but the Greek text (in which there are distinctive syntactic forms for reported speech) constantly reminds us that we are overhearing an account of a conversation, not hearing the words of the speakers directly. There are many possible explanations for Plato's choice to introduce his dialogue in this way. On one level, the frame invites us to see the party of Agathon as a window into the past: the demoralized city that limped to the end of the Peloponnesian War—and that would soon, in 399 B.C.E., execute Socrates—felt a nostalgia for the lost happiness of ten or fifteen years before. Perhaps, too, Plato is showing his readers that Socrates' activities and associates were less politically sinister than people might have suspected. Drinking parties were associated, in many people's minds, with clubs of antidemocratic, oligarchic aristocrats—such as Alcibiades. Athenian readers would have remembered that Alcibiades, who appears here as a besotted follower of Socrates, was disgraced and exiled from the city in 413 B.C.E. Far from plotting to overthrow the democracy, these friends just sit around talking about love—and so innocently that they neither have sex (with slave girls or each other) nor, for the most part, get drunk. On a thematic level, the frame introduces us to a central concern of the *Symposium*: the deep human desire for an absent, distant, perhaps unattainable object—whether that object is a long-gone drinking party, a sexy or puzzling person, or an abstract idea of beauty.

The *Symposium* develops into a series of speeches in praise of Eros. The themes of the speeches overlap, and each builds on what has gone before; but they are strikingly different in their approaches to the subject, and in their style and tone, as each is carefully modulated to the individual speaker. First we have Phaedrus, a young follower of Socrates, who defines Eros as one of the most ancient of the gods, and emphasizes his central place in traditional mythology and poetry. Then comes the older Pausanias, the lover of Agathon, who discusses the moral, social, and legal status of sexual relationships in contemporary Athens, and distinguishes between good, "heavenly" love, which works for the education and betterment of both parties, and bad, "common" love, which is motivated only by the desire for physical pleasure. The speakers are lying on couches arranged in a circle, leaning on their elbows to sip their wine, and the next in order is Aristophanes, the comic poet. But he has hiccups, so the doctor, Eryximachus, speaks in his place, after giving him some useful advice about how to cure himself. Eryximachus reinterprets *eros* in terms of a confused and technical version of contemporary scientific theory: not merely does it apply to the desire of one person for another, but it becomes the physical force that drives all aspects of the universe to harmony, from the balance of elements in the human body to music and astronomy. Then Aristophanes, recovered from his hiccups, gives the most famous speech of the evening: he tells a fantastical story about how, long ago, humans were spherical creatures, some both male and female, others all male, others all female; since being split in two by the gods, each person is constantly searching for his or her "other half." The speech of Agathon—the tragic poet at whose house the party is taking place—takes us full circle back to the speech of Phaedrus: speaking in an elevated, poetic style that echoes trends in contemporary rhetoric, Agathon claims that Eros is not old, as Phaedrus claimed, but ever young and beautiful; Agathon insists that Eros can inspire even the untalented to produce inspired poetry.

Now it is Socrates' turn to speak, but he claims to be unable to perform as the others have done, since he knows nothing about the subject. So instead of giving a formal encomium (a speech of praise), he begins by cross-questioning Agathon, and gets him to admit that Eros is the desire for beauty, but is not itself beautiful. Then Socrates tells of an encounter he once had with a mysterious, probably fictional woman called Diotima, who taught him what love is. According to Diotima, Eros is not ultimately about the desire for beautiful bodies; it may begin with physical lust, but there is a "ladder of love," which we climb toward our ultimate desire: immortality and divine, eternal beauty.

At this point, the party is interrupted: the infamous young playboy and general, Alcibiades, turns up very drunk, and is half-carried inside by a flute girl and some drunken friends. Instead of giving a speech in praise of Eros, Alcibiades gives a speech in praise—or condemnation—of Socrates. He tells how Socrates, extraordinarily by Athenian standards, practiced (what we call Platonic) love: although particularly appreciative of pretty young men, Socrates refused Alcibiades' sexual advances, even when they shared a blanket while out on a military campaign. In a reversal of the Athenian norm, Alcibiades, the younger man, tried to seduce the older Socrates; but Socrates remained unmoved. The relationship, or nonrelationship, of Alcibiades and Socrates forms the final test case through which we are asked to consider what we really want from one other. Does Alcibiades want the ugly old Socrates for his body, for his mind, for his wisdom, or for his beautiful soul? Is this apparently strange relationship really so different from other, more "normal" kinds of love? And what exactly does Socrates himself want?

Attitudes toward sex vary widely from one culture to another, and the *Symposium* is a vivid reminder of the fact that Athenian sexual norms were not quite like our own. All the speakers in the *Symposium* are male (with the exception of Diotima, the mysterious woman quoted by Socrates), and almost all of them (with a couple of interesting exceptions) assume that a discussion of *eros*—the whole set of emotions and behavior patterns that we might associate with falling in love—will apply primarily to men's love for younger males.

Modern readers may be tempted to apply modern categories to this kind of relationship: we call same-sex couples "homosexuals" and, depending on the age of the younger party, we might be anxious about child abuse. But these are not quite the right terms for the ancient Athenian social institution of pederasty ("boy love"). For one thing, we tend to think of homosexuality and heterosexuality as sexual identities, that is, as deep-seated, perhaps permanent inclinations; and we tend to assume that most people have either one or the other. By contrast, male Athenians seem to have assumed that most men will feel attraction both toward pretty boys and pretty women, and that in the normal course of events, a man in his early twenties will have highly public romantic relationships with adolescent boys, before he settles down with a wife. The relationship evoked in the *Symposium* between Agathon and Pausanias is presented as unusual, in that it involves a lifelong commitment between same-sex partners, rather than a passing phase. This relationship is also unusual because it suggests some degree of equality. In a culture where women were hardly ever allowed out of the house, and where they received little or no education, it is perhaps not surprising that men mostly fell in love with one another. But it is striking, from a modern perspective, that the ideal pederastic relationship is imagined as fundamentally unequal: there must be an older man, the *erastes*, and an adolescent boy, the *eromenos*, who is courted. The "boy" may often have been as old as eighteen or nineteen, since adolescence came later in the ancient world; but presumably he may sometimes have been younger. One of the most interesting challenges of this text is to try to disentangle the sexual and social assumptions it reveals. This is a difficult task, because Plato is not, of course, reporting a real conversation, and we always have to wonder how much his version of Athenian sexuality might be slanted by his own highly individual point of view.

The *Symposium*'s vision of love and human desire is both alien and deeply familiar. Readers may feel a shock of recognition when they realize that the myth told by Aristophanes is the original source for the idea that true love is reuniting with one's "other half." And despite the strangeness of some of the sexual behaviors evoked here, Plato prompts us to ask questions that are relevant to all our lives, even beyond the realm of sexuality. What drives us to try to connect with one another? Are some sexual relationships better for us, morally or spiritually, than others? Can love be the path to truth or enlightenment? What is it that we really want from our friends and our lovers? Is sex just about pleasure, or the desire for physical closeness, or do we have a drive to get, through physical intimacy, to something nonphysical, such as understanding? If human beings long for beauty and wisdom, what are the best means of getting them? Can one person teach another to be a wiser or better person, and, if so, how? The *Symposium* provides food for deep reflection on all these issues, as well as combining, in a single text, both comic and serious drama.

Symposium[1]

Apollodorus:[2] In fact, your question does not find me unprepared. Just the other day, as it happens, I was walking to the city from my home in Phaleron[3] when a man I know, who was making his way behind me, saw me and called from a distance:

"The gentleman from Phaleron!" he yelled, trying to be funny. "Hey, Apollodorus, wait!"

So I stopped and waited.

"Apollodorus, I've been looking for you!" he said. "You know there once was a gathering at Agathon's when Socrates, Alcibiades, and their friends had dinner together;[4] I wanted to ask you about the speeches they made on Love. What were they? I heard a version from a man who had it from Phoenix, Philip's son, but it was badly garbled, and he said you were the one to ask. So please, will you tell me all about it? After all, Socrates is your friend—who has a better right than you to report his conversation? But before you begin," he added, "tell me this: were you there yourself?"

"Your friend must have really garbled his story," I replied, "if you think this affair was so recent that I could have been there."

"I did think that," he said.

"Glaucon,[5] how could you? You know very well Agathon hasn't lived in Athens for many years, while it's been less than three that I've been Socrates' companion and made it my job to know exactly what he says and does each day. Before that, I simply drifted aimlessly. Of course, I used to think that what I was doing was important, but in fact I was the most worthless man on earth—as bad as you are this very moment: I used to think philosophy was the last thing a man should do."

"Stop joking, Apollodorus," he replied. "Just tell me when the party took place."

"When we were still children, when Agathon won the prize with his first tragedy.[6] It was the day after he and his troupe held their victory celebration."

"So it really was a long time ago," he said. "Then who told you about it? Was it Socrates himself?"

"Oh, for god's sake, of course not!" I replied. "It was the very same man who told Phoenix: a fellow called Aristodemus, from Cydatheneum, a real runt of a man, who always went barefoot. He went to the party because, I think, he was obsessed with Socrates[7]—one of the worst cases at that time. Naturally, I checked part of his story with Socrates, and Socrates agreed with his account."

"Please tell me, then," he said. "You speak and I'll listen, as we walk to the city. This is the perfect opportunity."

So this is what we talked about on our way; and that's why, as I said before, I'm not unprepared. Well, if I'm to tell *you* about it too—I'll be glad to. After all, my greatest pleasure comes from philosophical conversation, even if I'm only a listener, whether or not I think it will be to my advantage. All other talk, especially the talk of rich businessmen like you, bores me to tears, and I'm

1. Translated by Alexander Nehamas and Paul Woodruff.
2. A follower of Socrates, who was present at his trial and death.
3. A port town near Athens.
4. Agathon was a tragedian. Alcibiades was a notorious Athenian general. Both will appear later in the dialogue.
5. Probably Plato's brother, who was named Glaucon.
6. 416 B.C.E.
7. Literally, "was a lover (*erastes*) of Socrates."

sorry for you and your friends because you think your affairs are important when really they're totally trivial. Perhaps, in your turn, you think I'm a failure, and, believe me, I think that what you think is true. But as for all of you, I don't just *think* you are failures—I know it for a fact.

FRIEND: You'll never change, Apollodorus! Always nagging, even at yourself! I do believe you think everybody—yourself first of all—is totally worthless, except, of course, Socrates. I don't know exactly how you came to be called "the maniac," but you certainly talk like one, always furious with everyone, including yourself—but not with Socrates!

APOLLODORUS: Of course, my dear friend, it's perfectly obvious why I have these views about us all: it's simply because I'm a maniac, and I'm raving!

FRIEND: It's not worth arguing about this now, Apollodorus. Please do as I asked: tell me the speeches.

APOLLODORUS: All right. . . . Well, the speeches went something like this—but I'd better tell you the whole story from the very beginning, as Aristodemus told it to me.

He said, then, that one day he ran into Socrates, who had just bathed and put on his fancy sandals—both very unusual events. So he asked him where he was going, and why he was looking so good.

Socrates replied, "I'm going to Agathon's for dinner. I managed to avoid yesterday's victory party—I really don't like crowds—but I promised to be there today. So, naturally, I took great pains with my appearance: I'm going to the house of a good-looking man; I had to look my best. But let me ask you this," he added, "I know you haven't been invited to the dinner; how would you like to come anyway?"

And Aristodemus answered, "I'll do whatever you say."

"Come with me, then," Socrates said, "and we shall prove the proverb wrong; the truth is, 'Good men go uninvited to Goodman's feast.'[8] Even Homer himself, when you think about it, did not much like this proverb; he not only disregarded it, he violated it. Agamemnon, of course, is one of his great warriors, while he describes Menelaus as a 'limp spearman.' And yet, when Agamemnon offers a sacrifice and gives a feast, Homer has the weak Menelaus arrive uninvited at his superior's table."[9]

Aristodemus replied to this, "Socrates, I am afraid Homer's description is bound to fit me better than yours. Mine is a case of an obvious inferior arriving uninvited at the table of a man of letters. I think you'd better figure out a good excuse for bringing me along, because, you know, I won't admit I've come without an invitation. I'll say I'm your guest."

"Let's go," he said. "We'll think about what to say 'as we proceed, the two of us, along the way.'"[1]

With these words, they set out. But as they were walking, Socrates began to think about something, lost himself in thought, and kept lagging behind.

8. The real proverb was "Good men go uninvited to an inferior man's feast." Socrates is punning on Agathon's name, which means "good."

9. The visit is in book 2 of the *Iliad*; Menelaus is called a "limp spearman" in book 17. Agamemnon and Menelaus are brothers; Menelaus is the cuckolded husband of Helen, and Agamemnon is the leader of the forces who went to retrieve her and fight the Trojan War.

1. Another partial quotation from the *Iliad* (10.224).

Whenever Aristodemus stopped to wait for him, Socrates would urge him to go on ahead. When he arrived at Agathon's, he found the gate wide open, and that, Aristodemus said, caused him to find himself in a very embarrassing situation: a household slave saw him the moment he arrived and took him immediately to the dining room, where the guests were already lying down on their couches, and dinner was about to be served.

As soon as Agathon saw him, he called:

"Welcome, Aristodemus! What perfect timing! You're just in time for dinner! I hope you're not here for any other reason—if you are, forget it. I looked all over for you yesterday, so I could invite you, but I couldn't find you anywhere. But where is Socrates? How come you didn't bring him along?"

So I turned around (Aristodemus said), and Socrates was nowhere to be seen. And I said that it was actually Socrates who had brought *me* along as his guest.

"I'm delighted he did," Agathon replied. "But where is he?"

"He was directly behind me, but I have no idea where he is now."

"Go look for Socrates," Agathon ordered a slave, "and bring him in. Aristodemus," he added, "you can share Eryximachus' couch."

A slave brought water, and Aristodemus washed himself before he lay down. Then another slave entered and said: "Socrates is here, but he's gone off to the neighbor's porch. He's standing there and won't come in, even though I called him several times."

"How strange," Agathon replied. "Go back and bring him in. Don't leave him there."

But Aristodemus stopped him. "No, no," he said. "Leave him alone. It's one of his habits: every now and then he just goes off like that and stands motionless, wherever he happens to be. I'm sure he'll come in very soon, so don't disturb him; let him be."

"Well, all right, if you really think so," Agathon said, and turned to the slaves: "Go ahead and serve the rest of us. What you serve is completely up to you; pretend nobody's supervising you—as if I ever did! Imagine that we are all your own guests, myself included. Give us good reason to praise your service."

So they went ahead and started eating, but there was still no sign of Socrates. Agathon wanted to send for him many times, but Aristodemus wouldn't let him. And, in fact, Socrates came in shortly afterward, as he always did—they were hardly halfway through their meal. Agathon, who, as it happened, was all alone on the farthest couch, immediately called: "Socrates, come lie down next to me. Who knows: if I touch you, I may catch a bit of the wisdom that came to you under my neighbor's porch. It's clear *you've* seen the light. If you hadn't, you'd still be standing there."

Socrates sat down next to him and said, "How wonderful it would be, dear Agathon, if the foolish were filled with wisdom simply by touching the wise. If only wisdom were like water, which always flows from a full cup into an empty one when we connect them with a piece of yarn—well, then I would consider it the greatest prize to have the chance to lie down next to you. I would soon be overflowing with your wonderful wisdom. My own wisdom is of no account—a shadow in a dream—while yours is bright and radiant and has a splendid future. Why, young as you are, you're so brilliant I could call more than thirty thousand Greeks as witnesses."[2]

2. The audiences of Agathon's plays.

"Now you've gone *too* far, Socrates," Agathon replied. "Well, eat your dinner. Dionysus[3] will soon enough be the judge of our claims to wisdom!"

Socrates took his seat after that and had his meal, according to Aristodemus. When dinner was over, they poured a libation to the god, sang a hymn, and—in short—followed the whole ritual. Then they turned their attention to drinking. At that point Pausanias addressed the group:

"Well, gentlemen, how can we arrange to drink less tonight? To be honest, I still have a terrible hangover from yesterday, and I could really use a break. I daresay most of you could, too, since you were also part of the celebration. So let's try not to overdo it."

Aristophanes[4] replied: "Good idea, Pausanias. We've got to make a plan for going easy on the drink tonight. I was over my head last night myself, like the others."

After that, up spoke Eryximachus, son of Acumenus: "Well said, both of you. But I still have one question: How do *you* feel, Agathon? Are you strong enough for serious drinking?"

"Absolutely not," replied Agathon. "I've no strength left for anything."

"What a lucky stroke for us," Eryximachus said, "for me, for Aristodemus, for Phaedrus,[5] and the rest—that you large-capacity drinkers are already exhausted. Imagine how weak drinkers like ourselves feel after last night! Of course I don't include Socrates in my claims: he can drink or not, and will be satisfied whatever we do. But since none of us seems particularly eager to overindulge, perhaps it would not be amiss for me to provide you with some accurate information as to the nature of intoxication.[6] If I have learned anything from medicine, it is the following point: inebriation is harmful to everyone. Personally, therefore, I always refrain from heavy drinking; and I advise others against it—especially people who are suffering the effects of a previous night's excesses."

"Well," Phaedrus of Myrrhinus interrupted him, "I always follow your advice, especially when you speak as a doctor. In this case, if the others know what's good for them, they too will do just as you say."

At that point they all agreed not to get drunk that evening; they decided to drink only as much as pleased them.

"It's settled, then," said Eryximachus. "We are resolved to force no one to drink more than he wants. I would like now to make a further motion: let us dispense with the flute-girl who just made her entrance; let her play for herself or, if she prefers, for the women in the house. Let us instead spend our evening in conversation. If you are so minded, I would like to propose a subject."

They all said they were quite willing, and urged him to make his proposal. So Eryximachus said:

"Let me begin by citing Euripides' *Melanippe*: 'Not mine the tale.' What I am about to tell belongs to Phaedrus here, who is deeply indignant on this issue, and often complains to me about it:

3. God of both wine and the theater.
4. The comedian. Composer of, among other plays, *Lysistrata* and *Clouds*; the latter presents a hostile picture of Socrates as a Sophist, liable to talk nonsense and to teach morally corrupting ideas to the young.
5. An associate of Socrates who appears in other Platonic dialogues, including *Phaedrus*. He was, like Alcibiades, among the group of oligarchic aristocrats exiled from Athens in 415 B.C.E., for profaning a religious ritual (the Eleusinian Mysteries).
6. Eryximachus was a doctor.

"'Eryximachus,' he says, 'isn't it an awful thing! Our poets have composed hymns in honor of just about any god you can think of; but has a single one of them given one moment's thought to the god of love (*Erôs*), ancient and powerful as he is? As for our fancy intellectuals,[7] they have written volumes praising Heracles and other heroes (as did the distinguished Prodicus[8]). Well, perhaps *that's* not surprising, but I've actually read a book by an accomplished author who saw fit to extol the usefulness of salt! And you can find hymns of praise to many other, similar things. How *could* people pay attention to such trifles and never, not even once, write a proper hymn to Love? How could anyone ignore so great a god?'

"Now, Phaedrus, in my judgment, is quite right. I would like, therefore, to take up a contribution, as it were, on his behalf, and gratify his wish. Besides, I think this a splendid time for all of us here to honor the god. If you agree, we can spend the whole evening in discussion, because I propose that each of us give as good a speech in praise of Love as he is capable of giving, in proper order from left to right. And let us begin with Phaedrus, who is at the head of the table and is, in addition, the father of our subject."

"No one will vote against that, Eryximachus," said Socrates. "How could *I* vote 'No,' when the only thing I say I understand is the art of love? Could Agathon and Pausanias? Could Aristophanes, who thinks of nothing but Dionysus and Aphrodite?[9] No one I can see here now could vote against your proposal.

"And though it's not quite fair to those of us who have to speak last, if the first speeches turn out to be good enough and to exhaust our subject, I promise we won't complain. So let Phaedrus begin, with the blessing of Fortune; let's hear his praise of Love."

They all agreed with Socrates, and pressed Phaedrus to start. Of course, Aristodemus couldn't remember exactly what everyone said, and I myself don't remember everything he told me. But I'll tell you what he remembered best, and what I consider the most important points.

As I say, he said Phaedrus spoke first, beginning more or less like this:

Love is a great god, wonderful in many ways to gods and men, and most marvelous of all is the way he came into being. We honor him as one of the most ancient gods, and the proof of his great age is this: the parents of Love have no place in poetry or legend. According to Hesiod, the first to be born was Chaos,

> *. . . but then came*
> *Earth, broad-chested, a seat for all, forever safe,*
> *And Love.*[1]

And Acusilaus[2] agrees with Hesiod: after Chaos came Earth and Love, these two. And Parmenides[3] tells of this beginning:

> *The very first god [she] designed was Love.*

7. Sophists were wisdom teachers.
8. Famous Sophist; Socrates attended his lectures.
9. Aphrodite, goddess associated with sex and desire, is the mother of Eros (*eros* is Greek for "love" or "desire").
1. A quotation from the *Theogony* (116–20, with a line skipped).
2. Early 5th-century genealogical writer.
3. Pre-Socratic philosopher.

All sides agree, then, that Love is one of the most ancient gods. As such, he gives to us the greatest goods. I cannot say what greater good there is for a young boy than a gentle lover, or for a lover than a boy to love. There is a certain guidance each person needs for his whole life, if he is to live well; and nothing imparts this guidance—not high kinship, not public honor, not wealth—nothing imparts this guidance as well as Love. What guidance do I mean? I mean a sense of shame at acting shamefully, and a sense of pride in acting well. Without these, nothing fine or great can be accomplished, in public or in private.

What I say is this: if a man in love is found doing something shameful, or accepting shameful treatment because he is a coward and makes no defense, then nothing would give him more pain than being seen by the boy he loves—not even being seen by his father or his comrades. We see the same thing also in the boy he loves, that he is especially ashamed before his lover when he is caught in something shameful. If only there were a way to start a city or an army made up of lovers and the boys they love![4] Theirs would be the best possible system of society, for they would hold back from all that is shameful, and seek honor in each other's eyes. Even a few of them, in battle side by side, would conquer all the world, I'd say. For a man in love would never allow his loved one, of all people, to see him leaving ranks or dropping weapons. He'd rather die a thousand deaths! And as for leaving the boy behind, or not coming to his aid in danger—why, no one is so base that true Love could not inspire him with courage, and make him as brave as if he'd been born a hero. When Homer says a god 'breathes might' into some of the heroes, this is really Love's gift to every lover.

Besides, no one will die for you but a lover, and a lover will do this even if she's a woman. Alcestis is proof to everyone in Greece that what I say is true.[5] Only she was willing to die in place of her husband, although his father and mother were still alive. Because of her love, she went so far beyond his parents in family feeling that she made them look like outsiders, as if they belonged to their son in name only. And when she did this her deed struck everyone, even the gods, as nobly done. The gods were so delighted, in fact, that they gave her the prize they reserve for a handful chosen from the throngs of noble heroes—they sent her soul back from the dead. As you can see, the eager courage of love wins highest honors from the gods.

Orpheus,[6] the son of Oeagrus, however, they sent unsatisfied from Hades, after showing him only an image of the woman he came for. They did not give him the woman herself, because they thought he was soft (he was, after all, a cithara-player[7]) and did not dare to die like Alcestis for Love's sake, but contrived to enter, living, into Hades. So they punished him for that, and made him die at the hands of women.

The honor they gave to Achilles, the son of Thetis,[8] is another matter. They sent him to the Isles of the Blest because he dared to stand by his lover Patroclus

4. The Greek city of Thebes did create such an army, the Sacred Band, in 379–378 B.C.E., probably a little after the composition of the *Symposium*.

5. In myth, when Admetus was fated to die, his wife Alcestis agreed to die in his stead. Euripides' *Alcestis* tells the story.

6. Mythical poet who tried to get his dead wife, Eurydice, back from the underworld, but failed, and was eventually torn apart by female worshippers of Dionysus (known as Maenads or Bacchantes).

7. A cithara was a stringed instrument, somewhat like a guitar.

8. Achilles was a Greek hero of the Trojan War; Thetis was a sea goddess.

and avenge him, even after he had learned from his mother that he would die if he killed Hector, but that if he chose otherwise he'd go home and end his life as an old man.[9] Instead he chose to die for his lover Patroclus, and more than that, he did it for a man whose life was already over. The gods were highly delighted at this, of course, and gave him special honor, because he made so much of his lover. Aeschylus talks nonsense when he claims Achilles was the lover;[1] he was more beautiful than Patroclus, more beautiful than all the heroes, and still beardless. Besides he was much younger, as Homer says.

In truth, the gods honor virtue most highly when it belongs to Love. They are more impressed and delighted, however, and are more generous with a loved one who cherishes his lover, than with a lover who cherishes the boy he loves. A lover is more godlike than his boy, you see, since he is inspired by a god. That's why they gave a higher honor to Achilles than to Alcestis, and sent him to the Isles of the Blest.

Therefore I say Love is the most ancient of the gods, the most honored, and the most powerful in helping men gain virtue and blessedness, whether they are alive or have passed away.

That was more or less what Phaedrus said, according to Aristodemus. There followed several other speeches which he couldn't remember very well. So he skipped them and went directly to the speech of Pausanias.

Phaedrus (Pausanias began), I'm not quite sure our subject has been well defined. Our charge has been simple—to speak in praise of Love. This would have been fine if Love himself were simple, too, but as a matter of fact, there are two kinds of Love. In view of this, it might be better to begin by making clear which kind of Love we are to praise. Let me therefore try to put our discussion back on the right track and explain which kind of Love ought to be praised. Then I shall give him the praise he deserves, as the god he is.

It is a well-known fact that Love and Aphrodite are inseparable. If, therefore, Aphrodite were a single goddess, there could also be a single Love; but, since there are actually two goddesses of that name, there must also be two kinds of Love. I don't expect you'll disagree with me about the two goddesses, will you? One is an older deity, the motherless daughter of Uranus, the god of heaven: she is known as Urania, or Heavenly Aphrodite. The other goddess is younger, the daughter of Zeus and Dione: her name is Pandemos, or Common Aphrodite. It follows, therefore, that there is a Common as well as a Heavenly Love, depending on which goddess is Love's partner. And although, of course, all the gods must be praised, we must still make an effort to keep these two gods apart.

The reason for this applies in the same way to every type of action: considered in itself, no action is either good or bad, honorable or shameful. Take, for example, our own case. We had a choice between drinking, singing, or having a conversation. Now, in itself, none of these is better than any other: how it comes out depends entirely on how it is performed. If it is done honorably and properly, it turns out to be honorable; if it is done improperly, it is disgraceful.

9. In the *Iliad*, Achilles knows that he is fated to die if he stays at Troy. He chooses to stay, to kill the Trojan hero Hector, who killed Achilles' beloved friend Patroclus. In Homer, Achilles and Patroclus share a tent and are devoted to each other, but they do not seem to be physical lovers; later Athenian tradition reinterpreted the relationship in more sexual terms.

1. In a lost tragedy, *Myrmidons*.

And my point is that exactly this principle applies to being in love: Love is not in himself noble and worthy of praise; that depends on whether the sentiments he produces in us are themselves noble.

Now the Common Aphrodite's Love is himself truly common. As such, he strikes wherever he gets a chance. This, of course, is the love felt by the vulgar, who are attached to women no less than to boys, to the body more than to the soul, and to the least intelligent partners, since all they care about is completing the sexual act. Whether they do it honorably or not is of no concern. That is why they do whatever comes their way, sometimes good, sometimes bad; and which one it is, is incidental to their purpose. For the Love who moves them belongs to a much younger goddess, who, through her parentage, partakes of the nature both of the female and the male.

Contrast this with the Love of Heavenly Aphrodite. This goddess, whose descent is purely male (hence this love is for boys), is considerably older and therefore free from the lewdness of youth. That's why those who are inspired by her Love are attracted to the male: they find pleasure in what is by nature stronger and more intelligent. But, even within the group that is attracted to handsome boys, some are not moved purely by this Heavenly Love; those who are do not fall in love with little boys; they prefer older ones whose cheeks are showing the first traces of a beard—a sign that they have begun to form minds of their own.[2] I am convinced that a man who falls in love with a young man of this age is generally prepared to share everything with the one he loves—he is eager, in fact, to spend the rest of his own life with him. He certainly does not aim to deceive him—to take advantage of him while he is still young and inexperienced and then, after exposing him to ridicule, to move quickly on to someone else.

As a matter of fact, there should be a law forbidding affairs with young boys. If nothing else, all this time and effort would not be wasted on such an uncertain pursuit—and what is more uncertain than whether a particular boy will eventually make something of himself, physically or mentally? Good men, of course, are willing to make a law like this for themselves, but those other lovers, the vulgar ones, need external restraint. For just this reason we have placed every possible legal obstacle to their seducing our own wives and daughters. These vulgar lovers are the people who have given love such a bad reputation that some have gone so far as to claim that taking *any* man as a lover is in itself disgraceful. Would anyone make this claim if he weren't thinking of how hasty vulgar lovers are, and therefore how unfair to their loved ones? For nothing done properly and in accordance with our customs would ever have provoked such righteous disapproval.

I should point out, however, that, although the customs regarding Love in most cities are simple and easy to understand, here in Athens (and in Sparta[3] as well) they are remarkably complex. In places where the people are inarticulate, like Elis or Boeotia, tradition straightforwardly approves taking a lover in every case. No one there, young or old, would ever consider it shameful. The reason, I suspect, is that, being poor speakers, they want to save themselves the trouble of having to offer reasons and arguments in support of their suits.

2. "Little boys" does not mean small children but, rather, young teenagers. The signs of adolescence came later in the premodern world; beards often did not grow until about eighteen.

3. Major Greek city-state; enemy of Athens in the Peloponnesian War.

By contrast, in places like Ionia and almost every other part of the Persian empire, taking a lover is always considered disgraceful. The Persian empire is absolute; that is why it condemns love as well as philosophy and sport. It is no good for rulers if the people they rule cherish ambitions for themselves or form strong bonds of friendship with one another. That these are precisely the effects of philosophy, sport, and especially of Love is a lesson the tyrants of Athens learned directly from their own experience: Didn't their reign come to a dismal end because of the bonds uniting Harmodius and Aristogiton in love and affection?[4]

So you can see that plain condemnation of Love reveals lust for power in the rulers and cowardice in the ruled, while indiscriminate approval testifies to general dullness and stupidity.

Our own customs, which, as I have already said, are much more difficult to understand, are also far superior. Recall, for example, that we consider it more honorable to declare your love rather than to keep it a secret, especially if you are in love with a youth of good family and accomplishment, even if he isn't all that beautiful. Recall also that a lover is encouraged in every possible way; this means that what he does is not considered shameful. On the contrary, conquest is deemed noble, and failure shameful. And as for *attempts* at conquest, our custom is to praise lovers for totally extraordinary acts—so extraordinary, in fact, that if they performed them for any other purpose whatever, they would reap the most profound contempt. Suppose, for example, that in order to secure money, or a public post, or any other practical benefit from another person, a man were willing to do what lovers do for the ones they love. Imagine that, in pressing his suit, he went to his knees in public view and begged in the most humiliating way; that he swore all sorts of vows; that he spent the night at the other man's doorstep; that he were anxious to provide services even a slave would have refused—well, you can be sure that everyone, his enemies no less than his friends, would stand in his way. His enemies would jeer at his fawning servility, while his friends, ashamed on his behalf, would try everything to bring him back to his senses. But let a lover act in any of these ways, and everyone will immediately say what a charming man he is! No blame attaches to his behavior: custom treats it as noble through and through. And what is even more remarkable is that, at least according to popular wisdom, the gods will forgive a lover even for breaking his vows—a lover's vow, our people say, is no vow at all. The freedom given to the lover by both gods and men according to our custom is immense.

In view of all this, you might well conclude that in our city we consider the lover's desire and the willingness to satisfy it as the noblest things in the world. When, on the other hand, you recall that fathers hire attendants[5] for their sons as soon as they're old enough to be attractive, and that an attendant's main task is to prevent any contact between his charge and his suitors; when you recall how mercilessly a boy's own friends tease him if they catch him at it, and how strongly their elders approve and even encourage such mocking—when you take all this into account, you're bound to come to the conclusion that we Athenians consider such behavior the most shameful thing in the world.

In my opinion, however, the fact of the matter is this. As I said earlier, love is, like everything else, complex: considered simply in itself, it is neither honorable

4. Athenian lovers who tried to overthrow the tyrant Hippias, in 514 B.C.E.

5. Slaves who acted as both chaperone and tutor.

nor a disgrace—its character depends entirely on the behavior it gives rise to. To give oneself to a vile man in a vile way is truly disgraceful behavior; by contrast, it is perfectly honorable to give oneself honorably to the right man. Now, you may want to know who counts as vile in this context. I'll tell you: it is the common, vulgar lover, who loves the body rather than the soul; the man whose love is bound to be inconstant, since what he loves is itself mutable and unstable. The moment the body is no longer in bloom, "he flies off and away," his promises and vows in tatters behind him. How different from this is a man who loves the right sort of character, and who remains its lover for life, attached as he is to something that is permanent.

We can now see the point of our customs: they are designed to separate the wheat from the chaff, the proper love from the vile. That's why we do everything we can to make it as easy as possible for lovers to press their suits and as difficult as possible for young men to comply; it is like a competition, a kind of test to determine to which sort each belongs. This explains two further facts: First, why we consider it shameful to yield too quickly: the passage of time in itself provides a good test in these matters. Second, why we also consider it shameful for a man to be seduced by money or political power, either because he cringes at ill treatment and will not endure it or because, once he has tasted the benefits of wealth and power, he will not rise above them. None of these benefits is stable or permanent, apart from the fact that no genuine affection can possibly be based upon them.

Our customs, then, provide for only one honorable way of taking a man as a lover. In addition to recognizing that the lover's total and willing subjugation to his beloved's wishes is neither servile nor reprehensible, we allow that there is one—and only one—further reason for willingly subjecting oneself to another which is equally above reproach: that is subjection for the sake of virtue. If someone decides to put himself at another's disposal because he thinks that this will make him better in wisdom or in any other part of virtue, we approve of his voluntary subjection: we consider it neither shameful nor servile. Both these principles—that is, both the principle governing the proper attitude toward the lover of young men and the principle governing the love of wisdom and of virtue in general—must be combined if a young man is to accept a lover in an honorable way. When an older lover and a young man come together and each obeys the principle appropriate to him—when the lover realizes that he is justified in doing anything for a loved one who grants him favors, and when the young man understands that he is justified in performing any service for a lover who can make him wise and virtuous—and when the lover *is* able to help the young man become wiser and better, and the young man *is* eager to be taught and improved by his lover—then, and only then, when these two principles coincide absolutely, is it ever honorable for a young man to accept a lover.

Only in this case, we should notice, is it never shameful to be deceived; in every other case it is shameful, both for the deceiver and the person he deceives. Suppose, for example, that someone thinks his lover is rich and accepts him for his money; his action won't be any less shameful if it turns out that he was deceived and his lover was a poor man after all. For the young man has already shown himself to be the sort of person who will do anything for money—and that is far from honorable. By the same token, suppose that someone takes a lover in the mistaken belief that this lover is a good man and likely to make him better himself, while in reality the man is horrible, totally lacking in virtue; even so, it is noble for him to have been deceived. For he too has demonstrated something about himself: that he is the sort of person who will do anything for the sake of virtue—and what could be more honorable than that? It follows, therefore, that giving in to your lover for virtue's sake is honorable, whatever the outcome. And this, of course, is the Heavenly Love of the heavenly goddess. Love's value to the city as a whole and to the citizens is immeasurable, for he compels the lover and his loved one alike to make virtue their central concern. All other forms of love belong to the vulgar goddess.

Phaedrus, I'm afraid this hasty improvisation will have to do as my contribution on the subject of Love.

When Pausanias finally came to a pause (I've learned this sort of fine figure from our clever rhetoricians), it was Aristophanes' turn, according to Aristodemus. But he had such a bad case of the hiccups—he'd probably stuffed himself again, though, of course, it could have been anything—that making a speech was totally out of the question. So he turned to the doctor, Eryximachus, who was next in line, and said to him:

"Eryximachus, it's up to you—as well it should be. Cure me or take my turn."

"As a matter of fact," Eryximachus replied, "I shall do both.[6] I shall take your turn—you can speak in my place as soon as you feel better—and I shall also cure you. While I am giving my speech, you should hold your breath for as long as you possibly can. This may well eliminate your hiccups. If it fails, the best remedy is a thorough gargle. And if even this has no effect, then tickle your nose with a feather. A sneeze or two will cure even the most persistent case."

"The sooner you start speaking, the better," Aristophanes said. "I'll follow your instructions to the letter."

This, then, was the speech of Eryximachus:

Pausanias introduced a crucial consideration in his speech, though in my opinion he did not develop it sufficiently. Let me therefore try to carry his argument to its logical conclusion. His distinction between the two species of Love seems to me very useful indeed. But if I have learned a single lesson from my own field, the science of medicine, it is that Love does not occur only in the human soul; it is not simply the attraction we feel toward human beauty: it is a significantly broader phenomenon. It certainly occurs within the animal kingdom, and even in the world of plants. In fact, it occurs everywhere in the universe. Love is a deity of the greatest importance: he directs everything that occurs, not only in the human domain, but also in that of the gods.

Let me begin with some remarks concerning medicine—I hope you will forgive my giving pride of place to my own profession. The point is that our very bodies manifest the two species of Love. Consider for a moment the marked difference, the radical dissimilarity, between healthy and diseased constitutions and the fact that dissimilar subjects desire and love objects that are themselves dissimilar. Therefore, the love manifested in health is fundamentally distinct from the love manifested in disease. And now recall that, as Pausanias claimed, it is as honorable to yield to a good man as it is shameful to consort

6. *Eryximachus* could mean "belch fighter"—an appropriate name for a man who can cure hiccups.

with the debauched. Well, my point is that the case of the human body is strictly parallel. Everything sound and healthy in the body must be encouraged and gratified; that is precisely the object of medicine. Conversely, whatever is unhealthy and unsound must be frustrated and rebuffed: that's what it is to be an expert in medicine.

In short, medicine is simply the science of the effects of Love on repletion and depletion of the body, and the hallmark of the accomplished physician is his ability to distinguish the Love that is noble from the Love that is ugly and disgraceful. A good practitioner knows how to affect the body and how to transform its desires; he can implant the proper species of Love when it is absent and eliminate the other sort whenever it occurs. The physician's task is to effect a reconciliation and establish mutual love between the most basic bodily elements. Which are those elements? They are, of course, those that are most opposed to one another, as hot is to cold, bitter to sweet, wet to dry, cases like those. In fact, our ancestor Asclepius[7] first established medicine as a profession when he learned how to produce concord and love between such opposites—that is what those poet fellows say, and—this time—I concur with them.

Medicine, therefore, is guided everywhere by the god of Love, and so are physical education and farming as well. Further, a moment's reflection suffices to show that the case of poetry and music, too, is precisely the same. Indeed, this may have been just what Heraclitus[8] had in mind, though his mode of expression certainly leaves much to be desired. The one, he says, "being at variance with itself is in agreement with itself" "like the attunement of a bow or a lyre." Naturally, it is patently absurd to claim that an attunement or a harmony is in itself discordant or that its elements are still in discord with one another. Heraclitus probably meant that an expert musician creates a harmony by resolving the prior discord between high and low notes. For surely there can be no harmony so long as high and low are still discordant; harmony, after all, is consonance, and consonance is a species of agreement. Discordant elements, as long as they are still in discord, cannot come to an agreement, and they therefore cannot produce a harmony. Rhythm, for example, is produced only when fast and slow, though earlier discordant, are brought into agreement with each other. Music, like medicine, creates agreement by producing concord and love between these various opposites. Music is therefore simply the science of the effects of Love on rhythm and harmony.

These effects are easily discernible if you consider the constitution of rhythm and harmony in themselves; Love does not occur in both his forms in this domain. But the moment you consider, in their turn, the effects of rhythm and harmony on their audience—either through composition, which creates new verses and melodies, or through musical education, which teaches the correct performance of existing compositions—complications arise directly, and they require the treatment of a good practitioner. Ultimately, the identical argument applies once again: the love felt by good people or by those whom such love might improve in this regard must be encouraged and protected. This is the honorable, heavenly species of Love, produced by the melodies of Urania, the Heavenly Muse. The other, produced by Polyhymnia, the muse of many songs, is common and vulgar. Extreme caution is indicated here: we must be careful to enjoy his

7. God of medicine.

8. Pre-Socratic philosopher from Ephesus.

pleasures without slipping into debauchery—this case, I might add, is strictly parallel to a serious issue in my own field, namely, the problem of regulating the appetite so as to be able to enjoy a fine meal without unhealthy aftereffects.

In music, therefore, as well as in medicine and in all the other domains, in matters divine as well as in human affairs, we must attend with the greatest possible care to these two species of Love, which are, indeed, to be found everywhere. Even the seasons of the year exhibit their influence. When the elements to which I have already referred—hot and cold, wet and dry—are animated by the proper species of Love, they are in harmony with one another: their mixture is temperate, and so is the climate. Harvests are plentiful; men and all other living things are in good health; no harm can come to them. But when the sort of Love that is crude and impulsive controls the seasons, he brings death and destruction. He spreads the plague and many other diseases among plants and animals; he causes frost and hail and blights. All these are the effects of the immodest and disordered species of Love on the movements of the stars and the seasons of the year, that is, on the objects studied by the science called astronomy.

Consider further the rites of sacrifice and the whole area with which the art of divination is concerned, that is, the interaction between men and gods. Here, too, Love is the central concern: our object is to try to maintain the proper kind of Love and to attempt to cure the kind that is diseased. For what is the origin of all impiety? Our refusal to gratify the orderly kind of Love, and our deference to the other sort, when we should have been guided by the former sort of Love in every action in connection with our parents, living or dead, and with the gods. The task of divination is to keep watch over these two species of Love and to doctor them as necessary. Divination, therefore, is the practice that produces loving affection between gods and men; it is simply the science of the effects of Love on justice and piety.

Such is the power of Love—so varied and great that in all cases it might be called absolute. Yet even so it is far greater when Love is directed, in temperance and justice, toward the good, whether in heaven or on earth: happiness and good fortune, the bonds of human society, concord with the gods above—all these are among his gifts.

Perhaps I, too, have omitted a great deal in this discourse on Love. If so, I assure you, it was quite inadvertent. And if in fact I have overlooked certain points, it is now your task, Aristophanes, to complete the argument—unless, of course, you are planning on a different approach. In any case, proceed; your hiccups seem cured.

Then Aristophanes took over (so Aristodemus said): "The hiccups have stopped all right—but not before I applied the Sneeze Treatment to them. Makes me wonder whether the 'orderly sort of Love' in the body calls for the sounds and itchings that constitute a sneeze, because the hiccups stopped immediately when I applied the Sneeze Treatment."

"You're good, Aristophanes," Eryximachus answered. "But watch what you're doing. You are making jokes before your speech, and you're forcing me to prepare for you to say something funny, and to put up my guard against you, when otherwise you might speak at peace."

Then Aristophanes laughed. "Good point, Eryximachus. So let me 'unsay what I have said.' But don't put up your guard. I'm not worried about saying something funny in my coming oration. That would be pure profit, and it comes with the territory of my Muse. What I'm worried about is that I might say something ridiculous."

"Aristophanes, do you really think you can take a shot at me, and then escape? Use your head! Remember, as you speak, that you will be called upon to give an account. Though perhaps, if I decide to, I'll let you off."

"Eryximachus," Aristophanes said, "indeed I do have in mind a different approach to speaking than the one the two of you used, you and Pausanias. You see, I think people have entirely missed the power of Love, because, if they had grasped it, they'd have built the greatest temples and altars to him and made the greatest sacrifices. But as it is, none of this is done for him, though it should be, more than anything else! For he loves the human race more than any other god, he stands by us in our troubles, and he cures those ills we humans are most happy to have mended. I shall, therefore, try to explain his power to you; and you, please pass my teaching on to everyone else."

First you must learn what Human Nature was in the beginning and what has happened to it since, because long ago our nature was not what it is now, but very different. There were three kinds of human beings, that's my first point—not two as there are now, male and female. In addition to these, there was a third, a combination of those two; its name survives, though the kind itself has vanished. At that time, you see, the word "androgynous" really meant something: a form made up of male and female elements, though now there's nothing but the word, and that's used as an insult. My second point is that the shape of each human being was completely round, with back and sides in a circle; they had four hands each, as many legs as hands, and two faces, exactly alike, on a rounded neck. Between the two faces, which were on opposite sides, was one head with four ears. There were two sets of sexual organs, and everything else was the way you'd imagine it from what I've told you. They walked upright, as we do now, in whatever direction they wanted. And whenever they set out to run fast, they thrust out all their eight limbs, the ones they had then, and spun rapidly, the way gymnasts do cartwheels, by bringing their legs around straight.

Now here is why there were three kinds, and why they were as I described them: The male kind was originally an offspring of the sun, the female of the earth, and the one that combined both genders was an offspring of the moon, because the moon shares in both. They were spherical, and so was their motion, because they were like their parents in the sky.

In strength and power, therefore, they were terrible, and they had great ambitions. They made an attempt on the gods, and Homer's story about Ephialtes and Otus was originally about them: how they tried to make an ascent to heaven so as to attack the gods.[9] Then Zeus and the other gods met in council to discuss what to do, and they were sore perplexed. They couldn't wipe out the human race with thunderbolts and kill them all off, as they had the giants, because that would wipe out the worship they receive, along with the sacrifices we humans give them. On the other hand, they couldn't let them run riot. At last, after great effort, Zeus had an idea.

9. In the *Odyssey* (11.305–20), the giants tried to pile mountains on top of each other to reach the gods.

"I think I have a plan," he said, "that would allow human beings to exist and stop their misbehaving: they will give up being wicked when they lose their strength. So I shall now cut each of them in two. At one stroke they will lose their strength and also become more profitable to us, owing to the increase in their number. They shall walk upright on two legs. But if I find that they still run riot and do not keep the peace," he said, "I will cut them in two again, and they'll have to make their way on one leg, hopping."

So saying, he cut those human beings in two, the way people cut sorb-apples before they dry them or the way they cut eggs with hairs. As he cut each one, he commanded Apollo to turn its face and half its neck toward the wound, so that each person would see that he'd been cut and keep better order. Then Zeus commanded Apollo to heal the rest of the wound, and Apollo did turn the face around, and he drew skin from all sides over what is now called the stomach, and there he made one mouth, as in a pouch with a drawstring, and fastened it at the center of the stomach. This is now called the navel. Then he smoothed out the other wrinkles, of which there were many, and he shaped the breasts, using some such tool as shoemakers have for smoothing wrinkles out of leather on the form. But he left a few wrinkles around the stomach and the navel, to be a reminder of what happened long ago.

Now, since their natural form had been cut in two, each one longed for its own other half, and so they would throw their arms about each other, weaving themselves together, wanting to grow together. In that condition they would die from hunger and general idleness, because they would not do anything apart from each other. Whenever one of the halves died and one was left, the one that was left still sought another and wove itself together with that. Sometimes the half he met came from a woman, as we'd call her now, sometimes it came from a man; either way, they kept on dying.

Then, however, Zeus took pity on them, and came up with another plan: he moved their genitals around to the front! Before then, you see, they used to have their genitals outside, like their faces, and they cast seed and made children, not in one another, but in the ground, like cicadas. So Zeus brought about this relocation of genitals, and in doing so he invented interior reproduction, *by* the man *in* the woman. The purpose of this was so that, when a man embraced a woman, he would cast his seed and they would have children; but when male embraced male, they would at least have the satisfaction of intercourse, after which they could stop embracing, return to their jobs, and look after their other needs in life. This, then, is the source of our desire to love each other. Love is born into every human being; it calls back the halves of our original nature together; it tries to make one out of two and heal the wound of human nature.

Each of us, then, is a "matching half" of a human whole, because each was sliced like a flatfish, two out of one, and each of us is always seeking the half that matches him. That's why a man who is split from the double sort (which used to be called "androgynous") runs after women. Many lecherous men have come from this class, and so do the lecherous women who run after men. Women who are split from a woman, however, pay no attention at all to men; they are oriented more toward women, and lesbians come from this class. People who are split from a male are male-oriented. While they are boys, because they are chips off the male block, they love men and enjoy lying with men and being embraced by men; those are the best of boys and lads, because they are the most manly in their nature. Of course, some say such boys are shameless, but they're lying. It's not because they have no shame that such boys do this, you see, but because they are bold and brave and masculine, and they tend to cherish what is like themselves. Do you want me to prove it? Look, these are the only kind of boys who grow up to be real men in politics. When they're grown men, they are lovers of young men, and they naturally pay no attention to marriage or to making babies, except insofar as they are required by local custom. They, however, are quite satisfied to live their lives with one another unmarried. In every way, then, this sort of man grows up as a lover of young men and a lover of Love, always rejoicing in his own kind.

And so, when a person meets the half that is his very own, whatever his orientation, whether it's to young men or not, then something wonderful happens: the two are struck from their senses by love, by a sense of belonging to one another, and by desire, and they don't want to be separated from one another, not even for a moment.

These are the people who finish out their lives together and still cannot say what it is they want from one another. No one would think it is the intimacy of sex—that mere sex is the reason each lover takes so great and deep a joy in being with the other. It's obvious that the soul of every lover longs for something else; his soul cannot say what it is, but like an oracle it has a sense of what it wants, and like an oracle it hides behind a riddle. Suppose two lovers are lying together, and Hephaestus[1] stands over them with his mending tools, asking, "What is it you human beings really want from each other?" And suppose they're perplexed, and he asks them again: "Is this your heart's desire, then—for the two of you to become parts of the same whole, as near as can be, and never to separate, day or night? Because if that's your desire, I'd like to weld you together and join you into something that is naturally whole, so that the two of you are made into one. Then the two of you would share one life, as long as you lived, because you would be one being, and by the same token, when you died, you would be one and not two in Hades, having died a single death. Look at your love, and see if this is what you desire: wouldn't this be all the good fortune you could want?"

Surely you can see that no one who received such an offer would turn it down; no one would find anything else that he wanted. Instead, everyone would think he'd found out at last what he had always wanted: to come together and melt together with the one he loves, so that one person emerged from two. Why should this be so? It's because, as I said, we used to be complete wholes in our original nature, and now "Love" is the name for our pursuit of wholeness, for our desire to be complete.

Long ago we were united, as I said; but now the god has divided us as punishment for the wrong we did him, just as the Spartans divided the Arcadians.[2] So there's a danger that if we don't keep order before the gods, we'll be split in two again, and then we'll be walking around in the condition of people carved on gravestones in bas-relief, sawn apart between the nostrils, like half dice. We should encourage all men, therefore, to treat the gods with all due reverence, so that we may escape this fate and find wholeness instead. And we will, if

1. God of fire and metalworking.
2. After the Arcadian city of Mantinea opposed Sparta, Sparta retaliated and prevented further insurgency by dividing the population, in 385 B.C.E. This reference is therefore anachronistic in terms of the dramatic date of the dialogue.

Love is our guide and our commander. Let no one work against him. Whoever opposes Love is hateful to the gods, but if we become friends of the god and cease to quarrel with him, then we shall find the young men that are meant for us and win their love, as very few men do nowadays.

Now don't get ideas, Eryximachus, and turn this speech into a comedy. Don't think I'm pointing this at Pausanias and Agathon. Probably they both do belong to the group that are entirely masculine in nature. But I am speaking about everyone, men and women alike, and I say there's just one way for the human race to flourish: we must bring love to its perfect conclusion, and each of us must win the favors of his very own young man, so that he can recover his original nature. If that is the ideal, then, of course, the nearest approach to it is best in present circumstances, and that is to win the favor of young men who are naturally sympathetic to us.

If we are to give due praise to the god who can give us this blessing, then, we must praise Love. Love does the best that can be done for the time being: he draws us toward what belongs to us. But for the future, Love promises the greatest hope of all: if we treat the gods with due reverence, he will restore to us our original nature, and by healing us, he will make us blessed and happy.

"That," he said, "is my speech about Love, Eryximachus. It is rather different from yours. As I begged you earlier, don't make a comedy of it. I'd prefer to hear what all the others will say—or, rather, what each of them will say, since Agathon and Socrates are the only ones left."

"I found your speech delightful," said Eryximachus, "so I'll do as you say. Really, we've had such a rich feast of speeches on Love, that if I couldn't vouch for the fact that Socrates and Agathon are masters of the art of love, I'd be afraid that they'd have nothing left to say. But as it is, I have no fears on this score."

Then Socrates said, "That's because *you* did beautifully in the contest, Eryximachus. But if you ever get in my position, or rather the position I'll be in after Agathon's spoken so well, then you'll really be afraid. You'll be at your wit's end, as I am now."

"You're trying to bewitch me, Socrates," said Agathon, "by making me think the audience expects great things of my speech, so I'll get flustered."

"Agathon!" said Socrates, "How forgetful do you think I am? I saw how brave and dignified you were when you walked right up to the theater platform along with the actors and looked straight out at that enormous audience. You were about to put your own writing on display, and you weren't the least bit panicked. After seeing that, how could I expect you to be flustered by us, when we are so few?"

"Why, Socrates," said Agathon. "You must think I have nothing but theater audiences on my mind! So you suppose I don't realize that, if you're intelligent, you find a few sensible men much more frightening than a senseless crowd?"

"No," he said, "It wouldn't be very handsome of me to think you crude in any way, Agathon. I'm sure that if you ever run into people you consider wise, you'll pay more attention to them than to ordinary people. But you can't suppose we're in that class; we were at the theater too, you know, part of the ordinary crowd. Still, if you did run into any wise men, other than yourself, you'd certainly be ashamed at the thought of doing anything ugly in front of them. Is that what you mean?"

"That's true," he said.

"On the other hand, you wouldn't be ashamed to do something ugly in front of ordinary people. Is that it?"

At that point Phaedrus interrupted: "Agathon, my friend, if you answer Socrates, he'll no longer care whether we get anywhere with what we're doing here, so long as he has a partner for discussion. Especially if he's handsome. Now, like you, I enjoy listening to Socrates in discussion, but it is my duty to see to the praising of Love and to exact a speech from every one of this group. When each of you two has made his offering to the god, then you can have your discussion."

"You're doing a beautiful job, Phaedrus," said Agathon. "There's nothing to keep me from giving my speech. Socrates will have many opportunities for discussion later."

I wish first to speak of how I ought to speak, and only then to speak. In my opinion, you see, all those who have spoken before me did not so much celebrate the god as congratulate human beings on the good things that come to them from the god. But who it is who gave these gifts, what he is like—no one has spoken about that. Now, only one method is correct for every praise, no matter whose: you must explain what qualities in the subject of your speech enable him to give the benefits for which we praise him. So now, in the case of Love, it is right for us to praise him first for what he is and afterwards for his gifts.

I maintain, then, that while all the gods are happy, Love—if I may say so without giving offense—is the happiest of them all, for he is the most beautiful and the best. His great beauty lies in this: First, Phaedrus, he is the youngest of the gods. He proves my point himself by fleeing old age in headlong flight, fast-moving though it is (that's obvious—it comes after us faster than it should). Love was born to hate old age and will come nowhere near it. Love always lives with young people and is one of them: the old story holds good that like is always drawn to like. And though on many other points I agree with Phaedrus, I do not agree with this: that Love is more ancient than Cronus and Iapetus.[3] No, I say that he is the youngest of the gods and stays young forever.

Those old stories Hesiod and Parmenides tell about the gods—those things happened under Necessity, not Love, if what they say is true. For not one of all those violent deeds would have been done—no castrations, no imprisonments—if Love had been present among them. There would have been peace and brotherhood instead, as there has been now as long as Love has been king of the gods.

So he is young. And besides being young, he is delicate. It takes a poet as good as Homer to show how delicate the god is. For Homer says that Mischief is a god and that she is delicate—well, that her feet are delicate, anyway! He says:

. . . hers are delicate feet: not on the ground
Does she draw nigh; she walks instead upon the heads of men.[4]

A lovely proof, I think, to show how delicate she is: she doesn't walk on anything hard; she walks only on what is soft. We shall use the same proof about Love, then, to show that he is delicate. For he walks not on earth, not even on people's skulls, which are not really soft at all; but in the softest of all the things that are, there he walks, there he has his home. For he makes his home

3. Titans. Cronus was the father of Zeus; Iapetus was Cronus's brother. Zeus castrated, deposed, and imprisoned Cronus.

4. *Iliad* 19.92–93.

in the characters, in the souls, of gods and men—and not even in every soul that comes along: when he encounters a soul with a harsh character, he turns away; but when he finds a soft and gentle character, he settles down in it. Always, then, he is touching with his feet and with the whole of himself what is softest in the softest places. He must therefore be most delicate.

He is youngest, then, and most delicate; in addition he has a fluid, supple shape. For if he were hard, he would not be able to enfold a soul completely or escape notice when he first entered it or withdrew. Besides, his graceful good looks prove that he is balanced and fluid in his nature. Everyone knows that Love has extraordinary good looks, and between ugliness and Love there is unceasing war.

And the exquisite coloring of his skin! The way the god consorts with flowers shows that. For he never settles in anything, be it a body or a soul, that cannot flower or has lost its bloom. His place is wherever it is flowery and fragrant; there he settles, there he stays.

Enough for now about the beauty of the god, though much remains still to be said. After this, we should speak of Love's moral character. The main point is that Love is neither the cause nor the victim of any injustice; he does no wrong to gods or men, nor they to him. If anything has an effect on him, it is never by violence, for violence never touches Love. And the effects he has on others are not forced, for every service we give to love we give willingly. And whatever one person agrees on with another, when both are willing, that is right and just; so say "the laws that are kings of society."

And besides justice, he has the biggest share of moderation.[5] For moderation, by common agreement, is power over pleasures and passions, and no pleasure is more powerful than Love! But if they are weaker, they are under the power of Love, and *he* has the power; and because he has power over pleasures and passions, Love is exceptionally moderate.

And as for manly bravery: "Not even Ares can stand up to" Love![6] For Ares has no hold on Love, but Love does on Ares—love of Aphrodite, so runs the tale.[7] But he who has hold is more powerful than he who is held; and so, because Love has power over the bravest of the others, he is bravest of them all.

Now I have spoken about the god's justice, moderation, and bravery; his wisdom remains. I must try not to leave out anything that can be said on this. In the first place—to honor *our* profession as Eryximachus did his—the god is so skilled a poet that he can make others into poets: once Love touches him, *anyone* becomes a poet,

> . . . *howe'er uncultured he had been before.*[8]

This, we may fittingly observe, testifies that Love is a good poet, good, in sum, at every kind of artistic production. For you can't give to another what you don't have yourself, and you can't teach what you don't know.

And as to the production of animals—who will deny that they are all born and begotten through Love's skill?

5. "Moderation" is a translation of *sophrosyne*, which literally means "self-control" or "healthy-mindedness."
6. A quotation from Sophocles. Ares is god of war.
7. Ares and Aphrodite were adulterous lovers. Hephaestus, Aphrodite's husband, caught them in bed and trapped them in a net.
8. Quotation from a fragment by Euripides.

And as for artisans and professionals—don't we know that whoever has this god for a teacher ends up in the light of fame, while a man untouched by Love ends in obscurity? Apollo, for one, invented archery, medicine, and prophecy when desire and love showed the way. Even he, therefore, would be a pupil of Love, and so would the Muses in music, Hephaestus in bronze work, Athena in weaving, and Zeus in "the governance of gods and men."

That too is how the gods' quarrels were settled, once Love came to be among them—love of beauty, obviously, because love is not drawn to ugliness. Before that, as I said in the beginning, and as the poets say, many dreadful things happened among the gods, because Necessity was king. But once this god was born, all goods came to gods and men alike through love of beauty.

This is how I think of Love, Phaedrus: first, he is himself the most beautiful and the best; after that, if anyone else is at all like that, Love is responsible. I am suddenly struck by a need to say something in poetic meter, that it is he who—

> *Gives peace to men and stillness to the sea,*
> *Lays winds to rest, and careworn men to sleep.*

Love fills us with togetherness and drains all of our divisiveness away. Love calls gatherings like these together. In feasts, in dances, and in ceremonies, he gives the lead. Love moves us to mildness, removes from us wildness. He is giver of kindness, never of meanness. Gracious, kindly—let wise men see and gods admire! Treasure to lovers, envy to others, father of elegance, luxury, delicacy, grace, yearning, desire. Love cares well for good men, cares not for bad ones. In pain, in fear, in desire or speech, Love is our best guide and guard; he is our comrade and our savior. Ornament of all gods and men, most beautiful leader and the best! Every man should follow Love, sing beautifully his hymns, and join with him in the song he sings that charms the mind of god or man.

This, Phaedrus, is the speech I have to offer. Let it be dedicated to the god, part of it in fun, part of it moderately serious, as best I could manage.

When Agathon finished, Aristodemus said, everyone there burst into applause, so becoming to himself and to the god did they think the young man's speech.

Then Socrates glanced at Eryximachus and said, "Now, son of Acumenus, do you think I was foolish to feel the fear I felt before? Didn't I speak like a prophet a while ago when I said that Agathon would give an amazing speech and I would be tongue-tied?"

"You were prophetic about one thing, I think," said Eryximachus, "that Agathon would speak well. But you, tongue-tied? No, I don't believe that."

"Bless you," said Socrates. "How am I not going to be tongue-tied, I or anyone else, after a speech delivered with such beauty and variety? The other parts may not have been so wonderful, but that at the end! Who would not be struck dumb on hearing the beauty of the words and phrases? Anyway, I was worried that I'd not be able to say anything that came close to them in beauty, and so I would almost have run away and escaped, if there had been a place to go. And, you see, the speech reminded me of Gorgias,[9] so that I actually experienced what Homer describes: I was afraid that Agathon would end by sending the

9. Sophist and orator with a distinctively ornate style.

Gorgian head,[1] awesome at speaking in a speech, against my speech, and this would turn me to stone by striking me dumb. Then I realized how ridiculous I'd been to agree to join with you in praising Love and to say that I was a master of the art of love, when I knew nothing whatever of this business, of how anything whatever ought to be praised. In my foolishness, I thought you should tell the truth about whatever you praise, that this should be your basis, and that from this a speaker should select the most beautiful truths and arrange them most suitably. I was quite vain, thinking that I would talk well and that I knew the truth about praising anything whatever. But now it appears that this is not what it is to praise anything whatever; rather, it is to apply to the object the grandest and the most beautiful qualities, whether he actually has them or not. And if they are false, that is no objection; for the proposal, apparently, was that everyone here make the rest of us think he is praising Love—and not that he actually praise him. I think that is why you stir up every word and apply it to Love; your description of him and his gifts is designed to make him look better and more beautiful than anything else—to ignorant listeners, plainly, for of course he wouldn't look that way to those who knew. And your praise did seem beautiful and respectful. But I didn't even know the method for giving praise; and it was in ignorance that I agreed to take part in this. So 'the tongue' promised, and 'the mind' did not.[2] Goodbye to that! I'm not giving another eulogy using that method, not at all—I wouldn't be able to do it!—but, if you wish, I'd like to tell the truth my way. I want to avoid any comparison with your speeches, so as not to give you a reason to laugh at me. So look, Phaedrus, would a speech like this satisfy your requirement? You will hear the truth about Love, and the words and phrasing will take care of themselves."

Then Aristodemus said that Phaedrus and the others urged him to speak in the way he thought was required, whatever it was.

"Well then, Phaedrus," said Socrates, "allow me to ask Agathon a few little questions, so that, once I have his agreement, I may speak on that basis."

"You have my permission," said Phaedrus. "Ask away."

After that, said Aristodemus, Socrates began: "Indeed, Agathon, my friend, I thought you led the way beautifully into your speech when you said that one should first show the qualities of Love himself, and only then those of his deeds. I must admire that beginning. Come, then, since you have beautifully and magnificently expounded his qualities in other ways, tell me this, too, about Love. Is Love such as to be a love of something or of nothing? I'm not asking if he is born *of* some mother or father (for the question whether Love is love of mother or of father would really be ridiculous), but it's as if I'm asking this about a father—whether a father is the father *of* something or not. You'd tell me, of course, if you wanted to give me a good answer, that it's *of* a son or a daughter that a father is the father. Wouldn't you?"

"Certainly," said Agathon.

"Then does the same go for the mother?"

He agreed to that also.

"Well, then," said Socrates, "answer a little more fully, and you will understand better what I want. If I should ask, 'What about this: a brother, just insofar as he *is* a brother, is he the brother of something or not?'"

1. A pun. The monstrous Gorgon's head turned onlookers to stone.

2. Allusion to a line in Euripides' *Hippolytus*: "My tongue swore, not my mind."

He said that he was.

"And he's of a brother or a sister, isn't he?"

He agreed.

"Now try to tell me about love," he said. "Is Love the love of nothing or of something?"

"Of something, surely!"

"Then keep this object of love in mind, and remember what it is. But tell me this much: does Love desire that of which it is the love, or not?"

"Certainly," he said.

"At the time he desires and loves something, does he actually have what he desires and loves at that time, or doesn't he?"

"He doesn't. At least, that wouldn't be likely," he said.

"Instead of what's *likely*," said Socrates, "ask yourself whether it's *necessary* that this be so: a thing that desires, desires something of which it is in need; otherwise, if it were not in need, it would not desire it. I can't tell you, Agathon, how strongly it strikes me that this is necessary. But how about you?"

"I think so, too."

"Good. Now then, would someone who is tall want to be tall? Or someone who is strong want to be strong?"

"Impossible, on the basis of what we've agreed."

"Presumably because no one is in need of those things he already has."

"True."

"But maybe a strong man could want to be strong," said Socrates, "or a fast one fast, or a healthy one healthy: in cases like these, you might think people really do want to be things they already are and do want to have qualities they already have—I bring them up so they won't deceive us. But in these cases, Agathon, if you stop to think about them, you will see that these people are what they are at the present time, whether they want to be or not, by a logical necessity. And who, may I ask, would ever bother to desire what's necessary in any event? But when someone says 'I am healthy, but that's just what I want to be,' or 'I am rich, but that's just what I want to be,' or 'I desire the very things that I have,' let us say to him: 'You already have riches and health and strength in your possession, my man; what you want is to possess these things in time to come, since in the present, whether you want to or not, you have them. Whenever you say, *I desire what I already have,* ask yourself whether you don't mean this: *I want the things I have now to be mine in the future as well.*' Wouldn't he agree?"

According to Aristodemus, Agathon said that he would.

So Socrates said, "Then this is what it is to love something which is not at hand, which the lover does not have: it is to desire the preservation of what he now has in time to come, so that he will have it then."

"Quite so," he said.

"So such a man or anyone else who has a desire, desires what is not at hand and not present, what he does not have, and what he is not, and that of which he is in need; for such are the objects of desire and love."

"Certainly," he said.

"Come, then," said Socrates. "Let us review the points on which we've agreed. Aren't they, first, that Love is the love of something, and, second, that he loves things of which he has a present need?"

"Yes," he said.

"Now, remember, in addition to these points, what you said in your speech about what it is that Love loves. If you like, I'll remind you. I think you said something like this: that the gods' quarrels were settled by love of beautiful things, for there is no love of ugly ones. Didn't you say something like that?"

"I did," said Agathon.

"And that's a suitable thing to say, my friend," said Socrates. "But if this is so, wouldn't Love have to be a desire for beauty, and never for ugliness?"

He agreed.

"And we also agreed that he loves just what he needs and does not have."

"Yes," he said.

"So Love needs beauty, then, and does not have it."

"Necessarily," he said.

"So! If something needs beauty and has got no beauty at all, would you still say that it is beautiful?"

"Certainly not."

"Then do you still agree that Love is beautiful, if those things are so?"

Then Agathon said, "It turns out, Socrates, I didn't know what I was talking about in that speech."

"It was a beautiful speech, anyway, Agathon," said Socrates. "Now take it a little further. Don't you think that good things are always beautiful as well?"

"I do."

"Then if Love needs beautiful things, and if all good things are beautiful, he will need good things too."

"As for me, Socrates," he said, "I am unable to contradict you. Let it be as you say."

"Then it's the truth, my beloved Agathon, that you are unable to contradict," he said. "It is not hard at all to contradict Socrates."

Now I'll let you go. I shall try to go through for you the speech about Love I once heard from a woman of Mantinea, Diotima[3]—a woman who was wise about many things besides this: once she even put off the plague for ten years by telling the Athenians what sacrifices to make. She is the one who taught me the art of love, and I shall go through her speech as best I can on my own, using what Agathon and I have agreed to as a basis.

Following your lead, Agathon, one should first describe who Love is and what he is like, and afterward describe his works—I think it will be easiest for me to proceed the way Diotima did and tell you how she questioned me.

You see, I had told her almost the same things Agathon told me just now: that Love is a great god and that he belongs to beautiful things. And she used the very same arguments against me that I used against Agathon; she showed how, according to my very own speech, Love is neither beautiful nor good.

So I said, "What do you mean, Diotima? Is Love ugly, then, and bad?"

But she said, "Watch your tongue! Do you really think that, if a thing is not beautiful, it has to be ugly?"

"I certainly do."

"And if a thing's not wise, it's ignorant? Or haven't you found out yet that there's something in between wisdom and ignorance?"

3. *Mantinea* suggests "place of prophecy." Diotima is presumably a fantasy figure.

"What's that?"

"It's judging things correctly without being able to give a reason. Surely you see that this is not the same as knowing—for how could knowledge be unreasoning? And it's not ignorance either—for how could what hits the truth be ignorance? Correct judgment, of course, has this character: it is *in between* understanding and ignorance."

"True," said I, "as you say."

"Then don't force whatever is not beautiful to be ugly, nor whatever is not good to be bad. It's the same with Love: when you agree he is neither good nor beautiful, you need not think he is ugly and bad; he could be something in between," she said.

"Yet everyone agrees he's a great god," I said.

"Only those who don't know?" she said. "Is that how you mean 'everyone'? Or do you include those who do know?"

"Oh, everyone together."

And she laughed. "Socrates, how could those who say that he's not a god at all agree that he's a great god?"

"Who says that?" I asked.

"You, for one," she said, "and I for another."

"How can you say this!" I exclaimed.

"That's easy," said she. "Tell me, wouldn't you say that all gods are beautiful and happy? Surely you'd never say a god is not beautiful or happy?"

"Zeus! Not I," I said.

"Well, by calling anyone 'happy,' don't you mean they possess good and beautiful things?"

"Certainly."

"What about Love? You agreed he needs good and beautiful things, and that's why he desires them—because he needs them."

"I certainly did."

"Then how could he be a god if he has no share in good and beautiful things?"

"There's no way he could, apparently."

"Now do you see? You don't believe Love is a god either!"

"Then, what could Love be?" I asked. "A mortal?"

"Certainly not."

"Then, what is he?"

"He's like what we mentioned before," she said. "He is in between mortal and immortal."

"What do you mean, Diotima?"

"He's a great spirit, Socrates. Everything spiritual, you see, is in between god and mortal."

"What is their function?" I asked.

"They are messengers who shuttle back and forth between the two, conveying prayer and sacrifice from men to gods, while to men they bring commands from the gods, and gifts in return for sacrifices. Being in the middle of the two, they round out the whole and bind fast the all to all. Through them all divination passes, through them the art of priests in sacrifice and ritual, in enchantment, prophecy, and sorcery. Gods do not mix with men; they mingle and converse with us through spirits instead, whether we are awake or asleep. He who is wise in any of these ways is a man of the spirit, but he who is wise in any other way, in a profession or any manual work, is merely a mechanic. These spirits are many and various, then, and one of them is Love."

"Who are his father and mother?" I asked.

"That's rather a long story," she said. "I'll tell it to you, all the same."

"When Aphrodite was born, the gods held a celebration. Poros, the son of Metis, was there among them. When they had feasted, Penia came begging, as poverty does when there's a party, and stayed by the gates.[4] Now Poros got drunk on nectar (there was no wine yet, you see) and, feeling drowsy, went into the garden of Zeus, where he fell asleep. Then Penia schemed up a plan to relieve her lack of resources: she would get a child from Poros. So she lay beside him and got pregnant with Love. That is why Love was born to follow Aphrodite and serve her: because he was conceived on the day of her birth. And that's why he is also by nature a lover of beauty, because Aphrodite herself is especially beautiful.

"As the son of Poros and Penia, his lot in life is set to be like theirs. In the first place, he is always poor, and he's far from being delicate and beautiful (as ordinary people think he is); instead, he is tough and shriveled and shoeless and homeless, always lying on the dirt without a bed, sleeping at people's doorsteps and in roadsides under the sky, having his mother's nature, always living with Need. But on his father's side he is a schemer after the beautiful and the good; he is brave, impetuous, and intense, an awesome hunter, always weaving snares, resourceful in his pursuit of intelligence, a lover of wisdom[5] through all his life; a genius with enchantments, potions, and clever pleadings.

"He is by nature neither immortal nor mortal. But now he springs to life when he gets his way; now he dies—all in the very same day. Because he is his father's son, however, he keeps coming back to life, but then the resources he acquires always slip away, and for this reason Love is never completely without resources, nor is he ever rich.

"He is in between wisdom and ignorance as well. In fact, you see, none of the gods loves wisdom or wants to become wise—for they are wise—and no one else who is wise already loves wisdom; on the other hand, no one who is ignorant will love wisdom either or want to become wise. For what's especially difficult about being ignorant is that you are content with yourself, even though you're neither beautiful and good nor intelligent. If you don't think you need anything, of course you won't want what you don't think you need."

"In that case, Diotima, who *are* the people who love wisdom, if they are neither wise nor ignorant?"

"That's obvious," she said. "A child could tell you. Those who love wisdom fall in between those two extremes. And Love is one of them, because he is in love with what is beautiful, and wisdom is extremely beautiful. It follows that Love *must* be a lover of wisdom and, as such, is in between being wise and being ignorant. This, too, comes to him from his parentage, from a father who is wise and resourceful and a mother who is not wise and lacks resource.

"My dear Socrates, that, then, is the nature of the Spirit called Love. Considering what you thought about Love, it's no surprise that you were led into thinking of Love as you did. On the basis of what you say, I conclude that you thought Love was *being loved*, rather than *being a lover*. I think that's why Love

4. *Poros* means "way" or "resource." *Metis* means "intelligence" or "cunning." *Penia* means "poverty."

5. A philosopher, which literally means "lover of wisdom."

struck you as beautiful in every way: because it is what is really beautiful and graceful that deserves to be loved, and this is perfect and highly blessed; but being a lover takes a different form, which I have just described."

So I said, "All right then, Diotima. What you say about Love is beautiful, but if you're right, what use is Love to human beings?"

"I'll try to teach you that, Socrates, after I finish this. So far I've been explaining the character and the parentage of Love. Now, according to you, he is love for beautiful things. But suppose someone asks us, 'Socrates and Diotima, what is the point of loving beautiful things?'"

"It's clearer this way: 'The lover of beautiful things has a desire; what does he desire?'"

"That they become his own," I said.

"But that answer calls for still another question, that is, 'What will this man have when the beautiful things he wants have become his own?'"

I said there was no way I could give a ready answer to that question.

Then she said, "Suppose someone changes the question, putting 'good' in place of 'beautiful,' and asks you this: 'Tell me, Socrates, a lover of good things has a desire; what does he desire?'"

"That they become his own," I said.

"And what will he have, when the good things he wants have become his own?"

"This time it's easier to come up with the answer," I said. "He'll have happiness."

"That's what makes happy people happy, isn't it—possessing good things. There's no need to ask further, 'What's the point of wanting happiness?' The answer you gave seems to be final."

"True," I said.

"Now this desire for happiness, this kind of love—do you think it is common to all human beings and that everyone wants to have good things forever and ever? What would you say?"

"Just that," I said. "It is common to all."

"Then, Socrates, why don't we say that everyone is in love," she asked, "since everyone always loves the same things? Instead, we say some people are in love and others not; why is that?"

"I wonder about that myself," I said.

"It's nothing to wonder about," she said. "It's because we divide out a special kind of love, and we refer to it by the word that means the whole—'love'; and for the other kinds of love we use other words."

"What do you mean?" I asked.

"Well, you know, for example, that 'poetry' has a very wide range.[6] After all, everything that is responsible for creating something out of nothing is a kind of poetry; and so all the creations of every craft and profession are themselves a kind of poetry, and everyone who practices a craft is a poet."

"True."

"Nevertheless," she said, "as you also know, these craftsmen are not called poets. We have other words for them, and out of the whole of poetry we have marked off one part, the part the Muses give us with melody and rhythm, and we refer to this by the word that means the whole. For this alone is called 'poetry,' and those who practice this part of poetry are called poets."

6. In Greek, *poesis*, from which the term "poetry" derives, covers any kind of making.

"True."

"That's also how it is with love. The main point is this: every desire for good things or for happiness is 'the supreme and treacherous love' in everyone. But those who pursue this along any of its many other ways—through making money, or through the love of sports, or through philosophy—we don't say that *these* people are in love, and we don't call them lovers. It's only when people are devoted exclusively to one special kind of love that we use these words that really belong to the whole of it: 'love' and 'in love' and 'lovers.'"

"I am beginning to see your point," I said.

"Now there is a certain story," she said, "according to which lovers are those people who seek their other halves. But according to my story, a lover does not seek the half or the whole, unless, my friend, it turns out to be good as well. I say this because people are even willing to cut off their own arms and legs if they think they are diseased. I don't think an individual takes joy in what belongs to him personally unless by 'belonging to me' he means 'good' and by 'belonging to another' he means 'bad.' That's because what everyone loves is really nothing other than the good. Do you disagree?"

"Zeus! Not I," I said.

"Now, then," she said. "Can we simply say that people love the good?"

"Yes," I said.

"But shouldn't we add that, in loving it, they want the good to be theirs?"

"We should."

"And not only that," she said. "They want the good to be theirs forever, don't they?"

"We should add that too."

"In a word, then, love is wanting to possess the good forever."

"That's very true," I said.

"This, then, is the object of love," she said. "Now, how do lovers pursue it? We'd rightly say that when they are in love they do something with eagerness and zeal. But what is it precisely that they do? Can you say?"

"If I could, Diotima," I said, "I wouldn't be your student, filled with admiration for your wisdom, and trying to learn these very things."

"Well, I'll tell you," she said. "It is giving birth in beauty, whether in body or in soul."

"It would take divination to figure out what you mean. I can't."

"Well, I'll tell you more clearly," she said. "All of us are pregnant, Socrates, both in body and in soul, and, as soon as we come to a certain age, we naturally desire to give birth. Now no one can possibly give birth in anything ugly; only in something beautiful. That's because when a man and a woman come together in order to give birth, this is a godly affair. Pregnancy, reproduction—this is an immortal thing for a mortal animal to do, and it cannot occur in anything that is out of harmony, but ugliness is out of harmony with all that is godly. Beauty, however, is in harmony with the divine. Therefore the goddess who presides at childbirth—she's called Moira or Eilithuia—is really Beauty. That's why, whenever pregnant animals or persons draw near to beauty, they become gentle and joyfully disposed and give birth and reproduce; but near ugliness they frown and draw back in pain; they turn away and shrink back and do not reproduce, and because they hold on to what they carry inside them, the labor is painful. This is the source of the great excitement about beauty that comes to anyone who is pregnant and already teeming with life: beauty releases them from their great pain. You see, Socrates," she said, "what Love wants is not beauty, as you think it is."

"Well, what is it, then?"

"Reproduction and birth in beauty."

"Maybe," I said.

"Certainly," she said. "Now, why reproduction? It's because reproduction goes on forever; it is what mortals have in place of immortality. A lover must desire immortality along with the good, if what we agreed earlier was right, that Love wants to possess the good forever. It follows from our argument that Love must desire immortality."

All this she taught me, on those occasions when she spoke on the art of love. And once she asked, "What do you think causes love and desire, Socrates? Don't you see what an awful state a wild animal is in when it wants to reproduce? Footed and winged animals alike, all are plagued by the disease of Love. First they are sick for intercourse with each other, then for nurturing their young—for their sake the weakest animals stand ready to do battle against the strongest and even to die for them, and they may be racked with famine in order to feed their young. They would do anything for their sake. Human beings, you'd think, would do this because they understand the reason for it; but what causes wild animals to be in such a state of love? Can you say?"

And I said again that I didn't know.

So she said, "How do you think you'll ever master the art of love, if you don't know that?"

"But that's why I came to you, Diotima, as I just said. I knew I needed a teacher. So tell me what causes this, and everything else that belongs to the art of love."

"If you really believe that Love by its nature aims at what we have often agreed it does, then don't be surprised at the answer," she said. "For among animals the principle is the same as with us, and mortal nature seeks so far as possible to live forever and be immortal. And this is possible in one way only: by reproduction, because it always leaves behind a new young one in place of the old. Even while each living thing is said to be alive and to be the same—as a person is said to be the same from childhood till he turns into an old man—even then he never consists of the same things, though he is called the same, but he is always being renewed and in other respects passing away, in his hair and flesh and bones and blood and his entire body. And it's not just in his body, but in his soul, too, for none of his manners, customs, opinions, desires, pleasures, pains, or fears ever remains the same, but some are coming to be in him while others are passing away. And what is still far stranger than that is that not only does one branch of knowledge come to be in us while another passes away and that we are never the same even in respect of our knowledge, but that each single piece of knowledge has the same fate. For what we call *studying* exists because knowledge is leaving us, because forgetting is the departure of knowledge, while studying puts back a fresh memory in place of what went away, thereby preserving a piece of knowledge, so that it seems to be the same. And in that way everything mortal is preserved, not, like the divine, by always being the same in every way, but because what is departing and aging leaves behind something new, something such as it had been. By this device, Socrates," she said, "what is mortal shares in immortality, whether it is a body or anything else, while the immortal has another way. So don't be surprised if everything naturally values its own offspring, because it is for the sake of immortality that everything shows this zeal, which is Love."

Yet when I heard her speech I was amazed, and spoke: "Well," said I, "Most wise Diotima, is this really the way it is?"

And in the manner of a perfect sophist she said, "Be sure of it, Socrates. Look, if you will, at how human beings seek honor. You'd be amazed at their irrationality, if you didn't have in mind what I spoke about and if you hadn't pondered the awful state of love they're in, wanting to become famous and 'to lay up glory immortal forever,' and how they're ready to brave any danger for the sake of this, much more than they are for their children; and they are prepared to spend money, suffer through all sorts of ordeals, and even die for the sake of glory. Do you really think that Alcestis would have died for Admetus," she asked, "or that Achilles would have died after Patroclus, or that your Codrus would have died so as to preserve the throne for his sons,[7] if they hadn't expected the memory of their virtue—which we still hold in honor—to be immortal? Far from it," she said. "I believe that anyone will do anything for the sake of immortal virtue and the glorious fame that follows; and the better the people, the more they will do, for they are all in love with immortality.

"Now, some people are pregnant in body, and for this reason turn more to women and pursue love in that way, providing themselves through childbirth with immortality and remembrance and happiness, as they think, for all time to come; while others are pregnant in soul—because there surely *are* those who are even more pregnant in their souls than in their bodies, and these are pregnant with what is fitting for a soul to bear and bring to birth. And what is fitting? Wisdom and the rest of virtue, which all poets beget, as well as all the craftsmen who are said to be creative. But by far the greatest and most beautiful part of wisdom deals with the proper ordering of cities and households, and that is called moderation and justice. When someone has been pregnant with these in his soul from early youth, while he is still a virgin, and, having arrived at the proper age, desires to beget and give birth, he too will certainly go about seeking the beauty in which he would beget; for he will never beget in anything ugly. Since he is pregnant, then, he is much more drawn to bodies that are beautiful than to those that are ugly; and if he also has the luck to find a soul that is beautiful and noble and well-formed, he is even more drawn to this combination; such a man makes him instantly teem with speeches about virtue—about the qualities a virtuous man should have and the customary activities in which he should engage; and so he tries to educate him. In my view, you see, when he makes contact with someone beautiful and keeps company with him, he conceives and gives birth to what he has been carrying inside him for ages. And whether they are together or apart, he remembers that beauty. And in common with him, he nurtures the newborn; such people, therefore, have much more to share than do the parents of human children, and have a firmer bond of friendship, because the children in whom they have a share are more beautiful and more immortal. Everyone would rather

7. Codrus was the legendary last king of Athens; he gave his life when it was prophesied that the city would defeat the invading Dorians only if the king was killed.

have such children than human ones, and would look up to Homer, Hesiod, and the other good poets with envy and admiration for the offspring they have left behind—offspring, which, because they are immortal themselves, provide their parents with immortal glory and remembrance. "For example," she said, "those are the sort of children Lycurgus[8] left behind in Sparta as the saviors of Sparta and virtually all of Greece. Among you the honor goes to Solon[9] for his creation of your laws. Other men in other places everywhere, Greek or barbarian, have brought a host of beautiful deeds into the light and begotten every kind of virtue. Already many shrines have sprung up to honor them for their immortal children, which hasn't happened yet to anyone for human offspring.

"Even you, Socrates, could probably come to be initiated into these rites of love. But as for the purpose of these rites when they are done correctly—that is the final and highest mystery, and I don't know if you are capable of it. I myself will tell you," she said, "and I won't stint any effort. And you must try to follow if you can."

"A lover who goes about this matter correctly must begin in his youth to devote himself to beautiful bodies. First, if the leader leads aright, he should love one body and beget beautiful speeches there; then he should realize that the beauty of any one body is brother to the beauty of any other and that if he is to pursue beauty of form he'd be very foolish not to think that the beauty of all bodies is one and the same. When he grasps this, he must become a lover of all beautiful bodies, and he must think that this wild gaping after just one body is a small thing and despise it.

"After this he must think that the beauty of people's souls is more valuable than the beauty of their bodies, so that if someone is decent in his soul, even though he is scarcely blooming in his body, our lover must be content to love and care for him and to seek to give birth to such ideas as will make young men better. The result is that our lover will be forced to gaze at the beauty of activities and laws and to see that all this is akin to itself, with the result that he will think that the beauty of bodies is a thing of small importance. After customs he must move on to various kinds of knowledge. The result is that he will see the beauty of knowledge and be looking mainly not at beauty in a single example—as a servant would who favored the beauty of a little boy or a man or a single custom (being a slave, of course, he's low and small-minded)—but the lover is turned to the great sea of beauty, and, gazing upon this, he gives birth to many gloriously beautiful speeches, in unstinting love of wisdom,[1] until, having grown and been strengthened there, he catches sight of such knowledge, and it is the knowledge of such beauty. . . .

"Try to pay attention to me," she said, "as best you can. You see, the man who has been thus far guided in matters of Love, who has beheld beautiful things in the right order and correctly, is coming now to the goal of Loving: all of a sudden he will catch sight of something wonderfully beautiful in its nature; that, Socrates, is the reason for all his earlier labors:

"First, it always *is* and neither comes to be nor passes away, neither waxes nor wanes. Second, it is not beautiful this way and ugly that way, nor beautiful at one time and ugly at another, nor beautiful in relation to one thing and ugly in relation

8. Famous oligarchic lawgiver.
9. Athenian lawmaker.
1. I.e., unstinting philosophy.

to another; nor is it beautiful here but ugly there, as it would be if it were beautiful for some people and ugly for others. Nor will the beautiful appear to him in the guise of a face or hands or anything else that belongs to the body. It will not appear to him as a speech or a kind of knowledge does. It is not anywhere in another thing, as in an animal, or in earth, or in heaven, or in anything else, but itself by itself with itself, it is always one in form; and all the other beautiful things share in that, in such a way that when those others come to be or pass away, this does not become the least bit smaller or greater nor suffer any change. So when someone rises by these stages, through loving boys correctly, and begins to see this beauty, he has almost grasped his goal. This is what it is to go aright, or be led by another, into the art of Love: one goes always upwards for the sake of this Beauty, starting out from beautiful things and using them like rising stairs: from one body to two and from two to all beautiful bodies, then from beautiful bodies to beautiful customs, and from customs to learning beautiful things, and from these lessons he arrives in the end at this lesson, which is learning of this very Beauty, so that in the end he comes to know just what it is to be beautiful.

"And there in life, Socrates, my friend," said the woman from Mantinea, "there if anywhere should a person live his life, beholding that Beauty. If you once see that, it won't occur to you to measure beauty by gold or clothing or beautiful boys and youths—who, if you see them now, strike you out of your senses, and make you, you and many others, eager to be with the boys you love and look at them forever, if there were any way to do that, forgetting food and drink, everything but looking at them and being with them. But how would it be, in our view," she said, "if someone got to see the Beautiful itself, absolute, pure, unmixed, not polluted by human flesh or colors or any other great nonsense of mortality, but if he could see the divine Beauty itself in its one form? Do you think it would be a poor life for a human being to look there and to behold it by that which he ought, and to be with it? Or haven't you remembered," she said, "that in that life alone, when he looks at Beauty in the only way that Beauty can be seen—only then will it become possible for him to give birth not to images of virtue (because he's in touch with no images), but to true virtue (because he is in touch with the true Beauty). The love of the gods belongs to anyone who has given birth to true virtue and nourished it, and if any human being could become immortal, it would be he."

This, Phaedrus and the rest of you, was what Diotima told me. I was persuaded. And once persuaded, I try to persuade others too that human nature can find no better workmate for acquiring this than Love. That's why I say that every man must honor Love, why I honor the rites of Love myself and practice them with special diligence, and why I commend them to others. Now and always I praise the power and courage of Love so far as I am able. Consider this speech, then, Phaedrus, if you wish, a speech in praise of Love. Or if not, call it whatever and however you please to call it.

Socrates' speech finished to loud applause. Meanwhile, Aristophanes was trying to make himself heard over their cheers in order to make a response to something Socrates had said about his own speech. Then, all of a sudden, there was even more noise. A large drunken party had arrived at the courtyard door and they were rattling it loudly, accompanied by the shrieks of some flute-girl they had brought along. Agathon at that point called to his slaves:

"Go see who it is. If it's people we know, invite them in. If not, tell them the party's over, and we're about to turn in."

A moment later they heard Alcibiades shouting in the courtyard, very drunk and very loud. He wanted to know where Agathon was, he demanded to see Agathon at once. Actually, he was half carried into the house by the flute-girl and by some other companions of his, but, at the door, he managed to stand by himself, crowned with a beautiful wreath of violets and ivy and ribbons in his hair.

"Good evening, gentlemen. I'm plastered," he announced. "May I join your party? Or should I crown Agathon with this wreath—which is all I came to do, anyway—and make myself scarce? I really couldn't make it yesterday," he continued, "but nothing could stop me tonight! See, I'm wearing the garland myself. I want this crown to come directly from my head to the head that belongs, I don't mind saying, to the cleverest and best looking man in town. Ah, you laugh; you think I'm drunk! Fine, go ahead—I know I'm right anyway. Well, what do you say? May I join you on these terms? Will you have a drink with me or not?"

Naturally they all made a big fuss. They implored him to join them, they begged him to take a seat, and Agathon called him to his side. So Alcibiades, again with the help of his friends, approached Agathon. At the same time, he kept trying to take his ribbons off so that he could crown Agathon with them, but all he succeeded in doing was to push them further down his head until they finally slipped over his eyes. What with the ivy and all, he didn't see Socrates, who had made room for him on the couch as soon as he saw him. So Alcibiades sat down between Socrates and Agathon and, as soon as he did so, he put his arms around Agathon, kissed him, and placed the ribbons on his head.

Agathon asked his slaves to take Alcibiades' sandals off. "We can all three fit on my couch," he said.

"What a good idea!" Alcibiades replied. "But wait a moment! Who's the third?"

As he said this, he turned around, and it was only then that he saw Socrates. No sooner had he seen him than he leaped up and cried:

"Good lord, what's going on here? It's Socrates! You've trapped me again! You always do this to me—all of a sudden you'll turn up out of nowhere where I least expect you! Well, what do you want now? Why did you choose this particular couch? Why aren't you with Aristophanes or anyone else we could tease you about? But no, you figured out a way to find a place next to the most handsome man in the room!"

"I beg you, Agathon," Socrates said, "protect me from this man! You can't imagine what it's like to be in love with him: from the very first moment he realized how I felt about him, he hasn't allowed me to say two words to anybody else—what am I saying, I can't so much as look at an attractive man but he flies into a fit of jealous rage. He yells; he threatens; he can hardly keep from slapping me around! Please, try to keep him under control. Could you perhaps make him forgive me? And if you can't, if he gets violent, will you defend me? The fierceness of his passion terrifies me!"

"I shall never forgive you!" Alcibiades cried. "I promise you, you'll pay for this! But for the moment," he said, turning to Agathon, "give me some of these ribbons. I'd better make a wreath for him as well—look at that magnificent head! Otherwise, I know, he'll make a scene. He'll be grumbling that, though I crowned you for your first victory, I didn't honor him even though he has never lost an argument in his life."

So Alcibiades took the ribbons, arranged them on Socrates' head, and lay back on the couch. Immediately, however, he started up again:

"Friends, you look sober to me; we can't have that! Let's have a drink! Remember our agreement? We need a master of ceremonies; who should it be? . . . Well, at least till you are all too drunk to care, I elect . . . myself! Who else? Agathon, I want the largest cup around. . . . No! Wait! You! Bring me that cooling jar over there!"

He'd seen the cooling jar, and he realized it could hold more than two quarts of wine. He had the slaves fill it to the brim, drained it, and ordered them to fill it up again for Socrates.

"Not that the trick will have any effect on *him*," he told the group. "Socrates will drink whatever you put in front of him, but no one yet has seen him drunk."

The slave filled the jar and, while Socrates was drinking, Eryximachus said to Alcibiades:

"This is certainly most improper. We cannot simply pour the wine down our throats in silence: we must have some conversation, or at least a song. What we are doing now is hardly civilized."

What Alcibiades said to him was this:

"O Eryximachus, best possible son to the best possible, the most temperate father: Hi!"

"Greetings to you, too," Eryximachus replied. "Now what do you suggest we do?"

"Whatever you say. Ours to obey you, 'For a medical mind is worth a million others'. Please prescribe what you think fit."

"Listen to me," Eryximachus said. "Earlier this evening we decided to use this occasion to offer a series of encomia of Love. We all took our turn—in good order, from left to right—and gave our speeches, each according to his ability. You are the only one not to have spoken yet, though, if I may say so, you have certainly drunk your share. It's only proper, therefore, that you take your turn now. After you have spoken, you can decide on a topic for Socrates on your right; he can then do the same for the man to his right, and we can go around the table once again."

"Well said, O Eryximachus," Alcibiades replied. "But do you really think it's fair to put my drunken ramblings next to your sober orations? And anyway, my dear fellow, I hope you didn't believe a single word Socrates said: the truth is just the opposite! He's the one who will most surely beat me up if I dare praise anyone else in his presence—even a god!"

"Hold your tongue!" Socrates said.

"By god, don't you dare deny it!" Alcibiades shouted. "I would never—*never*—praise anyone else with you around."

"Well, why not just do that, if you want?" Eryximachus suggested. "Why don't you offer an encomium to Socrates?"

"What do you mean?" asked Alcibiades. "Do you really think so, Eryximachus? Should I unleash myself upon him? Should I give him his punishment in front of all of you?"

"Now, wait a minute," Socrates said. "What do you have in mind? Are you going to praise me only in order to mock me? Is that it?"

"I'll only tell the truth—please, let me!"

"I would certainly like to hear the truth from you. By all means, go ahead," Socrates replied.

"Nothing can stop me now," said Alcibiades. "But here's what you can do: if I say anything that's not true, you can just interrupt, if you want, and correct me; at worst, there'll be mistakes in my speech, not lies. But you can't hold it against me if I don't get everything in the right order—I'll say things as they come to mind. It is no easy task for one in my condition to give a smooth and orderly account of your bizarreness!"

I'll try to praise Socrates, my friends, but I'll have to use an image. And though he may think I'm trying to make fun of him, I assure you my image is no joke: it aims at the truth. Look at him! Isn't he just like a statue of Silenus?[2] You know the kind of statue I mean; you'll find them in any shop in town. It's a Silenus sitting, his flute or his pipes in his hands, and it's hollow. It's split right down the middle, and inside it's full of tiny statues of the gods. Now look at him again! Isn't he also just like the satyr Marsyas?[3]

Nobody, not even you, Socrates, can deny that you *look* like them. But the resemblance goes beyond appearance, as you're about to hear.

You are impudent, contemptuous, and vile! No? If you won't admit it, I'll bring witnesses. And you're quite a fluteplayer, aren't you? In fact, you're much more marvelous than Marsyas, who needed instruments to cast his spells on people. And so does anyone who plays his tunes today—for even the tunes Olympus played are Marsyas' work, since Olympus learned everything from him.[4] Whether they are played by the greatest flautist or the meanest flute-girl, his melodies have in themselves the power to possess and so reveal those people who are ready for the god and his mysteries. That's because his melodies are themselves divine. The only difference between you and Marsyas is that you need no instruments; you do exactly what he does, but with words alone. You know, people hardly ever take a speaker seriously, even if he's the greatest orator; but let anyone—man, woman, or child—listen to you or even to a poor account of what you say—and we are all transported, completely possessed.

If I were to describe for you what an extraordinary effect his words have always had on me (I can feel it this moment even as I'm speaking), you might actually suspect that I'm drunk! Still, I swear to you, the moment he starts to speak, I am beside myself: my heart starts leaping in my chest, the tears come streaming down my face, even the frenzied Corybantes[5] seem sane compared to me—and, let me tell you, I am not alone. I have heard Pericles[6] and many other great orators, and I have admired their speeches. But nothing like this ever happened to me: they never upset me so deeply that my very own soul started protesting that my life—*my* life!—was no better than the most miserable slave's. And yet that is exactly how this Marsyas here at my side makes me feel all the time: he makes it seem that my life isn't worth living! You can't

2. Drunken satyr—a mythical hairy, goatish creature, woodland follower of Dionysus, god of wine. Satyrs were often represented onstage and in art with large erections.
3. Marsyas competed with the god Apollo in music, and was flayed for his insolence.
4. Olympus was a legendary musician, loved by Marsyas.
5. Worshippers of the Mother Goddess, Cybele, Corybantes achieved divine ecstasy through music and dance.
6. Famous Athenian general, statesman, and orator.

say that isn't true, Socrates. I know very well that you could make me feel that way this very moment if I gave you half a chance. He always traps me, you see, and he makes me admit that my political career is a waste of time, while all that matters is just what I most neglect: my personal shortcomings, which cry out for the closest attention. So I refuse to listen to him; I stop my ears and tear myself away from him, for, like the Sirens,[7] he could make me stay by his side till I die.

Socrates is the only man in the world who has made me feel shame—ah, you didn't think I had it in me, did you? Yes, he makes me feel ashamed: I know perfectly well that I can't prove he's wrong when he tells me what I should do; yet, the moment I leave his side, I go back to my old ways: I cave in to my desire to please the crowd. My whole life has become one constant effort to escape from him and keep away, but when I see him, I feel deeply ashamed, because I'm doing nothing about my way of life, though I have already agreed with him that I should. Sometimes, believe me, I think I would be happier if he were dead. And yet I know that if he dies I'll be even more miserable. I can't live with him, and I can't live without him! What *can* I do about him?

That's the effect of this satyr's music—on me and many others. But that's the least of it. He's like these creatures in all sorts of other ways; his powers are really extraordinary. Let me tell you about them, because, you can be sure of it, none of you really understands him. But, now I've started, I'm going to show you what he really is.

To begin with, he's crazy about beautiful boys; he constantly follows them around in a perpetual daze. Also, he likes to say he's ignorant and knows nothing. Isn't this just like Silenus? Of course it is! And all this is just on the surface, like the outsides of those statues of Silenus. I wonder, my fellow drinkers, if you have any idea what a sober and temperate man he proves to be once you have looked inside. Believe me, it couldn't matter less to him whether a boy is beautiful. You can't imagine how little he cares whether a person is beautiful, or rich, or famous in any other way that most people admire. He considers all these possessions beneath contempt, and that's exactly how he considers all of us as well. In public, I tell you, his whole life is one big game—a game of irony. I don't know if any of you have seen him when he's really serious. But I once caught him when he was open like Silenus' statues, and I had a glimpse of the figures he keeps hidden within: they were so godlike—so bright and beautiful, so utterly amazing—that I no longer had a choice—I just had to do whatever he told me.

What I thought at the time was that what he really wanted was *me*, and that seemed to me the luckiest coincidence: all I had to do was to let him have his way with me, and he would teach me everything he knew—believe me, I had a lot of confidence in my looks. Naturally, up to that time we'd never been alone together; one of my attendants had always been present. But with this in mind, I sent the attendant away, and met Socrates alone. (You see, in this company I must tell the whole truth: so pay attention. And, Socrates, if I say anything untrue, I want you to correct me.)

So there I was, my friends, alone with him at last. My idea, naturally, was that he'd take advantage of the opportunity to tell me whatever it is that lovers

7. Magical female birdlike creatures whose singing lured sailors to their doom. Odysseus escaped their island by having his men tie him to the mast, in book 12 of the *Odyssey*.

say when they find themselves alone; I relished the moment. But no such luck! Nothing of the sort occurred. Socrates had his usual sort of conversation with me, and at the end of the day he went off.

My next idea was to invite him to the gymnasium with me. We took exercise together, and I was sure that this would lead to something. He took exercise and wrestled with me many times when no one else was present. What can I tell you? I got nowhere. When I realized that my ploy had failed, I decided on a frontal attack. I refused to retreat from a battle I myself had begun, and I needed to know just where matters stood. So what I did was to invite him to dinner, as if *I* were his lover and he my young prey! To tell the truth, it took him quite a while to accept my invitation, but one day he finally arrived. That first time, he left right after dinner: I was too shy to try to stop him. But on my next attempt, I started some discussion just as we were finishing our meal and kept him talking late into the night. When he said he should be going, I used the lateness of the hour as an excuse and managed to persuade him to spend the night at my house. He had had his meal on the couch next to mine, so he just made himself comfortable and lay down on it. No one else was there.

Now you must admit that my story so far has been perfectly decent; I could have told it in any company. But you'd never have heard me tell the rest of it, as you're about to do, if it weren't that, as the saying goes, 'there's truth in wine when the slaves have left'—and when they're present, too. Also, would it be fair to Socrates for me to praise him and yet to fail to reveal one of his proudest accomplishments? And, furthermore, you know what people say about snakebite—that you'll only talk about it with your fellow victims: only they will understand the pain and forgive you for all the things it made you do. Well, something much more painful than a snake has bitten me in my most sensitive part—I mean my heart, or my soul, or whatever you want to call it, which has been struck and bitten by philosophy, whose grip on young and eager souls is much more vicious than a viper's and makes them do the most amazing things. Now, all you people here, Phaedrus, Agathon, Eryximachus, Pausanias, Aristodemus, Aristophanes—I need not mention Socrates himself—and all the rest, have all shared in the madness, the Bacchic frenzy[8] of philosophy. And that's why you will hear the rest of my story; you will understand and forgive both what I did then and what I say now. As for the house slaves and for anyone else who is not an initiate, my story's not for you: block your ears!

To get back to the story. The lights were out; the slaves had left; the time was right, I thought, to come to the point and tell him freely what I had in mind. So I shook him and whispered:

"Socrates, are you asleep?"

"No, no, not at all," he replied.

"You know what I've been thinking?"

"Well, no, not really."

"I think," I said, "you're the only worthy lover I have ever had—and yet, look how shy you are with me! Well, here's how I look at it. It would be really stupid not to give you anything you want: you can have me, my belongings, anything my friends might have. Nothing is more important to me than becoming the best man I can be, and no one can help me more than you to reach that aim.

8. Madness inspired by Dionysus (Bacchus).

With a man like you, in fact, I'd be much more ashamed of what wise people would say if I did *not* take you as my lover, than I would of what all the others, in their foolishness, would say if I did."

He heard me out, and then he said in that absolutely inimitable ironic manner of his:

"Dear Alcibiades, if you are right in what you say about me, you are already more accomplished than you think. If I really have in me the power to make you a better man, then you can see in me a beauty that is really beyond description and makes your own remarkable good looks pale in comparison. But, then, is this a fair exchange that you propose? You seem to me to want more than your proper share: you offer me the merest appearance of beauty, and in return you want the thing itself, 'gold in exchange for bronze.'[9]

"Still, my dear boy, you should think twice, because you could be wrong, and I may be of no use to you. The mind's sight becomes sharp only when the body's eyes go past their prime—and you are still a good long time away from that."

When I heard this I replied:

"I really have nothing more to say. I've told you exactly what I think. Now it's your turn to consider what you think best for you and me."

"You're right about that," he answered. "In the future, let's consider things together. We'll always do what seems the best to the two of us."

His words made me think that my own had finally hit their mark, that he was smitten by my arrows. I didn't give him a chance to say another word. I stood up immediately and placed my mantle over the light cloak which, though it was the middle of winter, was his only clothing. I slipped underneath the cloak and put my arms around this man—this utterly unnatural, this truly extraordinary man—and spent the whole night next to him. Socrates, you can't deny a word of it. But in spite of all my efforts, this hopelessly arrogant, this unbelievably insolent man—he turned me down! He spurned my beauty, of which I was so proud, members of the jury—for this is really what you are: you're here to sit in judgment of Socrates' amazing arrogance and pride. Be sure of it, I swear to you by all the gods and goddesses together, my night with Socrates went no further than if I had spent it with my own father or older brother!

How do you think I felt after that? Of course, I was deeply humiliated, but also I couldn't help admiring his natural character, his moderation, his fortitude—here was a man whose strength of character and wisdom went beyond my wildest dreams! How could I bring myself to hate him? I couldn't bear to lose his friendship. But how could I possibly win him over? I knew very well that money meant much less to him than enemy weapons ever meant to Ajax,[1] and the only trap by means of which I had thought I might capture him had already proved a dismal failure. I had no idea what to do, no purpose in life; ah, no one else has ever known the real meaning of slavery!

All this had already occurred when Athens invaded Potidaea,[2] where we served together and shared the same mess. Now, first, he took the hardships of the campaign much better than I ever did—much better, in fact, than anyone in the whole army. When we were cut off from our supplies, as often happens in the field, no one else stood up to hunger as well as he did. And yet he was the one

9. Allusion to scene in the *Iliad* (6.232–36).
1. Strong Greek hero who carried a huge shield.
2. City besieged and defeated by Athens at the start of the Peloponnesian War.

man who could really enjoy a feast; and though he didn't much want to drink, when he had to, he could drink the best of us under the table. Still, and most amazingly, no one ever saw him drunk (as we'll straightaway put to the test).

Add to this his amazing resistance to the cold—and, let me tell you, the winter there is something awful. Once, I remember, it was frightfully cold; no one so much as stuck his nose outside. If we absolutely had to leave our tent, we wrapped ourselves in anything we could lay our hands on and tied extra pieces of felt or sheepskin over our boots. Well, Socrates went out in that weather wearing nothing but this same old light cloak, and even in bare feet he made better progress on the ice than the other soldiers did in their boots. You should have seen the looks they gave him; they thought he was only doing it to spite them!

So much for that! But you should hear what else he did during that same campaign,

The exploit our strong-hearted hero dared to do.[3]

One day, at dawn, he started thinking about some problem or other; he just stood outside, trying to figure it out. He couldn't resolve it, but he wouldn't give up. He simply stood there, glued to the same spot. By midday, many soldiers had seen him, and, quite mystified, they told everyone that Socrates had been standing there all day, thinking about something. He was still there when evening came, and after dinner some Ionians moved their bedding outside, where it was cooler and more comfortable (all this took place in the summer), mainly in order to watch if Socrates was going to stay out there all night. And so he did; he stood on the very same spot until dawn! He only left next morning, when the sun came out, and he made his prayers to the new day.

And if you would like to know what he was like in battle—this is a tribute he really deserves. You know that I was decorated for bravery during that campaign: well, during that very battle, Socrates single-handedly saved my life! He absolutely did! He just refused to leave me behind when I was wounded, and he rescued not only me but my armor as well. For my part, Socrates, I told them right then that the decoration really belonged to you, and you can blame me neither for doing so then nor for saying so now. But the generals, who seemed much more concerned with my social position, insisted on giving the decoration to me, and, I must say, you were more eager than the generals themselves for me to have it.

You should also have seen him at our horrible retreat from Delium.[4] I was there with the cavalry, while Socrates was a foot soldier. The army had already dispersed in all directions, and Socrates was retreating together with Laches.[5] I happened to see them just by chance, and the moment I did I started shouting encouragements to them, telling them I was never going to leave their side, and so on. That day I had a better opportunity to watch Socrates than I ever had at Potidaea, for, being on horseback, I wasn't in very great danger. Well, it was easy to see that he was remarkably more collected than Laches. But when I looked again I couldn't get your words, Aristophanes, out of my mind: in the midst of battle he was making his way exactly as he does around town,

. . . with swagg'ring gait and roving eye.[6]

3. Quotation from the *Odyssey* (4.242, 271).
4. The Athenians were routed by the Boeotians at Delium, a Boeotian town, in 424 B.C.E.
5. Famous Athenian general, who appears in an eponymous Platonic dialogue, on courage.
6. Aristophanes, *Clouds* 362.

He was observing everything quite calmly, looking out for friendly troops and keeping an eye on the enemy. Even from a great distance it was obvious that this was a very brave man, who would put up a terrific fight if anyone approached him. This is what saved both of them. For, as a rule, you try to put as much distance as you can between yourself and such men in battle; you go after the others, those who run away helter-skelter.

You could say many other marvelous things in praise of Socrates. Perhaps he shares some of his specific accomplishments with others. But, as a whole, he is unique; he is like no one else in the past and no one in the present—this is by far the most amazing thing about him. For we might be able to form an idea of what Achilles was like by comparing him to Brasidas or some other great warrior, or we might compare Pericles with Nestor or Antenor or one of the other great orators.[7] There is a parallel for everyone—everyone else, that is. But this man here is so bizarre, his ways and his arguments are so unusual, that, search as you might, you'll never find anyone else, alive or dead, who's even remotely like him. The best you can do is not to compare him to anything human, but to liken him, as I do, to Silenus and the satyrs, and the same goes for his arguments.

Come to think of it, I should have mentioned this much earlier: even his arguments are just like those hollow statues of Silenus. If you were to listen to his arguments, at first they'd strike you as totally ridiculous; they're clothed in words as coarse as the hides worn by the most vulgar satyrs. He's always going on about pack asses, or blacksmiths, or cobblers, or tanners; he's always making the same tired old points in the same tired old words. If you are foolish, or simply unfamiliar with him, you'd find it impossible not to laugh at his arguments. But if you see them when they open up like the statues, if you go behind their surface, you'll realize that no other arguments make any sense. They're truly worthy of a god, bursting with figures of virtue inside. They're of great—no, of the greatest—importance for anyone who wants to become a truly good man.

Well, gentlemen, this is my praise of Socrates, though I haven't spared him my reproach, either; I told you how horribly he treated me—and not only me but also Charmides, Euthydemus,[8] and many others. He has deceived us all: he presents himself as your lover, and, before you know it, you're in love with him yourself! I warn you, Agathon, don't let him fool you! Remember our torments; be on your guard: don't wait, like the fool in the proverb, to learn your lesson from your own misfortune.

Alcibiades' frankness provoked a lot of laughter, especially since it was obvious that he was still in love with Socrates, who immediately said to him:

"You're perfectly sober after all, Alcibiades. Otherwise you could never have concealed your motive so gracefully: how casually you let it drop, almost like an afterthought, at the very end of your speech! As if the real point of all this has not been simply to make trouble between Agathon and me! You think that I should be in love with you and no one else, while you, and no one else, should be in love with Agathon—well, we were *not* deceived; we've seen through your little satyr play. Agathon, my friend, don't let him get away with it: let no one come between us!"

7. Brasidas was a Spartan general in the Peloponnesian War. The mythical figures Nestor the Greek and Antenor the Trojan were counselors in the Trojan War.

8. Real people who appear in other Platonic dialogues. Charmides was Plato's uncle.

Agathon said to Socrates:

"I'm beginning to think you're right; isn't it proof of that that he literally came between us here on the couch? Why would he do this if he weren't set on separating us? But he won't get away with it; I'm coming right over to lie down next to you."

"Wonderful," Socrates said. "Come here, on my other side."

"My god!" cried Alcibiades. "How I suffer in his hands! He kicks me when I'm down; he never lets me go. Come, don't be selfish, Socrates; at least, let's compromise: let Agathon lie down between us."

"Why, that's impossible," Socrates said. "You have already delivered your praise of me, and now it's my turn to praise whoever's on my right. But if Agathon were next to you, he'd have to praise me all over again instead of having me speak in his honor, as I very much want to do in any case. Don't be jealous; let me praise the boy."

"Oh, marvelous," Agathon cried. "Alcibiades, nothing can make me stay next to you now. I'm moving no matter what. I simply *must* hear what Socrates has to say about me."

"There we go again," said Alcibiades. "It's the same old story: when Socrates is around, nobody else can get close to a good-looking man. Look how smoothly and plausibly he found a reason for Agathon to lie down next to him!"

And then, all of a sudden, while Agathon was changing places, a large drunken group, finding the gates open because someone was just leaving, walked into the room and joined the party. There was noise everywhere, and everyone was made to start drinking again in no particular order.

At that point, Aristodemus said, Eryximachus, Phaedrus, and some others among the original guests made their excuses and left. He himself fell asleep and slept for a long time (it was winter, and the nights were quite long). He woke up just as dawn was about to break; the roosters were crowing already. He saw that the others had either left or were asleep on their couches, and that only Agathon, Aristophanes, and Socrates were still awake, drinking out of a large cup which they were passing around from left to right. Socrates was talking to them. Aristodemus couldn't remember exactly what they were saying—he'd missed the first part of their discussion, and he was half asleep anyway—but the main point was that Socrates was trying to prove to them that authors should be able to write both comedy and tragedy: the skillful tragic dramatist should also be a comic poet.[9] He was about to clinch his argument, though, to tell the truth, sleepy as they were, they were hardly able to follow his reasoning. In fact, Aristophanes fell asleep in the middle of the discussion, and very soon thereafter, as day was breaking, Agathon also drifted off.

But after getting them off to sleep, Socrates got up and left, and Aristodemus followed him, as always. He said that Socrates went directly to the Lyceum,[1] washed up, spent the rest of the day just as he always did, and only then, as evening was falling, went home to rest.

9. This position would have sounded surprising to an ancient Athenian. Dramatists composed either comedy or tragedy, not both.

1. The Athenian Lyceum was an open-air gymnasium and meeting place.

82
7-14
509
92687

TRAVEL AND CONQUEST

Travel, either voluntary or under compulsion, has been a constant in human life: throughout history, humans have moved from one country to another, and formed new communities in places far from their homes. The inhabitants of the ancient Mediterranean and Near East had little or no knowledge of the most distant parts of the world (such as the Americas). But the various societies of this part of the ancient world were far from insular. People were highly conscious of differences between their own culture and those of their neighbors, and curious about worlds beyond their own. Without Internet or television, the primary means of understanding cultural difference came through stories.

Storytelling and travel have always had a close connection with one another. Literature itself takes us on a journey to another world. Travel plays a central part even in our earliest surviving literary texts, and the storytellers' attitudes toward these journeys are often complex. The literary technique of telling the story of a journey can allow ancient writers to create an exciting, surprising narrative, which includes elements that are far removed from the normal experience of most readers. Through a magical journey, a text may include a vision of the whole world. These texts can also use a literal journey as a way of representing psychological progress (as in the ***Odyssey*** and, later, Lucian's *True Story* and **Apuleius's *Golden Ass***). In these texts, the hero seems to learn and grow over the course of his journey. In studying literary narratives of spiritual journeys, we might also look forward to **Dante's *Divine Comedy*** and John Bunyan's *Pilgrim's Progress*.

Ancient peoples were aware that travel broadens the mind. Travel in the ancient world could be undertaken willingly, by curious tourists or scholars hoping to learn or to teach. Customs of other places could make people pause to reflect on life at home: travel gave some people the freedom to think about and criticize the established order. More often, merchants and pirates traveled for economic gain. Archaeological evidence shows us that material objects (such as ceramic pots, beads, and, later, coinage) were often traded over large distances. With trade came cultural exchange; one culture often learned from another, in areas as disparate as building techniques, philosophy, science, mathematics, religion, and mythology. Ancient peoples could be quite capable of treating one another's cultures with respect.

But most often, people traveled against their will. Travel could be the

This unusual Babylonian tablet features a unique map of the Mesopotamian world, ca. 700–500 B.C.E. Babylon is shown at the center of the map. Other places, including Assyria and Elam, are also named. A body of water identified as the "Salt Sea" encircles the central area, and outside this ring of water lie eight "regions" that are described in the accompanying inscription.

result of political necessity: the Athenians expelled (or "ostracized") unpopular citizens, and Rome forced many elite figures (including the poet **Ovid** and the philosopher **Seneca**) into exile. People might also be forced to leave home by bad economic conditions. But, as today, the most massive movements of people in antiquity were the result of war. Several cultures in the Mediterranean area tried to build an empire by invading and colonizing their neighbors, including the Babylonians, the Carthaginians, the Athenians, the Persians, the Macedonians, and, most successfully, the Romans. Often, those conquered and captured in war found themselves removed to the land of the victors, as slaves. Throughout antiquity, elite peoples lived with and depended on slaves, who were almost always nonnative people, captured in war or descended from captives. Since history is written by the winners, it can be difficult or impossible for us to recapture the experience of those who suffered in ancient wars, or to hear the voice of those enslaved and owned by the elite. Our vision of non-Egyptian, non-Greek, and non-Roman peoples is often filtered through sources that can only tell, at most, half the story. Sometimes literature—from **Homer's *Iliad*** onward—can seem to offer faint echoes of these lost voices, the peoples defeated and destroyed by war; but such texts are usually more illuminating about the mind-sets of the conquerors.

Like modern people, the ancients often felt the urge to define people from other cultures as essentially different from, and in some way less good than, themselves. Greeks, Romans, Hebrews, and Egyptians all defined their own cultures by contrasting themselves with the foreigners they encountered. A common theme in Greek and Roman texts is the clash between Eastern and Western civilizations, in which easterners—such as the Persians or Egyptians—may be presented as more effeminate, weaker, or less trustworthy than the strong, masculine Athenians or Romans. We can sometimes see the authors of these texts struggling to present foreigners as different from themselves, even in cases where the barbarians were not always easy to distinguish from the Greeks or Romans.

In the modern world, we do not have to travel in order to encounter peoples from other cultures; we can see people from many different ethnic backgrounds every day, in any large city of North America or Europe. Several ancient cultures were similarly cosmopolitan or multicultural and included peoples from a number of different ethnic and racial backgrounds. Multicultural societies were a common result of conquest and colonialism. For instance, from the fourth century B.C.E. onward (after Alexander the Great conquered Egypt in 332 B.C.E.), Greeks became the rulers of Egypt, creating a complex, multicultural society in the new city of Alexandria: it was in this period that the famous Rosetta Stone was produced, which helped decipher Egyptian hieroglyphics. The stone was inscribed with a bilingual tax decree in both Greek and Egyptian—a mark of a society in which people from different cultures, and speaking different languages, had to communicate with one another. Language—both in inscriptions and in literary texts—was an essential element in defining one culture against another, and in attempting to build bridges between them.

TALE OF THE SHIPWRECKED SAILOR

Tale of the Shipwrecked Sailor (ca. 1900 B.C.E.) is one of the oldest surviving fictional narratives from Egypt. It is an easy read and could appear at first sight like a folktale. A man consoles the returning leader of an expedition abroad, who is anxious about his reception at court. The speaker tells of his own failed journey to the Red Sea, which led to shipwreck and the loss of all his companions. He then encountered a giant snake that revealed itself to be a god, and we hear the snake tell its own story. The creature urges the sailor to practice self-control and to treasure his home and family. Despite the text's surface simplicity, it works on a number of different levels. The snake is not just an animal but also the Egyptian creator god, who existed as a snake in primeval times; this god emerges from the edge of the universe to address the man. The sailor promises to repay the snake with sacrifices, but it laughs at his presumption: the encounter seems to point to our failure to recognize the vast gulf between human and divine understanding. There is a surprising, perhaps humorous final twist in the tale: the man listening to the sailor entirely rejects his advice, sneering, "Don't act so clever, my friend!" The ending of the story is a reminder that the ancients may not have been unquestioning in their attitudes toward their own "wisdom" literature. Should we conclude that travel, of all kinds, is undesirable, since there's no place like home? Or is some kind of journey necessary, if only to remind us of the value of home and the need for endurance? This engaging text offers a thought-provoking example of how stories may blur the lines between a geographic and a spiritual journey.

Tale of the Shipwrecked Sailor[1]

A clever Follower[2] speaks:
'May your heart be well, my Count!
Look, we have reached home,[3]
and the mallet is taken, the mooring post driven in,
and the prow-rope has been thrown on the ground;
praises are given and God is thanked,[4]
every man is embracing his fellow,
and our crew has come back safe,
with no loss to our expedition.

1. Translated by Richard B. Parkinson.
2. The Follower is a subordinate official, the tale's narrator and protagonist. The Count is a high-ranking official and the leader of the expedition that has just returned to Egypt.
3. "Home" is a translation of a characteristic term for the period meaning either "Egypt" or the royal residence.
4. No particular deity is specified. This widespread usage accommodates the many different deities people worshiped.

We've reached the very end of Wawat, and passed Biga![5]
Look, we have arrived in peace!
Our own land, we've reached it!

Listen to me, my Count!
I am free ⟨from⟩ exaggeration.
Wash yourself![6] Pour water on your hands!
So you may reply when you are addressed,
and speak to the king with self-possession,
and answer without stammering.
A man's utterance saves him.[7]
His speech turns anger away from him.
But you do as you wish!
It is tiresome to speak to you!

I shall tell you something similar,
which happened to me myself:
I had gone to the Mining Region[8] of the sovereign.
I had gone down to the Sea,
in a boat 120 cubits long,[9]
40 cubits broad,
in which there were 120 sailors from the choicest of Egypt.
They looked at the sea, they looked at the land,
and their hearts were stouter than lions'.

Before it came, they could foretell a gale,
a storm before it existed;
but a gale came up while we were at sea, before we had reached land.
The wind rose, and made an endless howling,
and with it a swell of eight cubits.
Only the mast broke it for me.
Then the boat died.[1]
Those in it—not one of them survived.
Then I was given up onto an island
by a wave of the sea.
With my heart as my only companion,
I spent three days alone.
I spent the nights inside
a shelter of wood, and embraced the shadows.
Then I stretched out my legs to learn what I could put in my mouth.

5. Biga, an island in the first cataract of the Nile, marked the beginning of Egypt. Wawat is Lower Nubia, immediately to the south. The expedition has been returning from Nubia.
6. One should purify oneself before going into the presence of the king. The narrator is encouraging the Count to prepare himself properly for his expected audience with the king.
7. Probably a proverb. A related one comes at the end of the tale.
8. Most likely southwestern Sinai, reached by ship on the Red Sea.
9. A cubit is 525 millimeters, about 20 inches. The boat is very large by ancient Egyptian standards.
1. The verb *to die* could be used for an inanimate thing, rather as ships are called "she" in English.

I found figs and grapes there, and every fine vegetable;
and there were sycomore figs there, and also ripened ones,[2]
and melons as if cultivated;
fish were there, and also fowl:
there was nothing which was not in it.
Then I ate my fill, and put aside
what was too much for my arms.
I took a fire drill, made fire,
and made a burnt offering to the Gods.[3]

Then I heard a noise of thunder; I thought it was a wave of the sea,
for the trees were splintering,
the earth shaking;
I uncovered my face and found it was a serpent coming.
There were 30 cubits of him.
His beard was bigger than two cubits,[4]
his flesh overlaid with gold,
and his eyebrows of true lapis lazuli.
He was rearing upwards.

He opened his mouth to me, while I was prostrate in front of him.[5]
He said to me, "Who brought you?[6]
Who brought you, young man?
Who brought you?
If you delay in telling me
who brought you to this island,
I will make you know yourself to be ashes,
turned into invisibility!"

"You speak to me, without me hearing.[7]
I am in front of you, and do not know myself."
Then he put me in his mouth,
took me away to his dwelling place,
and laid me down without harming me.
I was safe, with no damage done to me.

He opened his mouth to me, while I was prostrate in front of him.[8]
Then he said to me: "Who brought you?
Who brought you, young man?

2. This shows that the island is cultivated, as is confirmed by the next line.
3. A fire drill is a stick spun against another piece of wood or a stone to produce a spark for lighting a fire. Burnt offerings were made to deities whose cult images were not present or who, like the sun god, were worshipped in their physical form.
4. The snake's beard shows that he has the form of a cult statue, as the precious materials mentioned in the next two lines also demonstrate.
5. The sailor has already identified that the snake is a god.
6. Probably a standard patronizing address to someone who seeks assistance. The snake then overawes the man with a threat that includes being consumed by his fiery breath.
7. The speaker shifts at this point. The absence of an indication of the change probably shows the sailor has lost consciousness from shock and on awaking cannot at first understand what is happening.
8. A gesture of supplication.

Who brought you to this island of the sea,
with water on all sides?"
Then I answered this to him, my arms bent in front of him.
I said to him, "It's because I was going down
to the Mining Region on a mission of the sovereign,
in a boat 120 cubits long,
40 cubits broad,
in which there were 120 sailors from the choicest of Egypt.
They looked at the sea, they looked at the land,
and their hearts were stouter than lions'.

Before it came, they could foretell a gale,
a storm before it existed;
each one of them—his heart was stouter,
his arm stronger, than his fellow's.
There was no fool among them.
And a gale came up while we were at sea, before we had reached land.
The wind rose, and made an endless howling,
and with it a swell of eight cubits.
Only the mast broke it for me.
Then the boat died.
Those in it—not one of them survived, except me.
And look, I am beside you.

Then I was brought to this island
by a wave of the sea."
And he said to me, "Fear not,
fear not, young man!
Do not be pale, for you have reached me!
Look, God has let you live,[9]
and has brought you to this island of the spirit;[1]
there is nothing which is not within it,
and it is full of every good thing.
Look, you will spend month upon month,
until you have completed four months in the interior of this island.
A ship will come from home,
with sailors in it whom you know,
and you will return home with them,
and die in your city.

How happy is he who can tell of his experience, so that the calamity passes![2]
I shall tell you something similar,
that happened on this island,
where I was with my kinsmen,
and with children amongst them.

9. The "God" evoked could also be understood as "providence."
1. This may indicate that the island is imaginary.
2. This inverts a proverbial saying known in various cultures. For example, Dante wrote, "There is no greater pain than to recall a time of happiness when in misery." The idea leads the snake to tell his own tale.

With my offspring and my kinsmen, we were 75 serpents in all[3]—
I shall not evoke the little daughter,
whom I had wisely brought away.

Then a star fell,[4]
and because of it they went up in flames.
Now this happened when I wasn't with them;
they were burnt when I wasn't among them.
Then I died for them,[5] when I found them as a single heap of corpses.
If you are brave, master your heart,[6]
and you will fill your embrace with your children,
kiss your wife, and see your house!
This is better than anything.
You will reach home, and remain there,
amongst your kinsmen."
Stretched out prostrate was I,
and I touched the ground in front of him.

I said to him, "I shall tell your power to the sovereign.[7]
I shall cause him to comprehend your greatness.
I shall have them bring you laudanum and malabathrum,
terebinth and balsam,[8]
and the incense of the temple estates with which every God is content.
I shall tell what has happened to me, as what I have seen of
your power.
They will thank God for you in the city
before the council of the entire land.

I shall slaughter bulls for you as a burnt offering.
I shall strangle fowls for you.
I shall have boats brought for you
laden with all the wealth of Egypt,
as is done for a God who loves mankind,
in a far land, unknown to mankind."

Then he laughed at me, at the things I had said,
which were folly to his heart.
He said to me, "Do you have much myrrh,
or all existing types of incense?
For I am the ruler of Punt;[9]

3. This number alludes to the 74 forms of the Egyptian sun god, perhaps with the addition of the snake himself. The "little daughter" is probably Maat ("Order"), known elsewhere as the sun god's daughter.
4. A falling star is known in other Egyptian sources as a portent. Here it strikes the group directly and annihilates them. This is probably a metaphor for the end of the world.
5. An extreme expression of grief.
6. The snake points out the moral the sailer should take from the cataclysm that he survived.
7. A deferential reference to the king of Egypt that is typical for this period.
8. The aromatics mentioned were all imported into Egypt, typically from the southwest, that is, the direction of the island where the man is.
9. A region reached from the Red Sea, probably on the latitude of modern Eritrea, from which Egypt imported aromatics and other African products. Punt also had a semimythical character as "God's Land" (the identity of the "God" is left open).

myrrh is mine;
that malabathrum you speak of bringing
is this island's plenty.
And once it happens that you have left this place,
you will never see this island again, which will have become water."[1]

Then that boat came,
as he had foretold previously.
Then I went and put myself up a tall tree,
and I recognized those inside it.
Then I went to report this,
and I found that he knew it.
Then he said to me, "Fare well,
fare well, young man,
to your house, and see your children!
Spread my renown in your city! Look, this is my due from you."[2]

Then I prostrated myself,
my arms bent in front of him.
Then he gave me a cargo
of myrrh and malabathrum,
terebinth and balsam,
camphor, *shaasekh*-spice, and eye-paint,
tails of giraffes,
a great mound of incense,
elephant tusks,
hounds and monkeys,
apes and all good riches.[3]

Then I loaded this onto the ship,
and it was then that I prostrated myself to thank God for him.
Then he said to me, "Look, you will arrive
within two months!
You will fill your embrace with your children.
You will grow young again at home, and be buried."
Then I went down to the shore nearby this ship.
Then I called to the expedition which was in this ship,
and I on the shore gave praises
to the lord of this island,
and those who were aboard did the same.[4]

We then sailed northwards,
to the Residence of the sovereign,
and we reached home
in two months, exactly as he had said.

1. The island exists only for the man's encounter with the snake and will vanish thereafter.
2. The god's desire to be known in Egypt mirrors hymns that extol the qualities of deities.
3. This list names products mentioned earlier, as well as various others that Egypt obtained through trade. Not all of them can be identified with certainty.
4. The praise of the snake by the ship's crew parallels the thanks offered to God by the expedition at the beginning of the tale.

Then I entered before the sovereign,
and I presented him with this tribute
from the interior of this island.
Then he thanked God for me before the council of the entire land.
Then I was appointed as a Follower;
I was endowed with 200 persons.[5]
Look at me, after I have reached land, and have viewed my past experience!
Listen to my [speech]!
Look, it is good to listen to men.'
Then he said to me,[6] 'Don't act clever, my friend!
Who pours water [for] a goose,
when the day dawns for its slaughter on the morrow?'[7]
So it ends, from start to finish,[8]
as found in writing,
[as] a writing of the scribe with clever fingers,
Ameny son of Amenyaa (l.p.h.!).[9]

5. This gift of people would have made the narrator into a rich man.
6. The "me" is the sailor who has been the narrator all along, while "he" is the Count whom he has been addressing. The last three lines are the Count's response to the tale.
7. This appears to be a proverb, which may imply either that the narrator is the one preparing the Count for a bad reception from the king, or that it is pointless to console him with the example of his recovery from shipwreck when the Count has no future.
8. The text concludes with a short passage in red, known as a colophon, that gives an assurance of a good copy and the identity of the copyist.
9. "Life, prosperity, health!" is a wish appended typically to a king's name but also to that of a superior in a letter. In this case the scribe has been presumptuous, and perhaps humorous, by writing it after his own name.

SEMNA STELA OF SENWOSRET III

In ancient Egypt, military campaigns were an essential part of a successful king's role, ideally leading to an expansion of Egypt's frontiers. This inscription, from ca. 1830 B.C.E., commemorates such expansion and reflects on the duty of later generations to defend conquered territory. It is known from two copies, both carved on granite stelae—large round-topped stone slabs—that were set up in the fortresses of Uronarti and Semna, in today's northern Sudan. The king briefly recounts his achievements and praises his own valor, proceeding to denigrate his Nubian enemies and exhort his successors to stand firm on the frontier. The text is part royal display and part exhortation to the occupying force in the fortresses; set up in an accessible place near a statue of Senwosret III, the stela would have provided a permanent inspiration for fortress personnel to honor the king and fight against his enemies.

Semna Stela of Senwosret III[1]

Horus: Divine of Forms;[2]
Two Ladies: Divine of Manifestations;
Dual King: Khakaure given life;
Golden Horus: Being;
Re's Bodily Son, whom he loves,
the Lord of the Two Lands: Senwosret,
given life, stability, power for all time!
Year 16, month 3 of Peret:[3]
his Person's making the southern boundary at Semna.

I have made my boundary, out-southing my forefathers.
I have exceeded what was handed down to me.
I am a king, whose speaking is acting;
what happens by my hand is what my heart plans;
one who is aggressive to capture,
swift to success;
who sleeps not with a matter (still) in his heart;
who takes thought for dependants, and stands by mercy;
who is unmerciful to the enemy that attacks him;
who attacks when attacked,
and is quiet when it is quiet;
who responds to a matter as it happens.
For he who is quiet after attack,
he is making the enemy's heart strong.
Aggression is bravery;
retreat is vile.
He who is driven from his boundary is a true back-turner,
since the Nubian only has to hear to fall at a word:[4]
answering him makes him retreat.
One is aggressive to him and he shows his back;
retreat and he becomes aggressive.
Not people to be respected—
they are wretches, broken-hearted!
My Person has seen it—it is not an untruth;
for I have plundered their women, and carried off their underlings,
gone to their wells,[5] driven off their bulls,
torn up their corn, and put fire to it.
As my father lives for me,[6]

1. Translated by Richard B. Parkinson.
2. The first seven lines of the text give the standard five-part titulary of Egyptian kings. "Horus" identifies the king as performing a divine role; the "Two Ladies" are the protective goddesses of the Two Lands (Upper and Lower Egypt); "Dual King" evokes two principal aspects of kingship: "Khakaure" means "the one who appears with the vital force of Re (the sun god)"; and "Lord of the Two Lands" precedes the king's birth name.
3. Peret is the middle of the three four-month seasons in the Egyptian calendar.
4. This passage asserts that one needs only to confront the Nubians to defeat them, but the next one tells how the king has pursued a scorched-earth policy in their land.
5. The land of Upper Nubia, which Senwosret III states he has raided, is mostly desert, so that the inhabitants would rely on wells.
6. A standard form of oath, in which the oath taker swears by the life of a higher being. The king's "father" is a god, perhaps Amun, who is not named here.

I speak true;
here is no boastful phrase
which has come from my mouth.

Now, as for any son of mine who shall make firm this boundary
my Person made,
he is my son, born of my Person;
the son who vindicates his father is a model,
making firm the boundary of his begetter.[7]
Now as for him who shall neglect it, shall not fight for it—
no son of mine, not born to me!
Now my Person has caused an image of my Person to be made,[8]
upon this boundary which my Person made,
so that you shall be firm for it, so that you shall fight for it.

7. The "son" evoked in this stanza is any successor of Senwosret III, and probably the higher-ranking officers who served at the fortress as well. This line is a proverb that is also known from literary instructions in wisdom.

8. This passage alludes to the statue set up near the stela.

HERODOTUS

The Greek Herodotus (ca. 484–425 B.C.E.), who is known as the "father of history," can also be seen as one of the world's earliest anthropologists. Scholars debate whether Herodotus actually traveled to all the places he describes, which include Egypt, Persia, and India; some of his accounts may well be based on hearsay, or "oral history." But his *Histories* certainly show an intense interest in trying to understand the diverse cultures of non-Greek peoples, whom he calls "barbarians." He is eager to incorporate multiple points of view into his narrative, and to study the vast diversity of human *nomos*—the Greek word for "culture," "law," or "custom." Herodotus's *Histories* begin from the premise that Europe and Asia have been at war with each other since before the time of the Trojan War. His goal is to uncover the roots of the conflict, both by tracing historical causes and by evoking cultural differences between, specifically, the Greeks, the Persians, and the Egyptians. In his discussion of Egypt, he acknowledges the great antiquity of Egyptian culture, and the influence of Egyptian thought on Greek myth, theology, and astronomy. The Persians, who were for many years the military enemies of the Greeks, are presented as distinctly alien, but in some respects superior, to the Greeks: for instance, they value truthfulness, and Herodotus expresses his approval of their law that even a king cannot put a person to death on the basis of just one charge.

From Histories[1]

From *Book I*

This is the publication of the research of Herodotus of Halicarnassus,[2] so that the actions of people shall not fade with time, so that the great and admirable monuments produced by both Greeks and barbarians shall not go unrenowned, and, among other things, to set forth the reasons why they waged war on each other.

Persian storytellers say that the Phoenicians[3] were the cause of the dispute, for they came from the so-called Red Sea to our sea,[4] inhabited the territory they now live in, and immediately set forth on long voyages. They shipped Egyptian and Assyrian merchandise to various places and they made a point of going to Argos. At that time, Argos was preeminent among the towns in the country which is now called Greece. Now, when the Phoenicians came to Argos, they laid out their cargo. On the fifth or sixth day after they arrived, when almost everything had been sold off, a large number of women—including the king's daughter—came down to the seashore. Her name (and the Greeks also agree in this) was Io, the daughter of Inachus.[5] While the women stood at the stern of the boat, buying the goods that appealed to them, the Phoenicians urged each other on and rushed them. Most of the women ran away, but Io was captured, along with some others. The Phoenicians put them in the boat and sailed away, bound for Egypt.

Although the Greeks do not agree, that is how the Persians say Io came to Egypt; and this act was the beginning of the violations of law. After this, they say that some Greeks, whose names I am unable to give you, though they would probably have been from Crete, put into port at Phoenician Tyre and abducted Europa,[6] the daughter of the king. This, though, was just a case of an eye for an eye, so the next crime, which the Greeks committed, was really the second in the series.

The Greeks sailed in a long warship to Colchian Aea, on the river Phasis.[7] After taking care of the business they had come about, they abducted Medea, the daughter of the king.[8] The Colchian king sent a messenger to Greece asking for his daughter back and demanding damages for the kidnapping. The

1. Translated by Walter Blanco.
2. "Research" is a translation of the Greek term *historia*, which literally means "investigation." Halicarnassus is a Greek city in Asia Minor, on the coast of modern Turkey.
3. Ancient Phoenicia was a maritime society known for its prominence in trade, located along the coast of modern Israel, Lebanon, and Syria. The main Phoenician cities were Tyre and Sidon.
4. The Red Sea, for the Greeks, covered the whole Indian Ocean, including what we now call the Red Sea, as well as the Persian Gulf. "Our sea" is the Mediterranean.
5. In Greek mythology, the god Zeus seduced Io and changed her into a heifer, so that he could have an affair with her in bull form, without his wife Hera finding out. But Hera discovered the truth, and Io was forced to wander all over the world, finally escaping to Egypt, where she was restored to her human form. Herodotus assumes knowledge of this myth, but eliminates its fantastical elements.
6. Europa was a Phoenician girl, also abducted by Zeus when he was in the form of a bull. He carried her on his back to the island of Crete.
7. Colchis was the area south of the Caucasus Mountains, overlapping with modern Georgia; its river, the Phasis, is now called the Rion.
8. Medea helped the Greek hero Jason steal the Golden Fleece from her father, the king, and fled back to Corinth with him.

Greeks answered that since the Phoenicians had not given damages for the kidnapping of Io, the girl from Argos, they would not give anything, either.

They say that two generations after this event, Alexander,[9] the son of Priam, heard about it and hankered to abduct a Greek woman for himself, fully persuaded that he would not have to pay any penalty. After all, no one else had. After he kidnapped Helen, it seemed to the Greeks that the first thing to do was to send messengers asking for Helen back and demanding damages for the kidnapping. In the face of these demands, the Trojans brought up the kidnapping of Medea: the Greeks had given neither damages nor the girl when they had been asked, and now they wanted damages to be given to them by others!

So far, say the Persians, they had merely been stealing women from each other, but after this the Greeks were most greatly to blame because they began to lead armies into Asia before the Asians began to lead them into Europe. The Persians believe that raping women is the work of evil men, but that making a great to-do about vengeance after women have been raped is the work of fools. Prudent men are not concerned about women who have been raped, since it is perfectly plain that they could not be raped if they didn't really want to be.[1] The Persians say that they paid no attention to the abduction of their women from Asia, while the Greeks, for the sake of a Lacedaemonian woman, assembled a huge army and then invaded Asia and destroyed the power of Priam.[2] Because of this, the Persians have always considered the Greeks to be their enemies. You see, the Persians regard Asia and the barbarian people who live in it as their domain, while they think of Europe and the Greeks as separate.

That is how the Persians say it happened, and they trace the beginning of their hatred of the Greeks to the conquest of Troy. The Phoenicians, however, do not agree with the Persians about Io. They say that they did not have to resort to kidnapping to take her to Egypt, but that she had been having sex in Argos with the captain of the ship. When she found out that she was pregnant, she was so ashamed for the sake of her parents that she willingly sailed away with the Phoenicians to avoid discovery. That is what the Persians and the Phoenicians say.

I am not going to say that these events happened one way or the other. Rather, I will point out the man[3] who I know for a fact began the wrongdoing against the Greeks, and then proceed with my story while giving detailed accounts of cities both great and small. Many that were great in the past have become small, and many that used to be small have become great in my lifetime, so I will mention both alike because I know very well that human prosperity never remains in the same place.

* * *

These are the customs I know the Persians to observe. They are not allowed to build statues, temples, and altars, and in fact they accuse those who do of

9. Paris of Troy. The abduction of the Spartan king Menelaus's wife, Helen, by Paris (Alexander), started the Trojan War.

1. The translation "rape" is somewhat misleading. The word used here means "capture"; it is the same word translated in earlier paragraphs as "kidnap," and in the next sentence as "abduction."

2. The Lacedaemonian (Spartan) woman is Helen. The invasion referred to is the Trojan War.

3. Croesus, ruler of Lydia, a kingdom adjacent to Persia.

silliness, in my opinion because unlike the Greeks, they don't think of the gods as having human form. It is their custom to climb to the mountaintops and sacrifice to Zeus, which is the name they give to the full circle of the sky. They sacrifice to the sun and the moon and the earth, as well as to fire, water, and air. At first, they sacrificed only to these, but they later learned to sacrifice to the Heavenly Aphrodite—they learned this from the Assyrians and the Arabians. The Assyrians call Aphrodite Mylitta, the Arabians call her Alilat, and the Persians call her Mitra.

This is the way the Persians sacrifice to the above-mentioned gods: they make no altars and light no fires when they are about to sacrifice. They don't pour libations or play the flute or wear garlands or sprinkle barley on their victims. Whenever someone wants to sacrifice to one of the gods, he leads the victim to a ritually pure place and invokes the god while wearing his turban wreathed, preferably, with myrtle. It is not allowed for the sacrificer to pray, in private, for good things for himself. Instead, he prays for the well-being of all the Persians and of the king, for the sacrificer, after all, is included among all the Persians. When he has cut up the sacrificial victim into pieces and then boiled the meat, he spreads out the tenderest grass—preferably clover—and then places all of the meat on top of it. When he has arranged the meat piece by piece, a Magus stands near and chants a hymn on the origin of the gods—anyway, that's the kind of hymn they say it is. It is not their custom to perform a sacrifice without a Magus. The sacrificer waits a little while, then carries away the meat and does whatever he wants with it.

The day of all days they celebrate the most is their own birthday. On that day, the right thing to do is to serve a bigger meal than on any other day. On that day, their rich people serve up oxen, horses, camels, and donkeys that have been roasted whole in ovens, while their poor people serve smaller cattle, like sheep and goats. They eat few main dishes, but lots of appetizers, one after another, and for this reason the Persians say that the Greeks eat a main course and then stop when they are still hungry since after dinner nothing worth mentioning is brought out, though they wouldn't stop eating if it was. They love wine, but they are not allowed to vomit or to urinate in front of someone else. But though they have to be careful about that, they are accustomed to deliberate about their most important affairs when they are drunk, and then, on the next day, when they are sober, the master of the house they have been deliberating in proposes the decision that pleased them most. If they like it even when they are sober, they adopt it, but if not, they let it go. If they ever come to a provisional decision while sober, though, they then get drunk and reconsider it.

This is how you can tell if people who happen to meet each other on the street are social equals: instead of a verbal greeting, they kiss each other on the lips. If one is of slightly lower rank, they kiss each other's cheeks. If one is of a much lower rank, though, he prostrates himself and pays homage to the other. After themselves, Persians have the highest respect for the people who live closest to them, and next highest for those next closest, and so on. In accordance with this principle, they have the least respect for those who live farthest away. They consider themselves to be the best of people by far and others to share worth proportionally, so the people who live the farthest away are the worst. Subject nations ruled each other even under Median rule. That is, the

Medes[4] ruled over everything, but especially over those nearest to them, while those, in turn, ruled their neighbors, and so on. The Persians rank nations according to the same principle, by which each nation has a surrogate rule over the next one.

Nevertheless, the Persians are more inclined than other people to adopt foreign customs. For example, they wear Median[4] clothes in the belief that they are more attractive than their own, and they wear Egyptian breastplates into war. They seek out and learn about all kinds of delights, and they even learned from the Greeks to have sex with boys. Each Persian man has many lawfully wedded wives, but many more mistresses.

Second only to being brave in battle, a man is considered manly if he has many sons to show for himself, and every year the king sends gifts to the man who shows off the most sons. They believe that there is strength in numbers. They educate their sons from the age of five to the age of twenty in only three things: horseback riding, archery, and telling the truth. The boy does not come into the presence of his father until he is five years old—until then he lives with the women. This is done so that if he should die while he is growing up he won't cause any grief to his father.

I approve of that custom, and I also approve of the one that forbids even the king to put someone to death on the basis of only one charge, and that forbids any Persian to do any of his household slaves any irreparable harm on the basis of one charge either. If, however, he finds on review that there are more and greater offenses than services, then he may give way to anger.

They say that no one has yet killed his own father or mother. It is inevitable, they say, that any such child who has ever been born will be found on investigation to have been either a changeling or a bastard. They say that it just isn't likely that a true parent will be killed by his own child.

Whatever they are not allowed to do, they are also not allowed to talk about. They consider lying to be the most disgraceful of all things. After that, it is owing money—for many reasons, but mostly, they say, because it is necessary for somebody who owes money to tell lies.

No citizen who is an albino or who has leprosy is allowed into the city or to mingle with other Persians. They say that he has committed some offense against the sun. Foreigners who catch these diseases are driven out of the country by posses. Even white doves are driven out, charged with the same offense.

They don't spit, urinate, or wash their hands in rivers, or allow anyone else to, for they especially revere rivers.

The Persians don't notice it, though we do, but this also happens to be true of them: their names, which refer to their physical characteristics or to their social importance, all end in the same letter, which the Dorians call san and which the Ionians call sigma. If you look into it, you will find that Persian names end in this letter—not some here and some there, but *all* of them.

I am able to say these things with certainty because I know them for a fact. There are things about the dead, though, which are concealed or referred to obliquely—for example that the corpse of a Persian man is not buried until it has been torn at by a bird or a dog. I know for sure, though, that the Magi

4. A people who lived in modern-day northwestern Iran, next to ancient Persia.

practice this—because they do it openly—and that the Persians cover a corpse with wax before putting it in the ground. The Magi are very different from other people, including the Egyptian priests. The Egyptian priests refrain from killing any living thing, except what they ritually sacrifice. The Magi, however, will kill everything but dogs and people with their own hands. In fact, they make a point of killing things, and go around killing ants and snakes and anything else that creeps, crawls, and flies. Well, that's how they've been practicing this custom since the beginning, so let it stay that way.

From *Book II*

As to the Egyptians, before Psammetichus[1] became king, they assumed that they were the very first people who ever existed. But when Psammetichus came to the throne, he wanted to know for sure who the first were, and ever since Psammetichus the Egyptians believe that the Phrygians preceded them, whereas they precede everybody else. Since Psammetichus could not find out who came first by asking questions, he devised this experiment: he gave two children chosen from the common people to a shepherd to raise among his sheep. He commanded that no one should make any sound in their presence, but that they should be kept to themselves in a solitary pen and should be brought she-goats from time to time, have their fill of milk, and be otherwise provided for. Psammetichus devised this experiment and gave this order because he wanted to find out—apart from meaningless babble—just what word first broke from the children.

And that's just what happened. After two years had gone by, this is what happened to the shepherd as he followed his routine: when he opened the door and went in, both children fell down before him and reached out their hands, saying "baakos!" The first time he heard this, the shepherd kept quiet about it, but since he heard the word every time he went there to do his chores, he mentioned it to his master and, at his master's command, led the children into his presence. When Psammetichus heard them for himself, he asked which people called something "baakos," and found out that it was what the Phrygians called bread. Calculating on the basis of this experiment, the Egyptians conceded that the Phrygians were older than they. I heard that is the way it was from the priests of the temple of Hephaestus in Memphis. (The Greeks talk a lot of nonsense, such as that Psammetichus cut out the tongues of some women and arranged for the children to live among these women.)

This is what they said about the upbringing of the children, but I heard other things in Memphis when I went there to confer with the priests of Hephaestus. I even went to Thebes and to Heliopolis since I wanted to know whether they would agree with the stories that came out of Memphis, because the Heliopolitans are said to be the most learned of all Egyptians when it comes to stories.

Now, I am not eager to relate what I heard about religion in these stories, except only for the names of the gods, since I believe that all men know the same things about gods, whatever they call them. If I do mention anything, it will be a necessary part of the story I am telling.

1. Ruler of Egypt from 663 to 609 B.C.E.

As to human affairs, however, all the priests agree about this: the Egyptians were the first of all mankind to discover the year, dividing the seasons into the twelve parts which make it up. They said that they figured this out from the stars. It seems to me that they went about this more intelligently than the Greeks, because the Greeks insert a month every other year on account of the seasons, whereas the Egyptians make up twelve thirty-day months and add five days to that number every year so that the circle of the seasons will come around to the same place every time. In addition, the priests said that the Egyptians were the first to regularly call the gods by twelve names, and that the Greeks adopted this practice from them. Furthermore, they were the first to assign altars and statues and temples to the gods, and to chisel pictures into stone. They outright proved to me that most of these things were so, but they merely asserted that the first human to rule Egypt was called Min.

AESCHYLUS

Aeschylus's *Persians* (472 B.C.E.) is our only surviving Greek tragedy with a real historical setting: it describes the wars between Greece and Persia, in which Aeschylus himself had fought. The play is set, surprisingly, in the Persian court, and represents an attempt to describe the war, which the Greeks won, from the other side. The Messenger Speech, included here, evokes the climactic battle of Salamis, presenting the event as a tragic disaster for Persia. It is noticeable that while individual Persians are named and mourned as individuals, the Greeks are an undifferentiated mass. But it is also noteworthy that this supposedly Persian messenger presents the Greeks as fighters for freedom, one of whom cries out, "Forward you sons of Hellas! Set your country free!" The destruction of the Persian Empire is the glory of democratic Athens. The play was clearly successful with its Athenian audience: it won first prize in the dramatic competition when it was first performed.

From Persians[1]

ATOSSA[2] To those whose sons are with the army now, your words
Bring fearful thoughts.
CHORUS If I mistake not, you will soon

1. Translated by Philip Vellacott.
2. Queen of Persia, wife of the dead king Darius and mother of the current ruler, Xerxes.

Know the whole truth. That runner's undeniably
A Persian courier; good or bad, he'll bring us news.

Enter a MESSENGER.

MESSENGER O cities of wide Asia! O loved Persian earth,
Haven of ample wealth! One blow has overthrown
Your happy pride; the flower of all your youth is fallen.
To bring the first news of defeat's an evil fate;
Yet I must now unfold the whole disastrous truth:
Persians, our country's fleet and army are no more.

CHORUS O grief, and grief again!
Weep, every heart that hears,
This cruel, unlooked-for pain.

MESSENGER Yes; all that mighty armament is lost; and I
Still see the light, beyond all hope, and have come back.

CHORUS Why have we lived so long?
The harvest of ripe years
Is new grief, sudden tears.

MESSENGER Sirs, I was there; what I have told I saw myself;
I can recount each detail of the great defeat.

CHORUS Lament and weep! In vain
Went forth our army, strong
In arrows, sabres, spears,
To Hellas' holy soil.[3]

MESSENGER The shores of Salamis,[4] and all the neighbouring coasts,
Are strewn with bodies miserably done to death.

CHORUS Weep and lament! Our dead
Are made the ocean's spoil,
Tossed on its restless bed,
Their folded cloaks spread wide
Over the drowning tide.

MESSENGER Our bows and arrows were no help; there, overwhelmed
By crashing prows, we watched a nation sink and die.

CHORUS Lament with loud despair
The cruel and crushing fate
Of those whom the gods' hate
Condemned to perish there.

MESSENGER What name more hateful to our ears than Salamis?
Athens—a name of anguish in our memory!

CHORUS Most hateful name of all—
Athens! Who can forget
Our Persian women's debt—
Innocent tears that fall
For husband lost, or son,
Long since at Marathon?[5]

3. Greece.
4. An island near Athens, the location of the climactic naval battle between Greece and the invading Persian army, in 480 B.C.E.
5. In its first invasion of Greece, the Persian army, led by Xerxes' father, Darius, was defeated at Marathon in 490 B.C.E.

ATOSSA Good councillors, I have kept silence all this while
Stunned with misfortune; this news is too terrible
For narrative or question. Yet, being mortal, we
Must endure grief when the gods send it. Therefore stand
And tell the whole disaster, though your voice be choked
With tears. Who is not dead? And whom have we to mourn
Among our generals, whose post death leaves unmanned?
MESSENGER Xerxes the king lives.
ATOSSA Then the light of hope shines forth
Like white dawn after blackest darkness, for my house.
MESSENGER But Artembares, marshal of ten thousand horse,
Floats, bruised by the hard rocks of the Silenian shore.
A spear struck Dadaces, captain of a thousand men,
And with an airy leap he hurtled from his ship.
Tenagon, a true Bactrian born, first in their ranks,
Now haunts the sea-worn fringe of Ajax' island home.[6]
Three more, Lilaeus, Arsames, and Argestes,
Struck down, were seen eddying round the Isle of Doves,[7]
Butting the granite rocks. Metallus the Chrysean,
Who led ten thousand foot and thirty thousand horse,
Called the Black Cavalry—when he was killed, the hair
Of his thick shaggy yellow beard was dyed blood-red,
Dipped in the crimson sea. Magus the Arabian
Is dead; and Bactrian Artames has stayed abroad,
A settler in a rugged land; and Tharybis,
Captain of five times fifty ships, a Lyrnean born,
Is dead – his handsome face met an unhandsome end,
Poor wretch, unburied. Syennesis, the bravest man
In the whole army, leader of the Cilician troops,
Who with his single arm destroyed more enemies
Than any other, won great glory, and is dead.
Such is the roll of officers who met their fate;
Yet I have told but few of many thousand deaths.
ATOSSA Alas! Here is the very crown of misery;
For Persia, shame and loss and anguish of lament.
But come, retrace your story now, and tell me this:
What was the number of the Hellene ships, that they
Dared to assault our fleet, and charge them prow to prow?
MESSENGER Had Fortune favoured numbers, we would have won the day.
Three hundred vessels made the total Hellene strength,
Not counting ten picked warships. Xerxes had, I know,
A thousand in command, of which two hundred and seven
Were special fast ships. That was the proportion. Now,
Do you say we entered battle with too weak a force?
No. The result shows with what partial hands the gods

6. Salamis, supposedly the homeland of the Homeric hero Ajax.

7. Salamis.

Weighed down the scale against us, and destroyed us all.
It is the gods who keep Athene's city[8] safe.
ATOSSA What—safe? Is Athens then not ravaged after all?
MESSENGER While she has men, a city's bulwarks stand unmoved.
ATOSSA Now tell me how the two fleets fell to the attack.
Who first advanced, struck the first blow? Was it the Greeks,
Or my bold son, exultant with his countless ships?
MESSENGER Neither, my queen. Some Fury, some malignant Power,
Appeared, and set in train the whole disastrous rout.
A Hellene[9] from the Athenian army came and told
Your son Xerxes this tale: that, once the shades of night
Set in, the Hellenes would not stay, but leap on board,
And, by whatever secret route offered escape,
Row for their lives. When Xerxes heard this, with no thought
Of the man's guile, or of the jealousy of gods,
He sent this word to all his captains: 'When the sun
No longer flames to warm the earth, and darkness holds
The court of heaven, range the main body of our fleet
Threefold, to guard the outlets and the choppy straits.'
Then he sent other ships to row right round the isle,
Threatening that if the Hellene ships found a way through
To save themselves from death, he would cut off the head
Of every Persian captain. By these words he showed
How ignorance of the gods' intent had dazed his mind.

Our crews, then, in good order and obediently,
Were getting supper; then each oarsman looped his oar
To the smooth rowing-pin; and when the sun went down
And night came on, the rowers all embarked, and all
The heavy-armed soldiers; and from line to line they called,
Cheering each other on, rowing and keeping course
As they were ordered. All night long the captains kept
Their whole force cruising to and fro across the strait.
Now night was fading; still the Hellenes showed no sign
Of trying to sail out unnoticed; till at last
Over the earth shone the white horses of the day,
Filling the air with beauty. Then from the Hellene ships
Rose like a song of joy the piercing battle-cry,
And from the island crags echoed an answering shout.

The Persians knew their error; fear gripped every man.
They were no fugitives who sang that terrifying
Paean, but Hellenes charging with courageous hearts
To battle. The loud trumpet flamed along their ranks.
At once their frothy oars moved with a single pulse,

8. Athens, whose patron goddess is Athena. 9. Greek.

Beating the salt waves to the bo'suns' chant; and soon
Their whole fleet hove clear into view; their right wing first,
In precise order, next their whole array came on,
And at that instant a great shout beat on our ears:
'Forward, you sons of Hellas! Set your country free!
Set free your sons, your wives, tombs of your ancestors,
And temples of your gods. All is at stake: now fight!'
Then from our side in answer rose the manifold
Clamour of Persian voices; and the hour had come.

At once ship into ship battered its brazen beak.
A Hellene ship charged first, and chopped off the whole stern
Of a Phoenician galley. Then charge followed charge
On every side. At first by its huge impetus
Our fleet withstood them. But soon, in that narrow space,
Our ships were jammed in hundreds; none could help another.
They rammed each other with their prows of bronze; and some
Were stripped of every oar. Meanwhile the enemy
Came round us in a ring and charged. Our vessels heeled
Over; the sea was hidden, carpeted with wrecks
And dead men; all the shores and reefs were full of dead.

Then every ship we had broke rank and rowed for life.
The Hellenes seized fragments of wrecks and broken oars
And hacked and stabbed at our men swimming in the sea
As fishermen kill tunnies or some netted haul.
The whole sea was one din of shrieks and dying groans,
Till night and darkness hid the scene. If I should speak
For ten days and ten nights, I could not tell you all
That day's agony. But know this: never before
In one day died so vast a company of men.

ATOSSA Alas! How great an ocean of disaster has
Broken on Persia and on every eastern race!

MESSENGER But there is more, and worse; my story is not half told.
Be sure, what follows twice outweighs what went before.

ATOSSA What could be worse? What could our armament endure,
To outweigh all the sufferings already told?

MESSENGER The flower of Persian chivalry and gentle blood,
The youth and valour of our choice nobility,
First in unmoved devotion to the king himself,
Are sunk into the mire of ignominious death.

ATOSSA My friends, this evil news is more than I can bear.—
How do you say they died?

MESSENGER Opposite Salamis
There is an island—small, useless for anchorage—
Where Pan the Dancer treads along the briny shore.
There Xerxes sent them, so that, when the enemy.
Flung from their ships, were struggling to the island beach,
The Persian force might without trouble cut them down,

And rescue Persian crews from drowning in the sea:
Fatal misjudgement! When in the sea-battle Heaven
Had given glory to the Hellenes, that same day
They came, armed with bronze shields and spears, leapt from their ships,
And made a ring round the whole island, that our men
Could not tell where to turn. First came a shower of blows
From stones slung with the hand; then from the drawn bowstring
Arrows leapt forth to slaughter; finally, with one
Fierce roar the Hellenes rushed at them, and cut and carved
Their limbs like butchers, till the last poor wretch lay dead.

This depth of horror Xerxes saw; close to the sea
On a high hill he sat, where he could clearly watch
His whole force both by sea and land. He wailed aloud,
And tore his clothes, weeping; and instantly dismissed
His army, hastening them to a disordered flight.
This, then, brings you new grief to mingle with the first.

ATOSSA Oh, what malign Power so deceived our Persian hopes?
My son, marching to taste the sweetness of revenge
On Athens, found it bitter. Those who died before
At Marathon were not enough; Xerxes has won
For us not vengeance but a world of suffering.
But tell me now, what of those ships that have escaped?
Where did you leave them? Have you any certain news?

MESSENGER The captains of surviving ships spread sail and fled
In swift disorder with a following wind. On land
The remnants of the army suffered fearful loss,
Tortured by hunger, thirst, exhaustion. Some of us
Struggled at last to Phocis and the Melian Gulf,
Where cool Spercheius wanders through the thirsty plain.
We came next to Achaea; then to Thessaly,
Half dead for want of food; and there great numbers died
Of thirst and hunger, for we suffered both. From there
We reached Magnesia, Macedonia, and the ford
Across the river Axius, and the reedy marsh
Of Bolbe, and Mount Pangaeus in Edonia.
That night some god woke Winter long before his time;
And holy Strymon was frost-bound. Men who before
Were unbelievers, then fell on their knees in worship
Of earth and heaven; and from the whole army rose
Innumerable prayers. Then over the firm ice
They made their way. Those of us who began to cross
Before the sun had shed abroad his sacred beams
Were saved. But soon his rays shone out like piercing flames,
Melting the ice in mid-stream. Helplessly they slipped,
Men heaped on men, into the water. He who died
Quickest, was luckiest. The handful who survived,

Suffering untold hardship, struggled on through Thrace
To safety, and now at last have reached their native earth.

So, well may Persia's cities mourn their young men lost.
I have spoken truth; yet all I have told is but a part
Of all the evil God sent to strike Persia down.

CHORUS O fatal Spirit of Destruction, cruelly
You have attacked and trampled the whole Persian race.

ATOSSA Our army is destroyed and gone. O bitter grief!
O vivid dream that lit the darkness of my sleep,
How clearly you forewarned me of calamity!
And, Councillors, how lightly you interpreted!
Yet, since you counselled me to pray, I am resolved
First to invoke the heavenly gods; then in my house
To prepare meal and oil and honey, and return
And offer them as gifts to Earth and to the dead.
What's done, I know, is done; yet I will sacrifice
In hope that time may bring about some better fate.
You meanwhile must take counsel on our present loss
With other faithful Councillors; and if my son
Returns while I am absent, comfort him, and bring him
Safe to the house, lest his despair heap grief on grief.

Exit ATOSSA *with her attendants, and the* MESSENGER.

CHORUS Thy hand, O Zeus our king, has swept from sight
The boastful pride of Persia's vast array,
And veiled the streets of Susa
In gloomy mists of mourning.

AIRS, WATERS, PLACES

The author of the anonymous Greek Hippocratic text *Airs, Waters, Places* (late fifth century B.C.E.) provides a fascinating analysis of how national character might be affected by geographic and climatic conditions. The writer subscribes to some stereotypes about Asiatic peoples, but does try to understand cultural difference and struggles with the important question of how physical environment and culture might inform one another. The word "Hippocratic" means that the text is part of a set of Greek medical writings associated with the famous doctor Hippocrates (ca. 460–370 B.C.E.), though probably not actually by him.

From Airs, Waters, Places[1]

I now want to show how different in all respects are Asia and Europe, and why races are dissimilar, showing individual physical characteristics. It would take too long to discuss this subject in its entirety but I will take what seem to me to be the most important points of difference.

Asia differs very much from Europe in the nature of everything that grows there, vegetable or human. Everything grows much bigger and finer in Asia, and the nature of the land is tamer, while the character of the inhabitants is milder and less passionate. The reason for this is the equable blending of the climate, for it lies in the midst of the sunrise facing the dawn. It is thus removed from extremes of heat and cold. Luxuriance and ease of cultivation are to be found most often when there are no violent extremes, but when a temperate climate prevails. All parts of Asia are not alike, but that which is centrally placed between the hot and the cold parts is the most fertile and well wooded; it has the best weather and the best water, both rain water and water from springs. It is not too much burnt up by the heat nor desiccated by parching drought; it is neither racked by cold nor drenched by frequent rains from the south or by snow. Crops are likely to be large, both those which are from seed and those which the earth produces of her own accord. But as the fruits of the latter are eaten by man, they have cultivated them by transplanting. The cattle raised there are most likely to do well, being most prolific and best at rearing their young. Likewise, the men are well made, large and with good physique. They differ little among themselves in size and physical development. Such a land resembles the spring time in its character and the mildness of the climate.

So much for the differences of constitution between the inhabitants of Asia and of Europe. The small variations of climate to which the Asiatics are subject, extremes both of heat and cold being avoided, account for their mental flabbiness and cowardice as well. They are less warlike than Europeans and tamer of spirit, for they are not subject to those physical changes and the mental stimulation which sharpen tempers and induce recklessness and hot-headedness. Instead they live under unvarying conditions. Where there are always changes, men's minds are roused so that they cannot stagnate. Such things appear to me to be the cause of the feebleness of the Asiatic race, but a contributory cause lies in their customs; for the greater part is under monarchical rule. When men do not govern themselves and are not their own masters they do not worry so much about warlike exercises as about not appearing warlike, for they do not run the same risks. The subjects of a monarchy are compelled to fight and to suffer and die for their masters, far from their wives, their children and friends. Deeds of prowess and valour redound to the advantage and advancement of their masters, while their own reward is danger and death. Moreover, such men lose their high-spiritedness through unfamiliarity with war and through sloth, so that even if a man be born brave and of stout heart, his character is ruined

1. Translated by G. E. R. Lloyd.

by this form of government. A good proof of this is that the most warlike men in Asia, whether Greeks or barbarians, are those who are not subject races but rule themselves and labour on their own behalf. Running risks only for themselves, they reap for themselves the rewards of bravery or the penalties of cowardice. You will also find that the Asiatics differ greatly among themselves, some being better and some worse. This follows from the variations of climate to which they are subject, as I explained before.

* * *

The remaining peoples of Europe differ widely among themselves both in size and appearance owing to the great and frequent climatic changes to which they are subject. Hot summers and hard winters, heavy rains followed by long periods of drought, all these occasion variations of every kind. It is reasonable that these changes should affect reproduction by variations in the coagulability of the semen so that its nature is different in summer and winter, in rainy weather and times of drought. I believe this to be the reason for the greater variation among individuals of the European races, even among the inhabitants of a single city, than is seen among Asiatics and also why they vary so much in size. When the weather changes often, abnormalities in the coagulation of the semen are more frequent than when the weather is constant. A variable climate produces a nature which is coupled with a fierce, hot-headed and discordant temperament, for frequent fears cause a fierce attitude of mind whereas quietness and calm dull the wits. Indeed, this is the reason why the inhabitants of Europe are more courageous than those of Asia. Conditions which change little lead to easy-going ways; variations to distress of body and mind. Calm and an easy-going way of living increase cowardice; distress and pain increase courage. That is one reason for the more warlike nature of Europeans. But another cause lies in their customs. They are not subjects of a monarchy as the Asiatics are and, as I have said before, men who are ruled by princes are the most cowardly. Their souls are enslaved and they are unwilling to risk their own lives for another's aggrandisement. On the other hand, those who govern themselves will willingly take risks because they do it for themselves. They are eager and willing to face even the worst of fates when theirs are the rewards of victory. It is clear, then, that the tradition of rule has no small influence on the courage of a people.

In general it may be said that these are the differences between Europe and Asia. There exist in Europe, then, people differing among themselves in size, appearance and courage, and the factors controlling those differences are those I have described. Let me summarize this plainly. When a race lives in a rough mountainous country, at a high elevation, and well watered, where great differences of climate accompany the various seasons, there the people will be of large physique, well-accustomed to hardihood and bravery, and with no small degree of fierceness and wildness in their character. On the other hand, in low-lying, stifling lands, full of meadows, getting a larger share of warm than cold winds, and where the water is warm, the people will be neither large nor slight, but rather broad in build, fleshy and black-haired. Their complexions are dark rather than fair and they are phlegmatic rather than bilious. Bravery and hardihood are not an integral part of their natural characters although these traits can be created by training. The people of a country where rivers drain the surface water and rain water have clear complexions and good health. But where there are no rivers and the drinking water is taken from lakes or marshes, the people will necessarily be more pot-bellied and splenetic. People who live in countries which are high, level, windswept and rainy tend to be of large stature and to show little variation among themselves. They are also of a less courageous and less wild disposition. In countries where there is a light waterless soil devoid of trees and where the seasons occasion but small changes in climate, the people usually have hard sinewy bodies, they are fair rather than dark and they are strong-willed and headstrong in temperament. Places where changes of weather are most frequent and of the greatest degree show the greatest individual differences in physique, temperament and disposition among the inhabitants.

The chief controlling factors, then, are the variability of the weather, the type of country and the sort of water which is drunk. You will find, as a general rule, that the constitutions and the habits of a people follow the nature of the land where they live. Where the soil is rich, soft and well-watered and where surface water is drunk, which is warm in summer and cold in winter, and where the seasons are favourable, you will find the people fleshy, their joints obscured, and they have watery constitutions. Such people are incapable of great effort. In addition, such a people are, for the most part, cowards. They are easy-going and sleepy, clumsy craftsmen and never keen or delicate. But if the land is bare, waterless and rough, swept by the winter gales and burnt by the summer sun, you will find there a people hard and spare, their joints showing, sinewy and hairy. They are by nature keen and fond of work, they are wakeful, headstrong and self-willed and inclined to fierceness rather than tame. They are keener at their crafts, more intelligent and better warriors. Other living things in such a land show a similar nature. These, then, are the most radically opposed types of character and physique. If you draw your deductions according to these principles, you will not go wrong.

HORACE

This ode by the Roman poet Horace (65–8 B.C.E.) deals with the defeat of the Roman general Antony and the Egyptian queen Cleopatra by Octavian (who would later become Augustus, the first Roman emperor). Horace makes use of a long tradition of Greek and Roman writers diminishing, and dismissing, their eastern, "barbarian" opponents, in order to justify Greco-Roman supremacy. In doing so, he covers up the fact that the battle in question was actually part of a civil war.

Ode 1.37[1]

Nunc est bibendum

Now we must drink, now we must
beat the earth with unfettered feet, now,
my friends, is the time to load the couches
of the gods with Salian feasts.[2]

Before this it was a sin to take the Caecuban[3]
down from its ancient racks, while the mad queen[4]
with her contaminated flock of men
diseased by vice was preparing

the ruin of the Capitol[5] and the destruction
of our power, crazed with hope
unlimited and drunk
with sweet fortune. But her madness

decreased when scarce a ship escaped the flames
and her mind, deranged by Mareotic wine,[6]
was made to face real fears
as she flew from Italy, and Caesar[7]

pressed on the oars (like a hawk
after gentle doves or a swift hunter
after a hare on the snowy plains
of Thrace) to put in chains

this monster sent by fate. But she looked
for a nobler death. She did not have a woman's fear
of the sword, nor did she make
for secret shores with her swift fleet.

Daring to gaze with face serene upon her ruined palace,
and brave enough to take deadly serpents
in her hand, and let her body
drink their black poison,

fiercer she was in the death she chose, as though
she did not wish to cease to be a queen, taken to Rome
on the galleys of savage Liburnians,[8]
to be a humble woman in a proud triumph.

1. Translated by David West. This poem has no title; West has used the first words of the Latin original as a title ("Now we must drink").
2. The Salii, priests of the war god Mars, were known for their energetic leaping, dancing, and feasting at their yearly festival, in March.
3. A type of wine.
4. Cleopatra, queen of Egypt, who aided her lover, the Roman general Antony, in his struggle against Octavian (later Augustus) in the last of the Roman civil wars. The poem celebrates Octavian's victory at Actium, in 31 B.C.E.
5. Hill in Rome, location of important Roman temples and center of Roman power.
6. A type of sweet wine.
7. Octavian.
8. Octavian used ships modeled on those of Liburnian pirates.

SENECA

Epistle 47 by the Roman philosopher Seneca (ca. 4 B.C.E.–65 C.E.), tutor to the emperor Nero, is a reminder of the brutality that many owners inflicted on their slaves. Seneca himself argues for a different approach: the slaveholder should insist on treating slaves "humanely," if only so that he can maintain his own psychological stability.

Epistle 47[1]

I'm glad to hear, from these people who've been visiting you,[2] that you live on friendly terms with your slaves. It is just what one expects of an enlightened, cultivated person like yourself. 'They're slaves,' people say. No. They're human beings. 'They're slaves.' But they share the same roof as ourselves. 'They're slaves.' No, they're friends, humble friends. 'They're slaves.' Strictly speaking they're our fellow-slaves, if you once reflect that fortune has as much power over us as over them.

This is why I laugh at those people who think it degrading for a man to eat with his slave. Why do they think it degrading? Only because the most arrogant of conventions has decreed that the master of the house be surrounded at his dinner by a crowd of slaves, who have to stand around while he eats more than he can hold, loading an already distended belly in his monstrous greed until it proves incapable any longer of performing the function of a belly, at which point he expends more effort in vomiting everything up than he did in forcing it down. And all this time the poor slaves are forbidden to move their lips to speak, let alone to eat. The slightest murmur is checked with a stick; not even accidental sounds like a cough, or a sneeze, or a hiccup are let off a beating. All night long they go on standing about, dumb and hungry, paying grievously for any interruption.

The result is that slaves who cannot talk before his face talk about him behind his back. The slaves of former days, however, whose mouths were not sealed up like this, who were able to make conversation not only in the presence of their master but actually with him, were ready to bare their necks to the executioner for him, to divert on to themselves any danger that threatened him; they talked at dinner but under torture they kept their mouths shut. It is just this high-handed treatment which is responsible for the frequently heard saying, 'You've as many enemies as you've slaves.' They are not our enemies when we acquire them; we make them so.

1. Translated by Robin Campbell.
2. Seneca's letters are addressed to a friend called Lucilius.

For the moment I pass over other instances of our harsh and inhuman behaviour, the way we abuse them as if they were beasts of burden instead of human beings, the way for example, from the time we take our places on the dinner couches, one of them mops up the spittle and another stationed at the foot of the couch collects up the 'leavings' of the drunken diners. Another carves the costly game birds, slicing off choice pieces from the breast and rump with the unerring strokes of a trained hand—unhappy man, to exist for the one and only purpose of carving a fat bird in the proper style—although the person who learns the technique from sheer necessity is not quite so much to be pitied as the person who gives demonstrations of it for pleasure's sake. Another, the one who serves the wine, is got up like a girl and engaged in a struggle with his years; he cannot get away from his boyhood, but is dragged back to it all the time; although he already has the figure of a soldier, he is kept free of hair by having it rubbed away or pulled out by the roots. His sleepless night is divided between his master's drunkenness and sexual pleasures, boy at the table, man in the bedroom. Another, who has the privilege of rating each guest's character, has to go on standing where he is, poor fellow, and watch to see whose powers of flattery and absence of restraint in appetite or speech are to secure them an invitation for the following day. Add to these the caterers with their highly developed knowledge of their master's palate, the men who know the flavours that will sharpen his appetite, know what will appeal to his eyes, what novelties can tempt his stomach when it is becoming queasy, what dishes he will push aside with the eventual coming of sheer satiety, what he will have a craving for on that particular day.

These are the people with whom a master cannot tolerate the thought of taking his dinner, assuming that to sit down at the same table with one of his slaves would seriously impair his dignity. 'The very idea!' he says. Yet have a look at the number of masters he has from the ranks of these very slaves.[3] Take Callistus' one-time master. I saw him once actually standing waiting at Callistus' door and refused admission while others were going inside, the very master who had attached a price-ticket to the man and put him up for sale along with other rejects from his household staff. There's a slave who has paid his master back—one who was pushed into the first lot, too, the batch on which the auctioneer is merely trying out his voice! Now it was the slave's turn to strike his master off his list, to decide that *he*'s not the sort of person he wants in *his* house. Callistus' master sold him, yes, and look how much it cost him!

How about reflecting that the person you call your slave traces his origin back to the same stock as yourself, has the same good sky above him, breathes as you do, lives as you do, dies as you do? It is as easy for you to see in him a free-born man as for him to see a slave in you. Remember the Varus disaster: many a man of the most distinguished ancestry, who was doing his military service as the first step on the road to a seat in the Senate, was brought low by fortune, condemned by her to look after a steading, for example, or a flock of sheep. Now think contemptuously of these people's lot in life, in whose very place, for all your contempt, you could suddenly find yourself.

3. Roman society allowed increasing numbers of slaves to gain their freedom and rise to high social positions.

I don't want to involve myself in an endless topic of debate by discussing the treatment of slaves, towards whom we Romans are exceptionally arrogant, harsh and insulting. But the essence of the advice I'd like to give is this: treat your inferiors in the way in which you would like to be treated by your own superiors. And whenever it strikes you how much power you have over your slave, let it also strike you that your own master has just as much power over you. 'I haven't got a master,' you say. You're young yet; there's always the chance that you'll have one. Have you forgotten the age at which Hecuba became a slave, or Croesus, or the mother of Darius, or Plato, or Diogenes?[4] Be kind and courteous in your dealings with a slave; bring him into your discussions and conversations and your company generally. And if at this point all those people who have been spoilt by luxury raise an outcry protesting, as they will, 'There couldn't be anything more degrading, anything more disgraceful,' let me just say that these are the very persons I will catch on occasion kissing the hand of someone else's slave.

Don't you notice, too, how our ancestors took away all odium from the master's position and all that seemed insulting or degrading in the lot of the slave by calling the master 'father of the household' and speaking of the slaves as 'members of the household' (something which survives to this day in the mime)? They instituted, too, a holiday on which master and slave were to eat together, not as the only day this could happen, of course, but as one on which it was always to happen. And in the household they allowed the slaves to hold official positions and to exercise some jurisdiction in it; in fact they regarded the household as a miniature republic.

'Do you mean to say,' comes the retort, 'that I'm to have each and every one of my slaves sitting at the table with me?' Not at all, any more than you're to invite to it everybody who isn't a slave. You're quite mistaken, though, if you imagine that I'd bar from the table certain slaves on the grounds of the relatively menial or dirty nature of their work—that muleteer, for example, or that cowhand. I propose to value them according to their character, not their jobs. Each man has a character of his own choosing; it is chance or fate that decides his choice of job. Have some of them dine with you because they deserve it, others in order to make them so deserving. For if there's anything typical of the slave about them as a result of the low company they're used to living in, it will be rubbed off through association with men of better breeding.

You needn't, my dear Lucilius, look for friends only in the City or the Senate; if you keep your eyes open, you'll find them in your own home. Good material often lies idle for want of someone to make use of it; just give it a trial. A man who examines the saddle and bridle and not the animal itself when he is out to buy a horse is a fool; similarly, only an absolute fool values a man according to his clothes, or according to his social position, which after all is only something that we wear like clothing.

4. All famous slaves. Hecuba, queen of Troy and wife of Priam, was enslaved when the Greeks captured the city. Croesus was the famously rich king of Lydia, who was eventually defeated and captured by Cyrus of Persia. Darius was emperor of Persia, who conducted an unsuccessful expedition against Greece. Plato, the philosopher, was about forty when he visited Sicily; he was deported by the tyrant of the country and sold into slavery. Diogenes, also a philosopher, was captured by pirates and enslaved.

'He's a slave.' But he may have the spirit of a free man. 'He's a slave.' But is that really to count against him? Show me a man who isn't a slave; one is a slave to sex, another to money, another to ambition; all are slaves to hope or fear. I could show you a man who has been a Consul who is a slave to his 'little old woman,' a millionaire who is the slave of a little girl in domestic service. I could show you some highly aristocratic young men who are utter slaves to stage artistes. And there's no state of slavery more disgraceful than one which is self-imposed. So you needn't allow yourself to be deterred by the snobbish people I've been talking about from showing good humour towards your slaves instead of adopting an attitude of arrogant superiority towards them. Have them respect you rather than fear you.

Here, just because I've said they 'should respect a master rather than fear him,' someone will tell us that I'm now inviting slaves to proclaim their freedom and bringing about their employers' overthrow. 'Are slaves to pay their "respects" like dependent followers or early morning callers? That's what he means, I suppose.' Anyone saying this forgets that what is enough for a god, in the shape of worship, cannot be too little for a master. To be really respected is to be loved; and love and fear will not mix. That's why I think you're absolutely right in not wishing to be feared by your slaves, and in confining your lashings to verbal ones; as instruments of correction, beatings are for animals only. Besides, what annoys us does not necessarily do us any harm; but we masters are apt to be robbed of our senses by mere passing fancies, to the point where our anger is called out by anything which fails to answer to our will. We assume the mental attitudes of tyrants. For they too forget their own strength and the helplessness of others and grow white-hot with fury as if they had received an injury, when all the time they are quite immune from any such danger through the sheer exaltedness of their position. Nor indeed are they unaware of this; but it does not stop them seizing an opportunity of finding fault with an inferior and maltreating him for it; they receive an injury by way of excuse to do one themselves.

But I won't keep you any longer; you don't need exhortation. It is a mark of a good way of life that, among other things, it satisfies and abides; bad behaviour, constantly changing, not for the better, simply into different forms, has none of this stability.

CATULLUS

ca. 84–ca. 54 B.C.E.

The poetry of Gaius Valerius Catullus conveys intense, and often conflicting, emotions. *Odi et amo*, he wrote: "I hate and love." These poems evoke the personal desires and enmities of a privileged but insecure and very young man: Catullus was only about thirty when he died. Reading Catullus, we feel in touch with raw feelings in a way that is rare in the literature of the ancient world. Catullus was also a technical master, who wrote in an impressive range of different verse patterns, and whose moods range from joy to grief, from vituperative obscenities to gentle teasing, and from self-pity to quiet nostalgia for lost and easier days. The pain, passion, lyricism, and humor in his poetry was a lasting inspiration for later love poets, both in ancient Rome and in modern times.

LIFE AND TIMES

Catullus was born in the northern Italian city of Verona, into a prominent aristocratic family (of the high social class called "equestrian"). He spent most of his life in Rome, making close friends and bitter enemies among his fellow Roman aristocrats. Perhaps he had an intense love affair (or several), which inspired the "Lesbia" poems. He does not seem to have married. Traditionally, Lesbia has been identified with Clodia Metella, an aristocratic, educated woman, whom Cicero cast as a sexual predator, a husband killer, and a drunk. But we have no contemporary evidence for the identification, and, of course, poets do not always base their love poems on real life. The name *Lesbia* is obviously designed to evoke literature as much as life: it alludes to the Greek poet **Sappho**, of Lesbos, who, like Catullus, wrote about the conflicting pains and pleasures of bittersweet love.

We know that in his late twenties, Catullus held a position in government that involved a trip to Bithynia, in Asia Minor; en route, he stopped at his brother's tomb, as he describes in a beautiful poem of quiet grief and farewell (poem 101). At some point after he returned to Rome, he died; we do not know the cause.

Catullus lived out his short life in the last century of the Roman Republic. It was a time of conflict, especially between populist and aristocratic factions in Rome. Catullus lived to see the rise of the populist general Julius Caesar, who won extensive victories in Britain and Gaul, although he died before Caesar was assassinated (44 B.C.E.). Catullus sometimes satirizes Caesar, and flaunts his lack of interest in Caesar's activities: "I've no great urge to find favor with you, Caesar," he declares (poem 93). Catullus can be read as a deliberately antipolitical writer, who forms a novel and personal interpretation of conventional Roman public virtues. Masculinity, for Catullus, is defined not by military exploits like Caesar's but by sexual prowess and emotional control; even duty (*pietas* in Latin) is redefined, applied to Catullus's love for his treacherous girlfriend. Catullus makes use of the values and norms of his society, but often turns them on their head.

POEMS

One hundred sixteen poems of Catullus survive, collected in a little book or "pamphlet." We do not know whether the arrangement as we have it represents Catullus's own authorial wishes. The poems are arranged by meter, not by subject, so that, for instance, the Lesbia poems do not all appear together. They are richly varied, including imitations of Greek poets, long poems on Greek mythological themes, personal and often obscene attacks on contemporaries ("Up yours and sucks!" one begins), lyrical celebrations of places and seasons, comic verse, and original love poems—some addressed to a woman named Lesbia, and a few to other love objects, such as the boy Juventius ("Youth").

The Lesbia poems are the most famous of Catullus's work. These poems present all the phases of a love affair, and their tone ranges from joy to torment to the depths of self-pity and back. Their direct and simple language seems to give readers immediate access to the experience of desire and betrayal and the feelings it arouses. Yet these are not diary entries but complex literary artefacts: it is one of the remarkable characteristics of Catullus's poetry that strong emotion and technical sophistication are not at odds with each other. Poem 51, for example, powerfully describes the physical symptoms of love in the speaker; but it is also a translation into Latin of one of Sappho's most passionate Greek lyrics, which achieves the feat of also imitating Sappho's rhythms in Latin.

Catullus is a highly self-conscious poet who achieves a dynamic dialogue with his readers. The first poem of the collection asks, What kind of reader does Catullus want for his work? And will the reader be worthy of the poet's trust? How are we to interpret what we hear? Catullus often puts his readers in a tempting but awkward position, as if they were eavesdropping on a private conversation—either between Catullus and another person, or between Catullus and himself. In poem 83, for example, when Lesbia seems to abuse Catullus in the presence of her husband, the speaker interprets this as a sign of love for himself to which the husband is obtusely oblivious. But we may also wonder whether this is a wishful interpretation. Who really is the dupe? The reader never gets access to Lesbia's feelings; instead, the poems present the speaker himself constantly struggling to understand the mixed signals in their changing relationship. The poet subjects his own persona to deep and sometimes damaging analysis: we see his defensive constructions and deconstructions of his own masculine identity, and his unresolved tensions and self-deceptions. In the brilliant poem 8, for example, a dialogue the speaker has with himself at the time of a break-up, he resolves, over and over, to "hang tough," to be a man and get over his beloved; but the reader, overhearing, is aware of how far he is from the goal.

One of the major themes that runs through much of Catullus's work is the vast distance between one era and another, one moment and the next, as well as between one person and another, or even between the same person at different times. The Lesbia poems celebrate moments of connection, which can be violently ruptured by betrayal—like the flower brutally cut down in its prime by a plough that never notices its existence (poem 11). Even in the best of times, the joys of connectedness can be fragile, and may depend on delicate threads—a mortal sparrow, a finite number of kisses: the beautiful celebration of arrival and homecoming, poem 31, emphasizes that this place of relaxation and joy is a "near-island," almost cut off from the mainland. Spring, in the lovely poem 46, is a time of "lush green meadows," but also a time for friends to say goodbye. The longest poem included here, poem 64, is a celebration of the marriage of Thetis and Peleus, the parents of Achilles. On one level, the subject allows Catullus to challenge the writers of epic, to reinterpret the themes of the *Iliad* from an original angle: it is an "epyllion," a mini-epic. On another, the poem is a joyful and sometimes funny celebration of a magical wedding at sea. But this poem also has surprisingly dark elements: the story embroidered on the comforter to be used on the marriage bed depicts a scene of betrayal, of the Greek hero Theseus abandoning his bride, Ariadne, and leaving her crying alone on the island of Naxos. At a time when Rome was expanding into an enormous empire, but when internal factions threatened to destroy the city's stability, the poems of Catullus express a deep awareness of how quickly, and with what devastating consequences, everything can change.

Poems[1]

1

Who's the dedicatee of my new witty
booklet, all fresh-polished with abrasive?[2]
You, Cornelius: for you always used to
feel my trivia possessed some substance,
even when you dared—the lone Italian!—
that great three-decker treatment of past ages:[3]
scholarly stuff, my god, and *so* exhaustive!
So take this little booklet, this mere trifle,
whatever it may be worth—and Patron Virgin,[4]
let it outlast at least *one* generation!

2

Sparrow, precious darling of my sweetheart,
always her plaything, held fast in her bosom,

1. Translated by Peter Green. Note that the translator has tried to reproduce the meters of the Latin, such as Catullus's most characteristic meter, the hendecasyllable (an eleven-syllable line).
2. This "booklet" of poems would have been a papyrus scroll, its ends rubbed smooth with pumice stone.
3. Cornelius Nepos, a Roman biographical writer and a friend of Catullus, apparently wrote a three-volume history of the world, from the beginning of time to the present, called the *Chronica* ("Times"). He was the "lone Italian" to have done so, because up to that point Romans had only written more limited histories of particular periods.
4. The Muse.

whom she loves to provoke with outstretched finger
tempting the little pecker[5] to nip harder
when *my* incandescent longing fancies
just a smidgin of fun and games and comfort
for the pain she's feeling (I believe it!),
something to lighten that too-heavy ardor—
how I wish I could sport with you as she does,
bring some relief to the spirit's black depression!

3

Mourn, Cupids all, every Venus,[6] and whatever
company still exists of caring people:
Sparrow lies dead, my own true sweetheart's sparrow,
Sparrow, the pet and darling of my sweetheart,
loved by her more than she valued her own eyesight.
Sweet as honey he was, and knew his mistress
no less closely than a child her mother;
nor from her warm lap's safety would he ever
venture far, but hopping this and that way
came back, cheeping, always to his lady.
Now he's travelling on that dark-shroud journey
whence, they tell us, none of the departed
ever returns. The hell with you, you evil
blackness of Hell, devouring all that's lovely—
such a beautiful sparrow you've torn from me!
Oh wicked deed! Oh wretched little sparrow!
It's your fault that now my sweetheart's eyelids
are sore and swollen red from all her weeping.

5

Let's live, Lesbia[7] mine, and love—and as for
scandal, all the gossip, old men's strictures,
value the lot at no more than a farthing!
Suns can rise and set ad infinitum—
for us, though, once our brief life's quenched, there's only
one unending night that's left to sleep through.
Give me a thousand kisses, then a hundred,
then a thousand more, a second hundred,
then yet another thousand then a hundred—
then when we've notched up all these many thousands,
shuffle the figures, lose count of the total,
so no maleficent enemy can hex us
knowing the final sum of all our kisses.

5. The translator's double entendre is deliberate; many scholars interpret the sparrow in phallic terms.
6. Cupid (the Greek Eros, god of desire) and his mother, Venus (the Greek Aphrodite, goddess of sex), usually exist only in the singular.
7. The name *Lesbia* alludes to the poet Sappho, who lived on the island of Lesbos.

7

You'd like to know how many of your kisses
would be enough and over, Lesbia, fór me?
Match them to every grain of Libyan sand in
silphium-rich[8] Cyrene, from the shrine of
torrid oracular Jupiter to the sacred
sepulchre of old Battus; reckon their total
equal to all those stars that in the silent
night look down on the stolen loves of mortals.
That's the number of times I need to kiss you,
That's what would satisfy your mad Catullus—
far too many for the curious to figure,
or for an evil tongue to work you mischief!

8

Wretched Catullus, stop this stupid tomfool stuff
and what you see has perished treat as lost for good.
Time was, every day for you the sun shone bright,
when you scurried off wherever *she* led *you*—
that girl you loved as no one shall again be loved.
There, when so many charming pleasures all went on,
things that *you* wanted, things *she* didn't quite turn down,
then for you truly every day the sun shone bright.
Now she's said *No*, so you too, feeble wretch, say *No*.
Don't chase reluctance, don't embrace a sad-sack life—
make up your mind, be stubborn, obdurate, hang tough!
So goodbye, sweetheart. Now Catullus *will* hang tough,
won't ask, "Where is she?" won't, since you've said *No*, beg, plead.
You'll soon be sorry, when you get these pleas no more—
bitch, wicked bitch, poor wretch, what life awaits *you* now?
Who'll now pursue you, still admire you for your looks?
Whom will you love now? Who will ever call you theirs?
Who'll get your kisses? Whose lips will you bite in play?
You, though, Catullus, keep your mind made up, *hang tough!*

11

Furius and Aurelius,[9] comrades of Catullus,
whether he'll penetrate the distant Indies[1]
where the shore's slammed by far-resounding Eastern
    thunderous breakers,

or make for Hyrcania, or the queening Arabs,
or the Sacae, or the Parthians with their quivers,

8. Silphium is an extinct plant known as giant fennel, which was used for cooking and medicine.

9. Marcus Furius Bibaculus was a poet, and Marcus Aurelius Cotta Maximus Messalinus was a politician; they seem to have been personal enemies of Catullus, so "comrades" is ironic. They have apparently tried to tag along with Catullus on his travels, in the hope of personal profit by association with Caesar.

1. India. The poem goes on to list the most distant parts of the Roman Empire at the time.

or that flat delta to which the seven-channelled
    Nile gives its color,

or toil across high-towering Alpine passes
to visit the monuments of mighty Caesar,[2]
the Gaulish Rhine, those rude back-of-beyonders
    the woad-dyed Britons—

All this, or whatever the high gods in heaven
may bring, you're both ready to face together;
just find my girl, deliver her this short and
    blunt little message:

Long may she live and flourish with her gallants,
embracing all three hundred in one session,
loving none truly, yet cracking each one's loins
    over and over.

Let her no more, as once, look for my passion,
which through her fault lies fallen like some flower
at the field's edge, after the passing ploughshare's
    cut a path through it.

16

Up yours both, and sucks to the pair of you,[3]
Queen Aurelius, Furius the faggot,[4]
who dared judge *me* on the basis of my verses—
they mayn't be manly: does that make *me* indecent?
Squeaky-clean, that's what every proper poet's
person should be, but not his bloody squiblets,
which, in the last resort, lack salt and flavor
if *not* "unmanly" and rather less than decent,
just the ticket to work a furious itch up,
I won't say in boys, but in those hirsute
clods incapable of wiggling their hard haunches.
Just because you've read about my countless
thousand kisses, you think I'm less than virile?
Up yours both, and sucks to the pair of you!

31

Of all near-islands, Sirmio,[5] and of islands
the jewel, of every sort that in pellucid
lakes or vast ocean fresh or salt Neptune bears—

2. Julius Caesar, who campaigned in Gaul and Britain.
3. This is, if anything, a fairly restrained translation. The Latin literally means, "I will fuck your asses and fuck your faces."
4. The politician and poet who were addressed in poem 11.
5. A promontary on Lake Garda, in Northern Italy.

how gladly, with what joy I now cast eyes
on you once more, can't believe I've left those flat,
endless Bithynian plains,[6] can see your safe haven.
What greater bliss than when, cares all dissolved,
the mind lays down its burden, and, exhausted
by our foreign labors we at last reach home
and sink into the bed we've so long yearned for?
This, this alone makes all our toil worthwhile.
Greetings, sweet Sirmio, and rejoice, your master's
here: and rejoice, you too, you lakeside ripples,
and all you joys of home, break out in laughter.

42

Come, you hendecasyllables, in force now,
each last one of you, from every quarter—
this vile slut seems under the impression
I'm a walking joke, won't give me back my
writing tablets—really, can you beat it?
Let's go after her, call for their surrender!
Which one is she, you ask? The one you see there,
her with the vulgar stride, the quite revolting
stage-door laugh, the face like a French poodle's.
Close in round her now, demand in chorus:
"Rotten slut, give back the writing tablets!
Give back, rotten slut, the writing tablets!"
Not one farthing she cares, the filthy scrubber
(fill in any nastier name you think of).
Still, don't let's make this our final effort—
even though we can't do more, let's raise a
burning blush on the bitch's brazen face, so
all shout one more time, and even louder,
"Rotten slut, give back the writing tablets!
Give back, rotten slut, the writing tablets!"
Still this gets us nowhere, she remains un-
moved, you'll need to change your tune and method.
Try this, then, see if it gets you further:
"Pure chaste maid, give back the writing tablets!"

46

Now spring fetches back the warmth, and winter's
chills die out; now raging equinoctial
storms are hushed by the west wind's pleasant breezes.
Leave these Phrygian plains, Catullus, leave the
lush green meadows of summer-hot Nicaea:[7]
let's decamp, move to Asia's famous cities.

6. Catullus had to go to the Roman province of Bithynia, in Asia Minor, as a civil servant.
7. Refers to Catullus's stay in the province of Bithynia (whose capital was Nicaea), as an underling of the provincial governor.

Now my heart's in a tizzy, yearns for action,
now my feet jitter, eager to be going—
so goodbye to my band of pleasant colleagues:
though we made the long trip from home together,
widely varying routes will take us back now.

48

Oh those honey-sweet eyes of yours, Juventius![8]
If they'd let me kiss them all I wanted
I'd go on three hundred thousand times, and
never feel I was getting near my limit,
even though our crop of osculations
ended tighter-packed than dried-out wheat ears.

51[9]

In my eyes he seems like a god's co-equal,
he, if I dare say so, eclipses godhead,
who now face to face, uninterrupted,
  watches and hears you

sweetly laughing—*that* sunders unhappy me from
all my senses: the instant I catch sight of
you now, Lesbia, dumbness grips my voice, it
  dies on my vocal

cords, my tongue goes torpid, and through my body
thin fire lances down, my ears are ringing
with their own thunder, while night curtains both my
  eyes into darkness.

Leisure, Catullus, is dangerous to you: leisure
urges you into extravagant behavior:
leisure in time gone by has ruined kings and
  prosperous cities.

58

Caelius,[1] Lesbia—*our* dear Lesbia, *that* one,
that Lesbia whom alone Catullus worshipped
more than himself, far more than all his kinsfolk—
now on backstreet corners and down alleys
jacks off Remus's generous descendants.[2]

8. A boyfriend: the name suggests youth.
9. This poem is a translation or adaptation of Sappho's poem 31. The last stanza corresponds to nothing in the original.
1. Marcus Caelius Rufus was a Roman politician who seems to have had an affair with Clodia, the woman on whom Lesbia may have been based.
2. Remus and his brother Romulus were the first builders of Rome. Romulus killed Remus.

64[3]

Once on a time pine trees from Pelion's summit
are said to have swum through Neptune's crystal ripples
to the breakers of Phasis and Aeëtes' territory,
when chosen young men, the strong core of Argive manhood,
eager to filch that gilded hide from the Colchians,
dared in their swift vessel to traverse the briny shoals,
sweeping blue, deep-sea vistas with their blades of fir-wood.[4]
For them the goddess whose realm's in high citadels[5]
herself made the craft that flew with the gentlest breeze,
conjoining pine-wood strakes to the curve of its hull—
the hull that was first to handsel those untouched waters.
And the moment its prow sheared through their wind-whipped surface,
and waves glistened spume white from the twist of the oar blades,
wild shy faces emerged from the foaming eddies,
deepwater Nereïds,[6] in wonder at this portent.
That was the day, never matched, when mere mortals witnessed
marine nymphs rising up from the dappled sea surge,
mother-naked to breasts and below. It was then that Peleus—
so goes the story—burned up with love for Thetis,
then that Thetis did not reject a human marriage,
then that the Father[7] himself felt Peleus and Thetis should wed.
O born in those days most missed through later ages,
you heroes, hail, gods' scions! noble offspring
of noble women, all hail! I shall have occasion
to invoke you often in the course of my poem,
and you first and foremost, so blest by beatitude's torches,
bulwark of Thessaly, Peleus, to whom Jove himself, no less,
himself, though Sire of the Gods, resigned his loved one.
Did Thetis, most lovely of Nereïds, then embrace you?
Did Tethys permit you to wed her granddaughter,
and Ocean, who rings the whole globe with his waters?[8]
When in due course this most eagerly awaited
wedding day dawns, guests from every distant quarter
of Thessaly throng the house, the palace is crowded
with a rejoicing multitude. All bear gifts, their faces
beam pleasure. Scyros is empty, they've deserted Phthiotic
Tempe, the houses of Crannon, the ramparts of Lárissa,
converging on Phársalus, packing Pharsalian rooftops.
Fieldwork's abandoned, draught oxen's necks get flabby,
no curved rake clears the weeds from the low-set ground vines,
no teams now split the sod with deep-thrusting ploughshares,

3. This is a narrative poem in epic meter (hexameter); the genre, known as *epyllion* ("little epic"), was popular in third-century Alexandria. Catullus here takes us back to a time in the distant mythological past, to the marriage of Achilles' parents, the human hero Peleus and the sea goddess Thetis.

4. Refers to the first-ever sea voyage, when the Argonauts from Greece crossed the ocean (ruled by the god Neptune) in search of the Golden Fleece, in Colchis, ruled by King Aeetes.

5. Athena, who supposedly made the ship, the Argo.

6. Sea nymphs.

7. Jupiter.

8. Tethys and Ocean are the oldest god and goddess of the sea, grandparents of Thetis.

no pruning hook lessens the shade of leaf-thick trees, while
the ploughs, deserted, are scarved with rust's scaly tetter.
But Peleus' seat, for the whole of its opulent rearward
length is a shining delight of gold and silver,
gleaming ivory thrones, cups glinting on their tables,
the entire house glittering proudly with royal treasure,
and there at its heart is set the goddess's own bridal
couch, all smoothly inlaid with Indian ivory,
its purple drapery dipped in the mollusc's blushing dye.

This coverlet, decorated with antique human figures,
portrays in marvelous art the brave deeds of heroes.
There, gazing out from Dia's surf-loud shoreline,[9]
eyes fixed on Theseus as he and his swift vessels
dwindle away to nothing, with uncontrollable passion
filling her heart, not yet able to credit the witness
of her own eyes, roused that moment from treacherous slumber,
Ariadne finds herself left on the lonely strand, poor creature,
while her heedless young lover vanishes, oar strokes flailing
the shallows, scattering broken promises galewards.
Him from afar, there on the wrack-strewn beach, eyes
agonized, Minos' daughter, a stony bacchant,[1] watches,
ah, watches, in breaking waves of grief unbounded,
lost the fine-woven net from her golden tresses,
lost the light garment veiling her torso, lost the
rounded breast-band that gathered her milk white bosom—
all of them, slipped from her body every which way, now
at her feet had become the salty ripples' playthings.
But at this moment neither net nor floating garment
were noticed by her: she with her whole heart, Theseus,
whole mind, whole spirit, was concentrated on *you*.
Ah wretched creature, in whose breast She of Eryx[2] planted
such thorny cares, whom She crazed with never-ending sorrows
from the day and hour when Theseus, that bold gallant,
setting forth from the curving shoreline of Piraeus[3]
arrived at the Cretan palace of that unjust monarch.
For long ago, the tale goes, in thrall to a pestilential
cruel demand for atonement after Androgeos' murder,
the city of Cecrops would send the pick of her young men,
the flower of her maidens, as a feast for the Minotaur.[4]

9. The Athenian hero Theseus met the princess Ariadne, daughter of Minos, on Crete, and she helped him defeat the monstrous Minotaur. He took her away with him, but then abandoned her on the way home, while she was napping on the beach. The abandoned Ariadne, waking up disheveled to discover her lover's ship departing, was a popular subject in ancient art. Bacchus (Dionysus) then rescued her, and her crown became a constellation. Ariadne was usually said to have been abandoned on the island of Naxos. Dia may be an alternative name for Naxos, or Catullus may be following an alternative tradition.

1. Bacchants are female worshippers of the wine god, Bacchus, usually imagined as frenzied in some way.

2. Venus.

3. Port in Athens.

4. In the myth, Crete demanded from Athens (the City of Cecrops) a yearly tribute of young boys and girls to be fed to the Minotaur. Theseus traveled to Crete himself to stop the slaughter.

With this evil hanging heavy over her narrow ramparts,
Theseus chose, for the sake of the Athens he loved, to
expose his own body rather than suffer these dead,
these living dead, to be shipped to Crete like cattle.
So trusting to his light vessel and following breezes
he came to haughty Minos and his palatial abode.
Him, the instant that with eyes of desire the royal
virgin spied him, though still confined to a single
sweet-scented bed and her mother's soft embraces,
like myrtle brought forth by the waters of Eurotas
or the dappled colors that vernal breezes conjure,
she did not lower her smoldering gaze from him till
through the length of her body the flame was kindled
deep at the core, and blazed up in her inmost marrow.
Ah, wretchedly stirring wild passions, ruthless at heart,
Sacred Boy, you who mingle joy with sorrow for mortals,
and you, Lady, ruler of Golgi and leaf-thick Idalium,[5]
on what rough surges you tossed that girl, mind flaring,
as over and over she sighed for the blond stranger:
what looming terrors with heavy heart she suffered,
how often she turned paler than gold's bright splendor
when Theseus, hot to contend with the savage monster,
courted either death or the rewards of glory!
Yet the giftlets she offered the gods, the vows she pledged
with silent lips—these were not in vain, not unpleasing.
For as on the peaks of Taurus, branches thrashing,
an oak or coniferous pine with gum-sweating cortex
has its strength wrenched round by a twister's all-powerful
blast, is torn up roots and all, crashes prostrate
all its great length, smashes everything in a wide swathe,
so Theseus brought down the monster, mastered its body
as it butted its horns in vain against airy emptiness,
then walked back out unhurt, in a cloud of glory, guiding
his fallible footsteps with that one slender thread, lest
during his emergence from the Labyrinth's windings
its deceptively mazed confusion should frustrate his purpose.
But why should I digress still further from my major
theme by relating how this daughter put behind her
her father's face, her consanguineous sister's
embraces, a mother lost in grief for her wretched offspring,
opting above all these for Theseus' sweet sweet love?
Or how aboard his vessel she came to Dia's surf-creamed
beaches, or how there he left her, eyes slumber-weighted,
to take himself off and vanish, a fickle-hearted husband?
Often (they tell us) heart burning, wild with passion,
she'd pour forth shrill cries fetched up from her innermost breast,
and then in her misery would scramble up steep mountains
from where she could see further across the sea's vast motion;

5. Cupid and Venus, who inspire desire.

then, again, would rush into the briny's toppling breakers,
light skirt hitched up, exposing her naked thighs,
and in the abyss of her sorrow heaving cold little sobs,
face streaked with tears, would cry: "Is *this* the way, then,
that—after taking me far from my ancestral altars—
you leave me on this lonely beach, perfidious, Theseus?
Is *this* how you vanish, the gods' will all neglected?
in blank indifference to divinity's own ruling
as you carelessly carry homeward your damnable perjuries?
Was there nothing that could deflect your cruel mind's
set purpose? Had you no compassion on hand
to nudge your hard heart into feeling pity for me?
These aren't the smooth-spoken promises you once made me,
this was not what you led my poor heart to expect,
but rather wedded bliss, the marriage I so yearned for—
all of which the intangible winds are shredding, making void.
Henceforth let no woman trust a man's sworn promise,
or hope that he'll ever be true to his given word,
for as long as his lustful heart is bent on possession
he'll shrink from no oath, stop short at no promises,
but the moment the urge of his ardent mind is sated
he forgets all he's said, breaks oaths without a tremor.
The truth is, when you were spinning in death's vortex
I pulled you clear, chose rather to lose a brother
than to fail you, you liar, when your need was greatest:
and in return I'll be left as a carcass for kites and jackals
to tear asunder, I'll get no proper burial. What
lioness was it whelped you under some lonely rock, what
sea conceived you, spat you up in the breakers' spume,
what Syrtes, what ravening Scylla, what bleak Charybdis,[6]
that you should make such return for your precious life?
If you failed to find marriage with me to your proper liking
through dread of an old-style father's merciless precepts,
you still could have brought me to your ancestral home,
to be your slave, to serve you with adoration,
washing your white-soled feet in crystal water, or
spreading and dressing your bed with a purple coverlet.
Oh, why do I uselessly plead to the indifferent breezes,
grief-stricken though I am? Being unendowed with senses
they can neither hear nor answer the words I utter—
while *he* by now has made nearly half his voyage,
and there's no other mortal in sight here on this lonely
wrack-strewn beach. That's cruel Fortune for you:
when we're down she kicks us, grudges hearers for our complaints.
Almighty Jove, how I wish in those early days no
Cecropian vessels had beached on Cnossos' strand,[7]
nor, bearing ghastly tribute for a bull yet unmastered,

6. All dangers of the ocean. Syrtes were quicksands; Scylla was a sea monster; Charybdis was a whirlpool.

7. Cnossos is in Crete, Ariadne's homeland. "Cecropian": Athenian.

had that perfidious sailor ever thrown hawser out on
a Cretan quayside, or evilly masking his cruel purpose
with a sweet show, had stayed as guest in our house, for
where now can I turn? I'm undone, I have no recourse.
Should I make for the mountains of Ida? There's a wide gulf lying
between, and the waters of a rough sea passage
divide us. Can I look for my father's help, when I left him
to follow a young man stained with the blood of my brother?
Can I solace myself with a faithful husband's love when
he's running away from me, urging tough oars through the water?
On top of which there's not one single house on this lonely
island, it's ringed by breakers, offers no loophole.
There's no way of escape, no hope, and, everywhere, silence:
everywhere's emptiness, everything signals death.
Yet my eyes shall not fade and grow still in dissolution,
nor the senses secede from my exhausted body,
till I've petitioned the gods for a befitting forfeit
for this betrayal, in my last hours have prayed that heaven
will keep faith. So, you whose vengeful exactions
answer men's crimes, you Furies whose snake-wreathed brows
announce the wrath gusting up from your secret hearts, I
summon you here to me now: give ear to the complaints
which I in my misery am forced to dredge up from the inmost
core of my being—helpless, burning, blinded
by mindless frenzy. But since they're the true products
of my private heart, don't let my grief all go for nothing:
rather in just such a mood as Theseus abandoned me
to my lonely fate, let him, goddesses, now doom both himself and his!"
After she'd poured out this speech from her grief-stricken heart,
desperately seeking requital for such heartless treatment,
the Celestial Ruler[8] nodded in final and absolute
assent, and at that gesture both earth and turbulent
ocean shook, and the firmament quaked with its glittering stars.
But Theseus himself, his mind a seedbed of blind darkness,
with forgetful heart let slip all the various commandments
that up to that moment he'd constantly kept in mind,
failed to hoist the happy signal for his grieving father
that would show he'd come safely in sight of Erechtheus' harbor.[9]
For when Aegeus, they say, was entrusting to the winds his
son and his son's fleet on departure from Athens's ramparts,
he embraced the young man and gave him these instructions:
"My only son, dearer to me than long life, my son
whom I'm forced to send forth to a perilous destiny,
though but lately restored to me in my extreme old age:
since my ill luck and your most fervid valor
now against my will take you from me—my dim old eyes
have not yet had their fill of my son's dear features—

8. Jupiter.
9. In Athens; Erechtheus was a legendary king of Athens. Aegeus was Theseus's father, the king of Athens.

I shall not send you forth gladly, with a rejoicing heart,
nor allow you to carry the signs of a fortunate destiny,
but shall first express my many heartfelt complaints,
fouling my old white hairs with handfuls of earth and dust,
and then hang your wanderer's mast with black-dyed sailcloth,
so that our grief and burning resentment of mind
may be declared by canvas darkened with Spanish rust.
But if She who dwells in sacred Itónus, the bestower
of security on our race and the seat of Erechtheus,[1]
should grant you to stain your right hand with bull's blood, then
take good care that your heart lays up and remembers
these commands of mine; keep them fresh, let time not erase them.
The instant your eyes catch sight of our hilly coastline,
let the yardarms lower all their funereal canvas
and the braided sheets haul up white sails as replacements
to let me know for certain, as early as may be,
bringing joy to my heart, the bright lot of your safe return."
These precepts, hitherto kept most constantly in mind,
now, like clouds whipped away from some snowy mountain top
by the gale's blast, abandoned Theseus. But his father,
scanning the horizon from the acropolis' summit,
anxious eyes worn out with constant weeping,
no sooner had glimpsed the canvas of the bellying sail
than he flung himself headlong from the height of the rock face,
believing Theseus destroyed by an unrelenting fate.
Thus when he entered the house now in mourning for his father's
death, haughty Theseus was himself faced with such grief
as by his thoughtless mind he'd left for Minos' daughter—
who, gazing in sorrow after his vanishing vessel,
and wounded at heart, now pondered a mass of troubles.

But in another quarter young Iacchus[2] went winging by
with his band of Satyrs and Nysa-bred Sileni,
searching for you, Ariadne, for you aflame with passion.
All about him with frenzied mind spun the crazy maenads,[3]
screaming "*euhoe, euhoe*," heads jerking madly,
some of them brandishing thyrsi with sheathed tips,
some tossing around the limbs of a dismembered
bullock, some decking themselves with writhing serpents,
others at secret rituals with hollow caskets—
rituals which the profane desire in vain to share.
Some again with flattened palms were beating on drumheads
or drawing thin rattle and clash from the rounded bronze.
Many were blowing horns, a raucous booming clamor,
while barbarous pipes skirled out their ghastly themes.

1. Athena, patron goddess of Athens, who had a shrine in the Boeotian city of Itonus.

2. Bacchus (Dionysus, god of wine and revelry). The Satyrs and Sileni, his companions, are half goat, half man.

3. Maenads ("madwomen") were inspired female followers of Bacchus. They traditionally chanted *euhoe euhoe*, carried sticks made of fennel twined with ivy (the *thyrsus*), and tore animals apart with their bare hands.

Such were the figures most amply adorning the coverlet
that lay the whole width of the couch, veiled and encompassed it.
So after Thessaly's youth had satisfied their eager
urge to inspect it, they now stood aside for the sacred gods.
Here, just as a calm sea's riffed by the matutinal
breath of the west wind, that catches the curling ripples
as dawn comes up at the threshold of the vagrant sun,
so that slowly at first, impelled by the gentle breeze,
they advance, to break with laughter's light plangency,
but then, as the wind increases, swell, swell in volume
and surging afar reflect the reddish sunlight,
so, pouring forth from the portals of the royal palace,
the crowd now scattered, each to his own abode.
Then, when they all were gone, there arrived, first, Chiron,[4]
from Pelion's ridges, bearing gifts of the forest:
for whatever flowers Thessaly grows, in the plain or on lofty
mountains, or beside the river's rippling passage,
nurtured by the west wind's warm and fecund breath,
all these he brought, in individual arrangements,
and the house laughed, happy in their fragrant perfume.
Next came Penios,[5] setting out from verdant Tempe,
Tempe enclosed above by overhanging woodlands,
the haunt of Haemonian dryads who dance in their honor;[6]
nor was he giftless, for he came bearing tall, uprooted
beeches and stately laurels, straight in the stem,
together with nodding plane trees, and the lithe poplar
sisters of cindered Phaëthon,[7] and tall airy
cypresses. These he set, all widely interwoven,
about the palace, to make a soft green leafy archway
for its portals. There followed him fox-hearted Prometheus,[8]
bearing the scars, now faded, of that ancient punishment
he once endured, limbs stapled to flint by metal shackles,
suspended over the void from a dizzying precipice.
Then the Father of Gods with his holy wife[9] and children
arrived from heaven, leaving you only, Phoebus,[1]
along with your sibling, haunter of Idrus' mountains,
since you and your sister both equally scorned Peleus
and would not attend the wedding of him and Thetis.
When the guests had settled themselves on the white-backed seating
the tables were piled high with an array of dishes;

4. A centaur (half man, half horse), who would be the tutor of Achilles.
5. God of the Peníos River.
6. Tempe is an area in Thessaly (Haemonia); dryads are tree nymphs.
7. Phaëthon, son of Helios (the sun god), begged his father to let him drive his chariot across the sky; he lost control of the reins and got burnt to a cinder. In their grief, his sisters were turned to poplar trees.
8. The Titan Prometheus stole fire from heaven, and was punished by being chained to a rock, to have his liver pecked out daily by wild birds.
9. Jupiter and his wife Juno.
1. Apollo; his sister is Diana, the huntress goddess. Apollo supported Troy, the city that Achilles would help to destroy, and caused Achilles' death by guiding Paris's arrow to his heel.

and meanwhile, old bodies prey to infirmity's tremors,
the trio of Fates began their prophetic chanting.
Each wore a long white robe that enfolded her tremulous
frame and fell to her ankles, purple-bordered; the three
had bandeaux of roses on their snow-white heads,
while their hands were properly busy with their unending labor,
the left gripping the distaff, all shrouded in soft wool,
while the right, first, teased out the threads with upturned
fingers and formed them, then twisting with down-turned thumb
spun the spindle, balanced on its rounded whorl,
while constantly with their teeth they nibbled and smoothed the work,
and to their thin lips nipped-off wool tufts adhered
which before were excrescences on the even thread line,
while before their feet the soft fleeces of bright white wool
were stored in little baskets of woven osier.
They now, still carding their fleeces, in clear articulate tones
poured forth in god-inspired song these prophecies—
a song no future age would accuse of falsehood.
"O you who augment high achievement with great virtues,
Emathia's safeguard, most dear to the son of Ops,[2]
accept what the Sisters reveal for you on this auspicious
day, a true oracle. But you which the fates follow,
run, drawing the weft out, run, you spindles!
Soon, soon there will come for you, granting all bridegrooms' longings,
Hesperus:[3] that beneficent star will be accompanied
by the partner who'll steep your awareness in mind-bending love
and be eager to share with you the sleep of exhaustion,
smooth arms pillowed beneath your sturdy neck.
Run, drawing the weft out, run, you spindles!
No house has ever embodied such a passion,
no love has ever joined lovers in such a compact,
as is the concord uniting Thetis and Peleus.
Run, drawing the weft out, run, you spindles!
There shall be born to you the fearless Achilles,
known to his foes not by back but by valiant front, who,
time and again victorious in the long-range footrace,
will outstrip the flame-swift tracks of the fleeting roebuck.
Run, drawing the weft out, run, you spindles!
Not one hero exists who'll be his equal in warfare
when the plains of Phrygia run with Teucrian blood
and in that long, long war and siege, Troy's ramparts
shall fall to the third in line from perjured Pelops.[4]

2. Ops, wife of Saturn, was the Roman goddess of plenty. Her son is Jupiter. Emathia is Thessaly. The addressee here is Peleus.
3. The evening star (the planet Venus).
4. Phrygia was the area in which the city of Troy was situated; the Teucrians are the Trojans. Agamemnon, leader of the Greek forces against Troy, is the grandson of Pelops, who is "perjured" because he bribed a charioteer to loosen a wheel of King Oenomaüs's chariot, so that Pelops could win the race and the hand of Hippodamia, the king's daughter; but after Pelops won the race, he refused to pay up and instead killed the charioteer.

Run, drawing the weft out, run, you spindles!
His virtues preeminent and most noble deeds
mothers shall ofttimes confess at their own sons' obsequies,
letting fall loose unkempt locks from their old white crowns
and with weak hands beating tattoo on their withered breasts.
Run, drawing the weft out, run, you spindles!
Just as a reaper, culling close-packed wheat ears
under a burning sun harvests the umber fields,
so with fierce steel shall he lay low his Trojans.
Run. drawing the weft out, run, you spindles!
Witness to his great virtues shall be Scamander's water,[5]
discharging every way in the swift Hellespont.
He'll choke its flow with piles of slaughtered bodies,
warm its deep channel with that slaughter's blood.
Run, drawing the weft out, run, you spindles!
Final witness shall be his recompense even in death
when stacked in a lofty barrow his rounded sepulchre
receives the snow-white limbs of a slaughtered virgin.[6]
Run, drawing the weft out, run, you spindles!
For as soon as Fortune grants the exhausted Achaeans
the means to loose Neptune's bonds from that Dardanian city,[7]
his high tomb will be drenched with the blood of Polyxena,
and she, like a victim undone by the two-edged steel,
shall slump down there, knees folding, a headless body.
Run, drawing the weft out, run, you spindles!
Come, therefore, unite the loves your hearts have longed for,
let your consort accept the goddess in happy compact,
and the bride be given at last to her ardent bridegroom.
Run, drawing the weft out, run, you spindles!
Her nurse, revisiting her tomorrow at sunrise,
won't be able to circle her neck with yesterday's ribbon,
nor shall her anxious mother, saddened by her cross daughter's
bedding apart, fail to hope for dear grandchildren."
Run, drawing the weft out, run, you spindles!
Predicting, far in the past, such blessings for Peleus
did the Fates from divine breast thus utter their chants, since
in those days, when pious belief was not yet held in scorn,
Heaven's denizens used to visit the chaste dwellings
of heroes in person, show themselves at mortals' meetings.
Often the Father of Gods, there in his gleaming temple,
when his annual feast day came round, with its sacred rites,
would watch while a hundred bulls were poleaxed for him.
Often wandering Bacchus from Parnassus' peaks would
drive his howling maenads, loose hair flying,

5. Scamander was a river in Troy, filled with dead bodies by Achilles.

6. Polyxena, youngest daughter of Priam, king of Troy, was sacrificed on the tomb of Achilles.

7. Troy. "Achaeans": Greeks. Neptune (Poseidon) was a divine enemy of Troy.

while the people of Delphi, all leaving town together,
would joyously welcome the god with smoking altars.
Often, too, during war's deadly struggle, Mavors
or speedy Triton's Lady or the Virgin of Amarynthus[8]
would be there to cheer on mere mortals' armed battalions.
But after Earth was imbued with unspeakable wrongdoing
and all sent justice packing from their covetous thoughts,
brothers now drenched their hands with the blood of brothers,
sons ceased to lament their parents' demise, a father
would hope for the premature death of his son, thus being
free himself to enjoy the bloom of son's teenage bride,
while an impious mother, couched supine under her ignorant son
did not let her impiety scruple to outrage the household's
domestic gods. By confusing good and bad in an evil frenzy
we alienated the gods' once-tolerant understanding,
which is why they neither deign to be present at such meetings
nor let themselves be exposed to open daylight.

70

My woman declares there's no one she'd sooner marry
than me, not even were Jove himself to propose.
She declares—but a woman's words to her eager lover
should be written on running water, on the wind.

72

You told me once, Lesbia, that Catullus alone understood you,
That you wouldn't choose to clasp Jupiter rather than me.
I loved you then, not just as the common herd their women,
but as a father loves his sons and sons-in-law.
Now, though, I *know* you. So yes, though I burn more fiercely,
yet for me you're far cheaper, lighter. "How,"
you ask, "can that be?" It's because such injury forces
a lover to love more, but to cherish less.

75

My mind has been brought so low by your conduct, Lesbia,
and so undone itself through its own goodwill
that now if you were perfect it couldn't like you,
nor cease to love you now, whatever you did.

8. Mavors is Mars (Ares), god of war. Triton's Lady is the goddess Athena. The Virgin of Amarynthus is the goddess Artemis, who had a sanctuary at Amarynthus.

76

If a man derives pleasure from recalling his acts of kindness,
from the thought that he's kept good faith,
never broken his sworn word, nor in any agreement
exploited the gods' favor to deceive
mortals, then many delights still wait for you, Catullus,
through the long years, from this most thankless love;
for whatever generous things men can say or do to
their fellows, these you have both said and done.
Yet the sum of them, entrusted to an ungrateful spirit,
is lost. Then why torment yourself any more?
Why not make a firm resolve, regain your freedom,
reject this misery that the gods themselves oppose?
It's hard to abruptly shrug off love long established:
hard, but this, somehow, you must do.
Here lies your only hope, you must win this struggle:
this, possible or not, must be your goal.
O gods, if it's in you to pity, or if you've ever rendered
help at the last to those on the verge of death,
look down on my misery, and if I've lived life cleanly,
pluck out of me this destruction, this plague,
which, creeping torpor-like into my inmost being
has emptied my heart of joy.
I no longer ask that she should return my love, or—
an impossibility—agree to be chaste.
What I long for is health, to cast off this unclean sickness.
O gods, if I have kept faith, please grant me this!

83

Lesbia keeps insulting me in her husband's presence:
this fills the fatuous idiot with delight.
Mule, you've no insight. If she shut up and ignored me
that'd show healthy indifference; all these insults mean
is, she not only remembers, but—words of sharper import—
feels angry. That is, the lady burns—and talks.

85

I hate and love. You wonder, perhaps, why I'd do that?
I have no idea. I just feel it. I am crucified.

92

Lesbia's always bad-mouthing me, never stops talking of me.
That means Lesbia loves me, or I'll be damned.
What proves it? I'm just the same still—praying nonstop
to lose her. But *I* love *her* still. Or I'll be damned.

93

I've no great urge to find favor with you, Caesar, nor to
discover whether, as man, you're black or white.

101

A journey across many seas and through many nations
has brought me here, brother, for these poor obsequies,
to let me address, all in vain, your silent ashes,
and render you the last service for the dead,
since fortune, alas, has bereft me of your person,
my poor brother, so unjustly taken from me.
Still, here now I offer those gifts which by ancestral custom
are presented, sad offerings, at such obsequies:
accept them, soaked as they are with a brother's weeping,
and, brother, forever now hail and farewell.

107

If anything ever came through for one who so longingly
yearned for it, yet without hope—that's balm for the soul.
So, there's balm for us too, than gold more precious,
Lesbia, in this: that you've brought yourself back to me
and my yearning for you: yes, back to my hopeless yearning,
to me, by your own choice. O brighter than white
day! Who lives happier than I do? Who can argue
that life holds any more desirable bliss?

109

You're suggesting, my life, that this mutual love between us
can be a delight—*and* in perpetuity?
Great gods, only let her promise be in earnest,
let her be speaking truly, and from the heart,
so that we can maintain, for the rest of our life together,
our hallowed friendship through this eternal pact!

VIRGIL

70–19 B.C.E.

Virgil's *Aeneid* is the greatest epic poem from ancient Rome. It has been one of the most profoundly influential works of all classical literature in the later Western cultural and literary tradition. The *Aeneid* can be described in ways that make it sound off-putting: as a work of nationalistic propaganda for a nation that no longer exists, or as a twelve-book poem about the importance of doing your duty. But such descriptions are entirely false to most readers' experience of this emotionally engaging and thought-provoking story. The *Aeneid* is an absorbing book, full of adventure, beauty, magic, dreams, love, loss, and violence. The characters make hard choices and have complex inner lives. The poem is also a profound meditation on the rights and wrongs of empire and colonialism that prompts us to ask whether civilizations, even the best of them, are ever founded without enormous personal and military cost.

LIFE AND TIMES

Virgil, whose full Roman name was Publius Vergilius Maro, was born near the peaceful northern Italian town of Mantua. His father probably owned land, and Virgil's poetry often shows a nostalgic appreciation for the quiet life of the Italian countryside. Before composing the *Aeneid*, Virgil wrote two books with a rural setting: the *Eclogues*, a set of ten poems featuring the songs and sorrows of fictional shepherds, and the *Georgics*, a four-book account of the struggles and triumphs of life on a farm. Ostensibly, neither of these texts has much to do with the subject of the *Aeneid*, which is about the quest to found an empire. But Virgil's poetic focus is surprisingly consistent throughout his career. Whether the setting is an empire or a village garden, he is interested in the value and pathos of the human struggle to build a home, even in hostile or near-impossible conditions. The farmer in the *Georgics*, whose hard work is washed away by a violent storm, is just as much a hero as the shipwrecked Trojans in the *Aeneid*.

When Virgil was young, the world beyond Mantua saw great political and military unrest. Rome had already, through its impressive military discipline, become the dominant power in the Mediterranean world; the city had defeated its main rival, the North African state of Carthage, some two generations before (in 146 B.C.E.). Now Rome was engaged in various further wars, struggling to expand the empire both eastward and westward. These wars generated greater glory for the nation, but also greater instability at home. In Virgil's childhood, Rome was still a Republic: no single man had control of the country; instead, government was divided among the people, the magistrates, and the Senate (an assembly of councilmen). But power was shifting away from the Senate and toward the military generals responsible for Rome's victories abroad. After a series of civil wars, Julius Caesar, one of these generals, became dictator of Rome. He was assassinated when Virgil was twenty-six (44 B.C.E.). More civil wars followed, and caused disruptions both at home and abroad: many country landowners—including some around Mantua, though apparently not Virgil's family—were forced to leave their homes, to make room for veterans returning from war. Finally, some twelve years after the assassination, Julius Caesar's adopted great-nephew Octavian defeated the joint forces of Antony and Cleopatra, and took control of Rome. In this volatile environment, Octavian was careful not to style himself "dictator," as Julius had done. Instead, he claimed to be restoring the old ways of the Republic. He named himself "Augustus" ("The Respected One"), the "Princeps" ("First Man") and "Emperor Caesar." Throughout his rule, Augustus was interested in controlling his public image: he knew that careful manipulation of information was essential if he were to avoid the fate of his great-uncle. In this context, it is not surprising that the emperor had a close personal relationship with the writers of Rome, who would, as Augustus knew, play an important part in his public image even after his death. Augustus hoped that Virgil would provide him with a great national epic, to justify, glorify, and immortalize Augustan Roman power.

We do not know how happy Augustus was with the poem that Virgil actually produced, although apparently the poet read parts of it aloud to the emperor and his sister, to great emotional effect: the sister fainted. It is possible that Augustus had hoped for a more direct account of his own glorious deeds. But perhaps he was smart enough to realize that direct propaganda never has much of a shelf life. We also do not know whether Virgil himself was satisfied with his creation. He was apparently a quiet man, moderate in his ways; thanks to Augustus's favor, he was given an expensive villa in Rome, but he seems to have preferred the quiet life of the country. He never married. As a poet, he was a perfectionist, willing to spend many hours editing his work. We are told that he compared himself to a mother bear who licks her cubs into shape. This process shows in the complex rhythms and careful patterns of Virgil's poetic style. He died of a fever at the age of fifty-one, returning from a trip to Greece. The *Aeneid* was still incomplete, and apparently he gave orders from his deathbed for it to be burned. Fortunately for us, Augustus countermanded the orders, and saved the poem for posterity.

THE *AENEID*

Virgil's masterpiece is about Rome, but only indirectly. The story takes us back in time, to a period well before the foundation of the city. It tells of how one civilization mutates into another, finding the origins of Rome in the destruction of Troy. The poem follows the Trojan Aeneas as he escapes with his father, son, and a few companions from the smoking ruins of his home. On the journey to find a new home in the "western land," he has many adventures, including an affair with Dido, the beautiful queen of Carthage, and a trip down to the underworld, to meet his dead father. When he arrives in Italy, he struggles to establish a base in his new land—where some of the native inhabitants are far from welcoming.

The *Aeneid* deals with universal themes, including the basic human need to find, or create, a home. The story is accessible even to those who know nothing about ancient history. But readers will find it helpful to think carefully about how Virgil incorporates his own times into this mythical story. When Virgil was writing, Rome had only recently emerged from a long, terrifying period of civil war. Aeneas, like Augustus, must show strong leadership to a people traumatized by years of violence. Virgil's account of the sack of Troy, including the horrible slaughter of old king Priam before the eyes of his family, is vivid and harrowing—and many contemporary readers will have witnessed similar scenes with their own eyes. But the historical parallels in this poem are complex, and one cannot simply identify Aeneas with

Augustus. The affair between Aeneas and Dido looks further back in history, to the Roman wars with Carthage. This episode also invites comparison with events of the more recent past: like Augustus's military and political rival Antony, Aeneas falls in love with a beautiful Eastern queen; Dido, in this interpretation, foreshadows Cleopatra, who also ended up killing herself. Once Aeneas has arrived in Italy, there are further questions. Is Aeneas a foreign invader, pushing the boundaries of his empire into new lands—as Augustus did? Or are these battles between different Italian peoples more like a civil war? Virgil's evocation of historical parallels is rich and fascinating precisely because it is so hard to pin down. Moreover, temporal paradoxes are created by telling "history in the future tense": from the Roman reader's point of view, Carthage has already been defeated; but from Dido's perspective, her city has just begun to be built.

Virgil's use of literary antecedents is equally interesting. His poem combines the themes of the ***Odyssey*** (the wanderer in search of home) and the ***Iliad*** (the hero in battle). He borrows Homeric turns of phrase, similes, sentiments, and whole incidents; for instance, his Aeneas, like Odysseus, passes the land of the Cyclops, and descends alive to the world of the dead; like Achilles, he receives a new set of armor from his goddess mother, and kills in rage to avenge a dead friend. But Virgil is not playing a sterile game of copying **Homer**. Rather, Homeric parallels are part of how the poem generates meaning. Virgil often uses several Homeric allusions at the same time. For instance, Turnus—the Italian prince who is originally engaged to Lavinia, the woman who will become Aeneas's wife—is in some ways like one of the suitors in the *Odyssey*: the rival who must be defeated and killed. But on another level, Turnus is like Hector, the doomed Trojan hero of the *Iliad*, who dies defending his city and his people. From Turnus's perspective, Aeneas himself is more like the suitors of the *Odyssey*: he is a usurper in a place he does not belong.

The *Aeneid*'s approach to storytelling is very different from that of the Homeric poems. Virgil often tells the parts of the story Homer left untold: for example, it is in Virgil, not Homer, that we get the full story of the Trojan Horse. On a more profound level, Virgil's presentation of war, peace, and human nature is quite unlike Homer's—it is both broader and deeper. Virgil is interested in communities that extend beyond the tribe or clan to the nation or the empire, and he evokes time that goes beyond the generations of a single family to the broad sweep of history. The characters, especially Aeneas, are more introspective and prone to ambivalent feelings than those in Homer; Virgil explores conflicts not just between one person and another but within an individual, between duty and the longings of the heart. In this way, Aeneas is a different kind of hero from any in Greek literature. The first time his name is mentioned, he is risking death by shipwreck and is overwhelmed by despair, wishing he could have died with his friends at Troy: he holds his hands to the sky and cries, "Three, four times blest, my comrades / lucky to die . . . before their parents' eyes!" Aeneas feels not only physical fear but also despair at being a survivor, with no home to go to. We can contrast this sense of being totally lost with the first mention of Odysseus in the *Odyssey*: he longs for a home that still exists, whereas Aeneas's home has been destroyed. A little later, we see a different Aeneas, when he talks to his men and tries to calm their fears, giving no hint of his own: "Bear up," he tells them, "dismiss your grief and fear." From the start of the poem, Aeneas will be put in situations where he cannot allow himself to show, or act on, his deepest feelings.

Virgil also seems to question the values of the Homeric warrior code. Aeneas is

This detail from a black figure vase by the "Louvre Painter" (6th century B.C.E.) shows Aeneas carrying his father, Anchises, on his shoulders as they escape Troy.

not, like Achilles, a man fighting for his personal honor, against even the leaders of his own side; rather, he is, and must be, a consensus builder, a team player. Odysseus (Romanized as *Ulysses*) is presented in the *Aeneid* as a cruel brute, lacking in the mercy for the defeated that Aeneas's father, Anchises, characterizes as an essential feature of the true Roman ("to spare the defeated, break the proud in war"). Moreover, Ulysses' cleverness—epitomized by the invention of the Trojan Horse—seems in this poem to be more like wicked dishonesty. Truthfulness is an essential element in the Roman code of honor: this is partly why Dido's accusation that Aeneas has deceived and betrayed her cuts so deeply.

Aeneas is often seen as the prototype of the ideal Roman ruler, devoted above all to *pietas*—a word from which we get *pity* and *piety*, and which covers both senses, though it is often translated as "duty." But whereas *duty* may suggest adherence to a set of abstract moral principles, the Latin word connotes devotion to particular people and entities: to the gods above all, but also to one's country, leaders, community, and family, especially father and sons. An iconic moment of Aeneas's *pietas* comes as he leaves his burning city, carrying his lame old father on his shoulders, holding the images of his household gods, and leading his little son by the hand. This scene reminds us that Aeneas is struggling to hold on to a community and create continuity even from the ruins of his old home. The *pietas* that holds families and cities together is contrasted in this poem with *furor* ("rage," "fury"), the wild passion that inspires bloodlust, both in Troy and on Italian shores.

But being good is not easy, and Virgil shows that Aeneas's repression of his own feelings for the sake of devotion comes at an enormous cost. Moreover, the poem seems to suggest that duty can even be harmful to other people. Aeneas, on the instructions of the gods, abandons the great passion of his life, his love for Dido, who had convinced herself that their relationship was equivalent to marriage. In despair, she kills herself. Virgil makes us admire and sympathize with Dido, and in doing so, we are forced to question whether Aeneas's mission is worthwhile. The *Aeneid* is not merely a celebration of Roman power; it is also an analysis of the costs of empire, both to the conquered and the conquerors. Moreover, we may wonder whether Rome itself—a city famously built by Romulus, who killed his brother Remus, a city defined by foreign and civil wars—is truly a civilization in which *pietas* is the defining value. This moral ambiguity continues up to the last lines of the poem, which many first-time readers will find shocking. We are left to wonder whether moderation or violence will be the truly defining quality of the future Roman Empire.

A NOTE ON THE TRANSLATION

Translation of this complex poem often reflects the ideological biases of the translator. Some versions make Virgil sound whole-heartedly enthusiastic about imperialism, eliminating much of his ambivalence; others make him sound unrelentingly gloomy about everything. Virgil's Latin is dignified, not colloquial, and has a beautiful, musical rhythm; but trying to reproduce this effect in modern English risks sounding merely pompous. Several excellent recent translations have steered clear of these dangers and given us readable, fast-paced versions of the *Aeneid*. We have chosen Robert Fagles's translation, because it is particularly good at evoking the psychological depth of Virgil's characters, and it allows readers to experience the sheer narrative pleasure of reading the *Aeneid*.

From The Aeneid[1]

BOOK I

[*Safe Haven after Storm*]

Wars and a man I sing—an exile driven on by Fate,
he was the first to flee the coast of Troy,
destined to reach Lavinian[2] shores and Italian soil,
yet many blows he took on land and sea from the gods above—
thanks to cruel Juno's[3] relentless rage—and many losses
he bore in battle too, before he could found a city,
bring his gods to Latium, source of the Latin race,
the Alban lords and the high walls of Rome.[4]
Tell me,
Muse, how it all began. Why was Juno outraged?
What could wound the Queen of the Gods with all her power?
Why did she force a man, so famous for his devotion,[5]
to brave such rounds of hardship, bear such trials?
Can such rage inflame the immortals' hearts?

There was an ancient city held by Tyrian settlers,[6]
Carthage, facing Italy and the Tiber River's mouth[7]
but far away—a rich city trained and fierce in war.
Juno loved it, they say, beyond all other lands
in the world, even beloved Samos,[8] second best.
Here she kept her armor, here her chariot too,
and Carthage would rule the nations of the earth
if only the Fates were willing. This was Juno's goal
from the start, and so she nursed her city's strength.
But she heard a race of men, sprung of Trojan blood,
would one day topple down her Tyrian stronghold,

1. Translated by Robert Fagles.
2. Lavinium is the city founded in Italy by Aeneas, near the later city of Rome. It is named after his Latin wife, Lavinia. "Lavinian" here means "Italian."
3. Juno is queen of the gods, wife of Jupiter.
4. According to legend, after Aeneas died, his son Ascanius moved from Latium and founded the city of Alba Longa; from there came Romulus and Remus, who built the walls of Rome.
5. The Latin word is *pietas:* "piety," "duty," "loyalty."
6. Tyre was the main city of the Phoenicians, an ancient seafaring merchant people.
7. The Tiber runs through Rome.
8. A Greek island famous for its cult of Hera.

breed an arrogant people ruling far and wide,
proud in battle, destined to plunder Libya.
So the Fates were spinning out the future . . .[9]
This was Juno's fear
and the goddess never forgot the old campaign
that she had waged at Troy for her beloved Argos.[1]
No, not even now would the causes of her rage,
her bitter sorrows drop from the goddess' mind.
They festered deep within her, galled her still:
the judgment of Paris, the unjust slight to her beauty,
the Trojan stock she loathed, the honors showered on Ganymede
ravished to the skies.[2] Her fury inflamed by all this,
the daughter of Saturn[3] drove over endless oceans
Trojans left by the Greeks and brute Achilles.[4]
Juno kept them far from Latium, forced by the Fates
to wander round the seas of the world, year in, year out.
Such a long hard labor it was to found the Roman people.

Now, with the ridge of Sicily barely out of sight,
they spread sail for the open sea, their spirits buoyant,
their bronze beaks churning the waves to foam as Juno,
nursing deep in her heart the everlasting wound,
said to herself: "Defeated, am I? Give up the fight?
Powerless now to keep that Trojan king from Italy?
Ah but of course—the Fates bar my way.
And yet Minerva could burn the fleet to ash
and drown my Argive crews in the sea, and all for one,
one mad crime of a single man, Ajax, son of Oileus![5]
She hurled Jove's all-consuming bolt from the clouds,
she shattered a fleet and whipped the swells with gales.
And then as he gasped his last in flames from his riven chest
she swept him up in a cyclone, impaled the man on a crag.
But I who walk in majesty, I the Queen of the Gods,
the sister and wife of Jove—I must wage a war,
year after year, on just one race of men!
Who will revere the power of Juno after this—
lay gifts on my altar, lift his hands in prayer?"

9. Refers to the Punic Wars of the third and second centuries B.C.E., in which Rome finally defeated Carthage; "Libya" is used as a generic term for the North African coast.

1. Argos is the homeland of Agamemnon and Menelaus; in the *Iliad,* Hera favors the Argives as they fight the Trojans and try to win back Helen, Menelaus's wife.

2. Paris, Prince of Troy, was asked to choose one of three goddesses: Hera, Athena (Minerva in Roman mythology), or Aphrodite (Venus to the Romans). He picked Aphrodite, and was rewarded with Helen, whom he took from her husband and led back to Troy. The second insult from the Trojans against Hera is that her husband, Zeus, once fell in love with a Trojan boy, Ganymede, and brought him up to heaven to be his cupbearer.

3. Saturn, the Roman god of agriculture, was the father of both Jupiter and Juno.

4. The greatest Greek warrior. These survivors are the few Trojans whom Achilles has not killed.

5. In the aftermath of the Greek victory at Troy, one of the Greek soldiers, this Ajax (who is not the same as the strong hero Telemonian Ajax) raped the Trojan princess Cassandra in the temple of Minerva. The goddess took revenge by setting light to the Greek fleet, and then overwhelming it with a storm.

With such anger seething inside her fiery heart
the goddess reached Aeolia, breeding-ground of storms,
their home swarming with raging gusts from the South.
Here in a vast cave King Aeolus[6] rules the winds,
brawling to break free, howling in full gale force
as he chains them down in their dungeon, shackled fast.
They bluster in protest, roaring round their prison bars
with a mountain above them all, booming with their rage.
But high in his stronghold Aeolus wields his scepter,
soothing their passions, tempering their fury.
Should he fail, surely they'd blow the world away,
hurling the land and sea and deep sky through space.
Fearing this, the almighty Father banished the winds
to that black cavern, piled above them a mountain mass
and imposed on all a king empowered, by binding pact,
to rein them back on command or let them gallop free.

Now Juno made this plea to the Lord of Winds:
"Aeolus, the Father of Gods and King of Men gave you
the power to calm the waves or rouse them with your gales.
A race I loathe is crossing the Tuscan Sea,[7] transporting
Troy to Italy, bearing their conquered household gods—
thrash your winds to fury, sink their warships, overwhelm them
or break them apart, scatter their crews, drown them all!
I happen to have some sea-nymphs, fourteen beauties,
Deiopea the finest of all by far . . .
I'll join you in lasting marriage, call her yours
and for all her years to come she will live with you
and make you the proud father of handsome children.
Such service earns such gifts."
Aeolus warmed
to Juno's offer: "Yours is the task, my queen,
to explore your heart's desires. Mine is the duty
to follow your commands. Yes, thanks to you
I rule this humble little kingdom of mine.
You won me the scepter, Jupiter's favors too,
and a couch to lounge on, set at the gods' feasts—
you made me Lord of the Stormwind, King of Cloudbursts."
With such thanks, swinging his spear around he strikes home
at the mountain's hollow flank and out charge the winds
through the breach he'd made, like armies on attack
in a blasting whirlwind tearing through the earth.
Down they crash on the sea, the Eastwind, Southwind,
all as one with the Southwest's squalls in hot pursuit,
heaving up from the ocean depths huge killer-breakers
rolling toward the beaches. The crews are shouting,
cables screeching—suddenly cloudbanks blotting out
the sky, the light of day from the Trojans' sight

6. Mythical king of the winds from the *Odyssey*.

7. Just west of central Italy; the Trojans have almost reached their destination.

as pitch-black night comes brooding down on the sea
with thunder crashing pole to pole, bolt on bolt
blazing across the heavens—death, everywhere
men facing instant death.
At once Aeneas, limbs limp in the chill of fear,
groans and lifting both his palms toward the stars
cries out: "Three, four times blest, my comrades
lucky to die beneath the soaring walls of Troy—
before their parents' eyes! If only I'd gone down
under your right hand—Diomedes, strongest Greek afield—
and poured out my life on the battle grounds of Troy![8]
Where raging Hector lies, pierced by Achilles' spear,
where mighty Sarpedon lies, where the Simois River
swallows down and churns beneath its tides so many
shields and helmets and corpses of the brave!"[9]
Flinging cries
as a screaming gust of the Northwind pounds against his sail,
raising waves sky-high. The oars shatter, prow twists round,
taking the breakers broadside on and over Aeneas' decks
a mountain of water towers, massive, steep.
Some men hang on billowing crests, some as the sea
gapes, glimpse through the waves the bottom waiting,
a surge aswirl with sand.
Three ships the Southwind grips
and spins against those boulders lurking in mid-ocean—
rocks the Italians call the Altars, one great spine
breaking the surface—three the Eastwind sweeps
from open sea on the Syrtes' reefs, a grim sight,
girding them round with walls of sand.
One ship
that carried the Lycian[1] units led by staunch Orontes—
before Aeneas' eyes a toppling summit of water
strikes the stern and hurls the helmsman overboard,
pitching him headfirst, twirling his ship three times,
right on the spot till the ravenous whirlpool gulps her down.
Here and there you can sight some sailors bobbing in heavy seas,
strewn in the welter now the weapons, men, stray spars
and treasures saved from Troy.
Now Ilioneus' sturdy ship,
now brave Achates', now the galley that carried Abas,
another, aged Aletes, yes, the storm routs them all,
down to the last craft the joints split, beams spring
and the lethal flood pours in.
All the while Neptune[2]

8. In the *Iliad,* Aeneas is wounded by the Greek hero Diomedes, and is rescued by his mother, Aphrodite.

9. Hector, the greatest Trojan hero, is killed by Achilles in the *Iliad*. Sarpedon is another fighter on the Trojan side, the favorite of Zeus, who is killed by Achilles' friend Patroclus. The Simois is the river at Troy, which in the *Iliad* becomes thick with the blood and bodies of those killed by Achilles.

1. Region in modern Turkey, allied with Troy in the *Iliad*.

2. God of the sea.

sensed the furor above him, the roaring seas first and
the storm breaking next—his standing waters boiling up
from the sea-bed, churning back. And the mighty god,
stirred to his depths, lifts his head from the crests
and serene in power, gazing out over all his realm,
he sees Aeneas' squadrons scattered across the ocean,
Trojans overwhelmed by the surf and the wild crashing skies.
Nor did he miss his sister Juno's cunning wrath at work.
He summons the East- and Westwind, takes them to task:
"What insolence! Trusting so to your lofty birth?
You winds, you dare make heaven and earth a chaos,
raising such a riot of waves without my blessings.
You—what I won't do! But first I had better set
to rest the flood you ruffled so. Next time, trust me,
you will pay for your crimes with more than just a scolding.
Away with you, quick! And give your king this message:
Power over the sea and ruthless trident is mine,
not his—it's mine by lot, by destiny. His place,
Eastwind, is the rough rocks where you are all at home.
Let him bluster there and play the king in his court,
let Aeolus rule his bolted dungeon of the winds!"

Quicker than his command he calms the heaving seas,
putting the clouds to rout and bringing back the sun.
Struggling shoulder-to-shoulder, Triton and Cymothoë[3]
hoist and heave the ships from the jagged rocks
as the god himself whisks them up with his trident,
clearing a channel through the deadly reefs, his chariot
skimming over the cresting waves on spinning wheels
to set the seas to rest. Just as, all too often,
some huge crowd is seized by a vast uprising,
the rabble runs amok, all slaves to passion,
rocks, firebrands flying. Rage finds them arms
but then, if they chance to see a man among them,
one whose devotion and public service lend him weight,
they stand there, stock-still with their ears alert as
he rules their furor with his words and calms their passion.
So the crash of the breakers all fell silent once their Father,
gazing over his realm under clear skies, flicks his horses,
giving them free rein, and his eager chariot flies.

Now bone-weary, Aeneas' shipmates make a run
for the nearest landfall, wheeling prows around
they turn for Libya's coast. There is a haven shaped
by an island shielding the mouth of a long deep bay, its flanks
breaking the force of combers pounding in from the sea
while drawing them off into calm receding channels.
Both sides of the harbor, rock cliffs tower, crowned
by twin crags that menace the sky, overshadowing

3. Triton is a lesser sea god; Cymothoë is a sea nymph.

reaches of sheltered water, quiet and secure.
Over them as a backdrop looms a quivering wood,
above them rears a grove, bristling dark with shade,
and fronting the cliff, a cave under hanging rocks
with fresh water inside, seats cut in the native stone,
the home of nymphs. Never a need of cables here to moor
a weathered ship, no anchor with biting flukes to bind her fast.

Aeneas puts in here with a bare seven warships
saved from his whole fleet. How keen their longing
for dry land underfoot as the Trojans disembark,
taking hold of the earth, their last best hope,
and fling their brine-wracked bodies on the sand.
Achates is first to strike a spark from flint,
then works to keep it alive in dry leaves,
cups it around with kindling, feeds it chips
and briskly fans the tinder into flame.
Then, spent as they were from all their toil,
they set out food, the bounty of Ceres,[4] drenched
in sea-salt, Ceres' utensils too, her mills and troughs,
and bend to parch with fire the grain they had salvaged,
grind it fine on stones.
While they see to their meal
Aeneas scales a crag, straining to scan the sea-reach
far and wide . . . is there any trace of Antheus now,
tossed by the gales, or his warships banked with oars?
Or Capys perhaps, or Caicus' stern adorned with shields?[5]
Not a ship in sight. But he does spot three stags
roaming the shore, an entire herd behind them
grazing down the glens in a long ranked line.
He halts, grasps his bow and his flying arrows,
the weapons his trusty aide Achates keeps at hand.
First the leaders, antlers branching over their high heads,
he brings them down, then turns on the herd, his shafts
stampeding the rest like rabble into the leafy groves.
Shaft on shaft, no stopping him till he stretches
seven hefty carcases on the ground—a triumph,
one for each of his ships—and makes for the cove,
divides the kill with his whole crew and then shares out
the wine that good Acestes,[6] princely man, had brimmed
in their casks the day they left Sicilian shores.

The commander's words relieve their stricken hearts:
"My comrades, hardly strangers to pain before now,
we all have weathered worse. Some god will grant us
an end to this as well. You've threaded the rocks
resounding with Scylla's howling rabid dogs,
and taken the brunt of the Cyclops' boulders, too.

4. Goddess of grain and harvest.
5. Names of lost Trojan leaders.
6. King in Sicily who gave the Trojans shelter and extra supplies.

Call up your courage again. Dismiss your grief and fear.
A joy it will be one day, perhaps, to remember even this.
Through so many hard straits, so many twists and turns
our course holds firm for Latium.[7] There Fate holds out
a homeland, calm, at peace. There the gods decree
the kingdom of Troy will rise again. Bear up.
Save your strength for better times to come."
Brave words.
Sick with mounting cares he assumes a look of hope
and keeps his anguish buried in his heart.
The men gird up for the game, the coming feast,
they skin the hide from the ribs, lay bare the meat.
Some cut it into quivering strips, impale it on skewers,
some set cauldrons along the beach and fire them to the boil.
Then they renew their strength with food, stretched out
on the beachgrass, fill themselves with seasoned wine
and venison rich and crisp. Their hunger sated,
the tables cleared away, they talk on for hours,
asking after their missing shipmates—wavering now
between hope and fear: what to believe about the rest?
Were the men still alive or just in the last throes,
forever lost to their comrades' farflung calls?
Aeneas most of all, devoted to his shipmates,
deep within himself he moans for the losses . . .
now for Orontes, hardy soldier, now for Amycus,
now for the brutal fate that Lycus may have met,
then Gyas and brave Cloanthus, hearts of oak.

Their mourning was over now as Jove[8] from high heaven,
gazing down on the sea, the whitecaps winged with sails,
the lands outspread, the coasts, the nations of the earth,
paused at the zenith of the sky and set his sights
on Libya, that proud kingdom. All at once,
as he took to heart the struggles he beheld,
Venus[9] approached in rare sorrow, tears abrim
in her sparkling eyes, and begged: "Oh you who rule
the lives of men and gods with your everlasting laws
and your lightning bolt of terror, what crime could my Aeneas
commit against you, what dire harm could the Trojans do
that after bearing so many losses, this wide world
is shut to them now? And all because of Italy.
Surely from them the Romans would arise one day
as the years roll on, and leaders would as well,
descended from Teucer's blood brought back to life,
to rule all lands and seas with boundless power—
you promised! Father, what motive changed your mind?
With that, at least, I consoled myself for Troy's demise,
that heart-rending ruin—weighing fate against fate.

7. Region of central Italy, home of the Latin race.

8. Alternative name of Jupiter.

9. Aeneas's mother; goddess of love and sex.

But now after all my Trojans suffered, still
the same disastrous fortune drives them on and on.
What end, great king, do you set to their ordeals?

"Antenor[1] could slip out from under the Greek siege,
then make his passage through the Illyrian gulfs and,
safe through the inlands where the Liburnians rule,
he struggled past the Timavus River's source.[2]
There, through its nine mouths as the mountain caves
roar back, the river bursts out into full flood,
a thundering surf that overpowers the fields.
Reaching Italy, he erected a city for his people,
a Trojan home called Padua—gave them a Trojan name,
hung up their Trojan arms and there, after long wars,
he lingers on in serene and settled peace.
"But we,
your own children, the ones you swore would hold
the battlements of heaven—now our ships are lost,
appalling! We are abandoned, thanks to the rage
of a single foe, cut off from Italy's shores.
Is this our reward for reverence,[3]
this the way you give us back our throne?"

The Father of Men and Gods, smiling down on her
with the glance that clears the sky and calms the tempest,
lightly kissing his daughter on the lips, replied:
"Relieve yourself of fear, my lady of Cythera,[4]
the fate of your children stands unchanged, I swear.
You will see your promised city, see Lavinium's walls
and bear your great-hearted Aeneas up to the stars on high.
Nothing has changed my mind. No, your son, believe me—
since anguish is gnawing at you, I will tell you more,
unrolling the scroll of Fate
to reveal its darkest secrets. Aeneas will wage
a long, costly war in Italy, crush defiant tribes
and build high city walls for his people there
and found the rule of law. Only three summers
will see him govern Latium, three winters pass
in barracks after the Latins have been broken.
But his son Ascanius, now that he gains the name
of Iulus—Ilus he was, while Ilium ruled on high[5]—
will fill out with his own reign thirty sovereign years,
a giant cycle of months revolving round and round,
transferring his rule from its old Lavinian home
to raise up Alba Longa's mighty ramparts.

1. Trojan leader who escaped the city's sack and settled in northern Italy.
2. Illyrium was a district, the Liburnians a people, and Timavus a river on the coast of the northern Adriatic sea.
3. *Pietas.*
4. Greek island where there was a cult of Aphrodite.
5. *Ilium* is another name for Troy. The Julian family, which included Julius Caesar and Augustus, claimed descent from Iulus (Julus).

There, in turn, for a full three hundred years
the dynasty of Hector will hold sway till Ilia,
a royal priestess great with the brood of Mars,
will bear the god twin sons.[6] Then one, Romulus,
reveling in the tawny pelt of a wolf that nursed him,
will inherit the line and build the walls of Mars
and after his own name, call his people Romans.[7]
On them I set no limits, space or time:
I have granted them power, empire without end.
Even furious Juno, now plaguing the land and sea and sky
with terror: she will mend her ways and hold dear with me
these Romans, lords of the earth, the race arrayed in togas.
This is my pleasure, my decree. Indeed, an age will come,
as the long years slip by, when Assaracus' royal house
will quell Achilles' homeland, brilliant Mycenae too,
and enslave their people, rule defeated Argos.[8]
From that noble blood will arise a Trojan Caesar,
his empire bound by the Ocean, his glory by the stars:
Julius, a name passed down from Iulus, his great forebear.
And you, in years to come, will welcome him to the skies,
you rest assured—laden with plunder of the East,
and he with Aeneas will be invoked in prayer.[9]
Then will the violent centuries, battles set aside,
grow gentle, kind. Vesta[1] and silver-haired Good Faith
and Romulus flanked by brother Remus will make the laws.
The terrible Gates of War with their welded iron bars
will stand bolted shut,[2] and locked inside, the Frenzy
of civil strife will crouch down on his savage weapons,
hands pinioned behind his back with a hundred brazen shackles,
monstrously roaring out from his bloody jaws."
So
he decrees and speeds the son of Maia[3] down the sky
to make the lands and the new stronghold, Carthage,
open in welcome to the Trojans, not let Dido,
unaware of fate, expel them from her borders.
Down through the vast clear air flies Mercury,
rowing his wings like oars and in a moment
stands on Libya's shores, obeys commands
and the will of god is done.
The Carthaginians calm their fiery temper

6. Ilia, also known as Rhea Silvia, was a priestess sworn to religious celibacy. She was raped by Mars, the god of war, and gave birth to twins, Romulus and Remus. Her brother, jealous of his own power, ordered that the babies be killed; but instead, his servant abandoned them in the wild, to be rescued by a wolf, who suckled them and raised them.

7. Virgil omits the fact that Romulus killed his brother, Remus, to gain sole power over the city.

8. Assaracus was an early king of Troy.

9. The "Trojan Caesar" is either Julius Caesar, who made Rome an empire, or Augustus himself, who had plundered "the East" by defeating the Egyptian queen Cleopatra.

1. Vesta is the goddess of the hearth, representative of home life.

2. There were real Gates of War in the temple of Janus, which Augustus shut in 25 B.C.E.—the first time they had been shut since 235 B.C.E.

3. Mercury (Roman version of Hermes), the messenger god.

and Queen Dido, above all, takes to heart
a spirit of peace and warm good will to meet
the men of Troy.
But Aeneas, duty-bound,
his mind restless with worries all that night,
reached a firm resolve as the fresh day broke.
Out he goes to explore the strange terrain . . .
what coast had the stormwinds brought him to?
Who lives here? All he sees is wild, untilled—
what men, or what creatures? Then report the news
to all his comrades. So, concealing his ships
in the sheltered woody narrows overarched by rocks
and screened around by trees and trembling shade,
Aeneas moves out, with only Achates at his side,
two steel-tipped javelins balanced in his grip.
Suddenly, in the heart of the woods, his mother
crossed his path. She looked like a young girl,
a Spartan girl decked out in dress and gear
or Thracian Harpalyce tiring out her mares,
outracing the Hebrus River's rapid tides.[4]
Hung from a shoulder, a bow that fit her grip,
a huntress for all the world, she'd let her curls
go streaming free in the wind, her knees were bare,
her flowing skirts hitched up with a tight knot.

She speaks out first: "You there, young soldiers,
did you by any chance see one of my sisters?
Which way did she go? Roaming the woods,
a quiver slung from her belt,
wearing a spotted lynx-skin, or in full cry,
hot on the track of some great frothing boar?"
So Venus asked and the son of Venus answered:
"Not one of your sisters have I seen or heard . . .
but how should I greet a young girl like you?
Your face, your features—hardly a mortal's looks
and the tone of your voice is hardly human either.
Oh a goddess, without a doubt! What, are you
Apollo's sister? Or one of the breed of Nymphs?
Be kind, whoever you are, relieve our troubled hearts.
Under what skies and onto what coasts of the world
have we been driven? Tell us, please. Castaways,
we know nothing, not the people, not the place—
lost, hurled here by the gales and heavy seas.
Many a victim will fall before your altars,
we'll slaughter them for you!"

4. The goddess Venus is dressed like a Spartan, a famously athletic and militaristic Greek people, or Harpalyce, a girl who lived in the wilds and devoted herself to hunting. The Hebrus is a river in Thrace. In Greco-Roman tradition, hunting was considered antithetical to sex and marriage.

But Venus replied:
"Now there's an honor I really don't deserve.
It's just the style for Tyrian girls to sport
a quiver and high-laced hunting boots in crimson.
What you see is a Punic[5] kingdom, people of Tyre
and Agenor's town, but the border's held by Libyans
hard to break in war. Phoenician Dido is in command,
she sailed from Tyre, in flight from her own brother.
Oh it's a long tale of crime, long, twisting, dark,
but I'll try to trace the high points in their order . . .

"Dido was married to Sychaeus, the richest man in Tyre,
and she, poor girl, was consumed with love for him.
Her father gave her away, wed for the first time,
a virgin still, and these her first solemn rites.
But her brother held power in Tyre—Pygmalion,
a monster, the vilest man alive.
A murderous feud broke out between both men.
Pygmalion, catching Sychaeus off guard at the altar,
slaughtered him in blood. That unholy man, so blind
in his lust for gold he ran him through with a sword,
then hid the crime for months, deaf to his sister's love,
her heartbreak. Still he mocked her with wicked lies,
with empty hopes. But she had a dream one night.
The true ghost of her husband, not yet buried,
came and lifting his face—ashen, awesome in death—
showed her the cruel altar, the wounds that pierced his chest
and exposed the secret horror that lurked within the house.
He urged her on: 'Take flight from our homeland, quick!'
And then he revealed an unknown ancient treasure,
an untold weight of silver and gold, a comrade
to speed her on her way.
"Driven by all this,
Dido plans her escape, collects her followers
fired by savage hate of the tyrant or bitter fear.
They seize some galleys set to sail, load them with gold—
the wealth Pygmalion craved—and they bear it overseas
and a woman leads them all. Reaching this haven here,
where now you will see the steep ramparts rising,
the new city of Carthage—the Tyrians purchased land as
large as a bull's-hide could enclose but cut in strips for size
and called it Byrsa, the Hide, for the spread they'd bought.
But you, who are you? What shores do you come from?
Where are you headed now?"
He answered her questions,
drawing a labored sigh from deep within his chest:
"Goddess, if I'd retrace our story to its start,
if you had time to hear the saga of our ordeals,
before I finished the Evening Star would close
the gates of Olympus, put the day to sleep . . .

5. Carthaginian.

From old Troy we come—Troy it's called, perhaps
you've heard the name—sailing over the world's seas
until, by chance, some whim of the winds, some tempest
drove us onto Libyan shores. I am Aeneas, duty-bound.
I carry aboard my ships the gods of house and home
we seized from enemy hands. My fame goes past the skies.
I seek my homeland—Italy—born as I am from highest Jove.
I launched out on the Phrygian sea with twenty ships,
my goddess mother marking the way, and followed hard
on the course the Fates had charted. A mere seven,
battered by wind and wave, survived the worst.
I myself am a stranger, utterly at a loss,
trekking over this wild Libyan wasteland,
forced from Europe, Asia too, an exile—"

Venus could bear no more of his laments
and broke in on his tale of endless hardship:
"Whoever you are, I scarcely think the Powers hate you:
you enjoy the breath of life, you've reached a Tyrian city.
So off you go now. Take this path to the queen's gates.
I have good news. Your friends are restored to you,
your fleet's reclaimed. The winds swerved from the North
and drove them safe to port. True, unless my parents
taught me to read the flight of birds for nothing.
Look at those dozen swans triumphant in formation!
The eagle of Jove[6] had just swooped down on them all
from heaven's heights and scattered them into open sky,
but now you can see them flying trim in their long ranks,
landing or looking down where their friends have landed—
home, cavorting on ruffling wings and wheeling round
the sky in convoy, trumpeting in their glory.
So homeward bound, your ships and hardy shipmates
anchor in port now or approach the harbor's mouth,
full sail ahead. Now off you go, move on,
wherever the path leads you, steer your steps."
At that,
as she turned away her neck shone with a rosy glow,
her mane of hair gave off an ambrosial fragrance,
her skirt flowed loose, rippling down to her feet
and her stride alone revealed her as a goddess.
He knew her at once—his mother—
and called after her now as she sped away:
"Why, you too, cruel as the rest? So often
you ridicule your son with your disguises!
Why can't we clasp hands, embrace each other,
speak out, and tell the truth?"

Reproving her so, he makes his way toward town
but Venus screens the travelers off with a dense mist,

6. The eagle, king of the birds, was associated with Jupiter.

pouring round them a cloak of clouds with all her power,
so no one could see them, no one reach and hold them,
cause them to linger now or ask why they had come.
But she herself, lifting into the air, wings her way
toward Paphos,[7] racing with joy to reach her home again
where her temples stand and a hundred altars steam
with Arabian incense, redolent with the scent
of fresh-cut wreaths.
Meanwhile the two men
are hurrying on their way as the path leads,
now climbing a steep hill arching over the city,
looking down on the facing walls and high towers.
Aeneas marvels at its mass—once a cluster of huts—
he marvels at gates and bustling hum and cobbled streets.
The Tyrians press on with the work, some aligning the walls,
struggling to raise the citadel, trundling stones up slopes;
some picking the building sites and plowing out their boundaries,
others drafting laws, electing judges, a senate held in awe.
Here they're dredging a harbor, there they lay foundations
deep for a theater, quarrying out of rock great columns
to form a fitting scene for stages still to come.
As hard at their tasks as bees in early summer,
working the blooming meadows under the sun
escorting a new brood out, young adults now,
or pressing oozing honey into the combs, the nectar
brimming the bulging cells, or gathering up the plunder
workers haul back in, or closing ranks like an army,
driving the drones, that lazy crew, from home.
The hive seethes with life, exhaling the scent
of honey sweet with thyme.
"How lucky they are,"
Aeneas cries, gazing up at the city's heights,
"their walls are rising now!" And on he goes,
cloaked in cloud—remarkable—right in their midst
he blends in with the crowds, and no one sees him.

Now deep in the heart of Carthage stood a grove,
lavish with shade, where the Tyrians, making landfall,
still shaken by wind and breakers, first unearthed that sign:
Queen Juno had led their way to the fiery stallion's head
that signaled power in war and ease in life for ages.
Here Dido of Tyre was building Juno a mighty temple,
rich with gifts and the goddess' aura of power.
Bronze the threshold crowning a flight of stairs,
the doorposts sheathed in bronze, and the bronze doors
groaned deep on their hinges.
Here in this grove
a strange sight met his eyes and calmed his fears
for the first time. Here, for the first time,

7. Greek island where there was a cult center of Aphrodite.

Aeneas dared to hope he had found some haven,
for all his hard straits, to trust in better days.
For awaiting the queen, beneath the great temple now,
exploring its features one by one, amazed at it all,
the city's splendor, the work of rival workers' hands
and the vast scale of their labors—all at once he sees,
spread out from first to last, the battles fought at Troy,
the fame of the Trojan War now known throughout the world,
Atreus' sons and Priam—Achilles, savage to both at once.[8]
Aeneas came to a halt and wept, and "Oh Achates,"
he cried, "is there anywhere, any place on earth
not filled with our ordeals? There's Priam, look!
Even here, merit will have its true reward . . .
even here, the world is a world of tears
and the burdens of mortality touch the heart.
Dismiss your fears. Trust me, this fame of ours
will offer us some haven."
So Aeneas says,
feeding his spirit on empty, lifeless pictures,
groaning low, the tears rivering down his face
as he sees once more the fighters circling Troy.
Here Greeks in flight, routed by Troy's young ranks,
there Trojans routed by plumed Achilles in his chariot.
Just in range are the snow-white canvas tents of Rhesus—
he knows them at once, and sobs—Rhesus' men betrayed
in their first slumber, droves of them slaughtered
by Diomedes splattered with their blood, lashing
back to the Greek camp their highstrung teams
before they could ever savor the grass of Troy
or drink at Xanthus' banks.[9]
Next Aeneas sees
Troilus[1] in flight, his weapons flung aside,
unlucky boy, no match for Achilles' onslaught—
horses haul him on, tangled behind an empty warcar,
flat on his back, clinging still to the reins, his neck
and hair dragging along the ground, the butt of his javelin
scrawling zigzags in the dust.
And here the Trojan women
are moving toward the temple of Pallas,[2] their deadly foe,
their hair unbound as they bear the robe, their offering,
suppliants grieving, palms beating their breasts
but Pallas turns away, staring at the ground.
And Hector—
three times Achilles has hauled him round the walls of Troy
and now he's selling his lifeless body off for gold.

8. That is, Achilles was angry with Greeks as well as Trojans.

9. Rhesus, king of Thrace, came to help the Trojans, but was slaughtered by Odysseus and Diomedes in a night raid. An oracle had proclaimed that if Rhesus's horses ate Trojan grass and drank from the river Xanthus, Troy would not fall.

1. Troilus was a young son of King Priam of Troy.

2. Athena, who was hostile to Troy.

Aeneas gives a groan, heaving up from his depths,
he sees the plundered armor, the car, the corpse
of his great friend, and Priam reaching out
with helpless hands . . . [3]
He even sees himself
swept up in the melee, clashing with Greek captains,
sees the troops of the dawn and swarthy Memnon's[4] arms.
And Penthesilea leading her Amazons bearing half-moon shields[5]—
she blazes with battle-fury out in front of her army,
cinching a golden breastband under her bared breast,
a girl, a warrior queen who dares to battle men.
And now
as Trojan Aeneas, gazing in awe at all the scenes of Troy,
stood there, spellbound, eyes fixed on the war alone,
the queen aglow with beauty approached the temple,
Dido, with massed escorts marching in her wake.
Like Diana urging her dancing troupes along
the Eurotas' banks or up Mount Cynthus' ridge[6]
as a thousand mountain-nymphs crowd in behind her,
left and right—with quiver slung from her shoulder,
taller than any other goddess as she goes striding on
and silent Latona[7] thrills with joy too deep for words.
Like Dido now, striding triumphant among her people,
spurring on the work of their kingdom still to come.
And then by Juno's doors beneath the vaulted dome,
flanked by an honor guard beside her lofty seat,
the queen assumed her throne. Here as she handed down
decrees and laws to her people, sharing labors fairly,
some by lot, some with her sense of justice, Aeneas
suddenly sees his men approaching through the crowds,
Antheus, Sergestus, gallant Cloanthus, other Trojans
the black gales had battered over the seas
and swept to far-flung coasts.
Aeneas, Achates,
both were amazed, both struck with joy and fear.
They yearn to grasp their companions' hands in haste
but both men are unnerved by the mystery of it all.
So, cloaked in folds of mist, they hide their feelings,
waiting, hoping to see what luck their friends have found.
Where have they left their ships, what coast? Why have they come?
These picked men, still marching in from the whole armada,
pressing toward the temple amid the rising din
to plead for some good will.

3. Having killed Hector, Achilles dragged his corpse around the city behind his chariot, until Priam came to ransom his son's body.

4. Memnon was king of the Ethiopians, and fought on the Trojan side.

5. The Amazons were a race of warrior women who fought for Troy.

6. Diana (Artemis in Greek mythology) is the virgin goddess associated with hunting. She was born on Delos, the island location of Mount Cynthus; Eurotas was a river in Sparta where she was worshipped.

7. Leto, Diana's mother.

Once they had entered,
allowed to appeal before the queen—the eldest,
Prince Ilioneus, calm, composed, spoke out:
"Your majesty, empowered by Jove to found
your new city here and curb rebellious tribes
with your sense of justice—we poor Trojans,
castaways, tossed by storms over all the seas;
we beg you: keep the cursed fire off our ships!
Pity us, god-fearing men! Look on us kindly,
see the state we are in. We have not come
to put your Libyan gods and homes to the sword,
loot them and haul our plunder toward the beach.
No, such pride, such violence has no place
in the hearts of beaten men.
"There is a country—
the Greeks called it Hesperia, Land of the West,
an ancient land, mighty in war and rich in soil.
Oenotrians[8] settled it; now we hear their descendants
call their kingdom Italy, after their leader, Italus.
Italy-bound we were when, surging with sudden breakers
stormy Orion[9] drove us against blind shoals and from the South
came vicious gales to scatter us, whelmed by the sea,
across the murderous surf and rocky barrier reefs:
We few escaped and floated toward your coast.
What kind of men are these? What land is this,
that you can tolerate such barbaric ways?
We are denied the sailor's right to shore—
attacked, forbidden even a footing on your beach.
If you have no use for humankind and mortal armor,
at least respect the gods. They know right from wrong.
They don't forget.
"We once had a king, Aeneas . . .
none more just, none more devoted to duty, none
more brave in arms. If Fate has saved that man,
if he still draws strength from the air we breathe,
if he's not laid low, not yet with the heartless shades,
fear not, nor will you once regret the first step
you take to compete with him in kindness.
We have cities too, in the land of Sicily,
arms and a king, Acestes, born of Trojan blood.
Permit us to haul our storm-racked ships ashore,
trim new oars, hew timbers out of your woods, so that,
if we are fated to sail for Italy—king and crews restored—
to Italy, to Latium we will sail with buoyant hearts.
But if we have lost our haven there, if Libyan waters
hold you now, my captain, best of the men of Troy,
and all our hopes for Iulus have been dashed,
at least we can cross back over Sicilian seas,

8. An ancient Italic people.
9. This constellation marks the approach of winter.

the straits we came from, homes ready and waiting,
and seek out great Acestes for our king."

So Ilioneus closed. And with one accord
the Trojans murmured Yes.
Her eyes lowered,
Dido replies with a few choice words of welcome:
"Cast fear to the winds, Trojans, free your minds.
Our kingdom is new. Our hard straits have forced me
to set defenses, station guards along our far frontiers.
Who has not heard of Aeneas' people, his city, Troy,
her men, her heroes, the flames of that horrendous war?
We are not so dull of mind, we Carthaginians here.
When he yokes his team, the Sun shines down on us as well.
Whatever you choose, great Hesperia—Saturn's fields—
or the shores of Eryx with Acestes as your king,[1]
I will provide safe passage, escorts and support
to speed you on your way. Or would you rather
settle here in my realm on equal terms with me?
This city I build—it's yours. Haul ships to shore.
Trojans, Tyrians: they will be all the same to me.
If only the storm that drove you drove your king
and Aeneas were here now! Indeed, I'll send out
trusty men to scour the coast of Libya far and wide.
Perhaps he's shipwrecked, lost in woods or towns."

Spirits lifting at Dido's welcome, brave Achates
and captain Aeneas had long chafed to break free
of the mist, and now Achates spurs Aeneas on:
"Son of Venus, what feelings are rising in you now?
You see the coast is clear, our ships and friends restored.
Just one is lost. We saw him drown at sea ourselves.
All else is just as your mother promised."

He'd barely ended when all at once the mist
around them parted, melting into the open air,
and there Aeneas stood, clear in the light of day,
his head, his shoulders, the man was like a god.
His own mother had breathed her beauty on her son,
a gloss on his flowing hair, and the ruddy glow of youth,
and radiant joy shone in his eyes. His beauty fine
as a craftsman's hand can add to ivory, or aglow
as silver or Parian marble[2] ringed in glinting gold.

Suddenly, surprising all, he tells the queen:
"Here I am before you, the man you are looking for,
Aeneas the Trojan, plucked from Libya's heavy seas.
You alone have pitied the long ordeals of Troy—unspeakable—

1. Hesperia is "the western land," that is, Italy. In Roman mythology, the Titan god Saturn, when driven out by Jupiter, fled to Italy and established the Golden Age. Eryx is a city in Sicily.

2. That is, marble from the island of Paros; famous for its whiteness.

and here you would share your city and your home with us,
this remnant left by the Greeks. We who have drunk deep
of each and every disaster land and sea can offer.
Stripped of everything, now it's past our power
to reward you gift for gift, Dido, theirs as well,
whoever may survive of the Dardan people still,
strewn over the wide world now. But may the gods,
if there are Powers who still respect the good and true,
if justice still exists on the face of the earth,
may they and their own sense of right and wrong
bring you your just rewards.
What age has been so blest to give you birth?
What noble parents produced so fine a daughter?
So long as rivers run to the sea, so long as shadows
travel the mountain slopes and the stars range the skies,
your honor, your name, your praise will live forever,
whatever lands may call me to their shores."
With that,
he extends his right hand toward his friend Ilioneus,
greeting Serestus with his left, and then the others,
gallant Gyas, gallant Cloanthus.
Tyrian Dido marveled,
first at the sight of him, next at all he'd suffered,
then she said aloud: "Born of a goddess, even so
what destiny hunts you down through such ordeals?
What violence lands you on this frightful coast?
Are you that Aeneas whom loving Venus bore
to Dardan Anchises on the Simois' banks at Troy?
Well I remember . . . Teucer[3] came to Sidon once,
banished from native ground, searching for new realms,
and my father Belus helped him. Belus had sacked Cyprus,
plundered that rich island, ruled with a victor's hand.
From that day on I have known of Troy's disaster,
known your name, and all the kings of Greece.
Teucer, your enemy, often sang Troy's praises,
claiming his own descent from Teucer's ancient stock.
So come, young soldiers, welcome to our house.
My destiny, harrying me with trials hard as yours,
led me as well, at last, to anchor in this land.
Schooled in suffering, now I learn to comfort
those who suffer too."
With that greeting
she leads Aeneas into the royal halls, announcing
offerings in the gods' high temples as she goes.
Not forgetting to send his shipmates on the beaches
twenty bulls and a hundred huge, bristling razorbacks
and a hundred fatted lambs together with their mothers:
gifts to make this day a day of joy.

3. A warrior who fought at Troy and was later exiled; he founded a city on the island of Cyprus.

Within the palace
all is decked with adornments, lavish, regal splendor.
In the central hall they are setting out a banquet,
draping the gorgeous purple, intricately worked,
heaping the board with grand displays of silver
and gold engraved with her fathers' valiant deeds,
a long, unending series of captains and commands,
traced through a line of heroes since her country's birth.

Aeneas—a father's love would give the man no rest—
quickly sends Achates down to the ships to take
the news to Ascanius, bring him back to Carthage.
All his paternal care is focused on his son.
He tells Achates to fetch some gifts as well,
plucked from the ruins of Troy: a gown stiff
with figures stitched in gold, and a woven veil
with yellow sprays of acanthus round the border.
Helen's glory, gifts she carried out of Mycenae,
fleeing Argos for Troy to seal her wicked marriage—
the marvelous handiwork of Helen's mother, Leda.
Aeneas adds the scepter Ilione used to bear,
the eldest daughter of Priam; a necklace too,
strung with pearls, and a crown of double bands,
one studded with gems, the other, gold. Achates,
following orders, hurries toward the ships.

But now Venus is mulling over some new schemes,
new intrigues. Altered in face and figure, Cupid[4]
would go in place of the captivating Ascanius,
using his gifts to fire the queen to madness,
weaving a lover's ardor through her bones.
No doubt Venus fears that treacherous house
and the Tyrians' forked tongues,
and brutal Juno inflames her anguish too
and her cares keep coming back as night draws on.
So Venus makes an appeal to Love, her winged son:
"You, my son, are my strength, my greatest power—
you alone, my son, can scoff at the lightning bolts
the high and mighty Father hurled against Typhoeus.[5]
Help me, I beg you. I need all your immortal force.
Your brother Aeneas is tossed round every coast on earth,
thanks to Juno's ruthless hatred, as you well know,
and time and again you've grieved to see my grief.
But now Phoenician Dido has him in her clutches,
holding him back with smooth, seductive words,
and I fear the outcome of Juno's welcome here . . .
She won't sit tight while Fate is turning on its hinge.
So I plan to forestall her with ruses of my own

4. Cupid (whose name means "desire") is the son of Venus and the god of sexual desire.

5. Jupiter hurled thunderbolts at the monster Typhoeus (Typhon), and finally trapped him under Mount Etna.

and besiege the queen with flames,
and no goddess will change her mood—she's mine,
my ally-in-arms in my great love for Aeneas.

"Now how can you go about this? Hear my plan.
His dear father has just sent for the young prince—
he means the world to me—and he's bound for Carthage now,
bearing presents saved from the sea, the flames of Troy.
I'll lull him into a deep sleep and hide him far away
on Cythera's heights or high Idalium,[6] my shrines,
so he cannot learn of my trap or spring it open
while it's being set. And you with your cunning,
forge his appearance—just one night, no more—put on
the familiar features of the boy, boy that you are,
so when the wine flows free at the royal board
and Dido, lost in joy, cradles you in her lap,
caressing, kissing you gently, you can breathe
your secret fire into her, poison the queen
and she will never know."
Cupid leaps at once
to his loving mother's orders. Shedding his wings
he masquerades as Iulus, prancing with his stride.
But now Venus distils a deep, soothing sleep
into Iulus' limbs, and warming him in her breast
the goddess spirits him off to her high Idalian grove
where beds of marjoram breathe and embrace him with aromatic
flowers and rustling shade.
Now Cupid is on the move,
under her orders, bringing the Tyrians royal gifts,
his spirits high as Achates leads him on.
Arriving, he finds the queen already poised
on a golden throne beneath the sumptuous hangings,
commanding the very center of her palace. Now Aeneas,
the good captain, enters, then the Trojan soldiers,
taking their seats on couches draped in purple.
Servants pour them water to rinse their hands,
quickly serving them bread from baskets, spreading
their laps with linens, napkins clipped and smooth.
In the kitchens are fifty serving-maids assigned
to lay out foods in a long line, course by course,
and honor the household gods by building fires high.
A hundred other maids and a hundred men, all matched in age,
are spreading the feast on trestles, setting out the cups.
And Tyrians join them, bustling through the doors,
filling the hall with joy, to take invited seats
on brocaded couches. They admire Aeneas' gifts,
admire Iulus now—the glowing face of the god
and the god's dissembling words—and Helen's gown
and the veil adorned with a yellow acanthus border.

6. Another town with a temple of Venus, in Cyprus.

But above all, tragic Dido, doomed to a plague
about to strike, cannot feast her eyes enough,
thrilled both by the boy and gifts he brings
and the more she looks the more the fire grows.
But once he's embraced Aeneas, clung to his neck
to sate the deep love of his father, deluded father,
Cupid makes for the queen. Her gaze, her whole heart
is riveted on him now, and at times she even warms him
snugly in her breast, for how can she know, poor Dido,
what a mighty god is sinking into her, to her grief?
But he, recalling the wishes of his mother Venus,
blots out the memory of Sychaeus bit by bit,
trying to seize with a fresh, living love
a heart at rest for long—long numb to passion.
Then,
with the first lull in the feast, the tables cleared away,
they set out massive bowls and crown the wine with wreaths.
A vast din swells in the palace, voices reverberating
through the echoing halls. They light the lamps,
hung from the coffered ceilings sheathed in gilt,
and blazing torches burn the night away.
The queen calls for a heavy golden bowl,
studded with jewels and brimmed with unmixed wine,
the bowl that Belus[7] and all of Belus' sons had brimmed,
and the hall falls hushed as Dido lifts a prayer:
"Jupiter, you, they say, are the god who grants
the laws of host and guest. May this day be one
of joy for Tyrians here and exiles come from Troy,
a day our sons will long remember. Bacchus,[8]
giver of bliss, and Juno, generous Juno,
bless us now. And come, my people, celebrate
with all good will this feast that makes us one!"

With that prayer, she poured a libation to the gods,
tipping wine on the board, and tipping it, she was first
to take the bowl, brushing it lightly with her lips,
then gave it to Bitias—laughing, goading him on
and he took the plunge, draining the foaming bowl,
drenching himself in its brimming, overflowing gold,
and the other princes drank in turn. Then Iopas,
long-haired bard, strikes up his golden lyre
resounding through the halls. Giant Atlas[9]
had been his teacher once, and now he sings
the wandering moon and laboring sun eclipsed,
the roots of the human race and the wild beasts,
the source of storms and the lightning bolts on high,
Arcturus, the rainy Hyades and the Great and Little Bears,[1]

7. Dido's father.
8. God of wine (Dionysus in Greek mythology).
9. A Titan condemned for his defiance of Jupiter to hold up the sky forever.
1. Constellations and stars.

and why the winter suns so rush to bathe themselves in the sea
and what slows down the nights to a long lingering crawl . . .
And time and again the Tyrians burst into applause
and the Trojans took their lead. So Dido, doomed,
was lengthening out the night by trading tales
as she drank long draughts of love—asking Aeneas
question on question, now about Priam, now Hector,
what armor Memnon, son of the Morning, wore at Troy,
how swift were the horses of Diomedes? How strong was Achilles?
"Wait, come, my guest," she urges, "tell us your own story,
start to finish—the ambush laid by the Greeks, the pain
your people suffered, the wanderings you have faced.
For now is the seventh summer that has borne you
wandering all the lands and seas on earth."

BOOK II

[*The Final Hours of Troy*]

Silence. All fell hushed, their eyes fixed on Aeneas now
as the founder of his people, high on a seat of honor,
set out on his story: "Sorrow, unspeakable sorrow,
my queen, you ask me to bring to life once more,
how the Greeks uprooted Troy in all her power,
our kingdom mourned forever. What horrors I saw,
a tragedy where I played a leading role myself.
Who could tell such things—not even a Myrmidon,
a Dolopian,[2] or comrade of iron-hearted Ulysses[3]—
and still refrain from tears? And now, too,
the dank night is sweeping down from the sky
and the setting stars incline our heads to sleep.
But if you long so deeply to know what we went through,
to hear, in brief, the last great agony of Troy,
much as I shudder at the memory of it all—
I shrank back in grief—I'll try to tell it now . . .

"Ground down by the war and driven back by Fate,
the Greek captains had watched the years slip by
until, helped by Minerva's superhuman skill,
they built that mammoth horse, immense as a mountain,
lining its ribs with ship timbers hewn from pine.
An offering to secure safe passage home, or so
they pretend, and the story spreads through Troy.
But they pick by lot the best, most able-bodied men
and stealthily lock them into the horse's dark flanks
till the vast hold of the monster's womb is packed
with soldiers bristling weapons.
"Just in sight of Troy
an island rises, Tenedos, famed in the old songs,

2. Myrmidons and Dolopians are companions of Achilles.
3. Odysseus.

powerful, rich, while Priam's realm stood fast.
Now it's only a bay, a treacherous cove for ships.
Well there they sail, hiding out on its lonely coast
while we thought—gone! Sped home on the winds to Greece.
So all Troy breathes free, relieved of her endless sorrow.
We fling open the gates and stream out, elated to see
the Greeks' abandoned camp, the deserted beachhead.
Here the Dolopians[4] formed ranks—
"Here savage Achilles
pitched his tents—
"Over there the armada moored
and here the familiar killing-fields of battle.
Some gaze wonderstruck at the gift for Pallas,
the virgin never wed[5]—transfixed by the horse,
its looming mass, our doom. Thymoetes leads the way.
'Drag it inside the walls,' he urges, 'plant it high
on the city heights!' Inspired by treachery now
or the fate of Troy was moving toward this end.
But Capys with other saner heads who take his side,
suspecting a trap in any gift the Greeks might offer,
tells us: 'Fling it into the sea or torch the thing to ash
or bore into the depths of its womb where men can hide!'
The common people are split into warring factions.

"But now, out in the lead with a troop of comrades,
down Laocoön runs from the heights in full fury,
calling out from a distance: 'Poor doomed fools,
have you gone mad, you Trojans?
You really believe the enemy's sailed away?
Or any gift of the Greeks is free of guile?
Is that how well you know Ulysses? Trust me,
either the Greeks are hiding, shut inside those beams,
or the horse is a battle-engine geared to breach our walls,
spy on our homes, come down on our city, overwhelm us—
or some other deception's lurking deep inside it.
Trojans, never trust that horse. Whatever it is,
I fear the Greeks, especially bearing gifts.'
"In that spirit, with all his might he hurled
a huge spear straight into the monster's flanks,
the mortised timberwork of its swollen belly.
Quivering, there it stuck, and the stricken womb
came booming back from its depths with echoing groans.
If Fate and our own wits had not gone against us,
surely Laocoön would have driven us on, now,
to rip the Greek lair open with iron spears
and Troy would still be standing—
proud fortress of Priam, you would tower still!

4. From Dolopia, a region in Greece.

5. The goddess Athena was famously a virgin.

"Suddenly, in the thick of it all, a young soldier,
hands shackled behind his back, with much shouting
Trojan shepherds were haling him toward the king.
They'd come on the man by chance, a total stranger.
He'd given himself up, with one goal in mind:
to open Troy to the Greeks and lay her waste.
He trusted to courage, nerved for either end,
to weave his lies or face his certain death.
Young Trojan recruits, keen to have a look,
came scurrying up from all sides, crowding round,
outdoing each other to make a mockery of the captive.
Now, hear the treachery of the Greeks and learn
from a single crime the nature of the beast . . .
Haggard, helpless, there in our midst he stood,
all eyes riveted on him now, and turning a wary glance
at the lines of Trojan troops he groaned and spoke:
'Where can I find some refuge, where on land, on sea?
What's left for me now? A man of so much misery!
Nothing among the Greeks, no place at all. And worse,
I see my Trojan enemies crying for my blood.'
"His groans
convince us, cutting all our show of violence short.
We press him: 'Tell us where you were born, your family.
What news do you bring? Tell us what you trust to,
such a willing captive.'
"'All of it, my king,
I'll tell you, come what may, the whole true story.
Greek I am, I don't deny it. No, that first.
Fortune may have made me a man of misery
but, wicked as she is,
she can't make Sinon a lying fraud as well.
"'Now,
perhaps you've caught some rumor of Palamedes,[6]
Belus' son, and his shining fame that rings in song.
The Greeks charged him with treason, a trumped-up charge,
an innocent man, and just because he opposed the war
they put him to death, but once he's robbed of the light,
they mourn him sorely. Now I was his blood kin,
a youngster when my father, a poor man, sent me
off to the war at Troy as Palamedes' comrade.
Long as he kept his royal status, holding forth
in the councils of the kings, I had some standing too,
some pride of place. But once he left the land of the living,
thanks to the jealous, forked tongue of our Ulysses—
you're no stranger to *his* story—I was shattered,
I dragged out my life in the shadows, grieving,
seething alone, in silence . . .
outraged by my innocent friend's demise until

6. A Greek warrior who advised the Greeks to return home from Troy. Odysseus persuaded them that he was a traitor, and had him killed. He was descended from the Egyptian king Belus.

I burst out like a madman, swore if I ever returned
in triumph to our native Argos, ever got the chance
I'd take revenge, and my oath provoked a storm of hatred.
That was my first step on the slippery road to ruin.
From then on, Ulysses kept tormenting me, pressing
charge on charge; from then on, he bruited about
his two-edged rumors among the rank and file.
Driven by guilt, he looked for ways to kill me,
he never rested until, making Calchas[7] his henchman—
but why now? Why go over that unforgiving ground again?
Why waste words? If you think all Greeks are one,
if hearing the name *Greek* is enough for you,
it's high time you made me pay the price.
How that would please the man of Ithaca,[8]
how the sons of Atreus would repay you!'
"Now, of course,
we burn to question him, urge him to explain—
blind to how false the cunning Greeks could be.
All atremble, he carries on with his tale,
lying from the cockles of his heart:
"'Time and again
the Greeks had yearned to abandon Troy—bone-tired
from a long hard war—to put it far behind and
beat a clean retreat. Would to god they had.
But time and again, as they were setting sail,
the heavy seas would keep them confined to port
and the Southwind filled their hearts with dread
and worst of all, once this horse, this mass of timber
with locking planks, stood stationed here at last,
the thunderheads rumbled up and down the sky.
So, at our wit's end, we send Eurypylus off
to question Apollo's oracle now, and back
he comes from the god's shrine with these bleak words:
"With blood you appeased the winds, with a virgin's sacrifice
when you, you Greeks, first sought the shores of Troy.[9]
With blood you must seek fair winds to sail you home,
must sacrifice one more Greek life in return."

"'As the word spread, the ranks were struck dumb
and icy fear sent shivers down their spines.
Whom did the god demand? Who'd meet his doom?
Just that moment the Ithacan haled the prophet,
Calchas, into our midst—he'd twist it out of him,
what was the gods' will? The army rose in uproar.
Even then our soldiers sensed that I was the one,
the target of that Ulysses' vicious schemes—
they saw it coming, still they held their tongues.

7. Greek prophet.
8. Ulysses.
9. Iphigenia was sacrificed by her father, Agamemnon, to allow the winds to blow the fleet to Troy.

For ten days the seer, silent, closed off in his tent,
refused to say a word or betray a man to death.
But at last, goaded on by Ulysses' mounting threats
but in fact conniving in their plot, he breaks his silence
and dooms me to the altar. And the army gave consent.
The death that each man dreaded turned to the fate
of one poor soul: a burden they could bear.

"'The day of infamy soon came . . .
the sacred rites were all performed for the victim,
the salted meal strewn, the bands tied round my head.
But I broke free of death, I tell you, burst my shackles,
yes, and hid all night in the reeds of a marshy lake,
waiting for them to sail—if only they would sail!
Well, no hope now of seeing the land where I was born
or my sweet children, the father I longed for all these years.
Maybe they'll wring from *them* the price for my escape,
avenge my guilt with my loved ones' blood, poor things.
I beg you, king, by the Powers who know the truth,
by any trust still uncorrupt in the world of men,
pity a man whose torment knows no bounds.
Pity me in my pain.
I know in my soul I don't deserve to suffer.'

"He wept and won his life—our pity, too.
Priam takes command, has him freed from the ropes
and chains that bind him fast, and hails him warmly:
'Whoever you are, from now on, now you've lost the Greeks,
put them out of your mind and you'll be one of us.
But answer my questions. Tell me the whole truth.
Why did they raise up this giant, monstrous horse?
Who conceived it? What's it for? its purpose?
A gift to the gods? A great engine of battle?'

"He broke off. Sinon, adept at deceit,
with all his Greek cunning lifted his hands,
just freed from their fetters, up to the stars
and prayed: 'Bear witness, you eternal fires of the sky
and you inviolate will of the gods! Bear witness,
altar and those infernal knives that I escaped
and the sacred bands I wore myself: the victim.
It's right to break my sworn oath to the Greeks,
it's right to detest those men and bring to light
all they're hiding now. No laws of my native land
can bind me here. Just keep your promise, Troy,
and if I can save you, you must save me too—
if I reveal the truth and pay you back in full.

"'All the hopes of the Greeks, their firm faith
in a war they'd launched themselves
had always hinged on Pallas Athena's help.

But from the moment that godless Diomedes,
flanked by Ulysses, the mastermind of crime,
attacked and tore the fateful image of Pallas[1]
out of her own hallowed shrine, and cut down
the sentries ringing your city heights and seized
that holy image and even dared touch the sacred bands
on the virgin goddess' head with hands reeking blood—
from that hour on, the high hopes of the Greeks
had trickled away like a slow, ebbing tide . . .
They were broken, beaten men,
the will of the goddess dead set against them.
Omens of this she gave in no uncertain terms.
They'd hardly stood her image up in the Greek camp
when flickering fire shot from its glaring eyes
and salt sweat ran glistening down its limbs
and three times the goddess herself—a marvel—
blazed forth from the ground, shield clashing, spear brandished.
The prophet spurs them at once to risk escape by sea:
"You cannot root out Troy with your Greek spears unless
you seek new omens in Greece and bring the god back here"—
the image they'd borne across the sea in their curved ships.
So now they've sailed away on the wind for home shores,
just to rearm, recruit their gods as allies yet again,
then measure back their course on the high seas and
back they'll come to attack you all off guard.

"'So Calchas read the omens. At his command
they raised this horse, this effigy, all to atone
for the violated image of Pallas, her wounded pride,
her power—and expiate the outrage they had done.
But he made them do the work on a grand scale,
a tremendous mass of interlocking timbers towering
toward the sky, so the horse could not be trundled
through your gates or hauled inside your walls
or guard your people if they revered it well
in the old, ancient way. For if your hands
should violate this great offering to Minerva,
a total disaster—if only god would turn it
against the seer himself!—will wheel down
on Priam's empire, Troy, and all your futures.
But if your hands will rear it up, into your city,
then all Asia in arms can invade Greece, can launch
an all-out war right up to the walls of Pelops.[2]
That's the doom that awaits our sons' sons.'

"Trapped by his craft, that cunning liar Sinon,
we believed his story. His tears, his treachery seized

1. An oracle stated that Troy could not be captured as long as the statue of Athena, the Palladium (after one of Athena's titles, Pallas), remained in place in her shrine.
2. Pelops was the grandfather of Agamemnon and Menelaus; his walls are the walls of Argos.

the men whom neither Tydeus' son[3] nor Achilles could defeat,
nor ten long years of war, nor all the thousand ships.

"But a new portent strikes our doomed people
now—a greater omen, far more terrible, fatal,
shakes our senses, blind to what was coming.
Laocoön, the priest of Neptune picked by lot,
was sacrificing a massive bull at the holy altar
when—I cringe to recall it now—look there!
Over the calm deep straits off Tenedos swim
twin, giant serpents, rearing in coils, breasting
the sea-swell side by side, plunging toward the shore,
their heads, their blood-red crests surging over the waves,
their bodies thrashing, backs rolling in coil on mammoth coil
and the wake behind them churns in a roar of foaming spray,
and now, their eyes glittering, shot with blood and fire,
flickering tongues licking their hissing maws, yes, now
they're about to land. We blanch at the sight, we scatter.
Like troops on attack they're heading straight for Laocoön—
first each serpent seizes one of his small young sons,
constricting, twisting around him, sinks its fangs
in the tortured limbs, and gorges. Next Laocoön
rushing quick to the rescue, clutching his sword—
they trap him, bind him in huge muscular whorls,
their scaly backs lashing around his midriff twice
and twice around his throat—their heads, their flaring necks
mounting over their victim writhing still, his hands
frantic to wrench apart their knotted trunks,
his priestly bands splattered in filth, black venom
and all the while his horrible screaming fills the skies,
bellowing like some wounded bull struggling to shrug
loose from his neck an axe that's struck awry,
to lumber clear of the altar . . .
Only the twin snakes escape, sliding off and away
to the heights of Troy where the ruthless goddess
holds her shrine, and there at her feet they hide,
vanishing under Minerva's great round shield.
"At once,
I tell you, a stranger fear runs through the harrowed crowd.
Laocoön deserved to pay for his outrage, so they say,
he desecrated the sacred timbers of the horse,
he hurled his wicked lance at the beast's back.
'Haul Minerva's effigy up to her house,' we shout,
'Offer up our prayers to the power of the goddess!'
We breach our own ramparts, fling our defenses open,
all pitch into the work. Smooth running rollers
we wheel beneath its hoofs, and heavy hempen ropes
we bind around its neck, and teeming with men-at-arms
the huge deadly engine climbs our city walls . . .

3. Diomedes.

And round it boys and unwed girls sing hymns,
thrilled to lay a hand on the dangling ropes
as on and on it comes, gliding into the city,
looming high over the city's heart.
"Oh my country!
Troy, home of the gods! You great walls of the Dardans[4]
long renowned in war!
"Four times it lurched to a halt
at the very brink of the gates—four times the armor
clashed out from its womb. But we, we forged ahead,
oblivious, blind, insane, we stationed the monster
fraught with doom on the hallowed heights of Troy.
Even now Cassandra[5] revealed the future, opening
lips the gods had ruled no Trojan would believe.
And we, poor fools—on this, our last day—we deck
the shrines of the gods with green holiday garlands
all throughout the city . . .
"But all the while
the skies keep wheeling on and night comes sweeping in
from the Ocean Stream, in its mammoth shadow swallowing up
the earth, and the Pole Star, and the treachery of the Greeks.
Dead quiet. The Trojans slept on, strewn throughout
their fortress, weary bodies embraced by slumber.
But the Greek armada was under way now, crossing
over from Tenedos, ships in battle formation
under the moon's quiet light, their silent ally,
homing in on the berths they know by heart—
when the king's flagship sends up a signal flare,
the cue for Sinon, saved by the Fates' unjust decree,
and stealthily loosing the pine bolts of the horse,
he unleashes the Greeks shut up inside its womb.
The horse stands open wide, fighters in high spirits
pouring out of its timbered cavern into the fresh air:
the chiefs, Thessandrus, Sthenelus, ruthless Ulysses
rappeling down a rope they dropped from its side,
and Acamas, Thoas, Neoptolemus, son of Achilles,
captain Machaon, Menelaus, Epeus himself,
the man who built that masterpiece of fraud.
They steal on a city buried deep in sleep and wine,
they butcher the guards, fling wide the gates and hug
their cohorts poised to combine forces. Plot complete.

"This was the hour when rest, that gift of the gods
most heaven-sent, first comes to beleaguered mortals,
creeping over us now . . . when there, look,
I dreamed I saw Prince Hector before my eyes,
my comrade haggard with sorrow, streaming tears,

4. Dardanus founded the city of Dardania, just above Troy; hence the Dardans or Dardanians are the Trojans.

5. Daughter of King Priam. Apollo fell in love with her and gave her the gift of unerring prophecy; but when she refused him, he turned the gift into a curse, by ensuring that nobody would ever believe her predictions.

just as he once was, when dragged behind the chariot,
black with blood and grime, thongs piercing his swollen feet—
what a harrowing sight! What a far cry from the old Hector
home from battle, decked in Achilles' arms—his trophies—
or fresh from pitching Trojan fire at the Greek ships.
His beard matted now, his hair clotted with blood,
bearing the wounds, so many wounds he suffered
fighting round his native city's walls . . .
I dreamed I addressed him first, in tears myself
I forced my voice from the depths of all my grief:
'Oh light of the Trojans—last, best hope of Troy!
What's held you back so long? How long we've waited,
Hector, for you to come, and now from what far shores?
How glad we are to see you, we battle-weary men,
after so many deaths, your people dead and gone,
after your citizens, your city felt such pain.
But what outrage has mutilated your face
so clear and cloudless once? Why these wounds?'

Wasting no words, no time on empty questions,
heaving a deep groan from his heart he calls out:
'Escape, son of the goddess, tear yourself from the flames!
The enemy holds our walls. Troy is toppling from her heights.
You have paid your debt to our king and native land.
If one strong arm could have saved Troy, my arm
would have saved the city. Now, into your hands
she entrusts her holy things, her household gods.
Take them with you as comrades in your fortunes.
Seek a city for them, once you have roved the seas,
erect great walls at last to house the gods of Troy!'

Urging so, with his own hands he carries Vesta forth
from her inner shrine, her image clad in ribbons,
filled with her power, her everlasting fire.[6]
"But now,
chaos—the city begins to reel with cries of grief,
louder, stronger, even though father's palace
stood well back, screened off by trees, but still
the clash of arms rings clearer, horror on the attack.
I shake off sleep and scrambling up to the pitched roof
I stand there, ears alert, and I hear a roar like fire
assaulting a wheatfield, whipped by a Southwind's fury,
or mountain torrent in full spate, flattening crops,
leveling all the happy, thriving labor of oxen,
dragging whole trees headlong down in its wake—
and a shepherd perched on a sheer rock outcrop
hears the roar, lost in amazement, struck dumb.
No doubting the good faith of the Greeks now,
their treachery plain as day.

6. In the temple of Vesta, the hearth goddess, was a fire that was never allowed to go out.

"Already, there,
the grand house of Deiphobus[7] stormed by fire,
crashing in ruins—
"Already his neighbor Ucalegon
up in flames—
"The Sigean straits[8] shimmering back the blaze,
the shouting of fighters soars, the clashing blare of trumpets.
Out of my wits, I seize my arms—what reason for arms?
Just my spirit burning to muster troops for battle,
rush with comrades up to the city's heights,
fury and rage driving me breakneck on
as it races through my mind
what a noble thing it is to die in arms!
"But now, look,
just slipped out from under the Greek barrage of spears,
Panthus, Othrys' son, a priest of Apollo's shrine
on the citadel—hands full of the holy things,
the images of our conquered gods—he's dragging along
his little grandson, making a wild dash for our doors.
'Panthus, where's our stronghold? our last stand?'—
words still on my lips as he groans in answer:
'The last *day* has come for the Trojan people,
no escaping this moment. Troy's no more.
Ilium, gone—our awesome Trojan glory.
Brutal Jupiter hands it all over to Greece,
Greeks are lording over our city up in flames.
The horse stands towering high in the heart of Troy,
disgorging its armed men, with Sinon in his glory,
gloating over us—Sinon fans the fires.
The immense double gates are flung wide open,
Greeks in their thousands mass there, all who ever
sailed from proud Mycenae. Others have choked
the cramped streets, weapons brandished now
in a battle line of naked, glinting steel
tense for the kill. Only the first guards
at the gates put up some show of resistance,
fighting blindly on.'

"Spurred by Panthus' words and the gods' will,
into the blaze I dive, into the fray, wherever
the din of combat breaks and war cries fill the sky,
wherever the battle-fury drives me on and now
I'm joined by Rhipeus, Epytus mighty in armor,
rearing up in the moonlight—
Hypanis comes to my side, and Dymas too,
flanked by the young Coroebus, Mygdon's son.
Late in the day he'd chanced to come to Troy
incensed with a mad, burning love for Cassandra:
son-in-law to our king, *he* would rescue Troy. Poor man,
if only he'd marked his bride's inspired ravings!

7. A son of Priam.

8. Promontory leading into the Aegean Sea.

Seeing their close-packed ranks, hot for battle,
I spur them on their way: 'Men, brave hearts,
though bravery cannot save us—if you're bent on
following me and risking all to face the worst,
look around you, see how our chances stand.
The gods who shored our empire up have left us,
all have deserted their altars and their shrines.
You race to defend a city already lost in flames.
But let us die; go plunging into the thick of battle.
One hope saves the defeated: they know they can't be saved!'
That fired their hearts with the fury of despair.
"Now
like a wolfpack out for blood on a foggy night,
driven blindly on by relentless, rabid hunger,
leaving cubs behind, waiting, jaws parched—
so through spears, through enemy ranks we plow
to certain death, striking into the city's heart,
the shielding wings of the darkness beating round us.
Who has words to capture that night's disaster,
tell that slaughter? What tears could match
our torments now? An ancient city is falling,
a power that ruled for ages, now in ruins.
Everywhere lie the motionless bodies of the dead,
strewn in her streets, her homes and the gods' shrines
we held in awe. And not only Trojans pay the price in blood—
at times the courage races back in their conquered hearts
and they cut their enemies down in all their triumph.
Everywhere, wrenching grief, everywhere, terror
and a thousand shapes of death.
"And the first Greek
to cross our path? Androgeos leading a horde of troops
and taking *us* for allies on the march, the fool,
he even gives us a warm salute and calls out:
'Hurry up, men. Why holding back, why now,
why drag your heels? Troy's up in flames,
the rest are looting, sacking the city heights.
But you, have you just come from the tall ships?'
Suddenly, getting no password he can trust,
he sensed he'd stumbled into enemy ranks!
Stunned, he recoiled, swallowing back his words
like a man who threads his way through prickly brambles,
pressing his full weight on the ground, and blindly treads
on a lurking snake and back he shrinks in instant fear
as it rears in anger, puffs its blue-black neck.
Just so Androgeos, seeing us, cringes with fear,
recoiling, struggling to flee but we attack,
flinging a ring of steel around his cohorts—
panic takes the Greeks unsure of their ground
and we cut them all to pieces.
Fortune fills our sails in that first clash
and Coroebus, flushed, fired with such success,
exults: 'Comrades, wherever Fortune points the way,

wherever the first road to safety leads, let's soldier on.
Exchange shields with the Greeks and wear their emblems.
Call it cunning or courage: who would ask in war?
Our enemies will arm us to the hilt.'
"With that he dons
Androgeos' crested helmet, his handsome blazoned shield
and straps a Greek sword to his hip, and comrades,
spirits rising, take his lead. Rhipeus, Dymas too
and our corps of young recruits—each fighter
arms himself in the loot that he just seized
and on we forge, blending in with the enemy,
battling time and again under strange gods,
fighting hand-to-hand in the blind dark
and many Greeks we send to the King of Death.
Some scatter back to their ships, making a run
for shore and safety. Others disgrace themselves,
so panicked they clamber back inside the monstrous horse,
burying into the womb they know so well.
"But, oh
how wrong to rely on gods dead set against you!
Watch: the virgin daughter of Priam, Cassandra,
torn from the sacred depths of Minerva's shrine,
dragged by the hair, raising her burning eyes
to the heavens, just her eyes, so helpless,
shackles kept her from raising her gentle hands.
Coroebus could not bear the sight of it—mad with rage
he flung himself at the Greek lines and met his death.
Closing ranks we charge after him, into the thick of battle
and face our first disaster. Down from the temple roof
come showers of lances hurled by our own comrades there,
duped by the look of our Greek arms, our Greek crests
that launched this grisly slaughter. And worse still,
the Greeks roaring with anger—we had saved Cassandra—
attack us from all sides! Ajax, fiercest of all and
Atreus' two sons and the whole Dolopian army,
wild as a rampaging whirlwind, gusts clashing,
the West- and the South- and Eastwind riding high
on the rushing horses of the dawn, and the woods howl
and Nereus[9] thrashing his savage trident, churns up
the sea exploding in foam from its rocky depths.
And those Greeks we had put to rout, our ruse
in the murky night stampeding them headlong on
throughout the city—back they come, the first
to see that our shields and spears are naked lies,
to mark the words on our lips that jar with theirs.
In a flash, superior numbers overwhelm us.
Coroebus is first to go,
cut down by Peneleus' right hand he sprawls

9. An old sea god.

at Minerva's shrine, the goddess, power of armies.[1]
Rhipeus falls too, the most righteous man in Troy,
the most devoted to justice, true, but the gods
had other plans.
"Hypanis, Dymas die as well,
run through by their own men—
"And you, Panthus,
not all your piety, all the sacred bands you wore
as Apollo's priest could save you as you fell.
Ashes of Ilium, last flames that engulfed my world—
I swear by you that in your last hour I never shrank
from the Greek spears, from any startling hazard of war—
if Fate had struck me down, my sword-arm earned it all.
Now we are swept away, Iphitus, Pelias with me,
one weighed down with age and the other slowed
by a wound Ulysses gave him—heading straight
for Priam's palace, driven there by the outcries.

"And there, I tell you, a pitched battle flares!
You'd think no other battles could match its fury,
nowhere else in the city were people dying so.
Invincible Mars[2] rears up to meet us face-to-face
with waves of Greeks assaulting the roofs, we see them
choking the gateway, under a tortoise-shell of shields,[3]
and the scaling ladders cling to the steep ramparts—
just at the gates the raiders scramble up the rungs,
shields on their left arms thrust out for defense,
their right hands clutching the gables.
Over against them, Trojans ripping the tiles
and turrets from all their roofs—the end is near,
they can see it now, at the brink of death, desperate
for weapons, some defense, and these, these missiles they send
reeling down on the Greeks' heads—the gilded beams,
the inlaid glory of all our ancient fathers.
Comrades below, posted in close-packed ranks,
block the entries, swordpoints drawn and poised.
My courage renewed, I rush to relieve the palace,
brace the defenders, bring the defeated strength.

There was a secret door, a hidden passage
linking the wings of Priam's house—remote,
far to the rear. Long as our realm still stood,
Andromache, poor woman, would often go this way,
unattended, to Hector's parents, taking the boy
Astyanax[4] by the hand to see grandfather Priam.
I slipped through the door, up to the jutting roof
where the doomed Trojans were hurling futile spears.

1. Minerva was a warrior goddess, often depicted carrying weapons.
2. God of war.
3. Position adopted by Roman soldiers: packed tightly together, they put their shields above their heads, making the army look like a tortoise.
4. Hector and Andromache's son.

There was a tower soaring high at the peak toward the sky,
our favorite vantage point for surveying all of Troy
and the Greek fleet and camp. We attacked that tower
with iron crowbars, just where the upper-story planks
showed loosening joints—we rocked it, wrenched it free
of its deep moorings and all at once we heaved it toppling
down with a crash, trailing its wake of ruin to grind
the massed Greeks assaulting left and right. But on
came Greek reserves, no letup, the hail of rocks,
the missiles of every kind would never cease.

"There at the very edge of the front gates
springs Pyrrhus, son of Achilles, prancing in arms,
aflash in his shimmering brazen sheath like a snake
buried the whole winter long under frozen turf,
swollen to bursting, fed full on poisonous weeds
and now it springs into light, sloughing its old skin
to glisten sleek in its newfound youth, its back slithering,
coiling, its proud chest rearing high to the sun,
its triple tongue flickering through its fangs.
Backing him now comes Periphas, giant fighter,
Automedon too, Achilles' henchman, charioteer
who bore the great man's armor—backing Pyrrhus,
the young fighters from Scyros raid the palace,
hurling firebrands at the roofs. Out in the lead,
Pyrrhus seizes a double-axe and batters the rocky sill
and ripping the bronze posts out of their sockets,
hacking the rugged oaken planks of the doors,
makes a breach, a gaping maw, and there, exposed,
the heart of the house, the sweep of the colonnades,
the palace depths of the old kings and Priam lie exposed
and they see the armed sentries bracing at the portals.

"But all in the house is turmoil, misery, groans,
the echoing chambers ring with cries of women,
wails of mourning hit the golden stars.
Mothers scatter in panic down the palace halls
and embrace the pillars, cling to them, kiss them hard.
But on he comes, Pyrrhus with all his father's force,
no bolts, not even the guards can hold him back—
under the ram's repeated blows the doors cave in,
the doorposts, prised from their sockets, crash flat.
Force makes a breach and the Greeks come storming through,
butcher the sentries, flood the entire place with men-at-arms.
No river so wild, so frothing in spate, bursting its banks
to overpower the dikes, anything in its way, its cresting
tides stampeding in fury down on the fields to sweep
the flocks and stalls across the open plain.
I saw him myself, Pyrrhus crazed with carnage
and Atreus' two sons just at the threshold—

"I saw
Hecuba with her hundred daughters and daughters-in-law,[5]
saw Priam fouling with blood the altar fires
he himself had blessed.
"Those fifty bridal-chambers
filled with the hope of children's children still to come,
the pillars proud with trophies, gilded with Eastern gold,
they all come tumbling down—
and the Greeks hold what the raging fire spares.

"Perhaps you wonder how Priam met his end.
When he saw his city stormed and seized, his gates
wrenched apart, the enemy camped in his palace depths,
the old man dons his armor long unused, he clamps it
round his shoulders shaking with age and, all for nothing,
straps his useless sword to his hip, then makes
for the thick of battle, out to meet his death.
At the heart of the house an ample altar stood,
naked under the skies,
an ancient laurel bending over the shrine,
embracing our household gods within its shade.
Here, flocking the altar, Hecuba and her daughters
huddled, blown headlong down like doves by a black storm—
clutching, all for nothing, the figures of their gods.
Seeing Priam decked in the arms he'd worn as a young man,
'Are you insane?' she cries, 'Poor husband, what impels you
to strap that sword on now? Where are you rushing?
Too late for such defense, such help. Not even
my own Hector, if *he* came to the rescue now . . .
Come to me, Priam. This altar will shield us all
or else you'll die with us.'
"With those words,
drawing him toward her there, she made a place
for the old man beside the holy shrine.
"Suddenly,
look, a son of Priam, Polites, just escaped
from slaughter at Pyrrhus' hands, comes racing in
through spears, through enemy fighters, fleeing down
the long arcades and deserted hallways—badly wounded,
Pyrrhus hot on his heels, a weapon poised for the kill,
about to seize him, about to run him through and pressing
home as Polites reached his parents and collapsed,
vomiting out his life blood before their eyes.
At that, Priam, trapped in the grip of death,
not holding back, not checking his words, his rage:
'You!' he cries, 'you and your vicious crimes!
If any power on high recoils at such an outrage,

5. Wife of Priam, king of Troy. He had fifty sons and fifty daughters—not all by Hecuba.

let the gods repay you for all your reckless work,
grant you the thanks, the rich reward you've earned.
You've made me see my son's death with my own eyes,
defiled a father's sight with a son's life blood.
You say you're Achilles' son? You lie! Achilles
never treated his enemy Priam so. No, he honored
a suppliant's rights, he blushed to betray my trust,
he restored my Hector's bloodless corpse for burial,
sent me safely home to the land I rule!'
With that
and with all his might the old man flings his spear—
but too impotent now to pierce, it merely grazes
Pyrrhus' brazen shield that blocks its way
and clings there, dangling limp from the boss,
all for nothing. Pyrrhus shouts back: 'Well then,
down you go, a messenger to my father, Peleus' son![6]
Tell him about my vicious work, how Neoptolemus
degrades his father's name—don't you forget.
Now—die!'
That said, he drags the old man
straight to the altar, quaking, slithering on through
slicks of his son's blood, and twisting Priam's hair
in his left hand, his right hand sweeping forth his sword—
a flash of steel—he buries it hilt-deep in the king's flank.

"Such was the fate of Priam, his death, his lot on earth,
with Troy blazing before his eyes, her ramparts down,
the monarch who once had ruled in all his glory
the many lands of Asia, Asia's many tribes.
A powerful trunk is lying on the shore.[7]
The head wrenched from the shoulders.
A corpse without a name.
"Then, for the first time
the full horror came home to me at last. I froze.
The thought of my own dear father filled my mind
when I saw the old king gasping out his life
with that raw wound—both men were the same age—
and the thought of my Creusa, alone, abandoned,
our house plundered, our little Iulus' fate.[8]
I look back—what forces still stood by me?
None. Totally spent in war, they'd all deserted,
down from the roofs they'd flung themselves to earth
or hurled their broken bodies in the flames.

6. Achilles was the son of Peleus. He was already dead at this point, killed by Paris with an arrow to the heel.

7. The detail that the body is left "on the shore"—which makes no narrative sense, since Priam is killed in the center of the city—is an allusion to the assassination of Pompey the Great. In the civil war of 49–45 B.C.E., Pompey, representing the more aristocratic party, was defeated by the more populist Julius Caesar, and eventually assassinated; his body was famously abandoned on the beach of Egypt.

8. Creusa is Aeneas's wife; Iulus is his son.

["So,[9]
at just that moment I was the one man left
and then I saw her, clinging to Vesta's threshold,
hiding in silence, tucked away—Helen of Argos.
Glare of the fires lit my view as I looked down,
scanning the city left and right, and there she was . . .
terrified of the Trojans' hate, now Troy was overpowered,
terrified of the Greeks' revenge, her deserted husband's rage—
that universal Fury, a curse to Troy and her native land
and here she lurked, skulking, a thing of loathing
cowering at the altar: Helen. Out it flared,
the fire inside my soul, my rage ablaze to avenge
our fallen country—pay Helen back, crime for crime.

"'So, this woman,' it struck me now, 'safe and sound
she'll look once more on Sparta, her native Greece?
She'll ride like a queen in triumph with her trophies?
Feast her eyes on her husband, parents, children too?
Her retinue fawning round her, Phrygian[1] ladies, slaves?
That—with Priam put to the sword? And Troy up in flames?
And time and again our Dardan shores have sweated blood?
Not for all the world. No fame, no memory to be won
for punishing a woman: such victory reaps no praise
but to stamp this abomination out as she deserves,
to punish her now, they'll sing my praise for *that*.
What joy, to glut my heart with the fires of vengeance,
bring some peace to the ashes of my people!'

"Whirling words—I was swept away by fury now]
when all of a sudden there my loving mother[2] stood
before my eyes, but I had never seen her so clearly,
her pure radiance shining down upon me through the night,
the goddess in all her glory, just as the gods behold
her build, her awesome beauty. Grasping my hand
she held me back, adding this from her rose-red lips:
'My son, what grief could incite such blazing anger?
Why such fury? And the love you bore me once,
where has it all gone? Why don't you look first
where you left your father, Anchises, spent with age?
Do your wife, Creusa, and son Ascanius still survive?
The Greek battalions are swarming round them all,
and if my love had never rushed to the rescue,
flames would have swept them off by now or
enemy sword-blades would have drained their blood.
Think: it's not that beauty, Helen, you should hate,
not even Paris, the man that you should blame, no,
it's the gods, the ruthless gods who are tearing down
the wealth of Troy, her toppling crown of towers.

9. This passage is bracketed because many scholars believe it does not belong in the poem, since it is contradicted by a passage in book 6 (573–623). The contradiction may be a sign of the *Aeneid*'s unfinished status at Virgil's death.

1. That is, Trojan.

2. Venus.

Look around. I'll sweep it all away, the mist
so murky, dark, and swirling around you now,
it clouds your vision, dulls your mortal sight.
You are my son. Never fear my orders.
Never refuse to bow to my commands.
“‘There,
yes, where you see the massive ramparts shattered,
blocks wrenched from blocks, the billowing smoke and ash—
it's Neptune himself,[3] prising loose with his giant trident
the foundation-stones of Troy, he's making the walls quake,
ripping up the entire city by her roots.
“‘There's Juno,
cruelest in fury, first to commandeer the Scaean Gates,[4]
sword at her hip and mustering comrades, shock troops
streaming out of the ships.
“‘Already up on the heights—
turn around and look—there's Pallas holding the fortress,
flaming out of the clouds, her savage Gorgon glaring.[5]
Even Father himself, he's filling the Greek hearts
with courage, stamina—Jove in person spurring the gods
to fight the Trojan armies!
“‘Run for your life, my son.
Put an end to your labors. I will never leave you,
I will set you safe at your father's door.'

“Parting words. She vanished into the dense night.
And now they all come looming up before me,
terrible shapes, the deadly foes of Troy,
the gods gigantic in power.
“Then at last
I saw it all, all Ilium settling into her embers,
Neptune's Troy, toppling over now from her roots
like a proud, veteran ash on its mountain summit,
chopped by stroke after stroke of the iron axe as
woodsmen fight to bring it down, and over and
over it threatens to fall, its boughs shudder,
its leafy crown quakes and back and forth it sways
till overwhelmed by its wounds, with a long last groan
it goes—torn up from its heights it crashes down
in ruins from its ridge . . .
Venus leading, down from the roof I climb
and win my way through fires and massing foes.
The spears recede, the flames roll back before me.

“At last, gaining the door of father's ancient house,
my first concern was to find the man, my first wish

3. The sea god (Poseidon in Greek mythology), who was hostile to the Trojans, since Laomedon, an early king of Troy, failed to repay him for helping to build the city walls.
4. The Scaean Gates are the main entrance to Troy.
5. Pallas Athena's shield displays the head of a Gorgon: the monster that turns those who look at it to stone.

to spirit him off, into the high mountain range,
but father, seeing Ilium razed from the earth,
refused to drag his life out now and suffer exile.
'You,' he argued, 'you in your prime, untouched by age,
your blood still coursing strong, you hearts of oak,
you are the ones to hurry your escape. Myself,
if the gods on high had wished me to live on,
they would have saved my palace for me here.
Enough—more than enough—that I have seen
one sack of my city, once survived its capture.[6]
Here I lie, here laid out for death. Come say
your parting salutes and leave my body so.
I will find my own death, sword in hand:
my enemies keen for spoils will be so kind.
Death without burial? A small price to pay.
For years now, I've lingered out my life,
despised by the gods, a dead weight to men,
ever since the Father of Gods and King of Mortals
stormed at me with his bolt and scorched me with its fire.'[7]

"So he said, planted there. Nothing could shake him now.
But we dissolved in tears, my wife, Creusa, Ascanius,
the whole household, begging my father not to pull
our lives down with him, adding his own weight
to the fate that dragged us down.
He still refuses, holds to his resolve,
clings to the spot. And again I rush to arms,
desperate to die myself. Where could I turn?
What were our chances now, at this point?
'What!' I cried. 'Did you, my own father,
dream that I could run away and desert you here?
How could such an outrage slip from a father's lips?
If it please the gods that nothing of our great city
shall survive—if you are bent on adding your own death
to the deaths of Troy and of all your loved ones too,
the doors of the deaths you crave are spread wide open.
Pyrrhus will soon be here, bathed in Priam's blood,
Pyrrhus who butchers sons in their fathers' faces,
slaughters fathers at the altar. Was it for this,
my loving mother, you swept me clear of the weapons,
free of the flames? Just to see the enemy camped
in the very heart of our house, to see my son, Ascanius,
see my father, my wife, Creusa, with them, sacrificed,
massacred in each other's blood?

6. Troy had been sacked by Hercules, when the previous king (Laomedon) cheated him.
7. When Anchises had his affair with Venus, he was sworn to secrecy. He broke his word and boasted about sleeping with the goddess, so Jupiter hurled a thunderbolt at him as punishment, making him lame.

'Arms, my comrades,
bring me arms! The last light calls the defeated.
Send me back to the Greeks, let me go back
to fight new battles. Not all of us here
will die today without revenge.'
"Now buckling on
my sword again and working my left arm through
the shieldstrap, grasping it tightly, just as I
was rushing out, right at the doors my wife, Creusa,
look, flung herself at my feet and hugged my knees
and raised our little Iulus up to his father.
'If you are going off to die,' she begged,
'then take us with you too,
to face the worst together. But if your battles
teach you to hope in arms, the arms you buckle on,
your first duty should be to guard our house.
Desert us, leave us now—to whom? Whom?
Little Iulus, your father and your wife,
so I once was called.'
"So Creusa cries,
her wails of anguish echoing through the house
when out of the blue an omen strikes—a marvel!
Now as we held our son between our hands
and both our grieving faces, a tongue of fire,
watch, flares up from the crown of Iulus' head,
a subtle flame licking his downy hair, feeding
around the boy's brow, and though it never harmed him,
panicked, we rush to shake the flame from his curls
and smother the holy fire, damp it down with water.
But Father Anchises lifts his eyes to the stars in joy
and stretching his hands toward the sky, sings out:
'Almighty Jove! If any prayer can persuade you now,
look down on us—that's all I ask—if our devotion
has earned it, grant us another omen, Father,
seal this first clear sign.'
"No sooner said
than an instant peal of thunder crashes on the left
and down from the sky a shooting star comes gliding,
trailing a flaming torch to irradiate the night
as it comes sweeping down. We watch it sailing
over the topmost palace roofs to bury itself,
still burning bright, in the forests of Mount Ida,
blazing its path with light, leaving a broad furrow,
a fiery wake, and miles around the smoking sulfur fumes.
Won over at last, my father rises to his full height
and prays to the gods and reveres that holy star:
'No more delay, not now! You gods of my fathers,
now I follow wherever you lead me, I am with you.
Safeguard our house, safeguard my grandson Iulus!
This sign is yours: Troy rests in your power.

I give way, my son. No more refusals.
I will go with you, your comrade.'
"So he yielded
but now the roar of flames grows louder all through Troy
and the seething floods of fire are rolling closer.
'So come, dear father, climb up onto my shoulders!
I will carry you on my back. This labor of love
will never wear me down. Whatever falls to us now,
we both will share one peril, one path to safety.
Little Iulus, walk beside me, and you, my wife,
follow me at a distance, in my footsteps.
Servants, listen closely . . .
Just past the city walls a gravemound lies
where an old shrine of forsaken Ceres stands
with an ancient cypress growing close beside it—
our fathers' reverence kept it green for years.
Coming by many routes, it's there we meet,
our rendezvous. And you, my father, carry
our hearthgods now, our fathers' sacred vessels.
I, just back from the war and fresh from slaughter,
I must not handle the holy things—it's wrong—
not till I cleanse myself in running springs.'
"With that,
over my broad shoulders and round my neck I spread
a tawny lion's skin for a cloak, and bowing down,
I lift my burden up. Little Iulus, clutching
my right hand, keeps pace with tripping steps.
My wife trails on behind. And so we make our way
along the pitch-dark paths, and I who had never flinched
at the hurtling spears or swarming Greek assaults—
now every stir of wind, every whisper of sound
alarms me, anxious both for the child beside me
and burden on my back. And then, nearing the gates,
thinking we've all got safely through, I suddenly
seem to catch the steady tramp of marching feet
and father, peering out through the darkness, cries:
'Run for it now, my boy, you must. They're closing in,
I can see their glinting shields, their flashing bronze!'

"Then in my panic something strange, some enemy power
robbed me of my senses. Lost, I was leaving behind
familiar paths, at a run down blind dead ends
when—
"Oh dear god, my wife, Creusa—
torn from me by a brutal fate! What then,
did she stop in her tracks or lose her way?
Or exhausted, sink down to rest? Who knows?
I never set my eyes on her again.
I never looked back, she never crossed my mind—
Creusa, lost—not till we reached that barrow

sacred to ancient Ceres where, with all our people
rallied at last, she alone was missing. Lost
to her friends, her son, her husband—gone forever.
Raving, I blamed them all, the gods, the human race—
what crueler blow did I feel the night that Troy went down?
Ascanius, father Anchises, and all the gods of Troy,
entrusting them to my friends, I hide them well away
in a valley's shelter, don my burnished gear
and back I go to Troy . . .
my mind steeled to relive the whole disaster,
retrace my route through the whole city now
and put my life in danger one more time.
"First then,
back to the looming walls, the shadowy rear gates
by which I'd left the city, back I go in my tracks,
retracing, straining to find my footsteps in the dark,
with terror at every turn, the very silence makes me cringe.
Then back to my house I go—if only, only she's gone there—
but the Greeks have flooded in, seized the entire place.
All over now. Devouring fire whipped by the winds
goes churning into the rooftops, flames surging
over them, scorching blasts raging up the sky.
On I go and again I see the palace of Priam
set on the heights, but there in colonnades
deserted now, in the sanctuary of Juno, there
stand the elite watchmen, Phoenix, ruthless Ulysses
guarding all their loot. All the treasures of Troy
hauled from the burning shrines—the sacramental tables,
bowls of solid gold and the holy robes they'd seized
from every quarter—Greeks, piling high the plunder.
Children and trembling mothers rounded up
in a long, endless line.
"Why, I even dared fling
my voice through the dark, my shouts filled the streets
as time and again, overcome with grief I called out
'Creusa!' Nothing, no reply, and again 'Creusa!'
But then as I madly rushed from house to house,
no end in sight, abruptly, right before my eyes
I saw her stricken ghost, my own Creusa's shade.
But larger than life, the life I'd known so well.
I froze. My hackles bristled, voice choked in my throat,
and my wife spoke out to ease me of my anguish:
'My dear husband, why so eager to give yourself
to such mad flights of grief? It's not without
the will of the gods these things have come to pass.
But the gods forbid you to take Creusa with you,
bound from Troy together. The king of lofty Olympus[8]

8. Jupiter.

won't allow it. A long exile is your fate . . .
the vast plains of the sea are yours to plow
until you reach Hesperian land, where Lydian Tiber[9]
flows with its smooth march through rich and loamy fields,
a land of hardy people. There great joy and a kingdom
are yours to claim, and a queen to make your wife.
Dispel your tears for Creusa, whom you loved.
I will never behold the high and mighty pride
of their palaces, the Myrmidons, the Dolopians,
or go as a slave to some Greek matron, no, not I,
daughter of Dardanus that I am, the wife of Venus' son.
The Great Mother of Gods[1] detains me on these shores.
And now farewell. Hold dear the son we share,
we love together.'
"These were her parting words
and for all my tears—I longed to say so much—
dissolving into the empty air she left me now.
Three times I tried to fling my arms around her neck,
three times I embraced—nothing . . . her phantom
sifting through my fingers,
light as wind, quick as a dream in flight.
"Gone—
and at last the night was over. Back I went to my people
and I was amazed to see what throngs of new companions
had poured in to swell our numbers, mothers, men,
our forces gathered for exile, grieving masses.
They had come together from every quarter,
belongings, spirits ready for me to lead them
over the sea to whatever lands I'd choose.
And now the morning star was mounting above
the high crests of Ida, leading on the day.
The Greeks had taken the city, blocked off every gate.
No hope of rescue now. So I gave way at last and
lifting my father, headed toward the mountains."

Summary of Book III Aeneas and his fleet travel across the Mediterranean. On the way, they meet the monstrous bird-women (Harpies) and visit Andromache, widow of Hector. Anchises dies, and the storm carries the Trojans to Carthage.

9. "Hesperian" is literally "western." The Tiber runs through Rome. "Lydian" is used as an alternative for "Etruscan," since the Etruscans were thought to come from Lydia.

1. Cybele is the mother goddess.

BOOK IV

[*The Tragic Queen of Carthage*]

But the queen—too long she has suffered the pain of love,
hour by hour nursing the wound with her lifeblood,
consumed by the fire buried in her heart.
The man's courage, the sheer pride of his line,
they all come pressing home to her, over and over.
His looks, his words, they pierce her heart and cling—
no peace, no rest for her body, love will give her none.

A new day's dawn was moving over the earth, Aurora's torch
cleansing the sky, burning away the dank shade of night
as the restless queen, beside herself, confides now
to the sister of her soul: "Dear Anna, the dreams
that haunt my quaking heart! Who is this stranger
just arrived to lodge in our house—our guest?
How noble his face, his courage, and what a soldier!
I'm sure—I know it's true—the man is born of the gods.
Fear exposes the lowborn man at once. But, oh, how tossed
he's been by the blows of fate. What a tale he's told,
what a bitter bowl of war he's drunk to the dregs.
If my heart had not been fixed, dead set against
embracing another man in the bonds of marriage—
ever since my first love deceived me, cheated me
by his death—if I were not as sick as I am
of the bridal bed and torch,[2] this, perhaps,
is my one lapse that might have brought me down.
I confess it, Anna, yes. Ever since my Sychaeus,
my poor husband met his fate, and my own brother
shed his blood and stained our household gods,
this is the only man who's roused me deeply,
swayed my wavering heart . . .
The signs of the old flame, I know them well.
I pray that the earth gape deep enough to take me down
or the almighty Father blast me with one bolt to the shades,
the pale, glimmering shades in hell, the pit of night,
before I dishonor you, my conscience, break your laws.
He's carried my love away, the man who wed me first—
may he hold it tight, safeguard it in his grave."

She broke off, her voice choking with tears
that brimmed and wet her breast.

But Anna answered:
"Dear one, dearer than light to me, your sister,
would you waste away, grieving your youth away, alone,
never to know the joy of children, all the gifts of love?
Do you really believe that's what the dust desires,
the ghosts in their ashen tombs? Have it your way.

2. Torches were used at weddings in antiquity.

But granted that no one tempted you in the past,
not in your great grief,
no Libyan suitor, and none before in Tyre,
you scorned Iarbas and other lords of Africa,
sons bred by this fertile earth in all their triumph:
why resist it now, this love that stirs your heart?
Don't you recall whose lands you settled here,
the men who press around you? On one side
the Gaetulian cities, fighters matchless in battle,
unbridled Numidians—Syrtes, the treacherous Sandbanks.
On the other side an endless desert, parched earth
where the wild Barcan marauders[3] range at will.
Why mention the war that's boiling up in Tyre,
your brother's deadly threats? I think, in fact,
the favor of all the gods and Juno's backing drove
these Trojan ships on the winds that sailed them here.
Think what a city you will see, my sister, what a kingdom
rising high if you marry such a man! With a Trojan army
marching at our side, think how the glory of Carthage
will tower to the clouds! Just ask the gods for pardon,
win them with offerings. Treat your guests like kings.
Weave together some pretext for delay, while winter
spends its rage and drenching Orion whips the sea—
the ships still battered, weather still too wild."

These were the words that fanned her sister's fire,
turned her doubts to hopes and dissolved her sense of shame.
And first they visit the altars, make the rounds,
praying the gods for blessings, shrine by shrine.
They slaughter the pick of yearling sheep, the old way,
to Ceres, Giver of Laws, to Apollo, Bacchus who sets us free
and Juno above all, who guards the bonds of marriage.[4]
Dido aglow with beauty holds the bowl in her right hand,
pouring wine between the horns of a pure white cow
or gravely paces before the gods' fragrant altars,
under their statues' eyes refreshing her first gifts,
dawn to dusk. And when the victims' chests are splayed,
Dido, her lips parted, pores over their entrails,
throbbing still, for signs . . . [5]
But, oh, how little they know, the omniscient seers.
What good are prayers and shrines to a person mad with love?
The flame keeps gnawing into her tender marrow hour by hour
and deep in her heart the silent wound lives on.
Dido burns with love—the tragic queen.
She wanders in frenzy through her city streets
like a wounded doe caught all off guard by a hunter

3. African groups living near Carthage.

4. Ceres: goddess of grain and agriculture. Apollo: god of the sun, associated with civilization. Bacchus: god of wine. Juno: queen of the gods, goddess of marriage. All were associated with the foundation of cities.

5. It was Roman custom to inspect the entrails of the sacrificial victim and interpret any unusual features as signs of the future.

stalking the woods of Crete, who strikes her from afar
and leaves his winging steel in her flesh, and he's unaware
but she veers in flight through Dicte's woody glades,
fixed in her side the shaft that takes her life.
And now
Dido leads her guest through the heart of Carthage,
displaying Phoenician power, the city readied for him.
She'd speak her heart but her voice chokes, mid-word.
Now at dusk she calls for the feast to start again,
madly begging to hear again the agony of Troy,
to hang on his lips again, savoring his story.
Then, with the guests gone, and the dimming moon
quenching its light in turn, and the setting stars
inclining heads to sleep—alone in the echoing hall,
distraught, she flings herself on the couch that he left empty.
Lost as he is, she's lost as well, she hears him, sees him
or she holds Ascanius back and dandles him on her lap,
bewitched by the boy's resemblance to his father,
trying to cheat the love she dare not tell.
The towers of Carthage, half built, rise no more,
and the young men quit their combat drills in arms.
The harbors, the battlements planned to block attack,
all work's suspended now, the huge, threatening walls
with the soaring cranes that sway across the sky.

Now, no sooner had Jove's dear wife perceived
that Dido was in the grip of such a scourge—
no thought of pride could stem her passion now—
than Juno approaches Venus and sets a cunning trap:
"What a glittering prize, a triumph you carry home!
You and your boy there, you grand and glorious Powers.
Just look, one woman crushed by the craft of two gods!
I am not blind, you know. For years you've looked askance
at the homes of rising Carthage, feared our ramparts.
But where will it end? What good is all our strife?
Come, why don't we labor now to live in peace?
Eternal peace, sealed with the bonds of marriage.
You have it all, whatever your heart desires—
Dido's ablaze with love,
drawing the frenzy deep into her bones. So,
let us rule this people in common: joint command.
And let her marry her Phrygian lover, be his slave
and give her Tyrians over to your control,
her dowry in your hands!"
Perceiving at once
that this was all pretense, a ruse to shift
the kingdom of Italy onto Libyan shores,
Venus countered Juno: "Now who'd be so insane
as to shun your offer and strive with you in war?
If only Fortune crowns your proposal with success!
But swayed by the Fates, I have my doubts. Would Jove
want one city to hold the Tyrians and the Trojan exiles?

Would he sanction the mingling of their peoples,
bless their binding pacts? You are his wife,
with every right to probe him with your prayers.
You lead the way. I'll follow."
"The work is mine,"
imperious Juno carried on, "but how to begin
this pressing matter now and see it through?
I'll explain in a word or so. Listen closely.
Tomorrow Aeneas and lovesick Dido plan to hunt
the woods together, soon as the day's first light
climbs high and the Titan's rays lay bare the earth.
But while the beaters scramble to ring the glens with nets,
I'll shower down a cloudburst, hail, black driving rain—
I'll shatter the vaulting sky with claps of thunder.
The huntsmen will scatter, swallowed up in the dark,
and Dido and Troy's commander will make their way
to the same cave for shelter. And I'll be there,
if I can count on your own good will in this—
I'll bind them in lasting marriage, make them one.
Their wedding it will be!"
So Juno appealed
and Venus did not oppose her, nodding in assent
and smiling at all the guile she saw through . . .

Meanwhile Dawn rose up and left her Ocean bed
and soon as her rays have lit the sky, an elite band
of young huntsmen streams out through the gates,
bearing the nets, wide-meshed or tight for traps
and their hunting spears with broad iron heads,
troops of Massylian horsemen galloping hard,
packs of powerful hounds, keen on the scent.
Yet the queen delays, lingering in her chamber
with Carthaginian chiefs expectant at her doors.
And there her proud, mettlesome charger prances
in gold and royal purple, pawing with thunder-hoofs,
champing a foam-flecked bit. At last she comes,
with a great retinue crowding round the queen
who wears a Tyrian cloak with rich embroidered fringe.
Her quiver is gold, her hair drawn up in a golden torque
and a golden buckle clasps her purple robe in folds.
Nor do her Trojan comrades tarry. Out they march,
young Iulus flushed with joy.
Aeneas in command, the handsomest of them all,
advancing as her companion joins his troop with hers.
So vivid. Think of Apollo leaving his Lycian haunts
and Xanthus in winter spate, he's out to visit Delos,
his mother's isle,[6] and strike up the dance again
while round the altars swirls a growing throng

6. The sun god Apollo is imagined leaving Lycia when the river Xanthus floods, and going to Delos, which was sacred to his mother, Leto.

of Cretans, Dryopians, Agathyrsians with tattoos,
and a drumming roar goes up as the god himself
strides the Cynthian ridge,[7] his streaming hair
braided with pliant laurel leaves entwined
in twists of gold, and arrows clash on his shoulders.
So no less swiftly Aeneas strides forward now
and his face shines with a glory like the god's.

Once the huntsmen have reached the trackless lairs
aloft in the foothills, suddenly, look, some wild goats
flushed from a ridge come scampering down the slopes
and lower down a herd of stags goes bounding across
the open country, ranks massed in a cloud of dust,
fleeing the high ground. But young Ascanius,
deep in the valley, rides his eager mount
and relishing every stride, outstrips them all,
now goats, now stags, but his heart is racing, praying—
if only they'd send among this feeble, easy game
some frothing wild boar or a lion stalking down
from the heights and tawny in the sun.
Too late—
The skies have begun to rumble, peals of thunder first
and the storm breaking next, a cloudburst pelting hail
and the troops of hunters scatter up and down the plain,
Tyrian comrades, bands of Dardans, Venus' grandson Iulus
panicking, running for cover, quick, and down the mountain
gulleys erupt in torrents. Dido and Troy's commander
make their way to the same cave for shelter now.
Primordial Earth and Juno, Queen of Marriage,
give the signal and lightning torches flare
and the high sky bears witness to the wedding,
nymphs on the mountaintops wail out the wedding hymn.
This was the first day of her death, the first of grief,
the cause of it all. From now on, Dido cares no more
for appearances, nor for her reputation, either.
She no longer thinks to keep the affair a secret,
no, she calls it a marriage,
using the word to cloak her sense of guilt.

Straightway Rumor flies through Libya's great cities,
Rumor, swiftest of all the evils in the world.
She thrives on speed, stronger for every stride,
slight with fear at first, soon soaring into the air
she treads the ground and hides her head in the clouds.
She is the last, they say, our Mother Earth produced.
Bursting in rage against the gods, she bore a sister
for Coeus and Enceladus:[8] Rumor, quicksilver afoot
and swift on the wing, a monster, horrific, huge
and under every feather on her body—what a marvel—

7. Mount Cynthus was on Delos.

8. Titans, the first children of Earth.

an eye that never sleeps and as many tongues as eyes
and as many raucous mouths and ears pricked up for news.
By night she flies aloft, between the earth and sky,
whirring across the dark, never closing her lids
in soothing sleep. By day she keeps her watch,
crouched on a peaked roof or palace turret,
terrorizing the great cities, clinging as fast
to her twisted lies as she clings to words of truth.
Now Rumor is in her glory, filling Africa's ears
with tale on tale of intrigue, bruiting her song
of facts and falsehoods mingled . . .
"Here this Aeneas, born of Trojan blood,
has arrived in Carthage, and lovely Dido deigns
to join the man in wedlock. Even now they warm
the winter, long as it lasts, with obscene desire,
oblivious to their kingdoms, abject thralls of lust."

Such talk the sordid goddess spreads on the lips of men,
then swerves in her course and heading straight for King Iarbas,
stokes his heart with hearsay, piling fuel on his fire.

Iarbas—son of an African nymph whom Jove had raped—
raised the god a hundred splendid temples across
the king's wide realm, a hundred altars too,
consecrating the sacred fires
that never died, eternal sentinels of the gods.
The earth was rich with blood of slaughtered herds
and the temple doorways wreathed with riots of flowers.
This Iarbas, driven wild, set ablaze by the bitter rumor,
approached an altar, they say, as the gods hovered round,
and lifting a suppliant's hands, he poured out prayers to Jove:
"Almighty Jove! Now as the Moors adore you, feasting away
on their gaudy couches, tipping wine in your honor—
do you see this? Or are we all fools, Father,
to dread the bolts you hurl? All aimless then,
your fires high in the clouds that terrify us so?
All empty noise, your peals of grumbling thunder?
That woman, that vagrant! Here in my own land
she founded her paltry city for a pittance.
We tossed her some beach to plow—on my terms—
and then she spurns our offer of marriage, she
embraces Aeneas as lord and master in her realm.
And now this second Paris . . .
leading his troupe of eunuchs, his hair oozing oil,
a Phrygian bonnet tucked up under his chin, he revels
in all that he has filched, while we keep bearing gifts
to your temples—yes, yours—coddling your reputation,
all your hollow show!"
So King Iarbas appealed,
his hand clutching the altar, and Jove Almighty heard

and turned his gaze on the royal walls of Carthage
and the lovers oblivious now to their good name.
He summons Mercury,[9] gives him marching orders:
"Quick, my son, away! Call up the Zephyrs,[1]
glide on wings of the wind. Find the Dardan captain
who now malingers long in Tyrian Carthage, look,
and pays no heed to the cities Fate decrees are his.
Take my commands through the racing winds and tell him
this is not the man his mother, the lovely goddess, promised,
not for *this* did she save him twice from Greek attacks.
Never. He would be the one to master an Italy
rife with leaders, shrill with the cries of war,
to sire a people sprung from Teucer's noble blood[2]
and bring the entire world beneath the rule of law.
If such a glorious destiny cannot fire his spirit,
if he will not shoulder the task for his own fame,
does the father of Ascanius grudge his son
the walls of Rome? What is he plotting now?
What hope can make him loiter among his foes,
lose sight of Italian offspring still to come
and all the Lavinian fields?[3] Let him set sail!
This is the sum of it. This must be our message."

Jove had spoken. Mercury made ready at once
to obey the great commands of his almighty father.
First he fastens under his feet the golden sandals,
winged to sweep him over the waves and earth alike
with the rush of gusting winds. Then he seizes the wand
that calls the pallid spirits up from the Underworld
and ushers others down to the grim dark depths,
the wand that lends us sleep or sends it away,
that unseals our eyes in death.[4] Equipped with this,
he spurs the winds and swims through billowing clouds
till in mid-flight he spies the summit and rugged flanks
of Atlas, whose long-enduring peak supports the skies.[5]
Atlas: his pine-covered crown is forever girded
round with black clouds, battered by wind and rain;
driving blizzards cloak his shoulders with snow,
torrents course down from the old Titan's chin
and shaggy beard that bristles stiff with ice.
Here the god of Cyllene[6] landed first,
banking down to a stop on balanced wings.
From there, headlong down with his full weight

9. The messenger god; Hermes in Greek mythology.
1. Personified winds. Zephyr is usually the gentle west wind.
2. Teucer was the first king of Troy.
3. Lavinium is the city Aeneas will found in Italy.
4. Mercury is the god who guides the dead to the underworld.
5. Atlas is a Titan who was condemned by Zeus to stand holding up the sky.
6. Mercury was born on Mount Cyllene, in Greece.

he plunged to the sea as a seahawk skims the waves,
rounding the beaches, rounding cliffs to hunt for fish inshore.
So Mercury of Cyllene flew between the earth and sky
to gain the sandy coast of Libya, cutting the winds
that sweep down from his mother's father, Atlas.
Soon
as his winged feet touched down on the first huts in sight,
he spots Aeneas founding the city fortifications,
building homes in Carthage. And his sword-hilt
is studded with tawny jasper stars, a cloak
of glowing Tyrian purple drapes his shoulders,
a gift that the wealthy queen had made herself,
weaving into the weft a glinting mesh of gold.
Mercury lashes out at once: "You, so now you lay
foundation stones for the soaring walls of Carthage!
Building her gorgeous city, doting on your wife.
Blind to your own realm, oblivious to your fate!
The King of the Gods, whose power sways earth and sky—
he is the one who sends me down from brilliant Olympus,
bearing commands for you through the racing winds.
What are you plotting now?
Wasting time in Libya—what hope misleads you so?
If such a glorious destiny cannot fire your spirit,
[if you will not shoulder the task for your own fame,][7]
at least remember Ascanius rising into his prime,
the hopes you lodge in Iulus, your only heir—
you owe him Italy's realm, the land of Rome!"
This order still on his lips, the god vanished
from sight into empty air.
Then Aeneas
was truly overwhelmed by the vision, stunned,
his hackles bristle with fear, his voice chokes in his throat.
He yearns to be gone, to desert this land he loves,
thunderstruck by the warnings, Jupiter's command . . .
But what can he do? What can he dare say now
to the queen in all her fury and win her over?
Where to begin, what opening? Thoughts racing,
here, there, probing his options, turning
to this plan, that plan—torn in two until,
at his wits' end, this answer seems the best.
He summons Mnestheus, Sergestus, staunch Serestus,
gives them orders: "Fit out the fleet, but not a word.
Muster the crews on shore, all tackle set to sail,
but the cause for our new course, you keep it secret."
Yet he himself, since Dido who means the world to him
knows nothing, never dreaming such a powerful love
could be uprooted—he will try to approach her,
find the moment to break the news gently,

7. Bracketed because some editors believe the line does not belong in the text.

a way to soften the blow that he must leave.
All shipmates snap to commands,
glad to do his orders.
True, but the queen—
who can delude a lover?—soon caught wind
of a plot afoot, the first to sense the Trojans
are on the move . . . She fears everything now,
even with all secure. Rumor, vicious as ever,
brings her word, already distraught, that Trojans
are rigging out their galleys, gearing to set sail.
She rages in helpless frenzy, blazing through
the entire city, raving like some Maenad[8]
driven wild when the women shake the sacred emblems,
when the cyclic orgy, shouts of "Bacchus!" fire her on
and Cithaeron echoes round with maddened midnight cries.

At last she assails Aeneas, before he's said a word:
"So, you traitor, you really believed you'd keep
this a secret, this great outrage?—steal away
in silence from my shores? Can nothing hold you back?
Not our love? Not the pledge once sealed with our right hands?
Not even the thought of Dido doomed to a cruel death?
Why labor to rig your fleet when the winter's raw,
to risk the deep when the Northwind's closing in?
You cruel, heartless—Even if you were not
pursuing alien fields and unknown homes,
even if ancient Troy were standing, still,
who'd sail for Troy across such heaving seas?
You're running away—from me? Oh, I pray you
by these tears, by the faith in your right hand—
what else have I left myself in all my pain?—
by our wedding vows, the marriage we began,
if I deserve some decency from you now,
if anything mine has ever won your heart,
pity a great house about to fall, I pray you,
if prayers have any place—reject this scheme of yours!
Thanks to you, the African tribes, Numidian warlords
hate me, even my own Tyrians rise against me.
Thanks to you, my sense of honor is gone,
my one and only pathway to the stars,
the renown I once held dear. In whose hands,
my guest, do you leave me here to meet my death?
'Guest'—that's all that remains of 'husband' now.
But why do I linger on? Until my brother Pygmalion
batters down my walls? Or Iarbas drags me off, his slave?
If only you'd left a baby in my arms—our child—
before you deserted me! Some little Aeneas

8. The Maenads (Bacchae) were female worshippers of Bacchus, who ran wild on Mount Cithaeron in a ritual held every other year—as depicted in Euripides' *Bacchae*, in which one such god-frenzied woman kills her own son.

playing about our halls, whose features at least
would bring you back to me in spite of all,
I would not feel so totally devastated,
so destroyed."
The queen stopped but he,
warned by Jupiter now, his gaze held steady,
fought to master the torment in his heart. At last
he ventured a few words: "I . . . you have done me
so many kindnesses, and you could count them all.
I shall never deny what you deserve, my queen,
never regret my memories of Dido, not while I
can recall myself and draw the breath of life.
I'll state my case in a few words. I never dreamed
I'd keep my flight a secret. Don't imagine that.
Nor did I once extend a bridegroom's torch
or enter into a marriage pact with you.
If the Fates had left me free to live my life,
to arrange my own affairs of my own free will,
Troy is the city, first of all, that I'd safeguard,
Troy and all that's left of my people whom I cherish.
The grand palace of Priam would stand once more,
with my own hands I would fortify a second Troy
to house my Trojans in defeat. But not now.
Grynean Apollo's oracle says that I must seize
on Italy's noble land, his Lycian lots say 'Italy!'[9]
There lies my love, there lies my homeland now.
If you, a Phoenician, fix your eyes on Carthage,
a Libyan stronghold, tell me, why do you grudge
the Trojans their new homes on Italian soil?
What is the crime if *we* seek far-off kingdoms too?

"My father, Anchises, whenever the darkness shrouds
the earth in its dank shadows, whenever the stars
go flaming up the sky, my father's anxious ghost
warns me in dreams and fills my heart with fear.
My son Ascanius . . . I feel the wrong I do
to one so dear, robbing him of his kingdom,
lands in the West, his fields decreed by Fate.
And now the messenger of the gods—I swear it,
by your life and mine—dispatched by Jove himself
has brought me firm commands through the racing winds.
With my own eyes I saw him, clear, in broad daylight,
moving through your gates. With my own ears I drank
his message in. Come, stop inflaming us both
with your appeals. I set sail for Italy—
all against my will."
Even from the start
of his declaration, she has glared at him askance,

9. Grynia was an Aeolian city sacred to Apollo. Lycia is another cult center of Apollo.

her eyes roving over him, head to foot, with a look
of stony silence . . . till abruptly she cries out
in a blaze of fury: "No goddess was your mother!
No Dardanus sired your line, you traitor, liar, no,
Mount Caucasus fathered you on its flinty, rugged flanks
and the tigers of Hyrcania gave you their dugs to suck![1]
Why hide it? Why hold back? To suffer greater blows?
Did *he* groan when *I* wept? Even look at me? Never!
Surrender a tear? Pity the one who loves him?
What can I say first? So much to say. Now—
neither mighty Juno nor Saturn's son, the Father,[2]
gazes down on this with just, impartial eyes.
There's no faith left on earth!
He was washed up on my shores, helpless, and I,
I took him in, like a maniac let him share my kingdom,
salvaged his lost fleet, plucked his crews from death.
Oh I am swept by the Furies, gales of fire![3] Now
it's Apollo the Prophet, Apollo's Lycian oracles:
they're his masters now, and now, to top it off,
the messenger of the gods, dispatched by Jove himself,
comes rushing down the winds with his grim-set commands.
Really! What work for the gods who live on high,
what a concern to ruffle their repose!
I won't hold you, I won't even refute you—go!—
strike out for Italy on the winds, your realm across the sea.
I hope, I pray, if the just gods still have any power,
wrecked on the rocks midsea you'll drink your bowl
of pain to the dregs, crying out the name of Dido
over and over, and worlds away I'll hound you then
with pitch-black flames, and when icy death has severed
my body from its breath, then my ghost will stalk you
through the world! You'll pay, you shameless, ruthless—
and I will hear of it, yes, the report will reach me
even among the deepest shades of Death!"
She breaks off
in the midst of outbursts, desperate, flinging herself
from the light of day, sweeping out of his sight,
leaving him numb with doubt, with much to fear
and much he means to say.
Catching her as she faints away, her women
bear her back to her marble bridal chamber
and lay her body down upon her bed.
But Aeneas
is driven by duty now. Strongly as he longs
to ease and allay her sorrow, speak to her,
turn away her anguish with reassurance, still,
moaning deeply, heart shattered by his great love,

1. Dardanus was the legendary founder of Troy. The Caucasus mountains, between the Black and Caspian Seas, and Hyrcania, south of the Caspian, were notoriously wild, uncivilized regions.

2. Jupiter was the son of Saturn.

3. The Furies are spirits of vengeance who carry flaming torches.

in spite of all he obeys the gods' commands
and back he goes to his ships.
Then the Trojans throw themselves in the labor,
launching their tall vessels down along the beach
and the hull rubbed sleek with pitch floats high again.
So keen to be gone, the men drag down from the forest
untrimmed timbers and boughs still green for oars.
You can see them streaming out of the whole city,
men like ants that, wary of winter's onset, pillage
some huge pile of wheat to store away in their grange
and their army's long black line goes marching through the field,
trundling their spoils down some cramped, grassy track.
Some put shoulders to giant grains and thrust them on,
some dress the ranks, strictly marshal stragglers,
and the whole trail seethes with labor.

What did you feel then, Dido, seeing this?
How deep were the groans you uttered, gazing now
from the city heights to watch the broad beaches
seething with action, the bay a chaos of outcries
right before your eyes?
Love, you tyrant!
To what extremes won't you compel our hearts?
Again she resorts to tears, driven to move the man,
or try, with prayers—a suppliant kneeling, humbling
her pride to passion. So if die she must,
she'll leave no way untried.
"Anna, you see
the hurly-burly all across the beach, the crews
swarming from every quarter? The wind cries for canvas,
the buoyant oarsmen crown their sterns with wreaths.
This terrible sorrow: since I saw it coming, Anna,
I can endure it now. But even so, my sister,
carry out for me one great favor in my pain.
To you alone he used to listen, the traitor,
to you confide his secret feelings. You alone
know how and when to approach him, soothe his moods.
Go, my sister! Plead with my imperious enemy.
Remind him I was never at Aulis, never swore a pact
with the Greeks to rout the Trojan people from the earth![4]
I sent no fleet to Troy, I never uprooted the ashes
of his father, Anchises, never stirred his shade.
Why does he shut his pitiless ears to my appeals?
Where's he rushing now? If only he would offer
one last gift to the wretched queen who loves him:
to wait for fair winds, smooth sailing for his flight!
I no longer beg for the long-lost marriage he betrayed,
nor would I ask him now to desert his kingdom, no,

4. The Greek forces mustered at Aulis before sailing to Troy. It was here that Agamemnon killed his daughter to make the wind blow. Now again, a woman must die to release a fleet.

his lovely passion, Latium.[5] All I ask is time,
blank time: some rest from frenzy, breathing room
till my fate can teach my beaten spirit how to grieve.
I beg him—pity your sister, Anna—one last favor,
and if he grants it now, I'll pay him back,
with interest, when I die."
So Dido pleads and
so her desolate sister takes him the tale of tears
again and again. But no tears move Aeneas now.
He is deaf to all appeals. He won't relent.
The Fates bar the way
and heaven blocks his gentle, human ears.
As firm as a sturdy oak grown tough with age
when the Northwinds blasting off the Alps compete,
fighting left and right, to wrench it from the earth,
and the winds scream, the trunk shudders, its leafy crest
showers across the ground but it clings firm to its rock,
its roots stretching as deep into the dark world below
as its crown goes towering toward the gales of heaven—
so firm the hero stands: buffeted left and right
by storms of appeals, he takes the full force
of love and suffering deep in his great heart.
His will stands unmoved. The falling tears are futile.[6]
Then,
terrified by her fate, tragic Dido prays for death,
sickened to see the vaulting sky above her.
And to steel her new resolve to leave the light,
she sees, laying gifts on the altars steaming incense—
shudder to hear it now—the holy water going black
and the wine she pours congeals in bloody filth.[7]
She told no one what she saw, not even her sister.
Worse, there was a marble temple in her palace,
a shrine built for her long-lost love, Sychaeus.
Holding it dear she tended it—marvelous devotion—
draping the snow-white fleece and festal boughs.
Now from its depths she seemed to catch his voice,
the words of her dead husband calling out her name
while night enclosed the earth in its dark shroud,
and over and over a lonely owl perched on the rooftops
drew out its low, throaty call to a long wailing dirge.
And worse yet, the grim predictions of ancient seers
keep terrifying her now with frightful warnings.
Aeneas the hunter, savage in all her nightmares,
drives her mad with panic. She always feels alone,
abandoned, always wandering down some endless road,
not a friend in sight, seeking her own Phoenicians
in some godforsaken land. As frantic as Pentheus

5. Region of central Italy, land of the Latins.

6. In the Latin, as here, it is unclear who is crying; it could be Anna, Dido, Aeneas, or all three.

7. Dido is trying to pour libations—liquid offerings to the gods.

seeing battalions of Furies, twin suns ablaze
and double cities of Thebes before his eyes.[8]
Or Agamemnon's Orestes hounded off the stage,
fleeing his mother armed with torches, black snakes,
while blocking the doorway coil her Furies of Revenge.[9]

So, driven by madness, beaten down by anguish,
Dido was fixed on dying, working out in her mind
the means, the moment. She approaches her grieving
sister, Anna—masking her plan with a brave face
aglow with hope, and says: "I've found a way,
dear heart—rejoice with your sister—either
to bring him back in love for me or free me
of love for him. Close to the bounds of Ocean,
west with the setting sun, lies Ethiopian land,
the end of the earth, where colossal Atlas turns
on his shoulder the heavens studded with flaming stars.
From there, I have heard, a Massylian priestess comes
who tended the temple held by Hesperian daughters.[1]
She'd safeguard the boughs in the sacred grove
and ply the dragon with morsels dripping loops
of oozing honey and poppies drowsy with slumber.
With her spells she vows to release the hearts
of those she likes, to inflict raw pain on others—
to stop the rivers in midstream, reverse the stars
in their courses, raise the souls of the dead at night
and make earth shudder and rumble underfoot—you'll see—
and send the ash trees marching down the mountains.
I swear by the gods, dear Anna, by your sweet life,
I arm myself with magic arts against my will.[2]
"Now go,
build me a pyre in secret, deep inside our courtyard
under the open sky. Pile it high with his arms—
he left them hanging within our bridal chamber—
the traitor, so devoted then! and all his clothes
and crowning it all, the bridal bed that brought my doom.
I must obliterate every trace of the man, the curse,
and the priestess shows the way!"
She says no more
and now as the queen falls silent, pallor sweeps her face.

8. Pentheus is the king of Thebes who, in Euripides' *Bacchae*, was driven mad so that he thought he saw two suns in the sky and was then killed by his own mother.

9. Agamemnon's son, Orestes, killed his mother in revenge for her killing his father. He was then driven mad by the Furies. The myth is the subject of Aeschylus's *Oresteia* and Euripides' *Orestes*.

1. The Massylians were a North African tribe. The daughters of Hesperus, the Evening Star, tended a garden containing the golden apples that belonged to Hera. A never-sleeping dragon with a hundred heads also guarded the apples.

2. These allusions to witchcraft make Dido sound like Medea, the princess of Colchis with magical powers, who helped Jason steal the Golden Fleece from her father and escape back to Greece. Later, after several years of marriage, Jason abandoned Medea; she then, according to Euripides' *Medea*, took revenge by killing their children.

Still, Anna cannot imagine these outlandish rites
would mask her sister's death. She can't conceive
of such a fiery passion. She fears nothing graver
than Dido's grief at the death of her Sychaeus.
So she does as she is told.
                                        But now the queen,
as soon as the pyre was built beneath the open sky,
towering up with pitch-pine and cut logs of oak—
deep in the heart of her house—she drapes the court
with flowers, crowning the place with wreaths of death,
and to top it off she lays his arms and the sword he left
and an effigy of Aeneas, all on the bed they'd shared,
for well she knows the future. Altars ring the pyre.
Hair loose in the wind, the priestess thunders out
the names of her three hundred gods, Erebus, Chaos
and triple Hecate, Diana the three-faced virgin.[3]
She'd sprinkled water, simulating the springs of hell,
and gathered potent herbs, reaped with bronze sickles
under the moonlight, dripping their milky black poison,
and fetched a love-charm ripped from a foal's brow,
just born, before the mother could gnaw it off.
And Dido herself, standing before the altar,
holding the sacred grain in reverent hands—
with one foot free of its sandal, robes unbound[4]—
sworn now to die, she calls on the gods to witness,
calls on the stars who know her approaching fate.
And then to any Power above, mindful, evenhanded,
who watches over lovers bound by unequal passion,
Dido says her prayers.
                                    The dead of night,
and weary living creatures throughout the world
are enjoying peaceful sleep. The woods and savage seas
are calm, at rest, and the circling stars are gliding on
in their midnight courses, all the fields lie hushed
and the flocks and gay and gorgeous birds that haunt
the deep clear pools and the thorny country thickets
all lie quiet now, under the silent night, asleep.
But not the tragic queen . . .
torn in spirit, Dido will not dissolve
into sleep—her eyes, her mind won't yield to night.
Her torments multiply, over and over her passion
surges back into heaving waves of rage—
she keeps on brooding, obsessions roil her heart:
"And now, what shall I do? Make a mockery of myself,
go back to my old suitors, tempt them to try again?
Beg the Numidians, grovel, plead for a husband—
though time and again I scorned to wed their likes?
What then? Trail the Trojan ships, bend to the Trojans'
every last demand? So pleased, are they, with all the help,

3. Erebus is Darkness, son of Chaos. Hecate, sometimes identified with Diana the moon goddess, was the goddess of witchcraft.
4. All magical practices.

the relief I lent them once? And memory of my service past
stands firm in grateful minds! And even if I were willing,
would the Trojans allow me to board their proud ships—
a woman they hate? Poor lost fool, can't you sense it,
grasp it yet—the treachery of Laomedon's breed?[5]
What now? Do I take flight alone, consorting
with crews of Trojan oarsmen in their triumph?
Or follow them out with all my troops of Tyrians
thronging the decks? Yes, hard as it was to uproot
them once from Tyre! How can I force them back to sea
once more, command them to spread their sails to the winds?
No, no, die!
You deserve it—
end your pain with the sword!
You, my sister, you were the first, won over by my tears,
to pile these sorrows on my shoulders, mad as I was,
to throw me into my enemy's arms. If only I'd been free
to live my life, untested in marriage, free of guilt
as some wild beast untouched by pangs like these!
I broke the faith I swore to the ashes of Sychaeus."

Such terrible grief kept breaking from her heart
as Aeneas slept in peace on his ship's high stern,
bent on departing now, all tackle set to sail.
And now in his dreams it came again—the god,
his phantom, the same features shining clear.
Like Mercury head to foot, the voice, the glow,
the golden hair, the bloom of youth on his limbs
and his voice rang out with warnings once again:
"Son of the goddess, how can you sleep so soundly
in such a crisis? Can't you see the dangers closing
around you now? Madman! Can't you hear the Westwind
ruffling to speed you on? That woman spawns her plots,
mulling over some desperate outrage in her heart,
lashing her surging rage, she's bent on death.
Why not flee headlong?
Flee headlong while you can! You'll soon see
the waves a chaos of ships, lethal torches flaring,
the whole coast ablaze, if now a new dawn breaks
and finds you still malingering on these shores.
Up with you now. Enough delay. Woman's a thing
that's always changing, shifting like the wind."
With that he vanished into the black night.

Then, terrified by the sudden phantom,
Aeneas, wrenching himself from sleep, leaps up
and rouses his crews and spurs them headlong on:
"Quick! Up and at it, shipmates, man the thwarts!
Spread canvas fast! A god's come down from the sky

5. Laomedon, father of Priam and previous king of Troy, broke a promise to repay Apollo and Neptune for building his city walls.

once more—I've just seen him—urging us on
to sever our mooring cables, sail at once!
We follow you, blessed god, whoever you are—
glad at heart we obey your commands once more.
Now help us, stand beside us with all your kindness,
bring us favoring stars in the sky to blaze our way!"

Tearing sword from sheath like a lightning flash,
he hacks the mooring lines with a naked blade.
Gripped by the same desire, all hands pitch in,
they hoist and haul. The shore's deserted now,
the water's hidden under the fleet—they bend to it,
churn the spray and sweep the clear blue sea.
By now
early Dawn had risen up from the saffron bed
of Tithonus,[6] scattering fresh light on the world.
But the queen from her high tower, catching sight
of the morning's white glare, the armada heading out
to sea with sails trimmed to the wind, and certain
the shore and port were empty, stripped of oarsmen—
three, four times over she beat her lovely breast,
she ripped at her golden hair and "Oh, by God,"
she cries, "will the stranger just sail off
and make a mockery of our realm? Will no one
rush to arms, come streaming out of the whole city,
hunt him down, race to the docks and launch the ships?
Go, quick—bring fire!
Hand out weapons!
Bend to the oars!
What am I saying? Where am I? What insanity's this
that shifts my fixed resolve? Dido, oh poor fool,
is it only *now* your wicked work strikes home?
It should have then, when you offered him your scepter.
Look at his hand clasp, look at his good faith now—
that man who, they say, carries his fathers' gods,
who stooped to shoulder his father bent with age!
Couldn't I have seized him then, ripped him to pieces,
scattered them in the sea? Or slashed his men with steel,
butchered Ascanius, served him up as his father's feast?[7]
True, the luck of battle might have been at risk—
well, risk away! Whom did I have to fear?
I was about to die. I should have torched their camp
and flooded their decks with fire. The son, the father,
the whole Trojan line—I should have wiped them out,
then hurled myself on the pyre to crown it all!

6. The goddess Dawn had a human lover named Tithonus, whom she had made immortal (though not ageless) and brought to live with her.

7. These horrible possibilities have mythic precedents. Medea, when she eloped with Jason, ripped up her little brother's body and scattered the pieces on the sea, to distract their father as he tried to pursue the boat. Atreus, father of Agamemnon and Menelaus, killed his brother's children and served them up to him at a feast.

"You, Sun, whose fires scan all works of the earth,[8]
and you, Juno, the witness, midwife to my agonies—
Hecate greeted by nightly shrieks at city crossroads—
and you, you avenging Furies and gods of dying Dido!
Hear me, turn your power my way, attend my sorrows—
I deserve your mercy—hear my prayers! If that curse
of the earth must reach his haven, labor on to landfall—
if Jove and the Fates command and the boundary stone is fixed,
still, let him be plagued in war by a nation proud in arms,
torn from his borders, wrenched from Iulus' embrace,
let him grovel for help and watch his people die
a shameful death! And then, once he has bowed down
to an unjust peace, may he never enjoy his realm
and the light he yearns for, never, let him die
before his day, unburied on some desolate beach!

"That is my prayer, my final cry—I pour it out
with my own lifeblood. And you, my Tyrians,
harry with hatred all his line, his race to come:
make that offering to my ashes, send it down below.
No love between our peoples, ever, no pacts of peace!
Come rising up from my bones, you avenger still unknown,
to stalk those Trojan settlers, hunt with fire and iron,
now or in time to come, whenever the power is yours.
Shore clash with shore, sea against sea and sword
against sword—this is my curse—war between all
our peoples, all their children, endless war!"

With that, her mind went veering back and forth—
what was the quickest way to break off from the light,
the life she loathed? And so with a few words
she turned to Barce, Sychaeus' old nurse—her own
was now black ashes deep in her homeland lost forever:
"Dear old nurse, send Anna my sister to me here.
Tell her to hurry, sprinkle herself with river water,
bring the victims marked for the sacrifice I must make.
So let her come. And wrap your brow with the holy bands.
These rites to Jove of the Styx that I have set in motion,
I yearn to consummate them, end the pain of love,
give that cursed Trojan's pyre to the flames."
The nurse bustled off with an old crone's zeal.
But Dido,
trembling, desperate now with the monstrous thing afoot—
her bloodshot eyes rolling, quivering cheeks blotched
and pale with imminent death—goes bursting through
the doors to the inner courtyard, clambers in frenzy
up the soaring pyre and unsheathes a sword, a Trojan sword
she once sought as a gift, but not for such an end.
And next, catching sight of the Trojan's clothes
and the bed they knew by heart, delaying a moment

8. The sun (Helios) was sometimes personified as a god; he was the grandfather of Medea.

for tears, for memory's sake, the queen lay down
and spoke her final words: "Oh, dear relics,
dear as long as Fate and the gods allowed,
receive my spirit and set me free of pain.
I have lived a life. I've journeyed through
the course that Fortune charted for me. And now
I pass to the world below, my ghost in all its glory.
I have founded a noble city, seen my ramparts rise.
I have avenged my husband, punished my blood-brother,
our mortal foe. Happy, all too happy I would have been
if only the Trojan keels had never grazed our coast."
She presses her face in the bed and cries out:
"I shall die unavenged, but die I will! So—
so—I rejoice to make my way among the shades.
And may that heartless Dardan, far at sea,
drink down deep the sight of our fires here
and bear with him this omen of our death!"

All at once, in the midst of her last words,
her women see her doubled over the sword, the blood
foaming over the blade, her hands splattered red.
A scream goes stabbing up to the high roofs,
Rumor raves like a Maenad through the shocked city—
sobs, and grief, and the wails of women ringing out
through homes, and the heavens echo back the keening din—
for all the world as if enemies stormed the walls
and all of Carthage or old Tyre were toppling down
and flames in their fury, wave on mounting wave
were billowing over the roofs of men and gods.

Anna heard and, stunned, breathless with terror,
raced through the crowd, her nails clawing her face,
fists beating her breast, crying out to her sister now
at the edge of death: "Was it all for *this,* my sister?
You deceived me all along? Is this what your pyre
meant for me—this, your fires—this, your altars?
You deserted me—what shall I grieve for first?
Your friend, your sister, you scorn me now in death?
You should have called me on to the same fate.
The same agony, same sword, the one same hour
had borne us off together. Just to think I built
your pyre with my own hands, implored our fathers' gods
with my own voice, only to be cut off from you—
how very cruel—when you lay down to die . . .
You have destroyed your life, my sister, mine too,
your people, the lords of Sidon and your new city here.
Please, help me to bathe her wounds in water now,
and if any last, lingering breath still hovers,
let me catch it on my lips."
With those words
she had climbed the pyre's topmost steps and now,

clasping her dying sister to her breast, fondling her
she sobbed, stanching the dark blood with her own gown.
Dido, trying to raise her heavy eyes once more, failed—
deep in her heart the wound kept rasping, hissing on.
Three times she tried to struggle up on an elbow,
three times she fell back, writhing on her bed.
Her gaze wavering into the high skies, she looked
for a ray of light and when she glimpsed it, moaned.

Then Juno in all her power, filled with pity
for Dido's agonizing death, her labor long and hard,
sped Iris[9] down from Olympus to release her spirit
wrestling now in a deathlock with her limbs.
Since she was dying a death not fated or deserved,
no, tormented, before her day, in a blaze of passion—
Proserpina had yet to pluck a golden lock from her head
and commit her life to the Styx and the dark world below.[1]
So Iris, glistening dew, comes skimming down from the sky
on gilded wings, trailing showers of iridescence shimmering
into the sun, and hovering over Dido's head, declares:
"So commanded, I take this lock as a sacred gift
to the God of Death, and I release you from your body."

With that, she cut the lock with her hand and all at once
the warmth slipped away, the life dissolved in the winds.

Summary of Books V–VII The Trojans sail back to Sicily, where they mark the death of Anchises with funeral rites and games. They journey to Cumae, Italy, where Aeneas consults the Sibyl, prophetess of Apollo, who helps him descend into the underworld. There, he meets his dead father, who fortells the future history of Rome up to the time of Augustus. Back in the upper world, Aeneas travels to the future site of Rome. He meets Latinus, king of the Latin race, who has just one daughter, Lavinia. An oracle has fortold that she must marry a stranger, and the Latin people welcome Aeneas as their future king. But Queen Amata, Latinus's wife, had hoped that her daughter would marry Turnus, a leader of the rival Rutulian tribe. Juno, jealous at Trojan success, rouses the people to war and leads the native Italians against the invading Trojans.

BOOK VIII

[*The Shield of Aeneas*]

Soon as Turnus hoisted the banner of war from Laurentum's heights[2]
and the piercing trumpets blared, soon as he whipped his horses
rearing for action, clashed his spear against his shield—
passions rose at once, all Latium stirred in frenzy

9. Iris is the goddess who sometimes acts as messenger between heaven and earth; she appears as a rainbow (hence "iridescence").
1. Proserpina, queen of the underworld, would normally have taken a lock of Dido's hair to release her life; since her death is premature, Iris does it.
2. Coastal city of Latium, home of King Latinus.

to swear the oath, and young troops blazed for war.
The chiefs in the lead, Messapus, Ufens, Mezentius,
scorner of gods, call up forces from all quarters
and strip the fields of men who worked the soil.
They send Venulus out to great Diomedes' city[3]
to seek reserves and announce that Trojan ranks
encamp in Latium: "Aeneas arrives with his armada,
bringing the conquered household gods of Troy,
claiming himself a king demanded now by Fate.
And the many tribes report to join the Dardan[4] chief
and his name rings far and wide through Latian country.
But where does the build-up end? What does he long to gain,
if luck is on his side, from open warfare? Clearly,
Diomedes would know—better than King Turnus,
better than King Latinus."

So things went in Latium. Watching it all,
the Trojan hero heaved in a churning sea of anguish,
his thoughts racing, here, there, probing his options,
shifting to this plan, that—as quick as flickering light
thrown off by water in bronze bowls reflects the sun
or radiant moon, now flittering near and far, now
rising to strike a ceiling's gilded fretwork.
The dead of night.
Over the earth all weary living things, all birds and flocks
were fast asleep when captain Aeneas, his heart racked
by the threat of war, lay down on a bank beneath
the chilly arc of the sky and at long last
indulged his limbs in sleep. Before his eyes
the god of the lovely river, old Tiber himself,[5]
seemed to rise from among the poplar leaves,
gowned in his blue-grey linen fine as mist
with a shady crown of reeds to wreathe his hair,
and greeted Aeneas to ease him of his anguish:

"Born of the stock of gods, you who bring back Troy
to us from enemy hands and save her heights forever!
How long we waited for you, here on Laurentine soil
and Latian fields. Here your home is assured, yes,
assured for your household gods. Don't retreat.
Don't fear the threats of war.
The swelling rage of the gods has died away.
I tell you now—so you won't think me an empty dream—
that under an oak along the banks you'll find a great sow
stretched on her side with thirty pigs just farrowed,
a snow-white mother with snow-white young at her dugs.
By this sign, after thirty years have made their rounds

3. The Greek hero Diomedes moved to Italy after the Trojan War.

4. Trojan (from *Dardanus*, the name of the founder of Troy).

5. The Tiber is the river that runs through Rome.

Ascanius will establish Alba, bright as the city's name.
All that I foresee has been decreed.
"But how to begin
this current struggle here and see it through,
victorious all the way?
I'll explain in a word or so. Listen closely.
On these shores Arcadians sprung from Pallas[6]—
King Evander's comrades marching under his banner—
picked their site and placed a city on these hills,
Pallanteum, named for their famous forebear, Pallas.
They wage a relentless war against the Latin people.
Welcome them to your camp as allies, seal your pacts.
I myself will lead you between my banks, upstream,
making your way against the current under oars—
I'll speed you on your journey. Up with you,
son of Venus! Now, as the first stars set,
offer the proper prayers to Juno, overcome
her anger and threats with vows and plead for help.
You will pay me with honors once you have won your way.
I am the flowing river that you see, sweeping the banks
and cutting across the tilled fields rich and green.
I am the river Tiber. Clear blue as the heavens,
stream most loved by the gods who rule the sky.
My great home is here,
my fountainhead gives rise to noble cities."
With that,
the river sank low in his deep pool, heading down
to the depths as Aeneas, night and slumber over,
gazing toward the sunlight climbing up the sky,
rises, duly draws up water in cupped hands
and pours forth this prayer to heaven's heights:
"You nymphs, Laurentine nymphs, you springs of rivers,
and you, Father Tiber, you and your holy stream,
embrace Aeneas, shield him from dangers, now at last.
You who pity our hardships—wherever the ground lies
where you come surging forth in all your glory—always
with offerings, always with gifts I'll do you honor,
you great horned king of the rivers of the West.
Just be with me. Prove your will with works."

So he prays and choosing a pair of galleys
from the fleet, he mans them both with rowers
while fitting out his troops with battle gear.
But look,
suddenly, right before his awestruck eyes, a marvel,
shining white through the woods with a brood as white,
lying stretched out on a grassy bank for all to see—

6. Pallas was a legendary king of Arcadia, in mainland Greece. Evander, a later Arcadian king, migrated to Italy and founded Pallanteum on the site of the future Rome. Evander was worshipped by Virgil's contemporaries; there was an altar in his honor on the Aventine Hill in Rome.

a great sow. Devout Aeneas offers her up to you,
Queen Juno on high, a blood sacrifice to you,
standing her at your altar with her young.
And all night long the Tiber lulled his swell,
checking his current so his waves would lie serene,
silent, still as a clear lagoon or peaceful marsh,
soothing its surface smooth, no labor there for oars.
So they embark with cheers to speed them on their way
and the dark tarred hulls go gliding through the river,
amazing the tides, amazing the groves unused to the sight
of warriors' shields, flashing far, and blazoned galleys
moving on upstream. And on and on they row, wearying
night and day as they round the long, winding bends,
floating under the mottled shade of many trees and
cleave the quiet stream reflecting leafy woods.
The fiery Sun had climbed to mid-career when,
off in the distance, they catch sight of walls,
a citadel, scattered roofs of houses: all that now
the imperial power of Rome has lifted to the skies,
but then what Evander held, his humble kingdom.
Quickly they swerve their prows and row for town.

As luck would have it, that day Arcadia's king
was holding solemn annual rites in honor of Hercules,
Amphitryon's powerful son,[7] and paying vows to the gods
in a grove before the city. Flanked by his son,
Pallas,[8] the ranking men and the lowly senate,
all were offering incense now, and warm blood
was steaming on the altars. As soon as they saw
the tall ships gliding through the shadowed woods
and the rowers bending to pull the oars in silence—
alarmed by the unexpected sight, all rise as one
to desert the sacred feast. But Pallas forbids them
to cut short the rites, and fearless, seizes a spear
and runs to confront the new arrivals by himself.
"Soldiers," he shouts from a barrow some way off,
"what drives you to try these unfamiliar paths?
Where are you going? Who are your people?
Where's your home? Do you bring peace or war?"

Then captain Aeneas calls from his high stern,
his hands extending the olive branch of peace:
"We're Trojans born. The weapons you see are honed
for our foes, the Latins. They drive us here—as exiles—
with all the arrogance of war. We look for Evander.
Tell him this: Leading chiefs of Dardania come,
pressing to be his friends-in-arms."

7. Hercules, the strongest Greek hero, who performed the Twelve Labors and was the child of Jupiter by Alcmena, whose human husband, Amphitryon, adopted the boy. Hercules was worshipped as a *heros* or demigod, and was a favorite of Augustus's.

8. Pallas is Evander's son.

Dardania . . .
Pallas, awestruck by the famous name, cries out:
"Come down onto dry land, whoever you are,
speak with my father face-to-face.
Come under our roofs—our welcome guest."
Clasping Aeneas' right hand, he held it long
and heading up to the grove they leave the river.

There Aeneas hails Evander with winning words:
"Best of the sons of Greece, Fortune has decreed
that I pray to you for help, extend this branch
of olive wound in wool.[9] I had no fear of you
as a captain of the Greeks, Arcadia-born
and bound by blood to Atreus' twin sons.
For I am bound to you by my own strength,
by oracles of the gods and by our fathers—
blood-kin—and your own fame that echoes
through the world. All this binds me to you,
and Fate drives me here, and glad I am to follow.
Dardanus, first and founding father of Ilium,[1]
came to the land of Troy. A son, as Greeks will tell,
of Electra, that Electra, daughter of Atlas, mighty Atlas
who bears the grand orb of the heavens on his shoulders.[2]
Your father is Mercury, conceived by radiant Maia
and born on a snow-capped peak of Mount Cyllene.
But Maia's father—to trust what we have heard—
is Atlas, the same Atlas who lifts the starry skies.[3]
So our two lines are branches sprung from the same blood.

"Counting on this, I planned my approach to you.
Not with envoys or artful diplomatic probes,
I come in person, put my life on the line,
a suppliant at your doors to plead for help.
The same people attack us both in savage war,
Rutulians under Turnus, and if they drive us out,
nothing, they do believe, can stop their forcing all
of Italy, all lands of the West beneath their yoke,
the masters of every seaboard north and south.
Take and return our trust. Brave hearts in war,
our tempers steeled, our armies proved in action."

Aeneas closed. While he spoke, Evander had marked
his eyes, his features, his whole frame, and now
he replies, pointedly: "Bravest of the Trojans,
how I welcome you, recognize you, with all my heart!

9. A sign of peace.
1. Troy.
2. Atlas, the Titan who holds up the sky, had seven daughters, the Pleiades, who included Maia and Electra. This Electra is not the daughter of Agamemnon and Clytemnestra, also called Electra.
3. Evander's parents were Maia, daughter of Atlas, and Mercury, the messenger god. Aeneas is also descended from Atlas, because Dardanus, his ancestor, was the son of Electra, daughter of Atlas.

How well I recall the face, the words, the voice
of your father, King Anchises.
"Once, I remember . . .
Priam, son of Laomedon, bound for Salamis,
out to visit his sister Hesione's kingdom,
continued on to see Arcadia's cold frontiers.
Then my cheeks still sported the bloom of youth
and I was full of wonder to see the chiefs of Troy,
wonder to see Laomedon's son, Priam himself, no doubt,
but one walked taller than all the rest—Anchises.
I yearned, in a boy's way, to approach the king
and take him by the hand. So up I went to him,
eagerly showed him round the walls of Pheneus.[4]
At his departure he gave me a splendid quiver
bristling Lycian arrows, a battle-cape shot through
with golden mesh, and a pair of gilded reins my son,
Pallas, now makes his. So the right hand you want
is clasping yours. We are allies bound as one.
Soon as tomorrow's sun returns to light the earth
I'll see you off, cheered with an escort and support
I'll send your way. But now for the rites,
since you have come as friends,
our annual rites it would be wrong to interrupt.
So, with a warm heart celebrate them with us now.
High time you felt at ease with comrades' fare."

That said, he orders back the food and cups already
cleared away, and the king himself conducts his guests
to places on the grass. Aeneas, the guest of honor,
he invites to a throne of maple, cushioned soft
with a shaggy lion's hide. Then picked young men
and the altar priest, outdoing themselves, bring on
the roasted flesh of bulls and heap the baskets high
with the gifts of Ceres, wheaten loaves just baked,
and in Bacchus'[5] name they keep the winecups flowing.
And now Aeneas and all his Trojan soldiers feast
on the oxen's long back cut and sacred vitals.
Once
their hunger was put aside, their appetites content,
King Evander began: "These annual rites, this feast,
a custom ages old, this shrine to a great spirit—
no hollow superstition, and no blind ignorance
of the early gods has forced them on us. No,
my Trojan guest, we have been saved from dangers,
brutal perils, and so we observe these rites,
we renew them year by year, and justly so.
"Now then,

4. Town in Arcadia.
5. God of wine. Ceres: goddess of grain.

first look up at this crag with its overhanging rocks,
the boulders strewn afar. An abandoned mountain lair
still stands, where the massive rocks came rumbling down
in an avalanche, a ruin. There once was a cavern here,
a vast unplumbed recess untouched by the sun's rays,
where a hideous, part-human monster made his home—
Cacus.[6] The ground was always steaming with fresh blood
and nailed to his high and mighty doors, men's faces
dangled, sickening, rotting, and bled white . . .
The monster's father was Vulcan,[7] whose smoky flames
he vomited from his maw as he hauled his lumbering hulk.
But even to us, at last, time brought the answer
to our prayers: the help, the arrival of a god.
That greatest avenger, Hercules! On he came,
triumphant in his slaughter and all the spoils
of triple-bodied Geryon.[8] The great victor,
driving those huge bulls down to pasture,
herds crowding these riverbanks and glens.
But Cacus, desperate bandit, wild to leave
no crime, no treachery undared, untested,
stole from their steadings four champion bulls
and as many head of first-rate, well-built heifers.
Ah, but to leave no hoofmarks pointing forward,
into his cave he dragged them by the tail,
turning their tracks backward—
the pirate hid his plunder deep in his dark rocks.
No hunter could spot a trace that led toward that cave.

"Meanwhile, Hercules was about to move his herds out,
full fed from their grazing, ready to go himself when
the cows began to low at parting, filling the woods
with protest, bellowing to the hills they had to leave.
But one heifer, deep in the vast cavern, lowed back
and Cacus' prisoner foiled its jailer's hopes.
Suddenly Hercules ignited in rage, in black fury
and seizing his weapons and weighted knotted club,
he made for the hill's steep heights at top speed.
And that was the first we'd seen of Cacus afraid,
his eyes aswirl with terror—off to his cave he flees,
swifter than any Eastwind, yes, his feet were winged with fear.
He shut himself in its depths, shattered the chains and
down the great rock dropped, suspended by steel and
his father's skill, to wedge between the doorposts,
block the entrance fast.
Watch Hercules on the attack. Scanning every opening,
tossing his head, this way, that way, grinding his teeth,

6. The name means "bad" in Greek.

7. God of fire, Roman counterpart to the Greek Hephaestos.

8. Monster with three bodies, three heads, and six arms, who owned a herd of cattle. Hercules killed Geryon and took the cattle.

blazing in rage, three times he circles the whole Aventine hill,[9]
three times he tries to storm the rocky gates—no use—
three times he sinks down in the lowlands, power spent.

"Looming over the cavern's ridge a spur reared up,
all jagged flint, its steep sides sheering away,
a beetling, towering sight, a favorite haunt
of nestling vultures. This crag jutting over
the ridge, leaning left of the river down below—
he charged from the right and rocked it, prised it
up from its bedrock, tore it free of its roots,
then abruptly hurled it down and the hurl's force
made mighty heaven roar as the banks split far apart.
and the river's tide went flooding back in terror.
But the cave and giant palace of Cacus lay exposed
and his shadowy cavern cleaved wide to its depths—
as if earth's depths had yawned under some upheaval,
bursting open the locks of the Underworld's abodes,
revealing the livid kingdom loathed by the gods,
and from high above you could see the plunging abyss
and the ghosts terror-struck as the light comes streaming in.

"So Cacus, caught in that stunning flood of light,
shut off in his hollow rock, howling as never before—
Hercules overwhelms him from high above, raining down
all weapons he finds at hand, torn-off branches, rocks
like millstones. A deathtrap, no way out for the monster now!
Cacus retches up from his throat dense fumes—unearthly,
I tell you—endless waves billowing through his lair,
wiping all from sight, and deep into his cave
he spews out tides of rolling, smoking darkness,
night and fire fused. Undaunted Hercules had enough—
furious, headlong down he leapt through the flames
where the thickest smoke was massing, black clouds
of it seething up and down the enormous cavern.
Here, as Cacus spouts his flames in the darkness,
all for nothing—Hercules grapples him, knots him
fast in a death-lock, throttling him, gouging out
the eyes in his head, choking the blood in his gullet dry.
He tears out the doors in a flash, opens the pitch-black den
and the stolen herds—a crime that Cacus had denied—
are laid bare to the skies, and out by the heels
he drags the ghastly carcass into the light.
No one can get his fill of gazing at those eyes,
terrible eyes, that face, the matted, bristling chest
of the brute beast, its fiery maw burnt out.

"From then on, we have solemnized this service
and all our heirs have kept the day with joy.
Potitius first, the founder of the rites,

9. One of the seven hills of Rome.

the Pinarian house too, that guards the worship
of Hercules. Potitius set this altar in the grove.
The Greatest Altar we shall always call it,
always the Greatest it will be.[1]
"So come,
my boys, in honor of his heroic exploits
crown your hair with leaves, hold high your cups,
invoke the god we share with our new allies,
offer him wine with all your eager hearts."

With that welcome, a wreath of poplar, hung
with a poplar garland's green and silver sheen
that shaded Hercules once,
shaded Evander's hair and crowned his head
and the sacred wooden winecup filled his hand.
In no time, all were tipping wine on the board
with happy hearts and praying to the gods.
Meanwhile
evening is coming closer, wheeling down the sky and
now the priests advance, Potitius in the lead,
robed in animal skins the old accustomed way
and bearing torches. They refresh the banquet,
bringing on the second course, a welcome savor,
weighing the altars down with groaning platters.
Then the Salii, dancing priests of Mars,[2] come
clustering, leaping round the flaming altars,
raising the chorus, brows wreathed with poplar:
here a troupe of boys and a troupe of old men there,
singing Hercules' praises, all his heroic feats.
How he strangled the first monsters, twin serpents
sent by his stepmother, Juno—crushed them in his hands.[3]
And the same in warfare: how he razed to the roots
those brilliant cities, Troy and Oechalia both.[4]
How under Eurystheus he endured the countless
grueling labors, Juno's brutal doom.[5]
"Hercules,
you the unvanquished one! You have slaughtered
Centaurs born of the clouds, half man, half horse,

1. The Greatest Altar (Ara Maxima) was an important site in Virgil's Rome, located in the cattle market (the Forum Boarium). It was dedicated to Hercules. The Potitii and Pinarii are two Roman clans.

2. These twelve dancing priests existed in Virgil's Rome. They wore strange, supposedly ancient military costumes and participated in religious festivals. They sang a special song, in archaic Latin, the *Carmen Saliare*. Augustus, who was interested in reviving the archaic religious practices of Rome, and in presenting himself as the fulfillment of ancient prophecies, had his own name inserted into the song.

3. Hercules was (like Aeneas) always hated by Juno, as the offspring of one of her husband's love affairs. When he was a baby, she sent snakes to kill him in his cradle, but the infant sat up and throttled them with his bare hands.

4. Hercules sacked Troy when King Laomedon reneged on a promise to reward him for killing a sea monster that was attacking the city. He sacked Oechalia after the king, Eurytus, similarly reneged on a promise to give him his daughter Iole's hand in marriage.

5. Eurystheus was the king who imposed the Labors on Hercules, supported by Juno.

Hylaeus and Pholus—the bull, the monster of Crete,
the tremendous Nemean lion holed in his rocky den.
The Stygian tide-pools trembled at your arrival,
Death's watchdog cringed, sprawling over the heaps
of half-devoured bones in his gory cave. But nothing,
no specter on earth has touched your heart with fear,
not even Typhoeus himself, towering up with weapons.
Nor did Lerna's Hydra, heads swarming around you,
strip you of your wits.[6] Hail, true son of Jove,
you glory added to all the gods! Come to us,
come to your sacred rites and speed us on
with your own righteous stride!"
So they sing
his praise, and to crown it sing of Cacus' cave,
the monster breathing fire, and all the woods resound
with the ringing hymns, and the hillsides echo back.

And then, with the holy rites performed in full,
they turned back to the city. The king, bent with years,
kept his comrades, Aeneas and his son, beside him,
moving on as he eased the way with many stories.
Aeneas marveled, his keen eyes gazing round,
entranced by the site, gladly asking, learning,
one by one, the legendary tales of the men of old.

King Evander, founder of Rome's great citadel, begins:
"These woods the native fauns and the nymphs once held[7]
and a breed of mortals sprung from the rugged trunks of oaks.
They had no notion of custom, no cultured way of life,
knew nothing of yoking oxen, laying away provisions,
garnering up their stores. They lived off branches,
berries and acorns, hunters' rough-cut fare. First
came Saturn, down from the heights of heaven, fleeing
Jove in arms: Saturn robbed of his kingdom, exiled.[8]
He united these wild people scattered over the hilltops,

6. All achievements of Hercules. The Centaurs were born when Ixion, who had been trying to rape Juno, instead had sex with a magic, goddess-shaped cloud. Hercules shot a centaur, Nessus, with a poisoned arrow when the latter tried to steal his wife. Hylaeus was one of the centaurs who tried to rape Atalanta. Hercules killed other centaurs, including Pholus, a wise centaur who was a friend of his, when the centaurs were on a drunken rampage. The Labors of Hercules included capturing the Cretan Bull; killing the Nemean Lion; capturing Cerberus, the three-headed guard dog of the underworld (through which ran the river Styx, hence "Stygian tide-pools"); and destroying the many-headed Lernean Hydra. Typhoeus was a rebellious fire-breathing monster whom Jupiter confined under Mount Etna; his continued presence there explains the mountain's volcanic activity.

7. Fauns are male woodland creatures with human faces and torsos but the horns and legs of goats. Nymphs are their female equivalents, though without the goat legs and horns: they are wild creatures associated with water, trees, or mountains.

8. Saturn, Jupiter's father, an important god in the Roman pantheon, who was often identified with the (less benign) Greek deity Kronos, father of Zeus. Jupiter overthrew his father and seized power for himself; in Roman myth, Saturn then fled to Italy, to the future site of Rome, and ruled over an ideal time on earth, the Golden Age. In Virgil's time, Romans held a yearly winter festival called the Saturnalia, commemorating the age of Saturn; this was one of the precursors to Christmas.

gave them laws and pitched on the name of Latium for the land,
since he'd lain hidden within its limits, safe and sound.
Saturn's reign was the Age of Gold, men like to say,
so peacefully, calm and kind, he ruled his subjects.
Ah, but little by little a lesser, tarnished age
came stealing in, filled with the madness of war,
the passion for possessions.
"Then on they came,
the Ausonian ranks in arms, Sicanian tribes and
time and again the land of Saturn changed its name.[9]
Then kings reared up and the savage giant Thybris,[1]
and since his time we Italians call our river Tiber.
The true name of the old river Albula's lost and gone.
And I, cast from my country, bound for the ocean's ends—
irresistible Fortune and inescapable Fate have planted me
in this place, spurred on by my mother's dire warnings,
the nymph Carmentis, and God Apollo's power."[2]

No sooner said than, moving on, he points out
the Altar of Carmentis, then the Carmental Gate
as the Romans call it: an ancient tribute paid
to the nymph Carmentis, seer who told the truth,
the first to foresee the greatness of Aeneas' sons
and Pallanteum's fame to come.[3] Next he displays
the grand grove that heroic Romulus restored
as a refuge—the Asylum—then shows him, under
its chilly rock, the grotto called the Lupercal,[4]
in the old Arcadian way, Pan of Mount Lycaeus.
And he shows him the grove of hallowed Argiletum too,
he swears by the spot, retells the Death of Argus,
once his guest.[5]
From there he leads Aeneas on
to Tarpeia's house and the Capitol, all gold now
but once in the old days, thorny, dense with thickets.[6]
Even then the awesome dread of the place struck fear
in the hearts of rustics, even then they trembled
before the woodland and the rock.
"This grove," he says,

9. The Ausonians were from southern Italy, Sicanians from Sicily.

1. Legendary Etruscan king, supposedly drowned in the river Tiber, which was then named for him; it was previously called Albula.

2. Evander's prophet-nymph mother, Carmentis, was inspired by Apollo, god of prophecy, to tell Evander to come to Italy.

3. Pallanteum was the city founded by Evander on the site of Rome.

4. Sacred grotto where, according to myth, Romulus and Remus were suckled by the wolf (*lupa* in Latin). This was, in Virgil's time, the location of a festival held in February, called the Lupercalia, in honor of the shepherd god Lupercus, identified with the Greek god Pan—who was worshipped on Mount Lycaeus, in Arcadia, Greece.

5. Argus was a guest of Evander, killed for plotting against him.

6. The Capitoline Hill was, in Virgil's time, crowned by a magnificent temple to Jupiter. Tarpeia was a legendary Roman girl who betrayed the city to the invading Sabines; she was thrown from a cliff on the Capitoline, which became the place of execution for criminals (the Tarpeian Rock).

"this hill with its crown of leaves is a god's home,
whatever god he is. My Arcadians think they've seen
almighty Jove in person, often brandishing high
his black storm-shield in his strong right hand
as he drives the tempest on. Here, what's more,
in these two towns, their walls razed to the roots,
you can see the relics, monuments of the men of old.
This fortress built by Father Janus,[7] that by Saturn:
this was called the Janiculum, that, Saturnia."
So,
conversing and drawing near Evander's humble home,
they saw herds of cattle, everywhere, lowing loud
in the Roman Forum and Carinae's elegant district.
"These gates," Evander says, as he reaches his lodge,
"Hercules in his triumph stooped to enter here.
This mansion of mine was grand enough for him.
Courage, my friend! Dare to scoff at riches.
Make yourself—you too—worthy to be a god.
Come into my meager house, and don't be harsh."

So he said, and under his narrow sloped roof
he led the great Aeneas, laid him down on a bed
of fallen leaves and the hide of a Libyan bear.
Night comes rushing down, embracing the earth
in its deep dark wings.
But his mother, Venus,
stirred by fear—no wonder—by all the threats
and the Latins' violent uproar, goes to Vulcan[8] now
and there in their golden bridal chamber whispers,
breathing immortal love through every word:
"When Greek kings were ravishing Troy in war,
her fated towers, her ramparts doomed to enemy fires,
I asked no help for the victims then, I never begged
for the weapons right within your skill and power.
No, my dearest husband, I'd never put you to work
in a lost cause, much as I owed to Priam's sons,
however often I wept for Aeneas' grueling labors.
Now, by Jove's command he lands on Rutulian soil,
so now I do come, kneeling before the godhead I adore,
begging weapons for my Aeneas, a mother for her son!
Remember Aurora, Tithonus' wife, and Nereus' daughter?[9]
Both wept and you gave way. Look at the armies massing,
cities bolting their gates, honing swords against me
to cut my loved ones down."
No more words.
The goddess threw her snow-white arms around him
as he held back, caressing him here and there,
and suddenly he caught fire—the same old story,

7. Janus is the two-headed god of change and transitions.
8. Vulcan (Hephaestus in Greek mythology) is Venus's husband, the fire god and master of metalwork.
9. Aurora asked Vulcan to make weapons for her son, Memnon; Thetis, Nereus's daughter, asked for weapons for Achilles.

the flame he knew by heart went running through him,
melting him to the marrow of his bones. As thunder
at times will split the sky and a trail of fire goes
rippling through the clouds, flashing, blinding light—
and his wife sensed it all, delighting in her bewitching ways,
she knew her beauty's power.
And father Vulcan,
enthralled by Venus, his everlasting love, replied:
"Why plumb the past for appeals? Where has it gone,
goddess, the trust you lodged in me? If only
you'd been so passionate for him, then as now,
we would have been in our rights to arm the Trojans,
even then. Neither Father Almighty nor the Fates
were dead against Troy's standing any longer or
Priam's living on for ten more years. But now,
if you are gearing up for war, your mind set,
whatever my pains and all my skills can promise,
whatever molten electrum and iron can bring to life,
whatever the bellows' fiery blasts can do—enough!
Don't pray to me now. Never doubt your powers."

With those words on his lips, he gave his wife
the embraces both desired, then sinking limp
on her breast he courted peaceful sleep
that stole throughout his body.
And then,
when the first deep rest had driven sleep away
and the chariot of Night had wheeled past mid-career,
that hour a housewife rises, faced with scratching out
a living with loom and Minerva's homespun crafts,[1]
and rakes the ashes first to awake the sleeping fires,
adding night to her working hours, and sets her women
toiling on at the long day's chores by torchlight—
and all to keep the bed of her husband chaste
and rear her little boys—so early, briskly,
in such good time the fire-god rises up
from his downy bed to labor at his forge.
Not far
from Aeolian Lipare flanked by Sicily's coast,
an island of smoking boulders surges from the sea.
Deep below it a vast cavern thunders, hollowed out
like vaults under Etna, forming the Cyclops' forges.
You can hear the groaning anvils boom with mighty strokes,
the hot steel ingots screeching steam in the cavern's troughs
and fires panting hard in the furnace—Vulcan's home,
it bears the name Vulcania.
Here the firegod dove from heaven's heights.

1. Minerva was the goddess linked to technology and handicrafts, including weaving and spinning.

The Cyclops were forging iron now in the huge cave:
Thunder and Lightning and Fire-Anvil stripped bare.
They had in hand a bolt they had just hammered out,
one of the countless bolts the Father rains on earth
from the arching sky—part buffed already, part still rough.
Three shafts of jagged hail they'd riveted on that weapon,
three of bursting stormclouds, three of blood-red flame
and the Southwind winging fast. They welded into the work
the bloodcurdling flashes, crackling Thunder, Terror
and Rage in hot pursuit. Others were pressing on,
forging a chariot's whirling wheels for Mars
to harrow men and panic towns in war.
Others were finishing off the dreaded aegis
donned by Pallas Athena blazing up in arms—
outdoing themselves with burnished gilded scales,
with serpents coiling, writhing around each other,
the Gorgon herself, the severed head, the rolling eyes,
the breastplate forged to guard the goddess' chest.[2]

"Pack it away!" he shouts. "Whatever you've started,
set it aside, my Cyclops of Etna, bend to this!
Armor must be forged for a man of courage!
Now for strength, you need it! Now for flying hands!
Now for mastery, all your skill! Cast delay to the winds!"

Enough said. At a stroke they all pitched into the work,
dividing the labors, share and share alike, and bronze
is running in rivers and flesh-tearing steel and
gold ore melting down in the giant furnace.
They are forging one tremendous shield, one
against all the Latin spears—welding seven plates,
circular rim to rim. And some are working the bellows
sucking the air in, blasting it out, while others
are plunging hissing bronze in the brimming troughs,
the ground of the cavern groaning under the anvils' weight,
and the Cyclops raising their arms with all their power,
arms up, arms down to the drumming, pounding beat
as they twist the molten mass in gripping tongs.

While Vulcan, the Lord of Lemnos, spurs the work
below that Aeolian coast, the life-giving light
and birdsong under the eaves at crack of dawn
awake Evander from sleep in his humble lodge.
The old man rises, pulls a tunic over his chest
and binds his Etruscan sandals round his feet.
Over his right shoulder, down his flank he straps
an Arcadian sword, swirling back the skin of a panther
to drape his left side. For company, two watchdogs
go loping on before him over the high doorsill,

2. Minerva carried a shield adorned with the snake-haired monster, the Gorgon, which could turn the onlooker to stone.

friends to their master's steps. He makes his way
to the private quarters of his guest, Aeneas,
the old veteran bearing in mind their recent talk
and the help that he had promised. Just as early,
Aeneas is stirring too. One comes with his son, Pallas,
the other brings Achates. They meet and grasp right hands
and sitting there in the open court, are free at last
to indulge in frank discussion.
                                        The old king starts in:
"Greatest chief of the Trojans—for while you are alive
I'll never consider Troy and its kingdom conquered—
our power to reinforce you in war is slight,
though I know our name is great. Here the Tiber
cuts us off and there the Rutulians close the vise,
the clang of their armor echoes round our walls.
But I mean to ally you now with mighty armies,
vast encampments filled with royal forces—
your way to safety revealed by unexpected luck.
It's Fate that called you on to reach our shores."

"Now, not far from here Agylla city stands,
founded on age-old rock by Lydian people once,
brilliant in war, who built on Etruscan hilltops.
The city flowered for many years till King Mezentius
came to power—his brutal rule, barbaric force of arms.
Why recount his unspeakable murders, savage crimes? The tyrant!
God store up such pains for his own head and all his sons!
Why, he'd even bind together dead bodies and living men,
couple them tightly, hand to hand and mouth to mouth—
what torture—so in that poison, oozing putrid slime
they'd die by inches, locked in their brute embrace.
Then, at last, at the end of their rope, his people
revolt against that raving madman, they besiege
Mezentius and his palace, hack his henchmen down
and fling fire on his roof. In all this slaughter
he slips away, taking flight to Rutulian soil,
shielded by Turnus' armies, his old friend.
So all Etruria rises up in righteous fury,
demanding the king, threatening swift attack.
Thousands, Aeneas, and I will put you in command.
Their fleet is massed on the shore and a low roar grows,
men crying for battle-standards now, but an aged prophet
holds them back, singing out his song of destiny:
'You elite Lydian troops, fine flower of courage
born of an ancient race, oh, what just resentment
whips you into battle! Mezentius makes you burn
with well-earned rage. But still the gods forbid
an Italian commander to lead a race so great—
choose leaders from overseas!'

"At that, the Etruscan fighting ranks subsided,
checked on the field of battle, struck with awe

by the warnings of the gods. Tarchon[3] himself
has sent me envoys, bearing the crown and scepter,
offering me the ensigns, urging: 'Join our camp,
take the Etruscan throne.' Ah, but old age,
sluggish, cold, played out with the years,
has me in its grip, denies me the command.
My strength is too far gone for feats of arms.
I'd urge my son to accept, but his blood is mixed,
half Sabine, thanks to his mother, and so, Italian.[4]
You are the one whose age and breed the Fates approve,
the one the Powers call. March out on your mission,
bravest chief of the Trojans, now the Italians too.
What's more, I will pair you with Pallas, my hope,
my comfort. Under your lead, let him grow hard
to a soldier's life and the rough work of war.
Let him get used to watching you in action,
admire you as his model from his youth.
To him I will give two hundred horsemen now,
fighting hearts of oak—our best—and Pallas
will give you two hundred more, in Pallas' name."

He had barely closed and Anchises' son, Aeneas,
and trusty Achates, their eyes fixed on the ground,
would long have worried deep in their anxious hearts
if Venus had not given a sign from the cloudless sky.
A bolt of lightning suddenly splits the heavens,
drumming thunder—the world seems to fall in a flash,
the blare of Etruscan trumpets blasting through the sky.
They look up—the terrific peals come crashing over and over—
and see blood-red in a brilliant sky, rifting a cloudbank,
armor clashing out. All the troops were dumbstruck,
all but the Trojan hero—well he knew that sound,
his goddess mother's promise—and he calls out:
"Don't ask, my friend, don't ask me, I beg you,
what these portents bring. The heavens call for me.
My goddess mother promised to send this sign
if war were breaking out, and bring me armor
down through the air, forged by Vulcan himself
to speed me on in battle. But, oh dear gods,
what slaughter threatens the poor Laurentine people!
What a price in bloodshed, Turnus, you will pay me soon!
How many shields and helmets and corpses of the brave
you'll churn beneath your tides, old Father Tiber!
All right then, you Rutulians,
beg for war! Break your pacts of peace!"

Fighting words. Aeneas rises from his high seat
and first he rakes the fires asleep on Hercules' altar,
then gladly goes to the lowly gods of hearth and home
he worshipped just the day before. Evander himself

3. Leader of the Etruscans.

4. The Sabines were a tribe of central Italy.

and his new Trojan allies, share and share alike,
slaughter yearling sheep as the old rite demands.
And next Aeneas returns to his ships and shipmates,
picks the best and bravest to take his lead in war
while the rest glide on at ease, no oars required
as the river's current bears them on downstream
to bring Ascanius news of his father and his affairs.
Horses go to the Trojans bound for Tuscan fields,
and marked for Aeneas, a special mount decked out
in a tawny lion's skin that gleams with gilded claws.

A sudden rumor flies through the little town:
"Horsemen are rushing toward the Tuscan monarch's gates!"
Mothers struck with terror pray and re-echo prayers,
the fear builds as the deadly peril comes closer,
the specter of War looms larger, ever larger . . .
Evander, seizing the hand of his departing son,
clinging, weeping inconsolably, cries out:
"If only Jove would give me back the years,
all gone, and make me the man I was, killing
the front ranks just below Praeneste's ramparts,
heaping up their shields, torching them in my triumph—
my right hand sent great King Erulus down to hell!
Three lives his mother Feronia gave him at his birth—
I shudder to say it now—three suits of armor for action.
Three times I had to lay him low but my right hand,
my right hand then, stripped him of all his lives
and all his armor too![5]
"Oh, if only! Then no force
could ever tear me *now* from your dear embrace,
my boy, nor could Mezentius ever have trod
his neighbor Evander down, butchered so many,
bereaved our city . . . so many widows left.
But you, you Powers above, and you, Jupiter,
highest lord of the gods: pity, I implore you,
a king of Arcadia, hear a father's prayers!
If your commands will keep my Pallas safe
and if the Fates intend to preserve my son,
and if I live to see him, join him again,
why then I pray for life—
I can suffer any pain on earth. But if
you are threatening some disaster, Fortune,
let me break this brutal life off now, now
while anxieties waver and hopes for the future fade,
while you, my beloved boy, my lone delight come lately,
I still hold you in my embrace. Oh, let no graver news
arrive and pierce my ears!"
So at their last parting
the words came pouring deep from Evander's heart.

5. King Erulus of Praeneste had three lives, from his divine mother Feronia; so he had to be killed three times over.

He collapsed, and his servants bore him quickly
into the house.
And even now the cavalry
had come riding forth through the open gates,
Aeneas out in the lead, flanked by trusty Achates,
then other Trojan captains, with Pallas in command
of the column's center, Pallas brilliant in battle cape
and glittering inlaid armor. Bright as the morning star
whom Venus loves above all the burning stars on high,
when up from his ocean bath he lifts his holy face
to the lofty skies and dissolves away the darkness.
Mothers stand on the ramparts, trembling, eyes trailing
the cloud of dust and the troops in gleaming bronze.
Over the brush, the quickest route, cross-country,
armored fighters ride. Cries go up, squadrons form,
galloping hoofbeats drum the rutted plain with thunder.

Next to Caere's icy river a huge grove stands,
held in ancestral awe by people far and wide,
on all sides cupped around by sheltering hills
and ringed by pitch-dark pines. The story goes
that ancient Pelasgians,[6] first in time long past
to settle the Latian borders, solemnized the grove
and a festal day to Silvanus, god of fields and flocks.
Not far from here, Tarchon and his Etruscans mustered,
all secure, and now from the hills his entire army
could be seen encamped on the spreading plain.
Down come captain Aeneas and all his fighters
picked for battle, water their horses well
and weary troops take rest.
But the goddess Venus,
lustrous among the cloudbanks, bearing her gifts,
approached and when she spotted her son alone,
off in a glade's recess by the frigid stream,
she hailed him, suddenly there before him: "Look,
just forged to perfection by all my husband's skill:
the gifts I promised! There's no need now, my son,
to flinch from fighting swaggering Latin ranks
or challenging savage Turnus to a duel!"

With that, Venus reached to embrace her son
and set the brilliant armor down before him
under a nearby oak.
Aeneas takes delight
in the goddess' gifts and the honor of it all
as he runs his eyes across them piece by piece.
He cannot get enough of them, filled with wonder,
turning them over, now with his hands, now his arms,
the terrible crested helmet plumed and shooting fire,

6. Greeks who were supposedly the first settlers in Latium.

the sword-blade honed to kill, the breastplate, solid bronze,
blood-red and immense, like a dark blue cloud enflamed
by the sun's rays and gleaming through the heavens.
Then the burnished greaves of electrum, smelted gold,
the spear and the shield, the workmanship of the shield,
no words can tell its power . . .
There is the story of Italy,
Rome in all her triumphs. There the fire-god forged them,
well aware of the seers and schooled in times to come,
all in order the generations born of Ascanius' stock
and all the wars they waged.
And Vulcan forged them too,
the mother wolf stretched out in the green grotto of Mars,
twin boys at her dugs, who hung there, frisky, suckling
without a fear as she with her lithe neck bent back,
stroking each in turn, licked her wolf pups
into shape with a mother's tongue.[7]
Not far from there
he had forged Rome as well and the Sabine women brutally
dragged from the crowded bowl when the Circus games were played
and abruptly war broke out afresh, the sons of Romulus
battling old King Tatius' hardened troops from Cures.[8]
Then when the same chiefs had set aside their strife,
they stood in full armor before Jove's holy altar,
lifting cups, and slaughtered a sow to bind their pacts.
Nearby,
two four-horse chariots, driven to left and right, had torn
Mettus apart—man of Alba, you should have kept your word—
and Tullus hauled the liar's viscera through the brush
as blood-drops dripped like dew from brakes of thorns.[9]
Porsenna,
there, commanding Romans to welcome banished Tarquin back,
mounted a massive siege to choke the city—Aeneas' heirs
rushing headlong against the steel in freedom's name.
See Porsenna to the life, his likeness menacing, raging,
and why? Cocles dared to rip the bridge down, Cloelia
burst her chains and swam the flood.[1]
Crowning the shield,
guarding the fort atop the Tarpeian Rock, Manlius
stood before the temple, held the Capitol's heights.
The new thatch bristled thick on Romulus' palace roof and
here the silver goose went ruffling through the gold arcades,
squawking its warning—Gauls attack the gates! Gauls

7. Romulus and Remus, first builders of Rome's walls, who were suckled by the wolf.

8. At the first games in the Roman arena (the Circus), Roman men seized the Sabine women, provoking their king, Tatius, to make war in revenge.

9. Mettus, king of Alba Longa, broke a promise to Tullus, third king of Rome, and was brutally punished.

1. When the Etruscan tyrant Tarquin was banished from Rome, the Etruscan general Lars Porsena attacked the city from a bridge, and took a girl—Cloelia—hostage; but a Roman, Cocles (better known as Horatius), tore down the bridge, and rescued both girl and city.

swarming the thickets, about to seize the fortress,
shielded by shadows, gift of the pitch-dark night.[2]
Gold their flowing hair, their war dress gold,
striped capes glinting, their milky necks ringed
with golden chokers, pairs of Alpine pikes in their hands,
flashing like fire, and long shields wrap their bodies.

Here Vulcan pounded out the Salii, dancing priests of Mars,
the Luperci,[3] stripped, their peaked caps wound with wool,
bearing their body-shields that dropped from heaven,
and chaste matrons, riding in pillowed coaches,
led the sacred marches through the city.
Far apart
on the shield, what's more, he forged the homes of hell,
the high Gates of Death and the torments of the doomed,
with you, Catiline,[4] dangling from a beetling crag,
cringing before the Furies' open mouths.
And set apart,
the virtuous souls, with Cato[5] giving laws.
And amidst it all
the heaving sea ran far and wide, its likeness forged
in gold but the blue deep foamed in a sheen of white
and rounding it out in a huge ring swam the dolphins,
brilliant in silver, tails sweeping the crests
to cut the waves in two.
And here in the heart
of the shield: the bronze ships, the battle of Actium,
you could see it all, the world drawn up for war,
Leucata Headland seething, the breakers molten gold.
On one flank, Caesar Augustus leading Italy into battle,
the Senate and People too, the gods of hearth and home
and the great gods themselves. High astern he stands,
the twin flames shoot forth from his lustrous brows and
rising from the peak of his head, his father's star.
On the other flank, Agrippa[6] stands tall as he steers
his ships in line, impelled by favoring winds and gods
and from his forehead glitter the beaks of ships
on the Naval Crown, proud ensign earned in war.

And opposing them comes Antony leading on
the riches of the Orient, troops of every stripe—
victor over the nations of the Dawn and blood-red shores
and in his retinue, Egypt, all the might of the East
and Bactra, the end of the earth, and trailing

2. In 390 B.C.E. Manlius defended Rome against the invading Gauls; he was woken by geese, who were the first to hear the attack.
3. Priests of Lupercus, the Roman equivalent of Pan, the countryside god.
4. Conspirator who tried to overthrow the Roman Republic in the first century B.C.E.
5. Cato the Younger, defender of the Republic, who killed himself after the victory of Julius Caesar at Utica.
6. Son-in-law of Augustus, and admiral.

in his wake, that outrage, that Egyptian wife![7]
All launch in as one, whipping the whole sea to foam
with tugging, thrashing oars and cleaving triple beaks
as they make a run for open sea. You'd think the Cyclades[8]
ripped up by the roots, afloat on the swells, or mountains
ramming against mountains, so immense the turrets astern
as sailors attack them, showering flaming tow and
hot bolts of flying steel, and the fresh blood running
red on Neptune's fields. And there in the thick of it all
the queen is mustering her armada, clacking her native rattles,
still not glimpsing the twin vipers hovering at her back,[9]
as Anubis[1] barks and the queen's chaos of monster gods
train their spears on Neptune, Venus, and great Minerva.
And there in the heart of battle Mars rampages on,
cast in iron, with grim Furies plunging down the sky
and Strife in triumph rushing in with her slashed robes
and Bellona[2] cracking her bloody lash in hot pursuit.
And scanning the melee, high on Actium's heights
Apollo bent his bow and terror struck them all,
Egypt and India, all the Arabians, all the Sabaeans
wheeled in their tracks and fled, and the queen herself—
you could see her calling, tempting the winds, her sails
spreading and now, now about to let her sheets run free.
Here in all this carnage the God of Fire forged her pale
with imminent death, sped on by the tides and Northwest Wind.
And rising up before her, the Nile immersed in mourning opens
every fold of his mighty body, all his rippling robes,
inviting into his deep blue lap and secret eddies
all his conquered people.
But Caesar[3] in triple triumph,
borne home through the walls of Rome, was paying
eternal vows of thanks to the gods of Italy:
three hundred imposing shrines throughout the city.
The roads resounded with joy, revelry, clapping hands,
with bands of matrons in every temple, altars in each
and the ground before them strewn with slaughtered steers.
Caesar himself, throned at brilliant Apollo's snow-white gates,
reviews the gifts brought on by the nations of the earth
and he mounts them high on the lofty temple doors
as the vanquished people move in a long slow file,
their dress, their arms as motley as their tongues.
Here Vulcan had forged the Nomad race, the Africans
with their trailing robes, here the Leleges, Carians,
Gelonian archers bearing quivers, Euphrates flowing now

7. Although Actium was a battle between two Roman factions in a civil war, it is presented here as a conflict between the disciplined West and the luxurious East. The "Egyptian wife" is Cleopatra, with whom the Roman general Antony was having an affair.

8. Greek islands.

9. Anticipating her death, since Cleopatra poisoned herself with snakes.

1. Dog-headed Egyptian god.

2. Goddess of war.

3. Augustus, who took on the title "Caesar."

with a humbler tide, the Morini brought from the world's end,
the two-horned Rhine and the Dahae never conquered,
Araxes River bridling at his bridge.
Such vistas
the God of Fire forged across the shield
that Venus gives her son. He fills with wonder—
he knows nothing of these events but takes delight
in their likeness, lifting onto his shoulders now
the fame and fates of all his children's children.

Summary of Books IX–XI The war becomes bloody and violent. Jupiter orders a council of the gods, reminding them that there was supposed to be peace between Trojans and Italians; but he ends up renouncing responsibility: "the Fates will find the way," he declares. Pallas, son of Evander, enters battle and is killed by Turnus. Aeneas longs to kill Turnus in revenge, but cannot find him; Juno has spirited him away. Attempts at peace-making fail, and many are killed on both sides, including a warrior princess named Camilla.

BOOK XII

[*The Sword Decides All*]

Once Turnus sees his ranks of Latins broken in battle,
their spirits dashed and the war-god turned against them,
now is the time, he knows, for him to keep his pledge.
All eyes are fixed on him—his blood is up
and nothing can quench the fighter's ardor now.
Think of the lion ranging the fields near Carthage . . .
the beast won't move into battle till he takes
a deep wound in his chest from the hunters, then
he revels in combat, tossing the rippling mane on his neck
he snaps the spear some stalker drove in his flesh and
roars from bloody jaws, without a fear in the world.
So Turnus blazes up into full explosive fury,
bursting out at the king with reckless words:
"Turnus spurns all delay! Now there's no excuse
for those craven sons of Aeneas to break their word,
to forsake the pact we swore. I'll take him on, I will!
Bring on the sacred rites, Father, draft our binding terms.
Either my right arm will send that Dardan down to hell,
that rank deserter of Asia—my armies can sit back
and watch, and Turnus' sword alone will rebut
the charge of cowardice trained against them all.
Or let him reign over those he's beaten down.
Let Lavinia go to him—his bride!"

Latinus replied in a calming, peaceful way:
"Brave of the brave, my boy, the more you excel
in feats of daring, the more it falls to me to weigh
the perils, with all my fears, the lethal risks we run.

The realms of your father, Daunus, are yours to manage,[4]
so are the many towns your right arm took by force.
Latinus, too, has wealth and the will to share it.
We've other unwed girls in Latian and Laurentine fields,
and no mean stock at that. So let me offer this,
hard as it is, yet free and clear of deception.
Take it to heart, I urge you. For me to unite
my daughter with any one of her former suitors
would have been wrong, forbidden:
all the gods and prophets made that plain.
But I bowed to my love of you, bowed to our kindred blood
and my wife's heartrending tears. I broke all bonds,
I tore the promised bride from her waiting groom,
I brandished a wicked sword.
"Since then, Turnus,
you see what assaults, what crises dog my steps,
what labors you have shouldered, you, first of all.
Beaten twice in major battles, our city walls
can scarcely harbor Italy's future hopes.
The rushing Tiber still steams with our blood,
the endless fields still glisten with our bones.
Why do I shrink from my decision? What insanity
shifts my fixed resolve? If, with Turnus dead,
I am ready to take the Trojans on as allies,
why not stop the war while he is still alive?
What will your Rutulians, all the rest of Italy
say if I betray you to death—may Fortune forbid!—
while you appeal for my daughter's hand in marriage?
Oh, think back on the twists and turns of war.
Pity your father, bent with years and grief,
cut off from you in your native city Ardea
far away."
Latinus' urgings deflect the fury
of Turnus not one bit—it only surges higher.
The attempts to heal enflame the fever more.
Soon as he finds his breath the prince breaks out:
"The anguish you bear for my sake, generous king,
for my sake, I beg you, wipe it from your mind.
Let me barter death as the price of fame.
I have weapons too, old father, and no weak,
untempered spears go flying from my right hand—
from the wounds we deal the blood comes flowing too.
His mother, the goddess, she'll be far from his side
with her woman's wiles, lurking in stealthy shadows,
hiding him in clouds when her hero cuts and runs!"

But the queen, afraid of the new rules of engagement,
wept, and bent on her own death embraced her ardent

4. Turnus's father ruled Daunia, in Apulia.

son-in-law to be: "Turnus, by these tears of mine,
by any concern for Amata that moves your heart,
you are my only hope, now, you the one relief
to my wretched old age. In your hands alone
the glory and power of King Latinus rest,
you alone can shore our sinking house.
One favor now, I pray you.
Refrain from going hand to hand with the Trojans!
Whatever dangers await you in that one skirmish,
Turnus, await me too. With you I will forsake
the light of this life I hate—never in shackles
live to see Aeneas as my son!"
As Lavinia heard
her mother's pleas, her warm cheeks bathed in tears,
a blush flamed up and infused her glowing features.
As crimson as Indian ivory stained with ruddy dye
or white lilies aglow in a host of scarlet roses,
so mixed the hues that lit the young girl's face.
Turnus, struck with love, fixing his eyes upon her,
fired the more for combat, tells Amata, briefly:
"Don't, I beg you, mother, send me off with tears,
with evil omens as I go into the jolting shocks of war,
since Turnus is far from free to defer his death.
Be my messenger, Idmon. Take my words to Aeneas,
hardly words to please that craven Phrygian[5] king!
Soon as the sky goes red with tomorrow's dawn,
riding Aurora's blood-red chariot wheels,
he's not to hurl his Trojans against our Latins,
he must let Trojan and Latian armies stand at ease.
Our blood will put an end to this war at last—
that's the field where Lavinia must be won!"
No more words.
Rushing back to the palace Turnus calls for his team
and thrills to see them neighing right before him,
gifts from Orithyia herself[6] to glorify Pilumnus,
horses whiter than snow, swifter than racing winds.
Restless charioteers flank them, patting their chests,
slapping with cupped hands, and groom their rippling manes.
Next Turnus buckles round his shoulders the breastplate,
dense with its golden mesh and livid mountain bronze,
and straps on sword, shield, and helmet with horns
for its bloody crest—that sword the fire-god forged
for Father Daunus, plunged red-hot in the river Styx.
And next with his powerful grip he snatches up
a burly spear aslant an enormous central column—

5. Trojan—with connotations of "oriental" effeminacy.

6. Daughter of Erechtheus, ancient king of Athens; wife of Boreas the north wind. Pilumnus is an ancestor of Turnus.

plunder seized from an enemy, Actor—shakes it hard
till the haft quivers and "Now, my spear," he cries,
"you've never failed my call, and now our time has come!
Great Actor wielded you once. Now you're in Turnus' hands.
Let me spill his corpse on the ground and strip his breastplate,
rip it to bits with my bare hands—that Phrygian eunuch—
defile his hair in the dust, his tresses crimped
with a white-hot curling-iron dripping myrrh!"
Frenzy drives him, Turnus' whole face is ablaze,
showering sparks, his dazzling glances glinting fire—
terrible, bellowing like some bull before the fight begins,
trying to pour his fury into his horns, he rams a tree-trunk,
charges the winds full force, stamping sprays of sand
as he warms up for battle.
At the same time, Aeneas,
just as fierce in the arms his mother gave him,
hones his fighting spirit too and incites his anger,
glad the war will end with the pact that Turnus offers.
Then he eases his friends' and anxious Iulus' fears,
explaining the ways of Fate, commanding envoys now
to return his firm reply to King Latinus,
state the terms of peace.
A new day was just
about to dawn, scattering light on the mountaintops,
the horses of the Sun just rearing up from the Ocean's depths,
breathing forth the light from their flaring nostrils when
the Latins and Trojans were pacing off the dueling-ground
below the great city's walls, spacing the braziers out
between both armies, mounding the grassy altars high
to the gods they shared in common. Others, cloaked
in their sacred aprons, brows wreathed in verbena,
brought out spring water and sacramental fire.
The Italian troops march forth, pouring out
of the packed gates in tight, massed ranks
and fronting them, the entire Trojan and Tuscan
force comes rushing up, decked out in a range of arms,
no less equipped with iron than if the brutal war-god
called them forth to battle. And there in the midst
of milling thousands, chiefs paraded left and right,
resplendent in all their purple-and-gold regalia:
Mnestheus, blood kin of Assaracus, hardy Asilas,
then Messapus, breaker of horses, Neptune's son.
The signal sounds. All withdraw to their stations,
plant spears in the ground and cant their shields against them.
Then in an avid stream the mothers and unarmed crowds
and frail old men find seats on towers and rooftops,
others take their stand on the high gates.
But Juno,
looking out from a ridge now called the Alban Mount—
then it had neither name, renown nor glory—gazed

down on the plain, on Italian and Trojan armies
face-to-face, and Latinus' city walls.
At once she called to Turnus' sister, goddess
to goddess, the lady of lakes and rilling brooks,
an honor the high and mighty king of heaven bestowed
on Juturna once he had ravished the virgin girl:[7]
"Nymph, beauty of streams, our heart's desire,
well you know how I have favored you, you
above all the Italian women who have mounted
that ungrateful bed of our warm-hearted Jove—
I gladly assigned you a special place in heaven.
So learn, Juturna, the grief that comes your way
and don't blame me. While Fortune seemed to allow
and Fate to suffer the Latian state to thrive,
I guarded Turnus, guarded your city walls.
But now I see the soldier facing unequal odds,
his day of doom, his enemy's blows approaching . . .
That duel, that deadly pact—I cannot bear to watch.
But if *you* dare help your brother at closer range,
go and do so, it becomes you. Who knows?
Better times may come to those in pain."
Juno
had barely closed when tears brimmed in Juturna's eyes
and three, four times over she beat her lovely breast.
"No time for tears, not now," warned Saturn's daughter.
"Hurry! Pluck your brother from death, if there's a way,
or drum up war and abort that treaty they conceived.
The design is mine. The daring, yours."
Spurring her on,
Juno left Juturna torn, distraught with the wound
that broke her heart.
As the kings come riding in,
a massive four-horse chariot draws Latinus forth,
his glistening temples ringed by a dozen gilded rays,
proof he owes his birth to the sun-god's line,
and a snow-white pair brings Turnus' chariot on,
two steel-tipped javelins balanced in his grip.
And coming to meet them, marching from the camp,
the great founder, Aeneas, source of the Roman race,
with his blazoned starry shield and armor made in heaven.
And at his side, his son, Ascanius, second hope of Rome's
imposing power, while a priest in pure white robes leads on
the young of a bristly boar and an unshorn yearling sheep
toward the flaming altars. Turning their eyes to face
the rising sun, the captains reach out their hands,
pouring the salted meal, and mark off the brows
of the victims, cutting tufts with iron blades,
and tip their cups on the sacred altar fires.

7. Turnus's sister, after being raped by Jupiter, was made a divine water nymph.

Then devoted Aeneas, sword drawn, prays:
"Now let the Sun bear witness here
and this, this land of Italy that I call.
For your sake I am able to bear such hardships.
And Jove almighty, and you, his queen, Saturnia[8]—
goddess, be kinder now, I pray you, now at last!
And you, Father, glorious Mars,[9] you who command
the revolving world of war beneath your sway!
I call on the springs and streams, the gods enthroned
in the arching sky and gods of the deep blue sea!
If by chance the victory goes to the Latin, Turnus,
we agree the defeated will depart to Evander's city,
Iulus will leave this land. Nor will Aeneas' Trojans
ever revert in times to come, take up arms again
and threaten to put this kingdom to the sword.
But if Victory grants our force-in-arms the day,
as I think she may—may the gods decree it so—
I shall not command Italians to bow to Trojans,
nor do I seek the scepter for myself.
May both nations, undefeated, under equal laws,
march together toward an eternal pact of peace.
I shall bestow the gods and their sacred rites.
My father-in-law Latinus will retain his armies,
my father-in-law, his power, his rightful rule.
The men of Troy will erect a city for me—
Lavinia will give its walls her name."

So Aeneas begins, and so Latinus follows,
eyes lifted aloft, his right hand raised to the sky:
"I swear by the same, Aeneas, earth and sea and stars,
by Latona's brood of twins,[1] by Janus facing left and right,
by the gods who rule below and the shrine of ruthless Death,
may the Father hear my oath, his lightning seals all pacts!
My hand on his altar now, I swear by the gods and fires
that rise between us here, the day will never dawn
when Italian men will break this pact, this peace,
however fortune falls. No power can bend awry
my will, not if that power sends the country
avalanching into the waves, roiling all in floods
and plunging the heavens into the dark pit of hell.
Just as surely as this scepter"—raising the scepter
he chanced to be grasping in his hand—"will never
sprout new green or scatter shade from its tender leaves,
now that it's been cut from its trunk's base in the woods,
cleft from its mother, its limbs and crowning foliage lost
to the iron axe. A tree, once, that a craftsman's hands
have sheathed in hammered bronze and given the chiefs
of Latium's state to wield."

8. Juno, daughter of Saturn.
9. God of war; counterpart of the Greek Ares.
1. Latona (Leto) is the mother of the twins Apollo and Diana.

So, on such terms
they sealed a pact of peace between both sides,
witnessed by all the officers of the armies.
Then they slash the throats of the hallowed victims
over the flames, and tear their pulsing entrails out
and heap the altars high with groaning platters.

But in fact the duel had long seemed uneven
to all the Rutulians, long their hearts were torn,
wavering back and forth, and they only wavered more
as they viewed the two contenders at closer range,
poorly matched in power . . .
Turnus adds to their anguish, quietly moving toward
the altar, eyes downcast, to pray. A suppliant now,
his fresh cheeks and his strong young body pallid.
Soon as his sister Juturna saw such murmurs rise
and the hearts of people slipping into doubt,
into the lines she goes like Camers to the life,
a soldier sprung from a grand ancestral clan:
his father a name for valor, brilliant deeds,
and he himself renowned for feats of arms.
Into the center lines Juturna strides,
alert to the work at hand,
and she sows a variety of rumors, urging:
"Aren't you ashamed, Rutulians, putting at risk
the life of one to save us all? Don't we match them
in numbers, power? Look, these are all they've got—
Trojans, Arcadians, and all the Etruscan forces,
slaves to Fate—to battle Turnus in arms! Why,
if only half of us went to war, each soldier
could hardly find a foe. But Turnus, think,
he'll rise on the wings of fame to meet the gods,
gods on whose altars he has offered up his life:
he will live forever, sung on the lips of men!
But we, if we lose our land, will bow to the yoke,
enslaved by our new high lords and masters—
we who idle on amid our fields!"
Stinging taunts
inflame the will of the fighters all the more
till a low growing murmur steals along the lines.
Even Laurentines, even Latins change their tune,
men who had just now longed for peace and safety
long for weapons, pray the pact be dashed
and pity the unjust fate that Turnus faces.
Then, crowning all, Juturna adds a greater power.
She displays in the sky the strongest sign that ever
dazed Italian minds and deceived them with its wonders.
The golden eagle of Jove, in flight through the blood-red sky,
was harrying shorebirds, routing their squadron's shrieking ranks
when suddenly down he swoops to the stream and grasps a swan,
out in the lead, in his ruthless talons. This the Italians

watch, enthralled as the birds all scream and swerving
round in flight—a marvel, look—they overshadow
the sky with wings, and forming a dense cloudbank,
force their enemy high up through the air until,
beaten down by their strikes and his victim's weight,
his talons dropped the kill in the river's run
and into the clouds the eagle winged away.
Struck,
the Italians shout out, saluting that great omen,
all hands eager to take up arms, and the augur
Tolumnius urges first: "This, this," he cries,
"is the answer to all my prayers! I embrace it,
I recognize the gods! I, I will lead you—
reach for your swords now, my poor people!
Like helpless birds, terrorized by the war
that ruthless invader brings you,
devastating your shores by force of arms.
He too will race in flight and wing away,
setting his sails to cross the farthest seas.
Close ranks. Every man of you mass with one resolve!
Fight to save your king the marauder seized!"
Enough.
Lunging out he whips a spear at the foes he faced
and the whizzing javelin hisses, rips the air dead-on—
and at that instant a huge outcry, ranks in a wedge
in disarray, lines buckling, hearts at a fever pitch
as the shaft wings on where a band of nine brothers
with fine bodies chanced to block its course. One
mother bore them all, a Tuscan, loyal Tyrrhena wed
to Gylippus, her Arcadian husband. And one of these,
in the waist where the braided belt chafes the flesh
and the buckle clasps the strap from end to end—
a striking, well-built soldier in burnished bronze—
the spear splits his ribs and splays him out on the sand.
But his brothers, a phalanx up in arms, enflamed by grief,
some tear swords from sheaths and some snatch up their spears
and all press blindly on. As the Latian columns charge them,
charging *them* come Agyllines and Trojans streaming up
with Arcadian ranks decked out in blazoned gear and
one lust drives them all: to let the sword decide.
Altars plundered for torches, down from menacing clouds
a torrent of spears, and the iron rain pelts thick-and-fast
as they carry off the holy bowls and sacred braziers.
Even Latinus flees, cradling his defeated gods and
shattered pact of peace. Others harness teams
to chariots, others vault up onto their horses,
swords brandished, tense for attack.
Messapus,
keen to disrupt the truce, whips his charger straight
at Tuscan Aulestes, king adorned with his kingly emblems,
forcing him back in terror. And back he trips, poor man,

stumbling, crashing head over shoulders into the altar
rearing behind him there, and Messapus, fired up now,
flies at him, looming over him, high in the saddle
to strike him dead with his rugged beamy lance,
the king begging for mercy, Messapus shouting:
"This one's finished! Here,
a choicer victim offered up to the great gods!"—
and the Latins rush to strip the corpse still warm.
Rushing to block them, Corynaeus grabs a flaming torch
from the altar—just so Ebysus can't strike first—and hurls
fire in the Latin's face and his huge beard flares up,
reeking with burnt singe. And following on that blow
he seizes his dazed foe's locks in his left hand and
pins him fast to the ground with a knee full force
and digs his rigid blade in Ebysus' flank.
Podalirius,
tracking the shepherd Alsus, hurtles through the front
where the spears shower down, he's rearing over him now
with his naked sword but Alsus, swirling his axehead back,
strikes him square in the skull, cleaving brow to chin
and convulsive sprays of blood imbrue his armor.
Grim repose and an iron sleep press down his eyes
and shut their light in a night that never ends.
But Aeneas,
bound to his oath, his head exposed and the hand unarmed
he was stretching toward his comrades, shouted out:
"Where are you running? Why this sudden outbreak,
why these clashes? Rein your anger in!
The pact's already struck, its terms are set.
Now I alone have the right to enter combat.
Don't hold me back. Cast your fears to the wind!
This strong right arm will put our truce to the proof.
Our rites have already made the life of Turnus mine."

Just in the midst of these, these outcries, look,
a winging arrow whizzes in and it hits Aeneas.
Nobody knows who shot it, whirled it on to bring
the Rutulians such renown—what luck, what god—
the shining fame of the feat is shrouded over now.
Nobody boasted he had struck Aeneas. No one.
Turnus,
soon as he saw Aeneas falling back from the lines,
his chiefs in disarray, ignites with a blaze of hope.
He demands his team and arms at once, in a flash of pride
he leaps up onto his chariot, tugging hard on the reins
and races on and droves of the brave he hands to death
and tumbles droves of the half-dead down to earth
or crushes whole detachments under his wheels or
seizing their lances, cuts down all who cut and run.
Amok as Mars by the banks of the Hebrus[2] frozen over—
splattered with blood, fired to fury, drumming his shield

2. River in Thrace, a region known for its wildness.

as he whips up war and gives his frenzied team free rein and
over the open fields they outstrip the winds from South and West
till the far frontiers of Thrace groan to their pounding hoofs
and round him the shapes of black Fear, Rage and Ambush,
aides of the war-god gallop on and on. Just so madly
Turnus whips his horses into the heart of battle,
chargers steaming sweat, trampling enemy fighters
killed in agony—kicking gusts of bloody spray,
their hoofs stamping into the sand the clotted gore.
Now he's dealing death to Sthenelus, Thamyris, Pholus:
Sthenelus speared at long-range, the next two hand-to-hand,
at a distance too both sons of Imbrasus, Glaucus and Lades.
Imbrasus had reared them himself in Lycia once and
equipped them both with matching weapons either
to fight close-up or outrace the winds on horseback.

Another sector. Eumedes charges into the melee,
grandson of old Eumedes, bearing that veteran's name
but famed for his father Dolon's heart and hand in war.
Dolon, who once dared to ask for Achilles' chariot,
his reward for spying out the Achaean camp
but Diomedes paid his daring a different reward—
now he no longer dreams of the horses of Achilles.[3]
Eumedes . . . spotting him far out on the open meadow,
Turnus hits him first with a light spear winged across
that empty space then races up to him, halts his team, and
rearing over the dying Trojan, plants a foot on his neck
and tears the sword from his grip—a flash of the blade—
he stains it red in the man's throat, and to top it off
cries out: "Look here, Trojan, here are the fields,
the great Land of the West you fought to win in war.
Lie there, take their measure. That's the reward
they all will carry off who risk my blade,
that's how they build their walls!"
A whirl of his spear
and Turnus sends Asbytes to join him, Chloreus too
and Sybaris, Dares, Thersilochus, then Thymoetes,
pitched down over the neck of his bucking horse.
Like a blast of the Thracian Northwind howling over
the deep Aegean, whipping the waves toward shore, wherever
the winds burst down the clouds take flight through the sky,
so Turnus, wherever he hacks his path, the lines buckle in
and the ranks turn tail and run as his own drive sweeps him on,
his rushing chariot charging the gusts that toss his crest.
Phegeus could not face his assault, his deafening cries;
he flung himself before the chariot, right hand wrestling
the horses' jaws around as they came charging into him,
frothing at their bits, then dragged him dangling down
from the yoke as Turnus' spearhead hit his exposed flank
and ripping the double links of his breastplate, there it stuck,

3. In the *Iliad*, book 10, the Trojan Dolon was promised Achilles' horses and chariot if he spied on the Greek camp, but Diomedes killed him.

just grazing the fighter's skin. But raising his shield,
swerving to brave his foe, he strained to save himself
with his naked sword—when the wheel and whirling axle
knocked him headlong, ground him into the dust. Turnus,
finishing up with a stroke between the helmet's base
and the breastplate's upper rim, hacked off his head
and left his trunk in the sand.
                                        And now, while Turnus
is spreading death across the plains in all his triumph,
Mnestheus and trusty Achates, Ascanius at their side,
are setting Aeneas down in camp—bleeding, propping
himself on his lengthy spear at every other step . . .
Furious, struggling to tear the broken arrowhead out,
he insists they take the quickest way to heal him:
"Cut the wound with a broadsword, open it wide,
dig out the point where it's bedded deep
and put me back into action!"

Now up comes Iapyx, Iasius' son, and dear
to Apollo, more than all other men, and once,
in the anguished grip of love, the god himself
gladly offered him all his own arts, his gifts,
his prophetic skills, his lyre, his flying shafts.
But he, desperate to slow the death of his dying father,
preferred to master the power of herbs, the skills that cure,
and pursue a healer's practice, silent and unsung. But Aeneas,
pressed by a crowd of friends and Iulus grieving sorely—
the fighter stood there bridling, fuming, hunched
on his rugged spear, unmoved by all their tears.
The old surgeon, his robe tucked back and cinched
in the healer's way, with his expert, healing hands
and Apollo's potent herbs he works for all he's worth.
No use, no use as his right hand tugs at the shaft
and his clamping forceps grip the iron point.
No good luck guides his probes,
Apollo the Master lends no help, and all the while
the ruthless horror of war grows greater, grimmer
throughout the field, a disaster ever closer . . .
Now they see a pillar of dust upholding the sky
and the horsemen riding on and dense salvos of weapons
raining down in the camp's heart, and the cries of torment
reach the heavens as young men fight and die beneath
the iron fist of Mars.
                                At this point, Venus,
shocked by the unfair pain her son endures,
culls with a mother's care some dittany fresh
from Cretan Ida, spear erect with its tender leaves
and crown of purple flowers. No stranger to wild goats
who graze it when flying arrows are planted in their backs.
This she bears away, her features veiled in a heavy mist,
this she distils in secret into the river water poured

in burnished bowls, and fills them with healing power
and sprinkles ambrosial juices bringing health,
and redolent cure-all too.[4] With this potion,
aged Iapyx laved the wound, quite unaware, and
suddenly all the pain dissolved from Aeneas' body, all
the blood that pooled in his wound stanched, and the shaft,
with no force required, slipped out in the healer's hand
and the old strength came back, fresh as it was at first.
"Quick, fetch him his weapons! Don't just stand there!"—
Iapyx cries, the first to inflame their hearts against the foe.
"This strong cure, it's none of the work of human skills,
no expert's arts in action. My right hand, Aeneas,
never saved your life. Something greater—
a god—is speeding you back to greater exploits."

Starved for war, Aeneas had cased his calves in gold,
left and right, and spurning delay, he shakes his glinting spear.
Once he has fitted shield to hip and harness to his back,
he clasps Ascanius fast in an iron-clad embrace
and kissing him lightly through his visor, says:
"Learn courage from me, my son, true hardship too.
Learn good luck from others.[5] My hand will shield you
in war today and guide you toward the great rewards.
But mark my words. Soon as you ripen into manhood,
reaching back for the models of your kin, remember—
father Aeneas and uncle Hector fire your heart!"

Urgings over, out of the gates he strode,
immense in strength, waving his massive spear.
Antheus and Mnestheus flank him closely, dashing on
and from the deserted camp roll all their swarming ranks.
The field is a swirl of blinding dust, the earth quaking
under their thundering tread. From the opposing rampart
Turnus saw them coming on, his Italians saw them too
and an icy chill of dread ran through their bones.
First in the Latin ranks, Juturna caught the sound,
she knew what it meant and, seized with trembling, fled.
But Aeneas flies ahead, spurring his dark ranks on and storming
over the open fields like a cloudburst wiping out the sun,
sweeping over the seas toward land, and well in advance
the poor unlucky farmers, hearts shuddering, know
what it will bring—trees uprooted, crops destroyed,
their labor in ruins far and wide—and the winds come first,
churning in uproar toward the shore. So the Trojans storm in,
their commander heading them toward the foe, their tight ranks
packed in a wedge, comrade linked with comrade massing hard.
A slash of a sword—Thymbraeus finished giant Osiris,

4. Ambrosia is a mythical magic liquid used as food, drink, and unguent by the immortal gods. Dittany and "cure-all" (panacea) are real herbs, used in medicine.

5. Sophocles' Ajax gives his son similar advice before killing himself.

Mnestheus kills Arcetius, Achates hacks Epulo down
and Gyas, Ufens. Even the seer Tolumnius falls,
the first to wing a lance against the foe.
Cries hit the heavens—now it's the Latins' time
to turn tail and flee across the fields in a cloud of dust.
Aeneas never stoops to leveling men who show their backs
or makes for the ones who fight him fairly, toe-to-toe,
or the ones who fling their spears at longer range.
No, it's Turnus alone he's tracking, eyes alert
through the murky haze of battle, Turnus alone
Aeneas demands to fight.
                                        Juturna, terror-struck
at the thought, the woman warrior knocks Metiscus,
Turnus' charioteer, from between the reins he grasps
and leaves him sprawling far from the chariot pole
as she herself takes over, shaking the rippling reins
like Metiscus to the life, his voice, his build, his gear.
Quick as a black swift darts along through the great halls
of a wealthy lord, and scavenging morsels, banquet scraps
for her chirping nestlings, all her twitterings echo now
in the empty colonnades, now round the brimming ponds.
So swiftly Juturna drives her team at the Trojan center,
darts along in her chariot whirling through the field,
now here, there, displaying her brother in his glory, true,
but she never lets him come to grips, she swerves far away.
But Aeneas, no less bent on meeting up with the enemy,
stalks his victim, circling round him, turn by turn
and his shrill cries call him through the broken ranks.
As often as he caught sight of his prey and strained
to outstrip the speed of that team that raced the wind,
so often Juturna wheeled the chariot round and swooped away.
What should he do? No hope. He seethes on a heaving sea
as warring anxieties call him back and forth.
                                        Then Messapus,
just sprinting along with a pair of steel-tipped spears
in his left hand, training one on the Trojan, lets it fly—
right on target. Aeneas stopped in his tracks and huddled
under his shield, crouching down on a knee but the spear
in its onrush swiped the peak of his helmet off and
swept away the plumes that crowned his crest.
Aeneas erupts in anger, stung by treachery now
and seeing Turnus' horses swing his chariot round
and speed away, over and over he calls out to Jove,
to the altars built for the treaty now a shambles.
Then, at last, he hurtles into the thick of battle
as Mars drives him on, and terrible, savage, inciting
slaughter, sparing none, he gives his rage free rein.

Now what god can unfold for me so many terrors?
Who can make a song of slaughter in all its forms—
the deaths of captains down the entire field,
dealt now by Turnus, now by Aeneas, kill for kill?

Did it please you so, great Jove, to see the world at war,
the peoples clash that would later live in everlasting peace?

Aeneas takes on Rutulian Sucro—here was the first duel
that ground the Trojan charge to a halt—and meets the man
with no long visit, just a quick stab in his flank and
the ruthless sword-blade splits the ribcage, thrusting
into the heart where death comes lightning fast.
Turnus,
hurling the brothers Amycus and Diores off their mounts,
attacks them on foot and one he strikes with a long spear,
rushing at Turnus, one he runs through with a sword and
severing both their heads, he dangles them from his car
as he carts them off in triumph dripping blood.
Aeneas
packs them off to death, Talos, Tanais, staunch Cethegus,
all three at a single charge, then grim Onites too,
named for his Theban line, his mother called Peridia.
Turnus
kills the brothers fresh from Apollo's Lycian fields
and next Menoetes who, in his youth, detested war
but war would be his fate. An Arcadian angler
skilled at working the rivers of Lerna stocked with fish,
his lodgings poor, a stranger to all the gifts of the great,
and his father farmed his crops on rented land.
Like fires
loosed from adverse sides into woodlands dry as tinder,
thickets of rustling laurel, or foaming rivers hurling
down from a mountain ridge and roaring out to sea,
each leaves a path of destruction in its wake.
Just as furious now those two, Aeneas, Turnus
rampaging through the battle, now their fury
boils over inside them, now their warring hearts
at the breaking point—they don't concede defeat—
and now they hack their wounding ways with all their force.

Here's Murranus sounding off the names of his forebears,
all his fathers' fathers' line from the start of time,
his entire race come down from the Latin kings . . .
Headlong down Aeneas smashes the braggart with a rock,
a whirling boulder's power that splays him on the ground,
snarled in the reins and yoke as the wheels roll him on
and under their thundering hoofbeats both his galloping horses—
all thought of their master vanished—trample him to death.
Here's Hyllus rushing in with his bloodcurdling rage
but Turnus rushing to block him whips a spear at his brow
that splits his gilded helmet, sticks erect in his brain.
And your sword-arm, Cretheus, bravest Greek afield—
it could not snatch you from Turnus,
nor did the gods he worshipped save Cupencus' life
when Aeneas came his way: he thrust his chest at the blade
but his brazen shield, poor priest, could not put off his death.

And Aeolus, you too, the Laurentine fields saw you go down
and your body spread across the earth. Down you went,
whom neither the Greek battalions could demolish,
nor could Achilles, who razed the realms of Priam.
Here was your finish line, the end of life.
Your halls lie under Ida, high halls at Lyrnesus
but here in Laurentine soil lies your tomb.
All on attack—
the armies wheeling around for combat, all the Latins,
all the Trojans—Mnestheus, fierce Serestus,
Messapus breaker of horses, brawny Asilas—
the Etruscan squadron, Evander's Arcadian wings,
each fighter at peak strength, all force put to the test
as they soldier on, no rest, no letup—total war.
And now
his lovely mother impelled Aeneas to storm the ramparts,
hurl his troops at the city—fast, frontal assault—
and panic the Latins faced with swift collapse.
And he, stalking Turnus through the moil of battle,
Aeneas' glances roving left and right, sights the town
untouched by this ruthless war, immune, at peace and
an instant vision of fiercer combat fires his soul.
He summons Mnestheus, Sergestus, staunch Serestus,
chosen captains, takes his stand on a high rise
where the rest of the Trojan fighters cluster round,
tight ranks that don't throw down their shields and spears
as Aeneas, rising amidst them, urges from the earthwork:
"No delay in obeying my orders—Jove backs us now!
No slowing down, I tell you, we must strike at once!
That city, the cause of the war, the heart of Latinus' realm—
unless they bow to the yoke, brought low this very day,
I'll topple their smoking rooftops to the ground.
What, wait till Turnus deigns to take me on?
Consents to fight me again, defeated as he is?
That city, my people, there's the core and crux
of this accursed war. Quick, bring torches!
Restore our truce with fire!"
A call to arms
and they pack in wedge formation bent on battle,
advancing toward the walls in a dense fighting mass—
in a moment you see ladders slanted, brands aflame.
Some charge at the gates and cut the sentries down
and others whirl their steel, blot out the sky with spears.
Aeneas himself, up in the lead beneath the ramparts,
raises his arm and thunders out, upbraiding Latinus,
calling the gods: "Bear witness, I've been dragged
into battle once again! The Latins are our enemies
twice over—this is the second pact they've shattered!"
And Discord surges up in the panic-stricken citizens,
some insisting the gates be flung wide to the Dardans,

yes, and they hale the king himself toward the walls.
Others seize on weapons, rush to defend the ramparts . . .
Picture a shepherd tracking bees to their rocky den,
closed up in the clefts he fills with scorching smoke
and all inside, alarmed by the danger, swarming round
through their stronghold walled with wax, hone sharp
their rage to a piercing buzz and the black reek
goes churning through their house and the rocks hum
with a blind din and the smoke spews out into thin air.

Now a new misfortune assailed the battle-weary Latins,
rocking their city to its roots with grief. The queen—
when from her house she sees the enemy coming strong,
walls assaulted, flames surging up to the roofs and no
Rutulian force in sight to block their way, no troops of Turnus,
then, poor woman, she thinks him killed in the press of war
and suddenly lost in the frenzied grip of sorrow, claims
that she's the cause, the criminal, source of disaster—
shrilling wild words in her crazed, grieving fit and
bent on death, ripping her purple gown for a noose,
she knots it high to a rafter, dies a gruesome death.
As soon as the wretched Latin women hear the worst,
the queen's daughter Lavinia is the first to tear
her golden hair and score her lustrous cheeks,
the rest of the women round her mad with grief and
the long halls resound with trilling wails of sorrow.
From here the terrible news goes racing through the city,
spirits plunge—Latinus, rending his robes to tatters,
stunned by his wife's death and his city's fall,
fouls his white hair with showers of dust.
Turnus
at this point, fighting off on the outskirts of the field,
is hunting a few stragglers. Yet he's less avid now,
exulting less and less when his horses win the day.
But the winds bring him a hint of hidden terrors,
mingled cries drifting out of the town in chaos.
A muffled din. He cocks his ears, listening . . .
hardly the sound of joy. "What am I hearing,
why this enormous grief that rocks the walls,
this clamor echoing from the city far away?"

So he wonders, madly tugging the reins back
and makes the chariot stop.
But his sister, changed
to look like his charioteer, Metiscus, handling the car
and team and reins, she faced him with this challenge:
"This way, Turnus! We'll hunt these Trojans down
where victory opens up the first way in.
Other hands can defend our city walls. Aeneas

hurtles down on the Latins—all-out assault—
but we can deal out savage death to his Trojans.
You'll return from the front no less than Aeneas
in numbers killed and battle honors won!"
"My sister,"
Turnus replies, "I recognized you long ago, yes,
when you first broke up our treaty with your wiles
and threw yourself into combat. No hiding your godhood,
you can't fool me now. But what Olympian wished it so,
who sent you down to bear such heavy labor? Why,
to witness your luckless brother's painful death?
What do I do now? What new twist of Fortune
can save me now? I've seen with my own eyes,
calling out to me 'Turnus!' as he fell . . .
Murranus—no one dearer to me survived,
a great soldier taken down by a great wound.
Unlucky Ufens died before he could see my shame
and the Trojans commandeered his corpse and weapons.
Must I bear the sight of Latinus' houses razed—
the last thing I needed—and not rebut
the ugly slander of Drances with my sword?
Shall I cut and run? Shall the country look
on Turnus in full retreat? To die, tell me,
is that the worst we face? Be good to me now,
you shades of the dead below, for the gods above
have turned away their favors. Down to you I go,
a spirit cleansed, utterly innocent as charged,
forever worthy of my great fathers' fame!"

The words were still on his lips when, look,
Saces, riding his lathered horse through enemy lines
and slashed where an arrow raked his face, comes racing up,
calling for help, crying the name of Turnus: "Turnus,
you are our last best hope! Pity your own people.
Aeneas strikes like lightning! Up in arms he threatens
to topple Italy's towers, bring them down in ruins,
already the flaming brands go winging toward the roofs.
The Latins, their eyes, their looks are trained on you.
Latinus, the king himself, moans and groans with doubt—
whom to call his sons? Which pact can he embrace?
And now the queen, whose trust lay all in you,
she's dead by her own hand,
terrified, she's fled the light of life.
Alone before the gates Messapus and brave Atinas
hold our front lines steady, ringed by enemy squadrons
packed tight, bristling a jagged crop of naked blades!
While look at you, wheeling your chariot round
the abandoned grassy fields!"
Stunned by pictures
of these disasters blurring through his mind,
Turnus stood there, staring, speechless, churning

with mighty shame, with grief and madness all aswirl
in that one fighting heart: with love spurred by rage
and a sense of his own worth too. As soon as the shadows
were dispersed and the light restored to his mind,
he turned his fiery glance toward the ramparts,
glaring back from his chariot to the town.
But now,
look, a whirlwind of fire goes rolling story to story,
billowing up the sky, and clings fast to a mobile tower,
a defense he built himself of wedged, rough-hewn beams,
fitting the wheels below it, gangways reared above.
"Now, now, my sister, the Fates are in command.
Don't hold me back. Where God and relentless
Fortune call us on, that's the way we go!
I'm set on fighting Aeneas hand-to-hand,
set, however bitter it is, to meet my death.
You'll never see me disgraced again—no more.
Insane as it is, I beg you, let me rage before I die!"

He leapt from his chariot, hit the ground at a run
through enemies, Trojan spears, and left his sister
grieving as he went bursting through the lines.
Wild as a boulder plowing headlong down from a summit,
torn out by the tempests—whether the stormwinds washed it free
or the creeping years stole under it, worked it loose,
down the cliff it crashes, ruthless crag of rock
bounding over the ground with enormous impact,
churning up in its onrush woods and herds and men.
So Turnus bursts through the fractured ranks, charging
toward the walls where the earth runs red with blood
and the winds hiss with spears and, hand flung up,
he cries with a ringing voice: "Hold back now,
you Rutulians! Latins, keep your arms in check!
Whatever Fortune sends, it's mine. Better
for me alone to redeem the pact for you
and let my sword decide!"
All ranks scattered,
leaving a no-man's-land between them both.
But Aeneas,
the great commander, hearing the name of Turnus,
deserts the walls, deserts the citadel's heights
and breaks off all operations, jettisons all delay—
he springs in joy, drums his shield and it thunders terror.
As massive as Athos, massive as Eryx or even Father
Apennine himself, roaring out with his glistening oaks,
elated to raise his snow-capped brow to the winds.[6] And then,
for a fact, the Rutulians, Trojans, all the Italians,
those defending the high ramparts, those on attack

6. Mount Athos is in Greece; Mount Eryx is in Sicily; the Apennine Mountains are a range extending all the way down Italy.

who batter the walls' foundations with their rams:
all armies strained to turn their glances round
and lifted their battle-armor off their shoulders.
Latinus himself is struck that these two giant men,
sprung from opposing ends of the earth, have met,
face-to-face, to let their swords decide.
                                                            But they,
as soon as the battlefield lay clear and level,
charge at speed, rifling their spears at long range,
then rush to battle with shields and clanging bronze.
The earth groans as stroke after stroke they land
with naked swords: fortune and fortitude mix
in one assault. Charging like two hostile bulls
fighting up on Sila's woods or Taburnus' ridges,
ramping in mortal combat, both brows bent for attack
and the herdsmen back away in fear and the whole herd
stands by, hushed, afraid, and the heifers wait and wonder,
who will lord it over the forest? who will lead the herd?—
while the bulls battle it out, horns butting, locking,
goring each other, necks and shoulders roped in blood
and the woods resound as they grunt and bellow out.
So they charge, Trojan Aeneas and Turnus, son of Daunus,
shields clang and the huge din makes the heavens ring.
Jove himself lifts up his scales, balanced, trued,
and in them he sets the opposing fates of both . . .
Whom would the labor of battle doom? Whose life
would weigh him down to death?
                                                   Suddenly Turnus
flashes forward, certain he's in the clear and
raising his sword high, rearing to full stretch
strikes—as Trojans and anxious Latins shout out,
with the gaze of both armies riveted on the fighters.
But his treacherous blade breaks off, it fails Turnus
in mid-stroke—enraged, his one recourse, retreat,
and swifter than Eastwinds, Turnus flies as soon
as he sees that unfamiliar hilt in his hand,
no defense at all. They say the captain, rushing
headlong on to harness his team and board his car
to begin the duel, left his father's sword behind
and hastily grabbed his charioteer Metiscus' blade.
Long as the Trojan stragglers took to their heels and ran,
the weapon did its work, but once it came up against
the immortal armor forged by the God of Fire, Vulcan,
the mortal sword burst at a stroke, brittle as ice,
and glinting splinters gleamed on the tawny sand.
So raging Turnus runs for it, scours the field,
now here, now there, weaving in tangled circles
as Trojans crowd him hard, a dense ring of them
shutting him in, with a wild swamp to the left
and steep walls to the right.
                                              Nor does Aeneas flag,
though slowed down by his wound, his knees unsteady,

cutting his pace at times but he's still in full fury,
hot on his frantic quarry's tracks, stride for stride.
Alert as a hunting hound that lights on a trapped stag,
hemmed in by a river's bend or frightened back by the ropes
with blood-red feathers[7]—the hound barking, closing, fast
as the quarry, panicked by traps and the steep riverbanks,
runs off and back in a thousand ways but the Umbrian hound,[8]
keen for the kill, hangs on the trail, his jaws agape—
and now, now he's got him, thinks he's got him, yes
and his jaws clap shut, stymied, champing the empty air.
Then the shouts break loose, and the banks and rapids round
resound with the din, and the high sky thunders back. Turnus—
even in flight he rebukes his men as he races, calling
each by name, demanding his old familiar sword.
Aeneas, opposite, threatens death and doom at once
to anyone in his way, he threatens his harried foes
that he'll root their city out and, wounded as he is,
keeps closing for the kill. And five full circles
they run and reel as many back, around and back,
for it's no mean trophy they're sporting after now,
they race for the life and the lifeblood of Turnus.

By chance a wild olive, green with its bitter leaves,
stood right here, sacred to Faunus,[9] revered by men
in the old days, sailors saved from shipwreck.
On it they always fixed their gifts to the local god
and they hung their votive clothes in thanks for rescue.
But the Trojans—no exceptions, hallowed tree that it was—
chopped down its trunk to clear the spot for combat.
Now here the spear of Aeneas had stuck, borne home
by its hurling force, and the tough roots held it fast.
He bent down over it, trying to wrench the iron loose and
track with a spear the kill he could not catch on foot.
Turnus, truly beside himself with terror—"Faunus!"
he cried, "I beg you, pity me! You, dear Earth,
hold fast to that spear! If I have always kept
your rites—a far cry from Aeneas' men
who stain your rites with war."
So he appealed,
calling out for the god's help, and not for nothing.
Aeneas struggled long, wasting time on the tough stump,
no power of *his* could loose the timber's stubborn bite.
As he bravely heaves and hauls, the goddess Juturna,
changing back again to the charioteer Metiscus,
rushes in and returns her brother's sword to Turnus.
But Venus, incensed that the nymph has had her brazen way,

7. Hunters used ropes and nets decorated with feathers.
8. A dog breed known for its skill in hunting.
9. An old Roman god associated with the countryside and forest.

steps up and plucks Aeneas' spear from the clinging root.
So standing tall, with their arms and fighting hearts refreshed—
one who trusted all to his sword, the other looming fiercely
with his spear—confronting each other, both men breathless,
brace for the war-god's fray.
Now at the same moment
Jove, the king of mighty Olympus, turns to Juno,
gazing down on the war from her golden cloud, and says:
"Where will it end, my queen? What is left at the last?
Aeneas the hero, god of the land: you know yourself,
you confess you know that he is heaven bound,
his fate will raise Aeneas to the stars.
What are you plotting? What hope can make you
cling to the chilly clouds? So, was it right
for a mortal hand to wound, to mortify a god?
Right to restore that mislaid sword to Turnus—
for without your power what could Juturna do?—
and lend the defeated strength? Have done at last.
Bow to my appeals. Don't let your corrosive grief
devour you in silence, or let your dire concerns come
pouring from your sweet lips and plaguing me forever.
We have reached the limit. To harass the Trojans
over land and sea, to ignite an unspeakable war,
degrade a royal house and blend the wedding hymn
with the dirge of grief: all that lay in your power.
But go no further. I forbid you now."
Jove said no more.
And so, with head bent low, Saturn's daughter replied:
"Because I have known your will so well, great Jove,
against my *own* I deserted Turnus and the earth.
Or else you would never see me now, alone
on a windswept throne enduring right and wrong.
No, wrapped in flames I would be up on the front lines,
dragging the Trojan into mortal combat. Juturna?
I was the one, I admit, who spurred her on
to help her embattled brother, true, and blessed
whatever greater daring it took to save his life,
but never to shower arrows, never tense the bow.
I swear by the unappeasable fountainhead of the Styx,[1]
the one dread oath decreed for the gods on high.
"So,
now I yield, Juno yields, and I leave this war I loathe.
But this—and there is no law of Fate to stop it now—
this I beg for Latium, for the glory of your people.
When, soon, they join in their happy wedding-bonds—
and wedded let them be—in pacts of peace at last,
never command the Latins, here on native soil,
to exchange their age-old name,

1. River in the underworld.

to become Trojans, called the kin of Teucer,
alter their language, change their style of dress.
Let Latium endure. Let Alban kings hold sway for all time.
Let Roman stock grow strong with Italian strength.
Troy has fallen—and fallen let her stay—
with the very name of Troy!"
Smiling down,
the creator of man and the wide world returned:
"Now there's my sister. Saturn's second child—
such tides of rage go churning through your heart.
Come, relax your anger. It started all for nothing.
I grant your wish. I surrender. Freely, gladly too.
Latium's sons will retain their fathers' words and ways.
Their name till now is the name that shall endure.
Mingling in stock alone, the Trojans will subside.
And I will add the rites and the forms of worship,
and make them Latins all, who speak one Latin tongue.
Mixed with Ausonian blood,[2] one race will spring from them,
and you will see them outstrip all men, outstrip all gods
in reverence. No nation on earth will match the honors
they shower down on you."
Juno nodded assent to this,
her spirit reversed to joy. She departs the sky
and leaves her cloud behind.
His task accomplished,
the Father turned his mind to another matter, set
to dismiss Juturna from her brother's battles.
They say there are twin Curses called the Furies . . .
Night had born them once in the dead of darkness,
one and the same spawn, and birthed infernal Megaera,
wreathing all their heads with coiled serpents,
fitting them out with wings that race the wind.
They hover at Jove's throne, crouch at his gates
to serve that savage king
and whet the fears of afflicted men whenever
the king of gods lets loose horrific deaths and plagues
or panics towns that deserve the scourge of war.
Jove sped one of them down the sky, commanding:
"Cross Juturna's path as a wicked omen!"

Down she swoops, hurled to earth by a whirlwind,
swift as a darting arrow whipped from a bowstring
through the clouds, a shaft armed by a Parthian,[3]
tipped with deadly poison, shot by a Parthian
or a Cretan archer—well past any cure—
hissing on unseen through the rushing dark.
So raced this daughter of Night and sped to earth.

2. Ausonian: Italian.
3. Parthia (a region in modern Iran) was known for its skillful archers.

Soon as she spots the Trojan ranks and Turnus' lines
she quickly shrinks into that small bird that often,
hunched at dusk on deserted tombs and rooftops, sings
its ominous song in shadows late at night. Shrunken so,
the demon flutters over and over again in Turnus' face,
screeching, drumming his shield with its whirring wings.
An eerie numbness unnerved him head to toe with dread,
his hackles bristled in horror, voice choked in his throat.

Recognizing the Fury's ruffling wings at a distance,
wretched Juturna tears her hair, nails clawing her face,
fists beating her breast, and cries to her brother:
"How, Turnus, how can your sister help you now?
What's left for me now, after all I have endured?
What skill do I have to lengthen out your life?
How can I fight against this dreadful omen?
At last, at last I leave the field of battle.
Afraid as I am, now frighten me no more,
you obscene birds of night! Too well I know
the beat of your wings, the drumbeat of doom.
Nor do the proud commands of Jove escape me now,
our great, warm-hearted Jove. Are these his wages
for taking my virginity? Why did he grant me life
eternal—rob me of our one privilege, death?
Then, for a fact, I now could end this agony,
keep my brother company down among the shades.
Doomed to live forever? Without you, my brother,
what do I have still mine that's sweet to taste?
If only the earth gaped deep enough to take me down,
to plunge this goddess into the depths of hell!"
With that,
shrouding her head with a gray-green veil and moaning low,
down to her own stream's bed the goddess sank away.

All hot pursuit, Aeneas brandishes high his spear,
that tree of a spear, and shouts from a savage heart:
"More delay! Why now? Still in retreat, Turnus, why?
This is no foot-race. It's savagery, swordplay cut-and-thrust!
Change yourself into any shape you please, call up
whatever courage or skill you still have left.
Pray to wing your way to the starry sky
or bury yourself in the earth's deep pits!"

Turnus shakes his head: "I don't fear you,
you and your blazing threats, my fierce friend.
It's the gods that frighten me—Jove, my mortal foe."

No more words. Glancing around he spots a huge rock,
huge, ages old, and lying out in the field by chance,
placed as a boundary stone to settle border wars.

A dozen picked men could barely shoulder it up, men
of such physique as the earth brings forth these days,
but he wrenched it up, hands trembling, tried to heave it
right at Aeneas, Turnus stretching to full height, the hero
at speed, at peak strength. Yet he's losing touch with himself,
racing, hoisting that massive rock in his hands and hurling,
true, but his knees buckle, blood's like ice in his veins
and the rock he flings through the air, plummeting under
its own weight, cannot cover the space between them,
cannot strike full force . . .
Just as in dreams
when the nightly spell of sleep falls heavy on our eyes
and we seem entranced by longing to keep on racing on,
no use, in the midst of one last burst of speed
we sink down, consumed, our tongue won't work,
and tried and true, the power that filled our body
fails—we strain but the voice and words won't follow.
So with Turnus. Wherever he fought to force his way,
no luck, the merciless Fury blocks his efforts.
A swirl of thoughts goes racing through his mind,
he glances toward his own Rutulians and their town,
he hangs back in dread, he quakes at death—it's here.
Where can he run? How can he strike out at the enemy?
Where's his chariot? His charioteer, his sister? Vanished.

As he hangs back, the fatal spear of Aeneas streaks on—
spotting a lucky opening he had flung from a distance,
all his might and main. Rocks heaved by a catapult
pounding city ramparts never storm so loudly, never
such a shattering bolt of thunder crashing forth.
Like a black whirlwind churning on, that spear
flies on with its weight of iron death to pierce
the breastplate's lower edge and the outmost rim
of the round shield with its seven plies and right
at the thick of Turnus' thigh it whizzes through,
it strikes home and the blow drops great Turnus
down to the ground, battered down on his bent knees.
The Rutulians spring up with a groan and the hillsides
round groan back and the tall groves far and wide
resound with the long-drawn moan.
Turnus lowered
his eyes and reached with his right hand and begged,
a suppliant: "I deserve it all. No mercy, please,"
Turnus pleaded. "Seize your moment now. Or if
some care for a parent's grief can touch you still,
I pray you—you had such a father, in old Anchises—
pity Daunus in his old age and send me back
to my own people, or if you would prefer,
send them my dead body stripped of life. Here,
the victor and vanquished, I stretch my hands to you,

so the men of Latium have seen me in defeat.
Lavinia is your bride.
Go no further down the road of hatred."

Aeneas, ferocious in armor, stood there, still,
shifting his gaze, and held his sword-arm back,
holding himself back too as Turnus' words began
to sway him more and more . . . when all at once
he caught sight of the fateful sword-belt of Pallas,
swept over Turnus' shoulder, gleaming with shining studs
Aeneas knew by heart. Young Pallas, whom Turnus had overpowered,
taken down with a wound, and now his shoulder flaunted
his enemy's battle-emblem like a trophy. Aeneas,
soon as his eyes drank in that plunder—keepsake
of his own savage grief—flaring up in fury,
terrible in his rage, he cries: "Decked in the spoils
you stripped from one I loved—escape my clutches? Never—
Pallas strikes this blow, Pallas sacrifices you now,
makes you pay the price with your own guilty blood!"
In the same breath, blazing with wrath he plants
his iron sword hilt-deep in his enemy's heart.
Turnus' limbs went limp in the chill of death.
His life breath fled with a groan of outrage
down to the shades below.[4]

4. The same lines are used in book 11 for the death of the woman warrior, Camilla.

OVID

43 B.C.E.–17 C.E.

Ovid (whose full name was Publius Ovidius Naso) was one of the smartest, most prolific, and most consistently entertaining of the Roman poets. During his long and productive career, he wrote funny, perceptive poems about sex and relationships in contemporary Rome, as well as vivid retellings of ancient myths. His way of telling stories remains extraordinary for its subtlety and its depth of psychological understanding. His work had a massive influence on the poets and artists of the Middle Ages, the Renaissance, and beyond, and it is one of our most important and accessible sources for the rich mythology of ancient Greece and Rome.

LIFE AND TIMES

Ovid was born into an aristocratic ("equestrian") family, in the provincial Roman town of Sulmo, east of Rome. His father wanted him to become a lawyer, and therefore had him trained in rhetoric. Ovid's writing shows the influence of rhetorical technique, in its polished, witty style. But Ovid had no real interest in the law. He was a natural poet, and at the age of twenty, to his father's disappointment and disapproval, he quit his legal training. He held various minor governmental posts, but eventually became a full-time poet, with the financial aid of a rich patron called Messalla. Ovid became part of the literary circles of Rome: he knew the poets Propertius and **Horace**, and met **Virgil**, who was some twenty-seven years older.

Ovid married three times; he had been divorced twice before the age of thirty. His third wife seems to have had a daughter by a previous husband, but Ovid had no children of his own. Beyond that, we know little of Ovid's personal life. He wrote a great deal about extramarital sex, but emphasized that his poetic persona should not be taken as autobiography, declaring, "My Muse is slutty, but my life is chaste."

Ovid's work included various collections of poems on mythological topics, such as the *Fasti* (never finished), on the Roman calendar, and a set of poetic letters, the *Heroides*, from mythical heroines like Helen of Troy to their boyfriends. But most notorious, in his own time and later, were his two books about sex and relationships: the *Amores* and the *Ars Amatoria*. These used the tradition of Roman love elegy, which had begun with **Catullus** and had been developed by Ovid's friend Propertius, who evoked the desperate, abject longing of a man for a beloved and unreliable girlfriend. Ovid's love poetry focuses less on feelings than on behavior, and less on love than on sex, which he treats in a light, knowing tone. He gives, for example, a titillating account of some hot afternoon sex; tells anecdotes about his girlfriend's bad experiences with hair dye and about her attempted abortion; and offers advice about the best places to go and best lines to use for picking up a date.

All this was guaranteed to irritate the more conservative members of Roman society, who included—unfortunately for Ovid—the emperor, Augustus. Having seized power after winning the battle of Actium (in 31 B.C.E.), at the end of a long civil war, Augustus was eager to impose order on the fragmented society of Rome. A key element in his domestic strategy was to reform the morals and increase the population of the Roman elite, by promoting marriage and traditional family structures. New laws were imposed in 19–18 B.C.E. to encourage married couples to have children, and to punish adultery with exile. In this context, Ovid's *Ars Amatoria* seems deliberately calculated to enrage the emperor. The poem points up the hypocrisy of Roman sexual mores and suggests that, in fact, having lots of extramarital sex is far more traditional than Augustan family values, since the Romans have been doing it ever since the foundation of the city: it was through the rape of the Sabine women that the male inhabitants of the new city acquired wives and were able to supply Rome with future citizens.

Ovid seems to have gotten himself into even worse trouble by what he calls a mistake. We do not know exactly what happened; Ovid suggests that he saw something he should not have seen, perhaps involving the emperor's daughter, Julia, who was having an adulterous affair. Combined with the *Ars Amatoria* and Ovid's generally provocative stance toward Augustus, this mistake was the last straw; in 8 C.E., the emperor—acting, unusually, on his own initiative, without input from the Senate—condemned Ovid to permanent exile from Rome to Tomis, a remote town on the Black Sea, in modern Romania. He lived out the remaining eight years of his life in grim isolation, far from family and friends, in a cold, bleak place where, he claims, nobody even spoke Latin. Ovid wrote a series of poems from exile, mostly letters bewailing his sufferings and pleading—to friends, family, acquaintances, the general public, and to the emperor himself—to be forgiven and to be allowed back home. All were unsuccessful; Ovid died in Tomis, alone and unforgiven.

METAMORPHOSES

At the time of his exile in 8 C.E., Ovid was finishing his greatest work, the *Metamorphoses* (Greek for "changes"). It is less obviously provocative than Ovid's love poetry, but it, too, provides a radical challenge both to Augustan moral and political values and to traditional poetic norms. Virgil had written what Augustus wanted to be the official epic of the new order. For all its innovations, the ***Aeneid*** focused on the deeds of a single hero, and it treated its culture's dominant values (such as duty, imperial power, and military honor) with respect. The *Metamorphoses* is recognizably epic; it is the only poem Ovid wrote in the epic meter, dactylic hexameter. But it can be seen as a critical response to Virgil, even an anti-*Aeneid*. Ovid produced a series of miniature stories strung together into a long narrative of fifteen books. The transitions between them, and the connections drawn by the narrator, are often transparently contrived—perhaps in mockery of the idea of narrative unity. There is no single hero, and no moral values are presented without irony. There is, however, an element common to these stories: change; and despite its leisurely and roundabout course, the narrative has a discernible direction—as Ovid says in his introduction, "from the world's beginning to the present day." Starting with the creation of the world, the transformation of matter into living bodies (the first great metamorphosis), Ovid tells of human beings changed into animals, flowers, and trees. He proceeds through Greek myth to stories of early Rome and so to his own time, culminating in the ascension of the murdered Julius Caesar to the heavens in the form of a star and the divine promise that Augustus too, far in the future, will become a god; it is tempting to speculate that Ovid hoped—vainly—to improve his relationship with the emperor by means of these few lines. The last change of all is that of Ovid himself, who will, he declares, be transformed from a mortal man into his own immortal poem.

Change underlies both the narrative style and the vision of the world the poem projects. Virgil also told of a transformation, the new (Roman) order arising from the ruins of the old (Troy). But once the transformation was completed by the Augustan order, there was to be stability, permanence. Ovid tells of a world ceaselessly coming to be in a process that never ends. Augustan Rome is not the culminating point of history here, as it was in the *Aeneid*; indeed, the whole idea of a historical end or goal seems, in the *Metamorphoses*, impossible and absurd. Ovid's epic without a hero presents shifting perspectives and offers the reader no single point of view from which to judge his complex narratives. Against the forced imposition of political and moral unity he sets change itself.

Change is also central to the narrative manner of the *Metamorphoses*. Ovid constantly shifts his point of view, telling a story first from one character's perspective, and then from another's. One story is embedded in another, so that one narrative voice is piled on top of another, as when Venus tells Adonis the story of Atalanta. This story is set within the tale of Venus's love for Adonis and of his death, which is one of a series of stories sung by Orpheus in the poem's main narrative. In such cases, the immediate and the larger contexts give the same story different shades of meaning. And there are thematic connections between stories, so that motifs and images also change their meaning from one story to another, or over the course of a single story. Daphne and Syrinx are turned into plants (the laurel and the reed) that are henceforth attributes of the gods who tried to rape them, a form of appropriation that substitutes for sexual violence.

A common element of many stories in books 1 and 2 is the lust of male gods for female humans. On one level, the gods' desire is presented as ridiculous: when Jupiter turns himself into a bull, the narrator comments, "Majestic power and erotic love / do not get on together very well." But these stories are also focused on rape, and, at least some of the time, the narrator shows the terror and suffering of the human victim. These stories of rape may have political implications, for rape is the ultimate imposition of control. When powerful gods force themselves on defenseless women, the reader is invited to remember how easily authority can be abused.

But male gods are not the only sexual agents in the poem: women and goddesses, too, can be overwhelmed by desire, and can themselves become sexual predators. The stories selected here from later in the *Metamorphoses* bring out the complexity of Ovid's presentation of gender and sexuality. The story of Iphis and Ianthe is a reminder that social gender roles for women and men are more or less arbitrary: girls usually look different from boys, but their feelings may be exactly the same. That story has a happy ending, but the tales from book 10 show various ways in which desire causes pain, distorts our perceptions, and ends in disaster. The tale of Pygmalion may seem an exception, but we should remember that it begins with the artist's hatred of women for their loose morals, and that the story as a whole, whatever it may say about the power of art, can also be read as a fable of man's fabrication of woman—her person and her functions—according to his desires. These stories are narrated by Orpheus, the archetypal poet, after his failure to bring Eurydice back from the underworld. The pathology of desire is fundamental to Ovid's poem, since the lover hopes to stop time, to achieve permanent possession of the beloved; but all these stories show us how impossible such a dream is. The girl is always running from the god; the boy is always running from the goddess; Orpheus's wife cannot be brought back from the land of the dead. Reaching for the body of another, the lover's own body is transformed. The closest any of these characters can get to permanence is to be transformed into a growing (living, changing) plant that will always represent their unfulfilled longings.

The Italian baroque sculptor Giovanni Bernini carved statue groups of Apollo and Daphne and of Hades and Proserpina—stunning translations of Ovid's poetry into marble. **Milton** and **Dante** frequently alluded to the *Metamorphoses*, and both used Ovid's version of the Proserpina story: Milton in book 9 of ***Paradise Lost***, as an image of death's entry into the world; Dante in the ***Purgatorio***, to emphasize redemption from death. It was surely not only the fact that the *Metamorphoses* draws into itself most of the major classical myths (and a number of lesser-known stories as well) that has made the poem a source of subjects for artists and poets ever since but also the memorable ways these stories are told and their rich potential for meaning. The poem shows, again and again, the irresistible power of a well-told narrative to hold the attention and shape the imagination of those who read or listen to it.

Giovanni Bernini's seventeenth-century interpretation in marble of the rape of Proserpina.

From Metamorphoses[1]

FROM BOOK I

[*Proem*]

My mind leads me to speak now of forms changed
into new bodies: O gods above, inspire
this undertaking (which you've changed as well)
and guide my poem in its epic sweep
from the world's beginning to the present day.

1. Translated by Charles Martin.

[*The Creation*]

Before the seas and lands had been created,
before the sky that covers everything,
Nature displayed a single aspect only
throughout the cosmos; Chaos was its name,
a shapeless, unwrought mass of inert bulk
and nothing more, with the discordant seeds
of disconnected elements all heaped
together in anarchic disarray.
The sun as yet did not light up the earth,
nor did the crescent moon renew her horns,
nor was the earth suspended in midair,
balanced by her own weight, nor did the ocean
extend her arms to the margins of the land.
Although the land and sea and air were present,
land was unstable, the sea unfit for swimming,
and air lacked light; shapes shifted constantly,
and all things were at odds with one another,
for in a single mass cold strove with warm,
wet was opposed to dry and soft to hard,
and weightlessness to matter having weight.
Some god (or kinder nature) settled this
dispute by separating earth from heaven,
and then by separating sea from earth
and fluid aether[2] from the denser air;
and after these were separated out
and liberated from the primal heap,
he bound the disentangled elements
each in its place and all in harmony.
The fiery and weightless aether leapt
to heaven's vault and claimed its citadel;
the next in lightness to be placed was air;
the denser earth drew down gross elements
and was compressed by its own gravity;
encircling water lastly found its place,
encompassing the solid earth entire.[3]
Now when that god (whichever one it was)
had given Chaos form, dividing it
in parts which he arranged, he molded earth
into the shape of an enormous globe,
so that it should be uniform throughout.
And afterward he sent the waters streaming
in all directions, ordered waves to swell
under the sweeping winds, and sent the flood
to form new shores on the surrounded earth;
he added springs, great standing swamps and lakes,

2. A region of refined air, fiery in nature, believed to be above the "denser air" that was closer to the earth and composed the breathable atmosphere.

3. From Homer on, the ancients conceived of Ocean as a stream that surrounded the earth.

as well as sloping rivers fixed between
their narrow banks, whose plunging waters (all
in varied places, each in its own channel)
are partly taken back into the earth
and in part flow until they reach the sea,
when they—received into the larger field
of a freer flood—beat against shores, not banks.
He ordered open plains to spread themselves,
valleys to sink, the stony peaks to rise,
and forests to put on their coats of green.
 And as the vault of heaven is divided
by two zones on the right and two on the left,
with a central zone, much hotter, in between,
so, by the care of this creator god,
the mass that was enclosed now by the sky
was zoned in the same way, with the same lines
inscribed upon the surface of the earth.
Heat makes the middle zone unlivable,
and the two outer zones are deep in snow;
between these two extremes, he placed two others
of temperate climate, blending cold and warmth.[4]
 Air was suspended over all of this,
proportionately heavier than aether,
as earth is heavier than water is.
He ordered mists and clouds into position,
and thunder, to make test of our resolve,[5]
and winds creating thunderbolts and lightning.
 Nor did that world-creating god permit
the winds to roam ungoverned through the air;
for even now, with each of them in charge
of his own kingdom, and their blasts controlled,
they scarcely can be kept from shattering
the world, such is the discord between brothers.
 Eurus[6] went eastward, to the lands of Dawn,
the kingdoms of Arabia and Persia,
and to the mountain peaks that lie below
the morning's rays; and Zephyr took his place
on the western shores warmed by the setting sun.
The frozen north and Scythia were seized
by bristling Boreas; the lands opposite,
continually drenched by fog and rain,
are where the south wind, known as Auster, dwells.
Above these winds, he set the weightless aether,
a liquid free of every earthly toxin.
 No sooner had he separated all

4. The sky, that is, is divided into five horizontal zones, and therefore so is the earth beneath it. On either side of the earth's uninhabitable torrid region, over which the sun passes, lies a temperate zone, and the northern one contains the inhabited, civilized lands on earth (ancient writers were vague about what the southern temperate zone contained). The two outermost zones, farthest from the sun, were too cold to live in.

5. Thunder was considered an omen.

6. The east wind. Zephyr, Boreas, and Auster were the west, north, and south winds, respectively.

within defining limits, when the stars,
which formerly had been concealed in darkness,
began to blaze up all throughout the heavens;
and so that every region of the world
should have its own distinctive forms of life,
the constellations and the shapes of gods
occupied the lower part of heaven;
the seas gave shelter to the shining fishes,
earth received beasts, and flighty air, the birds.
An animal more like the gods than these,
more intellectually capable
and able to control the other beasts,
had not as yet appeared: now man was born,
either because the framer of all things,
the fabricator of this better world,
created man out of his own divine
substance—or else because Prometheus[7]
took up a clod (so lately broken off
from lofty aether that it still contained
some elements in common with its kin),
and mixing it with water, molded it
into the shape of gods, who govern all.
And even though all other animals
lean forward and look down toward the ground,
he gave to man a face that is uplifted,
and ordered him to stand erect and look
directly up into the vaulted heavens
and turn his countenance to meet the stars;
the earth, that was so lately rude and formless,
was changed by taking on the shapes of men.

* * *

[*Apollo and Daphne*]

Daphne,[8] the daughter of the river god
Peneus, was the first love of Apollo;
this happened not by chance, but by the cruel
outrage of Cupid; Phoebus, in the triumph
of his great victory against the Python,[9]
observed him bending back his bow and said,
"What are *you* doing with such manly arms,
lascivious boy? That bow befits *our* brawn,[1]
wherewith we deal out wounds to savage beasts
and other mortal foes, unerringly:
just now with our innumerable arrows
we managed to lay low the mighty Python,
whose pestilential belly covered acres!

7. A god best known for stealing fire from the gods and giving it to mortals. In some stories he also created humans out of clay.
8. Literally, "Laurel" (Greek).
9. The enormous snake that Apollo (Phoebus) had to kill in order to found his oracle at Delphi. "Cupid": god of sexual desire.
1. The bow was one of Apollo's attributes.

Content yourself with kindling love affairs
with your wee torch—and don't claim *our* glory!"
The son of Venus[2] answered him with this:
"Your arrow, Phoebus, may strike everything:
mine will strike you: as animals to gods,
your glory is so much the less than mine!"
He spoke, and soaring upward through the air
on wings that thundered, in no time at all
had landed on Parnassus'[3] shaded height;
and from his quiver drew two arrows out
which operated at cross-purposes,
for one engendered flight, the other, love;
the latter has a polished tip of gold,
the former has a tip of dull, blunt lead;
with this one, Cupid struck Peneus' daughter,
while the other pierced Apollo to his marrow.
One is in love now, and the other one
won't hear of it, for Daphne calls it joy
to roam within the forest's deep seclusion,
where she, in emulation of the chaste
goddess Phoebe,[4] devotes herself to hunting;
one ribbon only bound her straying tresses.
Many men sought her, but she spurned her suitors,
loath to have anything to do with men,
and rambled through the wild and trackless groves
untroubled by a thought for love or marriage.
Often her father said, "You owe it to me,
child, to provide me with a son-in-law
and grandchildren!"
"Let me remain a virgin,
father most dear," she said, "as once before
Diana's father, Jove, gave her that gift."
Although Peneus yielded to you, Daphne,
your beauty kept your wish from coming true,
your comeliness conflicting with your vow:
at first sight, Phoebus loves her and desires
to sleep with her; desire turns to hope,
and his own prophecy deceives the god.
Now just as in a field the harvest stubble
is all burned off, or as hedges are set ablaze
when, if by chance, some careless traveler
should brush one with his torch or toss away
the still-smoldering brand at break of day—
just so the smitten god went up in flames
until his heart was utterly afire,
and hope sustained his unrequited passion.
He gazes on her hair without adornment:
"What if it were done up a bit?" he asks,

2. Goddess of love (Aphrodite in Greek).
3. Mountain in central Greece, near Delphi.
4. Diana (Artemis in Greek), Apollo's sister, virgin goddess of the hunt.

and gazes on her eyes, as bright as stars,
and on that darling little mouth of hers,
though sight is not enough to satisfy;
he praises everything that he can see—
her fingers, hands, and arms, bare to her shoulders—
and what is hidden prizes even more.
She flees more swiftly than the lightest breeze,
nor will she halt when he calls out to her:
"Daughter of Peneus, I pray, hold still,
hold still! I'm not a foe in grim pursuit!
Thus lamb flees wolf, thus dove from eagle flies
on trembling wings, thus deer from lioness,
thus any creature flees its enemy,
but I am stalking you because of love!
"Wretch that I am: I'm fearful that you'll fall,
brambles will tear your flesh because of me!
The ground you're racing over's very rocky,
slow down, I beg you, restrain yourself in flight,
and I will follow at a lesser speed.
"Just ask yourself who finds you so attractive!
I'm not a caveman, not some shepherd boy,
no shaggy guardian of flocks and herds—
you've no idea, rash girl, you've no idea
whom you are fleeing, that is why you flee!
"Delphi, Claros, Tenedos are all mine,
I'm worshiped in the city of Patara![5]
Jove is my father, I alone reveal
what was, what is, and what will come to be!
The plucked strings answer my demand with song!
"Although my aim is sure, another's arrow
proved even more so, and my careless heart
was badly wounded—the art of medicine
is my invention, by the way, the source
of my worldwide fame as a practitioner
of healing through the natural strength of herbs.
"Alas, there is no herbal remedy
for the love that I must suffer, and the arts
that heal all others cannot heal their lord—"
He had much more to say to her, but Daphne
pursued her fearful course and left him speechless,
though no less lovely fleeing him; indeed,
disheveled by the wind that bared her limbs
and pressed the blown robes to her straining body
even as it whipped up her hair behind her,
the maiden was more beautiful in flight!
But the young god had no further interest
in wasting his fine words on her; admonished
by his own passion, he accelerates,
and runs as swiftly as a Gallic hound[6]

5. All centers of Apollo's cult.

6. A hunting breed famous for speed.

chasing a rabbit through an open field;
the one seeks shelter and the other, prey—
he clings to her, is just about to spring,
with his long muzzle straining at her heels,
while she, not knowing whether she's been caught,
in one swift burst, eludes those snapping jaws,
no longer the anticipated feast;
so he in hope and she in terror race.
  But her pursuer, driven by his passion,
outspeeds the girl, giving her no pause,
one step behind her, breathing down her neck;
her strength is gone; she blanches at the thought
of the effort of her swift flight overcome,
but at the sight of Peneus, she cries,
"Help me, dear father! If your waters hold
divinity, transform me and destroy
that beauty by which I have too well pleased!"
  Her prayer was scarcely finished when she feels
a torpor take possession of her limbs—
her supple trunk is girdled with a thin
layer of fine bark over her smooth skin;
her hair turns into foliage, her arms
grow into branches, sluggish roots adhere
to feet that were so recently so swift,
her head becomes the summit of a tree;
all that remains of her is a warm glow.
  Loving her still, the god puts his right hand
against the trunk, and even now can feel
her heart as it beats under the new bark;
he hugs her limbs as if they were still human,
and then he puts his lips against the wood,
which, even now, is adverse to his kiss.
  "Although you cannot be my bride," he says,
"you will assuredly be my own tree,
O Laurel, and will always find yourself
girding my locks, my lyre, and my quiver too—
you will adorn great Roman generals
when every voice cries out in joyful triumph
along the route up to the Capitol;
you will protect the portals of Augustus,
guarding, on either side, his crown of oak;[7]
and as I am—perpetually youthful,
my flowing locks unknown to the barber's shears—
so you will be an evergreen forever
bearing your brilliant foliage with glory!"
  Phoebus concluded. Laurel shook her branches
and seemed to nod her summit in assent.

7. The laurel tree, sacred to Apollo, was the symbol of victory not only in athletic contests but also in war; victorious Roman generals honored with a triumphal procession through the city to the Capitol wore a laurel wreath. The oak was sacred to Jupiter.

[*Jove and Io*]

There is a grove in Thessaly,[8] enclosed
on every side by high and wooded hills:
they call it Tempe. The river Peneus,
which rises deep within the Pindus range,
pours its turbulent waters through this gorge
and over a cataract that deafens all
its neighbors far and near, creating clouds
that drive a fine, cool mist along, until
it drips down through the summits of the trees.
Here is the house, the seat, the inner chambers
of the great river; here Peneus holds court
in his rocky cavern and lays down the law
to water nymphs and tributary streams.
First to assemble were the native rivers,
uncertain whether to congratulate,
or to commiserate with Daphne's father:
the Sperchios, whose banks are lined with poplars,
the ancient Apidanus and the mild
Aeas and Amprysus; others came later—
rivers who, by whatever course they take,
eventually bring their flowing streams,
weary of their meandering, to sea.
Inachus[9] was the only river absent,
concealed in the recesses of his cave:
he added to his volume with the tears
he grimly wept for his lost daughter Io,
not knowing whether she still lived or not;
but since he couldn't find her anywhere,
assumed that she was nowhere to be found—
and in his heart, he feared a fate far worse.
For Jupiter had seen the girl returning
from her father's banks and had accosted her:
"O maiden worthy of almighty Jove
and destined to delight some lucky fellow
(I know not whom) upon your wedding night,
come find some shade," he said, "in these deep woods—"
(showing her where the woods were *very* shady)
"while the sun blazes high above the earth!
"But if you're worried about entering
the haunts of savage beasts all by yourself,
why, under the protection of a god
you will be safe within the deepest woods—
and no plebeian god, for I am he
who bears the celestial scepter in his hand,
I am he who hurls the roaming thunderbolt—
don't run from me!"
But run she did, through Lerna

8. A region of central Greece.
9. A river near Argos in the northeast Peloponnesus.

and Lyrcea,[1] until the god concealed
the land entirely beneath a dense
dark mist and seized her and dishonored her.
  Juno,[2] however, happened to look down
on Argos, where she noticed something odd:
swift-flying clouds had turned day into night
long before nighttime. She realized
that neither falling mist nor rising fog
could be the cause of this phenomenon,
and looked about at once to find her husband,
as one too well aware of the connivings
of a mate so often taken in the act.
  When he could not be found above, she said,
"Either I'm mad—or I am being had."
She glided down to earth from heaven's summit
immediately and dispersed the clouds.
  Having intuited his wife's approach,
Jove had already metamorphosed Io
into a gleaming heifer—a beauty still,
even as a cow. Despite herself,
Juno gave this illusion her approval,
and feigning ignorance, asked him whose herd
this heifer had come out of, and where from;
Jove, lying to forestall all inquiries
as to her origin and pedigree,
replied that she was born out of the earth.
Then Juno asked him for her as a gift.
  What could he do? Here is his beloved:
to hand her over is unnatural,
but not to do so would arouse suspicion;
shame urged him onward while love held him back.
Love surely would have triumphed over shame,
except that to deny so slight a gift
to one who was his wife and sister both
would make it seem that this was no mere cow!
  Her rival given up to her at last,
Juno feared Jove had more such tricks in mind,
and couldn't feel entirely secure
until she'd placed this heifer in the care
of Argus, the watchman with a hundred eyes:
in strict rotation, his eyes slept in pairs,
while those that were not sleeping stayed on guard.
No matter where he stood, he looked at Io,
even when he had turned his back on her.
  He let her graze in daylight; when the sun
set far beneath the earth, he penned her in
and placed a collar on her indignant neck.

1. A mountain on the border between Argos and Arcadia to the west. "Lerna": a marsh in the territory of Argos, near the coast.

2. Wife of Jupiter (Hera in Greek).

She fed on leaves from trees and bitter grasses,
and had no bed to sleep on, the poor thing,
but lay upon the ground, not always grassy,
and drank the muddy waters from the streams.
Having no arms, she could not stretch them out
in supplication to her warden, Argus;
and when she tried to utter a complaint
she only mooed—a sound which terrified her,
fearful as she now was of her own voice.
Io at last came to the riverbank
where she had often played; when she beheld
her own slack jaws and newly sprouted horns
in the clear water, she fled, terrified!
Neither her naiad sisters[3] nor her father
knew who this heifer was who followed them
and let herself be petted and admired.
Inachus fed her grasses from his hand;
she licked it and pressed kisses on his palm,
unable to restrain her flowing tears.
If words would just have come, she would have spoken,
telling them who she was, how this had happened,
and begging their assistance in her case;
but with her hoof, she drew lines in the dust,
and letters of the words she could not speak
told the sad story of her transformation.
"Oh, wretched me," cried Io's father, clinging
to the lowing calf's horns and snowy neck.
"Oh, wretched me!" he groaned. "Are you the child
for whom I searched the earth in every part?
Lost, you were less a grief than you are, found!
"You make no answer, unable to respond
to our speech in language of your own,
but from your breast come resonant deep sighs
and—all that you can manage now—you *moo*!
"But I—all unaware of this—was busy
arranging marriage for you, in the hopes
of having a son-in-law and grandchildren.
Now I must pick your husband from my herd,
and now must find your offspring there as well!
"Nor can I end this suffering by death;
it is a hurtful thing to be a god,
for the gates of death are firmly closed against me,
and our sorrows must go on forever."
And while the father mourned his daughter's loss,
Argus of the hundred eyes removed her
to pastures farther off and placed himself
high on a mountain peak, a vantage point
from which he could keep watch in all directions.
The ruler of the heavens cannot bear

3. River nymphs.

the sufferings of Io any longer,
and calls his son, born of the Pleiades,[4]
and orders him to do away with Argus.
  Without delay, he takes his winged sandals,
his magic, sleep-inducing wand, and cap;
and so equipped, the son of father Jove
glides down from heaven's summit to the earth,
where he removes and leaves behind his cap
and winged sandals, but retains the wand;
and sets out as a shepherd, wandering
far from the beaten path, driving before him
a flock of goats he rounds up as he goes,
while playing tunes upon his pipe of reeds.
  The guardian of Juno is quite taken
by this new sound: "Whoever you might be,
why not come sit with me upon this rock,"
said Argus, "for that flock of yours will find
the grass is nowhere greener, and you see
that there is shade here suitable for shepherds."
  The grandson of great Atlas takes his seat
and whiles away the hours, chattering
of this and that—and playing on his pipes,
he tries to overcome the watchfulness
of Argus, struggling to stay awake;
even though Slumber closes down some eyes,
others stay vigilant. Argus inquired
how the reed pipes, so recently invented,
had come to be, and Mercury responded:
  "On the idyllic mountains of Arcadia,[5]
among the hamadryads[6] of Nonacris,
one was renowned, and Syrinx[7] was her name.
Often she fled—successfully—from Satyrs,[8]
and deities of every kind as well,
those of the shady wood and fruited plain.
  "In her pursuits and in virginity
Diana was her model, and she wore
her robe hitched up and girt above the knees
just as her goddess did; and if her bow
had been made out of gold, instead of horn,
anyone seeing her might well have thought
she *was* the goddess—as, indeed, some did.
  "Wearing his crown of sharp pine needles, Pan[9]
saw her returning once from Mount Lycaeus,[1]

4. Mercury (Hermes in Greek) was the son of Maia, one of the Pleiades or daughters of Atlas. They were changed into stars when the hunter Orion was pursuing them along with their mother Pleione, whom he wanted to rape.
5. The rustic central region of the Peloponnesus. Nonacris was a town in its northern part.
6. Tree nymphs.
7. The name means "shepherd's pipe," a musical instrument made of reeds.
8. Woodland creatures—half man, half goat, bald, bearded, and highly sexed.
9. A god of the wild mountain pastures and woods, with goat's feet and horns. He was particularly associated with Arcadia.
1. A high mountain in Arcadia.

and began to say. . . ."
There remained to tell
of how the maiden, having spurned his pleas,
fled through the trackless wilds until she came
to where the gently flowing Ladon stopped
her in her flight; how she begged the water nymphs
to change her shape, and how the god, assuming
that he had captured Syrinx, grasped instead
a handful of marsh reeds! And while he sighed,
the reeds in his hands, stirred by his own breath,
gave forth a similar, low-pitched complaint!
The god, much taken by the sweet new voice
of an unprecedented instrument,
said this to her: "At least we may converse
with one another—I can have that much."
That pipe of reeds, unequal in their lengths,
and joined together one-on-one with wax,
took the girl's name, and bears it to this day.
Now Mercury was ready to continue
until he saw that Argus had succumbed,
for all his eyes had been closed down by sleep.
He silences himself and waves his wand
above those languid orbs to fix the spell.
Without delay he grasps the nodding head
and where it joins the neck, he severs it
with his curved blade and flings it bleeding down
the steep rock face, staining it with gore.
O Argus, you are fallen, and the light
in all your lamps is utterly put out:
one hundred eyes, one darkness all the same!
But Saturn's daughter[2] rescued them and set
those eyes upon the feathers of her bird,[3]
filling his tail with constellated gems.
Her rage demanded satisfaction, *now*:
the goddess set a horrifying Fury
before the eyes and the imagination
of her Grecian rival; and in her heart
she fixed a prod that goaded Io on,
driving her in terror through the world
until at last, O Nile, you let her rest
from endless labor; having reached your banks,
she went down awkwardly upon her knees,
and with her neck bent backward, raised her face
as only she could do it, to the stars;
and with her groans and tears and mournful mooing,
entreated Jove, it seemed, to put an end
to her great suffering.
Jove threw his arms
around the neck of Juno in embrace,

2. Juno.

3. The peacock.

imploring her to end this punishment:
"In future," he said, "put your fears aside:
never again will you have cause to worry—
about *this* one." And swore upon the Styx.[4]
The goddess was now pacified, and Io
at once began regaining her lost looks,
till she became what she had been before;
her body lost all of its bristling hair,
her horns shrank down, her eyes grew narrower,
her jaws contracted, arms and hands returned,
and hooves divided themselves into nails;
nothing remained of her bovine nature,
unless it was the whiteness of her body.
She had some trouble getting her legs back,
and for a time feared speaking, lest she moo,
and so quite timidly regained her speech.
She is a celebrated goddess now,
and worshiped by the linen-clad Egyptians.[5]
Her son, Epaphus, is believed to be
sprung from the potent seed of mighty Jove,
and temples may be found in every city
wherein the boy is honored with his parent.

* * *

FROM BOOK II

[*Jove and Europa*]

When Mercury had punished her for these
impieties of thought and word,[6] he left
Athena's city, and on beating wings
returned to heaven where his father Jove
took him aside and (without telling him
that his new passion was the reason) said:
"Dear son, who does my bidding faithfully,
do not delay, but with your usual
swiftness fly down to earth and find the land
that looks up to your mother[7] on the left,
called Sidon[8] by the natives; there you will see
a herd of royal cattle some way off
upon a mountain; drive them down to shore."
He spoke and it was done as he had ordered:
the cattle were immediately driven

4. One of the rivers of the underworld; the gods swore solemn oaths by it.
5. Io was identified with Isis, at least by the Greeks and Romans.
6. Mercury has been in Athens, where he tried to have a love affair with Herse, daughter of King Cecrops; promised help and then betrayed by her sister Aglauros, he took his revenge on Aglauros by turning her into a statue.
7. Maia, Mercury's mother, had been transformed into a star among the Pleiades in the constellation Taurus.
8. One of the principal cities of Phoenicia (in modern Lebanon).

down to a certain place along the shore
where the daughter of a great king used to play,
accompanied by maidens all of Tyre.[9]
  Majestic power and erotic love
do not get on together very well,
nor do they linger long in the same place:
the father and the ruler of all gods,
who holds the lightning bolt in his right hand
and shakes the world when he but nods his head,
now relinquishes authority and power,
assuming the appearance of a bull
to mingle with the other cattle, lowing
as gorgeously he strolls in the new grass.
  He is as white as the untrampled snow
before the south wind turns it into slush.
The muscles stand out bulging on his neck,
and the dewlap[1] dangles on his ample chest;
his horns are crooked, but appear handmade,
and flawless as a pair of matching gems.
His brow is quite unthreatening, his eye
excites no terror, and his countenance
is calm.
          The daughter of King Agenor[2]
admires him, astonished by the presence
of peacefulness and beauty in the beast;
yet even though he seems a gentle creature,
at first she fears to get too close to him,
but soon approaching, reaches out her hand
and pushes flowers into his white mouth.
  The lover, quite beside himself, rejoices,
and as a preview of delights to come,
kisses her fingers, getting so excited
that he can scarcely keep from doing it!
  Now he disports himself upon the grass,
and lays his whiteness on the yellow sands;
and as she slowly overcomes her fear
he offers up his breast for her caresses
and lets her decorate his horns with flowers;
the princess dares to sit upon his back
not knowing who it is that she has mounted,
and he begins to set out from dry land,
a few steps on false feet into the shallows,
then further out and further to the middle
of the great sea he carries off his booty;
she trembles as she sees the shore receding
and holds the creature's horn in her right hand
and with the other clings to his broad back,
her garments streaming in the wind behind her.

9. Another city of Phoenicia, but here used of Phoenicia itself.

1. A fold of loose skin hanging from the neck.

2. Europa. Agenor was the Phoenician king.

FROM BOOK V

[*Ceres and Proserpina*]

As the Muse spoke,[3] Minerva could hear wings
beating on air, and cries of greeting came
from high in the trees. She peered into the foliage,
attempting to discover where those sounds,
the speech of human beings to be sure,
were emanating from: why, from some birds!
Bewailing their sad fate, a flock of nine
magpies (which mimic anyone they wish to)
had settled in the branches overhead.
  Minerva having shown astonishment,
the Muse gave her a little goddess-chat:
"This lot has only recently been added
to the throngs of birds. Why? They lost a contest!
Their father was Pierus, lord of Pella,[4]
their mother was Evippe of Paeonia;
nine times she called upon Lucina's[5] aid
and nine times she delivered. Swollen up
with foolish pride because they were so many,
that crowd of simpleminded sisters went
through all Haemonia and through Achaea[6] too,
arriving here to challenge us in song:
  "'We'll show you girls just what real class is[7]
Give up tryin' to deceive the masses
Your rhymes are fake: accept our wager
Learn which of us is minor and which is major
There's nine of us here and there's nine of you
And you'll be nowhere long before we're through
Nothin's gonna save you 'cuz your songs are lame
And the way you sing 'em is really a shame
So stop with, "Well I *never*!" and "This *can't* be real!"
We're the newest New Thing and here is our deal
If we beat you, obsolete you, then you just get gone
From these classy haunts on Mount Helicon
We give you Macedonia—*if* we lose
An' that's an offer you just can't refuse
So take the wings off, sisters, get down and jam
And let the nymphs be the judges of our poetry slam!'
  "Shameful it was to strive against such creatures;
more shameful not to. Nymphs were picked as judges,

3. Minerva (Athena in Greek) has come to Mount Helicon in central Greece, the home of the nine Muses (daughters of Zeus and Memory, they are patronesses of poetry and the other arts). One of the Muses has told her of an attempt recently made to trap and rape them by the wicked Pyreneus.

4. City of Macedonia, in northern Greece. The Paeonians were a tribe living north of Macedonia.

5. Goddess of childbirth.

6. Regions of central Greece (*Haemonia* is another name for Thessaly). The sisters are traveling south toward Helicon.

7. Although there is no basis for it in the Latin text, the translator uses dialect and rhyme in the speeches and song of Pierus's daughters to show how they challenge, and partially deflate, the "high-culture" assumptions and language of the Muses.

sworn into service on their river banks,
and took their seats on benches made of tufa.
"And then—not even drawing lots!—the one
who claimed to be their champion commenced;
she sang of war between the gods and Giants,
giving the latter credit more than due
and deprecating all that the great gods did;
how Typhoeus,[8] from earth's lowest depths,
struck fear in every celestial heart,
so that they all turned tail and fled, until,
exhausted, they found refuge down in Egypt,
where the Nile flows from seven distinct mouths;
she sang of how earthborn Typhoeus
pursued them even here and forced the gods
to hide themselves by taking fictive shapes:[9]
"'In Libya the Giants told the gods to scram
The boss god they worship there has horns like a ram[1]
'Cuz Jupiter laid low as the leader of a flock
And Delius[2] his homey really got a shock
When the Giants left him with no place to go:
"Fuggedabout Apollo—make me a crow!"
And if you believe that Phoebus was a wuss
His sister Phoebe turned into a puss
Bacchus takes refuge in the skin of a goat
And Juno as a cow with a snow-white coat
Venus the queen of the downtown scene, yuh know what her wish is?
"Gimme a body just like a fish's"
Mercury takes on an ibis's shape
And that's how the mighty (**cheep cheep**) gods escape'
"And then her song, accompanied on the lute,
came to an end, and it was our turn—
but possibly you haven't got the time
to listen to our song?"
"Oh, don't think that,"
Minerva said. "I want it word for word:
sing it for me just as you sang it then."
The Muse replied: "We turned the contest over
to one of us, Calliope,[3] who rose,
and after binding up her hair in ivy
and lightly strumming a few plaintive chords,
she vigorously launched into her song:

"'Ceres[4] was first to break up the soil with a curved plowshare,
the first to give us the earth's fruits and to nourish us gently,
and the first to give laws: every gift comes from Ceres.

8. Monstrous son of Earth. Like the Earthborn Giants, he challenged Jupiter and the Olympian gods and was defeated.
9. An "explanation" of the Egyptian gods' animal forms.
1. Ammon, the chief Egyptian god, identified by the Greeks and Romans with Zeus/Jupiter. He had an important oracular cult in the Libyan desert (west of the Nile valley and part of Egypt under Roman rule).
2. Apollo, who was born on the island of Delos.
3. "Lovely Voice," the Muse of epic poetry.
4. Goddess of grain (Demeter).

The goddess must now be my subject. Would that I *could* sing
a hymn that is worthy of her, for she surely deserves it.
"'Vigorous Sicily sprawled across the gigantic body
of one who had dared aspire to rule in the heavens;
the island's weight held Typhoeus firmly beneath it.
Often exerting himself, he strives yet again to rise up,
but there in the north, his right hand is held down by Pelorus,
his left hand by you, Pachynus; off in the west, Lilybaeum[5]
weighs on his legs, while Mount Etna[6] presses his head, as
under it, raging Typhoeus coughs ashes and vomits up fire.
Often he struggles, attempting to shake off the earth's weight
and roll its cities and mountains away from his body.
"'This causes tremors and panics the Lord of the Silent,[7]
who fears that the earth's crust will crack and break open,
and daylight, let in, will frighten the trembling phantoms;
dreading disaster, the tyrant left his tenebrous kingdom;
borne in his chariot drawn by its team of black horses,
he crisscrossed Sicily, checking the island's foundation.
"'After his explorations had left him persuaded
that none of its parts were in imminent danger of falling,
his fears were forgotten, and Venus, there on Mount Eryx,[8]
observed him relaxing, and said, as she drew Cupid near her,
"My son, my sword, my strong right arm and source of my power,
take up that weapon by which all your victims are vanquished
and send your swift arrows into the breast of the deity
to whom the last part of the threefold realm[9] was allotted.
"'"You govern the gods and their ruler; you rule the defeated
gods of the ocean and govern the one who rules them, too;
why give up on the dead, when we can extend our empire
into their realm? A third part of the world is involved here!
And yet the celestial gods spurn our forbearance,
and the prestige of Love is diminished, even as mine is.
Do you not see how Athena and huntress Diana
have both taken leave of me?[1] The virgin daughter of Ceres
desires to do likewise—and will, if we let her!
But if you take pride in our alliance, advance it
by joining her to her uncle!"[2]
"'Venus ceased speaking and Cupid
loosened his quiver, and, just as his mother had ordered,
selected, from thousands of missiles, the one that was sharpest
and surest and paid his bow the closest attention,
and using one knee to bend its horn back almost double,
he pierces the heart of Dis with his barb-tipped arrow.

5. Mountains on the northeast, southeast, and western promontories of Sicily, respectively.
6. The large (and still active) volcano near the center of the east coast of Sicily.
7. Pluto or Hades, king of the dead.
8. Mountain in western Sicily with an important cult of Venus.
9. The underworld, ruled by Pluto. The other parts of the "threefold realm" are the sea (ruled by Neptune) and the sky or Mount Olympus (Jupiter).
1. Both were perpetual virgins.
2. Pluto (also called Dis) was the brother of Jupiter, the father by Ceres of Proserpina.

"'Near Henna's[3] walls stands a deep pool of water, called Pergus:
not even the river Cayster,[4] flowing serenely,
hears more songs from its swans; this pool is completely surrounded
by a ring of tall trees, whose foliage, just like an awning,
keeps out the sun and preserves the water's refreshing coolness;
the moist ground is covered with flowers of Tyrian purple;
here it is springtime forever. And here Proserpina
was playfully picking its white lilies and violets,
and, while competing to gather up more than her playmates,
filling her basket and stuffing the rest in her bosom,
Dis saw her, was smitten, seized her and carried her off;
his love was that hasty. The terrified goddess cried out
for her mother, her playmates—but for her mother most often,
since she had torn the uppermost seam of her garment,
and the gathered flowers rained down from her negligent tunic;
because of her tender years and her childish simplicity,
even this loss could move her to maidenly sorrow.

"'Her abductor rushed off in his chariot, urging his horses,
calling each one by its name and flicking the somber,
rust-colored reins over their backs as they galloped
through the deep lakes and the sulphurous pools of Palike
that boil up through the ruptured earth, and where the Bacchiadae,
a race sprung from Corinth, that city between the two seas,
had raised their own walls between two unequal harbors.[5]

"'There is a bay that is landlocked almost completely
between the two pools of Cyane and Pisaean Arethusa,
the residence of the most famous nymph in all Sicily,
Cyane, who gave her very own name to the fountain.
She showed herself now, emerged from her pool at waist level,
and recognizing the goddess, told Dis, "Go no further!
You cannot become the son-in-law of great Ceres
against her will: you should have asked and not taken!
If it is right for me to compare lesser with greater,
I accepted Anapis[6] when he desired to have me,
yielding to pleas and not—as in *this* case—to terror."
She spoke, and stretching her arms out in either direction,
kept him from passing. That son of Saturn could scarcely
hold back his anger; he urged on his frightening horses,
and then, with his strong right arm, he hurled his scepter
directly into the very base of the fountain;
the stricken earth opened a path to the underworld
and took in the chariot rushing down into its crater.

"'Cyane, lamenting not just the goddess abducted,
but also the disrespect shown for *her* rights as a fountain,

3. A city in central Sicily.
4. River in Lydia in Asia Minor, famous for its many swans.
5. Syracuse, on the southeastern coast of Sicily, founded by Corinthian colonists in the 8th century B.C.E. The Bacchiadae were a leading family who then ruled Corinth.
6. A river that empties into the sea near Syracuse.

tacitly nursed in her heart an inconsolable sorrow;
and she who had once been its presiding spirit,
reduced to tears, dissolved right into its substance.
You would have seen her members beginning to soften,
her bones and her fingertips starting to lose their old firmness;
her slenderest parts were the first to be turned into fluid:
her feet, her legs, her sea-dark tresses, her fingers
(for the parts with least flesh turn into liquid most quickly);
and after these, her shoulders and back and her bosom
and flanks completely vanished in trickling liquid;
and lastly the living blood in her veins is replaced by
springwater, and nothing remains that you could have seized on.
"'Meanwhile, the terrified mother was pointlessly seeking
her daughter all over the earth and deep in the ocean.
Neither Aurora, appearing with dew-dampened tresses,
nor Hesperus[7] knew her to quit; igniting two torches
of pine from the fires of Etna, the care-ridden goddess
used them to illumine the wintery shadows of nighttime;
and when the dear day had once more dimmed out the bright stars,
she searched again for her daughter from sunrise to sunset.

"'Worn out by her labors and suffering thirst, with no fountain
to wet her lips at, she happened upon a thatched hovel
and knocked at its humble door, from which there came forth
a crone who looked at the goddess, and, when asked for water,
gave her a sweet drink, sprinkled with toasted barley.
And, as she drank it, a boy with a sharp face and bold manner
stood right before her and mocked her and said she was greedy.
Angered by what he was saying, the goddess drenched him
with all she had not yet drunk of the barley mixture.
The boy's face thirstily drank up the spots as his arms were
turned into legs, and a tail was joined to his changed limbs;
so that he should now be harmless, the boy was diminished,
and he was transformed into a very small lizard.
Astonished, the old woman wept and reached out to touch him,
but the marvelous creature fled her, seeking a hideout.
He now has a name appropriate to his complexion,
Stellio, from the con*stella*tions spotting his body.
"'To speak of the lands and seas the goddess mistakenly searched
would take far too long; the earth exhausted her seeking;
she came back to Sicily; and, as she once more traversed it,
arrived at Cyane, who would have told her the story
had she not herself been changed; but, though willing in spirit,
her mouth, tongue, and vocal apparatus were absent;
nevertheless, she gave proof that was clear to the mother:
Persephone's girdle (which happened by chance to have fallen
into the fountain) now lay exposed on its surface.
"'Once recognizing it, the goddess knew that her daughter
had been taken, and tore her hair into utter disorder,

7. The evening star. "Aurora": goddess of the dawn.

and repeatedly struck her breasts with the palms of both hands.
With her daughter's location a mystery still, she reproaches
the whole earth as ungrateful, unworthy her gift of grain crops,
and Sicily more than the others, where she has discovered
the proof of her loss; and so it was here that her fierce hand
shattered the earth-turning plows, here that the farmers and cattle
perished alike, and here that she bade the plowed fields
default on their trust by blighting the seeds in their keeping.
Sicilian fertility, which had been everywhere famous,
was given the lie when the crops died as they sprouted,
now ruined by too much heat, and now by too heavy a rainfall;
stars and winds harmed them, and the greedy birds devoured
the seed as it was sown; the harvest of wheat was defeated
by thorns and darnels and unappeasable grasses.
"'Then Arethusa[8] lifted her head from the Elean waters
and swept her dripping hair back away from her forehead,
saying, "O Mother of Grain—and mother, too, of that virgin
sought through the whole world—here end your incessant labors,
lest your great anger should injure the earth you once trusted,
and which, unwillingly pillaged, has done nothing ignoble;
nor do I plead for my nation, since I am a guest here:
my nation is Pisa, I am descended from Elis,
and live as a stranger in Sicily—this land that delights me
more than all others on earth; here Arethusa
dwells with her household gods. Spare it, merciful goddess,
and when your cares and countenance both have been lightened,
there will come an opportune time to tell you the reason
why I was taken from home and borne off to Ortygia[9]
over a waste of waters. The earth gave me access,
showed me a path, and, swept on through underground caverns,
I raised my head here to an unfamiliar night sky.
But while gliding under the earth on a Stygian river,
I saw with my very own eyes your dear Proserpina;
grief and terror were still to be seen in her features,
yet she was nonetheless queen of that shadowy kingdom,
the all-powerful consort of the underworld's ruler."
"'The mother was petrified by the speech of the fountain,
and stood for a very long time as though she were senseless,
until her madness had been driven off by her outrage,
and then she set out in her chariot for the ethereal regions;
once there, with her face clouded over and hair all disheveled,
she planted herself before Jove and fiercely addressed him:
"Jupiter, I have come here as a suppliant, speaking
for my child—and yours: if you have no regard for her mother,
relent as her father—don't hold her unworthy, I beg you,
simply because *I* am the child's other parent!

8. A spring in Syracuse. Its waters are "Elean" because they were believed to originate in the district of Pisa in Elis, a region of the western Peloponnesus in mainland Greece.

9. The island on which Syracuse was originally built and on which the Arethusan spring was located.

The daughter I sought for so long is at last recovered,
if to recover means only to lose much more surely,
or if to recover means just to learn her location!
Her theft could be borne—if only he would return her!
Then let him do it, for surely *Jove's* daughter is worthy
of a mate who's no brigand, even if *my* daughter isn't."
"'Jupiter answered her, "She is indeed *our* daughter,
the pledge of our love and our common concern,
but if you will kindly agree to give things their right names,
this is not an injury requiring my retribution,
but an act of love by a son-in-law who won't shame you,
goddess, if you give approval; though much were lacking,
how much it is to be Jove's brother! But he lacks nothing,
and only yields to me that which the Fates have allotted.
Still, if you're so keen on parting them, your Proserpina
may come back to heaven—but only on one condition:
that she has not touched food, for so the Fates have required."

"'He spoke and Ceres was sure she would get back her daughter,
though the Fates were not, for the girl had already placated
her hunger while guilelessly roaming death's formal gardens,
where, from a low-hanging branch, she had plucked without thinking
a pomegranate, and peeling its pale bark off, devoured
seven of its seeds. No one saw her but Ascalaphus
(whom it is said that Orphne, a not undistinguished
nymph among those of Avernus, pregnant by Acheron,[1]
gave birth to there in the underworld's dark-shadowed forest);
he saw, and by his disclosure, kept her from returning.
"'Raging, the Queen of the Underworld turned that informer
into a bird of ill omen: sprinkling the waters
of Phlegethon[2] into the face of Ascalaphus,
she gave him a beak and plumage and eyes quite enormous.
Lost to himself, he is clad now in yellow-brown pinions,
his head increases in size and his nails turn to talons,
but the feathers that spring from his motionless arms scarcely flutter;
a filthy bird he's become, the grim announcer of mourning,
a slothful portent of evil to mortals—the owl.

"'That one, because of his tattling tongue, seems quite worthy
of punishment,—but you, daughters of Acheloüs,[3]
why do you have the plumage of birds and the faces of virgins?
Is it because while Proserpina gathered her flowers,
you, artful Sirens, were numbered among her companions?
No sooner had you scoured the whole earth in vain for her
than you desired the vast seas to feel your devotion,
and prayed to the gods, whom you found willing to help you,
that you might skim over the flood upon oars that were pinions,

1. Acheron ("Woe") is one of the rivers, and Avernus a lake, in the underworld. The name *Orphne* means "darkness" in Greek.
2. Fiery river of the underworld.
3. The Sirens, familiar from book 12 of the *Odyssey* and often associated with death in post-Homeric literature and art. Acheloüs is a large river in northwest Greece.

then saw your limbs turn suddenly golden with plumage.
And so that your tunefulness, which the ear finds so pleasing,
should not be lost, nor your gifts of vocal expression,
your maidenly faces remain, along with your voices.

"'But poised between his sorrowing sister and brother,
great Jove divided the year into two equal portions,
so now in two realms the shared goddess holds sway,
and as many months spent with her mother are spent with her husband.
She changed her mind then, and changed her expression to match it,
and now her fair face, which even Dis found depressing,
beams as the sun does, when, after having been hidden
before in dark clouds, at last it emerges in triumph.

"'Her daughter safely restored to her, kindhearted Ceres
wishes to hear *your* story now, Arethusa—
what did you flee from and what changed you into a fountain?
The splashing waters are stilled: the goddess raises
her head from their depths and wrings dry her virid tresses,
then tells the old tale of the river Alpheus'[4] passion.
"'"Once I was one of the nymphs who dwell in Achaea,"
she said, "and none had more zeal than I for traversing
the mountain pastures or setting out snares for small game.
But even though I did not seek to find fame as a beauty,
men called me that, my courage and strength notwithstanding;
nor was I pleased that my beauty was lauded so often,
and for my corporeal nature (which most other maidens
are wont to take pleasure in) I blushed like a rustic,
thinking it wrong to please men.
"'"Exhausted from hunting,
I was on my way back from the Stymphalian forest,[5]
and the fierce heat of the day was doubled by my exertions.
By chance I came on a stream, gently and silently flowing,
clear to the bottom, where you could count every pebble,
water so still you would scarcely believe it was moving.
Silvery willows and poplars, which the stream nourished,
artlessly shaded its banks as they sloped to the water.
"'"At once I approach and wiggle my toes in its wetness,
then wade in up to my knees—not satisfied wholly,
I strip off my garments and hang them up on a willow,
and, naked, merge with the waters. I strike and stroke them,
gliding below and thrashing about on the surface,
then hear a strange murmur that seems to come from the bottom,
which sends me scampering onto the near bank in terror:
'Why the great rush?' Alpheus cries from his waters,
then hoarsely repeating, 'Why the great rush, Arethusa?'
Just as I am, I flee without clothing (my garments
were on the bank opposite); aroused, Alpheus pursues me,

4. River that flows past Olympia in Elis.
5. The woods surrounding Lake Stymphalus in Arcadia.

my nakedness making me seem more ripe for the taking.
“‘“Thus did I run, and thus did that fierce one press after,
as doves on trembling pinions flee from the kestrel,
as kestrels pursue the trembling doves and assault them.
To Orchomenus and past, to Psophis, Cyllene,
the folds of Maenalia, Erymanthus,[6] and Elis,
I continued to run, nor was he faster than I was;
but since Alpheus was so much stronger, I couldn't
outrun him for long, given his greater endurance.
“‘“Nonetheless, I still managed to keep on running
across the wide fields, up wooded mountains,
on bare rocks, steep cliffs, in wastes wild and trackless;
with the sun at my back, I could see his shadow before me,
stretched out on the ground, unless my panic deceived me;
but surely I *did* hear those frightening footsteps behind me,
and felt his hot breath lifting the hair from my shoulders.
“‘“Worn with exertion, I cried out, ‘Help! Or I'm taken!
Aid your armoress, Diana—to whom you have often
entrusted your bow, along with your quiver of arrows!’
The goddess was moved by my plea and at once I was hidden
in a dense cloud of fine mist:[7] the river god, clueless,
circled around me, hidden in darkness, searching;
twice he unknowingly passed by the place where the goddess
had hidden me, and twice he called, ‘Yo! Arethusa!’
How wretched was I? Why, even as the lamb is,
at hearing the howling of wolves around the sheepfold,
or as the rabbit in the briar patch who glimpses
the dog's fierce muzzle and feels too frightened to tremble.
“‘“Alpheus remained there, for as he noticed no footprints
heading away from the cloud, he continued to watch it.
An icy sweat thoroughly drenched the limbs that he looked for,
and the dark drops poured from every part of my body;
wherever my foot had been, there was a puddle,
and my hair shed moisture. More swiftly than I can tell it,
I turned into liquid—even so, he recognized me,
his darling there in the water, and promptly discarded
the human form he had assumed for the occasion,
reverting to river, so that our fluids might mingle.
Diana shattered the earth's crust; I sank down,
and was swept on through sightless caverns, off to Ortygia,
so pleasing to me because it's the goddess's birthplace;[8]
and here I first rose up into the air as a fountain.”

“‘Here Arethusa concluded. The fruitful goddess summoned
her team of dragons and yoked them onto her chariot;
and guiding their heads with the reins, she was transported
up through the middle air that lies between earth and heaven

6. Towns and mountains of Arcadia.
7. Conventional means in ancient epic of making someone invisible.
8. The Ortygia where Arethusa ended up was in Syracuse, but Delos, the Aegean island where Diana was born, was also called Ortygia.

until she arrived in Athens, and, giving her carriage
to Triptolemus,[9] ordered him to go off and scatter
grain on the earth—some on land that had never been broken,
and some on land that had been a long time fallow.
"'The young man was carried high up over Europe and Asia
until at last he came to the kingdom of Scythia.
Lyncus was king here; he brought him into his palace,
and asked him his name, his homeland, the cause of his journey,
and how he had come there.
"'"My well-known homeland," he answered,
"is Athens; I am Triptolemus; neither by ship upon water
nor foot upon land have I come here; the air itself parted
to make me a path on which I coursed through the heavens.
I bear you the gifts of Ceres, which, sown in your broad fields,
will yield a bountiful harvest of nourishing produce."
"'This the barbarian heard with great envy, and wishing
that he himself might be perceived as the donor,
took him in as a guest, and while the young man was sleeping,
approached with a sword, and as he attempted to stab him,
Ceres changed *Lyncus* to *lynx*, and ordered Triptolemus
to drive her sacred team through the air back to Athens.'

"When our eldest sister had concluded
her superb performance, with one voice
the nymphs awarded victory to . . . the Muses!
"And when the others, in defeat, reviled us,
I answered them: 'Since you display such nerve
in challenging the Muses, you deserve
chastisement—even more so since you've added
insult to outrage: our wise forbearance
is not without its limits, as you'll learn
when we get to the penalties, and vent
our righteous anger on your worthless selves.'
"Then the Pierides[1] mock our threats,
and as they try to answer us by shouting
vulgarities and giving us the finger,
their fingers take on feathers and their arms
turn into pinions! Each one sees a beak
replace a sister's face, as a new bird
is added to the species of the forest;
and as they try to beat upon their breasts,
bewailing their new situation, they
all hang suspended, flapping in the air,
the forest's scandal—the P-Airides![2]
"And even though they are all feathered now,
their speech remains as fluent as it was,
and they are famous for their noisiness
as well as for their love of argument."

9. Son of the king of Eleusis, the great cult center of Demeter (Ceres) near Athens.

1. The daughters of Pierus.

2. The translator's pun on the name Pierides.

FROM BOOK IX

[*Iphis and Isis*]

Rumor might very well have spread the news
of this unprecedented transformation[3]
throughout the hundred towns of Crete, if they
had not just had a wonder of their own
to talk about—the change that came to Iphis.
  For, once upon a time, there lived in Phaestus,
not far from the royal capital at Cnossus,
a freeborn plebeian named Ligdus, who
was otherwise unknown and undistinguished,
with no more property than fame or status,
and yet devout, and blameless in his life.
  His wife was pregnant. When her time had come,
he gave her his instructions with these words:
"There are two things I pray to heaven for
on your account: an easy birth and a son.
The other fate is much too burdensome,
for daughters need what Fortune has denied us:
a dowry.
            "Therefore—and may God prevent
this happening, but if, by chance, it does
and you should be delivered of a girl,
unwillingly I order this, and beg
pardon for my impiety—*But let it die!*"
  He spoke, and tears profusely bathed the cheeks
of the instructor and instructed both.
Telethusa continued to implore
her husband, praying him not to confine
their hopes so narrowly—to no avail,
for he would not be moved from his decision.
  Now scarcely able to endure the weight
of her womb's burden, as she lay in bed
at midnight, a dream-vision came to her:
the goddess Io[4] stood (or seemed to stand)
before her troubled bed, accompanied
with solemn pomp by all her mysteries.
  She wore her crescent horns upon her brow
and a garland made of gleaming sheaves of wheat,
and a queenly diadem; behind her stood
the dog-faced god Anubis, and divine
Bubastis (who defends the lives of cats),
and Apis as a bull clothed in a hide
of varied colors, with Harpocrates,
the god whose fingers, pressed against his lips,
command our silence; and one often sought

3. The transformation of Byblis, who loved her brother Caunus, into a fountain.
4. Identified with the Egyptian Isis, goddess of fertility, marriage, and maternity, whose cult was widespread in the Roman world.

by his devoted worshipers—Osiris;[5]
and the asp, so rich in sleep-inducing drops.
She seemed to wake, and saw them all quite clearly.
These were the words the goddess spoke to her:
"O Telethusa, faithful devotee,
put off your heavy cares! Disobey your spouse,
and do not hesitate, when Lucina
has lightened the burden of your labor,
to raise this child, whatever it will be,
I am that goddess who, when asked, delivers,
and you will have no reason to complain
that honors you have paid me were in vain."
After instructing her, the goddess left.
The Cretan woman rose up joyfully,
lifted her hands up to the stars, and prayed
that her dream-vision would be ratified.
Then going into labor, she brought forth
a daughter—though her husband did not know it.
The mother (with intention to deceive)
told them *to feed the boy*. Deception prospered,
since no one knew the truth except the nurse.
The father thanked the gods and named the child
for its grandfather, Iphis; since this name
was given men and women both, his mother
was pleased, for she could use it honestly.
So from her pious lie, deception grew.
She dressed it as a boy—its face was such
that whether boy or girl, it was a beauty.
Meanwhile, the years went by, thirteen of them:
your father, Iphis, has arranged for you
a marriage to the golden-haired Ianthe,
the daughter of a Cretan named Telestes,
the maid most praised in Phaestus[6] for her beauty.
The two were similar in age and looks,
and had been taught together from the first.
First love came unexpected to both hearts
and wounded them both equally—and yet
their expectations were quite different:
Ianthe can look forward to a time
of wedding torches and of wedding vows,
and trusts that one whom she believes a man
will be *her* man. Iphis, however, loves
with hopeless desperation, which increases
in strict proportion to its hopelessness,
and burns—a maiden—for another maid!
And scarcely holding back her tears, she cries,
"Oh, what will be the end reserved for Iphis,
gripped by a strange and monstrous passion known

5. Husband of Isis, killed by his brother Set and restored to life by Isis; he is thus a figure of rebirth.
6. A city in Crete.

to no one else? If the gods had wished to spare me,
they should have; if they wanted to destroy me,
they should have given me a natural affliction.
"Cows do not burn for cows, nor mares for mares;
the ram will have his sheep, the stag his does,
and birds will do the same when they assemble;
there are no animals whose females lust
for other females! I wish that I were dead!
"That Crete might bring forth monsters of all kinds.
Queen Pasiphaë[7] was taken by a bull,
yet even *that* was male-and-female passion!
My love is much less rational than hers,
to tell the truth. At least she had the hope
of satisfaction, taking in the bull
through guile, and in the image of a cow,
thereby deceiving the adulterer!
"If every form of ingenuity
were gathered here from all around the world,
if Daedalus[8] flew back on waxen wings,
what could he do? Could all his learnèd arts
transform me from a girl into a boy?
Or could *you* change into a boy, Ianthe?
"But really, Iphis, pull yourself together,
be firm, cast off this stultifying passion:
accept your birth—unless you would deceive
yourself as well as others—look for love
where it is proper to, as a woman should!
Hope both creates and nourishes such love;
reality deprives you of all hope.
"No watchman keeps you from her dear embrace,
no husband's ever-vigilant concern,
no father's fierceness, nor does she herself
deny the gifts that you would have from her.
And yet you are denied all happiness,
nor could it have been otherwise if all
the gods and men had labored in your cause.
"But the gods have not denied me anything;
agreeably, they've given what they could;
my father wishes for me what *I* wish,
she and her father both would have it be;
but Nature, much more powerful than they are,
wishes it not—sole source of all my woe!
"But look—the sun has risen and the day
of our longed-for nuptials dawns at last!
Ianthe will be mine—and yet not mine:
we die of thirst here at the fountainside.
"Why do you, Juno, guardian of brides,

7. Wife of King Minos of Crete, and mother by a bull of the Minotaur.

8. Fabled craftsman who devised the heifer disguise that enabled Pasiphaë to seduce the bull and, later, built the labyrinth for the Minotaur. Forced to flee Crete, he made wings of feathers held together by wax, for himself and his son, Icarus.

and you, O Hymen, god of marriage, come
to these rites, which cannot be rites at all,
for no one takes the bride, and both are veiled?"
  She said no more. Nor did her chosen burn
less fiercely as she prayed you swiftly come,
O god of marriage.
                    Fearing what you sought,
Telethusa postponed the marriage day
with one concocted pretext and another,
a fictive illness or an evil omen.
But now she had no more excuses left,
and the wedding day was only one day off.
  She tears the hair bands from her daughter's head
and from her own, and thus unbound, she prayed
while desperately clinging to the altar:
"O holy Isis, who art pleased to dwell
and be worshiped at Paraetonium,
at Pharos, in the Mareotic fields,
and where the Nile splits into seven branches;
deliver us, I pray you, from our fear!
  "For I once saw thee and thy sacred emblems,
O goddess, and I recognized them all
and listened to the sound of brazen rattles[9]
and kept your orders in my memory.
  "And that my daughter still looks on the light,
and that I have not suffered punishment,
why, this is all your counsel and your gift;
now spare us both and offer us your aid."
  Warm tears were in attendance on her words.
The altar of the goddess seemed to move—
it *did* move, and the temple doors were shaken,
and the horns (her lunar emblem) glowed with light,
and the bronze rattles sounded.
                                Not yet secure,
but nonetheless delighted by this omen,
the mother left with Iphis following,
as was her wont, but now with longer strides,
darker complexion, and with greater force,
a keener countenance, and with her hair
shorter than usual and unadorned,
and with more vigor than a woman has.
  And you who were so recently a girl
are now a boy! Bring gifts to the goddess!
Now boldly celebrate your faith in her!
They bring the goddess gifts and add to them
a votive tablet with these lines inscribed:

GIFTS IPHIS PROMISED WHEN SHE WAS A MAID
TRANSFORMED INTO A BOY HE GLADLY PAID

9. Sistra, sacred rattles used in Isis's cult.

The next day's sun revealed the great wide world
with Venus, Juno, and Hymen all together
gathered beneath the smoking nuptial torches,
and Iphis in possession of Ianthe.

FROM BOOK X[1]

[*Pygmalion*]

"Pygmalion observed how these women[2] lived lives of sordid
indecency, and, dismayed by the numerous defects
of character Nature had given the feminine spirit,
stayed as a bachelor, having no female companion.
"During that time he created an ivory statue,
a work of most marvelous art, and gave it a figure
better than any living woman could boast of,
and promptly conceived a passion for his own creation.
You would have thought it alive, so like a real maiden
that only its natural modesty kept it from moving:
art concealed artfulness. Pygmalion gazed in amazement,
burning with love for what was in likeness a body.
"Often he stretched forth a hand to touch his creation,
attempting to settle the issue: *was* it a body,
or was it—this he would not yet concede—a mere statue?
He gives it kisses, and they are returned, he imagines;
now he addresses and now he caresses it, feeling
his fingers sink into its warm, pliant flesh, and
fears he will leave blue bruises all over its body;
he seeks to win its affections with words and with presents
pleasing to girls, such as seashells and pebbles, tame birds,
armloads of flowers in thousands of different colors,
lilies, bright painted balls, curious insects in amber;
he dresses it up and puts diamond rings on its fingers,
gives it a necklace, a lacy brassiere and pearl earrings,
and even though all such adornments truly become her,
she does not seem to be any less beautiful naked.
He lays her down on a bed with a bright purple cover
and calls her his bedmate and slips a few soft, downy pillows
under her head as though she were able to feel them.
"The holiday honoring Venus has come, and all Cyprus[3]
turns out to celebrate; heifers with gilded horns buckle
under the deathblow[4] and incense soars up in thick clouds;
having already brought his own gift to the altar,
Pygmalion stood by and offered this fainthearted prayer:

1. This selection of stories is part of the song sung by Orpheus, the legendary singer, after he has failed to redeem his wife, Eurydice, from the underworld. His theme, announced in the prologue of his song, is "young boys whom the gods have desired, / and . . . girls seized by forbidden and blameworthy passions."

2. Orpheus has just told of the Propoetides of Cyprus, who, as punishment for having denied Venus's divinity, became the first women to prostitute themselves.

3. Island in the eastern Mediterranean sacred to Venus.

4. I.e., as they are sacrificed.

'If you in heaven are able to give us whatever
we ask for, then I would like as my wife—' and not daring
to say, '—my ivory maiden,' said, '—one like my statue!'
Since golden Venus was present there at her altar,
she knew what he wanted to ask for, and as a good omen,
three times the flames soared and leapt right up to the heavens.
"Once home, he went straight to the replica of his sweetheart,
threw himself down on the couch and repeatedly kissed her;
she seemed to grow warm and so he repeated the action,
kissing her lips and exciting her breasts with both hands.
Aroused, the ivory softened and, losing its stiffness,
yielded, submitting to his caress as wax softens
when it is warmed by the sun, and handled by fingers,
takes on many forms, and by being used, becomes useful.
Amazed, he rejoices, then doubts, then fears he's mistaken,
while again and again he touches on what he has prayed for.
She is alive! And her veins leap under his fingers!
"You can believe that Pygmalion offered the goddess
his thanks in a torrent of speech, once again kissing
those lips that were not untrue; that she felt his kisses,
and timidly blushing, she opened her eyes to the sunlight,
and at the same time, first looked on her lover and heaven!
The goddess attended the wedding since she had arranged it,
and before the ninth moon had come to its crescent, a daughter
was born to them—Paphos,[5] who gave her own name to the island.

"She had a son named Cinyras, who would be regarded
as one of the blessèd, if he had only been childless.
I sing of dire events: depart from me, daughters,
depart from me, fathers; or, if you find my poems charming,
believe that I lie, believe these events never happened;
or, if you believe that they did, then believe they were punished.
"If Nature allows us to witness such impious misdeeds,
then I give my solemn thanks that the Thracian people
and the land itself are far away from those regions[6]
where evil like that was begotten: let fabled Panchaea[7]
be rich in balsam and cinnamon, costum and frankincense,
the sweat that drips down from the trees; let it bear incense
and flowers of every description: it also bears myrrh, and
too great a price was paid for that new creation.
"Cupid himself denies that his darts ever harmed you,
Myrrha, and swears that his torches likewise are guiltless;
one of the three sisters,[8] bearing a venomous hydra
and waving a Stygian firebrand, must have inspired your passion.
Hating a parent is wicked, but even more wicked
than hatred is this kind of love. Princes elected

5. One of the cities of Cyprus, whose name is often used for the island as a whole.

6. A reminder that Orpheus is singing in Thrace (the region stretching along the north coast of the Aegean Sea).

7. An imaginary island near Arabia, rich in spices.

8. The Furies.

from far and wide desire you, Myrrha; all Asia
sends its young men to compete for your hand in marriage:
choose from so many just one of these men for your husband,
so long as a certain one is not the one chosen.
"She understood and struggled against her perversion,
asking herself, 'What have I begun? Where will it take me?
May heaven and piety and the sacred rights of fathers
restrain these unspeakable thoughts and repel my misfortune,
if this indeed *is* misfortune; yet piety chooses
not to condemn this love outright: without distinctions
animals copulate; it is no crime for the heifer
to bear the weight of her father upon her own back;
daughters are suitable wives in the kingdom of horses;
the billy goats enter the flocks that they themselves sire,
and birds are inseminated by those who conceive them:
blessed, the ones for whom such love is permitted!
"'Human morality gives us such stifling precepts,
and makes indecent what Nature freely allows us!
But people say there are nations where sons and their mothers,
where fathers and daughters, may marry each other, increasing
the bonds of piety by their redoubled affections.
Wretched am I, who hadn't the luck to be born there,
injured by nothing more than mischance of location!
"'Why do I obsess? Begone, forbidden desires;
of course he is worthy of love—but love for a father!
So, then, if I were not the daughter of great Cinyras,
I would be able to have intercourse with Cinyras:
though he is mine, he is not mine, and our nearness
ruins me: I would be better off as a stranger.
"'It would be good for me to go far away from my country,
as long as I could escape from my wicked desires,
for what holds me here is the passion that I have to see him,
to touch and speak to Cinyras and give him my kisses—
if nothing more is permitted. You impious maiden,
what more can you imagine will ever be granted?
Are you aware how you confuse all rights and relations?
Would you be your mother's rival? The whore of your father?
Would you be called your son's sister? Your brother's own mother?
Do you not shudder to think of the serpent-coiffed sisters[9]
thrusting their bloodthirsty torches into the faces
of the guilty wretches that those three appear to and torture?
"'But you, while your body is undefiled, keep your mind chaste,
and do not break Nature's law with incestuous pairing.
Think what you ask for: the very act is forbidden.
and he is devout and mindful of moral behavior—
ah, how I wish that he had a similar madness!'
"She spoke and Cinyras, whom an abundance of worthy
suitors had left undecided, consulted his daughter,
ran their names by her and asked whom she wished for a husband;

9. Again, the Furies.

silent at first, she kept her eyes locked on her father,
seething until the hot tears spilled over her eyelids:
Cinyras, attributing this to the fears of a virgin,
bade her cease weeping, wiped off her cheeks, and kissed her;
Myrrha rejoiced overmuch at his gesture and answered
that she would marry a man 'just like you.' Misunderstanding
the words of his daughter, Cinyras approved them, replying,
'May you be this pious always.' Hearing that last word,
the virgin lowers her head, self-convicted of evil.
"Midnight: now sleep dissolves all the cares of the body;
Cinyras' daughter, however, lies tossing, consumed by
the fires of passion, repeating her prayers in a frenzy;
now she despairs, now she'll attempt it; now she is shamefaced,
now eager: uncertain: *What should she do now?* She wavers,
just like a tree that the axe blade has girdled completely,
when only the last blow remains to be struck, and the woodsman
cannot predict the direction it's going to fall in,
she, after so many blows to her spirit, now totters,
now leaning in one, and now in the other, direction,
nor is she able to find any rest from her passion
save but in death. Death pleases her, and she gets up,
determined to hang herself from a beam with her girdle:
'Farewell, dear Cinyras: may you understand why I do this!'
she said, as she fitted the noose around her pale neck.
"They say that, hearing her murmuring, her faithful old nurse
in the next chamber arose and entered her bedroom:
at sight of the grim preparations, she screams out, and striking
her breasts and tearing her garments, removes the noose from
around the girl's neck, and then, only then she collapses,
and weeping, embraces her, asking her why she would do it.
"Myrrha remained silent, expressionless, with her eyes downcast,
sorrowing only because her attempt was detected.
But the woman persists, baring her flat breasts and white hair,
and by the milk given when she was a babe in the cradle
beseeches her to entrust her old nurse with the cause of her sorrow.
The girl turns away with a groan; the nurse is determined
to learn her secret, and promises not just to keep it:
"'Speak and allow me to aid you,' she says, 'for in my old age,
I am not utterly useless: if you are dying of passion,
my charms and herbs will restore you; if someone wishes you evil,
my rites will break whatever spell you are under;
is some god wrathful? A sacrifice placates his anger.
What else could it be? I can't think of anything—Fortune
favors your family, everything's going quite smoothly,
both of your parents are living, your mother, your father—'
Myrrha sighed deeply, hearing her father referred to,
but not even then did the nurse grasp the terrible evil
in the girl's heart, although she felt that her darling
suffered a passion of some kind for some kind of lover.
"Nurse was unyielding and begged her to make known her secret.
whatever it was, pressing the tearful girl to her bosom;

and clasping her in an embrace that old age had enfeebled,
she said, 'You're in love—I am certain! I will be zealous
in aiding your cause, never you fear—and your father
will be none the wiser!'
"Myrrha in frenzy leapt up
and threw herself onto the bed, pressing her face in the pillows:
'Leave me, I beg you,' she said. 'Avoid my wretched dishonor;
leave me or cease to ask me the cause of my sorrow:
what you attempt to uncover is sinful and wicked!'
"The old woman shuddered: extending the hands that now trembled
with fear and old age, she fell at the feet of her darling,
a suppliant, coaxing her now, and now attempting to scare her;
threatening now to disclose her attempted self-murder,
but pledging to aid her if she confesses her passion.
"She lifted her head with her eyes full of tears spilling over
onto the breast of her nurse and repeatedly tried to
speak out, but repeatedly stopped herself short of confession,
hiding her shame-colored face in the folds of her garments,
until she finally yielded, blurting her secret:
'O mother,' she cried, 'so fortunate you with your husband!'
and said no more but groaned.
"The nurse, who now understood it,
felt a chill run through her veins, and her bones shook with tremor,
and her white hair stood up in stiff bristles. She said whatever
she could to dissuade the girl from her horrible passion,
and even though Myrrha knew the truth of her warning,
she had decided to die if she could not possess him.
'Live, then,' the other replied, 'and possess your—' Not daring
to use the word 'father,' she left her sentence unfinished,
but called upon heaven to stand by her earlier promise.
"Now it was time for the annual feast days of Ceres;
the pious, and married women clad in white vestments,
thronged to the celebration, offering garlands
of wheat as firstfruits of the season; now for nine nights
the intimate touch of their men is considered forbidden.
Among these matrons was Cenchreïs, wife of Cinyras,
for her attendance during these rites was required.
And so, while the queen's place in his bed was left vacant,
the overly diligent nurse came to Cinyras,
finding him drunk, and spoke to him of a maiden
whose passion for him was real (although her name wasn't)
and praising her beauty; when asked the age of this virgin,
she said, 'the same age as Myrrha.' Commanded to fetch her,
nurse hastened home, and entering, cried to her darling,
'Rejoice, my dear, we have won!' The unlucky maiden
could not feel joy in her heart, but only grim sorrow,
yet still she rejoiced, so distorted were her emotions.
"Now it is midnight, when all of creation is silent;
high in the heavens, between the two Bears, Boötes[1]

1. The Ox-herder, a constellation that was imagined as driving Ursa Major, the Great Bear.

had turned his wagon so that its shaft pointed downward;
Myrrha approaches her crime, which is fled by chaste Luna,[2]
while under black clouds the stars hide their scandalized faces;
Night lacks its usual fires; you, Icarus,[3] covered
your face and were followed at once by Erigone,
whose pious love of her father merited heaven.
"Thrice Myrrha stumbles and stops each time at the omen,
and thrice the funereal owl sings her his poem of endings;
nevertheless she continues, her shame lessened by shadows.
She holds the left hand of her nurse, and gropes with the other
blindly in darkness: now at the bedchamber's threshold,
and now she opens the door: and now she is led within,
where her knees fail her; she falters, nearly collapsing,
her color, her blood, her spirit all flee together.
"As she approaches the crime, her horror increases;
regretting her boldness, she wishes to turn back, unnoticed,
but even as she holds back, the old woman leads her
by the hand to the high bed, where she delivers her, saying,
'Take her, Cinyras—she's yours,' and unites the doomed couple.
The father accepts his own offspring in his indecent
bed and attempts to dispel the girl's apprehensions,
encouraging her not to be frightened of him, and
addressing her, as it happened, with a name befitting
her years: he called her 'daughter' while she called him 'father,'
so the right names were attached to their impious actions.
"Filled with the seed of her father, she left his bedchamber,
having already conceived, in a crime against nature
which she repeated the following night and thereafter,
until Cinyras, impatient to see his new lover
after so many encounters, brought a light in,
and in the same moment discovered his crime and his daughter;
grief left him speechless; he tore out his sword from the scabbard;
Myrrha sped off, and, thanks to night's shadowy darkness,
escaped from her death. She wandered the wide-open spaces,
leaving Arabia, so rich in palms, and Panchaea,
and after nine months, she came at last to Sabaea,[4]
where she found rest from the weariness that she suffered,
for she could scarcely carry her womb's heavy burden.
"Uncertain of what she should wish for, tired of living
but frightened of dying, she summed up her state in this prayer:
'O gods, if there should be any who hear my confession,
I do not turn away from the terrible sentence
that my misbehavior deserves; but lest I should outrage
the living by my survival, or the dead by my dying,
drive me from both of these kingdoms, transform me

2. The Moon, often associated with Diana, one of whose attributes was chastity.
3. More properly Icarius, a mythic Athenian. He received Dionysus into the city, and the god rewarded him with wine, which he shared with his countrymen. Feeling its effect, they thought they had been poisoned and killed him. His daughter Erigone hanged herself in grief, and both were changed into stars.
4. Arabia Felix, the southern tip of the Arabian Peninsula.

wholly, so that both life and death are denied me.'
"Some god *did* hear her confession, and heaven answered
her final prayer, for, even as she was still speaking,
the earth rose up over her legs, and from her toes burst
roots that spread widely to hold the tall trunk in position;
her bones put forth wood, and even though they were still hollow,
they now ran with sap and not blood; her arms became branches,
and those were now twigs that used to be called her fingers,
while her skin turned to hard bark. The tree kept on growing,
over her swollen belly, wrapping it tightly,
and growing over her breast and up to her neck; she
could bear no further delay, and, as the wood rose,
plunged her face down into the bark and was swallowed.
"Loss of her body has meant the loss of all feeling;
and yet she weeps, and the warm drops spill from her tree trunk;
those tears bring her honor: the distillate myrrh preserves and
will keep the name of its mistress down through the ages.
"But under the bark, the infant conceived in such baseness
continued to grow and now sought a way out of Myrrha;
the pregnant trunk bulged in the middle and its weighty burden
pressed on the mother, who could not cry out in her sorrow
nor summon Lucina with charms to aid those in childbirth.
So, like a woman exerting herself to deliver,
the tree groaned and bent over double, wet from its weeping.
Gentle Lucina stood by the sorrowing branches,
laid her hands onto the bark and recited the charms that
aid in delivery; the bark split open; a fissure
ran down the trunk of the tree and its burden spilled out,
a bawling boychild, whom naiads placed in soft grasses
and bathed in the tears of its mother. Not even Envy
could have found fault with his beauty, for he resembled
one of the naked cherubs depicted by artists,
and would have been taken as one, if you had provided
him with a quiver or else removed one from those others.

[*Venus and Adonis*]

"Time swiftly glides by in secret, escaping our notice,
and nothing goes faster than years do: the son of his sister
by his grandfather, the one so recently hidden
within a tree, so recently born, a most beautiful infant,
now is an adolescent and now a young man
even more beautiful than he was as a baby,
pleasing now even to Venus and soon the avenger
of passionate fires that brought his mother to ruin.
"For while her fond Cupid was giving a kiss to his mother,
he pricked her unwittingly, right in the breast, with an arrow
projecting out of his quiver; annoyed, the great goddess
swatted him off, but the wound had gone in more deeply
than it appeared to, and at the beginning deceived her.
"Under the spell of this fellow's beauty, the goddess

no longer takes any interest now in Cythera,[5]
nor does she return to her haunts on the island of Paphos,
or to fish-wealthy Cnidus or to ore-bearing Amathus;[6]
she avoids heaven as well, now—preferring Adonis,
and clings to him, his constant companion, ignoring
her former mode of unstrenuous self-indulgence,
when she shunned natural light for the parlors of beauty;
now she goes roaming with him through woods and up mountains
and over the scrubby rocks with her garments hitched up
and girded around her waist like a nymph of Diana,[7]
urging the hounds to pursue unendangering species,
hoppety hares or stags with wide-branching antlers,
or terrified does; but she avoids the fierce wild boars and
rapacious wolves and bears armed with sharp claws,
and shuns the lions, sated with slaughter of cattle.
"And she warns you also to fear the wild beasts, Adonis,
if only her warning were heeded. 'Be bold with the timid,'
she said, 'but against the daring, daring is reckless.
Spare me, dear boy, the risk involved in your courage;
don't rile the beasts that Nature has armed with sharp weapons,
lest I should find the glory you gain much too costly!
For lions and bristling boars and other fierce creatures
look with indifferent eyes and minds upon beauty
and youth and other qualities Venus is moved by;
pitiless boars deal out thunderbolts with their curved tusks,
and none may withstand the frenzied assault of the lions,
whom I despise altogether.'
"And when he asked why,
she said, 'I will tell you this story which will amaze you,
with its retribution delivered for ancient wrongdoing.
"'But this unaccustomed labor has left me exhausted—
look, though—a poplar entices with opportune shade, and
offers a soft bed of turf we may rest on together,
as I would like to.' And so she lay down on the grasses
and on her Adonis, and using his breast as a pillow,
she told this story, mixing her words with sweet kisses:

"'Perhaps you'll have heard of a maiden able to vanquish
the swiftest of men in a footrace; this wasn't a fiction,
for she overcame all contestants; nor could you say whether
she deserved praise more for her speed or her beauty.
She asked some god about husbands. "A husband," he answered,
"is not for you, Atalanta: flee from a husband!
But you will not flee—and losing yourself, will live on!"
"'Frightened by his grim prediction, she went to the forest
and lived there unmarried, escaping the large and persistent

5. Island south of the Peloponnesus, and like Cyprus sacred to Venus.

6. All three were important centers of Venus's cult: Paphos and Amathus were cities on the island of Cyprus, and Cnidus was a city in Asia Minor.

7. As a virgin and huntress, the antithesis of Venus.

throng of her suitors by setting out cruel conditions;
"You cannot have me," she said, "unless you outrun me;
come race against me! A bride and a bed for the winner,
death to the losers. Those are the rules of the contest."
"'Cruel? Indeed—but such was this young maiden's beauty
that a foolhardy throng of admirers took up the wager.
As a spectator, Hippomenes sat in the grandstand,
asking why anyone ever would risk such a danger,
just for a bride, and disparaging their headstrong passion.
However, as soon as he caught a glimpse of her beauty,
like mine or like yours would be if you were a woman,'
said Venus, 'her face and her body, both bared for the contest,
he threw up both hands and cried out, "I beg your pardons,
who only a moment ago disparaged your efforts,
but truly I had no idea of the trophy you strive for!"
"'Praises ignited the fires of passion and made him
hope that no young man proved to be faster than she was
and fear that one would be. Jealous, he asked himself why he
was leaving the outcome of this competition unventured:
"God helps those who improve their condition by daring,"
he said, addressing himself as the maiden flew by him.
Though she seemed no less swift than a Scythian arrow,
nevertheless, he more greatly admired her beauty,
and the grace of her running made her seem even more lovely;
the breezes blew back the wings attached to her ankles
while her loose hair streamed over her ivory shoulders
and her brightly edged knee straps fluttered lightly; a russet
glow fanned out evenly over her pale, girlish body,
as when a purple awning covers a white marble surface,
staining its artless candor with counterfeit shadow.
"'She crossed the finish line while he was taking it in, and
Atalanta, victorious, was given a crown and the glory;
the groaning losers were taken off: end of *their* story.
But the youth, undeterred by what had become of the vanquished,
stood on the track and fixed his gaze on the maiden:
"Why seek such an easy victory over these sluggards?
Contend with me," he said, "and if Fortune makes me the winner,
you will at least have been beaten by one not unworthy:
I am the son of Megareus, grandson of Neptune,
my great-grandfather; my valor is no less impressive
than is my descent; if you should happen to triumph,
you would be famous for having beaten Hippomenes."
"'And as he spoke, Atalanta's countenance softened:
she wondered whether she wished to win or to *be* won,
and asked herself which god, jealous of her suitor's beauty,
sought to destroy him by forcing him into this marriage:
"If *I* were judging, I wouldn't think I was worth it!
Nor am I moved by his beauty," she said, "though I could be,
but I *am* moved by his youth: his boyishness stirs me—
but what of his valor? His mind so utterly fearless?
What of his watery origins? His relation to Neptune?

What of the fact that he loves me and wishes to wed me,
and is willing to die if bitter Fortune denies him?
"'"Oh, flee from a bed that still reeks with the gore of past victims,
while you are able to, stranger; marrying *me* is
certain destruction! No one would wish to reject you,
and you may be chosen by a much wiser young lady!
"'"But why should I care for you—after so many have perished?
Now *he* will learn! Let him die then, since the great slaughter
of suitors has taught him nothing! He must be weary of living!
So—must he die then, because he wishes to wed me,
and is willing to pay the ultimate price for his passion?
He shouldn't have to! And even though it won't be *my* fault,
my victory surely will turn the people against me!
"'"If only you would just give it up, or if only,
since you're obsessed with it, you were a little bit faster!
How very girlish is the boy's facial expression!
O poor Hippomenes! I wish you never had seen me!
You're worthy of life, and if only *my* life had been better,
or if the harsh Fates had not prevented my marriage,
you would have been the one I'd have chosen to marry!"
"'She spoke, and, moved by desire that struck without warning,
loved without knowing what she was doing or feeling.
Her father and people were clamoring down at the racecourse,
when Neptune's descendent Hippomenes anxiously begged me:
"Cytherian Venus, I pray you preside at my venture,
aiding the fires that you yourself have ignited."
A well-meaning breeze brought me this prayer, so appealing
that, I confess, it aroused me and stirred me to action,
though I had scant time enough to bring off his rescue.
"'There is a field upon Cyprus, known as Tamasus,
famed for its wealth; in olden days it was given
to me and provides an endowment now for my temples;
and there in this field is a tree; its leaves and its branches
glisten and shimmer, reflecting the gold they are made of;
now, as it happened, I'd just gotten back from a visit,
carrying three golden apples that I had selected:
and showing myself there to Hippomenes only,
approached him and showed him how to use them to advantage.
"'Both of them crouched for the start; when horns gave the signal,
they took off together, their feet barely brushing the surface;
you would have thought they were able to keep their toes dry
while skimming over the waves, and could touch on the ripened
heads of wheat in the field without bending them under.
"'Cries of support and encouragement cheered on the young man;
"Now is the time," they screamed, "go for it, go for it, hurry,
Hippomenes, give it everything that you've got now!
Don't hold back! Victory!" And I am uncertain whether
these words were more pleasing to him or to his Atalanta,
for often, when she could have very easily passed him,
she lingered beside, her gaze full of desperate longing,
until she reluctantly sped ahead of his features.

"'And now Hippomenes, dry-mouthed, was breathlessly gasping,
the finish line far in the distance; he threw out an apple,
and the sight of that radiant fruit astounded the maiden,
who turned from her course and retrieved the glittering missile;
Hippomenes passed her: the crowd roared its approval.
"'A burst of speed now and Atalanta makes up for lost time:
once more overtaking the lad, she puts him behind her!
A second apple: again she falls back, but recovers,
now she's beside him, now passing him, only the finish
remains: "Now, O goddess," he cries, "my inspiration, be with me!"
"'With all the strength of his youth he flings the last apple
to the far side of the field: *this* will really delay her!
The maiden looked doubtful about its retrieval: I forced her
to get it and add on its weight to the burden she carried:
time lost and weight gained were equal obstructions: the maiden
(lest my account should prove longer than even the race was)
took second place: the trophy bride left with the victor.
"'But really, Adonis, wasn't I worthy of being
thanked for my troubles? Offered a gift of sweet incense?
Heedless of all I had done, he offered me neither!
Immediate outrage was followed by keen indignation;
and firmly resolving not to be spurned in the future,
I guarded against it by making this pair an example.
"'Now they were passing a temple deep in the forest,
built long ago by Echion to honor Cybele,[8]
Mother of Gods, and now the length of their journey
urged them to rest here, where unbridled desire
possessed Hippomenes, moved by the strength of my godhead.
There was a dim and cave-like recess near the temple,
hewn out of pumice, a shrine to the ancient religion,
wherein a priest of these old rites had set a great many
carved wooden idols. Hippomenes entered that place, and
by his forbidden behavior defiled it;[9] in horror,
the sacred images turned away from the act, and Cybele
prepared to plunge the guilty pair in Stygian waters,
but that seemed too easy; so now their elegant pale necks
are cloaked in tawny manes; curved claws are their fingers;
arms are now forelegs, and all the weight of their bodies
shifts to their torsos; and now their tails sweep the arena;
fierce now, their faces; growls supplant verbal expression;
the forest now is their bedroom; a terror to others,
meekly these lions champ at the bit of the harness
on either side of the yoke of Cybele's chariot.
"'My darling, you must avoid these and all other wild beasts,
who will not turn tail, but show off their boldness in battle;
flee them or else your courage will prove our ruin!'

8. A fertility goddess of Asia Minor known as the Great Mother. She was often pictured wearing a crown that resembled a city wall with towers, and flanked by lions or riding in a cart drawn by them.

9. It was considered sacrilege to have sexual intercourse in the precinct of a temple.

"And after warning him, she went off on her journey,
carried aloft by her swans; but his courage resisted
her admonitions. It happened that as his dogs followed
a boar they were tracking, they roused it from where it was hidden,
and when it attempted to rush from the forest, Adonis
pierced it, but lightly, casting his spear from an angle;
with its long snout, it turned and knocked loose the weapon
stained with its own blood, then bore down upon our hero,
and, as he attempted to flee for his life in sheer terror,
it sank its tusks deep into the young fellow's privates,
and stretched him out on the yellow sands, where he lay dying.
"Aloft in her light, swan-driven chariot, Venus
had not yet gotten to Cyprus; from a great distance
she recognized the dying groans of Adonis
and turned her birds back to him; when she saw from midair
his body lying there, lifeless, stained with its own blood,
she beat her breasts and tore at her hair and her garments,
and leapt from her chariot, raging, to argue with grim Fate:
"'It will not be altogether as you would have it,'
she said. 'My grief for Adonis will be remembered
forever, and every year will see, reenacted
in ritual form, his death and my lamentation;
and the blood of the hero will be transformed to a flower.
Or were *you* not once allowed to change a young woman[1]
to fragrant mint, Persephone? Do you begrudge me
the transformation of my beloved Adonis?'
"And as she spoke, she sprinkled his blood with sweet nectar,
which made it swell up, like a transparent bubble
that rises from muck; and in no more than an hour
a flower sprang out of that soil, blood red in its color,
just like the flesh that lies underneath the tough rind
of the seed-hiding pomegranate. Brief is its season,
for the winds from which it takes its name, the anemone,
shake off those petals so lightly clinging and fated to perish."

1. Mentha, Hades' mistress, trampled by the jealous Persephone and transformed into the mint (the meaning of her name).

SPEECH, WRITING, POETRY

Language is the most powerful tool possessed by human beings: it is our linguistic ability, more than anything else, that distinguishes us from animals. The development of writing was an enormously important development in the history of humanity, a leap second only to the development of language itself. Literacy allows for complex record keeping: a literate culture can have a far larger and more complex political and economic organization than is possible without writing. Through writing, we can communicate with people at a distance, over any expanse of space or time, and words can, in theory, be preserved forever. Moreover, written texts create the possibility of different kinds of communication, and even different kinds of thinking, from those available in an oral culture. Writing made way for the development of science and mathematics: it is impossible to solve a complex mathematical, scientific, or philosophical problem entirely in one's own head. It also allowed for new kinds of artistic composition—including history and other kinds of detailed narrative—that would be impossible to remember without the use of writing.

In the Mediterranean and Near East, the earliest people to develop systems of writing are the ancient Sumerians, who lived in the valley of Mesopotamia (between the Tigris and Euphrates rivers), and the ancient Egyptians. Sumerian cuneiform—"wedge-shape" markings inscribed on clay tablets—and Egyptian hieroglyphs both emerged in the latter half of the fourth millennium B.C.E. Variant writing systems were established by other ancient peoples much later in history: the Greeks invented their alphabet in the eighth century B.C.E., and their system was adapted by the Romans. Not surprisingly, ancient peoples were fully aware of the power of writing. The Sumerians showed legitimate pride in the fact that writing could be seen as their invention. In the poem ***Enmerkar and the Lord of Aratta*** (of which a section appears below), it is a Sumerian king who first molded clay and "put words on it," understanding that writing is a much more secure way to pass on an important message than merely telling your intentions to a messenger.

Both Sumer and Egypt were "scribal cultures," meaning that writing was an occupation for paid professionals, not something that everybody was expected to be able to do. Certain texts were used as models for novice scribes to copy, and some of these deal with the profession of the scribe itself—offering fascinating insight into how these early writers saw their task. The Sumerian ***Supervisor's Advice to a Young Scribe*** is a dialogue between a teacher and his young student, in which the older man first boasts about his own superior knowledge of the art, but then backs down, acknowledging that the scribal "graduate" is perfectly ready to begin writing and teaching for himself. The

---

This detail from a red figure kylix (drinking cup) by the "Eretria Painter" (fifth century B.C.E.) shows the poet Lino instructing his student Mousaios.

dialogue has some quiet humor, of a kind that would have been enjoyable to those who had to copy it: all students enjoy seeing a pompous teacher backing down. The Egyptian texts that follow show how long and difficult a journey it was to become a proficient scribe—often with humor, as in descriptions of unpromising trainee scribes who fritter away their time drinking and partying, when they should be studying. But the texts also emphasize the value of the goal: the scribe was rewarded both financially and socially, as an honored member of society. The god Thoth, who was the patron of human scribes and himself scribe to the other gods, was one of the most powerful members of the Egyptian pantheon: he was, unlike other gods, self-created (through the power of language), and associated with knowledge, wisdom, healing, order, and correct judgment.

The complex relation between writing and social, political, and economic power is explored in our other Egyptian text, ***The Tale of the Eloquent Peasant***. Here, a peasant goes to complain about the theft of his property to the magistrates, who record in writing his fluent but desperate, Job-like lament at the injustice he sees in his own life and in the world. The text seems to reflect an ambivalence toward writing. On the one hand, the poor man's words are conveyed through writing to the king, whose steward restores all the man's stolen property. On the other hand, the peasant's suffering is extended in order to provoke him to further eloquence and thereby generate more written literature. The text seems to suggest that writing can take on an aesthetic life of its own, and be valued—disturbingly enough—for reasons that may have nothing to do with morality.

Greek and Roman cultures were not primarily scribal: although people sometimes dictated to slaves (as a modern person might use a dictaphone), reading and writing were not seen as a specialty profession, and by the fifth century B.C.E., much of the elite male population could probably read and write, at least to some degree. But literacy did not, of course, become universal, and even those who could read encountered much of their "literature" orally, through recitation, singing, dramatic performance, and reading aloud; silent reading was almost unknown in the ancient world. Several Greek texts suggest anxiety about the transition from an oral to a literate culture. The only mention of writing in the ***Iliad***—a Greek poem based on an oral tradition—comes in book 6, in the story of Bellerophon, who is made to carry sinister "folded tablets" to a foreign king; unbeknown to the wronged hero, the tablets contain terrible lies against himself. The story depends on the fact that Bellerophon himself is presumably unable to read the tablets. In a culture where only a few can read

A black granite sculpture from the fourteenth century B.C.E. depicting an Egyptian scribe.

and write, the power of marks on clay or papyrus can seem akin to magic. Indeed, in the Egyptian pantheon, Thoth was lord of magic, as well as of science and mathematics.

Greek and Roman authors often celebrated the quasi-magical power of writing to preserve words across space and time, even after the speaker's death. **Theognis**, a Greek lyric poet, trumpets his ability to bring immortality to his addressee: a poem can make the boy live forever. Theognis was probably composing at a time when few of his Greek contemporaries were literate (in the sixth century B.C.E.), and his metaphors hover in interesting ways between literate and oral models of language. The poet describes himself as singing (not writing), and, indeed, Theognis's poetry probably was sung mostly at drinking parties (known as *symposia*, "where men dine and pass the cup"); but Theognis also emphasizes that his poetry is infinitely repeatable, sung again and again by many different lips but always ascribed to the same author, because the work is "sealed"—like a written letter, or a written book of poetry. Later in the Greco-Roman tradition, once literacy was more widespread, poets began to emphasize the physicality of the book they were producing: **Callimachus** presents himself as inspired by the god Apollo, but not, like the archaic poet Hesiod, while he was out on the hillside, but at the first moment that he sat down to write, "with the writing tablet on my lap." The Roman **Catullus** evokes the care he has taken over the content of his poetry by describing the nice polished appearance of his scroll (poem 1). **Horace** (in Ode 30) describes his poetic achievement in terms that are both physical and more than physical, since a book can be reproduced any number of times; the technology of writing allows the poet's work to defeat time and death ("I shall not wholly die"), and to last longer even than bronze or "the pyramids of kings."

But the power of writing could be seen as bad as well as good. In the ***Phaedrus,*** **Plato's** Socrates tells a fable about an ancient king of Thebes who was offered writing as a new gift by the Egyptian god Thoth. Thoth claims that the art of writing would improve human memory; but the king adamantly rejects this view, claiming that it is an "art of forgetfulness": when thoughts are stored outside the mind, on the page, people will no longer bother to remember them for themselves. And once ideas are written down, we may give them credit for wisdom; but in fact, books are less, not more, truthful than living human minds, since they are unable to change in response to new realizations. The possible disjunctions between literature and ethics, and between literature and truth, were of particular concern to the ancient Greeks, as we see in several texts collected here. Xenophanes criticizes the Homeric poems for misrepresenting the gods as setting a bad example to humanity. **Aristophanes**' comedy, the ***Frogs***, suggests that literature has an essential impact on the ethical and cultural life of a community: the premise of the play is that the city of Athens, in dire straits during its long war with Sparta, needs the help of a dead poet, who must be chosen and brought back to the world of the living by the theater god, Dionysus. Dionysus's choice comes down to the two tragedians, **Aeschylus** and **Euripides**, who represent two models for how a poet or writer might interact with society. Should literature inspire us to revere tradition, and rouse us to fight for our country—as Aeschylus's plays supposedly did? Or should it, rather, reflect people as they are, with all their flaws—even if, as some of Euripides' contemporaries claimed, the depiction of immoral behavior can inspire further wickedness? A version of this debate is still with us today.

One possible response is to claim that literature has nothing to do with morality, and to focus instead on the techniques that enable a work of literature to succeed or fail on its own terms. But good writing is not merely a matter of assembling correct words in the correct order: it also involves the heart. Even in Horace's ***Ars Poetica***, a work that stresses the concept of *decorum* ("appropriateness"), Horace sometimes veers away from his purely technical account of good writing, as when he suggests that the poet must first feel for himself the emotions that he hopes to inspire in his reader. ***Aristotle's Poetics***, too, despite its emphasis on technique, suggests that poetry has a deep emotional and ethical function. Writing in response to Plato's criticisms of poetry and writing, Aristotle suggests that good poetry actually helps us become better people, by recalibrating or healing our emotional responses. The art of writing is, then, far less distant from the art of good living than Aristotle's teacher Plato had believed.

None of these texts are "literary criticism" in a modern sense. Instead of analyzing specific written works, their ancient authors are interested in discussing how, why, and whether a person should write. Technique is at the forefront in some of these texts, while others focus on broader ethical, political, and psychological issues. It is worthwhile to think hard about how ancient conceptions of speech, writing, and poetry differ from our own notions of "literature"—as well as about how these writers and thinkers laid the foundation on which modern literature studies could be built.

MESOPOTAMIA: ENMERKAR AND THE LORD OF ARATTA

This ancient Sumerian mythological story, composed perhaps around 2000 B.C.E., celebrates Sumer, and one of its major cities, Uruk, as the birthplace of writing. The goddess Inana (known as Ishtar in ***The Epic of Gilgamesh***) permits Enmerkar, the king of the mighty city-state Uruk, to subjugate the people of Aratta—a mythical place rich in gold and jewels—and make them deliver tribute for her, to adorn her cult centers in Uruk. They resist, and after many exchanges of messengers, the Lord of Aratta proposes that the cities should each pick a champion, to fight it out. Enmerkar is willing to accept the challenge, on condition that the people of Aratta, if they lose, will pay even more tribute, or else face absolute destruction. At this point, the herald is overwhelmed and cannot remember the details of what he is to say. In response, Enmerkar invents writing, and sends the herald with clay tablets back to Aratta; this is the passage included here. The ending of the text is damaged and unclear, but it seems that the people of Aratta eventually submitted, sent tribute, and Enmerkar triumphed.

From Enmerkar and the Lord of Aratta[1]

From his throne he spoke to him like a raging torrent:[2]
"Messenger, when you speak to the lord of Aratta, say this:
"A cloth that is not black, a cloth that is not white,
"A cloth that is not brown, a cloth that is not red,
"A cloth that is not yellow, a cloth that is not pied—such a cloth
I will give him!
"My dog is embraced by Enlil;[3] this dog I will send to him.
"My dog will wrangle with his dog
"So that the stronger one be known. Tell him that!
"Second, when you speak to him, say also this:
"He must now stop prevaricating and come to a decision
"Those of his city shall walk before him like sheep,
"And he, like a shepherd, shall follow them.
"At his coming, the holy mound of lapis lazuli
"Shall humble itself before him like a crushed reed.
"They shall amass shining gold and silver
"For Inana of the Eana

1. Translated by Herman Vanstiphout.
2. The scene of the invention of writing by the king of Uruk opens with the king, Enmerkar, trying to instruct his messenger how to respond to the people of Aratta, who are not willing to pay tribute to Uruk.
3. One of the chief gods in the Mesopotamian pantheon. The messenger later calls Enmerkar a "son of Enlil."

"In the courtyard of Aratta in great piles.[4]
"Third, when you speak to him, say also this:
"Beware lest I make (the people/Aratta) flee from their city like a dove
from its tree,
"Lest I make them fly away like [a bird from its permanent nest].
"Lest I put a price on them [as on mere merchandise].
"[Lest I *make*] the wind carry them away!
"At his coming, when he holds the precious stones of the hills,
"He must build for me the shrines of Eridug, Abzu, and Enum;[5]
"He must adorn for me its architrave with a *slip of clay*;
"He must make it spread its shadow over the Land for me!
"When he speaks . . .
"Tell him this as a sign for him!"

Thereupon the lord . . .
on the throne dais, on the throne, the noble seed of princes,
grown all alone.
His speech was very grand, its meaning very deep;
The messenger's mouth was too *heavy*, he could not repeat it.
Because the messenger's mouth was too *heavy*, and he could not repeat it,
The lord of Kulab[6] patted some clay and put the words on it as on a tablet.
Before that day, there had been no putting words on clay;
But now, when the sun rose on that day—so it was:
The lord of Kulab had put words as on a tablet—so it was!

The messenger was like a bird flapping its wings.
Raging like a wolf chasing a kid
He crossed five, six, seven mountain ranges.
Lifting his head, he had reached Aratta.

Joyfully he stepped into the courtyard of Aratta
And proclaimed the preeminence of his king.
He spoke out what was in his heart
And transmitted it to the lord of Aratta:
"Your father, my king, has sent me;
"The lord of Unug;[7] and Kulab has sent me."

LORD OF ARATTA
"What is it to me what your king spoke, what he said?"

MESSENGER
"This is what my king spoke, what he said:
"My King is a tall MES-tree,[8] the son of Enlil.
"This tree has grown so tall that it links heaven and earth;
"Its crown reaches heaven;
"Its roots are set fast in the earth.

4. The king of Uruk requests tribute paid in gold and silver from the Lord of Aratta for adorning the temple of Inana. Eana is the goddess's abode.
5. Other shrines to be built and adorned; Eridug was a city in Southern Sumer.
6. Chancellor of King Enmerkar of Uruk.
7. Sumerian name for "Uruk," the city-state ruled by King Enmerkar.
8. Silvery tree of great worth.

"He who has manifested lordship and kingship,
"Enmerkar, son of the Sun, gave me this tablet.
"O lord of Aratta, when you have read this tablet, learned the gist of the message,
"When you will have replied to me whatever you want,
"To the scion of the one with the gleaming beard,
"To him whom the mighty cow bore on the hill of the lustrous power,
"To him who grew up on the soil of Aratta,
"To him who was suckled by the rear of the true cow,
"To him, suited for office in Kulab,[9] mountain of the great powers,
"To Enmerkar, son of the Sun,
"I will speak that word as glad tidings in the shrine Eana.
"In his Gipar, bearing fruit like a young MES-tree,
"I shall repeat it to my king, the lord of Kulab."

This having been said,
The lord of Arratta took from the messenger
The tablet (and held it) next to a brazier.
The lord of Aratta inspected the tablet.
The spoken words were mere wedges[1]—his brow darkened.
The lord of Aratta kept looking at the tablet (in the light of) the brazier.

9. Kulab was part of the city of Uruk, probably a temple quarter.
1. The Sumerian *gag* ("nail, wedge") is not the technical term for the wedge-shaped cuneiform writing. Thus, the passage is written from the perspective of the stunned Lord Aratta, who does not understand that the incisions on the clay tablet are spoken words recorded in the newly invented medium of writing.

EGYPT: THE TALE OF THE ELOQUENT PEASANT

Composed around 1850 B.C.E. during the Middle Kingdom, the classical age of Egyptian literature, this text is one of the longest Egyptian literary tales to survive complete. It tells the story of a poor merchant from an oasis near the Nile Delta, who is robbed and pleads for justice to the king's high steward. The steward recognizes the peasant's extraordinary gift for fine speech and detains him until he has declaimed nine extensive petitions that center on the theme of justice. Suspense in the tale rises with each round of declamation, since the peasant does not know that he has already won his case. The steward remains silent, thus goading the peasant into ever greater eloquence, which ranges from flattery to abuse and despair. At one point the steward even commands that the peasant be beaten, in order to stimulate him to yet higher flights of eloquence. The text is a complex meditation on the relation—or disjunction—of moral order and fine speech, as transcribed into fine writing.

From The Tale of the Eloquent Peasant[1]

And this peasant came to petition
the High Steward Meru's son Rensi,
and said, 'High Steward, my lord!
Great of the great,
leader of all that is not and all that is!

If you go down to the Sea of Truth,[2]
you will sail on it with true fair wind;
the bunt will not strip off your sails, nor your boat delay;
nor will misfortune come upon your mast, nor your yards break;
you will not go headlong, and be grounded;
nor will the flood carry you off;
nor will you taste the river's evil, nor stare in the face of fear.
But to you the fish will come caught;
you will catch fatted fowl.

For you are a father to the orphan[3]
and a husband to the widow,

1. Translated by Richard B. Parkinson.
2. A pun on the Sea of Maat, a waterway known from texts about the next world. The Egyptian for "truth," "justice," and "order" is *maat*, a different word from the name of the next-worldly stretch of water.
3. These lines give standard phrases describing the righteous behavior of high officials.

a brother to the divorced,
an apron to the motherless.
Let me make your name in this land, with every good law:
Leader free from selfishness!
Great one free from baseness!
Destroyer of Falsehood! Creator of Truth!
Who comes at the voice of the caller!

I speak so that you will hear.
Do Truth, praised one whom the praised praise!
Drive off my need—look, I am weighed down!
Examine me—look, I am at a loss!'

Now this peasant made this speech
in the reign of the Majesty of the Dual King Nebkaure, the justified.[4]
The High Steward Meru's son Rensi
then went before his Majesty
and said, 'My lord, I have found one of the peasants,
whose speech is truly perfect, and whose goods have been stolen.
And, look, he has come to me to appeal about it.'

And his Majesty said, 'As you wish to see me in health
you shall delay him here,
without answering anything he says!
For the sake of his speaking, be quiet!
Then we shall be brought it in writing, and we shall hear it.
But provide sustenance for his wife and children!
Look, one of these peasants only comes
to Egypt when his house is all but empty.
Also, provide sustenance for this peasant himself!
You shall have the provisions given to him
without letting him know that you are giving him them!'

And he was given ten loaves of bread,[5]
and two jars of beer daily.
The High Steward Meru's son
Rensi gave them—
gave them to his friend, and his friend gave them to him.
Then the High Steward Meru's son Rensi sent
to the mayor of the Wadi Natrun
about making provisions for this peasant's wife,
three gallons daily.

* * *

And this peasant came to appeal to him a third time
and said, 'High Steward, my lord!
You are a Sungod, lord of heaven, with your entourage.

4. A king of the tenth dynasty of Heracleopolis, ca. 2050 B.C.E. "The justified" is a standard epithet of the deceased.

5. A generous but not excessive ration. Rensi routes the provisions indirectly so that the peasant should not know who sent them.

Everyone's portion is with you, like a flood.
You are a Nileflood who revives the water-meadows, and restores
the ravaged mounds.
Punisher of the robber, protector of the poor—
become not a torrent against the appealer!

Take heed of eternity's approach! Wish to endure,[6]
as is said, "Doing Truth is the breath of life."
Deal punishment to the punishable!
May your standard never be equalled!
Do the scales wander?
Is the balance partial?
And is Thoth lenient?[7] If so, then you should do evil!
You should bestow yourself as the twin of these three!
If the three are lenient, then you can be lenient.
Do not answer good with bad!
Do not put one thing in another's place!
Or speech will grow, even more than weeds,
to reach the smeller with its answer.
The man who waters evil to make deception grow—
this is three times to make him act.

Steer according to the sail!
Remove the torrent to do Truth!
Beware turning back while at the tiller!
Maintaining earth's rightness is doing Truth.
Speak not falsehood, for you are great!
Be not light, for you are weighty!
Speak not falsehood, you are the scales!
Stray not, you are the standard!
Look, you yourself are the very scales:
if they tilt, then you can tilt.
Drift not, but steer!
Rescue with the tiller rope!
Seize not, but act against the seizer!
A selfish great one is not truly great.
But your tongue is the plummet;
your heart is the weight;
your lips are its arms.
So if you disregard the fierce, who will beat off wretchedness?

Look, you are a wretched washerman,[8]
a selfish one who destroys friendship,
and forsakes his faithful companion for his client—
anyone who comes and supplies him is his brother.
Look, you are a ferryman who ferries only fareholders,

6. In order to survive into the next life, Rensi should act justly.
7. Thoth, the assessor of the balance in judgment after death, is incorruptible and so not lenient.
8. The next stanza denigrates Rensi, whose role as a high official should include care for the indigent.

a doer of right whose righteousness is flawed.
Look, you are a storehouse keeper,
who does not let someone in penury escape a debt.

Look, you are a hawk to the folk,[9]
who lives on the wretched birds.
Look, you are a butcher
whose joy is slaughter, without feeling any of the carnage.
Look, you are a shepherd—
is it not a wrong for me that you cannot reckon?
If not, then you can create loss—a predatory crocodile,
a shelter which has abandoned the harbour of the whole land!

Hearer, you do not hear!
So why do you not hear?
Is it because the predator has today already been beaten off for me?
The crocodile retreats?
What use for you is this?
The mystery of Truth will be found, and Falsehood cast
  down on the ground!
Do not plan tomorrow before it comes; the evil in it cannot be known!'

Now the peasant spoke this speech
⟨to⟩ the High Steward Meru's son Rensi
at the entrance of the office.[1]
Then he set two attendants on him with whips.
Then they beat all his limbs with them.[2]

* * *

And this peasant came to appeal to him a ninth time,[3]
and said, 'High Steward, my lord!
The tongue of men is their balance;
and scales are what detect deficiency,
dealing punishment to the punishable: let the standard be like you!

Even when its portion exists, Falsehood [sallies forth],
but Truth turns back to confront it;
Truth is the property of Falsehood,
which lets it flourish, but Falsehood has never been gathered in.[4]
If Falsehood sets out, it strays;
it cannot cross in a ferry, and has not altered its course.

9. A perversion of an image of the king as a defender of his people.
1. The peasant never enters Rensi's office. Petitions are heard at doorways or other places of transition.
2. This passage takes the text forward; without it, the peasant would have exhausted his possibilities for recourse against Nemtinakht through Rensi. In the next stanza, not included here, the peasant accuses Rensi of abusing all the roles that he holds and exploiting them for his own ends.
3. This is the the peasant's final petition.
4. A metaphor of harvest that says that Truth is under the control of Falsehood, whose growth in an imperfect world cannot be checked.

He who is rich with it has no children,[5]
and no heirs on earth.
And he who sails with it cannot touch land,
his boat cannot moor in its harbour.

Be heavy no more, you have not yet been light!
Delay no more, you have not yet been swift!
Be not partial! Do not listen to the heart!
Do not disregard one you know!
Do not blind yourself against one who looks to you! Do not fend off a supplicator!

You should abandon this negligence, so that your sentence will be renowned!
Act for him who acts for you[6]
and listen to none against him,
so that a man will be summoned according to his true right!
There is no yesterday for the negligent,
no friend for him who is deaf to Truth,
no holiday for the selfish.
The accuser becomes wretched,[7]
more wretched than when a pleader,
and the opponent becomes a murderer.
Look, I am pleading to you, and you do not hear—
I will go and plead about you to Anubis.'[8]

And the High Steward Meru's son Rensi
sent two attendants to turn him back.
And this peasant was afraid, thinking this was done
to punish him for the speech he had made.
And this peasant said, 'The thirsty man
approaching water,
the nurseling reaching his mouth
for milk—they die,
while for him who longs to see it come,
death comes slowly.'
And the High Steward Meru's son Rensi said,
'Don't be afraid peasant!
Look, you will be dealing with me.'
And this peasant swore an oath,
'So, shall I live on your bread,[9]
and drink your beer for ever?'

5. In ancient Egypt, those who committed crimes could leave no inheritance. This idea is followed by a metaphor of navigation that makes the same point.
6. This is a common ideal. The peasant casts himself as acting for Rensi by articulating Truth.
7. The peasant has turned into Rensi's accuser, while Rensi is ultimately his murderer.
8. The peasant evokes his own god, Anubis, who aids the dead to reach the next world. He implies that he will commit suicide.
9. For the first time the peasant reveals that he knows Rensi has been providing for him while forcing him to make his petitions.

And the High Steward Meru's son Rensi said,
'Now wait here and hear your petitions!'
And he caused every petition to be read out
from a fresh roll according to [its] content.
And the High Steward Meru's son Rensi had them presented
before the Majesty of the Dual King Nebkaure, the justified.
And they seemed more perfect to his heart
than anything in this entire land.
And his Majesty said, 'Judge yourself, Meru's son!'

And the High Steward Meru's son Rensi
sent two attendants to [bring this Nemtinakht].
Then he was brought, and an inventory made [of his household].
Then he found six persons, as well as [his . . .],
his barley, his emmer,
his donkeys, his swine,[1] and his flocks.
And this Nemtinakht [was given] to this peasant,
[with all his property, all his] ser[vants],
[and all the belongings] of this Nemtinakht.

So it ends, [from start to finish,
as found in writing].

1. Pigs were commonly raised in ancient Egypt, but were subject to some sort of taboo and are almost absent from the pictorial and literary record. This is a rare exception.

EGYPT: TEXTS ON THE SCRIBAL PROFESSION

These texts on the scribal profession, composed in late New Kingdom Egypt (ca. 1300–1100 B.C.E.), were used by apprentice scribes as they practiced their writing skills. Many Egyptian literary texts exalted the calling of the scribe as administrator, rather than as magician, a characterization prominent in fictional tales. The texts selected here praise the life of the scribe, and mock students of writing who fail to concentrate on their studies. The texts also describe the hardships experienced by people who make their living in other ways. The scribe does not suffer as they do, and he may be the one who orders others to suffer when their dues are collected, generally in the form of rents. The last example is a prayer to Thot (or Thoth), the Egyptian god of scribes.

Reminder of the Scribe's Superior Status[1]

The overseer of the record-keepers of the treasury of Pharaoh, l.p.h.,[2] Amunemone speaks to the scribe Pentawere. This letter is brought to you saying: I have been told that you have abandoned writing and that you reel about in pleasures, that you have given your attention to work in the fields, and that you have turned your back on hieroglyphs. Do you not remember the condition of the field hand in the face of the registration of the harvest-tax, the snake having taken away half of the grain and the hippopotamus having eaten the remainder? The mice are numerous in the field, the locust descends, and the cattle eat. The sparrows bring want to the field hand. The remainder which is (on) the threshing floor is finished, and it is for the thieves. Its 'value in copper' is lost, and the yoke of oxen is dead from threshing and ploughing. The scribe has moored (at) the riverbank.[3] He reckons the tax, with the attendants bearing staffs and the Nubians[4] rods of palm. They [say]: Give the grain! There is none. They beat [him] vigorously. He is bound and cast into the well. They beat [him], drowning [him] head first, while his wife is bound in his presence. His children are manacled; his neighbors have abandoned them and fled. Their grain is gathered. But a scribe, he is the taskmaster of everyone. There is (no) taxing of the work of the scribe. He does not have dues. So take note of this.

Advice to the Youthful Scribe

O scribe, do not be idle, do not be idle, or you shall be curbed straight way. Do not give your heart to pleasures, or you shall fail. Write with your hand, recite with your mouth, and converse with those more knowledgeable than you. Exercise the office of magistrate, and then you will find it [advantageous] in old age. Fortunate is a scribe skilled in his office, the possessor of (a good) upbringing. Persevere in action daily, and you will gain mastery over them. Do not spend a day of idleness or you shall be beaten. The youth has a back and he hearkens to the beating of him.[1] Pay attention. Hearken to what I have said. You will find it advantageous. One teaches apes (to) dance, and one tames horses.[2] One can place a kite in a nest, and a falcon can be caught by the wings. Persevere in conversation. Do not be idle. Write. Do not feel distaste.

1. All selections translated by William Simpson.
2. In this period the living king was normally referred to by the name of the institution "Pharaoh" (literally "Great Estate"); l.p.h. is an abbreviation for "life, prosperity, health," a stereotyped wish formula written after a word for the king in documents and inscriptions.
3. Unlike the field hand, the scribe is brought by boat, so that he does not have to walk.
4. Nubians were widely employed in the police and the military.

1. The dull student learns by being beaten. A stronger form of this idea is to say that a pupil's ear is on his back.
2. If animals can learn, even a pupil scribe must be able to do so.

Prayer to Thot for Skill in Writing

Come to me, Thot, O noble Ibis, O god who longs for Khmun, O dispatch-writer of the Ennead, the great one of Unn.[1] Come to me that you may give advice and make me skillful in your office. Better is your profession than all professions. It makes (men) great. He who is skilled in it is found (fit) to exercise (the office of) magistrate. I have 'seen' many for whom you have acted, and they are in the Council of the Thirty,[2] they being strong and powerful through what you have done. You are the one who has given advice. You are the one who has given advice to the motherless man.[3] Shay and Renenwetet[4] are with you. Come to me that you may advise me. I am the servant of your house. Let me relate your prowess in whatever land I am. Then the multitude of men shall say: How great are the things that Thot has done. Then they shall come with their children to brand[5] them with your profession, a calling good to the lord of victory. Joyful is the one who has exercised it.

1. The ibis is the sacred bird of Thot (also spelled Thoth). Khmun (Hermopolis) is his sacred city, also known as Unu. Thot is the scribe of the gods, of whom the Ennead (group of nine) are the most important.
2. A legal and administrative body.
3. In addition to protecting scribes, Thot cares for the helpless.
4. The deities of fate and fortune.
5. This evokes the metaphor of human beings as the "cattle of the god."

XENOPHANES[1]

Xenophanes (ca. 570–475 B.C.E.), who came from the Greek city of Colophon on the Ionian coast (overlapping with modern Turkey), was a poet and philosopher whose work has survived only through quotation in later authors. He satirized the idea that gods are like human beings and criticized, on moral grounds, the representations of gods in the poetry of **Hesiod** and **Homer.**

[The myths of the theologians and poets] are full of every impiety;
hence Xenophanes, criticizing Homer and Hesiod, says:

Homer and Hesiod attributed to the gods everything
which among men is shameful and blameworthy—
theft and adultery and mutual deception.

—Sextus Empiricus, *Against the Mathematicians* IX

1. Translated by Jonathan Barnes. The work of Xenophanes does not survive, but we have quotations from him in other, much later authors. Here, the parts in regular font are summaries of his views, and the parts in italics are thought to be exact quotations.

Homer and Hesiod, according to Xenophanes of Colophon,
recounted many lawless deeds of the gods—
theft and adultery and mutual deception.
For Cronus, under whom they say was the golden age, castrated his father and ate his children. . . .

—Sextus Empiricus, *Against the Mathematicians* I

Xenophanes of Colophon, teaching that god is one and incorporeal, rightly says:
There is one god, greatest among gods and men,
similar to mortals neither in shape nor in thought.
And again:
But mortals think that gods are born,
and have clothes and speech and shape like their own.
And again:
But if cows and horses or lions had hands
and drew with their hands and made the things men make,
then horses would draw the forms of gods like horses, cows like cows,
and each would make their bodies
similar in shape to their own.

—Clement, *Miscellanies* 5.14

THEOGNIS

Theognis, who lived sometime in the sixth century B.C.E., was a Greek poet from the isthmus of Corinth. The collection that survives under his name includes many maxims, poems, and poem fragments, some of which are not by Theognis: some may have been composed one or two hundred years after his death. The poetry in this collection was probably sung at drinking parties for aristocratic young men and idealizes eloquence; it shows intense hostility to "the common man," and celebrates the love between an upper-class speaker and his beautiful boyfriend, Kyrnos.

From Elegies[1]

O Lord, the son of Leto, child of Zeus,[2]
I won't forget you now or at the end.
I'll sing you first and last and in between,
You, listen, and be favourable to me.

1. Translated by Dorothea Wender.
2. The god Apollo, who was associated with poetry.

I seal my words of wisdom with your name,[3]
Kurnos; no man can steal them now, nor try
To slip his trash in with my excellence,
And every man will say, 'This is a song
That great Theognis, the Megarian, sang.'

* * *

I give you wings. You'll soon be lifted up
Across the land, across the boundless crests
Of ocean; where men dine and pass the cup,
You'll light there, on the lips of all the guests,
Where lithe, appealing lads will praise you, swelling
Their song to match the piper's sweet, shrill tone.
At length, my boy, you'll enter Hades' dwelling,
That black hole where departed spirits moan,
But even then your glory will not cease,
Your well-loved name will stay alive, unworn;
You'll skim across the mainland, over Greece,
Over the islands and the sea, not borne
By horses, Kurnos; you'll be whirled along
By violet-crowned maids, the Muses; yours
Will be each practised singer's finest song,
As long as light exists and earth endures.
I give you this, for what? To be reviled—
To be betrayed and lied to, like a child.

3. The "seal" may be the title written on the scroll.

ARISTOPHANES

First performed in Athens in 405 B.C.E., *Frogs* is a comedy about the god Dionysus (associated with wine and theater) descending to the underworld to recover a dead tragic poet to save the city at a time of crisis in the war against Sparta. The choice comes down to two: the older, more traditional **Aeschylus**, author of ***Agamemnon***, who claims to be able to inspire his audience with patriotic, military fervor, but whose writing style is represented as pompous, wordy, and (literally) heavy; or the younger, more entertaining **Euripides**, author of ***Medea***, who writes in a more colloquial style and represents morally dubious behavior with realism and zing.

From Frogs[1]

EURIPIDES Don't anyone dare tell me to let go of this chair.[2]
With me—in the art of poetry—there's no one to compare.
DIONYSUS Aeschylus, you say nothing.
Don't you hear what this man's claiming?
EURIPIDES As always, he's being aloof—like his tragedies.
DIONYSUS That's a bit much, friend. Don't exaggerate.
EURIPIDES I've had this fellow's number for a long time.
The most boring primitives is what he likes to create:
unlettered, unfettered, unruly, uncouth, they froth at the mouth
in a flood of bombastical—diarrheical foam.
AESCHYLUS Really? You son of a vegetable-selling bitch?
This coming from you, you bleeding-burst-bubble-piece-of-bosh!
You beggermonger with an avocation to stitch
old sacks, you'll be sorry you said that.
DIONYSUS Hold on, Aeschylus. "Heap not the fuel on your fiery gall."[3]
AESCHYLUS No, I won't hold on. Not till I've laid bare
the impudence of this creator of spastics here.
DIONYSUS Hey, boys, a lamb, bring on a black lamb.[4]
I can see what's heading our way—a storm.
AESCHYLUS [*continuing his tirade against* EURIPIDES]
You connoisseur of dirty Cretan songs
fouling our art with incestuous intercourse.
DIONYSUS That's enough, illustrious Aeschylus,
and you, Euripides, poor fellow, it would be wise
to move out of range of this storm of hail.
He's so angry he might break your skull
with a crushing retort and your *Telephus*[5] would come to naught.
And you, Aeschylus,
do try to keep calm and free your repartee
from rancor and abuse.
It's simply not done for two well-known literary men
to wrangle like fishwives or go up in a blaze
like an oak tree on fire.
EURIPIDES I am ready to take him on if *he* is.
I'm not backing down
He can have the first go in this verbal bout
and pick away at the entire
gamut and guts of my songs and tragedies.

1. Translated by Paul Roche. This scene takes place in Hades, the underworld; Pluto, god of the underworld, is sitting onstage, on his throne. Dionysus, god of wine and theater, has come to take a dead tragic poet back up with him to Athens to save the city in its time of crisis at the end of the Peloponnesian War. He has to decide between Aeschylus and Euripides, so a competition is organized; the winner will be taken back to the upper world.
2. Euripides apparently grabs the place of honor, to the right of Pluto, the king.
3. Presumably a quotation from Aeschylus.
4. Apparently a good sacrifice for defense against bad weather.
5. A lost tragedy by Euripides.

I don't care which: my *Peleus*, my *Aeolus*,
my *Meleager*—yes, and even my *Telephus*.

DIONYSUS And, Aeschylus, what about you? Speak out.

AESCHYLUS I could have wished avoiding this altercation.
The odds are so uneven.

DIONYSUS How d'you mean?

AESCHYLUS My poetry hasn't died with me—
it's still alive up there,
whereas his is as moribund as he.
Still, if that's what you want, I don't care.

DIONYSUS Will someone go and get the incense and the fire
and I'll begin this display of supererogation with a prayer
that my decisions in this contest will be fair.
Meanwhile will the Chorus invoke the Muses with a hymn.

MEN AND WOMEN
Come, you holy maidens of Zeus,
You Muses nine, who activate the decisions and the minds
Of men along wonderfully clear and luminous lines
When they are pitted against each other in tough and abstruse
Debate, we invite you to come and admire the vigor and prowess
Of this couple of speakers, each of which is a master
Of handling enormous slabs of verb
As well as piddling chips of syllable. Look and observe
The mighty minds that are about to commence.

DIONYSUS Both of you now offer up a prayer before you say your piece.

AESCHYLUS Great Demeter, who sustains my faculties, let me be worthy of your Mysteries.[6]

DIONYSUS You now, Euripides.
Present your incense, make your prayer.

EURIPIDES Thanks, but I pray to a different set of deities.

DIONYSUS Your own personal ones? Brand-new, of course?

EURIPIDES Sure.

DIONYSUS Go on then. Have recourse to those personal gods of yours.

EURIPIDES Ether—you, my grazing pastures
As well as Nous and Nosey Parker[7]
Arm me with the words for argument.

Strophe[8]

MEN Now we're all agog to hear
Two literary geniuses at work
Who have decided to go to war
In a duel of words.

6. Demeter, goddess of harvest and fertility, was celebrated in a secret mystery cult at Eleusis.

7. Ether is the personification of the upper part of the sky; Nous is mind, which the philosopher Anaxagoras had claimed was the primary force in the physical world.

8. The first part of a choral ode, in a different meter from the dialogue in the original. It is echoed, metrically, by the antistrophe.

The tongues of both will go berserk.
Their spirits are not short of valor
Nor are their minds short of vigor.
So we may safely assume that soon
One will utter something smart,
Whetted, and keen,
The other score with a brilliant thrust
And reasons torn up by the roots
Scattering words in a cloud of dust.

LEADER Very well, begin your speechifying at once.
Don't fail to make it clever, but not pretentious
or commonplace with silly riddles.
EURIPIDES Good, but before I tell you the kind of creative writer I am
let me make clear what an impostor and sham my adversary is.
What he did was set himself up to diddle
the audiences he inherited from Phrynichus,[9]
Who were already pretty far gone in imbecility.
His Prologues always begin with some solitary soul,
an Achilles, say, or a Niobe,[1]
all muffled up so you can't see their faces
and not uttering a syllable.
Quite a travesty, I'd say, of dramatic tragedy.
DIONYSUS Yes, you've got it exactly.
EURIPIDES And while they sit there mute as dummies,
the Chorus lets go in a litany
of nonstop choral baloney.
DIONYSUS All the same, I quite enjoyed his silences.
They weren't as bad as today's babbling histrionics.
EURIPIDES That's because you're easily taken in.
DIONYSUS Perhaps you're right, but how else could he have written?
EURIPIDES Nevertheless, it's sheer chicanery.
He wants the audience to sit there interminably,
all ears cocked for the moment Niobe
utters a whimper. Meanwhile the play drags on.
DIONYSUS The rascal, he took me in!
Aeschylus, I'll thank you to stop fidgeting.
EURIPIDES It's because I'm showing him up. . . .
Then after he's bumbled along like this till the play's almost done,
he lets fly with a volley of words
as formidable as a beribboned bull
flaunting crests and a shaggy scowl,

9. A tragedian who was a little older than Aeschylus; his work is lost.

1. Achilles was the greatest Greek hero at Troy; Niobe was a woman whose fourteen children were all killed by Apollo and Artemis, in punishment for her pride. Each was featured in lost tragedies by Aeschylus.

which is followed by a whole string of scarecrow weirdies
designed to make your flesh crawl.

AESCHYLUS How cruel!

EURIPIDES And never does he utter a word that makes sense.

DIONYSUS Aeschylus, do stop grinding your molars.

EURIPIDES It's all river-Scamanders,[2]
fosses and bronze-bossed bucklers
emblazoned with eagle-griffins
and great rough-hewn declarations
for which there are never explanations.

DIONYSUS Don't I know it!
"I've lain awake all through the long leviathan of the night,[3] trying to tell
what is meant by a swooping hippocockerell.[4]

AESCHYLUS It's the figurehead painted on our ships at Troy, you cretin.

DIONYSUS And I was imagining it to be Eryxis,[5] son of Philoxenus.

EURIPIDES But honestly
do we really have to have cockerells in high tragedy?

AESCHYLUS All right, you god-detested,
in what sort of themes have you invested?

EURIPIDES Well, for a start,
no hippocockerells and not a single stag crossed with a goat,
the kind of freak you might expect to see
on a strip of Persian tapestry.
None of that!
When you passed on to me the tragic art
the poor thing was loaded to the ground with bombast and fat.
Immediately, I put her on a diet
and got her weight down by a course of long walks
and little mouthfuls of syllables in fricassee.
I also fed her chopped repartee
and a concoction of verbal juice pressed out of books.
Then as a pick-me-up I dosed her with a tincture
of monodies from Cephisophon.[6]
I never shambled along like you
with the first thing that entered my noggin,
or plunged ahead leaving the audience in a stew.
The first character to walk on
explained the nature of the play and—

AESCHYLUS A better nature than yours, any day!

EURIPIDES [*ignoring the interruption*] . . . from the opening lines
I got all the characters going:
wife speaking, servant speaking,

2. The river in Troy.
3. Parodic quotation from a line in Euripides' *Hippolytus*.
4. Apparently a word used in a lost play by Aeschylus.
5. Famously ugly man.
6. A friend of Euripides and fellow poet.

and of course the boss and young girl,
not to mention the old crone.
AESCHYLUS Such vulgarity! It calls for the death penalty.
EURIPIDES Not so. It's straightforward democracy.
DIONYSUS Be that as it may, pal,
but that's a topic I'd keep off if I were you.
EURIPIDES [*gesturing to the audience*] And I taught you people
the art of conversation and—
AESCHYLUS I'll say you did, and in my view
you should have been sliced down the middle.
EURIPIDES . . . some of the nicer subtleties
like how to make words tell;
how to think and observe and decide;
how to be quick off the mark and shrewd;
how to expect the worst and face reality in the round—
AESCHYLUS I'll say you did!
EURIPIDES . . . by re-creating the workaday world we know
and things that are part of our living,
things I couldn't sham without being shown up as a fraud
because they're common knowledge. So
I never tried to bamboozle them by fibbing
or by bombast and persiflage.
I never tried to frighten them with brutes like your Cycnus and your Memnon[7]
careering about in chariots with bells clanging.
And just look at the difference between his devotees and mine;
he's got Pussy-Beard Phormisius and Sidekick Megaenetus[8]
rip-'em-uppers-treetrunk-twisters
and bushy-bearded-bugle-blowing lancers
whereas I've got Cleitophon and the clever Theramenes.[9]
DIONYSUS Theramenes? Yes, he's supersmart,
surmounts every crisis and on the brink of disaster
always manages to land on his feet.
Whatever the fix, he always throws a six.
EURIPIDES That's exactly what I meant,
Teaching people how to think,
Putting logic into art
And making it a rational thing
Which enables them to grasp
And manage almost everything
Better than they've ever done,
Especially matters in the home,
Asking "Is everything all right?"

7. Trojan warriors, killed by Achilles; they apparently featured in a lost work of Aeschylus.
8. Athenian contemporaries, a politician and a soldier, respectively.
9. Two other Athenians, both prominent in politics.

"What happened to this?" "Oh, damn!
Who the deuce went off with that?"

DIONYSUS Ye gods, you're right!
When an Athenian comes home now
He starts to bawl the servants out:
"What's happened to that cooking pot?"
"Who bit the head off that sprat?"
"The basin I bought last year is shot."
"Where's the garlic? Do you know?"
"Who's been getting at the olives?" . . .
Whereas before Euripides
They sat like gawking dummies half alive.

Antistrophe

WOMEN "Renowned Achilles, do you behold this?"[1]
How will you respond to it?
Will you lose that famous temper?
Do take care.
And not go running amok.
His gibes certainly are no joke,
So, good sir, do take care.
Do not be consumed with bile,
Furl the canvas, slacken sheets,
Shorten sail.
Slowly, slowly cruise along
Till the breeze blows soft and strong
And bears you steadily along.

LEADER [*to* AESCHYLUS] You, first of Greeks to raise pinnacles of praise to adorn all tragic waffle, open up your throttle.

AESCHYLUS I'm furious matters have come to this. My stomach turns
that I have to demean myself by arguing with this man's
pretensions, but I must because otherwise
he'll say that I'm reduced to silence. . . . So tell me this:
What are the attributes that make a poet famous?

EURIPIDES Skill and common sense, by which we are able to make ordinary people better members of the State.

AESCHYLUS And say you've done the opposite—made honest folk into libertines—what punishment would you merit?

DIONYSUS Don't ask him—death.

AESCHYLUS Just give a thought to what they were like
when they came from my hand:
six-foot heroes all of them who never shirked,
unlike your loafers and your useless jerks,

1. This was the first line of Aeschylus's lost play *Myrmidons*, about Achilles (the Myrmidons were his companions in war).

these latter-day washouts we have now.
Those others were men of spears, men of darts, the very breath
of white-plumed helmets waving and ox-hide hearts.
DIONYSUS Heavens, it's helmets now! He'll wear me out.
EURIPIDES What method did you use to make them so elite?
DIONYSUS Come on, Aeschylus, lay off being aloof.
AESCHYLUS I did it by shoving Ares into everything.
DIONYSUS Exactly how?
AESCHYLUS In my *Seven Against Thebes* . . . I contrived
to make every male who saw it hot for war.
DIONYSUS Not very nice to have connived
in making Thebans braver in battle than us Athenians![2]
You ought to be chastised.
AESCHYLUS I think not.
You Athenians could have had the same training
but you didn't think it worth it. . . .
Then, when I produced my *Persians*,[3] it sent them raving
to annihilate the enemy. So you see,
in the end I didn't come off too badly.
DIONYSUS I love the part when they heard that Darius[4] was no more,
and they couldn't celebrate enough, clapping their hands and shouting,
"Hurrah! Hurrah!"
AESCHYLUS This is the sort of thing that poets should celebrate,
and this, you may remember, is what one finds
among the best of poets from earliest times.
Orpheus revealed to us the mysteries,
and also taught us to abhor murder as a crime.
Musaeus made us aware of things like clairvoyance
and also how to cure diseases.[5]
Hesiod taught us how to work the land, when to plow,
when to sow; and as to Homer, the divine,
did he not earn his fame and undying renown
by giving us lessons on how to esteem
military training, armory, and the discipline of men?
DIONYSUS That may be so but all the same
he did pretty dismally with that airhead Pantacles[6]
who only yesterday made a fool of himself on parade
trying to fix the plumes of his helmet while he had it on his head.
AESCHYLUS I know, but surely he did inspire other brave men,
for instance, the indomitable Lamachus,[7]
who was for me the role model in courage, like Patroclus

2. Thebes was on the Spartan side, against Athens, in the Peloponnesian War.
3. The only extant historical tragedy, based on the Athenian victory against the Persians in 480 B.C.E.
4. Darius was the emperor of Persia. In Aeschylus's play, he appears as a ghost.
5. Orpheus was a legendary poet whose name became associated with a mysterious religious cult (Orphism). Musaeus was another legendary poet.
6. Unknown figure.
7. Athenian general.

and the lion-hearted Teucer[8]—the role model for all of us,
inspiring valor and giving us courage to emulate them whenever
the bugle for battle blew. . . . I never did create
strumpets like Phaedra or Stheneboea, like you.[9]
  You'll never find anywhere in anything I wrote
a lascivious bitch.

EURIPIDES Don't I know it! You left poor Aphrodite[1] out.

AESCHYLUS I should think so, whereas you
have let her squash you and your whole household flat.

DIONYSUS He's got you there, Euripides, for you've been hit by the
same fate you invented for other people's wives.[2]

EURIPIDES [*ignoring the insult*] You tiresome man,
what harm to the community was ever done
by my *Stheneboea*?

AESCHYLUS You put decent women married to decent men
in a situation like that of Bellerephon
that drives them to suicide.

EURIPIDES All right, but I didn't invent the plot of Phaedra.

AESCHYLUS Worse luck, no! But the poet shouldn't side
with what is evil and display it on the stage like a demonstration.
  Children may have teachers but adults have the poet
and the poet ought to keep things on a higher plane.

EURIPIDES [*sarcastically*] As high as Mount Lycabettus, no doubt, or lofty
Parnassus, and they're to be our instructors in the good?
My word! Can't you do your teaching in the language of men?

AESCHYLUS Listen, you miserable heel, the lofty thought and the high ideal
call for a language to match,
and if the deities are clothed in rare attire
their language, too, should be out of the ordinary.
  This is where I blazed a trail,
which you've managed to undermine.

EURIPIDES How have I?

AESCHYLUS For a start, by the way you dress your royalty.
They're all in rags like any pitiful wretch.

EURIPIDES But whom do I hurt by that?

AESCHYLUS Well, to begin with,
it tempts the rich to shirk their responsibility:
a wealthy tycoon evades the funding of a warship
by dressing up in rags and whimpering about his poverty.[3]

DIONYSUS Yes, underneath the rags, by Demeter,
he's in lovely fleecy underwear
and you see him splashing out on fish in the market square.

8. Patroclus was Achilles' closest friend; Teucer was the best Greek archer at Troy.
9. Phaedra fell in love with her stepson, Hippolytus; Stheneboea, a married woman, tried to seduce the young hero Bellerophon, and when rejected, accused him of rape. Euripides wrote notorious tragedies about them, including *Stheneboea* (which is lost), and *Hippolytus* (which survives).
1. Goddess of sex.
2. Apparently there was a rumor that Euripides' wife was having an affair.
3. Rich Athenian citizens had an obligation to contribute to public works—for instance, by equipping warships.

AESCHYLUS What's more, you've taught people to prattle and gab,
emptying the wrestling schools and turning the young men's
bottoms into flab
as they prattle away—and you've encouraged the crew
of the *Paralus*[4] to answer their officers back.
But in the old days when I was alive all they knew
was how to clamor for their grub
and shout "Ship ahoy" and "Heave-to."

DIONYSUS That's exactly it, by Apollo.
Now they fart in the bottom bencher's face
shit on their messmates and go off with people's clothes when on shore.
What's more,
they give lip to their commanders and refuse to row,
so the ship goes drifting to and fro.

AESCHYLUS What bad behavior is he not responsible for?
Showing us a woman acting as a pander,
Or producing a baby in the very temple,
And others even coupling with their brothers
And saying that "something living's not alive,"[5]
The consequences naturally are simple:
A society swamped by lawyers' clerks
And buffoons lying their heads off to the people,
And, because nobody takes any exercise,
When it comes to running with a torch, no one tries.

DIONYSUS You couldn't be righter. I almost doubled up
At the Panathenaea[6] laughing when
A slow coach of a booby thumped along,
Stooped, white as a sheet, fat.
And when he got to the Gates by the potter's field
People whacked him on his belly and butt
And ribs and sides and all his miserable hide.
As he scurried along he began to fart
With gas enough to keep his torch alight.

Strophe

MEN Great is the struggle, grand the tussle,
The war's now under way.
One of them lands a hefty biff.
The other ducks with a swing
In counterattack. It's hard to say
Which of them will win. . . .

4. Ship used for official Athenian missions.
5. All events in plays by Euripides. The nurse in *Hippolytus* acts as a pander, trying to get Phaedra and her stepson together; Auge, in the lost *Auge*, had a baby in a temple; Canace had sex with her brother in the lost *Aeolus*. The source and significance of the quotation is unclear.
6. A huge citywide festival.

Hey, you two, you've not fought enough,
Many more buffetings are due
And plenty of cerebral stuff.
Whatever it is you're fighting about
Go at it hard and argue it out.
Flense the old and strip for the new.
Get down to the nitty-gritty
And something erudite.

Antistrophe

WOMEN And if you're afraid that people won't know
What it is all about
And have no inkling, are unable to follow
The twists of an argument,
Don't give it a thought; as a matter of fact
Things are different today.
Everyone's an expert now
And knows his book of rules by heart
And every nicety
Is fully briefed and clever as well,
And sharply honed, as we all know,
So that's not something to worry about.
Don't be afraid—enjoy it all.
People are primed to the hilt.[7]

7. The competition continues for some time, and includes a contest in which each poet weighs his words against the other's words on a big set of scales. In the end, Dionysus pronounces Aeschylus the winner.

PLATO

Composed around 370 B.C.E. by the brilliant Greek philosopher Plato, *Phaedrus* is a dialogue about love, passion, madness, and rhetoric, which features Plato's teacher, Socrates, and Socrates' young friend Phaedrus. The last passage of the text focuses on the arts of writing and of rhetoric, which Socrates claims are quite different from true wisdom.

From Phaedrus[1]

SOCRATES Well, do you know how best to please god when you either use words or discuss them in general?

PHAEDRUS Not at all. Do you?

SOCRATES I can tell you what I've heard the ancients said, though they alone know the truth. However, if we could discover that ourselves, would we still care about the speculations of other people?

PHAEDRUS That's a silly question. Still, tell me what you say you've heard.

SOCRATES Well, this is what I've heard. Among the ancient gods of Naucratis[2] in Egypt there was one to whom the bird called the ibis is sacred. The name of that divinity was Theuth,[3] and it was he who first discovered number and calculation, geometry and astronomy, as well as the games of checkers and dice, and, above all else, writing.

Now the king of all Egypt at that time was Thamus, who lived in the great city in the upper region that the Greeks call Egyptian Thebes; Thamus is what they call Ammon.[4] Theuth came to exhibit his arts to him and urged him to disseminate them to all the Egyptians. Thamus asked him about the usefulness of each art, and while Theuth was explaining it, Thamus praised him for whatever he thought was right in his explanations and criticized him for whatever he thought was wrong.

The story goes that Thamus said much to Theuth, both for and against each art, which it would take too long to repeat. But when they came to writing, Theuth said: "O King, here is something that, once learned, will make the Egyptians wiser and will improve their memory; I have discovered a potion[5] for memory and for wisdom." Thamus, however, replied: "O most expert Theuth, one man can give birth to the elements of an art, but only another can judge how they can benefit or harm those who will use them. And now, since you are the father of writing, your affection for it has made you describe its effects as the opposite of what they really are. In fact, it will introduce forgetfulness into the soul of those who learn it: they will not practice using their memory because they will put their trust in writing, which is external and depends on signs that belong to others, instead of trying to remember from the inside, completely on their own. You have not discovered a potion for remembering, but for reminding; you provide your students with the appearance of wisdom, not with its reality. Your invention will enable them to hear many things without being properly taught, and they will imagine that they have come to know much while for the most part they will know nothing. And they will be difficult to get along with, since they will merely appear to be wise instead of really being so."

1. Translated by Alexander Nehamas and Paul Woodruff. The philosopher Socrates and a young friend called Phaedrus have gone for a walk outside the city of Athens, eager to discuss a speech Phaedrus has just heard by the famous orator Lysias. After a discussion of rhetoric, in which Socrates questions the value of Lysias's work on the grounds that it is more about impressive appearances than truth, the conversation turns to writing.
2. A Greek trading colony.
3. The Egyptian god of writing, measurement, and calculation; also spelled Thot or Thoth.
4. Ammon is the king of the Egyptian gods.
5. The word for potion, *pharmakon*, can mean "drug," "medicine," "poison," or "cure."

PHAEDRUS Socrates, you're very good at making up stories from Egypt or wherever else you want!

SOCRATES But, my friend, the priests of the temple of Zeus at Dodona say that the first prophecies were the words of an oak. Everyone who lived at that time, not being as wise as you young ones are today, found it rewarding enough in their simplicity to listen to an oak or even a stone, so long as it was telling the truth, while it seems to make a difference to you, Phaedrus, who is speaking and where he comes from. Why, though, don't you just consider whether what he says is right or wrong?

PHAEDRUS I deserved that, Socrates. And I agree that the Theban king was correct about writing.

SOCRATES Well, then, those who think they can leave written instructions for an art, as well as those who accept them, thinking that writing can yield results that are clear or certain, must be quite naive and truly ignorant of Ammon's prophetic judgment: otherwise, how could they possibly think that words that have been written down can do more than remind those who already know what the writing is about?

PHAEDRUS Quite right.

SOCRATES You know, Phaedrus, writing shares a strange feature with painting. The offspring of painting stand there as if they are alive, but if anyone asks them anything, they remain most solemnly silent. The same is true of written words. You'd think they were speaking as if they had some understanding, but if you question anything that has been said because you want to learn more, it continues to signify just that very same thing forever. When it has once been written down, every discourse roams about everywhere, reaching indiscriminately those with understanding no less than those who have no business with it, and it doesn't know to whom it should speak and to whom it should not. And when it is faulted and attacked unfairly, it always needs its father's support; alone, it can neither defend itself nor come to its own support.

PHAEDRUS You are absolutely right about that, too.

SOCRATES Now tell me, can we discern another kind of discourse, a legitimate brother of this one? Can we say how it comes about, and how it is by nature better and more capable?

PHAEDRUS Which one is that? How do you think it comes about?

SOCRATES It is a discourse that is written down, with knowledge, in the soul of the listener; it can defend itself, and it knows for whom it should speak and for whom it should remain silent.

PHAEDRUS You mean the living, breathing discourse of the man who knows, of which the written one can be fairly called an image.

SOCRATES Absolutely right. And tell me this. Would a sensible farmer, who cared about his seeds and wanted them to yield fruit, plant them in all seriousness in the gardens of Adonis in the middle of the summer and enjoy watching them bear fruit within seven days? Or would he do this as an amusement and in honor of the holiday, if he did it at all? Wouldn't he use his knowledge of farming to plant the seeds he cared for when it was appropriate and be content if they bore fruit seven months later?

PHAEDRUS That's how he would handle those he was serious about, Socrates, quite differently from the others, as you say.

SOCRATES Now what about the man who knows what is just, noble, and good? Shall we say that he is less sensible with his seeds than the farmer is with his?

PHAEDRUS Certainly not.

SOCRATES Therefore, he won't be serious about writing them in ink, sowing them, through a pen, with words that are as incapable of speaking in their own defense as they are of teaching the truth adequately.

PHAEDRUS That wouldn't be likely.

SOCRATES Certainly not. When he writes, it's likely he will sow gardens of letters for the sake of amusing himself, storing up reminders for himself "when he reaches forgetful old age" and for everyone who wants to follow in his footsteps, and will enjoy seeing them sweetly blooming. And when others turn to different amusements, watering themselves with drinking parties and everything else that goes along with them, he will rather spend his time amusing himself with the things I have just described.

PHAEDRUS Socrates, you are contrasting a vulgar amusement with the very noblest—with the amusement of a man who can while away his time telling stories of justice and the other matters you mentioned.

SOCRATES That's just how it is, Phaedrus. But it is much nobler to be serious about these matters, and use the art of dialectic. The dialectician chooses a proper soul and plants and sows within it discourse accompanied by knowledge—discourse capable of helping itself as well as the man who planted it, which is not barren but produces a seed from which more discourse grows in the character of others. Such discourse makes the seed forever immortal and renders the man who has it as happy as any human being can be.

PHAEDRUS What you describe is really much nobler still.

SOCRATES And now that we have agreed about this, Phaedrus, we are finally able to decide the issue.

PHAEDRUS What issue is that?

SOCRATES The issue which brought us to this point in the first place: We wanted to examine the attack made on Lysias on account of his writing speeches, and to ask which speeches are written artfully and which not. Now, I think that we have answered that question clearly enough.

PHAEDRUS So it seemed; but remind me again how we did it.

SOCRATES First, you must know the truth concerning everything you are speaking or writing about; you must learn how to define each thing in itself; and, having defined it, you must know how to divide it into kinds until you reach something indivisible. Second, you must understand the nature of the soul, along the same lines; you must determine which kind of speech is appropriate to each kind of soul, prepare and arrange your speech accordingly, and offer a complex and elaborate speech to a complex soul and a simple speech to a simple one. Then, and only then, will you be able to use speech artfully, to the extent that its nature allows it to be used that way, either in order to teach or in order to persuade. This is the whole point of the argument we have been making.

PHAEDRUS Absolutely. That is exactly how it seemed to us.

SOCRATES Now how about whether it's noble or shameful to give or write a speech—when it could be fairly said to be grounds for reproach, and when not? Didn't what we said just a little while ago make it clear—

PHAEDRUS What was that?

SOCRATES That if Lysias or anybody else ever did or ever does write—privately or for the public, in the course of proposing some law—a political document which he believes to embody clear knowledge of lasting importance, then this writer deserves reproach, whether anyone says so or not. For to be unaware of the difference between a dream-image and the reality of what is just and unjust, good and bad, must truly be grounds for reproach even if the crowd praises it with one voice.

PHAEDRUS It certainly must be.

SOCRATES On the other hand, take a man who thinks that a written discourse on any subject can only be a great amusement, that no discourse worth serious attention has ever been written in verse or prose, and that those that are recited in public without questioning and explanation, in the manner of the rhapsodes[6] are given only in order to produce conviction. He believes that at their very best these can only serve as reminders to those who already know. And he also thinks that only what is said for the sake of understanding and learning, what is truly written in the soul concerning what is just, noble, and good can be clear, perfect, and worth serious attention: Such discourses should be called his own legitimate children, first the discourse he may have discovered already within himself and then its sons and brothers who may have grown naturally in other souls insofar as these are worthy; to the rest, he turns his back. Such a man, Phaedrus, would be just what you and I both would pray to become.

PHAEDRUS I wish and pray for things to be just as you say.

SOCRATES Well, then: our playful amusement regarding discourse is complete. Now you go and tell Lysias that we came to the spring which is sacred to the Nymphs and heard words charging us to deliver a message to Lysias and anyone else who composes speeches, as well as to Homer and anyone else who has composed poetry either spoken or sung, and third, to Solon[7] and anyone else who writes political documents that he calls laws: If any one of you has composed these things with a knowledge of the truth, if you can defend your writing when you are challenged, and if you can yourself make the argument that your writing is of little worth, then you must be called by a name derived not from these writings but rather from those things that you are seriously pursuing.

PHAEDRUS What name, then, would you give such a man?

SOCRATES To call him wise, Phaedrus, seems to me too much, and proper only for a god. To call him wisdom's lover—a philosopher—or something similar would fit him better and be more seemly.

PHAEDRUS That would be quite appropriate.

SOCRATES On the other hand, if a man has nothing more valuable than what he has composed or written, spending long hours twisting it around, pasting parts together and taking them apart—wouldn't you be right to call him a poet or a speech writer or an author of laws?

6. Performers who recited portions of poetry from memory for entertainment.

7. Famous Athenian lawmaker.

PHAEDRUS Of course.

SOCRATES Tell that, then, to your friend.

PHAEDRUS And what about you? What shall you do? We must surely not forget your own friend.

SOCRATES Whom do you mean?

PHAEDRUS The beautiful Isocrates.[8] What are you going to tell him, Socrates? What shall we say he is?

SOCRATES Isocrates is still young, Phaedrus. But I want to tell you what I foresee for him.

PHAEDRUS What is that?

SOCRATES It seems to me that by his nature he can outdo anything that Lysias has accomplished in his speeches; and he also has a nobler character. So I wouldn't be at all surprised if, as he gets older and continues writing speeches of the sort he is composing now, he makes everyone who has ever attempted to compose a speech seem like a child in comparison. Even more so if such work no longer satisfies him and a higher, divine impulse leads him to more important things. For nature, my friend, has placed the love of wisdom in his mind.

That is the message I will carry to my beloved, Isocrates, from the gods of this place; and you have your own message for your Lysias.

PHAEDRUS So it shall be. But let's be off, since the heat has died down a bit.

SOCRATES Shouldn't we offer a prayer to the gods here before we leave?

PHAEDRUS Of course.

SOCRATES O dear Pan[9] and all the other gods of this place, grant that I may be beautiful inside. Let all my external possessions be in friendly harmony with what is within. May I consider the wise man rich. As for gold, let me have as much as a moderate man could bear and carry with him.

Do we need anything else, Phaedrus? I believe my prayer is enough for me.

PHAEDRUS Make it a prayer for me as well. Friends have everything in common.

SOCRATES Let's be off.

8. Athenian teacher and orator.

9. God of the countryside.

ARISTOTLE

The Greek philosopher Aristotle (384–322 B.C.E.), a pupil of Plato's, founded a school of his own, and wrote on an enormous range of subjects, from ethics and politics to zoology, metaphysics, physics, logic, and mathematics. His extant works, unlike those of **Plato**, are based on lecture notes, and are therefore written in a somewhat dry style. His study of poetry (*Poetics*, one of his shorter treatises) focuses on the component features of the best tragedy, and offers a defense of good dramatic poetry against the Platonic charge that it can be morally and emotionally corrupting.

From Poetics[1]

* * * Thus, Tragedy is an imitation of an action that is serious, complete, and possessing magnitude; in embellished language, each kind of which is used separately in the different parts; in the mode of action and not narrated; and effecting through pity and fear [what we call] the *catharsis*[2] of such emotions. By "embellished language" I mean language having rhythm and melody, and by "separately in different parts" I mean that some parts of a play are carried on solely in metrical speech while others again are sung.

The constituent parts of tragedy. Since the imitation is carried out in the dramatic mode by the personages themselves, it necessarily follows, first, that the arrangement of Spectacle will be a part of tragedy, and next, that Melody and Language will be parts, since these are the media in which they effect the imitation. By "language" I mean precisely the composition of the verses, by "melody" only that which is perfectly obvious. And since tragedy is the imitation of an action and is enacted by men in action, these persons must necessarily possess certain qualities of Character and Thought, since these are the basis for our ascribing qualities to the actions themselves—character and thought are two natural causes of actions—and it is in their actions that men universally meet with success or failure. The imitation of the action is the Plot. By plot I here mean the combination of the events; Character is that in virtue of which we say that the personages are of such and such a quality; and Thought is present in everything in their utterances that aims to prove a point or that expresses an opinion. Necessarily, therefore, there are in tragedy as a whole, considered as a special form, six constituent elements, viz. Plot, Character, Language, Thought, Spectacle, and Melody. Of these elements, two [Language and Melody] are the

1. Translated by James Hutton, who has added bracketed text for clarity.
2. *Catharsis* is used elsewhere in Aristotle as a medical term, meaning "purgation." Tragedy "purges" the spectators' emotions. Aristotle does not explain exactly what this means.

media in which they effect the imitation, one [Spectacle] is the *manner*, and three [Plot, Character, Thought] are the *objects* they imitate; and besides these there are no other parts. So then they employ these six forms, not just some of them so to speak; for every drama has spectacle, character, plot, language, melody, and thought in the same sense, but the most important of them is the organization of the events [the plot].

Plot and character. For tragedy is not an imitation of men but of actions and of life. It is in action that happiness and unhappiness are found, and the end[3] we aim at is a kind of activity, not a quality; in accordance with their characters men are of such and such a quality, in accordance with their actions they are fortunate or the reverse. Consequently, it is not for the purpose of presenting their characters that the agents engage in action, but rather it is for the sake of their actions that they take on the characters they have. Thus, what happens—that is, the plot—is the end for which a tragedy exists, and the end or purpose is the most important thing of all. What is more, without action there could not be a tragedy, but there could be without characterization. * * *

Now that the parts are established, let us next discuss what qualities the plot should have, since plot is the primary and most important part of tragedy. I have posited that tragedy is an imitation of an action that is a whole and complete in itself and of a certain magnitude—for a thing may be a whole, and yet have no magnitude to speak of. Now a thing is a whole if it has a beginning, a middle, and an end. A beginning is that which does not come necessarily after something else, but after which it is natural for another thing to exist or come to be. An end, on the contrary, is that which naturally comes after something else, either as its necessary sequel or as its usual [and hence probable] sequel, but itself has nothing after it. A middle is that which both comes after something else and has another thing following it. A well-constructed plot, therefore, will neither begin at some chance point nor end at some chance point, but will observe the principles here stated. * * *

Contrary to what some people think, a plot is not ipso facto a unity if it revolves about one man. Many things, indeed an endless number of things, happen to any one man some of which do not go together to form a unity, and similarly among the actions one man performs there are many that do not go together to produce a single unified action. Those poets seem all to have erred, therefore, who have composed a *Heracleid*, a *Theseid*, and other such poems, it being their idea evidently that since Heracles was one man, their plot was bound to be unified. * * *

From what has already been said, it will be evident that the poet's function is not to report things that have happened, but rather to tell of such things as might happen, things that are possibilities by virtue of being in themselves inevitable or probable. Thus the difference between the historian and the poet is not that the historian employs prose and the poet verse—the work of Herodotus[4] could be put into verse, and it would be no less a history with verses than without them; rather the difference is that the one tells of things that have

3. Purpose.
4. Historian of the Persian Wars (ca. 480–430/425? B.C.E.).

been and the other of such things as might be. Poetry, therefore, is a more philosophical and a higher thing than history, in that poetry tends rather to express the universal, history rather the particular fact. A universal is: The sort of thing that (in the circumstances) a certain kind of person will say or do either probably or necessarily, which in fact is the universal that poetry aims for (with the addition of names for the persons); a particular, on the other hand is: What Alcibiades[5] did or had done to him. * * *

Among plots and actions of the simple type, the episodic form is the worst. I call episodic a plot in which the episodes follow one another in no probable or inevitable sequence. Plots of this kind are constructed by bad poets on their own account, and by good poets on account of the actors; since they are composing entries for a competitive exhibition, they stretch the plot beyond what it can bear and are often compelled, therefore, to dislocate the natural order. * * *

Some plots are simple, others complex; indeed the actions of which the plots are imitation are at once so differentiated to begin with. Assuming the action to be continuous and unified, as already defined, I call that action simple in which the change of fortune takes place without a reversal or recognition, and that action complex in which the change of fortune involves a recognition or a reversal or both. These events [recognitions and reversals] ought to be so rooted in the very structure of the plot that they follow from the preceding events as their inevitable or probable outcome; for there is a vast difference between following from and merely following after. * * *

Reversal (Peripety) is, as aforesaid, a change from one state of affairs to its exact opposite, and this, too, as I say, should be in conformance with probability or necessity. For example, in *Oedipus*, the messenger[6] comes to cheer Oedipus by relieving him of fear with regard to his mother, but by revealing his true identity, does just the opposite of this. * * *

Recognition, as the word itself indicates, is a change from ignorance to knowledge, leading either to friendship or to hostility on the part of those persons who are marked for good fortune or bad. The best form of recognition is that which is accompanied by a reversal, as in the example from *Oedipus*. * * *

Next in order after the points I have just dealt with, it would seem necessary to specify what one should aim at and what avoid in the construction of plots, and what it is that will produce the effect proper to tragedy.

Now since in the finest kind of tragedy the structure should be complex and not simple, and since it should also be a representation of terrible and piteous events (that being the special mark of this type of imitation), in the first place, it is evident that good men ought not to be shown passing from prosperity to misfortune, for this does not inspire either pity or fear, but only revulsion; nor evil men rising from ill fortune to prosperity, for this is the most untragic plot of all—it lacks every requirement, in that it neither elicits human sympathy nor stirs pity or fear. And again, neither should an extremely wicked man be seen falling from prosperity into misfortune, for a plot so constructed might indeed call forth human sympathy, but would not excite pity or fear, since the first is felt for a person whose misfortune is undeserved and the second for someone

5. A brilliant but unscrupulous Athenian statesman (ca. 450–404 B.C.E.).

6. The Corinthian herdsman in Sophocles' *Oedipus the King*.

like ourselves—pity for the man suffering undeservedly, fear for the man like ourselves—and hence neither pity nor fear would be aroused in this case. We are left with the man whose place is between these extremes. Such is the man who on the one hand is not pre-eminent in virtue and justice, and yet on the other hand does not fall into misfortune through vice or depravity, but falls because of some mistake;[7] one among the number of the highly renowned and prosperous, such as Oedipus and Thyestes[8] and other famous men from families like theirs.

It follows that the plot which achieves excellence will necessarily be single in outcome and not, as some contend, double, and will consist in a change of fortune, not from misfortune to prosperity, but the opposite from prosperity to misfortune, occasioned not by depravity, but by some great mistake on the part of one who is either such as I have described or better than this rather than worse. (What actually has taken place confirms this; for though at first the poets accepted whatever myths came to hand, today the finest tragedies are founded upon the stories of only a few houses, being concerned, for example, with Alcmeon, Oedipus, Orestes, Meleager, Thyestes, Telephus, and such others as have chanced to suffer terrible things or to do them.) So, then, tragedy having this construction is the finest kind of tragedy from an artistic point of view. And consequently, those persons fall into the same error who bring it as a charge against Euripides that this is what he does in his tragedies and that most of his plays have unhappy endings. For this is in fact the right procedure, as I have said; and the best proof is that on the stage and in the dramatic contests, plays of this kind seem the most tragic, provided they are successfully worked out, and Euripides, even if in everything else his management is faulty, seems at any rate the most tragic of the poets. * * *

In the characters and the plot construction alike, one must strive for that which is either necessary or probable, so that whatever a character of any kind says or does may be the sort of thing such a character will inevitably or probably say or do and the events of the plot may follow one after another either inevitably or with probability. (Obviously, then, the denouement of the plot should arise from the plot itself and not be brought about "from the machine," as it is in *Medea* and in the embarkation scene in the *Iliad*.[9] The machine is to be used for matters lying outside the drama, either antecedents of the action which a human being cannot know, or things subsequent to the action that

7. The Greek word is *hamartia*. It has sometimes been translated as "flaw" (hence the expression "tragic flaw") and thought of as a moral defect, but comparison with Aristotle's use of the word in other contexts suggests strongly that he means by it "mistake" or "error" (of judgment).

8. Brother of Atreus and his rival over the kingship of Argos. Pretending to be reconciled, Atreus gave a feast at which he served Thyestes' own sons to their father. Thyestes' only surviving son, Aegisthus, later helped murder Atreus's son Agamemnon.

9. The reference is to an incident in the second book of the *Iliad*: an attempt of the Greek rank and file to return home and abandon the siege is arrested by the intervention of Athena. If it were a drama, she would appear literally as the *deus ex machina* ("god from the machine"), the pulley that was employed in the theater to show the gods flying in space. It has come to mean any implausible way of solving complications of the plot. In Euripides' play, Medea escapes from Corinth on the machine, in her magic chariot.

have to be prophesied and announced; for we accept it that the gods see everything. Within the events of the plot itself, however, there should be nothing unreasonable, or if there is, it should be kept outside the play proper, as is done in the *Oedipus* of Sophocles.) * * *

The chorus in tragedy. The chorus ought to be regarded as one of the actors, and as being part of the whole and integrated into performance, not in Euripides' way but in that of Sophocles. In the other poets, the choral songs have no more relevance to the plot than if they belonged to some other play. And so nowadays, following the practice introduced by Agathon,[1] the chorus merely sings interludes. But what difference is there between the singing of interludes and taking a speech or even an entire episode from one play and inserting it into another?

1. A younger contemporary of Euripides; most of his plays were produced in the 4th century B.C.E.

CALLIMACHUS

The hyperlearned poet and librarian Callimachus (third century B.C.E.) was a Greek born in Libya who spent most of his life in the cosmopolitan Greek-Egyptian city of Alexandria. *Aetia* ("Causes")—a poem of which only part survives—was originally four books long, and told the mythical stories of the origins of various cults and traditions. The beginning, included here, is a poetic manifesto outlining Callimachus's commitment to short, careful, precise compositions over long, unwieldy, and derivative forms of poetry.

From Aetia[1]

The Telchines,[2] who know nothing
of poetry and hate the Muses, often
snipe at me, because it's not a monotonous
uninterrupted poem featuring kings
and heroes in thousands of verses
that I've produced, driving my song instead
for little stretches, like a child,

1. Translated by Frank Nisetich. Only parts of this poem survive.

2. Mythical monsters; the name is applied here to Callimachus's critics.

though the tale of my years
is not brief.
Well, here's what I say
to the Telchines:
'Born eaters
of your own hearts, [the Coan poet][3]
was not, admittedly, a man of few verses
but all the same his bountiful Demeter far
outweighs the woman he celebrated
at length.
And of the two books
Mimnermus[4] wrote, not the one that tells
of the big woman, but the one composed
with a delicate touch, displays
the poet at his sweetest.
Let the crane
who revels in the blood of Pygmies fly
far from Egypt, and the Massagetai
shoot at the Mede long range:[5] nightingales
are sweeter like this.
To hell with you, then,
spiteful brood of Jealousy: from now on
we'll judge poetry by the art,
not by the mile. And don't expect a song
to rush from my lips with a roar:
it's Zeus' job, not mine, to thunder.'
The very first time I sat down and put
a writing tablet on my lap, my own
Lykian[6] Apollo said to me:
'Make your sacrifice
as fat as you can, poet, but keep
your Muse on slender rations. And see that you go
where no hackneys plod: avoid the ruts
carved in the boulevard, even if it means
driving along a narrower path.'
And so I sing for those
who love the shrill cicada's cry, and hate
the clamour of asses. Let someone else,
loud as any long-eared brute, bray
for their amusement. As for me,
I would be small and winged—yes,
even so, to sing

3. Philitas, a scholar-poet a generation older than Callimachus. Apparently, he and Mimnermus (below) wrote both long and shorter works; these have not survived.

4. Greek elegiac poet from the 7th century B.C.E.

5. The Pygmies were a legendary race of tiny people who made war against cranes. The Massagetai were a northern race famous for their archery; the Mede were also known for skill in archery.

6. The epithet may suggest either "wolf killer" or "god of light." Apollo is the god of poetry.

with dew upon my lips, the food
of morning culled from air divine, shedding
the years that weigh on me
like Sicily on Enkelados.[7]
The Muses
won't repulse in grey old age
the man on whom they smiled in his youth.

7. Zeus threw the island of Sicily on top of the giant Enkelados.

HORACE

The Roman poet Horace (65–8 B.C.E.) was roughly contemporary with Virgil (whom he knew), and was the most prominent lyric poet during the time of Emperor Augustus. He was from a modest background (son of a freed slave), but made his way up the social ladder through education and talent. His *Odes* were a virtuosic technical achievement, transferring complex Greek meters into Latin. In the last poem (Ode 30) in the third book, he celebrates his own achievement, presenting poetry—usually written on papyrus scrolls—as more glorious and permanent than inscriptions on bronze tablets, which would have included legal and administrative documents. His *Ars Poetica* ("art of poetry") is a treatise in verse on the norms for successful poetry.

Ode 30[1]

[*Exegi Monumentum*]

I have built a monument more lasting than bronze
and set higher than the pyramids of kings.
It cannot be destroyed by gnawing rain
or wild north wind, by the procession

of unnumbered years or by the flight of time.
I shall not wholly die. A great part of me
will escape Libitina.[2] My fame will grow,
ever-renewed in time to come, as long as

1. Translated by David West. The *Odes* have no titles: the translator has used the first two words of the Latin original ("I have built a monument") as a title.
2. Goddess of death.

the priest climbs the Capitol with the silent Virgin.[3]
I shall be spoken of where fierce Aufidus thunders
and where Daunus, poor in water,
rules the country people.[4] From humble beginnings

I was able to be the first to bring Aeolian song
to Italian measures.[5] Take the proud honour
well-deserved, Melpomene, and be pleased
to circle my hair with the laurel of Delphi.[6]

From Ars Poetica[1]

Suppose a painter decided to set a human head
on a horse's neck, and to cover the body with coloured feathers,
combining limbs so that the top of a lovely woman
came to a horrid end in the tail of an inky fish—
when invited to view the piece, my friends, could you stifle your laughter?
Well, dear Pisos,[2] I hope you'll agree that a book containing
fantastic ideas, like those conceived by delirious patients,
where top and bottom never combine to form a whole,
is exactly like that picture.
'Painters and poets alike
have always enjoyed the right to take what risks they please.'
I know; I grant that freedom and claim the same in return,
but not to the point of allowing wild to couple with tame,
or showing a snake and a bird, or a lamb and tiger, as partners.

Often you'll find a serious work of large pretensions
with here and there a purple patch that is sewn on
to give a vivid and striking effect—lines describing
Diana's grove and altar,[3] or a stream which winds and hurries
along its beauteous vale, or the river Rhine, or a rainbow.
But here they are out of place. Perhaps you can draw a cypress;
what good is that, if the subject you've been engaged to paint
is a shipwrecked sailor swimming for his life? The job began
as a wine-jar; why as the wheel revolves does it end as a jug?
So make what you like, provided the thing is a unified whole.

3. Alludes to the religious rituals of Rome, which often involved a climb up the Capitoline hill, to the temple at the top, by the chief priest and the Vestal Virgins (holy girls vowed to religious chastity).
4. Aufidus is a river in Apulia, near Horace's home; Daunus is a legendary early king of the area.
5. Horace was the first Roman poet to adapt the Greek ("Aeolian") choral meters of Sappho and Alcaeus into Latin.
6. Melpomene is the name of the tragic muse, here used for any muse. Delphi and the laurel tree are sacred to Apollo, god of poetry.
1. Translated by Niall Rudd.
2. Roman noblemen, a father and two sons; apparently patrons of Horace's.
3. Diana (Artemis in Greek) is the goddess associated with the countryside, hunting, and the moon.

Poets in the main (I'm speaking to a father and his excellent sons)
are baffled by the outer form of what's right. I strive to be brief,
and become obscure; I try for smoothness, and instantly lose
muscle and spirit; to aim at grandeur invites inflation;
excessive caution or fear of the wind induces grovelling.
The man who brings in marvels to vary a simple theme
is painting a dolphin among the trees, a boar in the billows.
Avoiding a fault will lead to error if art is missing.

Any smith in the area round Aemilius' school[4]
will render nails in bronze and imitate wavy hair;
the final effect eludes him because he doesn't know how
to shape a whole. If I wanted to do a piece of sculpture,
I'd no more copy him than I'd welcome a broken nose,
when my jet black eyes and jet black hair had won admiration.

You writers must pick a subject that suits your powers,
giving lengthy thought to what your shoulders are built for
and what they aren't. If your choice of theme is within your scope,
you won't have to seek for fluent speech or lucid arrangement.
Arrangement's virtue and value reside, if I'm not mistaken,
in this: to say right now what has to be said right now,
postponing and leaving out a great deal for the present.

The writer pledged to produce a poem must also be subtle
and careful in linking words, preferring this to that.
When a skilful collocation renews a familiar word,
that is distinguished writing. If novel terms are demanded
to introduce obscure material, then you will have the
chance to invent words which the apron-wearing Cethegi[5]
never heard; such a right will be given, if it's not abused.
New and freshly created words are also acceptable
when channelled from Greek, provided the trickle is small. For why
should Romans refuse to Virgil and Varius what they've allowed
to Caecilius and Plautus?[6] And why should they grumble if I succeed
in bringing a little in, when the diction of Ennius and Cato[7]
showered wealth on our fathers' language and gave us unheard of
names for things? We have always enjoyed and always will
the right to produce terms which are marked with the current stamp.
Just as the woods change their leaves as year follows year
(the earliest fall, *and others spring up to take their place*)
so the old generation of words passes away,

4. A school for gladiators, near which craftsmen and artists worked.

5. An ancient Roman family who would have worn wraparound skirts rather than the togas worn by aristocrats in Horace's day.

6. Virgil (author of the *Aeneid*) and Varius were both writers contemporary with Horace; Caecilius and Plautus were older Roman writers, from the 2nd century B.C.E.

7. Ennius was an early Roman epic poet. Cato the Elder, a politician and moralist from the 3rd century B.C.E., is cited as an upholder of traditional Latin and of traditional Roman morality.

and the newly arrived bloom and flourish like human children.
We and our works are owed to death, whether our navy
is screened from the northern gales by Neptune[8] welcomed ashore—
a royal feat—or a barren swamp which knew the oar
feeds neighbouring cities and feels the weight of the plough,
or a river which used to damage the crops has altered its course
and learned a better way. Man's structures will crumble;
so how can the glory and charm of speech remain for ever?
Many a word long dead will be born again, and others
which now enjoy prestige will fade, if Usage requires it.
She controls the laws and rules and standards of language.

The feats of kings and captains and the grim battles they fought—
the proper metre for such achievements was shown by Homer.
The couplet of longer and shorter lines provided a framework,
first for lament, then for acknowledging a prayer's fulfilment.
Scholars, however, dispute the name of the first poet
to compose small elegiacs; the case is still undecided.
Fury gave Archilochus[9] her own missile—the iambus.
The foot was found to fit the sock and the stately buskin,[1]
because it conveyed the give and take of dialogue; also
it drowned the noise of the pit and was naturally suited to action.
The lyre received from the Muse the right to celebrate gods[2]
and their sons, victorious boxers, horses first in the race,
the ache of a lover's heart, and uninhibited drinking.
If, through lack of knowledge or talent, I fail to observe
the established genres and styles, then why am I hailed as a poet?
And why, from misplaced shyness, do I shrink from learning the trade?

A comic subject will not be presented in tragic metres.
Likewise Thyestes' banquet is far too grand a tale
for verse of an everyday kind which is more akin to the sock.[3]
Everything has its appropriate place, and it ought to stay there.
Sometimes, however, even Comedy raises her voice,
as angry Chremes[4] storms along in orotund phrases;
and sometimes a tragic actor grieves in ordinary language—
Peleus and Telephus (one an exile, the other a beggar)[5]
both abandon their bombast and words of a foot and a half
when they hope to touch the listener's heart with their sad appeals.

8. God of the sea.
9. Greek satirical poet (7th century B.C.E.), who wrote in iambic meter. The iamb ("iambus") is a metrical unit, or "foot."
1. Iambic meter was also, later, used for drama. The "sock" means comedy, the "stately buskin" means tragedy—particular types of footwear were characteristic of the two genres.
2. Lyric meters were used for hymns.
3. Thyestes was tricked by his brother into eating his own children. This story was treated in tragedy; Horace is arguing that it is not appropriate for comedy ("the sock").
4. A stock old-man character from comedy.
5. Characters from tragedy. Peleus was exiled after killing his brother; Telephus was wounded by Achilles and, in Euripides' version of the story, dressed as a beggar when he went to ask Clytemnestra for help.

Correctness is not enough in a poem; it must be attractive,
leading the listener's emotions in whatever way it wishes.
When a person smiles, people's faces smile in return;
when he weeps, they show concern. Before you can move me to tears,
you must grieve yourself. Only then will your woes distress me,
Peleus or Telephus. If what you say is out of character,
I'll either doze or laugh. Sad words are required
by a sorrowful face; threats come from one that is angry,
jokes from one that is jolly, serious words from the solemn.
Nature adjusts our inner feelings to every variety
of fortune, giving us joy, goading us on to anger,
making us sink to the ground under a load of suffering.
Then, with the tongue as her medium, she utters the heart's emotions.

II

India's Ancient Epics and Tales

The Indian subcontinent stretches from the borders of Iran and Afghanistan to those of Myanmar, and from the edges of Tibet and China to the Indian Ocean; also called South Asia, it covers an area as large as western Europe. From about the fifth century B.C.E. onward, the ancient Greeks knew this region as *Indos*, a term adapted from the Persians; after the seventh century C.E., Muslim societies came to refer to it as *al-Hind*. For much of its long history, the subcontinent has not been politically united, but it has been remarkably cohesive in its social and cultural practices: it has evolved as a distinct "cultural zone" within Asia, very different in language, religion, art, population, and ways of life from the comparable cultural zones of China and the Middle East.

THE PREHISTORIC ORIGINS OF INDIAN LITERATURE

The kinds of stories ancient Indian literature tells, the forms they take, and the themes they explore are connected to the subcontinent's past before the appearance of historical records. The earliest settled society in South Asia organized on a significant scale was that of the Indus Valley and Harappa

Kṛṣṇa battles the horse demon, Keshi. From a fifth-century C.E. terra-cotta carving.

(ca. 2600–1900 B.C.E.), which established a far-flung network of small towns and ports across what are now Pakistan and western India. This civilization had extensive contacts with Mesopotamia during the period in which the epic ***Gilgamesh*** was being composed in Sumerian. The Indus-Harappan people had a writing system of their own, but it remains undeciphered, even though we know a great deal about their material culture. Conquered or gradually displaced by the Indo-Aryans, or overcome by economic, political, or natural disasters, this population receded from the subcontinent's prehistory by about 1900 B.C.E., some segments perhaps surviving among the aboriginal and other ancient groups dispersed across the Indian peninsula down to modern times.

The Indo-Aryan people may have begun to arrive on the Indian subcontinent as early as 2000 B.C.E., and to create a new settled society over the next few centuries in what are now northern Pakistan and India. Originally a nomadic pastoral people who moved with vast herds of cattle in search of grazing land, the Indo-Aryans branched off from the Indo-Iranian people, who probably migrated from the Caucasus Mountains region (modern Chechnya) to the plateau of Iran late in the third millennium B.C.E. The Indo-Iranians were themselves one of the major groups of the Indo-European people, who spread in many stages from their Caucasian homeland westward into Europe and eastward into Asia. One western Indo-European group, roughly contemporaneous with the earliest Indo-Iranians and Indo-Aryans, migrated to the Mediterranean region also around 2000 B.C.E., initially establishing the Mycenaean civilization and subsequently emerging

An eighteenth-century watercolor depicting Kṛṣṇa protecting cowherds and cows during a fire.

in history as the ancient Greeks and Romans.

When the Indo-Aryans started settling in Punjab (now divided between India and Pakistan) in the second millennium B.C.E., they established an organized agrarian village society distinct from the urban society of their Indus-Harappan predecessors, who had focused on trade. This Indo-Aryan innovation, with its economic basis in agriculture (on small family farms) and animal husbandry (mainly of the domesticated cow), has proven to be the subcontinent's enduring social form of the past 3,500 years. In the mid-twentieth century, when it still had nearly 750,000 such villages, Mahatma Gandhi famously characterized India as a "land of villages"; and, in our own times, we still invoke the "holy cow"—an image that the Indo-Aryans created in their earliest poems on the subcontinent.

The Indo-Aryans brought with them the language that eventually became Sanskrit, the medium of the largest body of Indian literature, produced continuously from approximately 1200 B.C.E. to 1800 C.E. Sanskrit is intimately related to Greek and Latin: these languages share much of their grammar, use similar sentence structures, and draw on hundreds of common roots for their vocabularies. All three languages, along with ancient Persian, may therefore have evolved from a single source called proto-Indo-European, a language (lost since antiquity) presumably used by the ancestors of the Greeks, Romans, Indo-Iranians, and Indo-Aryans a few thousand years earlier.

But the connections among these scattered peoples are not merely linguistic. When they settled at the end of their respective migrations, they began to worship pantheons of gods, establish social hierarchies, practice rituals and customs, and adopt political models that strongly resembled one another. Most important, their songs, tales, and cycles of myths seemed to invoke a common stock of older memories, images, and narratives. By the first millennium B.C.E., Greek, Sanskrit, and Latin were highly differentiated from one another, and their emerging literatures—from, respectively, **Homer** (ca. eighth century B.C.E.); **Vālmīki** (ca. sixth century B.C.E.), the author of the original ***Rāmāyaṇa***; and **Virgil** (first century B.C.E.) onward—developed along independent trajectories. But they still contained remarkable echoes of one another that we cannot fully explain.

ORALITY AND WRITING IN INDIA

The first works on the subcontinent were hymns and ritual formulas (*mantras*) composed in Sanskrit, which were gathered with commentary and other theological material in four large groupings of discourse called the Vedas; these gave rise to an extensive, interconnected body of philosophy and mystical speculation called the Upaniṣads, fifty-two of which are important. Developed between approximately 1200 and 700 B.C.E., much of this literature was classified as scripture (*śruti*, revelation that is heard) and revealed knowledge (*veda*). Although the Vedic hymns are in verse, and some of them are poetry of the highest order, and even though the visionaries (*ṛṣis*) who "received them from the gods" are called *kavis* (poets), the texts themselves are not classified as *kāvya* (poetry): from this perspective, *mantras* are of divine origin and hence sacred, whereas poetry—no matter how beautiful and profound—is made by human authors and hence always mundane. Since divine revelation and knowledge need to be explained to human audiences, the Vedas and the Upaniṣads engendered many works of authoritative and specialized commentary (*śāstras*) as well as numerous compendiums and rule books (*sūtras*), which, by the latter half of the first millennium B.C.E., became part of the canon of Vedic religion and, centuries later, of classical Hinduism, one of the most important cultural forces on the subcontinent.

Although some of the essential commentaries and rule books were prepared after a writing system became available, the Hindu canon as a whole was transmitted orally throughout the ancient period. In this method of oral transmission, which is still practiced in our times, specialist priests and scholars belonging to the *brāhmaṇa* caste are trained from early childhood to memorize an entire work in multiple forms: by phoneme (sound unit), word, verse, chapter, and book; by mnemonic summaries of the whole work, and by its "indexed" words; and even by the reverse order of its verses. Taught orally for a dozen years, a good Vedic priest who specializes in the *Ṛg-veda* (ca. 1000 B.C.E.), for example, can recite all 1,028 hymns in its ten books, can confirm their correct order, can reproduce any individual verse at will, and can orally list every occurrence of a given word in the text. Unlike a bard, a Vedic reciter communicates divine revelation, and hence is not free to invent, embellish, or err. In post-Vedic times (starting ca. 500 B.C.E.), this method was extended to other kinds of composition in Sanskrit. In the classical period (ca. 400–1100 C.E.), for instance, poets and literary scholars memorized entire bodies of *kāvya*, so that their literature was always at hand—a practice that also continued well into the twentieth century.

Knowledge of the early writing system of the Indus-Harappan people did not survive the end of their civilization, around 1900 B.C.E. A new system of indigenous writing most likely reappeared around 500 B.C.E., and acquired its canonical form some 250 years later. This was the Brahmi script system, in which writing proceeds from left to right and uses alphabetical letters and diacritical marks to represent syllables (whole sounds), and hence is classified as an alpha-syllabary system, as distinct from the Greek and Latin scripts, which are strictly alphabetical. Brahmi migrated rapidly across South Asia after 250 B.C.E., spawning what would eventually become, over the next 1,500 years or so, the dozen distinct script systems in which most of the languages of the region are recorded. These include Sanskrit, Bengali, Hindi, Marathi, Kannada, and Tamil, among other languages, Urdu being among the few exceptions written in a modified Persian-Arabic script, which arrived from outside the subcontinent. During the same period, Brahmi also migrated out of India and became a transnational phenomenon of world importance: it engendered the scripts of Tibetan (Tibet), Burmese (Myanmar), Thai (Thailand), Javanese and Sumatran (Indonesia), Cham (Vietnam), and Tagalog (the Philippines), and hence launched literacy and literature across a wide swath of Asia.

This coin, from the late second-century B.C.E. kingdom of Satavahana, has a few characters of the Brahmī script on either side of the elephant.

By the beginning of the Common Era, professional scribes had begun to produce manuscripts with a metal stylus on prepared sheets of bark or palm leaves, tied together with string. Paper and ink first became common on the Indian subcontinent in the thirteenth century C.E.; until then, for more than a millennium, the principal form of a Sanskrit book was a palm-leaf manuscript: though highly perishable, it succeeded in recording an enormous quantity of literature, disseminating Indian epics, lyrics, stories, and plays all over the subcontinent, and well beyond its boundaries.

SOCIETY, POLITICS, AND RELIGION

The first Vedic hymns (ca. 1200 B.C.E.), and the first collection of hymns, the *Ṛg-veda saṃhitā* (ca. 1000 B.C.E.), were most likely composed in Punjab, "the land of five rivers" that are the tributaries of the Indus. Over the next few centuries, the Indo-Aryans pushed farther east, settling on the wider and equally fertile plains surrounding the Ganges river system, up to modern Bihar and Bengal. By the seventh century B.C.E., the expansion of agriculture and cattle breeding produced enough prosperity to support the first towns and cities across northern India, such as Banaras and Ayodhyā (which still flourish today). With this emerged the first recognizable political form in India: the small republic centered around an urban capital, not unlike a city-state, ruled by a lineage of hereditary monarchs. This became both the historical context and the narrative setting of the first Sanskrit epic, the *Rāmāyaṇa*, begun in the sixth century B.C.E. and composed on the central Gangetic plains.

A couple of centuries later, the small republics started to give way to bigger kingdoms that could garner sufficient surpluses from the land to maintain large armies, and control territories of several hundred square miles. Shortly after Alexander the Great invaded western and northern India, reaching Punjab in 327 B.C.E. and leaving behind a Greek colony in Gandhara (today's Peshawar and Swat Valley region, in Pakistan), the Maurya dynasty established the subcontinent's first empire—which stretched from Afghanistan to Bengal, and from the Himalayan foothills to the Deccan Plateau. Situated imaginatively in the transitional period between small republics and a vast empire, the other ancient Sanskrit epic, the ***Mahābhārata*** (ca. 400 B.C.E.–400 C.E.), represents a world of powerful monarchies and many medium-sized kingdoms, from which the older republican ideal was beginning to fade.

This evolving world was shaped by the religion we now call Hinduism. As we see from the *Rāmāyaṇa* and the *Mahābhārata*, one of the most influential ideas in Hinduism is that the universe, as it exists, is fashioned in a vast process of self-generation, in which all the primordial substance out of which it is made is godhead itself. Godhead, or "the god beyond god," is the absolute and undifferentiated original matter of the universe, and it divides itself into everything that exists; it is eternal and indestructible, and hence has no beginning or end in time. God in this view is not a creator god, or an anthropomorphic father, or a wrathful or vengeful deity; godhead is unknowable, unimaginable, and indescribable. Since everything that exists is made out of godhead (and there is no other elemental matter in the universe), god is everywhere and in everything—a view that constitutes pantheism. In some Vedic hymns, this all-pervading godhead is called *Puruṣa*, "spirit" (in the masculine gender); in the Upaniṣads, it is renamed *Brahman* (not to be confused

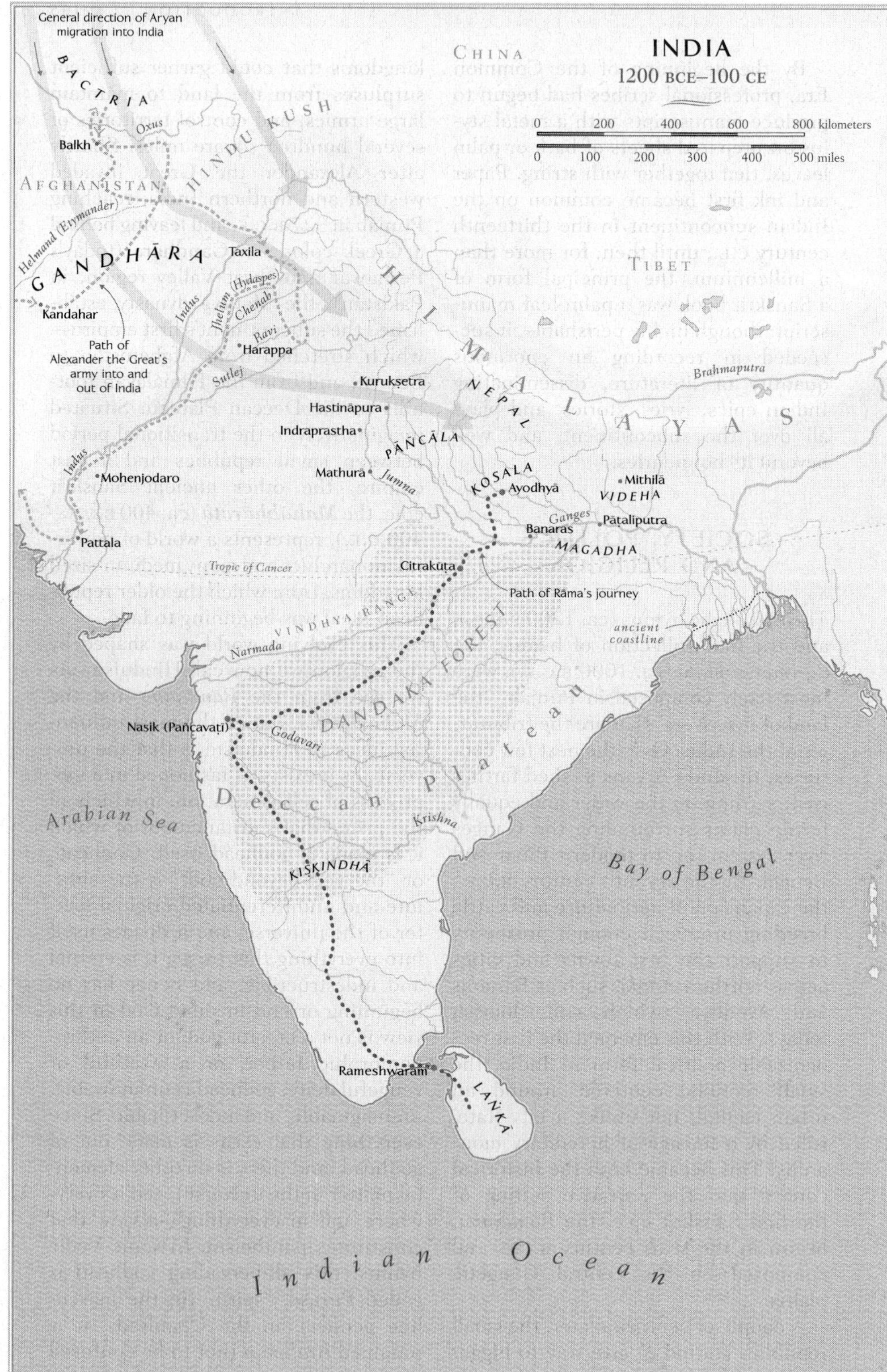

INDIA
1200 BCE–100 CE
0 200 400 600 800 kilometers
0 100 200 300 400 500 miles
General direction of Aryan migration into India
BACTRIA
Oxus
Balkh
HINDU KUSH
AFGHANISTAN
Helmand (Etymander)
GANDHĀRA
Taxila
Kandahar
Indus
Jhelum (Hydaspes)
Chenab
Ravi
Harappa
Sutlej
Path of Alexander the Great's army into and out of India
CHINA
TIBET
HIMALAYAS
NEPAL
Brahmaputra
Kurukṣetra
Hastināpura
Indraprastha
PĀÑCĀLA
Mathurā
Jumna
KOSALA
Ayodhyā
Mithilā
VIDEHA
Ganges
Pāṭaliputra
Banaras
MAGADHA
Mohenjodaro
Pattala
Tropic of Cancer
Citrakūṭa
Path of Rāma's journey
VINDHYA RANGE
Narmada
DANDAKA FOREST
ancient coastline
Nasik (Pañcavatī)
Godavari
Deccan Plateau
Krishna
Arabian Sea
KIṢKINDHĀ
Bay of Bengal
Rameshwaram
LAṄKĀ
Indian Ocean

with either *brāhmaṇa*, the priestly caste-group, or Brahmā, the later, anthropomorphic "god of creation"). The soul, spirit, or "self" (*ātman*) that animates every living creature is nothing but a piece of *Puruṣa* or *Brahman*, so it, too, is eternal and indestructible. The universe as we know it has a beginning in cosmic time, and therefore also comes to an end; since godhead cyclically differentiates itself into a particular universe, all its indestructible substance must return to it at the end of a cycle and be reintegrated into its primordial state. Any life-form's ultimate goal therefore is to be reunited with absolute godhead; for an individual soul or *ātman*, such a union with the elemental stuff of the universe is possible only if it can achieve *mokṣa*, or "liberation," from its differentiated existence.

Works such as the *Rāmāyaṇa* and the *Mahābhārata* further show us that many of Hinduism's characteristic doctrines follow from this theology of *Brahman* and *ātman*. Each of the popular gods in its pantheon becomes an aspect or a manifestation of godhead in an anthropomorphic or concrete form, which is especially useful in making divinity accessible to humans. The great gods Viṣṇu and Śiva are manifestations of godhead in equal measure; though Viṣṇu is often characterized as the god of preservation, and Śiva is distinguished as the god of destruction, each performs all the functions of creation, preservation, and destruction that only pure godhead can perform. The same is true of the anthropomorphic Brahmā, usually called the god of creation; and, by extension—because Hinduism, in the final analysis, does not attribute gender to godhead—it is equally true of the goddesses Lakṣmī, Pārvatī, and Sarasvatī (the consorts of Viṣṇu, Śiva, and Brahmā, respectively), each of whom also is a complete embodiment of godhead. Since godhead can thus take on countless forms, there cannot be any one true representation of divinity; from its earliest phase, Hinduism therefore consistently commits itself to polytheism, the belief that there are many gods. As a result, from its very beginnings in agrarian Indo-Aryan society in northern India, Hinduism emerges as a fundamentally pluralistic religion,

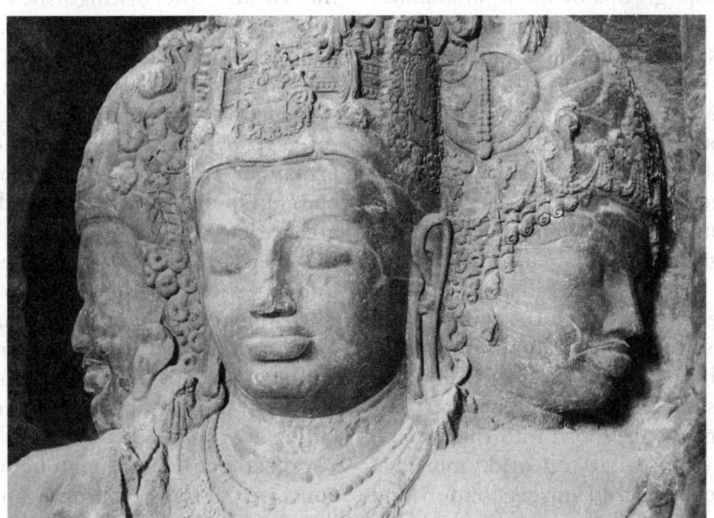

A sandstone sculpture at the Temple of Śiva, Elephanta (ca. seventh–eighth centuries C.E.), depicting the "Trimurti" of Hinduism: Śiva, Viṣṇu, and Brahmā.

tolerant (in principle) of the worship of many different gods in many different ways, and of the pursuit of divergent ways of life, each of which has the potential to discover a path to *mokṣa* for an individual *ātman*.

THE RELIGIOUS CONTEXTS OF EPIC AND TALE

Within this broad matrix, India's early epics and narrative traditions develop along specific religious lines, but also in keeping with the social world shaped by Hinduism. Vālmīki's *Rāmāyaṇa*, composed and transmitted orally at the outset, is classified as the first poem in Sanskrit because it emphasizes imaginative and aesthetic excellence outside a religious context; but it also takes the mythology of Viṣṇu and the practices of Hindu society for granted. In this framework, Viṣṇu is the "supreme god" who manifests all aspects of godhead; and Vedic rituals are essential for pleasing various gods and ensuring that individuals can pursue *mokṣa*. At the same time, the epic depicts a hierarchical society divided into four main caste-groups by birth: *brāhmaṇas* (priests), *kṣatriyas* (warriors), *vaiśyas* (traders), and *śūdras* (servants and cultivators). Theologically, this separation of castes is part of the primary differentiation of godhead into distinct categories of existence, and hence is divinely ordained and immutable; in most circumstances, an individual therefore cannot migrate from one caste to another on the basis of, say, talent or accomplishment. This structure is maintained by a system of endogamous marriage, in which legitimate spouses must belong to the same caste-group, so that their children are also born into their social category; in such a world, marriage is irrevocable, and miscegenation and adultery across castes can deeply destabilize not only the human order, but the cosmic moral order as well. The *Rāmāyaṇa* also depicts a society of villages and small republics, in which dynasties of kings do not yet pursue imperial ambitions: their role here is to preserve the divine order of things, in both the mundane world and the cosmos at large, which is populated by human beings, animal, plants, and inanimate things as well as demons, celestial beings, and gods.

In the *Mahābhārata*, composed a little later, village society coexists with a more complex urban world: the land is now divided into many sizable dynastic kingdoms on the verge of imperial formations. The four caste-groups (*varṇas*) have separated into five, with the addition of "untouchables" and foreigners (such as the Greeks left behind by Alexander's army); and each caste-group is differentiated into numerous specific castes (*jātīs*). While the *Rāmāyaṇa* upholds the ideal of monogamous marriage within caste boundaries, the *Mahābhārata* explores multiple marriages and reproductive relationships, overlaying polygamy with polyandry and complicating issues of legitimacy, illegitimacy, and legacy by birth. Whereas the earlier epic distinguishes sharply between good and evil, the later poem adopts more complex and varying views on how action (karma) can accord with divine law (*dharma*); as the laws revealed by the gods in the Vedas and explained in later authoritative discourse (such as the *śāstras* and *sūtras*) are intricate, many judgments regarding the rightness and wrongness of particular actions founder in uncertainty. The ***Bhagavad-gītā***, which is part of the *Mahābhārata*, tackles the dilemmas of *karma* in the most difficult of situations: when is war just, how can violence and killing ever be justified, and under what circumstances can human beings even conceive of taking up arms against family and loved ones? The philosophical and theological arguments about the human and the divine, and about social and political organization, launched by the Indo-Aryans toward the end of the second millennium B.C.E., thus reach a poetic culmination in the encyclopedic structure of the *Mahābhārata* a thousand years later.

By the sixth century B.C.E.—the likely date of Vālmīki's original *Rāmāyaṇa*—several indigenous responses to the Hindu theology of *Brahman* and *ātman* had already found historical expression. The strongest criticism and rejection came from two near contemporaries of Vālmīki: Mahāvīra, the last of Jainism's founders, and Siddhartha-Gautama Buddha, who launched Buddhism. Adopting a severe form of philosophical skepticism and atheism, Buddhism argued that there is no god beyond god (as postulated in Hinduism), no creation by differentiation, and that the universe therefore has no substantial reality. If *Brahman* does not exist, then living creatures have no eternal and indestructible *ātmans*; our perception that we possess an enduring self is therefore an illusion, and the only end of life can be a "snuffing out" or extinction of illusory identity. Such a snuffing out—the literal meaning of *nirvāṇa*—is the exact opposite of what the Hindus call *mokṣa*, the liberation of a substantial *ātman* from a material body for reunification with the ultimate, primordial substance, *Brahman*. And yet, perhaps paradoxically, Buddhism accepts the reality of karma and rebirth: even an illusory self is reborn numerous times, because it is deluded into believing that it has a persistent identity. This delusion ends only when the self reaches Enlightenment (the condition of being a Buddha), understands that it is not a substantial entity, and hence acquires the power to extinguish itself, attaining *nirvāṇa*. Such a rejection of Hinduism finds a narrative exposition in the ***Jātaka*** tales (ca. fourth century B.C.E.), which are part of the canon of Theravada Buddhism in the Pali language. The *Jātaka*'s vision, especially the playful irreverence and philosophical dissidence in a series of its short tales, offers us a profound cultural alternative to the heroic Hindu worlds of the *Rāmāyaṇa*, the *Mahābhārata*, and the *Bhagavad-gītā*.

As this historical overview suggests, for most of the ancient period the Indian subcontinent was not politically united. This pattern was to continue in the Common Era, down to modern times; since the end of British colonial rule (1757–1947), South Asia has come to be divided into seven nations, and its total population is now nearly 1.6 billion people, about three-fourths of whom live in contemporary India. The ancient period also witnessed internal religious division, with Jainism and Buddhism dissenting from Hinduism—a process that was repeated later with the arrival of other faiths, such as Zoroastrianism (ca. eleventh century) and Christianity, and the rise of Sikhism (both sixteenth century). Nevertheless, for the more than three millennia since the establishment of agrarian Indo-Aryan village society, the subcontinent has functioned as a cohesive cultural zone characterized by diversity and pluralism, which define the distinctive context of its early epics and tales.

THE RĀMĀYAṆA OF VĀLMĪKI

ca. 550 B.C.E.

The *Rāmāyaṇa* is many things to many people. It is a tale of adventure across a vast land, from palace to forest to sea; and a love story about an ideal prince and an ideal woman, whose relationship falters late in their marriage. It is a heroic epic about injustice and war, abduction and disinheritance, but also a wondrous tale involving gods, humans, animals, and demons with supernatural powers. It is a religious epic that explains the ways of the gods to human beings, and offers a model of justice and prosperity on earth. Moreover, it is great entertainment: like a roller coaster, it takes us up and down through many facets of human experience, from goodness, beauty, and romance to fear and tragedy.

CONTEXT

All we know about Vālmīki is the little he tells us about himself in his poem. He was an ascetic spiritual practitioner who had renounced normal life in human society, and lived in a small ashram, a hermit's enclave, on the banks of a river. One day he saw a pair of birds making love to each other, but a moment later a hunter shot and killed the male bird with an arrow. Incensed with this violent intrusion into a scene of great natural tenderness and beauty, Vālmīki pronounced an irrevocable curse on the hunter. Reflecting on what he had just uttered, the poet realized that he had spontaneously composed a *śloka*, an unrhymed metrical verse like a couplet, which fully expressed his compassionate grief for the slaughtered bird. Realizing that this verse form would be a perfect vehicle for story as well as song, Vālmīki set about using the *śloka* to compose the heroic and romantic tale of Rāma and Sītā, whose twin sons, Lava and Kuśa—by a twist of events—were then being raised in his ashram. Thus, the poet's life and character are fully integrated with the heroic world he creates and the tale he chooses to narrate. In the version of the epic we have inherited, and in the tradition since Vālmīki's time, he is celebrated as "the first poet," and his *Rāmāyaṇa* is known as "the inaugural poem" in Indian literature.

Vālmīki's epic tale—nearly one-and-a-half times the combined length of the ***Iliad*** and the ***Odyssey***—was originally composed in Sanskrit around the sixth century B.C.E. By that time, a settled society had been in place in northern India for at least a thousand years. Agriculture had become the principal economic activity on the fertile plains around the Indus and Ganges rivers, and it supported a network of prosperous villages, towns, and cities. Society was organized by caste, with priests (*brāhmaṇas*), warriors (*kṣatriyas*), and traders (*vaiśyas*) comprising the three main groups, and the large populace that served them (*śūdras*) constituting the fourth category in the hierarchy. The caste structure was maintained primarily by a system of arranged marriage, in which, ideally, the bridegroom and the bride belonged to the same caste but not the same clan. Each caste-group had its own laws and moral codes (*dharma*), which defined its members' duties and obligations, but it also had to obey laws that applied to all of society. These laws were not made by human beings: they were given by the gods, and were contained in scripture.

Hinduism, which was central to upholding this social order, had been established in its early form several centuries before Vālmīki; its scriptural canon included ritual texts (the Vedas) as well as philosophy and theology (the Upaniṣads). In this system of beliefs, human beings could find "salvation" only if they accumulated "good karma" by propitiating the gods and following *dharma* precisely. But moral laws and codes of conduct are always complex and subtle, and hence easy to violate; numerous rituals are therefore necessary to keep the gods happy, maintain the moral and social orders, and make up for ethical lapses.

The world of the *Rāmāyaṇa* is structured in a similar way, but it also contains many gods, among whom three are the most important: Brahmā, primarily a benign and paternalistic god of creation; Śiva, chiefly an angry and retributive god who engenders cycles of creation and destruction; and Viṣṇu, mainly a benevolent god who preserves the moral balance of the universe. Much of the flux and dynamism of the universe is due to the perpetual struggle for supremacy between Śiva and Viṣṇu. Śiva intervenes in the human world directly, in his multifaceted anthropomorphic form; Viṣṇu, in contrast, "comes down on earth" in a series of distinct avatars or incarnations, living temporarily among mortal creatures each time for the purpose of destroying a particular source of evil. A vital feature of the *Rāmāyaṇa* is that it tells the story of Lord Viṣṇu's seventh incarnation, when he embodied himself as prince Rāma, in order to end the demonic king Rāvaṇa's reign of terror on earth and beyond.

The mundane world that Vālmīki's characters inhabit is also a deeply political one, where the two upper caste-groups, the *brāhmaṇas* (priests) and the *kṣatriyas* (warriors and rulers), dominate society. The land is divided into small, autonomous republics with prosperous cities for their capitals. The king belongs to a dynasty of warriors, but is not an absolute monarch; his power is mediated by court priests and scholarly *brāhmaṇas*. He is defined as a "protector of *dharma*," and his ideal role is to ensure that he and his subjects follow all laws. He is also fully answerable to his subjects; as their moral caretaker, he is obliged to pay attention to their needs, their voices of affirmation and protest. Moreover, the king is further constrained by life in his palace: he is usually polygamous, and has several queens; he is therefore the head of an extended family whose members participate actively in affairs of state. The warrior-dynasties in these republics follow the law of primogeniture, so that the eldest son ascends the throne in the next generation; but the inheritance of the kingdom can be complicated by the protodemocratic politics of the royal family as well as of public opinion, or by the inability of the king and his queens to beget a son. All these aspects of early Indian society, religion, and politics come into play in the dramatic narrative of the *Rāmāyaṇa*.

WORK

While Vālmīki probably composed his poem around 550 B.C.E., it was expanded and polished anonymously by others over the next five or six hundred years. Since writing systems did not exist in his society, he must have composed the epic orally, using a large repertoire of formulaic expressions. During its first few centuries, the *Rāmāyaṇa* must have been transmitted with the sophisticated methods of memorization, preservation, and reproduction already used for Hindu scripture. In its modern canonical form, the Sanskrit *Rāmāyaṇa* contains about 24,000 couplets (*ślokas*) and is divided into seven books (*kāṇḍas*), each subdivided into a large number of chapters (*sargas*), most of which contain between twenty and fifty couplets. The first and last books seem to have been added later; they explicitly interpret Rāma as an avatar of Viṣṇu, and provide a multilayered narrative frame for the five books in the middle.

The English version of the *Rāmāyaṇa* reproduced here is not a translation but an adaptation and retelling of Vālmīki's poem. For the most part, it condenses the narrative of each chapter in a style that appeals to modern readers; but, in select passages, especially with important pieces of dialogue, its rendering is closer to the original. Our selection consists of excerpts from books 2 through 6 that capture the key moments of the tale; together, they convey the epic's essential story as Vālmīki probably imagined it.

To understand our selection, it is necessary to know what happens in book 1, *Bāla* ("Childhood"), which is not represented here. In that book, Rāvaṇa, the brilliant and highly accomplished king of Laṅkā (an island in the south, modern Sri Laṅkā), has become invincible, demonic, and evil. Lord Viṣṇu therefore has to descend to earth in a human form and destroy him, and so takes birth as Rāma, the eldest son of Daśaratha, king of Kosala, and his principal queen, Kausalyā. Daśaratha also has two other queens, who bear him sons (Rāma's half-brothers): Kaikeyī is the mother of Bharata, whereas Sumitrā has twins, Lakṣmaṇa and Śatrughna. All four boys are trained as warriors and future rulers; Rāma and Lakṣmaṇa, inseparable since childhood, become the pupils of the sage Viśvāmitra. As teenagers, they travel with Viśvāmitra to the neighboring Videha, where Rāma wins a suitors' contest for Sītā, the foster-daughter of that republic's king but actually a child of the goddess Earth.

Our selection begins with book 2, *Ayodhyā*, where Daśaratha follows the code of primogeniture and proclaims Rāma as heir apparent to Kosala's throne, and the republic's citizens celebrate the decision enthusiastically. But following an intrigue in the extended family, Daśaratha gives in to the demand that his second son, Bharata, be made king, and that Rāma be exiled for fourteen years. We then see how Rāma responds to this development, and what decisions he, Sītā, Lakṣmaṇa, and Bharata make under the circumstances. The chapters in this book are composed in a realistic style on the whole, and they give us vivid glimpses into the thoughts and feelings of the characters involved in the struggle for power.

The excerpts from the next four books focus on Rāma, Sītā, and Lakṣmaṇa's fourteen-year exile together, and the narrative now has the atmosphere of fairy tale and fantasy. In book 3, *Āraṇya* ("The Forest"), the trio pushes deeper into the vast Daṇḍaka forest, south of the River Ganges, whose only inhabitants are animals, ascetics, and demons. We discover how they learn to survive under hostile conditions, and what kinds of dangers and temptations they encounter. While the three are living peacefully in the Pañcavaṭī woodlands (in central India), Rāma and Lakṣmaṇa unwittingly initiate a conflict with Śūrpaṇakhā and her brother Rāvaṇa, the demonic king of Laṅkā. Enraged by their provocation, Rāvaṇa decides to destroy Rāma by abducting Sītā; how he carries out his plan constitutes a pivotal moment in the

A "Mughal"-style illustration from the *Rāmāyaṇa* dating from ca. 1600 C.E. shows Rāma chasing a golden deer.

epic. When Rāma realizes that Sītā is gone, he virtually goes mad with grief.

While searching desperately for Sītā, in book 4, *Kiṣkindhā* ("The Kingdom of the Monkeys"), Rāma and Lakṣmaṇa encounter a tribe of monkeys, whose citadel is at Kiṣkindhā (in southern India). Intervening in the political quarrels among their factions, the princes persuade the monkeys, and one of their powerful leaders, Hanumāna, to help them look for her. In book 5,

Sundara ("The Sundara Hill" [in Laṅkā]), Hanumāna spies on Rāvaṇa's capital, and discovers where Sītā is held captive. But she refuses to escape with Hanumāna for reasons that deepen the moral dimension of the story, and that leave him in a quandary. Hanumāna then sets fire to Rāvaṇa's city as a warning of impending war, and returns to apprise Rāma of the situation.

In book 6, *Yuddha* ("The War"), the monkeys build a bridge or causeway across the straits to Laṅkā with remarkable inventiveness. One of Rāvaṇa's brothers betrays him and joins the princes, helping them with their battle plans. After a lengthy conflict, in which Rāvaṇa's other brothers are killed and Lakṣmaṇa is wounded, Rāma finally confronts the demon king in single combat. When he recovers Sītā, however, he finds himself deeply troubled by the question of whether she has been faithful to him during her long captivity. Resolving his dilemma with a dramatic test of fidelity, Rāma returns to Ayodhyā with Sītā and Lakṣmaṇa, and is crowned king. His reign brings peace, prosperity, and justice to the republic of Kosala, and represents the ideal of kingship.

Our selection ends on this happy note, but the canonical version of Vālmīki's epic continues further. In book 7, *Uttara* ("The Final Book"), not included here, Rāma seems set to rule happily for the rest of his days; but people soon begin to gossip viciously about Sītā's probable infidelity with Rāvaṇa. In a misguided attempt to be morally answerable to his subjects, Rāma banishes Sītā, even though he knows that the rumors are false and that she is pregnant. Sītā takes refuge in the sage Vālmīki's ashram, where she gives birth to twin boys, Lava and Kuśa. Vālmīki composes a long poem about the life of Rāma; he trains the twins as bards, and teaches them to sing his epic beautifully. One day they sing the tale before the king, who does not know that they are his sons; when he recognizes them, he sends for his beloved queen. Overwhelmed by her suffering by then, however, Sītā asks her mother, the Earth, to take her back; the ground opens beneath her feet, and she disappears forever. Heartbroken, Rāma divides his kingdom between his sons, gives up his life on earth, and returns to heaven in his divine form as Viṣṇu, his task of destroying Rāvaṇa's evil accomplished.

Vālmīki's style in the original varies according to narrative mode. Many important events are narrated directly from an omniscient point of view; in contrast, when characters in the story tell a tale or engage in dialogue, the verse is adapted to capture their voices and personalities. In book 2, when the action is situated in the palace, the descriptions are frequently realistic; in books 3 through 5, when the action is set in the forest and focuses on animals, demons, and fantastic events—Rāvaṇa changing his form, Hanumāna flying over the sea—the atmosphere and effect are often fantastic. Even in the forest scenes, however, dream-like passages can be interspersed with flashes of realism, indicating how carefully the text is crafted throughout.

Vālmīki's poem articulates a strong moral vision. It offers us the ideals of Rāma as a son, husband, and king who is serene, courageous, and circumspect; Sītā as a vibrant, thoughtful, and selfless wife and mother; Lakṣmaṇa as a brother and brother-in-law whose first thought is always for his extended family; and Hanumāna as a loyal devotee. All these characters are larger than life, but each of them is also flawed or suffers great injustice. Moreover, in a polygamous society, Vālmīki's epic proposes the norm of monogamous marriage based on mutual love between husband and wife; in a world of political conflict, it portrays republics that build alliances for peace, and rulers and subjects who live by the law, aiming for social harmony. It explicitly promotes justice, goodness, balance, and morality in forms that remain valid today, even though we may not always agree on the details from a modern perspective.

As a literary narrative with scripture-like religious authority, the story of Rāma is special because it is fully integrated into the annual Hindu calendar, the way the story of Christ and the rituals of Christmas, Good Friday, and Easter are woven into the Christian calendar. Every year, in the weeks following the autumnal equinox, the public festivals of Dusehrā and Divālī mark the anniversaries, respectively, of Rāma's victory over Rāvaṇa and Rāma's return to Ayodhyā. Over the nine nights preceding Dusehrā, thousands of local Hindu communities throughout India perform the *Rāma-līlā*, "the play of Rāma"; in each community, children, teenagers, and adults enact the full story of Rāma in nightly installments on an amateur stage, culminating in a ritual burning of gigantic effigies representing Rāvaṇa and his brothers. On the next night of the new moon (usually in late October), every Indian village, town, and city celebrates Divālī, the festival of lights, a symbolic affirmation of Rāma's coronation as king and the cyclical restoration of goodness and justice in the world.

During the past two millennia, Vālmīki's *Rāmāyaṇa* has spread astonishingly far. In India, hundreds of translations, imitations, adaptations, and retellings have appeared in the dozens of languages that gradually replaced Sanskrit after the first millennium C.E. Many of these local and regional versions of the epic—such as Kamban's *Irāmavatāram* (Tamil, twelfth century) and Tulsīdās's *Rāmacaritamānasa* (Avadhi/Hindi, sixteenth century)—have become literary and religious classics in their own right; and many of them are transmitted orally, in a form called the *Rāma-kathā* ("the story of Rāma"), in public readings and recitations by professional performers sponsored annually by local communities. Outside India, the *Rāmāyaṇa* has migrated to the Persian, Arabic, and Chinese worlds; the central character of the Monkey King in ***Journey to the West***, one of the four major classical novels in Chinese, is modeled on Hanumāna. The epic has also reached every part of Southeast Asia, from Malaysia and Indonesia to the Philippines. Vālmīki's tale (originally a Hindu work) reappears with variations in the Thai *Rāmakien* (thirteenth century), the national epic of Thailand; in the relief sculptures at Angkor Wat, the Hindu temple complex in Cambodia (twelfth century onward); in Balinese classical and folk dance, dance drama, and pantomime; and in the spectacular puppet and shadow-puppet theaters of Malaysia and Indonesia (Muslim-majority societies) and Thailand and Cambodia (Buddhist-majority societies). The characters and stories of Rāma and Sītā, Lakṣmaṇa and Hanumāna and Rāvaṇa, are among the best known for almost half the world's population today.

The Rāmāyaṇa of Vālmīki[1]

From Book 2

Ayodhyā

AYODHYĀ 15–16

The brāhmaṇas[2] had got everything ready for the coronation ceremonies. Gold pots of holy water from all the sacred rivers, most of them gathered at their very source, were ready. All the paraphernalia like the umbrella, the chowries,[3] an elephant and a white horse, were ready, too.

But, the king did not emerge, though the sun had risen and the auspicious hour was fast approaching. The priests and the people wondered: "Who can awaken the king, and inform him that he had better hurry up!" At that moment, Sumantra[4] emerged from the palace. Seeing them, he told them: "Under the king's orders I am going to fetch Rāma." But, on second thought, knowing that the preceptors and the priests commanded even the king's respect, he returned to the king's presence to announce that they were awaiting him. Standing near the king, Sumantra sang: "Arise, O king! Night has flown. Arise and do what should be done." The weary king asked: "I ordered you to fetch Rāma, and I am not asleep. Why do you not do as you are told to do?" This time, Sumantra hurried out of the palace and sped to Rāma's palace.

Entering the palace and proceeding unobstructed through the gates and entrances of the palace, Sumantra beheld the divine Rāma, and said to him: "Rāma, the king who is in the company of queen Kaikeyī desires to see you at once." Immediately, Rāma turned to Sītā and announced: "Surely, the king and mother Kaikeyī wish to discuss with me some important details in connection with the coronation ceremony. I shall go and return soon." Sītā, for her part, offered a heartfelt prayer to the gods: "May I have the blessing of humbly serving you during the auspicious coronation ceremony!"

As Rāma emerged from his palace there was great cheer among the people who hailed and applauded him. Ascending his swift chariot he proceeded to the king's palace, followed by the regalia. Women standing at the windows of their houses and richly adorned to express their joy, showered flowers on Rāma. They praised Kausalyā, the mother of Rāma; they praised Sītā, Rāma's consort: "Obviously she must have done great penance to get him as her husband." The people rejoiced as if they themselves were being installed on the throne. They said to one another: "Rāma's coronation is truly a blessing to all the people. While he rules, and he will rule for a long time, no one will even have an unpleasant experience, or ever suffer." Rāma too was happy to see the huge crowds of people, the elephants and the horses—indicating that people had come to Ayodhyā from afar to witness the coronation.

1. Translated by Swami Venkatesananda.
2. Priests, members of the highest caste.
3. Yak-tail fans used to ward off flies; kings were attended by fan bearers.
4. King Daśaratha's charioteer and chief bard. The charioteer/bard (*sūta*) composed and narrated ancient epics and sagas.

AYODHYĀ 17–18

As Rāma proceeded in his radiant chariot towards his father's palace, the people were saying to one another: "We shall be supremely happy hereafter, now that Rāma will be king. But, who cares for all this happiness? When we behold Rāma on the throne, we shall attain eternal beatitude!" Rāma heard all this praise and the people's worshipful homage to him, with utter indifference as he drove along the royal road.[5] The chariot entered the first gate to the palace. From there on Rāma went on foot and respectfully entered the king's apartments. The people who had accompanied him eagerly waited outside.

Rushing eagerly and respectfully to his father's presence, Rāma bowed to the feet of his father and then devoutly touched the feet of his mother Kaikeyī, too. "O Rāma!" said the king: he could not say anything more, because he was choked with tears and grief. He could neither see nor speak to Rāma. Rāma sensed great danger: as if he had trodden on a most poisonous serpent. Turning to Kaikeyī, Rāma asked her: "How is it that today the king does not speak kindly to me? Have I offended him in any way? Is he not well? Have I offended prince Bharata or any of my mothers? Oh, it is agonizing: and incurring his displeasure I cannot live even for an hour. Kindly reveal the truth to me."

In a calm, measured and harsh tone, Kaikeyī now said to Rāma: "The king is neither sick nor angry with you. What he must tell you he does not wish to, for fear of displeasing you. He granted me two boons. When I named them, he recoiled. How can a truthful man, a righteous king, go back on his own word? Yet that is his predicament at the moment. I shall reveal the truth to you if you assure me that you will honor your father's promise." For the first time Rāma was distressed: "Ah, shame! Please do not say such things to me! For the sake of my father I can jump into fire. And, I assure you, Rāma does not indulge in double talk. Hence, tell me what the king wants to be done."

Kaikeyī lost no time. She said: "Long ago I rendered him a great service, and he granted me two boons. I claimed them now: and he promised. I asked for these boons: that Bharata should be crowned, and that you should go away to Daṇḍaka forest now. If you wish to establish that both you and your father are devoted to truth, let Bharata be crowned with the same paraphernalia that have been got ready for you, and go away to the forest for fourteen years. Do this, O best of men, for that is the word of your father; and thus would you redeem the king."

AYODHYĀ 19–20

Promptly and without the least sign of the slightest displeasure, Rāma said: "So be it! I shall immediately proceed to the forest, to dwell there clad in bark and animal skin.[6] But why does not the king speak to me, nor feel happy in my presence? Please do not misunderstand me; I shall go, and I myself will gladly give away to my brother Bharata the kingdom, wealth, Sītā and even my own life, and it is easier when all this is done in obedience to my father's command. Let

5. Rāma is an equanimous hero, one who is not affected by praise or blame.

6. Hermits and ascetics who lived in forests had to wear tree bark and animal skins. Queen Kaikeyī's demands included requiring Rāma to live the austere life of a hermit.

Bharata be immediately requested to come. But it breaks my heart to see that father does not say a word to me directly."

Kaikeyī said sternly: "I shall attend to all that, and send for Bharata. I think, however, that you should not delay your departure from Ayodhyā even for a moment. Even the consideration that the father does not say so himself, should not stop you. Till you leave this city, he will neither bathe nor eat." Hearing this, the king groaned, and wailed aloud: "Alas, alas!" and became unconscious again. Rāma decided to leave at once and he said to Kaikeyī: "I am not fond of wealth and pleasure: but even as the sages are, I am devoted to truth. Even if father had not commanded me, and you had asked me to go to the forest I would have done so! I shall presently let my mother and also Sītā know of the position and immediately leave for the forest."

Rāma was not affected at all by this sudden turn of events. As he emerged from the palace, with Lakṣmaṇa, the people tried to hold the royal umbrella over him: but he brushed them aside. Still talking pleasantly and sweetly with the people, he entered his mother's apartment. Delighted to see him, Kausalyā began to glorify and bless him and asked him to sit on a royal seat. Rāma did not, but calmly said to her: "Mother, the king has decided to crown Bharata as the yuvarājā[7] and I am to go to the forest and live there as a hermit for fourteen years." When she heard this, the queen fell down unconscious and grief-stricken. In a voice choked with grief, she said: "If I had been barren, I would have been unhappy; but I would not have had to endure this terrible agony. I have not known a happy day throughout my life. I have had to endure the taunts and the insults of the other wives of the king. Nay, even he did not treat me with kindness or consideration: I have always been treated with less affection and respect than Kaikeyī's servants were treated. I thought that after your birth, and after your coronation my luck would change. My hopes have been shattered. Even death seems to spurn me. Surely, my heart is hard as it does not break into pieces at this moment of the greatest misfortune and sorrow. Life is not worth living without you; so if you have to go to the forest, I shall follow you."

AYODHYĀ 21

Lakṣmaṇa said: "I think Rāma should not go to the forest. The king has lost his mind, overpowered as he is by senility and lust. Rāma is innocent. And, no righteous man in his senses would forsake his innocent son. A prince with the least knowledge of statesmanship should ignore the childish command of a king who has lost his senses." Turning to Rāma, he said: "Rāma, here I stand, devoted to you, dedicated to your cause. I am ready to kill anyone who would interfere with your coronation—even if it is the king! Let the coronation proceed without delay."

Kausalyā said: "You have heard Lakṣmaṇa's view. You cannot go to the forest because Kaikeyī wants you to. If, as you say, you are devoted to dharma, then it is your duty to stay here and serve me, your mother. I, as your mother, am as much worthy of your devotion and service as your father is: and I do not give you permission to go to the forest. If you disobey me in this, terrible will be

7. Crown prince.

your suffering in hell. I cannot live here without you. If you leave, I shall fast unto death."

Rāma, devoted as he was to dharma, spoke: "Among our ancestors were renowned kings who earned fame and heaven by doing their father's bidding. Mother, I am but following their noble example." To Lakṣmaṇa he said: "Lakṣmaṇa, I know your devotion to me, love for me, your prowess and your strength. The universe rests on truth: and I am devoted to truth. Mother has not understood my view of truth, and hence suffers. But I am unable to give up my resolve. Abandon your resolve based on the principle of might; resort to dharma;[8] let not your intellect become aggressive. Dharma, prosperity and pleasure are the pursuit of mankind here;[9] and prosperity and pleasure surely follow dharma: even as pleasure and the birth of a son follow a dutiful wife's service of her husband. One should turn away from that action or mode of life which does not ensure the attainment of all the three goals of life, particularly of dharma; for hate springs from wealth and the pursuit of pleasure is not praiseworthy. The commands of the guru, the king, and one's aged father, whether uttered in anger, cheerfully, or out of lust, should be obeyed by one who is not of despicable behavior, with a view to the promotion of dharma. Hence, I cannot swerve from the path of dharma which demands that I should implicitly obey our father. It is not right for you, mother, to abandon father and follow me to the forest, as if you are a widow. Therefore, bless me, mother, so that I may have a pleasant and successful term in the forest."

AYODHYĀ 22–23

Rāma addressed Lakṣmaṇa again: "Let there be no delay, Lakṣmaṇa. Get rid of these articles assembled for the coronation. And with equal expedition make preparations for my leaving the kingdom immediately. Only thus can we ensure that mother Kaikeyī attains peace of mind. Otherwise she might be worried that her wishes may not be fulfilled! Let father's promise be fulfilled. Yet, so long as the two objects of Kaikeyī's desire are not obtained, there is bound to be confusion in everyone's mind. I must immediately leave for the forest; then Kaikeyī will get Bharata here and have him installed on the throne. This is obviously the divine will and I must honor it without delay. My banishment from the kingdom as well as my return are all the fruits of my own doing (kṛtānta: end of action). Otherwise, how could such an unworthy thought enter the heart of noble Kaikeyī? I have never made any distinction between her and my mother; nor has she ever shown the least disaffection for me so far. The 'end' (reaction) of one's own action cannot be foreseen: and this which we call 'daiva' (providence or divine will) cannot be known and cannot be avoided by anyone. Pleasure, pain, fear, anger, gain, loss, life and death—all these are brought about by 'daiva.' Even sages and great ascetics are prompted by the divine will to give up their self-control and are subjected to lust and anger. It is

8. The religious and moral law, code of righteousness.
9. The phrase "dharma, prosperity and pleasure" refers to the first three goals of life for Hindu householders: "religious acts, wealth and public life, and sexual love and family life."

unforeseen and inviolable. Hence, let there be no hostility towards Kaikeyī; she is not to blame. All this is not her doing, but the will of the divine."

Lakṣmaṇa listened to all this with mixed feelings: anger at the turn events had taken, and admiration for Rāma's attitude. Yet, he could not reconcile himself to the situation as Rāma had done. In great fury, he burst forth: "Your sense of duty is misdirected, O Rāma. Even so is your estimation of the divine will. How is it, Rāma, that being a shrewd statesman, you do not see that there are self-righteous people who merely pretend to be good for achieving their selfish and fraudulent ends? If all these boons and promises be true, they could have been asked for and given long ago! Why did they have to wait for the eve of coronation to enact this farce? You ignore this aspect and bring in your argument of the divine will! Only cowards and weak people believe in an unseen divine will: heroes and those who are endowed with a strong mind do not believe in the divine will. Ah, people will see today how my determination and strong action set aside any decrees of the divine will which may be involved in this unrighteous plot. Whoever planned your exile will go into exile! And you will be crowned today. These arms, Rāma, are not handsome limbs, nor are these weapons worn by me ornaments: they are for your service."

AYODHYĀ 24–25

Kausalyā said again: "How can Rāma born of me and the mighty emperor Daśaratha live on food obtained by picking up grains and vegetables and fruits that have been discarded? He whose servants eat dainties and delicacies—how will he subsist on roots and fruits? Without you, Rāma, the fire of separation from you will soon burn me to death. Nay, take me with you, too, if you must go."

Rāma replied: "Mother, that would be extreme cruelty towards father. So long as father lives, please serve him: this is the eternal religion. To a woman her husband is verily god himself. I have no doubt that the noble Bharata will be very kind to you and serve you as I serve you. I am anxious that when I am gone, you should console the king so that he does not feel my separation at all. Even a pious woman who is otherwise righteous, if she does not serve her husband, is deemed to be sinner. On the other hand, she who serves her husband attains blessedness even if she does not worship the gods, perform the rituals or honor the holy men."

Seeing that Rāma was inflexible in his resolve, Kausalyā regained her composure and blessed him. "I shall eagerly await your return to Ayodhyā, after your fourteen years in the forest," said Kausalyā.

Quickly gathering the articles necessary, she performed a sacred rite to propitiate the deities and thus to ensure the health, safety, happy sojourn and quick return of Rāma. "May dharma which you have protected so zealously protect you always," said Kausalyā to Rāma. "May those to whom you bow along the roads and the shrines protect you! Even so, let the missiles which the sage Viśvāmitra[1] gave you ensure your safety. May all the birds and beasts of

1. "Missiles" (*astra*) are magical weapons bestowed on worthy heroes by gods and sages. The sage Viśvāmitra had presented the young Rāma and Lakṣmaṇa with such missiles when they protected his sacrificial rites in the forest from attacks by demons (Book 1, *Bāla*).

the forest, celestial beings and gods, the mountains and the oceans, and the deities presiding over the lunar mansions, natural phenomena and the seasons be propitious to you. May the same blessedness be with you that Indra enjoyed on the destruction of his enemy Vṛtra, that Vinatā bestowed upon her son Garuḍa, that Aditi pronounced upon her son Indra when he was fighting the demons, and that Viṣṇu enjoyed while he measured the heaven and earth.[2] May the sages, the oceans, the continents, the Vedas and the heavens be propitious to you."[3]

As Rāma bent low to touch her feet, Kausalyā fondly embraced him and kissed his forehead, and then respectfully went round him before giving him leave to go.

AYODHYĀ 26–27

Taking leave of his mother, Rāma sought the presence of his beloved wife, Sītā. For her part, Sītā who had observed all the injunctions and prohibitions connected with the eve of the coronation and was getting ready to witness the auspicious event itself, perceived her divine spouse enter the palace and with a heart swelling with joy and pride, went forward to receive him. His demeanor, however, puzzled her: his countenance reflected sorrow and anxiety. Shrewd as she was she realized that something was amiss, and hence asked Rāma: "The auspicious hour is at hand; and yet what do I see! Lord, why are you not accompanied by the regalia, by men holding the ceremonial umbrella, by the royal elephant and the horses, by priests chanting the Vedas, by bards singing your glories? How is it that your countenance is shadowed by sorrow?"

Without losing time and without mincing words, Rāma announced: "Sītā, the king has decided to install Bharata on the throne and to send me to the forest for fourteen years. I am actually on my way to the forest and have come to say good-bye to you. Now that Bharata is the yuvarājā, nay king, please behave appropriately towards him. Remember: people who are in power do not put up with those who sing others' glories in their presence: hence do not glorify me in the presence of Bharata. It is better not to sing my praises even in the presence of your companions. Be devoted to your religious observances and serve my father, my three mothers and my brothers. Bharata and Śatrughna should be treated as your own brothers or sons. Take great care to see that you do not give the least offense to Bharata, the king. Kings reject even their own sons if they are hostile, and are favorable to even strangers who may be friendly. This is my counsel."

Sītā feigned anger, though in fact she was amused. She replied to Rāma: "Your advice that I should stay here in the palace while you go to live in the forest is unworthy of a heroic prince like you, Lord. Whereas one's father,

2. The narrative of the heroic god Indra's victory over the dragonlike demon Vṛtra is an important myth in the *Ṛg-veda*, the oldest of the Hindu scriptures. Aditi is the mother of the gods. The eagle Garuḍa is the mount of Viṣṇu, the god of preservation. In the fifth of his ten incarnations, Viṣṇu took the form of a dwarf (Vāmana), who subsequently grew into the gigantic figure Trivikrama ("the god of three strides"), spanned earth and sky with two strides, then crushed the demon Bali with his third step.

3. The four Vedas are the ancient scriptures of the Hindus. The oceans, continents, and heavens of the Hindu universe are held to have sacred powers.

mother, brother, son and daughter-in-law enjoy their own good or misfortune, the wife alone shares the life of her husband. To a woman, neither father nor son nor mother nor friends but the husband alone is her sole refuge here in this world and in the other world, too. Hence I shall accompany you to the forest. I shall go ahead of you, clearing a path for you in the forest. Life with the husband is incomparably superior to life in a palace, or an aerial mansion, or a trip to heaven! I have had detailed instructions from my parents on how to conduct myself in Ayodhyā! But I shall not stay here. I assure you, I shall not be a burden, an impediment, to you in the forest. Nor will I regard life in the forest as exile or as suffering. With you it will be more than heaven to me. It will not be the least hardship to me; without you, even heaven is hell."

AYODHYĀ 28–29

Thinking of the great hardships they would have to endure in the forest, however, Rāma tried to dissuade Sītā in the following words: "Sītā, you come of a very wealthy family dedicated to righteousness. It is therefore proper that you should stay behind and serve my people here. Thus, by avoiding the hardships of the forest and by lovingly serving my people here, would you gladden my heart. The forest is not a place for a princess like you. It is full of great dangers. Lions dwell in the caves; and it is frightening to hear their roar. These wild beasts are not used to seeing human beings; the way they attack human beings is horrifying even to think about. Even the paths are thorny and it is hard to walk on them. The food is a few fruits which might have fallen on their own accord from the trees: living on them, one has to be contented all day. Our garments will be bark and animal skins: and the hair will have to be matted and gathered on the top of the head. Anger and greed have to be given up, the mind must be directed towards austerity and one should overcome fear even where it is natural. Totally exposed to the inclemencies of nature, surrounded by wild animals, serpents and so on, the forest is full of untold hardships. It is not a place for you, my dear."

This reiteration on the part of Rāma moved Sītā to tears. "Your gracious solicitude for my happiness only makes my love for you more ardent, and my determination to follow you more firm. You mentioned animals: they will never come anywhere near me while you are there. You mentioned the righteousness of serving your people: but, your father's command that you should go to the forest demands I should go, too; I am your half: and because of this, again I cannot live without you. In fact you have often declared that a righteous wife will not be able to live separated from her husband. And listen! This is not new to me: for even when I was in my father's house, long before we were married, wise astrologers had rightly predicted that I would live in a forest for some time. If you remember, I have been longing to spend some time in the forest, for I have trained myself for that eventuality. Lord, I feel actually delighted at the very thought that I shall at last go to the forest, to serve you constantly. Serving you, I shall not incur the sin of leaving your parents: thus have I heard from those who are well-versed in the Vedas and other scriptures, that a devoted wife remains united with her husband even after they leave this earth-plane. There is therefore no valid reason why you should wish to leave me here and go. If you still refuse to take me with you, I have no alternative but to lay down my life."

AYODHYĀ 30–31

To the further persuasive talk of Rāma, Sītā responded with a show of annoyance, courage and firmness. She even taunted Rāma in the following words: "While choosing you as his son-in-law, did my father Janaka realize that you were a woman at heart with a male body? Why, then are you, full of valor and courage, afraid even on my account? If you do not take me with you I shall surely die; but instead of waiting for such an event, I prefer to die in your presence. If you do not change your mind now, I shall take poison and die." In sheer anguish, the pitch of her voice rose higher and higher, and her eyes released a torrent of hot tears.

Rāma folded her in his arms and spoke to her lovingly, with great delight: "Sītā, I could not fathom your mind and therefore I tried to dissuade you from coming with me. Come, follow me. Of course I cannot drop the idea of going to the forest, even for your sake. I cannot live having disregarded the command of my parents. Indeed, I wonder how one could adore the unmanifest god, if one were unwilling to obey the commands of his parents and his guru whom he can see here. No religious activity nor even moral excellence can equal service of one's parents in bestowing supreme felicity on one. Whatever one desires, and whatever region one desires to ascend to after leaving this earth-plane, all this is secured by the service of parents. Hence I shall do as commanded by father; and this is the eternal dharma. And you have rightly resolved, to follow me to the forest. Come, and get ready soon. Give away generous gifts to the brāhmaṇas and distribute the rest of your possessions to the servants and others."

Lakṣmaṇa now spoke to Rāma: "If you are determined to go, then I shall go ahead of you." Rāma, however, tried to dissuade him: "Indeed, I know that you are my precious and best companion. Yet, I am anxious that you should stay behind and look after our mothers. Kaikeyī may not treat them well. By thus serving our mothers, you will prove your devotion to me." But Lakṣmaṇa replied quickly: "I am confident, Rāma, that Bharata will look after all the mothers, inspired by your spirit of renunciation and your adherence to dharma. If this does not prove to be the case, I can exterminate all of them in no time. Indeed, Kausalyā is great and powerful enough to look after herself: she gave birth to you! My place is near you; my duty to serve you."

Delighted to hear this, Rāma said: "Then let us all go. Before leaving I wish to give away in charity all that I possess to the holy brāhmaṇas. Please get them all together. Take leave of your friends and get our weapons ready, too."

* * *

From Book 3
Āraṇya

ĀRAṆYA 14–15

Rāma, Lakṣmaṇa and Sītā were proceeding towards Pañcavaṭī.[4] On the way they saw a huge vulture. Rāma's first thought was that it was a demon in disguise. The vulture said: "I am your father's friend!" Trusting the vulture's words, Rāma asked for details of its birth and ancestry.

The vulture said: "You know that Dakṣa Prajāpati[5] had sixty daughters and the sage Kaśyapa married eight of them. One day Kaśyapa said to his wives: 'You will give birth to offspring who will be foremost in the three worlds.' Aditi, Diti, Danu and Kālaka listened attentively; the others were indifferent. As a result, the former four gave birth to powerful offspring who were superhuman. Aditi gave birth to thirty-three gods. Diti gave birth to demons. Danu gave birth to Aśvagrīva. And, Kālaka had Naraka and Kālikā. Of the others, men were born of Manu, and the sub-human species from the other wives of Kaśyapa. Tāmra's daughter was Sukī whose granddaughter was Vinatā who had two sons, Garuḍa and Aruṇa. My brother Sampāti and I are the sons of Aruṇa. I offer my services to you, O Rāma. If you will be pleased to accept them, I shall guard Sītā when you and Lakṣmaṇa may be away from your hermitage. As you have seen, this formidable forest is full of wild animals and demons, too."

Rāma accepted this new friendship. All of them now proceeded towards Pañcavaṭī in search of a suitable place for building a hermitage. Having arrived at Pañcavaṭī, identified by Rāma by the description which the sage Agastya had given, Rāma said to Lakṣmaṇa: "Pray, select a suitable place here for building the hermitage. It should have a charming forest, good water, firewood, flowers and holy grass." Lakṣmaṇa submitted: "Even if we live together for a hundred years, I shall continue to be your servant. Hence, Lord, you select the place and I shall do the needful." Rejoicing at Lakṣmaṇa's attitude, Rāma pointed to a suitable place, which satisfied all the requisites of a hermitage. Rāma said: "This is holy ground; this is charming; it is frequented by beasts and birds. We shall dwell here." Immediately Lakṣmaṇa set about building a hermitage for all of them to live in.

Rāma warmly embraced Lakṣmaṇa and said: "I am delighted by your good work and devoted service: and I embrace you in token of such admiration. Brother, you divine the wish of my heart, you are full of gratitude, you know dharma; with such a man as his son, father is not dead but is eternally alive."

Entering that hermitage, Rāma, Lakṣmaṇa and Sītā dwelt in it with great joy and happiness.

ĀRAṆYA 16

Time rolled on. One day Lakṣmaṇa sought the presence of Rāma early in the morning and described what he had seen outside the hermitage. He said: "Winter, the season which you love most, has arrived, O Rāma. There is dry

4. "Five banyan trees," a grove in western India, toward which Rāma has been directed by the sage Agastya.

5. A progenitor god in ancient Hindu mythology.

cold everywhere; the earth is covered with foodgrains. Water is uninviting; and fire is pleasant. The first fruits of the harvest have been brought in; and the agriculturists have duly offered some of it to the gods and the manes, and thus reaffirmed their indebtedness to them. The farmer who thus offers the first fruits to gods and manes is freed from sin.

"The sun moves in the southern hemisphere; and the north looks lusterless. Himālaya, the abode of snow, looks even more so! It is pleasant to take a walk even at noon. The shade of a tree which we loved in summer is unpleasant now. Early in the morning the earth, with its rich wheat and barley fields, is enveloped by mist. Even so, the rice crop. The sun, even when it rises, looks soft and cool like the moon. Even the elephants which approach the water, touch it with their trunk but pull the trunk quickly away on account of the coldness of the water.

"Rāma, my mind naturally thinks of our beloved brother Bharata. Even in this cold winter, he who could command the luxury of a king, prefers to sleep on the floor and live an ascetic life. Surely, he, too, would have got up early in the morning and has perhaps had a cold bath in the river Sarayū. What a noble man! I can even now picture him in front of me: with eyes like the petals of a lotus, dark brown in color, slim and without an abdomen, as it were. He knows what dharma is. He speaks the truth. He is modest and self-controlled, always speaks pleasantly, is sweet-natured, with long arms and with all his enemies fully subdued.[6] That noble Bharata has given up all his pleasures and is devoted to you. He has already won his place in heaven, Rāma. Though he lives in the city; yet, he has adopted the ascetic mode of life and follows you in spirit.

"We have heard it said that a son takes after his mother in nature: but in the case of Bharata this has proved false. I wonder how Kaikeyī, in spite of having our father as her husband, and Bharata as her son, has turned out to be so cruel."

When Lakṣmaṇa said this, Rāma stopped him, saying: "Do not speak ill of our mother Kaikeyī, Lakṣmaṇa. Talk only of our beloved Bharata. Even though I try not to think of Ayodhyā and our people there, when I think of Bharata, I wish to see him."

ĀRAṆYA 17–18

After their bath and morning prayers, Rāma, Lakṣmaṇa and Sītā returned to their hermitage. As they were seated in their hut, there arrived upon the scene a dreadful demoness. She looked at Rāma and immediately fell in love with him! He had a handsome face; she had an ugly face. He had a slender waist; she had a huge abdomen. He had lovely large eyes; she had hideous eyes. He had lovely soft hair; she had red hair. He had a lovable form; she had a terrible form. He had a sweet voice; hers resembled the barking of a dog. He was young; she was haughty. He was able; her speech was crooked. He was of noble conduct; she was of evil conduct. He was beloved; she had a forbidding appearance. Such a demoness spoke to Rāma: "Who are you, young men; and what are both of you doing in this forest, with this lady?"

6. A list of the conventional attributes of a handsome, brave, and virtuous warrior.

Rāma told her the whole truth about himself, Lakṣmaṇa and Sītā, about his banishment from the kingdom, etc. Then Rāma asked her: "O charming lady,[7] now tell me who you are." At once the demoness replied: "Ah, Rāma! I shall tell you all about myself immediately. I am Śūrpaṇakhā, the sister of Rāvaṇa. I am sure you have heard of him. He has two other brothers, Kumbhakarṇa and Vibhīṣaṇa.[8] Two other brothers Khara and Dūṣaṇa live in the neighborhood here. The moment I saw you, I fell in love with you. What have you to do with this ugly, emaciated Sītā? Marry me. Both of us shall roam about this forest. Do not worry about Sītā or Lakṣmaṇa: I shall swallow them in a moment." But, Rāma smilingly said to her: "You see I have my wife with me here. Why do you not propose to my brother Lakṣmaṇa who has no wife here?" Śūrpaṇakhā did not mind that suggestion. She turned to Lakṣmaṇa and said: "It is all right. You please marry me and we shall roam about happily." She was tormented by passion.

Lakṣmaṇa said in a teasing mood: "O lady, you see that I am only the slave of Rāma and Sītā. Why do you choose to be the wife of a slave? You will only become a servant-maid. Persuade Rāma to send away that ugly wife of his and marry you." Śūpaṇakhā turned to Rāma again. She said: "Unable to give up this wife of yours, Sītā, you turn down my offer. See, I shall at once swallow her. When she is gone you will marry me; and we shall roam about in this forest happily." So saying, she actually rushed towards Sītā. Rāma stopped her in time, and said to Lakṣmaṇa: "What are you doing, Lakṣmaṇa? It is not right to jest with cruel and unworthy people. Look at the plight of Sītā. She barely escaped with her life. Come, quickly deform this demoness and send her away."

Lakṣmaṇa drew his sword and quickly cut off the nose and the ears of Śūpaṇakhā. Weeping and bleeding she ran away. She went to her brother Khara and fell down in front of him.

* * *

Summary Distraught and furious, Śūrpaṇakhā asks her brothers Khara and Dūṣaṇa, who live in nearby Janasthāna, to avenge her insult by killing Rāma and Lakṣmaṇa. However, Rāma and Lakṣmaṇa kill the brothers and all their troops.

ĀRAṆYA 32–33

Śūrpaṇakhā witnessed the wholesale destruction of the demons of Janasthāna,[9] including their supreme leader Khara. Stricken with terror, she ran to Laṅkā. There she saw her brother Rāvaṇa, the ruler of Laṅkā, seated with his ministers in a palace whose roof scraped the sky.[1] Rāvaṇa had twenty arms, ten heads, was broad chested and endowed with all the physical qualifications of a monarch. He had previously fought with the gods, even with their chief Indra. He was well versed in the science of warfare and knew the use of the celestial missiles in battle. He had been hit by the gods, even by the discus[2] of lord Viṣṇu,

7. This formulaic phrase used in addressing a lady is meant ironically here.

8. The names of the demons are suggestive: Śūrpaṇakhā means "woman with nails as large as winnowing baskets" and Kumbhakarṇa means "pot ear." Vibhīṣaṇa means "terrifying."

9. A region near Pañcavaṭī.

1. A conventional description of a palace or mansion.

2. A wheel with sharp points, Viṣṇu's weapon.

but he did not die. For, he had performed breathtaking austerities for a period of ten thousand years, and offered his own heads in worship to Brahmā the creator and earned from him the boon that he would not be killed by any superhuman or subhuman agency (except by man). Emboldened by this boon, the demon had tormented the gods and particularly the sages.

Śūrpaṇakhā entered Rāvaṇa's presence, clearly displaying the physical deformity which Lakṣmaṇa had caused to her. She shouted at Rāvaṇa in open assembly: "Brother, you have become so thoroughly infatuated and addicted to sense-pleasure that you are unfit to be a king any longer. The people lose all respect for the king who is only interested in his own pleasure and neglects his royal duties. People turn away from the king who has no spies, who has lost touch with the people and whom they cannot see, and who is unable to do what is good for them. It is the employment of spies that makes the king 'far-sighted' for through these spies he sees quite far. You have failed to appoint proper spies to collect intelligence for you. Therefore, you do not know that fourteen thousand of your people have been slaughtered by a human being. Even Khara and Dūṣaṇa have been killed by Rāma. And, Rāma has assured the ascetics of Janasthāna which is your territory, that the demons shall not do them any harm. They are now protected by him. Yet, here you are; reveling in little pleasures!

"O brother, even a piece of wood, a clod of earth or just dust, has some use; but when a king falls from his position he is utterly useless. But that monarch who is vigilant, who has knowledge of everything, through his spies, who is self-controlled, who is full of gratitude and whose conduct is righteous—he rules for a long time. Wake up and act before you lose your sovereignty."

This made Rāvaṇa reflect.

ĀRAṆYA 34–35

And, Rāvaṇa's anger was roused. He asked Śūrpaṇakhā: "Tell me, who is it that disfigured you thus? What do you think of Rāma? Why has he come to Daṇḍaka forest?"

Śūrpaṇakhā gave an exact and colorful description of the physical appearance of Rāma. She said: "Rāma is equal in charm to Cupid himself. At the same time, he is a formidable warrior. When he was fighting the demons of Janasthāna, I could not see what he was doing; I only saw the demons falling dead on the field. You can easily understand when I tell you that within an hour and a half he had killed fourteen thousand demons. He spared me, perhaps because he did not want to kill a woman. He has a brother called Lakṣmaṇa who is equally powerful. He is Rāma's right hand man and alter ego; Rāma's own life-force moving outside his body. Oh, you must see Sītā, Rāma's wife. I have not seen even a celestial nymph who could match her in beauty. He who has her for his wife, whom she fondly embraces, he shall indeed be the ruler of gods. She is a fit bride for you; and you are indeed the most suitable suitor for her. In fact, I wanted to bring that beautiful Sītā here so that you could marry her: but Lakṣmaṇa intervened and cruelly mutilated my body. If you could only look at her for a moment, you would immediately fall in love with her. If this proposal appeals to you, take some action quickly and get her here."

Rāvaṇa was instantly tempted. Immediately he ordered his flying chariot to be got ready. This vehicle which was richly adorned with gold, could move freely wherever its owner willed. Its front part resembled mules with fiendish heads. Rāvaṇa took his seat in this vehicle and moved towards the seacoast. The coastline of Laṅkā was dotted with hermitages inhabited by sages and also celestial and semi-divine beings. It was also the pleasure resort of celestials and nymphs who went there to sport and to enjoy themselves. Driving at great speed through them, Rāvaṇa passed through caravan parks scattered with the chariots of the celestials. He also drove through dense forests of sandal trees, banana plantations and cocoanut palm groves. In those forests there were also spices and aromatic plants. Along the coast lay pearls and precious stones. He passed through cities which had an air of opulence.

Rāvaṇa crossed the ocean in his flying chariot and reached the hermitage where Mārīca[3] was living in ascetic garb, subsisting on a disciplined diet. Mārīca welcomed Rāvaṇa and questioned him about the purpose of his visit.

ĀRAṆYA 36–37

Rāvaṇa said to Mārīca: "Listen, Mārīca. You know that fourteen thousand demons, including my brother Khara and the great warrior Triśira have been mercilessly killed by Rāma and Lakṣmaṇa who have now promised their protection to the ascetics of Daṇḍaka forest, thus flouting our authority. Driven out of his country by his angry father, obviously for a disgraceful action, this unrighteous and hard-hearted prince Rāma has killed the demons without any justification. And, they have even dared to disfigure my beloved sister Śūrpaṇakhā. I must immediately take some action to avenge the death of my brother and to restore our prestige and our authority. I need your help; kindly do not refuse this time.

"Disguising yourself as a golden deer of great beauty, roam near the hermitage of Rāma. Sītā would surely be attracted, and she would ask Rāma and Lakṣmaṇa to capture you. When they go after you, leaving Sītā alone in the hermitage, I shall easily abduct Sītā." Even as Rāvaṇa was unfolding this plot, Mārīca's mouth became dry and parched with fear. Trembling with fear, Mārīca said to Rāvaṇa:

"O king, one can easily get in this world a counselor who tells you what is pleasing to you; but hard it is to find a wise counselor who tells you the unpleasant truth which is good for you—and harder it is to find one who heeds such advice. Surely, your intelligence machine is faulty and therefore you have no idea of the prowess of Rāma. Else, you would not talk of abducting Sītā. I wonder: perhaps Sītā has come into this world to end your life, or perhaps there is to be great sorrow on account of Sītā, or perhaps maddened by lust, you are going to destroy yourself and the demons and Laṅkā itself. Oh, no, you were wrong in your estimation of Rāma. He is not wicked; he is righteousness incarnate. He is not cruel hearted; he is generous to a fault. He has not been disgraced and exiled from the kingdom. He is here to honor the promise his father had given his mother Kaikeyī, after joyously renouncing his kingdom.

"O king, when you entertain ideas of abducting Sītā you are surely playing with fire. Please remember: when you stand facing Rāma, you are standing face to face with your own death. Sītā is the beloved wife of Rāma, who is

3. An uncle of Rāvaṇa, expert in sorcery.

extremely powerful. Nay, give up this foolish idea. What will you gain by thus gambling with your sovereignty over the demons, and with your life itself? Please consult the noble Vibhīṣaṇa and your virtuous ministers before embarking upon such unwise projects. They will surely advise you against them."

* * *

ĀRAṆYA 42

Rāvaṇa was determined, and Mārīca knew that there was no use arguing with him. Hence, after the last-minute attempt to avert the catastrophe, Mārīca said to Rāvaṇa: "What can I do when you are so wicked? I am ready to go to Rāma's āśrama.[4] God help you!" Not minding the taunt, Rāvaṇa expressed his unabashed delight at Mārīca's consent. He applauded Mārīca and said: "That is the spirit, my friend: you are now the same old Mārīca that I knew. I guess you had been possessed by some evil spirit a few minutes ago, on account of which you had begun to preach a different gospel. Let us swiftly get into this vehicle and proceed to our destination. As soon as you have accomplished the purpose, you are free to go and to do what you please!"

Both of them got into the flying chariot and quickly left the hermitage of Mārīca. Once again they passed forests, hills, rivers and cities: and soon they reached the neighborhood of the hermitage of Rāma. They got down from that chariot which had been embellished with gold. Holding Mārīca by the hand, Rāvaṇa said to him: "Over there is the hermitage of Rāma, surrounded by banana plantations. Well, now, get going with the work for which we have come here." Immediately Mārīca transformed himself into an attractive deer. It was extraordinary, totally unlike any deer that inhabited the forest. It was unique. It dazzled like a huge gem stone. Each part of its body had a different color. The colors had an unearthly brilliance and charm. Thus embellished by the colors of all the precious stones, the deer which was the demon Mārīca in disguise, roamed about near the hermitage of Rāma, nibbling at the grass now and then. At one time it came close to Sītā; then it ran away and joined the other deer grazing at a distance. It was very playful, jumping about and chasing its tail and spinning around. Sītā went out to gather flowers. She cast a glance at that extraordinary and unusual deer. As she did so, the deer too, sensing the accomplishment of the mission, came closer to her. Then it ran away, pretending to be afraid. Sītā marveled at the very appearance of this unusual deer the like of which she had not seen before and which had the hue of jewels.

ĀRAṆYA 43

From where she was gathering flowers, Sītā, filled with wonder to see that unusual deer, called out to Rāma: "Come quick and see, O Lord; come with your brother. Look at this extraordinary creature. I have never seen such a beautiful deer before." Rāma and Lakṣmaṇa looked at the deer, and Lakṣmaṇa's suspicions were aroused: "I am suspicious; I think it is the same demon Mārīca

4. Hermitage.

in disguise. I have heard that Mārīca could assume any form at will, and through such tricks he had brought death and destruction to many ascetics in this forest. Surely, this deer is not real: no one has heard of a deer with rainbow colors, each one of its limbs shining resplendent with the color of a different gem! That itself should enable us to understand that it is a demon, not an animal."

Sītā interrupted Lakṣmaṇa's talk, and said: "Never mind, one thing is certain; this deer has captivated my mind. It is such a dear. I have not seen such an animal near our hermitage! There are many types of deer which roam about near the hermitage; this is just an extraordinary and unusual deer. It is superlative in all respects: its color is lovely, its texture is lovely, and even its voice sounds delightful. It would be a wonderful feat if it could be caught alive. We could use it as a pet, to divert our minds. Later we could take it to Ayodhyā: and I am sure all your brothers and mothers would just adore it. If it is not possible to capture it alive, O Lord, then it can be killed, and I would love to have its skin. I know I am not behaving myself towards both of you: but I am helpless; I have lost my heart to that deer. I am terribly curious."

In fact, Rāma was curious, too! And so, he took Sītā's side and said to Lakṣmaṇa: "It is beautiful, Lakṣmaṇa. It is unusual. I have never seen a creature like this. And, princes do hunt animals and cherish their skins.[5] By sporting and hunting kings acquire great wealth! People say that that is real wealth which one pursues without premeditation. So, let us try to get the deer or its skin. If, as you say, it is a demon in disguise, then surely it ought to be killed by me, just as Vātāpi who was tormenting and destroying sages and ascetics was justly killed by the sage Agastya.[6] Vātāpi fooled the ascetics till he met the sage Agastya. This Mārīca, too, has fooled the ascetics so far: till coming to me today! The very beauty of his hide is his doom. And, you, Lakṣmaṇa, please guard Sītā with great vigilance, till I kill this deer with just one shot and bring the hide along with me."

ĀRAṆYA 44–45

Rāma took his weapons and went after the strange deer. As soon as the deer saw him pursuing it, it started to run away. Now it disappeared, now it appeared to be very near, now it ran fast, now it seemed confused—thus it led Rāma far away from his hermitage. Rāma was fatigued, and needed to rest. As he was standing under a tree, intrigued by the actions of the mysterious deer, it came along with other deer and began to graze not far from him. When Rāma once again went for it, it ran away. Not wishing to go farther nor to waste more time, Rāma took his weapon and fitted the missile of Brahmā[7] to it and fired. This missile pierced the illusory deer-mask and into the very heart of the demon.

5. Hermits are required to take a vow of nonviolence, but Rāma, a warrior prince, is allowed to carry arms and to hunt.
6. The demon Vātāpi killed ascetics by tricking them. Disguising himself, he would invite innocent wayfarers to a meal. He would magically conceal himself in the food, thus entering his guests' bellies; he would then kill the men by splitting open their stomachs. The sage Agastya outwitted and killed Vātāpi by digesting his meal, and with it, the demon himself, before he could tear the sage's stomach open.
7. The creator god in the triad of Hindu great gods.

Mārīca uttered a loud cry, leapt high into the sky and then dropped dead onto the ground. As he fell, however, he remembered Rāvaṇa's instructions and assuming the voice of Rāma cried aloud: "Hey Sītā; Hey Lakṣmaṇa."

Rāma saw the dreadful body of the demon. He knew now that Lakṣmaṇa was right. And, he was even more puzzled by the way in which the demon wailed aloud before dying. He was full of apprehension. He hastened towards the hermitage.

In the hermitage, both Sītā and Lakṣmaṇa heard the cry. Sītā believed it was Rāma's voice. She was panic-stricken. She said to Lakṣmaṇa: "Go, go quickly: your brother is in danger. And, I cannot live without him. My breath and my heart are both violently disturbed." Lakṣmaṇa remembered Rāma's admonition that he should stay with Sītā and not leave her alone. He said to her: "Pray, be not worried." Sītā grew suspicious and furious. She said to him: "Ah, I see the plot now! You have a wicked eye on me and so have been waiting for this to happen. What a terrible enemy of Rāma you are, pretending to be his brother!" Distressed to hear these words, Lakṣmaṇa replied: "No one in the three worlds can overpower Rāma, blessed lady! It was not his voice at all. These demons in the forest are capable of simulating the voice of anyone. Having killed that demon disguised as a deer, Rāma will soon be here. Fear not." His calmness even more annoyed Sītā, who literally flew into a rage. She said again: "Surely, you are the worst enemy that Rāma could have had. I know now that you have been following us, cleverly pretending to be Rāma's brother and friend. I know now that your real motive for doing so is either to get me or you are Bharata's accomplice. Ah, but you will not succeed. Presently, I shall give up my life. For I cannot live without Rāma." Cut to the quick by these terrible words, Lakṣmaṇa said: "You are worshipful to me: hence I cannot answer back. It is not surprising that women should behave in this manner: for they are easily led away from dharma; they are fickle and sharp-tongued. I cannot endure what you said just now. I shall go. The gods are witness to what took place here. May those gods protect you. But I doubt if when Rāma and I return, we shall find you." Bowing to her, Lakṣmaṇa left.

ĀRAṆYA 46

Rāvaṇa was looking for this golden opportunity. He disguised himself as an ascetic, clad in ocher robes, carrying a shell water-pot, a staff and an umbrella, and approached Sītā who was still standing outside the cottage eagerly looking for Rāma's return. His very presence in that forest was inauspicious: and even the trees and the waters of the rivers were frightened of him, as it were. In a holy disguise, Rāvaṇa stood before Sītā: a deep well covered with grass; a death-trap.

Gazing at the noble Sītā, who had now withdrawn into the cottage and whose eyes were raining tears, Rāvaṇa came near her, and though his heart was filled with lust, he was chanting Vedic hymns. He said to Sītā in a soft, tender and affectionate tone: "O young lady! Pray, tell me, are you the goddess of fortune or the goddess of modesty, or the consort of Cupid himself?" Then Rāvaṇa described her incomparable beauty in utterly immodest terms, unworthy of an anchorite whose form he had assumed. He continued: "O charming lady! You have robbed me of my heart. I have not seen such a beautiful lady, neither a divine or a semi-divine being. Your extraordinary form and your youthfulness, and your living in this forest, all these together agitate my mind. It is not right that you should live in this forest. You should stay in palaces. In the forest monkeys, lions, tigers and other wild animals live. The forest is the natural habitat of demons who roam freely. You are living alone in this dreadful forest: are you not afraid, O fair lady? Pray, tell me, why are you living in this forest?"

Rāvaṇa was in the disguise of a brāhmaṇa. Therefore, Sītā offered him the worship and the hospitality that it was her duty to offer a brāhmaṇa. She made him sit down; she gave him water to wash his feet and his hands. Then she placed food in front of him.

Whatever she did only aggravated his lust and his desire to abduct her and take her away to Laṅkā.

ĀRAṆYA 47–48

Sītā, then, proceeded to answer his enquiry concerning herself. He appeared to be a brāhmaṇa; and if his enquiry was not answered, he might get angry and curse her.[8] Sītā said: "I am a daughter of the noble king Janaka; Sītā is my name. I am the beloved consort of Rāma. After our marriage, Rāma and I lived in the palace of Ayodhyā for twelve years." She then truthfully narrated all that took place just prior to Rāma's exile to the forest. She continued: "And so, when Rāma was twenty-five and I was eighteen, we left the palace and sought the forest-life.[9] And so the three of us dwell in this forest. My husband, Rāma, will soon return to the hermitage gathering various animals and also wild fruits. Pray, tell me who you are, O brāhmaṇa, and what you are doing in this forest roaming all alone."

Rāvaṇa lost no time in revealing his true identity. He said: "I am not a brāhmaṇa, O Sītā: I am the lord of demons, Rāvaṇa. My very name strikes terror in the hearts of gods and men. The moment I saw you, I lost my heart to you; and I derive no pleasure from the company of my wives. Come with me, and be my queen, O Sītā. You will love Laṅkā. Laṅkā is my capital, it is surrounded by the ocean and it is situated on the top of a hill. There we shall live together, and you will enjoy your life, and never even once think of this wretched forest-life."

Sītā was furious to hear this. She said: "O demon-king! I have firmly resolved to follow Rāma who is equal to the god of gods, who is mighty and charming, and who is devoted to righteousness.[1] If you entertain a desire for me, his wife, it is like tying yourself with a big stone and trying to swim across the ocean: you are doomed. Where are you and where is he: there is no comparison. You are like a jackal; he the lion.[2] You are like base metal; he gold."

8. Priestly *brāhmaṇas* and sages have the power to curse people as well as to bestow boons.

9. Rāma must have been thirteen and Sītā six years old when they were married. The practice of "child marriage" continued in India until very recently.

1. A special epithet of Rāma. "God of gods": an epithet used for warriors, kings, and heroes. It is a reference to Indra, king of heaven and all the gods.

2. King of animals, the lion represents regal majesty and courage, while the jackal is the embodiment of cunning and deceit.

But Rāvaṇa would not give up his desire. He repeated: "Even the gods dare not stand before me, O Sītā! For fear of me even Kubera the god of wealth abandoned his chariot and ran away to Kailāsa. If the gods, headed by Indra, even sense I am angry, they flee. Even the forces of nature obey me. Laṅkā is enclosed by a strong wall; the houses are built of gold with gates of precious stones. Forget this Rāma, who lives like an ascetic, and come with me. He is not as strong as my little finger!" Sītā was terribly angered: "Surely you seek the destruction of all the demons, by behaving like this, O Rāvaṇa. It cannot be otherwise since they have such an unworthy king with no self-control. You may live after abducting Indra's wife, but not after abducting me, Rāma's wife."

ĀRAṆYA 49–50

Rāvaṇa made his body enormously big and said to Sītā: "You do not realize what a mighty person I am. I can step out into space, and lift up the earth with my arms; I can drink up the waters of the oceans; and I can kill death itself. I can shoot a missile and bring the sun down. Look at the size of my body." As he expanded his form, Sītā turned her face away from him. He resumed his original form with ten heads and twenty arms. Again he spoke to Sītā: "Would you not like to be renowned in the three worlds? Then marry me. And, I promise I shall do nothing to displease you. Give up all thoughts of that mortal and unsuccessful Rāma."

Rāvaṇa did not wait for an answer. Seizing Sītā by her hair and lifting her up with his arm, he left the hermitage. Instantly the golden chariot appeared in front of him. He ascended it, along with Sītā. Sītā cried aloud: "O Rāma." As she was being carried away, she wailed aloud: "O Lakṣmaṇa, who is ever devoted to the elder brother, do you not know that I am being carried away by Rāvaṇa?" To Rāvaṇa, she said: "O vile demon, surely you will reap the fruits of your evil action: but they do not manifest immediately." She said as if to herself: "Surely, Kaikeyī would be happy today." She said to the trees, to the river Godāvarī, to the deities dwelling in the forest, to the animals and birds: "Pray, tell Rāma that I have been carried away by the wicked Rāvaṇa." She saw Jaṭāyu and cried aloud: "O Jaṭāyu! See, Rāvaṇa is carrying me away."

Hearing that cry, Jaṭāyu woke up. Jaṭāyu introduced himself to Rāvaṇa: "O Rāvaṇa, I am the king of vultures, Jaṭāyu. Pray, desist from this action unworthy of a king. Rāma, too, is a king; and his consort is worthy of our protection. A wise man should not indulge in such action as would disgrace him in the eyes of others. And, another's wife is as worthy of protection as one's own. The cultured and the common people often copy the behavior of the king. If the king himself is guilty of unworthy behavior what becomes of the people? If you persist in your wickedness, even the prosperity you enjoy will leave you soon.

"Therefore, let Sītā go. One should not get hold of a greater load than one can carry; one should not eat what he cannot digest. Who will indulge in an action which is painful and which does not promote righteousness, fame or permanent glory? I am sixty thousand years old and you are young. I warn you. If you do not give up Sītā, you will not be able to carry her away while I am alive and able to restrain you! I shall dash you down along with that chariot."

ĀRAṆYA 51

Rāvaṇa could not brook this insult: he turned towards Jaṭāyu in great anger. Jaṭāyu hit the chariot and Rāvaṇa; Rāvaṇa hit Jaṭāyu back with terrible ferocity. This aerial combat between Rāvaṇa and Jaṭāyu looked like the collision of two mountains endowed with wings. Rāvaṇa used all the conventional missiles, the Nālikas, the Nārācas and the Vikarṇis. The powerful eagle shrugged them off. Jaṭāyu tore open the canopy of the chariot and inflicted wounds on Rāvaṇa himself.

In great anger, Jaṭāyu grabbed Rāvaṇa's weapon (a cannon) and broke it with his claws. Rāvaṇa took up a more formidable weapon which literally sent a shower of missiles. Against these Jaṭāyu used his own wings as an effective shield. Pouncing upon this weapon, too, Jaṭāyu destroyed it with his claws. Jaṭāyu also tore open Rāvaṇa's armor. Nay, Jaṭāyu even damaged the gold-plated propellers of Rāvaṇa's flying chariot, which had the appearance of demons, and thus crippled the craft which would take its occupant wherever he desired and which emitted fire. With his powerful beak, Jaṭāyu broke the neck of Rāvaṇa's pilot.

With the chariot thus rendered temporarily useless, Rāvaṇa jumped out of it, still holding Sītā with his powerful arm. While Rāvaṇa was still above the ground, Jaṭāyu again challenged him: "O wicked one, even now you are unwilling to turn away from evil. Surely, you have resolved to bring about the destruction of the entire race of demons. Unknowingly or wantonly, you are swallowing poison which would certainly kill you and your relations. Rāma and Lakṣmaṇa will not tolerate this sinful act of yours: and you cannot stand before them on the battlefield. The manner in which you are doing this unworthy act is despicable: you are behaving like a thief not like a hero." Jaṭāyu swooped on Rāvaṇa and violently tore at his body.

Then there ensued a hand-to-hand fight between the two. Rāvaṇa hit Jaṭāyu with his fist; but Jaṭāyu tore Rāvaṇa's arms away. However, new ones sprang up instantly. Rāvaṇa hit Jaṭāyu and kicked him. After some time, Rāvaṇa drew his sword and cut off the wings of Jaṭāyu. When the wings were thus cut, Jaṭāyu fell, dying. Looking at the fallen Jaṭāyu, Sītā ran towards him in great anguish, as she would to the side of a fallen relation. In inconsolable grief, Sītā began to wail aloud.

ĀRAṆYA 52–53

As Sītā was thus wailing near the body of Jaṭāyu, Rāvaṇa came towards her. Looking at him with utter contempt, Sītā said: "I see dreadful omens, O Rāvaṇa. Dreams as also the sight and the cries of birds and beasts are clear indicators of the shape of things to come.[3] But you do not notice them! Alas, here is Jaṭāyu, my father-in-law's friend who is dying on my account. O Rāma, O Lakṣmaṇa, save me, protect me!"

Once again Rāvaṇa grabbed her and got into the chariot which had been made airworthy again. The Creator, the gods and the celestials who witnessed

3. See the description of Trijaṭā's dream, below (p. 1221). Dreams and omens play a comparable role in the culture of the Greeks and Romans.

this, exclaimed: "Bravo, our purpose is surely accomplished."[4] Even the sages of the Daṇḍaka forest inwardly felt happy at the thought, "Now that Sītā has been touched by this wicked demon, the end of Rāvaṇa and all the demons is near." As she was carried away by Rāvaṇa, Sītā was wailing aloud: "O Rāma, O Lakṣmaṇa."

Placed on the lap of Rāvaṇa, Sītā was utterly miserable. Her countenance was full of sorrow and anguish. The petals of the flowers that dropped from her head fell and covered the body of Rāvaṇa for a while. She was of beautiful golden complexion; and he was of dark color. Her being seated on his lap looked like an elephant wearing a golden sash, or the moon shining in the midst of a dark cloud, or a streak of lightning seen in a dense dark cloud.

The chariot streaked through the sky as fast as a meteor would. On the earth below, trees shook as if to reassure Sītā: "Do not be afraid," the waterfalls looked as if mountains were shedding tears, and people said to one another, "Surely, dharma has come to an end, as Rāvaṇa is carrying Sītā away."

Once again Sītā rebuked Rāvaṇa: "You ought to feel ashamed of yourself, O Rāvaṇa. You boast of your prowess; but you are stealing me away! You have not won me in a duel, which would be considered heroic. Alas, for a long, long time to come, people will recount your ignominy, and this unworthy and unrighteous act of yours will be remembered by the people. You are taking me and flying at such speed: hence no one can do anything to stop you. If only you had the courage to stop for a few moments, you would find yourself dead. My lord Rāma and his brother Lakṣmaṇa will not spare you. Leave me alone, O demon! But, you are in no mood to listen to what is good for your own welfare. Even as, one who has reached death's door loves only harmful objects. Rāma will soon find out where I am and ere long you will be transported to the world of the dead."

Rāvaṇa flew along, though now and then he trembled in fear.

ĀRAṆYA 54–55

The chariot was flying over hills and forests and was approaching the ocean. At that time, Sītā beheld on the ground below, five strong vānaras[5] seated and watching the craft with curiosity. Quickly, Sītā took off the stole she had around her shoulders and, removing all her jewels and putting them in that stole, bundled them all up and threw the bundle into the midst of the vānaras, in the hope that should Rāma chance to come there they would give him a clue to her whereabouts.

Rāvaṇa did not notice this but flew on. And now the craft, which shot through space at great speed, was over the ocean; a little while after that, Rāvaṇa entered Laṅkā along with his captive Sītā. Entering his own apartments, Rāvaṇa placed Sītā in them, entrusting her care to some of his chief female attendants. He said to them: "Take great care of Sītā. Let no male approach these apartments without my express permission. And, take great care to let Sītā have whatever she wants and asks for. Any neglect on your part means instant death."

4. We are reminded here that Viṣṇu incarnated himself as Rāma at the request of the gods, who wished Rāvaṇa to be killed.

5. Some scholars have suggested that *vānaras*, usually translated as "monkeys" or "apes," refers to tribal people or apelike human beings. This translator has left the word untranslated.

Rāvaṇa was returning to his own apartments: on the way he was still considering what more could be done to ensure the fulfilment of his ambition. He sent for eight of the most ferocious demons and instructed them thus: "Proceed at once to Janasthāna. It was ruled by my brother Khara; but it has now been devastated by Rāma. I am filled with rage to think that a mere human being could thus kill Khara, Dūṣaṇa and all their forces. Never mind: I shall put an end to Rāma soon. Keep an eye on him and keep me informed of his movements. You are free to bring about the destruction of Rāma." And, the demons immediately left.

Rāvaṇa returned to where Sītā was and compelled her to inspect the apartments. The palace stood on pillars of ivory, gold, crystal and silver and was studded with diamonds. The floor, the walls, the stairways—everything was made of gold and diamonds. Then again he said to Sītā: "Here at this place there are over a thousand demons ever ready to do my bidding. Their services and the entire Laṅkā I place at your feet. My life I offer to you; you are to me more valuable than my life. You will have under your command even the many good women whom I have married. Be my wife. Laṅkā is surrounded by the ocean, eight hundred miles on all sides. It is unapproachable to anybody; least of all to Rāma. Forget the weakling Rāma. Do not worry about the scriptural definitions of righteousness: we shall also get married in accordance with demoniacal wedding procedure. Youth is fleeting. Let us get married soon and enjoy life."

ĀRAṆYA 56

Placing a blade of grass between Rāvaṇa and herself,[6] Sītā said: "O demon! Rāma, the son of king Daśaratha, is my lord, the only one I adore. He and his brother Lakṣmaṇa will surely put an end to your life. If they had seen you lay your hands on me, they would have killed you on the spot, even as they laid Khara to eternal rest. It may be that you cannot be killed by demons and gods; but you cannot escape being killed at the hands of Rāma and Lakṣmaṇa. Rāvaṇa, you are doomed, beyond doubt. You have already lost your life, your good fortune, your very soul and your senses, and on account of your evil deeds Laṅkā has attained widowhood.[7] Though you do not perceive this, death is knocking at your door, O Rāvaṇa. O sinner, you cannot under any circumstances lay your hands on me. You may bind this body, or you may destroy it: it is after all insentient matter, and I do not consider it worth preserving, nor even life worth living—not in order to live a life which will earn disrepute for me."

Rāvaṇa found himself helpless. Hence, he resorted to threat. He said: "I warn you, Sītā. I give you twelve months in which to make up your mind to accept me as your husband. If within that time you do not so decide, my cooks will cut you up easily for my breakfast." He had nothing more to say to her. He turned to the female attendants surrounding her and ordered them: "Take this Sītā away to the Aśoka grove. Keep her there. Use every method of persuasion that you know of to make her yield to my desire. Guard her vigilantly. Take her and break her will as you would tame a wild elephant."

6. The magical power of Sītā's virtue allows her to use even a blade of grass as an effective barrier between herself and her abductor.
7. The ancient Indian king was considered to be the husband of the land he ruled, and kingdoms were often personified as a goddess (e.g., Laṅkā, pp. 1211–12).

The demonesses thereupon took Sītā away and confined her to the Aśoka grove, over which they themselves mounted guard day and night. Sītā did not find any peace of mind there, and stricken with fear and grief, she constantly thought of Rāma and Lakṣmaṇa.

It is said that at the same time, the creator Brahmā felt perturbed at the plight of Sītā. He spoke to Indra, the chief of gods: "Sītā is in the Aśoka grove. Pining for her husband, she may kill herself. Hence, go reassure her, and give her the celestial food to sustain herself till Rāma arrives in Laṅkā." Indra, thereupon, appeared before Sītā. In order to assure her of his identity he showed that his feet did not touch the ground and his eyes did not wink.[8] He gave her the celestial food, saying: "Eat this, and you will never feel hunger or thirst, nor will fatigue overpower you." While Indra was thus talking to Sītā, the goddess of sleep (Nidrā) had overpowered the demonesses.

ĀRAṆYA 57–58

Mārīca, the demon who had disguised himself as a unique deer, had been slain. But Rāma was intrigued and puzzled by the way in which Mārīca died, after crying: "O Sītā, O Lakṣmaṇa." Rāma sensed a deep and vicious plot. Hence he made haste to return to his hermitage. At the same time, he saw many evil omens. This aggravated his anxiety. He thought: "If Lakṣmaṇa heard that voice, he might rush to my aid, leaving Sītā alone. The demons surely wish to harm Sītā; and this might well have been a plot to achieve that purpose."

As he was thus brooding and proceeding towards his hermitage, he saw Lakṣmaṇa coming towards him. The distressed Rāma met the distressed Lakṣmaṇa; the sorrowing Rāma saw the sorrowful Lakṣmaṇa. Rāma caught hold of Lakṣmaṇa's arm and asked him, in an urgent tone: "O Lakṣmaṇa, why have you left Sītā alone and come? My mind is full of anxiety and terrible apprehension. When I see all these evil omens around us, I fear that something terrible has happened to Sītā. Surely Sītā has been stolen, killed or abducted."

Lakṣmaṇa's silence and grief-stricken countenance added fuel to the fire of anxiety in Rāma's heart. He asked again: "Is all well with Sītā? Where is my Sītā, the life of my life, without whom I cannot live even for an hour? Oh, what has happened to her? Alas, Kaikeyī's desire has been fulfilled today. If I am deprived of Sītā, I shall surely die. What more could Kaikeyī wish for? If, when I enter my hermitage, I do not find Sītā alive, how shall I live? Tell me, Lakṣmaṇa; speak. Surely, when that demon cried: 'O Lakṣmaṇa' in my voice, you were afraid that something had happened to me. Surely, Sītā also heard that cry and in a state of terrible mental agony, sent you to me. It is a painful thing that thus Sītā has been left alone; the demons who were waiting for an opportunity to hit back have been given that opportunity. The demons were sore distressed by my killing of the demon Khara. I am sure that they have done some great harm to Sītā, in the absence of both of us. What can I do now? How can I face this terrible calamity?"

Still, Lakṣmaṇa could not utter a word concerning what had happened. Both of them arrived near their hermitage. Everything that they saw reminded them of Sītā.

8. Attributes of the immortals.

ĀRAṆYA 59–60

And, once again before actually reaching the hermitage, and full of apprehension on account of Sītā, Rāma said to Lakṣmaṇa: "Lakṣmaṇa, you should not have come away like this, leaving Sītā alone in the hermitage. I had entrusted her to your care." When Rāma said this again and again, Lakṣmaṇa replied: "I have not come to you, leaving Sītā alone, just because I heard the demon Mārīca cry: 'O Lakṣmaṇa, O Sītā in your voice. I did so only upon being literally driven by Sītā to do so. When she heard the cry, she immediately felt distressed and asked me to go to your help. I tried to calm her saying: 'It is not Rāma's voice; it is unthinkable that Rāma, who is capable of protecting even the gods, would utter the words, 'save me.' She, however, misunderstood my attitude. She said something very harsh, something very strange, something which I hate even to repeat. She said: 'Either you are an agent of Bharata or you have unworthy intentions towards me and therefore you are happy that Rāma is in distress and do not rush to his help.' It is only then that I had to leave."

In his anxiety for Sītā, Rāma was unimpressed by this argument. He said to Lakṣmaṇa: "Swayed by an angry woman's words, you failed to carry out my words; I am not highly pleased with what you have done, O Lakṣmaṇa."

Rāma rushed into their hermitage. But he could find no trace of Sītā in it. Confused and distressed beyond measure, Rāma said to himself, as he continued to search for Sītā: "Where is Sītā? Alas, she could have been eaten by the demons. Or, taken away by someone. Or, she is hidden somewhere. Or, she has gone to the forest." The search was fruitless. His anguish broke its bounds. Not finding her, he was completely overcome by grief and he began to behave as if he were mad.[9]

Unable to restrain himself, he asked the trees and the birds and the animals of the forest; "Where is my beloved Sītā?" The eyes of the deer, the trunk of the elephant, the boughs of trees, the flowers—all these reminded Rāma of Sītā. "Surely, you know where my beloved Sītā is. Surely, you have a message from her. Won't you tell me? Won't you assuage the pain in my heart?" Thus Rāma wailed. He thought he saw Sītā at a distance and going up to 'her,' he said: "My beloved, do not run away. Why are you hiding yourself behind those trees? Will you not speak to me?" Then he said to himself: "Surely it was not Sītā. Ah, she has been eaten by the demons. Did I leave her alone in the hermitage only to be eaten by the demons?" Thus lamenting, Rāma roamed awhile and ran around awhile.

ĀRAṆYA 61–62

Again Rāma returned to the hermitage, and, seeing it empty, gave way to grief again. He asked Lakṣmaṇa: "Where has my beloved Sītā gone, O Lakṣmaṇa? Or, has she actually been carried away by someone?" Again, imagining that it

9. The description of the lover maddened by grief, searching for his beloved, is a theme in many literary traditions: examples include the Greek myth of Orpheus's search for Eurydice and the Persian story of Majnun ("the mad lover"), who wanders in the wilderness looking for Laila.

was all fun and a big joke which Sītā was playing, he said: "Enough of this fun, Sītā; come out. See, even the deer are stricken with grief because they do not see you." Turning to Lakṣmaṇa again, he said: "Lakṣmaṇa, I cannot live without my Sītā. I shall soon join my father in the other world. But, he may be annoyed with me and say: 'I told you to live in the forest for fourteen years; how have you come here before that period?' Ah Sītā, do not forsake me."

Lakṣmaṇa tried to console him: "Grieve not, O Rāma. Surely, you know that Sītā is fond of the forest and the caves on the mountainside. She must have gone to these caves. Let us look for her in the forest. That is the proper thing to do; not to grieve."

These brave words took Rāma's grief away. Filled with zeal and eagerness, Rāma along with Lakṣmaṇa, began to comb the forest. Rāma was distressed: "Lakṣmaṇa, this is strange; I do not find Sītā anywhere." But Lakṣmaṇa continued to console Rāma: "Fear not, brother; you will surely recover the noble Sītā soon."

But this time, these words were less meaningful to Rāma. He was overcome by grief, and he lamented: "Where shall we find Sītā, O Lakṣmaṇa, and when? We have looked for her everywhere in the forest and on the hills, but we do not find her." Lamenting thus, stricken with grief, with his intelligence and his heart robbed by the loss of Sītā, Rāma frequently sighed in anguish, muttering: "Ah my beloved."

Suddenly, he thought he saw her, hiding herself behind the banana trees, and now behind the karnikara trees. And, he said to 'her': "My beloved, I see you behind the banana trees! Ah, now I see you behind the karnikara tree: my dear, enough, enough of this play: for your fun aggravates my anguish. I know you are fond of such play; but pray, stop this and come to me now."

When Rāma realized that it was only his hallucination, he turned to Lakṣmaṇa once more and lamented: "I am certain now that some demon has killed my beloved Sītā. How can I return to Ayodhyā without Sītā? How can I face Janaka, her father? Oh, no: Lakṣmaṇa, even heaven is useless without Sītā; I shall continue to stay in the forest; you can return to Ayodhyā. And you can tell Bharata that he should continue to rule the country."

ĀRAṆYA 63–64

Rāma was inconsolable and even infected the brave Lakṣmaṇa. Shedding tears profusely, Rāma continued to speak to Lakṣmaṇa who had also fallen a prey to grief by this time: "No one in this whole world is guilty of as many misdeeds as I am, O Lakṣmaṇa: and that is why I am being visited by sorrow upon sorrow, grief upon grief, breaking my heart and dementing me. I lost my kingdom, and I was torn away from my relations and friends. I got reconciled to this misfortune. But then I lost my father. I was separated from my mother. Coming to this hermitage, I was getting reconciled to that misfortune. But I could not remain at peace with myself for long. Now this terrible misfortune, the worst of all, has visited me.

"Alas, how bitterly Sītā would have cried while she was carried away by some demon. May be she was injured; may be her lovely body was covered with blood. Why is it that when she was subjected to such suffering, my body did not split into pieces? I fear that the demon must have cut open Sītā's neck and drunk her blood. How terribly she must have suffered when she was dragged by the demons.

"Lakṣmaṇa, this river Godāvarī was her favorite resort. Do you remember how she used to come and sitting on this slab of stone talk to us and laugh? Probably she came to the river Godāvarī in order to gather lotuses? But, no: she would never go alone to these places.

"O sun! You know what people do and what people do not do. You know what is true and what is false. You are a witness to all these. Pray, tell me, where has my beloved Sītā gone. For, I have been robbed of everything by this grief. O wind! You know everything in this world, for you are everywhere. Pray, tell me, in which direction did Sītā go?"

Rāma said: "See, Lakṣmaṇa, if Sītā is somewhere near the river Godāvarī." Lakṣmaṇa came back and reported that he could not find her. Rāma himself went to the river and asked the river: "O Godāvarī, pray tell me, where has my beloved Sītā gone?" But the river did not reply. It was as if, afraid of the anger of Rāvaṇa, Godāvarī kept silent.

Rāma was disappointed. He asked the deer and the other animals of the forest: "Where is Sītā? Pray, tell me in which direction has Sītā been taken away." He then observed the deer and the animals; all of them turned southwards and some of them even moved southwards. Rāma then said to Lakṣmaṇa: "O Lakṣmaṇa, see, they are all indicating that Sītā has been taken in a southerly direction."

ĀRAṆYA 64

Lakṣmaṇa, too, saw the animals' behavior as sure signs indicating that Sītā had been borne away in a southerly direction, and suggested to Rāma that they should also proceed in that direction. As they were thus proceeding, they saw petals of flowers fallen on the ground. Rāma recognized them and said to Lakṣmaṇa: "Look here, Lakṣmaṇa, these are petals from the flowers that I had given to Sītā. Surely, in their eagerness to please me, the sun, the wind and the earth, have contrived to keep these flowers fresh."

They walked further on. Rāma saw footprints on the ground. Two of them he immediately recognized as those of Sītā. The other two were big—obviously the footprints of a demon. Bits and pieces of gold were strewn on the ground. Lo and behold, Rāma also saw blood which he concluded was Sītā's blood: he wailed again: "Alas, at this spot, the demon killed Sītā to eat her flesh." He also saw evidence of a fight: and he said: "Perhaps there were two demons fighting for the flesh of Sītā."

Rāma saw on the ground pieces of a broken weapon, an armor of gold, a broken canopy, and the propellers and other parts of a flying chariot. He also saw lying dead, one who had the appearance of the pilot of the craft. From these he concluded that two demons had fought for the flesh of Sītā, before one carried her away. He said to Lakṣmaṇa: "The demons have earned my unquenchable hate and wrath. I shall destroy all of them. Nay, I shall destroy all the powers that be who refuse to return Sītā to me. Look at the irony of fate, Lakṣmaṇa: we adhere to dharma, but dharma could not protect Sītā who has been abducted in this forest! When these powers that govern the universe witness Sītā being eaten by the demons, without doing anything to stop it, who is there to do what is pleasing to us? I think our meekness is misunderstood to be weakness. We are full of self-control, compassion and devoted to the welfare of all beings: and yet these virtues have become as good as vices in us now. I shall set aside all these virtues and the universe shall witness my supreme glory which will bring about the destruction of all creatures, including the demons. If Sītā is not immediately brought back to me, I shall destroy the three worlds—the gods, the demons and other creatures will perish, becoming targets of my most powerful missiles. When I take up my weapon in anger, O Lakṣmaṇa, no one can confront me, even as no one can evade old age and death."

ĀRAṆYA 65–66

Seeing the world-destroying mood of Rāma, Lakṣmaṇa endeavored to console him. He said to Rāma:

"Rāma, pray, do not go against your nature. Charm in the moon, brilliance in the sun, motion in the air, and endurance in the earth—these are their essential nature: in you all these are found and in addition, eternal glory. Your nature cannot desert you; even the sun, the moon and the earth cannot abandon their nature! Moreover, being king, you cannot punish all the created beings for the sin of one person. Gentle and peaceful monarchs match punishment to crime: and, over and above this, you are the refuge of all beings and their goal. I shall without fail find out the real criminal who has abducted Sītā; I shall find out whose armor and weapons these are. And you shall mete out just punishment to the sinner. Oh, no, no god will seek to displease you, O Rāma: Nor these trees, mountains and rivers. I am sure they will all eagerly aid us in our search for Sītā. Of course, if Sītā cannot be recovered through peaceful means, we shall consider other means.

"Whom does not misfortune visit in this world, O Rāma? And, misfortune departs from man as quickly as it visits him. Hence, pray, regain your composure. If you who are endowed with divine intelligence betray lack of endurance in the face of this misfortune, what will others do in similar circumstances?

"King Nahuṣa, who was as powerful as Indra, was beset with misfortune.[1] The sage Vasiṣṭha, our family preceptor, had a hundred sons and lost all of them on one day! Earth is tormented by volcanic eruptions, and earthquakes. The sun and the moon are afflicted by eclipses. Misfortune strikes the great ones and even the gods.

"For, in this world people perform actions whose results are not obvious; and these actions which may be good or evil, bear their own fruits. Of course, these fruits are evanescent. People who are endowed with enlightened intelligence know what is good and what is not good. People like you do not grieve over misfortunes and do not get deluded by them.

"Why am I telling you all this, O Rāma? Who in this world is wiser than you? However, since, as is natural, grief seems to veil wisdom, I am saying all this.

1. King Nahuṣa, an ancestor of Rāma, became so powerful that he claimed the throne of Indra, king of gods, but an arrogant act soon effected his fall from his exalted position.

All this I learnt only from you: I am only repeating what you yourself taught me earlier. Therefore, O Rāma, know your enemy and fight him."

ĀRAṆYA 67–68

Rāma then asked Lakṣmaṇa: "O Lakṣmaṇa, tell me, what should we do now?" Lakṣmaṇa replied: "Surely, we should search this forest for Sītā."

This advice appealed to Rāma. Immediately he fixed the bayonet to his weapon and with a look of anger on his face, set out to search for Sītā. Within a very short time and distance, both Rāma and Lakṣmaṇa chanced upon Jaṭāyu, seriously and mortally wounded and heavily bleeding. Seeing that enormous vulture lying on the ground, Rāma's first thought was: "Surely, this is the one that has swallowed Sītā." He rushed forward with fixed bayonet.

Looking at Rāma thus rushing towards him, and rightly inferring Rāma's mood, Jaṭāyu said in a feeble voice: "Sītā has been taken away by Rāvaṇa. I tried to intervene. I battled with the mighty Rāvaṇa. I broke his armor, his canopy, the propellers and some parts of his chariot. I killed his pilot. I even inflicted injuries on his person. But he cut off my wings and thus grounded me." When Rāma heard that the vulture had news of Sītā, he threw his weapon away and kneeling down near the vulture embraced it.

Rāma said to Lakṣmaṇa: "An additional calamity to endure, O Lakṣmaṇa. Is there really no end to my misfortune? My misfortune plagues even this noble creature, a friend of my father's." Rāma requested more information from Jaṭāyu concerning Sītā, and also concerning Rāvaṇa. Jaṭāyu replied: "Taking Sītā with him, the demon flew away in his craft, leaving a mysterious storm and cloud behind him. I was mortally wounded by him. Ah, my senses are growing dim. I feel life ebbing away, Rāma. Yet, I assure you, you will recover Sītā." Soon Jaṭāyu lay lifeless. Nay, it was his body, for he himself ascended to heaven. Grief-stricken afresh, Rāma said to Lakṣmaṇa: "Jaṭāyu lived a very long life; and yet has had to lay down his life today. Death, no one in this world can escape. And what a noble end! What a great service this noble vulture has rendered to me! Pious and noble souls are found even amongst subhuman creatures, O Lakṣmaṇa. Today I have forgotten all my previous misfortunes: I am extremely tormented by the loss of this dear friend who has sacrificed his life for my sake. I shall myself cremate it, so that it may reach the highest realms."

Rāma himself performed the funeral rites, reciting those Vedic mantras[2] which one recites during the cremation of one's own close relations. After this, Rāma and Lakṣmaṇa proceeded on their journey in search of Sītā.

* * *

Summary The monkey hordes sent to search for Sītā in the southern direction by Sugrīva, king of the monkeys, are disheartened and take refuge in a cave near the southern ocean to discuss their course of action.

2. Sacred chants, usually from the scriptures.

From Book 4

Kiṣkindhā

KIṢKINDHĀ 56, 57, 58

The sound, the gust of wind and dust preceded the arrival near the cave of a huge vulture. The vānaras who were seated on a flat surface outside the cave saw the vulture perched on a big rock. The vulture was known as Sampāti and was the brother of Jaṭāyu. It said to itself: "Surely, unseen providence is in control of the whole world. By that benign providence it has been decreed that my food should thus arrive at my very door, as it were. As and when each one of these vānaras dies I shall eat the flesh." The vānaras, however, heard this and were greatly disturbed.

With a mind agitated by intense fear, Aṅgada[3] said to Hanumān: "Death has come to us, disguised as a vulture. But, then, did not the noble Jaṭāyu give up his life in the service of Rāma. Even so we shall die in his service. Jaṭāyu suffered martyrdom while actually trying to help Sītā; but we, unfortunately, have not been able to find where she is."

Sampāti heard this. His mind was now disturbed. He asked: "Who is there who mentioned the name of my dearly beloved brother Jaṭāyu? I have not heard from him or of him for a very long time. Hearing of his murder my whole being is shaken. How did it happen?"

Even after this, the vānaras were skeptical: however, they helped Sampāti get down from the rock. Aṅgada then related the whole story of Rāma, including his friendship with Sugrīva and the killing of Vāli. He concluded: "We were sent in search of Sītā. We cannot find her. And the time-limit set by Sugrīva has expired. Afraid to face him, we have decided to fast unto death, lying here."

Sampāti said: "Jaṭāyu was my brother. Both of us flew to the abode of Indra when the latter had killed the demon Vṛtra. Jaṭāyu was about to faint, while we were near the sun. And I shielded him. By the heat of the sun my wings were burnt and I fell down here.[4] Though wingless and powerless, I shall help you in my own way, O vānaras, for the sake of Rāma. Some time ago, I saw a beautiful lady being carried away by Rāvaṇa: she was crying: 'O Rāma, O Lakṣmaṇa.' He dwells in Laṅkā, an island eight hundred miles from here. There, I can actually see Rāvaṇa and also Sītā living in Laṅkā, on account of the strength of my vision. I can also see through intuition that you will find Sītā before returning to Kiṣkindhā. Now, take me to the seaside so that I can offer libations for the peace of my brother's soul." The vānaras gladly obliged Sampāti.

KIṢKINDHĀ 59–60

Jāmbavān who heard Sampāti mention that he had seen Sītā, approached Sampāti and asked: "Pray, tell me in detail where Sītā is and who has seen her?" Sampāti replied:

"Indeed, my son Supārśva had an even more direct encounter with Rāvaṇa and Sītā than I had. I shall narrate the story to you in detail. Please listen.

3. Son of Vāli, brother of Sugrīva, king of the monkeys.

4. This narrative is similar to the Greek myth of Icarus. Endowed with wings made by his father, Daedalus, Icarus flew too close to the sun; his wings melted, and he plunged to his death.

"I told you that in a foolhardy attempt to fly to the sun, my wings got burnt. I fell down wingless on this mountain. Just as the celestials are excessively lustful, snakes possess terrible anger, deer are easily frightened, and we vultures are voracious eaters. How could I appease insatiable hunger when I had no wings? My son Supārśva volunteered to supply me with food regularly. One day, recently, he failed to appear at the usual time, and I was tormented by hunger. When I took him to task for that lapse, he narrated what had happened that day. He said: 'I was looking for some meat to bring to you for your meal. At that time I saw a big demon flying away with a lady in his arms. I stopped him wishing to bring both of them for your meal today. But he begged of me to let him go: who could deny such a request? So I let him go. Later, some of the sages in the region exclaimed: "By sheer luck has Sītā escaped alive today." After they had flown away, I went on looking in that direction for a considerable time, and I saw that lady dropping ornaments on the hills. I was delayed by all this, O father!' It was from my son Supārśva that I heard about the abduction of Sītā in the first place. I could not challenge and kill Rāvaṇa, because I had neither wings nor the strength for it. But I shall render service to Rāma in my own way.

"There lived on this mountain a great sage named Niśākara. On the day that Jaṭāyu and I flew towards the sun and on which my wings had been completely burnt, I fell down here. I remained unconscious for some time. Later I regained consciousness. With great difficulty I reached the hermitage of the sage, as I was eager to see him. After some time I saw him coming to the hermitage, surrounded by bears, deer, tigers, lions and snakes! When he entered the hermitage, they returned to the forest. He merely greeted me and went in. But soon he came back to where I was and said: 'Are you not Sampāti? Was not Jaṭāyu your brother? Both of you used to come here in human forms, to salute me. Ah, I recognize you. But tell me: who has burnt your wings and why have they been burnt?' "

KIṢKINDHĀ 61, 62, 63

Sampāti continued: "My physical condition and the loss of wings and vitality prevented me from giving a complete account of our misadventure. However, I said to the sage: 'Determined to pursue the sun, we flew towards it. We soared high into the sky. From there we looked at the earth: the cities looked like cartwheels! We heard strange noises in the space. The mountains on earth looked like pebbles; the rivers looked like strings which bound the earth! The Himālaya and the Vindhya[5] appeared to be elephants bathing in a pond. And our sense of sight was playing tricks with us. It looked as if the earth were on fire. We then concentrated on the sun to get our bearings right. It looked as big as the earth. Jaṭāyu decided to return. I followed him. I tried to shield him against the fierce rays of the sun; and my wings were burnt. Jaṭāyu fell in Janasthāna, I think. I am here on the Vindhya.[6] What shall I do now? I have lost everything. My heart seeks death which I shall meet by jumping off a peak.'

5. The Himalaya mountain range spans the northern and northeastern borders of the Indian subcontinent. The Vindhya Mountains are located in the northern part of central India.

6. The location of Sampāti's cave in the "Vindhya" is problematic since soon after the monkeys meet the old vulture, they reach the shore of the southern ocean, across which Hanumān leaps to the island of Laṅkā.

"The sage, however, contemplated for a while and said: 'Do not despair. You will get back your wings, sight, life force and strength. A prediction have I heard: soon the earth will be ruled by king Daśaratha whose son Rāma will go to the forest in obedience to his father's will, and there Rāma will lose his wife Sītā in search of whom he will send vānaras. When you inform the vānaras where Sītā is kept in captivity, you will gain new wings. In fact, I can make your wings grow now: but it is better you get them after rendering a great service to Rāma.' Soon afterwards, the sage left this world.

"I have impatiently been waiting for you all, all these hundreds of years. I have often thought of committing suicide; but I have abandoned the idea every time, knowing that I have an important mission in life. I even scolded my son the other day for his having let Rāvaṇa get away with Sītā; but I myself could not pursue Rāvaṇa."

As Sampāti was speaking thus, new wings sprouted from his sides, even as the vānaras were looking on. The vānaras were delighted. Sampāti continued: "It is by the grace of the sage Niśākara that I have regained these wings, O vānaras. And, the sprouting of these wings is positive proof that you will be successful in finding Sītā."

Sampāti flew away, in an attempt to see if he could still fly! The vānaras had abandoned the idea of fasting unto death. They had regained their enthusiasm and their morale. They set out once again in search of Sītā.

KIṢKINDHĀ 64–65

Sampāti's words inspired confidence in the vānaras, but that enthusiasm lasted only till they actually faced the ocean itself. They reached the northern shore of the southern ocean, and stopped there. When they saw the extent of the ocean, their hearts sank. All of them wailed with one voice: "How can we get beyond this and search for Sītā?"

Aṅgada said to them: "Do not despair, O vānaras! He who yields to despondency is robbed of his strength and valor, and he does not reach his goal." Upon hearing this, all the vānaras surrounded Aṅgada, awaiting his plan. He continued: "Who can cross this ocean? Who will fulfill the wish of Sugrīva? Surely, it is by the grace of that vānara who is able to cross this ocean that we shall all be able to return home and behold our wives and children: it is by his grace that Rāma and Lakṣmaṇa can experience great joy." No one answered. Aṅgada said again: "Surely, you know that you have immeasurable strength. No one can obstruct your path. Come on, speak up. Let me hear how far each one of you can go."

One by one the mightiest amongst the vānaras answered: "I can go eighty miles." "I can go double that distance." "I can cover treble that distance." And so on till Jāmbavān's turn[7] came. He said: "In days of yore I had great strength and I could easily have gone across and returned. But on account of my great age I have grown weak. Once upon a time when lord Viṣṇu assumed the gigantic form (to measure the whole earth with one foot, and the sky with the other) I went round him. But now, alas, I am incapable of crossing this little ocean."

7. Jāmbavān is a *ṛkṣa*, a word usually translated as "bear."

Aṅgada himself declared: "I can surely cross this ocean and go to Laṅkā. But I am not sure if I can make the return journey. And, if I do not return, my going to Laṅkā would have been in vain." But Jambavān intervened and said: "Oh, no: you should not undertake this task. When an expedition is organized the commander himself should not participate in it. You are the very root of this whole expedition. And, the wise say that one should always protect the root; for so long as the root is preserved one can always expect to reap the harvest. You are our respected leader, and you should therefore not risk your own life in this venture."

Aṅgada said: "If no one else can cross the ocean and I should not, then we are all doomed to die here. What shall we do?" Jambavān, however, had other ideas: he said: "O prince, there is someone amongst us who can do this."

KIṢKINDHĀ 66–67

Jāmbavān said to Hanumān: "What about you, O mighty hero? Why don't you speak up? Your might is equal to that of Sugrīva, nay even to that of Rāma and Lakṣmaṇa; and yet you are quiet.

"I shall remind you of your birth and your ancestry. There once was a nymph called Puñjikasthalā. She was once cursed by a sage as a result of which she was reborn as Añjanā, the daughter of a vānara chief called Kuñjara. Añjanā married Kesari. This nymph who had the body of a human woman was once resting on the top of a hill. It is said that the wind-god, by whom her clothes had been blown up revealing her attractive legs, fell in love with her. Her body was, as it were, embraced by the wind-god. But she was furious and exclaimed: 'Who dares to violate my chastity?' The wind-god replied: 'Nay, I shall not violate you, O vānara lady! However, since as wind I have entered your body, you will bear a child who will vie with me in power.'

"Añjanā gave birth to you, O Hanumān! When you were a baby, you once saw the sun in the sky. You thought it was a fruit, and jumped up to pluck it from the sky. But, Indra struck you down with his thunderbolt and you fell down.[8] Your left chin was broken; and hence you came to be known as hanu-man. It is said that when you were thus injured, the wind-god was angered; there was no movement of wind in the world. The frightened gods propitiated the wind-god; and Brahmā the creator then gave you the boon of invincibility in battle. When Indra came to know that you did not die on being hit by the thunderbolt, he conferred a boon on you, that you will die only when you wish to.

"There is no one equal to you in strength or in the ability to cross this ocean, nay, an ocean far wider than this. All others are despondent; the mission surely depends upon you."

When his glory was thus sung and he was reminded of his own power, Hanumān grew in stature, as it were. Seeing him thus filled with enthusiasm, the other vānaras jumped for joy. Hanumān grew in size; and shook his tail in great delight. He said: "Of course I can cross this ocean! With the strength of my arms I can push this ocean away. Stirred by my legs, the ocean will overflow its bounds. I can break up mountains. I can leap into the sky and sail along. I am equal to the wind-god in strength and valor. No one is equal to me other

8. A thunderbolt-wielding king of the gods, Indra is the Indian counterpart of the Greek god Zeus.

than Garuḍa of divine origin. I can even lift up the island of Laṅkā and carry it away."

Greatly inspired by Hanumān's words, the vānaras exclaimed with one voice: "Bravo, O Hanumān. You have saved us all. We shall pray for the success of your mission, standing on one leg till you return." Hanumān ascended the mountain, ready to leap.

From Book 5

Sundara

Hanumān was preparing to jump across the ocean and to cross the ocean to go to Laṅkā. Before undertaking this momentous and vital advanture, he offered prayers to the sun-god, to Indra, to the wind-god, to the Creator and to the elements. He turned to the east and offered his salutations to the wind-god, his own divine parent. He turned his face now to the south, in order to proceed on his great mission.

As he stood there, with his whole being swelling with enthusiasm, fervor and determination, and as he pressed his foot on the mountain before taking off from there, the whole mountain shook. And the shock caused the trees to shed their flowers, birds and beasts to leave their sheltered abodes, subterranean water to gush forth, and even the pleasure-loving celestials and the peace-loving ascetics to leave the mountain resorts, to fly into the sky and watch Hanumān's adventure from there. Giving proof of their scientific skill and knowledge, these celestials and sages remained hovering over the hill, eager to witness Hanumān's departure to Laṅkā. They said to one another: "This mighty Hanumān who is the god-child of the wind-god himself, will swiftly cross this ocean; for he desires to cross the ocean in order to achieve the mission of Rāma and the mission of the vānaras."

Hanumān crouched on the mountain, ready to go. He tensed his body in an effort to muster all the energy that he had. He held his breath in his heart and thus charged himself with even more energy.

He said to the vānaras who surrounded him: "I shall proceed to Laṅkā with the speed of the missile discharged by Rāma. If I do not find Sītā there, I shall with the same speed go to the heaven to search for her. And, if I do not see her even there, I shall get hold of Rāvaṇa, bind him and bring him over to the presence of Rāma. I shall definitely return with success. If it is difficult to bind Rāvaṇa and bring him, I shall uproot Laṅkā itself and bring it to Rāma."

After thus reassuring the vānaras, Hanumān took to the sky. The big trees that stood on the mountain were violently drawn into the slip-stream. Some of these trees flew behind Hanumān; others fell into the ocean; and yet others shed their blossoms on the hill tops, where they lay as a colorful carpet, and on the surface of the ocean where they looked like stars in the blue sky.

SUNDARA I

The mighty Hanumān was on his way to Laṅkā. He flew in the southerly direction, with his arms outstretched. One moment it looked as if he would soon drink the ocean; at another as if he desired to drink the blue sky itself. He followed the course of wind, his eyes blazing like fire, like lightning.

Hanumān flying in the air with his tail coiled up behind looked like a meteor with its tail flying from north to the south. His shadow was cast on the surface of the ocean: this made it appear as if there were a big ship on the ocean. As he flew over the surface of the ocean, the wind generated by his motion greatly agitated the ocean. He actually dashed the surface of the ocean with his powerful chest. Thus the sea was churned by him as he flew over it. Huge waves arose in his wake with water billowing high into fine spray which looked like clouds. Flying thus in the sky, without any visible support, Hanumān appeared to be a winged mountain.

Hanumān was engaged in the mission of Rāma: hence the sun did not scorch him. Rāma was a descendant of the solar dynasty. The sages who were present there in their ethereal forms showered their blessings upon him.

Sāgara, the deity presiding over the ocean, bethought to himself: "In days of yore, Rāma's ancestors the sons of king Sagara, rendered an invaluable service to me.[9] And it therefore behoves me to render some service to this messenger of Rāma who is engaged in the service of Rāma. I should see that Hanumān does not tire himself and thus fail in his mission. I should arrange for him to have some rest before he proceeds further."

Thus resolved, Sāgara summoned the deity presiding over the mountain named Maināka which had been submerged in the ocean, and said to Maināka: "O Maināka, Indra the chief of gods has established you here in order to prevent the denizens from the subterranean regions from coming up. You have the power to extend yourself on all sides. Pray, rise up and offer a seat to Hanumān who is engaged on an important mission on behalf of Rāma, so that he can refresh himself before proceeding further."

SUNDARA I

Readily agreeing to this request, the mountain Maināka rose from the bed of the ocean. As Hanumān flew towards Laṅkā he saw this mountain actually emerge from the ocean and come into his view. However, he considered that it was an obstacle to his progress towards Laṅkā, an obstruction on his path, to be quickly overcome. Hanumān actually flew almost touching the peak of the mountain and by the force of the motion, the peak was actually broken.

Assuming a human-form the deity presiding over the Maināka mountain addressed Hanumān who was still flying: "O Hanumān, pray accept my hospitality. Rest a while on my peak. Refresh yourself. The ocean was extended by the sons of king Sagara, an ancestor of Rāma. Hence the deity presiding over the ocean wishes to return the service as a token of gratitude: thus to show one's gratitude is the eternal dharma. With this end in view, the ocean-god has commanded me to rise to the surface and offer you a resting place. It is our tradition to welcome and to honor guests, even if they are ordinary men: how much more important it is that we should thus honor men like you! There is yet another reason why I plead that you should accept my hospitality! In ancient times, all the mountains were endowed with wings. They used to fly

9. Looking for the horse that was stolen from their father's royal sacrifice, the 60,000 sons of Rāma's ancestor Sagara dug up the entire earth and its surrounding continents and seas, thus expanding the ocean's domain.

around and land where they liked; thus, they terrorized sages and other beings. In answer to their prayer, Indra the chief of gods, wielded his thunderbolt and clipped off the wings of the mountains. As Indra was about to strike me, the wind-god bore me violently away and hid me in the ocean—so that I escaped Indra's wrath. I owe a debt of gratitude to the wind-god who is your god-father. Pray, allow me to discharge that debt by entertaining you."

Hanumān replied politely: "Indeed, I accept your hospitality, in spirit. Time is passing; and I am on an urgent mission. Moreover, I have promised not to rest till my task is accomplished. Hence, forgive my rudeness and discourtesy: I have to be on my way." As a token acceptance of Maināka's hospitality, Hanumān touched the mountain with his hand and was soon on his way. The gods and the sages who witnessed this scene were greatly impressed with Maināka's gesture of goodwill and Hanumān's unflagging zeal and determination. Indra, highly pleased with the Maināka mountain, conferred upon it the boon of fearlessness.

SUNDARA I

The gods and the sages overseeing Hanumān's flight to Laṅkā had witnessed his first feat of strength when he took off from the Mahendra mountain, and his second feat of strength and enthusiasm when he declined even to rest and insisted on the accomplishment of the mission. They were eager to assure themselves still more conclusively of his ability to fulfill the task he had undertaken.

The gods and the sages now approached Surasā (mother of the Nāgas)[1] and said to her: "Here is Hanumān, the god-child of the wind-god, who is flying across the ocean. Pray, obstruct his path just a short while. Assume a terrible demoniacal form, with the body as big as a mountain, with terrible looking teeth and eyes, and mouth as wide as space. We wish to ascertain Hanumān's strength. And we therefore wish to see whether when he is confronted by you, he triumphs over you or becomes despondent."

In obedience to their command, Surasā assumed a terrible form and confronted Hanumān with her mouth wide open. She said to him, as he approached her mouth while flying in the air: "Ah, fate has decreed that you should serve as my food today! Enter my mouth and I shall eat you up."

Hanumān replied: "O lady, I am on an important mission. Rāma, the son of king Daśaratha, came to the forest to honor his father's promise. While he was in the forest with his wife, Sītā, and his brother, Sītā was abducted by Rāvaṇa, the ruler of Laṅkā. I am going to Laṅkā to find her whereabouts. Do not obstruct my path now. Let me go. If the gods have ordained that I should enter your mouth, I promise that as soon as I discover Sītā and inform Rāma of her whereabouts, I shall come back and enter your mouth."

But, Surasā could not be put off. She repeated: "No one can escape me; and it has been decreed that you shall enter my mouth." She opened her mouth wide. Hanumān, by his yogic power, made himself minute, quickly entered her mouth and as quickly got out! He then said to her: "O lady, let me now proceed. I have fulfilled your wish and honored the gods' decree: I have entered your mouth! Salutations to you! I shall go to where Sītā is kept in captivity."

1. A class of serpents or demigods.

Surasā abandoned her demoniacal form and resumed her own form which was pleasant to look at. She blessed Hanumān: "Go! You will surely find Sītā and re-unite her with Rāma." The gods and the sages were thrilled to witness this third triumph of Hanumān.

SUNDARA 1

Hanumān continued to fly towards Laṅkā, along the aerial route which contains rain-bearing clouds, along which birds course, where the masters of music[2] move about, and along which aerial cars which resemble lions, elephants, tigers, birds and snakes, fly—the sky which is also the abode of holy men and women with an abundant store of meritorious deeds, which serves as a canopy created by the creator Brahmā to protect living beings on earth, and which is adorned with planets, the moon, the sun and the stars.

As he flew onwards, he left behind him a black trail which resembled black clouds, and also trails which were red, yellow and white. He often flew through cloud-formations.

A demoness called Simhikā saw Hanumān flying fearlessly in the sky and made up her mind to attack him. She said to herself: "I am hungry. Today I shall swallow this big creature and shall appease my hunger for some time." She caught hold of the shadow cast by Hanumān on the surface of the ocean. Immediately, Hanumān's progress was arrested and he was violently pulled down. He wondered: "How is it that suddenly I am dragged down helplessly?" He looked around and saw the ugly demoness Simhikā. He remembered the description which Sugrīva had given of her and knew it was Simhikā without doubt.

Hanumān stretched his body and the demoness opened her mouth wide. He saw her mouth and her inner vital organs through it. In the twinkling of an eye, he reduced himself to a minute size and dropped into her mouth. He disappeared into that wide mouth. The gods and the sages witnessing this were horrified. But with his adamantine nails he tore open the vital parts of the demoness and quickly emerged from her body. Thus, with the help of good luck, firmness and dexterity Hanumān triumphed over this demoness. The gods applauded this feat and said: "He in whom are found (as in you) these four virtues (firmness, vision, wisdom and dexterity) does not despair in any undertaking."

Hanumān had nearly covered the eight hundred miles, to his destination. At a short distance he saw the shore of Laṅkā. He saw thick forests. He saw the mountains known as Lamba. And he saw the capital city Laṅkā built on the mountains. Not wishing to arouse suspicion, he softly landed on the Lamba mountains which were rich in groves of Ketaka, Uddalaka and cocoanut trees.

SUNDARA 2

Though Hanumān had crossed the sea, covering a distance of eight hundred miles, he felt not the least fatigue nor exhaustion. Having landed on the mountain range close to the shore of the ocean, Hanumān roamed the forests for some time. In them he saw trees of various kinds, bearing flowers and fruits.

2. *Gandharvas*, a class of demigods.

He saw the city of Laṅkā situated on the top of a hill, surrounded by wide moats and guarded by security forces of demons. He approached the northern gate to the city and quietly surveyed it. That gate was guarded by the most ferocious looking demons armed to the teeth with the most powerful weapons. Standing there, he thought of Rāvaṇa, the abductor of Sītā.

Hanumān thought: "Even if the vānara forces do come here, of what use would that be? For Rāvaṇa's Laṅkā cannot be conquered even by the gods. Only four of us can cross the ocean and come here—Aṅgada, Nīla, Sugrīva and myself. And that is totally useless. One cannot negotiate with these demons and win them over by peaceful means. Anyhow, I shall first find out if Sītā is alive or not, and only then consider the next step."

In order to find out where Sītā was kept in captivity, he had to enter Laṅkā. The wise Hanumān considered that aspect of his mission. He thought: "Surely, I must be very careful, cautious and vigilant. If I am not, I might ruin the whole mission. An undertaking even after it has been carefully deliberated and decided upon will fail if it is mishandled by an ignorant or inefficient messenger. Therefore I should consider well what should be done and with due regard to all the pros and cons, I should vigilantly ensure that I do nothing which ought not to be done. I should enter the city in such a way that my presence and my movements are not detected; and I see that Rāvaṇa's security forces are so very efficient that it will not be easy to escape detection."

Thus resolved, Hanumān reduced himself to a small size, to the size of a cat as it were, and when darkness had fallen, proceeded towards the city. Even from a distance he could see the affluence that the city enjoyed. It had buildings of many stories. It had archways made of gold. It was brilliantly lit and tastefully decorated. The city was of unimaginable beauty and glory. When Hanumān saw it, he was filled with a mixture of feelings, feelings of despondence, and joy—joy at the prospect of seeing Sītā, and despondency at the thought of the difficulty involved in it.

Unnoticed by the guards, Hanumān entered the gateway.

SUNDARA 3

Hanumān was still contemplating the difficulties of the imminent campaign for the recovery of Sītā. Conquering Laṅkā by force seemed to him to be out of the question. He thought: "Possibly only Kumuda, Aṅgada, Suṣena, Mainda, Dvivida, Sugrīva, Kuśaparva, Jāmbavān and myself may be in a position to cross the ocean and come here. However, in spite of the heavy odds against such a campaign, there is the immeasurable prowess of Rāma and Lakṣmaṇa: surely they can destroy the demons without any difficulty whatsoever."

As he was entering the city, he was intercepted by Laṅkā, the guardian of the city. She questioned him: "Who are you, O vānara? This city of Laṅkā cannot be entered by you!" Hanumān was in no mood to reveal his identity: and he questioned her, in his turn: "Who are you, O lady? And why do you obstruct my path?" Laṅkā replied: "At the command of the mighty Rāvaṇa, I guard this city. No one can ignore me and enter this city: and you, O vānara, will soon enter into eternal sleep, slain at my hands!"

Hanumān said to her: "I have come as a visitor to this city, to see what is to be seen here. When I have seen what I wish to see, I shall duly return to where

I have come from. Pray, let me proceed." But Laṅkā continued to say: "You cannot enter without overpowering me or winning my permission," and actually hit Hanumān on his chest with her hand.

Hanumān's anger was aroused. Yet, he controlled himself: for he did not consider it right to kill a woman! He clenched his fist and struck Laṅkā. She fell down, and then revealed: "Compose yourself, O vānara! Do not kill me. The truly strong ones do not violate the code of chivalry, and they do not kill a woman. I am Laṅkā, and he who has conquered me has conquered Laṅkā. That was what Brahmā the creator once said: 'When a vānara overpowers you, know that then the demons have cause for great fear.' I am sure that this prophecy refers to you, O vānara! I realize now that the inevitable destruction of the demons of Laṅkā has entered the territory in the form of Sītā who has been forcibly brought here by Rāvaṇa. Go, enter the city: and surely you will find Sītā and accomplish all that you desire to accomplish."

SUNDARA 4–5

Hanumān did not enter the city through the heavily guarded main gate, but climbed over the wall. Then he came to the main road and proceeded towards his destination—the abode of Rāvaṇa. On the way Hanumān saw the beautiful mansions from which issued the sound of music, and the sound of the citizens' rejoicing. He saw, too, prosperous looking mansions of different designs calculated to bring happiness and greater prosperity to the owners of the mansions. He heard the shouts of wrestling champions. Here and there he heard bards and others singing the glories of Rāvaṇa, and he noticed that these bards were surrounded by citizens in large numbers, blocking the road.

Right in the heart of the city, Hanumān saw in the main square numerous spies of Rāvaṇa: and these spies looked like holy men, with matted hair, or with shaven heads, clad in the hides of cows or in nothing at all. In their hands they carried all sorts of weapons, right from a few blades of grass to maces and sticks. They were of different shapes and sizes and of different appearance and complexions. Hanumān also saw the garrison with a hundred thousand soldiers right in front of the inner apartments of Rāvaṇa.

Hanumān approached the palace of Rāvaṇa himself. This was a truly heavenly abode. Within the compound of the palace and around the building there were numerous horses, chariots, and also flying chariots. The palace was built of solid and pure gold and the inside was decorated with many precious stones, fragrant with incense and sandalwood which had been sprinkled everywhere: Hanumān entered the palace.

It was nearly midnight. The moon shone brilliantly overhead. From the palace wafted the strains of stringed musical instruments; good-natured women were asleep with their husbands; the violent night-stalkers[3] also emerged from their dwellings to amuse themselves. In some quarters, Hanumān noticed wrestlers training themselves. In some others, women were applying various cosmetic articles to themselves. Some other women were sporting with their husbands. Others whose husbands were away looked unhappy and pale, though they were still beautiful. Hanumān saw all these: but he did not see Sītā anywhere.

3. A class of demons. The word is also used more generally for "demons."

Not seeing Sītā, the beloved wife of Rāma, Hanumān felt greatly distressed and unhappy and he became moody and dejected.

SUNDARA 6, 7, 8

Hanumān was greatly impressed by the beauty and the grandeur of Rāvaṇa's palace which he considered to be the crowning glory of Laṅkā itself. He did not all at once enter Rāvaṇa's inner apartments. First he surveyed the palaces of the other members of the royal family and the leaders of the demons, like Prahasta. He surveyed the palaces of Rāvaṇa's brothers Kumbhakarṇa and Vibhīṣaṇa, as also that of Rāvaṇa's son Indrajīt. He was greatly impressed by the unmistakable signs of prosperity that greeted him everywhere. After thus looking at the palaces of all these heroes, Hanumān reached the abode of Rāvaṇa himself.

Rāvaṇa's own inner apartments were guarded by terrible looking demons, holding the most powerful weapons in their hands. Rāvaṇa's own private palace was surrounded by more armed forces; and even these garrisons were embellished by gold and diamonds. Hanumān entered the palace and saw within it palanquins, couches, gardens and art galleries, special chambers for enjoying sexual pleasures and others for indulging in other pastimes during the day. There were also special altars for the performance of sacred rituals. The whole palace was resplendent on account of the light emitted by precious stones which were found everywhere. Everywhere the couches, the seats and the dining vessels were of gold; and the floor of the whole palace was fragrant with the smell of wine and liquor. In fact Hanumān thought that the palace looked like heaven on earth, resplendent with the wealth of precious gems, and fragrant with the scent of a variety of flowers which covered its dome making it look like a flower-covered hill.

There were swimming pools with lotuses and lilies. In one of them there was the carved figure of a lordly elephant offering worship to Lakṣmī, the goddess of wealth.

Right in the center of the palace stood the best of all flying chariots, known as Puṣpaka. It had been painted with many colors and provided with numerous precious gems. It was decorated with lovely figures of snakes, birds, and horses fashioned of gems, silver and coral. Every part of that flying chariot had been carefully engineered, only the very best materials had been used, and it had special features which even the vehicles of the gods did not have—in fact, in it had been brought together only special features! Rāvaṇa had acquired it after great austerities and effort.

Hanumān saw all this. But, he did not see Sītā anywhere!

SUNDARA 9

Hanumān ascended the chariot Puṣpaka from which he could easily look into the inner apartments of Rāvaṇa! As he stood on the chariot, he smelled the extraordinary odor emanating from Rāvaṇa's dining room—the odor of wines and liquors, the smell of excellent food. The smell was appetizing and Hanumān thought the food should be nourishing. And, he saw at the same time the beautiful hall of Rāvaṇa which had crystal floors, with inlaid figures made of ivory, pearls, diamonds, corals, silver and gold. The hall was resplendent with pillars of gems. There was on the floor, a carpet of extraordinary beauty and design. On the walls were murals of several countries' landscapes. This hall thus provided all the five senses with the objects for their utmost gratification! A soft light illumined this hall.

On the carpet beautiful women lay asleep. With their mouths and their eyes closed, they had fallen asleep, after drinking and dancing, and from their bodies issued the sweet fragrance of lotuses. Rāvaṇa, sleeping there surrounded by these beautiful women, looked like the moon surrounded by the stars in the night sky. They were all asleep in beautiful disorder. Some were using their own arms as the pillow, others used the different parts of yet others' bodies as their pillow. Their hair was in disarray. Their dress was in disarray, too. But none of these conditions diminished the beauty of their forms. From the breath of all the women there issued the smell of liquor.

These women had come from different grades of society. Some of them were the daughters of royal sages, others those of brāhmaṇas, yet others were the daughters of gandharvas (celestial artists), and, of course, some were the daughters of demons: and all of them had voluntarily sought Rāvaṇa, for they loved him. Some he had won by his valor; others had become infatuated with him. None of these women had been carried away by Rāvaṇa against their wish. None of them had been married before. None of them had desire for another man. Rāvaṇa had never before abducted any woman, except Sītā.

Hanumān thought for a moment: Rāvaṇa would indeed have been a good man if he had thus got Sītā too, to be his wife: that is, before she had married Rāma and if he had been able to win her by his valor or by his charm. But, Hanumān contemplated further: by abducting the wife of Rāma, Rāvaṇa had certainly committed a highly unworthy action.

SUNDARA 10–11

In the center of that hall, Hanumān saw the most beautiful and the most luxurious bed: it was celestial in its appearance, built entirely of crystal and decked with gems. The lord of the demons, Rāvaṇa himself was asleep on it. The sight of this demon was at first revolting to Hanumān; so he turned his face away from Rāvaṇa. But then he turned his gaze again to Rāvaṇa. He saw that the two arms of Rāvaṇa were strong and powerful, and they were adorned with resplendent jewelry. His face, his chest, in fact his whole body was strong and radiant. His limbs shone like the lightning.

Around this bed were others on which the consorts of Rāvaṇa were asleep. Many of them had obviously been entertaining the demon with their music; and they had fallen asleep with the musical instruments in their arms. On yet another bed was asleep the most charming of all the women in that hall: she surpassed all the others in beauty, in youth and in adornment. For a moment Hanumān thought it was Sītā: and the very thought that he had seen Sītā delighted him.

But that thought did not last long. Hanumān realized: "It cannot be. For, separated from Rāma, Sītā will not sleep, nor will she enjoy herself, adorn herself or drink anything. Nor will Sītā ever dwell with another man, even if he be a celestial: for truly there is none equal to Rāma." He turned away from the hall, since he did not see Sītā there.

Next, Hanumān searched the dining hall and the kitchen: there he saw varieties of meats and other delicacies, condiments and a variety of drinks. The dining hall floor had been strewn with drinking vessels, fruits and even anklets and armlets which had obviously fallen from their wearers as they were drinking and getting intoxicated.

While he was thus inspecting the palace and searching for Sītā, a thought flashed in Hanumān's mind: was he guilty of transgressing the bounds of morality, in as much as he was gazing at the wives of others, while they were asleep with their ornaments and clothes in disarray? But, he consoled himself with the thought: "True, I have seen all these women in Rāvaṇa's apartment. But, no lustful thought has entered my mind! The mind alone is the cause of good and evil actions performed by the senses; but my mind is devoted to and established in righteousness. Where else can I look for Sītā, except among the womenfolk in Rāvaṇa's palace: shall I look for a lost woman among a herd of deer? I have looked for Sītā in this place with a pure mind; but she is not to be seen."

SUNDARA 12–13

Hanumān had searched the whole palace of Rāvaṇa. But he could not find Sītā. He reflected: "I shall not yield to despair. For, it has been well said that perseverance alone is the secret of prosperity and great happiness; perseverance alone keeps all things going, and crowns all activities with success. I shall search those places which I have not yet searched." He then began to search for Sītā in other parts of the palace. He saw many, many other women, but not Sītā.

Hanumān then searched for Sītā outside the palace. Yet, he could not find her. Once again dejection gripped him. He thought: "Sītā is to be found nowhere; yet Sampāti did say that he saw Rāvaṇa and he saw Sītā, too. Perhaps it was mistaken identity. It may be that slipping from the control of Rāvaṇa, Sītā dropped her body into the sea. Or, it may be she died of shock. Or, perhaps when she did not yield to him, Rāvaṇa killed her and ate her flesh. But it is impossible that she had consented to be Rāvaṇa's consort. Whether she is lost, or she has perished or has died, how can I inform Rāma about it? On the other hand, to inform Rāma and not to inform Rāma—both these appear to be objectionable. What shall I do now?" He also reflected on the consequence of his returning to Kiṣkindhā with no news of Sītā. He felt certain that: "When Rāma hears the bad news from me, he will give up his life. So will Lakṣmaṇa. And then their brothers and mothers in Ayodhyā. Nor could Sugrīva live after Rāma departs from this world. He will be followed to the other world by all the vānaras of Kiṣkindhā. What a terrible calamity will strike Ayodhyā and Kiṣkindhā if I return without news of Sītā's safety!" He resolved: "It is good that I should not return to Kiṣkindhā. Like an ascetic I shall live under a tree here. Or, I can commit suicide by jumping into the sea. However, the wise ones say that suicide is the root of many evils, and that if one lives one is sure to find what one seeks."

The consciousness of his extraordinary strength suddenly seized Hanumān! He sprang up and said to himself: "I shall at once kill this demon Rāvaṇa. Even if I cannot find Sītā, I shall have avenged her abduction by killing her abductor. Or, I shall kidnap him and take him to Rāma." Then he thought of a few places in Laṅkā he had not yet searched: one of them was Aśoka-grove. He resolved to go there. Before doing so, he offered a prayer: "Salutations to Rāma and Lakṣmaṇa; salutations to Sītā, the daughter of Janaka. Salutations to Rudra, Indra, Yama, the wind-god, to the moon, fire, and the Maruts." He turned round in all directions and invoked the blessings of all. He knew he needed them for he felt that demons of superhuman strength were guarding the Aśoka-grove.

SUNDARA 14–15

Hanumān then climbed the palace wall and jumped into the Aśoka-grove. It was most beautiful and enchanting, with trees and creepers of innumerable types.

In that grove, Hanumān also saw the bird sanctuary, the ponds and artificial swimming pools hemmed by flights of steps which had been paved with expensive precious and semi-precious stones. He also saw a hill with a waterfall flowing from its side. Not far from there, he saw a unique Aśoka or Simśapā tree which was golden in its appearance. The area around this tree was covered with trees which had golden leaves and blossoms, giving the appearance that they were ablaze.

Climbing up that unique Simśapā tree, Hanumān felt certain that he would soon see Sītā. He reasoned: "Sītā was fond of the forests and groves, according to Rāma. Hence, she will doubtless come to this yonder lotus-pond. Rāma did say that she was fond of roaming the forest: surely, then, she would wish to roam this grove, too. It is almost certain that the grief-stricken Sītā would come here to offer her evening prayers. If she is still alive, I shall surely see her today."

Seated on that Aśoka or Simśapā tree, Hanumān surveyed the whole of the grove. He was enthralled by the beauty of the grove, of the trees, and of the blossoms which were so colorful that it appeared as if the whole place were afire. There were numerous other trees, too, all of which were delightful to look at. While he was thus surveying the scene, he saw a magnificent temple, not far from him. This temple had a hall of a thousand pillars, and looked like the Kailāsa.[4] The temple had been painted white. It had steps carved out of coral. And its platforms were all made of pure gold.

And, then, Hanumān saw a radiant woman with an ascetic appearance. She was surrounded by demonesses who were apparently guarding her. She was radiant though her garments were soiled. She was beautiful in form, though emaciated through sorrow, hunger and austerity. Hanumān felt certain that it was Sītā, and that it was the same lady whom he had momentarily seen over the Ṛṣymūka hill. She was seated on the ground. And, she was frequently sighing, surely on account of her separation from Rāma. With great difficulty, Hanumān recognized her as Sītā: and in this he was helped only by the graphic and vivid description that Rāma had given him.

Looking at her, thus pining for Rāma, and recollecting Rāma's love for her, Hanumān marveled at the patience of Rāma in that he could live without Sītā even for a short while.

4. The Himalayan peak on which the god Śiva dwells.

SUNDARA 16–17

Hanumān contemplated the divine form of Sītā for a few minutes; and he once again gave way to dejection. He reflected: "If even Sītā who is highly esteemed by the noble and humble Lakṣmaṇa, and who is the beloved of Rāma himself, could be subjected to such sorrow, indeed one should conclude that Time is all-powerful. Surely, Sītā is utterly confident in the ability of Rāma and Lakṣmaṇa to rescue her; and hence she is tranquil even in this misfortune. Only Rāma deserves to be her husband, and she to be Rāma's consort." How great was Rāma's love for Sītā! And, what an extraordinary person Sītā was! Hanumān continued to "weigh" her in his own mind's balance: "It was for the sake of Sītā that thousands of demons in the Daṇḍaka forest were killed by Rāma. It was for her sake alone that Rāma killed Vāli and Kabandha. Khara, Dūṣaṇa, Triśira—so many of these demons met their end because of her. And, why not: she is such a special person that if, for her sake, Rāma turned the whole world upside down it would be proper. For, she was of extraordinary birth, she is of extraordinary beauty and she is of extraordinary character. She is unexcelled in every way. And, what an extraordinary love she has for Rāma, in that she patiently endures all sorts of hardships living, as she does, as a captive in Laṅkā. Again, Rāma pines for her and is eagerly waiting to see her, to regain her. Here she is, constantly thinking of Rāma: she does not see either these demonesses guarding her, nor the trees, flowers or fruits, but with her heart centered in Rāma, she sees him alone constantly." He was now certain that that lady was in fact Sītā.

The moon had risen. The sky was clear and the moonlight enabled Hanumān to see Sītā clearly. He saw the demonesses guarding Sītā. They were hideous-looking and deformed in various parts of their bodies. Their lips, breasts and bellies were disproportionately large and hanging. Some were very tall; others were very short. They were mostly dark-complexioned. Some of them had ears, etc., that made them look like animals. They were querulous, noisy, and fond of flesh and liquor. They had smeared their bodies with meat and blood; and they ate meat and blood. Their very sight was revolting and frightening. There in their midst was Sītā.

Sītā's dress and her appearance reflected her grief. At the foot of the tree whose name, Aśoka, meant free of sorrow, was seated Sītā immersed in an ocean of sorrow, surrounded by these terrible demonesses! It was only her confidence in the prowess and the valor of her lord Rāma that sustained her life. Hanumān mentally prostrated to Rāma, to Lakṣmaṇa and to Sītā and hid himself among the branches of the tree.

SUNDARA 18, 19, 20

Night was drawing to a close. In his palace, Rāvaṇa was being awakened by the Vedic recitation of brāhmaṇa-demons who were well versed in the Vedas and other scriptural texts, and also by musicians and bards who sang his praises. Even before he had time to adorn himself properly, Rāvaṇa thought of Sītā and longed intensely to see her. Quickly adorning himself with the best of ornaments and clad in splendid garments, he entered the Aśoka-grove, accompanied by a hundred chosen women who carried golden torches, fans, cushions and other articles. They were still under the influence of alcohol: and Rāvaṇa, though mighty and powerful, was under the influence of passion for Sītā.

Hanumān recognized the person he had seen asleep in the palace the previous night.

Seeing him coming in her direction, the frightened Sītā shielded her torso with her legs and hands, and began to weep bitterly. Pining for Rāma, distressed on account of her separation from him and stricken with grief, the most beautiful and radiant Sītā resembled eclipsed fame, neglected faith, enfeebled understanding, forlorn hope, ruined prospect, disregarded command, and obstructed worship; eclipsed moon, decimated army, fuelless flame, river in drought. She was constantly engaged in the prayer that Rāma might soon triumph over Rāvaṇa and rescue her.

Rāvaṇa appeared to be chivalrous in his approach to Sītā, and his words were meaningful and sweet: he said to Sītā, "Pray, do not be afraid of me, O charming lady! It is natural for a demon to enjoy others' wives and abduct them forcibly; it is the demon's own dharma. But, I shall not violate you against your wishes. For, I want to win your love; I want to win your esteem. I have enough strength to restrain myself. Yet, it breaks my heart to see you suffer like this; to see you, a princess, dressed like this in tattered and dirty garments. You are born to apply the most delightful cosmetic articles, to wear royal attire, and to adorn yourself with the most expensive jewels. You are young, youthful: this is the time to enjoy yourself, for youth is passing. There is none in the three worlds who is as beautiful as you are, O princess: for, having fashioned you, the Creator has retired. You are so beautiful that no one in the three worlds—not even Brahamā the creator—could but be overcome by passion. When you accept me, all that I have will become yours. Even my chief wives will become your servants. Let me warn you: no one in the three worlds is my match in strength and valor. Rāma, even if he is alive, does not even know where you are: he has no hope of regaining you. Give up this foolish idea of yours. Let me behold you appropriately dressed and adorned. And, let us enjoy life to your heart's content."

SUNDARA 21–22

Rāvaṇa's words were extremely painful to the grief-stricken Sītā. She placed a blade of grass in front of her, unwilling even to speak to Rāvaṇa directly, and said: "You cannot aspire for me any more than a sinful man can aspire for perfection! I will not do what is unworthy in the eyes of a chaste wife. Surely, you do not know dharma, nor do you obviously listen to the advice of wise counselors. Set an example to your subjects, O demon: and consort with your own wives; desire for others' wives will lead to infamy. The world rejoices at the death of a wicked man: even so it will, soon, on your death. But do not desire for me. You cannot win me by offering me power or wealth: for I am inseparable from Rāma even as light from the sun. He is the abode of righteousness, of dharma; take me back to him and beg his pardon. He loves those who seek his refuge. If you do not, you will surely come to grief: for no power on earth can save you from Rāma's weapon. His missiles will surely destroy the entire Laṅkā. In fact, if you had not stolen me in the absence of Rāma and Lakṣmaṇa, you would not be alive today: you could not face them, you coward!"

Rāvaṇa's anger was roused, and he replied: "Normally, women respond to a pleasant approach by a man. But you seem to be different, O Sītā. You rouse my anger; but my desire for you subdues that anger. My love for you prevents me from killing you straight away; though you deserve to be executed, for all the insulting and impudent words you utter. Well, I had fixed one year as the time-limit for you to make up your mind. Ten months have elapsed since then. You have two more months in which to decide to accede to my wish. If you fail to do so, my cooks will prepare a nice meal of your flesh for me to eat."

But, Sītā remained unmoved. She said to Rāvaṇa: "You are prattling, O wicked demon: I can by my own spiritual energy reduce you to ashes: but I do not do so on account of the fact that I have not been so ordered by Rāma and I do not want to waste my own spiritual powers."

The terrible demon was greatly enraged by these words of Sītā. He threatened her: "Wait, I shall destroy you just now." But he did not do so. However, he said to the demonesses guarding Sītā: "Use all your powers to persuade Sītā to consent to my proposal." Immediately, Rāvaṇa's consorts embraced him and pleaded: "Why don't you enjoy our company, giving up your desire for Sītā? For, a man who seeks the company of one who has no love for him comes to grief, and he who seeks the company of one who loves him enjoys life." Hearing this and laughing aloud, Rāvaṇa walked away.

SUNDARA 23–24

After Rāvaṇa had left the grove, the demonesses said: "How is it that you do not value Rāvaṇa's hand? Perhaps you do not know who he is. Of the six Prajāpatis who were the sons of the creator himself, Pulastya is the fourth; of Pulastya was the sage Viśrava born, and he was equal to Pulastya himself in glory. And this Rāvaṇa is the son of Viśrava. He is known as Rāvaṇa because he makes his enemies cry.[5] It is a great honor to accept his proposal. Moreover, this Rāvaṇa worsted in battle the thirty-three deities presiding over the universe. Hence he is superior even to the gods. And, what is most important: he surely loves you so much that he is prepared to abandon his own favorite wives and give you all his love."

Sītā was deeply pained by these words uttered by the demonesses. She said: "Enough of this vulgar and sinful advice. A human being should not become the wife of a demon. But, even that is irrelevant. I shall not under any circumstance abandon my husband and seek another." The demonesses were enraged and began to threaten Sītā. And, Hanumān was witnessing all this.

The demonesses said again: "You have shown enough affection to the unworthy Rāma. Excess of anything is undesirable and leads to undesirable result. You have so far conformed to the human rules of conduct. It is high time that you abandoned that code, abandoned the human Rāma and consented to be Rāvaṇa's wife. We have so far put up with the rude and harsh words you have uttered; and we have so far offered you loving and wholesome advice, intent as we are on your welfare. But you seem to be too stupid to see the truth. You have been brought here by Rāvaṇa; you have crossed the ocean. Others cannot cross the ocean and come to your rescue. We tell you this, O Sītā: even Indra cannot rescue you from here. Therefore, please do as we tell you, in your interest. Enough of your weeping. Give up this sorrow which is destructive.

5. *Rāvaṇa*, from the verb *ru*, "to roar," "to cry."

Abandon this wretched life. Attain love and pleasure. Make haste, O Sītā: for youth, especially of women, is but momentary and passes quickly. Make up your mind to become Rāvaṇa's wife. If, however, you are obstinate, we shall ourselves tear your body and eat your heart."

Other demonesses took up the cue and began to threaten Sītā. They said: "When I first saw this lovely woman brought into Laṅkā by Rāvaṇa the desire arose in me that I should eat her liver and spleen, her breasts and her heart. I am waiting for that day. . . . What is the delay? Let us report to the king that she died and he will surely ask us to eat her flesh! . . We should divide her flesh equally and eat it, there should be no quarrel amongst us. . . . After the meal, we shall dance in front of the goddess Bhadrakāli."

SUNDARA 25–26

In utter despair, Sītā gave vent to her grief by thinking aloud: "The wise ones have rightly said that untimely death is not attained here either by man or a woman. Hence though I am suffering intolerable anguish on account of my separation from my beloved husband, I am unable to give up my life. This grief is slowly eating me. I can neither live nor can I die. Surely, this is the bitter fruit of some dreadful sin committed in a past birth. I am surrounded by these demonesses: and how can Rāma reach me here? Fie upon human birth, and fie upon the state of dependence upon others, as a result of which I cannot even give up my life.

"What a terrible misfortune it was that even though I was living under the protection of Rāma and Lakṣmaṇa, I was abducted by Rāvaṇa, in their absence. Even more terrible it is that having been separated from my beloved husband I am confined here surrounded by these terrible demonesses. And, the worst part of it is: in spite of all these misfortunes, my heart does not burst with anguish thus letting me die. Of course, I shall never allow Rāvaṇa to touch me, so long as I am alive.

"I wonder why Rāma has not taken steps to come to my aid. For my sake he killed thousands of demons while we were in the forest. True I am on an island; but Rāma's missiles have no difficulty crossing oceans and finding their target. Surely, he does not know where I am. Alas, even Jaṭāyu who could have informed Rāma of what had happened was killed by Rāvaṇa. If only he knew I was here, Rāma would have destroyed Laṅkā and dried up the ocean with his missiles. All the demonesses of Laṅkā would weep then, as I am weeping now; all the demons would be killed by Rāma. Laṅkā would be one huge crematorium.

"I see all sorts of evil portents. I shall be re-united with Rāma. He will come. He will destroy all these demons. If only Rāma comes to know where I am, Laṅkā will be turned desolate by him, burnt by his terrible missiles. On the other hand, the time is fast running out: the time limit that Rāvaṇa had fixed for me to decide. Two more months: and I shall be cut into pieces for Rāvaṇa's meal. May it be that Rāma himself is no more, having succumbed to grief on account of my separation? Or, may it be that he has turned an ascetic? Usually, people who love each other forget each other when they are separated: but not so Rāma whose love is eternal. Blessed indeed are the holy sages who have reached enlightenment and to whom the pleasant and the unpleasant are non-different. I salute the holy ones. And, fallen into this terrible misfortune, I shall presently give up my life."

SUNDARA 27

Hearing the words of Sītā, some of the demonesses grew terribly angry. They threatened: "We shall go and report all this to Rāvaṇa; and then we shall be able to eat you at once." Another demoness named Trijaṭā just then woke up from her slumber and announced: "Forget all this talk about eating Sītā, O foolish ones! I have just now dreamt a dream which forewarns that a terrible calamity awaits all of you." The demonesses asked: "Tell us what the dream was."

Trijaṭā narrated her dream in great detail: "I saw in my dream Rāma and Lakṣmaṇa, riding a white chariot. Sītā was sitting on a white mountain, clad in shining white robes. Rāma and Sītā were re-united. Rāma and Lakṣmaṇa then got on a huge elephant which Sītā, too, mounted. Sītā held out her arms and her hands touched the sun and the moon. Rāma, Lakṣmaṇa and Sītā later mounted the Puṣpaka chariot and flew away in a northerly direction. From all these I conclude that Rāma is divine and invincible.

"Listen to me further. In another dream I saw Rāvaṇa. His head had been shaven. He was covered with oil. He wore crimson clothes. He was drunk. He had fallen from the Puṣpaka chariot. Later, I saw him dressed in black but smeared in a red pigment and dragged by a woman riding a vehicle drawn by donkeys. He fell down from the donkey. He was prattling like a mad man. Then he entered a place which was terribly dark and foul-smelling. Later a dark woman with body covered in mud bound Rāvaṇa's neck and dragged him away in a southerly direction.[6] I saw Kumbhakarṇa as also the sons of Rāvaṇa in that dream; all of them undergoing the same or similar treatment. Only Vibhīṣaṇa's luck was different. He was clad in a white garment, with white garlands, and had a royal white umbrella held over his head.[7]

"I also saw in that dream that the whole of Laṅkā had been pushed into the sea, utterly destroyed and ruined. I also saw a rather strange dream. I saw Laṅkā burning furiously: though Laṅkā is protected by Rāvaṇa who is mighty and powerful, a vānara was able to set Laṅkā ablaze, because the vānara was a servant of Rāma.

"I see a clear warning in these dreams, O foolish women! Enough of your cruelty to Sītā; I think it is better to please her and win her favor. I am convinced that Sītā will surely achieve her purpose and her desire to be re-united with Rāma."

Hearing this, Sītā felt happy and said: "If this comes true, I shall certainly protect all of you."

SUNDARA 28, 29, 30

But, the demonesses did not pay heed to Trijaṭā. And, Sītā thought:

"Truly have the wise ones declared that death never comes to a person before the appointed time. My time has come. Rāvaṇa has said definitely that if I do not agree to him I will be put to death. Since I can never, never love him, it is certain that I shall be executed. Hence, I am condemned already. I shall, therefore, incur no blame if I voluntarily end my life today. O Rāma! O Lakṣmaṇa!

6. The south is the direction of misfortune, the ancestors, and death.

7. In this context, the color white symbolizes virtue, purity, and sovereignty.

O Sumitrā! O Kausalyā! O Mother! Caught helplessly and brought to this dreadful place, I am about to perish. Surely it was my own 'bad-time' that approached me in the form of that golden deer, and I, a foolish woman sent the two princes in search of it. Maybe, they were killed by some demon. Or, maybe they are alive and do not know where I am.

"Alas, whatever virtue I practiced and the devotion with which I served my own lord and husband, all these have come to naught; I shall presently abandon this ill-fated life of mine. O Rāma, after you complete the fourteen-year term of exile, you will return to Ayodhyā and enjoy life with the queens you might marry. But, I who loved you and whose heart is forever fastened to you, shall soon be no more.

"How shall I end this life? I have no weapon; nor will anyone here give me a weapon or poison to end my life. Ah, I shall use this string with which my hair has been tied and hang myself from this tree."

Thinking aloud in this manner, Sītā contemplated the feet of Rāma and got ready to execute herself. At the same time, however, she noticed many auspicious omens which dissuaded her from her wish to end her life. Her left eye, left arm and left thigh throbbed.[8] Her heart was gladdened, her sorrow left her for the moment, her despair abated, and she became calm and radiant once again.

Hanumān, sitting on the tree, watched all this. He thought: "If I meet Sītā in the midst of these demonesses, it would be disastrous. In fact, she might get frightened and cry and before I could make the announcement concerning Rāma, I might be caught. I can fight all the demons here; but then I might be too weak to fly back. I could speak to her in the dialect of the brāhmaṇa; but she might suspect a vānara speaking Sanskrit to be Rāvaṇa himself![9] To speak to Sītā now seems to be risky; yet, if I do not, she might commit suicide. If one does not act with due regard to place and time, the contrary results ensue. I shall sing the glories of Rāma softly and thus win Sītā's confidence. Then I shall deliver Rāma's message to her in a manner which will evoke her confidence."

SUNDARA 31, 32, 33

After deep deliberation, Hanumān decided upon the safest and the wisest course! Softly, sweetly, clearly and in cultured accents, he narrated the story of Rāma. He said: "A descendant of the noble Ikṣvāku was the emperor Daśaratha, who was a royal sage in as much as he was devoted to asceticism and righteousness, while yet ruling his kingdom. His eldest son Rāma was equally powerful, glorious and righteous. To honor his father's promise to his step-mother, Rāma went to the Daṇḍaka forest along with his brother Lakṣmaṇa, and his wife Sītā. There, Rāma killed thousands of demons. A demon disguised as a deer tricked Rāma and Lakṣmaṇa away, and at that time, the wicked Rāvaṇa abducted Sītā. Rāma went searching for her; and while so wandering the forest cultivated the friendship of the vānara Sugrīva. Sugrīva commissioned millions

8. In the case of men, the throbbing of the right eye, arm, or thigh signifies good fortune.

9. Women in all castes and men in castes lower than those of the *brāhmaṇas* and the *kṣatriyas* often spoke languages or dialects other than Sanskrit. Sītā can speak Sanskrit because she has been educated as a princess of the *kṣatriya* caste-group.

of vānaras to search for Sītā. Endowed with extraordinary energy, I crossed the ocean; and blessed I am that I am able to behold that Sītā."

Sītā was supremely delighted to hear that speech. She looked up and down, around and everywhere, and saw the vānara Hanumān. But, seeing the vānara seated on the tree, Sītā was frightened and suspicious. She cried aloud. "O Rāma, O Lakṣmaṇa." She was terror-stricken as the vānara approached her; but she was pleasantly surprised to see that he came humbly and worshipfully. She thought: "Am I dreaming? I hope not; it forebodes ill to dream of a vānara. Nay, I am not dreaming. Maybe, this is hallucination. I have constantly been thinking of Rāma. I have constantly uttered his name, and talked about him. Since my whole being is absorbed in him, I am imagining all this. But, I have reasoned out all this carefully within myself; yet, this being here is not only clearly seen by me, but it talks to me, too! I pray to the gods, may what I have just heard be true."

With his palms joined together in salutation over his head, Hanumān humbly approached Sītā and asked: "Who are you, O lady? Are you indeed the wife of that blessed Rāma?"

Highly pleased with this question, Sītā thereupon related her whole story: "I am the daughter-in-law of king Daśaratha, and the daughter of king Janaka. I am the wife of Rāma. We lived happily in Ayodhyā for twelve years. But when Rāma was about to be crowned, his step-mother Kaikeyī demanded the boon from her husband that Rāma should be banished to the forest. The king swooned on hearing this; but Rāma took it upon himself to fulfill that promise. I followed him; and Lakṣmaṇa, too, came with us. One day when they were away, Rāvaṇa forcibly carried me and brought me here. He has given me two more months to live; after which I shall meet my end."

SUNDARA 34–35

Once again bowing down to Sītā, Hanumān said to her: "O divine lady, I am a messenger sent by Rāma. He, as also his brother Lakṣmaṇa, send their greetings and hope that you are alive and well." Sītā rejoiced and thought to herself: "Surely, there is a lot of truth in the old adage: 'Happiness is bound to come to the man who lives, even though after a long time.'" But, as Hanumān came near her, she grew suspicious and would not even look at him: she thought, and said to him: "O Rāvaṇa! Previously you assumed the disguise of a mendicant and abducted me. Now, you have come to torment me in the guise of a vānara! Pray, leave me alone." But, on the other hand, she reasoned to herself: "No this cannot be; for on seeing this vānara, my heart rejoices."

Hanumān, however, reassured her: "O blessed Sītā, I am a messenger sent by Rāma who will very soon kill these demons and rescue you from their captivity. Rāma and Lakṣmaṇa constantly think of you. So does king Sugrīva whose minister Hanumān, I am. Endowed with extraordinary energy I crossed the sea. I am not what you suspect me to be!"

At her request, Hanumān recounted the glories of Rāma:[1] "Rāma is equal to the gods in beauty, charm and wisdom. He is the protector of all living beings,

1. In the description that follows, Hanumān reiterates many of the qualities and attributes ascribed to Rāma throughout the epic. This conventional portrait of the ideal man blends physical characteristics and character traits.

of his own people, of his work and of his dharma; he is the protector of people of different occupations, of good conduct, and he himself adheres to good conduct and makes others do so, too. He is mighty, friendly, well-versed in scriptures and devoted to the holy ones. He is endowed with all the characteristics of the best among men, which are: broad shoulders, strong arms, powerful neck, lovely face, reddish eyes, deep voice, dark-brown colored skin; he has firm chest, wrist and fist; he has long eyebrows, arms and scrotum; he has symmetrical locks, testicles and knees; he has strong bulging chest, abdomen and rim of the navel; reddish in the corner of his eyes, nails, palms and soles; he is soft in his glans, the lines of his feet and hair; he has deep voice, gait and navel; three folds adorn the skin of his neck and his abdomen; the arch of his feet, the lines on his soles, and the nipples are deep; he has short generative organ, neck, back and shanks; three spirals adorn the hair on his head; there are four lines at the root of his thumb; and four lines on his forehead; he is four cubits tall; the four pairs of his limbs (cheeks, arms, shanks and knees) are symmetrical; even so the other fourteen pairs of limbs; his limbs are long. He is excellent in every way. Lakṣmaṇa, Rāma's brother, is also full of charm and excellences."

SUNDARA 35–36

Hanumān then narrated in great detail all that had happened. He mentioned in particular how Rāma was moved to tears when Hanumān showed him the pieces of jewelry that Sītā had dropped on the hill. He concluded that narrative by affirming: "I shall certainly attain the glory of having seen you first; and Rāma too will soon come here to take you back." He also revealed to Sītā his own identity: "Kesari, my father, lived on the mountain known as Malayavān. Once he went to the Gokarṇa mountain at the command of the sages to fight and to kill a demon named Sāmbasadana who tormented the people. I was born of the wind-god and my mother Añjanā. I tell you again, O divine lady, that I am a vānara, and I am a messenger sent by Rāma; here, behold the ring which has been inscribed with the name of Rāma. Whatever might have been the cause of your suffering captivity, it has almost come to an end."

When she saw the signet ring, Sītā felt the presence of Rāma himself; she was filled with joy. Her attitude to Hanumān, too, immediately and dramatically changed. She exclaimed: "You are heroic, capable, and wise, too, O best among vānaras. What a remarkable feat you have accomplished by crossing this vast ocean, a distance of eight hundred miles.[2] Surely, you are not an ordinary vānara in that you are not afraid of even Rāvaṇa. I am delighted to hear that Rāma and Lakṣmaṇa are well. But why has he not rescued me yet: he could dry up the ocean, in fact he could even destroy the whole earth with his missiles if he wanted to. Perhaps, they had to wait for the propitious moment, and that moment which would mean the end of my suffering has not yet arrived.

"O Hanumān, tell me more about Rāma. Does he continue to rely on both self-effort and divine agency in all that he undertakes? Tell me, O Hanumān, does he still love me as before? And, I also hope that, pining for me, he does not waste away. And also tell me: how will Rāma rescue me from here. Will

2. Not a realistic estimate of the distance between Laṅkā and the southern tip of India, which is much shorter than this.

Bharata send an army? When he renounced the throne and when he took me to the forest, he displayed extraordinary firmness: is he still as firm in his resolves? Oh, I know that he loves me more than anyone else in this world."

Hanumān replied: "You will soon behold Rāma, O Sītā! Stricken with grief on account of his separation from you, Rāma does not eat meat, nor drink wine; he does not even wish to ward off flies and mosquitoes that assail him. He thinks of you constantly. He hardly sleeps; and if he does, he wakes up calling out 'Ah Sītā.' When he sees a fruit or flower, he thinks of you." Hearing the glories of Rāma, Sītā was rid of sorrow; hearing of his grief, Sītā grew equally sorrowful.

SUNDARA 37

Sītā replied to Hanumān: "Your description of Rāma's love for me comes to me like nectar mixed with poison. In whatever condition one may be, whether one is enjoying unlimited power and prosperity or one is in dreadful misery, the end of one's action drags a man as if he were tied with a rope. Look at the way in which Rāma, Lakṣmaṇa and I have been subjected to sorrow: surely, no one can overcome destiny. I wonder when the time will come when I shall be united with Rāma once again. Rāvaṇa gave me one year, of which ten months have passed and only two are left. At the end of those two months, Rāvaṇa will surely kill me. There is no alternative. For, he does not fancy the thought of taking me back to Rāma. In fact, such a course was suggested by Rāvaṇa's own brother Vibhīṣaṇa: so his own daughter Kalā told me. But Rāvaṇa turns a deaf ear upon such wise counsel."

Hanumān said to Sītā: "I am sure that Rāma will soon arrive here, with an army of forest-dwellers and other tribes, as soon as I inform him of your whereabouts. But, O divine lady, I have another idea. You can rejoin your husband this very day. I can enable you to end this sorrow instantly. Pray, do not hesitate; get on my back, and seek union (yogam) with Rāma now. I have the power to carry you, or even Laṅkā, Rāvaṇa and everything in it! No one will be able to pursue me or to overcome me. What a great triumph it will be if I return to Kiṣkindhā with you on my back!"

For a moment Sītā was thrilled at this prospect. But she remarked almost in jest: "You are speaking truly like a vānara, an ignorant tribesman. You are so small: and you think you can carry me over the ocean!" Hanumān, thereupon, showed Sītā his real form. Seeing him stand like a mountain in front of her, Sītā felt sure that his confidence was justified, but said to him: "O mighty Hanumān, I am convinced that you can do as you say. But I do not think it is proper for me to go with you. You may proceed at great speed; but I may slip and fall into the ocean. If I go with you, the demons will suspect our relationship and give it an immoral twist. Moreover, many demons will pursue you: how will you, unarmed as you are, deal with them and at the same time protect me? I might once again fall into their hands. I agree you have the power to fight them: but if you kill them all, it will rob Rāma of the glory of killing them and rescuing me. Surely, when Rāma and Lakṣmaṇa come here with you, they will destroy the demons and liberate me. I am devoted to Rāma: and I will not of my own accord touch the body of another man. Therefore, O Hanumān, enable Rāma and Lakṣmaṇa to come here with greatest expedition."

SUNDARA 38

Hanumān, the wise vānara, was highly impressed and thoroughly convinced of the propriety of Sītā's arguments. He applauded them, and prayed: "If you feel you should not come, pray, give me a token which I might take back with me and which Rāma might recognize."

This suggestion revived old memories and moved Sītā to tears. She said to Hanumān: "I shall give you the best token. Please remind my glorious husband of a delightful episode in our forest-life which only he and I know. This happened when we were living near Citrakooṭa hill. We had finished our bath; and we had had a lot of fun playing in water, Rāma was sitting on my lap. A crow began to worry me. I kept it away threatening it with stones. It hid itself. When I was getting dressed and when my skirt slipped a little, the crow attacked me again: but I defended myself angrily. Looking at this Rāma laughed, while sweetly pacifying me.

"Both of us were tired. I slept on Rāma's lap for sometime. Later Rāma slept with his head resting on my lap. The crow (who was Indra's son in disguise) attacked me again and began to inflict wounds on my body. A few drops of blood trickled from my chest and fell on Rāma who awoke. Seeing the vicious crow perched on a nearby tree, Rāma picked up the missile named after the creator and hurled it at the crow. That crow flew round to the three worlds but found no asylum anywhere else.

"Eventually it sought refuge with Rāma himself. Rāma was instantly pacified. Yet, the missile could not be neutralized. The crow sacrificed its right eye and saved its life." As she was narrating the story, Sītā felt the presence of Rāma and addressed him: "O Rāma, you were ready to use the Brahmā-missile towards a mere crow for my sake; why do you suffer my abduction with patience? Though I have you as my lord and master, yet I live here like a destitute! Have you no compassion for me: it was from you I learnt that compassion is the greatest virtue!" She said to Hanumān again: "No power on earth can confront Rāma. It is only my ill-luck that prevents them from coming to my rescue."

Hanumān explained: "It was only ignorance of your whereabouts that has caused this delay, O divine lady. Now that we know where you are, the destruction of the demons is at hand." Sītā said: "The fulfillment of this mission depends upon you; with your aid, Rāma will surely succeed in his mission. But, please tell Rāma that I shall be alive only for a month more." Then as a further token, Sītā took off a precious jewel from her person and gave it to Hanumān. Receiving that jewel, and with Sītā's blessings Hanumān was ready to depart.

* * *

From Book 6

Yuddha

YUDDHA 109, 110, 111

When Rāma and Rāvaṇa began to fight, their armies stood stupefied, watching them! Rāma was determined to win; Rāvaṇa was sure he would die: knowing this, they fought with all their might. Rāvaṇa attacked the standard on Rāma's car: and Rāma similarly shot the standard on Rāvaṇa's car. While Rāvaṇa's standard fell; Rāma's did not. Rāvaṇa next aimed at the "horses" of Rāma's car: even though he attacked them with all his might, they remained unaffected.

Both of them discharged thousands of missiles: these illumined the skies and created a new heaven, as it were! They were accurate in their aim and their missiles unfailingly hit the target. With unflagging zeal they fought each other, without the least trace of fatigue. What one did the other did in retaliation.

Rāvaṇa shot at Mātali[3] who remained unaffected by it. Then Rāvaṇa sent a shower of maces and mallets at Rāma. Their very sound agitated the oceans and tormented the aquatic creatures. The celestials and the holy brāhmaṇas witnessing the scene prayed: "May auspiciousness attend to all the living beings, and may the worlds endure forever. May Rāma conquer Rāvaṇa." Astounded at the way in which Rāma and Rāvaṇa fought with each other, the sages said to one another: "Sky is like sky, ocean is like ocean; the fight between Rāma and Rāvaṇa is like Rāma and Rāvaṇa—incomparable."

Taking up a powerful missile, Rāma correctly aimed at the head of Rāvaṇa; it fell. But another head appeared in its place. Every time Rāma cut off Rāvaṇa's head, another appeared! Rāma was puzzled. Mātali, Rāma's driver, said to Rāma: "Why do you fight like an ordinary warrior, O Rāma? Use the Brahmā-missile; the hour of the demon's death is at hand."

Rāma remembered the Brahmā-missile which the sage Agastya had given him. It had the power of the wind-god for its "feathers"; the power of fire and sun at its head; the whole space was its body; and it had the weight of a mountain. It shone like the sun or the fire of nemesis. As Rāma took it in his hands, the earth shook and all living beings were terrified. Infallible in its destructive power, this ultimate weapon of destruction shattered the chest of Rāvaṇa, and entered deep into the earth.

Rāvaṇa fell dead. And the surviving demons fled, pursued by the vānaras. The vānaras shouted in great jubilation. The air resounded with the drums of the celestials. The gods praised Rāma. The earth became steady, the wind blew softly and the sun was resplendent as before. Rāma was surrounded by mighty heroes and gods who were all joyously felicitating him on the victory.

YUDDHA 112, 113

Seeing Rāvaṇa lying dead on the battlefield, Vibhīṣaṇa burst into tears. Overcome by brotherly affection, he lamented thus: "Alas, what I had predicted has come true: and my advice was not relished by you, overcome as you were by lust and delusion. Now that you have departed, the glory of Laṅkā has departed. You were like a tree firmly established in heroism with asceticism for its strength, spreading out firmness in all aspects of your life: yet you have been cut down. You were like an elephant with splendor, noble ancestry, indignation, and pleasant nature for parts: yet you have been killed. You, who were like blazing fire have been extinguished by Rāma."

Rāma approached the grief-stricken Vibhīṣaṇa and gently and lovingly said to him: "It is not right that you should thus grieve, O Vibhīṣaṇa, for a mighty warrior fallen on the battlefield. Victory is the monopoly of none: a hero is either slain in battle or he kills his opponent. Hence our ancients decreed that the

3. Indra, king of the gods, has sent his own charioteer, Mātali, to drive Rāma's chariot in battle.

warrior who is killed in combat should not be mourned. Get up and consider what should be done next."

Vibhīṣaṇa regained his composure and said to Rāma: "This Rāvaṇa used to give a lot in charity to ascetics; he enjoyed life; he maintained his servants well; he shared his wealth with his friends, and he destroyed his enemies. He was regular in his religious observances; learned he was in the scriptures. By your grace, O Rāma, I wish to perform his funeral in accordance with the scriptures, for his welfare in the other world." Rāma was delighted and said to Vibhīṣaṇa: "Hostility ends at death. Take steps for the due performance of the funeral rites. He is your brother as he is mine, too."

The womenfolk of Rāvaṇa's court, and his wives, hearing of his end, rushed out of the palace, and, arriving at the battlefield, rolled on the ground in sheer anguish. Overcome by grief they gave vent to their feelings in diverse heart-rending ways. They wailed: "Alas, he who could not be killed by the gods and demons, has been killed in battle by a man standing on earth. Our beloved lord! Surely when you abducted Sītā and brought her to Laṅkā, you invited your own death! Surely it was because death was close at hand that you did not listen to the wise counsel of your own brother Vibhīṣaṇa, and you ill-treated him and exiled him. Even later if you had restored Sītā to Rāma, this evil fate would not have overtaken you. However, it is surely not because you did what you liked, because you were driven by lust, that you lie dead now: God's will makes people do diverse deeds. He who is killed by the divine will dies. No one can flout the divine will, and no one can buy the divine will nor bribe it."

* * *

YUDDHA 115, 116

Rāma returned to the camp where the vānara troops had been stationed. He turned to Lakṣmaṇa and said: "O Lakṣmaṇa, install Vibhīṣaṇa on the throne of Laṅkā and consecrate him as the king of Laṅkā. He has rendered invaluable service to me and I wish to behold him on the throne of Laṅkā at once."

Without the least loss of time, Lakṣmaṇa made the necessary preparations and with the waters of the ocean consecrated Vibhīṣaṇa as king of Laṅkā, in strict accordance with scriptural ordinance. Rāma, Lakṣmaṇa and the others were delighted. The demon-leaders brought their tributes and offered them to Vibhīṣaṇa who in turn placed them all at Rāma's feet.

Rāma said to Hanumān: "Please go, with the permission of king Vibhīṣaṇa, to Sītā and inform her of the death of Rāvaṇa and the welfare of both myself and Lakṣmaṇa." Immediately Hanumān left for the Aśoka-grove. The grief-stricken Sītā was happy to behold him. With joined palms Hanumān submitted Rāma's message and added: "Rāma desires me to inform you that you can shed fear, for you are in your own home as it were, now that Vibhīṣaṇa is king of Laṅkā." Sītā was speechless for a moment and then said: "I am delighted by the message you have brought, O Hanumān; and I am rendered speechless by it. I only regret that I have nothing now with which to reward you; nor is any gift equal in value to the most joyous tidings you have brought me." Hanumān submitted: "O lady, the very words you have uttered are more precious than all the jewels of the world! I consider myself supremely blessed to have witnessed Rāma's victory and Rāvaṇa's destruction." Sītā was even more delighted: she said, "Only you can utter such sweet words, O Hanumān, endowed as you are with manifold excellences. Truly you are an abode of virtues."

Hanumān said: "Pray, give me leave to kill all these demonesses who have been tormenting you so long." Sītā replied: "Nay, Hanumān, they are not responsible for their actions, for they were but obeying their master's commands. And, surely, it was my own evil destiny that made me suffer at their hands. Hence, I forgive them. A noble man does not recognize the harm done to him by others: and he never retaliates, for he is the embodiment of goodness. One should be compassionate towards all, the good and the wicked, nay even towards those who are fit to be killed: who is free from sin?" Hanumān was thrilled to hear these words of Sītā, and said: "Indeed you are the noble consort of Rāma and his peer in virtue and nobility. Pray, give me a message to take back to Rāma." Sītā replied: "Please tell him that I am eager to behold his face." Assuring Sītā that she would see Rāma that very day, Hanumān returned to Rāma.

YUDDHA 117, 118, 119

Hanumān conveyed Sītā's message to Rāma who turned to king Vibhīṣaṇa and said: "Please bring Sītā to me soon, after she has had a bath and has adorned herself." Immediately Vibhīṣaṇa went to Sītā and compelled her to proceed seated in a palanquin, to where Rāma was. Vānaras and demons had gathered around her, eager to look at Sītā. And Vibhīṣaṇa, in accordance with the tradition, wished to ensure that Sītā was not seen by these and rebuked them to go away. Restraining him, Rāma said: "Why do you rebuke them, O Vibhīṣaṇa? Neither houses nor clothes nor walls constitute a veil for a woman; her character alone is her veil. Let her descend from the palanquin and walk up to me." So she did.

Rāma said sternly: "My purpose has been accomplished, O Sītā. My prowess has been witnessed by all. I have fulfilled my pledge. Rāvaṇa's wickedness has been punished. The extraordinary feat performed by Hanumān in crossing the ocean and burning Laṅkā[4] has borne fruit. Vibhīṣaṇa's devotion has been rewarded." Rāma's heart was in a state of conflict, afraid as he was of public ridicule. Hence, he continued: "I wish to let you know that all this was done not for your sake, but for the sake of preserving my honor. Your conduct is open to suspicion, hence even your sight is displeasing to me. Your body was touched by Rāvaṇa: how then can I, claiming to belong to a noble family, accept you? Hence I permit you to go where you like and live with whom you like—either Lakṣmaṇa, Bharata, Śatrughna, Sugrīva or even Vibhīṣaṇa. It is difficult for me to believe that Rāvaṇa, who was so fond of you, would have been able to keep away from you for such a long time."

Sītā was shocked. Rāma's words wounded her heart. Tears streamed down her face. Wiping them, she replied: "O Rāma, you are speaking to me in the language of a common and vulgar man speaking to a common woman. That which was under my control, my heart, has always been yours; how could I

4. When Hanumān destroys the groves of Laṅkā, Rāvaṇa's henchmen capture him and set his tail on fire. Hanumān sets fire to Laṅkā's mansions with his fiery tail and himself escapes unhurt.

prevent my body from being touched when I was helpless and under another person's control? Ah, if only you had conveyed your suspicion through Hanumān when he came to meet me, I would have killed myself then and saved you all this trouble and the risk involved in the war." Turning to Lakṣmaṇa, she said: "Kindle the fire, O Lakṣmaṇa: that is the only remedy. I shall not live to endure this false calumny." Lakṣmaṇa looked at Rāma and with his approval kindled the fire. Sītā prayed: "Even as my heart is ever devoted to Rāma, may the fire protect me. If I have been faithful to Rāma in thought, word or deed, may the fire protect me. The sun, the moon, the wind, earth and others are witness to my purity; may the fire protect me." Then she entered into the fire, even as an oblation poured into the fire would. Gods and sages witnessed this. The women who saw this screamed.

YUDDHA 120, 121

Rāma was moved to tears by the heart-rending cries of all those women who witnessed the self-immolation of Sītā. At the same time, all the gods, including the trinity—the Creator, the Preserver, and the Redeemer (or Transformer)[5]—arrived upon the scene in their personal forms. Saluting Rāma, they said: "You are the foremost among the gods, and yet you treat Sītā as if you were a common human being!"

Rāma replied to these divinities: "I consider myself a human being, Rāma the son of Daśaratha. Who I am, and whence I am, may you tell me!"

Brahmā the creator said: "You are verily lord Nārāyaṇa.[6] You are the imperishable cosmic being. You are the truth. You are eternal. You are the supreme dharma of the worlds. You are the father even of the chief of the gods, Indra. You are the sole refuge of perfected beings and holy men. You are the Om,[7] and you are the spirit of sacrifice. You are that cosmic being with infinite heads, hands and eyes.[8] You are the support of the whole universe. The whole universe is your body. Sītā is Lakṣmī[9] and you are lord Viṣṇu, who is of a dark hue, and who is the creator of all beings. For the sake of the destruction of Rāvaṇa you entered into a human body. This mission of ours has been fully accomplished by you. Blessed it is to be in your presence; blessed it is to sing your glories; they are truly blessed who are devoted to you, for their life will be attended with success."

As soon as Brahmā finished saying this, the god of fire emerged from the fire in his personal form, holding up Sītā in his hands. Sītā shone in all her radiance. The god of fire who is the witness of everything that takes place in the world, said to Rāma: "Here is your Sītā, Rāma. I find no fault in her. She has not erred in thought, word or deed. Even during the long period of her detention in the abode of Rāvaṇa, she did not even think of him, as her

5. The triad of the three great gods, Brahmā (Creator), Viṣṇu (Preserver), and Śiva (Redeemer or Transformer).
6. Viṣṇu in his primeval cosmic form.
7. A sacred chant (mantra) of the Vedas.
8. The cosmic being described here is Puruṣa, or "Man," a primeval being with innumerable heads, arms, and eyes who was offered as the sacrificial victim by the gods and sages in the first sacrifice, described in a hymn of the *Ṛg-veda*.
9. Goddess-consort of Viṣṇu.

heart was set on you. Accept her: and I command you not to treat her harshly."

Rāma was highly pleased at this turn of events. He said: "Indeed, I was fully aware of Sītā's purity. Even the mighty and wicked Rāvaṇa could not lay his hands upon her with evil intention. Yet, this baptism by fire was necessary, to avoid public calumny and ridicule, for though she was pure, she lived in Laṅkā for a long time. I knew, too, that Sītā would never be unfaithful to me: for we are non-different from each other even as the sun and its rays are. It is therefore impossible for me to renounce her."

After saying so, Rāma was joyously reunited with Sītā.

YUDDHA 122, 123

Lord Śiva then said to Rāma: "You have fulfilled a most difficult task. Now behold your father, the illustrious king Daśaratha who appears in the firmament to bless you and to greet you."

Rāma along with Lakṣmaṇa saw that great monarch, their father clad in a raiment of purity and shining by his own luster. Still seated in his celestial vehicle, Daśaratha lifted up Rāma and placing him on his lap, warmly embraced him and said: "Neither heaven nor even the homage of the gods is as pleasing to me as to behold you, Rāma. I am delighted to see that you have successfully completed the period of your exile and that you have destroyed all your enemies. Even now the cruel words of Kaikeyī haunt my heart; but seeing you and embracing you, I am rid of that sorrow, O Rāma. You have redeemed my word and thus I have been saved by you. It is only now that I recognize you to be the supreme person incarnated as a human being in this world in order to kill Rāvaṇa."

Rāma said: "You remember that you said to Kaikeyī, 'I renounce you and your son'? Pray, take back that curse and may it not afflict Kaikeyī and Bharata." Daśaratha agreed to it and then said to Lakṣmaṇa: "I am pleased with you, my son, and you have earned great merit by the faithful service you have rendered to Rāma."

Lastly, king Daśaratha said to Sītā: "My dear daughter, do not take to heart the fire ordeal that Rāma forced you to undergo: it was necessary to reveal to the world your absolute purity. By your conduct you have exalted yourself above all women." Having thus spoken to them, Daśaratha ascended to heaven.

Before taking leave of Rāma, Indra prayed: "Our visit to you should not be fruitless, O Rāma. Command me, what may I do for you?" Rāma replied: "If you are really pleased with me, then I pray that all those vānaras who laid down their lives for my sake may come back to life. I wish to see them hale and hearty as before. I also wish to see the whole world fruitful and prosperous." Indra replied: "This indeed is an extremely difficult task. Yet, I do not go back on my word, hence I grant it. All the vānaras will come back to life and be restored to their original form, with all their wounds healed. Even as you had asked, the world will be fruitful and prosperous."

Instantly, all the vānaras arose from the dead and bowed to Rāma. The others who witnessed this marveled and the gods beheld Rāma who had all his wishes fulfilled. The gods returned to their abodes.

* * *

Summary After crowning Vibhīṣana king of Laṅkā, Rāma, Lakṣmaṇa and Sītā fly to Ayodhyā in Rāvaṇa's flying chariot, accompanied by Vibhīṣaṇa, Sugrīva, Hanumān, and the monkey hordes.

YUDDHA 130

Bharata immediately made the reception arrangements. He instructed Śatrughna: "Let prayers be offered to the gods in all temples and houses of worship with fragrant flowers and musical instruments."

Śatrughna immediately gave orders that the roads along which the royal procession would wend its way to the palace should be leveled and sprinkled with water, and kept clear by hundreds of policemen cordoning them. Soon all the ministers, and thousands of elephants and men on horse-back and in cars went out to greet Rāma. The royal reception party, seated in palanquins,[1] was led by the queen-mother Kausalyā herself; Kaikeyī and the other members of the royal household followed—and all of them reached Nandigrāma.[2]

From there Bharata headed the procession with the sandals of Rāma placed on his head, with the white royal umbrella and the other regalia.[3] Bharata was the very picture of an ascetic though he radiated the joy that filled his heart at the very thought of Rāma's return to the kingdom.

Bharata anxiously looked around but saw no signs of Rāma's return! But, Hanumān reassured him: "Listen, O Bharata, you can see the cloud of dust raised by the vānaras rushing towards Ayodhyā. You can now hear the roar of the Puṣpaka flying chariot."

"Rāma has come!"—these words were uttered by thousands of people at the same time. Even before the Puṣpaka landed, Bharata humbly saluted Rāma who was standing on the front side of the chariot. The Puṣpaka landed. As Bharata approached it, Rāma lifted him up and placed him on his lap. Bharata bowed down to Rāma and also to Sītā and greeted Lakṣmaṇa. And he embraced Sugrīva, Jāmbavān, Aṅgada, Vibhīṣaṇa and others. He said to Sugrīva: "We are four brothers, and with you we are five. Good deeds promote friendship, and evil is a sign of enmity."

Rāma bowed to his mother who had become emaciated through sorrow, and brought great joy to her heart. Then he also bowed to Sumitrā and Kaikeyī. All the people thereupon said to Rāma: "Welcome, welcome back, O Lord."

Bharata placed the sandals in front of Rāma, and said: "Rāma here is your kingdom which I held in trust for you during your absence. I consider myself supremely blessed in being able to behold your return to Ayodhyā. By your grace, the treasury has been enriched tenfold by me, as also the storehouses and the strength of the nation." Rāma felt delighted. When the entire party had disembarked, he instructed that the Puṣpaka be returned to its original owner, Kubera.[4]

1. Litters in which people were carried by bearers.
2. The village outside the city of Ayodhyā, from which Bharata ruled the kingdom on behalf of Rāma.
3. By carrying Rāma's sandals on his head, Bharata indicates his subservience to and reverence for Rāma as his sovereign, elder brother, and teacher.
4. God of wealth.

YUDDHA 131

The coronation proceedings were immediately initiated by Bharata. Skilled barbers removed the matted locks of Rāma. He had a ceremonial bath and he was dressed in magnificent robes and royal jewels. Kausalyā herself helped the vānara ladies to dress themselves in royal robes; all the queens dressed Sītā appropriately for the occasion. The royal chariot was brought; duly ascending it, Rāma, Lakṣmaṇa and Sītā, went in a procession to Ayodhyā, Bharata himself driving the chariot. When he had reached the court, Rāma gave his ministers and counselors a brief account of the events during his exile, particularly the alliance with the vānara chief Sugrīva, and the exploits of Hanumān. He also informed them of his alliance with Vibhīṣaṇa.

At Bharata's request, Sugrīva despatched the best of the vānaras to fetch water from the four oceans, and all the sacred rivers of the world. The aged sage Vasiṣṭha thereupon commenced the ceremony in connection with the coronation of Rāma. Rāma and Sītā were seated on a seat made entirely of precious stones. The foremost among the sages thereupon consecrated Rāma with the appropriate Vedic chants. First the brāhmaṇas, then the virgins, then the ministers and warriors, and later the businessmen poured the holy waters on Rāma.[5] After that the sage Vasiṣṭha placed Rāma on the throne made of gold and studded with precious stones, and placed on his head the dazzling crown which had been made by Brahmā the creator himself. The gods and others paid their homage to Rāma by bestowing gifts upon him. Rāma also gave away rich presents to the brāhmaṇas and others, including the vānara chiefs like Sugrīva. Rāma then gave to Sītā a necklace of pearls and said: "You may give it to whom you like, Sītā." And, immediately Sītā bestowed that gift upon Hanumān.

After witnessing the coronation of Rāma, the vānaras returned to Kiṣkindhā. So did Vibhīṣaṇa return to Laṅkā. Rāma looked fondly at Lakṣmaṇa and expressed the wish that he should reign as the prince regent. Lakṣmaṇa did not reply: he did not want it. Rāma appointed Bharata as prince regent. Rāma thereafter ruled the earth for a very long time.

During the period of Rāma's reign, there was no poverty, no crime, no fear, and no unrighteousness in the kingdom. All the people constantly spoke of Rāma; the whole world had been transformed into Rāma. Everyone was devoted to dharma. And Rāma was highly devoted to dharma, too. He ruled for eleven thousand years.

YUDDHA 131

Rāma's rule of the kingdom was characterized by the effortless and spontaneous prevalence of dharma. People were free from fear of any sort. There were no widows in the land: people were not molested by beasts and snakes, nor did they suffer from diseases. There was no theft, no robbery nor any violence. Young people did not die making older people perform funeral services for them. Everyone was happy and everyone was devoted to dharma; beholding

5. The *brāhmaṇas*, ministers and warriors, and businessmen represent the three highest caste-groups in Hindu society.

Rāma alone, no one harmed another. People lived long and had many children. They were healthy and they were free from sorrow. Everywhere people were speaking all the time about Rāma; the entire world appeared to be the form of Rāma. The trees were endowed with undying roots, and they were in fruition all the time and they flowered throughout the year. Rain fell whenever it was needed. There was a pleasant breeze always. The brāhmaṇas (priests), the warriors, the farmers and businessmen, as also the members of the servant class, were entirely free from greed, and were joyously devoted to their own dharma and functions in society. There was no falsehood in the life of the people who were all righteous. People were endowed with all auspicious characteristics and all of them had dharma as their guiding light. Thus did Rāma rule the world for eleven thousand years, surrounded by his brothers.

This holy epic Rāmāyaṇa composed by the sage Vālmīki, promotes dharma, fame, long life and in the case of a king, victory. He who listens to it always is freed from all sins. He who desires sons gets them, and he who desires wealth becomes wealthy, by listening to the story of the coronation of Rāma. The king conquers the whole world, after overcoming his enemies. Women who listen to this story will be blessed with children like Rāma and his brothers. And they, too, will be blessed with long life, after listening to the Rāmāyaṇa. He who listens to or reads this Rāmāyaṇa propitiates Rāma by this; Rāma is pleased with him; and he indeed is the eternal lord Viṣṇu.

LAVA AND KUŚA said: Such is the glorious epic, Rāmāyaṇa. May all recite it and thus augment the glory of dharma, of lord Viṣṇu. Righteous men should regularly listen to this story of Rāma, which increases health, long-life, love, wisdom and vitality.

THE MAHĀBHĀRATA

ca. fourth century B.C.E.–fourth century C.E.

The *Mahābhārata* is the longest poem in the world, about eight times the combined length of the ***Iliad*** and the ***Odyssey***. It is one of the oldest compositions in world literature to offer us a sustained reflection on the possibilities of a just war and a harmonious society, and it does so by telling the story of a dynasty of kings in northern India deeply divided by the pursuit of power and wealth. The division leads to a tragic conflict on an epic scale, which destroys several generations of men and women, and lays a whole land waste. The *Mahābhārata* seeks to explain these events by mapping out their place within ancient India as a whole, and by reflecting on the nature of law, right, and political power and on the intricate connections between power, violence, and good and evil.

CONTEXT

The *Mahābhārata* attributes its own authorship to Kṛṣṇa Dvaipāyana, who is said to have originally composed or compiled it as a "poetic history" of the dynasty that came to rule a major kingdom in northern India in the ancient period. This was a time when the small republics that dotted the political landscape of the ***Rāmāyaṇa*** (the older Sanskrit epic) gradually gave way to larger republican kingdoms and imperial formations. Dvaipāyana, who is also commonly known in Indian tradition as Vyāsa (editor or compiler), was commissioned by a late descendant of the ruling dynasty to narrate the history of his ancestors, and particularly to explain the great war that had divided and devastated his family a few generations earlier. Dvaipāyana composed his tale as a long poem and taught it to a protégé, who became the main narrator in the text of the epic.

Many aspects of the society depicted in the *Mahābhārata* resemble the world in which it was composed, which is more crowded and complex than that in the *Rāmāyaṇa*. Large parts of the plains surrounding the River Ganges have been cleared of forests to make room for a multifaceted, settled society. While the majority of people live in small villages in the countryside, cultivating the land, a sizable urban population has emerged in towns and cities that serve as market and administrative centers. Capital cities are large and prosperous; the palaces of the kings are enormous, and royal households contain hundreds of occupants.

In the place and time of the *Mahābhārata*, both inside and outside the story, Indian society is highly differentiated. The four main caste-groups (*varṇas*)—consisting of the *brāhmaṇas* (priests), *kṣatriyas* (warriors), *vaiśyas* (traders), and *śūdras* (peasants and those who serve the three higher groups)—have diversified internally into numerous specific and local castes (*jātīs*). Each of these smaller castes, containing many lineages and clans, tends to have its own distinctive occupation, rituals, codes of conduct, marriage customs, dress, and cuisine. In addition, three other groups have become visible in this society: a fifth caste-group, comprising the so-called untouchables, has been clearly separated from the others; various aboriginal tribes, living in particular regions, have acquired distinct identities; and groups of foreign origin have migrated to specific parts of the country. The *Mahābhārata* gives us characters who are drawn from or interact with all these social groups, and portrays a wide variety of lifestyles: thus, for example, we encounter polygamous as well as polyandrous families, male as well as female warriors, warriors who have become scholars, and priests who have become warriors.

In this world surrounding the epic tale but also present within it, the priestly and warrior castes have joined forces to constitute a distinct ruling class. The *brāhmanas* here are scholars and spiritual practitioners, but they are also worldly participants in court politics, at home in statecraft and factional infighting, policy making and warfare. The warriors are statesmen, familiar with the intricacies of diplomacy and governance; they rule extensive territories, form and break alliances, and negotiate elaborate treaties. As members of a composite class pursuing power and wealth, these *kṣatriyas* and *brāhmaṇas* are fully engaged with war and conquest; with building large kingdoms; and with establishing long-term dynastic rule. The dynasties we see in Dvaipāyana's poem span many generations; they comprise clans rather than families, so two or more branches of a common lineage sometimes compete—often violently and unscrupulously—for territory and dominance.

In a dynamic and unstable political order of this sort, in which the material and practical stakes are high, the central problems often revolve around the nature of the law. What constitutes right and wrong, good and evil, justice and injustice, legitimacy and illegitimacy? How can or should power and violence be constrained, and by whom, and why? When are war and violence justified? The *Mahābhārata* narrates its long tale in the context of these questions, focusing on the concept of *dharma*, which refers at once to law (as given by the gods), to the moral and ethical basis of order in the universe as well as the human world, and to the duties and obligations of an individual acting and making choices in everyday society. In this worldview, an individual or a society practicing *dharma* is good, and one violating it is evil. But law, specific moral and ethical codes, and practical rules of conduct are subtle, confusing, and even inconsistent; following them is never easy, and the probability of breaking them—and hence of perpetrating evil—is high.

Responding to the world inside and outside his poem, Dvaipāyana suggests that human beings on their own cannot resolve the moral dilemmas of *dharma*; they need the intervention of the gods. His epic therefore represents a time when Viṣṇu, the god who preserves the moral order of the universe, descends on earth as Lord Kṛṣṇa, in order to destroy evil. Kṛṣṇa is Viṣṇu's eighth avatar, just as Rāma in the *Rāmāyaṇa* is the seventh avatar (in a series of ten major incarnations); Kṛṣṇa is a king of the warrior caste-group in western India, and he enters the story as a friend and political ally of its heroes. Dvaipāyana's epic, like Vālmīki's in a slightly earlier period, is thus not only a literary work but also an authoritative religious text.

WORK

The *Mahābhārata* raises its universal, philosophical questions in the form of a narrative, the story of one large dynasty with a long history of ruling a significant region of northern India, which includes what is now the city of Delhi (the capital of modern India). The epic's main events center around a generation in the dynasty, in which the burden of governing the kingdom falls upon three brothers, Dhṛtarāṣṭra, Pāṇḍu, and Vidura. The eldest, Dhṛtarāṣṭra, is born blind, and hence cannot rule; Pāṇḍu, second in line, becomes the king.

The difficulties of succession to the throne arise with the next generation because Pāṇḍu is cursed to die the moment he touches either of his queens with sexual desire, and hence cannot father any children. But his two queens are able to invoke a special divine power: the elder queen has three sons and the younger one has twins, each magically engendered by a god. These five "surrogate" sons of Pāṇḍu are the Pāṇḍavas, the heroes of the epic: Yudhiṣṭhira, begotten by Dharma (the god of law); Bhīma, begotten by the Wind; Arjuna, begotten by Indra (the Indian equivalent of Zeus); and Nakula and Sahadeva, begotten by the twin gods, the Aśvins. In the meantime, Pāṇḍu's blind elder brother Dhṛtarāṣṭra also has children; his queen bears him one hundred sons (and one daughter), collectively called the Kauravas—the eldest of whom is Duryodhana, the epic's "villain." Duryodhana is born the same day as his cousin Bhīma, and hence is younger than Yudhiṣṭhira.

A folio from a seventeenth-century C.E. manuscript of the *Mahābhārata* that depicts Bhīma (center) fighting with Kichaka (right) after Kichaka has violated Draupadī (left). This episode, not included in the excerpts here, occurs in book 4.

By the law of primogeniture, Yudhiṣṭhira, the eldest in his generation among the Pāṇḍavas and the Kauravas, ought to be the next king. But, by the same law, Dhṛtarāṣṭra is the eldest son in the previous generation (and hence the original inheritor of the kingdom), and his eldest son, Duryodhana, therefore ought to ascend to the throne. The irresolvable conflict between these two equally valid applications of the *dharma* of succession creates the lifelong tensions between the Pāṇḍavas and the Kauravas; each line of cousins feels that their eldest member has the true right to rule in their generation. When the conflict intensifies, the Pāṇḍavas suggest a division of the realm; but when Duryodhana, the leader of the Kauravas, rejects any such compromise, war becomes inevitable. Even the divine Kṛṣṇa, intervening on behalf of the Pāṇḍavas, cannot prevent the violence, which results in a widespread destruction of both families, their property, and the land at large; the Pāṇḍavas win, but their victory comes at an enormous price, and proves to be hollow in the end.

The canonical version of the *Mahābhārata* in Sanskrit contains about 100,000 verses composed in a variety of meters. The epic is divided into eighteen major books, which in turn are subdivided into a total of one hundred minor books. The first five major books deal with the origins and earlier history of the dynasty, and with the events leading up to the conflict between the Kauravas and the Pāṇḍavas; books 6 through 9 cover the war itself (which lasts for eighteen days); and the nine remaining books then narrate the aftermath of the violence over decades, which brings an entire age to a close.

The style and narrative structure of the *Mahābhārata* stand in contrast to those of the *Rāmāyaṇa*. While the *Rāmāyaṇa* is stylistically more uniform and more linear in its narrative progression (in spite of its many tales within tales), the *Mahābhārata* gives the impression of being more varied in its texture and more roughly hewn. The latter is especially notable for pushing the use of tales within tales to an extreme: it tells several stories at once, interweaving them at many levels. Thus its outer narrative frame itself—which identifies the poet and the narrators of the text—consists of three frames successively embedded inside each other, each with its own narrator or narrators; and in the actual telling of the tale, which is attributed to one of Dvaipāyana's bardic pupils, there are approximately four hundred major and minor narrators, each of whom is also a character in the epic, or a participant in its action. The story is therefore delivered to us in many interacting voices, speaking from distinct perspectives about the characters, events, and situations that make up the whole.

The excerpts included here are of two different kinds. All but one are from a condensed but reliable modern retelling, which includes more-literal translations of some key verses; the readings from this retelling enable us to follow the epic tale in its broad developments, without being distracted by every detail or digression. The one exception in our readings is a full translation of a central episode in the epic (the dice game in book 2); this selection enables us to "zoom in" on the original and to experience the narrative as it unfolds verse by verse (though our translation is in English prose).

The passages from book 1, *Ādi* ("Origins") introduce us to the large cast of characters who play important roles in the epic: among them are Dhṛtarāṣṭra and Pāṇḍu and their brother Vidura; their grand-uncle Bhīṣma, who raises them; and the brothers' various wives, who bear the children that become the principal figures in the epic's action in the next generation. We learn about the supernatural births of the five Pāṇḍavas—including Yudhiṣṭhira, Bhīma, and Arjuna—and the one hundred Kauravas, including Duryodhana, and about their shared upbringing and education in the royal household.

The verse-by-verse translation from book 2, *Sabhā* ("The Assembly Hall"), offers us a glimpse into the episode that sets up the protracted conflict between these two sets of cousins. The episode's background, omitted from our selection, is as follows. The struggle for power between the two families pits Duryodhana and the Kauravas against Yudhiṣṭhira and his four brothers, who as Pāṇḍu's successors claim their rightful share of the kingdom. Knowing that Yudhiṣṭhira has one tragic flaw in his character—he cannot resist gambling at dice games, even though he is a poor player—Duryodhana challenges the eldest Pāṇḍava to a gambling match in a full assembly at court, with the kingdom at stake: if Yudhiṣṭhira wins the dice game, he and his brothers can have their kingdom. Our excerpt from book 2 opens in the middle of the gambling match, whose outcome will determine the fate of the Pāṇḍavas as well as the land itself.

The next excerpt leaps forward in time. Duryodhana has gained the power he desires but refuses to divide the kingdom with the Pāṇḍavas as promised. The segments from book 5, *Udyoga* ("The Preparation for War"), then begin in the middle of Lord Kṛṣṇa's embassy to the Kauravas, in which Kṛṣṇa—as the god Viṣṇu's avatar and as the Pāṇḍavas' divine friend and counselor—attempts to find a peaceful diplomatic resolution. Here we discover how Duryodhana responds to Kṛṣṇa, and why war between the two branches of the dynasty becomes inevitable.

Thereafter, the excerpts from book 8, *Karṇa*, and book 9, *Śalya*, take us to the final stages of the war, in which we witness two famous moments on the battlefield: the confrontation between Arjuna (the third Pāṇḍava) and his illegitimate elder half-brother, Karṇa (who sides with the Kauravas); and the final duel between Bhīma (the second Pāṇḍava) and Duryodhana. The last two excerpts, from book 11, *Strī* ("Women"), and book 12, *Śānti* ("Peace"), round off the main story of the epic. They depict the effects of the destructive conflict on those who survive it: among the grieving survivors are Dhṛtarāṣṭra and his queen, who have lost their hundred sons, and the Pāṇḍavas themselves, who now have to set their hard-won kingdom in order.

Ever since its completion around 400 C.E., the *Mahābhārata* has been a constant reference point in Indian culture. With its numerous stories, involving several hundred major and minor characters, the epic has served as a general reservoir of stories to live by: individual episodes illustrate situations that we typically encounter, mirror many of the ethical dilemmas we ourselves face, and offer solutions that we can apply to our own lives. Many of the poem's characters and events are memorable and entertaining at the imaginative level: Bhīma, the impetuous strongman among the Pāṇḍavas, is a perennial children's favorite, like Hanumāna in the *Rāmāyana*. Most important, the *Mahābhārata* provides its audiences with a comprehensive education in politics, ethics, and morality.

Largely because of their many-sided significance, the stories of the *Mahābhārata* have traveled widely across Asia over the past sixteen hundred years, becoming an integral part of folklore, literature, and performance traditions from Indonesia and Malaysia to the Philippines. In particular, during the past two centuries, the ***Bhagavad-gīta***—which is a part of book 6 of Dvaipāyana's epic—has been translated into all the major languages of the world, and has become an indispensable part of world literature.

The Mahābhārata

From Book 1[1]

Ādi [*Origins*]

7

From their birth, Bhīṣma brought up Dhṛtarāṣṭra and Pāṇḍu and the wise Vidura as if they were his own sons. In accordance with the usual rites of their order, they engaged themselves in study and the observance of vows; by the time they had grown to young manhood, they were expert in athletic feats, adept in archery, learned in the scriptures, and skilfull in fighting with club, sword, and shield. They were skilled in horsemanship and in the management of elephants; they were learned in the science of morality. They shone equally in history, mythology, and many other branches of learning, and mastered the inner meaning of the scriptures. In all these activities they became proficient with practice. Pāṇḍu excelled all men in the science of archery, and Dhṛtarāṣṭra in personal strength. There was none in the three worlds to equal Vidura in his devotion to religion and virtue, and in his knowledge of the science of morality.

1. Translated by C. V. Narasimhan.

Bhīṣma heard from the Brāhmaṇas[2] that Gāndhārī, daughter of Subala, had been worshiping the bountiful deity Śiva, and obtained the boon that she would bear one hundred sons. He then sent emissaries to the king of Gāndhāra, seeking her hand on behalf of Dhṛtarāṣṭra. Subala hesitated on account of the blindness of the bridegroom. But taking into consideration his noble blood and the fame of the Kurus, he bestowed the virtuous Gāndhārī on Dhṛtarāṣṭra.

Gāndhārī was informed of the blindness of Dhṛtarāṣṭra, and of her parents' wish notwithstanding to bestow her upon him. Devoted to her husband, Gāndhārī bandaged her own eyes with a cloth, gathered into many folds, out of her desire not to excel her husband in any way. In due course Śakuni, the son of the king of Gāṇdhāra, brought his sister, endowed with great wealth, to the Kurus, and gave her away in the proper manner to Dhṛtarāṣṭra. He then returned to his own capital. The beautiful Gāndhārī pleased all the Kurus by her exemplary conduct and respectful attentions.

One day Gāndhārī pleased Vyāsa, who had arrived at the palace hungry and fatigued. He granted her a boon, and she expressed her desire to have one hundred sons like her husband. Some time afterwards, she became pregnant, but bore the burden in her womb for two years without being delivered, and was therefore much afflicted with grief.

Meanwhile she heard that Pāṇḍu's queen Kuntī had borne a son, bright as the morning sun. She could not help feeling that in her case the time of bearing the child in the womb was too long. Deprived of reason by her grief, she struck her womb with force, without the knowledge of Dhṛtarāṣṭra. Thereupon she brought forth a hard mass of flesh like an iron ball which had been in her womb for two years. On learning this, Vyāsa, best of ascetics, soon came to her and saw that mass of flesh. He asked Gāndhārī, "What have you done?" She revealed the truth to him, saying "Having heard that Kuntī had first given birth to a prince, bright as the sun, I struck at my womb in grief. You gave me the boon that I should bear one hundred sons. But only this ball of flesh has emerged instead."

Vyāsa said, "O Gāndhārī, it shall be as I said. I have never uttered a lie even in jest. Let one hundred jars, filled with ghee, be brought quickly and let cool water be sprinkled on this ball of flesh." The ball of flesh, being thus cooled with water, split into parts, each about the size of a thumb. These were then placed in the jars, which were stationed in a concealed spot and carefully watched. The holy one bade Gāndhārī open the lids of the jars only after two years. Having given these instructions and made these arrangements, the holy and wise Vyāsa went to the Himālaya mountains to perform penance.

It was thus that Prince Duryodhana was born. According to the order of birth, however, Yudhiṣṭhira, the eldest son of Pāṇḍu, was senior to him. As soon as a son had been born to him, Dhṛtarāṣṭra said: "Summon the Brāhmaṇas, as well as Bhīṣma and Vidura. The prince Yudhiṣṭhira is the eldest of our line. There is no doubt that he should succeed to the kingdom in his own right."

At that time beasts of prey, jackals, and crows[3] made ominous noises everywhere. Seeing these frightful portents, the assembled Brāhmaṇas and the wise Vidura said to Dhṛtarāṣṭra, "It is clear that your son will be the exterminator of your race. The peace of the family depends upon his being abandoned. There will be great calamity in keeping him." Though he was thus adjured by Vidura

2. Priests, members of the highest caste.

3. The howling of jackals is inauspicious; jackals are associated with cunning, cowardice, and treachery. Crows are scavengers, and hence associated with death.

and by all those learned Brāhmaṇas, the king did not heed their advice, because of his natural love for his son. There were born within a month one hundred sons to Dhṛtarāṣṭra, and also a daughter, Duḥśalā.

8

The chief of the Yadus, named Śūra, had a son, Vasudeva, and a daughter, Pṛthā, whose beauty was matchless on earth. As had been promised, Śūra gave Pṛthā in adoption to his childless cousin and close friend, the high-souled Kuntibhoja. Hence she also came to be known as Kuntī. In her adopted father's house Kuntī's duties were to worship the family deities and look after the guests.

One day, by her solicitude, she pleased the terrible and notoriously short-tempered sage Durvāsa, who was learned in the mysteries. Through his foresight, Durvāsa could see that Kuntī would have difficulty in conceiving sons. He therefore taught her an invocatory spell, saying to her, "Through the radiance of those celestials whom you invoke by this spell, you will obtain progeny."

After a while the virtuous Kuntī out of curiosity tried the spell and invoked the sun god. That brilliant deity the Sun, who sees everything in the world, immediately appeared before her, and the beautiful Kuntī was overcome by astonishment at this wondrous sight. The light of the universe, the Sun, got her with child. Thus was born the hero of divine ancestry, known all over the world by the name of Karṇa, the foremost of warriors. He was born wearing armor and earrings.[4] Thereafter the Sun restored Kuntī's maidenhood and returned to heaven.

Afraid of her friends and relatives, Kuntī resolved to hide her transgression. She accordingly threw her handsome son into the river, from which he was rescued by a charioteer. He and his wife Rādhā brought up the infant as their own son, giving him the name of Vasuṣeṇa,[5] because he was endowed with wealth even at birth, namely armor and earrings. Vasuṣeṇa grew up to be very strong and energetic, and adept in the use of all weapons. He used to worship the Sun until the afternoon sun scorched his back. When he was thus engaged in worship, the heroic, truthful, and high-souled Vasuṣeṇa would give away to the Brāhmaṇas anything on earth which they requested of him.

Once Indra,[6] the protector of all living things, came to him for alms, adopting the guise of a Brāhmaṇa, and asked him for his armor and the earrings. Perplexed though he was at Indra's request, he cut off the armor from his body, and also his earrings from his ears, and gave them, dripping with blood, to Indra with joined hands. Greatly surprised at his generosity, Indra gave him the Śakti weapon, saying, "Be your foe a celestial, asura, human being, Gandharva, Nāga, or Rākṣasa, if you hurl this missile at him, it will certainly kill him."[7] The son of Sūrya, who till then was known by the name of Vasuṣeṇa, came to be called Karṇa [the cutter] after this act of unequaled generosity.

4. As we shall learn from the incidents narrated below, Karṇa was born with armor and earrings bonded to his body.
5. "Endowed with wealth."
6. King of the gods.
7. Asuras, Gandharvas, Nāgas, and Rākṣasas are various classes of supernatural beings.

9

Kuṅtibhoja held a svayaṁvara[8] for his beautiful and virtuous daughter. There she saw that tamer of lions and elephants,[9] the mighty Pāṇḍu, in the midst of all the kings present. She chose him for her husband, even as Paulomī chose Iṅdra.

Bhīṣma also obtained for Pāṇḍu, in exchange for much wealth, the daughter of the king of Madra, Mādrī, who was famous for her beauty in all the three worlds, after which he solemnized the marriage of the high-souled[1] Pāṇḍu.

One day, while roaming in the forest, Pāṇḍu saw two deer in the act of mating, and hit both of them with five sharp and swift arrows, embellished with golden feathers. They were an ascetic, the son of a sage, and his wife, with whom he was thus disporting in the form of a deer. "I am the sage Kiṇdama, without equal in austerity," said the deer. "You have killed me in the act of mating in the form of a deer, a form I have assumed out of modesty. Though you will not be visited with the sin of killing a Brāhmaṇa, since you did not know who I was, you shall however be punished similarly: when you are overcome by desire in the company of your wife, you shall also die!"

Thus cursed, Pāṇḍu returned to his capital, and explained his predicament to his queens, after which he said to Kuṅtī: "At my request, you should have children endowed with all good qualities by the grace of a Brāhmaṇa who is a great sage; if you do so, I shall go the same way as those with sons." To this request, Kuṅtī, ever interested in her husband's welfare, replied to Pāṇḍu, "O king, since you so desire, I shall invoke a god as taught me by Durvāsa, so that we may have issue." Pāṇḍu said: "Among the gods Dharma is the one who bestows spiritual merit. Hence I request you to invoke the god Dharma this very day."

Gāṅdhārī had been pregnant for a year when Kuṅtī invoked the eternal Dharma[2] for progeny, worshiping him and repeating in the proper form the invocation which Durvāsa had taught her. She was then united with Dharma in his spiritual form and, in time, gave birth to a fine boy. As soon as the child was born, a voice with no visible source said: "This child will certainly be virtuous. He will be known as Yudhiṣṭhira; he will be famous over the three worlds.[3] He will be splendid, determined, and renowned."

Having been blessed with this virtuous son, Pāṇḍu bade Kuṅtī ask for a son of great physical strength, since the Kṣatriyas were the foremost in strength. In response to her husband's request, Kuṅtī invoked Vāyu,[4] who begot the mighty Bhīma, of great strength. On his birth, the supernatural voice said: "This child will be the greatest of all strong men." Duryodhana was born on the very day on which Bhīma was born.

Thereafter the illustrious Pāṇḍu consulted with the great sages and asked Kuṅtī to observe certain vows for one full year. At the end of the period Pāṇḍu said, "O beautiful one, Iṅdra the king of the celestials is pleased. Invoke him and conceive a son." In response, the illustrious Kuṅtī invoked Iṅdra, the lord of the celestials, who came to her and begot Arjuna. As soon as the prince was

8. The assembly or contest in which a princess or other high-born lady chose a bridegroom for herself.
9. Epic epithet for a brave warrior.
1. Noble, virtuous (*mahātmā*).
2. God personifying the cosmic and moral law.
3. Heaven, earth, and the underworld.
4. The wind god.

born, a supernatural voice boomed over the whole sky with a loud and deep roar, saying: "O Kuṅtī, this child will be as strong as Kārtavīrya and Śibi,[5] invincible in battle as Iṅdra himself. He will spread your fame everywhere, and will acquire many celestial weapons."

After the birth of Kuṅtī's sons, and those of Dhṛtarāṣṭra, Mādrī privately spoke to Pāṇḍu thus, "It is my great grief that, though we are of equal rank, my husband should have sons by Kuṅtī alone. If the princess Kuṅtī will arrange that I may have sons, she will do me a great kindness, and it will also be of benefit to you."

Thereupon Pāṇḍu again spoke to Kuṅtī privately. He said, "O blessed lady, give me some more sons, and ensure the funeral oblations for myself and my ancestors. O blameless one, aid Mādrī, as though with a raft across the river, by helping her to obtain progeny. Thus you will obtain great renown."

Kuṅtī then said to Mādrī, "Think of some celestial by whose grace you may obtain worthy offspring." Thereupon Mādrī reflected a little and invoked the twin Aśvins.[6] Both of them came to her and sired twin sons, namely Nakula and Sahadeva, unmatched for beauty on earth. On their birth, the supernatural voice said: "The twins will be handsome and good, and will excel all men in beauty, energy, and wealth. They will glow with splendor."

The sages living in Śataśṛṅga invoked blessings on the princes and performed their birth rites with devotion. They named the eldest of Kuṅtī's sons Yudhiṣṭhira, the second Bhīmasena, and the third Arjuna. Mādrī's twin sons they named Nakula and Sahadeva. The five sons of Pāṇḍu and the hundred sons of Dhṛtarāṣṭra, the ornaments of the Kuru race, bloomed like lotuses in a lake.

One day Pāṇḍu saw Mādrī adorned with jewels, and his desire was aroused. But as soon as he touched her, he died. Thereupon Mādrī ascended Pāṇḍu's funeral pyre, asking Kuṅtī to bring up her children with kindness and love. Then Vidura, King Dhṛtarāṣṭra, Bhīṣma, and other relatives performed the last rites of Pāṇḍu and Mādrī and offered the funeral oblations.

Thereafter the sons of Pāṇḍu were brought by the citizens to Hāstinapura. There the Pāṇḍavas performed all the purifying rites prescribed in the scriptures. They grew up in royal style in their father's house, sporting with the sons of Dhṛtarāṣṭra, whom they excelled in all the boyish games. Bhīma vanquished all the sons of Dhṛtarāṣṭra in various feats. Seeing his extraordinary strength, Duryodhana, the mighty son of Dhṛtarāṣṭra, conceived a lasting enmity towards him.

10

Once the great sage Bharadvāja happened to see the beautiful nymph Dhṛtācī in the sacrificial place, when her dress was accidentally blown aside by the wind. Aroused by this sight, the sage dropped his seed in a vessel [droṇa], in which the wise Droṇa was born. He read all the Scriptures.

Bharadvāja had a royal friend, named Pṛṣata, who had a son named Drupada. Prince Drupada went every day to Bharadvāja's hermitage, where he played and studied with Droṇa. When Pṛṣata died, the mighty Drupada succeeded to the kingdom of the Northern Pāñcālas.

5. Legendary heroes.

6. The gods known as the "twin horsemen."

At about the same time the illustrious Bharadvāja also passed away; thereupon, in accordance with his late father's wishes, and being desirous of offspring, Droṇa married Kṛpī, the daughter of Śaradvata. Ever engaged in sacrifices and penance, the pious Kṛpī bore Droṇa a son, named Aśvatthāmā. As soon as he was born, he neighed like a horse. Thereupon a voice from the skies said, "As this child neighed like a horse and could be heard over a great distance, he will be known by the name of Aśvatthāmā [the horse-voiced]."

Droṇa, who was extremely pleased at having a son, then became deeply interested in the study of archery. He heard that the great-souled Paraśurāma was giving away all his wealth to Brāhmaṇas.[7] Seeing Paraśurāma as he was leaving for the forest, Droṇa said, "Know me to be Droṇa, best of Brāhmaṇas, who has come to you seeking wealth."

Paraśurāma said, "O treasury of penance! I have already given away to the Brāhmaṇas my gold and whatever wealth I had." "O Paraśurāma," said Droṇa, "give me then all your arms and weapons, and teach me the secrets of launching and withdrawing them." Paraśurāma said: "So be it!" He gave away all his weapons to Droṇa and taught him the science of arms and all its secrets. Droṇa, considering himself amply rewarded and feeling well pleased, went to see his dear friend Drupada.

In due course approaching Drupada, the son of Pṛṣata, Droṇa said, "Know me as your friend." Drupada said: "Our former friendship was based on the bonds of skill; but time, that erodes everything, wears out friendship too." Thus rebuffed by Drupada, the mighty Droṇa was filled with wrath. He reflected for a moment, while he made up his mind as to his course of action, and then went to Hāstinapura, the city of the foremost of the Kurus.

11

Anxious to give his grandsons a superior education, Bhīṣma inquired about tutors who were brave and well skilled in the science of arms. He decided that the preceptor of the Kurus should be strong, intelligent, and illustrious, and complete master of the science of arms.

When he heard that a stranger had arrived [in Hāstinapura], Bhīṣma knew that this must be Droṇa and decided that he was the right tutor for his grandsons. Welcoming Droṇa, he asked him why he had come to Hāstinapura. Droṇa told him everything. Bhīṣma then appointed Droṇa as the preceptor and gave him various gifts. He presented his grandsons, including the sons of Pāṇḍu, according to custom, and handed them over to Droṇa, who accepted them all as his pupils.

Droṇa called them aside when they saluted him, and said privately to them: "O princes, in my heart I have one special yearning; promise me that you will fulfill it when you have become proficient in arms." To these words the Kuru princes made no reply. Arjuna, however, gave his promise.

Thereupon Droṇa taught Arjuna how to fight from the back of a horse, on an elephant, on a chariot or on the ground, in single combat or in a crowd. He taught him how to fight with the club, the sword, the spear, and the dart. Two of Droṇa's pupils, Duryodhana and Bhīma, became highly proficient in club

7. The *brāhmaṇa* Paraśurāma had vowed to exterminate the *kṣatriya* class.

fighting; Aśvatthāmā surpassed the others in the mysteries of the science of arms; the twins Nakula and Sahadeva outshone everybody in swordsmanship; Yudhiṣṭhira was first among car[8]-warriors.

Arjuna reigned supreme in every field; he excelled all in intelligence, in concentration, in strength, and in zest, and was famous unto the limits of the ocean as the foremost of car-warriors. He was unequaled not only in the use of arms but also in his love and regard for his preceptor. Though all the royal pupils received the same instruction, yet the mighty Arjuna by his excellence became the only Atiratha[9] among all the princes. The wicked sons of Dhṛtarāṣṭra became jealous of Bhīma's strength and Arjuna's many accomplishments.

When the sons of Dhṛtarāṣṭra and Pāṇḍu had thus become proficient in arms, Droṇa said to King Dhṛtarāṣṭra, "O king, your sons have completed their studies. Permit them to display their skill." The king replied, with joy in his heart: "O Droṇa, O best of Brāhmaṇas, great is your achievement!" By order of the king, the masons built a huge arena according to the rules, with a grandstand for the king and the royal ladies. Then, with Yudhiṣṭhira at their head, the heroic princes followed each other in the order of their age and began to display their wonderful skill in arms.

At the command of the preceptor, the youthful Arjuna, equipped with leather protector for the finger, his quiver full of arrows, bow in hand, and wearing golden armor, performed the initial rites of propitiation and entered the arena like the evening cloud reflecting the rays of the setting sun. His very entrance caused a stir among the spectators. When they had calmed down a little, Arjuna displayed before his preceptor his easy mastery of arms and his great skill in the use of the sword, the bow, and the club.

While the spectators were watching Arjuna's feats in wide-eyed wonder, that conqueror of hostile cities, Karṇa, entered the spacious arena. The entire assembly of people remained motionless staring at the newcomer. Curious to know his name, they asked one another in agitation, "Who is he?" Then, in a voice deep as thunder, Karṇa, foremost of eloquent men, said to Arjuna, whom he did not know to be his brother: "O Arjuna, I shall repeat before these spectators all that you have just done. Do not be surprised." Thus challenged, Arjuna was abashed and angry, but Duryodhana was touched with affection for the challenger. With the permission of Droṇa, the powerful Karṇa, ever fond of battle, duplicated all the feats that Arjuna had displayed a little earlier.

Thereupon Duryodhana with his brothers embraced Karṇa with joy and spoke to him thus: "O mighty hero, welcome to you! Your arrival is our good fortune. The entire Kuru kingdom and I myself are at your service." Karṇa replied, "I desire only your friendship."

Karṇa then challenged Arjuna to a duel. When the two heroes were ready with their great bows, Kṛpa, the son of Śaradvata, who knew all the rules governing such duels, said: "O mighty hero, tell us of your father and mother, of your family, and of the royal line which you adorn. It is only after knowing your lineage that Arjuna can decide whether or not to fight with you." Duryodhana announced, "O preceptor, it is said that royalty may be claimed by three classes of men,

8. Car = chariot.

9. A champion at chariot fighting.

namely, by a person of noble birth, by a hero, and by a leader of soldiers. If Arjuna is unwilling to engage in a duel with one who is not a king, I shall install Karṇa at once as the king of Añga."

Without delay the mighty car-warrior Karṇa was seated on a golden seat, and crowned as the king of Añga by those learned in the rites, with unhusked rice, flowers, waterpots, gold, and much wealth. When the cheers subsided, Karṇa said to the Kaurava king, Duryodhana, "What can I give you compared with your gift of a kingdom? O great king, I shall do your bidding." Duryodhana replied, "I seek only your friendship." Then Karṇa said, "So be it!" They thereupon joyfully embraced each other and felt very happy.

Having obtained Karṇa, Duryodhana forgot his fears aroused by Arjuna's skill in arms. The heroic Karṇa, accomplished in arms, spoke words of comfort to Duryodhana. Yudhiṣṭhira too was impressed with the conviction that there was no bowman on earth like Karṇa.

12

One day the preceptor Droṇa called his pupils together and asked for his dakṣiṇā[1] from them all. He said, "I want you to capture the king of Pāñcāla, Drupada, in battle and bring him securely to me. That will be the most precious dakṣiṇā you can give me." Saying "So be it!" and armed with quivers of arrows, the princes mounted their cars and went with Droṇa to win wealth for their preceptor. They attacked the Pāñcālas and killed them, and then besieged the capital of the famous Drupada. Successful in capturing Drupada, along with his ministers, they brought him to Droṇa.

Droṇa, remembering his former enmity towards Drupada, now humiliated, bereft of wealth, and completely subdued, spoke thus to him, "I have quickly laid waste your kingdom and your capital. Do you wish to renew our old friendship and to receive your life at my hands?" Smiling, he added, "O king, be not afraid for your life. We Brāhmaṇas are lenient. I seek your friendship again. I shall grant you one half of your kingdom. You may rule the territory lying to the south of the Gāngā, and I shall rule the northern part. O king of Pāñcāla, if it pleases you, know that I am your friend from now on." Drupada said, "O Brāhman, such generosity is not surprising in men of noble soul and great strength. I am pleased to accept your friendly offer and I desire your eternal friendship."

Then Droṇa released Drupada, and with a pleased heart he bestowed upon him half the kingdom. Drupada, however, was unable to recover his peace of mind, being obsessed by his hatred of Droṇa. He knew he could not hope to avenge his defeat by superior force, nor by spiritual power, in which too he was aware of being weak. Hence King Drupada desired the birth of a son, who would be the instrument of his revenge.[2]

1. The fee given by students to their preceptors (*gurus*) at the completion of their studies.
2. King Drupada performs a special fire sacrifice to the gods, seeking the birth of a son who would be an invincible warrior. Born out of Drupada's sacrificial fire, Prince Dhṛṣṭadyumna, fighting on the Pāṇḍava side during the great war between the Pāṇḍavas and their cousins, does kill Droṇa. Drupada's daughter Draupadī is also born from his sacrificial fire.

From Book 2[3]

Sabhā [*The Assembly Hall*]

58

ŚAKUNI[4] SAID:

You have lost vast wealth of the Pāṇḍavas, Yudhiṣṭhira. Tell me what wealth you have left, Kaunteya,[5] what you have not yet lost!

YUDHIṢṬHIRA SAID:

I know of untold riches that I possess, Saubala. But, Śakuni, pray, why do you ask about my wealth? Myriad, ton, million, crore,[6] a hundred million, a billion, a hundred thousand crores, an ocean count of drops I can stake! That is my stake, king, play me for it!

VAIŚAṂPĀYANA[7] SAID:

At these words Śakuni decided, tricked, and cried "Won!" at Yudhiṣṭhira.[8]

YUDHIṢṬHIRA SAID:

I have countless cattle and horses and milch cows and sheep and goats, whatever belongs to our color of people east of the Indus, Saubala.[9] That is my stake, king, I play you for it!

VAIŚAṂPĀYANA SAID:

At these words Śakuni decided, tricked, and cried "Won!" at Yudhiṣṭhira.

YUDHIṢṬHIRA SAID:

My city, my country, the wealth of all my people, excepting brahmins, all my people themselves, excepting brahmins, are the wealth I have left, king. That is my stake, king, I play you for it!

VAIŚAṂPĀYANA SAID:

At these words Śakuni decided, tricked, and cried "Won!" at Yudhiṣṭhira.

YUDHIṢṬHIRA SAID:

Here are the ornaments with which the princes glitter, the earrings and breastplates and all the adornment of their bodies. That is my stake, king, I play you for it!

3. Translated by J. A. B. van Buitenen. Forced to accept Duryodhana's challenge to a dice match, which is properly a part of the rite of the consecration of the ancient "universal monarch," Yudhiṣṭhira arrives at Hāstinapura, accompanied by his brothers and Draupadī. The Kuru nobles have assembled at the Hāstinapura court to watch the dice match. Duryodhana's uncle Śakuni, trickster and expert at dice, plays the game on Duryodhana's behalf. At each play of the dice, Yudhiṣṭhira stakes his valuable possessions, including gold, precious jewels, elephants and chariots, a splendid horse, and many male and female servants. Each time, Śakuni plays deceitfully, winning the stake on Duryodhana's behalf.

4. Śakuni Saubala, son of the king of Gandhāra, brother of Queen Gāndhāri, and maternal uncle to the Kauravas.

5. Son of Kuntī.

6. Ten million.

7. The bard who recounts the story of the Mahābhārata war to King Janamejaya, descendant of the Pāṇḍavas.

8. This refrain is spoken by the bard-narrator. We do not know how the *Mahābhārata*'s game of dice was actually played, but it may have been a game in which a number of dice (*akṣa*) were placed in a cup or a pile, and the players drew one or more dice from there. The epic does not describe the rules of the game, but the following things are suggested: the dice were rearranged, and one of the players had to make a guess (as to the number? odds and evens?); if the drawer won, he continued to lead the play.

9. The Indus River flows in the northwest region of the Indian subcontinent, in modern Pakistan. "Color": Although the basic meaning of the word *varṇa* is "color," here, as elsewhere, it does not denote skin color, but indicates one of the four major social classes (*varṇa*) of ancient Indian society (priest, warrior, merchant, servant). Here the warrior class is meant.

VAIŚAṂPĀYANA SAID:
At these words Śakuni decided, tricked, and cried "Won!" at Yudhiṣṭhira.
YUDHIṢṬHIRA SAID:
This dark youth with the bloodshot eyes and the lion shoulders and the large arms,[1] this Nakula and all he owns shall be one throw.
ŚAKUNI SAID:
But Prince Nakula is dear to you, King Yudhiṣṭhira! If we win this stake, what more do you have to gamble?
VAIŚAṂPĀYANA SAID:
Having said this, Śakuni addressed those dice and cried "Won!" at Yudhiṣṭhira.
YUDHIṢṬHIRA SAID:

> This Sahadeva preaches the Laws,[2]
> And has in the world earned the name of a scholar:
> For this loving prince who does not deserve it,
> I play with you like an enemy!

VAIŚAṂPĀYANA SAID:
At these words Śakuni decided, tricked, and cried "Won!" at Yudhiṣṭhira.
ŚAKUNI SAID:
I have now won, king, these two dear sons of Mādrī. Yet methinks Bhīmasena and Arjuna are dearer to you.
YUDHIṢṬHIRA SAID:
Surely this is an Unlaw[3] that you are perpetrating, without looking to propriety! You want to pluck us like flowers!
ŚAKUNI SAID:
A drunk falls into a hole, a distracted man walks into a tree trunk, you are our elder and better, king—farewell to you, bull of the Bharatas![4] When gamblers play, Yudhiṣṭhira, they prattle like madmen of things they have not seen asleep or awake!
YUDHIṢṬHIRA SAID:

> Like a ferry he carried us over in battle,
> Defeater of foes, a prince of vigor;
> For this world hero who does not deserve it,
> For Phalguna[5] I play you, Śakuni!

VAIŚAṂPĀYANA SAID:
At these words Śakuni decided, tricked, and cried "Won!" at Yudhiṣṭhira.
ŚAKUNI SAID:

> Here I have won the Pāṇḍavas' bowman,
> The left-handed archer,[6] of Pāṇḍu the son!
> Now gamble, O king, your beloved Bhīma,
> If that's what you, Pāṇḍava, have left to throw!

1. Characteristics of an ideal warrior.
2. *Dharma.* Stanzas in the *triṣṭubh* meter, such as this one, have been translated in a four-line verse format.
3. The opposite of *dharma.*
4. "Superior (mighty as a bull) warrior in the family of Bharata" (a formulaic phrase). The bull represents might and virility.
5. Arjuna.
6. Arjuna, who could shoot with both hands.

YUDHIṢṬHIRA SAID:

Who led us, who guided us to the battle,
Like the Thunderbolt-wielder[7] the Dānavas' foe,
Looking down, great-spirited, knitting his brow,
With a lion's shoulders and lasting wrath,
Whose equal in might is nowhere to be found,
The first of club warriors, enemy-killer—
For this good prince who does not deserve it
I play you, king, for Bhīmasena!

VAIŚAṂPĀYANA SAID:

At these words Śakuni decided, tricked, and cried "Won!" at Yudhiṣṭhira.

ŚAKUNI SAID:

You have lost great wealth, you have lost your brothers, your horses and elephants. Now tell me, Kaunteya, if you have anything left to stake!

YUDHIṢṬHIRA SAID:

I myself am left, dearly loved by all my brothers. When won, we shall slave for you to our perdition.

VAIŚAṂPĀYANA SAID:

At these words Śakuni decided, tricked, and cried "Won!" at Yudhiṣṭhira.

ŚAKUNI SAID:

This is the worst you could have done, losing yourself! If there is something left to stake, it is evil to stake oneself!

VAIŚAṂPĀYANA SAID:

Thus spoke the man so dexterous at dicing, who had won in the gaming all those brothers arrayed there, the champions of the world, each with one throw.

ŚAKUNI SAID:

Yet there is your precious queen, and one throw is yet unwon. Stake Kṛṣṇā of Pāñcāla,[8] and win yourself back with her!

YUDHIṢṬHIRA SAID:

She is not too short or too tall, not too black or too red, and her eyes are red with love[9]—I play you for her! Eyes like the petals of autumn lotuses, and fragrance as of autumn lotuses, a beauty that waits on autumn lotuses—the peer of the Goddess of Fortune![1] Yes, for her lack of cruelty, for the fullness of her body, for the straightness of her character does a man desire a woman. Last she lies down who was the first to wake up, who knows what was done or left undone, down to the cowherds and goatherds. Her sweaty lotuslike face shines like a lotus. Her waist shaped like an altar,[2] hair long, eyes the color of copper, not too much body hair . . . such is the woman, king, such is the slender-waisted Pāñcālī, for whom I now throw, the beautiful Draupadī! Come on, Saubala!

VAIŚAṂPĀYANA SAID:

When the King Dharma had spoken this word, Bhārata,[3] the voices that were raised by the elders spelled of "Woe! Woe!" The hall itself shook, king, and talk

7. The Vedic hero-god Indra wields the thunderbolt and leads the gods in battle against the Dānavas (demons).
8. Kṛṣṇā ("dark lady," from *kṛṣṇā*, "dark" or "black") is a name of Draupadī, princess of Pāñcāla.
9. Bloodshot eyes, suggesting passion and intoxication, are a sign of beauty in women.
1. Goddess of Fortune and consort of the god Viṣṇu and of kings, Śrī is associated with the red lotus.
2. The altar of the Vedic sacrifice is narrow at the middle.
3. Descendant of Bharata.

started among the kings. Bhīṣma, Droṇa, Kṛpa, and others broke out in sweat.[4] Vidura buried his face in his hands and looked as though he had fainted; he sat, head down, brooding, wheezing like a snake.[5] But Dhṛtarāṣṭra, exhilarated, kept asking, "Has he won, has he won?" for he did not keep his composure. Karṇa, Duḥśāsana,[6] and their cronies were mightily pleased, but of others in the hall the tears flowed freely. But Saubala, without hesitation, with the glow of the winner and high with passion, again addressed the dice and cried, "We have won!"

59

DURYODHANA SAID:

All right, you Steward,[7] bring Draupadī,
The beloved wife whom the Pāṇḍava honor,
Let her sweep the house and run on our errands—
What a joy to watch!—with the serving wenches!

VIDURA SAID:

The incredible happens through people like you,
You don't know it, nitwit, you are tied in a noose!
You hang over a chasm and do not grasp it,
You dumb deer to anger tigers!

You are carrying poisonous snakes on your head, their pouches full of venom! Don't infuriate them, fool, lest you go to Yama![8] Kṛṣṇā is not a slave yet, Bhārata! I think she was staked when the king was no longer his own master.

Dhṛtarāṣṭra's son the prince bears fruit,
Like the bamboo, only to kill himself:[9]
He is ripe for death, but he fails to see
That dicing leads to a dangerous feud.

Be never hurtful or speak cruelly,
Nor extort the last from a penniless man,
Nor speak the wounding, hell-earning words
That when voiced hurt another man.
Those words beyond need fly from the mouth,
And the one they hurt grieves day and night:
Those words that strike where the other hurts
No wise man will loose on another man.

For this goat, they say, dug up a knife,
When a knife was missing, by pawing the ground.
It became a means to cut its own throat:
So dig up no feud with Pāṇḍu's sons!

4. Son of King Śantanu and the river goddess Gaṅgā (Ganges), Bhīṣma is the granduncle of the Pāṇḍavas and Kauravas. Droṇa is their *guru* (teacher) in the martial arts.
5. Born to Vyāsa and a maidservant at the Hāstinapura court, Vidura the Steward is a half brother of Dhṛtarāṣṭra and Pāṇḍu.
6. Younger brother of Duryodhana.
7. Vidura.
8. God of death.
9. Bamboo bears fruit only after many years and then dies.

They don't speak either good or ill
Of the forest-dweller or householder,
But of the ascetic of mature wisdom,
The same people bark like the curs they are.

This dreadful crooked door tilts toward hell—
You know it not, Dhṛtarāṣṭra's son;
There are many will follow you down that road,
Now the game has been won, with Duḥśasana!

The gourds will sink and the rocks will float,
And the ships will forever be lost on the seas.
Before the fool prince, Dhṛtarāṣṭra's son,
Will lend his ear to my apt words!

For this to be sure spells the end of the Kurus,
A grisly end, the perdition of all.
The words of the sage, so apt, and his friends
Are no longer heard, and greed just grows!

60

VAIŚAMPĀYANA SAID:

"A plague on the Steward," he said and rose,
Maddened with pride, Dhṛtarāṣṭra's son,
And he looked at his usher in the hall
And to him he spoke amidst those grandees,

"Go, usher, and bring me Draupadī here!
You have nothing to fear from the Pāṇḍavas.
The Steward is timid and speaks against it,
But never did he wish that *we* should prosper!"

The usher, a bard, at his master's word
Went quickly out upon hearing the king,
And he entered, a dog in a lion's den,
Crawling up to the Queen of the Pāṇḍavas.

THE USHER SAID:

Yudhiṣṭhira, crazed by the dicing game,
Has lost you to Duryodhana, Draupadī.
Come enter the house of Dhṛtarāṣṭra,
To your chores I must lead you, Yājñasenī!

DRAUPADĪ SAID:

How dare you speak so, an usher, to me?
What son of a king would hazard his wife?
The king is befooled and crazed by the game—
Was there nothing left for him to stake?

THE USHER SAID:

When nothing was left for him to stake,
Ajātaśatru[1] wagered you.

1. "Invincible," an epithet of Yudhiṣṭhira.

Already the king had thrown for his brothers,
And then for himself—then. Princess, for you.

DRAUPADĪ SAID:

Then go to the game and, son of a bard, ask in the assembly, "Bhārata, whom did you lose first, yourself or me?" When you have found out, come and take me, son of a bard!

VAIŚAṂPĀYANA SAID:

He went to the hall and asked Draupadī's question. "As the owner of whom did you lose us?" so queries Draupadī. "Whom did you lose first, yourself or me?" But Yudhiṣṭhira did not stir, as though he had lost consciousness, and made no reply to the bard, whether good or ill.

DURYODHANA SAID:

Let Kṛṣṇā of the Pāñcālas come here and ask the question herself. All the people here shall hear what she or he has to say.

VAIŚAṂPĀYANA SAID:

As he was in Duryodhana's service; the usher, who was the son of a bard, went to the king's lodgings and, as though shuddering, said to Draupadī.

The men in the hall are summoning, Princess!
Methinks that the fall of the Kurus has come.
That fool will not protect our fortunes
If *you* have to come to the hall, O Princess.

DRAUPADĪ SAID:

That is how he disposes, the All-Disposer,[2]
Both touches touch the sage and the fool:
He said, "In this world only Law is supreme":
He shall bring us peace when the Law is obeyed!

VAIŚAṂPĀYANA SAID:

But Yudhiṣṭhira, on hearing what Duryodhana wanted to do, sent an acceptable messenger to Draupadī, O bull of the Bhāratas. In her one garment, knotted below, weeping and in her courses,[3] she went to the hall, the Pāñcāla princess, and stood before her father-in-law.

Watching the courtiers' faces, the Prince
Duryodhana said gleefully to the bard,
"Bring her here, good usher, right here on this spot,
So the Kauravas may speak up to her face!"

So the *sūta* who was in Duryodhana's service,
But afraid of the wrath of the Drupada Princess,
Shed all his pride and asked the assembled,
"Who am I to speak to a Draupadī?"

DURYODHANA SAID:

Duḥśāsana, he is a fool, this bard's son,
He is terrified of the Wolf-Belly![4]

2. God.
3. She is menstruating. In observing the menstrual taboos of women of her class, she has been secluded, her hair is not dressed, and she wears only one garment (the lower?) instead of the customary two cloths (an upper and a lower one).
4. Bhīma's enormous appetite earns him this epithet.

Fetch and bring yourself Yajñasena's daughter,
How can our powerless rivals prevent you?

VAIŚAMPĀYANA SAID:

Thereupon the son of the king rose up,
On hearing his brother, eyes reddened with wrath,
And entered the dwelling of those great warriors,
And he said to Draupadī, daughter of kings,

"All right now, come, Pāñcālī, you're won!
Look upon Duryodhana, without shame!
You shall now love the Kurus, long-lotus-eyed one,[5]
You've been won under Law, come along to the hall!"

In bleak spirits did she rise,
And wiped with her hand her pallid face.
In despair she ran where the women sat
Of the aged king, the bull of the Kurus.

And quickly the angry Duḥśāsana
Came rushing to her with a thunderous roar;
By the long-tressed black and flowing hair
Duḥśāsana grabbed the wife of a king.

The hair that at the concluding bath
Of the king's consecration had been sprinkled
With pure-spelled water, Dhṛtarāṣṭra's son
Now caressed with force, unmanning the Pāṇḍus.[6]

Duḥśāsana, stroking her, led her and brought her,
That Kṛṣṇā of deep black hair, to the hall,
As though unprotected amidst her protectors,
And tossed her as wind tosses a plantain tree.

And as she was dragged, she bent her body
And whispered softly, "It is now my month!
This is my sole garment, man of slow wit,
You cannot take me to the hall, you churl!"

But using his strength and holding her down,
By her deep black locks, he said to Kṛṣṇā,
"To Kṛṣṇā and Jiṣṇu, to Hari and Nara,[7]
Cry out for help! I shall take you yet!

"Sure, you be in your month, Yajñasena's daughter,
Or wear a lone cloth, or go without one!
You've been won at the game and been made a slave,
And one lechers with slaves as the fancy befalls!"

Her hair disheveled, her half skirt drooping,
Shaken about by Duhśāsana,

5. Woman with elongated eyes shaped like a lotus petal, a mark of beauty.
6. As an important part of the royal consecration of Yudhiṣthira, the queen's hair had been anointed with sacred waters to the accompaniment of sacred chants ("pure spells"). By laying hands on the Pāṇḍavas' wife and desecrating Yudhiṣṭhira's sovereignty, Duḥśāsana is doubly *unmanning* them.
7. Both pairs refer to Arjuna and Kṛṣṇā, who rescue Draupadī whenever she is in trouble.

Ashamed and burning with indignation,
She whispered again, and Kṛṣṇā said,

"In the hall are men who have studied the books,
All follow the rites and are like unto Iṅdras.
They are all my *gurus*[8] or act for them:
Before their eyes I cannot stand thus!

"You ignoble fool of cruel feats,
Don't render me nude, do not debase me!
These sons of kings will not condone you,
Were Iṅdra and Gods to be your helpmates!

"The king, son of Dharma,[9] abides by the Law,
And the Law is subtle, for the wise to find out:
But even at his behest I would not
Give the least offense and abandon my virtue.

"It is *base* that amidst the Kaurava heroes
You drag me inside while I am in my month;
There is no one here to honor you for it,
Though surely they do not mind your plan.

"Damnation! Lost to the Bhāratas
Is their Law and the ways of sagacious barons,
When all these Kauravas in their hall
Watch the Kuru Law's limits overstridden!

"There is no mettle in Droṇa and Bhīṣma,
Nor to be sure in this good man;
The chiefs of the elders amongst the Kurus
Ignore this dread Unlaw of this king."

As she piteously spoke the slim-waisted queen
Threw a scornful glance at her furious husbands
And inflamed with the fall of her sidelong glances,
The Pāṇḍavas, wrapped with wrath in their limbs.

Not the kingdom lost, nor the riches looted,
Nor the precious jewels plundered did hurt
As hurt that sidelong glance of Kṛṣṇā,
That glance of Kṛṣṇā sent in fury.

Duhśāsana, though, watched only Kṛṣṇā
Who was looking down on her wretched lords,
And shaking her wildly—she was close to fainting—
Cried cruelly "Slave!" and laughed aloud.

And Karṇa applauded his word to the full
And heartily laughing acknowledged it,
And Subala's son, king of Gāndhāra,
Likewise cheered on Duhśāsana.

Apart from these two and Duryodhana,
All other men who sat in the hall,

8. Teachers, elders.

9. Yudhiṣṭhira.

On seeing Kṛṣṇā dragged into the hall,
Were filled with misery beyond measure.

BHĪṢMA SAID:

As the Law is subtle, my dear, I fail
To resolve your riddle the proper way:
A man without property cannot stake another's—
But given that wives are the husband's chattels?

Yudhiṣṭhira may give up all earth
With her riches, before he'd give up the truth.
The Pāṇḍava said, "I have been won,"
Therefore I cannot resolve this doubt.

No man is Śakuni's peer at the dice,
And he left Yudhiṣṭhira his own choice.
The great-spirited man does not think he was cheating,
Therefore I cannot speak to the riddle.

DRAUPADĪ SAID:

In the meeting hall he was challenged, the king,
By cunning, ignoble, and evil tricksters
Who love to game; he had never much tried it.
Why then do you say he was left a choice?

Pure, the best of Kurus and Pāṇḍavas,
He did not wake up to the playing of tricks,
He attended the session and when he'd lost all,
Only then he agreed to hazard me.

They stand here, the Kurus, they stand in their hall,
Proud owners of sons and daughters-in-law:
Examine ye all this word of mine,
And resolve my riddle the proper way!

VAIŚAMPĀYANA SAID:

So she piteously spoke and flowing with tears
Kept looking at those who were her husbands;
Meanwhile Duḥśāsana said many words
That were bitter and mean and none that were gentle.

The Wolf-Belly looked and watched how she
Was dragged, in her courses, with upper cloth drooping,[1]
Who so little deserved it, in desperate pain;
He looked at his brother and gave voice to his rage.

61

BHĪMA SAID:

There are a lot of whores in the country of gamblers, Yudhiṣṭhira, but they never throw for them, for they have pity even for women of that stripe. The

1. The mention of the upper cloth suggests that this verse might belong to a different version of the narrative than the one we have been following. The other verses indicate that Draupadī is wearing a single (lower) cloth.

tribute that the king of the Kāśīs[2] brought and all our vast wealth, the gems that the other kings of the earth brought in, the mounts and prizes, the armor and weaponry, the kingdom, yourself and we have all been staked and lost to others. This I didn't mind much, for you are the master of all we possess. But you went too far, I think, when you staked Draupadī. She did not deserve this! After she had won Pāṇḍavas as a girl, she is now because of you plagued by Kauravas, mean and cruel tricksters! It is because of her that I hurl my fury at you! I shall burn off your arms! Sahadeva![3] Bring the fire!

ARJUNA SAID:

Never before have you said words like these, Bhīmasena! Surely your respect for the Law has been destroyed by our harsh enemies! Don't fall in with the enemy's plans, obey your highest Law: no one may overreach his eldest brother by Law. The king was challenged by his foes, and, remembering the baronial Law,[4] he played at the enemy's wish. *That* is our great glory!

BHĪMASENA SAID:

If I'd thought he'd done it for his own glorification, I'd have forced his arms together and burned them in the blazing fire, Dhanaṃjaya![5]

VAIŚAMPĀYANA SAID:

Hereupon, seeing the grief of the Pāṇḍavas and the torment of Pāñcālī, Vikarṇa, a son of Dhṛtarāṣṭra's,[6] spoke out: "Ye kings! Answer the question that Yajñasena's daughter has asked! We must decide or we shall go to hell! Bhīṣma and Dhṛtarāṣṭra are the eldest of the Kurus; they are here but say nought, nor does the sagacious Vidura. Droṇa Bhāradvāja is here, the teacher of us all, and so is Kṛpa, yet even they, most eminent of brahmins, do not speak to the question! All the other kings, assembled here from every horizon, should shed all partisan feelings and speak up as they think. Consider the question that the beautiful Draupadī has raised repeatedly, kings, and whatever your side, make your answer!"

Thus did he speak many times to all the men who were sitting in the hall, but none of the kings said aught, whether good or bad. Vikarṇa spoke again and again to all those kings, and sighing, kneading his hands, he finally said, "Make your answer, kings, or do not. But I shall tell you, Kaurava, what I think is right in this matter. Ye best of men, they recount four vices that are the curse of a king: hunting, drinking, dicing, and fornicating. A man with those addictions abandons the Law, and the world does not condone his immoderate deeds. The Pāṇḍava was under the sway of his vice when the gamblers challenged him and he staked Draupadī. The innocent woman is held in common by all the Pāṇḍavas, and the Pāṇḍava staked her when he already had gambled away his own freedom. It was Saubala who mentioned Kṛṣṇā when he wanted a stake. Considering all this I do not think she has been won."

When they heard this, there was a loud outcry from the men in the hall as they praised Vikarṇa and condemned Saubala. When the noise died down, the son of Rādhā,[7] fairly fainting with fury, grasped his shining arm and said, "Are

2. The ruler of Benares (Kāśī) and surrounding kingdoms, one of many kings who brought tribute to Yudhiṣṭhira at his royal consecration.
3. Sahadeva is the keeper of the Pāṇḍavas' ritual fires.
4. The code of the *kṣatriya* or warrior class.
5. "Winner of wealth," an epithet of Arjuna.
6. Thus, Duryodhana's brother.
7. Karṇa, half brother of the Pāṇḍavas, abandoned by his mother Kuntī at birth, and brought up by the charioteer Adhiratha and his wife Rādhā.

there not many mockeries of the truth found in Vikarṇa? As the fire burns the block from which it was drilled, so the fire he generates will lead to his perdition! All these men here have failed to reply despite Kṛṣṇā's urging. I hold that Draupadī has been won, and so do they hold. You are torn to pieces by your own folly, Dhārtarāṣṭra,[8] for, still a child, you announce in the assembly what should be said by your elders. A younger brother of Duryodhana's, you do not know the true facts of the Law, if you stupidly maintain that Kṛṣṇā, who has been won, has not in fact been won. How, son of Dhṛtarāṣṭra, can you hold that Kṛṣṇā has not been won when the eldest Pāṇḍava staked all he owned in the assembly hall? Draupadī is part of all he owns, bull of the Bharatas, then how can you hold that Kṛṣṇā, won by Law, has not been won? Draupadī was mentioned by name and the Pāṇḍavas allowed her to be staked—then by what reasoning do you hold that she has not been won?

"Or if you think that it was against the Law to bring her into the hall clad in one piece of clothing, listen to what I have to say in reply to that. The Gods have laid down that a woman shall have one husband, scion of Kuru. She admits to many men and assuredly is a whore![9] Thus there is, I think, nothing strange about taking her into the hall, or to have her in one piece of clothing, or for that matter naked! She, the Pāṇḍava's wealth, and the Pāṇḍavas themselves have all been won by Saubala here according to the Law.

"Duḥśāsana, this Vikarṇa is only a child, blabbing of wisdom! Strip the clothes from the Pāṇḍavas and Draupadī!"

Hearing this, all the Pāṇḍavas shed their upper clothes[1] and sat down in the assembly hall. Then Duḥśāsana forcibly laid hold of Draupadī's robe, O king, and in the midst of the assembly began to undress her. But when her skirt was being stripped off, lord of the people, another similar skirt appeared every time. A terrible roar went up from all the kings, a shout of approval, as they watched that greatest wonder on earth. And in the midst of the kings Bhīma, lips trembling with rage, kneading hand in hand, pronounced a curse in a mighty voice: "Take to heart this word of mine, ye barons that live on this earth, a word such as never has been spoken before nor any one shall ever speak hereafter! May I forfeit my journey to all my ancestors, if I do not carry out what I say, if I not tear open in battle the chest of this misbegotten fiend, this outcaste of the Bharatas, and drink his blood!"

When they heard this curse, which exhilarated all the world, they offered him much homage and reviled Dhṛtarāṣṭra's son. A pile of clothes was heaped up in the middle of the hall, when Duḥśāsana, tired and ashamed, at last desisted and sat down. The gods among men[2] in the hall raised the hair-raising cry of "Fie!" as they watched the sons of Kuntī. The people shouted, "The Kauravyas[3] refuse to answer the question," and condemned the Dhārtarāṣṭras.

Thereupon, raising his arms and stopping the crowd in the hall, Vidura, who knew all the Laws, made his speech.[4]

8. Son of Dhṛtarāṣṭra.
9. Karṇa's hatred of the Pāṇḍavas comes across very clearly in this speech. This is one of the few places in the epic in which Draupadī's marriage to five men is condemned as being immoral.
1. A gesture of subordination, here equivalent to stripping. The Pāṇḍavas are wearing two loose cloths, one tied around the waist and the other draped over the shoulders.
2. Kings, chiefs.
3. Kauravas.
4. Despite his partially low birth (his mother was a maidservant), Vidura is respected for his knowledge of the law.

VIDURA SAID:

Draupadī, having raised the question, now weeps piteously as though she has none left to protect her. If you do not resolve it, men in this hall, the Law will be offended. The man who comes to the hall with a grievance is like a blazing fire: the men in the hall must appease him with true Law. If a man comes with a grievance and raises a question of Law with the men in the hall, they must resolve the question and shed all partiality. Vikarṇa has answered the question according to his lights, kings of men; you too must speak to the question according to yours. If a person sits in the hall and fails to answer a question, although he sees the Law, he incurs half the guilt that accrues if the answer is false. And he who has gone to the hall, knows the Law, yet resolves it falsely, certainly incurs the full guilt of the falsehood.

Summary Vidura recounts a lengthy story portraying the fall of those who fail to answer a question of dharma in a public assembly. Draupadī and Bhīṣma urge the assembled noblemen to answer Draupadī's challenge.

62

VAIŚAMPĀYANA SAID:

Upon witnessing all those many events
And Draupadī screeching, a winged osprey,
The kings said nought, neither good nor bad,
For they feared for Dhṛtarāṣṭra's son.

And seeing the sons and grandsons of kings
Keep silent, the son of Dhṛtarāṣṭra
Began to smile and said this word
To the daughter of the Pāñcāla king:

"Let the question now rest with the mettlesome Bhīma,
With Arjuna and with Sahadeva,
And your husband Nakula, Draupadī:
Let them speak the word that you have begotten.

"In the midst of these nobles they must declare
For thy sake that Yudhiṣṭhira's not thy master,
And thus they must make King Dharma a liar.
Pāñcalī, so you escape servitude!

"King Dharma, great-spirited, firm in the Law,
The peer of Indra, himself must declare
Whether he owns you or does not own you;
At his word you must choose, the one or the other.

"For all the Kauravas in the assembly
Are caught inside your misery:
They cannot resolve it, the noble-hearted,
And they look to your unfortunate masters."

The men in the hall all loudly approved
The word that the king of the Kurus had spoken;
There were those who cheeringly waved their clothes,

But also cries of "Woe!" were heard.
And all the kings in cheerful spirits
Applauded the Law of the first of the Kurus.

All the kings looked at Yudhiṣṭhira, their faces turned sideways: "What will the law-wise prince say? What will the Terrifier[5] say, the Pāṇḍava undefeated in battle? And Bhīmasena and the twins?" thus they wondered, greatly curious. When the noise had died down, Bhīmasena spoke, grasping his broad, sandal-scented[6] arm.

"Had Yudhiṣṭhira the King Dharma not been our own guru and lord of our family we should never have suffered this! He owns our merit and our austerities, he commands our lives. If he holds himself defeated, so are we defeated. No mortal who walks the earth would have escaped me with his life, for touching the hair of Pāñcālī! Look at my arms, long and round like iron-studded bludgeons: once caught in them not the God of the Hundred Sacrifices[7] could escape from them! But now, like this, tied by the noose of the Law, constrained by his gravity and held back by Arjuna, I wreak no havoc! But if the King Dharma unleashes me, I shall crush the evil band of Dhṛtarāṣṭra with the swordlike flats of my hands, as a lion flattens small game!" And at once Bhīṣma and Droṇa and Vidura spoke: "Bear with it! With you anything is possible!"

63

KARṆA SAID:

There are three who own no property,
A student, a slave, a dependent woman:
The wife of a slave, you are his now, my dear;
A masterless slave wench, you are now slave wealth!

Come in and serve us with your attentions:
That is the chore you have left in this house.
Dhṛtarāṣṭra's men, and not the Pārthas,[8]
Are now your masters, child of a king!

Now quickly choose you another husband
Who will not gamble your freedom away:
For license with masters is never censured:
That is the slave's rule, remember it!

Won have been Nakula, Bhīmasena,
Yudhiṣṭhira, Sahadeva, Arjuna!
Become a slave, come inside, Yājñasenī!
The ones who are won are no longer your men.

What use are now to the Pārtha[9] himself,
His gallantry and his manliness?
In the midst of the hall he has gambled away
The daughter of Drupada, king of Pāñcāla!

5. Arjuna.
6. Scented with a fragrant paste made from sandalwood.
7. Indra. Vedic Aryans gave him one hundred sacrificial offerings.
8. Sons of Pṛthā (Kuntī).
9. Son of Pṛthā (Kuntī), here an epithet of Yudhiṣṭhira.

VAIŚAṂPĀYANA SAID:

Hearing this, Bhīma bore it no longer;
A man tormented, he panted hard;
But avowed to the king and trapped by the Law,
Burning him down with wrath-shot eye,

BHĪMA SAID:

I do not anger at a sūta's son,[1]
For the Law of serfdom is surely upon us:
But could our enemies now have held me,
If you had not thrown for her, my liege?

VAIŚAṂPĀYANA SAID:

When he had heard the words of Rādheya,[2] Prince Duryodhana said to Yudhiṣṭhira, who was sitting silent and mindless, "Bhīma and Arjuna and the twins follow your orders, king. Answer the question, whether you think she has been won!" This he said to the Kaunteya,[3] and crazed by his ascendancy, he took his cloth[4] and looked invitingly at Pāñcālī. Then, smiling up at Rādheya, and taunting Bhīma, he exposed to Draupadī who was watching him his left thigh, soft like a banana tree and auspiciously marked—an elephant trunk and a thunderbolt in one.[5] The Wolf-Belly saw it and, widening his bloodshot eyes, spoke up in the midst of the kings, willing the assembly to listen: "May the Wolf-Belly never share the world of his fathers, if I fail to break that thigh with my club in a great battle!" And as he raged, flames of the fire burst forth from all the orifices of his body, as from the hollows of a tree that is on fire.

VIDURA SAID:

Kings! Watch for the ultimate danger from Bhīma!
Kings! Watch it as if it were Varuṇa's noose![6]
For surely the hostile fate has emerged
That the Gods set of old for the Bhāratas.

This has been an overplay, Dhārtarāṣṭras.
Who fight over a woman in this hall!
Your security now seems much imperiled,
For evil counsels the Kurus now spell.

Kurus, quickly decide on the Law of the case.
If it's wrongly perceived the assembly will suffer.
If this gamester here had staked her before,
He'd have been undefeated and still been her master.

Like a stake that is won in a dream is the stake,
If the stake is put up by one who does not own it!

1. Karṇa is the adopted son of a charioteer-bard, and his real birth (as Kuntī's son and thus half brother of the Pāṇḍavas) is unknown even to him.
2. Karṇa, son of Rādhā (the charioteer's wife).
3. Yudhiṣṭhira, son of Kuntī.
4. He either waves his upper cloth or picks up an end of the cloth at his waist.
5. A sexual suggestion need not be ruled out; however, Duryodhana is inviting Draupadī to become *his* queen. In sculpture and painting, the queen consort is portrayed as sitting on the king's left thigh.
6. As the Vedic god of law, Varuṇa binds people with his noose.

You have listened to Gāndhārī's son,[7]
Now Kurus, don't run from the Law of the case!

DURYODHANA SAID:

I stay with the word of Bhīmasena
And Arjuna's word and the word of the twins:
If they say Yudhiṣṭhira wasn't their master,
Then Yājñasenī, you won't be a slave!

ARJUNA SAID:

The king was our master when first he played us,
Great-spirited Dharma, the son of Kuntī:
But whose master is he who has lost himself?
That you should decide, ye Kurus assembled!

VAIŚAMPĀYANA SAID:

And there in the house of the King Dhṛtarāṣṭra
At the agnihotra[8] a jackal barked,
The donkeys, they brayed in response, O king,
And so on all sides the grisly birds.[9]

And Vidura, sage of all portents, listened
To the horrible sound, so did Saubala;
And Bhīṣma and Droṇa and wise Gautama
Made loud declarations of "Peace!" and "Peace!"

Thereupon Gāndhārī and Vidura the wise,
Who both had observed that ghastly omen,
At once unhappily told the king;
Whereupon the king gave voice to his word:

"You're lost, Duryodhana, shallow-brain,
Who in this hall of the bulls of the Kurus
Berated a woman most uncouthly,
And her a Draupadī, married by Law!"

Having spoken the wise Dhṛtarāṣṭra withdrew,
For he wished for the weal of his allies-in-law;
Kṛṣṇā Pāñcālī he pacified,
And thinking with insight, informed of the facts,

DHṚTARĀṢṬRA SAID:

Choose a boon for me, Pāñcālī, whatever you wish;[1] for you are to me the most distinguished of my daughters-in-law, bent as you are on the Law!

DRAUPADĪ SAID:

If you give me a boon, bull of the Bhāratas, I choose this: the illustrious Yudhiṣṭhira, observer of every Law, shall be no slave! Do not let these little boys, who do not know my determined son, say of Prativindhya[2] when he happens to

7. Duryodhana.
8. A Vedic rite in which an offering of milk is made to the sun god at dawn and dusk.
9. Evil omens.
1. Frightened by the evil omens, Dhṛtarāṣṭra tries to compensate for his sons' treachery by granting a wish (boon) to the aggrieved Draupadī.
2. His father is Yudhiṣṭhira.

come in, "Here comes the son of a slave!" He has been a *king's* son, as no man has been anywhere. Spoiled as he is, he shall die, Bhārata, when he finds out that he has been a slave's son!

DHṚTARĀṢṬRA SAID:

I give you a second boon, good woman, ask me! My heart has convinced me that you do not deserve only a single boon.

DRAUPADĪ SAID:

With their chariots and bows I choose Bhīmasena and Dhanaṃjaya, Nakula and Sahadeva, as my second boon!

DHṚTARĀṢṬRA SAID:

Choose a third boon from us; two boons do not honor you enough. For of all of my daughters-in-law you are the best, for you walk in the Law.

DRAUPADĪ SAID:

Greed kills Law, Sir, I cannot make another wish. I am not worthy to take a third boon from you, best of kings. As they say, the commoner has one boon, the baron and his lady two, but three are the king's, great king, and a hundred the brahmin's. They were laid low, my husbands, but they have been saved: and they will find the good things, king, with their own good acts!

64

KARṆA SAID:

Of all the women of mankind, famous for their beauty, of whom we have heard, no one have we heard accomplished such a deed! While the Pārthas and the Dhārtarāṣṭra are raging beyond measure, Kṛṣṇā Draupadī has become the salvation of the Pāṇḍavas! When they were sinking, boatless and drowning, in the plumbless ocean, the Pāñcālī became the Pāṇḍavas' boat, to set them ashore!

VAIŚAMPĀYANA SAID:

Hearing this amidst the Kurus, that a woman had become the refuge of the sons of Pāṇḍu, resentful Bhīmasena said glumly, "Devala has declared that there are three stars in man—offspring, deeds, and knowledge; for creatures live on through them. When the body has become impure, void of life, emptied, and cast off by the kinsmen, it is these three that survive of a man. Our light has been darkened, for our wife has been defiled, Dhanaṃjaya: how can offspring be born from one defiled?"

ARJUNA SAID:

Bhāratas never babble of the insults, spoken or unspoken, from a lower man. The best people always remember only the good acts, not the hostilities they have been shown, acknowledging them because they have confidence in themselves.

BHĪMA SAID:

I shall here and now kill all the enemies that have assembled! Or you go outside, Bhārata, lord among the kings, and cut them to their roots! What is the use for us to argue here, why suffer, Bhārata? I am going to kill them here and now, and you sway this world!

VAIŚAMPĀYANA SAID:

When Bhīmasena had spoken, surrounded by his younger brothers like a lion amidst deer, he kept glancing at his club. While the Pārtha of unsullied deeds sought to appease and cool him off, the powerful strong-armed Bhīma began to sweat with his inner heat. From the ears and the other orifices of the raging man fire issued forth, smoking and sparking. His face became fierce to behold, with its folds of knitted brows, as the face of Yama himself when the end of the Eon has come. Yudhiṣṭhira restrained the strong-armed Bhīma with his arm, O Bhārata. "Don't!" he said. "Stay quiet!" And when he had restrained the strong-armed man, whose eyes were bloodshot with rage, Yudhiṣṭhira went up to his father Dhṛtarāṣṭra and folded his hands.

65

YUDHIṢṬHIRA SAID:

King, what should we do? Command us, you are our master. For we always wish to obey your behest, Bhārata.

DHṚTARĀṢṬRA SAID:

Ajātaśatru, good luck to you! Go ye in peace and comfort. I give you my leave: rule your own kingdom with your own treasures. But keep in mind this admonition that I, an old man, utter; I have thought it through with my mind, as it is proper and beneficent above all.

Yudhiṣṭhira, my wise son, you know the subtle course of the Laws, you are courteous and you attend to your elders. Where there is wisdom there is serenity: become serene, Bhārata. An ax does not sink in if it is not on wood, but on wood it cuts. The best among men do not remember hostilities; they see the virtues, not the faults, and they do not stoop to enmity. It is the lowliest that hurl insults in a quarrel, Yudhiṣṭhira; the middling ones return the insults, but the best and the steady ones never babble about hostile insults, spoken or unspoken. The good only remember the good that was done, not the hostile deeds, acknowledging it because they have confidence in themselves.

You have behaved nobly in this meeting of good people, therefore, my son, do not brood in your heart on Duryodhana's offensiveness. Look at your mother Gāndhārī, and at me, your old blind father before you, who longs for your virtues. It was from affection that I allowed this dicing game, as I wished to see my friends and find out the strengths and weaknesses of my sons. King, the Kurus whose ruler you are and whose councillor is the sagacious Vidura, expert in all the fields of knowledge, are they to be pitied? In you there is Law, in Arjuna prowess, in Bhīmasena might, in the twins, foremost among men, there is faith and obedience to their elders.

Ajātaśatru, good luck to you! Return to the Khāṇḍava Tract. May you have brotherly bonds with your brethren, and may your mind abide by the Law!

VAIŚAṂPĀYANA SAID:

At his words Yudhiṣṭhira the King Dharma, first of the Bhāratas, having fulfilled the full covenant of the nobles, departed with his brothers. Riding their cloudlike chariots they started with Kṛṣṇā, and in cheerful spirits, for their good city Indraprastha.[3]

Summary At the end of the Pāndava exile, the Kauravas refuse to hand over the kingdom to Yudhiṣthira as promised. Kṛṣna, the divine incarnation, approaches the Kauravas on

3. Duryodhana succeeds in arranging a replay of the dice game, with the outcome to be decided by a single throw of the dice. Yudhiṣṭhira loses, and the Pāṇḍavas are exiled for thirteen years.

Yudhiṣṭhira's behalf with a proposal for a peaceful settlement between the feuding cousins. Duryodhana rejects the proposal and opts for all-out war.

From Book 5[4]

Udyoga [The Preparation for War]

42

Dhṛtarāṣṭra said to Kṛṣṇa, "O Kṛṣṇa, I agree with what you have said to me. It will lead to the attainment of heaven, besides being beneficial to the world, as well as virtuous and just. But I am not my own master and I cannot do what I would like to do. O Kṛṣṇa, try and persuade my wicked son Duryodhana, who disregards the injunctions of the scriptures. Then you will have discharged a great duty as a friend."

So Kṛṣṇa addressed himself to the wrathful Duryodhana, in sweet words pregnant with virtue and worldly profit, "O Duryodhana, listen to these words of mine, which are meant for your benefit and that of your followers. Born as you are in a family of very wise men, and endowed as you are with learning and good conduct and with all good qualities, it is right and proper that you should behave honorably. In this case your obstinacy is perverse and unrighteous, and it will result in great and terrible loss of life. O tiger among men, be reconciled with the Pāṇḍavas, who are wise, heroic, energetic, self-restrained, and greatly learned. It is beneficial to you, and will be appreciated by the wise Dhṛtarāṣṭra, as well as by the grandfather Bhīṣma, Droṇa, and the intelligent Vidura. Let there be some survivors of the Kuru race and let not the whole race be destroyed, and do not let yourself, O king, become notorious as the exterminator of the race."

Duryodhana became enraged on hearing the words of Kṛṣṇa. Bhīṣma said to him, "Kṛṣṇa has spoken as a friend wishing peace; listen to his words, my dear son, and do not follow the lead of anger." But Duryodhana did not heed Bhīṣma's advice. He remained under the influence of wrath, breathing hard. Then Droṇa told him, "Kṛṣṇa said words to you which are filled with virtue and profit, my dear son; so did Bhīṣma, the son of Śaṅtanu; heed them, O ruler of men." At the end of Droṇa's speech, Vidura spoke in similar terms to Duryodhana, the irate son of Dhṛtarāṣṭra. "Duryodhana," he said, "I do not grieve for you, but for these two old people, your father and Gāṅdhārī your mother." Dhṛtarāṣṭra then said to Duryodhana, who was seated along with his brothers and surrounded by other kings, "O Duryodhana, listen to this advice given by the great-souled Kṛṣṇa; accept his words which are beneficial, of eternal validity and conducive to our salvation."

So, among the assembled Kurus, Duryodhana had to listen to this counsel which he little liked. Finally he said in reply to Kṛṣṇa, "No doubt, as is proper, you have spoken to me after due consideration; but you find fault only with me. I have not committed the slightest fault, nor do I see even the smallest misconduct on my side after a searching examination. I may recall that the

4. Books 5, 8, 9, 11, and 12 translated by C. V. Narasimhan.

Pāṇḍavas were defeated at a game of dice in which they engaged of their own free will and in the course of which their kingdom was won by Śakuni; what misconduct was there on my part? Indeed, you will remember that I ordered at the time the return of the wealth which the Pāṇḍavas had lost. It is not our fault that the Pāṇḍavas were defeated at another game of dice and were then banished to the forest. The principal duty of a Kṣatriya is that he should lie down on a bed of arrows in the battlefield. I am ready to do so. I shall not, during my lifetime, allow the Pāṇḍavas to regain the share of the kingdom that was given them by our ancestors in early days."

After reflecting on Duryodhana's speech, Kṛṣṇa, his eyes red with anger, spoke these words to Duryodhana in that assembly of the Kurus: "It is your desire to get the bed of a hero, and it will be fulfilled; you and your advisers will not have to wait long. Soon there will be a great massacre. O fool, you think that there is nothing blameworthy in your conduct towards the Pāṇḍavas. All the kings here know the truth of what I am now going to say. Being jealous of the prosperity of the great Pāṇḍavas, you arranged for a game of dice in evil cabal with Śakuni. Who save yourself could have treated the wife of your brothers in the way you did? After dragging Draupadī to the council hall, who else could have spoken to her as you did? You went to great trouble to burn the Pāṇḍavas alive when they were mere boys, and were staying with their mother at Vāraṇāvata, but that attempt of yours did not succeed. By poison, by snake, and by rope, in fact by every means, you have attempted the destruction of the sons of Pāṇḍu, but you have not been successful. You have been urged again and again, by your mother and by your father and also by Bhīṣma, Droṇa, and Vidura, to make peace but you do not wish to do so."

When Kṛṣṇa had thus charged the wrathful Duryodhana, Duḥśāsana said these words in the assembly of the Kurus, "If you do not make peace of your own free will with the Pāṇḍavas, it looks as if the Kauravas will make you over to Yudhiṣṭhira bound hand and foot." Hearing these words of his brother, Duryodhana could no longer restrain himself. He got up from his seat hissing like a huge serpent. Disregarding all those present—Vidura, King Dhṛtarāṣṭra, Bāhlika, Kṛpa, Somadatta, Bhīṣma, Droṇa, and Kṛṣṇa—that shameless and wicked prince walked out of the court.

43

Dhṛtarāṣṭra then said to Vidura, "Go, my friends, to the wise Gāṅdhārī; get her here; along with her I shall try to persuade our son." In response to the request of Dhṛtarāṣṭra, Vidura brought the farsighted Gāṅdhārī. By command of Dhṛtarāṣṭra and also at the request of Gāṅdhārī, Vidura had the wrathful Duryodhana brought back. Seeing her son, who was following the wrong course, Gāṅdhārī spoke these significant words, "O Duryodhana, my dear son, listen to these words of mine which will be to your benefit and that of your followers, and which will bring you all happiness. It is my fond and earnest wish, as well as that of Bhīṣma, your father, and other well-wishers, the chief of whom is Droṇa, that you should make peace."

Disregarding those sensible words spoken by his mother, the obstinate Duryodhana again went to his own palace burning with rage. Then he consulted King Śakuni, the expert in the game of dice, as well as Karṇa and Duḥśāsana. The four, namely, Duryodhana, Karṇa, Śakuni, and Duḥśāsana, reached the following conclusion: "Kṛṣṇa means to waste no time, and wants to capture us first in concert with Dhṛtarāṣṭra and Bhīṣma. We shall, however, capture Kṛṣṇa by force, before he can carry out his plan."

Coming to know of this plan through Sātyaki, Vidura said to Dhṛtarāṣṭra, "O king, your sons are approaching the hour of doom, because they are ready to perpetrate an infamous act, even though they are incapable of doing it." He then informed the king of Duryodhana's nefarious plot. On hearing this, Dhṛtarāṣṭra said to Vidura, "Bring here again the sinful Duryodhana, who covets the kingdom." Therefore Vidura made the reluctant Duryodhana return once more to the council chamber, along with his brothers.

King Dhṛtarāṣṭra addressed Duryodhana, Karṇa, Duḥśāsana, and the kings who surrounded them, "O you of inhuman conduct, of exceeding sinfulness, having for your supporters only petty men, I know of your secret desire to commit a wicked deed. Kṛṣṇa cannot be captured by force, even as air cannot be held by the hand, as the moon cannot be touched, and as the earth cannot be supported on the head." Vidura's warning was: "If you try to use force on the mighty Kṛṣṇa, you, along with your advisers, will perish like an insect falling into the flame."

When Vidura had finished speaking, Kṛṣṇa said to Duryodhana, "O Duryodhana! since, out of your folly, you suppose me to be alone, you think you can effect my capture by overpowering me." So saying, he laughed aloud. And at his laughter the body of the great-souled one became like lightning. From his body issued forth gods only as big as the thumb but bright as rays of fire. Brahmā was found to be on his brow and Rudra on his breast. On his arms appeared the regents of the earth and from his mouth issued forth the god of fire. When Kṛṣṇa thus showed himself on the floor of the assembly hall, celestial drums were sounded and there was a shower of flowers. After a moment he discarded that celestial and wonderful form. Taking Sātyaki by the hand, Kṛṣṇa went out, with the permission of the sages present in the court.

As he was about to depart on the chariot which was ready for him, the great king Dhṛtarāṣṭra again said to Kṛṣṇa, "You have seen, O Kṛṣṇa, what little influence I wield over my sons; you have been a witness to that; nothing has happened behind your back." Then Kṛṣṇa said to Dhṛtarāṣṭra, and to Droṇa and the grandfather Bhīṣma, and to Vidura, and to Bāhlika and Kṛpa, "Your exalted selves are witnesses to what went on in the assembly of the Kurus; how today that fool, like an uneducated and unmannerly fellow, walked out. Now you have heard the ruler of the earth Dhṛtarāṣṭra say that he is powerless in the matter. With the permission of all of you I shall go to Yudhiṣṭhira."

Then in that large, white chariot, furnished with tinkling bells, Kṛṣṇa went first to see his aunt Kuṅtī. Entering her abode, he bowed at her feet, after which he briefly described to her what had happened in the assembly of the Kurus. Having completed his report he respectfully circumambulated her, and took leave of her.

When Kṛṣṇa had left, Bhīṣma and Droṇa said to Duryodhana, "The sons of Kuṅtī will do what Kṛṣṇa advises, and they will not be pacified without the restoration of the kingdom. The Pāṇḍavas and Draupadī too were persecuted by you in the assembly hall, but they were bound by the ties of virtue at that time. Now they have in Arjuna a master of all weapons and in Bhīma a giant of firm determination. They have the Gāṇḍīva bow and the two quivers and the chariot and the flag, and they have Kṛṣṇa as their ally. The Pāṇḍavas will not forgive the past."

44

Before leaving Hāstinapura, Kṛṣṇa met Karṇa and said to him: "O Karṇa, you know the eternal instruction of the holy books and are fully conversant with all their subtleties. The two classes of sons called Kānīna and Sahoḍha who are borne by a girl before her marriage have for their father the man who marries their mother subsequently—so it is said by people conversant with the holy books. You were born in that way and you are therefore morally the son of Pāṇḍu; so come with me and be a king in your own right. Let us go together to the Pāṇḍava camp, and let the sons of Pāṇḍu know you to be the son of Kuṅtī born before Yudhiṣṭhira. The five Pāṇḍava brothers will clasp your feet, as will the five sons of Draupadī, and the invincible son of Subhadrā.[5] Enjoy the kingdom in company with your brothers, the sons of Pāṇḍu, who are ever engaged in prayer and sacrifice and other auspicious ceremonies. Let your friends rejoice and in the same way let your enemies suffer; be reconciled today with your brothers, the sons of Pāṇḍu."

Karṇa replied: "I have no doubt, O Kṛṣṇa, that you have spoken these words out of good will, love, and friendship, and also out of the desire to do me good. Before her wedding with Pāṇḍu, Kuṅtī conceived me by the Sun-god, and at his command she abandoned me as soon as I was born. I know I was born in this way and I am therefore morally the son of Pāṇḍu. I was however left destitute at birth by Kuṅtī, who had no thought of my welfare. On the other hand, I have been practically a member of the family of Dhṛtarāṣṭra and, under the protection of Duryodhana, I have enjoyed sovereignty for thirteen years without let or hindrance. Relying on me, Duryodhana has made preparations for war with the Pāṇḍavas. At this stage, I cannot behave treacherously towards Duryodhana out of fear of being slain or captured, or from covetousness."

Kṛṣṇa said, "I fear that this world will surely come to an end, O Karṇa, since my advice does not seem acceptable to you." "O Kṛṣṇa," replied Karṇa, "I shall see you again if I survive this great battle which has come upon us. Otherwise we shall surely meet in heaven. I now feel that I shall meet you only there, O sinless one."

Having learnt of the failure of Kṛṣṇa's mission, Kuṅtī decided to make a personal appeal to Karṇa. Thus resolved, she went towards the river Gāṅgā for the attainment of her object. On the banks of the river she heard the sound of the chanting of hymns by her son, the kind and truthful Karṇa. That austere lady waited behind Karṇa, whose arms were raised and whose face was turned to the east, till the end of his devotions, which continued till his back had been scorched by the rays of the sun. Karṇa then turned and, seeing Kuṅtī, did her honor by saluting her and folding his hands before her, according to proper form.

Karṇa first introduced himself, by saying, "I am Karṇa, the son of Rādhā and of Adhiratha, and I salute you. Why are you come here? Tell me what I may do for you." Kuṅtī replied, "You are the son of Kuṅtī and not the son of Rādhā; nor

5. Abhimanyu, son of Arjuna and Subhadrā.

is Adhiratha your father. O Karṇa, you are not born in the race of Sūta;[6] know this word of mine to be true. I conceived you illegitimately when I was an unmarried girl and you were the first in my womb; you were born in the palace of Kuṅtibhoja, my dear son. The maker of brightness, the Sun-god, begot you on me, O Karṇa. O my son, you were born in my father's palace, wearing earrings, clad in a coat of mail, like a divine being. But, owing to ignorance of your true birth, you are now serving the sons of Dhṛtarāṣṭra, without recognizing your brothers. That is not proper, my son. Let the Kurus witness today the union between Karṇa and Arjuna; and seeing that true reconciliation among brothers let dishonest men bow down!"

Then Karṇa heard an affectionate voice issue from the solar disc from afar. It was Sūrya himself, speaking with the affection of a father. The voice said, "O Karṇa, Kuṅtī has spoken the truth. Act according to the advice of your mother; by doing so, you will benefit greatly." But in spite of this entreaty both by his mother and by his father, Karṇa's attitude did not waver.

"O Kṣatriya[7] lady," he said, "I cannot heed the words you have spoken and I do not feel that the way to virtue lies in my doing as you urge me to do. What you did to me was sinful, and I have thereby suffered what is tantamount to the destruction of my fame. Though I was born as a Kṣatriya I did not get the baptismal rites of a Kṣatriya; it was all your sinful doing; what enemy can possibly do me a greater injury? Without having shown me any mercy at that time, you come today to urge me, who was deprived of the rites of my order as a Kṣatriya at birth, to be reconciled to my brothers. You did not think as a mother of my good and you have now come to me purely out of desire for your own good. Unknown as a brother before, and recognized as such now, by whom shall I be called a Kṣatriya if I go over to the side of the Pāṇḍavas on the eve of battle?

"This is the time for those who have obtained their living from Duryodhana to show their fidelity," Karṇa continued, "and I shall do so even at the risk of my life. I shall stay on the side of the sons of Dhṛtarāṣṭra, and I shall fight your sons with all my might and prowess; I do not speak falsely to you. I promise you this: it is with Arjuna alone, among all the forces of Yudhiṣṭhira, that I shall fight. Killing Arjuna in battle, I shall obtain great merit. Slain by him, I shall obtain great glory. O illustrious lady, you will thus always be left with five sons; with Arjuna dead and me alive, or with me slain and Arjuna alive."

When she heard Karṇa's words, Kuṅtī trembled with grief. Embracing her son, who was unmoved in his fortitude, she said, "Indeed, what you say is possible. As you say, fate is all-powerful." Before leaving him, Kuṅtī said to Karṇa, "May you be blessed and may all be well with you." Karṇa also saluted her, and the two went their own ways.

45

Kṛṣṇa returned to Yudhiṣṭhira and reported the failure of his mission. The virtuous and just Yudhiṣṭhira, after hearing Kṛṣṇa's account, said to his brothers, "You have heard what happened in that assemblage of the Kurus and you have no doubt understood what Kṛṣṇa has said. Therefore let us make a division of our army; here are the seven Akṣauhiṇis[8] which are gathered for our victory.

6. Charioteer.
7. The class of warriors.
8. Battalions.

Listen to the names of those famous men who are to be their respective commanders. Drupada, Virāṭa, Dhṛṣṭadyumna and Śikhaṇḍī, Sātyaki, Cekitāna, and Bhīma endued with strength, these heroes, who are prepared to sacrifice their lives if necessary, will be the commanders of my army."

There was a speedy gathering of the soldiers and there was everywhere the trumpeting of elephants, the neighing of horses, and the clatter of chariot wheels, which mingled with the noise caused by the blare of the conch and the sound of the drum. The mobilization of that army caused a roar like that of the sea at high tide. Indeed, the tumult of those happy warriors seemed to reach the very heavens.

Forty thousand chariots, five times that number of horses, ten times that number of foot soldiers, and sixty thousand elephants were gathered there. Anādhṛṣṭi and Cekitāna, the king of Cedi, and Sātyaki surrounded Yudhiṣṭhira along with Kṛṣṇa and Arjuna. Finally, they reached Kurukshetra with their army ready for action and they then blew their conches. All the soldiers of the army became cheerful on hearing the thunderous sound of Kṛṣṇa's conch, the Pāñcajanya.

The next morning, King Duryodhana surveyed his forces, which consisted of eleven Akṣauhiṇis. Dividing his men, elephants, chariots, and horses into superior, inferior, and indifferent, he distributed them among his forces. He selected men who were wise and also heroic to be the leaders of his army. They were Kṛpa, Droṇa, Śalya, Jayadratha the king of the Siṅdhus, Sudakṣiṇa the king of the Kāṁbojas, Kṛtavarmā, Aśvatthāmā the son of Droṇa, Karṇa, Bhūriśravas, Śakuni the son of Subala, and Bāhlika the great car-warrior.

Then, with clasped hands, Duryodhana went to Bhīṣma along with the other kings, and said to him, "Without a commander in chief even a large army is broken up like a swarm of ants when engaged in battle. You are like the sun among the luminous bodies, the moon among deciduous herbs,[9] Kubera among the Yakṣas,[1] Iṅdra among the gods. If you lead and protect us, we shall be like the gods protected by Iṅdra, and we shall surely be invincible even if faced by the denizens of heaven."

Bhīṣma replied, "I am at your disposal. O Duryodhana; but as you are dear to me, so are the Pāṇḍavas. It is my duty to look after their welfare too, but I shall fight on your side since I have promised to do so. In a moment I can make this world destitute of men, gods, asuras, and rākṣasas by the strength of my weapons. But I cannot kill these sons of Pāṇḍu. Instead, I shall slay ten thousand of the opposing warriors every day. In this way, I shall try to bring about their defeat, if indeed they do not kill me before I have time to carry out my plans in the battle."

"There is another condition," Bhīṣma continued, "on which I shall be commander in chief of your army; it is only fair that I should tell you about it now. Either let Karṇa fight first or I myself, but not both, since Karṇa always compares his prowess in battle with mine." Karṇa replied, "O king, I shall not fight as long as Bhīṣma the son of Gāngā[2] lives. Should Bhīṣma be slain, I shall fight with Arjuna, the wielder of the Gāṇḍīva bow."

9. The moon is the "lord of plants."
1. The Yakṣa is a type of demigod; Kubera is the guardian of wealth.
2. The river goddess Ganges.

Meanwhile, in the Pāṇḍava camp, Yudhiṣṭhira summoned before him Drupada, Virāṭa, Sātyaki, Dhṛṣṭadyumna, Dhṛṣṭaketu, Śikhaṇḍī, and the king of Magadha, and made these heroes, who were eager for battle, the leaders of his army. Finally he installed Dhṛṣṭdyumna, who had emerged from the sacrificial fire for causing the death of Droṇa, as commander in chief.[3] The curly-haired Arjuna was made supreme commander over all those great men, while Kṛṣṇa was chosen as the guide of Arjuna and the driver of his horses.

Seeing that a very destructive battle was about to take place, Balarāma, elder brother of Kṛṣṇa, entered the encampment of the royal Pāṇḍavas. He said, "There will be a very fierce massacre; it is surely ordained by fate and cannot be averted. Both these heroes, Bhīma and Duryodhana, well skilled in fighting with the mace, are my pupils and I bear the same affection for both of them. I shall now go on a pilgrimage to the sacred waters of the Sarasvatī for ablutions, for I cannot stay and look on with indifference while this destruction of the Kurus takes place."

From Book 8

Karṇa [*The Book of Karṇa*]

47

When the mighty bowman Droṇa was slain, the Kaurava host became pale-faced and gloomy. Seeing his own forces standing as if paralyzed and lifeless, King Duryodhana said to them, "Relying on the strength of your arms, I have challenged the Pāṇḍavas to this battle. Victory or death is the lot of all warriors. Why wonder then at the fall of Droṇa? Let us resume the fighting in all directions, encouraged by the sight of the lofty-minded Karṇa, the son of Vikartana, mighty bowman and wielder of celestial weapons, who is roving about in the field of battle. Permit me to remind you that it was he who slew Ghaṭotkaca, that creator of illusions, with the indomitable Śakti weapon." Then all those kings, headed by Duryodhana, quickly installed Karṇa as commander in chief, and bathed him according to rites with golden and earthen pitchers of holy water.

As the sixteenth day dawned, Karṇa summoned the Kaurava forces to battle with loud blasts on his conch. He arranged his army in the form of a makara,[4] and proceeded to attack the Pāṇḍavas, desirous of victory. On the Pāṇḍava side, Arjuna, whose car was drawn by white horses, formed a counter-array in the shape of a half-moon.

The day's fighting was marked by many duels, between Bhīma and Aśvatthāmā, Sahadeva and Duḥśāsana, Nakula and Karṇa, Ulūka and Yuyutsu, Kṛpa and Dhṛṣṭadyumna, and Śikhaṇḍī and Kṛtavarmā. While they were thus engaged, the sun disappeared behind the western mountains. Then both sides retired from the field and proceeded to their own encampments.

Before the fighting began on the seventeenth day, Karṇa said to Duryodhana, "Today, O king, I will go forth and battle with the famous Pāṇḍava,

3. The son won through a sacrifice to the gods by King Drupada, Droṇa's sworn enemy, in order to avenge the insult he had suffered at Droṇa's hands.

4. A crocodile or other aquatic animal.

Arjuna. Either I shall slay that hero, or he shall slay me. You are aware of his energy, weapons, and resources. My bow, known by the name of Vijaya,[5] is the greatest of all weapons. It was made by Viśvakarmā[6] in accordance with Indra's wishes, and is a celestial and excellent weapon. On this count I believe I am superior to Arjuna."

"Now you must know," continued Karṇa, "in what respect Arjuna is superior to me. Kṛṣṇa, born of the Dāśārha race, who is revered by all people, is the holder of the reins of his horses. He who is verily the creator of the universe thus guards Arjuna's car. On our side Śalya, who is the ornament of all assemblies, is of equal heroism. Should he take over the duties of my charioteer, then victory will surely be yours. Let the irresistible Śalya, therefore, act as my charioteer."

Duryodhana thereupon went to see Śalya. Humbly approaching the Madra prince, he affectionately spoke these words to him: "You have heard what Karṇa has said, namely that he chooses you, foremost of princes, as his charioteer. Therefore, for the destruction of the Pāṇḍavas, and for my own good, be pleased to become Karṇa's charioteer. As that foremost of charioteers, Kṛṣṇa, counsels and protects Arjuna, so should you support Karṇa at all times."

Śalya replied, "You are insulting me, O Duryodhana, or surely you must doubt my loyalty, since you so readily request me to do the work of a charioteer. You praise Karṇa and consider that he is superior to us. But I do not consider him to be my equal in the field of battle. Knowing that I can strike down the enemy, why do you wish to employ me in the office of charioteer to the lowborn Karṇa?"

Duryodhana replied to Śalya with great affection and high respect. Desirous of achieving his main objective, he addressed him in a friendly manner, saying sweetly, "O Śalya, what you say is doubtless true. However, in making this request I have a certain purpose. Even as Karṇa is reckoned to be superior to Arjuna in many ways so are you, in the opinion of the whole world, superior to Kṛṣṇa. As the high-souled Kṛṣṇa is expert in the handling of horses, even so, O Śalya, are you doubly skilled. There is no doubt about it."

Thus flattered, Śalya said, "O Duryodhana! As you tell me that amongst all these troops there is none but myself who is more accomplished than Kṛṣṇa, I am pleased with you. I therefore agree to act as the charioteer of the famous Karṇa while he is engaged in battle with Arjuna, foremost of the Pāṇḍavas. But there is one condition on which I accept your proposal: that I shall give vent in Karṇa's presence to such expressions as I may wish."[7] Duryodhana, who was accompanied by Karṇa, readily accepted this condition, saying, "So be it."

48

After Śalya had taken over as his charioteer, Karṇa said to him, "Today I shall fearlessly fight Kṛṣṇa and Arjuna, foremost among all wielders of weapons. My mind is, however, troubled by the curse of Paraśurāma, the best of Brāhmaṇas. In my early days, desirous of obtaining a celestial weapon, I lived with him in the

5. "Victor."
6. The smith of the gods.
7. That is, to address him in an insulting manner.

disguise of a Brāhmaṇa.[8] But, O Śalya, in order to benefit Arjuna, Indra,[9] the king of the gods, took on the horrible form of an insect and stung my thigh. Even so, I remained motionless for fear of disturbing my preceptor. When he woke up, he saw what had happened. He subsequently learnt the deception I had practiced on him, and cursed me, that the invocation for the weapon I had obtained by such trickery would not come to my memory at the time of dire need."

"Once while wandering in the forest," Karṇa continued, "I accidentally killed the sacrificial cow of a Brāhmaṇa.[1] Although I offered him seven hundred elephants with large tusks, and many hundreds of male and female slaves, the best of Brāhmaṇas was still not pleased, and although I begged for forgiveness, he said: 'O sūta, what I have prophesied will happen. It cannot be otherwise.' He had said, 'Your wheel[2] shall fall into a hole.' In this battle, while I am fighting, that will be my only fear."

During the fighting on that day there was a dreadful and thrilling battle between Karṇa and the Pāṇḍavas which increased the domain of the god of Death. After that terrible and gory combat only a few of the brave Samśaptakas survived. Then Dhṛṣṭadyumna and the rest of the Pāṇḍavas rushed towards Karṇa and attacked him. As a mountain receives heavy rainfall, so Karṇa received those warriors in battle. Elsewhere on the battlefield Duḥśāsana boldly went up to Bhīma and shot many arrows at him. Bhīma leapt like a lion attacking a deer, and hurried towards him. The struggle that took place between those two, incensed against each other and careless of life, was truly superhuman.

Fighting fiercely, Prince Duḥśāsana achieved many difficult feats in that duel. With a single shaft he cut off Bhīma's bow; with six shafts he pierced Bhīma's driver. Then, without losing a moment, he pierced Bhīma himself with many shafts discharged with great speed and power, while Bhīma hurled his mace at the prince. With that weapon, from a distance of ten bow-lengths, Bhīma forcibly dislodged Duḥśāsana from his car. Struck by the mace, and thrown to the ground, Duḥśāsana began to tremble. His charioteer and all his steeds were slain, and his car too was smashed to pieces by Bhīma's weapon.

Then Bhīma remembered all the hostile acts of Duḥśāsana towards the Pāṇḍavas. Jumping down from his car, he stood on the ground, looking steadily on his fallen foe. Drawing his keen-edged sword, and trembling with rage, he placed his foot upon the throat of Duḥśāsana and, ripping open the breast of his enemy, drank his warm lifeblood, little by little. Then, looking at him with wrathful eyes, he said, "I consider the taste of this blood superior to that of my mother's milk, or honey, or ghee, or wine, or excellent water, or milk, or curds, or buttermilk."

All those who stood around Bhīma and saw him drink the blood of Duḥśāsana fled in terror, saying to each other, "This one is no human being!" Bhīma then said, in the hearing of all those heroes, "O wretch among men, here I drink your lifeblood. Abuse us once more now, 'Beast, beast,' as you did before!"

Having spoken these words, the victorious Bhīma turned to Kṛṣṇa and Arjuna, and said, "O you heroes, I have accomplished today what I had vowed in respect

8. The *brāhmaṇa* Paraśurāma had vowed to exterminate the *kṣatriyas* and had mastered the science of magical weapons, which could be discharged and retracted with the help of incantations.

9. Indra is Arjuna's father.

1. Cows are sacred animals, and the lowborn Karṇa's offense is doubly serious since the sacred cow belonged to a *brāhmaṇa*.

2. Chariot wheel.

of Duḥśāsana! I will soon fulfill my other vow by slaying that second sacrificial beast,[3] Duryodhana! I shall kick the head of that evil one with my foot in the presence of the Kauravas, and I shall then obtain peace!" After this speech, Bhīma, drenched with blood, uttered loud shouts and roared with joy, even as the mighty Indra of a thousand eyes after slaying Vṛtra.[4]

49

Fleeing in the face of Arjuna's onslaught, the broken divisions of the Kauravas saw Arjuna's weapon swelling with energy and careering like lightning. But Karṇa destroyed that fiery weapon of Arjuna with his own weapon of great power[5] which he had obtained from Paraśurāma. The encounter between Arjuna and Karṇa became very fierce. They attacked each other with arrows like two fierce elephants attacking each other with their tusks.

Karṇa then fixed on his bowstring the keen, blazing, and fierce shaft which he had long polished and preserved with the object of destroying Arjuna. Placing in position that shaft of fierce energy and blazing splendor, that venomous weapon which had its origin in the family of Airāvata[6] and which lay within a golden quiver covered by sandal dust,[7] Karṇa aimed it at Arjuna's head. When he saw Karṇa aim that arrow, Śalya said, "O Karṇa, this arrow will not succeed in hitting Arjuna's neck! Aim carefully, and discharge another arrow that may succeed in striking the head of your enemy!" His eyes burning in wrath, Karṇa replied, "O Śalya, Karṇa never aims an arrow twice!"

Thereupon Karṇa carefully let loose that mighty snake in the form of an arrow, which he had worshiped for many long years, saying, "You are slain, O Arjuna!" Seeing the snake aimed by Karṇa, Kṛṣṇa, strongest among the mighty, exerted his whole strength and pressed down Arjuna's chariot with his feet into the earth. When the car itself had sunk into the ground the steeds, too, bent their knees and laid themselves down upon the earth. The arrow then struck and dislodged Arjuna's diadem, that excellent ornament celebrated throughout the earth and the heavens.

The snake said, "O Kṛṣṇa! Know me as one who has been wronged by Arjuna. My enmity towards him stems from his having slain my mother!"

Then Kṛṣṇa said to Arjuna, "Slay that great snake which is your enemy." Thus urged by Kṛṣṇa, Arjuna asked, "Who is this snake that advances of his own accord against me, as if right against the mouth of Garuḍa?"[8] Kṛṣṇa replied, "While you were worshiping the fire-god at the Khāndava forest, this snake was ensconced within his mother's body, which was shattered by your arrows." As the snake took a slanting course across the sky, Arjuna cut it to pieces with six keen shafts, so that it fell down on the earth.

Then, because of the curse of the Brāhmaṇa, Karṇa's chariot wheel fell off, and his car began to reel. At the same time, he forgot the invocation for the weapon he had obtained from Paraśurāma. Unable to endure these calamities, Karṇa waved his arms and began to rail at righteousness, saying, "They that are

3. The animal offered as a victim in a sacrifice.
4. In an important Vedic myth the god Indra slays the dragonlike demon Vṛtra.
5. A magical weapon.
6. Celestial white elephant, mount of Indra, king of gods.
7. Fragrant sandalwood powder.
8. Garuḍa, the celestial eagle, is the enemy of snakes.

conversant with virtue say that righteousness protects the righteous! But today righteousness does not save me."

Speaking thus, he shed tears of wrath, and said to Arjuna, "O Pāṇḍava! Spare me for a moment while I extricate my wheel from the earth! You are on your car while I am standing weak and languid on the ground. It is not fair that you should slay me now! You are born in the Kṣatriya order. You are the scion of a high race. Recollect the teachings of righteousness, and give me a moment's time!"

Then, from Arjuna's chariot, Kṛṣṇa said, "It is fortunate, O Karṇa, that you now remember virtue. It is generally true that those who are mean rail at Providence when they are afflicted by distress, but forget their own misdeeds. You and Duryodhana and Duḥśāsana and Śakuni caused Draupadī, clad in a single garment, to be brought into the midst of the assembly. On that occasion, O Karṇa, this virtue of yours was not in evidence! When Śakuni, skilled in dicing, vanquished Yudhiṣṭhira who was unacquainted with it, where was this virtue of yours? Out of covetousness, and relying on Śakuni, you again summoned the Pāṇḍavas to a game of dice. Whither then had this virtue of yours gone?"

When Kṛṣṇa thus taunted Karṇa, Arjuna became filled with rage. Remembering the incidents to which Kṛṣṇa alluded, he blazed with fury and, bent upon Karṇa's speedy destruction, took out of his quiver an excellent weapon. He then fixed on his bow that unrivaled arrow, and charged it with mantras. Drawing his bow Gāṇḍīva, he quickly said, "Let this shaft of mine be a mighty weapon capable of speedily destroying the body and heart of my enemy. If I have ever practiced ascetic austerities, gratified my preceptors, and listened to the counsels of well-wishers, let this sharp shaft, so long worshiped by me, slay my enemy Karṇa by that Truth!"

Having uttered these words, Arjuna discharged for the destruction of Karṇa, that terrible shaft, that blazing arrow fierce and efficacious as a rite prescribed in the Atharva of Aṅgiras,[9] and invincible against the god of Death himself in battle. Thus sped by that mighty warrior, the shaft endowed with the energy of the Sun caused all the points of the compass to blaze with light. The head of the commander of the Kaurava army, splendid as the Sun, fell like the Sun disappearing in the blood-red sunset behind the western hills. Cut off by Arjuna's arrow and deprived of life, the tall trunk of Karṇa, with blood gushing from every wound, fell down like the thunder-riven summit of a mountain of red chalk with crimson streams running down its sides after a shower of rain.

Then from the body of the fallen Karṇa a light, passing through the atmosphere, illumined the sky. This wonderful sight was seen by all the warriors on the battlefield. After the heroic Karṇa was thus thrown down and stretched on the earth, pierced with arrows and bathed in blood, Śalya, the king of the Madras, withdrew with Karṇa's car. The Kauravas, afflicted with fear, fled from the field, frequently looking back on Arjuna's lofty standard which blazed in splendor.

Summary Śalya is appointed Marshal of the Kaurava army on the eighteenth and last day of the war.

9. The *Atharva Veda*, the fourth Veda, consisting mainly of magical spells, composed by the sage Aṅgiras.

From Book 9

Śalya [*The Book of Śalya*]

71

After the fall of Ulūka and Śakuni, their followers were enraged. Prepared to sacrifice their lives in that fierce encounter, they began to oppose the Pāṇḍavas. Duryodhana too was filled with rage. Collecting his remaining chariots, still many hundreds in number, as well as his elephants, horses, and foot soldiers, he said these words to those warriors: "Kill the Pāṇḍavas with their friends and allies in this battle, and also the Pāñcāla prince with his own army. Then you may turn back from the field."

Respectfully obeying that mandate, the invincible warriors proceeded once more against the Pāṇḍavas. But because it had no leader, that army was destroyed in an instant by those great warriors the Pāṇḍavas. Thus all the eleven akṣauhiṇis[1] of troops which had been collected by Duryodhana were killed by the Pāṇḍavas and the Sṛñjayas.

Looking on all sides, Duryodhana saw the field empty, and himself deprived of all his troops. Meanwhile the Pāṇḍavas, greatly pleased at having attained all their objects, were roaring aloud in joy. Overcome by despair, and bereft of troops and animals, Duryodhana decided to flee from the field. Taking up his mace, he fled on foot towards a lake.

In Duryodhana's army, which had consisted of many hundreds of thousands of warriors, not one single car-warrior was alive, save Aśvatthāmā the heroic son of Droṇa, Kṛtavarmā, Kṛpa, and Duryodhana himself. Duryodhana said to Sañjaya, "Tell the blind king that his son Duryodhana has entered into the lake." He then entered the waters of the lake, which he charmed by his power of wizardry.

Then the old men, who had been engaged to look after the ladies of the royal household, started for the city, followed by the princesses, who wept aloud when they heard of the destruction of the whole army. After the flight of the royal ladies the Kaurava camp was entirely empty, except for the three car-warriors. Filled with anxiety, and hoping to rescue Duryodhana, they too proceeded towards the lake.

Meanwhile Yudhiṣṭhira and his brothers felt happy, and ranged over the field with the desire to kill Duryodhana. Though they searched carefully for him everywhere, they could not discover the Kuru king who, mace in hand, had fled quickly from the field of battle, entered the lake, and solidified the water by his magic.

Not seeing Duryodhana who had thus concealed himself, and wishing to put an end to that sinful man's evil courses, the Pāṇḍavas sent spies in all directions on the field of battle. Some hunters brought news of Duryodhana's whereabouts to Bhīma. Rewarding them with immense wealth, Bhīma disclosed this news to the righteous King Yudhiṣṭhira, saying, "Duryodhana, O king, has been found by the hunters who supply me with meat. He for whom you feel sorry now lies within a lake whose waters have been turned solid by him."

Thereupon, with Kṛṣṇa in the lead, Yudhiṣṭhira proceeded toward that lake, accompanied by Arjuna, the twins, Dhṛṣṭadyumna, the invincible Śikhaṇḍī,

1. Battalions.

Uttamaujus, Yudhāmanyu, the great car-warrior Sātyaki, the five sons of Draupadī, and those amongst the Pāñcālas who had survived, with all their elephants, and infantry by the hundreds.

72

Having arrived at the banks of the Dvaipāyana lake, they saw the reservoir enchanted by Duryodhana. Then Yudhiṣṭhira said to Kṛṣṇa, "Behold, the son of Dhṛtarāṣṭra has charmed these waters by his power of wizardry, and lives within them, without fear of injury." Kṛṣṇa replied, "With your own power of wizardry, O Bhārata, destroy this illusion of Duryodhana."

Then Yudhiṣṭhira derisively said to Duryodhana, who was still within the waters of the lake, "Why, O Duryodhana, have you charmed these waters, after having caused the death of all the Kṣatriyas, as well as your own family? Why have you entered this lake today, in order to save your own life? Arise and fight us, O Suyodhana!"

From the depths of the lake, Duryodhana replied, "It was not for the sake of saving my life, nor from fear, nor from grief, that I entered this lake. It was only out of fatigue that I did so. The Kurus for whose sake I desired sovereignty, those brothers of mine, all lie dead on the battlefield. This empty earth is now yours. Who could wish to rule a kingdom bereft of allies? As for myself, clad in deerskins I shall retire to the forest. Friendless as I am, I have no desire to live."

"You may now be willing, O Suyodhana," said Yudhiṣṭhira, "to make a gift of the earth to me. However, I do not wish to rule the earth as a gift from you. Before this, you would not agree to give me even so much of the earth as could be covered by the point of a needle. Either rule the earth after having defeated us, or go to the celestial regions after being slain by us."

Duryodhana said, "You Pāṇḍavas have friends, cars, and animals. I, however, am alone now, without a car or a mount. Alone as I am, and devoid of weapons, how can I venture to fight on foot against countless foes, all well armed and having cars? O Yudhiṣṭhira, fight one at a time with me. It is not fair that one should be called upon to fight with many, especially when that one is without armor, tired and wounded, and devoid of both animals and troops."

Thus challenged, Yudhiṣṭhira replied, "Fight any one of us, choosing whatever weapon you like. The rest of us will remain spectators. I grant you also this other wish of yours, that if you kill any one of us, you shall then become king. Otherwise, you shall be killed, and go to heaven."

"Brave as you are," answered Duryodhana, "if you allow me the option of fighting only one of you, I choose to fight with this mace that I have in my hand. Let any of you who thinks that he is a match for me come forward and fight me on foot, armed with mace." So saying, Duryodhana emerged from the water and stood there, mace in hand, his limbs covered with blood.

At the conclusion of this parley Kṛṣṇa, worked up with wrath, said to Yudhiṣṭhira, "Planning to kill Bhīma, O king, Duryodhana has practiced with the mace upon a statue of iron for thirteen years. Except for Bhīma, I do not at this moment see any match for Duryodhana. However, Bhīma has not practiced as hard as Duryodhana. I do not see any man in the world today, nor even a god, who can defeat the mace-armed Duryodhana in battle. In a fair fight between Duryodhana and Bhīma, our victory will be in doubt because Duryodhana is powerful, practiced, and skillful."

Bhīma was, however, more confident. He said, "I shall surely kill Duryodhana in battle. I feel that the victory of the righteous Yudhiṣṭhira is certain. This mace of mine is one and a half times as heavy as Duryodhana's. Do not give way to anxiety. I dare to fight him, selecting the mace as the weapon. All of you, O Kṛṣṇa, witness this encounter!"

After Bhīma had said these words, Kṛṣṇa joyfully applauded him and said, "Thanks to you, O mighty Bhīma, the righteous King Yudhiṣṭhira will regain prosperity after achieving the destruction of all his foes. You should, however, always fight with care against Duryodhana. He is endowed with skill and strength and loves to fight."

When the fierce duel was about to start, and when all the great Pāṇḍavas had taken their seats, Balarāma[2] came there, having heard that a battle between those two heroes, both of whom were his disciples, was about to start. Seeing him, the Pāṇḍavas and Kṛṣṇa were filled with joy. They greeted him and saluted him with due rites. They then said to him, "Witness, O Rāma, the skill in battle of your two disciples."

73

The duel then began. Duryodhana and Bhīma fought like two bulls attacking each other with their horns. The clash of their maces produced loud peals like those of thunderbolts. After the fierce and terrible battle had lasted for some time, both contenders were exhausted. They rested for some time and then, taking up their maces, they once again began to ward off each other's attacks.

While the fight was thus raging between those two heroes, Arjuna said to Kṛṣṇa, "Who, in your opinion, is the better of these two? What is their respective merit? Tell me this, O Kṛṣṇa!"

Kṛṣṇa replied, "They are equally well instructed. Bhīma is possessed of greater strength while Duryodhana has greater skill and has practiced harder. If he fights fairly, Bhīma will never succeed in gaining victory. If, however, he fights unfairly, he will surely be able to kill Duryodhana. At the time of the gambling Bhīma promised to break the thighs of Duryodhana with his mace in battle. Let him now fulfill his vow. Let him, by deception, kill the Kuru king who is the master of deception! If Bhīma does not kill him by unfair means, the son of Dhṛtarāṣṭra will surely retain the kingdom!"

Thereupon Arjuna, before Bhīma's sight, struck his own left thigh. Understanding that sign, Bhīma began to move about with his mace raised, making many kinds of maneuvers. Seeing the energetic and angry Bhīma rushing towards him and desiring to thwart his blow, Duryodhana thought of the maneuver called avasthāna, and prepared to jump upwards.

Bhīma fully understood the object of his opponent. Rushing at him, with a loud roar, he fiercely hurled his mace at Duryodhana's thighs, as the latter jumped into the air. The mace, hurled by Bhīma, broke the thighs of Duryodhana, and he fell down, so that the earth resounded.

2. Kṛṣṇa's brother, an expert mace fighter.

Having struck Duryodhana down, Bhīma approached the Kuru chief and said, "O wretch, formerly you laughed at Draupadī who had only one bit of cloth in the midst of the assembly, and you called us cows. Bear now the consequences of that insult." Saying this, he kicked the head of his fallen foe with his left foot.[3]

Balarāma became highly incensed when he saw Duryodhana thus brought down by a blow aimed at his thighs. Raising his arms, he sorrowfully said in the midst of those kings, "Oh, fie on Bhīma, that in such a fair fight a blow should have been inflicted below the navel! Never before has such a foul blow been seen in an encounter with the mace!

"Having unfairly killed the righteous King Duryodhana," Balarāma continued, "Bhīma shall be known in the world as an unfair fighter! The righteous Duryodhana, on the other hand, shall acquire eternal blessedness!"

Kṛṣṇa then said to Yudhiṣṭhira, "O king of virtue, why do you permit such a wrong act? Why do you suffer the head of the insensible and fallen Duryodhana to be thus kicked by Bhīma with his foot? Conversant as you are with the rules of morality, why do you look on this deed with indifference?"

Yudhiṣṭhira said, "O Kṛṣṇa, Bhīma's action in angrily touching the head of the fallen king with his foot does not please me, nor am I glad at this extermination of my race! But remember how we were cheated by the sons of Dhṛtarāṣṭra! Remember too the many harsh words they addressed to us, and how they sent us in exile into the forest. On account of all those things Bhīma has been nursing a great grief in his heart! Bearing all this in mind, O Kṛṣṇa, I looked on his actions with indifference!"

* * *

From Book 11

Strī [*The Book of the Women*]

81

Having lost all his sons, King Dhṛtarāṣṭra was grief-stricken. Looking like a tree shorn of its branches, he was overcome by depression and lost his power of speech. The wise Sañjaya approached the king and said to him, "Why do you grieve, O monarch? Forget your sorrow, and arrange for the due performance of the obsequial rites of your fathers, sons, grandsons, kinsmen, preceptors, and friends."

Dhṛtarāṣṭra lamented, "Deprived as I am of sons and counselors and all my friends, I shall have to wander in sorrow over the earth. In the midst of the assembly, Kṛṣṇa told me what was for my good. He said, 'Let us end hostilities, O king! Let your son take the entire kingdom, except for five villages.' Foolishly I disregarded that advice, and I am now forced to repent. I must have committed great sins in my previous births, and hence the Creator has made me suffer such grief in this life. Ask the Pāṇḍavas to come and see me this very day, determined as I am upon following the long way that leads to the regions of Brahmā."

3. The left foot and hand have sinister associations.

Though he too was grief-stricken because of the death of his own sons, Yudhiṣṭhira, accompanied by his brothers, set out to see Dhṛtarāṣṭra. He was followed by Kṛṣṇa and Sātyaki, and by Yuyutsu. The grieving princess Draupadī too, accompanied by the Pāñcāla ladies, sorrowfully followed.

Having duly saluted their sire, the Pāṇḍavas announced themselves to him, each uttering his own name. Dhṛtarāṣṭra first greeted the eldest son of Pāṇḍu, Yudhiṣṭhira, who was the cause of the slaughter of all his sons. Having embraced Yudhiṣṭhira, and spoken a few comforting words to him, the wicked Dhṛtarāṣṭra sought Bhīma, like a fire ready to burn everything that would approach it. Understanding his wicked intentions towards Bhīma, Kṛṣṇa dragged away the real Bhīma, and presented an iron statue of the second son of Pāṇḍu to the old king. Grasping with his two arms that iron statue, the powerful king broke it into pieces, taking it for the real Bhīma.

His passion gone, the king then cast off his anger and became normal. Overcome by grief, he began to weep aloud, "Alas, O Bhīma! Alas!" Knowing that he was no longer under the influence of anger, and that he was truly sorry for having, as he believed, slain Bhīma, Kṛṣṇa said, "Do not grieve, O Dhṛtarāṣṭra, for you have not killed Bhīma. What you broke was only an iron statue."

82

Then, at the request of Dhṛtarāṣṭra, the Pāṇḍava brothers, accompanied by Kṛṣṇa, went to see Gāndhārī. The innocent Gāndhārī was grief-stricken at the death of her hundred sons. Recalling that Yudhiṣṭhira had killed all his enemies, she wished to curse him. Knowing her evil intentions, Vyāsa prepared to keep them from being fulfilled.

He said to her, "Do not be angry with the Pāṇḍavas, O Gāndhārī! May you have peace! Control the words you are about to say! Listen to my counsel." Gāndhārī said, "Thanks to the folly of Duryodhana and Śakuni, of Karṇa and Duḥśāsana, this extinction of the Kurus has taken place. But in the very presence of Kṛṣṇa, Bhīma did something that excites my anger. Having challenged Duryodhana to a deadly duel with the mace, and knowing that my son was superior to him in skill, he struck him below the navel. It is this that provokes my wrath. Why should heroes forget their duties to save their lives?"

Hearing these words of Gāndhārī, Bhīma was afraid, and tried to soothe her. He said, "Whether the deed was fair or unfair, I did it through fear and to protect my own self! Please forgive me now! Your son was incapable of being killed by anybody in a fair fight. And therefore I did what was unfair."

Gāndhārī then said, "When Vṛṣasena had deprived Nakula of his horses, you drank Duḥśāsana's blood in battle. That was an act of cruelty which is censured by the good, becoming only to an unworthy person. It was an evil act, O Bhīma!"

"It is wrong to drink the blood of even a stranger," Bhīma replied. "One's brother is like one's own self, and there is no difference between them. The blood, however, did not pass my lips and teeth, as Karṇa knew well. Only my hands were covered with Duḥśāsana's blood. When Draupadī was seized by the hair after the gambling match, in my anger I gave vent to certain words which I still remember. For all the years to come I would have been deemed to have neglected the duties of a Kṣatriya if I had left that promise unfulfilled. It was for this reason, O queen, that I committed that act." Gāndhārī wailed, "You have killed a hundred sons of this old man [Dhṛtarāṣṭra]! Why did you not spare even one son of this old couple, deprived of their kingdom, who had committed only a minor offense?"

83

Filled with anger at the slaughter of all her sons and grandsons, Gāndhārī then inquired after Yudhiṣṭhira, saying, "Where is the king?" After she had asked for him, Yudhiṣṭhira approached her, trembling and with joined hands, and said these soft words, "Here is Yudhiṣṭhira, O queen, that cruel destroyer of your sons! I deserve your curses, for I am the real cause of this universal destruction! Curse me! I do not care for life, for kingdom, or for wealth, having killed such friends."

Sighing heavily, Gāndhārī could say nothing to Yudhiṣṭhira as, overcome with fear, he stood in her presence. When Yudhiṣṭhira, with body bent, was about to prostrate himself at her feet, the far-sighted Kuru queen, conversant as she was with righteousness, directed her eyes from within the folds of the cloth that covered them to the tip of Yudhiṣṭhira's toe. Thereupon, the king whose nails had till then been perfect came to have a scorched nail on his toe.[4]

Seeing this, Arjuna moved behind Kṛṣṇa, and the other Pāṇḍavas too became restless. Meanwhile Gāndhārī shook off her anger, and comforted the Pāṇḍavas as a mother should. With her permission those heroes then proceeded to see their mother.

Seeing her sons after a long time, Kuntī, who had been filled with anxiety for them, covered her face with a fold of her garment and shed copious tears. She then repeatedly embraced and patted each of her sons. Next she consoled Draupadī who had lost all her children and who was lying on the bare earth, wailing piteously. Raising the grief-stricken princess of Pāñcāla who was weeping thus, Kuntī began to comfort her.

Accompanied by Draupadī, and followed by her sons, Kuntī then proceeded towards the sorrowful Gāndhārī, though she herself was in greater sorrow. Seeing that illustrious lady with her daughter-in-law, Gāndhārī said, "Do not grieve thus, O daughter. I too am much afflicted with grief. I think this universal destruction has been caused by the irresistible course of Time. Since it was not brought about by human agency, this dreadful slaughter was inevitable. What the wise Vidura foretold, after Kṛṣṇa's supplication for peace had failed, has now come to pass!"

Gāndhārī then said to Kṛṣṇa, "The Pāṇḍavas and the sons of Dhṛtarāṣṭra have destroyed each other. Why did you look on while they were thus exterminating each other? Because you were deliberately indifferent to their destruction, you shall obtain the fruit of this act. O Kṛṣṇa, by constant service to my husband I have acquired a little merit. By that merit, which was so difficult to obtain, I now curse you. Since you remained indifferent while the Kauravas and Pāṇḍavas slew each other, O Kṛṣṇa, you shall be the slayer of your own kinsmen. Thirty-six years hence you shall, after causing the death of your kinsmen, friends, and son, perish by ignoble means in the wilderness."[5]

4. The queen's righteous anger has the power to reduce her sons' killer to ashes.

5. Gāndhārī's curse comes true, becoming the means by which the divine Kṛṣṇa ends his incarnation.

From Book 12

Śānti [*The Book of Peace*]

84

Along with Vidura, Dhṛtarāṣṭra, and all the Bhārata ladies, the Pāṇḍavas offered oblations of water to all their departed kinsmen and friends. The noble descendants of the Kurus then passed a month of purification outside the city. Many famous sages came there to see the virtuous King Yudhiṣṭhira. Among them were Vyāsa, Nārada, the great sage Devala, Devasthāna, and Kaṇva, and their worthy disciples.

Yudhiṣṭhira said, "I am haunted by grief because of the death in battle of young Abhimanyu, the sons of Draupadī, Dhṛṣṭadyumna, Virāṭa, King Drupada, Vasuṣeṇa, King Dhṛṣṭaketu, and other kings coming from various countries. I feel that, through my desire to recover my kingdom, I caused the destruction of my kinsmen and the extermination of my own race. I am an evildoer and a sinner and the cause of the destruction of the earth. Seated as I am now, I shall starve myself to death."

Vyāsa consoled Yudhiṣṭhira, saying, "You should not, O king, grieve so. I shall repeat what I have once said. All this is Destiny. Do what you have been created to do by your Maker. That is your fulfillment. Remember, O king, you are not your own master.

"O king, do not indulge in grief!" Vyāsa continued. "Remember the duties of a Kṣatriya. All those fighters were killed while performing their legitimate duties. You too have performed the duties of a Kṣatriya and obtained the kingdom blamelessly. Do your duty now, O son of Kuntī, and you shall obtain happiness in the next world." Thus was Yudhiṣṭhira comforted, and persuaded to return to his kingdom.

When the Pāṇḍavas reentered the city, many thousands of citizens came out to greet them. Entering the interior of the palace, the illustrious Yudhiṣṭhira approached the deities and worshiped them with offerings of gems and incense and garlands of all kinds.

Freed of his grief and his sickness of heart, Yudhiṣṭhira cheerfully sat facing eastward on an excellent seat made of gold. Those two heroes, Sātyaki and Kṛṣṇa, sat facing him on a seat covered by a rich carpet. On either side of the king sat the great-minded Bhīma and Arjuna upon two soft seats set with gems. Upon a white ivory couch, decked with gold, sat Kuntī with Sahadeva and Nakula.

Then by Kṛṣṇa's leave the priest Dhaumya consecrated, according to rule, an altar facing the east and the north. He next seated the great Yudhiṣṭhira and Draupadī upon a soft seat covered with a tiger-skin, called Sarvatobhadra. Thereafter he began to pour libations of clarified butter upon the sacrificial fire while chanting the prescribed incantations. King Dhṛtarāṣṭra was first to anoint Yudhiṣṭhira and all the others followed him. Thus worshiped by those pious men, Yudhiṣṭhira the king of virtue, with his friends, was restored to his kingdom.

Accepting the greetings of his subjects, King Yudhiṣṭhira answered them, saying: "Blessed are the sons of Pāṇḍu, whose merits, deservedly or otherwise, are thus recited in this world by the foremost of Brāhmaṇas assembled together. King Dhṛtarāṣṭra, however, is our father and supreme deity. Those who wish to please me should obey his commands and respect his every wish. The whole world is his, as are the Pāṇḍavas, and everybody else. These words of mine should be borne in mind by all of you."

Having given the citizens and the villagers leave to depart, the Kuru king appointed his brother Bhīma as yuvarāja.[6] He gladly appointed the highly intelligent Vidura to help him with advice and to look after the sixfold requirements[7] of the state. The venerable Sañjaya, wise and thoughtful and endued with every accomplishment, was designated as the superintendent of finances.

Nakula was placed in charge of the forces, to give them food and pay and to look after the other affairs of the army. Yudhiṣṭhira made Arjuna responsible for resisting hostile forces and punishing the wicked. Dhaumya, the foremost of priests, was asked to attend to the Brāhmaṇas and to perform all Vedic rites and all other rites. Sahadeva was always to remain by Yudhiṣṭhira's side, as his protector.

6. Crown prince.
7. Peace, war, military expeditions, cease-fire, instigating strife among enemies, and the defense of the kingdom.

THE BHAGAVAD-GĪTĀ

ca. fourth century B.C.E.–fourth century C.E.

The *Bhagavad-gītā* asks the most difficult of questions. What is a just war, and when can the use of armed conflict to resolve a political stalemate be justified? Under what circumstances is it possible to engage in a violent conflict with family members, clansmen, teachers, and friends—the very people who have nurtured us since infancy—and claim a victory that is morally right? What is such a victory worth if, in the name of life, wealth, or truth, it destroys what we love? As a philosophical poem, the *Bhagavad-gītā* does not provide simple answers but offers explanations that are appropriately difficult because they involve dilemmas that cannot be resolved once and for all.

CONTEXT

During the past two centuries, it has become commonplace to treat the *Bhagavad-gītā* as an independent poem, which can be read and understood by itself for its philosophical message as a meditation on universal issues. But the work is actually an integral part of the *Mahābhārata*, and was originally composed as the sixty-third minor book of that epic, and included in its sixth major book, *Bhīṣma*. Since it is a poem within a poem, the *Bhagavad-gītā* is best interpreted in relation to the epic's larger narrative, setting, and background.

The *Mahābhārata* is attributed to a single poet or compiler named Kṛṣṇa Dvaipāyana, but it was composed collaboratively by many generations of poets in Sanskrit between about 400 B.C.E. and 400 C.E. Its main story concerns a protracted conflict between two branches of a royal dynasty in northern India, over the inheritance of a kingdom and the succession to its throne. The embattled groups are the Kauravas and the

Pāṇḍavas, who are paternal cousins; the Kauravas are one hundred brothers, led by their eldest, Duryodhana, whereas the Pāṇḍavas are five half brothers, the three eldest being Yudhiṣṭhira, Bhīma, and Arjuna. Both branches have strong and legitimate claims to the kingdom, and one possible settlement is a division of the dominion, so that each set of cousins can rule its own territory without conflict. But Duryodhana and his brothers, the Kauravas, resist such a solution; using a variety of strategies, they deny the Pāṇḍavas' claim, and send the five brothers and their shared wife (in a polyandrous marriage) into a thirteen-year exile, with the promise to restore their share of territory if they meet several conditions. The Pāṇḍavas complete their exile as required, but when they return to Duryodhana's court, he refuses to honor his word.

At this point in the main narrative, Lord Kṛṣṇa—a human avatar of Viṣṇu, the god who primarily preserves the moral order of the universe—intervenes on behalf of the Pāṇḍavas. In the course of his life in human form, Kṛṣṇa became a close friend of the third Pāṇḍava, Arjuna, in his youth; now, many years later, when Arjuna and his half brothers find themselves in an impossible situation with their cousins, Kṛṣṇa agrees to serve as their ambassador to Duryodhana. Even though Kṛṣṇa (whose divinity is evident to the other characters in the epic) offers the Kauravas a peaceable solution in accordance with *dharma* (law, morality, duty, obligation), Duryodhana refuses to give the Pāṇḍavas even five small villages as their share of the kingdom. In consultation with Kṛṣṇa, the Pāṇḍavas decide that the only way in which they can now assert their legitimate claim to the kingdom is by going to war with the Kauravas. This is a just war because their claim is based strictly on the *dharma* of succession and inheritance; and it is a justifiable war because they have exhausted every possibility of a peaceful resolution of the stalemate with the Kauravas.

The Kauravas and Pāṇḍavas then prepare for armed conflict, and their respective armies gather on the battlefield of Kurukṣetra (about sixty-five miles north of modern Delhi). Arjuna, the most skilled and feared archer of his times, enters the battlefield on a chariot, with Kṛṣṇa serving as his charioteer. But in the moments just before the battle begins, Arjuna looks at the forces arrayed on the enemy side, and sees in their midst all his cousins as well as many people he grew up with—teachers, friends, and members of his clan, people he has known and loved much of his life. Faced with the prospect of shedding their blood, he throws down his weapons and refuses to fight; he cannot imagine how any such war could possibly be good or right. But, in doing so, he immediately places himself in moral jeopardy as a warrior, because *dharma* requires that a *kṣatriya* be prepared to wage war whenever necessary, and in this case his cause is just. Caught between his fundamental duty as a warrior and his equally powerful obligation to preserve the lives of those he loves, Arjuna turns to Kṛṣṇa—his friend, aide, and counselor—and asks for his divine advice under the circumstances. The *Bhagavad-gītā* is the poetic record of that moment of crisis in Arjuna's mind, and of the conversation he has with God on the brink of war.

WORK

The *Bhagavad-gītā* is divided into eighteen chapters or cantos composed in verse, and its total length runs to seven hundred couplets. In the translation from which our selection of passages is drawn, each canto is called a "chapter"; it contains, in part, Kṛṣṇa's instruction to Arjuna about what is involved in war, violence, duty, courage, life, and death (among other things), and why it is essential to fight a just war, even if it means destroying precious lives.

The structure of the *Bhagavad-gītā* as a whole has two layers of interspersed dialogue: one between Sañjaya and Dhṛtarāṣṭra, which defines the outer frame of the book, and the other between Arjuna and Kṛṣṇa, which occurs in an inner frame. Dhṛtarāṣṭra is the father of the Kauravas and the current head of the dynasty; he is blind and old, and cannot participate in or even observe the battle. He sits in his chariot on the edge of the battlefield with his charioteer, a youth named Sañjaya; on the eve of the war, Dvaipāyana, the original author of the *Mahābhārata*, grants Sañjaya "celestial vision," so that he can omnisciently observe everything in the past, present, and future, and everything that happens on the battlefield, in public and in private; throughout the eighteen days of the war, Sanjaya tells the blind Dhṛtarāṣṭra what happens in the war, and we, the readers, also witness the entire conflict through Sañjaya's "visionary eye." Our excerpts here mostly omit the dialogue between Sañjaya and Dhṛtarāṣṭra in the various cantos; the main exception is the passage from Chapter Eleven, which ends with a portion of Sañjaya's narrative.

In the excerpt from Chapter One we hear Arjuna's voice, explaining to Kṛṣṇa at length why he is unable to take up arms against his blood relatives, mentors, and friends. In the segments from Chapter Two, Kṛṣṇa begins his response to Arjuna's dilemma by explaining the nature of the imperishable self or soul embodied in every human being. In the portions reproduced from Chapter Three, Arjuna raises fresh questions about human action in relation to the inner self and to evil, and Kṛṣṇa teaches him the yoga or discipline of action, especially as it should be practiced by a warrior. In the next excerpt, which jumps ahead to Chapter Six, Kṛṣṇa then explains what self-discipline in general is, and what a man who establishes complete control over himself can accomplish. In the final passage, drawn from Chapter Eleven, Arjuna achieves a comprehensive, new understanding of his task as a warrior, and asks Kṛṣṇa to reveal his full divine form; Kṛṣṇa does so, but the vision is so intense that a merely human eye cannot experience it. The narrator Sanjaya, talking to King Dhṛtarāṣṭra, therefore intercedes with his extraordinary visual capacity, and reports, in part, what Kṛṣṇa reveals to Arjuna.

The passages from the *Bhagavad-gītā* reproduced here cover only a small portion of Lord Kṛṣṇa's advice to Arjuna on the battlefield of Kurukṣetra. In the course of the eighteen cantos of the book, Kṛṣṇa constructs a long argument, containing many strands, about the justification for violence in the context of a war that is morally right and in complete accordance with all applicable aspects of *dharma*. Especially when encountered in excerpts, this argument can be, and often has been, easily misunderstood. Kṛṣṇa emphatically does *not* offer a general justification for violence under all circumstances; the use of violence to settle a major dispute can be justified only when every possible option for a peaceful resolution has been explored within the full scope of the law, and all such options have failed. Moreover, in a just war, only the thoroughly trained and disciplined warrior can use violence, and even he can do so only when he is in complete control of himself, and selflessly pursues his duty as defined by *dharma*.

From The Bhagavad-gītā[1]

CHAPTER ONE[2]

* * *

20 "Now Monkey-Bannered Arjuna,[3]
seeing his foes drawn up for war,
raised his bow, that Son of Pandu,
as the weapons began to clash.

21 "Then he said these words to Krishna:[4]
'Lord of the Earth, Unshaken One,
bring my chariot to a halt
between the two adverse armies,

22 'so I may see these men, arrayed
here for the battle they desire,
whom I am soon to undertake
a warrior's delight in fighting!

23 'I see those who have assembled,
the warriors prepared to fight,
eager to perform in battle
for Dhritarashtra's evil son!'[5]

24 "When Arjuna had spoken so
to Krishna, O Bharata,[6]
he, having brought their chariot
to a halt between the armies,

25 "in the face of Bhishma, Drona,[7]
and the other Lords of the Earth,[8]
said, 'Behold, O Son of Pritha,[9]
how these Kurus[1] have assembled!'

26 "And there the son of Pritha saw
rows of grandfathers and grandsons;

1. Translated by Gavin Flood and Charles Martin. Verse numbers run to the left of the text.
2. Most of the *Bhagavad-gītā* is narrated by Sañjaya; the double quotation marks throughout these excerpts represent Sanjaya's direct speech, addressed to Dhṛtarāṣtra. For an explanation of these two characters, who define the outer narrative frame of the poem, see the "Work" section of the headnote. The single quotation marks represent the dialogue between Arjuna and Kṛṣṇa, which takes place within Sanjaya's narrative.
3. The third of the five sons of Pāṇḍu.
4. An incarnation of Viṣṇu, the preserver god.
5. Duryodhana, the leader of the Kauravas, who is the eldest son of Dhṛtarāṣṭra.
6. An alternate name or epithet for Dhṛtarāṣṭra, who, like his brother Pāṇḍu and their respective sons, is a descendant of Bhārata, the founder of their dynasty of kings.
7. Droṇa was the teacher or guru of both the Kauravas and the Pāṇḍavas; Bhīṣma is the granduncle of both these branches of the family.
8. "Lord of the earth" is a common epithet for a king in epic Sanskrit.
9. Another name for Kuṅtī, the mother of Arjuna and the Pāṇḍavas.
1. Another name for the Kauravas.

sons and fathers, uncles, in-laws;
teachers, brothers and companions,

27 "all relatives and friends of his
in both of the assembled armies.
And seeing them arrayed for war,
Arjuna, the Son of Kunti,

28 "felt for them a great compassion,
as well as great despair, and said,
'O Krishna, now that I have seen
my relatives so keen for war,

29 'I am unstrung: my limbs collapse
beneath me, and my mouth is dry,
there is a trembling in my body,
and my hair rises, bristling;

30 'Gandiva, my immortal bow,[2]
drops from my hand and my skin burns,
I cannot stand upon my feet,
my mind rambles in confusion—

31 'All inauspicious are the signs
that I see, O Handsome-Haired One![3]
I foresee no good resulting
from slaughtering my kin in war!

32 'I have no wish for victory,
nor for kingship and its pleasures!
O Krishna, what good is kingship?
What good even life and pleasure?

33 'Those for whose sake we desire
kingship, pleasures and enjoyments,
are now drawn up in battle lines,
their lives and riches now abandoned:

34 'fathers, grandfathers; sons, grandsons;
my mother's brothers and the men
who taught me in my youth; brothers-
and fathers-in-law, kinsmen all!

35 'Though they are prepared to slay us,
I do not wish to murder them,
not even to rule the three worlds—
how much less one earthly kingdom?

2. A powerful celestial bow of great antiquity and renown that Arjuna won from the fire god, Agni.

3. Kṛṣṇa is often depicted with long, flowing hair.

36 'What joy for us in murdering
Dhritarashtra's sons, O Krishna?
for if we killed these murderers,
evil like theirs would cling to us!

37 'So we cannot in justice slay
our kinsmen, Dhritarashtra's sons,
for, having killed our people, how
could we be pleased, O Madhava?[4]

38 'Even if they, mastered by greed,
are blind to the consequences
of the family's destruction,
of friendships lost to treachery,

39 'how are we not to comprehend
that we must turn back from evil?
The wrong done by this destruction
is evident, O Shaker of Men.

40 'For with the family destroyed,
its eternal laws must perish;
and when they perish, lawlessness
overwhelms the whole family.

41 'Whelmed by lawlessness, the women
of the family are corrupted;
from corrupted women comes
the intermingling of classes.[5]

42 'Such intermingling sends to hell
the family and its destroyers:
their ancestors fall then, deprived
of rice and water offerings.[6]

43 'Those who destroy the family,
who institute class-mingling,
cause the laws of the family
and laws of caste to be abolished.

44 'Men whose familial laws have been
obliterated, O Krishna,
are damned to dwell eternally
in hell, as we have often heard.

4. One of Viṣṇu's 1,008 names in Hindu ritual and mythology, meaning "the one sweet as honey."

5. "Intermingling" here refers to miscegenation, and "classes" to caste-groups. The caste system is based on endogamy, or marriage within a caste-group (*varṇa*) or caste (*jātī*); only if both partners come from the same social category can that category be reproduced in the next generation. Here Kṛṣṇa affirms that if two spouses belong to different social categories (*varṇa* or *jātī*), then their children do not belong to the same category as their parents, and hence undermine the "laws of caste."

6. Hindus are required to make these ritual offerings to their ancestors.

45 'It grieves me that as we intend
to murder our relatives
in our greed for pleasures, kingdoms,
we are fixed on doing evil!

46 'If the sons of Dhritarashtra,
armed as they are, should murder me
weaponless and unresisting,
I would know greater happiness!'

47 "And having spoken, Arjuna
collapsed into his chariot,
his bow and arrows clattering,
and his mind overcome with grief."

CHAPTER TWO

* * *

"The Lord[7] said:

11 'Although you seem to speak wisely,
you have mourned those not to be mourned:
the wise do not grieve for those gone
or for those who are not yet gone.

12 'There was no time when I was not,
nor you, nor these lords around us,
and there will never be a time
henceforth when we shall not exist.

13 'The embodied one passes through
childhood, youth, and then old age,
then attains another body;
in this the wise are undeceived.[8]

14 'Contacts with matter by which we
feel heat and cold, pleasure and pain,
are transitory, come and go:
these you must manage to endure.

15 'Such contacts do not agitate
a wise man, O Bull among Men,
to whom pleasure and pain are one.
He is fit for immortality.

16 'Non-being cannot come to be,
nor can what is come to be not.
The certainty of these sayings
is known by seers of the truth.

7. Lord Kṛṣṇa, who now addresses Arjuna.

8. Here Kṛṣṇa explains the process of reincarnation, emphasizing the identity of the seemingly finite embodied soul (*ātman*) with the infinite and imperishable universal spirit or godhead (*Brahman*).

17 'Know it as indestructible,
that by which all is pervaded;
no one may cause the destruction
of the imperishable one.

18 'Bodies of the embodied one,
eternal, boundless, all-enduring,
are said to die; the one cannot:
therefore, take arms, O Bharata!

19 'This man believes the one may kill;
That man believes it may be killed;
both of them lack understanding:
it can neither kill nor be killed.

20 'It is not born, nor is it ever mortal,
and having been, will not pass from existence;
ancient, unborn, eternally existing,
it does not die when the body perishes.

21 'How can a man who knows the one
to be eternal (both unborn
and without end) murder or cause
another to? Whom does he kill?

22 'Someone who has abandoned worn-out garments
sets out to clothe himself in brand new raiment;
just so, when it has cast off worn-out bodies,
the embodied one will encounter others.

23 'This may not be pierced by weapons,
nor can this be consumed by flames;
flowing waters cannot drench this,
nor blowing winds desiccate this.

24 'Not to be pierced, not to be burned,
neither drenched nor desiccated—
eternal, all-pervading, firm,
unmoving, everlasting this!

25 'This has been called unmanifest,
unthinkable and unchanging;
therefore, because you know this now,
you should not lament, Arjuna.

26 'But even if you think that this
is born and dies time after time,
forever, O great warrior,
not even then should you mourn this.

27 'Death is assured to all those born,
and birth assured to all the dead;

you should not mourn what is merely
inevitable consequence.

28 'Beginnings are unmanifest,
but manifest the middle-state,
and ends unmanifest again;
so what is your complaint about?

29 'Somebody looks upon this as a marvel,
and likewise someone tells about this marvel,
and yet another hears about this marvel,
but even having heard it, no one knows it.

30 'The one cannot ever perish
in a body it inhabits,
O Descendent of Bharata;
and so no being should be mourned.

31 'Nor should you tremble to perceive
your duty as a warrior;
for him there is nothing better
than a battle that is righteous.

32 'And if by chance they will have gained
the wide open gate of heaven,
O Son of Pritha, warriors
rejoice in fighting such as that!

33 'If you turn from righteous warfare,
your behavior will be evil,
for you will have abandoned both
your duty and your honored name.

34 'People will speak of your disgrace
forever, and an honored man
who falls from honor into shame
suffers a fate much worse than death.

* * *

47 "'Your concern should be with action,
never with an action's fruits;
these should never motivate you,
nor attachment to inaction.

48 'Established in this practice, act
without attachment, Arjuna,
unmoved by failure or success!
Equanimity is yoga.

49 'Action is far inferior
to the practice of higher mind;

seek refuge there, for pitiful
are those moved by fruit of action!

50 'One disciplined by higher mind
here casts off good and bad actions;
therefore, be yoked to discipline;
discipline is skill in actions.

51 'Having left the fruit of action,
the wise ones yoked to higher mind
are freed from the bonds of rebirth,
and go where no corruption is.

52 'When your higher mind has crossed
over the thicket of delusion,
you will become disenchanted
with what is heard in the Vedas.[9]

53 'When, unvexed by revelation,
your higher mind is motionless
and stands fixed in meditation,
then you will attain discipline.'

"Arjuna asked,

54 'Tell me, Krishna, how may I know
the man steady in his wisdom,
who abides in meditation?
How should that one sit, speak and move?'

"The Blessed Lord replied,

55 'When he renounces all desires
entering his mind, Arjuna,
and his self rests within the Self,[1]
then his wisdom is called steady.

56 'He who is not agitated
by suffering or by desires,
freed from anger, fear and passions,
is called a sage of steady mind.

57 'Who is wholly unimpassioned,
not rejoicing in the pleasant,
nor rejecting the unpleasant,
is established in his wisdom.

9. Kṛṣṇa suggests here that the older ritualistic knowledge embodied in the Vedas is useless for the liberation of the individual self or soul from the bondage of karma.
1. This is a play on the word *ātman*, which means both "the self" (soul) and "oneself." Kṛṣṇa now begins to describe the techniques for and effects of "withdrawing" one's senses from interaction with the external world and focusing them instead on the interior self.

58 'And when this one wholly withdraws
all his senses from their objects,
as a tortoise draws in its limbs,
his wisdom is well-established.'"

* * *

CHAPTER THREE

"Arjuna said:

1 'If you regard the intellect
as superior to action,
why urge me, O Handsome-Haired One,
into actions so appalling?

2 'By your equivocating speech,
my mind is, as it were, confused.
Tell me this one thing, and clearly:
By what means may I reach the best?'

"The Blessed Lord said:

3 'As I have previously taught,
there are two paths, O Blameless One:
there is the discipline of knowledge
and the discipline of action.

4 'Not by not acting in this world
does one become free from action,
nor does one approach perfection
by renunciation only.

5 'Not even for a moment does
someone exist without acting.
Even against one's will, one acts
by the nature-born qualities.[2]

6 'He who has restrained his senses,
but sits and summons back to mind
the sense-objects, is said to be
a self-deluding hypocrite.

7 'But he whose mind controls his senses,
who undertakes the discipline
of action by the action-organs,
without attachment, is renowned.

2. There are three such primary qualities: *sattva* (purity, light), *rajas* (passion, heat), and *tamas* (inertia, darkness).

8 'You must act as bid, for action
is better than non-action is:
not even functions of the body
could be sustained by non-action.

9 'This world is bound by action, save
for action which is sacrifice;
therefore, O Son of Kunti, act
without attachment to your deeds.

10 'When Prajapati brought forth life,
he brought forth sacrifice as well,
saying, "By this may you produce,
may this be your wish-fulfilling cow."[3]

11 'Nourish the gods with sacrifice,
and they will nourish you as well.
By nourishing each other, you
will realize the highest good.

12 'Nourished by sacrifice, the gods
will give the pleasures you desire.
One who enjoys such gifts without
repaying them is just a thief.

13 'The good, who eat of the remains
from sacrifice, rise up faultless.
But the wicked, who cook only
for their own sakes, eat their own filth.

14 'Beings come to exist by food,
which emanates from the rain god,
who comes to be by sacrifice,
which arises out of action.

15 'Know that action comes from Brahman,
Brahman comes from the eternal;
so the all-pervading Brahman
is based in sacrifice forever.

16 'One who in this world does not turn
the wheel, thus setting it in motion,
lives uselessly, O Son of Pritha,
a sensual, malicious life.

3. In Vedic religion, Prajapati is the god (creator) of all mortal creatures. In Hindu mythology generally, *kāmadhenu* is a celestial cow who has the power to fulfill the wishes of anyone who worships her. Here Prajāpatī suggests that the act of sacrificing is itself like a wish-granting *kāmadhenu*. In the Vedic worldview, the preservation of the universe depends on the sacrifices made to the gods, and such ritual was at the center of the religion.

17 'But the man whose only pleasure
and satisfaction is the self,
which is his sole contentment too,
has no task he must accomplish.

18 'That man finds no significance
in what has, or has not, been done;
moreover, he does not depend
on any being whatsoever.

19 'Therefore, act without attachment
in whatever situation,
for by the practice of detached
action, one attains the highest.

20 'Only by action Janaka[4]
and the others reached perfection.
In order to maintain the world,
your obligation is to act.

21 'Whatever the best leader does
the rank and file will also do;
everyone will fall in behind
the standard such a leader sets.

22 'O Son of Pritha, there is nought
that I need do in the three worlds,[5]
nor anything I might attain;
and yet I take part in action.

23 'For if I were not always to
engage in action ceaselessly,
men everywhere would soon follow
in my path, O Son of Pritha.

24 'Should I not engage in action,
these worlds would perish, utterly;
I would cause a great confusion,
and destroy all living beings.

25 'The unwise are attached to action
even as they act, Arjuna;
so, for the welfare of the world,
the wise should act with detachment.'"

* * *

4. Celebrated character in the dialogues of the *Bṛhadāraṇyaka Upaniṣad;* an exemplar of the warrior-king who is also a man of discipline (a yogi).

5. Heaven, earth, and the underworld.

"Arjuna said:

36 'Say what impels a man to do
such evil, Krishna, what great force
urges him, forces him into it,
even if he is unwilling?'

"The Blessed Lord said:

37 'Know that the enemy is this:
desire, anger, whose origins
are in the quality of passion,
all consuming, greatly harmful.

38 'As fire is obscured by smoke,
or by dust, a mirror's surface,
or an embryo by its membrane,
so this is covered up by that.

39 'Knowledge is constantly obscured
by this enemy of the wise,
by this insatiable fire
whose form, Arjuna, is desire.

40 'The senses, mind, and intellect
are its abode, as it is said.
Having obscured knowledge with these,
it deludes the embodied one.

41 'When you have subdued your senses,
then, O Bull of the Bharatas,
kill this demon, the destroyer
of all knowledge and discernment.

42 'Senses are said to be important,
but mind is higher than they are,
and intellect is above mind;
but Self is greater than all these.

43 'So knowing it to be supreme,
and sustaining the self with Self,
slay the foe whose form is desire,
so hard to conquer, Arjuna.'"

CHAPTER SIX

* * *

10 "'The yogi should be self-subdued
always, and stand in solitude,
alone, controlled in thought and self,
without desires or possessions.

11 'Having established for himself
a steady seat in a pure place,
neither too high nor yet too low,
covered with grass, deer hide and cloth,

12 'with his mind sharpened to one point,
with thought and senses both subdued,
there he should sit, doing yoga
so as to purify the self,

13 'keeping his head, neck and body
aligned, erect and motionless,
gaze fixed on the tip of his nose,
not looking off distractedly,

14 'now fearless and with tranquil self,
firm in avowed celibacy,
with his thought focused on myself,
he should sit, devoted to me.

15 'Thus always chastening himself
the yogi's mind, subdued, knows peace,
whose farthest point is cessation;
thereafter, he abides in me.

16 'Yoga is not for the greedy,
nor yet for the abstemious;
not for one too used to sleeping,
nor for the sleepless, Arjuna.

17 'Yoga destroys the pain of one
temperate in his behavior,
in his food and recreation,
and in his sleep and waking too.

18 'After his thought has been subdued,
and abides only in the Self,
free from all longing and desire,
then he is said to be steadfast.

19 '"Like a lamp in a windless place
unflickering," is the likeness
of the yogi subdued in thought,
performing yoga of the Self.

20 'Where all thought comes to cease, restrained
by the discipline of yoga,
where, by the self, the Self is seen,
one is satisfied in the Self.

21 'When he knows that eternal joy
grasped only by the intellect,

beyond the senses where he dwells,
he does not deviate from truth;

22 'having attained it, he believes
there is no gain superior;
abiding there, he is unmoved
even by profound suffering.

23 'Let him know that the dissolving
of the union with suffering
is called yoga, to be practiced
with persistence, mind undaunted.

24 'Having abandoned all desires
born to satisfy intentions,
and having utterly restrained
the many senses by the mind,

25 'Gradually let him find rest,
his intellect under control,
his mind established in the Self,
not thinking about anything.

26 'Having subdued the unsteady
mind in motion, he should lead it
back from wherever it strays to,
into the domain of the Self.

27 'Supreme joy comes to the yogi
of calm mind and tranquil passion,
who has become one with Brahman
and is wholly free of evil.

28 'Constantly controlling himself,
the yogi, freed from evil now,
swiftly attains perpetual
joy of contact here with Brahman.

29 'He whose self is yoked by yoga
and who perceives sameness always,
will see the Self in all beings
and see all beings in the Self.

30 'I am not lost for someone who
perceives my presence everywhere,
and everything perceives in me,
nor is that person lost for me.

31 'The yogi firmly set in oneness
who worships me in all beings,
whatever the path that he takes,
will nonetheless abide in me.

32 'The yogi who sees all the same
analogous to his own Self
in happiness or suffering
is thought supreme, O Arjuna.'"

Summary In Chapters Seven through Ten, Krishna explains diverse aspects of the nature of the infinite spirit, gradually unveiling the mystery of his own identity as the highest manifestation of that universal spirit and thus leading up to the revelation of his cosmic form in Chapter Eleven.

CHAPTER ELEVEN

"Arjuna said,

1 'As a result of your kindness
in speaking of that greatest secret
recognized as the Supreme Self,
I have been left undeluded.

2 'I have, in detail, heard you speak
Of creatures' origins and ends,
and of your eternal greatness,
O One of Lotus-Petal-Eyes.

3 'This is just as you have spoken
about yourself, O Supreme Lord.
I desire to behold your
lordly form, O Supreme Spirit.

4 'If you think it is possible
for me to see this, then, O God,
O Lord of Yoga, allow me
to behold your eternal Self!'

"The Blessed Lord said,

5 'O Son of Pritha, look upon
my hundredfold, no, thousandfold
forms various and celestial,
forms of diverse shapes and colors!

6 'Behold the Adityas and Vasus,
the Rudras, Ashvins and Maruts,[6]
many unseen previously!
Behold these wonders, Arjuna!

7 'Here behold all the universe,
beings moving and motionless,

6. Groups of Hindu deities: Adityas are sun gods; Vasus are elemental deities; Rudras are wind gods; the Ashvins are twin gods of sunrise and sunset; and the Maruts are storm gods.

standing as one in my body,
and all else that you wish to see!

8 'Because you are unable to
behold me with your mortal eye,
I give you one that is divine:
Behold my majestic power!'"

Sanjaya[7] said,

9 "And after saying this, O King,
Vishnu, the great Lord of Yoga,
revealed his supreme, majestic
form to him, the Son of Pritha.

10 "That form has many eyes and mouths,
and many wonders visible,
with many sacred ornaments,
and many sacred weapons raised.

11 "Clothed in sacred wreaths and garments,
with many sacred fragrances,
and comprising every wonder,
the infinite, omniscient god!

12 "If in the sky a thousand suns
should have risen all together,
the brilliance of it would be like
the brilliance of that Great-Souled One.

13 "And then the Son of Pandu saw
the universe standing as one,
divided up in diverse ways,
embodied in the god of gods."

* * *

"Arjuna said:

43 'Father of all the world, the still and moving,
you are what it worships and its teacher;
with none your match, how could there be one greater
in the three worlds, O Power-Without-Equal?

44 'Making obeisance, lying in prostration,
I beg your indulgence, praiseworthy ruler;
as father to son, as one friend to another,
as lover to beloved, show your mercy!

7. The bard who is narrating the events of the battle to King Dhṛtarāṣṭra.

45 'I am pleased to have seen what never has been
seen before, yet my mind quakes in its terror:
show me, O God, your human form; have mercy,
O Lord of Gods, abode of all the cosmos!

46 'I wish to see you even as I did once,
wearing a diadem, with mace and discus;
assume that form now wherein you have four arms,
O thousand-armed, of every form the master!'

"The Blessed Lord said,

47 'For you, Arjuna, by my grace and favor,
this highest form is brought forth by my power,
of splendor made, universal, endless, primal,
and never seen before by any other.

48 'Not Vedic sacrifice nor recitation,
gifts, rituals, strenuous austerities,
will let this form of mine be seen by any
mortal but you, O Hero of the Kurus!

49 'You should not tremble, nor dwell in confusion
at seeing such a terrible appearance.
With your fears banished and your mind now cheerful,
look once again upon my form, Arjuna.'

Sanjaya said,

50 "So Krishna, having spoken to Arjuna,
stood before him once more in his own aspect;
having resumed again a gentle body,
the Great Soul calmed the one who had been frightened.

"Arjuna said,

51 'Seeing once again your gentle,
human form now, I am composed,
O Agitator of Mankind;
my mind is restored to normal.'

"The Blessed Lord said,

52 'It is difficult to see this
aspect of me that you have seen;
even the gods are forever
desirous of seeing it.

53 'Not by studying the Vedas,
nor even by austerities,
and not by gifts or sacrifice,
may I be seen as you saw me;

54 'but by devotion undisturbed
can I be truly seen and known,
and entered into, Arjuna,
O Scorcher of the Enemy!

55 'Who acts for me, depends on me,
devoutly, without attachment
or hatred for another being,
comes to me, O Son of Pandu!' "

THE JĀTAKA

fourth century B.C.E.

In the fable of the goose with golden eggs, a farmer finds that one of his geese lays a golden egg each day; wanting to get rich faster, he kills the bird for all the gold inside it, but finds nothing, and hence loses even his daily income. This story comes to us from one of ***Aesop*'s fables** in ancient Greece, but it also has an astonishing parallel in the *Jātaka* tale "The Golden Goose," told by Buddhists in ancient India. Greeks and Indians seem to have invented a narrative with the same ideas (a goose, an unlimited supply of gold) and the same moral (greed undoes itself), at almost the same time—the middle of the first millennium B.C.E., before they had any direct contact with each other in historical times.

CONTEXT

The *Jātaka,* a set of 547 tales, is one of the books in the canon of Buddhist scripture. The canon of Theravada Buddhism, composed in Pali, and known as the *Tipiṭaka,* is divided into three main parts: Vinaya (texts concerning discipline, for monks and nuns), Sutta (texts of sermons or sayings, mostly of Siddhartha-Gautama Buddha), and Abhidhamma (texts of speculative philosophy or "higher teaching"). The *Jātaka* is included in the Sutta, because it is believed to be a record of the Buddha's actions in the world in his previous lives. Like other texts in the canon, it is an anonymous work of collective authorship, composed over several generations after the Buddha's death (fifth century B.C.E.).

Theravada Buddhists use Pali as the uniform language of their scripture and its accompanying commentary. Pali emerged in the first millennium B.C.E. as one of several distinct Prakrits ("natural languages"), which are closely related to refined Sanskrit but much simpler than it; unlike Sanskrit, which was not usually spoken, except by priests, scholars, and courtiers under special circumstances, the Prakrits were the common spoken languages of the ancient period. Pali could therefore be used to preach to ordinary people, and it became central to the egalitarian mission of Theravada Buddhism as a "way of life" that can be adopted by anybody. As narratives recorded in a colloquial medium, the *Jātaka* tales have performed several essential functions in this context. They have been used in sermons to engage audiences, much like the parables from the life of Jesus in Christianity, and they have been the objects of meditation as well as philosophical analysis. They have also enabled the Buddha's common followers to commemorate and reflect on his exemplary life (or many lives), even as they have circulated like popular folktales and fables, bringing his message to the populace at large.

The *Jātaka* tales take it for granted that living creatures transmigrate from one life to another, as a consequence of the law of karma. According to this law, every act that a human being performs in the world "bears fruit," or has a good or bad moral effect; the cumulative good and evil from a person's lifetime of deeds supposedly attach to his or her *ātman*, inner self or soul. If, at the moment of physical death, the sum of a person's good deeds outweighs the sum of evil actions, the self is ready for "salvation"; but if evil exceeds goodness, the self is reborn in the world in a new body (and, possibly, as a different life-form), with an opportunity to perform good and earn salvation over a whole new lifetime.

When a self is reborn—or transmigrates into another life—it carries with it all the residual good and evil from the previous life; the reborn person therefore has to do enough good in the new life not only to exceed the evil that he or she will inevitably do in the present, but also to wipe out the excess of evil from the preceding lifetime. So, even as a new lifetime offers an opportunity to do good and achieve salvation, it also substantially increases the chances of failure, because it is notoriously difficult to do good in the world even without a backlog of evil to overcome. Most human selves in the world therefore are likely to be reborn again and again, trapped in their karma. But, as "The Hare's Self-Sacrifice" tells us below, whether human selves do or do not break free of transmigration, their existence is determined "according to their deeds."

WORK

The *Jātaka* tales consistently adopt the view that all living creatures seek liberation from the cycle of lifetimes by pursuing goodness. To this purpose, it depicts the Buddha (Siddhartha-Gautama) in numerous human and animal forms in his lifetimes before he finally attained Enlightenment (a state of complete understanding of the nature of reality, the created universe, and human life), which gave him the means to break through the "bondage" of karma and rebirth. In the first story reproduced here, he is born as a *brāhmaṇa* and then reborn as a golden goose; in the second story, he is a hare; in the third, a monkey; and, in each case, the form he takes is "endowed with consciousness of its former existences." Each tale is then about the goodness that the Buddha conscientiously accumulated in a particular form and life, preparatory to the lifetime in which he became the Enlightened One.

As represented in our selection, the *Jātaka* tales vary in their narrative organization, imaginative effect, and cultural complexity. "The Golden Goose," perhaps the simplest of the stories, resembles an animal fable, in which the Buddha (as a goose) gives his golden feathers, one by one, to his widow and daughters from a former life, who have been living on the charity of neighbors and friends since his death (as a human). The story can be understood as a cautionary tale against greed; but, in a Buddhist context, it can also be interpreted as a reminder of the necessity of detachment from, and ultimately renunciation of, family.

The other two stories are more complicated in their structure as well as message. "The Hare's Self-Sacrifice" involves not only the Buddha, reborn as a hare, and three other animals in the wild—a monkey, a jackal, and an otter—with whom he tries to live in harmony. It also involves the Hindu god Indra (called Sakka in the Pali canon), a symbolic competition between him and the Buddha for moral authority over the universe, and a victory for the Buddha, who lets out "a cry of exultation like a lion roaring." At the same time, the tale suggests that the spots we see on the moon every night are daubed in the shape of a hare, in order to commemorate this lifetime of the Buddha and his victory over Indra. "The Monkey's Heroic Self-Sacrifice" then takes us deeper into the natural world and the world of animals, to show us how the Buddha, reborn as a monkey who leads eighty thousand of his fellow creatures, selflessly gives up his life for them while helping them escape from avaricious humans. It also creates a myth about how human beings discovered the delicious fruit called the mango, and offers a parable about a king's responsibilities to his subjects.

In all three tales, the Buddha (then still a *bodhisattava,* one who has the potential for enlightenment but has not yet attained it) makes an elemental sacrifice, risking his own life and limb for the benefit of others. In each case, he maintains the right "mindfulness," keeping his intentions clear of selfish considerations; and his will is focused on the accumulation of goodness across many lifetimes, without which he cannot be ready for Enlightenment. These tales therefore are much more than entertaining stories, or even fables with moral lessons that can be summed up in a phrase or two; they are narratives whose meanings cannot be deciphered only at the level of "story," or only in an aesthetic context.

The tradition of Indian animal fables that grow out of the *Jātaka* tales in later centuries, as in the ***Pañcatantra*** and the *Hitopdeśa,* shifts toward practical wisdom and common sense in everyday life. The *Jātaka* tales resist this tendency; they remain tied closely to the ideal of a *bodhisattva*'s "six perfections": selfless giving to others; moral clarity and firmness; patience or forbearance; unstinting effort in the pursuit of the right goals; meditation; and wisdom. The tales thus become a means not only to entertain a storyteller's audience, but also to educate children and common people (who may not have access to literacy), and to communicate the abstract message of a scriptural canon.

The Golden Goose[1]

Once upon a time when Brahmadatta[2] was reigning in Benares,[3] the Bodhisatta[4] was born a brahmin,[5] and growing up was married to a bride of his own rank, who bore him three daughters named Nandā, Nandavatī and Sundarinandā.

1. Translated by H. T. Francis and E. J. Thomas.
2. A mythical king; many *Jātaka* tales begin with the formulaic phrase "Once upon a time."
3. Modern Banaras or Varanasi, also called Kashi; oldest and most famous holy city in India, on the River Ganges. Banaras is associated mainly with Hinduism and its major god, Śiva; but it is also vital to Buddhism, because the Buddha preached his first sermon in its deer park.
4. Pali term, equivalent to Sanskrit *bodhisattva;* used for "a being on the path to enlightenment" or a Buddha-to-be. Since the *Jātaka* tells stories about Siddhartha-Gautama's lives previous to the one in which he attained enlightenment, they refer to him as a Bodhisatta rather than as the Buddha.
5. A brāhmaṇa; a member of the Hindu caste-group of hereditary priests and scholars.

The Bodhisatta dying, they were taken in by neighbours and friends, whilst he was born again into the world as a golden goose endowed with consciousness of its former existences.[6] Growing up, the bird viewed his own magnificent size and golden plumage, and remembered that previously he had been a human being. Discovering that his wife and daughters were living on the charity of others, the goose bethought him of his plumage like hammered and beaten gold and how by giving them a golden feather at a time he could enable his wife and daughters to live in comfort. So away he flew to where they dwelt and alighted on the top of the central beam of the roof. Seeing the Bodhisatta, the wife and girls asked where he had come from; and he told them that he was their father who had died and been born a golden goose, and that he had come to visit them and put an end to their miserable necessity of working for hire. "You shall have my feathers," said he, "one by one, and they will sell for enough to keep you all in ease and comfort." So saying, he gave them one of his feathers and departed. And from time to time he returned to give them another feather, and with the proceeds of their sale these brahmin-women grew prosperous and quite well-to-do. But one day the mother said to her daughters, "There's no trusting animals, my children. Who's to say your father might not go away one of these days and never come back again? Let us use our time and pluck him clean next time he comes, so as to make sure of all his feathers." Thinking this would pain him, the daughters refused. The mother in her greed called the golden goose to her one day when he came, and then took him with both hands and plucked him. Now the Bodhisatta's feathers had this property that if they were plucked out against his wish, they ceased to be golden and became like a crane's feathers. And now the poor bird, though he stretched his wings, could not fly, and the woman flung him into a barrel and gave him food there. As time went on his feathers grew again (though they were plain white ones now), and he flew away to his own abode and never came back again.

The Hare's Self-Sacrifice[1]

Once upon a time when Brahmadatta was reigning in Benares, the Bodhisatta came to life as a young hare and lived in a wood. On one side of this wood was the foot of a mountain, on another side a river, and on the third side a border-village. The hare had three friends—a monkey, a jackal and an otter. These four wise creatures lived together and each of them got his food on his own hunting-ground, and in the evening they again came together. The hare in his wisdom by way of admonition preached the Truth[2] to his three companions, teaching that alms are to be given, the moral law to be observed, and holy days to be kept. They accepted his admonition and went each to his own part of the jungle and dwelt there.

6. In both Hinduism and Buddhism, an individual "self" or soul that is reborn due to a net accumulation of "bad karma" in previous lives carries forward memories of those actions into its current life. Such memories enable it to seek liberation by aiming for a net accumulation of "good karma."

1. Translated by H. T. Francis and E. J. Thomas.

2. Most likely an early version of the moral law that the Buddha systematized in his doctrine of Four Noble Trurhs.

And so in the course of time the Bodhisatta one day observing the sky, and looking at the moon knew that the next day would be a fast-day,[3] and addressing his three companions he said, "To-morrow is a fast-day. Let all three of you take upon you the moral precepts, and observe the holy day. To one that stands fast in moral practice, almsgiving brings a great reward. Therefore feed any beggars[4] that come to you by giving them food from your own table." They readily assented, and abode each in his own place of dwelling.

On the morrow quite early in the morning, the otter sallied forth to seek his prey and went down to the bank of the Ganges. Now it came to pass that a fisherman had landed seven red fish, and stringing them together on a withe, he had taken and buried them in the sand on the river's bank. And then he dropped down the stream, catching more fish. The otter, scenting the buried fish, dug up the sand till he came upon them, and pulling them out cried thrice, "Does anyone own these fish?" And not seeing any owner he took hold of the withe with his teeth and laid the fish in the jungle where he dwelt, intending to eat them at a fitting time. And then he lay down, thinking how virtuous he was! The jackal too sallied forth in quest of food and found in the hut of a field-watcher two spits, a lizard and a pot of milk-curd. And after thrice crying aloud, "To whom do these belong?" and not finding an owner, he put on his neck the rope for lifting the pot, and grasping the spits and the lizard with his teeth, he brought and laid them in his own lair, thinking, "In due season I will devour them," and so lay down, reflecting how virtuous he had been.

The monkey also entered the clump of trees, and gathering a bunch of mangoes laid them up in his part of the jungle, meaning to eat them in due season, and then lay down, thinking how virtuous he was. But the Bodhisatta in due time came out, intending to browse on the kusa-grass,[5] and as he lay in the jungle, the thought occurred to him, "It is impossible for me to offer grass to any beggars that may chance to appear, and I have no sesame, rice, and such like. If any beggar shall appeal to me, I shall have to give him my own flesh to eat." At this splendid display of virtue, Sakka's[6] white marble throne manifested signs of heat. Sakka on reflection discovered the cause and resolved to put this royal hare to the test. First of all he went and stood by the otter's dwelling-place, disguised as a brahmin, and being asked why he stood there, he replied, "Wise Sir, if I could get something to eat, after keeping the fast, I would perform all my ascetic duties." The otter replied, "Very well, I will give you some food," and as he conversed with him he repeated the first stanza:[7]

> Seven red fish I safely brought to land from Ganges flood,
> O brahmin, eat thy fill, I pray, and stay within this wood.

3. In the lunisolar calendar followed by Buddhism, Hinduism, and Jainism, some days, corresponding to particular phases of the moon, are set aside for keeping fasts.
4. Begging is part of the vow of poverty observed by Buddhist monks and many Hindu ascetics.
5. Used in Hindu rituals.
6. Indra, king of gods, who rewards those who display extraordinary virtue.
7. The traditional stanza known as *gāthā*. The formula by which the stanzas are introduced shows that they were meant to be memorized. The Pali stanzas in the *Jātaka* tales are very old, stylistically more archaic than the stanzas of the Hindu epics, and seem to have been used by monks as keys to memorize and summarize the tales.

The brahmin said, "Let be till to-morrow. I will see to it by and by." Next he went to the jackal, and when asked by him why he stood there, he made the same answer. The jackal, too, readily promised him some food, and in talking with him repeated the second stanza:

> A lizard and a jar of curds, the keeper's evening meal,
> Two spits of roasted flesh withal I wrongfully did steal:
> Such as I have I give to thee: O brahmin, eat, I pray,
> If thou shouldst deign within this wood a while with us to stay.

Said the brahmin, "Let be till to-morrow. I will see to it by and by." Then he went to the monkey, and when asked what he meant by standing there, he answered just as before. The monkey readily offered him some food, and in conversing with him gave utterance to the third stanza:

> An icy stream, a mango ripe, and pleasant greenwood shade,
> Tis thine to enjoy, if thou canst dwell content in forest glade.

Said the brahmin, "Let be till to-morrow. I will see to it by and by." And he went to the wise hare, and on being asked by him why he stood there, he made the same reply. The Bodhisatta on hearing what he wanted was highly delighted, and said, "Brahmin, you have done well in coming to me for food. This day will I grant you a boon that I have never granted before, but you shall not break the moral law by taking animal life.[8] Go, friend, and when you have piled together logs of wood, and kindled a fire, come and let me know, and I will sacrifice myself by falling into the midst of the flames, and when my body is roasted, you shall eat my flesh and fulfil all your ascetic duties." And in thus addressing him the hare uttered the fourth stanza:

> Nor sesame, nor beans, nor rice have I as food to give,
> But roast with fire my flesh I yield, if thou with us wouldst live.

Sakka, on hearing what he said, by his miraculous power caused a heap of burning coals to appear, and came and told the Bodhisatta. Rising from his bed of kusa-grass and coming to the place, he thrice shook himself that if there were any insects within his coat, they might escape death. Then offering his whole body as a free gift he sprang up, and like a royal swan, alighting on a cluster of lotuses, in an ecstasy of joy he fell on the heap of live coals. But the flame failed even to heat the pores of the hair on the body of the Bodhisatta, and it was as if he had entered a region of frost. Then he addressed Sakka in these words: "Brahmin, the fire you have kindled is icy-cold: it fails to heat even the pores of the hair on my body. What is the meaning of this?" "Wise Sir," he replied, "I am no brahmin. I am Sakka, and I have come to put your virtue to the test." The Bodhisatta said, "If not only thou, Sakka, but all the inhabitants of the world were to try me in this matter of almsgiving, they would not find in me any unwillingness to give," and with this the Bodhisatta uttered a cry of exultation

8. According to the Buddha, the taking of life results in evil karma; therefore, he stressed extreme nonviolence.

like a lion roaring. Then said Sakka to the Bodhisatta, "O wise hare, be thy virtue known throughout a whole aeon."[9] And squeezing the mountain, with the essence thus extracted, he daubed the sign of a hare on the orb of the moon.[1] And after depositing the hare on a bed of young kusa-grass, in the same wooded part of the jungle, Sakka returned to his own place in heaven. And these four wise creatures dwelt happily and harmoniously together, fulfilling the moral law and observing holy days, till they departed to fare according to their deeds.

The Monkey's Heroic Self-Sacrifice[1]

Once upon a time when Brahmadatta was reigning in Benares, the Bodhisatta was born as a monkey.[2] When he grew up and attained stature and stoutness, he was strong and vigorous, and lived in the Himalaya with a retinue of eighty thousand[3] monkeys. Near the Ganges bank there was a mango tree (others say it was a banyan), with branches and forks, having a deep shade and thick leaves, like a mountain-top.[4] Its sweet fruits, of divine fragrance and flavour, were as large as water-pots: from one branch the fruits fell on the ground, from one into the Ganges water, from two into the main trunk of the tree. The Bodhisatta, while eating the fruit with a troop of monkeys, thought, "Someday danger will come upon us owing to the fruit of this tree falling on the water"; and so, not to leave one fruit on the branch which grew over the water, he made them eat or throw down the flowers at their season from the time they were of the size of a chick-pea. But notwithstanding, one ripe fruit, unseen by the eighty thousand monkeys, hidden by an ant's nest, fell into the river, and stuck in the net above the king of Benares who was bathing for amusement with a net above him and another below. When the king had amused himself all day and was going away in the evening, the fishermen, who were drawing the net, saw the fruit and not knowing what it was, shewed it to the king. The king asked, "What is this fruit?" "We do not know, sire." "Who will know?" "The foresters, sire." He had the foresters called, and learning from them that it was a mango, he cut it with a knife, and first making the foresters eat of it, he ate of it himself and had some of it given to his seraglio and his ministers. The flavour of the ripe mango remained, pervading the king's whole body. Possessed by desire[5] of the flavour, he asked the foresters where that tree stood, and hearing that it was on a river bank in the Himalaya quarter, he had many rafts joined together and sailed upstream by the route shewn by the foresters.

9. A unit of cosmic time, consisting of a thousand cycles of four ages.

1. Throughout India the markings on the moon are recognized as being in the shape of a hare, and this *Jātaka* is one of the tales that explains its origin. Folklorists have discovered legends about a hare on the moon among other peoples, including the Kalmuks, the Hottentots, and some Native American groups.

1. Translated by H. T. Francis and E. J. Thomas.

2. As demonstrated by the role of Hanumān, Rāma's monkey helper in the *Rāmāyaṇa*, monkeys are beloved characters in Indian folklore; there are several *Jātaka*s about the Bodhisattva's births as a monkey.

3. A large number or a multitude.

4. The tree is gigantic. A banyan tree (a kind of fig tree with spreading aerial roots) of that size would have made a suitable home for a large monkey troop, but its fruit hardly compares with the sweet mango, the allure of which is a crucial point in this tale.

5. Identified as the root cause of existential suffering.

The exact account of days is not given. In due course they came to the place, and the foresters said to the king, "Sire, there is the tree." The king stopped the rafts and went on foot with a great retinue, and having a bed prepared at the foot of the tree, he lay down after eating the mango fruit and enjoying the various excellent flavours. At every side they set a guard and made a fire. When the men had fallen asleep, the Bodhisatta came at midnight with his retinue. Eighty thousand monkeys moving from branch to branch ate the mangoes. The king, waking and seeing the herd of monkeys, roused his men and calling his archers said, "Surround these monkeys that eat the mangoes so that they may not escape, and shoot them: to-morrow we will eat mangoes with monkey's flesh." The archers obeyed, saying, "Very well," and surrounding the tree stood with arrows ready. The monkeys seeing them and fearing death, as they could not escape, came to the Bodhisatta and said, "Sire, the archers stand round the tree, saying, 'We will shoot those vagrant monkeys': what are we to do?" and so stood shivering. The Bodhisatta said, "Do not fear, I will give you life"; and so comforting the herd of monkeys, he ascended a branch that rose up straight, went along another branch that stretched towards the Ganges, and springing from the end of it, he passed a hundred bow-lengths and lighted on a bush on the bank. Coming down, he marked the distance, saying, "That will be the distance I have come": and cutting a bamboo shoot at the root and stripping it, he said, "So much will be fastened to the tree, and so much will stay in the air," and so reckoned the two lengths, forgetting the part fastened on his own waist. Taking the shoot he fastened one end of it to the tree on the Ganges bank and the other to his own waist, and then cleared the space of a hundred bow-lengths with a speed of a cloud torn by the wind. From not reckoning the part fastened to his waist, he failed to reach the tree: so seizing a branch firmly with both hands he gave signal to the troop of monkeys, "Go quickly with good luck, treading on my back along the bamboo shoot." The eighty thousand monkeys escaped thus, after saluting the Bodhisatta and getting his leave. Devadatta[6] was then a monkey and among that herd: he said, "This is a chance for me to see the last of my enemy," so climbing up a branch he made a spring and fell on the Bodhisatta's back. The Bodhisatta's back broke and great pain came on him. Devadatta having caused that maddening pain went away: and the Bodhisatta was alone. The king being awake saw all that was done by the monkeys and the Bodhisatta: and he lay down thinking, "This animal, not reckoning his own life, has caused the safety of his troop." When day broke, being pleased with the Bodhisatta, he thought, "It is not right to destroy this king of the monkeys: I will bring him down by some means and take care of him": So turning the raft down the Ganges and building a platform there, he made the Bodhisatta come down gently, and had him clothed with a yellow robe on his back and washed in Ganges water, made him drink sugared water, and had his body cleansed and anointed with oil refined a thousand times; then he put an oiled skin on a bed and making him lie there, he set himself, on a low seat, and spoke the first stanza:

> You made yourself a bridge for them to pass in safety through:
> What are you then to them, monkey, and what are they to you?

6. Gautama Buddha's evil cousin, who appears in many *Jātakas*.

Hearing him, the Bodhisatta instructing the king spoke the other stanzas:

Victorious king, I guard the herd, I am their lord and chief,
When they were filled with fear of thee and stricken sore with grief.

I leapt a hundred times the length of bow outstretched that lies,
When I had bound a bamboo-shoot firmly around my thighs:

I reached the tree like thunder-cloud sped by the tempest's blast;
I lost my strength, but reached a bough: with hands I held it fast.

And as I hung extended there held fast by shoot and bough,
My monkeys passed across my back and are in safety now.

Therefore I fear no pain of death, bonds do not give me pain,
The happiness of those was won o'er whom I used to reign.

A parable for thee, O king, if thou the truth would'st read:
The happiness of kingdom and of army and of steed
And city must be dear to thee, if thou would'st rule indeed.

The Bodhisatta, thus instructing and teaching the king, died. The king, calling his ministers, gave orders that the monkey-king should have obsequies like a king, and he sent to the seraglio, saying, "Come to the cemetery, as retinue for the monkey-king, with red garments, and dishevelled hair, and torches in your hands." The ministers made a funeral pile with a hundred waggon loads of timber. Having prepared the Bodhisatta's obsequies in a royal manner, they took his skull, and came to the king. The king caused a shrine to be built at the Bodhisatta's burial-place, torches to be burnt there and offerings of incense and flowers to be made; he had the skull inlaid with gold, and put in front raised on a spearpoint: honouring it with incense and flowers, he put it at the king's gate when he came to Benares, and having the whole city decked out he paid honour to it for seven days. Then taking it as a relic and raising a shrine, he honoured it with incense and garlands all his life; and established in the Bodhisatta's teaching he did alms and other good deeds, and ruling his kingdom righteously became destined for heaven.

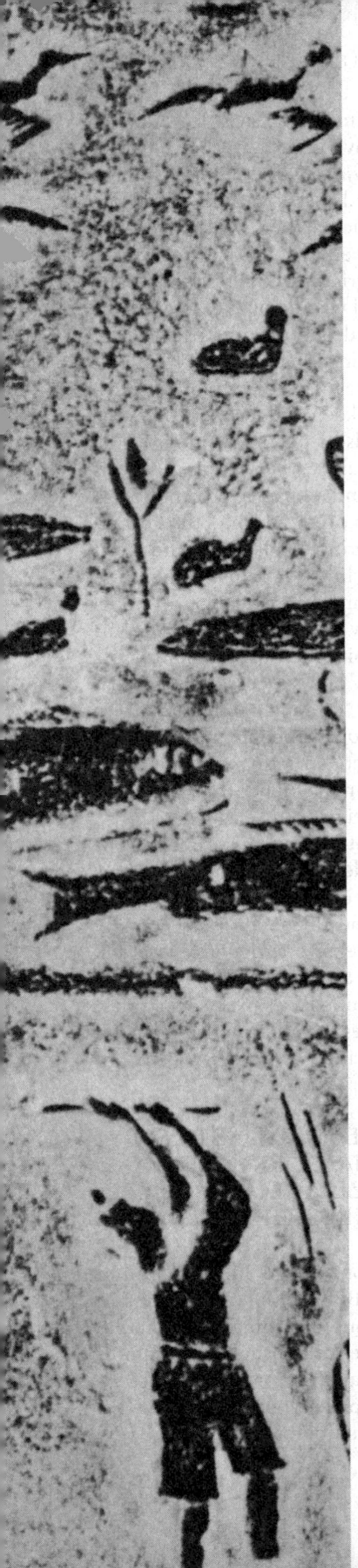

III

Early Chinese Literature and Thought

Many great civilizations have perished with little consequence. What we know of them comes from the imaginative reconstructions of scholars, from inscriptions, and from the accounts of early travelers. Civilizations like those of ancient Egypt and Mesopotamia left extensive written records that were swept aside by other civilizations; the very names by which we refer to them—Egypt and Mesopotamia—are Greek. This is not the case with China, the oldest surviving civilization, whose literary tradition stretches over more than three thousand years. Its earliest literature set patterns and posed questions that shaped the actions and values of the Chinese people for thousands of years, serving as the connective tissue that gave its civilization a sense of unity and continuity.

Throughout China's long history, its territories, ruling classes, capitals, religions, and customs kept changing with the rise and fall of ruling dynasties; and its peoples have spoken a great number of widely divergent Chinese dialects as well as many non-Chinese languages from the Turkic, Mongolian, and even Indo-European language families. Thus, China might easily have become fragmented by regional interests and linguistic differences like

A contemporary rubbing made from a Han Dynasty (206 B.C.E.–220 C.E.) earthenware tile that depicts scenes of hunting and harvesting.

Europe after the fall of the Roman Empire. But whereas Rome was truly a conquest empire, a political center that ruled over many peoples, each with its own sense of distinct ethnic identity, traditional China was an idea tied to cultural values and the power of the written word. Certainly, Chinese emperors did at certain times in history conquer territories as remote as Korea, Vietnam, Tibet, and Taiwan. But China could survive periods of turmoil and even rule by non-Chinese conquerors such as the Mongols and the Manchus because peoples on the margins of the ancient heartland had for centuries been adopting China's writing, cultural values, and institutions, and had thus become "Chinese." Many times in China's history, regional identity has become subordinate to a belief in cultural and political unity.

BEGINNINGS: EARLY SAGE RULERS

Although China has always been in contact with western parts of the Eurasian landmass, it developed independently from the earlier Mesopotamian, Egyptian, and Indus Valley city civilizations. By the third millennium B.C.E. at least a dozen Neolithic (New Stone Age) cultures flourished along the Yellow River in the north and the Yangzi River in the south. By the second millennium B.C.E. most settlements had defensive walls made of rammed earth, a sign of the increasing influence of military elites, who defended the populace against other rising city-states. Later Chinese historians placed into this early period a lineage of sage rulers who laid the foundations for Chinese civilization. Fu Xi reputedly taught people how to raise silkworms. He also invented the eight trigrams, symbols consisting of three broken or unbroken (Yin and Yang) lines each, which became the basis for China's canonical divination text, the *Classic of Changes (Yijing)*. Shennong invented the plow and instructed people in the use of medicinal herbs. Huangdi, the "Yellow Emperor," was a patron of medicine and agriculture. His scribe, Cang Jie, invented writing by creating graphs that imitated the articulate tracks of birds, realizing that the new technology "could regulate the various professions and keep under scrutiny the various kinds of people." Among three later sage rulers, Yao disinherited his inept son and chose a commoner to succeed him on the throne, thus establishing the principle of virtue and merit over blood lineage. This commoner, Shun, was an ideal ruler and a model of filial piety (he remained true to his parents despite their repeated attempts to kill him). His successor, the Great Yu, showed exemplary dedication to the welfare of his people and invented irrigation, constructing channels to tame the Great Flood that occurred during his reign.

Encapsulated in this lineage of legendary rulers are fundamental values of Chinese civilization: the importance of writing and divination; an economy based on intensive agriculture and silk production; a political philosophy of virtue that emphasizes fixed social roles; and practices of self-cultivation and herbal medicine.

EARLIEST DYNASTIES: CHINA DURING THE BRONZE AGE AND THE BEGINNING OF WRITING

China's Bronze Age began around 2000 B.C.E. By 1200 B.C.E., cultures in several regions of China made ample use of bronze for the molding of more-effective weapons, for the new technology of spoke-wheel chariots, and for the production of ritual bronze ves-

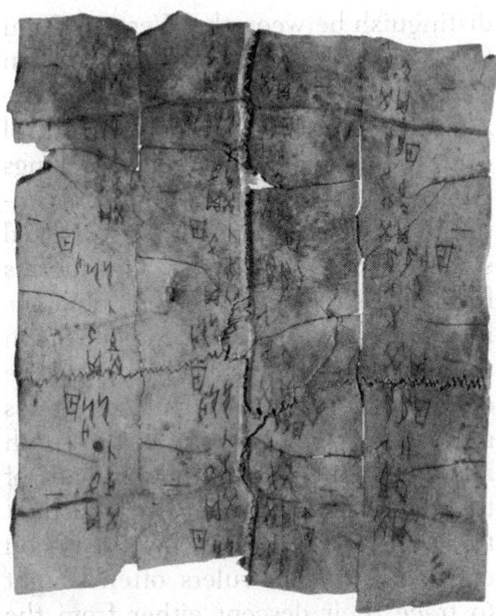

This tortoiseshell, inscribed with writing dating from ca. 1200 B.C.E., was used for ceremonial divination.

sels used in ceremonies for gods and ancestors. A small area in the Yellow River basin of north-central China is the best known of these Bronze Age cultures: thanks to the groundbreaking archeological discovery of inscriptions on tortoiseshells and cattle bones in 1898, this area could be identified as the so-called second dynasty—the Shang (ca. 1500–1045 B.C.E.). The first dynasty is traditionally identified as the Xia, whose name and list of kings are recorded in later texts, but whose existence hasn't been linked to any of the known Bronze Age archeological sites.

The Shang was a loose confederation of city-states with a complex state system, large settlements, and, most important, a common writing system. Although it remains unclear when the Chinese script began to be developed, it appeared as a fully functional writing system during the later period of the Shang dynasty. To date, more than 48,000 fragments of inscribed shells and bones have been found. These so-called oracle bone inscriptions are usually short records of divination rituals. Ritual specialists and the Shang kings would apply heat to the bones and use the resulting cracks to interpret or predict events: determining weather, harvest, floods, or tribute payments; divining the outcome of imminent war or the birth of male offspring; or even finding the causes for the toothache of a royal family member. Thus, writing was part of ritual practices that guided political decision making and harmonized the relation between human beings and the world of unpredictable spiritual forces in the cosmos. Its use was a prerogative of the Shang king and his elites.

From the inscriptions we can see that the Shang kings paid meticulous attention to the veneration of their dead ancestors and various gods, including the highest god, *Di*, who also commanded rain and thunder. They used war captives as slaves and sacrificial victims and employed conscript workers for monumental labor projects. For example, the sumptuous grave

Among the many objects fashioned out of bronze during the Shang Dynasty were "fangding," ritual vessels for cooking and presenting food. This fangding is the only extant example that is decorated with a human face.

site of Lady Hao, one of the prominent Shang king Wu Ding's many wives, contained hundreds of bronze objects.

THE ZHOU CONQUEST AND THE "MANDATE OF HEAVEN"

Around 1045 B.C.E. the Zhou people overthrew the Shang. The Zhou were an agrarian people and former allies of the Shang. Their justification of the conquest set the model for subsequent dynastic shifts in Chinese history. Texts recorded during the first centuries of Zhou rule claimed that a new power, "Heaven," transferred the mandate to rule to the Zhou, because the moral worth of the Shang had declined and the last Shang rulers were decadent tyrants without regard for the people. In turn, the first rulers of the Zhou, King Wen (the "cultured" or "civilized" king) and his son King Wu (the "martial" king), who completed the conquest, were praised as paragons of virtue and "sons of Heaven" deserving of the mandate. After the Zhou conquest, the claim to power in China depended on the claim to virtuous rule, which in large measure meant holding to the statutes and models of the earliest sage rulers and the virtuous early Zhou kings.

THE DECLINE OF THE EASTERN ZHOU AND THE AGE OF CHINA'S PHILOSOPHICAL MASTERS

After their conquest, the early Zhou kings rewarded their allies with gifts of land. But initially strong personal ties between the Zhou kings and their allies weakened over the centuries, and in 771 B.C.E. some vassals joined forces with nomadic tribesmen and killed the king. The Zhou court fled and moved the capital to the east. Historians thus distinguish between the Western Zhou (1045–771 B.C.E.) and the Eastern Zhou (770–256 B.C.E.) periods. The Zhou kings never regained full control over their vassals. Although its kings continued to rule for another five centuries, the Eastern Zhou Dynasty lacked strong central authority, allowing its former vassals to build up their domains into belligerent independent states. On the southern and western borders of the old Zhou domain, powerful new states arose: Chu, Wu, and Yue in the south and Qin in the west. Although many of these new kingdoms had their distinct traditions, they gradually absorbed Zhou culture, and their rulers often sought to trace their descent either from the Zhou royal house or from more ancient, northern Chinese ancestors. Just before the defeat of the Western Zhou, there were around two hundred lords with domains of varying size, all under the titular rule of the Zhou king. By the third century B.C.E., only seven powerful states were left in the struggle over supremacy, and in 256 B.C.E. the last Zhou king was killed.

The Eastern Zhou Period was one of the most formative periods in Chinese history. The Eastern Zhou rulers built new institutions, and among its vassal states a lively interstate diplomacy unfolded; new military technology revolutionized warfare, and the old aristocracy was gradually dismantled and replaced by a new class of advisers and strategists. During the earlier part of the Eastern Zhou Period, the so-called Spring and Autumn Annals Period (722–481 B.C.E., named after the court chronicle of Confucius's home state of Lu in eastern China), the old aristocracy in their chariots were still central to combat, and an honor code of military conduct was respected. Battles started with an agreement on both sides, states that were in mourning for their rulers were not attacked, and, if a state was defeated, the conqueror respectfully continued the ancestral sacrifices for the vanquished ruling lineage. This changed dramatically during the latter half of the Eastern Zhou, the so-called Warring States Period (403–221 B.C.E., named after a collection of stories about political intrigues between the Zhou states): mass infantry armies built on coercive drafts replaced the old aristocracy; raw power politics and strategic deception became the norm; the newly invented crossbow allowed soldiers to kill their enemies at greater distance, not in noble close combat; and rulers of the larger Zhou states started to call themselves kings, indicating that they not only defied the authority of the Zhou king but also intended to replace him as ruler over all of China.

It was in this climate that **Confucius**, and the philosophical masters who followed in his wake, formulated visions of how to live and govern well in a corrupt world. Chinese call this the period when "a hundred schools of thought bloomed." The Eastern Zhou Period coincides with the period when the religions and philosophies of ancient India, Greece, Persia, and Israel took shape, and scholars have compared the social and political conditions facilitating this flourishing in these different civilizations. In China, rulers of the feudal states employed able advisers, or "masters," to help them gain more resources, territory, and power, and the Chinese masters often moved between states in search for employment and patronage.

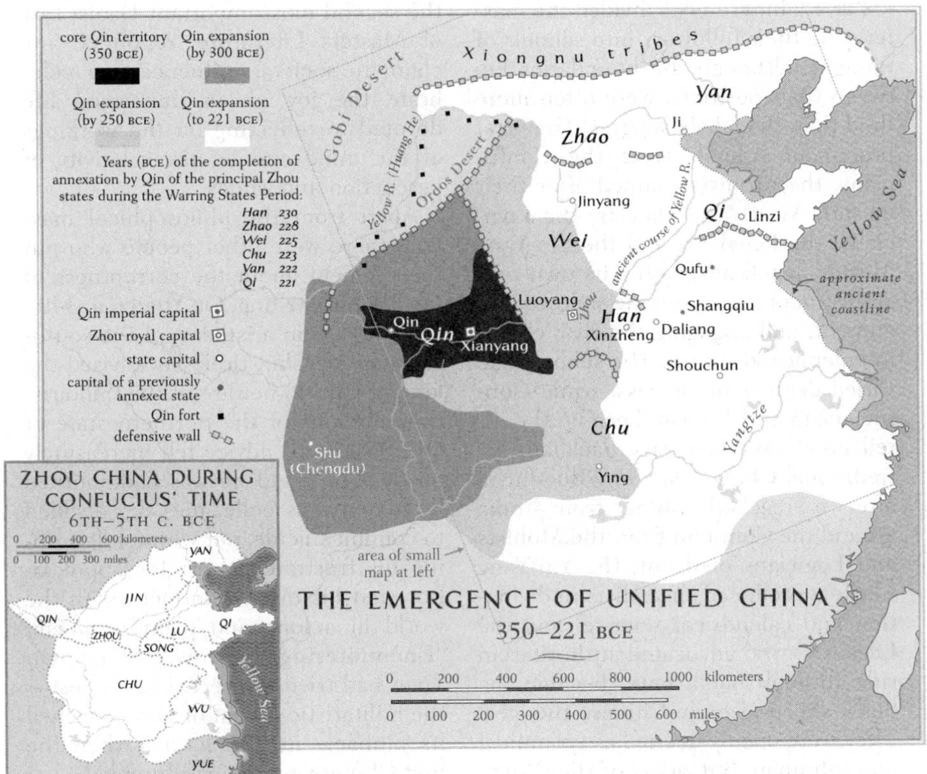

Chinese call the texts written by masters or compiled by their disciples "Masters Literature." This name derives from scenes that show a charismatic master in vivid conversation with disciples, rulers, or other contemporaries. Masters Literature flourished from the time of Confucius through the Han Dynasty (206 B.C.E.–220 C.E.). This rich corpus of texts, represented in this anthology by selections from the ***Analects***, and from ***Laozi*** and ***Zhuangzi***, reveals the broad spectrum of opinions on fundamental questions: How can we create social order in a society that is incessantly at war? How can we become exemplary, fulfilled human beings in a less-than-ideal society? How can we make use of history and existing precedents to create a better future? How should we use words, and what impact can words and ideas have on social reality?

Later Chinese texts divided the masters and their followers into schools of thought, although the boundaries between their positions were often more fluid than the labels suggest. The most prominent schools were the Confucians, the Mohists (named after their master, Mozi), the Daoists, the Logicians, the Legalists, and the Yin-Yang Masters, each advocating its own programs, adopting different styles of argument, and engaging the rival camps in polemical disputes. The schools had varied degrees of success: while Confucianism and Daoism became the intellectual and religious backbone of traditional China (joined by Buddhism after it reached China from India around the Common Era), the Mohists and Logicians died out, the Yin-Yang Masters produced specialists in divination and calendrical science, and the Legalists, who advocated authoritarian rule through harsh laws, became the black sheep of early Chinese thought. They were openly decried as tyrannical and inhuman, but many of their ideas and methods were used by the architects of the Chinese empire throughout the centuries.

Confucius, the first and most exemplary master whose sayings are preserved in the *Analects*, believed that a return to the values of the virtuous early Zhou kings, a respect for social hierarchies, self-cultivation through proper ritual behavior, and the study of ancient texts could bring order. The most radical opponents of Confucius and his followers were thinkers who advocated passivity and following of the natural "way," or *dao*. The Daoists had a deep mistrust of human-made things: conscious effort, artifice, and words. *Laozi*, a collection of poems and the foundational text of Daoism, proposed passivity as a means of ultimately prevailing over one's opponents and gaining spiritual and political control. By contrast, many passages in *Zhuangzi*, the second most important Daoist text of Masters Literature, renounce any claim to societal influence and celebrate the joy of an unharmed life devoted to reflecting on the workings of the mind and on the relativity of perception and values.

Apart from the philosophical masters, there were other people who put their lament about the corruptness of the age into writing. Qu Yuan (ca. 340–278 B.C.E.), an aristocrat of the southern state of Chu, tirelessly advised the king of Chu to beware of the militaristic ambitions of the northern state of Qin. When his advice fell increasingly on deaf ears and he was badmouthed by his envious colleagues, he decided to commit suicide, not without describing his frustrated quest for appreciation and his disenchantment with the world in a long and plaintive poem, "**Encountering Sorrow**." What Qu Yuan had tried to prevent at all cost—the militaristic ascent of Qin—reached its pinnacle in 221 B.C.E., when the first Chinese empire was founded.

FOUNDATIONS OF IMPERIAL CHINA: THE QIN AND THE HAN

The state of Qin, which had a reputation for ruthlessness and untrustworthiness, but whose armies were well disciplined and well supplied, destroyed the Zhou royal domain in 256 B.C.E. and conquered the last of the independent states in 221 B.C.E. That year is one of the most important dates in Chinese history. Conscious of the historical moment's weight, the king of Qin conferred the title "First Emperor of Qin" upon himself to mark the novelty of his achievement. Although the Qin was a short-lived dynasty, many of its measures—designed to create a new type of state with a strong centralized bureaucracy—were adopted and adapted by the rulers of the subsequent Han Dynasty (206 B.C.E.–220 C.E.). With the Qin unification, China was finally an empire. Imperial China, with its upheavals, dynastic shifts, and momentous changes, would last another 2,100 years—until the Republican Revolution of 1911.

Some scholars credit the Qin Dynasty's policy reforms with the success of the Chinese empire. Since the fourth century B.C.E. ministers associated with the Legalist school advised the kings of Qin to reduce the power of the old nobility and to base governance on a direct connection between ruler and bureaucrats controlled by the strict rule of written law codes and policies. In the decades before the Qin unification, the Legalist thinker **Han Feizi** (d. ca. 233 B.C.E.) had found particular favor with the king of Qin. Although Han Feizi was ultimately forced into suicide by the slander of suspicious colleagues, his vision of governance was adopted for the new empire.

The First Emperor's megalomania became legendary in later Chinese history, exerting as much fascination as horror. Though much of his statecraft

Perhaps the most illustrative symbol of the First Emperor's megalomania and imperial ambitions is the vast terra-cotta army, unearthed in 1974, that the emperor had buried with him. Over 7,000 life-size sculptures fill the burial site.

was subtle, many of his most famous policies had a chilling simplicity. Some, such as unifying the currency, the various scripts, and the weights and measures used in different states, deserve credit. But his solution to intellectual disagreement was the suppression of scholars and the burning of all books except for practical manuals of medicine, agriculture, and divination and for the historical records of Qin. The "Qin Burning of the Books," of 213 B.C.E., was one of the most traumatic events in Chinese history.

After the death of the First Emperor, rebellions broke out. Many of the rebels tried to restore the old pre-Qin states, but the final winner, a simple commoner named Liu Bang, became the first emperor of the Han Dynasty and continued the centralized government strategy of the Qin, while eliminating its unpopular features, loosening some particularly cruel laws, cutting taxes, and refraining from the constant labor mobilizations that the Qin emperor had forced on his people.

The Han Dynasty lasted more than four hundred years. The Han was the crucial phase of imperial consolidation that set patterns for future Chinese dynasties. During this period China expanded its boundaries into Central Asia and parts of modern Korea and Vietnam. Han emperors learned to deal with the challenging threat of northern frontier tribes, developing strategies that proved effective for subsequent empires: fight them, pay them off, or appease them with marriage alliances, offering Chinese princesses as brides to the tribal chieftains.

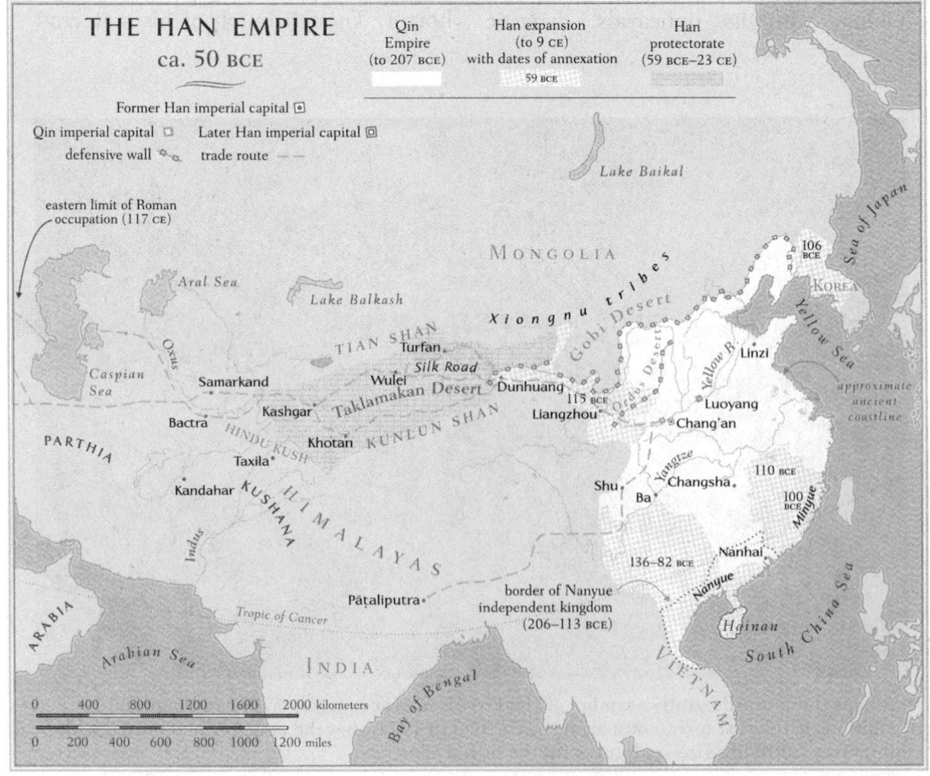

The most influential Han ruler was Emperor Wu, whose long reign lasted from 141 to 87 B.C.E. He undertook costly campaigns to expand the empire and established government monopolies on the production of iron, salt, and liquor to finance them. He was a generous patron of the arts, of music, and of scholarship. Although he was intrigued by immortality techniques, portents, and the occult, he was the first emperor to privilege Confucian scholars, founding a state academy for the education of government officials and setting up positions for professors to teach the so-called Five Classics: the *Classic of Changes*, used for divination; the *Classic of Documents*, a collection of proclamations by early sage kings and ministers; the ***Classic of Poetry***, a collection of poetry including hymns to the Zhou ancestors and ballads recounting the history of the Zhou; the *Spring and Autumn Annals*, a historical chronicle, and the *Record of Rites*, the most important of several works on ritual. During Emperor Wu's reign the first comprehensive history of China was written, by a court historian and his son, **Sima Qian** (ca. 145–86 B.C.E.), who suffered the punishment of castration for a minor disagreement with Emperor Wu but persisted in finishing his monumental history, which became the model for subsequent dynastic histories of China into the twentieth century.

Early China was a groundbreaking period of enduring influence on all subsequent periods of Chinese history. These first 1,500 years of Chinese history, from the Shang Dynasty to the end of the Han Dynasty, saw the emergence of enduring political institutions and ideologies, of moral standards and social manners. The literature produced during this period encapsulates these values and formative patterns and is still the canonical foundation of Chinese civilization.

CLASSIC OF POETRY

ca. 1000–600 B.C.E.

Standing at the beginning of China's three-millennia-long literary tradition, the *Classic of Poetry* (also *Book of Songs* or *Book of Odes*) is the oldest poetry collection of East Asia. Its poems reflect the breadth of early Chinese society. Some poems convey the history and values of the earlier part of the Zhou Dynasty (ca. 1045–256 B.C.E.), whose founding kings set a standard of ideal governance for later generations. Others treat themes familiar from folk ballads: courtship, marriage and love, birth and death, and the stages of the agricultural cycle such as planting and harvesting. Filled with images of nature and the plain life of an agricultural society, the *Classic of Poetry* offers a distinctive, fresh simplicity. Because of the collection's canonical status, centuries of commentary and interpretation have accrued around it, adding to its meaning and significance and endowing the simple scenes in the poems with moral or political purpose. The anthology has had a profound impact on the literatures of Korea, Japan, and Vietnam and was an important element of the traditional curriculum throughout East Asia until the beginning of the twentieth century.

THE ANTHOLOGY AND ITS SIGNIFICANCE

While other ancient literary traditions were founded on epics about gods and heroes, or sprawling legends about the origins of the cosmos, the *Classic of Poetry* provided a different sort of foundation for Chinese literature, made up of the compact and evocative form of lyric poetry. Because Chinese literature originated with the *Classic of Poetry*, short verse gained a degree of political, social, and pedagogical importance in East Asia that it has not enjoyed anywhere else in the world.

The *Classic of Poetry* contains 305 poems and consists of three parts, the "Airs of the Domains" (*Guofeng*, 160 poems), the "Odes/Elegances" (*Ya*, 105 poems), and the "Hymns" (*Song*, 40 poems). The "Hymns" are the oldest part and contain songs used in ritual performances to celebrate the Zhou royal house. Next are the "Odes," narrative ballads about memorable historical events. The youngest poems are the "Airs of the Domains," based on folk ballads from some fifteen domains of the Zhou kingdom. (The early Zhou kings gave lands to their loyal vassals and gradually built a multistate system of "domains" extending from modern-day Beijing far beyond the Yangtze River in the south.) Tradition credited **Confucius**, the most important of the early philosophical masters, with the compilation of the *Classic of Poetry*. He allegedly selected the poems in the collection from three thousand poems he found in the archives of the Zhou kingdom. Therefore, the choice and arrangement of the poems were seen as an expression of Confucius's philosophy. Confucius believed that political order depended on the ability of individuals in society to cultivate their moral virtue and thus contribute to social order. We know from the ***Analects***, a collection containing Confucius's sayings, that Confucius thought highly of the *Classic of Poetry*. He advised his own son to study the *Classic of Poetry* to enhance his ability to express his opinions, he praised disciples who quoted passages from the *Classic of Poetry* to make a particular point, and he saw a comprehensive educational program in the anthology: "The *Classic of Poetry* can provide you with stimulation and with observation, with a capacity for communion, and with a vehicle for grief. At home, they [the poems] enable you to serve your father, and abroad, to serve your lord. Also, you will learn there the names of many birds, animals, plants, and trees." Confucius's high opinion of the *Classic of Poetry* led to its inclusion in the canon of "Confucian Classics." The other classics are the *Classic of Changes*, used for divination; the *Classic of Documents*, a collection of sayings by early kings and ministers; the *Spring and Autumn Annals*, a historical chronicle of Confucius's home state of Lu; and the *Record of Rites*, the most important of a few books on ritual. The Confucian Classics became the curriculum of the state academy that Emperor Wu of the Han Dynasty founded in 124 B.C.E.

As a further sign of the *Classic of Poetry*'s canonization during the Han Dynasty, a **"Great Preface"** written for the anthology became the single most fundamental statement about the nature and function of poetry in East Asia. Written more than half a millennium after the anthology's compilation, the "Great Preface" claimed that there were "six principles" (*liu yi*) of poetry: the three categories in which the poems were placed ("Airs of the Domains," "Odes," and "Hymns") and the three rhetorical devices of "enumeration" (*fu*), "comparison" (*bi*), and "evocative image" (*xing*). Scholars and poets have debated the usefulness and precise meaning of these principles for the last two millennia, but on a basic level the principles illuminate rhetorical patterns that distinguish the *Classic of Poetry* and even later Chinese poetry. The concept of *feng* is a good case in point: it refers to the "Airs of the Domains" section of the anthology, but it also contains a rich web of associations that grew up around its literal meaning, "wind": Like wind that causes grass to sway, the ruler can "influence" (*feng*) his people and instill virtuous behavior in them through poetry. For their part, his subjects can express their dissatisfaction with their ruler through "criticism" (*feng*). In reality, most poems in the anthology contain at best indirect criticism. But the idea that poetry and song can bridge the gulf between social classes, that they can serve as a tool for mutual "influence" and "criticism" and give the people a voice, helping them keep bad rulers in check, was central to the Confucian understanding of poetry and society. Poetry made room for social critique and created the institution of "remonstration," the duty of officials in the bureaucracy to speak out against abuses of power.

THE POEMS

Our selections come from the "Odes" section ("She Bore the Folk") and the "Airs" section (all other poems). Although almost all poems in the *Classic of Poetry* are anonymous, they give voice to many different players in Zhou society, such as kings, aristocrats and peasants, men and women in love, and, collectively, to communities as they celebrate harvest or worship their ancestors. Poems put into the mouths of peasants or soldiers show considerable literary skill, which suggests that a member of the educated elite at the courts of the Zhou domains must have given them their final shape.

The constraints imposed by society and the conflict between individual desire and social expectations are important themes in the "Airs" section. Marriage is often praised as a sanctioned form of sexual relation, but some poems also celebrate the pleasures of transgression. "Boat of Cypress" is a remarkable outcry of a heart that refuses to bend to society's wishes. Unlike the virtuous Zhou Dynasty, the domain of Zheng and its music were associated with sensual pleasures: "Zhen and Wei," for example, depicts a festival scene along two rivers. Although its frolicking man and woman do not go beyond politely exchanging flowers as courtship gifts, the scene is highly charged with eroticism.

The protagonists in the romantic plots that appear in the poems of the "Airs of the Domains" could be from any culture past or present, but the extensive tradition of commentaries endowed these poems with specific moral and historical significance. According to the canonical "Mao commentary," "Fishhawk," the first poem of the *Classic of Poetry*, in which a young man is tormented by his desire for a girl, is not a simple romantic folk song. Instead, the commentary claims that the poem praises the consort of King Wen for being free from jealousy when her husband takes a new consort, a typical situation in traditional Chinese society, where men could have several wives. This counterintuitive reading of the poem established "Fishhawk" as a model of exemplary female behavior for all times and embedded it in the history of the early Zhou kings.

The central stylistic device of the *Classic of Poetry* is repetition with variation. Many of the poems consist of three rhyming stanzas of four or six lines with four syllables each. The stanza format encourages line repetitions, which give the poems melodic rhythm and, with the introduction of small variations, additional meaning. In "Plums Are Falling," the fruits become fewer with each repetition until the woman has finally decided whom among her suitors she wants to marry. In "Peach Tree Soft and Tender," the peach tree goes through the natural cycle of bearing blossoms, fruits, and leaves while a new bride, who it is hoped will bear many descendants for the family line, is introduced into the household. Far from being a simplistic rhetorical device, repetition with variation gives compelling shape to a suitor's intrusive desire and his lover's fear of scandal in "Zhongzi, Please." As the insolent Zhongzi systematically advances stanza by stanza from the village wall to the family's fence and through the garden towards his lover's bedchamber, the helpless woman, fearing her parents' and brothers' reproach and society's disapproval, fends her lover off by promising to keep him in her thoughts.

Among the rhetorical devices listed in the "Great Preface" to the *Classic of Poetry*, "enumeration" and "evocative image" are particularly interesting. Enumeration, the telling of sequences of events in straightforward narrative fashion, structures longer odes like "She Bore the Folk," a poem on the miraculous birth of Lord Millet, the inventor of agriculture and legendary ancestor of the Zhou people. Lord Millet's birth by a resourceful mother who steps into a god's footprint and his subsequent development into the Zhous' ancestor and cultural hero are recounted through vivid enumeration. Enumeration also lists the order of the ritual acts that the Zhou people perform to celebrate the harvest and commemorate their ancestor. Poems from the "Airs" section, by contrast, mostly employ "comparisons" and "evocative images." Comparisons are like similes: "Huge Rat" compares an exploitative lord directly to a voracious rodent. Evocative images are much more elusive and do not easily translate into any rhetorical trope in the Western tradition. *Xing*, the term rendered as "evocative image," literally means "stimulus" or "excitement." *Xing* brings natural images into suggestive resonance with human situations, stimulating the imagination and pushing perception beyond a simple comparison of one thing to another. Often, the animals or plants used to evoke human situations appear in the same scene with the human protagonists, but the relation between the animals or plants and the humans is mysterious. For example, in "Dead Roe Deer" the reader sees a landscape in which a girl, a "maiden white as marble," who has just been seduced by a man, hovers next to a dead deer "wrapped in white rushes."

The resonant, elusive imagery of the *Classic of Poetry* has enticed readers through the ages. The poet and critic Ezra Pound (1885–1972), attracted to and inspired by the use of imagery in Chinese poetry, spearheaded the new movement of "imagism" in the 1910s, experimenting with the poetic power that sparse juxtaposition of images whose relation remains obscure can produce. His adoption of such poetic techniques in turn profoundly influenced modernist writers such as T. S. Eliot and James Joyce. Although Pound did not know Chinese, he eventually produced a poetic rendering of the *Classic of Poetry* in collaboration with the Harvard sinologist Achilles Fang. Because of their divergence from the wording of the originals, Pound's versions might better be conceived as English poems in their own right than translations. Yet they can come close to the Chinese originals in other ways. In Pound's version, the second stanza of "Dead Roe Deer" reads, "Where the scrub elm skirts the wood, be it not in white mat bound, as a jewel flawless found, dead as doe is maidenhood." Death hovers ominously over the deer, the woman, and her maidenhood. Here we see the drama of the distinctive Chinese trope of *xing* in full play, transposed into the English language.

The *Classic of Poetry* has left deep traces in the literary cultures of East Asia into the modern period. Because its compilation was attributed to Confucius and its traditional interpretations emphasized Confucian values, it was part and parcel of the education of political elites. Yet, despite the dominant moralizing interpretations, the poems of the *Classic of Poetry* have retained their pristine simplicity and have lost nothing of their evocative power to voice fundamental human emotions and challenges.

CLASSIC OF POETRY[1]

I. Fishhawk

The fishhawks sing *guan guan*
on sandbars of the stream.
Gentle maiden, pure and fair,
fit pair for a prince.

Watercress grows here and there,
right and left we gather it.
Gentle maiden, pure and fair,
wanted waking and asleep.

Wanting, sought her, had her not,
waking, sleeping, thought of her,

1. Translated by Stephen Owen.

on and on he thought of her,
he tossed from one side to another.

Watercress grows here and there,
right and left we pull it.
Gentle maiden, pure and fair,
with harps we bring her company.

Watercress grows here and there,
right and left we pick it out.
Gentle maiden, pure and fair,
with bells and drums do her delight.

VI. Peach Tree Soft and Tender

Peach tree soft and tender,
how your blossoms glow!
The bride is going to her home,
she well befits this house.

Peach tree soft and tender,
plump, the ripening fruit.
The bride is going to her home,
she well befits this house.

Peach tree soft and tender,
its leaves spread thick and full.
The bride is going to her home,
she well befits these folk.

XX. Plums Are Falling

Plums are falling,
seven are the fruits;
many men want me,
let me have a fine one.

Plums are falling,
three are the fruits;
many men want me,
let me have a steady one.

Plums are falling,
catch them in the basket;
many men want me,
let me be bride of one.

XXIII. Dead Roe Deer

A roe deer dead in the meadow,
all wrapped in white rushes.
The maiden's heart was filled with spring;
a gentleman led her astray.

Undergrowth in forest,
dead deer in the meadow,
all wound with white rushes,
a maiden white as marble.

Softly now, and gently, gently,
do not touch my apron, sir,
and don't set the cur to barking.

XXVI. Boat of Cypress

That boat of cypress drifts along,
it drifts upon the stream.
Restless am I, I cannot sleep,
as though in torment and troubled.
Nor am I lacking wine
to ease my mind and let me roam.

This heart of mine is no mirror,
it cannot take in all.
Yes, I do have brothers,
but brothers will not be my stay.
I went and told them of my grief
and met only with their rage.

This heart of mine is no stone;
you cannot turn it where you will.
This heart of mine is no mat;
I cannot roll it up within.
I have behaved with dignity,
in this no man can fault me.

My heart is uneasy and restless,
I am reproached by little men.
Many are the woes I've met,
and taken slights more than a few.
I think on it in the quiet,
and waking pound my breast.

Oh Sun! and you Moon!
Why do you each grow dim in turn?
These troubles of the heart

are like unwashed clothes.
I think on it in the quiet,
I cannot spread wings to fly away.

XLII. Gentle Girl

A gentle girl and fair
awaits by the crook of the wall;
in shadows I don't see her;
I pace and scratch my hair.

A gentle girl and comely
gave me a scarlet pipe;
scarlet pipe that gleams—
in your beauty I find delight.

Then she brought me a reed from the pastures,
it was truly beautiful and rare.
Reed—the beauty is not yours—
you are but beauty's gift.

LXIV. Quince

She cast a quince to me,
a costly garnet I returned;
it was no equal return,
but by this love will last.

She cast a peach to me,
costly opal I returned;
it was no equal return,
but by this love will last.

She cast a plum to me,
a costly ruby I returned;
it was no equal return,
but by this love will last.

LXXVI. Zhongzi, Please

Zhongzi, please
don't cross my village wall,
don't break the willows planted there.
It's not that I care so much for them,

but I dread my father and mother;
Zhongzi may be in my thoughts,
but what my father and mother said—
that too may be held in dread.

Zhongzi, please
don't cross my fence,
don't break the mulberries planted there.
It's not that I care so much for them,
but I dread my brothers;
Zhongzi may be in my thoughts,
but what my brothers said—
that too may be held in dread.

Zhongzi, please
don't cross into my garden,
don't break the sandalwood planted there.
It's not that I care so much for them,
but I dread others will talk much;
Zhongzi may be in my thoughts,
but when people talk too much—
that too may be held in dread.

XCV. Zhen and Wei

O Zhen and Wei together,
swollen now they flow.
Men and maids together,
chrysanthemums in hand.
The maid says, "Have you looked?"
The man says, "I have gone."
"Let's go then look across the Wei,
it is truly a place for our pleasure."
Man and maid together
each frolicked with the other
and gave as gift the peony.

O Zhen and Wei together,
flowing deep and clear.
Men and maids together,
teeming everywhere.
The maid says, "Have you looked?"
The man says, "I have gone."
"Let's go then look across the Wei,
it is truly a place for our pleasure."
Man and maid together
each will frolic with the other
and give as gift the peony.

CXIII. Huge Rat

Huge rat, huge rat,
eat my millet no more,
for three years I've fed you,
yet you pay me no heed.

I swear that I will leave you
and go to a happier land.
A happy land, a happy land,
and there I will find my place.

Huge rat, huge rat,
eat my wheat no more,
for three years I've fed you
and you show no gratitude.

I swear that I will leave you
and go to a happier realm.
A happy realm, a happy realm,
there I will find what I deserve.

Huge rat, huge rat,
eat my sprouts no more,
for three years I have fed you,
and you won't reward my toil.

I swear that I will leave you
and go to happy meadows.
Happy meadows, happy meadows
where none need wail and cry.

CCXLV. She Bore the Folk

She who first bore the folk—
Jiang it was, First Parent.
How was it she bore the folk?—
she knew the rite and sacrifice.
To rid herself of sonlessness
she trod the god's toeprint
  and she was glad.
She was made great, on her luck settled,
the seed stirred, it was quick.
She gave birth, she gave suck,
and this was Lord Millet.

When her months had come to term,
her firstborn sprang up.
Not splitting, not rending,

working no hurt, no harm.
He showed his godhead glorious,
the high god was greatly soothed.
He took great joy in those rites
and easily she bore her son.

She set him in a narrow lane,
but sheep and cattle warded him.
She set him in the wooded plain,
he met with those who logged the plain.
She set him on cold ice,
birds sheltered him with wings.
Then the birds left him
and Lord Millet wailed.
This was long and this was loud;
his voice was a mighty one.

And then he crept and crawled,
he stood upright, he stood straight.
He sought to feed his mouth,
and planted there the great beans.
The great beans' leaves were fluttering,
the rows of grain were bristling.
Hemp and barley dense and dark,
the melons, plump and round.

Lord Millet in his farming
had a way to help things grow:
He rid the land of thick grass,
he planted there a glorious growth.
It was in squares, it was leafy,
it was planted, it grew tall.
It came forth, it formed ears,
it was hard, it was good.
Its tassels bent, it was full,
he had his household there in Dai.

He passed us down these wondrous grains:
our black millets, of one and two kernels,
Millets whose leaves sprout red or white,
he spread the whole land with black millet,
And reaped it and counted the acres,
spread it with millet sprouting red or white,
hefted on shoulders, loaded on backs,
he took it home and began this rite.

And how goes this rite we have?—
at times we hull, at times we scoop,
at times we winnow, at times we stomp,
we hear it slosh as we wash it,
we hear it puff as we steam it.

Then we reckon, then we consider,
take artemisia, offer fat.
We take a ram for the flaying,
then we roast it, then we sear it,
to rouse up the following year.

We heap the wooden trenchers full,
wooden trenchers, earthenware platters.
And as the scent first rises
the high god is peaceful and glad.
This great odor is good indeed,
for Lord Millet began the rite,
and hopefully free from failing or fault,
it has lasted until now.

CONFUCIUS

551–479 B.C.E.

To this day there is virtually no aspect of East Asia on which Confucius and his ideas have not had some impact. When Confucius died in 479 B.C.E., he was a relatively little-known figure, having failed to find a ruler willing to implement his philosophical vision. Although he had attracted quite a few followers and had even established a school toward the end of his life, nobody could have anticipated then how this man's legacy would shape the destiny of China, East Asia, and the world. About 350 years later, Confucian values were not only widely known and revered but had also become the basis for official Chinese state ideology during the Han Dynasty (206 B.C.E.–220 C.E.). Twenty-five hundred years later, Confucius is a national icon for China's venerable past, although Confucianism, the system of beliefs and practices that developed on the basis of Confucius's ideas, took a severe beating in mainland China during much of the twentieth century.

LIFE AND TIMES

Confucius was born in the northeastern state of Lu in today's Shandong Province. Confucius came from the lower ranks of hereditary nobility. Like other masters during the fifth to the third centuries B.C.E., a period of heated intellectual debates comparable to the contemporary flourishing of Greek philosophy, he was eager to put his talents at the disposal of an able ruler who would implement his ideas. But the rulers of Lu were often at the mercy of powerful clans whose arrogance scandalized Confucius. For example, Confucius took offence when one of the great local clans in Lu used eight rows of dancers for the ceremonies at their ancestral temple, a lavish number that only the Zhou king had the prerogative to use. In Confucius's mind, this was not a simple breach of superficial protocol but a blatant symptom of the rottenness of the political system. Disgusted with the situation in his home state, Confucius left Lu and spent many years wandering from court to court, in search of a ruler who would appreciate his talents and political vision. He finally returned to Lu and lived out his life as a teacher, gathering a considerable following.

THE ZHOU HERITAGE AND CONFUCIUS'S INNOVATION

Confucius's philosophical vision brims with admiration for the values of the early Zhou rulers. The Zhou Dynasty (ca. 1045–256 B.C.E.), by Confucius's time already five centuries old, began with two exemplary rulers, King Wen and King Wu. King Wu had destroyed the last remnants of the reputedly despised Shang Dynasty in the eleventh century B.C.E., and instituted a new government that took pride in showing concern for the people and enforcing wise policies. After King Wu's death his brother, the Duke of Zhou, conducted government affairs for the duke's young nephew, King Cheng, who was still a child. Besides King Wen, the Duke of Zhou had particular importance for Confucius, not just because he was the ancestor of the ducal family of Confucius's home state. The Duke of Zhou also protected his nephew from rebellions and challenges to the newly founded dynasty and was an exemplary regent, with an eye on the welfare of the dynasty, not on his personal ambitions. But the splendor of the dynastic founders vanished over the next half millennium, as the Zhou kings increasingly lost control over the feudal lords, who had started out as their allies in the war against the Shang. By Confucius's time the Zhou kings had only nominal power and China consisted of rival states, whose rulers competed for territory and power. In the *Analects* Confucius often sharply criticizes the irreverent behavior of the feudal lords toward the Zhou king and showcases

This rubbing on paper, copied from an engraved stone slab, shows how later ages imagined Confucius. It is from Qufu, Shandong Province, Confucius's birthplace.

their corruption to explain his vision of proper government.

Although Confucius claims in the *Analects* that he is merely the "transmitter" of Zhou values and not an "innovator," he actually built a new tradition. Confucius's conviction that the political chaos he perceived around him could be avoided by returning to the moral values of the venerable founders of the Zhou Dynasty, Kings Wu and Wen and the Duke of Zhou, paid homage to tradition but was also visionary, even revolutionary. His emphasis on the importance of social roles and rituals could reinforce existing hierarchies, but at the same time it allowed individuals to develop their inner potential and find a meaningful place in society. His pedagogical program, which promoted the reading of a group of texts, later called "Confucian Classics," and their application to life's challenges, could lead to mindless memorization designed merely for career advancement, but it also enabled people to better understand and take control of their lives by following the moral models, historical precedents, and words of wisdom contained in these canonical texts.

DIVERSITY AND CORE VALUES IN THE *ANALECTS*

Confucius's vision has been extraordinarily influential over the past two and a half millennia and has profoundly shaped the societies not just of China but also of Korea, Japan, and Vietnam. The *Analects*, best translated as "Collected Sayings," convey the power of Confucius's vision. A collection of brief quotations, conversations, and anecdotes from the life of Confucius, the *Analects* were not written by the master himself, but compiled by later generations of disciples. They probably reached their current form only during the second century B.C.E., when Confucius's ideas were gaining influence and it became necessary to create a representative collection of his sayings out of the vast body of Confucius lore that circulated in various other books. Later it became the key text to understanding the great master's character and ideas. The *Analects* throw light on people, concrete situations, and above all the exemplary model of Confucius himself, instead of supplying systematic expositions of his ideas or abstract definitions of moral philosophy. When commenting on central concepts such as "goodness" or "humanity" (*ren*), "ritual" (*li*), and "respect for one's parents" (*xiao*), Confucius might utter different, even contradictory maxims: sometimes he claims that anybody who wants to can become "humane" in a moment, but at other times he turns the concept into a distant ideal. He also explains that his answers sometimes differ, because an overeager disciple needs to be held back, while a timid one needs to be encouraged. Another explanation for the widely divergent pieces of advice to be found in the *Analects* is that it was compiled over several centuries and thus includes the changing opinions of the compilers.

RITUAL

Despite the diversity of views expounded in the *Analects*, it is possible to identify a core set of values. First, there is Confucius's emphasis on ritual. Everything we do in life is a ritual, whether we greet each other with a handshake or mark life's important moments, such as birth and death, with special observances. Although Confucius briefly refers to earlier notions of the powers of Heaven and declares that he respects the gods and spirits, his concern is with our world, the world of human society. Rituals are thus used not to communicate with divine powers, but instead to make social life meaningful. One learns and perfects these rituals in one's community through continuous practice and self-cultivation. The person who has perfected himself in this manner is the *junzi*—the "superior person," or "gentleman." The word referred originally to a prince of aristocratic birth, but Confucius boldly applies it to moral, not hereditary, superiority. Although Confucius at times denies having reached the stage of *junzi* himself, he makes clear that anybody can become a *junzi*, and that everyone should strive to reach that ideal. The *Analects* also idealize historical figures whom Confucius considers models of exemplary moral conduct. Even before the sage rulers of the Zhou, there were the sage emperors of highest antiquity, including Emperor Shun, whose moral charisma was so overwhelming that it sufficed for him to sit in proper ritual position on his throne to induce spontaneous order in his empire. In Confucianism, models of proper ritual behavior are crucial to guiding one's moral self-cultivation, and book 10 of the *Analects* enshrines the master himself as such a model actor: it is the only book in which the master does not speak, but is simply shown in silent ritual action. That the compilers of the *Analects* placed this book at the heart of the *Analects*' twenty books shows that they admired Confucius not just for what he said, but for his exemplary conduct throughout his life.

SOCIAL ROLES

A second recurrent concern in the *Analects* is Confucius's attention to social roles. In his words humans owe each other "goodness" or "humanity" (*ren*)—that is, empathy and reciprocal concern, mutual respect and obligation. Some later Confucians, such as Mencius (ca. 372–289 B.C.E.), believed that this natural ability for empathy was even more important than ritual. The natural and spontaneous basis for respect is the relation between child and parent. From this experience, respect is extended to other figures, such as elder siblings, seniors, and rulers.

Although Confucius endorses social hierarchies, he abhorred any form of force and coercion. Because Confucianism and its canonical texts became the basis for the recruitment of bureaucrats and part of the ideology of government in imperial China, it is sometimes portrayed as a philosophy that, in contrast to Daoism, puts social duty over natural desires. Yet the stance of Confucius in the *Analects* is much more complex. He often navigates between the instincts of inborn nature and the need for cultivation, the power of spontaneous action and the importance of patient learning, the pleasures of a life in harmony with one's wishes and the duties of a life devoted to political service. In book 18 we see Confucius attracted to recluses, dropouts who reject life in society; another time Confucius praises the view of a disciple who values ritual celebration and joyful singing with friends over petty state service. At yet another point Confucius recommends avoiding government service unless a virtuous ruler is on the throne.

EFFICIENT ACTION

Goodness, ritual, and attention to social roles create order in society; efficient action, another major Confucian concern, helps to maintain it and to effect change in the world. One of Confucius's most attractive ideas is his promise that it is possible to harmonize one's natural impulses with social norms and thus become an efficient, harmonious agent in society. He himself apparently reached this balance only in old age: "At seventy I followed my heart's desire without overstepping the line." Throughout the *Analects*, Confucius is fascinated with various kinds of efficiency. Emperor Shun, facing south on his throne and thereby creating order in the world, is the prime incarnation of minimalist action put to great effect. The notion that the moral charisma of a sage ruler can be so powerful that there is no need to resort to lowly means of war and violence became the basis of the traditional Chinese view of rulership. Confucius's admiration for efficient thinking is best exemplified by his praise of his favorite disciple Yan Hui: "When he is told one thing he understands ten." The master of efficient speech, Confucius himself seems always to know more than he says: his utterances can be so short that they verge on the obscure. Sometimes he even speaks of his desire to reject language altogether.

THE IMPORTANCE OF CANONICAL TEXTS IN CONFUCIANISM

Confucius and his followers, called *Ru*, or "traditionalist scholars," considered the study of the ancient texts that contained the legacy of the Zhou as paramount to self-cultivation. Confucius is traditionally associated with the composition of the ***Classic of Poetry***, *Classic of History*, *Record of Ritual*, *Spring and Autumn Annals*, and *Classic of Changes*, which were later called the "Confucian Classics." Today hardly anybody believes that they were written or compiled by Confucius. These books became the curriculum in the first Chinese state university, founded in 124 B.C.E. by Emperor Wu of the Han Dynasty. Later the Confucian Classics and other canonical Confucian texts such as the *Analects* formed the basis for the all-important civil service examination system, which allowed hundreds of thousands of individuals to attain office in the expansive bureaucracy of the Chinese empire. For more than two millennia these texts were the backbone of the training of political and cultural elites throughout East Asia and Confucius was venerated in temples as "the foremost teacher," a deity of moral perfection and learning.

Throughout its long history, Confucianism has served many political, social, and religious causes, and it has therefore also met with strident criticism. Already in the late fifth century B.C.E., Mozi, the first forceful critic of Confucius, wrote a devastating piece, "Against the Confucians," in which he parodied Confucians as "beggars, greedy hamsters, and staring he-goats who puff themselves up like wild boars." Their clothes, cries Mozi, are hopelessly old-fashioned, and they cling to the importance of ritual only because they hope to get a good meal out of the sacrificial food prepared for the occasion.

In the twentieth century, Chinese intellectuals and the Communist Party waged mass campaigns against Confucianism, considering it the utmost evil and blaming it for everything that supposedly went wrong with China's modernization. Yet many public intellectuals in Taiwan and the United States have been propagating "Neo-Confucianism" and are convinced that it can help renew humanistic values in today's harsh and cynical world. Since the 1990s the Confucius temples in mainland China have been rebuilt. Confucius is now discussed on television talk shows in China, and the Chinese government uses his name to represent China in the world. References to Confucius hovered over the Beijing Olympics of 2008, and in the first decade of the twenty-first century the government founded several hundred "Confucius Institutes" around the world and thus uses the old sage as an icon for the propagation of Chinese language and culture. The future of Confucius's legacy is as bright as ever.

From Analects[1]

From *Book I*

1.1. The Master said: "To learn something and then to put it into practice at the right time: is this not a joy? To have friends coming from afar: is this not a delight? Not to be upset when one's merits are ignored: is this not the mark of a gentleman?"

1. Translated by Simon Leys.

1.4. Master Zeng said: "I examine myself three times a day. When dealing on behalf of others, have I been trustworthy? In intercourse with my friends, have I been faithful? Have I practiced what I was taught?"

1.11. The Master said: "When the father is alive, watch the son's aspirations. When the father is dead, watch the son's actions. If three years later, the son has not veered from the father's way, he may be called a dutiful son indeed."

From *Book II*

2.1. The Master said: "He who rules by virtue is like the polestar, which remains unmoving in its mansion while all the other stars revolve respectfully around it."

2.2. The Master said: "The three hundred *Poems*[2] are summed up in one single phrase: 'Think no evil.' "

2.4. The Master said: "At fifteen, I set my mind upon learning. At thirty, I took my stand. At forty, I had no doubts. At fifty, I knew the will of Heaven. At sixty, my ear was attuned. At seventy, I follow all the desires of my heart without breaking any rule."

2.7. Ziyou asked about filial piety. The Master said: "Nowadays people think they are dutiful sons when they feed their parents. Yet they also feed their dogs and horses. Unless there is respect, where is the difference?"

2.11. The Master said: "He who by revising the old knows the new, is fit to be a teacher."

2.19. Duke Ai[3] asked: "What should I do to win the hearts of the people?" Confucius replied: "Raise the straight and set them above the crooked, and you will win the hearts of the people. If you raise the crooked and set them above the straight, the people will deny you their support."

From *Book III*

3.5. The Master said: "Barbarians who have rulers are inferior to the various nations of China who are without."

3.21. Duke Ai asked Zai Yu which wood should be used for the local totem. Zai Yu replied: "The men of Xia used pine; the men of Yin used cypress; the men of Zhou used *fir*, for (they said) the people should *fear*."[4]

The Master heard of this; he said: "What is done is done, it is all past; there would be no point in arguing."

2. Another name for the *Classic of Poetry*.
3. Ruler of the dukedom of Lu, Confucius's home state.
4. Zai Yu, one of Confucius's disciples, replies to the duke with a pun: in the original text the chestnut tree (*li*), translated here as "fir," puns on "fear" (*li*).

3.24. The officer in charge of the border at Yi requested an interview with Confucius. He said: "Whenever a gentleman comes to these parts, I always ask to see him." The disciples arranged an interview. When it was over, the officer said to them: "Gentlemen, do not worry about his dismissal. The world has been without the Way for a long while. Heaven is going to use your master to ring the tocsin."

From *Book IV*

4.8. The Master said: "In the morning hear the Way; in the evening die content."

4.15. The Master said: "Shen, my doctrine has one single thread running through it." Master Zeng Shen replied: "Indeed."

The Master left. The other disciples asked: "What did he mean?" Master Zeng said: "The doctrine of the Master is: Loyalty and reciprocity, and that's all."

From *Book V*

5.9. The Master asked Zigong: "Which is the better, you or Yan Hui?"[5]—"How could I compare myself with Yan Hui? From one thing he learns, he deduces ten; from one thing I learn, I only deduce two." The Master said: "Indeed, you are not his equal, and neither am I."

5.10. Zai Yu was sleeping during the day. The Master said: "Rotten wood cannot be carved; dung walls cannot be troweled. What is the use of scolding him?"

The Master said: "There was a time when I used to listen to what people said and trusted that they would act accordingly, but now I listen to what they say and watch what they do. It is Zai Yu who made me change."

5.20. Lord Ji Wen[6] always thought thrice before acting. Hearing this, the Master said: "Twice is enough."

5.26. Yan Hui and Zilu were in attendance. The Master said: "How about telling me your private wishes?"

Zilu said: "I wish I could share my carriages, horses, clothes, and furs with my friends without being upset when they damage them."

Yan Hui said. "I wish I would never boast of my good qualities or call attention to my good deeds."

Zilu said: "May we ask what are our Master's private wishes?"

The Master said: "I wish the old may enjoy peace, friends may enjoy trust, and the young may enjoy affection."

5. Confucius's most beloved disciple.

6. Grand officer of the state of Lu, who lived before Confucius's time.

From *Book VI*

6.3. Duke Ai asked: "Which of the disciples has a love of learning?" Confucius replied: "There was Yan Hui who loved learning; he never vented his frustrations upon others; he never made the same mistake twice. Alas, his allotted span of life was short; he is dead. Now, for all I know, there is no one with such a love of learning."

6.12. Ran Qiu said: "It is not that I do not enjoy the Master's way, but I do not have the strength to follow it." The Master said: "He who does not have the strength can always give up halfway. But you have given up before starting."

6.13. The Master said to Zixia: "Be a noble scholar, not a vulgar pedant."

6.18. The Master said: "When nature prevails over culture, you get a savage; when culture prevails over nature, you get a pedant. When nature and culture are in balance, you get a gentleman."

6.20. The Master said: "To know something is not as good as loving it; to love something is not as good as rejoicing in it."

6.22. Fan Chi asked about wisdom. The Master said: "Secure the rights of the people; respect ghosts and gods, but keep them at a distance—this is wisdom indeed."

Fan Chi asked about goodness. The Master said: "A good man's trials bear fruit—this is goodness indeed."

6.23. The Master said: "The wise find joy on the water, the good find joy in the mountains. The wise are active, the good are quiet. The wise are joyful, the good live long."

From *Book VII*

7.1. The Master said: "I transmit, I invent nothing. I trust and love the past. In this, I dare to compare myself to our venerable Peng."[7]

7.3. The Master said: "Failure to cultivate moral power, failure to explore what I have learned, incapacity to stand by what I know to be right, incapacity to reform what is not good—these are my worries."

7.5. The Master said: "I am getting dreadfully old. It has been a long time since I last saw in a dream the Duke of Zhou."[8]

7. Identifications of this figure vary, but venerable Peng might have been a virtuous official of the Shang Dynasty (ca. 1500–1045 B.C.E.).
8. Son of King Wen, who together with King Wu founded the Zhou Dynasty (1045–256 B.C.E.). He laid the groundwork for basic institutions of the Zhou Dynasty and is the founding ancestor of the state of Lu, Confucius's home state.

7.16. The Master said: "Even though you have only coarse grain for food, water for drink, and your bent arm for a pillow, you may still be happy. Riches and honors without justice are to me as fleeting clouds."

7.21. The Master never talked of: miracles; violence; disorders; spirits.

From *Book VIII*

8.5. Master Zeng said: "Competent, yet willing to listen to the incompetent; talented, yet willing to listen to the talentless; having, yet seeming not to have; full, yet seeming empty; swallowing insults without taking offense—long ago, I had a friend who practiced these things."

8.8. The Master said: "Draw inspiration from the *Poems;* steady your course with the ritual; find your fulfillment in music."

8.13. The Master said: "Uphold the faith, love learning, defend the good Way with your life. Enter not a country that is unstable: dwell not in a country that is in turmoil. Shine in a world that follows the Way; hide when the world loses the Way. In a country where the Way prevails, it is shameful to remain poor and obscure; in a country which has lost the Way, it is shameful to become rich and honored."

8.17. The Master said: "Learning is like a chase in which, as you fail to catch up, you fear to lose what you have already gained."

From *Book IX*

9.5. The Master was trapped in Kuang. He said: "King Wen is dead: is civilization not resting now on me? If Heaven intends civilization to be destroyed, why was it vested in me? If Heaven does not intend civilization to be destroyed, what should I fear from the people of Kuang?"[9]

9.6. The Grand Chamberlain asked Zigong: "Is your Master not a saint? But then, why should he also possess so many particular aptitudes?" Zigong replied: "Heaven indeed made him a saint; but he also happens to have many aptitudes."

Hearing of this, the Master said: "The Grand Chamberlain truly knows me. In my youth, I was poor; therefore, I had to become adept at a variety of lowly skills. Does such versatility befit a gentleman? No, it does not."

9.12. The Master was very ill. Zilu organized the disciples in a retinue, as if they were the retainers of a lord. During a remission of his illness, the Master said: "Zilu, this farce has lasted long enough. Whom can I deceive with these sham retainers? Can I deceive Heaven? Rather than die amidst retainers,

9. Kuang was a border town where Confucius nearly fell into the hands of a lynch mob who mistook him for an adventurer who had ransacked the region. Confucius uses a pun in making his point: the name of King Wen, the founder of the Zhou Dynasty, also means "civilization" (*wen*).

I prefer to die in the arms of my disciples. I may not receive a state funeral, but still I shall not die by the wayside."

9.14. The Master wanted to settle among the nine barbarian tribes of the East. Someone said: "It is wild in those parts. How would you cope?" The Master said: "How could it be wild, once a gentleman has settled there?"

9.17. The Master stood by a river and said: "Everything flows like this, without ceasing, day and night."

9.23. The Master said: "One should regard the young with awe: how do you know that the next generation will not equal the present one? If, however, by the age of forty or fifty, a man has not made a name for himself, he no longer deserves to be taken seriously."

From *Book X*

10.2. At court, when conversing with the under ministers, he was affable; when conversing with the upper ministers, he was respectful. In front of the ruler, he was humble yet composed.

10.4. When entering the gate of the Duke's palace, he walked in discreetly. He never stood in the middle of the passage, nor did he tread on the threshold.

When he passed in front of the throne, he adopted an expression of gravity, hastened his step, and became as if speechless. When ascending the steps of the audience hall, he lifted up the hem of his gown and bowed, as if short of breath; on coming out, after descending the first step, he expressed relief and contentment.

At the bottom of the steps, he moved swiftly, as if on wings. On regaining his place, he resumed his humble countenance.

From *Book XI*

11.9. Yan Hui died. The Master said: "Alas! Heaven is destroying me. Heaven is destroying me!"

11.10. Yan Hui died. The Master wailed wildly. His followers said: "Master, such grief is not proper." The Master said: "In mourning such a man, what sort of grief would be proper?"

11.26. Zilu, Zeng Dian, Ran Qiu, and Gongxi Chi were sitting with the Master. The Master said: "Forget for one moment that I am your elder. You often say: 'The world does not recognize our merits.' But, given the opportunity, what would you wish to do?"

Zilu rushed to reply first: "Give me a country not too small,[1] but squeezed between powerful neighbors; it is under attack and in the grip of a famine. Put

1. Literally "a country of a thousand chariots."

me in charge: within three years, I would revive the spirits of the people and set them back on their feet."

The Master smiled. "Ran Qiu, what about you?"

The other replied: "Give me a domain of sixty to seventy—or, say, fifty to sixty leagues; within three years I would secure the prosperity of its people. As regards their spiritual well-being, however, this would naturally have to wait for the intervention of a true gentleman."

"Gongxi Chi, what about you?"

"I don't say that I would be able to do this, but I would like to learn: in the ceremonies of the Ancestral Temple, such as a diplomatic conference for instance, wearing chasuble and cap, I would like to play the part of a junior assistant."

"And what about you, Zeng Dian?"

Zeng Dian, who had been softly playing his zithern, plucked one last chord and pushed his instrument aside. He replied: "I am afraid my wish is not up to those of my three companions." The Master said: "There is no harm in that! After all, each is simply confiding his personal aspirations."

"In late spring, after the making of the spring clothes has been completed, together with five or six companions and six or seven boys, I would like to bathe in the River Yi, and then enjoy the breeze on the Rain Dance Terrace, and go home singing." The Master heaved a deep sigh and said: "I am with Dian!"

The three others left; Zeng Dian remained behind and said: "What did you think of their wishes?" The Master said: "Each simply confided his personal aspirations."

"Why did you smile at Zilu?"

"One should govern a state through ritual restraint; yet his words were full of swagger."

"As for Ran Qiu, wasn't he in fact talking about a full-fledged state?"

"Indeed; have you ever heard of 'a domain of sixty to seventy, or fifty to sixty leagues'?"

"And Gongxi Chi? Wasn't he also talking about a state?"

"A diplomatic conference in the Ancestral Temple! What could it be, if not an international gathering? And if Gongxi Chi were there merely to play the part of a junior assistant, who would qualify for the main role?"

Silence - Maxims of Good Discourse

From *Book XII*

12.2. Ran Yong asked about humanity. The Master said: "When abroad, behave as if in front of an important guest. Lead the people as if performing a great ceremony. What you do not wish for yourself, do not impose upon others. Let no resentment enter public affairs; let no resentment enter private affairs."

Ran Yong said: "I may not be clever, but with your permission I shall endeavor to do as you have said."

12.5. Sima Niu was grieving: "All men have brothers; I alone have none." Zixia said: "I have heard this: life and death are decreed by fate, riches and honors are allotted by Heaven. Since a gentleman behaves with reverence and diligence, treating people with deference and courtesy, all within the Four Seas are his brothers. How could a gentleman ever complain that he has no brothers?"

12.7. Zigong asked about government. The Master said: "Sufficient food, sufficient weapons, and the trust of the people." Zigong said: "If you had to do without one of these three, which would you give up?—"Weapons."—"If you had to do without one of the remaining two, which would you give up?"—"Food; after all, everyone has to die eventually. But without the trust of the people, no government can stand."

12.11. Duke Jing of Qi asked Confucius about government. Confucius replied: "Let the lord be a lord; the subject a subject; the father a father; the son a son." The Duke said: "Excellent! If indeed the lord is not a lord, the subject not a subject, the father not a father, the son not a son, I could be sure of nothing anymore—not even of my daily food."

12.18. Lord Ji Kang was troubled by burglars. He consulted with Confucius. Confucius replied: "If you yourself were not covetous, they would not rob you, even if you paid them to."

12.19. Lord Ji Kang asked Confucius about government, saying: "Suppose I were to kill the bad to help the good: how about that?" Confucius replied: "You are here to govern, what need is there to kill? If you desire what is good, the people will be good. The moral power of the gentleman is wind, the moral power of the common man is grass. Under the wind, the grass must bend."

From *Book XIII*

13.1. Zilu asked about government. The Master said: "Guide them. Encourage them." Zilu asked him to develop these precepts. The Master said: "Untiringly."

13.3. Zilu asked: "If the ruler of Wei were to entrust you with the government of the country, what would be your first initiative?" The Master said: "It would certainly be to rectify the names." Zilu said: "Really? Isn't this a little farfetched? What is this rectification for?" The Master said: "How boorish can you get! Whereupon a gentleman is incompetent, thereupon he should remain silent. If the names are not correct, language is without an object. When language is without an object, no affair can be effected. When no affair can be effected, rites and music wither. When rites and music wither, punishments and penalties miss their target. When punishments and penalties miss their target, the people do not know where they stand. Therefore, whatever a gentleman conceives of, he must be able to say; and whatever he says, he must be able to do. In the matter of language, a gentleman leaves nothing to chance."

13.10. The Master said: "If a ruler could employ me, in one year I would make things work, and in three years the results would show."

13.11. The Master said: " 'When good men have been running the country for a hundred years, cruelty can be overcome, and murder extirpated.' How true is this saying!"

13.12. The Master said: "Even with a true king, it would certainly take one generation for humanity to prevail."

13.20. Zigong asked: "How does one deserve to be called a gentleman?" The Master said: "He who behaves with honor, and, being sent on a mission to the four corners of the world, does not bring disgrace to his lord, deserves to be called a gentleman."

"And next to that, if I may ask?"

"His relatives praise his filial piety and the people of his village praise the way he respects the elders."

"And next to that, if I may ask?"

"His word can be trusted; whatever he undertakes, he brings to completion. In this, he may merely show the obstinacy of a vulgar man; still, he should probably qualify as a gentleman of lower category."

"In this respect, how would you rate our present politicians?"

"Alas! These puny creatures are not even worth mentioning!"

From *Book XIV*

14.24. The Master said: "In the old days, people studied to improve themselves. Now they study in order to impress others."

14.35. The Master said: "No one understands me!" Zigong said: "Why is it that no one understands you?" The Master said: "I do not accuse Heaven, nor do I blame men; here below I am learning, and there above I am being heard. If I am understood, it must be by Heaven."

14.38. Zilu stayed for the night at the Stone Gate. The gatekeeper said: "Where are you from?" Zilu said: "I am from Confucius's household."—"Oh, is that the one who keeps pursuing what he knows is impossible?"

14.43. Yuan Rang sat waiting, with his legs spread wide. The Master said: "A youth who does not respect his elders will achieve nothing when he grows up, and will even try to shirk death when he reaches old age: he is a parasite." And he struck him across the shin with his stick.

From *Book XV*

15.3. The Master said: "Zigong, do you think that I am someone who learns a lot of things and then stores them all up?"—"Indeed; is it not so?" The Master said: "No. I have one single thread on which to string them all."

15.5. The Master said: "Shun[2] was certainly one of those who knew how to govern by inactivity. How did he do it? He sat reverently on the throne, facing south—and that was all."

15.7. The Master said: "How straight Shi Yu was! Under a good government, he was straight as an arrow: under a bad government, he was straight as an arrow. What a gentleman was Qu Boyu![3] Under a good government, he displayed his talents. Under a bad government, he folded them up in his heart."

2. Emperor of high antiquity known for his exemplary virtue. The throne usually faced south.

3. Shi Yu and Qu Boyu were both high officials in the state of Wei. Confucius was once hosted by Qu Boyu.

15.31. The Master said: "In an attempt to meditate, I once spent a whole day without food and a whole night without sleep: it was no use. It is better to study."

From *Book XVII*

17.4. The Master went to Wucheng, where Ziyou was governor. He heard the sound of stringed instruments and hymns. He was amused and said with a smile: "Why use an ox-cleaver to kill a chicken?" Ziyou replied: "Master, in the past I have heard you say: 'The gentleman who cultivates the Way loves all men; the small people who cultivate the Way are easy to govern.'" The Master said: "My friends, Ziyou is right. I was just joking."

17.9. The Master said: "Little ones, why don't you study the *Poems*? The *Poems* can provide you with stimulation and with observation, with a capacity for communion, and with a vehicle for grief. At home, they enable you to serve your father, and abroad, to serve your lord. Also, you will learn there the names of many birds, animals, plants, and trees."

17.19. The Master said: "I wish to speak no more." Zigong said: "Master, if you do not speak, how would little ones like us still be able to hand down any teachings?" The Master said: "Does Heaven speak? Yet the four seasons follow their course and the hundred creatures continue to be born. Does Heaven speak?"

17.21. Zai Yu asked: "Three years mourning for one's parents—this is quite long. If a gentleman stops all ritual practices for three years, the practices will decay; if he stops all musical performances for three years, music will be lost. As the old crop is consumed, a new crop grows up, and for lighting the fire, a new lighter is used with each season. One year of mourning should be enough." The Master said: "If after only one year, you were again to eat white rice and to wear silk, would you feel at ease?"—"Absolutely."—"In that case, go ahead! The reason a gentleman prolongs his mourning is simply that, since fine food seems tasteless to him, and music offers him no enjoyment, and the comfort of his house makes him uneasy, he prefers to do without all these pleasures. But now, if you can enjoy them, go ahead!"

Zai Yu left. The Master said: "Zai Yu is devoid of humanity. After a child is born, for the first three years of his life, he does not leave his parents' bosom. Three years mourning is a custom that is observed everywhere in the world. Did Zai Yu never enjoy the love of his parents, even for three years?"

From *Book XVIII*

18.5. Jieyu, the Madman of Chu, went past Confucius, singing:

Phoenix, oh Phoenix!
The past cannot be retrieved,
But the future still holds a chance
Give up, give up!
The days of those in office are numbered!

Confucius stopped his chariot, for he wanted to speak with him, but the other hurried away and disappeared. Confucius did not succeed in speaking to him.

18.6. Changju and Jieni were ploughing together. Confucius, who was passing by, sent Zilu to ask where the ford was. Changju said: "Who is in the chariot?" Zilu said: "It is Confucius." "The Confucius from Lu?" "Himself."—"Then he already knows where the ford is."

Zilu then asked Jieni, who replied: "Who are you?"—"I am Zilu."—"The disciple of Confucius, from Lu?"—"Yes."—"The whole universe is swept along by the same flood; who can reverse its flow? Instead of following a gentleman who keeps running from one patron to the next, would it not be better to follow a gentleman who has forsaken the world?" All the while he kept on tilling his field.

Zilu came back and reported to Confucius. Rapt in thought, the Master sighed: "One cannot associate with birds and beasts. With whom should I keep company, if not with my own kind? If the world were following the Way, I would not have to reform it."

DAODEJING / LAOZI

sixth–third centuries B.C.E.

Attributed to a master called Laozi, the *Daodejing* ("The Classic of the Way and Its Virtue") is the most often translated early Chinese text. It is also the most paradoxical, because it uses logical contradictions to articulate its vision. The *Daodejing* exhorts its readers in pithy, simple language to return to the natural way of things, to reject the corruptions of human civilization, and to adopt a productive passiveness, a stance of "nonaction," that promises unexpected success. It claims that those who understand it will preserve their lives in a dangerous world, reach their goals, and gain political power. The *Daodejing* declares at one point that its message is easy to understand, but the fact that more than seven hundred commentaries have been written on the *Daodejing* over the past 2,200 years shows that it is hardly self-explanatory. The lack of agreement among readers about the *Daodejing*'s message has only increased its popularity. It has become familiar to readers around the world thanks to the great number of translations, which sometimes differ so considerably that readers wonder whether they are all reading the same source text.

The *Daodejing* contains eighty-one short chapters written in rhythmic verse. It is divided into two main parts: one part on the "Way" (*dao*) and one part on "Virtue" (*de*). The Way refers to a natural, uncorrupted way of being that pervades everything in heaven and earth, from all beings in the cosmos to humans. Virtue is the power inherent in each thing in its natural state and the force that allows humans to reach their full potential. Both concepts were central to the intense philosophical debates initiated by **Confucius** (551–479 B.C.E.), and they remained important during the so-called Warring States Period (403–221 B.C.E.), when China was divided into small rival states. During this time thinkers traveled from state to state to offer political advice to rulers hungry for territory and power. The rich corpus of so-called Masters Literature, philosophical texts centered around charismatic master figures, allows us to follow these masters' arguments in great detail. Much of the debate focused on how rulers should govern their states, and how individuals can live the best possible life. Although the thinkers of the Warring States Period did not agree about the meaning of the Way and of Virtue, they all considered these concepts important, and they discussed and debated them at length. Yet the *Daodejing* placed so much emphasis on the concept of *dao* that, together with ***Zhuangzi***, it became the foundational text of Daoism, the "School of the Way." Recent excavations that produced copies of the *Daodejing* from a tomb datable to around 300 B.C.E. confirm that the text existed by that time in its more or less finished form, though the order of chapters differs.

Many Masters Texts argue for good government and a good life by referring to memorable historical events and people. But the *Daodejing* boldly projects its message beyond any specific time and place. Instead, it evokes cosmic categories such as the Way and relies on the power not of history but of universal natural imagery: the "uncarved block," the "spirit of the valley," the "gateway of the manifold secrets," or "the mysterious female." There is no identifiable speaker, except for an indefinite "I" that delivers words of wisdom as if talking from the "cosmic void." Claiming that the Way cannot be named or explained, many chapters define it negatively. They criticize conventional wisdom and elevate the values that contradict it. The *Daodejing* teaches that weakness, softness, and passivity, not force, rigidity, and assertive action, are qualities key to surviving in a dangerous world. It preaches that emptiness, not fullness; the female, not the male principle; and counterintuitive, not conventional wisdom are needed to succeed. Unlike most early Chinese texts that hurl their attacks directly against their opponents, the *Daodejing* cleverly abstains from naming rival schools of thought and thus places itself above the heated intellectual strife that surrounds it. It does not mention Confucius by name, but its polemical attack on Confucian values such as moral virtue, positive action, and refinement through education, which leads away from the state of nature, leaves no doubt that the *Daodejing* was partly written as a refutation of Confucius and his followers.

Despite its praise of weakness and nonaction, the *Daodejing* contains a powerful political philosophy and provides recipes of how to "win the empire" and how to succeed in a world of political competition and intrigue. This aspect of its message is addressed to those aspiring to become both sages and rulers: they should preserve their power by keeping the populace ignorant and manipulating them imperceptibly from above, giving the impression of not interfering but ultimately exercising absolute power.

In traditional China, the *Daodejing* was attractive because it provided a radical alternative to the Confucian vision of human morality and cultivation and was couched in poignant paradoxical formulations. Instead of arguing against the Confucian vision, it built an alternative universe that seemed to transcend the intellectual disputes of the centuries during which it was written. Although its political teachings appear abstract to the point of becoming impractical, the *Daodejing* has lost nothing of its influence. It is present in ever new editions on bookshelves around the world and variously praised as a manual of self-actualization, professional success, and leadership training in a postindustrial world.

Daodejing[1]

I

The way that can be spoken of
Is not the constant way;
The name that can be named
Is not the constant name.
The nameless was the beginning of heaven
and earth;
The named was the mother of the myriad creatures.
Hence always rid yourself of desires in order to
observe its secrets;
But always allow yourself to have desires in order
to observe its manifestations.
These two are the same
But diverge in name as they issue forth.
Being the same they are called mysteries,
Mystery upon mystery—
The gateway of the manifold secrets.

II

The whole world recognizes the beautiful as the beautiful, yet this is
only the ugly; the whole world recognizes the good as the good,
yet this is only the bad.
Thus Something and Nothing produce each other;
The difficult and the easy complement each other;
The long and the short off-set each other;
The high and the low incline towards each other;
Note and sound harmonize with each other;
Before and after follow each other.
Therefore the sage keeps to the deed that consists in taking no action
and practises the teaching that uses no words.
The myriad creatures rise from it yet it claims no authority;
It gives them life yet claims no possession;
It benefits them yet exacts no gratitude;
It accomplishes its task yet lays claim to no merit.
It is because it lays claim to no merit
That its merit never deserts it.

1. Translated by D. C. Lau.

III

Not to honor men of worth will keep the people from contention; not to value goods which are hard to come by will keep them from theft; not to display what is desirable will keep them from being unsettled of mind.
Therefore in governing the people, the sage empties their minds but fills their bellies, weakens their wills but strengthens their bones. He always keeps them innocent of knowledge and free from desire, and ensures that the clever never dare to act.
Do that which consists in taking no action, and order will prevail.

IV

The way is empty, yet use will not drain it.
Deep, it is like the ancestor of the myriad creatures.
Blunt the sharpness;
Untangle the knots;
Soften the glare;
Let your wheels move only along old ruts.
Darkly visible, it only seems as if it were there.
I know not whose son it is.
It images the forefather of God.

V

Heaven and earth are ruthless, and treat the myriad creatures as straw dogs;[2] the sage is ruthless, and treats the people as straw dogs.
Is not the space between heaven and earth like a bellows?
It is empty without being exhausted:
The more it works the more comes out.
Much speech leads inevitably to silence.
Better to hold fast to the void.

VI

The spirit of the valley never dies.
This is called the mysterious female.
The gateway of the mysterious female
Is called the root of heaven and earth.
Dimly visible, it seems as if it were there,
Yet use will never drain it.

2. Straw dogs were sometimes used in rituals. They were treated with great respect during the ceremony, only to be trampled on and discarded afterward.

VII

Heaven and earth are enduring. The reason why heaven and earth can be enduring is that they do not give themselves life. Hence they are able to be long-lived.
Therefore the sage puts his person last and it comes first,
Treats it as extraneous to himself and it is preserved.
Is it not because he is without thought of self that he is able to accomplish his private ends?

VIII

Highest good is like water. Because water excels in benefiting the myriad creatures without contending with them and settles where none would like to be, it comes close to the way.
In a home it is the site that matters;
In quality of mind it is depth that matters;
In an ally it is benevolence that matters;
In speech it is good faith that matters;
In government it is order that matters;
In affairs it is ability that matters;
In action it is timeliness that matters.
It is because it does not contend that it is never at fault.

XI

Thirty spokes
Share one hub.
Adapt the nothing therein to the purpose in hand, and you will have the use of the cart. Knead clay in order to make a vessel. Adapt the nothing therein to the purpose in hand, and you will have the use of the vessel. Cut out doors and windows in order to make a room. Adapt the nothing[3] therein to the purpose in hand, and you will have the use of the room.
Thus what we gain is Something, yet it is by virtue of Nothing that this can be put to use.

XII

The five colors make man's eyes blind;
The five notes make his ears deaf;
The five tastes injure his palate;
Riding and hunting

3. "Nothing" in these instances refers to the empty spaces of wheels, vessels, and rooms.

Make his mind go wild with excitement;
Goods hard to come by
Serve to hinder his progress.
Hence the sage is
For the belly
Not for the eye.
Therefore he discards the one and takes the other.

XVI

I do my utmost to attain emptiness;
I hold firmly to stillness.
The myriad creatures all rise together
And I watch their return.
The teaming creatures
All return to their separate roots.
Returning to one's roots is known as stillness.
This is what is meant by returning to one's destiny.
Returning to one's destiny is known as the constant.
Knowledge of the constant is known as discernment.
Woe to him who wilfully innovates
While ignorant of the constant,
But should one act from knowledge of the constant
One's action will lead to impartiality,
Impartiality to kingliness,
Kingliness to heaven,
Heaven to the way,
The way to perpetuity,
And to the end of one's days one will meet with no danger.

XVII

The best of all rulers is but a shadowy presence to his subjects.
Next comes the ruler they love and praise;
Next comes one they fear;
Next comes one with whom they take liberties.
When there is not enough faith, there is lack of good faith.
Hesitant, he does not utter words lightly.
When his task is accomplished and his work done
The people all say, 'It happened to us naturally.'

XVIII

When the great way falls into disuse
There are benevolence and rectitude;
When cleverness emerges

There is great hypocrisy;
When the six relations[4] are at variance
There are filial children;
When the state is benighted
There are loyal ministers.

XIX

Exterminate the sage, discard the wise,
And the people will benefit a hundredfold;
Exterminate benevolence, discard rectitude,
And the people will again be filial;
Exterminate ingenuity, discard profit,
And there will be no more thieves and bandits.
These three, being false adornments, are not enough
And the people must have something to which they
 can attach themselves:
Exhibit the unadorned and embrace the uncarved
 block,
Have little thought of self and as few desires as
 possible.

XX

Exterminate learning and there will no longer be worries.
Between yea and nay
How much difference is there?
Between good and evil
How great is the distance?
What others fear
One must also fear.
And wax without having reached the limit.
The multitude are joyous
As if partaking of the *tai lao*[5] offering
Or going up to a terrace in spring.
I alone am inactive and reveal no signs,
Like a baby that has not yet learned to smile,
Listless as though with no home to go back to.
The multitude all have more than enough.
I alone seem to be in want.
My mind is that of a fool—how blank!
Vulgar people are clear.

4. One commentator takes them as the relation between father and son, elder and younger brother, and husband and wife.

5. A ritual feast, where three kinds of animals—ox, sheep, and pig—were sacrificed.

I alone am drowsy.
Vulgar people are alert.
I alone am muddled.
Calm like the sea:
Like a high wind that never ceases.
The multitude all have a purpose.
I alone am foolish and uncouth.
I alone am different from others
And value being fed by the mother.

XXV

There is a thing confusedly formed,
Born before heaven and earth.
Silent and void
It stands alone and does not change,
Goes round and does not weary.
It is capable of being the mother of the world.
I know not its name
So I style it 'the way'.
I give it the makeshift name of 'the great'.
Being great, it is further described as receding,
Receding, it is described as far away,
Being far away, it is described as turning back.
Hence the way is great; heaven is great; earth is great; and the king is also great. Within the realm there are four things that are great, and the king counts as one.
Man models himself on earth,
Earth on heaven,
Heaven on the way,
And the way on that which is naturally so.

XXVIII

Know the male
But keep to the role of the female
And be a ravine to the empire.
If you are a ravine to the empire,
Then the constant virtue will not desert you
And you will again return to being a babe.
Know the white
But keep to the role of the black
And be a model to the empire.
If you are a model to the empire,
Then the constant virtue will not be wanting
And you will return to the infinite.
Know honor

But keep to the role of the disgraced
And be a valley to the empire.
If you are a valley to the empire,
Then the constant virtue will be sufficient
And you will return to being the uncarved block.
When the uncarved block shatters it becomes vessels.
The sage makes use of these and becomes the lord over the officials.
Hence the greatest cutting
Does not sever.

XXXVII

The way never acts yet nothing is left undone.
Should lords and princes be able to hold fast to it,
The myriad creatures will be transformed of their own accord.
After they are transformed, should desire raise its head,
I shall press it down with the weight of the nameless uncarved block.
The nameless uncarved block
Is but freedom from desire,
And if I cease to desire and remain still,
The empire will be at peace of its own accord.

XXXVIII

A man of the highest virtue does not keep to virtue and that is why he has virtue. A man of the lowest virtue never strays from virtue and that is why he is without virtue. The former never acts yet leaves nothing undone. The latter acts but there are things left undone. A man of the highest benevolence acts, but from no ulterior motive. A man of the highest rectitude acts, but from ulterior motive. A man most conversant in the rites acts, but when no one responds rolls up his sleeves and resorts to persuasion by force.
Hence when the way was lost there was virtue; when virtue was lost there was benevolence; when benevolence was lost there was rectitude; when rectitude was lost there were the rites.
The rites are the wearing thin of loyalty and good faith
And the beginning of disorder;
Foreknowledge is the flowery embellishment of the way
And the beginning of folly.
Hence the man of large mind abides in the thick not in the thin, in the fruit not in the flower.
Therefore he discards the one and takes the other.

XLII

The way begets one; one begets two; two begets three; three begets the myriad creatures.
The myriad creatures carry on their backs the *yin* and embrace in their arms the *yang* and are the blending of the generative forces of the two.
There are no words which men detest more than 'solitary', 'desolate', and 'hapless', yet lords and princes use these to refer to themselves.
Thus a thing is sometimes added to by being diminished and diminished by being added to.
What others teach I also teach. 'The violent will not come to a natural end.' I shall take this as my precept.

XLVIII

In the pursuit of learning one knows more every day; in the pursuit of the way one does less every day. One does less and less until one does nothing at all, and when one does nothing at all there is nothing that is undone.
It is always through not meddling that the empire is won. Should you meddle, then you are not equal to the task of winning the empire.

LXIV

It is easy to maintain a situation while it is still secure;
It is easy to deal with a situation before symptoms develop;
It is easy to break a thing when it is yet brittle;
It is easy to dissolve a thing when it is yet minute.
Deal with a thing while it is still nothing;
Keep a thing in order before disorder sets in.
A tree that can fill the span of a man's arms
Grows from a downy tip;
A terrace nine storeys high
Rises from hodfuls of earth;
A journey of a thousand miles
Starts from beneath one's feet.
Whoever does anything to it will ruin it; whoever lays hold of it will lose it.
Therefore the sage, because he does nothing, never ruins anything; and, because he does not lay hold of anything, loses nothing.
In their enterprises the people
Always ruin them when on the verge of success.
Be as careful at the end as at the beginning
And there will be no ruined enterprises.
Therefore the sage desires not to desire
And does not value goods which are hard to come by;

Learns to be without learning
And makes good the mistakes of the multitude
In order to help the myriad creatures to be natural
and to refrain from daring to act.

LXX

My words are very easy to understand and very easy to put into practice, yet no one in the world can understand them or put them into practice.
Words have an ancestor and affairs have a sovereign. It is because people are ignorant that they fail to understand me.
Those who understand me are few;
Those who imitate me are honoured.
Therefore the sage, while clad in homespun, conceals on his person a priceless piece of jade.

LXXVI

A man is supple and weak when living, but hard and stiff when dead. Grass and trees are pliant and fragile when living, but dried and shrivelled when dead. Thus the hard and the strong are the comrades of death; the supple and the weak are the comrades of life.
Therefore a weapon that is strong will not vanquish;
A tree that is strong will suffer the axe.
The strong and big takes the lower position,
The supple and weak takes the higher position.

LXXXI

Truthful words are not beautiful; beautiful words are not truthful. Good words are not persuasive; persuasive words are not good. He who knows has no wide learning; he who has wide learning does not know.
The sage does not hoard.
Having bestowed all he has on others, he has yet more;
Having given all he has to others, he is richer still.
The way of heaven benefits and does not harm; the way of the sage is bountiful and does not contend.

SONGS OF THE SOUTH

ca. fourth century B.C.E.–second century C.E.

Whether in language or landscape, temperament or culture, the regional differences between north and south in today's China are significant. Although this north-south dynamic has taken different forms over the last three millennia, its earliest manifestation in literature is the poetry anthology *Songs of the South* (literally called *Chuci* or *Lyrics of Chu*). This collection contains a genre of poetry that flourished from the Warring States Period (403–221 B.C.E.) to the Han Dynasty (206 B.C.E.–220 C.E.) in the region of Chu, a powerful southern state on the margins of the territory controlled by the Zhou Dynasty (ca. 1045–256 B.C.E.), whose center of power was located in the north. The early Chinese dynasties developed along the Yellow River in the north: China's earliest poetry anthology, the ***Classic of Poetry*** (ca. 600 B.C.E.), contained hymns in praise of the early rulers of the Zhou Dynasty, and interpretations of this classic emphasized Confucian values of moral virtue and wise statecraft. Although the state of Chu had close links to the north, the *Songs of the South* are remarkably distinct from the northern tradition of poetry. In contrast to the unadorned, earthy poems of the *Classic of Poetry*, the *Songs of the South* seduce the reader into a mythical realm where shamans, gods, and rulers of high antiquity mingle freely, surrounded by exotic flora or flying through the air on dragons with floating rainbow banners, unencumbered by gravity or historical chronology. The poetic geography of the *Songs of the South* gave southern China a lush and vibrant face for ages to come.

While the poems in the *Classic of Poetry* are anonymous, the central poems of the *Songs of the South* have been attributed to the tragic hero Qu Yuan (ca. 340–278 B.C.E.). He is considered the first lyric poet of China. Eight of the seventeen poetry cycles included in the *Songs of the South* are attributed to this aristocratic statesman, who was slandered by envious rivals. He lost the favor of King Huai, was banished under Huai's successor, and ultimately drowned himself in the Miluo River in despair.

Our knowledge of Qu Yuan is based on two wildly different accounts. We have **Sima Qian**'s (ca. 145–85 B.C.E.) historical biography of Qu Yuan (included in this volume), which portrays Qu Yuan as a loyal minister with political foresight, someone entangled in the unification conquests launched by the state of Qin. Qu Yuan understands the military ambitions of Qin and predicts Chu's downfall. The kings of Chu ignore Qu Yuan's repeated warnings against Qin's aggressive militarism, but half a century after Qu Yuan's death his prophecy comes true: Qin completes the conquest of the remaining Zhou feudal states, and establishes an unprecedented autocratic regime.

But there is also the image of Qu Yuan that can be derived from "Encountering Sorrow," the longest poem in the *Songs of the South*. Here, Qu Yuan is a superhuman being who moves smoothly through time and space: he expounds on his moral worth (expressed for example in the fragrance of flowers), revels in spirit travel through the cosmos, and, in the end, abruptly announces his wish to die. The intensely lyric lament of "Encountering

Sorrow" lacks a historical or political setting. Its urgent expression of despair comes from the voice of a human, but the methods of this voice's attempt to gain recognition in a corrupt world are supernatural and allegorical. Comparing the Qu Yuan in the poem "Encountering Sorrow" and the Qu Yuan in Sima Qian's historical biography gives insight into the remarkable life of one extraordinary person—both historical and supernatural. It also shows the emergence of the figure of the unsuccessful, loyal scholar-official, who suffers injustice and uses writing as an alternative means to gain immortality. This figure became tremendously successful in Chinese history and resonates still today with intellectuals who feel at odds with Chinese society.

Qu Yuan lived in the waning days of the Zhou Dynasty, when seven larger states, which were only nominally subservient to the weak Zhou kings, engaged in constant warfare with mass armies that grew ever more technologically advanced. The southern state of Chu became one of the largest and most powerful among them. But it was ultimately unable to resist the militaristic northern state of Qin, which managed to conquer all other Chinese states by 221 B.C.E., leading to the foundation of the first unified Chinese empire. Although the state of Chu was thus integrated into the Qin and Han empires, it remained a distinctive cultural force, and the southern princely courts became a lively stage for thinkers and poets as well as for adepts of Daoism. By the second century C.E., a certain Wang Yi (d. 158 C.E.), who had access to the Han imperial library, compiled the poems attributed to Qu Yuan and his later followers into the *Songs of the South.* He also added a detailed commentary and included his own poetry at the end of the anthology, as a closure to four centuries of poetic production in the style of Qu Yuan.

No one will ever fully understand the nature and origin of the oldest pieces in the *Songs of the South,* and the debates about Qu Yuan's historical identity and his relation to the poems in the anthology are not likely to reach any firm conclusions. It is best to think of the poems as part of a dramatic repertoire, which grew out of liturgical songs performed at shamanistic rituals. The main elements of the Qu Yuan narrative correspond to the stages of the relationship between a shaman-lover and a deity: the lover laments being neglected by the deity, makes a case for his beauty and worth, and then goes on a spirit quest through the cosmos. The oldest works in the *Songs of the South,* the "Nine Songs" (three are represented in our selections), portray ritual celebrations, whose speakers perform the role of deities or take a shamanistic mediator role to communicate with deities. Many plot elements from the "Nine Songs" resurface in "Encountering Sorrow." Flowers feature in the "Nine Songs" as adornments of deities or as decoration used during ritual celebrations; cosmic travels of (or in pursuit of) the beloved play an important role, as do tantalizing erotic encounters with a deity who turns his back on the anxious lover.

"Encountering Sorrow," by far the longest piece of the *Songs of the South*, is an idiosyncratic and seductive poem that puts considerable strains on its readers. Although the speaker tells of his plight with captivating intimacy, "Encountering Sorrow" does not have a unified voice. We can only make sense of this plaintive monologue once we discern the multiple personalities inhabiting its voice: there is the humiliated aristocrat, who seeks employment and recognition by a worthy ruler—this voice resonates with Sima Qian's historical account of Qu Yuan. But there is also the spirit traveler who is able to hitch dragons to tour the heavens and meet sage rulers who lived many centuries ago—this voice is closer to the fantastic portrait of deities in the "Nine Songs." Also, the speaker alternates between pursuing worthy rulers and beautiful women. He speaks as a passionate gardener, real and metaphorical: the Qu Yuan of "Encountering Sorrow" with his aristocratic pride is linked to notions of fragrance and purity. He plants exquisite flowers like orchids and sweet angelica, feeds on petals of chrysanthemums, wears waterlily robes, and even uses lotus as tissue paper to wipe his tears. (The plant names are translated for poetic flavor rather than botanical precision, since much of the early Chinese flora has no correlative in literary English.) The speaker claims to possess a sort of "moral perfume," which he contrasts with the stinky vulgarity of envious weeds and treacherous plants, kennings for his enemies at court. Thus, what is considered the first individual lyric voice of the Chinese literary tradition is, ironically, a polyphony of identities, some of them not even human.

It is hard to overstate the importance of the *Songs of the South*. They furnished themes, styles, and imagery for China's oldest properly literary genre, the rhapsody (a sample of which by the poet **Lu Ji** is included in Volume B). They provided religious metaphors for immortality techniques, propagated by Daoists who promised the possibility of physical transformation into winged immortals through a combination of bodily control, alchemy, and diet; and they profoundly shaped the way later poetry and landscape writing translated visual imagination into text.

The *Songs of the South* are enthrallingly visual. Over the last few decades, the traditional literary image of Chu has been complemented in unexpected ways by thousands of objects dating to the Warring States Period and Han Dynasty that archeologists have unearthed in the region of the ancient state of Chu. The mysterious mythological scenes and entangled patterns of plants and fabled animals—dragons, phoenixes, tigers, serpent-shaped deities—are reminiscent of Qu Yuan's entourage on his travel through the cosmos. Although they do not solve the many riddles of this complex text, these newly discovered remainders of Chu culture confirm the strong cultural identity conveyed by the extraordinary *Songs of the South*.

From The Nine Songs[1]

Lord in the Clouds

In orchid baths bathed, hair washed in blooms' scent,
our robes are resplendent, with lavender flowers.
The holy one writhes, he lingers within her,
she glows with a nimbus, his light is unbounded.
He shall be here transfixed in the Temple of Life,
He whose rays are the equal of sun and the moon;
in his dragon-drawn cart, the garb of the god,
he soars in his circles around and around.

1. Translated by and with notes adapted from Stephen Owen.

The holy one glistens, for he has come down;
he lifts up in a gust, afar into clouds.
He scans all the heartland and far off beyond,
across seas on each side; where does he end?
We yearn for our Lord and heave a great sigh,
hearts greatly troubled, and fretful within.

The Lord of the East

"I glow coming forth in the eastlands,
I shine on my porch by the tree Fusang,[2]
then slapping my steeds to a steady gallop,
the night is lit up, and the day breaks.

My dragon team hitched, I ride on the thunder,
bearing banners of cloud streaming behind.
But I heave a great sigh on the point of ascending;
there the heart falters, I look back with care:
for the sounds and beauty so give a man joy
those who watch are transfixed and forget to go.

Harps tightly strung, the drums alternating,
bells being rung, chime frames shaking,
fifes sing out, pipes are blown;
those who act holy ones, wholesome and comely,
hover here winging, suddenly mount,
reciting the lyrics joining in dance.

Catching the pitch, matching the rhythms,
the holy ones come, they cover the sun.
In gown of green cloud and white rainbow mantle,
I raise the long arrow, I shoot Heaven's Wolf,
with yew-bow in hand I now sink back under,
and seize the North Dipper to pour cinnamon wine,
then clutching my reins, I rush soaring high,
off far through darkness voyaging east."

The Hill Wraith

It seemed there was someone in the cleft of the hills,
her mantle was hanging moss, she was girded with ivy,
her eyes glanced upon me, her mouth formed a smile;
"You who yearn for me, who am so comely—

I ride the red leopard, striped lynxes attend me,
with magnolia-wood wagon, my flags, plaited cassia,
my cloak is stone-orchid, my sash is asarum,
I snap the sweet fragrance, gift for him that I love."

2. The sun rose from the Fusang tree in the east.

She dwells in bamboo's darkness, she never sees sky;
the way was steep and hard, late she came and alone.

Alone she stands forth, high on the hill,
with clouds' rolling billows there down below her;
it grows dim and blacker, daylight turns dark,
and in gustings of east wind the goddess rains.
I remain for the holy one, transfixed, forget going,
the year has grown late, who will clothe me in flowers?

I picked three-bloom asphodel out in the hills,
on slopes rough and rocky, through tangles of vines;
reproaching the Lady, I in grief forget going,
for though she may love me, she does not find time.

In the hills there is someone, sweet smell of lavender,
she drinks from the stone-springs in shadow of pines.

and though she may love me, she holds back unsure.
The sky shakes in thunder, with darkness comes rain,
the apes are all wailing, in the night monkeys moan;
the whistling of winds that howl through the trees;
I long for the Lady, fruitless torment I find.

Encountering Sorrow[1]

1

Of the god-king Gaoyang I am the far offspring,[2]
my late honored sire bore the name of Boyong.
The *sheti* stars[3] aimed to the year's first month;
gengyin was the day that I came down.[4]

2

He scanned and he delved into my first measure,
from the portents my sire gave these noble names:
The name that he gave me was Upright Standard;
and my title of honor was Godly Poise.[5]

1. Translated by and with notes adapted from Stephen Owen.
2. Gaoyang was one of the mythic emperors of high antiquity, from whom the Chu royal house claimed ancestry. Though not the ruling family, Qu Yuan's clan, the Qu, was one of the three royal clans of Chu and descended from Gaoyang.
3. A constellation by whose position early astronomers determined the beginning of the year.
4. *Gengyin* is the precise day in the sixty-day cycle, which the Chinese used to count time.
5. To choose a name, the father reads his son's "measure," based either on astronomical conjunctions of his birth or on his physiognomy. These "auspicious names" are not usually associated with Qu Yuan.

3

Such bounty I had of beauty within,
and to this was added fair countenance.
I wore mantles of river rush and remote angelica,
strung autumn orchids to hang from my sash.

4

They fled swiftly from me, I could not catch them—
I feared the years passing would keep me no company.
At dawn I would pluck magnolia on bluffs,
in the twilight on isles I called undying herbs.

5

Days and months sped past, they did not long linger,
springtimes and autumns altered in turn.
I thought on things growing, on the fall of their leaves,
and feared for the Fairest, her drawing toward dark.[6]

6

Cling to your prime, forsake what is rotting—
why not change from this measure of yours?
Mount a fine steed, go off at a gallop—
I will now take the lead, ride ahead on the road.

7

The Three Kings of old were pure and unblemished,[7]
all things of sweet scent indeed were theirs.
Shen's pepper was there, together with cassia,
white angelica, sweet clover were not strung alone.

8

Such shining grandeur had Kings Yao and Shun;
they went the true way, they held to the path.
But sloven and scruffy were Kings Jie and Zhou;
they walked at hazard on twisted trails.[8]

6. The "fairest" is the Chu king in the figure of a beautiful woman. Thus Qu Yuan's later quest for a mate is taken as a search for a prince who will appreciate his worth and employ him.

7. This might refer to three earlier kings of Chu, although interpretations vary.

8. Yao and Shun were two sage kings of high antiquity much revered in northern China. In the southern Chu tradition they play a quasi-religious role. The speaker later goes to visit Shun, or Zhonghua, who was supposedly buried at Cangwu in Chu (stanza 47), in order to lodge his plaint. Yao's two daughters married Shun and became river goddesses after Shun's death. Jie and Zhou were the last kings of two early dynasties and known as exemplarily bad rulers.

9

Those men of faction had ill-gotten pleasures,
their paths went in shadow, narrow, unsafe.
Not for myself came this dread of doom—
I feared my king's chariot soon would be tipped.

10

In haste I went dashing in front and behind,
till I came to the tracks of our kings before.
Lord Iris[9] did not fathom my nature within,
he believed ill words, he glowered in rage.

11

I knew well my bluntness had brought me these woes,
yet I bore through them, I could not forswear.
I pointed to Heaven to serve as my warrant,
it was all for the cause of the Holy One.

12

To me at first firm word had been given,
she regretted it later, felt otherwise.
I made no grievance at this break between us,
but was hurt that the Holy One so often changed.

13

I watered my orchids in all their nine tracts,
and planted sweet clover in one hundred rods;
I made plots for peonies and for the wintergreen,
mixed with asarum and sweet angelica.

14

I wished stalks and leaves would stand high and flourish,
I looked toward the season when I might reap.
If they withered and dried, it would cause me no hurt,
I would grieve if such sweetness went rotting in weeds.

15

Throngs thrust themselves forward in craving and want,
they never are sated in things that they seek.
They show mercy to self, by this measure others,
in them the heart stirs to malice and spite.

9. Kenning for the king, now figured as a male deity.

16

Such a headlong horse race, each hot in pursuit,
is not a thing that thrills my own heart.
Old age comes on steadily, soon will be here,
I fear my fair name will not be fixed firmly.

17

At dawn I drank dew that dropped on magnolia,
in twilight ate blooms from chrysanthemums shed.
If my nature be truly comely, washed utterly pure,
what hurt can I have in long wanness from hunger?

18

I plucked tendrils of trees to knot white angelica,
pierced fallen pistils of flowering ivy.
I reached high to cassia for stringing sweet clover,
and corded the coilings of the rope vine.

19

Yes, I took as my rule those fair men before me,
it was not the garb worn in the ways of our age.
Though it did not agree with men of these days,
I would rest in the pattern left by Peng and by Xian.[1]

20

Long did I sigh and wipe away tears,
sad that men's lives lay in such peril.
Though love of the fair was the halter that guided me,
at dawn I was damned and by twilight, undone.

21

Yes, I was undone for sash hung with sweet clover,
then I added to it the angelica and orchid.
Still my heart will find goodness in these—
though I die many times, I will never regret.

22

I reproach the Holy One's unbridled rashness,
never discerning what lies in men's hearts.

1. Peng and Xian were two legendary shaman ancestors. Here and in the poem's last line traditional commentators often took them as a single name. Peng Xian, a worthy adviser to a king of the Shang Dynasty (ca. 1500–1045 B.C.E.), drowned himself in despair, thus suffering a fate similar to Qu Yuan's.

Women-throngs envied my delicate brows,
they made scurrilous songs, they said I loved lewdness.

23

Of these times the firm folkways: to be skillful in guile;
facing compass and square, they would alter the borehole.
They forswear the straight line, go chasing the crooked;
rivals for false faces, such is their measure.

24

A woe wells within me, to be so hapless,
alone at an impasse in times such as these.
Best to die promptly, to vanish away,
for I cannot bear to show myself thus.

25

The great bird of prey does not go in flocks,
so it has been from times long ago.
The square and the circle can never be matched,
what man can find peace on a way not his own?

26

Bending one's heart, quelling one's will,
abiding faults found, submitting to shame,
embracing pure white, death for the right—
these indeed were esteemed by wise men before us.

27

I regretted my course was not well discerned,
long I stood staring, about to go back.
I turned my coach round along the same path—
it was not yet too far I had strayed in my going.

28

I let horses walk through meadows of orchids,
to a hill of pepper trees I raced, there rested the while,
I drew close, did not reach him, I met with fault-finding,
I withdrew to restore that garb I first wore.

29

Waterlilies I fashioned to serve as my robe,
I gathered the lotus to serve as my skirt.
Let it be over then, no man knows me,
my nature in truth has a scent sweet and steadfast.

30

High was my hat, above me it loomed,
well strung, the pendants that swung from my sash.
Sweet scent and stench were all intermingled,
this gleaming flesh only suffered no dwindling.

31

All at once I looked back, and I let my eyes roam,
I would go off to view the wild lands around.
Pendants in bunches, I was richly adorned,
their sweet fragrance spread, ever more striking.

32

Each man has a thing in which he finds joy:
I alone love the fair, in that I abide.
Though my limbs be cut from me, I still will not change,
for how could my heart be made to cower?

33

Then came the Sister, tender and distressed,[2]
mild of manner she upbraided me thus,
she said: "Gun was unyielding, he fled into hiding,
at last died untimely on moors of Mount Yu.[3]

34

"Why such wide culling, such love of the fair,
in you alone bounty of beautiful raiment?
Haystacks of stinkweed are heaped in their rooms;
you alone stand aloof and refuse such attire.

35

"No swaying the throngs person by person;
None says: 'Come, discern this my nature within!'
Now men rise together, each favors his friends,
why do you stand alone— why not listen to me?"

36

I trust sages before us for moderate judgment,
my heart swelled in torment, it had come now to this,

2. Although "Sister" was often interpreted as Qu Yuan's actual sister, it might be a title rather than a proper name. It is unclear whether to read this in the literal or figurative sense.
3. Gun, here a figure of fatal stubbornness, was a son of Gao Yang, who was charged by the sage-king Yao with controlling the great flood. When he failed, he was executed and his body abandoned on Mount Yu.

I crossed Xiang and Yuan, faring on southward,
reached Zhonghua, King Shun, to state him my case:

37

"King Qi had Nine Stanzas and the Nine Songs—
extreme in wild pleasures, he did as he pleased.
He was heedless of troubles, made no plans for the morrow,
whereby the five sons brought strife to his house.[4]

38

"Yi recklessly ventured, he was lavish in hunts,
he also loved shooting the great foxes.
Such turbulent wickedness rarely ends well:
and Han Zhuo was lusting to seize his bride.[5]

39

"Guo Ao garbed himself in the stiffened leather;
he followed his wants, he failed to forbear.
He lost himself daily in wild pleasures,
whereby his own head was toppled and fell.[6]

40

"Xia's Jie was steadfast in his misdeeds,
in pursuit of these he met with his doom.
Shang's Zhow, the Lord Xin, minced men to stew,
whereby Yin's great lineage could not last long.[7]

41

"Yu the Mighty was stern, respectful and godly;[8]
the right way was Zhou's norm, it thus did not err.
They raised men of worth, rewarded the able,
they kept the straight line, they did not veer.

42

"Sovereign Heaven is slanted in favor of none;
it discerns a man's virtues, puts helpers beside him.

4. King Qi was the son of Gun's son, the Great Yu, who finally tamed the great flood and founded the Xia Dynasty. He brought back the "Nine Songs" from Heaven.
5. Yi the Archer seized the kingship after King Qi's death, but was subsequently killed by his retainer Han Zhuo.
6. Yet a further step in the genealogy of the Xia Dynasty: Guo Ao was a son of Han Zhuo and Yi the Archer's stolen bride. He was killed by Shao Gang, who restored the Xia Dynasty.
7. Jie was the last ruler of the Xia Dynasty and notorious for his misrule. Zhow was the depraved last ruler of the subsequent dynasty, the Shang (also called Yin).
8. The speaker returns to the Great Yu, Gun's son and founder of the Xia Dynasty.

When wisdom and sense do deeds that are splendid,
they may then act their will in this land down below.

43

"I scanned times before us, looked to times yet to come,
read the measures of men, and the ends of their plans:
who found wanting in virtue may be put to use?
who found wanting in good may be still retained?

44

"By the brink stands my body, I am in death's peril,
I discern my first nature and still regret not.
Not judging the drillhole, they squared the peg:
indeed, fair men of old came to mince in a stew.

45

"Sighs come from me often, the heart swells within,
sad that I and these times never will be matched.
I plucked sage and lotus to wipe away tears,
that soak my gown's folds in their streaming."

46

I knelt with robes open, thus stated my case,
having grasped so clearly what is central and right,
I teamed jade white dragons, rode the Bird that Hides Sky,
waiting on winds to fleetly fare upward.

47

At dawn I loosed wheel-block there by Cangwu
and by twilight I reached the Gardens of Air.[9]
I wished to bide a while by the windows of gods,
but swift was the sun and it soon would be dusk.

48

I bade sun-driver Xihe, to pause in her pace,
to stand off from Yanzi and not to draw nigh.[1]
On and on stretched my road, long it was and far,
I would go high and go low in this search that I made.

9. Cangwu was the mountain where the sage-king Shun was buried. Shun was the successor of the sage-king Yao, who had employed Gun to fight the great flood. On his cosmic travels Qu Yuan had just visited Shun (also called Zhonghua) in the preceding ten stanzas to state his case. The "Gardens of Air" were a section of the Kunlun Mountain Range in western China, a region associated with immortals.

1. Xihe is the goddess who drives the sun's chariot across the sky. Mount Yanzi is located in the extreme west, where the sun goes down; thus, the poet is ordering the sun not to set.

49

I watered my horses in the Pools of Xian,
and twisted the reins on the tree Fusang,
snapped a branch of the Ruo Tree to block out the sun,
I roamed freely the while and lingered there.[2]

50

Ahead went Wang Shu to speed on before me,
behind came Fei Lian, he dashed in my train.[3]
Phoenix went first and warned of my coming,
Thunder Master told me that all was not set.

51

I bade my phoenixes mount up in flight,
to continue their going both by day and by night.
Then the whirlwinds massed, drawing together,
they marshaled cloud-rainbows, came to withstand me.

52

A bewildering tumult, first apart, then agreeing,
and they streamed flashing colors, high and then low.
I bade the God's gatekeeper open the bar;
he stood blocking gateway and stared at me.

53

The moment grew dimmer, light soon would be done,
I tied signs in orchids, standing there long.
An age foul and murky cannot tell things apart;
it loves to block beauty from malice and spite.

54

At dawn I set to fare across the White Waters,
I climbed Mount Langfeng, there tethered my horses.[4]
All at once I looked back, my tears were streaming,
sad that the high hill lacked any woman.

55

At once I went roaming to the Palace of Spring,
I broke sprays of garnet to add to my pendants.

2. When rising the sun is bathed in the Pools of Xian and comes out at the base of the Fusang tree. The Ruo tree is at the opposite side of the world, where the sun sets.

3. Wang Shu was the driver of the moon, Fei Lian the god of winds.

4. White Waters and Mount Langfeng are sections of the Kunlun Range.

Before the blooms' glory had fallen away,
I would seek a woman below to whom I might give them.[5]

56

Feng Long I bade to go riding the clouds,
to seek out Fufei down where she dwells.[6]
I took pendant-sash, I tied there a message,
and bade Lady Mumbler act as my envoy.

57

A bewildering tumult, first apart, then agreeing,
she suddenly balked, she could not be swayed.
She went twilights to lodge at Farthest-of-Rocks,
and at dawn bathed her hair in Weiban Stream.[7]

58

She presumed on her beauty, she was scornful and proud,
in wild pleasures daily she wantonly strayed.
Though beautiful truly, she lacked right behavior—
I let her go then, I sought for another.

59

I let my gaze sweep over all the world's ends,
I roamed throughout Sky, then I came down.
I viewed the surging crest of a terrace of onyx,
there saw a rare woman, the You-Song's daughter.[8]

60

I bade the venom-owl make match between us,
and the venom-owl told me she was not fair.
Early summer's dove-cock went away singing,
and I still loathe its petty wiles.

61

My heart then faltered, doubts overcame me,
I wanted to go myself; it was not allowed.

5. "Woman below" probably refers here to Fufei as a river goddess.
6. Feng Long was the god of clouds and thunder, Fufei the goddess of the river Luo, near Luoyang in the northeast, the capital of the Zhou Dynasty (ca. 1045–256 B.C.E.), during which Qu Yuan lived.
7. The goddess has apparently wandered to the far west, to the Weiban Stream next to the Ruo Stream, where the sun sets.
8. The mother of the ancestor of the royal house of the Shang Dynasty. She was a gift from the You-Song, the main clan of the Song tribes, to Gao Xin.

Already the phoenix   had given my troth gifts,
still I feared that Gao Xin   had come before me.[9]

62

I wanted to alight far away,   there was no place to halt,
so I drifted the while   and roamed at my ease.
If still not yet married   to Shaokang the Prince,
there remained the two Yao girls   of the clan You-Yu.[1]

63

My envoy was feeble,   my matchmaker bumbling;
I feared words to charm them   would not hold fast.
An age foul and murky,   it spites a man's worth,
it loves to block beauty,   it acclaims what is ill.

64

Remote and far   are the chambers of women;
and the wise king also   is not yet aware.
I keep feelings within me,   do not bring them forth,
yet how can I bear   that it be thus forever?

65

I sought stalks of milfoil,   and slips to cast lots,
and bade Holy Fen   to divine the thing for me.
I said:
"Two lovely beings   must surely be matched;
whose fairness is steadfast   that I may adore her?

67

"Consider the wide sweep   of these Nine Domains—
can it be only here   that a woman be found?"
He said:
"Undertake to fare far,   be not full of doubts;
none who seeks beauty   would let you slip by.

67

"Is there any place lacking   in plants of sweet fragrance?
why must you cherish   your former abode?
This age is a dark one,   eyes are dazzled and blinded,
no man can discern   our good or our bad.

9. Gao Xin married the woman from the Song tribes. The speaker's courtship of "You-Song's daughter" fails because, in high antiquity long before Qu Yuan's time, she married Gao Xin.

1. Ousted by a rival, Shaokang, rightful heir to the Xia throne, fled to the You-Yu, the main clan of the Yu tribes, whose ruler gave him his two daughters in marriage.

68

"What men love and loathe   is never the same—
only these men of faction   alone stand apart.
Each person wears mugwort,   stuffed in their waists,
they declare that the orchid   may never be strung.

69

"If in judgment of plants   they still cannot grasp it,
can they ever be right   on the beauty of gems?
They seek shit and mire   to stuff their sachets,
and say that Shen's pepper   lacks any sweet smell."

70

I wished to follow Holy Fen's   lot of good fortune,
yet still my heart faltered,   doubts overcame me.
The Shaman Xian   would descend in the twilight,[2]
I clasped pepper and rice   to beseech him.

71

The gods blotted sky,   their full hosts descending,
spirit vassals of Many Doubts   joined to go greet them.[3]
In a light-burst the Sovereign   sent forth his spirit,
giving me word   of a lucky outcome.

72

He said:
"Undertake to fare high   and then to fare low,
find one who agrees   with the yardstick and square.
Yu the Mighty was stern,   he sought one who matched him,
he held to Gao Yao   as one able to suit him.[4]

73

"If one's nature within   loves what is fair,
what need to make use   of matchmaker or envoy?
Yue held an earth-ram   upon Fu's cliff;
Wuding employed him   and did not doubt.[5]

74

"Once there was Lü Wang   who swung a butcher's knife,
yet he met Zhou's King Wen   and he was raised up.

2. The Shaman Xian mentioned in stanza 19.
3. "Many Doubts" (literally "Nine Doubts") was the mountain range in the south where the sage-king Shun was supposedly buried.
4. Again, the Great Yu, who tamed the flood and founded the Xia Dynasty. Gao Yao was a worthy minister of the Great Yu.
5. King Wuding of the Shang Dynasty found a labor convict named Yue on Fu Cliff and recruited him as minister.

And there was Ning Qi, a singer of songs;
Huan of Qi heard him; he served as the helper.[6]

75

"Yet act now before the year grows too late,
now while the season has not yet passed.
I fear only cries early from summer's nightjar,
making all plants lose their sweet scent."

76

My pendants of garnet, how they dangle down from me—
yet the throngs would dim them, cover them up.
These men of faction are wanting in faith,
I fear their malice, that they will break them.

77

The times are in tumult, ever transforming—
how then may a man linger here long?
Orchid, angelica change, they become sweet no more;
Iris, sweet clover alter, they turn into straw.

78

These plants that smelled sweet in days gone by
have now become nothing but stinking weeds.
Can there be any reason other than this?—
the harm that is worked by no love for the fair.

79

I once thought that orchid could be steadfast:
it bore me no fruit, it was all show.
Forsaking its beauty, it followed the common;
it wrongly is ranked in the hosts of sweet scent.

80

Pepper is master of fawning, it is swaggering, reckless,
only mock-pepper stuffs sachets hung from waists.
It pressed hard to advance, it struggled for favor,
what sweet scent remains that is able to spread?

6. Like Yue these are figures of worthy officials recruited in unexpected places. Lü Wang was first a butcher, then a fisherman before being discovered by a king of the Zhou Dynasty in old age and made a minister. Ning Qi was a petty merchant who would perform songs as he rapped the horns of his buffalo. Duke Huan of Qi heard of his worth and made him his aide.

81

Truly, ways of these times are willful and loose,
who now is able to avoid being changed?
Look on orchid and pepper, see them like this—
will less be true of river rush and wintergreen?

82

Only these my own pendants are still to be prized;
forsaken is loveliness, and I come to this.
Yet their sweet scent spreads, it is not diminished,
an aroma that even now has still not abated.

83

In their blending's balance I take my delight,
I will drift and will roam, seeking the woman.
And while such adornment is still in its glory,
I will range widely looking, both high and low.

84

Since Holy Fen told me my fortunate lot,
I will choose a luck-day, and I will set out.
I snap sprays of garnet to serve as my viands,
fine garnet meal will serve as my fare.

85

For me have been hitched those dragons that fly,
mixed onyx and ivory serve as my coach.
How can a mind set apart be ever like others?
I will go away far, keep myself removed.

86

I bent my way round at Kunlun Mountain,
long and far was the road, there I ranged widely.
I raised my cloud-rainbows, dimming and darkening,
jade phoenix chimes rang with a jingling voice.

87

At dawn I loosed the wheel-block at Ford-of-the-Sky,[7]
by twilight I came to the ends of the west.
Phoenix spread its wings, and bore up my banners,
high aloft it soared, its wingbeats were steady.

7. The narrowest point in the Milky Way.

88

All at once I was facing across Drifting Sands,
I went down the Red Waters, there took my ease.[8]
I signaled the dragons to make me a bridge,
I called to West's Sovereign to take me across.

89

Long and far was the road, it was filled with perils,
I passed word to my hosts: drive straight and attend me.
I made way to Mount Buzhou, there turned to the left,
toward the Sea of the West, my appointed goal.[9]

90

Then I massed all my chariots, a thousand strong,
jade hubs lined even, we galloped together.
I hitched my eight dragons, heaving and coiling,
and bore my cloud banners streaming behind.

91

I then quelled my will and paused in my pace;
the gods galloped high far to the distance,
they were playing "Nine Songs" and dancing "the Shao,"[1]
making use of this day to take their delight.

92

I was mounting aloft to such dazzling splendor—
all at once I glanced down to my homeland of old.
My driver grew sad, my horses felt care,
they flexed looking backward and would not go on.

The Ending Song

It is done now forever!
in all the kingdom there is no man, no man who knows me,
then why should I care for that city, my home?
Since no one can join me in making good rule,
I will go off to seek where Peng and Xian dwell.[2]

8. "Drifting Sands" is a general term for the imagined terrors of China's northwestern deserts. The Red Waters flowed off to the Kunlun Range in the far west.
9. Mount Buzhou is a mythical mountain in the far west.
1. Ancient ceremonial music and dance. These "Nine Songs" are a legendary repertoire and not the shamanistic hymns given earlier in this poem.
2. As in stanza 19, this refers either to Peng and Xian, two legendary shamans, or to Peng Xian, a worthy adviser to a king of the Shang Dynasty.

ZHUANGZI
fourth–second centuries B.C.E

The *Zhuangzi,* a text attributed to a figure called Zhuangzi (ca. 369–286 B.C.E), is the most iridescent example of early Chinese Masters Literature. Conveying wisdom about how to live a good life in a world filled with violence and conceit, the rich philosophical genre of Masters Literature flourished for half a millennium, beginning at the time of **Confucius** (551–479 B.C.E). Next to the ***Daodejing*** ("The Classic of the Way and Its Virtue," attributed to a master called **Laozi**), the *Zhuangzi* is considered the second most foundational text of Daoist philosophy. For Zhuangzi the good life was one of freedom from societal bounds, spent far away from political obligation, in blissful accordance with the *dao,* the "natural Way." As Zhuangzi claims at one point, he preferred happily "dragging his tail in the mud" like a giant tortoise to getting involved in current affairs. *Zhuangzi*'s wit and literary versatility is playful, while always giving his readers the sense that something fundamental is being said, and this makes the *Zhuangzi* fresh and thought provoking even today.

Little is known about the philosopher Zhuangzi beyond what we hear about him in *Zhuangzi.* Many masters of his time traveled from state to state and offered political advice to rulers during the contentious Warring States Period (fourth–third centuries B.C.E), which preceded the unification of China under the Qin Dynasty (221 B.C.E.). They relied on the patronage of these fickle rulers in return. Zhuangzi did not seek patronage or office, but seemed content to tell his stories and write. He did, however, gather admirers: only the first seven of the *Zhuangzi*'s thirty-three chapters are attributed to him, while the remaining chapters were probably written over several centuries by later followers.

The *Zhuangzi* is written in a prose of constantly changing styles, with embedded verse passages. It moves from wise jokes and funny parables to moments of passionate seriousness, to tight philosophical arguments that turn imperceptibly into parodies. It hovers between hilarious anecdotes and complex philosophical treatises, between deriding and celebrating the power of language, between humiliating proponents of clever logic and brilliantly mobilizing their tools against them, and between rhetorical pyrotechnics and gestures toward some grand truth. This grand truth is often conveyed by fantastic creatures, such as monstrous birds, ocean spirits, or remarkable trees, that populate a gigantic universe that dwarfs our human world and teaches—and laughs at—the ultimate relativity of our perspective. The structure of the first seven chapters is intricate: what seems at first to be a discontinuous series of parables gradually reveals itself as an echoing interplay of themes, sometimes bending a thought in a new direction or standing an earlier argument on its head.

This changeable form of narrative and argument allows Zhuangzi to unmask our lack of understanding and to ask fundamental questions about human life. Humans, he claims, do not understand what is really useful: in one parable, Huizi, a clever proponent of the contemporary school of logicians and both a dear friend of Zhuangzi and a frequent target of his parodic jibes, destroys a large gourd because he finds it useless as a water container, but lacks the imagination to make it into a boat that would allow him to leisurely roam the lakes and rivers. Similarly, people do not understand the usefulness of the physical deformity of "Crippled Shu," another character Zhuangzi introduces to make his point: the deformity protects him from being drafted for war and secures him social-welfare grain payments. But most people fail to understand that preserving one's life is more precious than serving in office or acquiring fame in society. And they fail to understand that death is a liberating pleasure. In *Zhuangzi* we see repeatedly how those with deeper understanding of the world rejoice over a beloved's passing, to the outrage of everybody else. One master muses at his friend's deathbed about the wonderful schemes of the creator of the universe and asks enthusiastically, "Where is he going to send you? Will he make you into a rat's liver? Will he make you into a bug's arm?" In another chapter a speaking skull lying by the wayside instructs Zhuangzi that death and liberation from the world are better than a king's life. Sometimes, existence itself becomes a puzzling miracle. In one episode Zhuangzi awakes from a dream in which he was a butterfly and comes to wonder whether he is Zhuangzi dreaming of being a butterfly or a butterfly dreaming of being Zhuangzi. Life is full of pleasures, says Zhuangzi, but so is death because it liberates us from our earthly cares in this life. Moreover, it allows us to return to the flow of the *dao* and become somebody—or more often something—new and exciting in the grander scheme of the "Ten Thousand Things" that make up the cosmos.

For Zhuangzi the greatest sources of misunderstanding are words. Words acquire meaning through human convention and are therefore limited to a human scale and human problems. In chapter 2 he moves into a logical argument on the relativity of the terms *this* and *that* as well as *right* and *wrong*. The argument is intricate and stylized, and at some point readers begin to suspect that they are reading the parody of an argument, a suspicion confirmed when Zhuangzi's grand summation culminates in a joke. But then again, this is perhaps the only proper conclusion for an argument against the absolute validity of arguments and of the meaning of words. In another chapter a wheelwright named Pian teaches his lord the radical emptiness of words, something he has learned from his profession. When Pian dares to point out that the book his lord is reading contains only "chaff and dregs of the men of old," his lord gets so angry that he demands the wheelwright defend his claim or face execution. The eloquent wheelwright explains quickly that supreme skill and wisdom cannot be transmitted in words but die with the person who has acquired them through intuition, training, and insight. Just as he cannot teach his art of wheel making to his sons, books are merely the empty traces of their writers' wisdom: their meaning has left them and they have no lessons to teach.

That Zhuangzi chooses a lowly artisan to teach his arrogant lord a lesson is no coincidence. Figures of authority and conventional wisdom, such as Confucius, appear as either fools or humble disciples aspiring to some grasp of Zhuangzian wisdom. Criminals and freaks, artisans and animals, and other outsiders embody and understand the *dao*; they constitute a colorful group of countermasters. Gigantic animals allow Zhuangzi to remind his readers that proportions, like values and words, are linked to a particular viewpoint: many anecdotes set their happy protagonists flying, riding the clouds, or sailing the oceans and winds. In chapter 1, "Free and Easy Wandering," he begins with a monstrous sea creature, whose name is Kun ("Fish Eggs"). Kun is transformed into the Peng, a bird that is so large its wings hang over the sky to both horizons. The Peng flies so high that when it looks down all it sees is blue. Suddenly the focus shifts to a tiny hollow in a floor to explain how the Peng can fly at all. Then a little quail twitters jealously, "Where does he think *he's* going?" In dizzying sequence Zhuangzi shifts scales and observers, exercising the readers' imaginations to break down their habitual perspectives.

Alongside the *Daodejing*, the *Zhuangzi* is one of the foundational texts of Daoist philosophy. While these two texts share a general outlook—a rejection of conventional wisdom, a pleasure in paradox, a call to return to a natural Way, and a polemical stance against Confucianism—their visions diverge on crucial points. Zhuangzi's happy abstention from any will to rule is foreign to the *Daodejing*'s advice on how to gain power and become a successful ruler. His joyful embrace of death contrasts with the notion in the *Daodejing* that death is a state of alienation and rigidity, and runs completely counter to the pursuit of immortality through bodily practices and drugs in later Daoism. Most important, while the *Daodejing* repeats its pithy paradoxes in short verse over and over again, Zhuangzi revels in the pleasure of storytelling, sometimes adding narrative flesh to the abstract cosmic arguments of the *Daodejing*, and sometimes varying or contradicting them.

In the intellectual world of China and beyond, the *Zhuangzi* is unique: its anecdotes and parables shimmer with comic playfulness and wear their weighty philosophical themes with unbearable lightness. The uncertainty of whether Zhuangzi is the butterfly or the butterfly is Zhuangzi does not create the intellectual pessimism or existential angst of a radical skeptic who solemnly doubts everything in the world. Rather, there is an exuberant joy in being part of the "great transformation of things." With this philosophical style, his sophisticated reflection on language, and his whiff of iconoclasm, Zhuangzi has been popular with ancients and moderns alike: Oscar Wilde, the famous Irish wit, was attracted to the text and reviewed one of its early translations into English in 1889. For all his readers, nobody can quite pin Zhuangzi down. As his earliest followers said: "Above he wandered with the Creator, below he made friends with those who had gone beyond life and death. . . . So veiled and arcane! He has never been completely comprehended."

Zhuangzi[1]

CHAPTER I

Free and Easy Wandering

In the northern darkness there is a fish and his name is Kun.[2] The Kun is so huge I don't know how many thousand li[3] he measures. He changes and becomes a bird whose name is Peng. The back of the Peng measures I don't know how many thousand li across and, when he rises up and flies off, his

1. Translated by and with notes adapted from Burton Watson.
2. Kun means fish roe, a figure for something tiny.
3. A unit of distance; in this period it was roughly a quarter of a mile.

wings are like clouds all over the sky. When the sea begins to move, this bird sets off for the southern darkness, which is the Lake of Heaven.

The *Universal Harmony*[4] records various wonders, and it says: "When the Peng journeys to the southern darkness, the waters are roiled for three thousand li. He beats the whirlwind and rises ninety thousand li, setting off on the sixth-month gale." Wavering heat, bits of dust, living things blowing each other about—the sky looks very blue. Is that its real color, or is it because it is so far away and has no end? When the bird looks down, all he sees is blue too.

If water is not piled up deep enough, it won't have the strength to bear up a big boat. Pour a cup of water into a hollow in the floor and bits of trash will sail on it like boats. But set the cup there and it will stick fast, for the water is too shallow and the boat too large. If wind is not piled up deep enough, it won't have the strength to bear up great wings. Therefore when the Peng rises ninety thousand li, he must have the wind under him like that. Only then can he mount on the back of the wind, shoulder the blue sky, and nothing can hinder or block him. Only then can he set his eyes to the south.

The cicada and the little dove laugh at this, saying, "When we make an effort and fly up, we can get as far as the elm or the sapanwood tree, but sometimes we don't make it and just fall down on the ground. Now how is anyone going to go ninety thousand li to the south!"

If you go off to the green woods nearby, you can take along food for three meals and come back with your stomach as full as ever. If you are going a hundred li, you must grind your grain the night before; and if you are going a thousand li, you must start getting the provisions together three months in advance. What do these two creatures understand? Little understanding cannot come up to great understanding; the short-lived cannot come up to the long-lived.

How do I know this is so? The morning mushroom knows nothing of twilight and dawn; the summer cicada knows nothing of spring and autumn. They are the short-lived. South of Chu there is a caterpillar which counts five hundred years as one spring and five hundred years as one autumn. Long, long ago there was a great rose of Sharon that counted eight thousand years as one spring and eight thousand years as one autumn. They are the long-lived. Yet Pengzu alone is famous today for having lived a long time, and everybody tries to ape him. Isn't it pitiful!

Among the questions of Tang to Qi we find the same thing. In the bald and barren north, there is a dark sea, the Lake of Heaven. In it is a fish which is several thousand li across, and no one knows how long. His name is Kun. There is also a bird there, named Peng with a back like Mount Tai and wings like clouds filling the sky. He beats the whirlwind, leaps into the air, and rises up ninety thousand li, cutting through the clouds and mist, shouldering the blue sky, and then he turns his eyes south and prepares to journey to the southern darkness.

The little quail laughs at him, saying, "Where does he think *he's* going? I give a great leap and fly up, but I never get more than ten or twelve yards before I come down fluttering among the weeds and brambles. And that's the best kind

4. Identified variously as the name of a man or the name of a book. Probably Zhuangzi intended it as the latter, and is poking fun at the philosophers of other schools who cite ancient texts to prove their assertions.

of flying anyway! Where does he think *he's* going?" Such is the difference between big and little.

Therefore a man who has wisdom enough to fill one office effectively, good conduct enough to impress one community, virtue enough to please one ruler, or talent enough to be called into service in one state, has the same kind of self-pride as these little creatures. Song Rongzi[5] would certainly burst out laughing at such a man. The whole world could praise Song Rongzi and it wouldn't make him exert himself; the whole world could condemn him and it wouldn't make him mope. He drew a clear line between the internal and the external, and recognized the boundaries of true glory and disgrace. But that was all. As far as the world went, he didn't fret and worry, but there was still ground he left unturned.

Liezi[6] could ride the wind and go soaring around with cool and breezy skill, but after fifteen days he came back to earth. As far as the search for good fortune went, he didn't fret and worry. He escaped the trouble of walking, but he still had to depend on something to get around. If he had only mounted on the truth of Heaven and Earth, ridden the changes of the six breaths, and thus wandered through the boundless, then what would he have had to depend on?

Therefore I say, the Perfect Man has no self; the Holy Man has no merit; the Sage has no fame.

Yao wanted to cede the empire to Xu You.[7] "When the sun and moon have already come out," he said, "it's a waste of light to go on burning the torches, isn't it? When the seasonal rains are falling, it's a waste of water to go on irrigating the fields. If you took the throne, the world would be well ordered. I go on occupying it, but all I can see are my failings. I beg to turn over the world to you."

Xu You said, "You govern the world and the world is already well governed. Now if I take your place, will I be doing it for a name? But name is only the guest of reality—will I be doing it so I can play the part of a guest? When the tailor-bird builds her nest in the deep wood, she uses no more than one branch. When the mole drinks at the river, he takes no more than a bellyful. Go home and forget the matter, my lord. I have no use for the rulership of the world! Though the cook may not run his kitchen properly, the priest and the impersonator of the dead at the sacrifice do not leap over the wine casks and sacrificial stands and go take his place."

Jian Wu said to Lian Shu, "I was listening to Jie Yu's talk—big and nothing to back it up, going on and on without turning around. I was completely dumfounded at his words—no more end than the Milky Way, wild and wide of the mark, never coming near human affairs!"

"What were his words like?" asked Lian Shu.

"He said that there is a Holy Man living on faraway Gushe Mountain, with skin like ice or snow, and gentle and shy like a young girl. He doesn't eat the

5. He taught a doctrine of social harmony, frugality, and the rejection of conventional standards of honor and disgrace.
6. A Daoist sage who appears frequently in the *Zhuangzi*. A book attributed to him was compiled around the 3rd or 4th century C.E.
7. A famous hermit. Yao was a legendary sage-king of great antiquity.

five grains, but sucks the wind, drinks the dew, climbs up on the clouds and mist, rides a flying dragon, and wanders beyond the four seas. By concentrating his spirit, he can protect creatures from sickness and plague and make the harvest plentiful. I thought this was all insane and refused to believe it."

"You would!" said Lian Shu. "We can't expect a blind man to appreciate beautiful patterns or a deaf man to listen to bells and drums. And blindness and deafness are not confined to the body alone—the understanding has them too, as your words just now have shown. This man, with this virtue of his, is about to embrace the ten thousand things and roll them into one. Though the age calls for reform, why should he wear himself out over the affairs of the world? There is nothing that can harm this man. Though flood waters pile up to the sky, he will not drown. Though a great drought melts metal and stone and scorches the earth and hills, he will not be burned. From his dust and leavings alone you could mold a Yao or a Shun![8] Why should he consent to bother about mere things?"

A man of Song who sold ceremonial hats made a trip to Yue, but the Yue people cut their hair short and tattoo their bodies and had no use for such things. Yao brought order to the people of the world and directed the government of all within the seas. But he went to see the Four Masters of the faraway Gushe Mountain, [and when he got home] north of the Fen River, he was dazed and had forgotten his kingdom there.

Huizi[9] said to Zhuangzi, "The king of Wei gave me some seeds of a huge gourd. I planted them, and when they grew up, the fruit was big enough to hold five piculs.[1] I tried using it for a water container, but it was so heavy I couldn't lift it. I split it in half to make dippers, but they were so large and unwieldy that I couldn't dip them into anything. It's not that the gourds weren't fantastically big—but I decided they were no use and so I smashed them to pieces."

Zhuangzi said, "You certainly are dense when it comes to using big things! In Song there was a man who was skilled at making a salve to prevent chapped hands, and generation after generation his family made a living by bleaching silk in water. A traveler heard about the salve and offered to buy the prescription for a hundred measures of gold. The man called everyone to a family council. 'For generations we've been bleaching silk and we've never made more than a few measures of gold,' he said. 'Now, if we sell our secret, we can make a hundred measures in one morning. Let's let him have it!' The traveler got the salve and introduced it to the king of Wu, who was having trouble with the state of Yue. The king put the man in charge of his troops, and that winter they fought a naval battle with the men of Yue and gave them a bad beating.[2] A portion of the conquered territory was awarded to the man as a fief. The salve had the power to prevent chapped hands in either case; but one man used it to get a fief, while the other one never got beyond silk bleaching—because they used

8. Another legendary sage-king of great antiquity.

9. A famous logician, who often appears as an interlocutor in dialogues with Chuang Chou.

1. A picul is a measure of volume.

2. Because the salve, by preventing the soldiers' hands from chapping, made it easier for them to handle their weapons.

it in different ways. Now you had a gourd big enough to hold five piculs. Why didn't you think of making it into a great tub so you could go floating around the rivers and lakes, instead of worrying because it was too big and unwieldly to dip into things! Obviously you still have a lot of underbrush in your head!"

Huizi said to Zhuangzi, "I have a big tree of the kind men call *shu*. Its trunk is too gnarled and bumpy to apply a measuring line to, its branches too bent and twisty to match up to a compass or square. You could stand it by the road and no carpenter would look at it twice. Your words, too, are big and useless, and so everyone alike spurns them!"

Zhuangzi said, "Maybe you've never seen a wildcat or a weasel. It crouches down and hides, watching for something to come along. It leaps and races east and west, not hesitating to go high or low—until it falls into the trap and dies in the net. Then again there's the yak, big as a cloud covering the sky. It certainly knows how to be big, though it doesn't know how to catch rats. Now you have this big tree and you're distressed because it's useless. Why don't you plant it in Not-Even-Anything Village, or the field of Broad-and-Boundless, relax and do nothing by its side, or lie down for a free and easy sleep under it? Axes will never shorten its life, nothing can ever harm it. If there's no use for it, how can it come to grief or pain?"

CHAPTER 2

Discussion on Making All Things Equal

Ziqi of south wall sat leaning on his armrest, staring up at the sky and breathing—vacant and far away, as though he'd lost his companion.[3] Yan Cheng Ziyou, who was standing by his side in attendance, said, "What is this? Can you really make the body like a withered tree and the mind like dead ashes? The man leaning on the armrest now is not the one who leaned on it before!"

Ziqi said, "You do well to ask the question, Yan. Now I have lost myself. Do you understand that? You hear the piping of men, but you haven't heard the piping of earth. Or if you've heard the piping of earth, you haven't heard the piping of Heaven!"

Ziyou said, "May I venture to ask what this means?"

Ziqi said, "The Great Clod[4] belches out breath and its name is wind. So long as it doesn't come forth, nothing happens. But when it does, then ten thousand hollows begin crying wildly. Can't you hear them, long drawn out? In the mountain forests that lash and sway, there are huge trees a hundred spans around with hollows and openings like noses, like mouths, like ears, like jugs, like cups, like mortars, like rifts, like ruts. They roar like waves, whistle like arrows, screech, gasp, cry, wail, moan, and howl, those in the lead calling out *yeee!*, those behind calling out *yuuu!* In a gentle breeze they answer faintly, but in a full gale the chorus is gigantic. And when the fierce wind has passed on, then all the hollows are empty again. Have you never seen the tossing and trembling that goes on?"

3. Interpreted variously to mean his associates, his wife, or his own body.
4. The earth.

Ziyou said, "By the piping of earth, then, you mean simply [the sound of] these hollows, and by the piping of man [the sound of] flutes and whistles. But may I ask about the piping of Heaven?"

Ziqi said, "Blowing on the ten thousand things in a different way, so that each can be itself—all take what they want for themselves, but who does the sounding?"

Great understanding is broad and unhurried; little understanding is cramped and busy. Great words are clear and limpid; little words are shrill and quarrelsome. In sleep, men's spirits go visiting; in waking hours, their bodies hustle. With everything they meet they become entangled. Day after day they use their minds in strife, sometimes grandiose, sometimes sly, sometimes petty. Their little fears are mean and trembly; their great fears are stunned and overwhelming. They bound off like an arrow or a crossbow pellet, certain that they are the arbiters of right and wrong. They cling to their position as though they had sworn before the gods, sure that they are holding on to victory. They fade like fall and winter—such is the way they dwindle day by day. They drown in what they do—you cannot make them turn back. They grow dark, as though sealed with seals—such are the excesses of their old age. And when their minds draw near to death, nothing can restore them to the light.

Joy, anger, grief, delight, worry, regret, fickleness, inflexibility, modesty, willfulness, candor, insolence—music from empty holes, mushrooms springing up in dampness, day and night replacing each other before us, and no one knows where they sprout from. Let it be! Let it be! [It is enough that] morning and evening we have them, and they are the means by which we live. Without them we would not exist; without us they would have nothing to take hold of. This comes close to the matter. But I do not know what makes them the way they are. It would seem as though they have some True Master, and yet I find no trace of him. He can act—that is certain. Yet I cannot see his form. He has identity but no form.

The hundred joints, the nine openings, the six organs, all come together and exist here [as my body]. But which part should I feel closest to? I should delight in all parts, you say? But there must be one I ought to favor more. If not, are they all of them mere servants? But if they are all servants, then how can they keep order among themselves? Or do they take turns being lord and servant? It would seem as though there must be some True Lord among them. But whether I succeed in discovering his identity or not, it neither adds to nor detracts from his Truth.

Once a man receives this fixed bodily form, he holds on to it, waiting for the end. Sometimes clashing with things, sometimes bending before them, he runs his course like a galloping steed, and nothing can stop him. Is he not pathetic? Sweating and laboring to the end of his days and never seeing his accomplishment, utterly exhausting himself and never knowing where to look for rest—can you help pitying him? I'm not dead yet! he says, but what good is that? His body decays, his mind follows it—can you deny that this is a great sorrow? Man's life has always been a muddle like this. How could I be the only muddled one, and other men not muddled?

If a man follows the mind given him and makes it his teacher, then who can be without a teacher? Why must you comprehend the process of change and form your mind on that basis before you can have a teacher? Even an idiot has his teacher. But to fail to abide by this mind and still insist upon your rights and wrongs—this is like saying that you set off for Yue today and got there yesterday.[5] This is to claim that what doesn't exist exists. If you claim that what doesn't exist exists, then even the holy sage Yu couldn't understand you, much less a person like me!

Words are not just wind. Words have something to say. But if what they have to say is not fixed, then do they really say something? Or do they say nothing? People suppose that words are different from the peeps of baby birds, but is there any difference, or isn't there? What does the Way rely upon, that we have true and false? What do words rely upon, that we have right and wrong? How can the Way go away and not exist? How can words exist and not be acceptable? When the Way relies on little accomplishments and words rely on vain show, then we have the rights and wrongs of the Confucians and the Mo-ists.[6] What one calls right the other calls wrong; what one calls wrong the other calls right. But if we want to right their wrongs and wrong their rights, then the best thing to use is clarity.

Everything has its "that," everything has its "this." From the point of view of "that" you cannot see it, but through understanding you can know it. So I say, "that" comes out of "this" and "this" depends on "that"—which is to say that "this" and "that" give birth to each other. But where there is birth there must be death; where there is death there must be birth. Where there is acceptability there must be unacceptability; where there is unacceptability there must be acceptability. Where there is recognition of right there must be recognition of wrong; where there is recognition of wrong there must be recognition of right. Therefore the sage does not proceed in such a way, but illuminates all in the light of Heaven.[7] He too recognizes a "this," but a "this" which is also "that," a "that" which is also "this." His "that" has both a right and a wrong in it; his "this" too has both a right and a wrong in it. So, in fact, does he still have a "this" and "that"? Or does he in fact no longer have a "this" and "that"? A state in which "this" and "that" no longer find their opposites is called the hinge of the Way. When the hinge is fitted into the socket, it can respond endlessly. Its right then is a single endlessness and its wrong too is a single endlessness. So, I say, the best thing to use is clarity.

To use an attribute to show that attributes are not attributes is not as good as using a nonattribute to show that attributes are not attributes. To use a horse to show that a horse is not a horse is not as good as using a non-horse to show that a horse is not a horse,[8] Heaven and earth are one attribute; the ten thousand things are one horse.

What is acceptable we call acceptable; what is unacceptable we call unacceptable. A road is made by people walking on it; things are so because they are called so. What makes them so? Making them so makes them so. What makes them not so? Making them not so makes them not so. Things all must have that which is so; things all must have that which is acceptable. There is nothing that is not so, nothing that is not acceptable.

5. A typical paradox of the logician Huizi.

6. Followers of a utilitarian philosophical school who opposed the traditional ceremonies that the Confucians saw as essential to a good society.

7. Nature or the Way.

8. Zhuangzi pokes fun at the logician Gongsun Long and his treatises "A White Horse Is Not a Horse" and "Attributes Are Not Attributes in and of Themselves."

For this reason, whether you point to a little stalk or a great pillar, a leper or the beautiful Xishi, things ribald and shady or things grotesque and strange, the Way makes them all into one. Their dividedness is their completeness; their completeness is their impairment. No thing is either complete or impaired, but all are made into one again. Only the man of far-reaching vision knows how to make them into one. So he has no use [for categories], but relegates all to the constant. The constant is the useful; the useful is the passable; the passable is the successful; and with success, all is accomplished. He relies upon this alone, relies upon it and does not know he is doing so. This is called the Way.

But to wear out your brain trying to make things into one without realizing that they are all the same—this is called "three in the morning." What do I mean by "three in the morning"? When the monkey trainer was handing out acorns, he said, "You get three in the morning and four at night." This made all the monkeys furious. "Well, then," he said, "you get four in the morning and three at night." The monkeys were all delighted. There was no change in the reality behind the words, and yet the monkeys responded with joy and anger. Let them, if they want to. So the sage harmonizes with both right and wrong and rests in Heaven the Equalizer. This is called walking two roads.

The understanding of the men of ancient times went a long way. How far did it go? To the point where some of them believed that things have never existed—so far, to the end, where nothing can be added. Those at the next stage thought that things exist but recognized no boundaries among them. Those at the next stage thought there were boundaries but recognized no right and wrong. Because right and wrong appeared, the Way was injured, and because the Way was injured, love became complete. But do such things as completion and injury really exist, or do they not?

There is such a thing as completion and injury—Mr. Zhao playing the lute is an example. There is such a thing as no completion and no injury—Mr. Zhao not playing the lute is an example.[9] Zhao Wen played the lute; Music Master Kuang waved his baton; Huizi leaned on his desk. The knowledge of these three was close to perfection. All were masters, and therefore their names have been handed down to later ages. Only in their likes they were different from him [the true sage]. What they liked, they tried to make clear. What he is not clear about, they tried to make clear, and so they ended in the foolishness of "hard" and "white."[1] Their sons, too, devoted all their lives to their fathers' theories, but till their death never reached any completion. Can these men be said to have attained completion? If so, then so have all the rest of us. Or can they not be said to have attained completion? If so, then neither we nor anything else have ever attained it.

9. Zhao Wen was a famous lute (*qin*) player. But the best music he could play (i.e., complete) was only a pale and partial reflection of the ideal music, which was thereby injured and impaired, just as the unity of the Way was injured by the appearance of love—i.e., someone's likes and dislikes. Hence, when Mr. Zhao refrained from playing the lute, there was neither completion nor injury.

1. The logicians Huizi and Gongsun Long spent much time discussing paradoxes involving the relation between attributes such as "hard" and "white" and the things to which they pertain.

The torch of chaos and doubt—this is what the sage steers by. So he does not use things but relegates all to the constant. This is what it means to use clarity.

Now I am going to make a statement here. I don't know whether it fits into the category of other people's statements or not. But whether it fits into their category or whether it doesn't, it obviously fits into some category. So in that respect it is no different from their statements. However, let me try making my statement.

There is a beginning. There is not yet beginning to be a beginning. There is a not yet beginning to be a not yet beginning to be a beginning. There is being. There is nonbeing. There is a not yet beginning to be nonbeing. There is a not yet beginning to be a not yet beginning to be nonbeing. Suddenly there is nonbeing. But I do not know, when it comes to nonbeing, which is really being and which is nonbeing. Now I have just said something. But I don't know whether what I have said has really said something or whether it hasn't said something.

There is nothing in the world bigger than the tip of an autumn hair,[2] and Mount Tai is tiny. No one has lived longer than a dead child, and Pengzu died young. Heaven and earth were born at the same time I was, and the ten thousand things are one with me.

We have already become one, so how can I say anything? But I have just *said* that we are one, so how can I not be saying something? The one and what I said about it make two, and two and the original one make three. If we go on this way, then even the cleverest mathematician can't tell where we'll end, much less an ordinary man. If by moving from nonbeing to being we get to three, how far will we get if we move from being to being? Better not to move, but to let things be!

The Way has never known boundaries; speech has no constancy. But because of [the recognition of a] "this," there came to be boundaries. Let me tell you what the boundaries are. There is left, there is right, there are theories, there are debates, there are divisions, there are discriminations, there are emulations, and there are contentions. These are called the Eight Virtues. As to what is beyond the Six Realms,[3] the sage admits its existence but does not theorize. As to what is within the Six Realms, he theorizes but does not debate. In the case of the *Spring and Autumn*,[4] the record of the former kings of past ages, the sage debates but does not discriminate. So [I say,] those who divide fail to divide; those who discriminate fail to discriminate. What does this mean, you ask? The sage embraces things. Ordinary men discriminate among them and parade their discriminations before others. So I say, those who discriminate fail to see.

The Great Way is not named; Great Discriminations are not spoken; Great Benevolence is not benevolent; Great Modesty is not humble; Great Daring does not attack. If the Way is made clear, it is not the Way. If discriminations are put into words, they do not suffice. If benevolence has a constant object, it

2. Figure for something extremely tiny. The strands of animal fur were believed to grow particularly fine in autumn.
3. The universe: heaven, earth, and the four directions.
4. Probably a reference to the *Spring and Autumn Annals*, a history of the state of Lu said to have been compiled by Confucius.

cannot be universal. If modesty is fastidious, it cannot be trusted. If daring attacks, it cannot be complete. These five are all round, but they tend toward the square.[5]

Therefore understanding that rests in what it does not understand is the finest. Who can understand discriminations that are not spoken, the Way that is not a way? If he can understand this, he may be called the Reservoir of Heaven. Pour into it and it is never full, dip from it and it never runs dry, and yet it does not know where the supply comes from. This is called the Shaded Light.

So it is that long ago Yao said to Shun, "I want to attack the rulers of Zong Kuai and Xu'ao. Even as I sit on my throne, this thought nags at me. Why is this?"

Shun replied, "These three rulers are only little dwellers in the weeds and brush. Why this nagging desire? Long ago, ten suns came out all at once and the ten thousand things were all lighted up. And how much greater is virtue than these suns!"[6]

Nie Que asked Wang Ni, "Do you know what all things agree in calling right?"

"How would I know that?" said Wang Ni.

"Do you know that you don't know it?"

"How would I know that?"

"Then do things know nothing?"

"How would I know that? However, suppose I try saying something. What way do I have of knowing that if I say I know something I don't really not know it? Or what way do I have of knowing that if I say I don't know something I don't really in fact know it? Now let me ask *you* some questions. If a man sleeps in a damp place, his back aches and he ends up half paralyzed, but is this true of a loach? If he lives in a tree, he is terrified and shakes with fright, but is this true of a monkey? Of these three creatures, then, which one knows the proper place to live? Men eat the flesh of grass-fed and grain-fed animals, deer eat grass, centipedes find snakes tasty, and hawks and falcons relish mice. Of these four, which knows how food ought to taste? Monkeys pair with monkeys, deer go out with deer, and fish play around with fish. Men claim that Maoqiang and Lady Li were beautiful, but if fish saw them they would dive to the bottom of the stream, if birds saw them they would fly away, and if deer saw them they would break into a run. Of these four, which knows how to fix the standard of beauty for the world? The way I see it, the rules of benevolence and righteousness and the paths of right and wrong are all hopelessly snarled and jumbled. How could I know anything about such discriminations?"

Nie Que said, "If you don't know what is profitable or harmful, then does the Perfect Man likewise know nothing of such things?"

Wang Ni replied, "The Perfect Man is godlike. Though the great swamps blaze, they cannot burn him; though the great rivers freeze, they cannot chill him; though swift lightning splits the hills and howling gales shake the sea,

5. All are originally perfect, but may become "squared"—i.e., impaired by the misuses mentioned.

6. Here virtue is to be understood in a positive sense, as the power of the Way.

they cannot frighten him. A man like this rides the clouds and mist, straddles the sun and moon, and wanders beyond the four seas. Even life and death have no effect on him, much less the rules of profit and loss!"

Ju Quezi said to Zhang Wuzi, "I have heard Confucius say that the sage does not work at anything, does not pursue profit, does not dodge harm, does not enjoy being sought after, does not follow the Way, says nothing yet says something, says something yet says nothing, and wanders beyond the dust and grime. Confucius himself regarded these as wild and flippant words, though I believe they describe the working of the mysterious Way. What do you think of them?"

Zhang Wuzi said, "Even the Yellow Emperor would be confused if he heard such words, so how could you expect Confucius to understand them? What's more, you're too hasty in your own appraisal. You see an egg and demand a crowing cock, see a crossbow pellet and demand a roast dove. I'm going to try speaking some reckless words and I want you to listen to them recklessly. How will that be? The sage leans on the sun and moon, tucks the universe under his arm, merges himself with things, leaves the confusion and muddle as it is, and looks on slaves as exalted. Ordinary men strain and struggle; the sage is stupid and blockish. He takes part in ten thousand ages and achieves simplicity in oneness. For him, all the ten thousand things are what they are, and thus they enfold each other.

"How do I know that loving life is not a delusion? How do I know that in hating death I am not like a man who, having left home in his youth, has forgotten the way back?

"Lady Li was the daughter of the border guard of Ai.[7] When she was first taken captive and brought to the state of Jin, she wept until her tears drenched the collar of her robe. But later, when she went to live in the palace of the ruler, shared his couch with him, and ate the delicious meats of his table, she wondered why she had ever wept. How do I know that the dead do not wonder why they ever longed for life?

"He who dreams of drinking wine may weep when morning comes; he who dreams of weeping may in the morning go off to hunt. While he is dreaming he does not know it is a dream, and in his dream he may even try to interpret a dream. Only after he wakes does he know it was a dream. And someday there will be a great awakening when we know that this is all a great dream. Yet the stupid believe they are awake, busily and brightly assuming they understand things, calling this man ruler, that one herdsman—how dense! Confucius and you are both dreaming! And when I say you are dreaming, I am dreaming, too. Words like these will be labeled the Supreme Swindle. Yet, after ten thousand generations, a great sage may appear who will know their meaning, and it will still be as though he appeared with astonishing speed.

"Suppose you and I have had an argument. If you have beaten me instead of my beating you, then are you necessarily right and am I necessarily wrong? If I have beaten you instead of your beating me, then am I necessarily right and are

7. She was taken captive by Duke Xian of Jin in 671 B.C.E., and later became his consort.

you necessarily wrong? Is one of us right and the other wrong? Are both of us right or are both of us wrong? If you and I don't know the answer, then other people are bound to be even more in the dark. Whom shall we get to decide what is right? Shall we get someone who agrees with you to decide? But if he already agrees with you, how can he decide fairly? Shall we get someone who agrees with me? But if he already agrees with me, how can he decide? Shall we get someone who disagrees with both of us? But if he already disagrees with both of us, how can he decide? Obviously, then, neither you nor I nor anyone else can decide for each other. Shall we wait for still another person?

"But waiting for one shifting voice [to pass judgment on] another is the same as waiting for none of them. Harmonize them all with the Heavenly Equality, leave them to their endless changes, and so live out your years. What do I mean by harmonizing them with the Heavenly Equality? Right is not right; so is not so. If right were really right, it would differ so clearly from not right that there would be no need for argument. If so were really so, it would differ so clearly from not so that there would be no need for argument. Forget the years; forget distinctions. Leap into the boundless and make it your home!"

Penumbra said to Shadow, "A little while ago you were walking and now you're standing still; a little while ago you were sitting and now you're standing up. Why this lack of independent action?"

Shadow said, "Do I have to wait for something before I can be like this? Does what I wait for also have to wait for something before it can be like this? Am I waiting for the scales of a snake or the wings of a cicada? How do I know why it is so? How do I know why it isn't so?"

Once Zhuang Zhou dreamt he was a butterfly, a butterfly flitting and fluttering around, happy with himself and doing as he pleased. He didn't know he was Zhuang Zhou. Suddenly he woke up and there he was, solid and unmistakable Zhuang Zhou. But he didn't know if he was Zhuang Zhou who had dreamt he was a butterfly, or a butterfly dreaming he was Zhuang Zhou. Between Zhuang Zhou and a butterfly there must be *some* distinction! This is called the Transformation of Things.

CHAPTER 3
The Secret of Caring for Life

Your life has a limit but knowledge has none. If you use what is limited to pursue what has no limit, you will be in danger. If you understand this and still strive for knowledge, you will be in danger for certain! If you do good, stay away from fame. If you do evil, stay away from punishments. Follow the middle; go by what is constant, and you can stay in one piece, keep yourself alive, look after your parents, and live out your years.

Cook Ding was cutting up an ox for Lord Wenhui. At every touch of his hand, every heave of his shoulder, every move of his feet, every thrust of his knee—zip! zoop! He slithered the knife along with a zing, and all was in perfect rhythm, as though he were performing the dance of the Mulberry Grove or keeping time to the Jingshou music.[8]

"Ah, this is marvelous!" said Lord Wenhui. "Imagine skill reaching such heights!"

Cook Ding laid down his knife and replied, "What I care about is the Way, which goes beyond skill. When I first began cutting up oxen, all I could see was the ox itself. After three years I no longer saw the whole ox. And now—now I go at it by spirit and don't look with my eyes. Perception and understanding have come to a stop and spirit moves where it wants. I go along with the natural makeup, strike in the big hollows, guide the knife through the big openings, and follow things as they are. So I never touch the smallest ligament or tendon, much less a main joint.

"A good cook changes his knife once a year—because he cuts. A mediocre cook changes his knife once a month—because he hacks. I've had this knife of mine for nineteen years and I've cut up thousands of oxen with it, and yet the blade is as good as though it had just come from the grindstone. There are spaces between the joints, and the blade of the knife has really no thickness. If you insert what has no thickness into such spaces, then there's plenty of room—more than enough for the blade to play about it. That's why after nineteen years the blade of my knife is still as good as when it first came from the grindstone.

"However, whenever I come to a complicated place, I size up the difficulties, tell myself to watch out and be careful, keep my eyes on what I'm doing, work very slowly, and move the knife with the greatest subtlety, until—flop! the whole thing comes apart like a clod of earth crumbling to the ground. I stand there holding the knife and look all around me, completely satisfied and reluctant to move on, and then I wipe off the knife and put it away."

"Excellent!" said Lord Wenhui. "I have heard the words of Cook Ding and learned how to care for life!"

When Gongwen Xuan saw the Commander of the Right,[9] he was startled and said, "What kind of man is this? How did he come to be footless? Was it Heaven? Or was it man?"

"It was Heaven, not man," said the commander. "When Heaven gave me life, it saw to it that I would be one-footed. Men's looks are given to them. So I know this was the work of Heaven and not of man. The swamp pheasant has to walk ten paces for one peck and a hundred paces for one drink, but it doesn't want to be kept in a cage. Though you treat it like a king, its spirit won't be content."

When Lao Dan[1] died, Qin Shi went to mourn for him; but after giving three cries, he left the room.

"Weren't you a friend of the Master?" asked Laozi's disciples.

8. The Mulberry Grove is identified as a rain dance from the time of King Tang of the Shang Dynasty, and the Jingshou music as part of a longer composition from the time of the sage-king Yao.

9. Probably the ex–Commander of the Right, since he has been punished by having one foot amputated, a common penalty in ancient China.

1. Laozi, the reputed author of the *Daodejing*. In Zhuangzi he appears as a contemporary of Confucius.

"Yes."

"And you think it's all right to mourn him this way?"

"Yes," said Qin Shi. "At first I took him for a real man, but now I know he wasn't. A little while ago, when I went in to mourn, I found old men weeping for him as though they were weeping for a son, and young men weeping for him as though they were weeping for a mother. To have gathered a group like *that,* he must have done something to make them talk about him, though he didn't ask them to talk, or make them weep for him, though he didn't ask them to weep. This is to hide from Heaven, turn your back on the true state of affairs, and forget what you were born with. In the old days this was called the crime of hiding from Heaven. Your master happened to come because it was his time, and he happened to leave because things follow along. If you are content with the time and willing to follow along, then grief and joy have no way to enter in. In the old days, this was called being freed from the bonds of God.

"Though the grease burns out of the torch, the fire passes on, and no one knows where it ends."

FROM CHAPTER 4

In the World of Men

Carpenter Shi went to Qi and, when he got to Crooked Shaft, he saw a serrate oak standing by the village shrine. It was broad enough to shelter several thousand oxen and measured a hundred spans around, towering above the hills. The lowest branches were eighty feet from the ground, and a dozen or so of them could have been made into boats. There were so many sightseers that the place looked like a fair, but the carpenter didn't even glance around and went on his way without stopping. His apprentice stood staring for a long time and then ran after Carpenter Shi and said, "Since I first took up my ax and followed you, Master, I have never seen timber as beautiful as this. But you don't even bother to look, and go right on without stopping. Why is that?"

"Forget it—say no more!" said the carpenter. "It's a worthless tree! Make boats out of it and they'd sink; make coffins and they'd rot in no time; make vessels and they'd break at once. Use it for doors and it would sweat sap like pine; use it for posts and the worms would eat them up. It's not a timber tree—there's nothing it can be used for. That's how it got to be that old!"

After Carpenter Shi had returned home, the oak tree appeared to him in a dream and said, "What are you comparing me with? Are you comparing me with those useful trees? The cherry apple, the pear, the orange, the citron, the rest of those fructiferous trees and shrubs—as soon as their fruit is ripe, they are torn apart and subjected to abuse. Their big limbs are broken off, their little limbs are yanked around. Their utility makes life miserable for them, and so they don't get to finish out the years Heaven gave them, but are cut off in mid-journey. They bring it on themselves—the pulling and tearing of the common mob. And it's the same way with all other things.

"As for me, I've been trying a long time to be of no use, and though I almost died, I've finally got it. This is of great use to me. If I had been of some use, would I ever have grown this large? Moreover you and I are both of us things. What's the point of this—things condemning things? You, a worthless man about to die—how do you know I'm a worthless tree?"

When Carpenter Shi woke up, he reported his dream. His apprentice said, "If it's so intent on being of no use, what's it doing there at the village shrine?"[2]

"Shhh! Say no more! It's only *resting* there. If we carp and criticize, it will merely conclude that we don't understand it. Even if it weren't at the shrine, do you suppose it would be cut down? It protects itself in a different way from ordinary people. If you try to judge it by conventional standards, you'll be way off!"

* * *

There's Crippled Shu—chin stuck down in his navel, shoulders up above his head, pigtail pointing at the sky, his five organs on the top, his two thighs pressing his ribs. By sewing and washing, he gets enough to fill his mouth; by handling a winnow and sifting out the good grain, he makes enough to feed ten people. When the authorities call out the troops, he stands in the crowd waving good-by; when they get up a big work party, they pass him over because he's a chronic invalid. And when they are doling out grain to the ailing, he gets three big measures and ten bundles of firewood. With a crippled body, he's still able to look after himself and finish out the years Heaven gave him. How much better, then, if he had crippled virtue!

When Confucius visited Chu, Jie Yu, the madman of Chu, wandered by his gate crying, "Phoenix, phoenix, how his virtue failed! The future you cannot wait for; the past you cannot pursue. When the world has the Way, the sage succeeds; when the world is without the Way, the sage survives. In times like the present, we do well to escape penalty. Good fortune is light as a feather, but nobody knows how to hold it up. Misfortune is heavy as the earth, but nobody knows how to stay out of its way. Leave off, leave off—this teaching men virtue! Dangerous, dangerous—to mark off the ground and run! Fool, fool—don't spoil my walking! I walk a crooked way—don't step on my feet. The mountain trees do themselves harm; the grease in the torch burns itself up. The cinnamon can be eaten and so it gets cut down; the lacquer tree can be used and so it gets hacked apart. All men know the use of the useful, but nobody knows the use of the useless!"

FROM CHAPTER 6

The Great and Venerable Teacher

Master Si, Master Yu, Master Li, and Master Lai were all four talking together. "Who can look upon nonbeing as his head, on life as his back, and on death as his rump?" they said. "Who knows that life and death, existence and annihilation, are all a single body? I will be his friend!"

The four men looked at each other and smiled. There was no disagreement in their hearts and so the four of them became friends.

All at once Master Yu fell ill. Master Si went to ask how he was. "Amazing!" said Master Yu. "The Creator is making me all crookedly like this! My back

2. The shrine, or altar of the soil, was always situated in a grove of beautiful trees. The oak was therefore serving a purpose by lending an air of sanctity to the spot.

sticks up like a hunchback and my vital organs are on top of me. My chin is hidden in my navel, my shoulders are up above my head, and my pigtail points at the sky. It must be some dislocation of the yin and yang!"[3]

Yet he seemed calm at heart and unconcerned. Dragging himself haltingly to the well, he looked at his reflection and said, "My, my! So the Creator is making me all crookedy like this!"

"Do you resent it?" asked Master Si.

"Why no, what would I resent? If the process continues, perhaps in time he'll transform my left arm into a rooster. In that case I'll keep watch on the night. Or perhaps in time he'll transform my right arm into a crossbow pellet and I'll shoot down an owl for roasting. Or perhaps in time he'll transform my buttocks into cartwheels. Then, with my spirit for a horse, I'll climb up and go for a ride. What need will I ever have for a carriage again?

"I received life because the time had come; I will lose it because the order of things passes on. Be content with this time and dwell in this order and then neither sorrow nor joy can touch you. In ancient times this was called the 'freeing of the bound.' There are those who cannot free themselves, because they are bound by things. But nothing can ever win against Heaven—that's the way it's always been. What would I have to resent?"

Suddenly Master Lai grew ill. Gasping and wheezing, he lay at the point of death. His wife and children gathered round in a circle and began to cry. Master Li, who had come to ask how he was, said, "Shoo! Get back! Don't disturb the process of change!"

Then he leaned against the doorway and talked to Master Lai. "How marvelous the Creator is! What is he going to make of you next? Where is he going to send you? Will he make you into a rat's liver? Will he make you into a bug's arm?"

Master Lai said, "A child, obeying his father and mother, goes wherever he is told, east or west, south or north. And the yin and yang—how much more are they to a man than father or mother! Now that they have brought me to the verge of death, if I should refuse to obey them, how perverse I would be! What fault is it of theirs? The Great Clod burdens me with form, labors me with life, eases me in old age, and rests me in death. So if I think well of my life, for the same reason I must think well of my death. When a skilled smith is casting metal, if the metal should leap up and say, 'I insist upon being made into a Moye![4] he would surely regard it as very inauspicious metal indeed. Now, having had the audacity to take on human form once, if I should say, 'I don't want to be anything but a man! Nothing but a man!', the Creator would surely regard me as a most inauspicious sort of person. So now I think of heaven and earth as a great furnace, and the Creator as a skilled smith. Where could he send me that would not be all right? I will go off to sleep peacefully, and then with a start I will wake up."

Master Sanghu, Mengzi Fan, and Master Qinzhang, three friends, said to each other, "Who can join with others without joining with others? Who can do with others without doing with others? Who can climb up to heaven and

3. The female and male principles, respectively; darkness and light, the duality by which all things function. Medical disorders were often described as imbalances of the yin and yang.

4. A famous sword of King Helü (ruled 514–496 B.C.E.) of the southern state of Wu.

wander in the mists, roam the infinite, and forget life forever and forever?" The three men looked at each other and smiled. There was no disagreement in their hearts and so they became friends.

After some time had passed without event, Master Sanghu died. He had not yet been buried when Confucius, hearing of his death, sent Zigong[5] to assist at the funeral. When Zigong arrived, he found one of the dead man's friends weaving frames for silkworms, while the other strummed a lute. Joining their voices, they sang this song:

> Ah, Sanghu!
> Ah, Sanghu!
> You have gone back to your true form
> While we remain as men, O!

Zigong hastened forward and said, "May I be so bold as to ask what sort of ceremony this is—singing in the very presence of the corpse?"

The two men looked at each other and laughed. "What does this man know of the meaning of ceremony?" they said.

Zigong returned and reported to Confucius what had happened. "What sort of men are they anyway?" he asked. "They pay no attention to proper behavior, disregard their personal appearance and, without so much as changing the expression on their faces, sing in the very presence of the corpse! I can think of no name for them! What sort of men are they?"

"Such men as they," said Confucius, "wander beyond the realm; men like me wander within it. Beyond and within can never meet. It was stupid of me to send you to offer condolences. Even now they have joined with the Creator as men to wander in the single breath of heaven and earth. They look upon life as a swelling tumor, a protruding wen, and upon death as the draining of a sore or the bursting of a boil. To men such as these, how could there be any question of putting life first or death last? They borrow the forms of different creatures and house them in the same body. They forget liver and gall, cast aside ears and eyes, turning and revolving, ending and beginning again, unaware of where they start or finish. Idly they roam beyond the dust and dirt; they wander free and easy in the service of inaction. Why should they fret and fuss about the ceremonies of the vulgar world and make a display for the ears and eyes of the common herd?"

Zigong said, "Well then, Master, what is this 'realm' that you stick to?"

Confucius said, "I am one of those men punished by Heaven. Nevertheless, I will share with you what I have."

"Then may I ask about the realm?"[6] said Zigong.

Confucius said, "Fish thrive in water, man thrives in the Way. For those that thrive in water, dig a pond and they will find nourishment enough. For those that thrive in the Way, don't bother about them and their lives will be secure. So it is said, the fish forget each other in the rivers and lakes, and men forget each other in the arts of the Way."

Zigong said, "May I ask about the singular man?"

5. One of Confucius's disciples.
6. The word *fang*, translated here as "realm," may also mean "method" or "procedure," and Confucius's answer seems to stress this latter meaning.

"The singular man is singular in comparison to other men, but a companion of Heaven. So it is said, the petty man of Heaven is a gentleman among men; the gentleman among men is the petty man of Heaven."

Yan Hui said to Confucius, "When Mengsun Cai's mother died, he wailed without shedding any tears, he did not grieve in his heart, and he conducted the funeral without any look of sorrow. He fell down on these three counts, and yet he is known all over the state of Lu for the excellent way he managed the funeral. Is it really possible to gain such a reputation when there are no facts to support it? I find it very peculiar indeed!"

Confucius said, "Mengsun did all there was to do. He was advanced beyond ordinary understanding and he would have simplified things even more, but that wasn't practical. However, there is still a lot that he simplified. Mengsun doesn't know why he lives and doesn't know why he dies. He doesn't know why he should go ahead; he doesn't know why he should fall behind. In the process of change, he has become a thing [among other things], and he is merely waiting for some other change that he doesn't yet know about. Moreover, when he is changing, how does he know that he is really changing? And when he is not changing, how does he know that he hasn't already changed? You and I, now—we are dreaming and haven't waked up yet. But in his case, though something may startle his body, it won't injure his mind; though something may alarm the house [his spirit lives in], his emotions will suffer no death. Mengsun alone has waked up. Men wail and so he wails, too—that's the reason he acts like this.

"What's more, we go around telling each other, I do this, I do that—but how do we know that this 'I' we talk about has any 'I' to it? You dream you're a bird and soar up into the sky; you dream you're a fish and dive down in the pool. But now when you tell me about it, I don't know whether you are awake or whether you are dreaming. Running around accusing others is not as good as laughing, and enjoying a good laugh is not as good as going along with things. Be content to go along and forget about change and then you can enter the mysterious oneness of Heaven."

FROM CHAPTER 7

Fit for Emperors and Kings

The emperor of the South Sea was called Shu [Brief], the emperor of the North Sea was called Hu [Sudden], and the emperor of the central region was called Hundun [Chaos]. Shu and Hu from time to time came together for a meeting in the territory of Hundun, and Hundun treated them very generously. Shu and Hu discussed how they could repay his kindness. "All men," they said, "have seven openings so they can see, hear, eat, and breathe. But Hundun alone doesn't have any. Let's trying boring him some!"

Every day they bored another hole, and on the seventh day Hundun died.

FROM CHAPTER 12

Heaven and Earth

Zigong traveled south to Chu, and on his way back through Jin, as he passed along the south bank of the Han, he saw an old man preparing his fields for planting. He had hollowed out an opening by which he entered the well and from which he emerged, lugging a pitcher, which he carried out to water the fields. Grunting and puffing, he used up a great deal of energy and produced very little result.

"There is a machine for this sort of thing," said Zigong. "In one day it can water a hundred fields, demanding very little effort and producing excellent results. Wouldn't you like one?"

The gardener raised his head and looked at Zigong. "How does it work?"

"It's a contraption made by shaping a piece of wood. The back end is heavy and the front end light and it raises the water as though it were pouring it out, so fast that it seems to boil right over! It's called a well sweep."

The gardener flushed with anger and then said with a laugh, "I've heard my teacher say, where there are machines, there are bound to be machine worries; where there are machine worries, there are bound to be machine hearts. With a machine heart in your breast, you've spoiled what was pure and simple; and without the pure and simple, the life of the spirit knows no rest. Where the life of the spirit knows no rest, the Way will cease to buoy you up. It's not that I don't know about your machine—I would be ashamed to use it!"

Zigong blushed with chagrin, looked down, and made no reply. After a while, the gardener said, "Who are you, anyway?"

"A disciple of Kong Qiu."[7]

"Oh—then you must be one of those who broaden their learning in order to ape the sages, heaping absurd nonsense on the crowd, plucking the strings and singing sad songs all by yourself in hopes of buying fame in the world! You would do best to forget your spirit and breath, break up your body and limbs—then you might be able to get somewhere. You don't even know how to look after your own body—how do you have any time to think about looking after the world! On your way now! Don't interfere with my work!"

Zigong frowned and the color drained from his face. Dazed and rattled, he couldn't seem to pull himself together, and it was only after he had walked on for some thirty li that he began to recover.

One of his disciples said, "Who was that man just now? Why did you change your expression and lose your color like that, Master, so that it took you all day to get back to normal?"

"I used to think there was only one real man in the world," said Zigong. "I didn't know there was this other one. I have heard Confucius say that in affairs you aim for what is right, and in undertakings you aim for success. To spend little effort and achieve big results—that is the Way of the sage. Now it seems that this isn't so. He who holds fast to the Way is complete in Virtue; being complete in Virtue, he is complete in body; being complete in body, he is complete in spirit; and to be complete in spirit is the Way of the sage. He is content to live among the people, to walk by their side, and never know where he is going. Witless, his purity is complete. Achievement, profit, machines, skill—they have no place in this man's mind! A man like this will not go where he has no will to go, will not do what he has no mind to do. Though the world might praise him and say he had really found something, he would look unconcerned and never turn his head; though the world might condemn him and say he had lost something, he would look serene and pay no heed. The praise and blame

7. Confucius.

of the world are no loss or gain to him. He may be called a man of Complete Virtue. I—I am a man of the wind-blown waves."

When Zigong got back to Lu, he reported the incident to Confucius. Confucius said, "He is one of those bogus practitioners of the arts of Mr. Chaos. He knows the first thing but doesn't understand the second. He looks after what is on the inside but doesn't look after what is on the outside. A man of true brightness and purity who can enter into simplicity, who can return to the primitive through inaction, give body to his inborn nature, and embrace his spirit, and in this way wander through the everyday world—if you had met one like that, you would have had real cause for astonishment. As for the arts of Mr. Chaos, you and I need not bother to find out about them."

FROM CHAPTER 17

Autumn Floods

Once, when Zhuangzi was fishing in the Pu River, the king of Chu sent two officials to go and announce to him: "I would like to trouble you with the administration of my realm."

Zhuangzi held on to the fishing pole and, without turning his head, said, "I have heard that there is a sacred tortoise in Chu that has been dead for three thousand years. The king keeps it wrapped in cloth and boxed, and stores it in the ancestral temple. Now would this tortoise rather be dead and have its bones left behind and honored? Or would it rather be alive and dragging its tail in the mud?"

"It would rather be alive and dragging its tail in the mud," said the two officials.

Zhuangzi said, "Go away! I'll drag my tail in the mud!"

When Huizi was prime minister of Liang, Zhuangzi set off to visit him. Someone said to Huizi, "Zhuangzi is coming because he wants to replace you as prime minister!" With this Huizi was filled with alarm and searched all over the state for three days and three nights trying to find Zhuangzi. Zhuangzi then came to see him and said, "In the south there is a bird called the Yuanchu—I wonder if you've ever heard of it? The Yuanchu rises up from the South Sea and flies to the North Sea, and it will rest on nothing but the Wutong tree, eat nothing but the fruit of the Lian and drink only from springs of sweet water. Once there was an owl who had gotten hold of a half-rotten old rat, and as the Yuanchu passed by, it raised its head, looked up at the Yuanchu, and said, 'Shoo!' Now that you have this Liang state of yours, are you trying to shoo me?"

Zhuangzi and Huizi were strolling along the dam of the Hao River when Zhuangzi said, "See how the minnows come out and dart around where they please! That's what fish really enjoy!"

Huizi said, "You're not a fish—how do you know what fish enjoy?"

Zhuangzi said, "You're not I, so how do you know I don't know what fish enjoy?"

Huizi said, "I'm not you, so I certainly don't know what you know. On the other hand, you're certainly not a fish—so that still proves you don't know what fish enjoy!"

Zhuangzi said, "Let's go back to your original question, please. You asked me *how* I know what fish enjoy—so you already knew I knew it when you asked the question. I know it by standing here beside the Hao."

FROM CHAPTER 18

Perfect Happiness

When Zhuangzi went to Chu, he saw an old skull, all dry and parched. He poked it with his carriage whip and then asked, "Sir, were you greedy for life and forgetful of reason, and so came to this? Was your state overthrown and did you bow beneath the ax, and so came to this? Did you do some evil deed and were you ashamed to bring disgrace upon your parents and family, and so came to this? Was it through the pangs of cold and hunger that you came to this? Or did your springs and autumns pile up until they brought you to this?"

When he had finished speaking, he dragged the skull over and, using it for a pillow, lay down to sleep.

In the middle of the night, the skull came to him in a dream and said, "You chatter like a rhetorician and all your words betray the entanglements of a living man. The dead know nothing of these! Would you like to hear a lecture on the dead?"

"Indeed," said Zhuangzi.

The skull said, "Among the dead there are no rulers above, no subjects below, and no chores of the four seasons. With nothing to do, our springs and autumns are as endless as heaven and earth. A king facing south on his throne could have no more happiness than this!"

Zhuangzi couldn't believe this and said, "If I got the Arbiter of Fate to give you a body again, make you some bones and flesh, return you to your parents and family and your old home and friends, you would want that, wouldn't you?"

The skull frowned severely, wrinkling up its brow. "Why would I throw away more happiness than that of a king on a throne and take on the troubles of a human being again?" it said.

FROM CHAPTER 20

The Mountain Tree

Zhuang Zhou was wandering in the park at Diaoling when he saw a peculiar kind of magpie that came flying along from the south. It had a wingspread of seven feet and its eyes were a good inch in diameter. It brushed against Zhuang Zhou's forehead and then settled down in a grove of chestnut trees. "What kind of bird is that!" exclaimed Zhuang Zhou. "Its wings are enormous but they get it nowhere; its eyes are huge but it can't even see where it's going!" Then he hitched up his robe, strode forward, cocked his crossbow and prepared to take aim. As he did so, he spied a cicada that had found a lovely spot of shade and had forgotten all about [the possibility of danger to] its body. Behind it, a praying mantis, stretching forth its claws, prepared to snatch the cicada, and it too had forgotten about its own form as it eyed its prize. The peculiar magpie was close behind, ready to make off with the praying mantis, forgetting its own true self as it fixed its eyes on the prospect of gain. Zhuang Zhou, shuddering at the sight, said, "Ah!—things do nothing but make trouble for each other—one creature calling down disaster on another!" He threw down his crossbow, turned about, and hurried from the park, but the park keeper [taking him for a poacher] raced after him with shouts of accusation.

Zhuang Zhou returned home and for three months looked unhappy. Lin Ju, in the course of tending to his master's needs, questioned him, saying, "Master, why is it that you are so unhappy these days?"

Zhuang Zhou said, "In clinging to outward form I have forgotten my own body. Staring at muddy water, I have been misled into taking it for a clear pool. Moreover, I have heard my Master say, 'When you go among the vulgar, follow their rules!' I went wandering at Diaoling and forgot my body. A peculiar magpie brushed against my forehead, wandered off to the chestnut grove, and there forgot its true self. And the keeper of the chestnut grove, to my great shame, took me for a trespasser! That is why I am unhappy."

Yangzi, on his way to Song, stopped for the night at an inn. The innkeeper had two concubines, one beautiful, the other ugly. But the ugly one was treated as a lady of rank, while the beautiful one was treated as a menial. When Yangzi asked the reason, a young boy of the inn replied, "The beautiful one is only too aware of her beauty, and so we don't think of her as beautiful. The ugly one is only too aware of her ugliness, and so we don't think of her as ugly."

Yangzi said, "Remember that, my students! If you act worthily but rid yourself of the awareness that you are acting worthily, then where can you go that you will not be loved?"

FROM CHAPTER 22

Knowledge Wandered North

Master Dongguo asked Zhuangzi, "This thing called the Way—where does it exist?"

Zhuangzi said, "There's no place it doesn't exist."

"Come," said Master Dongguo, "you must be more specific!"

"It is in the ant."

"As low a thing as that?"

"It is in the panic grass."

"But that's lower still!"

"It is in the tiles and shards."

"How can it be so low?"

"It is in the piss and shit!"

Master Dongguo made no reply.

Zhuangzi said, "Sir, your questions simply don't get at the substance of the matter. When Inspector Huo asked the superintendent of the market how to test the fatness of a pig by pressing it with the foot, he was told that the lower down on the pig you press, the nearer you come to the truth. But you must not expect to find the Way in any particular place—there is no thing that escapes its presence! Such is the Perfect Way, and so too are the truly great words. 'Complete,' 'universal,' 'all-inclusive'—these three are different words with the same meaning. All point to a single reality.

"Why don't you try wandering with me to the Palace of Not-Even-Anything—identity and concord will be the basis of our discussions and they will never come to an end, never reach exhaustion. Why not join with me in inaction, in tranquil quietude, in hushed purity, in harmony and leisure? Already my will is vacant and blank. I go nowhere and don't know how far I've gotten. I go and come and don't know where to stop. I've already been there and back, and I don't know when the journey is done. I ramble and relax in unbordered vastness; Great Knowledge enters in, and I don't know where it will ever end.

"That which treats things as things is not limited by things. Things have their limits—the so-called limits of things. The unlimited moves to the realm of limits; the limited moves to the unlimited realm. We speak of the filling and emptying, the withering and decay of things. [The Way] makes them full and empty without itself filling or emptying; it makes them wither and decay without itself withering or decaying. It establishes root and branch but knows no root and branch itself; it determines when to store up or scatter but knows no storing or scattering itself."

SIMA QIAN

ca. 145–85 B.C.E.

Sima Qian's life was cursed with a smoldering sense of shame: when condemned for offending Emperor Wu, Sima Qian chose to be castrated and serve in the women's quarters of the palace as a eunuch rather than commit an honorable suicide, which would have been the appropriate choice by the standards of his time. He devoted himself thereafter to finishing the *Historical Records*, a monumental history begun by his father that covered China from its beginnings up to his own time. His fascination with the best and worst impulses in the human psyche and his conviction that his *Historical Records* would survive him as an immortal achievement gave him the strength to endure his shameful circumstances. His confidence in the project was ultimately justified: the *Historical Records* laid the foundations for the tradition of Chinese official history writing; influenced the work of court historians for more than two millennia, from Sima Qian's death until the end of the last imperial dynasty in the twentieth century; and served as a model for historiography in Korea, Japan, and Vietnam.

LIFE

Sima Qian was born into a family of "grand historians" serving at the court of the Han Dynasty (206 B.C.E.–220 C.E.). The office of grand historian combined responsibility for astronomical observations and regulation of the calendar with the duty of keeping records of court events and overseeing the imperial library, which had greatly expanded during the transition from the short-lived Qin Dynasty to the Han Dynasty, when many historical records from far-flung locations were brought to the new Han capital and archived in the imperial library. The privileged access that Sima Qian (and his father before him) had to this greatly expanded library was part of the reason he was able to write a history of unprecedented scope and depth.

The moment that was to change Sima's life came when a general named Li Ling was captured during embittered fights with the Xiongnu, a confederation of nomadic people on China's northern frontier. The Han Dynasty had suffered humiliating defeats at the hands of the Xiongnu and had tried to appease the frontier peoples with a diplomacy of gifts and marriage alliances. When Emperor Wu assumed power, however, he pursued a more aggressive foreign policy: not only did he conquer parts of Vietnam and Korea, he also undertook repeated campaigns against the Xiongnu. During one such campaign, his general, Li Ling, lacking the support of delayed backup troops, was forced to surrender in the face of an overwhelmingly superior Xiongnu army. Emperor Wu was enraged and had Li Ling's entire family executed. Although Sima Qian was not a close friend of Li Ling, he admired his valor and sense of justice and spoke to the emperor on his behalf. The emperor took offence and offered Sima Qian the fateful choice between suicide and castration. Although Sima Qian was later pardoned, a sense of deep injustice pervaded his life and writings until the end of his life.

THE *HISTORICAL RECORDS*

The *Historical Records* were not the first work of historiography in China: **Confucius** (551–479 B.C.E.) had supposedly written the *Spring and Autumn Annals*, a year-by-year chronicle of events in his home state of Lu, and court historians of other states recorded major events in the political sphere and natural world. Sima Qian followed the fashion of this annalistic court tradition and included chronological accounts of successive rulers and of the ruling families of the various states before China's unification. He also added treatises on topics such as astronomy, the calendar, and music. But he decided to write half of the 130 chapters of the *Historical Records* in a radically new format: biographies. Fascinated by the complexities of human psychology, he was not just interested in the famous generals and ministers, scholars and thinkers who made history. He also wrote collective biographies of assassins, flatterers, court jesters, and foreign peoples. And he deeply empathized with his heroes when he had the chance to visit the key sites associated with their lives and to reimagine their trials and tribulations.

The biographical format allowed Sima Qian to introduce crucial innovations: history became populated with protagonists, men and women with complex and often contradictory desires, values, and ambitions. The historian had to explain their motivations and choices, and judge their character and the successes and failures of their lives. The biographical format also allowed Sima Qian to inject individual perspectives into historical truth: when pairing the biographies of opponents he could describe the same set of events in different ways, true to the eyes of each historical actor.

THE *LETTER IN REPLY TO REN AN*

Our selections start with Sima Qian's riveting account of his own life and his decision to endure the shame of castration in order to complete the *Historical Records*. Sima Qian wrote the *Letter in Reply to Ren An* as a response to someone who had apparently accused Sima Qian of cowardice for not taking the honorable route of suicide after his conviction in the Li Ling case. Sima Qian had long hesitated to respond, but finally did so in the fateful moment when Ren An himself had been accused of some crime and was awaiting death. Although Ren An's letter to Sima Qian does not survive, Sima Qian's reply to Ren An was preserved in the *Han History*, an official history of the Han Dynasty that was compiled almost two centuries after Sima Qian's *Historical Records* and largely adopted Sima Qian's model of history writing. *The Letter in Reply to Ren An* was included in the biography devoted to Sima Qian in the *Han History* as a moving testimony of the life of China's most influential historian.

In his letter Sima Qian justifies his behavior in the Li Ling case, but he also resorts to grander schemes to defend his decision against suicide: he inserts his name into a list of grand historical figures who produced masterpieces when imprisoned, threatened, or banished, including King Wen, the virtuous founder of the Zhou Dynasty; Confucius, the ultimate master; and Qu Yuan, the model of the virtuous minister whose worth goes unrecognized by his age. In the company of these towering figures, Sima Qian felt confident that posterity would judge him and his *Historical Records* more favorably than his contemporaries did.

THE BIOGRAPHIES

"The Biography of Bo Yi and Shu Qi" and "The Biography of Qu Yuan and Jia Yi" (of which only the section on Qu Yuan is included here) come from the large biographies sections of the *Historical Records*. They are devoted to four individuals whose willpower and high moral principles Sima Qian admired and who lost their lives because they refused to compromise their principles. The opening chapter to the biographies section, "The Biography of Bo Yi and Shu Qi" contains a manifesto of Sima Qian's vision of the historian's task. Bo Yi and Shu Qi were the sons of a lord who served the last king of the Shang Dynasty (ca. 1500–1045 B.C.E.). When the Shang were overthrown by King Wu, who founded the Zhou Dynasty (ca. 1045–256 B.C.E.), Bo Yi and Shu Qi criticized the new king for his violent conquest, refused to serve the new dynasty, and retreated into the mountains to starve themselves to death. Reflecting on the fact that we know about these two noble recluses only from Confucius's scattered references to them, Sima Qian questions the justness of the historical record, and ultimately the justice of heaven: how reliable are historical records really and why do certain people make it into history books, while other, equally remarkable individuals leave no traces? Where can we find justice in a world where the likes of Yan Hui, the most exemplary student of Confucius, die senselessly early, while the likes of the despicable robber Zhi live a long and happy life off their pilfered goods?

The first part of "The Biography of Qu Yuan and Jia Yi" shows us another tragic hero with whom Sima Qian could empathize. Qu Yuan (ca. 340–278 B.C.E.) was a brilliant minister serving King Huai in the southern state of Chu, one of the most powerful states on the eve of China's unification under the militaristic northern state of Qin in 221 B.C.E.. He lived during the time when the Zhou Dynasty was reduced to symbolic power and its former vassal states had set themselves up as independent states constantly competing over territory, resources, and power. Qu Yuan lost favor when slandered by envious colleagues, was exiled, and ended up drowning himself in the Miluo River on the way to exile. Sima Qian leaves no doubt that the unjust banishment of Qu Yuan led to political disaster: with prophetic foresight, Qu Yuan took every occasion to warn the king against the power-hungry Qin, but his advice went unheeded, and Chu, like the other states under the nominal Zhou Dynasty, fell victim to Qin's relentless conquests and became part of the first Chinese empire, the Qin Dynasty, in 221 B.C.E. However, it is unclear whether Sima Qian, perhaps with his own fate in mind, sided with Qu Yuan's choice of death over humiliation or preferred the advice of the fisherman who admonished Qu Yuan before his suicide to go into exile and adapt to new circumstances.

Qu Yuan's poetry of lament, which is represented by the poem **"Encountering Sorrow"** in our selection from the ***Songs of the South***, is considered the beginning of intensely personal lyric poetry in China. "Encountering Sorrow" tells of Qu Yuan's attempts to find an appreciative ruler and explains why he ultimately decided to commit suicide. Sima Qian's Qu Yuan hardly resembles the superhuman speaker of "Encountering Sorrow," who rides on clouds, meets with shamans and long-dead rulers of high antiquity, and knocks on heaven's door to find an appreciative lord. But both Qu Yuans consider staying true to one's principles an ultimate value, although one is clothed in superhuman myth, and the other is shaped into a historical individual by Sima Qian. Qu Yuan became one of the most poignant figures in Chinese history. People around the world still celebrate the yearly Dragon Boat Festival in honor of his death; and as a model of the brilliant adviser destroyed by a foolish ruler, he became the consoling ideal of generations of aspiring officeholders in Chinese history who failed to realize their hopes to find employment and participate in the government of their country.

A conscientious and erudite historian, Sima had an insatiable desire to understand the larger patterns of historical events. At the same time, he had an uncanny ability to put himself—and the reader—under the skin of his individual protagonists and was at least as interested in the losers of history as he was in the winners. Sima Qian wrote the first comprehensive history of China, but his powerful portrayals of people's motivations, desires, and obsessions make the *Historical Records* into a gripping study of the universals and peculiarities of the human psyche.

Letter in Reply to Ren An[1]

The Lord Historian, your obedient servant Sima Qian to Ren An

Some time ago you were so kind as to grace me with a letter, instructing me to observe caution in my associations and to devote myself to recommending worthy gentlemen.[2] Your manner then was earnest and forthright, as if anticipating that I would not do as you directed, but would rather be swayed by what ordinary people said. I would never dare to act in such a way. I may be an old horse that has outlived its usefulness, but I always harkened to the influences from my seniors. When I consider how my body has been mutilated, how fault has been found in whatever I have done, and how my desire to be of benefit has brought ruin to me instead, my heart bursts and I have no one to tell.

1. Translated by Stephen Owen.
2. This is a polite way of saying that Sima Qian should not have supported the cause of Li Ling.

There is a saying: "For whom do you act, and who will pay attention to you?" When Zhongzi Qi died, Bo Ya never played his harp again.[3] Why was that? A man does something for the sake of someone who understands him, as a woman adorns herself for someone who is attracted to her. Some like me, whose flesh is now missing a part, can never be thought to flourish, even if I had qualities within me like Sai's pear or Bian He's jade, or even if my actions were like those of Xu You or Bo Yi.[4] In fact, all they could do is win me ridicule and humiliation.

I should have answered your letter immediately, but at the time I was coming back from the east with His Majesty and I was also beset by minor problems. Few were the days when we could meet, and I was always in such a hurry that there was never even a moment when I could tell you everything that was on my mind.

Now you yourself stand accused of the gravest crimes. As the weeks and months pass, the last month of winter draws near;[5] and I am again constrained to accompany His Majesty to Yong. I fear that ultimately there will be no escaping your swift death. Were I never to have the opportunity to reveal all that torments me and make things clear to you, then in death your soul would harbor an unceasing resentment against me. Let me then tell you my thoughts, and please do not take it amiss that I have been negligent in replying.

I have learned that cultivating one's person is the treasurehouse of wisdom, that a love of offering things is the beginning of feeling for others, that taking and giving is the counterpart of a sense of right, that feeling shame determines courage, and that making one's name known is the ultimate end of action. Only after having all five of these may a man give himself to public life and be ranked among the best. There is no misfortune so miserable as desire for advantage, no grief so painful as a wound that festers within, no action more loathsome than one that brings dishonor upon one's ancestors, and no degradation greater than castration. Those who live on after castration are comparable to no one else. Nor is this true only of the present age—it has been this way from long ago in the past. In olden times when Duke Ling of Wei shared his carriage with the eunuch Yongqu, Confucius left for Chen; Shang Yang arranged an audience through Eunuch Jing, and Zhao Lang's heart sank; when the eunuch Zhao Tan joined the Emperor in his coach, Yuan Si turned pale. This has been considered shameful ever since antiquity. When a man of even middling qualities has business to conduct with a eunuch, he always feels ill at ease—not to mention a gentleman of strong spirit! The court may need capable men these days, but would you have a person who has been gelded recommend the outstanding gentlemen of the world for service!

It has been more than twenty years since I took over my father's profession, and though unworthy, I have had the opportunity to serve the throne. When I think it over, on the most important level I have not been able to contribute my loyalty or show my good faith, winning esteem for remarkable plans and the power of my talents, thus forming a natural bond with my wise lord. On the next

3. Bo Ya was a famous harpist, and his friend Zhongzi Qi was the only person who truly understood what was in his heart when he played. When Zhongzi Qi died, Bo Ya broke his harp and never played again.

4. Objects of great value and persons with a reputation for purity of behavior.

5. The last month of winter was the time for executions, including Ren An's.

level I have not been able to catch matters that have been overlooked, summoning worthy men to court and recommending those with abilities, bringing to the public eye those who live hidden in caves in the cliffs. On a still lower level I have not been able to take a place in the ranks and in assaults on cities or in battles in the open, to win glory by beheading generals and seizing the enemy's colors. Finally, on the lowest level, I have not been able to accumulate a stock of merit through continuous service, getting high office and a good salary, thus bringing honor and favor to family and friends. Having been successful in none of these, it is obvious that I have merely followed expedience and tried to please others, achieving nothing that deserves either praise or blame.

Previously, among the ranks of minor grandees, I took part in lesser deliberations of the outer court. On those occasions I brought in no grand plans, nor did I give matters their fullest consideration. Now, as a castrated servant who sweeps up, as the lowest of the low, if I were to try to lift my head, arch my brows, and hold forth with judgments, wouldn't that be showing contempt for the court and offering insult to those gentlemen now in power? What more is there for somebody like me to say!

It is not easy to explain the sequence of events clearly. When I was young I had an ungovernable disposition, and as I grew older I won no esteem from the people of my locale. I was fortunate that, on account of my father, His Majesty allowed me to offer him my meager skills and to frequent the royal apartments. I felt that I could never gaze on Heaven with a bowl covering my head, so I cut off contact with my friends and gave up all thought of the family property; day and night I tried to exercise my miserable talents to their utmost, striving single-mindedly to carry out my office and thus to please His Majesty and win his affection. Yet one thing happened that was a great mistake and had a very different effect.

Li Ling and I had both been in residence in the palace, but we were never good friends. Our interests led us in different directions, so we never even shared a cup of beer or had a direct and earnest relation. Nevertheless, I observed that he was a remarkable person, showing a son's proper devotion to his parents, true to his word with other gentlemen, scrupulous in matters of property, possessed of a sense of right in matters of giving and taking; in questions of status he would yield place, and he behaved deferentially, demonstrating respect and temperance. Always he longed to put his life on the line in responding to some crisis of the empire. He had always harbored these virtues, and to my mind he possessed the qualities of one of the great men of the state. When a subject would brave death thousands of times without thinking to save his own life, going forth to meet threats to the commonwealth, it is remarkable indeed. It truly pained me personally that those courtiers who keep themselves and their families out of harm's way plotted to do him mischief when one thing went wrong out of all that he had done.

The foot soldiers that Li Ling took with him were less than five thousand, and they marched deep into the lands of the nomads; on foot they crossed the khan's own preserve to dangle bait in the tiger's mouth; they brazenly flaunted a stronger force of barbarians and stood face to face against an army of millions.[6] For more than ten days they did continuous battle with the khan and killed

6. The enemies were people of the Xiongnu tribes on the unruly northeastern frontier of Han Dynasty China.

more than their own number. When the tribesmen tried to rescue the dead and carry back the wounded, they couldn't take care of themselves, and their chieftains, dressed in wool and furs, were all quaking in terror. Then the Good Princes of the Right and Left were called up and anyone among the folk who could draw a bow; the whole nation surrounded them and attacked. They fought on the move across a thousand leagues, until their arrows were used up and they had nowhere to go. The relief column did not come; dead and wounded troops lay in heaps. Nevertheless, Li Ling gave a shout to cheer up his army, and not a soldier failed to rise; he was weeping, swallowing the tears running down his bloodied face. They drew their empty crossbows and faced down naked blades; facing north, they fought with the enemy to the death.

Before Li Ling was destroyed, a messenger brought word of him; and all the great lords, princes, and counts of Han lifted their goblets in a toast to his health. Several days afterward, the letter bearing news of Li Ling's defeat became known, and on this account His Majesty found no savor in his meals and took no pleasure in holding court. The great officers of the court were worried and fearful, not knowing what to do.

Without giving due consideration to my lowly position, I saw that His Majesty was despondent and distressed, and I truly wanted to offer him my sincere thoughts on the matter. I held that Li Ling always gave up fine food and shared meager fare with his attendant gentlemen, that he was able to get men to die for him to a degree that was unsurpassed even by the famous generals of antiquity. Though he was defeated, if one but considered his intentions, they should make up for it and repay what he owes the Han. Nothing could be done about what had happened, but those he had defeated were an accomplishment sufficient to make him famous in the empire. I had it in mind to make this case, but had not yet had the means. Then it happened that I was summoned and questioned; and I spoke highly of Li Ling's accomplishments in this way, wanting to set His Majesty's mind to rest and stop malicious comments.

I was not able to be entirely persuasive. Our wise ruler did not fully understand, thinking that I was trying to injure the Nishi general, Li Guangli,[7] and acting as a personal advocate of Li Ling. I was subsequently sent to prison. And never was I able to demonstrate the depth of my loyalty. In the end I was convicted of having tried to deceive the Emperor. My family was poor, and I didn't have the means to buy my way out. None of my friends came to my rescue. My colleagues, kin, and close friends did not say a single word on my behalf. The body is not a thing of wood or stone; and alone in the company of jailers, in the hidden depths of a dungeon, to whom could I complain? This you can see for yourself now, Ren An—was what happened to me any different? Since Li Ling surrendered alive, he ruined the good name of his family. Yet I too, in my turn, came to the silken chambers,[8] where the knife is used, and I am the laughingstock of the world. Oh, the misery of it!

The matter is not easy to explain in a few words to ordinary people. My father's accomplishments were not such as would bring the imperial seal of investiture among the nobility; writers of history and astronomical calculations are close in status to diviners and soothsayers. His Majesty finds amusement in such, and we are kept by him on a par with singers and acrobats, thus held in

7. Head of one of the larger armies that failed to meet up with Li Ling.

8. Place where castrations were performed.

contempt by the common opinion. Suppose that I had bowed to the law and accepted execution; it would have been like the loss of a single hair from a herd of cattle, a death no different from that of an ant or a cricket. And the world would never have granted that I might be compared to those who could die for principle. They would have considered it nothing more than a person finally accepting death because he could think of no way out of the gravity of his crime, someone with no other choice. Why is this? It would have been the consequence of the position in which I had so long established myself.

Human beings truly have but one death. There are deaths that seem heavier than Mount Tai,[9] but to some death seems lighter than a piece of swans-down. The difference lies in what is done by dying. Uppermost is not to bring dishonor upon one's forebears; next is not to bring dishonor upon oneself; next is not to dishonor the right or appearances; next is not to dishonor one's own words; next is to bear the dishonor of bending in submission; next is to bear the dishonor of changing into the uniform of a prisoner; next is to bear the dishonor of being flogged, tied with a rope to the pillory; next is to bear the dishonor of having one's head shaved and bound in metal chains; next is to bear the dishonor of having one's flesh cut and one's limbs amputated; but the worst of all is castration—that is the ultimate.

Tradition says: "Physical punishments are not applied to grandees." This means that a gentleman has no choice but to be severe in guarding his honor. The fierce tiger dwells in the depths of the mountains, and all creatures there quake in fear of him; but when he falls into a pit, he wags his tail for food—this follows gradually from constraining his fearsome power. Thus if you mark out the form of a prison cell on the ground, a gentleman will not enter it, and if you cut a piece of wood to represent the warden, he will not speak to it in his own defense; he has made of his mind to show who he is [by suicide]. But let him cross his hands and feet to receive the manacles and rope, let him expose his flesh to receive the blows of the rod, hide him away in an enclosed cell—and in a situation like this he will knock his head to the ground when he sees the warden and he will breathe hard in terror when he catches sight of the guards. Why is this? It is the natural outcome of constraining fearsome power. And brought to such a state, anyone who says that there is no dishonor is putting up a false front and deserves no esteem.

Yet King Wen[1], the Earl of the West, may have been an earl, but he was held in the prison at Youli; Li Si was a minister, yet he endured each of the five punishments; Han Xin of Huaiyin was a prince, yet he endured the stocks in Chen; of Peng Yue and Zhang Ao, who sat on the throne and called themselves rulers, one went bound to prison, and the other, to death; Jianghou Zhoubo executed all the members of the Lu clan and his power was greater than that of the five earls, yet he was imprisoned in a dungeon awaiting death; Wei Qi was a great general, yet he wore the prisoner's uniform and was bound head, hands, and feet; Ji Bu became a slave of the Zhu clan; Guanfu bore dishonor in the guest chambers.

All these men had reached the positions of prince, count, general, or minister, and their fame was known far and wide; but when they were accused and

9. One of China's sacred mountains and here a symbol of weight and importance.
1. The founder of the Zhou Dynasty (ca. 1045–256 B.C.E.), first an earl under the previous dynasty and later King Wen.

brought before the law, they could not summon the resolution to kill themselves. When one is lying in the dirt, it is the same thing, both in ancient times and in the present—how could one think they were not dishonored! Judging from these examples, courage and fearfulness depend on the situation; resolution and weakness are circumstantial. Reflect on it—there's nothing strange about it! For if a man cannot commit suicide before he is brought to the law, he is already slowly slipping down to the whips and rods. And if he wants to assert his honor then, it is already far out of reach. Certainly this is the reason why the ancients thought it a grave matter to apply physical punishments to grandees.

By their very nature all human beings are greedy for life and hate death, care about their parents, are concerned for their wives and children. But it is otherwise for those who are stirred up by their sense of right, and in fact they cannot help themselves. I had the misfortune to lose both my parents early in life; and not having brothers to be my close family, I was all alone. And you can see how much I took wife and children into consideration! Yet a man of courage does not necessarily die for honor; and when fearful man aspires to the right, he will strive in any way he can. I may have been fearful and weak in choosing life at any cost, but I also recognize quite well the proper measure in how to act. How then could I come to the dishonor of letting myself sink into prison bonds? If even a captive slave girl can take her own life, certainly someone like me could do the same when all was lost. The reason I bore through it in silence and chose to live at any cost, the reason I did not refuse to be covered in muck was because I could not stand to leave something of personal importance to me unfinished, because I despised perishing without letting the glory of my writings be shown to posterity.

The number of rich and noble men in ancient times whose names have been utterly wiped away is beyond reckoning; the only ones who are known are the exceptional, those outside the norm. King Wen of Zhou, when Earl of the West, was in captivity and elaborated the *Classic of Changes;* Confucius was in a desperate situation and wrote *The Springs and Autumns of Lu;* Qu Yuan was banished, and only then composed the *Li Sao;*[2] Zuo Qiuming lost his sight, and he wrote *The Discourses of the Domains;* Sunzi had his feet amputated, and then his *Techniques of War* was drawn up; Lü Bowei was demoted to Shu, from which has been preserved the *Synopticon of Lu;* Han Fei was imprisoned by Qin and wrote "Troubles of Persuasion" and "Solitary Outrage." The three hundred *Poems*[3] were for the most part written as the expression of outrage by good men and sages. All of these men had something eating away at their hearts; they could not carry through their ideas of the Way, so they gave an account of what had happened before while thinking of those to come. In cases like Zuo Qiuming's sightlessness or Sunzi's amputated feet, these men could never be employed; they withdrew and put their deliberations into writing in order to give full expression to their outrage, intending to reveal themselves purely through writing that would last into the future.

Being, perhaps, too bold, I have recently given myself over to writing that lacks ability. I have compiled neglected knowledge of former times from all over the world; I have examined these for veracity and have given an account of the principles behind success and defeat, rise and fall. In all there are one hun-

2. "Encountering Sorrow," included above in the selections from *Songs of the South.*

3. Alternative name for *Classic of Poetry.*

dred and thirty chapters. In it I also wanted to fully explore the interaction between Heaven and Man, and to show the continuity of transformations of past and present. It will become an independent discourse that is entirely my own. The draft version was not yet completed when this misfortune happened to me; I could not bear that it not be completed, so I submitted to the most extreme punishment without showing my ire. When I have actually completed this book, I will have it stored away on some famous mountain, left for someone who will carry it through all the cities. Then I will have made up for the blame that I earlier incurred by submitting to dishonor. I could die thousands of deaths without feeling regret. This, however, may be said only to a wise man; you can't explain it to an ordinary person.

It is not easy to live enduring contempt, and the inferior sort of people usually put a malicious interpretation on things. It was by the spoken word that I met this misfortune; and if I am also exposed to the ridicule of the people of my native region, dishonoring my ancestors, how could I ever again face the tomb mound of my parents? The blot on our name would grow worse and worse, even after a hundred generations. Thus every day I feel a pang in the heart again and again. When I'm in the house, I am distracted, as though I am not there; when I'm outside, I don't know where I'm going. My thoughts keep returning to this shame, and I always break into a sweat that soaks my clothes. I am fit to serve only in the women's quarters, and I would rather take myself off to hide deep away in the caves of the cliffs. But I keep on following the ordinary world, rising and sinking, moving with the times, keeping in communication with fools.

Now you, Ren An, instructed me to recommend worthy men—would not that be the wrong thing to do, considering my private aims? Even if I wanted to give myself refinement and explain myself with gracious words, it would do no good, because ordinary people would not credit me and I would only earn more humiliation. Only when I am dead will the final judgment be made.

Writing cannot say all that is in a person's mind, thus I give you only the rough account of my thoughts.

From Historical Records[1]

The Biography of Bo Yi and Shu Qi

Texts by men of learning range most widely in what they include, yet we look into the Six Classics[2] for what is reliable. Although works were omitted from the *Poems* and *Documents*, still we can read writings from the times of Shun and Yu.[3]

Sage-King Yao planned to cede the throne and yielded his place to Shun. Between Shun's accession and that of Yu, governors and prefects all recommended men. Shun tested them in posts and let them perform their offices over several decades; only after there was ample evidence of merit and ability did he hand over the reins of government. This testifies to the fact that the empire is a weighty vessel, and the kingship is the supreme office. Thus it is no easy thing to pass the empire from one person to another.

1. Translated by Stephen Owen.
2. The Confucian Classics, canonized during the Han Dynasty, under which Sima Qian lived.
3. Sage-kings of high antiquity.

And yet tellers of tales say that Yao offered up the empire to Xu You, but Xu You would not take it and fled out of shame into hiding. Bian Sui and Wu Guang did the same in the time of Xia. But how did these men become widely known?

This is my opinion as Lord Historian: I personally climbed Mount Ji, on whose summit was reputed to be the grave of Xu You. When Confucius named the gentle, the good, and the sagely men of antiquity, he went into some detail in cases like Wu Taibo and Bo Yi.[4] Now from what I have heard, Xu You and Wu Guang were supposed to have had the highest sense of right—why is it, then, that they are not even mentioned in passing in Confucius' writing?

Confucius said: "Bo Yi and Shu Qi did not brood on old hatreds, and thus they felt little bitterness of spirit." He also said: "They sought feeling for their fellow man and achieved it—so how could they have known bitterness of spirit?" I myself am moved by Bo Yi's sense of purpose, and when I look at his poem that has come down to us, I find it remarkable. This is the story about them.

> Bo Yi and Shu Qi were two sons of the Lord of Guzhu. Their father wanted Shu Qi to take his place, but when their father died, Shu Qi yielded to Bo Yi. Bo Yi said: "Those were our father's orders," and he fled into hiding. But Shu Qi also refused to become Lord of Guzhu and fled into hiding. Then the people of the domain made the middle son lord.
>
> Then Bo Yi and Shu Qi heard that the Earl of the West [King Wen of the Zhou] took good care of the elderly, and they considered going to put themselves under his protection. But when they arrived, the Earl of the West had died; and King Wu had taken his father's Spirit Tablet, given his father the title "King Wen," and gone east to attack King Zhow of the Shang. Bo Yi and Shu Qi stopped King Wu's horse and criticized him: "Can this be considered the right way for a son to behave, taking up arms even before your father's funeral rites have been completed? And can a subject murdering his ruler be considered feeling for one's fellow man?" The king's party wanted to put them to the sword, but his Counselor Taigong said: "These men have a sense of right." And he helped them up and sent them away.
>
> When King Wu had settled the lawlessness of the Shang, all the world gave their allegiance to the Zhou; yet Bo Yi and Shu Qi thought that to be something shameful, and out of their sense of right they refused to eat the grain of Zhou. They lived as hermits on Shouyang Mountain and picked bracken ferns to eat. As they were dying of hunger, they composed a song, whose words go:
>
> We climbed West Hill,
> we picked its bracken.
> Brute force for brute force—
> he knew not it was wrong.
> Shennong, Yu, and Xia
> gone in a flash,
> where can we turn?
> Ah, let us depart now,
> our lifespans are done.
>
> And then they died of hunger on Shouyang Mountain.

4. Wu Taibo was an uncle of King Wen. He fled when his father made his younger brother ruler, virtuously giving up his right as the first-born to inherit the rulership. Bo Yi also fled, since his father wished his younger brother to succeed him.

Considered in this light, did they or did they not feel bitterness of spirit?

There are those who say: "The Way of Heaven shows no personal favorites and always provides for good men." Can we or can we not consider people like Bo Yi and Shu Qi good men? To have such a history of kindness to one's fellow men and to be so pure in actions, yet to die from hunger! Of his seventy disciples, Confucius singled out Yan Hui for praise for his love of learning. Yet Yan Hui lived in dire poverty and never ate his fill even of grain mash or bran. And he died before his time. How is it then that Heaven repays good men with its gifts?

Zhi the Outlaw killed innocent men every day and fed on their flesh. A brutal, savage man, he committed every kind of outrage and gathered a band of several thousand men who wreaked havoc all over the world. In the end he died at a ripe old age. From what virtue did this follow?

These are particularly clear and obvious cases. And if we come down to more recent times, conduct beyond the rules of morality and willful transgressions have brought lifetimes of carefree pleasures and great wealth passed on for endless generations. Others take care where they tread, speak up only when it is timely, take no dark byways, and are stirred only for justice and the common good; yet the number of such people who have met with disaster is beyond reckoning. I cannot understand this at all. Is this what is meant by the "Way of Heaven"?

Confucius said: "Men who follow different ways cannot make judgments for one another." Each person follows his own aims in life. He further said: "If wealth and noble station could be properly sought, I would seek them, even if it meant being the king's meanest servant; but since they cannot be sought, I will follow what I love." And: "Only in the cold of the year can you know that pine and cypress are the last to turn brown." When all the world is foul and corrupt, the pure man appears most clearly. Obviously what is considered so important by some is despised by others.

"The man of virtue is pained by the thought of dying without his name being known." [*Analects*]

Jia Yi[5] wrote:

> Grasping men spend themselves for goods;
> brash warriors spend themselves for glory.
> The man overweening will die for power,
> and the common man covets his life.

"Things of equal light reveal one another; things of the same kind seek one another." [*Classic of Changes*]

"Clouds follow the dragon; winds follow the tiger; the Sage arises and all things are perspicuous." [*Classic of Changes*]

Although Bo Yi and Shu Qi were virtuous men, it was through Confucius that their names became more widely known. Though Yan Hui was devoted to learning, like the fly on the tail of a fine steed, his actions became more widely famed. It is most sad that men who live in caves in the cliffs may have an equal sense of appropriateness in their decisions, yet their good names are obliterated and never known. How can folk of the villages who wish to perfect their behavior and establish their names be known to later generations unless through some gentleman who rises high in the world?

5. Han Dynasty writer who lived before Sima Qian's time.

From *The Biographies of Qu Yuan and Master Jia*[1]

In fine phrases he censured the actions of the king, and with examples and analogies argued for the right. Such is the nature of Qu Yuan's poem, "Encountering Sorrow."[2] Thus I made "The Biographies of Qu Yuan and Master Jia."

QU YUAN

Qu Yuan, whose familiar name was Qu Ping, bore the same surname as one of the royal families of the state of Chu. He acted as aide to King Huai of Chu (328–299 BC). Possessed of wide learning and a strong will, he was wise in affairs of government and skilled in the use of words. In the inner palace he deliberated with the king on national affairs and the issuing of orders, and in the outer court he received visitors and held audience with the feudal lords. The king put the greatest trust in him, and the chief minister, the lord of Shangguan, who was thus forced to share the same rank with Qu Yuan, vied with him for the king's favour and was secretly disturbed by his great ability.

King Huai set Qu Yuan the task of drawing up a code of laws. While Qu Yuan was still working on the rough draft the chief minister got a glimpse of it and tried to get it away from Qu Yuan so he could steal the ideas for himself, but Qu Yuan refused to give it to him. Thereupon the minster began to slander Qu Yuan, saying, "The king has given Qu Yuan the task of drawing up laws, the sort of thing that anyone could do and yet, when each new law is finished, he goes about boasting of his acheivement and saying that 'in my opinion no one but myself could have done this.'"

The king, angered by these reports, grew cold toward Qu Yuan. Qu Yuan grieved that the king should be so deceived in what he heard and that his understanding should be clouded by idle slander, that petty evil should be allowed to injure the public good and justice should be without a hearing. Plunged into melancholy thought because of the affair, he composed his poem entitled "Li Sao," which means "encountering sorrow."

Heaven is the beginning of man, and father and mother the root from which he springs. When a man finds his way blocked he will turn again to the source of his being. Therefore, when he is troubled and weary, he will always cry to Heaven, and when he is grieved and in pain, he will call upon his father and mother. Qu Yuan conducted himself with justice and forthrightness, displaying the ulmost loyalty and exhausting his wisdom in the service of his lord, and yet libellous men came between them. This is indeed what it means to find one's way blocked. To be faithful and yet doubted, to be loyal and yet suffer slander—can one bear this without anger? Qu Yuan's composition of the "Li Sao" sprang, I am sure, from this very anger. The "Airs from the States" in the *Book of Odes*[3] sing of romantic love but are never lewd; the "Lesser Odes" in the same work are full of anger and censure, but never of insubordination. A work

1. Translated by and with notes adapted from Burton Watson. Sima Qian includes the biographies of two officials and writers—namely, Qu Yuan (3rd century B.C.E.) and Jia Yi (201–169 B.C.E.), who were both slandered, banished, and lamented their fate in writing of not being appreciated by a worthy ruler. These selections only feature the biography of Qu Yuan.
2. Central text of the poetry anthology *Songs of the South*.
3. *Classic of Poetry*.

like the "Li Sao," however, may be said to combine the best qualities of both of these. In it the poet praises the Sage Emperor Ku of ancient times, relates the deeds of Kings Tang and Wu of a later age and, coming to more recent times, describes Duke Huan of Qi, in order to censure his own age and make clear the worth of virtue and the form and principles of good government, leaving no point untouched. His phrases are brief and his words subtle; his will is pure and his conduct virtuous. Though he appears to speak of small matters, his meaning is profound; though he chooses examples from close at hand, he uses them to illustrate far-reaching principles. Since his will is pure, he speaks often of fragrant plants and trees; and because his conduct was virtuous, he chose to die rather than seek a place in the world. He took himself off from the stagnant pools and fens; like a cicada slipping from its shell, he shook off the filth that surrounded him and soared far beyond its defilement. He would not allow himself to be soiled by the dust of the world but, shining pure amidst its mire, kept himself free from stain. Such a will as his is fit to vie for brilliance with the very sun and moon themselves!

Sometime after Qu Yuan had lost his position at court the state of Qin began to make plans to attack the state of Qi. But Qi and Chu were both members of the Vertical Alliance,[4] and King Hui, the king of Qin, was afraid that if he attacked Qi, Chu would come to its aid. He therefore ordered his minister Zhang Yi to leave Qin and, bearing lavish gifts, to visit the king of Chu and attempt to deceive him by saying, "Qin bears a deep hatred for Qi, but Qi and Chu are joined in an alliance of friendship. If you are willing, however, to break off relations with Qi, then Qin will be happy to present you with the cities of Shang and Wu and their surrounding lerritories of 600 *li*." King Huai of Chu was greedy for land and trusted Zhang Yi's words, and so he broke off his alliance with Qi and sent an envoy to Qin to receive the title to the lands. But when the envoy from Chu appeared before Zhang Yi the latter falsely denied his promise, saying, "I agreed to give the king of Chu six *li*. I have no recollection of any talk of 600 *li*!"

The Chu envoy left Qin in great anger and returned to report to King Huai what had happened. King Huai was furious and raised a huge army to attack Qin. Qin sent out its troops to meet the attack and inflicted a severe defeat on the Chu army between the Dan and Xi rivers, cutting off 80,000 heads and capturing the Chu general Chu Gai. The Qin troops proceeded to seize the Chu territory of Hanzhong.

King Huai then called up all the troops in the state of Chu and marched deep into the state of Qin, engaging the Qin forces at Lantian. When the state of Wei heard of the expedition, it launched a surprise attack on Chu, invading it as far as Deng. The Chu forces, afraid for the safety of their own land, withdrew from Qin, and Qi, angered at Chu's behaviour, refused to come to its aid, so that Chu found itself in grave difficulties.

The following year Qin offered to divide the region of Hanzhong and return part of it to Chu in order to bring peace between the two states, but the king of Chu replied, "I do not want land. I only want Zhang Yi so that I may have my revenge on him!"

4. Alliance of Zhou states in the east, such as Qi and Chu, formed against the rapidly expanding militaristic western state of Qin.

When this was reported to Zhang Yi he said, "If I alone am worth as much to the king of Chu as the region of Hanzhong, then I beg to be sent to Chu!" Zhang Yi once more journeyed to Chu and, bringing lavish gifts for the king's trusted minister Jin Shang, had him plead by artful means with the king's favourite concubine, Zheng Xiu, for her intervention.[5] King Huai eventually gave in to Zheng Xiu's requests and pardoned Zhang Yi and allowed him to return to Qin.

At this time Qu Yuan, already out of favour, had not been restored to his former position but had instead been sent as an envoy to Qi. When he returned to Chu he admonished King Huai saying, "Why did you not kill Zhang Yi?" King Huai began to regret that he had let Zhang Yi go free, and sent men to pursue him, but they were unable to overtake him in time. After this a number of the feudal lords joined in attacking Chu, inflicting a severe defeat and killing the Chu general Tang Mei.

At this time King Zhao, who had succeeded King Hui as king of Qin and allied himself with Chu by marriage, asked King Huai to come to Qin to meet with him. King Huai was about to depart for Qin when Qu Yuan advised him that "Qin is a nation of tigers and wolves and cannot be trusted. It would be better not to make the journey!" But King Huai's youngest son Zilan encouraged his father to go, saying that it would not do to disrupt the friendly relations which had been established between Chu and Qin. King Huai accordingly set out but, after he had entered the Wu Pass, the Qin soldiers ambushed his party and, blocking their escape, detained the king, demanding that he cede part of his territory to Qin. King Huai was infuriated and refused to listen to their demands. He fled to the border of the state of Zhao, but Zhao refused to admit him and he was forced to return to Qin. Eventually he died in Qin and his body was returned to Chu for burial.

King Huai's eldest son, posthumously known as King Qingxiang, ascended the throne of Chu and appointed his younger brother Zilan as prime minister. The people of Chu blamed Zilan for encouraging his father to make the journey to Qin from which he never returned.

Qu Yuan had always disliked Zilan and, though he had fallen from favour and been sent to Qi, he had anxiously watched the proceedings in Chu and had been gravely concerned for King Huai, never forgetting his desire to awaken the king to the danger that faced him. He hoped to be fortunate enough eventually to enlighten his lord and reform the ways of the state. Repeatedly in his poems he expressed this desire to save the ruler and aid his country, but in the end his wishes proved vain. He was unable to remedy the situation and eventually it became apparent that King Huai would never wake to the danger that awaited him if he journeyed to Qin.

Any ruler, whether he be wise or foolish, worthy or unworthy, will invariably seek for loyal men to aid him, and wise men to be his assistants. And yet the fact that we see endless examples of kingdoms lost and ruling families ruined, while generation after generation passes without showing us a sage ruler who can bring order to his country, is simply because the so-called loyal men are not really loyal, and the so-called wise ones are not wise. It was because King

5. Jin Shang persuaded the concubine to intervene on Zhang Yi's behalf by making her believe that, if Zhang Yi were not quickly pardoned, the king of Qin would present beautiful women to the king of Chu as a diplomatic gift, so that she would lose favor with the king. The concubine thus made all efforts to have Zhang Yi released.

Huai could not distinguish the truly loyal that he was misled by his own concubine Zheng Xiu and deceived in foreign affairs by Zhang Yi, that he drove Qu Yuan from the court and trusted the lord of Shangguan and his son Zilan instead, that his soldiers were driven back and his territory seized, and that he lost six provinces to his enemies and died a stranger's death in Qin, the mockery of the world! This is the fate of those who do not know how to judge men! The *Book of Changes* says:

> Though the well is pure, men do not drink;
> My heart is filled with grief at it.
> If the king is wise and will dip up the water,
> We will all share his blessings![6]

But if the king is not wise, how can he be worthy to receive blessings?

When the prime minister Zilan heard of Qu Yuan's opposition to him he was very angry and eventually persuaded the lord of Shangguan to criticize Qu Yuan to King Qingxiang. The king was incensed and banished Qu Yuan to the south.

When Qu Yuan reached the banks of the Yangtze he was one day wandering along the river embankment lost in thought, his hair unbound, his face haggard with care, his figure lean and emaciated, when a fisherman happened to see him and asked, "Are you not the high minister of the royal family? What has brought you to this?"

"All the world is muddied with confusion," replied Qu Yuan. "Only I am pure! All men are drunk, and I alone am sober! For this I have been banished!"

"A true sage does not stick at mere things, but changes with the times," said the fisherman. "If all the world is a muddy turbulence, why do you not follow its current and rise upon its waves? If all men are drunk, why do you not drain their dregs and swill their thin wine with them? Why must you cling so tightly to this jewel of virtue and bring banishment upon yourself?"

Qu Yuan replied, "I have heard it said that he who has newly washed his hair should dust off his cap, and he who had just bathed his body should shake out his robes. What man can bear to soil the cleanness of his person with the filth you call 'mere things'? Better to plunge into this never-ending current beside us and find an end in some river fish's belly! Why should radiant whiteness be clouded by the world's vile darkness?"

Then he composed a poem in the rhyme-prose style entitled "Embracing the Sands":

> Warm, bright days of early summer,
> When shrubs and trees grow rich with green,
> And I, in anguish and endless sorrow,
> Hasten on my way to a southern land.
> My eyes are dazed by darkness,
> Deep stillness lies all around me;
> Bound by injustice, grieved by wrong,
> I bear the long torment of this pain.

6. From the explanation to the hexagram "well," one of sixty-four hexagrams in *The Classic of Changes*. Hexagrams consist of six stacked horizontal lines, which are either yang lines (continuous) or yin lines (broken in the middle). These symbols were used in the divination of the future. Sima Qian is likening the wise and loyal minister to the pure water of the well.

I still my heart and follow my will:
Bowing before injustice, I humble myself.
They would round the corners of my squareness,
But I will not change my constant form.
To abandon the course he has set out upon:
This is a disgrace to a worthy man.
As a builder with his line, I have laid out my plan:
I will not alter my former course.
To be forthright in nature and of loyal heart:
This is the pride of a great man.
If the skilled carpenter never carves,
Who can tell how true he cuts?
Dark patterns in a hidden place
The ill of sight call a formless nothing:
The subtle glance of the keen-eyed Li Lou
The ignorant mistake for blindness.
They have changed white into black,
Toppled "up" and made it "down".
Phoenixes they pen in cages,
While common fowl soar aloft;
Jewels and stones they mix together,
And weigh them in the same balance.
The men in power, with their petty envies,
Cannot recognize my worth.
I could bear high office and bring glory to the world,
Yet I am plunged to the depths and deprived of success.
So I must embrace this jewel of virtue
And to the end share it with no one.
As the packs of village dogs bark,
So they bark at what is strange;
To censure greatness and doubt the unusual,
Such is the nature of the herd.
Though I have abundance of talent,
No one acknowledges my possessions.
I have honoured benevolence and upheld duty,
Been diligent and faithful in full degree;
Yet, since I cannot meet Emperor Shun of old,[7]
Who is there to appreciate my actions?
Many men have been born in an ill age,
But I cannot tell the reason.
The sages Tang and Yu have long departed:
Though I yearn for them, they are far away.
I will calm my wrath and mend my anger,
Still my heart, and be strong.
Though I meet darkness, I will not falter;
Let my determination serve as a model to men!
I walk the road to my lodge in the north:[8]
The day grows dark; night is falling.

7. Sage-king of high antiquity. The Qu Yuan in "Encountering Sorrow" does actually visit Emperor Shun to lodge his plaint.

8. The direction of winter and death.

I will cast off sorrow and delight in woe,
For all will have an end in the Great Affair of death.

Reprise:

Broad flow the waters of the Yuan and the Xiang:
Their two streams roar on to the Yangtze.
Long is the road and hidden in shadow:
The way I go is vast and far.
I sing to myself of my constant sorrow,
Lost in lamentation.
In the world no one knows me;
There is none to tell my heart to.
I must embrace my thoughts, hold fast my worth:
I am alone and without a mate.
Bo Luo, judge of fine steeds, has long passed away;
Who now can tell the worth of a thoroughbred?[9]
Man at his birth receives his fate,
And by it each life must be disposed.
I will calm my heart and pluck up my will;
What more have I to fear?
I know that death cannot be refused:
May I love life no longer!
This I proclaim to all worthy men:
I will be an example for you!

With this he grasped a stone in his arms and, casting himself into the Miluo River, drowned.

After the death of Qu Yuan there were a number of his followers such as Song Yu, Tang Le, and Jing Cha, who were fond of fine writing and won fame by their compositions in the rhyme-prose style. But although they all imitated Qu Yuan's actions and fine phrases, none of them dared to remonstrate openly with the king. The state of Chu continued to lose territory day by day until, some twenty or thirty years later, it was finally destroyed by Qin.

* * *

The Grand Historian remarks: At first when I read Qu Yuan's "Encountering Sorrow", "Heavenly Questions", "Summons of the Soul", and "Grieving for Ying", I was moved to pity by his determination, and at times when I visited Changsha and viewed the deep waters where he had drowned himself, I could never keep from shedding tears and trying to imagine what sort of person he was. Later, when I read the lament which Jia Yi wrote for him, I began to wonder why a man with the ability of Qu Yuan who, if he had chosen to serve some other lord, would have been welcomed anywhere, should have brought such an end upon himself! Faced with the rhyme-prose on the owl, in which Jia Yi regards death as the same as life and makes light of all worldly success, I find myself utterly at a loss for words![1]

9. Exquisite horses are often used as a metaphor for men of superior talent and virtue.

1. When Jia Yi was on his way to exile and passed through the area where Qu Yuan was said to have committed suicide, he empathized with Qu Yuan and wrote "Lament for Qu Yuan." He also wrote a "Rhymeprose on the Owl," which is not included here.

SPEECH, WRITING, AND POETRY IN EARLY CHINA

Along with Egypt, Mesopotamia, and Mesoamerica, China is one of the world's regions where writing was invented. Unlike the Egyptian hieroglyphs, Babylonian cuneiform characters, or Mayan glyphs, which fell out of use with the destruction of their civilizations, Chinese script is still used today. This writing system thrived not only on the Chinese mainland but also in Korea, Vietnam, and Japan, all of which gradually adopted the Chinese writing system as they came under Chinese influence during the centuries around the beginning of the Common Era. In large parts of East Asia, Chinese characters were prominently used until the twentieth century alongside vernacular scripts that were developed during the intervening centuries: Japanese *kana*, Vietnamese *chu'nom*, and Korean *hangul*. In the twenty-first century, Chinese characters remain an indispensible part of the language only in China and Japan.

THE CHINESE WRITING SYSTEM

The Chinese characters used today have a history of more than 3,200 years. It remains unclear when Chinese script began to be developed, but it appears as a fully functional writing system during the later period of the Shang Dynasty (ca. 1500–1045 B.C.E.). The earliest texts in Chinese script are found on animal bones and tortoise-shells. These so-called oracle-bone inscriptions are short records of divination rituals that the Shang kings conducted to guide their political decision making and to restore harmony between humans and the world inhabited by unpredictable spiritual forces. Unlike the scripts that dominate today's world, the Chinese script is nonalphabetic. It does not represent a sound syllable with the same invariable set of phonetic letters as alphabetic languages do. Some sounds, for example *yi*, can have dozens of different meanings, written with dozens of different characters which record the same sound in writing. Only if you see the character will you know whether this *yi* means, for example, "art," "different," "translate," "justice," or "epidemics." The complexity of the Chinese writing system and the difficulties associated with learning and mastering it have repeatedly inspired calls for a switch to an alphabet or a syllabary, a system in which a fixed set of characters represents not individual sounds but individual syllables, but the great number of characters that sound alike but have different meanings has proven an obstacle to such attempts. Also, Chinese characters have been a perfect means to communicate efficiently in writing despite the lack of a common spoken language. This holds for the many dialects in China and for different languages across East Asia. Today, basic literacy in Chinese requires knowing about two to three thousand common characters; well-educated people know a few thousand more.

A detail from the bronze backing of a Han Dynasty mirror, ca. second century B.C.E.

Because the Chinese writing system is so different from the alphabetic languages that became dominant in the western part of Eurasia, it fostered a rich lore of fantasies. The more direct relation in Chinese between script and meaning, in contrast to alphabetic scripts that work through the sound of the word, fascinated early modern European scholars who learned about China through the reports of Christian missionaries active in Asia. Some believed that Chinese represented a kind of universal language—written as a string of ideas and symbols rather than words. In one of the earliest comprehensive accounts of China, the Jesuit historian Jean-Baptiste du Halde (1674–1743) wrote, "Chinese has no resemblance with any dead or living language we know. . . . The Chinese have only figures to express their thoughts. . . . Their characters are in this respect like the figures of arithmetic, they are used by several nations with different names, but their meaning is everywhere the same. . . . In the beginning of their monarchy, they communicated their ideas by drawing on paper the natural images of the things they would express: for instance, a bird, mountains, trees, wavy lines, to express birds, mountains, a forest, and water."

The misconception that Chinese is a "pictographic" or "ideographic" language, in which characters depict things or ideas directly instead of referring to words in a specific language, continues to this day. Some characters might indeed have had a pictographic origin, like, for example, *ri* 日 ("sun"), which on the oracle bones appears as a circle with a dot in the middle. But most characters combine an element that indicates the sound and an element, called a radical, that indicates a conceptual category: for example, 昭 (*zhao*), "shining, bright," consists of the sound element *zhao*, on the right, and the sun radical, on the left. Therefore, the Chinese script is now usually called "logographic" (from the Greek *logos*, meaning "word"), since each sound syllable stands for a word.

The great advantage of the nonalphabetic-character script is that the written characters remained the same, although they were pronounced differently at different times and in different regions of China and East Asia. This contributed significantly to the coherence of Chinese civilization, which covered a large area of many mutually unintelligible dialects, even languages. Until the twentieth century it also enabled the Chinese to communicate directly with their East Asian neighbors: the Korean, Japanese, and Vietnamese elites were all trained in Literary Chinese. And while they would pronounce the characters differently, and would be unable to understand each other's speech, they could all communicate with one another by writing back and forth on a sheet of paper and engaging in what was called "brush talk": sophisticated conversation in the absence of a common spoken language.

WRITINGS ABOUT POETRY

The four Chinese texts that follow all comment on the power and effects of words in poetry and in oral persuasion. In the first text we see **Confucius** (551–479 B.C.E.), the first and foremost of China's philosophical masters, praise the versatility of poetry and explain its usefulness for education and society. Confucius emphasized in particular the study of the ***Classic of Poetry***, China's earliest anthology of verse, and he valued the collection's importance for moral education so highly that tradition ascribed the compilation of the anthology to him. In the centuries after Confucius, ideas about the *Classic of Poetry* continued to develop and were finally fixed in the

"Great Preface" to the *Classic of Poetry*, the next selection below. The preface has been the most authoritative statement in China and East Asia about the nature, function, and composition of poetry, and about its indispensible role in human society. It shaped the poetic traditions of Korea, Japan, and Vietnam. In tenth-century Japan, with the first imperial anthology, the ***Kokinshū***, the preface even became the basis for theories about Japanese vernacular poetry, *waka* verse in thirty-one syllables, and lives on today in the way modern Japanese poets of traditional verse forms like *waka* and *haiku* think about their art. Although the "Great Preface" was attributed to a specific author, either Confucius's disciple Zixia or the first-century-C.E. scholar Wei Hong, it is best to think of this text as a compilation of broadly shared truths about poetry that had accumulated in the centuries between the compilation of the *Classic of Poetry*, around 600 B.C.E., and the first century C.E., when the preface reached its final shape.

The "Great Preface" could hardly make greater claims for the power of poetry. Poetry becomes a universal tool for individual self-expression: impressions from the outside world induce intentions in the mind, which then become manifest in words as poetry. In this flow from inside intentions to outside manifestation, poetry is part of a chain of release of emotional intensity, or vital breath (*qi*): if words are insufficient to express the intentions, they are followed by sighs, then songs, then dance and body movement. In inverse direction to the self-expression of individual intention, poetry can serve later readers as a diagnostic tool: like amber in which insects have been captured, the poem preserves traces of the age of its composition and shows whether the poet lived in well-governed or troubled times.

WRITINGS ABOUT SPEECH AND PERSUASION

Belief in the power of speech is already evident in the earliest Chinese texts. The *Classic of Documents* contains records of speeches of early kings and ministers: here speech is a sign of political authority and charisma. Confucius and the philosophical masters in his wake who disputed about the secrets of proper government and a fulfilled life appropriate this previously courtly authority of speech for their own purposes. Like Socrates, Confucius did not write down his ideas, but his disciples compiled a collection of his sayings that shows the master in conversation with his followers and rulers of his time. While Confucius believed in the power of the written word and the educational value of the study of canonical texts, Daoist thinkers sometimes doubted the reliability of words, both written and spoken. The foundational Daoist text ***Laozi*** (or ***Daodejing***) starts with the paradox "The Way that can be spoken of is not the constant Way," shattering the Confucian trust in the meaning of words. In "The Way of Heaven," an anecdote in our third selection below, taken from the Daoist text ***Zhuangzi***, a simple wheelwright explains to Duke Huan, a literate aristocrat, that his reading of old books is worthless. Here as elsewhere the *Zhuangzi* voices tantalizing doubts about words, while expertly wielding their power.

In addition to early Chinese schools with different views on governance and life, like the Confucians and Daoists, there was a class of persuaders who offered their services to the rulers of the feudal domains that were nominally vassals of the Zhou king but waged incessant wars against one another to enhance the wealth and territory of their domains. Not unlike the sophists in Ancient Greece, these persuaders were often depicted as brilliant and opportunistic experts of argument who would persuade you of whatever point they were paid to argue. The anecdote "Of Swords" from the book *Zhuangzi*, included here, can be considered both an example and a veiled parody of this world of persuaders.

Han Feizi's (ca. 280–233 B.C.E.) ***Difficulties of Persuasion***, our fourth selection below, is the earliest longer reflection on the art of persuasion from early China. It captures the connection between persuasion and lethal danger in a suggestive image: the ruler, whom the persuader faces, is like a dragon with scales on the underside of his throat, who kills whoever brushes against them.

The veneration of the written word has run deep in Chinese culture since earliest times. It complemented and enhanced the importance of speech and oral persuasion for political, diplomatic, and literary purposes. Overall, a thorough, applicable knowledge of a shared canon of poetry was a requisite for both effective speech and sophisticated writing in early China.

CONFUCIUS

The ***Analects*** is a collection of Confucius's sayings recorded by his disciples. (See pp. 1330–44, above, for a full presentation of Confucius and the *Analects*.) Confucius (551–479 B.C.E.) was among the first to emphasize the social and ethical importance of poetry, in particular the poetry contained in the ***Classic of Poetry***. The political elites of the time were well versed in the *Classic of Poetry* and were able to strengthen their arguments regarding policy decisions by alluding to famous lines from the poetry collection. In his remarks in the *Analects*, Confucius adds to the status of the collection by endowing it with farther-reaching efficacy. Confucius claims that it contains models for how to find your role in society, that it stimulates your creative engagement with the world and enhances your perceptiveness toward the outside world. He also believes that the *Classic of Poetry* shapes your skills of analytic and synthetic thinking and that it enables you to effectively voice misgivings and criticism. Last but not least, it enriches your encyclopedic knowledge of animals' and plants' names, which occur often in the poems.

From Analects[1]

2.2. The Master said: "The three hundred *Poems*[2] are summed up in one single phrase: 'Think no evil.'"

8.8. The Master said: "Draw inspiration from the *Poems*; steady your course with the ritual; find your fulfillment in music."

1. Translated by Simon Leys.

2. Alternative name for the *Classic of Poetry*.

17.9. The Master said: "Little ones, why don't you study the *Poems*? The *Poems* can provide you with stimulation and with observation, with a capacity for communion, and with a vehicle for grief. At home, they enable you to serve your father, and abroad, to serve your lord. Also, you will learn there the names of many birds, animals, plants, and trees."

1.15. Zigong said: "'Poor without servility; rich without arrogance.' How is that?" The Master said: "Not bad, but better still: 'Poor, yet cheerful; rich, yet considerate.'" Zigong said: "In the *Poems*, it is said: 'Like carving horn, like sculpting ivory, like cutting jade, like polishing stone.' Is this not the same idea?" The Master said: "Ah, one can really begin to discuss the *Poems* with you! I tell you one thing, and you can figure out the rest."

THE GREAT PREFACE TO THE *CLASSIC OF POETRY*

"The Great Preface" claims that poetry is the perfect means to give expression to one's innermost thoughts and that, conversely, later readers can reconstruct the poet's political and social circumstances from each poem. Yet more spectacular than the claim of poetry's expressive and diagnostic function is the conviction that poetry possesses the power to create and maintain political order in society and harmony with the spirit world. The argument hinges on a subtle manipulation of the manifold meanings of one term, *feng*. *Feng*'s basic meaning is "wind." By extension it also means folk songs or "airs" that show *feng*, the "customs" of the people. Like "wind" bending the grasses, *feng* is also "influence." Influence can proceed along social hierarchies in two directions: from rulers and superiors who through the influence of poetry can instill proper behavior in their subjects, and from subjects who use poetry to voice their "criticism," yet another meaning of *feng*, of their superiors. This is a classical formulation of the principle of "remonstration"—the outspoken criticism of superiors who neglect their duties or abuse their power—which has been a crucial feature of traditional Chinese political culture. *Feng* means all these things and processes at once. It has no direct equivalent in other literary cultures but is distinctively linked to Chinese conceptions about the physiology of the body, the structure of society, and the power of language.

The Great Preface[1]

"Fishhawk" is the virtue of the Queen Consort and the beginning of the "Airs" [*Feng*, the first large section of the *Classic of Poetry*].[2] It is the means by which the world is influenced *(feng)* and by which the relations between husband and wife are made correct. Thus it is used in smaller communities, and it is used in larger domains. "Airs" *(Feng)* are "Influence" *(feng);* it is to teach. By influence it stirs them; by teaching it transforms them.[3]

The poem is that to which what is intently on the mind *(zhi)* goes. In the mind, it is "being intent" *(zhi);* coming out in language, it is a "poem."

The affections are stirred within and take on form in words. If words alone are inadequate, we speak it out in sighs. If sighing is inadequate, we sing it. If singing is inadequate, unconsciously our hands dance it and our feet tap it.[4]

Feelings emerge in sounds; when those sounds have patterning, they are called "tones." The tones of a well-managed age are at rest and happy: its government is balanced. The tones of an age of turmoil are bitter and full of anger: its government is perverse. The tones of a ruined state are filled with lament and brooding: its people are in difficulty.[5]

Thus to correctly present achievements and failures, to move Heaven and Earth, to stir the gods and spirits, there is nothing more appropriate than poetry. By it the former kings managed the relations between husbands and wives, perfected the respect due to parents and superiors, gave depth to human relations, beautifully taught and transformed the people, and changed local customs.

Thus there are six principles in the poems: (1) Airs *(Feng);* (2) "exposition" *(fu);* (3) "comparison" *(bi);* (4) "affective image" *(xing);* (5) Odes *(Ya);* (6) Hymns *(song).*[6]

By *feng*, those above transform those below; also by *feng*, those below criticize those above. When an admonition is given that is governed by patterning, the one who speaks it has no culpability, yet it remains adequate to warn those who hear it. In this we have *feng.*[7]

1. Translated by Stephen Owen.
2. "The Great Preface" is attached to "Fishhawk," the first poem of the *Classic of Poetry*. In traditional Confucian interpretations, the poem was understood as celebrating the virtue of the queen consort of King Wen of the Zhou Dynasty.
3. *Feng*, a central term of "The Great Preface," literally means "wind." By extension, it means "influence" (like wind bending the grasses) and "Airs," the poetry in the first part of the *Classic of Poetry* that was understood as a means to positively influence people's behavior.
4. Although *qi*, "vital breath," is not directly mentioned, the psychology of poetic composition described here relies on the notion that a release of vital breath results in ever stronger forms of outward expression: words, sighs, songs, or dance.
5. Since the poems in the *Classic of Poetry* were performed to music, the "tones" that reveal the social and political conditions under which the poems were composed became manifest in both the words and the music.
6. The "six principles" consist of the three main parts of the *Classic of Poetry* (the "Airs," "Odes," and "Hymns") and three modes of expression ("exposition," "comparison," and "affective image"). "Exposition" describes poems with a longer narrative of events, "comparison" describes poems that use similes, and "affective image" describes poems that use natural imagery that parallels a human situation and should stir the emotions. The "six principles" became staple terms in discussions of poetry in East Asia.
7. A last addition to the many meanings of *feng*: ministers or simple people can "criticize" their rulers or superiors through this kind of poetry.

When the Way of the Kings declined, rites and moral principles were abandoned; the power of government to teach failed; the government of the domains changed; the customs of the family were altered. And at this point the changed *Feng* ("Airs") and the changed *Ya* ("Odes") were written. The historians of the domains understood clearly the marks of success and failure; they were pained by the abandonment of proper human relations and lamented the severity of punishments and governance. They sang their feelings to criticize *(feng)* those above, understanding the changes that had taken place and thinking about former customs. Thus the changed *Feng* emerge from the affections, but they go no further than rites and moral principles. That they should emerge from the affections is human nature; that they go no further than rites and moral principles is the beneficent influence of the former kings.

Thus the affairs of a single state, rooted in the experience of a single person, are called *Feng*. To speak of the affairs of the whole world and to describe customs *(feng)* common to all places is called *Ya*. *Ya* means "proper." These show the source of either flourishing or ruin in the royal government. Government has its greater and lesser aspects: thus we have a "Greater *Ya*" and a "Lesser *Ya*." The "Hymns" give the outward shapes of praising full virtue, and they inform the spirits about the accomplishment of great deeds. These are called the "Four Beginnings" and are the ultimate perfection of the Poems.

ZHUANGZI

Several anecdotes from the Masters Text *Zhuangzi*, more extensive selections of which are included elsewhere in this anthology, show the verbal wit with which the Daoist master Zhuangzi exposed both the power and weakness of words. The first anecdote shows how the words of the venerable *Classic of Poetry* can be abused for the basest purposes, such as making profit on robbing graves.

In the second anecdote, a simple craftsman challenges Duke Huan, a literate aristocrat, by discrediting the worth of written words. The irate duke threatens to execute the wheelwright unless he can explain his challenge. The wheelwright persuades the duke by proceeding from his own experience as a craftsman and showing that a person's intuitive experience and knowledge cannot be communicated in words. Yet in the end it is the power of the spoken word that saves the eloquent wheelwright from death.

In the third anecdote, Master Zhuangzi himself, in full persuader mode, has the difficult task of dissuading a king from neglecting government duties to indulge his obsession for swordplay. Zhuangzi is not the typical greedy persuader: he refuses the crown prince's promise of a fat reward. Posing in swordsman clothes, he approaches the king and succeeds in dealing a deathblow to his addiction simply by unleashing his weapons of persuasion. The king is healed when realizing that he craves the power of imperial rule by the "emperor's sword," instead of the foolish carnage that hair-raising gladiators effect with the "sword of the ordinary man." In this anecdote death, blood, and persuasion are linked to dramatic effect. Many early Chinese anecdotes about persuaders make the potentially lethal blade of persuasion into a central plot device.

From Zhuangzi[1]

From *The Way of Heaven*

Duke Huan was reading in his hall. Wheelwright Pian, who was cutting a wheel just outside the hall, put aside his hammer and chisel and went in. There he asked Duke Huan, "What do those books you are reading say?" The duke answered, "These are the words of the Sages." The wheelwright said, "Are the Sages still around?" And the duke answered, "They're dead." Then the wheelwright said, "Well, what you're reading then is no more than the dregs of the ancients." The duke: "When I, a prince, read, how is it that a wheelwright dares come and dispute with me? If you have an explanation, fine. If you don't have an explanation, *you* die!" Then Wheelwright Pian said, "I tend to look at it in terms of my own work: when you cut a wheel, if you go too slowly, it slides and doesn't stick fast; if you go too quickly, it jumps and doesn't go in. Neither too slowly nor too quickly—you achieve it in your hands, and those respond to the mind. I can't put it into words, but there is some fixed principle there. I can't teach it to my son, and my son can't get instruction in it from me. I've gone on this way for seventy years and have grown old in cutting wheels. The ancients have died, and along with them, that which cannot be transmitted. Therefore what you are reading is nothing more than the dregs of the ancients."

* * *

From *Outer Things*

Traditionalists[2] break into tombs using the *Poems*[3] and Ceremony.

The chief Traditionalist deigned to convey these words, "It beginneth to grow light in the east. How's it going?"

The subordinate Traditionalist responded, "I haven't got the skirt and jacket off yet, but there's a pearl in his mouth."

The high Traditionalist: "Verily it is even as the *Poems* say:

> Green, green groweth grain
> upon the slopes of the mound.
> The man ungenerous alive,
> in death his mouth will hold no pearl.[4]

I'll grab the whiskers and pull down on the beard; you take a metal bar, break through his cheeks, and slowly part his jaws, but don't damage the pearl in his mouth."

1. Translated by Stephen Owen.
2. Confucian scholars well versed in the Classics.
3. *Classic of Poetry*.
4. Because these verses are not included in the current version of the *Classic of Poetry*, they were probably invented here to parody the behavior of Confucian scholars.

Of Swords

A long time ago King Wen of Zhao took great pleasure in swordplay, and over three thousand men thronged his gates to receive his patronage as swordsmen. In his presence they would hack at each other day and night, and every year more than a hundred died of their wounds. But the king loved it dearly and never tired of it. It went on like this for three years, and as the kingdom's fortunes slid into decline, the nobility debated what to do about it.

Crown Prince Kui was appalled by the situation, and summoned his entourage. "I will offer a reward of a thousand pieces of gold to anyone who can dissuade the king from this mania of his and put a stop to these swordsmen."

Members of his entourage said, "Zhuangzi can certainly do it."

The crown prince then sent a messenger with a thousand pieces of gold to offer to Zhuangzi. But Zhuangzi refused to accept the gold and went back with the messenger to see the crown prince. "What is it that the Crown Prince wants of me, presenting me a thousand pieces of gold?"

The crown prince said, "I have heard of your sagely understanding, and out of respect I offered you a thousand pieces of gold so that you could distribute it to your followers. Since you have refused to accept it, what more can I say?"

Zhuangzi said, "I have heard of the purpose for which you want to employ me, which is to put an end to the king's amusements. Now let us suppose, on the one hand, that I try to persuade the king and in doing so, offend him, thus not satisfying you; in that case, I will be executed. What would I do with gold then? On the other hand, let us suppose that I persuade the king and do satisfy you. In that case, I could have anything I wanted in the Kingdom of Zhao."

The crown prince said, "True. However, our king will see only swordsmen."

Zhuangzi: "Understood. But I am rather good with the sword."

The crown prince: "Be that as it may, the swordsmen that our king-sees all have messy hair with bristling locks and slouched caps, plain, rough cap-strings, robes hitched up in the back, bulging eyes, and stumbling speech. This is the sort the king prefers. Since you will no doubt visit the king wearing your scholar's clothes, the whole thing will inevitably be a complete failure."

Zhuangzi: "Would you please have a swordsman's clothes prepared for me?"

Three days later, after the swordsman's clothes had been prepared, he met with the crown prince, and the crown prince presented him to the king, who waited for him with a bare blade drawn. Zhuangzi entered the gate of the great hall without hurrying; and when he saw the king, he did not bow.

The king, "Now that you have had the Crown Prince put you forward, what do you expect to do for me?"

"I've heard that the king enjoys swordplay, so I've come to see the king by way of swordplay."

The king said, "How can that sword of yours defend you?"

"If I had an opponent every ten paces, I could go a thousand leagues without pausing."

The king liked that very much. "Then there's no match for you in the whole world."

Zhuangzi said, "In swordplay one

displays himself as vacant,
initiates by advantage,

is the second to swing the blow,
is the first to strike home.

And I wish to have the chance to put this to the test."

The king said, "Stop now. Go to your lodgings and await my bidding. I'll invite you when I have arranged a contest to the death."

Then the king tried his swordsmen against one another for seven days, during which over sixty died of their wounds. Of these he got five or six men, whom he had bring their swords into the great hall. Then he summoned Zhuangzi.

"Today I'm going to have my men match swords."

Zhuangzi: "I've been looking forward to this for a long time."

The king: "Which would you use as your weapon, the long or the short?"

"For my own use, anything is fine. However, I have three swords that may be used only by a king. Let me tell you about these first, and then we will have the trial."

The king said, "Tell me about these three swords."

"There is an Emperor's sword, a sword of the great nobility, and the sword of an ordinary man."

The king said, "What is the Emperor's sword like?"

Zhuangzi said, "The sword of an Emperor:

has as its point Yan Valley and Mount Stonewall,
has as its blade Tai Mountain in Qi,
has its blunt edge in the kingdoms of Jin and Wei,
has as its guard the kingdoms Zhou and Song,
has as its hilt the kingdoms Han and Wei;
its wrappings are the barbarians that surround us,
its sheath is the four seasons,
it is wound about by the Sea of Bo,
Mount Heng is the sash from which it hangs,
it is governed by the five phases,
it makes judgments of punishment or virtue;
it is brought forth through Dark and Light,
it is held through spring and summer,
and is used in autumn and winter.
This sword, when held straight, has nothing before it,
pointed up, has nothing above it,
pressed downward, has nothing below it,
and swung, has nothing around it.
It slashes the clouds that drift above,
it cuts to Earth's axis below.
Use this sword but once,
and the nobility will all be brought in line,
and the whole world will yield—
for this is the sword of an Emperor."

As if in a daze, King Wen was completely absorbed. He said, "What is the sword of the great nobility like?"

Zhuangzi said, "The sword of the great nobility:

has as its point shrewd and valiant gentlemen,
has as its blade honest and unassuming gentlemen,

has its blunt edge in good and worthy gentlemen,
has as its guard loyal and wise gentlemen,
has as its hilt daring and outstanding gentlemen.
And this sword too, when held straight, has nothing before it,
pointed up, has nothing above it,
pressed downward, has nothing below it,
and swung, has nothing around it.
It takes model from the roundness of Heaven above,
whereby it moves with sun, moon, and stars.
It takes model from the squareness of Earth below,
whereby it moves with the four seasons.
From the center it knows the people's will,
by which it brings peace to lands all around.
Use this sword but once,
and it is like a rumbling quake of thunder.
Within the boundaries all around,
there is no man but yields to it
and obeys the bidding of their lord.
This is a sword of the great nobility."

The king then asked, "And what is the sword of the ordinary man like?"

Zhuangzi said, "The sword of the ordinary man belongs to one with messy hair, with bristling locks and slouched cap, plain, rough cap-strings, robes hitched up in the back, bulging eyes, and stumbling speech, men who hack at each other in front of you. A high hack will chop off a neck, and a low one cuts liver or lungs. This is the sword of the ordinary man, and it is no different from cockfighting, with a life cut off in a single morning. It has no use at all in the workings of a kingdom. We have here a king, to whom belongs the position of an Emperor, and yet who is in love with the sword of the ordinary man. And for this king's sake I have taken the liberty of disparaging it."

The king then drew him up into the hall where the Master of the Kitchens was having food set out. The king kept circling the table, until Zhuangzi said, "Sit calmly and settle your spirit. I have finished my expostulation on swords." Thereafter the king did not leave his palace for three months, and his swordsmen all perished on their own swordpoints in their places.

HAN FEIZI

Han Feizi was the most prominent proponent of Legalism, a vision of government that was based on authoritarian rule and the power of law. Although Han Feizi was a student of the Confucian thinker Xunzi, his vision of good government contrasted strongly with the Confucian emphasis on the moral virtue of rulers and officials. Han Feizi belonged to the royal lineage of the tiny state of Han. The king of Qin, on his way to become the megalomaniac

"First Emperor" of China in 221 B.C.E., was so impressed with Han Feizi's writings that he employed him. Yet in the end Han Feizi was slandered by colleagues who considered him partial to his homeland Han and dangerous to Qin's relentless thirst for conquest: Han Feizi was forced into suicide a decade before Qin completed his bloody unification of China. Thus his art of persuasion unfolded in a Machiavellian world of intrigues, mutual suspicion, and secrecy.

Han Feizi has a sober vision of human nature: thirst for power, fame, gain, reputation, merit, and reward is what drives humans in their thoughts and actions. In *The Difficulties of Persuasion*, the first extensive treatise on the power of speech in China, he proposes a psychology of persuading an audience comparable to Aristotle's rhetoric, which emphasizes the role of appealing to the emotions. Yet unlike Aristotle, Han Feizi finds flattery and counterintuitive praise the most effectively persuasive tools to use when facing the absolute power of an authoritarian ruler. Although Han Feizi died of the consequences of political suspicion, which his skills of persuasion could apparently not disperse, his essay does express the hope that the art of persuasion can sway a ruler's opinion and that, ideally, it can create room for a fruitful collaboration between a ruler and his government officials.

From The Difficulties of Persuasion[1]

On the whole, the difficult thing about persuading others is not that one lacks the knowledge needed to state his case nor the audacity to exercise his abilities to the full. On the whole, the difficult thing about persuasion is to know the mind of the person one is trying to persuade and to be able to fit one's words to it.

If the person you are trying to persuade is out to establish a reputation for virtue, and you talk to him about making a fat profit, then he will regard you as low-bred, accord you a shabby and contemptuous reception, and undoubtedly send you packing. If the person you are trying to persuade is on the contrary interested in a fat profit, and you talk to him about a virtuous reputation, he will regard you as witless and out of touch with reality, and will never heed your arguments. If the person you are trying to persuade is secretly out for big gain but ostensibly claims to be interested in a virtuous name alone, and you talk to him about a reputation for virtue, then he will pretend to welcome and heed you, but in fact will shunt you aside; if you talk to him about making a big gain, he will secretly follow your advice but ostensibly reject you. These are facts that you must not fail to consider carefully.

Undertakings succeed through secrecy but fail through being found out. Though the ruler himself has not yet divulged his plans, if you in your discussions happen to hit upon his hidden motives, then you will be in danger. If the ruler is ostensibly seeking one thing but actually is attempting to accomplish something quite different, and you perceive not only his ostensible objective but the real motives behind his actions as well, then you will likewise be in danger. If you happen to think up some unusual scheme for the ruler which meets with his approval, and some other person of intelligence manages by

1. Translated by Burton Watson.

outside means to guess what it is and divulges the secret to the world, then the ruler will suppose that it was you who gave it away and you will be in danger. If you have not yet won substantial reward and favor and yet your words are extremely apt and wise, then if the ruler heeds them and the undertaking is successful, he will forget to reward you; and if he does not heed them and the undertaking fails, he will regard you with suspicion and you will be in danger. If some person of eminence takes a brief step in the wrong direction and you immediately launch into a lecture on ritual principles and challenge his misdeed, then you will be in danger. If some eminent person gets hold of a good scheme somewhere and plans to use it to win merit for himself, and you happen to know where he got it, then you will be in danger. If you try forcibly to talk a person into doing what he cannot do, or stopping what he cannot stop, then you will be in danger.

If you talk to the ruler about men of real worth, he will think you are implying that he is no match for them; if you talk to him of petty men, he will think you are attempting to use your influence to get your friends into office; if you talk to him about what he likes, he will suspect you of trying to utilize him; if you talk about what he hates, he will suspect you of trying to test his patience. If you speak too bluntly and to the point, he will consider you unlearned and will shun you; if you speak too eloquently and in too great detail, he will consider you pretentious and will reject you. If you are too sketchy in outlining your ideas, he will think you a coward who is too fainthearted to say what he really means; if you are too exuberant and long-winded in stating your proposals, he will think you an uncouth bumpkin who is trying to talk down to him. These are the difficulties of persuasion; you cannot afford to be ignorant of them!

The important thing in persuasion is to learn how to play up the aspects that the person you are talking to is proud of, and play down the aspects he is ashamed of. Thus, if the person has some urgent personal desire, you should show him that it is his public duty to carry it out and urge him not to delay. If he has some mean objective in mind and yet cannot restrain himself, you should do your best to point out to him whatever admirable aspects it may have and to minimize the reprehensible ones. If he has some lofty objective in mind and yet does not have the ability needed to realize it, you should do your best to point out to him the faults and bad aspects of such an objective and make it seem a virtue not to pursue it. If he is anxious to make a show of wisdom and ability, mention several proposals which are different from the one you have in mind but of the same general nature in order to supply him with ideas; then let him build on your words, but pretend that you are unaware that he is doing so, and in this way abet his wisdom.

* * *

Praise other men whose deeds are like those of the person you are talking to; commend other actions which are based upon the same policies as his. If there is someone else who is guilty of the same vice he is, be sure to gloss it over by showing that it really does no great harm; if there is someone else who has suffered the same failure he has, be sure to defend it by demonstrating that it is not a loss after all. If he prides himself on his physical prowess, do not antagonize him by mentioning the difficulties he has encountered in the past; if he considers himself an expert at making decisions, do not anger him by pointing out his past errors; if he pictures himself a sagacious planner, do not tax him with his failures. Make sure that there is nothing in your ideas as a whole that will vex your listener, and nothing about your words that will rub him the wrong way, and then you may exercise your powers of rhetoric to the fullest. This is the way to gain the confidence and intimacy of the person you are addressing and to make sure that you are able to say all you have to say without incurring his suspicion.

* * *

If you are able to fulfill long years of service with the ruler, enjoy his fullest favor and confidence, lay long-range plans for him without ever arousing suspicion, and when necessary oppose him in argument without incurring blame, then you may achieve merit by making clear to him what is profitable and what is harmful, and bring glory to yourself by your forthright judgments of right and wrong. When ruler and minister aid and sustain each other in this way, persuasion may be said to have reached its fulfillment.

* * *

In ancient times Mi Zixia won favor with the ruler of Wei.[2] According to the laws of the state of Wei, anyone who secretly made use of the ruler's carriage was punished by having his feet amputated. When Mi Zixia's mother fell ill, someone slipped into the palace at night to report this to Mi Zixia. Mi Zixia forged an order from the ruler, got into the ruler's carriage, and went off to see her, but when the ruler heard of it, he only praised him, saying, "How filial! For the sake of his mother he forgot all about the danger of having his feet cut off!" Another day Mi Zixia was strolling with the ruler in an orchard and, biting into a peach and finding it sweet, he stopped eating and gave the remaining half to the ruler to enjoy. "How sincere is your love for me!" exclaimed the ruler. "You forget your own appetite and think only of giving me good things to eat!" Later, however, when Mi Zixia looks had faded and the ruler's passion for him had cooled, he was accused of committing some crime against his lord. "After all," said the ruler, "he once stole my carriage, and another time he gave me a half-eaten peach to eat!" Mi Zixia was actually acting no differently from the way he always had; the fact that he was praised in the early days, and accused of a crime later on, was because the ruler's love had turned to hate.

If you gain the ruler's love, your wisdom will be appreciated and you will enjoy his favor as well; but if he hates you, not only will your wisdom be rejected, but you will be regarded as a criminal and thrust aside. Hence men who wish to present their remonstrances and expound their ideas must not fail to ascertain the ruler's loves and hates before launching into their speeches.

The beast called the dragon can be tamed and trained to the point where you may ride on its back. But on the underside of its throat it has scales a foot in diameter that curl back from the body, and anyone who chances to brush against them is sure to die. The ruler of men too has his bristling scales. Only if a speaker can avoid brushing against them will he have any hope for success.

2. Duke Ling of Wei (6th century B.C.E.).

Selected Bibliographies

I. Ancient Mediterranean and Near Eastern Literature

On the early history of writing, an excellent starting point is Walter Ong, *Orality and Literacy: Technologizing of the Word* (1982), which teases out the cultural and psychological implications of the shift from an oral to a literate culture. Those with a particular interest in Near Eastern cultures can begin with James Pritchard's classic anthology of texts in translation, containing many illustrations: *The Ancient Near East: An Anthology of Texts and Pictures* (reissued 2010). A good illustrated survey of Greek and Roman culture by a number of different specialists is John Boardman, Jasper Griffin, and Oswyn Murray, *The Oxford History of the Classical World* (1986). Introductory texts that combine discussion of Greek, Roman, and Near Eastern cultures include *An Introduction to the Ancient World* (2008), by Lukas de Blois and R. J. van der Spek, and the less scholarly but lively *The History of the Ancient World: From the Earliest Accounts to the Fall of Rome*, by Susan Wise Bauer (2007). Reliable general introductions to Greek and Roman literature include Albin Lesky, *Greek Literature* (reissued 1996), and G. B. Conte, *Latin Literature: A History* (reissued 1999). For more information about the ancient world, including images of ancient art, architecture, and artifacts, as well as ancient Greek and Roman texts, a wonderful resource is Tufts University's website *Perseus* (www.perseus.tufts.edu).

Aeschylus

Simon Goldhill, *Aeschylus: The* Oresteia (1992), is a clearly written introduction to the whole trilogy and includes both discussion of metaphor and other literary techniques, and an account of the political and social background. There is more on Aeschylus's staging in an older but still useful study, Oliver Taplin, *The Stagecraft of Aeschylus: The Dramatic Use of Entrances and Exits in Greek Tragedy* (1977). Further discussion of Aeschylus's literary techniques appears in D. J. Conacher, *Aeschylus'* Oresteia: *A Literary Commentary* (1987). A good recent collection of important essays is Michael Lloyd, ed., *Aeschylus* (2007).

Aesop

The introduction to Laura Gibb, trans., *Aesop's Fables* (2008), draws attention to the complex tradition by which these fables came to be written down, in many different forms. The ancient, anonymous *Life of Aesop* appears in Lloyd Daly, trans., *Anthology of Greek Popular Literature* (1998). The Loeb edition of Babrius, reputed author of a set of fables in Greek verse, from the first century C.E., and Phaedrus, a Macedonian slave who wrote Latin verse fables in the first century C.E., in English translation, includes a survey of parallels between the Aesopic fable and the traditions of ancient Mesopotamia (1965). A useful scholarly survey of the genre is Gert-Jan van Dijk, *Ainoi, Logoi, Mythoi: Fables in Archaic, Classical, and Hellenistic Greek Literature: With a Study of the Theory and Terminology of the Genre* (1997).

Ancient Athenian Drama

A good introduction to the genre of Athenian tragedy, which includes discussions of all the extant plays and is particularly strong on social context, is Edith Hall, *Greek Tragedy: Suffering under the Sun* (2010). Marianne McDonald and J. Michael Walton, eds., *Cambridge Companion to Greek and Roman Theatre* (2007), includes essays on both tragedy and comedy, and also has some discussion of staging. Another fine collection of introductory essays, on tragedy, comedy, and satyr plays, is Ian C. Storey and Arlene Allan, *A Guide to Ancient Greek Drama* (2005). Further information on performance contexts, in the fifth century and also in modern revivals, can be found in David Wiles, *Mask and Performance in Greek Tragedy: From Ancient Festival to Modern Experimentation* (2007). Many pieces of visual evidence of Greek theater, including vase paintings, statues, and photographs of remaining theater sites, are collected in Richard Green and Eric Handley, *Images of the Greek Theater* (1995).

Ancient Egyptian Literature

The material and cultural background to ancient Egyptian civilization is presented in John Baines and Jaromir Malek, *Cultural Atlas of Ancient Egypt* (2000). Ian Shaw, ed., *The Oxford History of Ancient Egypt* (2000), is a useful treatment with broad cultural coverage for some periods. Marc van de Mieroop, *A History of Ancient Egypt* (2011), is the most up-to-date and reliable history. Alan K. Bowman, *Egypt after the Pharaohs, 332 BC–AD 642: From Alexander to the Arab Conquest* (1996), is an excellent presentation of the post-Pharaonic period. Two reliable surveys of Egyptian religion are Byron E. Shafer, ed., *Religion in Ancient Egypt: Gods, Myths, and Personal Practice* (1991), and Stephen Quirke, *Ancient Egyptian Religion* (1995). Donald B. Redford, ed., *The Oxford Encyclopedia of Ancient Egypt*, 3 vols. (2001), has articles on most major topics relating to ancient Egypt. The *UCLA Encyclopedia of Egyptology* (www.uee.ucla.edu) is an online resource that will gradually supersede print materials in its area.

There is no broad, general study of all periods of ancient Egyptian literature, but the works detailed in this paragraph have introductions setting the ancient works in context, in addition to prefatory remarks and notes on the individual texts. The largest and richest collection of translations is Miriam Lichtheim, *Ancient Egyptian Literature: A Book of Readings* (1973–80; reprinted with new forewords, 2006), 3 vols. A one-volume work that concentrates on fictional texts is William Kelly Simpson, ed., *The Literature of Ancient Egypt* (3rd ed., 2003). R. B. Parkinson, *Voices from Ancient Egypt* (1991), gives an excellent, more diverse selection from the Middle Kingdom. Parkinson has also provided an outstanding full translation of Middle Kingdom texts, The Tale of Sinuhe *and Other Ancient Egyptian Poems, 1940–1640 BC* (1998), and his *Reading Ancient Egyptian Poetry: Among Other Histories* (2009) is a detailed study of the context and background of the principal Middle Kingdom tales and includes questions of performance and new translations of the oldest surviving manuscripts.

For those wishing to explore Egyptian literature in relation to other Near Eastern literatures, William W. Hallo and K. Lawson Younger, eds., *The Context of Scripture: Canonical Compositions, Monumental Inscriptions, and Archival Documents from the Biblical World* (2003), 3 vols., is a rich resource. Susan Walker and Peter Higgs, eds., *Cleopatra of Egypt: From History to Myth* (2001), places *Stela of Taimhotep* in the context of the art and religion of its period (184–87).

Aristophanes

A prose translation of *Lysistrata*, along with Aristophanes' two other comedies about women, appears in Jeffrey Henderson, trans. and ed., *Three Plays by Aristophanes: Staging Women* (1996, 2010); this collection has a useful introduction to the plays and to Athenian comedy in general. A good general introduction to Aristophanes is D. M. MacDowell, *Aristophanes and Athens: An Introduction to the Plays* (1995). More on the genre can be found in Gregory Dobrov, ed., *Brill's Companion to the Study of Greek Comedy* (2010). The political context of the plays is discussed in Keith C. Sidwell, *Aristophanes the Democrat: The Politics of Satirical Comedy during the Peloponnesian War* (2009). A good discussion of staging is Martin Revermann, *Comic Business: Theatricality, Dramatic Technique and Performance Contexts of Aristophanic Comedy* (2006).

Catullus

A good general literary introduction is Charles Martin, *Catullus* (1992). An important study of Catullus's masculine, macho persona is David Wray, *Catullus and the Poetics of Roman Manhood* (2001). To know more about Clodia, on whom Lesbia may have been based, read Cicero's *Pro Caelio*, which is included in Michael Grant, trans., *Selected Political Speeches* (1977). Maria Wyke, *The Roman Mistress: Ancient and Modern Representations* (2002), mostly focuses on authors later than Catullus, but has important implications for interpretation of the Lesbia poems; Wyke reads the poet's girlfriend as a literary creation and stresses that she need not be based on any real person.

Creation and the Cosmos

A useful survey of ancient Near Eastern literature is J. M. Sasson, *Civilizations of the Ancient Near East* (1995), vol. 4, a large part of which is dedicated to the literatures of Egypt. In Markham J. Geller and Mineke Schipper, eds., *Imagining Creation* (2008), W. G. Lambert's article "Mesopotamian Creation Stories" (15–59) includes a general survey of Mesopotamian creation myths and a new translation of the *Enuma Elish*. Introductions to Sumerian and Akkadian literature can also be found in J. Black et al., *The Literature of Ancient Sumer* (2004), and B. R. Foster, *Before the Muses* (2005). Martin West's introduction to his prose translation of *Theogony* and *Works and Days* (1999), draws useful parallels between Hesiodic and Near Eastern myths. Jenny Strauss Clay, *Hesiod's Cosmos* (2003), is an intelligent literary account of Greek myth. Catherine Osborne, *Presocratic Philosophy: A Very Short Introduction* (2004), gives a good overview of Thales and the other pre-Socratics and points the reader to further secondary sources. Stuart Gillespie and Philip Hardie, eds., *The Cambridge Companion to Lucretius* (2007), contains essays by prominent Lucretius scholars on both literary and philosophical questions.

Euripides

A good collection of scholarly essays on Euripides is Judith Mossman, ed., *Euripides* (2003). For representations of "barbarians" in tragedy, including in *Medea*, see Edith Hall, *Inventing the Barbarian: Greek Self-Definition through Tragedy* (1989). Ruby Blondell, ed., *Women on the Edge: Four Plays* (1999), includes a translation of *Medea* and three other Euripides plays focused on women, as well as a useful introduction that discusses representations of gender in these plays. A good general introduction to Euripides, with brief discussions of all nineteen extant plays and a focus on their reception after ancient times is Michael Walton, *Euripides Our Contemporary* (2010). William Allan, *Euripides: Medea* (2002), surveys the most important literary themes of the play.

Gilgamesh

The most recent scholarly translations of *The Epic of Gilgamesh* are Stephanie Delany, *Myths from Mesopotamia: Creation, the Flood, Gilgamesh, and Others* (1989); Maureen Kovacs, *The Epic of Gilgamesh* (1989); Andrew George, *The Epic of Gilgamesh: The Babylonian Epic Poem and Other Texts in Akkadian and Sumerian* (1999) and *The Babylonian Gilgamesh Epic: Introduction, Critical Edition, and Cuneiform Texts* (2003); and Benjamin Foster, *The Epic of Gilgamesh* (2001). They contain ample commentary and important introductory articles that aid in the interpretation of the epic. The poet Stephen Mitchell's *Gilgamesh: A New English Version* (2004) is a smooth verse retelling of the epic. David Ferry, *Gilgamesh: A New Rendering into English Verse* (1992) is also recommended. For a study of the evolution of the story over time, see Geffrey Tigay, *The Evolution of the Gilgamesh Epic* (1982). Alexander Heidel shows the importance of *Gilgamesh* for biblical studies in *The Gilgamesh Epic and Old Testament Parallels* (1963). Rivkah Harris, *Gender and Aging in Mesopotamia: The Gilgamesh Epic and Other Ancient Literature* (2000), discusses the gender dynamic in the epic in the light of other ancient texts. John Maier, *Gilgamesh: A Reader* (1997), contains seminal articles on *Gilgamesh* and an extensive bibliography. David Damrosch, *The Buried Book: The Loss and Rediscovery of the Great Epic of Gilgamesh* (2007), tells the story of the colonial adventurers, scholars, and contemporary writers involved in the rediscovery of *Gilgamesh*.

For those wishing to discover the riches of Mesopotamian literature beyond *Gilgamesh*, Benjamin Foster's voluminous *Before the Muses: An Anthology of Akkadian Literature* (1993, 2005) and *From Distant Days: Myths, Tales, and Poetry of Ancient Mesopotamia* (1995) contain a wealth of material. Jack Sasson et al., *Civilizations of the Ancient Near East* (1995), vol. 4, is devoted to languages and literatures of the region. For vivid presentations of Mesopotamian civilization, see Jean Bottéro, *Mesopotamia: Writing, Reasoning, and the Gods* (1992); J. N. Postgate, *Early Mesopotamia: Society and*

Economy at the Dawn of History (1992); and Benjamin Foster and Karen Polinger Foster, *Civilizations of Ancient Iraq* (2009).

The Hebrew Bible

Richard Elliott Friedman, *Who Wrote the Bible?* (1987), is a clear introduction to the idea that each of the first books of the Bible is composed from several narrative strands (the "documentary hypothesis"). The *Anchor Bible*, in multiple volumes, has useful introductions and notes to each book of the Bible, including historical information. More on the historicity of the Bible can be found in Ronald Hendel, *Remembering Abraham: Culture, History and Memory in Ancient Israel* (2004). Robert Alter and Frank Kermode, eds., *The Literary Guide to the Bible* (1987), has useful essays on approaching the stylistic and narrative structures of the Bible. James L. Crenshaw, *Defending God: Biblical Responses to the Problem of Evil* (2005), is an interesting attempt to grapple with the central moral problems raised by the Hebrew Bible.

Homer

The first chapter of Erich Auerbach's *Mimesis: The Representation of Reality in Western Literature* (1953), trans. Willard Trask, gives a stimulating account of how Homeric narrative technique might differ from that of the Hebrew Bible. Essential works on the relation of the Homeric poems to the Greek oral tradition include Albert Lord, *The Singer of Tales* (1960), and Milman Parry, *The Making of Homeric Verse* (1973). Jenny Strauss Clay, *The Wrath of Athena: Gods and Men in the* Odyssey (1983), provides a useful overview of the gods in the epic. Female characters, human and divine, are discussed in Beth Cohen, ed., *The Distaff Side: Representing the Female in Homer's* Odyssey (1995). A good collection of classic essays on the *Odyssey* is Seth Schein, ed., *Reading the* Odyssey: *Selected Interpretative Essays* (1996). Those interested in the history of Homeric Greece will find useful information in M. I. Finley, *Early Greece: The Bronze and Archaic Ages* (1981). James Tatum, *The Mourner's Song: War and Remembrance from the* Iliad *to Vietnam* (2003), is a moving account of the *Iliad* in the context of later representations of war. Sheila Murnaghan's introductory essays to Stanley Lombardo's translations of the *Odyssey* (2000) and the *Iliad* (1997) provide rich interpretations of important literary themes, such as disguise, hospitality, heroism, and death.

Ovid

Sarah Mack, *Ovid* (1988), is a good general introduction, with a long chapter on the *Metamorphoses*. Philip Hardie, *Ovid's Poetics of Illusion* (2002), is an important guide to Ovid's poetic technique; metapoetic aspects are also discussed in R. A. Smith, *Poetic Allusion and Poetic Embrace in Ovid and Virgil* (1997), which includes a fine reading of the Pygmalion episode. Garth Tissol, *The Face of Nature* (1997), provides a useful close reading of the poem, including discussion of Ovid's puns, and looks in particular at the Myrrha episode. Charles Martindale, *Ovid Renewed: Ovidian Influences on Literature and Art from the Middle Ages to the Twentieth Century* (1988), gives some idea of the importance of Ovid for later literature.

Plato

An interesting collection of scholarly essays on both philosophical and literary themes, with some discussion of postclassical reception, is J. H. Lesher, Debra Nails, and Frisbee C. C. Sheffield, eds., *Plato's Symposium: Issues in Interpretation and Reception* (2006). A good introduction to themes in the text is Richard Hunter, *Plato's Symposium* (2004). Those interested in studying Plato more broadly can find pointers in Julia Annas, *Plato: A Very Short Introduction* (2003). A provocative philosophical discussion of Plato's use of the dialogue form can be found in Charles Kahn, *Plato and the Socratic Dialogue: The Philosophical Use of a Literary Form* (1996). The extensive scholarly and theoretical work on Athenian sexuality includes David M. Halperin, John J. Winkler, and Froma I. Zeitlin, eds., *Before Sexuality: The Construction of Erotic Experience in the Ancient Greek World* (1990), which explores sexuality as a cultural construct; Kenneth Dover's introduction to his edition of the *Symposium* (1980) and his *Greek Homosexuality* (1989), which assumes, controversially, that the term "homosexuality" can be applied back to the Greeks; and the equally controversial work of James Davidson, *The Greeks and Greek Love* (2009).

Sappho

A useful collection of scholarly essays is Ellen Greene, ed., *Reading Sappho: Contemporary Approaches* (1996). Marguerite Johnson, *Sappho* (2007), is a clear, short introduction to some important literary themes in the poet's work. Sappho is read alongside two male, contemporary lyric poets in A. P. Burnett, *Three Archaic Poets: Archilochus, Alcaeus, Sappho* (1983). The reception of Sappho is particularly interesting; Margaret Reynolds, ed., *The Sappho Companion* (2000), is a collection of translations, imitations, and adaptations of Sappho's poems by postclassical poets and writers.

Sophocles

A good literary introduction to Sophocles, which draws on psychoanalytic and anthropological ideas to emphasize pairs of concepts (such as civilization versus wildness) is Charles Segal, *Tragedy and Civilization: An Interpretation of Sophocles* (1981). Important essays by various scholars on *Oedipus the King*, including a classic article by E. R. Dodds on common student misinterpretations of the play, are collected in Michael O'Brien, ed., *Twentieth-Century Interpretations of* Oedipus Rex (1968). Mary Blundell, *Helping Friends and Harming Enemies* (1989), reads Sophocles through the maxim of Greek popular morality alluded to in its title; one chapter is devoted to *Antigone*. The city of Thebes in Greek tragedy in general, and in these plays in particular, is discussed by Froma Zeitlin in her essay in Zeitlin and John J. Winkler, eds., *Nothing to Do with Dionysos?* (1990). In two editions of the plays in Greek, scholars have written introductions that are accessible and useful even to the nonspecialist reader: R. D. Dawe on *Oedipus Tyrannos*, and Mark Griffith on *Antigone* (1982 and 1999 respectively). The political dimensions of the plays are particularly difficult for modern readers to grasp; an interesting attempt to apply the specifics of Athenian political history to the plays is Michael Vickers, *Sophocles and Alcibiades: Athenian Politics in Ancient Greek Literature* (2008). Both plays have been adapted in many different ways for the modern stage; one important example is Seamus Heaney's version of *Antigone*, set in Northern Ireland, *The Burial at Thebes* (2004).

Speech, Writing, Poetry

Walter Ong, *Orality and Literacy: The Technologizing of the Word* (2002), is essential reading. On the social contexts of scribal life in Mesopotamia, see L. E. Pearce, "The Scribes and Scholars of Ancient Mesopotamia," in J. M. Sasson et al., eds., *Civilizations of the Ancient Near East* (1995). More ancient Greek and Roman texts expressing ideas about speech, literacy, and literature can be found in D. Russell and M. Winterbottom, eds. and trans., *Ancient Literary Criticism* (1972). An important close reading of Aristotle's *Poetics* is S. Halliwell, *Aristotle's* Poetics (1986); see also his translation with commentary (1987). An introduction to the *Ars Poetica* is Bernard Frischer, *Shifting Paradigms: New Approaches to Horace's* Ars poetica (1991). Andrew Ford, *The Origins of Criticism* (2002), is an important account of how literary criticism came into being. A groundbreaking discussion of ancient modes of reading, including the importance of allegorical reading, is Peter Struck, *Birth of the Symbol* (2004). A. Richard Hunter, *Critical Moments in Classical Literature: Studies in the Ancient View of Literature and Its Uses* (2009), also offers insights into how the ancient Greeks and Romans imagined their literature.

Travel and Conquest

Two controversial accounts of racial identity and power in the ancient world, and in modern understandings of the ancient world, are Martin Bernal, *Black Athena: The Afroasiatic Roots of Classical Civilization* (1987), which emphasizes Egyptian influence on Greek myth and culture; and Edward Said, *Orientalism* (1978), which traces modern "occidentalist" bias back to the ancient Greeks and includes a reading of Aeschylus's *Persians*. A more recent, also controversial account is Benjamin Isaac, *The Invention of Racism in Classical Antiquity* (2004). A good collection of essays on Herodotus can be found in the *Cambridge Companion to Herodotus* (2006). Page DuBois, *Slavery: Antiquity and Its Legacy* (2009), juxtaposes ancient and modern experiences of slavery. The introduction to Sandra R. Joshel and Sheila Murnaghan, eds., *Women and Slaves in Greco-Roman Culture: Differential Equations* (1998), gives good insights into how we might look at these non-elite groups in classical cultures. Carol Doherty, *The Poetics of Colonization* (1993), is an interesting attempt to read archaic Greek poetry in the light of ancient experiences of colonization.

Amanda Podany, *Brotherhood of Kings: How International Relations Shaped the Ancient Near East* (2010), provides a broad vista of intercultural and diplomatic contacts in the Ancient Near East. Muzhou Pu (or Mu-chou Poo), *Enemies of Civilization: Attitudes toward Foreigners in Ancient Mesopotamia, Egypt, and China* (2005), compares how three of the world's most ancient civilizations defined themselves against their neighbors.

To read more tales from the Middle Kingdom like *The Tale of the Shipwrecked Sailor*, Richard B. Parkinson, The Tale of Sinuhe *and Other Ancient Egyptian Poems, 1940–1640 BC* (1997), contains outstanding full translations. John H. Taylor, *Egypt and Nubia* (1991), further explores relations between Egypt and Nubia. On royal inscriptions and their relation to other Egyptian literary genres, see Christopher Eyre, "The Semna Stelae: Quotation, Genre and Functions of Literature," in Sarah Israelit-Groll, ed., *Studies in Egyptology Presented to Miriam Lichtheim*, vol. 1 (1990).

Virgil

The structure of the whole poem is discussed in David O. Ross, *Virgil's* Aeneid: *A Reader's Guide* (2007). S. Harrison, ed., *Oxford Readings in Virgil's* Aeneid (1990) has useful articles on many aspects of the poem. A good literary introduction to the whole poem is Michael C. J. Putnam, *Virgil's* Aeneid: *Interpretation and Influence* (1995). Yasmin Syed, *Virgil's* Aeneid *and the Roman Self* (2005), gives an interesting account of how the poem participated in, and formed, Roman cultural values. A good short discussion of Virgilian allusion to earlier literature, why it works and why it matters, is R. O. A. M. Lyne, *Further Voices in Virgil's* Aeneid (1987). S. Quinn, ed., *Why Virgil?* (2000), includes literary essays and some examples of modern literature imitating or responding to Virgil. David Quint, *Epic and Empire* (1993), provides an important model for reading Virgil and later epics in terms of the losers and winners of history.

II. India's Ancient Epics and Tales

Burton Stein, *A History of India* (1998), and Stanley Wolpert, *A New History of India* (2008), offer good, complementary historical overviews of ancient India; Upinder Singh, *A History of Ancient and Early Medieval India* (2009), provides a more detailed, up-to-date account. Romila Thapar, *Cultural Pasts: Essays in Early Indian History* (2000), contains the best critical analyses of specific aspects of the ancient period. Thomas R. Trautmann, *The Aryan Debate* (2005), surveys recent controversies on India's prehistory, and includes a selection of important texts from the eighteenth century onward. Patrick Olivelle, *Upaniṣads* (1996), provides an excellent overview of Vedic religion, with translations of some canonical texts; Gavin Flood, *An Introduction to Hinduism* (1996), explains both early and later forms of the religion. Peter Harvey, *An Introduction to Buddhism* (1990), covers history, doctrine, and practice, with a focus on Mahayana Buddhism; Joseph M. Kitagawa and Mark D. Cummings, *Buddhism and Asian History* (1989), offers greater depth as well as a broader sweep, with specialist essays by many scholars.

The Bhagavad-Gītā

Among the world's canonical religious texts, the *Bhagavad-gītā* is second only to the Bible in the number of times it has been translated, and the range of languages into which it has been rendered. Of the many modern translations available in English, Barbara Stoler Miller, *The* Bhagavad-gītā: *Krishna's Counsel in Time of War* (1986), is one of the most reliable and accessible. R. C. Zaehner, *The Bhagavad-gītā* (1969), includes the original Sanskrit text in English transcription, along with a literal rendering, a more polished version, and a commentary on each verse. The most useful Indian translation into English is S. Radhakrishnan's older *The Bhagavad-gītā*—1948 and later editions. For a discussion of Indian interpretations of the poem, see Robert Minor, *Modern Interpreters of the* Bhagavadgītā (1986); and for an account of its reception in the West, consult Eric Sharpe, *The Universal Gītā: Western Images of the* Bhagavad Gītā, *a Bicentennial Survey* (1985).

The Jātaka
A complete English translation is available in E. B. Cowell, *The* Jātaka: *Or Stories of the Buddha's Former Births*, 6 vols. (1981). A good selection is provided in H. T. Francis and E. J. Thomas, eds., *Jātaka Tales* (1956). On the wide influence of this work from Afghanistan to China, see M. Cummings, *The Lives of the Buddha in the Art and Literature of Asia* (1982). The fascinating story of the *Jātaka*'s transmission to Europe is recounted in T. W. Rhys David's introduction to *Buddhist Birth Stories* (1880). An excellent translation of the canonical Sanskrit version of this work is offered in Peter Khoroche, *Once the Buddha Was a Monkey: Aryasura's Jātakamala* (1989).

The Mahābhārata
The best condensed version of the epic in English, which enables readers to grasp it as a whole and also to become familiar with many of its details, is C. V. Narasimhan, Mahābhārata: *An English Version Based on Selected Verses* (1965). A complete rendering of the poem that is still useful is Manmatha Nath Dutt, *A Prose English Translation of the* Mahābhārata (1895–1905), in six volumes. A full scholarly translation of the first five major books of the epic, with notes and critical commentary, is available in the three volumes of J. A. B. Van Buitenen, *The Mahābhārata* (1975–). Important modern Indian interpretations include V. S. Sukhtankar, *The Meaning of the* Mahābhārata (1957), and Irawati Karve, *Yuganta: The End of an Epoch* (1971).

The Rāmāyaṇa of Vālmīki
The Rāmāyaṇa *of Vālmīki: An Epic of Ancient India* (1984–), translated, annotated, and introduced by various scholars led by Robert Goldman, is the best recent version in English; five volumes, representing books 1 through 5, have appeared so far. Swami Venkatesanand, *The Concise* Rāmāyaṇa (1988), the source of our text, is a condensed prose version, which emphasizes the religious message of Vālmīki's epic, interpreted from a conservative modern perspective. A particularly readable literary prose rendering of Kamban's twelfth-century Tamil version of the poem appears in R. K. Narayan, *The* Rāmāyaṇa (1972). Important scholarly essays on most aspects of "the story of Rāma" are collected in Paula Richman, *Many* Rāmāyaṇas: *The Diversity of a Narrative Tradition in South Asia* (1991).

III. Early Chinese Literature and Thought

Jacques Gernet, *A History of Chinese Civilization* (1982), is a commanding survey history of China. Patricia Ebrey, Anne Walthall, and James Palais, *Pre-Modern East Asia to 1800: A Cultural, Social and Political History* (2009), is an excellent shorter account of Chinese history in the broader context of East Asia. Michael Loewe and Edward Shaughnessy, eds., *The Cambridge History of Ancient China* (1999), is a comprehensive reference work for early Chinese history and culture. For a vivid account of thought and society in early imperial China, see Mark Lewis, *The Early Chinese Empires: Qin and Han* (2007).

For those wishing to explore more early Chinese texts, Stephen Owen, *Anthology of Chinese Literature, Beginnings to 1911* (1996), presents a rich selection of Chinese literature with ample introductory material and commentary. Cyril Birch, *Anthology of Chinese Literature* (1965), and Victor Mair, *The Columbia Anthology of Traditional Chinese Literature* (1994), which is organized by genre and not chronology, are also recommended. For early Chinese thought and religion, see William Theodore de Bary, *Sources of Chinese Tradition* (2nd ed. 1999), a two-volume anthology covering a broad variety of original texts in translation from the beginnings to the modern period.

For broader explorations of Chinese Masters Literature, see Benjamin Schwartz, *The World of Thought in Ancient China* (1985); A. C. Graham, *Disputers of the Tao: Philosophical Argument in Ancient China* (1989); Chad Hansen, *A Daoist Theory of Chinese Thought: A Philosophical Interpretation* (1992); and Wiebke Denecke, *The*

Dynamics of Masters Literature: Early Chinese Thought from Confucius to Han Feizi (2010). To explore comparisons between Ancient Greece and China, see Lisa Raphals, *Knowing Words: Wisdom and Cunning in the Classical Traditions of China and Greece* (1992), and Steven Shankman and Stephen Durrant, *The Siren and the Sage: Knowledge and Wisdom in Ancient Greece and China* (2000).

Classic of Poetry

Other translations for comparison include Arthur Waley, *The Book of Songs* (1937), and Ezra Pound, *The Classic Anthology Defined by Confucius* (1954). Anecdotes by the Han Dynasty scholar Han Ying (fl. 150 B.C.E.) that show how poems from the *Classic of Poetry* were applied to concrete situations and moral questions can be found in James R. Hightower, *Han Shih Wai Chuan: Han Ying's Illustrations of the Didactic Application of the* Classic of Songs (1952). For stimulating studies of the anthology and its interpretation, see Steven Van Zoeren, *Poetry and Personality: Reading, Exegesis and Hermeneutics in Traditional China* (1991), and Haun Saussy, *The Problem of a Chinese Aesthetic* (1993). Pauline Yu, *The Reading of Imagery in the Chinese Poetic Tradition* (1987), is a compelling study of imagery in the *Classic of Poetry* and other Chinese texts.

Confucius

There are many translations of the *Analects*. The selections in this anthology are from Simon Leys's complete translation, *The* Analects *of Confucius* (1997). Arthur Waley's resonant translation of 1938 has recently been reprinted with an explanatory introduction by Sarah Allan (2000). D. C. Lau, *Analects* (1979), is a solid translation and contains a lucid introduction to Confucius and his ideas. Roger T. Ames and Henry Rosemont, *The* Analects *of Confucius: A Philosophical Translation* (1998), provides the classical Chinese text alongside an English version. Herbert Fingarette, *Confucius—The Secular as Sacred* (1972), remains one of the most persuasive accounts of the appeal of the *Analects*. David L. Hall and Roger T. Ames, *Thinking through Confucius* (1987), is an innovative reading of the *Analects* inspired by American pragmatic philosophy. John Makeham, *Transmitters and Creators: Chinese Commentators and Commentaries on the* Analects (2003), gives insight into later commentators' understanding of the *Analects*. For a compelling account of early Confucianism, see Robert Eno, *The Confucian Creation of Heaven: Philosophy and the Defense of Ritual Mastery* (1990). Thomas A. Wilson, *On Sacred Grounds: Culture, Society, Politics, and the Formation of the Cult of Confucius* (2002), is a collection of articles about the religious dimensions of Confucianism and the Confucius cult. Lionel Jensen, *Manufacturing Confucianism: Chinese Traditions and Universal Civilization* (1997), discusses how the image of Confucianism created by European missionaries working in China during the sixteenth and seventeenth centuries has influenced modern understandings. John Makeham, *Lost Soul: "Confucianism" in Contemporary Chinese Academic Discourse* (2008), surveys the significance of Confucianism in today's intellectual debates.

Daodejing

Among the many translations of the *Daodejing*, D. C. Lau, *Tao Te Ching* (1963); Roger Ames and David L. Hall, Daodejing*—Making This Life Significant—A Philosophical Translation* (2003); and Red Pine, *Lao-tzu's* Taoteching: *With Selected Commentaries of the Past 2000 Years* (1997), are especially recommended. Robert G. Henricks, *Lao-Tzu's* Tao Te Ching: *A New Translation Based on the Recently Discovered Ma-wang-tui Texts* (1989) and *Lao Tzu's* Tao Te Ching: *A Translation of the Startling New Documents Found at Guodian* (2000), are based on excavated manuscripts of the *Daodejing* and are interesting to compare to the received text.

For a broader view on the *Daodejing* within the context of Early Chinese intellectual debates, see the chapters on the *Daodejing* in the books on Chinese Masters Literature indicated in the regional introduction to "Early Chinese Thought and Literature." Arthur Waley, *The Way and Its Power: A Study of the* Tao Te Ching *and Its Place in Chinese Thought* (1958), is still a classic study of the *Daodejing*. Michael LaFargue, *Tao and Method: A Reasoned Approach to the* Tao Te Ching (1994), is a compelling reconstruction of what the text might have meant to its earliest readers. For interpretations of one of the most influential commentators of the *Daodejing*, see Rudolf Wagner, *The Craft of the Chinese Commentator: Wang Bi on the* Laozi (2000) and *A Chinese Reading of the* Daodejing: *Wang Bi's Commentary on the* Laozi *with Critical Text and Translation* (2003). For views on the *Daodejing* and its relation to the *Laozi* and Daoism, see Livia Kohn and Michael LaFargue, Lao-tzu *and the* Tao-te-ching (1998), and Mark Csikszentmihalyi and Philip J. Ivanhoe, *Religious and Philosophical Aspects of the* Laozi (1999).

Sima Qian

Due to its length, there is to date no comprehensive translation of the *Historical Records*. Burton Watson, *Records of the Grand Historian: Han Dynasty*, 2 vols. (1993), and *Records of the Grand Historian: Qin Dynasty* (1993), cover the Qin and Han parts of the *Historical Records*. The multivolume series *The Grand Scribe's Records* (1994–), edited by William H. Nienhauser, includes translations of parts on pre-Qin Chinese history.

For compelling studies of Sima Qian's work, see Stephen W. Durrant, *The Cloudy Mirror: Tension and Conflict in the Writings of Sima Qian* (1995); Grant Hardy, *Worlds of Bronze and Bamboo: Sima Qian's Conquest of History* (1999); and Michael Puett, ed., *Narrative, Authorship, and Historiography: Studies on Sima Qian's* Shiji (forthcoming). Nicola Di Cosmo, *Ancient China and Its Enemies: The Rise of Nomadic Power in East Asian History* (2002), explores the rise of the Xiongnu and analyzes Sima Qian's ethnographic depiction of nomadic peoples on China's border.

Songs of the South

David Hawkes, The Songs of the South: *An Anthology of Poems by Qu Yuan and Other Poets* (1985), contains a complete translation with a detailed introduction. You can compare the translation to Hsien-yi Yang and Gladys Yang, *Li sao, and Other Poems of Qu Yuan* (1955). Zong-Qi Cai, ed., *How To Read Chinese Poetry: A Guided Anthology* (2008), contains an annotated bilingual translation of parts of the "Nine Songs" and of "Encountering Sorrow." On the "Nine Songs," see Arthur Waley's classic work *The Nine Songs: A Study of Shamanism in Ancient China* (1973). On the allegorical interpretation of the *Songs of Chu*, see Geoffrey R. Waters, *Three Elegies of Ch'u: An Introduction to the Traditional Interpretation of the 'Ch'u Tz'u'* (1985), and the relevant chapter in Pauline Yu's *The Reading of Imagery in the Chinese Poetic Tradition* (1987). The essays in Constance Cook and John S. Major, *Defining Chu: Image and Reality in Ancient China* (1999), portray the culture of Chu in the light of the recent archaeological discoveries.

Speech, Writing, and Poetry in Early China

Mark Lewis, *Writing and Authority* (1999), is an extensive exploration of the role of writing in early Chinese society. To explore Chinese writing and the languages of China, see John DeFrancis, *The Chinese Language: Fact and Fantasy* (1984); S. Robert Ramsey, *The Languages of China* (1987); Jerry Norman, *Chinese* (1988); and Xigui Qiu, *Chinese Writing* (2000). Steven van Zoeren, *Poetry and Personality: Reading, Exegesis and Hermeneutics in Traditional China* (1991), surveys the interpretation of the *Classic of Poetry*. For witty anecdotes about early Chinese persuaders and strategists, see J. I. Crump, *Legends of the Warring States: Persuasions, Romances, and Stories from Chan-kuo ts'e* (1999). Lisa Raphals, *Knowing Words: Wisdom and Cunning in the Classical Traditions of China and Greece* (1992), compares Chinese and Ancient Greek cultures of persuasion, as does Xing Lu, *Rhetoric in Ancient China, Fifth to Third Century B.C.E.: A Comparison with Classical Greek Rhetoric* (1998).

Zhuangzi

There are a number of good English translations, including Burton Watson, *The Complete Works of Chuang Tzu* (1968); A. C. Graham, Chuang-tzu: *The Inner Chapters* (1981); Sam Hamill and J. P. Seaton, *The Essential* Chuang Tzu (1998); and Brook Ziporyn, Zhuangzi: *The Essential Writings with Selections from Traditional Commentaries* (2009). For situating *Zhuangzi* in the context of early Chinese intellectual debates see the chapters on *Zhuangzi* in the books on Chinese Masters Literature indicated in the regional introduction to "Early Chinese thought and literature." *Zhuangzi* has inspired many interpretive essays and personal reflections, some of which can be found in Roger T. Ames, *Wandering at Ease in the* Zhuangzi (1998); Paul Kjellberg and Philip J. Ivanhoe, *Essays on Skepticism, Relativism and Ethics in the* Zhuangzi (1996); and Victor H. Mair, *Experimental Essays on Chuang-tzu* (1983).

Timeline

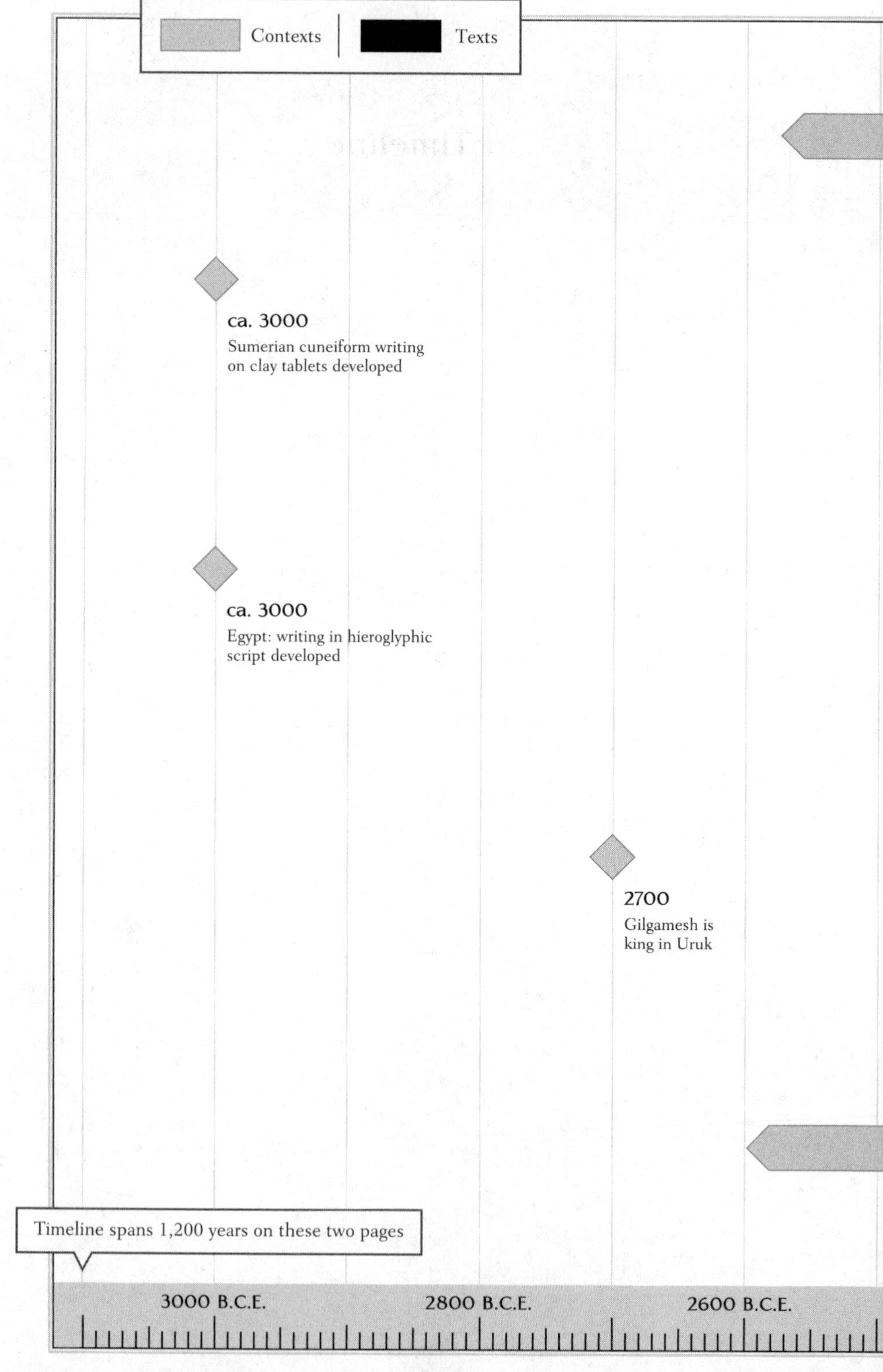
Contexts
Texts
ca. 3000
Sumerian cuneiform writing on clay tablets developed
ca. 3000
Egypt: writing in hieroglyphic script developed
2700
Gilgamesh is king in Uruk
Timeline spans 1,200 years on these two pages
3000 B.C.E.
2800 B.C.E.
2600 B.C.E.

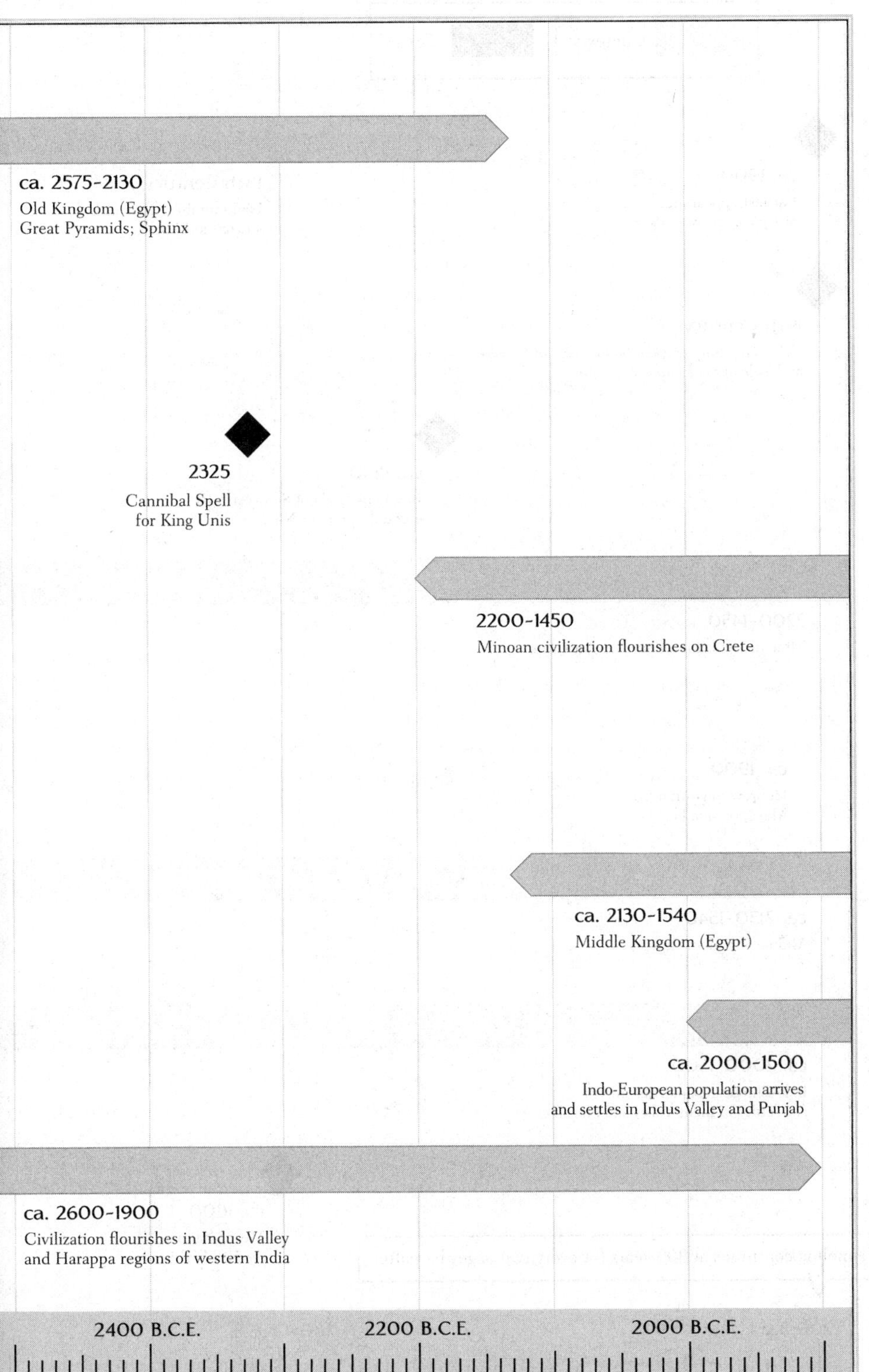
ca. 2575–2130
Old Kingdom (Egypt)
Great Pyramids; Sphinx
2325
Cannibal Spell
for King Unis
2200–1450
Minoan civilization flourishes on Crete
ca. 2130–1540
Middle Kingdom (Egypt)
ca. 2000–1500
Indo-European population arrives
and settles in Indus Valley and Punjab
ca. 2600–1900
Civilization flourishes in Indus Valley
and Harappa regions of western India
2400 B.C.E.
2200 B.C.E.
2000 B.C.E.

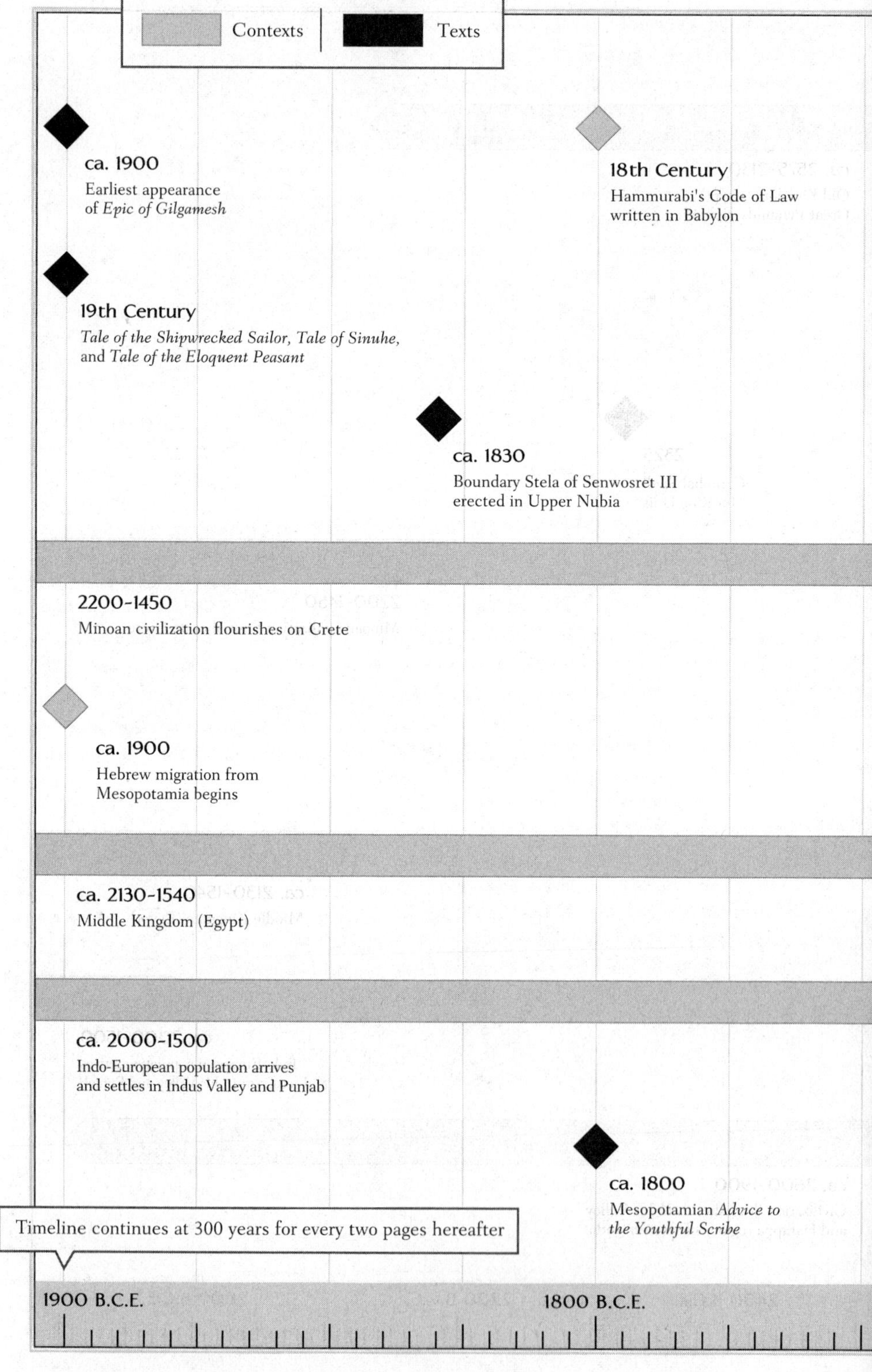
Contexts
Texts
ca. 1900
Earliest appearance of *Epic of Gilgamesh*
18th Century
Hammurabi's Code of Law written in Babylon
19th Century
Tale of the Shipwrecked Sailor, Tale of Sinuhe, and *Tale of the Eloquent Peasant*
ca. 1830
Boundary Stela of Senwosret III erected in Upper Nubia
2200–1450
Minoan civilization flourishes on Crete
ca. 1900
Hebrew migration from Mesopotamia begins
ca. 2130–1540
Middle Kingdom (Egypt)
ca. 2000–1500
Indo-European population arrives and settles in Indus Valley and Punjab
ca. 1800
Mesopotamian *Advice to the Youthful Scribe*
Timeline continues at 300 years for every two pages hereafter
1900 B.C.E.
1800 B.C.E.

1700 B.C.E.

1600 B.C.E.

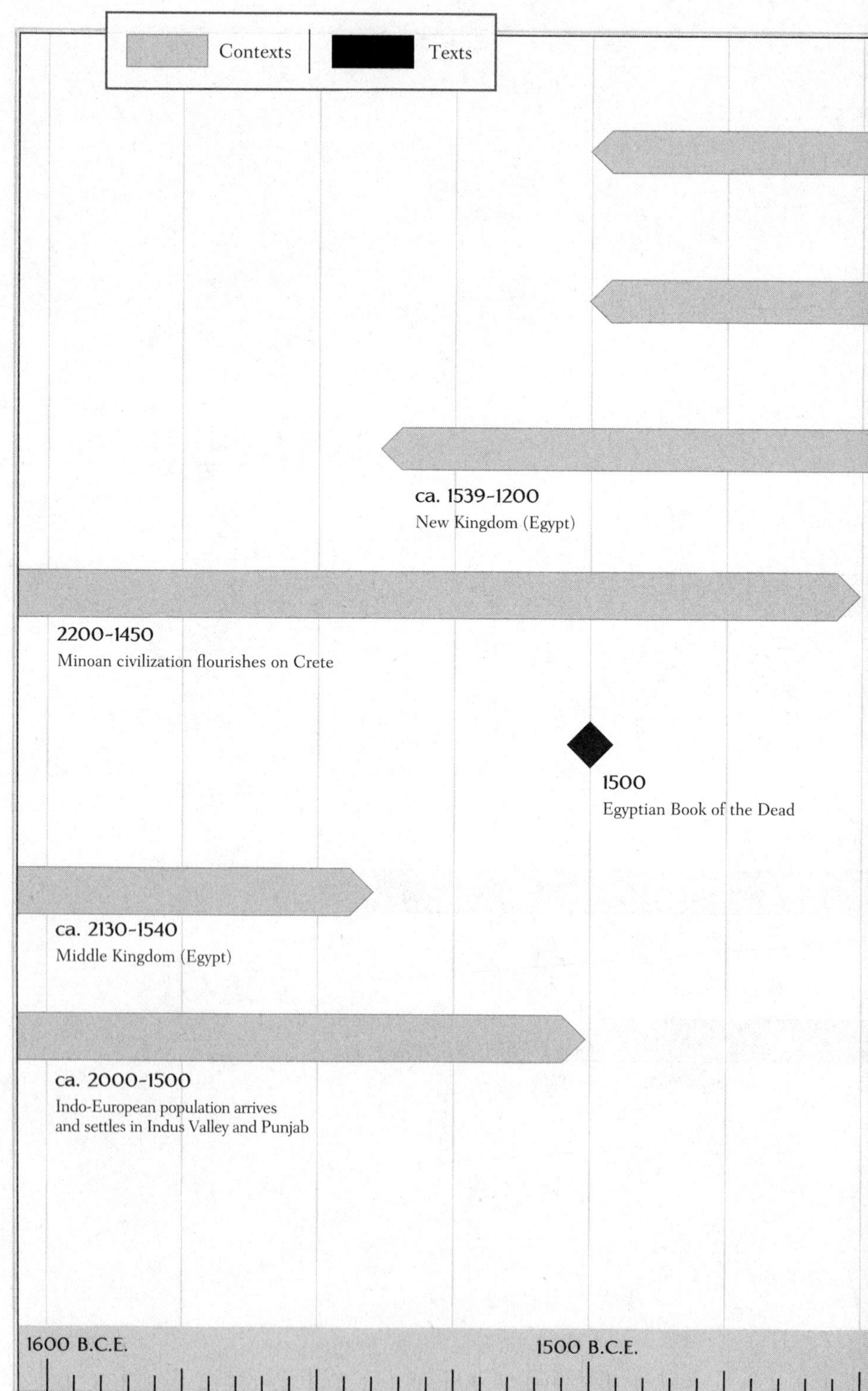
Contexts
Texts
ca. 1539–1200
New Kingdom (Egypt)
2200–1450
Minoan civilization flourishes on Crete
1500
Egyptian Book of the Dead
ca. 2130–1540
Middle Kingdom (Egypt)
ca. 2000–1500
Indo-European population arrives and settles in Indus Valley and Punjab
1600 B.C.E.
1500 B.C.E.

ca. 1500-1200
Earliest form of Sanskrit developed

ca. 1500-1200
Indo-European settlers establish agrarian village society in northwestern India

ca. 1350
Akhenaten's *Great Hymn to Aten*

ca. 1450
Mycenaeans from mainland Greece occupy Crete

ca. 1375-1354
Egyptian king Akhenaten dedicates his capital to Aten, the sun god

1400 B.C.E.

1300 B.C.E.

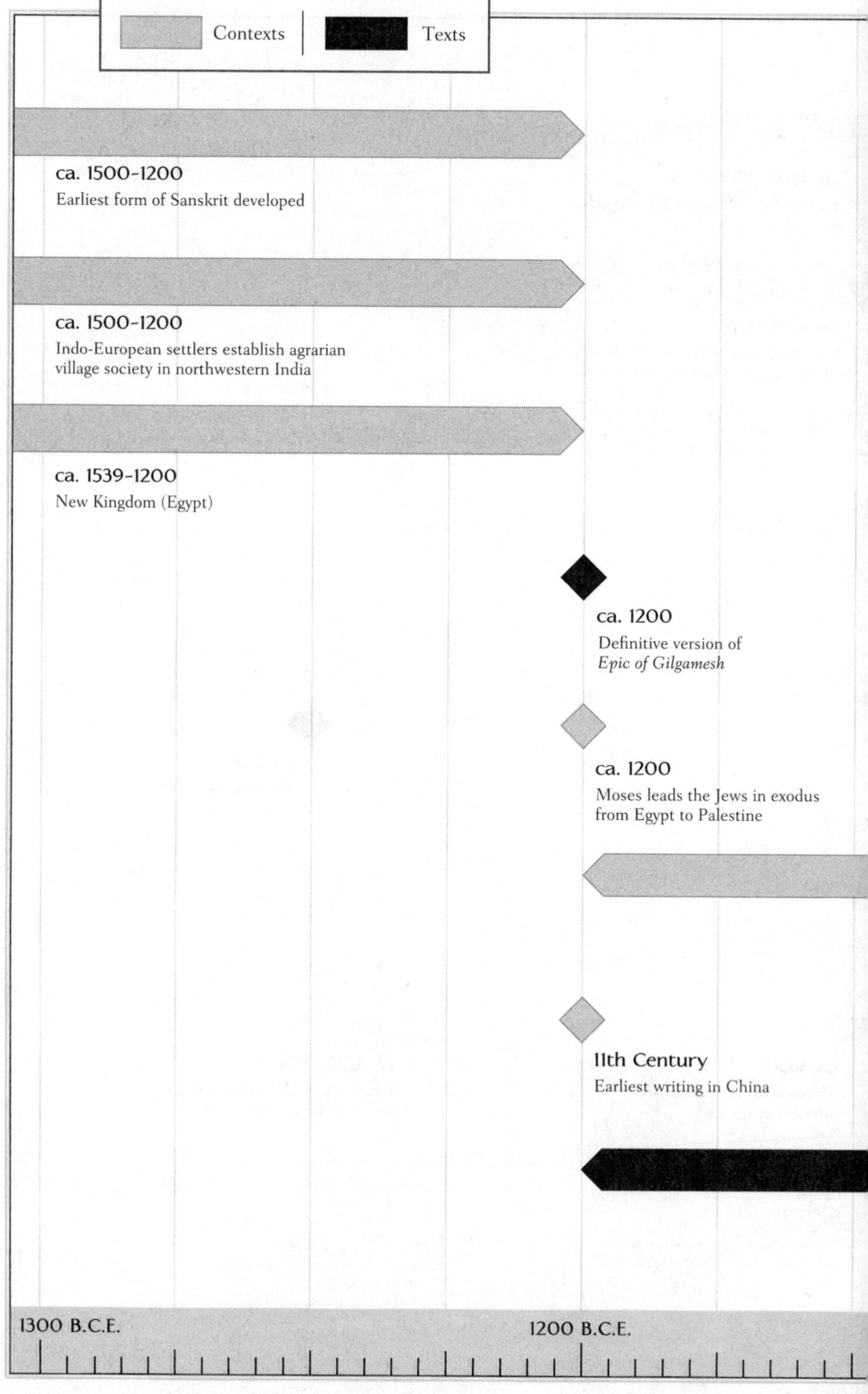
Contexts
Texts
ca. 1500–1200
Earliest form of Sanskrit developed
ca. 1500–1200
Indo-European settlers establish agrarian village society in northwestern India
ca. 1539–1200
New Kingdom (Egypt)
ca. 1200
Definitive version of *Epic of Gilgamesh*
ca. 1200
Moses leads the Jews in exodus from Egypt to Palestine
11th Century
Earliest writing in China
1300 B.C.E.
1200 B.C.E.

1045
King Wen and King Wu found the Zhou Dynasty in China

ca. 1200–900
Emergence of Hindu beliefs and rituals in India. Caste system develops

ca. 1200–700
The Vedas (Hindu scripture) and early Upaniṣads (philosophical and mystical texts) composed in the Punjab region of India

1100 B.C.E. 1000 B.C.E.

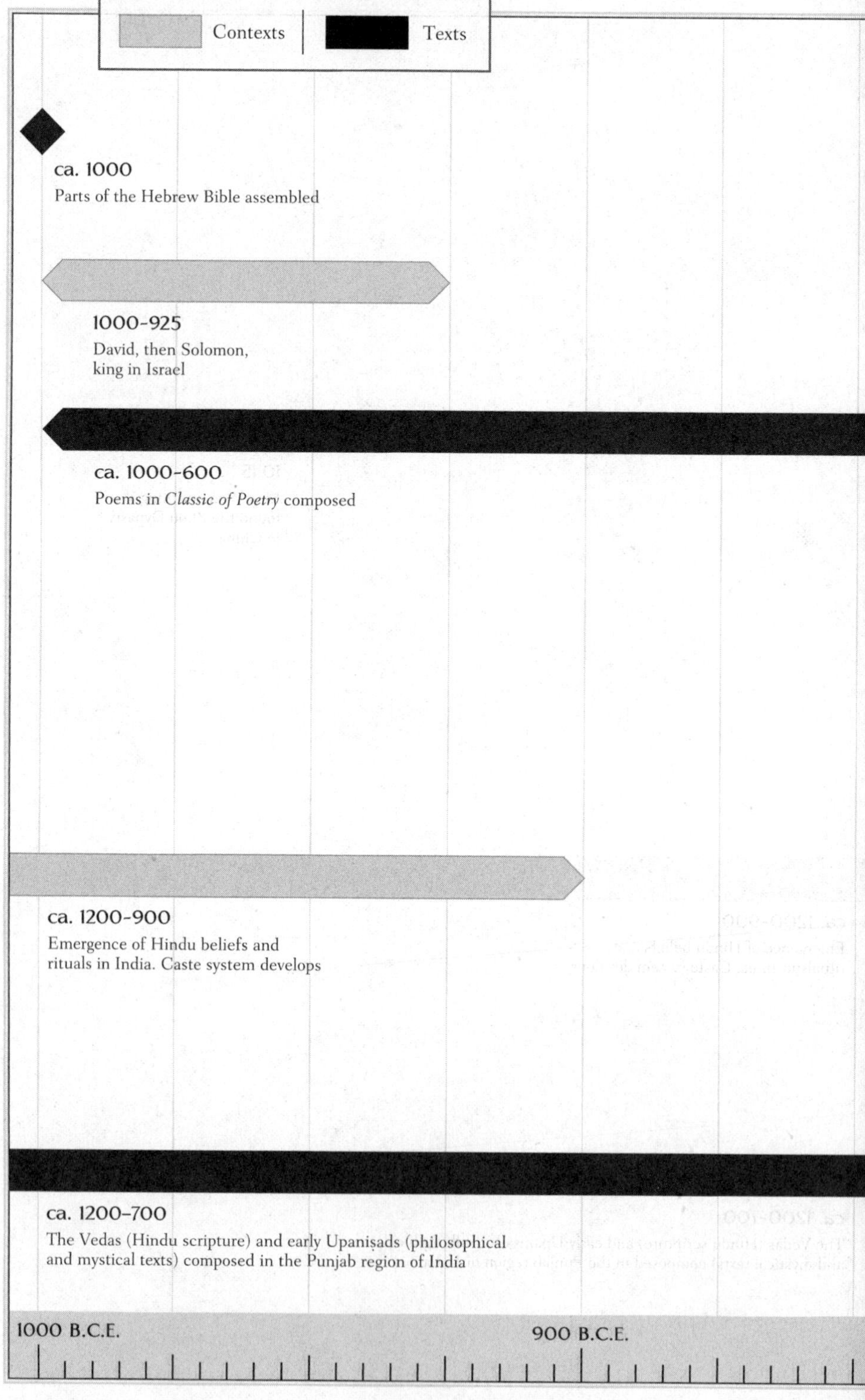
Contexts
Texts
ca. 1000
Parts of the Hebrew Bible assembled
1000–925
David, then Solomon, king in Israel
ca. 1000–600
Poems in *Classic of Poetry* composed
ca. 1200–900
Emergence of Hindu beliefs and rituals in India. Caste system develops
ca. 1200–700
The Vedas (Hindu scripture) and early Upaniṣads (philosophical and mystical texts) composed in the Punjab region of India
1000 B.C.E.
900 B.C.E.

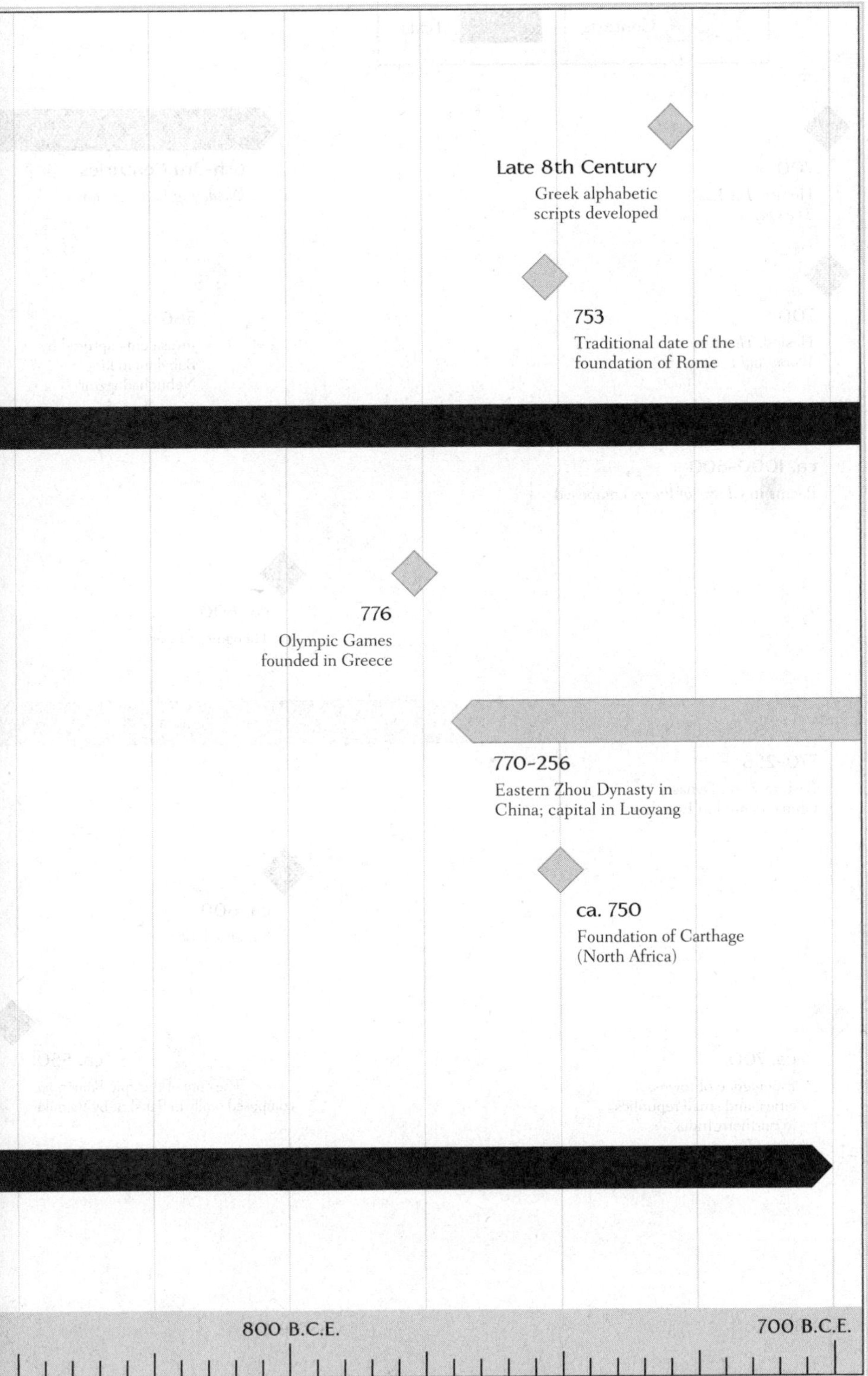
Late 8th Century
Greek alphabetic scripts developed
753
Traditional date of the foundation of Rome
776
Olympic Games founded in Greece
770–256
Eastern Zhou Dynasty in China; capital in Luoyang
ca. 750
Foundation of Carthage (North Africa)
800 B.C.E.
700 B.C.E.

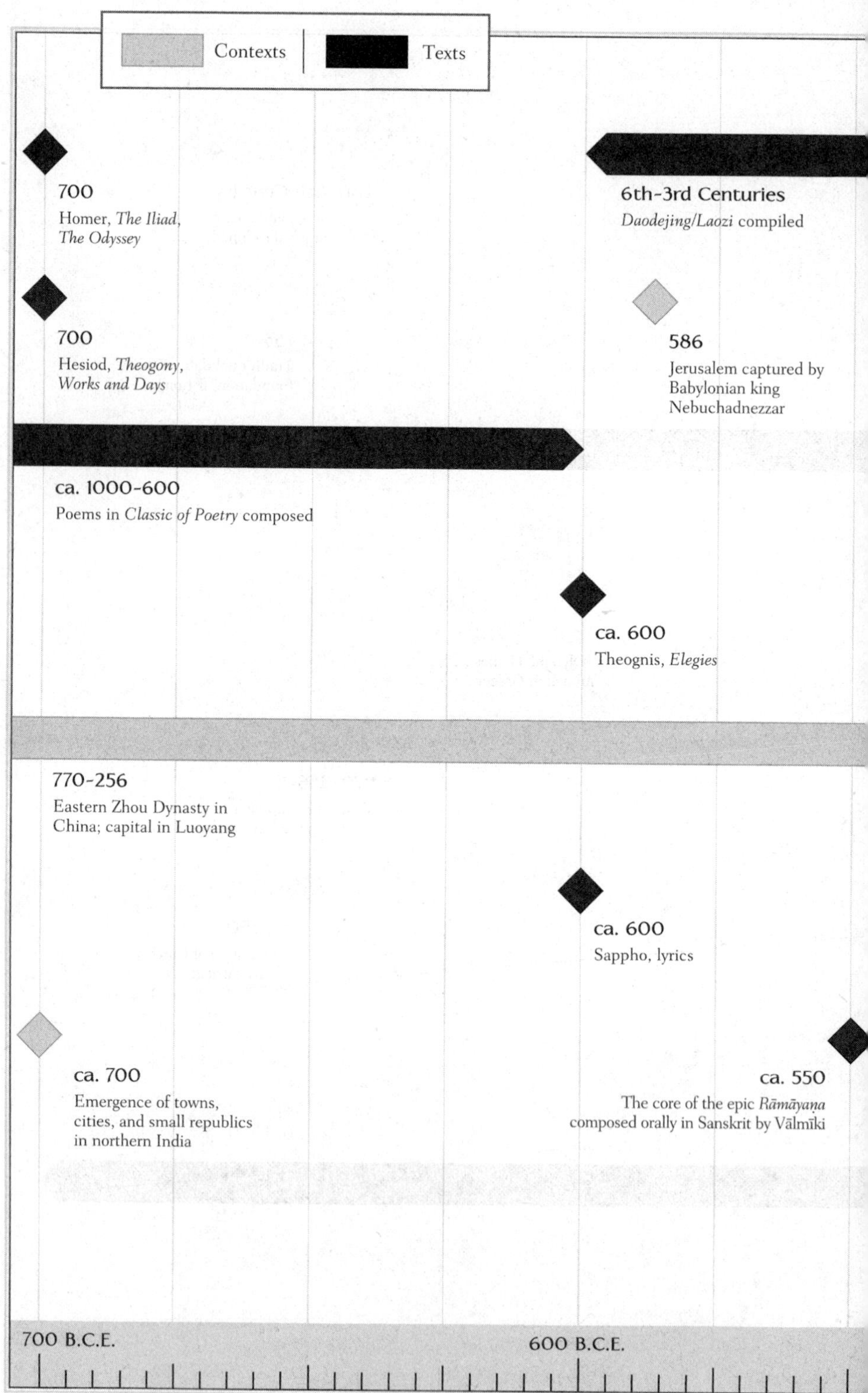
Contexts
Texts
700
Homer, *The Iliad*, *The Odyssey*
6th–3rd Centuries
Daodejing/Laozi compiled
700
Hesiod, *Theogony*, *Works and Days*
586
Jerusalem captured by Babylonian king Nebuchadnezzar
ca. 1000–600
Poems in *Classic of Poetry* composed
ca. 600
Theognis, *Elegies*
770–256
Eastern Zhou Dynasty in China; capital in Luoyang
ca. 600
Sappho, lyrics
ca. 700
Emergence of towns, cities, and small republics in northern India
ca. 550
The core of the epic *Rāmāyaṇa* composed orally in Sanskrit by Vālmīki
700 B.C.E.
600 B.C.E.

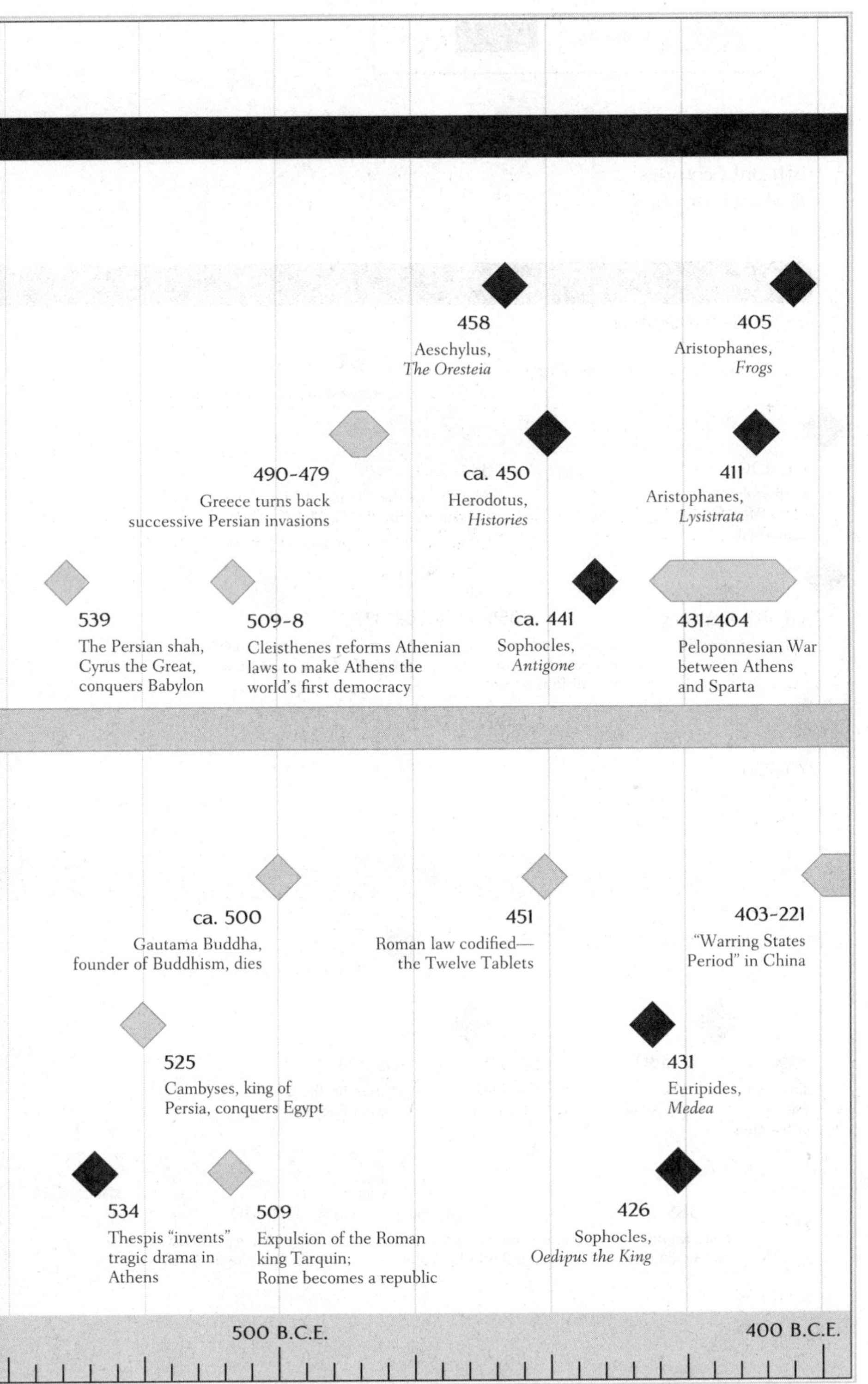
458
Aeschylus,
The Oresteia
405
Aristophanes,
Frogs
490–479
Greece turns back
successive Persian invasions
ca. 450
Herodotus,
Histories
411
Aristophanes,
Lysistrata
539
The Persian shah,
Cyrus the Great,
conquers Babylon
509–8
Cleisthenes reforms Athenian
laws to make Athens the
world's first democracy
ca. 441
Sophocles,
Antigone
431–404
Peloponnesian War
between Athens
and Sparta
ca. 500
Gautama Buddha,
founder of Buddhism, dies
451
Roman law codified—
the Twelve Tablets
403–221
"Warring States
Period" in China
525
Cambyses, king of
Persia, conquers Egypt
431
Euripides,
Medea
534
Thespis "invents"
tragic drama in
Athens
509
Expulsion of the Roman
king Tarquin;
Rome becomes a republic
426
Sophocles,
Oedipus the King
500 B.C.E.
400 B.C.E.

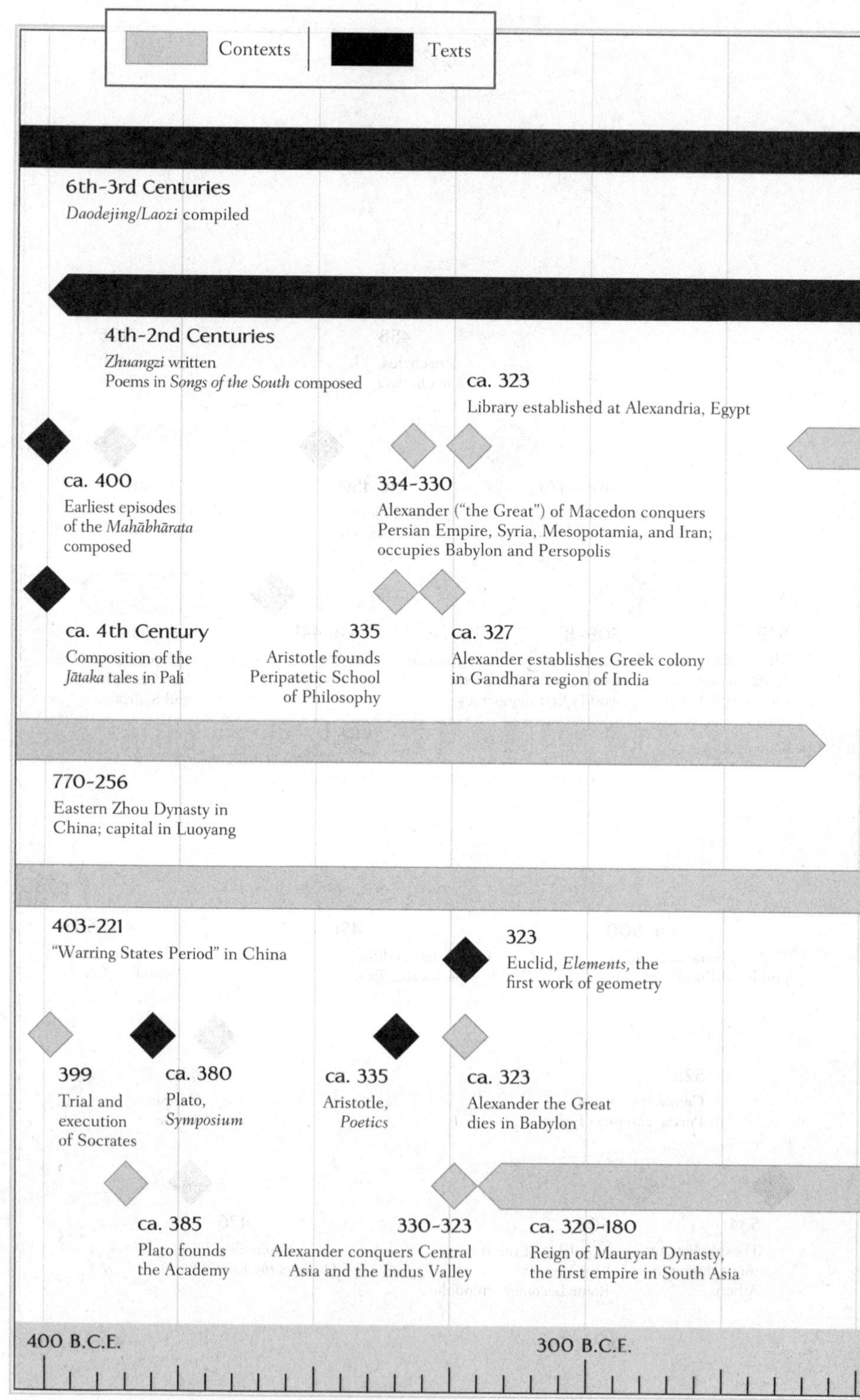
Contexts
Texts
6th–3rd Centuries
Daodejing/Laozi compiled
4th–2nd Centuries
Zhuangzi written
Poems in *Songs of the South* composed
ca. 323
Library established at Alexandria, Egypt
ca. 400
Earliest episodes of the *Mahābhārata* composed
334–330
Alexander ("the Great") of Macedon conquers Persian Empire, Syria, Mesopotamia, and Iran; occupies Babylon and Persopolis
ca. 4th Century
Composition of the *Jātaka* tales in Pali
335
Aristotle founds Peripatetic School of Philosophy
ca. 327
Alexander establishes Greek colony in Gandhara region of India
770–256
Eastern Zhou Dynasty in China; capital in Luoyang
403–221
"Warring States Period" in China
323
Euclid, *Elements,* the first work of geometry
399
Trial and execution of Socrates
ca. 380
Plato, *Symposium*
ca. 335
Aristotle, *Poetics*
ca. 323
Alexander the Great dies in Babylon
ca. 385
Plato founds the Academy
330–323
Alexander conquers Central Asia and the Indus Valley
ca. 320–180
Reign of Mauryan Dynasty, the first empire in South Asia
400 B.C.E.
300 B.C.E.

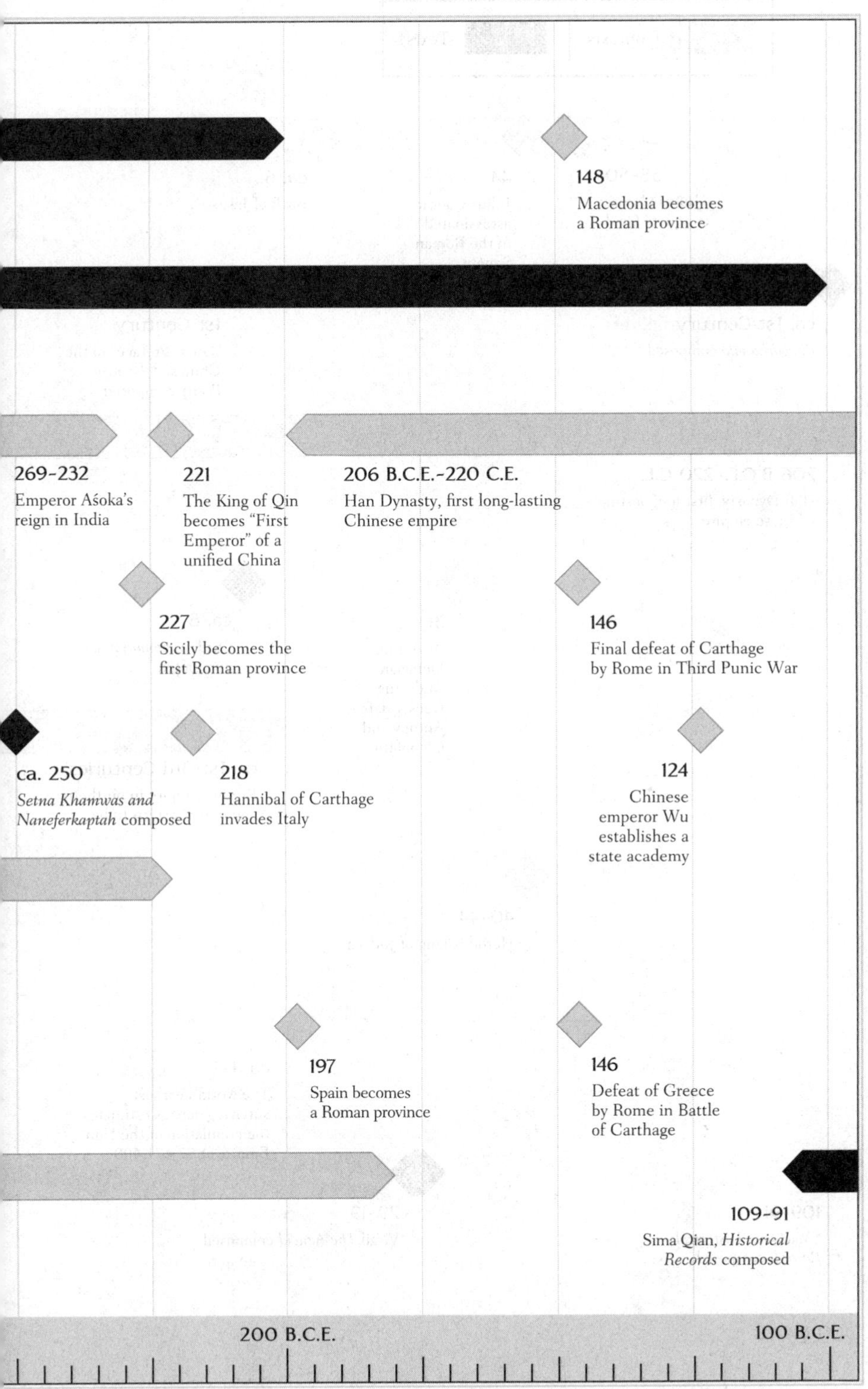
148
Macedonia becomes a Roman province
269–232
Emperor Aśoka's reign in India
221
The King of Qin becomes "First Emperor" of a unified China
206 B.C.E.–220 C.E.
Han Dynasty, first long-lasting Chinese empire
227
Sicily becomes the first Roman province
146
Final defeat of Carthage by Rome in Third Punic War
ca. 250
Setna Khamwas and Naneferkaptah composed
218
Hannibal of Carthage invades Italy
124
Chinese emperor Wu establishes a state academy
197
Spain becomes a Roman province
146
Defeat of Greece by Rome in Battle of Carthage
109–91
Sima Qian, *Historical Records* composed
200 B.C.E.
100 B.C.E.

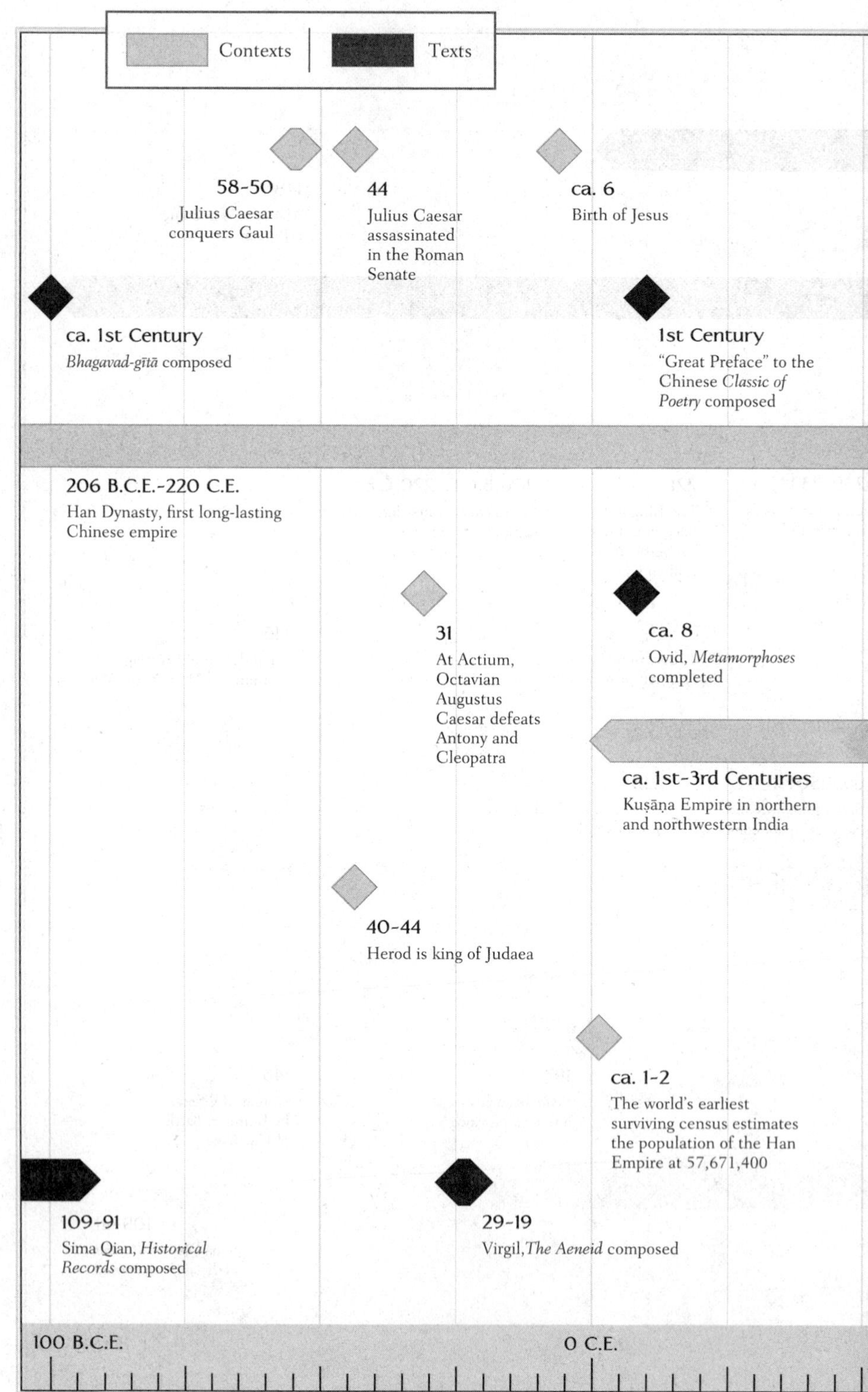
Contexts
Texts
58-50
Julius Caesar conquers Gaul
44
Julius Caesar assassinated in the Roman Senate
ca. 6
Birth of Jesus
ca. 1st Century
Bhagavad-gītā composed
1st Century
"Great Preface" to the Chinese *Classic of Poetry* composed
206 B.C.E.-220 C.E.
Han Dynasty, first long-lasting Chinese empire
31
At Actium, Octavian Augustus Caesar defeats Antony and Cleopatra
ca. 8
Ovid, *Metamorphoses* completed
ca. 1st-3rd Centuries
Kuṣāṇa Empire in northern and northwestern India
40-44
Herod is king of Judaea
ca. 1-2
The world's earliest surviving census estimates the population of the Han Empire at 57,671,400
109-91
Sima Qian, *Historical Records* composed
29-19
Virgil, *The Aeneid* composed
100 B.C.E.
0 C.E.

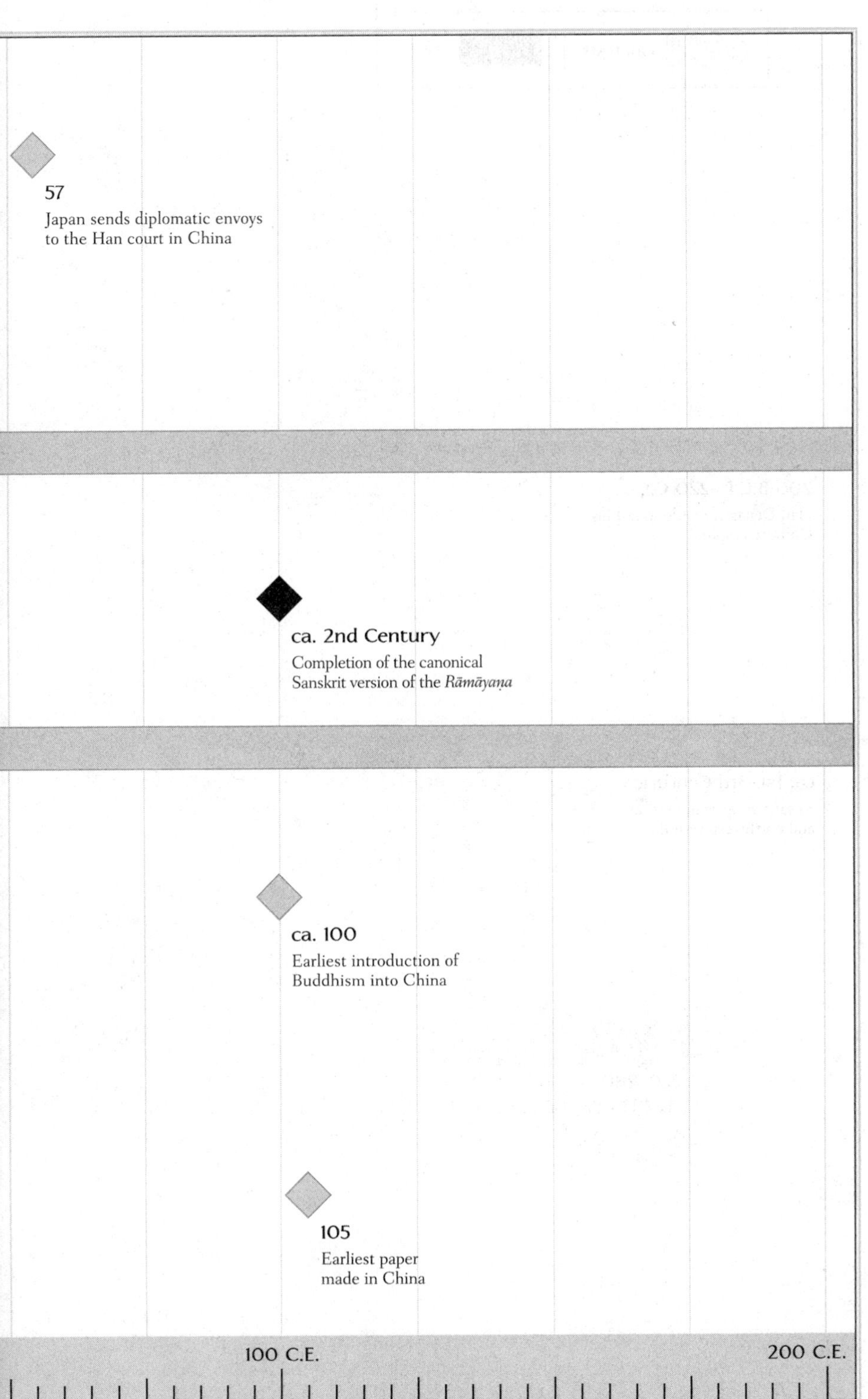
57
Japan sends diplomatic envoys to the Han court in China
ca. 2nd Century
Completion of the canonical Sanskrit version of the *Rāmāyaṇa*
ca. 100
Earliest introduction of Buddhism into China
105
Earliest paper made in China
100 C.E.
200 C.E.

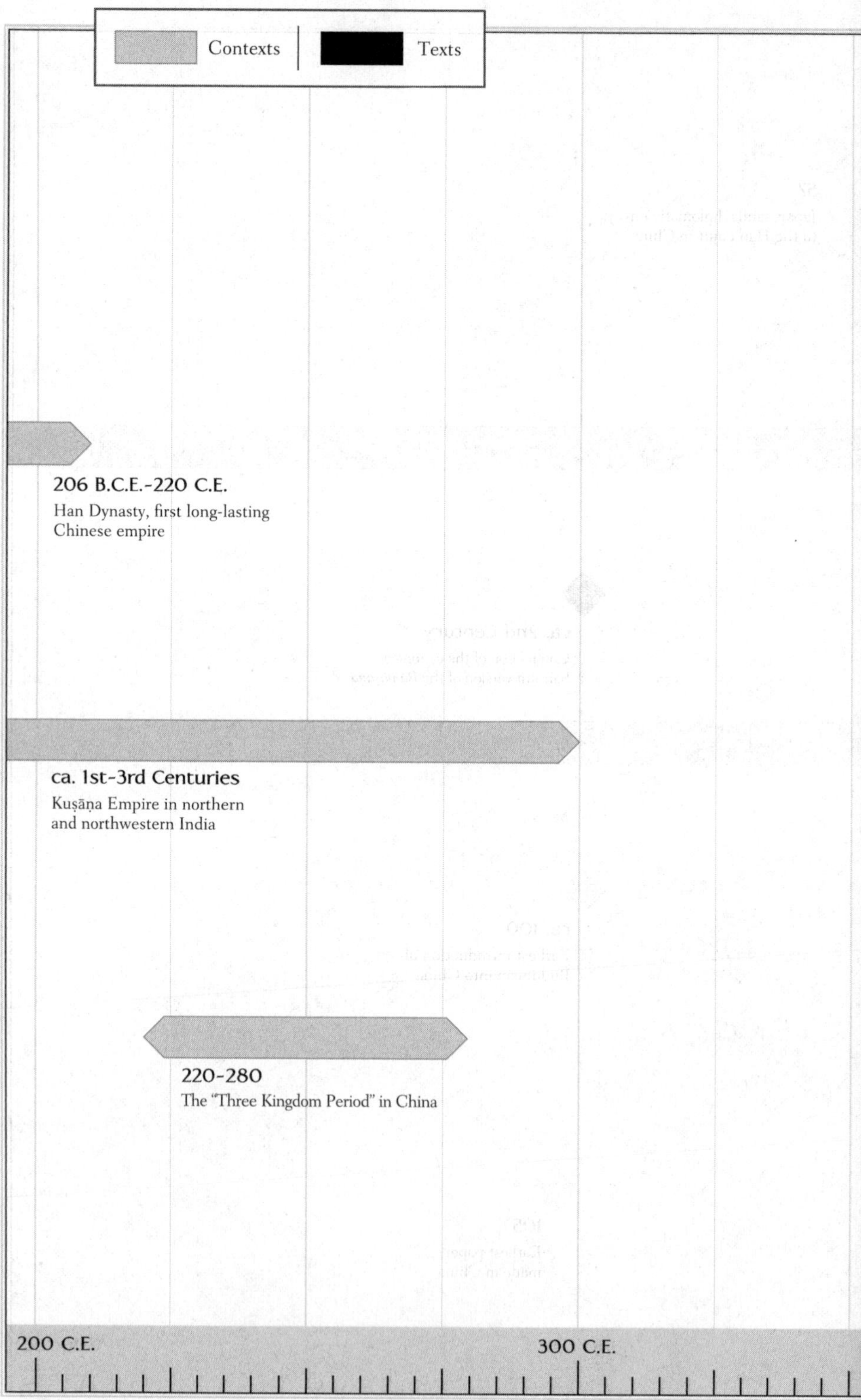
Contexts
Texts
206 B.C.E.–220 C.E.
Han Dynasty, first long-lasting Chinese empire
ca. 1st–3rd Centuries
Kuṣāṇa Empire in northern and northwestern India
220–280
The "Three Kingdom Period" in China
200 C.E.
300 C.E.

ca. 400

Completion of the canonical Sanskrit version of the *Mahābhārata*

400 C.E.

500 C.E.

Permissions Acknowledgments

Aeschylus: *Agamemnon* from THE ORESTEIA by Aeschylus, trans. by Robert Fagles, copyright © 1966, 1967, 1975, 1977 by Robert Fagles. Used by permission of Viking Penguin, a division of Penguin Group (USA) Inc. From *The Persians* from PROMETHEUS BOUND AND OTHER PLAYS, trans. with an introduction by Philip Vellacott (Penguin Classics 1961). Copyright © 1961 Philip Vellacott. Reproduced by permission of Penguin Books Ltd.

Aesop: From AESOP'S FABLES, trans. by Laura Gibbs (2002). By permission of Oxford University Press.

***Airs, Waters, Places*:** An anonymous Hippocratic text from HIPPOCRATIC WRITINGS, ed. with an introduction by G. E. R. Lloyd, trans. by J. Chadwick and W. N. Mann (Penguin Classics 1983). Introduction copyright © 1978 by G. E. R. Lloyd. Translation copyright © 1950 by J. Chadwick and W. N. Mann. Reproduced by permission of Penguin Books Ltd.

Ancient Egyptian Poems: From "The Tale of Sinuhe," from "The Tale of the Shipwrecked Sailor," and from "The Tale of the Eloquent Peasant," from THE TALE OF SINUHE AND OTHER ANCIENT EGYPTIAN POEMS 1940–1640 B.C., trans. by Richard B. Parkinson (1997). By permission of Oxford University Press.

Aristophanes: LYSISTRATA, trans. by Sarah Ruden. Copyright © 2003 by Hackett Publishing Company, Inc. All rights reserved. Reprinted by permission of Hackett Publishing Company, Inc. From FROGS from THE COMPLETE PLAYS, trans. by Paul Roche, copyright © 2004, 2005 by Paul Roche. Used by permission of Dutton Signet, a division of Penguin Group (USA) Inc.

Aristotle: From POETICS, trans. by James Hutton. Copyright © 1982 by W. W. Norton & Company, Inc. Used by permission of W. W. Norton & Company, Inc.

Babylonian Creation Myth: From "Enuma Elish" from BEFORE THE MUSES (2005), trans. by Benjamin R. Foster, is reprinted by permission of CDL Press.

***Bhagavad-Gītā*:** From *The Bhagavad-Gītā: A New Translation*, translated by Gavin Flood and Charles Martin. Copyright © 2012 by Gavin Flood and Charles Martin. Used by permission of W. W. Norton & Company, Inc.

Callimachus: From "Aetia 1–2" from THE POEMS OF CALLIMACHUS, trans. by Frank Nisetich (2001). By permission of Oxford University Press.

Cannibal Spell for Pharaoh Unis: "Spells for the Spirit's Rebirth" from THE ANCIENT EGYPTIAN PYRAMID TEXTS, trans. by James P. Allen (2005). Reprinted by permission of the Society of Biblical Literature.

Catullus: From THE POEMS OF CATULLUS: A BILINGUAL EDITION, trans. by Peter Green. Copyright © 2005 by Peter Green. Reprinted by permission of the University of California Press.

***Classic of Poetry*:** Poems from *The Classic of Poetry* and an excerpt from "The Great Preface" to *The Classic of Poetry* from AN ANTHOLOGY OF CHINESE LITERATURE: BEGINNINGS TO 1911, ed. and trans. by Stephen Owen. Copyright © 1996 by Stephen Owen and the Council for Cultural Planning and Development of the Executive Yuan of the Republic of China. Used by permission of W. W. Norton & Company, Inc.

Confucius: From THE ANALECTS OF CONFUCIUS, trans. by Simon Leys. Copyright © 1997 by Pierre Ryckmans. Used by permission of W. W. Norton & Company, Inc.

Early Greek Philosophy: Thales, Xenophanes, Heraclitus, Empedocles, Anaxagoras, from EARLY GREEK PHILOSOPHY, trans. and ed. with an introduction by Jonathan Barnes (Penguin Classics 1987). Copyright © 1987 Jonathan Barnes. Reproduced by permission of Penguin Books Ltd.

Egyptian Love Poems: From THE SONG OF SONGS AND THE ANCIENT EGYPTIAN LOVE SONGS by Michael V. Fox (The University of Wisconsin Press 2005); reprinted by permission of the author.

***Enmerkar and the Lord of Aratta*:** From EPICS OF SUMERIAN KINGS: THE MATTER OF ARATTA by Herman Vanstiphout (2003). Reprinted by permission of the Society of Biblical Literature.

Euripides: MEDEA from ALCESTIS, MEDEA, HIPPOLYTUS, trans. D. Arnson Svarlien. Copyright © 2008 by Hackett Publishing Company, Inc. All rights reserved. Reprinted by permission of Hackett Publishing Company, Inc.

***Gilgamesh*:** From THE EPIC OF GILGAMESH, trans. by Benjamin R. Foster. Copyright © 2001 by W. W. Norton & Company, Inc. Used by permission of W. W. Norton & Company, Inc.

The Great Hymn to the Aten: From ANCIENT EGYPTIAN LITERATURE, Vol. II, THE NEW KINGDOM, by Miriam Lichtheim. Copyright © 1976 by the Regents of the University of California. Reprinted by permission of the University of California Press via the Copyright Clearance Center.

Han Feizi: From "The Difficulties of Persuasion," trans. by Burton Watson from BASIC WRITINGS OF MO TZU, HSUN TZU, and HAN FEI TZU. Copyright © 1963, 1964 by Columbia University Press. Reprinted with permission of the publisher.

The Hebrew Bible: From THE FIVE BOOKS OF MOSES: A TRANSLATION WITH COMMENTARY, trans. by Robert Alter. Copyright © 2004 by Robert Alter. Used by permission of W. W. Norton & Company, Inc. Visual adaptation of Genesis, Chapter 25, from THE BOOK OF GENESIS ILLUSTRATED by Robert Crumb. Copyright © 2009 by Robert Crumb, with text from GENESIS: TRANSLATION AND COMMENTARY, trans. by Robert Alter. Copyright © 1996 by Robert Alter. Used by permission of W. W. Norton & Company, Inc. From Job from THE WISDOM BOOKS: JOB, PROVERBS, AND ECCLESIASTES, trans. by Robert Alter. Copyright © 2010 by Robert Alter. Used by permission of W. W. Norton & Company.

Herodotus: From THE HISTORIES: A NORTON CRITICAL EDITION, ed. by Walter Blanco and Jennifer Tolbert Roberts, trans. by Walter Blanco. Copyright © 1992 by W. W. Norton & Company, Inc. Used by permission of W. W. Norton & Company, Inc.

Hesiod: From HESIOD: THEOGONY, WORKS AND DAYS, trans. by Apostolos N. Athanassakis. Copyright © 1983, 2004 The Johns Hopkins University Press. Reprinted with permission of The Johns Hopkins University Press.

Homer: THE ODYSSEY, trans. by Stanley Lombardo. Copyright © 2000 by Hackett Publishing Company, Inc. Reprinted by permission of Hackett Publishing Company, Inc. All rights reserved. From THE ILIAD, trans. by Stanley Lombardo. Copyright © 1997 by Hackett Publishing Company, Inc. All rights reserved. Reprinted by permission of Hackett Publishing Company, Inc.

Horace: Book One, Ode 37, and Book Three, Ode 30, from COMPLETE ODES AND EPODES, trans. by David West (1997). By permission of Oxford University Press.

Lao Zi: From TAO TE CHING by Lao Tzu, trans. with an introduction by D. C. Lau (Penguin Classics 1963). Copyright © 1963 by D. C. Lau. Reproduced by permission of Penguin Books Ltd.

Lucretius: From ON THE NATURE OF THINGS: DE RERUM NATURA, trans. by Anthony M. Esolen. Copyright © 1995 The Johns Hopkins University Press. Reprinted with permission of The Johns Hopkins University Press.

The Mahābhārata: From THE MAHĀBHĀRATA, from Books 1, 5, 8, 9, 11, and 12, trans. by Chakravarthi V. Narasimhan. Copyright © 1965 Columbia University Press. Reprinted by permission of the publisher. From THE MAHĀBHĀRATA, from Book 2, trans. and ed. by J. A. B. van Buitenen. Copyright © 1975 by The University of Chicago. Reprinted by permission of the University of Chicago Press.

Ovid: From METAMORPHOSES, trans. by Charles Martin. Copyright © 2004 by Charles Martin. Used by permission of W. W. Norton & Company, Inc.

Plato: *Symposium* and from *Phaedrus* from PLATO ON LOVE, trans. by Alexander Nehamas and Paul Woodruff, ed. C. D. C. Reeve. Copyright © 2006 by Hackett Publishing Company, Inc. Reprinted by permission of Hackett Publishing Company, Inc. All rights reserved.

The Rāmāyaṇa of Valimiki: Reprinted by permission from CONCISE RĀMĀYAṆA OF VALMIKI, ed. by Swami Venkatesananda, the State University of New York Press. © 1988, State University of New York. All rights reserved.

Sappho of Lesbos: "Deathless Aphrodite of the spangled mind," "Some men say an army of horse and some men say an army on foot," "He seems to me equal to gods that man," "Kypros," "I simply want to be dead," "You came and I was crazy for you," "I don't know what to do," "Dead you will lie and never memory of you," "Sweet mother I cannot work the loom," "Eros the melter of limbs (now again) stirs me," "Moon has set," "Eros shook my" from IF NOT, WINTER by Anne Carson. Copyright © 2002 by Anne Carson. Used by permission of Alfred A. Knopf, a division of Random House, Inc. "[(You for) the Fragrant-Bosomed (Muses') Lovely Gifts]," translated by Martin West, as published in *Zeitschrift für Papyrologie und Epigraphik*, vol. 151, 2005. Reprinted by permission of Martin West.

Scribal Traditions: "Reminder of the Scribe's Superior Status," "Advice to the Youthful Scribe," and "Prayer to Thot for Skill in Writing" from THE LITERATURE OF ANCIENT EGYPT, ed. by William Kelly Simpson. Copyright © 2003 by Yale University. Reprinted by permission of Yale University Press.

Semna Stela of Senwosret III: From VOICES FROM ANCIENT EGYPT: AN ANTHOLOGY OF MIDDLE KINGDOM WRITINGS, trans. by Richard B. Parkinson. Published by the British Museum Press, 1991. Reprinted by permission of The British Museum Company Ltd.

Seneca: From LETTERS FROM A STOIC, selected and trans. with an introduction by Robin Campbell (Penguin Classics 1969). Copyright © 1969 Robin Alexander Campbell. Reproduced by permission of Penguin Books Ltd.

***Setne Khamwas and Naneferkaptah* (Setne 1)**: From ANCIENT EGYPTIAN LITERATURE, vol. III, The Late Period, by Miriam Lichtheim. Copyright © 1980 by the Regents of the University of

California. Reprinted by permission of the University of California Press via the Copyright Clearance Center.

Sima Qian: From "The Biographies of Qu Yuan and Master Jia" from RECORDS OF THE GRAND HISTORIAN: HAN DYNASTY 1, rev. ed., trans. by Burton Watson. Copyright © 1961, 1993 by Columbia University Press. Reprinted with permission of the publisher. "Letter in Reply to Ren An," from "Historical Records," and "The Biography of Bo Yi and Shu Qi," from AN ANTHOLOGY OF CHINESE LITERATURE: BEGINNINGS TO 1911, ed. and trans. by Stephen Owen. Copyright © 1996 by Stephen Owen and the Council for Cultural Planning and Development of the Executive Yuan of the Republic of China. Used by permission of W. W. Norton & Company, Inc.

***Songs of the South*:** From "The Nine Songs" and "The Li Sao [Encountering Sorrow]" from AN ANTHOLOGY OF CHINESE LITERATURE: BEGINNINGS TO 1911, ed. and trans. by Stephen Owen. Copyright © 1996 by Stephen Owen and the Council for Cultural Planning and Development of the Executive Yuan of the Republic of China. Used by permission of W. W. Norton & Company, Inc.

Sophocles: Translations by Robert Bagg of *Oedipus the King* and *Antigone* from THE COMPLETE PLAYS OF SOPHOCLES: TRANSLATIONS by Robert Bagg and James Scully. Copyright © 2011 by Robert Bagg and James Scully. Reprinted by permission of HarperCollins Publishers.

Theognis: From ELEGIES by Theognis, trans. by Dorothea Wender (Penguin Classics 1973). Copyright © 1973 by Dorothea Wender.

Virgil: From THE AENEID, trans. by Robert Fagles, copyright © 2006 by Robert Fagles. Used by permission of Viking Penguin, a division of Penguin Group (USA), Inc.

***Zhuangzi*:** From THE COMPLETE WORKS OF CHUANG TZU, trans. by Burton Watson. Copyright © 1968 by Columbia University Press. Reprinted with permission of the publisher. From AN ANTHOLOGY OF CHINESE LITERATURE: BEGINNINGS TO 1911, ed. and trans. by Stephen Owen. Copyright © 1996 by Stephen Owen and the Council for Cultural Planning and Development of the Executive Yuan of the Republic of China. Used by permission of W. W. Norton & Company, Inc.

IMAGES

2–3 bpk, Berlin /Antikensammlung, Staatliche Museen/ / Art Resource, NY; **4** © The Metropolitan Museum of Art / Art Resource, NY; **6** Gianni Dagli Orti/Corbis; **8** Marie Mauzy / Art Resource, NY; **9** DEA/Getty Images; **12** DEA/Getty Images; **14** Vanni / Art Resource, NY; **18** Gianni Dagli Orti/ Corbis; **19** DEA/Gianni Dagli Orti/Getty Images; **22** Bildarchiv Preussischer Kulturbesitz / Art Resource, NY; **25** Oriental Insititute of the University of Chicago; **30** Erich Lessing / Art Resource, NY; **58** bpk, Berlin / Aegyptisches Museum / Art Resource, NY; **93** The Trustees of the British Museum / Art Resource, NY; **97** Werner Forman / Art Resource, NY; **171–74** From The Book of Genesis © 2009 by Robert Crumb; **225** © The Trustees of the British Museum / Art Resource, NY; **645** Museo Archeologico Nazionale, Naples, Italy / Scala / Art Resource, NY; **646** Marie Mauzy / Art Resource, NY; **647** Theater and Playhouse by Richard and Helen Leacroft, Methuen Publishing, Ltd; **908** © The Trustees of The British Museum / Art Resource, NY; **963** Réunion des Musées Nationaux / Art Resource, NY; **1076** Andrea Jemolo/Scala / Art Resource, NY; **1116** Réunion des Musées Nationaux / Art Resource, NY; **1118** Giraudon / Art Resource, NY; **1160–61** © The Metropolitan Museum of Art / Art Resource, NY; **1162** Victoria & Albert Museum, London / Art Resource, NY; **1164** © The Trustees of the British Museum / Art Resource, NY; **1167** Werner Forman / Art Resource, NY; **1173** Angelo Hornak / Corbis; **1237** Brooklyn Museum/Corbis; **1310–11** The Granger Collection, NY; **1313 top** Réunion des Musées Nationaux / Art Resource, NY; **1313 bottom** Bridgeman-Giraudon / Art Resource, NY; **1317** HIP / Art Resource, NY; **1331** AKG-images; **1416** Réunion des Musées Nationaux / Art Resource, NY; **1418** Richard G. Rudolph East Asian Library.

COLOR INSERT

Egyptian Statue of Seated Scribe. Gianni Dagli Orti / Corbis; **Clay tablet with cuneiform letter.** The Trustees of the British Museum / Art Resource, NY; **Shang dynasty oracle bone.** Royal Ontario Museum / Corbis; **Detail of Book of the Dead of Maiherperi.** Sandro Vannini/ Corbis; **Ostrakon. Greek potsherd.** Scala / Art Resource, NY; **Pillar edict of Emperor Asoka.** The Trustees of The British Museum / Art Resource, NY; **Portrait of girl, Roman fresco.** Vanni / Art Resource, NY; **Battle scene from Homer's *Iliad*.** Heritage Images / Corbis.

Index